the

M000285583

Contents

WORLD'S END

darkest hour

always for

WORLD'S END

BOOK ONE OF THE AGE OF MISRULE

MARK
CHADBOURN

For Elizabeth, Betsy, Joe and Eve

PROLOGUE

And now the world turns slowly from the light. Not with the cymbal clash of guns and tanks, but with the gently plucked harp of shifting moods and oddly lengthening shadows, the soft tread of a subtle invasion, not here, then here, and none the wiser. Each morning the sun still rises on supermarket worlds of plastic and glass, on industrial estates where slow trucks lumber in belches of diesel, on cities lulled by the whirring of disk drives breaking existence down into digitised order. People still move through their lives with the arrogance of rulers who know their realms will never fall. Several weeks into the new Dark Age, life goes on as it always has, oblivious to the passing of the Age of Reason, of Socratic thought and Apollonian logic.

No one had noticed. But they would. And soon.

CHAPTER ONE

Misty Morning, Albert Bridge

It was just before dawn, when the darkness was most oppressive. London was blanketed by an icy, impenetrable, February mist that rolled off the Thames, distorting the gurgle and lap of the water and the first tentative calls of the birds in the trees along the embankment as they sensed the impending sunrise. The hour and atmosphere were unfriendly, but Church was oblivious to both as he wandered, directionless, lost to thoughts that had turned from discomfort to an obsession, and had soured him in the process. If anyone had been there to see his passing, they might have thought him a ghost: tall and slim, with too-pale skin emphasised by the blackness of his hair and a dark expression which added to the air of disquieting sadness which surrounded him. The night-time walks had become increasingly regular over the past two years. During the routines of the day he could lose himself, but when evening fell the memories returned in force, too realistic by far, forcing him out on to the streets in the futile hope he could walk them off, leave them behind. It was as futile as any childhood wish; when he returned home he could never escape her things or her empty space. The conundrum was almost more than he could bear: to recover meant he would have to forget her, but the mystery and confusion made it impossible to forget; it seemed he was condemned to live in that dank, misty world of not-knowing. And until he did know he felt he would not be whole again.

But that night the routine had been different. It wasn't just the memories that had driven him out, but a dream that God had decided His work, the world, had gone irrevocably wrong and He had decided to wipe it away and start again. Inexplicably, it had disturbed Church immeasurably.

There was a clatter of dustbins nearby, some dog scavenging for food. But just to be sure, he paused, tense and alert, until a russet shape padded soundlessly out of the fog. The fox stopped in its tracks when it saw him, eyed him warily for a second, until it seemed to recognise some similar trait, and then continued across the road until it was lost again. Church felt a *frisson* of some barely remembered emotion that he gradually recognised as a sense of wonder. Something wild and untamed in a place shackled by concrete and tarmac, pollution and regulations. Yet after the initial excitement it served only to emphasise the bleak view of the world he had established since Marianne. Perhaps his dream had been right. He had never really been enticed by the modern world. Perhaps that was why he was so drawn to archaeology as a child. But now everything seemed so much worse. If there *was* a God, what would he want with a world where such a vital force as a sense of wonder was so hard to come by? Although most people seemed to hark back to some golden age where things were *felt* so much more vibrantly, it seemed to Church, with his new eyes, that they didn't even seem to have the passion to hate the world they lived in; they were simply bowed by the boredom of it: a place of routine and rules, where daily toil was the most important thing and the only rewards that really counted were the ones that came in currency. There wasn't anything to get excited about any more; nothing to believe in. You couldn't even count on God. Churches of all denominations seemed to be in decline, desperately stripping out the supernatural wonder for some modernist sense of *community* that made them seem like dull Oxfam working parties. But he had no time for God anyway. And that brought him in an ironic full circle: God was preparing to wipe the world clean and God didn't exist.

He snorted a bitter laugh. Away in the mist he could hear the fox's eerie barking howl and for a hopeful second he considered pursuing it to a better place. But he knew in his heart he wasn't nimble enough; his legs felt leaden and there seemed to be an unbearable weight crushing down on his shoulders.

And then all the thoughts of God got him thinking about himself and his miserable life, as if there were any other subject. Was he a good person? Optimistic? Passionate? He had been once, he was sure of it, but that was before Marianne had turned everything on its head. How could one event sour a life so completely?

It wasn't the damp that drew his shiver, but he pulled his overcoat tighter nonetheless. Sometimes he wondered what the future held for him. Two years ago there had been so much hope stitched into the direction he had planned for his life: more articles for the learned magazines, a book, something witty and incisive about the human condition, which also instigated a quiet revolution in archaeological thinking, building on the promise he had shown at Oxford when he had become the first member of his family to attain a degree. At twenty-six, he had known everything about himself. Now, at twenty-eight, he knew nothing. He was flailing around, lost in a strange world where nothing made sense. Any insight he thought he might have had into the human condition had been expunged, and poking about in long-dead things suddenly hadn't seemed as attractive as it had when he'd been the leading light of his archaeology course. It sounded pathetic to consider it in such bald terms, and that made it even more painful. He had never been pathetic. He had been strong, funny, smart, confident. But never pathetic. He had potential, ambitions, dreams, things that he thought were such a vital part of him he would never be able to lose them, yet there he was without any sign of them at all. Where had they all gone?

The only work of which he had felt capable was hack journalism, turning technical manuals into plain English and writing PR copy, bill-paying rather than future-building. And all because of Marianne. Sometimes he wished he could channel his feelings into bitterness, maybe even hate, anything that would allow him to move on, but he just wasn't capable of it. She'd dragged him out of life and left him on a mountaintop, and he felt he would never be able to climb down again.

With a relief that was almost childlike in its intensity, his thoughts were disturbed by a splashing of water which jarred against the sinuous sounds of the river. At first Church thought it might have been a gull at the river's edge, another sign of raw nature intruding on his life, but the intermittent noise suggested something larger. Leaning on the cold, wet wall, he waited patiently for the folds of mist to part as the splashing ebbed and flowed.

For several minutes he couldn't see anything, but as he was about to leave, the mist unfurled in a manner that reminded him of a theatre curtain rolling back. Framed in the white clouds at the river's edge was a hunched black shape, like an enormous crow. As it dipped into the eddies, then rose shakily, Church glimpsed a white, bony hand. An old woman, in a long, black dress and a black shawl, was washing something he couldn't see; it made him think of pictures of peasants in the Middle East doing their laundry in muddy rivers. The strangeness of a woman in the freezing water before dawn didn't strike him at first, which was odd in itself, but the more he watched, the more he started to feel disturbed by the way she dipped and washed, dipped and washed. Finally the jangling in his mind began to turn to panic and he started to pull away from the sight. At that moment the woman stopped her washing and turned, as if she had suddenly sensed his presence. Church glimpsed a terrible face, white and gaunt, and black, piercing eyes, but it was what she held that filled his thoughts as he ran away along the footpath towards Albert Bridge. For the briefest instant it appeared to be a human head, dripping blood from the severed neck into the cold Thames. And it had his face.

Ruth Gallagher had a song in her head that she couldn't quite place; something by The Pogues, she thought. Then she considered the holiday she hoped to take in the South of France that summer, before admiring the pearly luminescence of the mist as it rolled across the surface of the Thames. And when she opened her ears again Clive was still whining irritatedly.

'And another thing, why do you always have to act so superior?'

Clive gesticulated like he was berating a small child. He didn't even look at her; he had been lost in his rant for so long that she was no longer needed in the conversation.

'I don't act superior, I am.' It was the wrong thing to say, but Ruth couldn't resist it. She had to stifle a smile when a sound like a boiler venting steam erupted from his throat. It didn't help that at nearly six foot, she towered above him. Such nastiness wasn't normally in her nature, but he had treated her so badly throughout the evening she felt justified, while still acknowledging the whiff of childishness in her response.

When they had met at the Law Society dinner six weeks earlier, she went into the relationship with the same hope and optimism as always; it wasn't her fault that it hadn't worked out. In fact, after so many previous failed relationships, she had tried especially hard, but Clive was like so many other men she had met in recent times: self-obsessed, nervous of her intellect and wit while professing the opposite, quickly becoming insecure when they realised she wasn't so desperate to hold on to them that she'd kowtow to their every whim and turn a blind eye to their many insufferable qualities. It didn't take her long to see that Clive equated long, dark, curly hair and refined, attractive features with some pre-war view of femininity which he could easily control.

That sort of attitude could have made her blood boil, but the simple truth was she had realised that night that she felt so far removed from him it was hardly worth losing sleep over.

But Clive was just symptomatic of a wider malaise. Nothing in her life seemed fixed down, as she had expected it would be by the time she approached thirty; the job, her great ambition since her father had instilled it in her at thirteen, left her feeling empty and weary, but it was too late to go back and start over; she was ambivalent about London; the best word she could find for her friends and social life was *pleasant*. It was as if she was holding her breath, waiting for something to happen.

She hummed The Pogues' song in her head, trying to recall the chorus, then turned her attention once more to the marvellous way the mist smothered the echoes of their footsteps. Not far to go until she was home, she thought with relief.

'And another thing—'

'If you say that one more time, Clive,' Ruth interjected calmly, 'I'll be forced to perform an emergency tracheotomy on you with my fountain pen.'

Clive threw his arms in the air. 'That's it! I've had enough! You can make your way home alone.'

He spun on his heels and Ruth watched him march off into the fog with his head thrust down like some spurned, spoiled child. 'The perfect gentleman,' she muttered ironically.

As his footsteps faded away, Ruth became acutely aware of the stifling silence. She wished she'd left the club earlier, or at least countermanded Clive's order for the cab to pull over so they could have a 'quiet chat' as they walked the last few hundred yards to her flat. London wasn't a safe place for a woman alone. Her heels click-clacked on the slick pavement as she speeded up a little. The rhythm was soothing in the unnerving quiet, but as she approached Albert Bridge other sounds broke through: scuffles, gasps, the smack of flesh on flesh.

Ruth paused. Her every instinct told her to hurry home, but if someone was in trouble she knew her conscience wouldn't allow her to ignore it. She was spurred into life by a brief cry, quickly strangled, that seemed to come from the river's edge in the lonely darkness beneath the bridge. Two itinerants fighting over the remnants of a cheap bottle of wine, she supposed, but she had seen too many police reports to know the other possibilities were both many and disturbing. She located the steps to the river and moved cautiously down until the mist had swallowed up the street lights behind her.

When he heard the same struggle, Church's heartrate had just about returned to normal, but his nerves still jangled alarmingly. The image of the woman's terrible face wouldn't go, but he had almost managed to convince himself he had been mistaken in his view of what she was holding. Just a bundle of dirty clothes, a trick of the light and the fog. That was all.

He had been approaching Albert Bridge from the opposite direction to Ruth when the scuffling sounds provided a welcome distraction. Negotiating the treacherously slick steps down to the river, he found himself on a rough stone path that ran next to the slim, muddy beach at the water's edge, where an oppressive smell of rotting vegetation filled the dank air. A slight change in the quality of light signalled that somewhere above the mist, dawn was finally beginning to break, but the gloom beneath the bridge was impenetrable.

With only the soothing lapping of the Thames around him, he wondered if he had misheard the source of the fight. He paused, listening intently, and then a muffled cry broke and was instantly stifled. Cautiously he advanced towards the dark.

Keeping close to the wall so he wouldn't be seen, odd sounds gradually emerged: heavy boots on stones, a grunt, a choke. Finally, at the edge of the darkness, his eyes adjusted enough to see what lay beneath the bridge.

A giant of a man with his back to Church grasped a smaller man by the lapels. The victim looked mousily weak, with tiny, wire-framed spectacles on a grey face, his frame slight beneath a dark suit. There was a briefcase lying on the ground nearby.

The taller man, who must have been at least 7ft 6ins tall, turned suddenly, although Church was sure he hadn't made a sound. The giant had a bald head and long, animalistic features contorted by a snarl of rage. In the shadows, his pale, hooded eyes seemed to glow with a cold, grey fire. Church shivered unconsciously at the aura of menace that washed off him in a black wave.

'Put him down.'

Church started at the female voice. A woman with long dark hair and a beautiful, pale face was standing on the other side of the bridge, framed against the background of milky mist.

The tall man's breath erupted in a plume of white as it hit the cold; there was a sound like a horse snorting. He looked slowly from Church to the woman and back, effortlessly holding his victim like a rag doll, his gaze heavy and hateful. Church felt his heart begin to pound again; something in the scene was frightening beyond reason.

'If you don't put him down, I'm going for the police,' the woman continued in a calm, firm voice.

For a moment Church thought the victim was dead, but then his head lolled and he muttered something deliriously. There was contempt in the attacker's face as he glanced once more at Church and the woman, and then he hauled the smaller man off the ground with unnatural ease. Transferring his left hand to his victim's chin, he braced himself, ready to snap the neck.

'Don't!' Church yelled, moving forward.

In that instant, for no reason he could pinpoint, Church felt fear explode in every fibre of his being. The giant glared at him and Church had the disorienting sensation that the mugger's face was shifting like oil poured on water. He flashed back to the old woman at the water and what she was holding, and then his thoughts devolved into an incomprehensible jumble. His brain desperately tried to comprehend the retinal image of the giant's face becoming something else, and for a moment he almost grasped it, but the merest touch of the sight was like staring into the heart of the sun. His mind flared white, then shut down in shock, and he slumped to the ground unconscious.

Dawn had finally come when Church woke to the sensation of hands pulling him into a sitting position. There was a spinning moment of horror when he thought he was still staring at the changing face, and then he became dimly aware of the dampness of his clothes from the wet ground and a flurry of movement and sound around him. He grappled for some kind of understanding, but there was a yawning hole in his memory from the moment of his collapse, as raw as if he had been slashed with a razor.

'Are you okay?' A paramedic crouched in front of him, shining a light into his eyes. When the flare cleared, Church saw uniformed police and what were obviously plain-clothes detectives hovering near the river's edge.

Church remembered the mugger and his victim and suddenly lurched forward. The paramedic held him back with a steady hand. 'Did you see what happened?' he asked.

Church struggled for the words. 'Some kind of fight. Then . . .' He glanced around him curiously. 'I suppose I fainted. Pathetic, isn't it?'

The paramedic nodded. 'She said the same thing.'

Nearby was the woman Church had seen earlier. A blanket was draped around her shoulders; a medic checked her over while a detective tried to make sense of her replies. As Church watched, she looked up at him. In the second when their eyes met, Church had a sudden sensation of connection that went beyond the shared experience: a recognition of a similar soul. It was so intimate that it made him uncomfortable, and he looked away.

'Do you feel up to a few questions, sir?' The detective offered a hand and Church allowed himself to be hauled to his feet. The CID man seemed unnaturally calm for the activity going on around them, but there was an intensity in his eyes that was disturbing. As they headed towards the water's edge, Church saw the body in the glare of a camera flash; the neck had been broken.

'How long was I out?' Church asked.

The detective shrugged. 'Can't have been long. Some postman on his bike heard the commotion and we had a car here within five minutes of his call. What did you see?'

11

Church described hearing the noise of the fight and then seeing the tall man mugging his victim. The detective eyed him askance, a hint of suspicion in his face. 'And then he attacked you?'

Church shook his head. 'I don't think so.'

'So what happened to you and the young lady?'

There was an insectile skittering deep in his head as he fought to recall what he had seen; he was almost relieved when the memory refused to surface. 'I was tired, the ground looked so comforting . . .' The detective gave him the cold eye. 'How should I know?' Church looked round for a way to change the subject. 'Where's his briefcase?'

'We didn't find one.' The detective scribbled a line in his notebook and seemed brighter, as if the disappearance of the briefcase explained everything; a simple mugging after all.

Church spent the next hour at the station, growing increasingly disturbed as he futilely struggled to express his fears in some form the police could understand. In reception, he bumped into his fellow witness, whose expression suggested she had had a similar experience.

'Look, can we go and grab a coffee? I need to talk about this,' she said without any preamble. She ran her fingers through her hair, then lightened. 'Sorry. Ruth Gallagher.' She stuck out a hand.

Church took it; her grip was strong and confident. 'Jack Churchill. Church. They weren't having any of it, were they?'

Ruth sighed wearily. 'No surprise there. I'm a solicitor, in court every day. I found out pretty early on that once the police have discovered the most simplistic idea out there, they're like a dog with a bone. If they want to file this under M for Mugging, by God they're going to, and nothing I'm going to say will change their minds.'

'A mugging. Right. And JFK got roughed up that day in Dallas.' Church watched her features intently, trying to discern her true thoughts.

She looked away uncomfortably, disorientation and worry reflected in her face.

There was an intensity about her that Church found impossible to resist. They went to a little place on St John's Hill at Clapham Junction, filled with hissing steam from the cappuccino machine, the sizzle of frying food and the hubbub of local workers taking an early breakfast. They sat opposite each other at a table in the window and within seconds all the noise had faded into the background.

Sipping her coffee hesitantly, Ruth began. 'What did we see?'

Church chewed on his lip, trying to find the words that would tie down the errant memory. 'It seemed to me that his face began to change.'

'Impossible, of course,' Ruth said unconvincingly. 'So there has to be a rational explanation.'

'For a changing face?'

'A mask?'

'Did it look like a mask to you?' He tapped his spoon in his saucer. The merest attempt at recollection made him uncomfortable. 'This is what I saw: a man, much bigger than average, picked up someone with a strength he shouldn't have had, even at that size. Then he turned to us and his features started to flow away like they were melting. And what lay beneath—' He swallowed. '—I have no idea.'

'And then we both went out at exactly the same time.'

'Because of what we saw next.'

Ruth gave an uncomfortable smile. 'I'm not the kind of person who has hallucinations in a moment of tension.'

Church glanced out of the window, as if an answer would somehow present itself to him, but all he could see was a tramp on the opposite side of the road watching them intently. There was something about the unflinching stare that disturbed him. He turned back to his coffee and when he looked again the tramp was gone.

'This whole business is making me paranoid,' he said. 'Maybe we should leave it at that. We're not going to discover what happened. Just put it down to one of those inexplicable things that happen in life.'

'How can you say that?' Ruth exclaimed. 'This was real! We were right at the heart of it. We can't just dismiss it.' She leaned forward with such passion Church thought she was going to grab his jacket. 'You must have some intellectual curiosity.'

'I find it difficult to get curious about anything these days.' There was a hint of surgical dissection in the way she eyed him; he almost felt his ego unpeeling.

'At least give me your number in case one of us remembers any more details,' she said. It was too firm to be a request. Church scribbled the digits on a paper serviette and then took Ruth's business card for her practice in Lincoln's Inn Fields with her home number on the back.

As he rose, she said, in a quiet voice that demanded reassurance, 'Were you frightened?'

He smiled falsely, said nothing.

The days passed bleakly. Winter receded a little more, but there was still an uncomfortable chill in the air that even the suffocating central heating of Church's flat seemed unable to dispel. Once spring was just around the corner, he always used to feel an urge to get his hands dirty in some dig or other, grubbing around for flaking bits of pottery or corroded nails which used to instil in some people a depression for the fleeting nature of life, but always filled him with a profound sense of the strength of humanity. At that moment, as he dredged deeply for any remaining vestige of enthusiasm to help him complete a manual for spreadsheet software, the feeling seemed further away than ever. It was compounded by a terrible uneasiness brought on by what he now called *that night*; whatever secret his mind held pressed at the back of his head like a tumour, sometimes feeling so malign it unleashed a black depression of such strength he found himself considering suicide, a feeling he had never countenanced before, even in the worst days after Marianne had left.

Dale, one of his few friends from before (he always saw his life as two distinct units, Before Marianne and After Marianne), was so shocked by his latest state of mind he almost attempted to pressgang Church into getting some kind of medical help. After a wearying struggle, Church had convinced him it was simply a passing phase, while secretly knowing neither Prozac nor EST could put him back on the road to wellbeing. The only option was to lance the boil, unleash the memory, and how could he do that when it was so unbearable in the first place?

'You've got to start getting out, you know.' Dale, always the most irresponsible of his friends, suddenly sounded like some geriatric relative. Church, seeing how he was infecting others, winced with guilt.

'It's not as simple as that.'

'I know it's not as simple as that. I'm not stupid,' Dale bristled. He swigged from his beer bottle, then suddenly flicked it in a loop in the air and caught it without spilling a drop. 'Hey! That was good, wasn't it?'

'Marvellous.'

'Okay. This weekend. We get a bootful of cans and take off for Brighton. Drink them all under the pier, a few burgers, a mountain of candy floss, then off to the pleasure beach and see who's first to vomit on the rides. You know it has to be done.'

Church smiled wanly; two years ago he would never have guessed Dale would have been the one to stick around. 'It's a good idea, but I've got too much work on. Financial planning software, for my sins. It's got to be in by Monday.'

Dale said, resignedly, 'You remember the time you cancelled your holiday in Cyprus and bundled us all into the car for a week in Devon to cheer up Louise after her dad died? That was spontaneous fun.'

Church shrugged. 'Cyprus would have been too hot that time of year, anyway.'

'You don't fool me. You'd been planning for that holiday for months. Years probably, knowing you. And you gave it up in an instant.'

14

'I'm so selfless,' Church said sarcastically. He caught Dale examining him as if searching for the person he remembered. 'Of course, I've still got the photo of you at that gig we drove up to in Oxford.'

Dale blanched. 'Not the one where I lost my trousers when I was stage-diving?'

'Boxers too. Jesus, that was a horrible sight.'

'I was expecting you to catch me, not take photos!' Dale said indignantly. 'If I ever find out who pulled my keks down—'

'Serves you right for stage-diving. The rest of us were respectfully enjoying the music,' Church mocked.

'Yeah, you were a real muso, weren't you? You were like the bleedin' HMV computer. Name a CD and you'd list every track on it. And you could play the guitar *and* the drums. Bloody show-off.'

'You know you needed me. I provided the intellectual conversation while the rest of you were drinking your own weight in alcohol.'

Dale chuckled at the memories. 'We had some laughs too, right? You, me, Pete, Kate, Louise, Billy . . .'

And Marianne.

'That was a long time ago,' Church said.

Dale visibly winced at his *faux pas*. 'Listen to me. I sound like some old git reminiscing about the war.' His voice trailed off, and he looked Church in the eye a little uncomfortably. 'We can't keep talking around it, you know.'

'I'm okay,' Church protested. Here it was, as he feared, coming up on him from his blindside. 'I'm not some sap mooning around who can't accept his girlfriend's gone. It's been two years!'

'Bollocks. We both know it's not about the fact she's not here. It's the *way* it happened. And what you saw. That would be enough to screw anybody up.'

'Are you saying I'm screwed up?'

'Are you telling me you're not?' Dale dropped his bottle and the contents flooded out. 'Shit. Now look what you've made me do.'

'Forget it.'

Dale scrubbed the beer into the carpet with his boot. 'You shouldn't tear yourself apart. It wasn't your fault, you know.'

'You think she'd have gone like that for no reason? Of course it was my fault.'

'Listen, you're a good bloke. I'll never repeat this in company, but you're probably the most decent bloke I've ever met.' He paused thoughtfully. 'I know about your doctorate, you know.'

'What are you talking about?' Church looked away.

'Billy's a screw-up – he always was. But you gave him that money

15

you'd been working round the clock for a year to save so you could go back and get that qualification you'd been dreaming about ever since you were a kid. Don't deny it, Church – he told me, even though you tried to keep it a secret. I know your family never had much and you had to get a job to send some cash back to them. And then you saved Billy from all that disgrace and now look at him – the fattest of fat-cat accountants in the West End. Thanks to you. And all it cost you was your life's dream – to be a doctor of digging-up-crap. Not much to anybody else, but I know how much it meant to you. So don't go beating yourself up thinking you're some little shit because of Marianne.'

Church shook his head dismissively. Dale didn't understand – how could he?

'I'm only saying these things because I'm a mate.' Dale was on a roll now; Church recognised the gleam in his eye. 'I remember what you used to be like. You used to enjoy yourself, all the time, even when the rest of us were miserable and it was pissing down with rain and some club wouldn't let us in because Billy was dressed like a stiff again. When Louise and Pete had one of their irritating arguments, you'd always find something positive to get them back together. You used to read more books and see more films and hear more music than anybody I knew. And now—'

'I don't.'

'Exactly. Now you don't do anything. You've lost all focus. What's done is done. You've got to start living again.'

Church made some concilatory sounds, but it didn't convince Dale; he'd heard it all before. In the end he departed in irritation, but Church knew he'd be back to try again. He was good like that. But Dale couldn't be expected to understand the depth of the problem, how many futile hours had been spent looking at it from every angle; if there was an easy solution he would have found it long ago. The worst thing was he felt so bad about how he'd made Dale feel over the months, he couldn't bring himself to talk about the experience under Albert Bridge.

For the rest of the evening he kept flashing back to the moment before he fainted that night, interspersed with too many memories of Marianne: on the banks of Loch Ness, at her birthday in Covent Garden, the Sunday morning she brought him a champagne breakfast in bed for no reason apart from the fact that she loved him. Finally sleep crept up on him.

'Ruth. My office. Now!'

Ruth dropped the pile of files at Milton's barked order and then cursed under her breath as she scrambled to collect them. What was wrong with her? She wasn't the nervous type, but since that morning by the river she had been permanently on edge, jumping at shadows, snapping at colleagues. Her work had always been the calm centre of her life where she could do no wrong, but now it seemed dangerously askew.

Dumping the files on her desk, she marched into Milton's glass-walled office, sensing the atmosphere before she had crossed the threshold. The senior partner glowered behind his desk.

'Close the door,' he growled, his repressed anger bringing out his Highland brogue. That was always a bad sign. Ruth waited for the fireworks.

'What's wrong with you, Ruth?' he asked. 'Is it drugs? Drink?'

'I don't know what you mean, Ben.'

He tapped a letter that was placed precisely in the centre of his blotter. 'Sir Anthony is absolutely livid. He says you hung up on him yesterday.'

'It was an accident,' she lied. She'd always been able to cope with the peer's toffee-nosed pomposity and condescension, but, for some reason, yesterday she'd had enough. She knew at the time she should have called him back, but she couldn't bear to listen to any more of his bluster.

'He's our top client, for God's sake! Do you know how much money he brings into this firm? And he was *your* client because you were the best and you could be trusted.'

Ruth didn't like the sound of the past tense. 'It won't happen again, Ben.'

'It's not the only thing, Ruth. Not by a long shot.' He angrily flicked open a thin file. 'During the last two weeks you've overcharged three clients, undercharged two. Your brief to the barrister in the Mendeka case was so incompetent it's possibly actionable. You were so late in court on Friday the case had to be rescheduled. Two weeks for at least three sackable offences. Jesus Christ, what kind of a firm do you think this is?' Her ears burned. 'To be honest, I don't want to know what's wrong,' he continued. 'I just want it sorted out. Anybody else would have been out on their ear by now, but your past record has been exemplary, Ruth. I hope you've not simply become aware of that and you're resting on your laurels.'

'No, Ben—'

'—Because even our best man can't go about pissing off the clients who make this a premier league firm thanks to their patronage and their money. At your best you're still an asset to us. I want you to find out where that best has gone.'

'Ben?'

'You've got some time off, unpaid of course. The next time you're here I want it to be the old Ruth.'

He lowered his attention to the paper on the desk in a manner that was both irritating and insulting. Ruth had never liked him, but at that moment she wanted to grab him by the lapels and punch him in the face. The only thing that stopped her was that every word had been true.

In the toilet, she blinked away tears of frustration and rage and kicked the cubicle door so hard it almost burst off its hinges; her hatred for the job made her feel even worse. It had never been what she wanted to do, but her father had been so keen she hadn't been able to refuse him. But that wasn't the real cause of her sudden bout of incompetence; it was the scurrying, black lizard-thing that had taken up residence in her head.

For the first time she had an inkling how the victims of abuse suffered in later life from the hideous repressed memories that manipulated their subconscious. Whatever had truly happened that early morning beneath Albert Bridge had turned her into a different person: depressive, anxious, underconfident, hesitant, pathetic.

She put her hands over her eyes and tried to hold the emotions back.

Church was spending too long surfing the web and he knew his phone bill would be horrendous, but there was something almost soothing in the crashing waves of information. It was zen mediation for the new age; every time he felt an independent thought enter his head he would click on the hotlink and jump to a new site with new images and words to hypnotise him. He had been around a score of different subjects – cult TV, music, new science, even delving into some of the archaeology sites, but somehow he had found himself at www.forteantimes.com – and everything had gone horribly wrong.

He knew vaguely of the magazine the website represented. The journal of strange phenomena, *Fortean Times* it called itself, an erudite publication which examined every odd happening, from crop circles and UFOs to contemporary folklore, bizarre deaths to crazy coincidences, with a ready wit and a sharp intellect. He always flicked through copies in Smiths, but he'd never gone so far as buying one.

On the lead page was a brief story:

In the last few weeks the world has gone totally weird! As you know, we continually compile all reports of strange phenomena from around the globe for an annual index to show if the world is getting weirder. Since Christmas the number of reports has increased twentyfold. Postings on the Fortean news-group {alt.misc.forteana} indicate an astonishing increase in all categories, from electronic voice phenomena and hauntings via amazing cryptozoological sightings to UFOs and accounts of more big cats in the wilderness. What's going on!?!

Church went through the report twice, feeling increasingly unnerved for reasons he couldn't explain. Briefly he considered how he should have read it – as cranky but fun – but it sparked disturbing connections in his mind. He clicked on the hotlink to Usenet. When alt.misc.forteana appeared, he scrolled slowly through the postings. In Nottingham, a sound engineer for Central TV had recorded strange giggling voices when his microphone should have been picking up white noise from a radio. A rain of fish had fallen on Struy in the Scottish Highlands. Mysterious lights had been seen moving slowly far beneath the surface of Ennerdale Water in the Lake District. A postmistress from Norwich wrote passionately about a conversation with her dead father late one evening. Unconnected incidents, but as he worked his way down the neverending list of messages he was staggered by the breathtaking diversity of unbelievable things happening around the country, to people from all walks of life, in all areas. The accounts were heartfelt, which made them even more disturbing. It put his own odd experience into some kind of context.

One posting leapt out at him from LauraDuS@legion.com. It said simply:

All this is linked. And I have proof.
Email me if you want to know more.

He vacillated for a moment or two, then rattled off a quick reply requesting more information.

Further down the list there was a message from one of the *Fortean Times* editors, Bob Rickard, talking in general terms about the magazine's philosophy. With a certain apprehension, Church typed out the details of his experience at Albert Bridge and sent it off for Rickard's views. Then he returned to the list and immersed himself in the tidal wave of weirdness.

With bleary eyes and a dry mouth, he eventually came offline at 1 a.m. feeling an odd mixture of excitement, agitation, concern, and curiosity that left his head spinning. It was a pleasure to feel anything after two years of hermetically sealed life.

Away from the computer, he became aware once again of the hidden memory's horrible presence at the back of his head; his mood dampened instantly and he knew there would be no relief for him until that desperate event was put into some kind of perspective. He was so lost in his introspection that at first he didn't notice the figure outside as he began to draw the curtains. But a passing car disturbed him and within seconds he had grown rigid and cold. From his first-floor vantage point, the figure was half-hidden by the overhanging branches of the tree across the road, but the subtle way the body was held was as unmistakable to him as his own reflection.

And a second later he was running through the flat and down the stairs, feeling the first tremors of shock ripple through his body, wincing as the cold night air froze the sweat that seemed to be seeping from every pore. Desperation and disbelief propelled him out into the road, but the figure was gone, and although he went a hundred yards in both directions, there was no sign of the person who had been watching his window. Finally he sagged to his knees at the front gate and held his head, wondering if he had gone insane, feeling his thoughts stumble out of control. There were tears where he thought he had exhausted the well. It had been Marianne, as surely as the sun came up at dawn.

And Marianne had been dead for two years.

CHAPTER TWO

Different Views from the Same Window

Inactivity did not sit well with Ruth and it seemed only right that her enforced absence from work should be put to good use. Although she knew the buried trauma of Albert Bridge was responsible for her day-time confusions, black moods and constantly disturbed nights, she was determined she would not be paralysed by it; practicality was one of the strengths which had seen her rise so rapidly in the firm.

No one had been arrested for the Albert Bridge murder, although photofits based on Ruth and Church's descriptions had been given wide circulation throughout the media; the suspect had appeared so grotesque that Ruth found it hard to believe he hadn't been picked up within hours. Yet the investigation had drawn repeated blanks and as the days turned to weeks it became increasingly apparent it wasn't going anywhere. One advantage of Ruth's position with Cooper, Sedgwick & Tides was her direct access to the Met, where she found plenty of contacts who weren't averse to allowing her a glimpse into a restricted file or digging up some particular snippet of information. So it was relatively easy to find herself that morning in an empty room, bare apart from a rickety table, with the murder file.

The victim was a low-grade Ministry of Defence civil servant named Maurice Gibbons, a fact which had at first raised suspicion of some shadier motive beyond a simple mugging. When it became apparent the only secrets Gibbons had access to centred on the acquisition of furniture for MoD property, all conspiracy scenarios were quickly discarded. He was forty-eight and lived with his wife in Crouch End; both their children had left home. The only gap in the information was exactly what he was doing at Albert Bridge at that time of night. He had told his wife he was calling in at his local for a pint and she had gone to bed early, not realising he hadn't returned home. She didn't remember him leaving with his briefcase, although it was possible he had picked it up from the hall on the way out; why he had felt the need to take a briefcase to the pub was not discussed. And that was about it. He had no enemies; everything pointed to a random killing. Ruth jotted down Gibbons' address, phone number and his wife's name and slipped out, pausing to flash a thankful smile at the detective lounging by the coffee machine.

While there could be a completely reasonable explanation for his appearance at Albert Bridge – an illicit liaison, hetero or homo – to ignore it wasn't the correct way to conduct an investigation. Ruth knew she would have to interview the wife.

Her decision to take action had raised her mood slightly, but it seemed morbidity and depression were still waiting at the flat door, emotions so unnatural to her she had no idea how to cope. Bitterly, she set off for the kitchen to make a strong coffee in the hope that a shock of caffeine would sluice it from her system. As she passed the answer machine, the red light was flashing and she flicked it to play.

It was Church. 'We need to talk,' he said.

They met in the Nag's Head pub in Covent Garden just before the lunchtime rush. Church had a pint of Winter Warmer and Ruth a mineral water, which they took to a table at the back where they wouldn't be disturbed. Church felt in turmoil; he had barely slept since the shock of seeing – or thinking he had seen – Marianne outside the flat. He had tried to convince himself it was a hallucination brought on by all the turbulence in his subconscious, but it added to the queasy unreality that had infected his life. It had had one good effect, though: it had shocked him so severely that he could no longer passively accept what had happened to him.

'I didn't think I'd be hearing from you again. The last time we spoke you didn't sound too enthusiastic about opening this can of worms any further,' Ruth said.

'You can only bury your head in the sand for so long. That is, if it's been affecting you the same way it's affected me,' Church began cautiously. He tapped the side of his head. 'I can't remember a thing about what happened, but my subconscious can see it in full, glorious Technicolor, and that little bastard at the back of my head won't let me rest until I sort it out.' Ruth nodded. 'So,' he added, almost dismissively, 'what I'm saying is, you were right.'

'I do love to hear people say that.' Ruth appraised Church carefully behind her smile. She instinctively felt he was a man she could trust; more than that, she felt he was someone she could actually like, although she couldn't put her finger on exactly what it was that attracted her. There was an intensity about him that hinted at great depths, but an intriguing darkness too. 'So what do you suggest?'

Church took out a folded printout of the email he had received from Bob Rickard, the *Fortean Times* editor. 'I made a few enquiries online about what options are available for people with repressed memories.'

'This happens all the time, does it?'

'You'd be surprised. Apparently, it's *de rigueur* if you've been abducted by aliens. You thought that aching rectum was just haemorrhoids? Here's how you find out you've really had a nocturnal anal probe. Regression hypnosis. To be honest, the expert I contacted wasn't, let's say, *enthusiastic* about its effectiveness. Some people think it can screw you up even more. There's something called False Memory Syndrome where your memory's been polluted by stuff that's leaked in from your imagination, things you've read, other memories, so your mind actually creates a fantasy that it believes is real. The Royal College of Psychiatrists has banned its members from using any hypnotic method to recover memories, so this guy says. But then there're a whole bunch of other experts who claim it does work.'

'And the alternative?'

'Years, maybe decades, of therapy.'

Ruth sighed. 'I'm not too sure I'm comfortable with someone stomping around with hobnail boots in the depths of my mind.'

'So we'd only do it if we were desperate, right?' Church's statement hung in the air for a moment before he turned over the printout to reveal several scrawled names and numbers. 'I've got a list of qualified people here.'

Ruth closed her eyes and jabbed her finger down at random. 'They say a leap of faith can cause miracles.'

'Don't go getting all religious on me,' Church said as he circled the name. 'I have enough trouble sleeping as it is. The last thing I need is you telling me it was the Devil we saw.'

The appointment was fixed for three days hence. As the time grew closer, Church and Ruth found themselves growing increasingly anxious, as if whatever lay deep in their heads sensed its imminent removal and fought to stay in the comforting dark. Church received his first email from LauraDuS@legion.com. She was Laura DuSantiago, a software designer at a computer games company in Bristol. She didn't actually say how the strange phenomena were connected, but she dropped some broad hints of a personal experience which had given her a unique insight. The ever more disturbing aspects of his own life had left Church oddly intrigued by what she had to say and he fired back an email straight away.

The day was bleakly cold, with depressing sheets of rain sweeping along Kensington High Street as Church and Ruth made their way west from the tube. There was no hint of spring around the corner. The street scene was a muddy mess of browns and greys, with the occasional red plastic sign adding a garish dash of colour. A heavy smog of car fumes had been dampened down to pavement level by the continuous downpour.

'When you're a kid the world never looks like this. What happened to all the magic?' Church said as they negotiated the honking, steaming traffic which was backed up in both directions for no apparent reason.

'Didn't they pass a law or something? It was putting the workers off their toil.' Ruth led them to shelter in W.H. Smiths' doorway for a while in the hope that the cloudburst would blow over, but their anxiety to reach the therapist's office soon drove them out again with Ruth holding a copy of *Marie Claire* over her head.

Their destination lay up a side road just off the High Street. They buzzed the entryphone and dashed in out of the rain. 'The pubs are open now,' Church suggested. Ruth smiled wanly; for a second she almost turned back.

The reception smelled of new carpets and polished furniture. It was functional and blandly decorated, with a blonde Sloane smiling behind a low desk. Stephen Delano, the therapist, stepped out of the back room the moment they entered, as if they had tripped some silent alarm. He was in his forties, with light brown hair that had been blow-dried back from a high forehead and a smile that wasn't exactly insincere, but which made Church uneasy nonetheless. He strode over and shook their hands forcefully.

'Good to see you. Come on through.' He led them into the rear office which was dark, warm and filled with several deep, comfortable chairs. The blinds were down and it was lit ambiently by a couple of small, well-placed lamps. Several pieces of recording equipment were sitting near the chairs. 'Welcome to the womb,' Delano said. 'I think you'll feel comfortable and secure here. You need to feel at ease.'

Ruth slipped into one of the chairs, put her head back and closed her eyes. 'Wake me when it's over.'

'You're absolutely sure you want to go through this together?' Delano continued. 'I think it would be more effective to do it separately, if only to prevent what one is saying influencing the other. This isn't like surgery. Memories are delicate, easily corrupted by outside sources.'

'We do it together,' Church said firmly. When they had discussed it earlier, they both instinctively felt it was something they could only face up to together.

'Well, you're the bosses.' Delano clapped his hands, then ushered Church into a chair next to Ruth's and manoeuvred a reel-to-reel recorder between them. 'So we have a good record of what you say,' he explained. 'I can transfer it to a cassette for you to take away, and I'll store the master here.'

After a brief explanation of the principle, he dimmed the lights even further with a hand-held remote control. Church expected to feel sleepy in the gloomy warmth, but the anxiety had set an uncomfortable resonance which seemed to be buzzing around his body. He turned to look at Ruth, her face pale in the dark. She smiled at him, but the unease was apparent in her eyes. Delano pulled up a chair opposite and began to talk in measured tones that were so low Church occasionally had trouble hearing him. After a minute or two, the words were rolling in and out of his consciousness like distant thunder and he was suspended in time.

For what could have been one minute or ten, the sensation was pleasurable, but then Church began to get an odd feeling of disquiet. On a level he couldn't quite grasp, he was sensing they were not alone in the room. He wanted to shout out a warning to Ruth and Delano, but his mouth wouldn't respond, nor would his neck muscles when he tried to turn his head so he could look around. He was convinced there was a presence somewhere in the shadows in the corner of the room, malign, watching them balefully, waiting for the right moment to make its move. When the sensation faded a moment later, Church convinced himself it was just a by-product of Delano's hypnosis, but it didn't go away completely.

'It is the morning of February 7,' Delano intoned calmly. 'Where are you, Jack?'

Church found himself talking even though he wasn't consciously aware of moving his mouth. 'I can't sleep. I've gone out for a walk to wear myself out so I'll drop off quickly. I have bad dreams.' He swallowed; his throat felt like it was closing up. 'It's foggy, a real pea-souper. I've never seen it like that before, like something out of Dickens. I see a woman washing something in the river . . .' A spasm convulsed him. 'No . . .'

'It's okay, Jack. You rest a moment,' Delano said quickly. 'Ruth, where are you?'

Ruth's chest grew tighter; she sucked in a deep breath until her lungs burned. 'I've been to The Fridge. Clive is whining on. He realises we've got nothing in common.' Her voice turned spontaneously singsong: ' "Why don't you do this? Why don't you do that?" He doesn't really want me, just the woman he thinks I am. He gets wound up . . . blows his top . . . walks off. I'm a bit frightened – it's so quiet, so still – but I try not to show it. I can make it home in a few minutes if I walk quickly. Then I hear the sound of . . . a fight? . . . coming from under the bridge.' Her breath became more laboured. She wondered obliquely if she was having a heart attack.

'Jack, do you hear the fight now?' Delano's voice seemed to be floating away from both of them.

'Yes. I was frightened by the old woman, but when I hear them fighting I forget her. I could walk on . . . ignore it . . . but that's not right. I've got to try to help. Somebody might be in trouble.'

'Are you afraid for yourself?'

'A little. But if I could do something to help I've got to try. Too many people walk by. I find the steps down to the river. They're wet . . . I go down slowly. There're more scuffling noises. A grunt. I wonder if there's an animal down there. Maybe a dog or . . . something. I can smell the river. Everywhere's so damp. My heart's beating so loud. I edge along the wall.' Another spasm. He thought he almost saw something; was it in the room or in his head?

'Take a rest, Jack. Ruth?'

'I go down the steps. I'm ready to run at any moment, but I'm aware I've got heels on. If the worst comes to the worst I'll have to kick them off. They're expensive though . . . I don't want to lose them. It's dark under the bridge. I can't see anything. I move closer. I think I've bitten my lip . . . I can taste blood.' She heaved in another juddering breath; each one was getting harder and harder. 'There're two men. They just look like shadows at first. One of them's big, the biggest man I've ever seen. He's shaking the smaller one. I look over and there's another man there watching the fight. I can see he's come from the other side. I'm relieved . . . I'm not alone.'

'Is it Jack?' Delano asked quietly.

'Yes, yes, it's Church. He's got a strong face. He looks decent. He makes me feel safer. We both look at the two men—'

'Is he dead?' Church suddenly interjected, his voice too loud. 'Christ, I think he's dead! No . . . he's moving. But the giant's picking him up. How can he be so strong? Just one arm . . . what's going on? . . . he's going to break his neck!'

'Calm down,' Delano hushed.

'Don't do it or I'm going to call the police!' Ruth yelled. She snapped forward in her seat, then slumped back.

'Take it easy now,' Delano said soothingly. 'Be peacef—'

'Stop!' Church thrashed to one side. Delano placed a comforting hand on Church's forearm, but Church knocked it away wildly.

'He's looking—' Ruth was wheezing, but she couldn't seem to draw any breath into her lungs.

'—at us!' Church continued.

Delano was alarmed at the paleness of her face. 'I think that's enough now,' he began. 'It's time to take a break. We can come back to this.'

'My God! Look at—' Church gasped.

'—his face! It's changing—'

'—melting—'

They were convulsing in their seats. Delano grabbed both their wrists, gripped by anxiety that he was losing control; they were all losing control. He stood up so he could place his head between them. 'On the count of three . . .'

'Not human!'

'His eyes—'

'—red—'

'—a demon!' Ruth gasped. 'Twisted . . . monstrous . . .' She leaned to one side and vomited on to the carpet.

'One . . .'

'Evil!' Jack cried. 'I feel evil coming off it! It's looking at me!'

'Two . . .'

Ruth vomited again, then stumbled off the chair to her knees.

'I can't bear to look at its face!'

'Three . . .'

For a second, Delano was terrified he wouldn't be able to bring them out of it, but gradually they seemed to come together, as if he were watching them swim up from deep water. Church bobbed forward and put his face in his hands. He felt like he was burning up, his hair slick with sweat. Ruth levered herself back into the chair and sat there with her eyes shut.

Delano was visibly shaken. There was sweat on his own brow and his hands were trembling as he switched off the tape recorder. Frantically he thumbed the remote control until the light flared up too bright and drove the shadows from the room. 'Well that was an unusual experience,' he mumbled bathetically. He fetched them both water, which they sipped in silence. Then called in his assistant to clean up the carpet. It was a full ten minutes until they had recovered.

'That was unbelievable,' Church said eventually. His voice was like sandpaper in the arid stillness of the room.

'You're right,' Ruth responded, 'because it's not true.'

'What do you mean?' Church eyed her curiously. 'We saw the same thing.'

Ruth shook her head emphatically. 'Think about it, Church. There must be a rational explanation. We have to use a little intellectual rigour here – the first answer isn't always the right one. We were talking about how memories can be corrupted by other aspects of the mind's working. That can happen, can't it?' she said to Delano. He nodded. 'Remember in the pub you made some throwaway comment about us seeing the Devil, so that's exactly what we did see. You placed that thought in both our heads and our subconscious turned it into reality. It was self-fulfilling.' She looked to Delano for support.

'Your reactions were very extreme, which suggests a serious trauma buried away, but if you witnessed a particularly brutal murder, as you told me on the phone, that would explain it,' the therapist said. 'What you recalled today is known as a screen memory. You create it yourself to protect your own mind from further trauma. Yes, it was quite horrible, but the unbelievable elements allow you to dismiss it within the context of reality as you perceive it so it's not as threatening as it first appears. The *true* memory that lies beneath is much more of a threat to you. I think we'll need a few more sessions to get to it, to be honest.' Delano's smile suggested he was relieved by his own explanation. 'I must admit, I was a little worried. I've never come across anything quite like that before.'

Church wasn't convinced. 'It was pretty real.'

'Sorry about the carpet,' Ruth said sheepishly. Church thought she was going to burst into a fit of embarrassed giggles.

'Don't worry,' Delano said. 'Let me just check the recording and I'll make arrangements to get your cassette copy.'

He knelt down and rewound the tape. When he pressed play there was a blast of white noise and what sounded like an ear-splitting shriek of hysterical laughter. Delano's brow furrowed. He ran the tape forward a little and tried again. The white noise hissed from the speakers. A second later the giggling started, fading in and out as if it was a badly tuned radio signal, the laughter growing louder and louder until Church's ears hurt; it made him feel sick and uncomfortable. Delano snapped off the recorder in dismay.

'I'm terribly sorry. That's never happened before,' he said in bafflement. 'It must have picked up some stray signal.'

'Remind me not to book with that mini-cab service,' Church said.

Outside, the rain had stopped briefly to allow a burst of insipid sunlight, but the oppressive experience with Delano clung to them. Their reclaimed memories, even if false, were now free, scurrying round, insect-like, in the back of their heads, making them feel queasy and disoriented.

'I feel much better after that, even if we didn't find out exactly what happened,' Ruth said, trying to put a brave face on it. She gave Church a comforting pat on the back. 'Come on, don't let it get to you. It was a bad dream, that's all.'

Church looked round at the black office windows above the shops, unable to shake the feeling they were being watched. 'I need a drink.'

'Let's see what we can do about that.'

She took him for lunch to Wodka, a Polish restaurant nestling in the hinterland of well-heeled apartment blocks on Kensington High Street's south side. Over blinis and cream and ice-cold honey vodka, they discussed the morning's events and what lay ahead. Church was taken by Ruth's brightly efficient manner and sharp sense of humour which helped her see the inherent farce in even the bleakest moment.

'You always seem like you've got something on your mind,' Ruth said when she felt comfortable enough to talk a little more personally.

'You know how it is.' Church sipped at the strong Polish coffee, but if Ruth noticed his discomfort she didn't pay it any heed.

'Anything you want to talk about?'

'Nothing I should burden you with.'

'Go on, I'm a good listener. Besides, after an experience like that we're a minority of two. We have to stick together.'

It would have been easy to bat her questions away, but there was something in her which made him feel like unburdening himself; a warmth, an *understanding*. He took a deep breath, surprised he even *felt* like talking about it. 'I had a girlfriend. Marianne Leedham. She was a graphic designer – magazine work, some book covers, that kind of thing. We met soon after I'd left university. I had a seedy flat in Battersea, just off Lavender Hill, and Marianne lived round the corner. We'd see each other in the local Spar or in the newsagents. You know how it is when you see someone and you know it's inevitable that sooner or later you're going to get together, even if you haven't spoken?' Ruth nodded, her eyes bright. 'I felt like that, and I could tell she did too. The local pub, the Beaufoy Arms, used to hire a boat to go along the Thames each year. It was an overnight thing, lots of Red Stripe, jerk pork and dancing, up to the Thames Barrier and then back again for dawn. I went with my mates and Marianne was there with hers. We both knew something was going to happen. Then just before sunrise we found ourselves on deck alone.' He smiled. 'Not by chance. We talked a little. We kissed a lot. It was like some stupid romantic film.'

Ruth watched his smile grow sad. 'What happened, Church?'

His sigh seemed like the essence of him rushing out. 'It was all a blur after that. We saw each other, moved in together. You know, people think I'm lying when I say this, but we never argued. Not once. It was just the best. It was so serious for both of us we never even thought about getting married, but Marianne's mum was getting a bit antsy, as they do, so we started muttering about getting engaged. Everything was fine, and then—' His voice drifted away; the words felt like heavy stones at the back of his throat, but somehow he forced them out. 'Two years ago, it was. I'd been out for the night. When I came back the flat was so silent, I knew there was something wrong. Marianne always had some kind of music on. And there was this odd smell. To this day I don't know what it was. I called out for her – there was nowhere else she could have been at that time of night – and my heart started beating like it was going to explode. I knew, you see. I knew. I found her face down in a pool of blood on the bathroom floor. She'd slashed her wrists.'

'Oh, God, I'm sorry,' Ruth said in dismay. 'I shouldn't have pried.'

'Don't worry, it's okay. It doesn't hurt me to think about her any more. I've got over all that grief thing, although sometimes I feel a little . . .' His voice trailed off, but her smile told him she understood what he was trying to say. 'It's how she died that I can't cope with. There hasn't been a single day gone by since then when I haven't tried to make sense of it. There was no reason for it. She hadn't been depressed. We'd never, ever argued. As far as I was concerned, everything in our lives was perfect. Can you imagine what that's like? To discover your partner had this whole secret world of despair that you never knew existed? Enough despair to kill herself. How could I have been so wrapped up in myself not to have even the slightest inkling?' He couldn't find the words to tell her what it was that had soured his life since that night: not grief, but guilt; the only possible explanation was that he, in some way, was complicit.

But Ruth seemed to know exactly what he was thinking. She leaned across the table and said softly, 'There could be a hundred and one explanations. A sudden chemical inbalance in her brain—'

'I've been through them all. I've weighed it up and turned it inside out and investigated every possibility, so much that I can't think of anything else. To answer your original question, that's why I always seem so preoccupied. Nothing else seems important beside that.'

'I'm sorry—'

'No, *I'm* sorry. It's selfish of me to be so wrapped up in myself. We've all got problems.' He looked out into the puddled street. Briefly he considered telling Ruth about Marianne's appearance outside his home, but to give voice to it would mean he would have to face up to the reality of the experience and everything that came with it; besides, it was too close to his heart right now. 'I wish I could put it all behind me, but there are so many things about it that don't make sense. Only hours before, she'd been making plans for the wedding.' Church grew silent as the waitress came over to pour more coffee; it broke his introspective mood and when she left it was obvious he didn't want to talk about it any more. 'This is a good lunch. Thanks.'

Ruth smiled affectionately. 'My philosophy is eat yourself out of a crisis.'

'Yet you stay so thin!' he said theatrically. They laughed together, but gradually the conversation turned to what they had seen beneath the bridge, as they had known it would. 'So whose face lies behind the Devil?' he asked.

Ruth's expression darkened. 'I don't know. Why should our reactions in the trance have been so extreme, and identical?' Church understood her confusion. 'But it's strange. For the first time in months, I feel like I've got some kind of direction. I really want to keep going until we get to the heart of it.'

Church was surprised to realise he felt the same way. 'How ironic can you get? It takes a brutal murder to give us some purpose in life.'

'Of course, there's also the danger that if we let it drop now that awful memory will start its destabilisation again, and I could really do without wrecking my career at this stage in my life.' She called for the bill and paid it with a gold Amex.

'So where do we go from here?' Church asked.

Ruth smiled. 'Elementary, my dear Watson.'

Maurice Gibbons had lived in a three-storey terrace in a tree-lined avenue; not too imposing, but certainly comfortable; it looked like it could have done with a lick of paint and a touch of repointing here and there. The lights were already ablaze in the twilight as Church and Ruth opened the front gate and walked up to the door, shivering from the chill; the night was going to be icy. They'd spent the afternoon quietly at Ruth's flat, drinking coffee, talking about comfortingly bland topics, but now they were both feeling apprehensive. Susan Gibbons was a quiet woman who looked older than her years. Her grief still lay heavy on her, evident in the puffiness of her eyes, her pallor and her timidity as she led them into the lounge where condolence cards still gathered dust on the mantelpiece. She accepted at face value Ruth's statement that they were looking into her husband's murder and sat perched on an armchair listening to their questions with a blankness which Church found unnerving, if only because he recognised something of himself in her.

'I know you've probably been through all this before, Mrs Gibbons,

31

but we have to go over old ground in case there's anything we've missed,' Ruth began.

Mrs Gibbons smiled without a hint of lightness or humour. 'I understand.'

'Your husband had no enemies?'

'None at all. Maurice wasn't what you would call a passionate man. He enjoyed his job and he did it well, but he didn't really have any ambition to move on, and everyone recognised that and accepted it. No one felt threatened by him.' Her hands clutched at each other in her lap every time she mentioned her husband's name.

'I know he told you he was going to the pub. Do you have any idea how or why he ended up south of the river?'

'No.'

A look of panic crossed her face, and Church moved quickly to change the subject. 'Had your husband been acting any differently in the days or weeks leading up to his death?'

There was a long pause when Mrs Gibbons appeared to have drifted off into a reverie, but then she said quietly, 'Now that you mention it, Maurice was a little . . . skittish, perhaps. He was jumping at the slightest thing.'

'He was frightened of something?' Church pressed.

'Oh, I wouldn't go that far. Not frightened, just . . . uneasy.' She let out a deep sigh that seemed to fill the room. 'He went to church on the Sunday before he passed on. That was so unlike Maurice. Do you think he might have sensed something, wanted to make his peace with God?'

'Perhaps he did,' Ruth said soothingly. Church was impressed with her manner; her caring was from the heart, and he could see Mrs Gibbons being visibly calmed.

'Would you like to see his room?' Mrs Gibbons asked. 'Maurice had so many interests and he had a room where he could be alone to think and read. That's where he kept all his things. You might find something of interest there. Lord knows, there's nothing I can tell you.'

She led them up two flights to a little box room lit by a bare bulb. It was quite tidy, uncluttered by any kind of decoration; just a cheap desk and chair, a filing cabinet and a bookshelf. A pair of plaid slippers were tucked in the corner.

'I'll leave you to it. Make a cup of tea, how about that?' Mrs Gibbons slipped out, closing the door behind them.

'Why do you think he was *uneasy* just before he was killed?' Church said as he sank on to the chair and opened the desk.

'Don't start extrapolating. You'll end up with all sorts of hideous conspiracy theories.'

' "Just the facts, ma'am." '

'Exactly.' Ruth crouched down to examine the bookshelf. 'I think one of us should pay a visit to the local vicar. You never know, Maurice might have seen fit to bare his soul.'

'Wouldn't that be nice and simple. He fingers his murderer to the vicar and everything falls into place.' He started to go through the sparse contents of the desk aloud. 'Pens, envelopes, writing paper. Look at this, typical anally retentive civil servant – a big pile of receipts, most of them for cabs.'

'Nothing wrong with being anal retentive,' Ruth said tartly.

'Hoping for some tax deduction, I suppose,' Church continued. 'A notebook—'

'A lot of these books are new,' Ruth mused. 'UFOs, Von Daniken, *The Occult* by Colin Wilson, *Messages from the Dead: A Spiritualists' Guide.* Looks like he's been reading that magazine you were rambling on about.'

'That's a bit of a coincidence.'

'Sure. Life's full of them. Anything in the notebook?'

'The first few pages have been torn out. There's only one thing in it: a phone number. Barry Riggs. Crouch End UFO Association.'

'Great. Little Green Men got him,' Ruth said wryly. 'We should check it out anyway. You never know.'

They caught a cab back to South London and dropped Ruth off first. Church felt chastened by Mrs Gibbons' grief. Afraid that the depression would come back to ruin the first halfway-normal mood he had felt in a long time, he quickly switched on the computer and went online. There was an email waiting for him from Laura DuSantiago.

Greetings, Churchill-Dude (No relation, I hope. I don't want to picture you with a big, fat cigar.)

I get the impression from your last email that you think I'm full of hot air, but you're too polite to say so. Well, I'll stop teasing, big boy – I wouldn't want a *premature* withdrawal on your behalf. Everyone else who emailed me has scarpered before I had the chance to get down to the *meat*. And I better stop now before this becomes a bad Carry On film . . .

Here's the dope: the increase in paranormal activity that all the net-nerds noticed started on the same day. Coincidence? I don't think so. There's stuff happening around the globe, but the epicentre is the UK – and most of it is happening around places of significance to our pagan/Celtic ancestors. Now, statistically, I know that's not difficult in an island like ours, but look at the big picture, not the details. I'm not going too fast for you, am I?

And here's the big story, Morning Glory. I saw something that changed my life. Me, technohead, feet-on-the-ground Laura DuS. Something that all the crazies and geeks of the UFO/Spirit World would give their right arms to see. And losing their right arms would really hamper those types. This was a drug-free, alcohol-free experience, and it talked to me. You want to know what it said, you'll have to meet me on my own turf. I'm not spreading this stuff around online so I can be branded as another nut.

But here's a tip: don't go making plans for the next millennium . . .

Your new best friend, Laura.

And there, at the end, was the thing that hooked him and made his blood run cold.

PS Before we meet I need to know if this name means anything to you: Marianne.

Church read the line three times, trying to work out if he was going insane, then wondering if someone was playing a nasty trick on him. It could have been another coincidence, but the way they were piling up gave him an eerie feeling of some power behind the scenes manipulating his life. He turned off the computer and busied himself with mundane tasks for the better part of an hour, but it wouldn't leave him alone and it was only a matter of time before he returned to the keyboard to type out his reply. Then he retired to bed without once looking out of the window into the dark, quiet street.

Ruth reached the church shortly after 9 a.m. It was a bracing morning, with the wind sending the clouds streaking across the blue sky. Standing in the sun, peering at the skeletal trees through screwed-up eyes that cropped out the buildings, Ruth could almost believe she wasn't in London, away from the smog and the traffic noise and the omnipresent background threat. Sometimes she hated the modern world with a vengeance.

The vicar was in the churchyard, in his shirt-sleeves despite the chill, trimming the hedge with an electric cutter. He was tall with a red face – although that might have been from the exertion – and a balding head with white hair swept back around his ears. The drone of the cutter drowned out Ruth's first attempt at an introduction, but she eventually caught his eye.

'I said, shouldn't you have a gardener to do that?' she said.

'Oh, I like to get my hands dirty every now and then. What can I do for you?'

'My name's Ruth Gallagher. A solicitor. I'm looking into the death of

Maurice Gibbons. I was told you knew him.' She was still surprised how quickly people parted with information once she announced her legal background; it was almost as if they considered her a policewoman-in-waiting.

The vicar nodded ruefully. 'Poor Maurice. Still no suspect, I suppose.'

'Not yet, but no one's giving up. There was one particular line of enquiry I wanted to discuss with you. It might be nothing, but Mrs Gibbons mentioned he came to church the week before his death which was unusual—'

'He was a very troubled man,' the vicar interjected. 'He came round to the rectory after the service for a chat. I can't betray the confidences of the people who come to me . . .' He paused, weighing up his options. 'But with Maurice dead, I don't see the harm, especially if it gives an insight into his state of mind.' Folding his arms, he stared up at the steeple. 'Maurice was concerned about spiritual matters. We discussed, amongst other things, the return of the spirits of the dead, ghosts, you know, and possession by demonic entities. He wanted to know how easy it would be to arrange an exorcism if necessary, and I told him something of that magnitude would have to be sanctioned by the bishop.'

'He thought he was possessed!' Ruth said incredulously.

'No, I didn't feel that. It was more as if he was talking in general terms, but he was certainly very anxious. He seemed to fear being tormented by the more malignant aspects of the spiritual realm.'

The memory unleashed by the therapist returned in force, and Ruth stifled a shudder.

'Are you feeling all right?' the vicar asked, concerned.

'Fine. Just a chill.' She forced a smile. She didn't believe in those kind of things, but the coincidence was hard to ignore.

The Victorian house could have been stately, but it had been indelibly scarred by thoughtless *improvement*: cheap UPVC window frames and door, grey plastic guttering, an obtrusive aluminium flue for a gas boiler. Barry Riggs smiled broadly when he answered the door to Church, but it seemed forced, almost gritted. He was around forty, slightly overweight, with a doughy face and glasses that were a little too large. He smelled of cheap aftershave fighting to mask body odour. Inside, he seemed to have the builders in. Planks leaned against the stairs, an empty paint can stood in the hall, there were dust sheets everywhere and a pristine toilet bowl stood in the lounge, but he made no mention of the mess and there was no sound from anywhere else in the house.

'I know why you're here,' Riggs said conspiratorially as Church was ushered on to the sheet that covered the sofa.

'I did tell you on the phone,' Church replied dryly.

'No, the *real* reason. Something much bigger than Maurice Gibbons.' He nodded knowingly.

'You better fill me in from the beginning, Barry.' Church was already harbouring doubts about the validity of his visit. As 'chief investigator' of the Crouch End UFO Association, Riggs had sounded more authoritative on the phone than he appeared in his natural habitat.

'Maurice heard of my investigations on the grapevine,' Riggs began, sitting a little too close to Church for comfort. 'People talk. There's never any coverage in the media, but you talk to people in the street and they know of the importance of my work. It's the future, isn't it? Anyway, I digress. Maurice knew I'd uncovered some unarguable evidence about Government knowledge of the UFO threat. I'm not going to go into details now, but let me just say *secret base* and *St Albans*. We can talk about that later if you want.'

'Why did Maurice come to you, Barry?'

'Alien infiltration, Jack. Plain and simple. Maurice was a Government employee. He knew he was a target. He was frightened, Jack, very frightened, and he came to me looking for any information that might protect him. "They walk among us," he said. I remember it well. He was sitting just where you are, with his little briefcase. He'd got classified information in it, but he wasn't ready to show me just then. It was a matter of building trust, but they got to him before he could divulge what he knew.'

'Who got to him?'

'The aliens! In the future, Maurice will be seen as a hero. He was a whistleblower, ready to open up the whole can of worms about the Government selling us down the line for alien experiments.'

Church stared out of the window at the sinking afternoon sun, wishing he had opted for the vicar. 'And he told you this? That aliens were after him?'

Riggs paused. 'Not in so many words. But he wanted to know everything about my investigations. We ran through the dates and times of sightings, witness reports, everything. He was particularly interested in the descriptions of different races, the Greys and the Nordics and all that. And alien abduction scenarios. What the abductees experienced in real detail. What they heard, lights in the sky. I tell you, Jack, he was here for hours.'

Church stood up quickly before he was overpowered by Riggs' body odour. 'Thank you, Barry. You've been very helpful.'

Riggs grinned. 'You know, that's just what Maurice said. "People need to know what's out there, Barry. They're sleepwalking into a disaster."'

'So here are the options. Maurice was crazy. Maurice was overworked and suffering from stress-induced psychosis. Or Maurice was crazy. Either way, it's a good explanation for why he was wandering along by the river at the crack of dawn.' Church sprawled on the sofa in Ruth's lounge, looking out at the city lights against the early evening sky.

'Do you think you could possibly be a little more glib?' Ruth said ironically.

Over a take-out curry and a bottle of Chilean red, they had spent half an hour trading information and finding there was no common ground whatsoever.

'You were the sceptical one,' Church replied. 'This was supposed to be taking us away from the Devil living under Albert Bridge. Now we have one man thinking Gibbons is being hunted by aliens, another convinced our man is being haunted by ghosts and demons.'

'You're still skating on the surface, Church. Dig a little deeper.'

'Do you think you can patronise me a little more? I haven't had my fill yet.'

She laughed and topped up his glass. 'The important fact is that Maurice Gibbons was a frightened man. Something was disturbing him enough to seek out the vicar and your UFO loon for information. He knew something.'

'Or he was crazy.'

'He was a civil servant, down-to-earth. If he was frightened, why was he keeping it to himself? There must have been hundreds of people he could have discussed it with, not least his wife.'

'Perhaps he was waiting until he was sure.' Church took a deep swig of his wine and then said out of the blue, 'Do you believe in ghosts?'

Ruth looked at him in surprise. 'Why do you ask?'

'It doesn't matter. So where do we go from here? I can't think of any other lines of enquiry . . . hang on a minute.' He suddenly stared into the middle distance, ordering his thoughts, then he snapped his fingers. 'There's something we've missed.'

Susan Gibbons welcomed them in forty-five minutes later after Church's phone call had convinced her their visit would only take a few minutes. In Maurice's room, he went straight to the desk and pulled out the pile of taxi receipts, riffling through them quickly. They were all for a Monday evening and for the same amount.

'So where was he going on a regular basis?' Church asked pointedly. Mrs Gibbons had no idea. 'I think the police looked into this, but didn't get anywhere,' she said. Church wasn't deterred. He called the minicab firm. The receptionist asked around in the office and a few minutes later came back with an address.

The house was a small semi in High Barnet; half-rendered, with more UPVC windows and a paved-over front garden where a few yellow weeds forced their way among the cracks. The light that glared through the glass of the front door seemed unpleasantly bright. They rang the bell and it was answered immediately by a woman with dyed black hair and sallow skin. She dragged on a cigarette, eyeing them suspiciously while Ruth ran through her patter. She reluctantly allowed them into the hall, which smelled of cigarettes and bacon fat.

'He came round to see my uncle every week,' she said, glancing at a photo of Gibbons which his wife had lent them. 'Queer duck, but he used to perk the old man up. He's not well, you know. Hasn't left his bed in weeks. I got lumbered looking after him.' She wrinkled her nose in what could have been disgust or irritation.

'Can we see him?' Church asked.

The woman nodded, then added combatively, 'I'm going out soon.'

'Don't worry, we can let ourselves out,' Ruth said disarmingly. 'What's your uncle's name?'

'Kraicow,' the woman snapped as if that was all she knew.

She led the way up the stairs and swung open a bedroom door on to a painfully thin old man, his limbs just bone draped in skin. He lay on the top of his bed in striped pyjamas with one arm thrown across his eyes. His hair was merely tufts of silver on his pillow.

'Is it okay if we talk to him?' Church said.

'Just one of you,' the woman said. 'He gets very confused if there's more than one person speaking.' She added obliquely, 'He's an artist, you know. Used to be quite well known.'

The woman left them alone, and Church went to sit by the bed while Ruth watched from the door. Church remained quiet as Kraicow twitched and moaned beneath his arm, but eventually the old man removed it from his face and looked at Church with clear grey eyes, as if he had known he had a visitor all along.

'Hello, I'm Jack Churchill,' Church said quietly. 'I hope you don't mind me coming to see you.'

Kraicow looked away and mumbled something; Church wondered if he'd be able to get any sense out of him at all. But when Kraicow looked

38

back he spoke in a clear, deep voice. 'I'm pleased to see any human face after looking at that miserable bitch all day long. She never leaves me alone.'

'You don't know me,' Church continued, 'but I wanted to talk to you about Maurice Gibbons.'

Church wondered how he would be able to discuss the matter without upsetting Kraicow about Gibbons' death, but the old man said simply, 'He's dead, isn't he?'

Church nodded.

'I warned him.'

A hush seemed to descend on the house. 'Warned him about what?'

Kraicow levered himself up on his elbows so he could look Church in the face. For a moment the old man's eyes ranged across Church's features as if he was searching for something he could trust, before slowly lowering himself down with a wheeze. 'Maurice saw my break-down . . . what the bastards at the health centre call my breakdown,' he began in a voice so low Church had to bend forward to hear him. 'It was in the street, in Clerkenwell – where I work. I was making too much noise. Ranting, I suppose. Not surprising under the circumstances. Maurice overheard some of the things I said, and he knew straight away I was telling the truth because he'd seen the same thing too.'

'What had you seen?' Church whispered.

Kraicow licked his dry lips. 'You know much about the old myths and legends?'

'It depends which ones.'

'The final battle between Good and Evil. The end of this cycle and the start of something new.' The front door slammed loudly; Kraicow's niece had gone. 'The legend is the same all over the world. The End-Time.' Kraicow grabbed Church's wrist with fingers which seemed too strong for his feeble state. 'They're coming back.'

'Who are?' Church's mood dampened; more craziness. 'Aliens? Demons?'

'No!' Kraicow said emphatically. 'I told you, the old myths. Not fairytales, no, no, not folklore!' His eyes rolled back until all Church could see were the whites. 'The legends are true.'

'Are you okay?'

Kraicow threw his arm across his face again. 'The legends said they'd be back for the final battle and they were right! Do you think we stand a chance against them?'

'Take it easy,' Church said calmly. 'Why did Maurice come to see you?'

'He knew they were back! He'd seen them too. He knew they were biding their time, but they'll be making their move soon – they won't wait long. The doors are open!'

'Did Maurice say—'

'He wanted to know what to do! He was so frightened. So frightened. He knew they wouldn't let him have the knowledge for long . . . they'd get to him. But who could he tell? The bastards put me in here!'

Church sat back in his chair in disappointment; he was getting nowhere. Was Gibbons as crazed as Kraicow, or were his visits some kind of altruistic act? He glanced at Ruth, about to take his leave, but Kraicow grabbed his shirt and dragged him forward.

'Remember the old legend: *In England's darkest hour, a hero shall arise.* It's there. It's been written.' He took a deep breath and some degree of normalcy returned to him. 'You don't believe me, do you?'

'I'm sorry—'

'No, no, it's crazy talk. I've spent too long breathing in those paint fumes.' He chuckled throatily. 'Look in the top drawer.'

Curiously Church followed his nod to the bedside cabinet. In the drawer was an envelope; an address was scribbled on the front. 'That's my studio. You go there, you'll see.'

'I can't—'

'You'll find what you're looking for. Peace of mind. Direction. You'll know what happened to Maurice. It's up to you now.' He pushed Church away roughly and rolled over. 'Go!'

Church glanced at the envelope one more time, then reluctantly took it. At the door, he silenced Ruth's questions with a simple, 'Later.' Downstairs was in darkness. In the gloom, Church felt eyes on his back although he knew the place was empty, and he didn't feel safe until they were outside, dialling a cab on Ruth's mobile.

Kraicow's studio was at the top of a Victorian warehouse in one of the many unredeemed backstreets that formed the heart of Clerkenwell. From the outside it seemed almost derelict: smashed windows filthy with dust, graffiti and posters for bands that had long since split up. Unidentified hulks of machinery were scattered around the ground floor, which stank of engine oil and dirt. But when they climbed out of the service lift at the summit, Kraicow's room presented itself to them in a burst of colour and a smell of oil paint and solvent. An enormous, half-completed canvas was suspended over the centre of the floor, but it was impossible to tell from the splashes of colour exactly what it would eventually be. Other canvases of all sizes were stacked against various walls. The floor was bare boards, but clean, and there was a small camp bed in one corner where the artist obviously snatched a rest during his more intense periods of work. On an uneven table was a collection of tubes of oil, dirty rags, a palette and a jar filled with brushes.

'Do you ever get the feeling you're wasting your time?' Ruth said as she looked around at the disarray.

'You were the one who insisted we go down every avenue, however ridiculous,' Church replied. 'Personally, I think you've been reading way too much Sherlock Holmes.'

Ruth began to search through the stacked canvases. 'What are we looking for?'

'God knows.' Church busied himself with an investigation of a pile of rags and empty paint pots near the window. On the top was a sheet of sketch paper where Kraicow had written *El sueño de la Razon Produce monstruos*. Church read it aloud, then asked, 'What does that mean?'

Ruth paused in her search and dredged her memory for a translation. ' "The sleep of reason brings forth monsters." It's the title of—'

'—a painting by Goya. Yes, I remember.'

Ruth leaned on the canvases and mused, 'It's strange, isn't it? We go about our lives thinking the world is normal and then we stumble across all these people who obviously have a completely different view of reality, indulging in their paranoid fantasies.'

'Are you including the vicar in that?'

Ruth laughed. 'The UFO guy and Kraicow and obviously Gibbons, all feeding each other. And obviously Mrs Gibbons had no idea what was going on in her husband's head.'

Church moved on to another collection of canvases, older, judging by the thick layer of dust that lay on the top. 'Well, paranoia's like a fire. It quickly gets out of control and suddenly the norm looks weird and the weird becomes perfectly acceptable.'

'You'd know, would you?' Ruth jibed. Church didn't respond.

Their search continued for fifteen minutes more, becoming increasingly aimless as the futility of the task overcame them. Church, for his part, was afraid to stop; he didn't want to return to his empty flat with its bleak memories. Their hunt for meaning in their experience had released a whole host of emotions with which he hadn't had time to come to terms.

Ruth let the final canvas drop back with a clatter. 'We should call it a day,' she said. Church noted a hint of gloom in her voice. After a second she added morosely, 'I don't think we're getting anywhere and I'm afraid if we don't sort out what happened I'm never going to get back to who I was. That morning was so destabilising I feel like every support for my life has been kicked away.' She wandered over to the window and hauled up the blind to look out over the city.

'I know exactly what you mean,' Church said, remembering the morning after Marianne's terrible death with an awful intensity. 'Sometimes you never get straight again.' He checked the final canvas, a surreal landscape with hints of Dali. 'Nothing here. I don't know what Kraicow was talking about. Serves us right for listening to the views of a mental patient. So what do we do next?'

There was no reply. Church turned slowly. Ruth was standing at the window with her back to him, so immobile she could have been a statue. 'Did you hear me?'

Still no answer. He could tell from her frozen body something was wrong. A hum of anxiety rose at the back of his head, growing louder as he moved towards her. Before he had crossed the floor, her voice came up small, still and frightened. 'He was right.'

Church felt his heart begin to pound; somewhere, doors were opening.

When he came up behind her, he could see what it was that had caught her attention. On the window ledge was a small sculpture in clay, rough and unfinished, but detailed in the upper part. It was a figure with a face so hideous in its deformity and evil they could barely bring themselves to look at it.

And it was the perfect representation of the *devil* they had recalled during Delano's therapy session. Kraicow had seen it too.

It existed.

CHAPTER THREE

On the Road

For the rest of the night they sat in Ruth's lounge, talking in the quiet, clipped tones of people who had suffered the massive shock of a sudden bereavement. The discovery of the desperately crafted statue left them with nowhere to turn. Suddenly the shadows were alive, and life had taken on the perspective of a bottle-glass window.

'What the hell's going on?' Ruth looked deep into the dregs of her wine. She had drunk too much too quickly, but however much she told herself it was an immature reaction, she couldn't face up to the immensity of what the statue meant and what they had truly seen that night. For someone immersed on a daily basis in the logic and reason of the law, it was both too hard to believe and impossible to deny; the conflict made her feel queasy.

Church rubbed his tired eyes, at once deflated and lost. 'We can't walk away from it—'

'I know that.' There was an edge to her voice. 'I never thought one moment could change your life so fundamentally.' She walked over to the window and looked out at the lights of the city in the pre-dawn dark. 'We're so alone now – nobody knows what we know. It's a joke! How can we tell anybody? We'll end up getting treated like Kraicow.'

'And what do we know? That there's some kind of supernatural creature out there that looks like a man one moment and something too hideous to look at the next?'

'We know,' she said dismally, 'that nothing is how we imagined it. That if something like that can exist, anything is possible. What are the rules now, Church? What's going on?'

Church paused; he had no idea how to answer her question. He drained the remainder of his wine, then played with the glass thoughtfully. 'At least we've got each other,' he said finally.

Ruth looked round suddenly, a faint smile sweeping away the darkness in her face. 'That's right. You and me against the world, kid.'

Church mused for a moment. 'Kraicow must know more. He'd seen something, the same as Gibbons.'

'Then,' Ruth said pointedly, 'we should pay him another visit.'

Unable to sleep, they arrived at Kraicow's house at first light and sat outside in Church's old Nissan Bluebird until a reasonable hour, dozing fitfully. His niece answered the door, her recognition giving way instantly to anger.

'Did you two have something to do with it?' she barked. Church and Ruth were taken aback by her fury, their speechlessness answering the woman's question. 'He's gone,' she snapped.

Church's puzzlement showed on his face; Kraicow had seemed too weak to move. 'Where—'

'I don't know where, that's the problem!' Anxiously, she looked past them into the empty street. 'They came for him in the night. I had the fright of my life when I opened the door.'

'Who was it?' Church asked.

'I don't know! They didn't tell me!' She back-pedalled, suddenly aware they might judge her for not questioning the men further. 'They were coppers,' she said unconvincingly. 'Looked like a bloody funeral party, all dressed in smart suits and ties. I don't know what the old man's done. He never tells me anything.'

Church and Ruth looked at each other uneasily. 'Do you know where they took him?' Ruth said.

The woman shook her head. 'They said they'd let me know. They told me it was in his best interests!' she protested pathetically before slamming the door.

'What was that all about?' Ruth asked once they were comfortably in heavy traffic heading back into town.

'Could be the murder squad. They might have linked Kraicow to Maurice Gibbons.'

'Could be.' Her voice suggested she didn't believe it. 'Seems more like the kind of thing Special Branch would do. Or the security services.'

'What would they want with Kraicow?' The question hung uncomfortably in the air for a moment until Church added, 'Let's not get paranoid about this.'

'If this whole episode isn't a case for paranoia, I don't know what is. We haven't got any more leads now. Where do we go from here?'

They crawled forward through the traffic for another fifteen minutes before Church found an answer. 'There's a lot of weird stuff going on around the country just like this. I mean, not people turning into devils, but things that shouldn't be happening.' Church explained to her at length about the massive upsurge in supposed paranormal events he

44

had read about on the net. 'I don't know . . .' He shrugged. 'It may be nothing. All the nuts coming out of the woodwork at once. But it seems to me too much of a coincidence.'

Ruth sighed heavily and stared out of the passenger window at the dismal street scene; no one seemed happy, their shoulders bowed beneath an invisible weight as they headed to the tube for another dreary day at work. It depressed her even more. 'I can't get my head round this at all.'

'Let's just pretend it's not happening,' Church snapped, then instantly regretted it; he was tired and sick of nothing in his life making sense.

Ruth glared at him, then looked back out of the window.

'Sorry.'

She ignored his apology frostily; Church could see she was tired herself. 'Gibbons was killed to prevent him telling what he'd seen,' she mused almost to herself. 'But what did he see?'

'I've had some emails from a woman who says she saw something which could throw some light on what's going on,' Church ventured. He considered telling her about Laura's mention of Marianne, but thought better of it; he could barely handle the implications himself.

'You really think all that stuff's linked to what we're dealing with?'

'Who knows?' he said wearily. 'These days, everything's a leap in the dark.'

'So is she going to tell you what she knows?'

'She wants to do it face to face. I was going to see her anyway, you know, just out of curiosity.' He winced inwardly at the lie about his motivations. Ruth didn't deserve it, but how could he tell her he wanted to find out how this woman knew about his dead girlfriend? It sounded a little pathetic, worse, like an obsession.

'Why the hell not. Where is she?'

'Bristol.'

Ruth moaned. 'Oh well, I've got no job to keep me here. Just give me a couple of hours to pack. Looks like we've got us a road trip.'

Although it had been two years since he had last felt the warmth of her skin, Marianne's presence still reverberated throughout the flat. On the wall of the hall hung the grainy black and white photo of the two of them staggering out of the sea at Bournemouth, fully clothed, laughing; Marianne had had it framed to remind them both how carefree life could be if they ever faced any hardship. In the kitchen, in the glass-fronted cabinet, stood her blue-and-white-hooped mug with the chip out of the side. Church couldn't bear to throw it away. He saw it every

45

day when he made his first cup of tea, and his last. The dog-eared copy of *Foucault's Pendulum* which they had both read and argued about intensely sat on the shelf in the lounge, next to the pristine edition of *Walking on Glass* which Marianne had given him and which he had promised her he would read and had never got round to. The paperweight of a plastic heart frozen in glass which they had bought together in Portobello. The indelible stain of Marianne's coffee on the carpet next to her seat. A hundred tiny lies ready to deceive him in every corner of his home. Sometimes he even thought he could smell her perfume.

With the TV droning in the background and the holdall still half-packed on the bed, Church suddenly found himself taking stock of it all in a way he had not done since the immediate aftermath of her death. For months the reminders had simply been there, like the drip of a distant tap, but as he trailed around the flat, they seemed acute and painfully lucid once more. Perhaps it was the bizarre, disturbing mention of her name in the email, or what he thought he had seen in the street, but he had to visit each one in turn with an imperative which he found disturbing.

But he was sure he could give it all up, turn back to the future, if he could somehow understand what had driven her to suicide and how he had been so blind to the deep undercurrents that must have been in place months before. He had played over every aspect of their relationship in minute detail until he was sick of it, but the mystery held as strong as ever, trapping him in the misery of not-knowing, a limbo where he could not put the past and all its withered, desperate emotions to rest. No wonder he was seeing her ghost; he was surprised it hadn't come sooner, lurching out of his subconscious to drive him completely insane.

In the lounge, the TV news had made an incongruous link from an account of a bizarre multiple slasher murder in Liverpool to details of a religious fervour which seemed to be sweeping the country; the Blessed Virgin Mary had allegedly appeared to three young children on wasteland in Huddersfield; a statue of the Hindu god Ganesh had given forth milk in Wolverhampton, and there were numerous reports of the name of Allah spelled out in the seeds of tomatoes and aubergines when they were cut open in Bradford, Bristol and West London. Church watched the item to the end, then switched off the TV and put on a CD. The jaunty sound of Johnny Mercer singing Ac-cent-tchu-ate the Positive filled the flat as he returned to his packing.

He picked up Laura's email confirming the details of their meeting and then checked the road atlas. Church hoped his car would make the

46

trip to Bristol. It had seen better days and very few long journeys, but he had bought it with Marianne and hadn't been able to give it up.

A haze of chill drizzle had descended on the city just after he had dropped Ruth off and by the time he began to load up the car, it seemed to have settled in for the day. The world appeared different somehow; there was a smell in the air which he didn't recognise and the quality of light seemed weird as if it was filtering through glass. Even the people passing by looked subtly changed, in their expressions or the strange, furtive glances which he occasionally glimpsed. He felt oddly out of sorts and apprehensive about what lay ahead.

When he stepped out of the front gate, a group of children splashing in the gutter across the road stopped instantly and turned to face him as one, their eyes glassy and unfocused. Slowly, eerily, they each raised their left arm and held up the index finger. 'One!' they shouted together. Then they splayed out their fingers and thumb. 'Of five!' Some stupid catchphrase from a kids' cartoon, Church thought, but he still felt a shiver run down his spine as he hurried up the street to the car.

As he threw his bag into the boot, he heard the shuffle of feet on the pavement behind him. He whirled, expecting to catch the children preparing to play a prank, only to see a homeless man in a filthy black suit, his long hair and beard flattened by the rain. He walked up to Church, shaking as if he had an ague, and then he leaned forward and snapped his fingers an inch away from Church's face.

'You have no head,' he said. Church felt an icy shadow fall over him, an image of the woman at the riverside; by the time he had recovered the man had wandered away, humming some sixties tune as if he hadn't seen Church at all.

On his way to Ruth's, Church passed through five green lights and halted at one red. Nearby was a poster of a man selling mobile phones; the top of the poster was torn off and the man's head was missing. Further down the road, he glanced in a clothes shop to see five mannequins; four were fine, one was headless.

And as he rounded the corner into Ruth's street, a woman looked into the car, caught his eye, then suddenly and inexplicably burst into tears.

He finally reached Ruth's flat just before 1 p.m. She was ready, with a smart leather holdall and Mulberry rucksack. 'I can't help believing all this will have a perfectly reasonable explanation and we'll both end up with egg on our faces. God help me if the people at work find out,' she said.

'Let's hope, eh.'

Church drummed his fingers anxiously on the steering wheel as they sat in the steaming traffic in the bottleneck of Wandsworth High Street. Ruth looked out at the rain-swept street where a man in a business suit hurried, head bent, into the storm with a copy of the *FT* over his head – as if it could possibly offer any protection. 'You know,' she mused, 'I have the strangest feeling. Like we're leaving one life behind and moving into a different phase.'

'Too much Jack Kerouac.' Church's attention was focused on the rearview mirror; he had the sudden, uncomfortable feeling they were being followed.

'It's frightening, but it's liberating too,' Ruth continued. 'Everything was set in stone before – my job, where I was going. Now it feels like anything is possible. Isn't that weird? The world has turned on its head and I feel like I'm going on holiday.'

'Sunny Bristol, paradise playground of the beautiful people. I hope you packed your string bikini.'

'Have you got any music in this heap?' Ruth flicked open the glove compartment and ferreted among the tapes, screwing up her nose as she inspected each item. 'Sinatra. Crosby. Louis Armstrong. Billie Holiday. Anything from this century?'

'Old music makes me feel secure.' He snatched *Come Fly With Me* out of her fingers and slipped it into the machine. Sinatra began to sing the title track. 'And old films and old books. *Top Hat*, now there's a great movie. Astaire and Rogers, the perfect partnership, elegance and sexuality. Or *A Night At The Opera*—'

'The Marx Brothers. Yeuckk!' Ruth mimed sticking her fingers down her throat.

'Or *It Happened One Night*. Clark Gable and Claudette Colbert. Romance, passion, excitement, great clothes, great cars. You can't get better than that.'

Ruth smiled secretly when she saw Church's grin; he didn't do it enough.

'Life was great back then.' He waved his hand dismissively at the jumble of shops on Upper Richmond Road. 'Where did it all go wrong? When did style get banned from life?'

'When they decided big money and vacuous consumption were much more important.'

'We need more magic. That's what life is all about.'

Ruth flicked her seat into the reclining position and closed her eyes while Sinatra serenaded the joys of Moonlight in Vermont. The traffic crept forward.

The journey through south-west London was long and laborious. In rain, the capital's archaic transport system ground to a halt, raising clouds of exhaust, steam from hissing engines and tempers. By the time they reached the M4 more than an hour later, Church and Ruth were already tired of travelling. As the planes swooped down in a never-ending procession to Healthrow, they agreed to pull in at Heston Services for a coffee before embarking on the monotonous drag along the motorway. By the time they rolled into the near-empty car park, Church's paranoia had reached fever pitch; at various stages on the journey he had been convinced that several different cars had been following them, and when a grey Transit that had been behind them since Barnes proceeded on to the services too, it had taken all of Ruth's calm rationality to keep him from driving off.

Beneath the miserable grey skies, the services seemed a bleak place. Pools of water puddled near the doors and slickly followed the tramp of feet to the newsagents or toilets where the few travellers who hung around had a uniform expression of irritation; at the weather, at travelling, at life in general.

As Church and Ruth entered, they could see through the glass wall on their right that the restaurant was nearly empty. They proceeded round to the serving area where a couple of bored assistants waited for custom and bought coffee and Danishes before taking a seat near the window where they could see the spray flying up from the speeding traffic. Through the glass, distant factory towers lay against the grey sheet of sky, while beneath the fluorescent lighting the cafeteria had a listless, melancholy air. Despite the constant drone from the motorway which thrummed like the bleak soundtrack to some French arthouse film, they spoke quietly, although there were only three other travellers in the room and none of them close enough to hear.

'This is killing me,' Church mused. 'Every time I look behind I think someone's following us.'

Ruth warmed her hands around her coffee mug; she didn't meet his eyes. 'A natural reaction.'

Near the door, a tall, thin man was casting furtive glances in their direction, the hood of his plastic waterproof pulled so tightly around his face that the drawstrings were biting into the flesh. At a table on the other side of the room, an old hippie with wiry, grey hair fastened in a ponytail was also watching them. Church fought his anxiety and turned his attention back to Ruth.

'When I was a boy this would all have seemed perfectly normal,' he said. 'You know how it is – you're always convinced the world is stranger than it seems.'

'That just goes to show we *lose* wisdom as we get older, doesn't it,' Ruth replied edgily. 'We've obviously been spending all our adult lives lying to ourselves.'

'When I was seven or eight I had these bizarre dreams, really colourful and realistic,' Church began. 'There was a woman in them, and this strange world. They were so powerful I think I had trouble distinguishing between the dreams and reality, and it worried my mother: she dragged me off to the doctor at one point. They faded after I reached puberty, but I know they affected the way I looked at the world. And I'm getting the same kind of feeling now – that all we see around us is some kind of cheap scenery and that the real business is happening behind it.' He glanced around; the man in the waterproof had gone, but the hippie was still watching them.

'I'm finding it hard to deal with, to be honest,' Ruth said. 'I've always believed this is all there is. I've never had much time for ghosts or God.'

Church nodded. 'I always thought there was something there. An instinct, really. You know, you'd look around . . . sometimes it's hard to believe there's not something behind it all. But these days . . . I don't have much time for the Church . . . any churches. After Marianne died, they weren't much help, to say the least.'

Ruth sipped her coffee thoughtfully. 'My dad was a member of the Communist Party and a committed atheist. I remember him saying one day, "The Bible's a pack of lies, written by a bunch of power-hungry men who wanted their own religion."'

'Christmas must have been a bundle of fun in your house.'

'No, it was great. It was a really happy, loving home.' She smiled wistfully. 'He died a couple of years ago.'

'I'm sorry.'

'It was sudden, a heart attack. His brother, my uncle, was murdered and it just destroyed my dad. It was the unfairness of it . . . the complete randomness. Uncle Jim was in the wrong place at the wrong time, and some desperate, pathetic idiot killed him. You know, I work in the law and I see all the motivations for crime, but if I came across that bastard today I'd probably kill him with my bare hands. No jury, no legal arguments.' She bit her lip. 'Dad just couldn't cope with it. It didn't fit in with the ordered world view, you see. He tore himself apart for a couple of days and then his heart gave out. And in one instant I could understand the need for religion.' Emotions flickered across her face. 'Of course, by that stage it was too late to suddenly start believing.'

Church felt an urge to comfort her, but he didn't know how. 'The time when the Church had any relevance to people's lives is long gone, yet we all still have these spiritual needs. So where do we turn when things get dark?'

'We look into ourselves, I suppose,' Ruth said quietly.

The hippie's unwavering stare was beginning to unnerve Church; behind his wire-rimmed spectacles, his eyes were cold and grey, sharply intelligent and incisive. One hand rested protectively on a faded, olive-coloured haversack bearing a large peace symbol and a CND badge.

Ruth drained her coffee and stood up. 'I had better go to the toilet or we'll be stopping all the way to Bristol.'

As she wandered out, the hippie watched her intently. Church gnawed on his Danish while keeping one eye out to make sure Ruth wasn't followed. The man didn't have an unpleasant face; the skin was the kind of brown that only came from an outdoor life, the lines around the mouth suggested more smiles than tears or rage. But there was a world-weariness to him that had added a touch of bitterness or cynicism around the eyes. A large gold ring hung in his left ear and he wore a tie-dyed and faded pink T-shirt, old army fatigues and a pair of rugged walking boots.

He did nothing further to arouse suspicion and after a while Church's attention wandered, but when ten minutes had passed he began to grow anxious. He finished his coffee and went to stand outside the toilets, but although he tried to wait patiently, alarm bells were ringing in his head. He swung open the door and called Ruth's name. When there was no reply, he headed to the newsagents, but she wasn't there either. The car park was deserted. She hadn't slipped by him and returned to the cafeteria. Suddenly his heart was pounding as his uneasiness worried into a pearl of panic in his gut.

He decided the best option was to get security to put out an announcement, or at the very worst he could check to see if they had seen her on the surveillance cameras. The office lay at the furthest point of the thoroughfare, through a windowless door and up a short flight of stairs. Church stepped on to the stairs, desperately trying not to think the worst. But he had barely climbed three steps when he became starkly aware the temperature was dropping rapidly. By the time he reached the top, his breath was pluming and shivers rippled through him. The main office door creaked open noisily. Against one wall there was a curved desk with a bank of black-and-white monitors showing scenes from the car park, the Travelodge, the cafeteria and others. An uncomfortable silence lay heavy over everything, punctuated occasionally by sudden bursts of static from the radio speaker on the desk. But what caught Church's eye first was the glittering cobweb of frost that dappled everything – the desk, the equipment, the walls and floor. His head was spinning as he advanced slowly; it didn't make sense. A high-backed leather chair was turned away from him at the desk; he could just make out the tip of the head of a man sitting in it.

'Hello?' he said hesitantly.

His voice echoed hollowly; all remained still and quiet. He stared at the man's unmoving head, hoping the guard hadn't heard him, knowing in his heart that wasn't the answer. And suddenly he wanted to run out of there, not turn the chair around, not find any answers at all, but he forced himself to move forward. His footsteps sounded crisp, his breath was clouds of white. He spun the chair round in one movement and his stomach contracted instantly. The guard was frozen as solidly as if he had been left out in an Antarctic night; frost rimed his eyebrows and hair. His stare was glassy, his bloodless skin blueish beneath the unforgiving striplight. Church backed away, unable to come to terms with a situation that both terrified and baffled him. But as he turned, another shock brought him up sharp. Behind the door, hidden from his initial view, several bodies had been stacked. He recognised one of the women he had seen working in the cafeteria; the others also seemed to be staff from the services. Church felt like his head was fizzing as ideas banged into one another without forming one coherent thought. He rushed through the door and down the stairs two steps at a time.

When he crashed through the door into the main thoroughfare, the hippie from the cafeteria was waiting for him. 'They've taken her,' he said, with a faint Scottish brogue. He glanced around furtively. 'Outside. Don't draw attention from any of the staff.'

'Who's got her?' Church snapped, the anxiety cracking his voice.

'Quiet,' the man said sharply. 'They want you both dead. They already know who you are.'

'Ruth—'

'—is not dead yet. But she will be soon and you'll be next. Now, come.' He led the way to the car park, Church following like a sheep, confused, but slowly regaining his equilibrium. The hippie gazed around the bleak, puddled car park until his eyes settled on the grey Transit Church had earlier believed was following them. 'There,' he said.

Church looked into the man's face, wondering if he should trust him, and then he threw caution to the wind and set off weaving among the parked cars. As he neared the Transit, he could see it shift slightly on its suspension, although the windows were too dirty to see who was in the back. Without a second thought, Church grabbed the handle and yanked the rear door open.

There was a roar that wasn't human and a stink that reminded him of the monkey house at the zoo. Ruth was unconscious on the floor of the van. Standing over her, his face wild with rage, was the man in the waterproof Church had seen at the door of the café, his beady, darting eyes like an ape's behind the mask of his face, which had a strange waxy sheen. The man snarled and lashed out. Church caught a glimpse of a silver-bright knife that almost curved into a crescent near the end, and then he was yanked back suddenly.

Church's new associate stepped to his side. 'Stay out of his reach. He's too strong for you.'

Church was overwhelmed with sensations; the stench coming off the man making his head spin; the way the black-pebble eyes were filled with a monstrous anger Church couldn't begin to comprehend; the rasp of breath deep in the man's throat; the flash and glimmer as the blade danced in the air between them; and then the instinctive knowledge that *this* was what he had seen under the bridge. Ruth's captor jabbed the knife at Church and said what sounded like, 'Arith Urkolim.'

'What did he say?' Church snapped.

At Church's voice, Ruth stirred slightly, and his relief that she was okay surprised Church with its force. He edged to one side, looking for an opening, but there didn't seem any way he could get past the knife, and Ruth's captor was already trying to manoeuvre into a position to close the rear doors; strangely, he seemed wary of Church, ensuring the knife was always between the two of them, when he could probably have snapped Church's neck with one flex of his fingers. At the same time, he was changing; his skin seemed milky, then translucent and Church thought he could glimpse scales glistening just below the surface, while his tongue had grown forked at the tip like a snake's; when it wriggled out over his thin, dry lips it was accompanied by that deep, disturbing rasp from the back of his throat.

Ruth's eyes flickered open and briefly met his. Church saw an instant of panic as she took in the surroundings and then her natural control reasserted itself. At that moment her attacker lunged forward to grab the door handle. Knowing all would be lost if it shut, Church fumbled, then grasped the edge, feeling his knuckles pop and his tendons stretch to breaking as, effortlessly, Ruth's captor began to drag it closed.

'Get away!' the hippie barked. 'He's going to use the knife!'

Church looked up to see the blade at throat level, drawn back to strike. The snake-man said something in the same guttural language, his eyes now black with a red-slit pupil.

Suddenly Ruth's boot struck her attacker's calf with such force he overbalanced. Before he could recover, she had tangled both her feet among his legs. Church seized the moment, shifting his weight to fling the door shut so that with the force of the snake-man's pull it slammed into his face like a hammer. The dirty window glass exploded in a shower of crystals as the attacker crashed backwards over Ruth. In a sudden burst, Ruth scrambled out from under him, kicked open the door and tumbled out on to the wet tarmac, but Church's attention was still focused on the knife. He half thought about grabbing it when it clattered on to the floor of the van, but before his eyes it shimmered, then changed shape into something that resembled a silver spider which scurried away into the shadows.

'Let's get away from here,' the hippie hissed, dragging them both by their jackets. 'Where's your car?' The snake-man was already pulling himself to his feet, his face a mess of blood and torn flesh. An ear-splitting, inhuman roar erupted from its throat as they ran to the Nissan, and for a second of pure terror, Church thought it was coming after them. As he pushed the key in the lock, Church couldn't help glancing back, and instantly wished he hadn't; framed in the open van doors, he saw the snake-man howling terrible monkey cries as he tore at his clothes and face which was transforming, melting, shifting into something so awful Church gagged and turned away.

When they were safely inside, he fired up the engine, gunning the accelerator, and then they were lurching forward in a screech of tyres.

Only when they had pulled off the slip road into traffic did Church's heart start to return to normal. He turned to Ruth in the passenger seat. 'Are you okay?'

She nodded, her face pale and drawn.

'That thing in the van,' he stuttered, 'it was the same as whatever we saw under the bridge. Not the same one, though. So there's more of—'

'They can put on human faces,' the hippie interrupted from the back seat.

'They'd taken the place of all the staff there!' Church said, finally accepting what he'd seen.

'Waiting for you,' he continued. 'I think, if we took the time to investigate, we would find something similar at the airport and at other sites on all the arterial routes out of the capital.'

Church felt queasily like things were running out of control. 'They're after us?' he said dumbfoundedly.

'I was in one of the cubicles when I heard someone else come into the toilet and hang around outside. When I started to come out, the door burst in. Caught me a right one.' Ruth tenderly touched the ripening

54

bruise on her temple. 'The first thing I thought was, "What a geek", because he had that hood pulled so tightly round his face you could only see the little circle of his features. He looked like a mental patient. And then I thought, "You'd better make some noise because this bastard is going to try to rape you." And then his face changed. Just a bit, like a flicker in transmission or something, but I got a hint of what was behind it.'

Church shook his head in disbelief. 'They're after us?' he repeated stupidly. 'I thought we were after them?' Gradually his thoughts started to come together and he turned and briefly examined the hippie before returning his gaze to the road. 'And who are *you*?' he asked then. The man's cold eyes had been impossible to read; Church thought he might have done too many drugs, something to take him one step away from normal human experience.

'Tom,' he replied. 'I've never had much need for any other name. But Learmont is my family name.'

'That wasn't what I meant. You'd better start explaining.'

Tom removed his glasses and cleaned them, then checked through the window at the quality of light; although it was mid-afternoon, night did not seem far away. He smiled inscrutably. 'Life is a poem and a new verse is about to start.'

Ruth saw the anger flare in Church's face and calmed him with a hand on his forearm. She turned round in her seat and stared at the hippie coldly. 'You've been speaking like you know what's happening. You've been acting like you were waiting for us, even though we didn't even know we were going to stop here. I've just had the most frightening experience of my life. Don't play games with us.'

Tom removed a small tin from his haversack and began to roll himself a thin cigarette. To Church's irritation, he remained silent until the blue smoke clouded his face, and then he said, 'The world you grew up in is dead. It simply doesn't know it yet. This society is like some dumb animal that's had its throat cut and is still wandering around as if nothing has happened. You see, the most enormous conceit of this time is that the rules of the game are known. The scientists have fooled the populace – and themselves – that the universe is like clockwork, and that grand lie will cost everyone dearly. The universe is not like clockwork. The universe is like stoats fighting in a sack, bloody and chaotic, and any rules there might be could never be glimpsed by you or I.'

He sucked on his cigarette, choked a cough in his throat. Church felt odd licks of anxiety, while Ruth waited for the punchline.

'The one true law of the universe is duality,' Tom continued. 'You would think even the most confused of philosophers would see that, but it seems to have eluded all the apologists for this so-called Age of Reason. Hot and cold. Life and death. Good and evil. And what would be the flipside of science?'

He addressed the question to Ruth, but it was Church who answered: 'Magic?'

Tom smiled slyly. 'The seasons have turned. The Age of Reason has passed. We're on the cusp of a new age.'

Church laughed dismissively. 'I thought all that Age of Aquarius rubbish went out with flower children and love-ins.'

'The Age of Aquarius is one way of making sense of it, but it isn't the whole of it. Yes, we are entering an era of spirituality, wisdom and magic. But there will also be blood and brutality. All I'm saying is you must let go of old certitudes, keep an open mind. That's the only way you'll be able to face the trials that lie ahead.'

'You're not telling us anything,' Church protested.

'This isn't the time or the place. We need to move quickly. What happened back there wasn't the end of it. They won't be happy till you're both dead.'

When Church looked in the rearview mirror he could tell from Tom's set face that he was not about to reveal any more. A small nugget of anger made him want to drop the man off at the next services in retaliation, but he knew he couldn't dismiss the one person who seemed to know something about what was happening in his suddenly chaotic life. He glanced at Ruth, who smiled back as warmly as she could muster, but her eyes were still terribly scared.

They hadn't gone much further when Ruth's mobile phone rang. She answered it, then said to Church, 'It's someone called Dale for you.'

'He's a friend. I gave him your number for emergencies.' He nursed the phone against his shoulder as he drove. 'What's wrong, Dale?'

'You tell me.' Dale's voice was drawn and worried. There was a long pause, then he said, 'You've had some trouble at your flat.'

'What do you mean?'

Dale sighed. 'Well, there's no easy way to say this . . . It's been burnt out.'

'What?' Church almost dropped the phone.

'Someone broke down the door, then set fire to it. The fire brigade got there before it took out the rest of the house, but . . . well, I'm sorry, Church, everything's a write-off.' Another pause. 'That's not all. I've had the cops round here asking after you. I don't know how they found out where I worked, how they even knew we were friends . . .'

Dale's voice faded; he sounded disorientated, worried. 'They wanted to know where you were. I got the feeling it was about more than the fire.'

'What did you tell them?'

'Nothing, honest. Listen, if you're in any trouble—'

'Don't worry, Dale. It's probably just a mix-up. But I'd appreciate it if you didn't tell them where we are.'

'I don't know where you are!'

'Then you won't have to lie.'

After he'd switched off the phone, he told Ruth what Dale had told him. 'They have probably done the same to your home too,' Tom said to Ruth. 'And if either of you had been there you would be lying in the ashes now.'

'Who are *they*?' Church snapped; he felt at breaking point.

Tom sniffed at Church's tone, then lay across the seat and closed his eyes. 'Later,' he said dismissively. However much Church protested, he wouldn't respond, and in the end Church and Ruth were forced into a desperate silence as the sun slipped towards the horizon.

the purifying fire

Twilight was upon them. The traffic was growing heavier as the weekend rush from London to country homes in the west gathered force. The lights of Reading were now behind and the featureless landscape they had been passing through since they left the capital had given way to more wooded countryside, the trees eventually pressing in so that at times it was impossible to see beyond the edges of the motorway. Church adjusted the rearview mirror to check on Tom, who was still asleep on the back seat.

'Perfect. He sleeps, we worry.'

Ruth glanced at him askance. They had barely spoken since they had restarted the journey, lost in their own thoughts. 'Patience is a virtue,' she said.

'I don't trust him,' Church said quietly. 'I don't like being manipulated and that's what he's doing with all his talk that says nothing.' When he glanced at Ruth for a response, he saw how exhausted she looked; her experience at the service station was taking its toll. 'Why don't you close your eyes for a while?' he suggested.

She shook her head. 'Every time I do that, all I can see is that bastard coming at me in the toilets.'

'You'll get over it. I've seen you in action – you can cope with anything.'

'Is that what it looks like? In my head I feel like I've fought every step of the way through my life to keep it all from falling apart.' She watched the grey light disappearing over the horizon ahead. 'My dad always expected great things from me. He was the one who pushed me into the law. I think he had this idea I'd be some bigshot barrister.'

'Don't you like the job?'

'There were other things I could have done,' she said noncommittally. 'But I suppose my dad's attitude made me focused. Now I don't think I could loosen up if I tried.'

'You can never shake off those chains that keep you tied to the past, can you?' He thought of Marianne and the night swept in.

The driving was hard. There were too many lorries winding their way to

Bristol, too many coaches with weekend trippers, cars bumper-to-bumper, filled with anxious, irritable people desperate to get out of the city for a breath of fresh air, even though they were destroying it with each piston pump and exhaust belch. Drivers threw themselves in front of Church in suicidal bids to win the race, forcing him to slam on the brakes, cursing through gritted teeth. There were a thousand accidents waiting to happen in sleepy eye and stressed hand; the desire to escape was voracious, coloured by all sorts of ancient impulses. Church put on *London Calling* by The Clash to drown out the noise of the traffic, but Ruth had turned it down before Strummer had barely started to sing so as not to wake Tom; Church couldn't tell if it was through kindness or because she was afraid of what their new companion might have to say.

Newbury and Hungerford were long gone and they were on the flat, unspoiled stretch of countryside somewhere near the Ridgway. Swindon's lights burned orange in the sky ahead. Church flexed his aching fingers off the steering wheel. It would be late by the time they reached Bristol and they still had to find somewhere to stay. In the back seat, Tom stirred, mumbled something, then hauled himself upright to lean on Church and Ruth's seats. 'We need to find something to eat,' he said bluntly.

'Right away, Tom,' Church replied acidly. 'Have to keep you well-fed after your long sleep.'

'Can we try to get along?' Ruth asked. 'This is a very small car for—' She paused suddenly.

'What's wrong?' Church asked.

Ruth leaned forward to peer through the windscreen. 'What's that?'

'What's what?' The traffic was too heavy for Church to take his eyes off the road.

'A flash of light in the sky over to the south-west.'

'A UFO? I can give you Barry Riggs' number if you like. I'm sure he'd like to take you to his secret base.'

'Maybe it was lightning,' Ruth mused, still searching the skies.

'Actually, Salisbury Plain's over there somewhere,' Church continued. 'They had a big UFO flap down near Warminster in the sixties when all the believers and hippies used to gather on the hilltops to wait for the mothership to come.' He glanced in the mirror to see if Tom would rise to the bait, but the man ignored his gaze.

There was another flash and this time they all saw it: among the clouds, lighting them in an orange burst like a firework. 'That's not lightning,' Church said. 'It's more like a flare.' His attention had wavered from the road and he had to brake sharply to avoid hitting the car in front, which had slowed down as the driver also saw the lights.

'How long until you can get off this road?' Tom asked sharply.

'We don't need to get off this road.'

'How long?'

The tone of his voice snapped Church alert. 'Not long. I remember a junction somewhere on the outskirts of Swindon. Why?' Church glanced in the mirror, but Tom had his face pressed against the passenger window scanning the night sky.

There was another burst of light somewhere above them, so bright that Church saw the ruddy glare reflected on the roofs of the cars around. Ruth gasped in shock.

'What's going on?' Church thumped the horn as another distracted driver strayed across the line into his lane. 'There's going to be a pile-up in a minute!'

Ruth tried to crane her neck to see upwards through the windscreen. 'I think there's something up there,' she said.

'Probably the army on helicopter manoeuvres with no thought for anyone else as usual,' Church said. 'Jesus Christ!' He swung the wheel to avoid hitting a motorbike weaving in and out of the traffic. The rider kept glancing up at the sky in panic as he gunned the machine. Cold water washed up Church's spine. The traffic had become more dense, with no space to overtake. He was glad he was in the slow lane, with the hard shoulder available for any drastic evasive action.

Tom was becoming more anxious by the second. 'We must leave this traffic as soon as possible,' he stressed.

'I'm doing the best I can,' Church snapped. 'Do you think I can pick up the car and run with it?'

Ahead of them something big swept across the motorway about thirty feet off the ground. It was just a blur, a block of darkness against the lighter night sky, but its size and speed made Church catch his breath.

'What the hell was that?' he exclaimed.

'My God,' Ruth whispered in awe. 'Was that alive?'

The shock rippled back through the vehicles in a slewing of wheels and a sparking of brake lights. A red Fiesta gouged a furrow along the side of a Beetle before righting itself. There was a burst of exploding glass as a car in the centre lane clipped the one in front. Both cars fishtailed, but miraculously kept going.

Church was afraid to take his eyes off the road, but he had the awful feeling that something terrible was about to happen. He wound down the window; above the rumble of the traffic he could hear an odd noise,

60

rhythmic, loud, like the rending of thick cloth. After a second or two he suddenly realised what it sounded like: the beating of enormous wings.

He shifted the rearview mirror. Reflected in it was Tom's troubled face, his jaw set hard. 'What's going on?' Church barked. 'You know, don't you?'

Before Tom could answer, a column of fire blazed from the black sky on to a blue Orion, shattering all the windows with one tremendous blast and, a split second later, igniting the petrol tank. The car went up like it had been bombed. And then all hell erupted.

A shockwave exploded out, driving chunks of twisted metal and burning plastic like guided missiles, shattering windscreens, careening off roofs and bonnets, imbedding in doors and wings. The vehicles closest to the blast were the first to go. Some were travelling too fast and simply ploughed into the inferno. Others, attempting to avoid it, swerved, clipped other vehicles and set off a complex pattern of ricochets that rippled across the motorway. A lorry, its windscreen a mass of frosted glass, crushed a Peugeot before slamming into the side of a coach. The coach driver fought with the wheel as his vehicle went over on two wheels, then back on the other two, before toppling over completely in a bone-juddering impact that crushed two more cars. Church caught sight of terrified white faces through glass and felt his stomach churn.

And then there was chaos as vehicles thundered into each other, smashing through the central reservation, piling up twisted wreckage in a deafening Wagnerian cacophony of exploding glass, screeching tyres and rending metal, until it seemed all six lanes were filled with death and destruction. The flames leapt from collision to collision, feeding on ruptured petrol tanks, until a wall of fire blazed across the whole of the motorway. Another column of fire lanced down from the heavens, blowing up a living fountain of flame that soared high above their heads.

Their ears rang from the noise, and the sudden, awful smell of thick smoke and petrol engulfed them as Church threw the car on to the hard shoulder; the accident had happened too fast for the vehicles ahead to attempt the same route. Behind them and to the side, cars were still smashing into the carnage. Ruth thought she could hear terrible screams buried in the sounds of wreckage, but she convinced herself it was just an illusion. A juggernaut jackknifed and was lost to the fire. A motorcyclist skidded along at ground level, his arms raised in a futile attempt to ward off the inevitable. And more, and more, too much to bear. They turned their heads away as one, and Church hit the accelerator, launching the car forward. The nearside wheels churned up mud and grass on the bank; the rear end skidded wildly, but he kept his foot to the floor. As they approached the inferno at breakneck speed, Ruth screamed and threw her arms across her face, Tom dropped flat on the seat and Church closed his eyes and whispered a prayer.

The heat made his skin bloom and he half-expected the glass to implode, but then they were through it and racing across the empty motorway ahead.

'God,' Ruth said in shock. She clasped her hands together in her lap to stop them shaking.

Church slowed down and headed towards one of the emergency phones on the hard shoulder.

'Don't stop!' Tom yelled. 'The worm will still be here. It doesn't give up easily!' Then he added with exasperation, 'Don't you see? It's after us.'

Church swung the car in a wide arc until they faced the wall of fire. Vehicles had backed up on the other side of the central barrier. In the distance came the sound of sirens.

'What are you doing?' Tom snapped.

'I have to see for myself.' Church leaned forward over the wheel and searched the skies. He and Ruth saw it at the same moment, just a glimmer at first, high above the billowing grey smoke. But as it came lower it fell into focus and they both froze in their seats. They saw glints of copper and gold and green as the red glare of the fire burnished its scales. A scarlet eye as bright as a brake light. Enormous, leathery wings that beat the air with a slow, heavy rhythm, and a long tail that writhed and twisted behind it as if it had a separate existence. As it swooped low, it opened its mouth wide and belched a gush of golden-orange fire that sprayed into the inferno and sent another torrent of flames spouting high. Its movements were fluid as it soared on the air currents, terrifying and majestic at the same time.

'I don't believe it,' Ruth said in hushed, incredulous tones. Church's head was spinning.

'They have been away too long, excluded against their will. They miss their old places,' said Tom.

'I don't believe it,' Church echoed in a mix of wonder and fear.

Tom rested a hand on his shoulder. 'We have to be away. It will soon realise we've escaped its first strike.'

'What the hell's going on?' Church spun round in a rage. 'You know. Tell us!'

'I told you.' Tom's tone was darker than he intended. 'They've recognised you. They won't let you live.'

'Stop procrastinating—'

Ruth caught his arm, signalling that it wasn't the time or the place. 'Where will we go?' she said in dismay. 'Look at the speed of it. It won't take long to catch us, however fast we're driving.'

'There's only one place we can be assured of safety until dawn comes,' Tom replied. 'But it's still a long journey from here. We have to get the wind behind us and pray to God we reach there first.'

Following Tom's directions, Church put the pedal to the floor until they reached the next exit, where they took the A346 south. An oppressive silence lay on them as they each struggled with the terrible sights they had witnessed. Even with the window down, Church couldn't clear the stink of burning from his nose, and when he glanced at Ruth, he saw in the flicker of the street lamps her cheeks were wet. Behind all the churning emotions was an incomprehension at how they had suddenly found themselves in a situation where terrible, unbelievable forces had emerged from the shadows to target them alone. There seemed no reason for the magnitude of the power ranged against them, or for the unflinching focus of its cold eye.

Tom barely removed his head from the rear window shelf, where he was pressing his face against the glass in numerous contortions to search the skies. The thick cloud cover made it impossible to get a clear view, but the wind had blown the rain away and the driving was easier.

'I don't believe what we saw there,' Church said quietly. 'What's going on?' He glanced in the mirror at Tom. 'I said, what's going on? You weren't surprised by that thing—'

'I've seen one before,' Tom replied. 'And I'll tell you all about it when we get where we're going. If we get there.'

Church shook his head incredulously, then glanced at Ruth for support. She caught his eye for a second, then looked away.

The road was straight, but slow after the motorway, and seemed very old. Grassy banks and ancient wire fences lined it, punctuated at intervals by bursts of elder and bushy hawthorn. There seemed little habitation on either side away in the dark where fields stretched up to the downy hills. The route dipped and rose so it was always hard to see too far ahead and Church had to temper his speed accordingly. They eventually passed a golf club and two large thatched cottages with lights burning brightly in the windows; Church felt oddly warmed by the sight.

After a while they burst from the dark, worrying countryside into

Marlborough, the road sweeping down through its age-old buildings, jumbled topsy-turvy in a mix of pastel shades.

'Have we lost it?' Church asked anxiously. 'We must have by now.'

'We won't be able to evade it,' Tom said distractedly. 'All we can hope is we reach our destination before it.'

'You're telling me it can recognise the make and model of a dark-coloured car at night, from hundreds of feet overhead?' Church said.

'She isn't *looking*,' Tom replied obliquely. 'The Fabulous Beasts are highly sensitive. She knows our signature. She can locate us from miles distant.'

'*She?*' Church said incredulously. 'How do you know so much about something that shouldn't exist? Christ, tell me something! This is driving me insane!'

There was a long silence until Ruth said, 'You're wasting your breath, Church. Just keep your eyes on the road.'

Still heading south, Tom directed them through Pewsey alongside the Avon, guarded by the stone bulk of its twelfth century church. In the countryside beyond, the road was so dark the driving became even more difficult. Trees clustered in tightly, with only the occasional light of a farm off in the distance breaking through the branches. But through Upavon they became aware of a change in the countryside as Salisbury Plain rolled in, bleak and uncompromising. The military presence was unmissable, with signs for armoured vehicle crossings and tank tracks tearing up the landscape on both sides. There were high, chainlink fences topped with barbed wire and a checkpoint for the forces off to the left.

The sight sparked an idea in Church. 'Why haven't the RAF scrambled to shoot it down? There's an early warning base at Lyneham.'

Tom was distracted and nervous, glancing repeatedly out of the window to ascertain their relative position. 'They won't know it's there unless they happen to glance up to see it. And then they wouldn't believe their eyes.'

'It must register on radar at that size.'

'It belongs to the old world. Technology can't comprehend it.' As they passed Figheldean in a blur of sodium glare, he said darkly, 'I see her. She is circling up high, trying to find us.'

For a while the trees offered some cover, but then Tom caught his breath. 'She's seen us. Drive faster!'

'I'm just about blowing a piston now!' Church grunted.

Ruth wound down the window and hung her head out, fighting against the buffeting slipstream. At first she could see nothing, but then the clouds parted to reveal the moon and the Fabulous Beast caught in its milky luminescence, its scales glinting like polished metal; for the briefest instant, it appeared to be made out of silver. Its wings, at full stretch, could span a football pitch. They looked like dark leather which at times seemed scarlet, and then emerald, sparkling as if dusted with gold. Occasionally Ruth could make out its eyes glowing like the landing lights of a plane. She pulled her head in and said in hushed awe, 'It's magnificent.'

'What's it doing now?' Church felt the sweat pooling in the small of his back.

'Circling like a bird of prey.' Ruth turned to Tom. 'If we could get off the open road, under cover somewhere—'

There was a roar like a jet taking off, a concentrated burst of orange-yellow light that illuminated the interior of the car as brightly as day, and then the hedge on their side of the road disintegrated in a firestorm. Church fought to keep the car on the road against the sudden shockwave of superheated air.

They crashed across a roundabout, narrowly avoiding another car, and then Tom ordered Church to take the next right. For the first stretch it was a dual carriageway, allowing Church to floor the accelerator; the car complained under the sudden pull. But then the road narrowed to a single carriageway and Church feared the worst. At Tom's instruction he took a right fork on the wrong side of the road, his shirt wet with sweat.

'Turn right when I say!' Tom yelled. Church's eyes were constantly drawn to the sky, but he steeled himself for the order. 'Now!'

Church swung the wheel, clipping the kerb as another pillar of fire erupted from the heavens. Behind them the tarmac exploded in molten gouts. They swung round in a massive car park, the plain rolling off flatly ahead of them.

'Where do we go from here?' Church shouted, suddenly confronted by a huddle of low buildings and a barrier with a turnstile.

'Out of the car,' Tom ordered, wrenching the door open.

Before Church could protest, Tom was moving rapidly for someone in his late fifties. He vaulted the barrier, and by the time they had caught up with him he was turning into a tunnel which cut back under the road. Overhead, the slow beat of the creature's wings was almost deafening. They felt the surge of air currents as it swooped by, but by the time it had rounded to emit another blast of fire they were already deep in the tunnel.

Ruth slumped against the wall to catch her breath. 'Thank God,' she gasped.

'Not here,' Tom stressed, grabbing her arm and pulling her on. A few seconds later, a wall of flame roared along the tunnel to the point where she had been standing, the wave of scorching air knocking them to the ground.

Coughing and choking, with lungs that seemed to burn from the inside, they scrambled forward and emerged into the cool night. Church was instantly transfixed by a view of black megaliths crowded squat and ancient beneath the light of the moon.

'Stonehenge?' Ruth gasped.

They ran forward and clawed their way over the perimeter fence, only pausing once they were amongst the stones.

'It can see us here as easily as anywhere else,' Ruth protested as she watched the creature soar and turn high overhead, a black shape blocking out the stars as it passed.

'I told you, she senses.' Tom knelt and patted the scrubby grass affectionately. 'The land is filled with power. Earth Magic. Tremendous alchemical energy that flows among the old places and sacred spots. The Fabulous Beasts feed on it, use the lines for guidance when they are flying. We can't see it, but to them it appears like a network of blue fire on the land. And here, in a powerful nexus of that energy, we're lost in the glare.'

There was a moment of silence as Ruth gaped at Tom, then she turned to Church; he shook his head dismissively.

Tom shrugged and turned away. 'Believe what you will. You have seen one of the Fabulous Beasts. You cannot wish your way back to your old life.' He wandered off amongst the stones and was soon lost in the shadows.

Ruth and Church watched the sky, ready to run at any second.

'Well, he's right about one thing,' Ruth said after a tense few moments. 'It's not attacking.' She watched it circling, the arc growing wider and wider.

Church followed her gaze. 'What the hell's going on?'

Gradually the creature disappeared from view. The wind picked up, blustering over the sweeping plain, driving the few remaining clouds ahead of it until the night sky was clear and burning with the beacons of a thousand stars. Church couldn't remember the last time he had seen the sweep of the heavens in such a virginal, breathtaking state.

'Beautiful,' Ruth whispered in a state of dazed incomprehension. 'I knew there was a reason to move out of the city.'

The enormity of their experience made it almost impossible to consider so Church focused on the mundane. 'What do you make of him?'

Ruth thought for a while, her face hidden in shadows. 'I think he could help us.'

'But you don't trust him.'

'No.' She chewed on her lip thoughtfully, then said, 'I don't like the way he's not telling us what's happening. You can see he knows more. But it's like he's using it to control us.'

The wind that had been rushing around the henge died down and for a second there was just peace and quiet. 'Who is he, Church? How can he know these things?'

'I've given up trying to make any sense of it,' he replied morosely. 'I'll just be happy getting out the other end in one piece.'

They found a spot on one of the fallen stones where they could lie without getting damp and simply watched the stars, almost touching, aware only of their presence in the universe, the noise of their chaotic thoughts shut down for a brief moment of tranquillity. A shooting star streaked brightly across the arc of the sky, and the last thought Church remembered having was, 'That's an omen.'

The tramp of Tom's boots disturbed them some time later as they floated half in and out of sleep.

'I feel like I've slept for hours,' Church said, scrubbing his face to wake himself. 'Must be the stress.'

'The blue fire,' Tom corrected. 'It heals and invigorates if you open yourself up to it.' Something landed on the ground before them. 'Dinner,' he said. A rabbit lay there, its tufts of white fur ghostly in the dark.

'How did you catch that?' Ruth asked.

'You pick up a few tricks when you're hungry on the road.'

'We're going to eat it raw?' Church said in disgust.

'You can if you like. I'm lighting a fire.'

'And have every security guard in the county here in five minutes. I'm surprised they haven't picked us up already,' Church said.

'Their technology is blind to us. And there's no need to worry about the fire, either. I'll make sure of that.'

Church lay back and closed his eyes again. 'I'm not even going to ask.'

Tom looked around for some fuel; the land was just grassy scrub in all directions so he tore up a walkway of wooden pallets that kept the tourists out of the mud in wet weather. It was enough to build a decent fire, and even though the kindling was damp he was able to get it alight with relative ease. He skinned, gutted, trimmed and jointed the rabbit with a Swiss Army knife, then stuffed the various pieces in packets of turf and placed them in the embers around the edge of the fire.

'It will not be long,' he said when he'd finished. 'A hedgehog would have been quicker, but I could not find one.'

'Mmmm,' Church said acidly. 'Vermin.'

'It's a tasty dish. You're soft.'

'That's why God invented pizza parlours.'

Tom smiled wryly. 'And what will you do when all the pizza parlours have gone?'

'More doom and gloom. The end of the world is nigh.'

'You're starting to sound like an idiot who can't count the fingers held in front of his face,' Tom countered.

Tom and Church glared at each other until Ruth interjected. 'Don't argue – I haven't got the energy.' Her face seemed too pale in the firelight and her eyes brimmed with tears. 'I keep thinking of all those people who died on the motorway. Everywhere there was something horrible – somebody's face screaming. I can't get it out of my head.'

Compassion lit Tom's face, softening the lines and the set of his jaw that gave a hardness to his appearance.

'And we caused it!' Ruth continued.

'You didn't cause it,' Tom said flatly. 'What you saw this evening is just the first of many outrages. Some you will be at the heart of, many will happen without your involvement.'

Church had reached his limit. 'You're driving me mad, saying things like, "Oh, that's because of the blue fire", whatever *that* means, or pretending you have intimate knowledge of the habits of mythical creatures. Why should we believe anything you say?'

There was no outburst in response. Tom merely stared into the middle distance thoughtfully as he gently rubbed his chin. 'How can I explain things to you when you have no frame of reference to understand them?' Then: 'Unfortunately I don't have any credentials to show you. All I can say is that I've seen unmistakable evidence of what's occurring. You'll have to accept me on trust until we know each other well enough to discuss the past.' He held up his hand to silence Church's protests. 'But if you're looking for some kind of proof, there is something I *can* show you.' He dipped into a hidden pocket and pulled out his tobacco tin and a small block of hash which he used to roll a joint.

'I don't think this is the time to get off your face,' Church said.

'This isn't for pleasure,' Tom replied. He lit the joint and inhaled deeply. 'Before the Christian era, psychoactive substances were used by most cultures to put them in touch with the sacred. And that's what I'm about to do now, to show you so you understand what lies behind it all.' He closed his eyes in meditation for a short while, then said, in a gentle voice barely audible over the wind and the fire, 'The people who put up these stones were smoking as they sat here, looking at the stars. In the fougous and under the barrows, beneath the cromlechs, in the circles and the chambered cairns, they were eating sacred mushrooms and ingesting hallucinogens thousands of years before the so-called Summer of Love. It helped man touch the heart of the universe.' He blew a fragrant cloud into the breeze. Then he said in a strong, powerful voice: 'You have to understand that magic works.'

'Magic as in spells and funny hand movements and all that mumbo jumbo,' Church said tartly. 'Sure, why not? A few hits on that and I'll believe in anything.'

'Magic as in influencing people and events without having any obvious direct contact with them,' Tom said, calmly but forcefully. 'Magic as in beings with abilities you can only dream of. An old word for something that may lie just beyond science, that has its own strict rules, that operates with subtle energy flows and fields. A completely different way of looking at how the world works.' Church's expression remained unchanged, so Tom walked over to the nearest standing stone. 'Science says this is just a lump of rock stuck in the earth. Magic says it's something more. Look at it closely, along the edge silhouetted against the sky.'

'What am I supposed to be looking for?' Church said.

'Look close and look hard. Dismiss nothing as a trick of your eyes. Believe.'

Ruth and Church stared at the point Tom was indicating and after a few minutes Ruth said, 'I think I can see a light.'

'Keep looking,' Tom pressed.

Church shook his head dismissively, but then he squinted and after a second or two he seemed to make out a faint blue glow limning the edge of the menhir. The more he stared, the more it came into focus, until tiny azure flames appeared to be flickering all around the ancient stone. 'What is that?' he asked in amazement.

'Magic,' Tom replied softly. He slowly held out his right index finger to the stone and an enormous blue spark jumped from the rock to his hand; a second later the force, whatever it was, was running to him directly, infusing him with a soft sapphire glow. Still smiling, he raised his left hand palm upwards; shimmering shapes danced in the air above it. Church thought he glimpsed faces and bodies, but nothing stayed in focus.

'Static electricity,' Church ventured without believing it himself. 'An electromagnetic field given off by geological stresses.'

Tom simply smiled.

'Does it hurt?' Ruth asked.

'I feel like I could run a hundred miles.' He drew in a deep, peaceful breath. 'This is the power in the land. Earth Magic. The Fiery Network. Science can't measure it so science says it doesn't exist. But you see it.'

Church felt his mood altering in proximity to the crackling display; he was overcome with an exuberation that made him want to shout and jump around. Negative thoughts sloughed off him like mud in the rain; he couldn't stop himself grinning like an idiot.

Tom broke off the display and returned to his seat by the fire. 'Belief in a new way – the true way – won't happen in a night, but all things flow from this and once you accept it you'll truly understand.'

'But what is it exactly?' Church's intellectual curiosity had been piqued alongside the buzz his emotions had received.

'The vital force of the world, the thing that binds humanity and the planet together. An energy unlike any other, spiritual in essence. If you look closely enough you'll find it within you as well as within the earth.'

'The New Agers always said there was something like this.' Church felt a shiver wash through him; he felt deeply affected in a way he couldn't understand.

'The ancients knew about it. The Chinese call it *chi*, the dragon energy, for it's always been linked with the Fabulous Beasts who are both its symbol and its guardians. That's why the standing stones were raised, the old stone chambers, the earliest churches. To mark the sacred sites where the energy was strongest, to channel it, to keep it flowing freely. But when the so-called Age of Reason came, it was discounted by the new generation of thinkers – it couldn't be quantified, bottled, replicated in a laboratory. And as that new way of seeing the world took hold, the people forgot it too. Over time it became dormant. For centuries no one could have stirred it, however hard they tried. But with the change that came over the world at the turn of the year, it awoke again. Now a few of us know how to raise it briefly, but it still needs to be woken completely, to become the vital force once more. And this,' he added, 'is the first sign that the world is now a very different place.'

'How do you know all this?' Ruth asked.

'I was called. Informed—'

'Called by whom?'

He smiled at the insistence in her voice. 'If you must know, by a gentleman called the Bone Inspector. Any the wiser?'

'That's an odd name.'

'He's an odd man. His people have been linked to the land for millennia, the custodians of secret knowledge and ancient ritual. He guards the old places where the blue fire burns the brightest. He felt the changes first. Perhaps you'll meet him one day and then you can ask him all these questions yourself.'

'This is making my head hurt,' Church said. 'People who guard the old places?'

'The best way to approach this is to forget everything you thought you knew,' Tom said bluntly.

'Okay,' Church said, 'you've convinced me you've got some sort of insight, but there are still a lot of questions to be answered—'

'At least I have your attention now,' Tom said acidly.

'Then what is going on?' Ruth asked. Beyond the ruddy glow cast by the fire, the night seemed too dark; past the comforting bulk of the stones the shadows seemed to rise up from the plain. 'Why are all these things happening now?'

Tom crimped out the joint. 'Everything changed, suddenly, dramatically, sometime around the New Year.' He prodded the fire with a broken branch, sending a shower of sparks skyward. 'The world's turning away from the light. History is cyclical, you should know that. Empires rise and fall, knowledge is learned then lost, and sometimes things that seem gone for ever return unannounced. There's a basis for all legends, folklore, fairytales—'

'Symbolism, rites of passage, religion,' Church interrupted. 'A way to pass important wisdom down the generations so it can be easily understood by those learning it.'

'All true, of course. How very erudite of you. But some of it is *literal*. As I understand it, the world used to be a very different place. You saw the Fabulous Beast so this is undeniable – creatures of myth once walked this land, old gods, ancient races, things you would think existed only in the imagination. And the old stories are our way of remembering this time of wonder and miracles.'

Church glanced at Ruth; Tom's words were an echo of what Kraicow had begun to say. 'There's no archaeological record—' he began, but Tom waved him silent.

'Somehow, for some reason, all these things were swept away to' – he made an expansive gesture – 'some other place. But now—'

'They're back.' Ruth shivered. Somewhere nearby an owl's forlorn hoot keened over the wind. She searched the darkness, but it was impossible to see anything beyond the circle of the fire. 'And this man you called the Bone Inspector told you all this?'

'Some of it.'

'And you believed him straight away?' Church put his head in his hands and closed his eyes for a moment. But having seen what Tom called the Fabulous Beast, he knew there was no rational explanation for it. 'So where did all these creatures of myth go for the last millennia or so?'

Church couldn't tell if Tom's silence was because he didn't know or because he didn't want to tell them.

'And what we saw under the bridge and at the service station were some of the things from those days?' Ruth asked hesitantly.

Tom searched for the right words. 'This is how it was told to me: long ago, long before mankind had established itself, there were old races. Beings of tremendous power, understanding of all the secret forces in the universe. They were so incomprehensible to us in their appearance and their actions they could have been gods. They were the source of all our legends. In the Celtic stories, in the sacred traditions of other races and cultures. Even in the Christian heritage.'

'Demons,' Ruth ventured.

'And angels,' Tom continued. 'Folklore is the secret history of this land. There's a bright truth in every story. Look at mediaeval wood carvings. Illustrated religious texts. The stone creatures on some of the churches. Once seen, never forgotten. Over time the old races went into decline and soon the season came for them to move on. They disappeared beyond the veil, supposedly for ever. There have been echoes of them down the years – some of the old gods could not leave well alone. Other times their power leaked through, into the ancient places, the sacred places. In all but that they were gone, and the world breathed again, and mankind prospered.' He stared deep into the heart of the flames. 'But now their season has come round again.'

The wind picked up as if in response to his words; Church shivered and pulled his jacket tightly around him. 'If what you're saying is true, and I'm not saying it is, why have they returned now?'

Tom shrugged. 'As I said, everything is cyclical. Perhaps it is simply their time. And perhaps the time of mankind has now passed. Who knows? The rules remain hidden; life is a mystery.'

Church tried to read Tom's face in the hope that he could see the lie, any sign that it was all just a fantasy made up to frighten them; he looked away a moment later in failure.

'But how many of them are there?' Ruth asked.

Tom shrugged. 'Of the larger creatures, the Fabulous Beasts, a handful, I would guess. Many of the wilder mythical creatures, probably the same. I haven't seen an outcry in the media over the last few weeks, so they must be so few as to be able to find hiding places in this over-populated island.'

'And the things that are after us?'

Tom looked down. 'They seem to be everywhere. You saw them – they're shapeshifters. They hide in plain sight. But their skills aren't perfect. If you look close enough, you can see.'

'The skin was too waxy,' Church noted. 'The face looked like a mask.'

'And Gibbons and Kraicow stumbled across them among us,' Ruth said. 'And they both paid the price.'

'They seem to be going to any lengths to prevent themselves being discovered.'

'Like setting a fire-breathing monster on us just because we went to see Kraicow. With that kind of overreaction they must be scared of being uncovered. What are they planning to do?' Church asked. 'Stay in hiding?'

'I don't think,' Tom mused, 'it's in their nature to stay hidden for long.'

'Then what?' Church said insistently.

'Your guess is as good as mine. But I think there will be some kind of conflict. They appear more powerful than us.'

'Even so,' Church said dismissively, 'what could they do?'

'There's one thing I don't understand,' Ruth said. 'You seemed to be waiting for us at the services, yet we didn't even know we were going to be stopping there ourselves until the last minute.'

'I had a feeling I had to be there.'

'What? You're psychic now?' Church shook his head dismissively.

'Things have changed more than you think,' Tom said coldly. 'How can the rigid laws of physics exist after what we've discussed this evening? Science and magic are incompatible. When the doors opened, it wasn't just the stuff of legends that flooded back into our world – it was a new way of thinking, of existing.'

Ruth looked particularly uncomfortable at that prospect. 'What do you mean?'

'There are some Eastern religions that believe the world is the way it is because we wish it that way,' Tom continued. 'In this new age it will be wished another way. Do you think there will be a place for the old, masculine, ultra-logical, highly-structured way of thinking that has dominated for so long? This will be a time of instinct, of the feminine aspect, of wonder and awe. Science and technology, certainly, will suffer.'

Tom's voice was lulling, hypnotic. In the crackle of the flames, Church could almost hear whispers echoing down the centuries, in their dance he seemed to see faces, dark and alien. It disturbed him too much and he looked back into the impenetrable night.

'You're saying it could be the end of the world as we know it?' Ruth said fearfully.

'It will be a time of change, certainly.' He didn't sound very reassuring.

A cold wind blasted into the clearing, making the fire roar, showering a cascade of sparks upwards. Church had the sudden impression they were being watched. He looked round quickly, trying to see beyond the pathetic circle of light, but the darkness was too dense. Tom threw some more wood on the fire and listened to it sputter and sizzle for a while.

Church eyed Tom suspiciously. 'Sitting here, having seen what we've seen, this all makes a stupid kind of sense. But there's still a part of me that says—'

'That I'm lying? I never lie.' He poked the fire. 'The food should be ready now. Let's eat.'

'It hasn't been in long enough,' Ruth said.

'I think it will be ready.'

'More magic?' Church said.

'That, or good cooking technique.' Tom's smile was inscrutable, and Church was instantly aware he had no idea what was going on behind the man's eyes.

The rabbit was steaming hot, fragrant and tender. They gnawed the meat off the bone with the fire hot on their faces and the chill of the night at their backs. Although it may have been the aftermath of the strange energy, Church was convinced it was one of the best meals he had ever eaten.

Afterwards, as the night grew colder, they huddled closer to the fire, relaxed and replete, the uneasiness forgotten, at least for the moment. Tom picked the remaining meat from his teeth with a twig while he surveyed the position of the stars.

Eventually, he said, 'Everything is changing. You have to be prepared for the new ways . . . the new, *old* ways . . . if you're to be of any use in the coming struggle.'

'But what could we possibly do,' Ruth began, 'if things are as dire as you say? We could try to warn the Government, the police, the army, but I think we'd pretty much be laughed out and locked up.'

'They will not be able to do anything anyway,' Tom said. 'This is a time for individuals, not institutions, for passion not planning.'

'Very poetic,' Church noted. 'But, with all due respect to Ruth . . . look at us. We're not exactly people of action.'

'Adaptation is the key, and people adapt quicker than groups. If you can learn to work within the new rules, then . . . perhaps something can be done.' Tom eyed them both with a dissecting look which made Church feel uncomfortable.

Ruth wasn't convinced. 'Two people against the sort of powers that you're talking about? Get real.'

'But we have to do something,' Church said passionately. 'We have a responsibility—'

'A good word,' Tom interjected.

'Don't be so patronising!' Church felt his emotions were on the edge of swinging out of control.

'I apologise,' Tom said, without seeming in the least contrite.

Church grunted with irritation and marched over to lean on the great trilithon. Ruth watched him affectionately as he gazed up at the stars.

'It would help if you were a little less smug,' she said to Tom diplomatically. 'He's a good man. He wants to do something. You shouldn't be so hard on him.'

He shrugged. 'We all have our flaws.'

'There's so much more we need to know—'

'We can discuss it tomorrow, when we're all a little more receptive. I've given you plenty to chew over – a whole new way of looking at life, a new belief system, things that at first glance seem impossible. Isn't that enough to be going on with?'

'How much more is there?'

'There's always more.' He yawned and stretched. 'It's late. We need to sleep. We've got a great deal ahead of us, and we may not always have such a fortuitous place to rest our heads.'

'You expect me to sleep after all this?'

'You will sleep.' Tom brushed her forehead with his fingertips and she went out as if he had flicked a switch. He caught her and laid her down next to the fire, removing her coat and pulling it over her like a blanket.

'It is a magnificent place, isn't it?'

Church hadn't heard Tom approach behind him. 'I wish I'd seen it under other circumstances.'

'You should see it on June 21, at the solstice at sunrise. If you stand at the centre of the circle, there comes a moment when the sun appears to be suspended on the heel stone and the whole place is painted gold. Beautiful.'

'I wish I hadn't got dragged into all this. Life was complicated enough as it was.'

'It's too late for that.'

'Yes. I know.'

Tom lit another joint, took the smoke down deep, then exhaled into the wind. 'There are journeys without and within to make,' he said softly, 'and many mysteries to be uncovered before the end of the road. We are surrounded by them, all the time, every day, and when we think we are trying to expose one, it often turns out we are delving into another. Take this place. They *think* Neolithic man dug the outer circle more than four and a half thousand years ago. They *think* the Beaker People erected the bluestones eight hundred years later and the Wessex People put in the sarsen blocks in 1,500 BC. But who did it is not as important as why. Why did different peoples value this place so highly they returned to it over all those years? Simply because it aligned with the sun, moon and stars? Would they have put so much effort into it if it was simply a tool? Or a metaphor for some religious experience?'

Church drew his fingers across the surface of the stone, feeling the years heavy under his touch. 'They were searching for some meaning,' he said.

'That's right. They were trying to find the magic at the heart of reality. And they found it, the most valuable thing mankind could ever possess. But somehow we lost it again, and during the twentieth century it got as far away from us as it could possibly get. But if one good thing can come out of all the terrible things that lie ahead, it will be that we, as a race, will get back in touch with it again.'

Church scanned the dark horizon. 'That's tomorrow taken care of. What do we do on the day after?'

'You're no longer the person you used to be.' Church couldn't tell if it were an admonition or a pep talk. 'The path away from that person began with your alchemical experience under the bridge, and there are plenty of changes on the road ahead, for you and Ruth.' Tom rested one hand on Church's shoulder and pointed towards the heel stone. 'You see that star there? Wait five minutes until it touches the stone.'

They stood in silence watching the gradual descent until, at the exact moment of alignment, Church felt a tingling at the base of his spine. A second later it felt like heaven had exploded around him. The blue energy Tom had summoned earlier erupted upwards from the top of the stones, forming a structure that soared at least a hundred feet above their heads. The lines of force met at the pinnacle and sheets of paler blue, shifting between opaque and clear, crackled among them. Church had the sudden sensation of standing in a cathedral, magnified by a feeling of overwhelming transcendental awe and mystery that left him trembling. Ahead, lines of azure fire raced out across the land, criss-crossing into a network as they reached other ancient sites, where they exploded upwards in glory. To Church, it seemed like the whole of Britain was coming alive with magnificence and wonder. Tears of emotion stung his eyes and there was a yearning in his heart that he hadn't experienced since childhood.

After five minutes the flames shimmered then dwindled until all was as it had been, but Church knew he would keep the moment with him for the rest of his days.

Still lost in the spell, he started suddenly when Tom touched his hand. 'Before you passed under the bridge that night, you would never have seen that. It's a mark of how much you have already changed, and a hint of the potential ahead.'

As they wandered back to the fire, Church felt calm and energised by the experience. 'Make the most of this night,' Tom said as they lay down and looked up at the stars. 'This is a safe place, but from here on, things are going to get wild and dangerous.'

'We'll cope,' Church said, surprising himself at his confidence.

The last words of Tom's he heard were almost lost on the edge of sleep: 'One more thing – do not leave the circle before sunrise.'

Church awoke some time in the early hours. Tom and Ruth were still sleeping, cast in the faintest reddish glow from the embers of the fire. His soft back muscles ached from the hard ground, but as he rolled around trying to get comfortable, he became aware of an uneasy feeling in the pit of his stomach and the sensation that he was being watched. Over the next five minutes it grew gradually stronger until he had to stand up to look warily around. Beyond the small circle lit by the dim mantle of the fire, the night seemed uncommonly dark.

He waited for a minute or two, but when the sensation didn't diminish he cautiously edged towards the shadows. Beyond the reach of the fire's luminescence, his eyes grew accustomed to the dark and he began to make out the shapes of hedges and trees on the plains that rolled away from the henge. There was no sign of movement and his ears, tuned for the tramp of a foot, could only pick up the bleak moan of the wind as it swept across the lowlands.

When he reached the outer stones, Church paused, his heart

thumping madly from the discomfort of invisible eyes. 'Who's there?' he hissed.

There was a lull, as if the night were waiting for him to progress further, then he heard what appeared to be the faintest reply on the edge of his hearing, barely more than a rustle of grass.

After a few seconds he caught a glimpse of movement, like a dark shape separating itself from the lighter dark of the night. His skin seemed to grow taut across his body. A figure, slim and tall, moved towards him, gradually developing an inner light as if tiny fireflies were buzzing around within it. Long before it had coalesced into any recognisable form, Church was overcome. And when it finally halted twenty feet away from him, his eyes burned with tears and his trembling knees threatened to buckle.

'Marianne,' he whispered.

She was pale and fragile, her eyes dark and hollow, as if she had gone days without sleep; Church couldn't bear to look into their depths. Her skin had an opaque quality that seemed to shimmer and for the briefest instant become transparent. Her arms hung limply at her sides, her shoulders slouched from an unseen burden. Church felt an overwhelming wave of despair and longing washing off her, sluicing away the *frisson* of fear he felt at her terrible appearance.

And all he could remember was that moment when the last dregs of life drained away and the intelligence died in her eyes, leaving him with just an armful of hope and chattering images of promised futures now lost and, worse, the certain knowledge he would never know why everything he ever needed or believed in had been taken away from him.

He thought he might die if he heard the truth, but he asked anyway, in a hoarse voice that didn't sound like his own: 'Just tell me why.'

If she heard, she gave no sign; her blank features still radiated that sense of terrible loss. Church couldn't bear to look at her; he closed his burning eyes and stifled the sobs that threatened to rack him.

When he did finally look again, she had raised her arms, beckoning.

His breath froze in his throat. Tom's warning flickered for an instant, then was driven away. He took a step and passed the edge of the stones.

But as he moved forward, Marianne began to recede, still holding her arms in front of her, faster and faster, however quickly he advanced, eerily gliding an inch or two above the ground. And then he was running madly down the slope and Marianne was whisking away from him, growing smaller until she was just a glowing spot on the horizon that eventually winked out.

Heartbroken, Church fell to his knees, his loss as raw as in the days just after her death. Somehow he managed to compose himself enough to trudge back to the stones, but as he passed the spot where she had waited he noticed something unusual. On the ground lay a rose, its petals as black as the night, perfectly formed, with a stem that had been neatly clipped. As he picked it up, he felt a whisper in his head that said *Roisin Dubh*, and he knew in a way he couldn't explain that it was the flower's name; and that it was a gift from Marianne.

Although he couldn't fathom its meaning, he felt a rush of elation. He tucked the flower secretly into his jacket and made his way back to the dying fire.

CHAPTER FIVE

Where the Black Dog Runs

They woke early with the sun heavy and red on the horizon. A thick dew sparkled on the ground and on their jackets and there was a chill in the air that made their bones ache, but they soon stamped the warmth back into their limbs. As soon as they had properly woken, Church and Ruth realised they felt strangely refreshed; new and clean like they had been reborn; Church could not remember having slept so deeply in the last two years.

'It's the healing and energising effect of the earth energy,' Tom told them as they made their way back to the car.

'The NHS should get a franchise,' Ruth replied with a relaxed smile. Church was pleased to see her face clear of the anxiety and worry that had transformed her the previous evening.

In the tunnel they stopped to examine the black crust scorching the concrete and were instantly reminded of how close their escape had been. And before they could depart, Church had to scrape the car windows free of a thick layer of ash made tacky by the dew; the air smelled like the aftermath of a house fire.

'I still do not understand how the Fabulous Beast was marshalled in our pursuit,' Tom mused as Church cursed quietly in his labour. 'They are supposed to be wildly independent, uncontrollable.'

'Maybe that's one bit of your lore that's wrong,' Church said sourly. 'A good council Fabulous Beast training course . . . sit . . . beg . . . roll over. They'll do anything for a treat.'

Tom muttered something under his breath and wandered off to take the air while Church finished the windows.

'Doesn't he speak funny?' Ruth found a clean part of the wing to perch on. 'Like some bad historical novel.'

'He's a strange fish all round. I still don't trust him. It feels like he's just throwing out enough titbits to keep us interested while he works on his own agenda.'

'As long as we're aware of it.' Ruth closed her eyes and put her head back to feel the sun on her face.

Church was glad of the silence that followed. He could barely contain the emotional upheaval he felt after his encounter with

Marianne; it resonated confusingly through every thought. Why was she visiting him – to torment him further or to pass on some message? Was it linked to all the other high strangenesses that had descended on the country? And what was the significance of the Black Rose which was secreted in the inside pocket of his jacket close to his heart? Instinctively, he felt he ought to tell Ruth about it, but there was a niggling part of his mind that forced him to hold back. *Maybe later*, he promised himself.

Their first aim was to find somewhere to eat. At the A345 they came across a Little Chef surrounded by trees and were the first inside once the doors opened. Over full English breakfasts and tea looking out over the sun-drenched car park, they tried to make some sense of what was happening.

'I still don't see what we can possibly do,' Ruth said as she dunked her toast into her egg.

'Probably nothing apart from find some way to raise the alarm. But we do have a responsibility to do *something*.' Still distracted, Church sipped on his tea; he knew *exactly* what he wanted to do: discovering what the mysterious email woman knew about Marianne was still the driving force. At the moment that dovetailed with their search for more information about the imminent crisis Tom had described, but if he ever had to make a choice between the two, he didn't know how he would react.

Ruth suddenly glanced down at her hand in surprise. 'Look at this: I cut my hand scrambling through the fence last night, and this morning there's no sign of it. It's completely healed.'

'Make the most of it,' Tom mumbled grumpily. He seemed preoccupied, constantly glancing around the room.

'Expecting guests?' Church said.

'Just because we survived last night doesn't mean it's the end of it.'

'There's a cheery thought,' Ruth said breezily, but Church could see she was disturbed by it.

'So now we're on the run,' he said. Tom didn't answer.

They went to the checkout, but as the waitress totted up their bill the till suddenly started spewing out reams of receipt paper. Her eyes flashed irritation while she attempted to maintain a pleasant smile as she wrestled with the snaking roll. Eventually the register jammed and she tore off the streamer with restrained anger. On it was the same thing printed over and over again:

1 OF 5

It bore no relation to what she had keyed in. When Church noticed it, he felt strangely uneasy. He was immediately thrown back to his journey to collect Ruth and the odd sequence of coincidences.

Church leaned on the car bonnet in the sun with Ruth's mobile phone after struggling for ten minutes to find a signal. Laura's sleepy voice told him he'd woken her.

'It's Jack Churchill. I'm sorry we didn't make the meeting with you last night. We got delayed in Wiltshire.'

There was a long pause, then: 'It's Sunday. Mornings have been banned. What's the matter? The missus thrown you out of bed?'

'I'm sorry.'

'Yeah, yeah.' She yawned. 'So what's the score? You still want to meet?'

'Yes, and soon. We can get up to Bristol by—'

'Don't worry, I'll come to you. If you're in Wiltshire then you might as well head to Salisbury. That's where it happened. You can take the ghost train with me, see if you get the full Fright Night treatment too. Or maybe I really have done too many drugs.' The line threatened to break up, but then her voice came through clear once more. '—king mobiles! I'll meet you tomorrow at Poultry Cross in the city centre. 10 a.m. You'll find it.'

'What about your work?'

'Yeah, like it matters any more.'

They reached Salisbury just after 10.30 a.m. The March sun was strong enough to catch the historic cathedral town in an unseasonable light, bright and buzzing with tourists through the main shopping area and Market Square. Ruth used her credit card to check them into a hotel in the centre of town, selected by Tom for its olde worlde appeal: a thirteenth century coaching inn, half-timbered in black on white, with hanging eaves, high chimneys and diamond window panes which, from the pavement, made the interior seem mysteriously murky. They managed to get rooms side by side. They were fitted with all mod cons, but the sloping floors and oddly angled ceilings still gave them a time-lost feeling.

With the threat of so much darkness looming on the horizon, they agreed to take a break, from each other and, hopefully, from the stresses of the events sweeping in around them, until early evening. Ruth and Church both felt they needed time to assimilate all that Tom had shown and told them at Stonehenge.

In the sun outside the hotel, amongst the bustle of everyday life, they could easily have pretended nothing had changed. But as they walked away, Tom called out, 'Be on your guard.'

For some reason he couldn't quite explain, Church found himself drawn to the cathedral which stood on the south of the city, an imposing vision of majesterial white stone in acres of greenery bounded by the River Avon. As he stood in The Close looking up at the soaring spire, he had a sudden impression of it as a symbol of all that was under threat. Seven hundred years of British history, built on solid foundations that not even an earthquake could throw down. It had overseen the coming of the Age of Enlightenment, of the establishment of a civilisation based on science, reason and logic. And more than that, it represented the glory of a God who had created that world; a religion which allowed no space for the truth that was slowly being unpeeled before their eyes. The magnitude of what could be swept away dwarfed him.

It was too much. He hurried in through the south-west entrance as if he were seeking sanctuary and walked slowly up the nave to take a seat in the pews. For long minutes, he couldn't bear to think, instead losing himself in the quiet beauty of the surroundings. Organ music played gently in the background, adding to the air of reverent tranquillity which soothed him a little, and eventually his attention fell upon the altar and its intricately worked cloth. The central image showed a crown of thorns in gold and red surrounding the Holy Grail. There was something about the image which seemed to speak to him, whispering insistently at the back of his head until he became disturbed by the suggestion of a subconscious connection which he couldn't make. In the end he had to force himself to look away.

Then there was no other choice but to let his mind turn to Marianne, as he knew it would. Carefully, as if he were handling a fragile piece of pottery, he drew out the Roisin Dubh, wondering how he knew what he guessed was the Gaelic, marvelling at how the rose had survived so immaculately. The petals were like velvet, the black so rich it seemed to have numerous depths. He lifted it to his nose, but surprisingly it had no fragrance at all. Was it, as he hoped, a sign from her of their enduring love?

The thought filled him with such a swell of desperate emotion he had to close his eyes, and in that instant he almost prayed. But since Marianne's death, nothing any religion preached made sense any more; however much he hoped her essence lived on in some kind of afterlife, the mundanity of everyday life had almost convinced him that death was an end. Now he couldn't even wallow in that existentialist purgatory. Two years of weighing up every option, trying to find some common ground between hope and reality, had left him sick and mentally worn down. He was too tired to have faith. He just wanted to *know.*

His sense of alienation on the sacred ground drove him to his feet, but as he turned to go he glimpsed someone watching him from across the nave. The figure seemed unreal, oddly proportioned and hazy. It darted behind a pillar when it saw him look, but it left him with a sudden chill, as if its gaze had transmitted a hoarfrost. Suddenly he had to see who it was.

Cautiously, he made his way along the pews to the pillar. His footsteps sounded uncommonly loud, although an elderly couple passed by immersed in their guidebook, oblivious to him. The space behind the pillar was empty, but in the corner of his eye he saw a shimmer away to the right; someone was moving unfeasibly quickly along the south aisle. Church had an impression of a man, yet he was almost mist, as if he were radiating a grey light. In his trail there was a claustrophobic sense of threat.

Get out of here, he told himself. But running away seemed a weak thing to do, and after Marianne's death he didn't want to be pathetic again. He moved quickly in pursuit.

He slipped through an exit near the refectory and found himself in the cloisters, a square of wide corridors with low, vaulted ceilings surrounding a brightly sunlit lawned area which only served to make the other legs of the cloisters seem impenetrably shadowed. His first impression was that it was eerily still, as if he had stepped through time into after-hours. There were no tourists, even near the entrance to the Magna Carta exhibition in the Chapter House, and the sound of the organ had mysteriously disappeared. His skin prickled as he watched for any sign of movement. Gradually he became aware of an atmosphere of disquiet lying across the area. A cloying scent of lavender hovered in the air.

Slowly Church left the protection of the door. He hadn't progressed far when the stillness was broken by a deep, guttural growling that raised the hairs on the back of his neck. He froze, then turned slowly in a circle. Still nothing. It was impossible to see through the sunlight of the square into the darkness beyond.

The growl rang off the stone once more, filled with menace, hinting at some enormous beast. He glanced down one corridor, then another, unable to tell from where it was coming. There was no sign of the shadowy figure either. Slowly he advanced along the north corridor, but with each step the sensation of unease grew more intense until he felt an unbearable urge to get out of that lonely place.

But as he rounded the corner into the east corridor, it was there, waiting for him, halfway along: a black dog, bigger than any he had ever seen before; it was only when it took a step forward on its heavy, sinewy limbs that he·realised it was the size of a small pony. And then Church noticed its eyes, red as blood, with an inner light that burned with a cruel, demonic intelligence. A long strand of saliva drooled from its yellow fangs to splatter on the stone flags, where it sizzled like acid. It was so monstrous he knew it was no earthly creature.

The dog growled once more, rumbling menacingly deep in its throat. Then it lowered its head and took a slow step forward. Church knew if he turned it would be on him in a second. He noted the power in its jaws; he would have no protection if they were tearing at his throat. He took a tentative step backwards.

Deep in his head he felt a buzzing like a swarm of flies, sickening in its intensity, and he knew that in some way it was the creature's alien, terrible thoughts interfering with his own; there was nothing there he could make sense of, just a primal feeling of threat and devouring. His stomach churned at the contact. *What is it doing?* he thought.

Slowly it moved forwards, each heavy paw echoing as it thudded on the stone. Powerful muscles rippled beneath the sleek black fur. Its eyes ranged across his face with a terrible, malign force, scarlet pools surrounding a circle of black like the drop into the abyss; the buzz of its thoughts crackled louder in his head. And in that moment he knew this was no chance encounter; it wanted him.

Church backed away a little further, but he realised the door was too far away to run. Slowly the muscles on the dog's back began to pull together as it lowered its enormous head. The deep, rattling growl dropped a notch into its throat. It was preparing to attack.

Church felt the cold wash of fear. He had an instant to decide what to do, but there were no options. Hopelessly, he decided he should turn and run. The dog's nails clicked loudly on the stone.

This is it, he thought.

But just as he was about to launch himself, the door into the cloisters crashed open and a guide leading a column of tourists marched in, his voice echoing out with the history of the site. Church was about to yell out for them to flee when he noticed a sudden, subtle change in the atmosphere. Out of the corner of his eye he saw the beast pause on the cusp of its attack, its eyes falling sullenly in the direction of the tourists. Briefly, it seemed to consider whether to continue its assault, but then it closed its jaws with a faint snick and padded away with a heavy step. Church remained frozen, unable to tear his eyes from it. When it was twenty feet from him, it turned its head and surveyed him balefully before losing itself in the shadows.

The column of tourists trooped past him, clicking their cameras, muttering in foreign languages. Church rested back against the stone wall in relief, his heart pounding madly, the stink of the dog all around. 'Are you all right?' the guide asked in concern.

Church smiled weakly, but he couldn't bring himself to reply. He had the sudden feeling that events were closing in around them.

Ruth wandered through the city, staring into shop windows without really seeing, her head swimming with the bizarre experiences that had impacted on her life. She felt completely at odds with herself. Everything she had seen and heard filled her with a feeling of dread for what might lie ahead, yet at the same time she was overcome with a sense of freedom that was remarkably uplifting; the office was just a bad dream; from a distance the career seemed like shackles preventing her living her life. Now she was able to do what her heart told her. At the same time, these feelings ignited a tinge of guilt, as if she was betraying the memory of her father. He had always dreamed of her establishing a great career in law and he had been so happy when she was offered her job. It was all a mess of conflicting emotions and for the first time she felt she didn't know herself at all.

But she had been intrigued by Tom's manipulation of the blue fire; more than that, she decided, she wanted to be able to do it for herself. Now *there* was freedom. The thought of it raised her spirits enough that with the sun and the crowds she finally began to feel optimistic, for the first time since she had left her flat.

After a while she found herself crossing a gushing stretch of the Avon to The Maltings shopping centre, a modernist slab of brown brick at odds with the age of the rest of the city. As she mused whether there would be anything in it worth her attention, she suddenly caught sight of an old woman watching her intently. She had a sun-browned, wizened face with diamond-sparkle eyes and tight grey curls, and although she was slightly hunched with age, she was still tall and slim. Her smile reminded Ruth of the richness of autumn, while the crisp, golden-brown of her long dress was like fallen leaves. Ruth smiled in return, but the way the woman was focusing on her alone unnerved her and she hurried quickly by.

She picked up an alley that took her around the squat, grey mound of St Thomas's Church, but as she glanced over into the churchyard, she felt a sudden tingling deep in her belly. A woman was standing amongst the stones watching her. If Ruth didn't know better she would have sworn it was the woman she had just seen; the same proud line to her jaw, the same sparkling eyes, the same body shape. Only this woman was years younger; the face had no wrinkles and was rounder, with the apple cheeks of middle age. The dress was the same design too, but the colour was the deep, dark green of summer vegetation. And then she smiled and Ruth felt the tingling turn into a cold shiver; it was the same smile.

Suddenly it was as if her eyes had opened. She felt an odd, unearthly atmosphere around the woman, as if the air was shifting between opaque and translucent. And no one else passing by seemed to notice the woman standing there, staring at Ruth with such eerie intensity. Fearing the worst, Ruth hurried on aimlessly, following the crowds back to the city centre before somehow turning back on herself to arrive at the gently undulating greenery of Queen Elizabeth Gardens along the banks of the Avon.

She glanced around anxiously before flopping on to a bench, where she rested for a moment with her head in her hands, trying to understand what she had experienced. She hadn't felt any sense of threat from the woman; if anything, she was warm and comforting, almost motherly. But how could she know that was not a deception? Everything was wild and unfamiliar; there was nothing to get a handle on.

After a while Ruth began to relax and watch the children laughing and running in the play area while their mothers chatted secretively nearby. Ducks splashed in the river, then waddled over to sun themselves on the grass, while the air was filled with the intoxicating scents of spring wafting in from the woods and hills that lay just beyond the river's floodplain. Everything seemed so incongruously peaceful and normal, it was hard even to begin to grasp what was happening.

Then, inexplicably, her left hand began to shake uncontrollably. She gripped the wrist with her right hand to steady it, and when she looked up and around she gasped in shock. The woman now stood directly behind her, her hands resting on the back of the bench. Ruth leapt to her feet, her heart thundering; she hadn't heard even the slightest sound of the stranger's approach. And it was the same woman, except now she was in her teens, her face beautiful and pale like the moon, her long, lustrous hair glinting in the sun. The familiar dress was now the bright green of early spring shoots. Her eyes, though, still sparkled with great age and unnerving mystery, and there was a terrible aspect to her face that made Ruth shiver in fear, although there was no malice that she could see; she felt in the presence of something so inhuman, she couldn't begin to comprehend what it was that stood before her.

'He is missing. The night to my day, the winter to my summer. We must be joined and then you must join us, daughter.' The tone of her voice was eerie, part rustle of wind in the branches, part splash of water on rock.

Ruth backed away slowly, that awful, unblinking stare heavy upon her. 'Leave me alone,' she said hoarsely.

Slowly the girl who was not a girl raised her arms in a beckoning gesture. It was too much for Ruth. She turned and hurried away several yards. But when she glanced back, confused and troubled, the girl had gone and in her place was an odd effect, as if gold dust had been sprinkled in a sunbeam. After a few seconds something began to form in the glimmering; light shifted and blazed from nowhere, forming an intense halo around a dark figure which gradually became the Virgin Mary.

Someone called out, 'Look! It's a miracle!' and then people were running from all over the park to the bench where the vision was already beginning to fade. Ruth watched the joy and amazement infuse the crowd for a while longer before walking slowly back to the city centre, the burden of her thoughts heavy upon her.

The Haunch of Venison was almost empty at 7 p.m. when Church and Ruth arrived within minutes of each other. The pub had all the twisty-turny nooks and crannies one would expect of fourteenth century architecture and it took them a while to locate Tom at a table in a shadowy corner. He appeared tired and irritable, nodding emotionlessly when they sat down with their drinks.

Church looked from Ruth to Tom. 'I saw something this afternoon.'

'So did I.' Ruth shifted in her seat uncomfortably. She had spent the rest of the day walking, but she still hadn't been able to escape the memory of what she had seen in the woman's eyes.

Tom made sure no one was watching, then folded down the upright collar of his jacket to reveal four livid scars on the soft flesh of his neck.

Ruth stared in horror. 'My God, what happened?'

'The Baobhan Sith.' Tom winced as he gingerly raised his collar.

'What's that?' Church asked although he wasn't sure he wanted to hear the answer.

'In the old tales, they are the sentries of the night. Terrible things that take on the shape of beautiful women to lure passers-by. Get too close and they'll tear out your throat and drink your blood.'

'And now they're here too,' Church said, before adding, 'You seem to have a good knowledge of folklore.'

'I thought, if the worst came to the worst, we might be able to go back to Stonehenge for the night,' Tom continued. 'But I wanted to be sure the road would be open to us so I went out on foot for a couple of miles to check the route. I presumed they would have moved to bar our retreat in some way, but not . . .' He paused to touch his neck tenderly. 'One of the Baobhan Sith was lying in a ditch, waiting. She rose up when I passed.' His face seemed to drain in the halflight. 'There were more, I'm sure. We would never get past them.'

'They're bad, then?' Church asked facetiously. Tom's expression gave him all the answer he needed.

'How many more things are there going to be?' Ruth fidgeted with her glass, slopping vodka and tonic on to the table. 'This afternoon I was followed by a woman, only she wasn't, she was something more, pretending to be a woman. She kept changing age. There was no sense of threat, but . . . It was me she wanted. To do something for her. What's that all about?'

Church took a long draught of his Guinness while he thought. 'Is this how it's going to be from now on?'

'I think it probably is,' Tom replied dismally.

'I suppose only a few people have seen them so far,' Ruth mused. 'But what will the response be when it becomes so widespread that everyone realises what's going on?'

'Chaos. The kind of supernatural fear you used to get in mediaeval times,' Church said.

'What bothers me is the intelligence behind it,' Ruth said. 'What do these things want?'

'At the moment most of them seem to want you and me wiped off the face of the earth,' Church said. 'And that's another thing. A lot of effort is being expended on two people who aren't very much of a threat. Why should they be even bothering to hunt us down because we know something – and not much at that – when it's bound to become common knowledge sooner or later? Christ, I'm surprised it's not all over the media now after a big, scaly monster blitzed the M4!'

'It's not – I checked,' Ruth said. 'I can't understand why nothing's appeared – you'd have thought the *Sun* at least would have gone for dragons tearing up the motorway, wouldn't you?'

Church turned to Tom. 'Well? You're the man with all the answers.'

'I wish I *was* the man with all the answers.' Tom cupped his cider with both hands and stared into its depths.

The pub had started to fill up quickly, but they still felt alone in their gloomy corner. 'Should we be sitting here?' Ruth asked. 'If those bloodsuckers that took a bite out of you are on their way, shouldn't we be hitting the road again?'

'We haven't heard what Laura has to say yet!' Church protested. 'We can't just keep running until we hit the sea.'

'The Baobhan Sith are supposed to have little intelligence or guile. They're more like animals, I suppose . . . hunting dogs . . . point them in the right direction and they'll bring you down. But it's possible to hide from them.'

'And you're basing this knowledge on, what?' Church said sharply. 'Some old fairytale you read? There might be some truths in the folklore and legends and myths, but we can't take them as gospel. People add bits to spice them up. Take things out. Mis-tell them.'

'And what do *you* suggest we do?' Tom snapped.

'Okay, we should calm down.' Ruth raised her hands between them. 'Same team and all that. I vote we sleep together tonight and take it in turns to keep watch. You're right, we need to check out what that Laura woman has to say and we've only got to get through the night.'

They agreed, but before they could return to their drinks, Ruth turned to Church and asked, 'And what did you see?'

'A black dog, but like no—'

Tom froze with his glass halfway to his lips. 'My God,' he said in a thin voice.

As Church related what had happened that afternoon in the cathedral cloisters, Tom's face grew darker. 'Black Shuck,' he said when Church had finished. 'The Devil Dog. I hoped it would just be the Baobhan Sith—'

'What is it?' Ruth said.

'A demon, some claim. And the precursor of something far worse. It was here long before the first settlement was hacked out, trailing disaster in its wake. I remember once, in Scotland, lying awake one night listening to its awful howling above the raging of the worst storm of the year, and I knew some poor bastard was about to die horribly.' Tom took a deep swig of his cider. 'Before you encountered it, or just after, did you see something – like a shadow flitting across your vision, or a misty figure passing nearby?'

Church nodded. 'In the cathedral. It seemed to be watching.'

Tom took a breath and said, 'Black Shuck marks the way for the Grey Walker. The Erl-King, the leader of the Wild Hunt.'

Church stared into his Guinness, recalling a snippet from the reading he had done for a strand of his degree. 'The hunt that hounds lost souls to damnation.'

There was a commotion at the bar as a tall, thin man with swept-back silver hair and a hollow face was berated by a group of drinkers. He was smiling obsequiously, but one woman seemed on the verge of attacking him.

Ruth raised her glass. 'Here's to the end of the world.'

'Now there's a toast to which one can really drink.' The silver-haired man had slid up behind her, clutching the dregs of a half-pint. His broad smile revealed a gap between his middle teeth, which were stained with nicotine. His black suit had the grey sheen of overuse, but it was offset with a red brocade waistcoat. His boots were dusty and worn; the smell of the road came off him, of muddy verges and damp hedges, a hint of sweat and the bloom of being caught in too many downpours. Despite the colour of his hair, he couldn't have been more than forty-five. Tom eyed him suspiciously; Church finished his drink.

'Knock it all down and start again, I say. Deconstruction before reconstruction.' He raised his glass heartily. 'Cheers!' Ruth smiled in return, and the man gave her a wink.

Church picked up his empty glass and offered the others a refill with a nod. As he turned towards the bar, the silver-haired man quickly drained his glass and held it out. 'As you're going, old boy, do me a favour and fill this up. I'll get the next one in.'

A sarcastic comment at the stranger's audacity sprang to Church's lips, but it seemed more trouble than it was worth. Grudgingly, he snatched the glass as he passed.

'Cider, please,' the man said, slipping into Church's seat. 'And thank you kindly.' He turned to Ruth and took her hand. 'Charmed to meet you, my dear. I have many names, though the one I like the most is Callow. I hope you don't mind me resting my old bones. It's been a long day's travelling. The romance of the open road is a fine thing, but no one talks about the exhaustion at the end of the day.'

'Where are you going?' Ruth asked politely.

Callow laughed. 'Oh, from here to there and back again. There's too much to see on this beautiful, beautiful island of ours to be resting in one place for too long. I've done all that, you see. Worn a strangling tie in an office prison, filed the papers, counted the paper clips, watched the clock mark the passing of my life. Slow death for a poor wage. But how much could they pay you to make it worth dying? One needs to hear oneself think. In the words of Longfellow, "Not in the clamour of the crowded street, Not in the shouts and plaudits of the throng, But in ourselves, are triumph and defeat." And if you can't find a reason for being in one place, or even for being, then you have to look elsewhere.'

'I know what you're saying.' Ruth was entertained by his attitude. It was an act he had obviously perfected over time, a mix of music hall comedian and slightly fey theatre ham. If it managed to get him a few free drinks, who was she to judge?

'Ah, a kindred spirit. And have you broken the shackles of mundanity for the life of quicksilver heels?'

'We're just touring around,' Tom interjected coldly before Ruth could answer.

Callow reached across the table. 'Pleased to meet you.' He nodded towards the badges on Tom's holdall at the edge of the table. 'A veteran of the road too, I see. Ah, the Isle of Wight Festival. I remember it well. Hendrix played guitar like an angel. And Glastonbury, so many weeks there in the summer. The mud! You must remember the mud! Terrible. But fun. If you know what I mean. The Stonehenge Free Festivals too! Ah, how I miss them. The Battle of the Beanfield. I was there, I was there. Took a truncheon from a stormtrooper in blue. Saved some poor young girl from getting her head stove in.' He shook his head sadly. 'Ah me, the end of the world. And not a day too soon.'

Church placed the others' drinks before them, then pointedly held Callow's cider up high for him to vacate his seat. Callow stood up to take it, then sat down quickly and snatched a thirsty sip. 'And cheers to all of you!'

'That's my seat,' Church snapped.

'There's one over there, old boy.' Callow waved his hand dismissively to a stool next to Tom. 'Don't interrupt us now. We're reminiscing about the good old days.'

Ruth couldn't help a giggle at the irritation on Church's face. It deflated the moment, making it churlish for him to have stood his ground. With obvious annoyance, he took up his new position.

Callow didn't leave a gap in the conversation long enough for the others to throw him out, and soon his constant spiel mingling with the effects of the alcohol had almost lulled them into a hypnotic acceptance. As their guards dropped, they loosened up and the conversation became fourway. There was no doubting that Callow was entertaining, with a knowledge of every subject, it seemed, and a colourful use of language that was bizarrely at odds with his lifestyle, although, if they had been sober, they would have admitted to themselves he was accepted more because he was a distraction from the worries that lay heavily upon them.

When Callow finally felt comfortable enough to go to the toilet, Church said, 'How did we get lumbered with that freak?'

'Oh, he's harmless,' Ruth said, 'and entertaining, which is a relief after listening to you and Tom go at each other with knives.'

'I'd be happier if he stood his round,' Church said. 'He's freeloading his way to getting well and truly pissed.'

Ruth punched him on the shoulder a little harder than she intended. 'Don't be so miserable. You can afford it – spread a little happiness.'

As the night progressed, the pub became more and more crowded, the air filling with smoke, shouts and laughter. Ruth surprised them all with a tale of her engagement to a political activist whom her father had admired and whom she had jilted on her wedding day after a panic attack that had almost resulted in a call for an ambulance. Church related the story of his brief, aborted career as a guitarist in a band which ended at his debut gig in a pub backroom when he vomited on stage through a mixture of nerves and too much drink. And Tom, loosened by several pints of cider, had several outlandish tales of his wanderings, most of them involving drug abuse: to Goa, and a frantic escape from the local police; to California, and a trip over the border to Mexico in search of the fabled hallucinogenic cactus; how he had raised the alarm about the brown acid at Woodstock; and his brief time as a 'spiritual advisor' to The Grateful Dead which seemed to involve little more than handing out vast quantities of drugs.

As drinking-up time rolled around, Church leaned across the table to Tom and said drunkenly, 'So when will we get the Wild Hunt knocking at our door?'

Tom waved him away with a dismissive snort, but Callow's eyes sparkled and his brow furrowed curiously. 'The Wild Hunt?'

'Don't you know?' Church slurred. 'Every fairytale you ever heard is true! Bloody goblins and bogles and beasties are real – they've just been hiding away! And now they've come back!'

Callow laughed, although he didn't get the joke, but when he looked around the table he saw there was obviously some truth in what Church was saying. 'What do you mean, old boy?'

'It's the end of the world, right. That's why we're all sitting here drinking. For tomorrow we may die.'

'Don't mind him,' Ruth said, who was nowhere near as inebriated as Church. 'He talks rubbish when he's drunk.'

'No, no, please tell me. I love a good tale,' Callow said. 'I once met a man in a pub in Greenock who swore the fairies were real. He claimed he'd seen them one Midsummer's Eve.'

Tom finished his drink. 'It's late. We better be on our way.' He added pointedly, 'We've got an early start in the morning.'

'Oh? A little sightseeing?'

'We're meeting a woman who's going to tell us about it,' Church said. Tom helped him to his feet a little too roughly.

'If you don't mind, I'll walk with you a while. It's a nice night,' Callow said. He sidled up next to Church. 'So tell me all about it, old boy.'

The evening was surprisingly mild. As they walked, Church poured out everything he knew, not caring if Callow believed him or not, while Ruth chipped in wry comments every now and then. Tom trailed behind, cautiously watching the shadows off the main road.

'Why, it seems to me that this could be a time of great opportunity for people like us,' Callow said in a tone which suggested he didn't entirely believe them, but was going along with the joke anyway. 'Forward thinkers and dazzling iconoclasts who have shaken off the shackles of a society which only wants to keep us locked away! *We* are free to adapt while the sheep mutate into lemmings and rush towards the cliff! Magic – now there is a great leveller. Power on tap for all! Raising the lowly up to the level of the great and good!' He paused thoughtfully. 'If one doesn't get eaten first, of course.'

Church and Ruth both laughed at this, the first time they had found humour in anything for too long, and, coupled with the act of unburdening, it provided a greater release than they could have imagined.

'Where are you staying?' Ruth asked Callow. Unselfconsciously, she slipped her arm through Church's and leaned against him.

'Here and there,' the stranger replied. 'A different night, a different billet. But enough of that. Look at the sky! Look at the stars! What a world we live in, eh? We are all in the gutter, but not enough of us look at the stars, to paraphrase Wilde. And where are you staying, my dear?' Ruth told him and he smiled broadly. 'A fine establishment. I could tell you appreciated quality and I am rarely wrong when it comes to character. Let's be off, then!'

'Be off where?' Church asked.

'Surely you're not going to abandon me now?' the stranger asked with a hurt expression. 'On such a fine night, and with it being so early and all. We still have stories to tell, experiences to share! The end of the world is nigh! We must make the most of what we have left. There must be a bar in your hotel that serves libations after hours to guests?'

'No—' Church began to protest.

'Go on,' Ruth laughed. 'Let him get another drink. We don't have to stay up.'

94

Callow took her hand and kissed it. 'You are a lifesaver, my dear, and I am eternally in your debt!'

In the bar, Ruth set Callow up with a pint of cider and a whisky. He wrung her hand, praised her to the roof and tried to entreat all three of them to stay with him drinking.

Finally retreating to a table in the corner, he called out jovially, 'Remember the words of T. S. Eliot, fellow travellers: "We shall not cease from exploration, And the end of all our exploring Will be to arrive where we started And know the place for the first time." Philosophy does not come easily at this time of the night and that, unfortunately, is the best I can do.'

They left him there, attacking his drinks with a gusto that suggested not a drop had passed his lips all night.

'I shouldn't have got drunk,' Church groaned. He was slumped in a chair in a corner. 'Bloody stupid!'

'We did it to forget. Don't criticise yourself for being human.' Ruth sprawled on the bed against the plumped-up pillows, her eyes closed, while Tom leaned against the wall near the window, occasionally peeking out behind the curtains. 'You know, I'm not a wilting flower. I don't *have* to have the bed just because I'm a woman,' she continued. They had chosen Church's room to spend the night; it was slightly bigger and it had a better view of the street.

'Indulge us.' Tom nodded towards Church. 'I wouldn't want him to have the bed if I have to sleep on the floor, and I'm sure he would feel the same about me. You're the compromise candidate.'

'In that case, you won't catch me arguing.' Ruth's laugh faded quickly. 'Do you think we're going to be safe?'

'We can hope.' Tom glanced outside again. 'No sign of anything yet.'

'Do you think they'll keep sending bigger and bigger things after us until they get us?'

'The Wild Hunt is coming,' he replied darkly. 'There *is* nothing after that.'

'Yeah, but we'll be safe tonight,' Church mumbled. He crawled on to the mat at the side of the bed, threw his coat over him and was asleep within seconds.

When he awoke in the deep still of the night, Church at first wondered if Marianne had come to him again. His head was thick with the alcohol, but he soon realised he had been disturbed by a strange grating noise, faint yet insistent. It seemed to be coming from the window. And it sounded like fingernails on glass.

'What's that?' he hissed to himself.

'Be still.' Church started at Tom's strained whisper; Church hadn't noticed Tom was awake, but he was sitting up, staring at the drawn curtains. 'The Baobhan Sith are here.'

'But we're on the first floor.'

Suddenly Church was filled with an overwhelming desire to see what was on the other side of the thick drapes, high above the ground; the fingernails scraped gently, chinking on the glass, calling to whoever was inside. He began to crawl towards the window. He could just peek through the gap, get some final proof that he'd left one world behind and entered another one which had no rules he could grasp. And what would he see? he wondered. What would he feel finally looking into the face of the unknown? He reached out to peel the curtains aside.

Tom's arm crashed on to his shoulder and thrust him to the floor, his nails biting almost to the bone. Tom's breath was hot in his ear. 'Don't,' he hissed, 'if you want to live a second longer.'

There was a pause in the scratching, as if whatever was outside had heard them. Tom and Church froze, their breath hard in their chests. Church half-expected the glass suddenly to burst inward, but then the scratching resumed and they both exhaled slowly and painfully. Tom gripped Church's upper arm relentlessly and dragged him back to the other side of the bed.

'They only know we're *somewhere* in the vicinity, but they can't pinpoint us, or they would have had us in our sleep,' Tom whispered. 'The scratching is to draw the occupant of the room. If you had pulled back the curtains, you wouldn't have seen anything, but they would have seen you.'

'Sorry,' Church said, 'I don't know what came over me.'

A noise in the corridor outside made them both catch their breath again. Tom's face was pale in the dark, his cold eyes fearful. 'I think they're coming in,' he said.

Before Church could speak, he had leapt across the room and was kneeling next to the bed where Ruth was still sleeping soundly. He roused her gently, then clasped a hand across her mouth before she could speak; her eyes grew wide and frightened, but Tom silenced her with a finger to his lips.

He summoned Church to his side, then said, 'Hide under the sheets with Ruth. I'll get into the wardrobe. When they come into the room, don't make a sound. Don't move a muscle.'

'But they'll see us under the covers,' Church protested.

'If they don't see you move or hear you they won't investigate further. They have little intellect. They simply respond,' Tom said. 'Trust me. Now, quickly.'

He held up the sheets so Church could wriggle down next to Ruth, then pulled them over their heads. It was hot and stifling, emphasising the swirl of alcohol in Church's head and the steadily increasing rumble of his heart; for the first time in his life, he had a sudden twist of claustrophobia. The wardrobe door clicked and then there was silence. In the dark he couldn't see Ruth's face, but he could feel the bloom of her breath. Her fingers found his hand and gave it a confident squeeze.

They didn't have to wait long. A dim clunk echoed hollowly; the tumblers of the lock turning although Church had sealed it on the inside. The faint creak of the hinges as the door swung open. A soft tread on the carpet, deceptively light as if it was a child, moving to the foot of the bed.

Church held his breath; Ruth's stopped too. Her fingers around his hand were rigid. Together they listened. It seemed the intruder was watching the heap of covers on the bed for any movement, listening for a barely audible rustle. Suddenly every nerve on Church's body came alive. A tic was developing in his calf, a spasm in his forearm; he didn't know how much longer he could hold it. Somehow Ruth seemed to sense his discomfort for her fingernails started to bite into the soft flesh at the base of his thumb, drawing his attention to the pain.

After what seemed like a lifetime, they heard movement again. The quiet tread progressed around the bed to the head and with his blood ringing in his ears, Church waited for the sheets to be snatched back. Instead, the tread continued to the wardrobe door, where it waited again, then to the window and finally back to the door. Even when they'd heard the click of the door closing, they remained in hiding for five more minutes, not daring to move.

Finally they heard the wardrobe door open tentatively and Tom stepped out. 'Gone,' he whispered.

Church threw back the covers and sucked in a breath of cool air. Ruth rolled over and gave him a hug in relief and he was surprised at how comforting it felt; he responded, and she nestled her head into the crook of his neck briefly before getting up.

'Will they be back?' she said.

'I doubt it. They'll continue to search the area until dawn, but we should be out of here before sunset tomorrow.' Tom stretched and cracked his knuckles.

Despite Tom's earlier warning, Church couldn't resist peeking behind the curtains. All along the street shadows flitted in and out of doorways or shimmered in the streetlights like ghosts. It wasn't as if they were insubstantial; Church had the feeling they simply didn't want to be seen. And high over the rooftops there were others, floating like leaves caught in the wind. It was an alien infestation that made him shudder and he returned to the others dreading what the forthcoming days would bring.

They slept fitfully, but awoke with a sense of purpose driven as much by what was at their backs as what lay ahead. They made the most of a heavy breakfast of bacon, sausages and eggs and tea, not knowing when the next meal would be, and then went to check out. Church carried out the formalities and got the credit card slip for Ruth to sign, while Ruth and Tom watched the street outside, but when he came back over to them there was anger in his face.

'What's wrong?' Ruth asked.

He waved the bill at them. 'That sneaky bastard from the pub stiffed us! It looks like he was drinking till sun-up, plus food from the kitchen, and he signed it all on to our bill! I knew he was a conman the moment I laid eyes on him!'

'He was quite sweet in his own way.' Ruth laughed. 'He stopped us wallowing in our misery so we owe him something for that.'

'Fifty quid! That's Harley Street rates!' He screwed up the bill angrily. 'If I see him again I'm going to take this out of his hide.'

At first there was a shock of colour glimpsed through the throng; white-blonde hair, short at the sides, spiky on top, expensively cut to look like a mess. Then there were the sunglasses, round, hi-tech and, again, expensive, on a morning when the sun was as pallid as a watercolour; the clothes, shabby, long overcoat, jeans and engineer boots, designed to look hard and uncompromising; the portable computer tucked under her arm; and finally the air of confidence that seemed, at least to Ruth, to border on arrogance. They knew it was Laura DuSantiago long before she spoke. She looked as out of place in the crowd of shoppers and business people as if she had beamed down from another planet.

'You brought the posse,' she said to Church after they'd exchanged introductions.

'They're both trustworthy. Within reason.'

'They better be. I don't want my insanity made public. I have enough trouble getting a loan as it is. So, you fancy something hot, wet and sweet?' The sunglasses prevented Church reading her eyes to tell how he should take the innuendo so he simply nodded. 'Yeah, I bet you do. Face it, tiger, you just hit the jackpot.'

She led them down a side street off the main drag to a café called Mr C's Brasserie that was quiet enough to talk and not too empty to be overheard. They took a seat in the window and once the espressos and cappuccinos had arrived, Laura plugged her computer into a mobile phone and logged on to the net. The forteana newsgroup was so jammed with postings it seemed to take forever to load.

'It's getting worse,' she said. 'All over the country, an epidemic of bozo-ness. Claims of alien abductions, hauntings, UFOs, sightings of the Loch Ness Monster, even fairies, for God's sake. Now don't get me wrong, not so long ago I wouldn't have acknowledged these geeks if they'd painted themselves red and were doing naked handstands in Cross Keys Shopping Centre. Anybody who believed in the super-natural was dead between the ears. But we're talking smoke and fire here, if you know what I mean.'

'You said something happened to you.' Church had to restrain himself not to ask her about Marianne.

'I'm getting to that. Slowly. Because I don't want to talk about it, but I do.' Her confidence seemed to waver for a moment. 'Listen to me. I sound like I've got Alzheimer's.'

'If it makes you feel better, we've seen things too—' Ruth began.

'Does one crazy make another seem better? Look, I'm doing this because somebody has to, because there's something important going down, but all I see is dull sheep going about their lives either blind to it or pretending things are just how they were. And I'm doing it for me. To make sense of my experience before it eats its way out of my head.' She sipped her espresso, watching Church over the top of her sunglasses with eyes that were cold and unreadable. 'So, you ready to get screwed in the head?'

He met her eyes without flinching. 'Tell us what you know.'

'It happened back here in Salisbury, the city that made me into the woman I am today. I was staying with friends for the weekend and we went out to a party on the Saturday night. Talk about dull. I thought I'd gone into the Incontinence Home for the Elderly. But I made sure I enjoyed myself, even if *they* didn't know how to, and the next morning I needed to chill out so I took a walk. Ended up on this industrial estate. Right in the middle there's a depot for something or other – cogs or shit, I don't know. Anyway, it's pretty rundown, grass pushing up through the tarmac, the odd broken window, you know what I mean. I was standing outside looking at it thinking it would be a good place to hold a party when I heard . . . I mean, I thought I heard . . . it could have been the wind . . . I heard my name. Now I don't want you thinking I'm the kind of person who always follows imaginary voices, but I thought I ought to check it out. I've seen enough slasher flicks to be on my guard in that kind of situation, but, you know, it bothered me. I had to see.'

She looked from one face to the other as if searching for validation, but not wanting them to think she needed it.

'You don't have to explain yourself,' Church said. 'We've been through the same thing – trying to deal with something your head tells you can't be true, but your heart tells you is.'

'Sorry? Do you think I'm interested? Quiet, bud, this is my story.' Her attitude was antagonistic, but there was something, a flicker of a facial muscle, perhaps, that told Church his words had given her some comfort. 'So, I went through the wire and had a look around. It was deserted, Sunday morning, but I still thought there might be some social inadequate with a uniform and a dog so I moved out of the open sharpish. Then I heard it again. Laura. Definitely, Laura. It seemed to be coming from this route between two buildings where lots of yellow oil drums had been stacked. By that time even I was thinking I was crazy – there could have been any psycho down there – but it was like I was being *pulled* in by something. I picked my way through the drums, and then . . . Can I get another coffee?'

Church could tell she'd done it for effect. Even though her face remained impassive, she seemed pleased at the grumble she'd elicited from Tom; Church could see Ruth wasn't wholly warming to her either, but there was something in her obviously *faux* obnoxiousness that he quite liked. Tom ordered her another espresso which she took without thanks, and then she continued.

'I walked past the last heap of oil drums and it was like the air opened up in front of me.' She fumbled for the right words. 'Like the depot and everything around was some kind of stage scenery and somebody had peeled it back to show what really lay behind. I tried to back off, until I realised it was coming towards me quicker than I could move. And then it swallowed me up.'

Ruth looked at her incredulously. 'It was alive?'

'No, it was like some *Star Trek* effect – with no Scotty to pull me out at the last minute. There was this weird, spangly shit like I was having beads of oil sprayed on me, and then it was like I was tripping. I'm not going to start to describe the sensations – I don't want to sound like some burnt out acid case.' She nodded to Tom. 'No offence, space cadet. And then I saw things, heard things—'

'What kind of things?' Church interjected.

'Images. Sounds. It was a trip. And a half.'

'But what did you *see*?' Church stressed.

'Enough to know that this whole world's in deep trouble. And I was told—'

'Who told you?'

'—I was told that all this strange, supernatural shit that's been going on all over the country is tied into it. The basic message was: don't go getting any longterm mortgages.' Before Church could complain about her reticence, she added, 'Anything I say won't do it justice. But I can show you.'

a View into the Dark

Churchfields Industrial Estate lay on the western outskirts of the city. It was a maze of low, flat buildings in bleak, sixties design, each enclosed by chainlink fence or barbed wire. The entrance was through a dark, long tunnel under a railway bridge, which added to the sense of grim isolation. There was a constant smell of petrol fumes and engine oil, claustrophobic in the growing heat of the day, but despite the many builders' merchants and car lots, there was no sign of life.

Church parked the car round the corner and they sauntered up to the depot on foot. It comprised a large warehouse surrounded by smaller units, with a wide turning area for lorries at the front; the tarmac was cracked and tufts of yellowing grass poked through. As they neared, a fork-lift truck whizzed by carrying a pallet full of yellow oil drums, and through an open slide-door they could see movement deep within the building. Twelve-foot-high gates barred the way; they seemed to be opened electronically.

'We've got no chance of getting in there unseen,' Church said.

'Don't be defeatist, Church-dude. Where's your ninja training?' Laura waited patiently and when a lorry pulled up at the gate five minutes later, she slipped through in its wake and motioned for the others to follow. The rumble of the lorry's engines drowned their footsteps as they sprinted across the wide open space to the shelter of the depot. Laura led the way along the wall and then dived down the alley she had described. Once they were out of sight of the main entrance, they rested briefly behind a pile of oil drums while Laura checked her bearings.

'This is the place.' She turned back to the others. 'I hope you're set. There's no turning back now.'

'We're set.' Church steeled himself, but the apprehension he felt was increasing with each moment.

Laura picked her way among the oil drums with the others close behind, the air thick with the stink of chemicals. Finally they came to a clearing among the stacks.

'Here we are,' she said.

'What do we do? Say abracadabra?' Church could see nothing out of the ordinary.

'This is the place,' Laura repeated defiantly, but there was a note of anxiety in her voice, as if she were afraid it really had all been in her mind.

Tom and Ruth hung back, keeping watch as Laura and Church investigated, but the moment they stepped into the clearing there was a sudden drop in temperature and a rushing sound like water cascading over rapids. Tom and Ruth turned in time to see the air opening, not like a door as Laura had described it, but like someone slashing silk with a razor blade. They moved forward together, but they were too slow. The gap in the air folded around Church and Laura then sealed, leaving only a faint aroma of pine forests and lemon.

Ruth and Tom had just a second to wonder what had happened. There was movement at the end of the alley; an oil drum clanged, then rolled over noisily. Three depot workers appeared, moving menacingly towards them. At first Ruth thought they would be able to talk their way out of the corner until she saw the wild look in their eyes and smelled the choking stench of animals' cages. Their faces began to move like oil on water.

Tom put an arm across Ruth's chest, forcing her to back away, but another sound from the other end of the alley brought them to a halt. More were coming from the other direction. Tom cursed under his breath. 'She's led us into a trap.'

There was a brief sensation of floating in water and then Church was suddenly somewhere else. The odour of chemicals and diesel fumes was replaced by more natural smells, of clean, fresh air and damp stone. He was standing in a corridor with a flagged floor and rough-hewn stone walls. Torches burned at intervals, but they didn't cast enough light to dispel the gloom. It was too sudden a transition to comprehend and for a second he felt as if the ground was violently moving under his feet; desperately he flailed around until he found a wall on which to cling. With his eyes clamped shut and his chest feeling as if it were being crushed by an anvil, his mind screamed out for some kind of explanation. Feebly, he tried to tell himself he had fallen through a hole in the ground into some structure beneath; it was such a ridiculous assertion it didn't hold for a second. He hadn't fallen at all. Beyond the floating, he couldn't describe what *had* happened to him. With dread acceptance, he opened his eyes and looked around. It was true; somehow he had gone from there to here – wherever here was – in the blink of an eye. All at once his gorge rose and he turned to one side and vomited.

It took him several minutes to reach some kind of equilibrium, but he knew there was no point pathetically trying to deny the truth; and after all, over the past five weeks he had seen enough impossible things simply to start to accept without trying to understand.

His initial worry was what had happened to Laura. She had been at his side when the strange effect had begun to happen in front of them, but there was no sign of her along the stretch of corridor. Briefly he considered calling her name; but who knew what else might answer?

Certainly there was no point staying where he was. He was about to choose a direction at random when he heard someone singing, though faintly, as if it were filtered through numerous layers of stone. It hadn't just started, he was sure of it, but neither had he been aware of it before. It had a quality that made the hairs on his neck prickle. He weighed his options for a moment, decided he had none, and then started to move towards the music.

His footsteps echoed louder than he would have liked, and he remained permanently alert for any sound of someone approaching, but at the same time his mind was working overtime: where was he? There were few clues in his surroundings, but his deliberations took a new turn as he rounded a corner into another branch of the corridor.

On his right was a window, the first he had seen. He approached it in hope that it would allow him to get his bearings, but the moment he glanced out, an icy cold rushed through him. The view was of an infinite black void where occasional flashes of fire like distant explosions flared then subsided. There was no sign of surrounding land; whatever building he was in seemed to be floating in space.

Panic came first, like spiders in his mind; it was worse than he had feared. But somehow he managed to damp it down and continue on his way with a stoic acceptance; there would be time enough for explanations. He hoped. Tom had been right when he suggested Church's experiences had changed him; certainly if he had been presented with the same situation a few months ago he would not have remained so calm.

Although the singing didn't grow any louder, he found it increasingly entrancing, soothing even. Round another bend, he came to an oaken door, studded with black iron. It didn't seem particularly special, but after what he had seen he was filled with apprehension at what might lie behind; still, the safe option would get him nowhere. Throwing caution to the wind, he grasped the iron handle and threw the door open.

Church didn't know what he had expected, but it certainly wasn't the bedroom he had occupied as a seven-year-old. It was there in detail, down to the blue bedspread adorned with a picture of a cowboy on horseback, the annuals and comics, the lamp with the mosaic base on the bedside table: everything he could remember, and some things he couldn't. And there he was, asleep in his cowboy pyjamas, his pale face so innocent and untroubled it made him feel like crying; he could barely remember being that way. It seemed almost like he was watching the scene through glass. When he reached out, his hand came up against resistance and the air sparkled and shimmered around it.

The sparkling continued after he removed his hand until he realised that now it was coming from within the room. Something was gradually coalescing out of the glimmering at the foot of the bed. Eventually he saw it was a woman with long auburn hair and a beautiful, fine-boned face that reminded him of the idealised females in classical paintings. Her dress was long and of the darkest green, and it was embroidered with the finest filigree of gold in an astonishingly intricate pattern which, disturbingly, seemed to be moving as if it had a life of its own. Church had a sudden sense of majesty that took his breath away. Slowly she raised her arms and the sleeping Church woke as if she had called his name. He blinked once, twice, then a broad smile of wonder crept across his face. The woman smiled in return, then said three words softly.

In that instant, Church knew the scene that was happening *had* happened. The memory clawed its way from the back of his head where it had been dismissed as a dream and buried by reality; and it had happened not once, but several times over a short period.

The tableau slowly grew dark and then disappeared into inky blackness. Church closed the door and turned back to the corridor, trying to understand the tears that had sprung to his eyes. There was one other thing he did remember; the phrase she had uttered as a greeting:

Brother of Dragons.

This time Laura managed to control the nausea. As the stone corridor settled into focus, her biggest fear returned in force: that she would be compelled to look once again upon the things she had faced during her previous visit. Of all she had seen then, it was not the glimpses into her past that had been the worst, although that had been bad enough, but what she had to accept was a vista on to her future. It had been more than anyone should be expected to bear.

For a moment she wondered what had happened to Church, but in that place nothing was a surprise. The ethereal singing filtered through the walls; at least this time she knew what to expect. She set off purposefully, wishing there was some direct route, recalling how the maze had changed, even when she had tried carefully retracing her steps. She guessed it wasn't even as simple as stumbling across the right path; she felt instinctively that the maze *allowed* her through when she was ready.

The windows tempted her to peer out, but she resisted; it disturbed her too much. Instead she turned her thoughts to Church and the others. She hadn't made up her mind about them yet. Church was impossible to read at first glance; he was all dark water moving deeply, but she liked that in people. Superficiality was boring; the fun came in stripping away the layers, like unwrapping a surprise birthday present, until the real person was revealed, good or bad. Ruth seemed a little too nicey-nice, and, if she admitted it to herself, Ruth's easy confidence made her uncomfortable. The hippie disturbed her on some deeper level. When he looked at her she felt like squirming, as if he were mentally dissecting her with a cold contempt.

Deep in the building a rumbling began which sounded like the breathing of some mighty beast. Laura picked up her step, hoping against hope that Church and the others were the right ones and she wouldn't have to come here again.

'Follow me,' Tom urged, clambering on to a heap of oil drums. He held out a hand and hauled Ruth behind him and then he was scrambling to the top of the precarious pile like a monkey. Ruth was more cautious, but the sight of the approaching men-who-weren't-men spurred her on.

The top of the heap was level with a dusty window which Tom smashed with his elbow, turning away to shield his face from the flying glass. Beneath them, their pursuers were already tearing at the drums in an attempt to unbalance them, roaring in the guttural language Ruth had first heard in the service station car park. Out of the corner of her eye she caught the merest glimpse of their true faces before she had snapped her attention away, but it was enough to make her head swim to the verge of blacking out.

Tom grabbed her as he knocked out the remaining shards of glass from the frame before hauling her through on to a metal walkway. 'Sorry, I couldn't help looking,' she gasped as she slowly regained control.

'Their faces are too much to bear until you're used to it.' Ruth had an instant to wonder how Tom knew this before he grabbed her arm and pressed his palm against her forehead. At first it was cool, but then she felt a warmth spread out into her brain. 'There. It won't be pleasant, but at least you'll be able to deal with them now.'

Ruth glanced down and felt her gorge rise, but she didn't black out. It was still too much for her mind to register, as if she were looking at a TV where the signal was distorting and breaking up; misshapen bone and scales, things writhing both on the skin and underneath it. But the horror that assailed her didn't even come from the appearance; it was as if it were part of their existence, radiating out from deep within them. She turned quickly and pushed Tom away from the window.

'What's happened to Church?' she cried. Her heart jumped when she thought of him.

'I don't know where the door leads. We can come back for him later. First we have to save ourselves.'

The walkway overlooked the depot's loading bay. A lorry had its rear door down and had been half-filled with the oil drums. A fork-lift truck was abandoned nearby. There was no one around, but they could hear an insane cacophany of roars drawing closer.

'They've been put here to guard the door. They let us in, knowing we wouldn't get out again. They'll tear us apart if they catch us.' Tom stopped suddenly, then climbed on to the walkway's railing. 'Come on.'

His leap carried him on to the roof of the lorry, where he landed awkwardly. Ruth moaned when she saw him lie there for a second or two, but then he was up and limping along to the cab. She swayed on the railings for an instant, afraid to follow, but then she saw the creatures swarming in through the main door like insects, their forms thankfully blurred into grey shadows by her mind. Her landing was graceless, but she managed only to wind herself and then she was scrambling and sliding behind Tom, who was already lowering himself over the side through the cab's open window.

The creatures were moving astonishingly quickly for their size. One of them picked up an oil drum as easily as if it had been a paper cup and hurled it at the truck which Tom was already gunning into life. It smashed against the front just below the windscreen and bounced off to one side where it leaked foul-smelling chemicals.

The lorry was already moving forward jerkily so she lay flat on the cab roof, gripping the edge tightly, her eyes closed, praying she wouldn't fall off. It built up speed rapidly. There was a loud bump as it hit one of the creatures and then it was rolling out of the doors.

She heard Tom shout a warning and looked up to see a long, sinewy arm reaching out for her ankle from the side of the cab where one of the things was clinging on. She snatched her foot away at the last moment and the talons dug into the metal, tearing furrows through it like paper.

Before it could have another go, Ruth kicked out wildly. Her boot slammed against the creature's head with a jarring impact that felt like she had kicked granite, but it did enough to loosen its grip. It fell away and a second later the lorry jumped as the wheels went over it. The sound behind them was awful to hear, a screeching chorus of animal noises filled with threat.

Suddenly Ruth could smell smoke. The chemicals in the drum must have been highly volatile because the heat from the engine had ignited the residue on the front of the lorry and flames were licking up the windscreen. It wouldn't be long before the whole thing was alight.

Tom headed for the chainlink fence, then slammed on the brakes at the last moment. Ruth desperately tried to hold on, but the momentum was too great; it propelled her over the top. She hit the pavement hard, the shock winding her, bringing tears to her eyes. When she looked up, Tom had slammed the lorry into reverse and was heading back into the depot at speed.

At the last moment, he threw open the door and leapt out. She saw his head hit the tarmac, but somehow he rolled over and came to his feet, and then he was limping as fast as he could towards her with blood streaming down his face.

The lorry careered into the depot, showering sparks as it passed too close to the door, and then it hit the piles of oil drums waiting to be loaded. For the briefest instant there was a sound like a huge inhalation of breath and then the whole place went up, a rapid series of firecracker bursts as each drum exploded, merging into a gigantic conflagration. The depot was ripped apart, debris erupting like missiles as a tempest of heat-blasted air roared out. Ruth's head rang with the furious noise. An enormous piece of roofing narrowly missed her, embedding itself in the tarmac. The rest of the building rained down in fiery chunks for what seemed like an age as Ruth rolled up into a foetal ball.

When it subsided, she jumped to her feet, unable to believe her luck. Where the depot had stood, an inferno blazed up so high she could feel the heat on her face from fifty feet away, blackening the midday sky. Nothing could have survived.

Relief mingled with worry about what had happened to Church, but then another realisation surfaced. Slowly she scanned around the blasted site: Tom was nowhere to be seen.

Church no longer had any idea which way he was going. The corridor twisted and turned, often folding back on itself as if it had been designed by some insane architect. Nor was he helped by the unending array of stone walls, flickering torches, occasional windows on to nothing and, every now and then, a door, although most of them had been locked. Of the two that had been open, he had received more startlingly clear visions, seemingly of his life. The first showed him sitting on a hill watching the burning of a city which looked disturbingly like London. Billowing clouds of black smoke turned the sky almost as dark as night, although somehow he was sure it was daytime. Yet it was the way he looked that affected him the most: though he didn't appear much older, his face was burdened with trouble and suffering that made him seem closer to forty. He was hunched over as he scanned the horizon, clutching an ornate sword to his chest like one of those characters who spent their weekends re-enacting ancient battles. His hair was longer and he had a tightly clipped goatee; there were tears in his eyes at what he saw.

The second door showed him pale and broken, alone in the flat the day after Marianne had died. Seeing the terrible torment frozen in a face that had never experienced such depths before brought back the intensity of the emotions and he slammed the door and ran down the corridor before any more of the tableau could present itself to him.

What could it all mean? He suspected that wherever he was lay outside of the existence he knew; time seemed to flow back and forth randomly and he wondered if it were possible to see any point in the past or the future. If he opened a door at the exact right moment, would he see Marianne in the weeks or days or hours that led up to her making her tragic decision to take her life? The thought brought with it a blast of such hope it made his head spin.

As if in answer, he rounded a corner and came upon another door. Nervously he stood before it for a full minute until he found the courage, and then he swung it open.

He was instantly deflated when the scene was unfamiliar: a green bank running down to a fast-flowing stream that passed under a stone bridge. Someone lay on his back in its shadow, the head and shoulders submerged in the foam, unmistakably dead. Church knew who it was before the white water cleared for a second to allow him to see the pale skin and staring eyes.

This was how he would die.

He threw the door shut and pressed his back against it, his head in his hands. He hadn't looked much older than he was now.

How he kept going he didn't know; his head was spinning and his emotions were so raw he wondered if he were having a breakdown. Nothing made sense. There was just a queasy disorientation and a sense of growing despair.

He wandered on in a daze until he realised something had changed: there was a faint trail of incense in the air, like the hint of a lover's perfume in an empty room. Then, as he progressed, the music grew noticeably louder − for the first time since he had been in that place. The melody was powerfully evocative, of warm summer nights beneath a full moon, of the smell of pine forests and the taste of a cool mountain stream; yet despite the images that flashed through his mind the words seemed to be in some alien language, so exquisitely formed they wove in and out of the music to create something greater than the sum.

It made Church's heart quicken until a sudden joy overcame all the negative thoughts that had been consuming him. He broke into a jog and then a sprint, any reticence left behind in the rush.

When the corridor opened into a wide, lofty room he almost tumbled into it. Ahead of him, windows twice as tall as a man ranged in a semi-circle, offering a prospect out into the void. An ornate, gold telescope stood in front of them. On either side of the hemisphere, braziers burned, filling the air with the sweet, soothing incense. Intricately designed tapestries hung on the walls showing a vast range of scenes like a more exquisite Bayeux Tapestry, while thick rugs lay on the stone flags. And looking through the telescope with her back to him was the woman who had appeared in his childhood bedroom.

She turned as he entered and her beautiful face was even more potent than in the vision through the door. Her cheekbones were high, her lips full and her skin seemed to glow with an inner, golden light that mesmerised him; her cool, blue eyes, filled with wisdom and passion, were so deep he felt he could never reach the bottom of them.

'Who are you?' In his head his voice sounded weak and pathetic.

She smiled and he instantly felt like his veins had been flooded with honey. 'A friend.'

'Was that you singing?'

She nodded gently. 'It is a song from the old world, from the time before times, about two star-crossed lovers capturing one night for themselves before they are torn apart. It is sad but beautiful, like all things that move the soul. Come closer.'

She held out one delicate hand and Church descended the three steps into the room. 'You came to me when I was a boy.'

'Many times, always on the edge of dreams.'

'Why?'

'To convince myself you are who you are.'

'Which is what?'

'A Brother of Dragons.' She looked at him with a faint, curious smile, as if it was the most obvious thing in the world.

Church shrugged. 'I don't know what that means.' But at that moment it didn't seem important. What mattered was the tint of her skin, the faint emotion that flickered around the edges of her mouth, the musical timbre of her voice, the smell of her, like lemongrass and cardamon, so seductive he was mesmerised. Right then she could have said anything of importance to him and it wouldn't have registered. Finally he became aware that he was staring and he blushed, looking around uncomfortably. 'Where is this place?'

'It is called the Watchtower. A place between the worlds, neither human nor faery, neither sun nor moon, neither sand nor water. Time flows around it.'

'Is it your home?'

Her laugh was as musical as her voice. 'It is a refuge for now. And, if you like, it is an adequate stepping stone for someone from your land. I would not wish to present the majesty of my true home to you until you were fully adjusted.'

'I'm sorry. I shouldn't be here. I was curious—'

She took his hand and her fingers were as cool as a stream in summer. 'You *should* be here,' she said forcefully, leading him to two carved wooden chairs, between which was a table on which was a jug with a thin neck and twin pewter goblets. 'I have been waiting for you.'

Church looked at her curiously. 'I didn't know I was coming here until today.'

'*I* knew you were coming here.' She sat him down and poured him a drink from the tall jug. 'Do not worry. The laws of my home do not apply here. You are free to take of this place what you will.' It looked like water, but the taste was heavenly, so complex on the palate that Church experienced a new flavour every instant until he gave up and just let it slip down his throat; it felt like liquid gold, glowing bright as it infused him.

'That's amazing,' he said.

She nodded. Then her face slowly darkened. 'There are many things of which we must talk, and time is growing rare. Your world is turning from the light.' Church felt a sudden *frisson*; Tom had used the same phrase. 'The old Covenant has been broken and now the Night Walkers have returned to the land of man to shape it to their own way. They must not be allowed to succeed. In the time before time they defeated my people and brought in the Season of Eternal Night, a rule so bitterly malign the Filid's lays can bring tears from the coldest heart. The land was blighted, the people lived in permanent shadow and no corner of the world was free from suffering and despair. Never again.'

'The Night Walkers.' He knew whom she meant without questioning her further.

'They have always existed in darkness, crawling along the edge of the light, envying it and fearing it.' She looked down so Church couldn't see her eyes. 'They were the worst of the old races. The Great Destroyers, leeching the heat of life, leaving only the cold of the void. Their corrupt power laid waste to all before them.'

There was an odd tone in her voice that filled him with a creeping dread. If the creatures were as powerful as she intimated, it didn't sound like all the military might of humanity stood a chance against them. 'Then who are your people?' he asked.

When she looked up her face was filled with such sadness he winced. 'Most Glorious of the old races, known as the Golden Ones, Shining People of the Light, raised above all others.'

Suddenly Church could feel some of the pieces falling into place. 'Your people and the Night Walkers were on our world sometime in the distant past? And you interracted with humanity in some way—'

'We ruled peacefully until the Night Walkers came,' she said proudly. 'They defeated my people through trickery, not power, but only for a while. And when we struck back they fell before us and were made to pay for their deception.' Her flashing eyes were frightening in their intensity. Church knew he would not want to have her as an enemy.

But here was something that made Church give pause: an age-old story stitched into the very fabric of human understanding. Two immensely powerful races, one of the light, the other of the dark, opposing each other in a war that shook the world while humanity trembled beneath them. He wondered how this woman and the terrible creatures they had seen under the bridge and at the services must have seemed to the ancient people who first encountered them. It was hardly surprising they had resonated down the millennia in legends and race memories, spawning the archetypes that were buried deep in the human subconscious. Suddenly he felt on the edge of something monumental, transcendental; the source of everything that mattered to mankind. He felt humbled by it all. 'But where did you come from? Some other galaxy? A different planet?'

Her expression suggested she didn't seem able to comprehend what he was saying. 'We came from the Far Lands.'

'The Far Lands?'

She nodded. 'And after the Covenant was forged, in the days of sorrow and joy that followed the second great battle, we returned to the

Far Lands once more. The Night Walkers accepted their bleak purgatories beneath the lakes and seas. As victors, we occupied all that remained, the cloud-topped mountains, the thick, dark forests, the lush fields. We returned to our courts glittering with wonders.'

'And you left our world behind?'

'That was the Covenant.'

'And now it's been broken. But then your people could help us! You have the power to—'

'The Night Walkers unleashed the Wish-Hex.' There was fire in her voice. 'My brethren were swept away. A few of us escaped, to places like this, or to your world. Some were tainted by the Night Walkers.' Whatever this meant, it seemed to fill her with horror.

'And the rest?'

'In some empty place beyond the land, hidden from all our searching, prisoners—'

'Isn't there anything that can be done?' he asked passionately.

She smiled at his display of emotion. 'That is why you are here, Jack Churchill.'

'What can *I* do?' It seemed such a ridiculous question he had trouble restraining the self-contempt in his voice, but he instinctively knew she would not accept any disrespect.

'You are not yet in tune with your heritage. When you find your true heart, the strength to act will come with it. Yet it is true, even then the Brothers and Sisters of Dragons would not have the power to defeat the Night Walkers alone. Yet you do have the power to free my people—'

'How?'

'—given the right calling, given the correct conjunction of important things. And that is your task, Jack Churchill, should you accept my patronage. Indeed, it is your destiny, and if truth be told, you have little choice in the matter. Assemble the five Brothers and Sisters of Dragons who are one in spirit, the quincunx that make the hero foretold by the Faithi, who will save the Age of Man from the final threat. Locate the objects of power that will make the summoning.'

'This is all moving too fast. I don't understand—' Church's right hand began to shake uncontrollably and he had to replace the goblet on the table; he couldn't tell if it was the weight of her words that had triggered the violent tremor or his subconscious rebellion at the threat of what lay ahead if he did as she said.

'Tell me,' he said, staring off into space, 'those things I saw in the rooms—'

'They will come to pass.'

'Even if I refuse to take part in this?'

'They will come to pass.'

Church could still see his pale, dead face submerged in the water, his torment as he watched the burning city, and it seemed whatever life stretched ahead was bleak and despairing; but then, was that any different to the days since Marianne had died? Deep within him, something stirred; if he knew his burden, he would shoulder it as best he could, and if he could do some good for others then that would be enough. The woman was smiling as if she could sense his thoughts. 'I'll do what I can,' he said.

'The fire burns strong within you, Jack Churchill, though you cannot see it yourself.'

He sighed. 'I wish I could say that gave me some comfort.'

He was surprised when the woman took his hand and wrapped her own around it, even more surprised when he felt some strange succour from the act; his heartbeat subsided, the stress seeped from his muscles, his shoulders relaxed gradually. Her voice, when she began speaking, was quieter than before, as if she were afraid the walls would overhear the secrets she was about to reveal. Church looked into her eyes, entranced.

'When my people first came to your land, they brought with them four objects of the most remarkable strangeness and power. They were touchstones for my people, prized above all else, celebrating our origins and our power, the culmination of our great tradition. Though our beginnings are lost to time, for we are an ancient race, the Filid tell of our days in four marvellous cities of the northland: Falias, Gorias, Finias and Murias. There, buildings of glass and gold soared to the clouds; the days were filled with glory, the nights with wonder. There, we learned magic, craft and knowledge, became aware of the weft and weave of nature and, eventually, transcended our humble beginnings to become gods. When we ventured abroad, we took a talisman from each of the magical cities so we would never forget our transformation and grow arrogant in our power. And finally, for we are a nomadic people, our journeying brought us to your land.'

There was a sadness in her smile as she recounted her tale; the heart of her melancholy, Church guessed, lay in whatever had encouraged her people to leave paradise, for having seen heaven, how could they truly know peace again? 'And you want me to find these four talismans?'

She nodded slowly. 'They will be like a candle in the night, leading my people across the void.'

'What are they?' Church asked.

'There is a stone which can recognise the true king of your land. The sword of our great war leader, which inflicts only a fatal blow. The

Spear of the Lord of the Sun, for ever exalted as the slayer of the Adversary, bringer of victory over the Night Walkers. And finally, and most importantly, the Cauldron of our Allfather, an object filled with such power to heal or destroy that few can survive in its presence.

'When we left your land for our new home, the talismans were hidden, for we knew the Night Walkers envied them and we could not risk them falling into their hands. And by then the talismens were too tied to the land to take with us,' she continued. 'The Night Walkers would never have been able to use them, for they would have been consumed by the light the talismans contained, but they were such a vital part of my people's tradition and pride that they *were* my people. And to see them in the hands of the enemy would have been more than we could bear.'

Something stirred deep in Church's memory at her description of the artefacts, but the details wouldn't come forth. 'A stone, a sword, a spear and a cauldron. They seem familiar.'

'They have played important roles in the history of your land. Found, then lost again, they have been used to shape momentous events by some of the most consequential mortals to walk your world. Indeed, they are now as much a part of your tradition and pride as mine. They have become infused with the very essence of your world. And that is why only the Brothers and Sisters of Dragons can find them.' She paused as a shadow flickered across her face; in that moment, Church had the sense that she was something more than just the woman he saw before him, something alien and terrifying. 'These are the forms you can understand. They are objects of pure power, their shapes defined by the stories. They have existed under other names, but at their heart, in your terms, this is what they are: a stone, a sword, a spear and a cauldron. But they have been missing for an age and though many have searched, none have found.'

'Then how will I find them? You said time is short, so surely you can't expect me to spend years wandering the country, digging holes.'

She led him to a large oak chest in one corner which he hadn't noticed before. The hinges creaked as if it hadn't been opened for centuries, and from within came a strong azure light which he recognised from Stonehenge. Carefully she removed an iron lantern on a short chain with a hook on the end. The light glowed from a blue flame which flickered through the tiny bottle-glass panes on the lamp's four sides. She held it out to Church, who took it gingerly.

'You must take this back with you. It will light the way.'

'How?'

'Follow the flame. It is the essence of your world and is drawn to the talismans. Trust your instinct.'

A feeling of wellbeing flowed up the arm that was holding the lantern aloft. 'Thank you,' Church said honestly. 'I'll do what I can.'

'Now—' she began.

'Wait,' Church said anxiously. 'There's so much more I need to know. Who are the five?'

'You will know them when they come together.'

At that moment, Laura emerged cautiously from the shadows of the doorway. She looked from Church to the woman.

'You did well,' the woman said to her. 'He is the one.'

Church eyed Laura suspiciously. 'Wait a minute, you were *supposed* to bring me here?'

'Don't get antsy, Church-dude. I couldn't take the chance you were going to get all yellow-bellied on me.' She seemed to be shying away from the woman as if she was afraid of her.

Church felt a bolt of awareness that made his palms sweat. 'When you mentioned Marianne—'

'She told me the one I had to bring here would know the name and it would be reason enough to make him come.' Laura glanced at the woman, unsure she had said the right thing.

The woman's expression was impassive. 'You would have been drawn here in time—'

'But you knew that would get me here quickly.' Church felt his hands shaking and he hid them behind his back; he was almost afraid to ask the question. 'This place looks out over all time, you said.' He swallowed; his mouth was too dry. 'Do you know—' There was a flicker across the woman's face that told him he didn't have to continue the question; he could see she knew something.

'Once you have done as I asked, all will be revealed to you.'

The lack of emotion in her face disturbed him; it was a mask to hide the truth, but he couldn't tell if it was because it would destroy him, or because she felt suspending the answer would drive him on to succeed. 'You must tell me now,' he pleaded. He hated the desperation in his voice – it seemed so weak – but he couldn't control it.

She shook her head, said nothing. But for the first time he had real hope of finding out what really drove Marianne to take her own life; real hope of ending his own purgatory. If it was all he could take away with him, it would be enough.

The woman motioned for Church to move towards Laura. 'You must locate my people before the Beltane fires light the land or they

116

will be lost to you for another year, and by then . . .' Her voice trailed away.

Church felt a surprising twinge of sadness that he was leaving the mysterious woman behind. 'You still haven't told me your name.'

She smiled. 'When we become friends, then we will know each other.' She touched his shoulder so briefly he barely felt it, but in that instant energy crackled between them. He thought he glimpsed something in her face then, but before he could be sure, she had turned away, by chance or on purpose. Then she made an odd, convoluted movement with her hand and the next second the woman, and the Watchtower, were gone.

The air was foul with the stink of burning, melted plastics and charred metal. Where the depot had stood was a broken outline, blackened and dripping water on the sodden, scorched ground; trails of smoke drifted up into the twilight sky from the twisted girder framework that was still too hot to touch. Three fire engines were parked in what had been the forecourt, their firemen, exhausted and sooty, standing around in small gaggles surveying the wreckage or spraying bursts of water on to pockets that were still burning.

'My God!' Church said, turning slowly to examine the carnage; the shock on their re-entry had taken any conscious thought away for a moment. Then: 'We couldn't have been gone for more than a couple of hours.'

'Time's different over there,' Laura said distractedly.

They both stood for five minutes trying to come to terms with the upheaval until Church noticed a group of men in suits standing among the wreckage examining something on the ground before them. He squinted, but the haze made the object difficult to discern. Then a gust of wind cleared the smoke away and he saw it was a skeleton charred by the fire. But it was clearly not human; the bones were enormous, twisted into such monstrous forms he couldn't imagine what it would have looked like when it was alive.

Laura saw where he was staring. 'What is that?' There was a note of sick disbelief in her voice.

'A Night Walker,' he said quietly.

Suddenly one of the men spotted them and said something hurriedly to his colleagues. They looked towards Church and Ruth, their faces cold and serious, and then they started to advance. They weren't police, Church was sure; something in their manner suggested a higher authority.

'We had better get out of here,' he said.

As one of the men called out harshly for them to stop, they turned and ran through the smouldering wreckage towards the gates which had been blown down. As they crossed the forecourt, they heard a cry and then saw Ruth waving from the other side of the fence.

'What in heaven happened to you?' she said; the strain was evident on her pale face.

There wasn't time to answer. The men were yelling furiously, but the three of them had enough of a head start. By the time their pursuers had reached the gates, Church was already behind the wheel of the car, the engine roaring.

'Who the hell were they?' Laura said as they pulled away at speed.

Ruth ignored her and turned towards Church. 'We should dump her now,' she said. 'She led us into a trap. And now Tom's missing.'

In the rearview mirror, Church watched the smoke obscure the angry red glare of the sunset. Laura spent several minutes denying trying to cause them harm, but her ironic manner made it difficult for them to accept anything she said at face value.

'Look, I tumbled through that hole to God knows where by accident,' she said to Church. 'I spent hours wandering around those corridors getting my head well and truly screwed, and then I met Lady Freakzone who insisted I'd be cóntacted by some Brother of Dragons and I had to bring him straight to her. She didn't have to say *or else* – I'm not stupid, and I'm not about to mess with someone who lives on a big floating castle in space. I had no idea if you were the right one. I hoped, because I didn't want to keep jumping on the Nightmare Shuttle. But I didn't *know*. And I certainly didn't have any idea about whoever those geeks were who jumped the old guy and Miss Smarty Pants here.'

Ruth glanced at her coldly, then said, 'The point's moot now. We need to find what's happened to Tom and move on.'

'You're not leaving me behind,' Laura said. 'I'm in on this now.'

Ruth turned to Church. 'We can't take someone with us we can't trust. And she's just excess baggage—'

'Who made you—'

Church silenced Laura with his hand. 'The woman on the Watch-tower told me there had to be five of us – the right five, the chosen ones, I suppose – involved in this mess and I don't reckon she would have involved Laura if she wasn't one of us.'

Ruth chewed on her lip. Reluctantly she said, 'You had better tell me what else you were told.'

For the next fifteen minutes, Church related everything that had happened to him on the Watchtower, detailing the four items they needed to find and showing them both the lantern with the blue flame.

'This is getting crazier by the minute,' Ruth said. 'Soon we aren't going to have any frames of reference at all. But in our current insane world I suppose it makes a certain kind of sense. So we have a deadline? What's this Beltane?'

'A Celtic festival,' Church said. 'It falls on May 1 and celebrates the onset of summer.'

'Barely two months! How the hell are we supposed to find things that have been missing for eons in that short time? And why is it down to us?' Ruth seemed irritable and exhausted after the shock of her experiences. 'And what's happened to Tom?'

Church recalled the blasted site; if Tom had been caught in the explosion there wouldn't have been much hope for him.

'The last thing I saw he was running away from the depot, then the explosion hit,' Ruth continued. 'I searched everywhere. Questioned the firemen . . .' Her voice trailed away dismally.

Only a sliver of red sun was visible on the horizon, painting Salisbury scarlet and ruddy browns. With the flakes of soot whisked up by the wind and the choking smell of burning, it felt like a scene from hell.

'We can't wait here for him,' Church said eventually. 'You heard what he said about the Baobhan Sith. They'll be hunting tonight.'

'But we can't just abandon him,' Ruth protested.

'He's smart enough to lie low if he's okay.' Church felt a tinge of guilt at not discovering what had happened to Tom, but they had no other choice but to press on. 'We need to get out of town by dark, see where this takes us. The roads might not be safe at night, but we don't have much choice, do we?' He turned to Laura. 'What about an overnight bag—'

'I travel light. I'll pick up some things along the way – that's the wonder of credit cards. And the way things are going, I'll never have to pay them back.'

The lantern flame was already leaning heavily in one direction, as if it was caught in an air current. With a certain apprehension, Church eased the car through the winding streets until they were heading the same way: north.

Yet his emotions were in such turmoil it was almost impossible to concentrate on the driving. Now he knew what the old woman on the banks of the Thames had meant: it was a premonition of his death. He would have thought the knowledge would have destroyed him, but he couldn't quite work out what he felt: disbelief, despite what the woman had said, hope that it would all work out differently, even some relief that the tiring struggle of the last two years was coming to an end. But it was too soon to consider that. In the brief time he had spoken to the woman she had given him so much information his head was spinning. What did it all mean, and why was he involved? And was he finally going to find out the answer to the only question that mattered to him: why Marianne had taken her life? He switched on the radio in the hope that it would drown out his chattering thoughts.

As the music filled the car, he knew it would prevent Laura hearing any conversation, so he said quietly to Ruth, 'Do you ever think about dying?'

She looked at him suspiciously, as if she could see right through his question. 'Not if I can help it.'

'But you never know how much time you've got, do you?'

'Did something happen to you in that place that you're not telling me?'

He kept his eyes firmly on the road ahead. 'I think if I knew I was going to die, I'd like to do something good, something unselfish for once.'

Ruth could see the heaviness of his thoughts echoed on his face and it upset her that he didn't feel he could open up to her.

Suddenly it didn't seem right to talk any more. The sun slid beneath the horizon and they fell into an uneasy silence as the car headed out into the night.

ῃeʀe Be ɒʀᴀʓoɴs

Church wanted to keep to the well-lit roads while following the lantern's general direction, but that would have meant heading back towards Stonehenge, where Tom had said the Baobhan Sith had posted sentries. Instead he had to follow a looping route which took them on to an unlit road across Salisbury Plain. As they left the sodium haze behind and the night closed around them, they all thought they could see strange things moving off across the plain; odd lights flickered intermittently, will o' the wisps trying to draw their attention, and at one point a large shadow loomed at the side of the road. Church floored the accelerator to get past it and didn't look in the rearview mirror until they were far away.

It was a disturbing journey; they all felt the countryside had somehow become a no-man's land filled with peril. At first, hedges were high and trees clustered against the road oppressively, but as they moved on to the plain it opened out and they were depressed to see there were no welcoming lights anywhere. They passed a sign for Ministry of Defence land where a red flag warned of military manoeuvres; Church wondered briefly if they were already having to cope with things that shouldn't exist; whether they *could* cope.

They felt relief when they reached the outskirts of Devizes. The lantern pointed them towards the north-east as they passed through the town and they found themselves on another quieter road, although there was not the same sense of foreboding they felt on Salisbury Plain. The landscape on either side was ancient, dotted with hill figures and prehistoric mounds. By 10 p.m. they had wound through numerous tiny villages and eventually found themselves in Avebury, where the lantern flame relaxed into an upright position. The village was protectively encircled by the famous stone circle, its lights seeming a pitiful defence against the encroaching night. Church pulled into the car park in the centre where they could see a handful of the rocks silhouetted against the night sky; he felt oddly unnerved by the synchronicity of long lost times shouting down the years.

'More standing stones,' Ruth said, peering through the windscreen at the squat, irregular shapes. 'What are we supposed to do now?'

'It's too late to do anything now.' Church stretched out the kinks in his back.

Laura leaned forward between the two of them. 'Looks like we've just driven into the dead zone. Any danger this place has a pub?'

'We're not here for the night life,' Ruth said sourly.

'No reason why we can't enjoy ourselves while we're waiting for the world to end.' Laura picked up her computer and mobile phone and climbed out.

Although it was only just March, the night was not unduly cold. An occasional breeze blew from the Downs, filled with numerous subtle fragrances, and the lack of any traffic noise added to the time-lost feeling which was, oddly, both comforting and disconcerting. The Red Lion pub lay only a short walk along the road, an enormous, many-roomed inn whose black timbers creaked beneath the weight of a thatched roof.

'I can't help feeling we should be digging out a foxhole instead of sitting down for a quiet drink like nothing was wrong,' Ruth said as they settled at a table.

'When everything is going insane, it's reassuring to do normal things,' Church replied. 'Pubs have a lot of power in situations like this. It's all about humanity coming together, celebrating in the face of—'

'Do you two always talk bollocks like this?' Laura took a swig of her beer from the bottle, then leaned back in her chair. 'Because, you know, I'm starting to see an upside to Armageddon.'

Ruth bristled. 'You're still on probation. It would be a shame if you made us dump you here in the dead zone.'

Laura smiled mockingly which irritated Ruth even more, then directed her comments at Church. 'Mystic Meg wouldn't have told you all that information if she didn't think you could do something with it.'

Church nodded. 'You're right. *She* thought we were capable of it.' He took a long draught of his beer, then looked at Laura curiously. 'You've got a good job, a life. Why did you decide to come with us?'

Laura shrugged, then glanced around the bar with studied distraction. 'I can't go back to my life and wait for the world to go to hell in a handcart.'

'No, you want to give it a helping hand down the slope,' Ruth said acidly.

'And let's face it, I'm a different person now,' Laura continued. 'I've done a few drugs in my time. It's not big or clever, but, hey, I enjoyed myself. And if you've done drugs you know they change you. Suddenly you find yourself apart from all your old friends who haven't done them. They couldn't ever understand what you've been through without experiencing it themselves. After crossing over to that castle, that's how I feel now. It was such a big thing, such a life-changing experience, bigger than the wildest trip, there isn't a single person on earth who understands me now. Except you. We've got an affinity, Church-dude. We're beyond everyone else. Could you go back to your life after that?'

Church felt Ruth stiffen beside him. He couldn't tell if Laura was specifically trying to annoy her by making her feel excluded, but he guessed she was. 'We've all experienced weird things,' he said. 'I suppose that puts us on common ground.'

'But we don't have to like each other,' Ruth said coldly.

Laura looked away; nothing seemed to concern her.

'So what's all this nonsense about Brothers and Sisters of Dragons?' Ruth said directly to Church. 'It sounds like some ridiculous secret society.'

'She was implying we were important somehow. Different. Special.' He wrinkled his nose; it didn't make sense to him either.

Ruth snorted ironically. 'The way you told it suggested it was some kind of destiny thing. But we wouldn't be here now if we hadn't been under Albert Bridge at that particular moment in time, and that was chance. A big coincidence. If I hadn't had that row with Clive and got out of the taxi, if you'd stayed in bed for five minutes longer, none of this would have happened to us. So how can it be destiny?'

Church shrugged. 'Well, she wasn't *lying* to me – at least it didn't seem that she was. Maybe she was mistaken.'

'She wasn't lying,' Laura said emphatically.

'How do you know?'

'I just feel it.'

'But maybe that explains why those things have been going for the nuclear option in trying to stop us,' Church mused. 'It would have helped if the mystery woman had told us exactly what our little dragon group is supposed to do. Something about our *heritage*, she said—'

'If Tom were here I bet he'd have something to say about it,' Ruth mused.

'Yeah, he'd be sitting back dispensing enigmatic wisdom like Yoda,' Church said. 'He was obviously keeping stuff from us – we couldn't trust him. Maybe we're better off without him.'

'Do you reckon he's scattered in bits and pieces across Salisbury?' Laura stared out some elderly local who was watching her curiously.

'Who knows where he is. Maybe he fell through another of those holes in the air. Maybe he's hiding out and doing this just to wind us up.'

'Oh, he helped us out, Church. He was just selective in what he said.' Ruth pondered for a moment, before adding, 'He seemed a little scared when you told him about that black dog.'

'You should have seen it.'

Ruth glanced out of the window, but the lights were too bright within to see anything clearly. 'I wonder how much longer we've got?'

'What do you mean?'

'Before the next thing comes after us. The Wild Hunt, Tom said. The worst thing we could expect.'

Outside the pub, while they waited for Church to return from the toilet, Ruth could no longer contain herself. Laura was chewing on some gum and kicking stones at the parked cars.

'You ought to know I don't trust you,' Ruth said, 'and I'm going to be keeping an eye on you.'

'Ask me if I'm bothered.' Laura continued to boot the stones; one rattled on the side of a brand new BMW.

'You should be.'

'What do you want me to do, cry myself to sleep because you don't like me? Wake up, it's never going to happen.'

Ruth wanted to slap her, but she controlled herself. 'What's wrong with you? This is a nightmare. We could die at any moment. You could at least make the effort to get on.'

'I am who I am, Miss Boring Pants. Like it or lump it.'

'Really? You expect me to believe DuSantiago is your real name? Lots of South Americans in Salisbury, I suppose. And you really haven't tried hard to build up that cool, hard exterior? Yeah, right.'

'Nice sermon. Pity you're talking out of your arse. You don't know anything about me.'

'That's the problem. If you opened up, we could start trusting you . . . if you really want to help.'

'Don't go getting all touchy-feely, New Agey on me. I'm not one for hugs and baring my soul.' A stone bounced off the bonnet of a Volvo and set the car alarm blaring. Laura turned back to Ruth, her face lit by the flashing indicator lights. 'I'm as committed to this as you are. That's all you need to know.'

'No, it's—' Ruth caught her tongue as Church emerged from the pub.

'So . . . a night in the car. Should be very restful,' he said ironically.

'Lucky me. I get the bijou back seat.' When Laura dropped into step next to Church, Ruth felt an odd twinge of loneliness, as if she were slowly being cut out.

'You think we'll be safe there?' she said.

'As safe as anywhere. At least we'll be able to drive off if anything happens.' He laughed quietly to himself.

Ruth trailed behind them, overcome by the sudden knowledge that her friendship with Church had become deeper than she realised. How had that happened? she wondered. Their situation was complicated enough without bringing emotions into the fray, but somehow the whole stupid mess had blindsided her. She looked at Laura and hated herself for feeling a twinge of jealousy that the cosy relationship she had with Church was being interrupted. She just hoped she was level-headed enough to prevent her feelings getting in the way during the difficult times ahead.

Church woke at first light. His joints ached, his feet felt like ice and there was a band of pain across his thigh where his leg had been jammed under the steering wheel. Sleep had been intermittent, troubled by the discomfort of his quarters, nightmares and fears of things off in the dark. He resolved to buy a tent for any future emergencies. But the moment he wiped the condensation from the window with the back of his hand, any grumbles were swept away by the beauty of the early spring day. The sun was just breaking above the horizon, painting the few clouds golden beneath a sky that was slowly turning blue. Among the stones a faint mist rose and drifted, and a stillness lay across the whole area. From his viewpoint, there was no sign of the twentieth century; it could have been anytime. The thought sent prickles down his spine, adding to the haunting quality of the moment that left him feeling like he had been cut adrift from the life he once knew.

Ruth and Laura were still sleeping. He was instantly struck by how beautiful they both looked, in their own ways, once the troubles of the day were stripped from their faces.

But as he wondered if he should wake them, he caught sight of something out of the corner of his eye that jolted him alert. A man was perched on a fencepost next to a hawthorn hedge, eyeing the car intently. Church had to look twice to convince himself it was what he had seen; the watcher was old, thin and angular with skin so sun-browned he seemed almost like a spindly tree growing out of the hedge. He was holding a long, gnarled wooden staff that must have been at least six feet tall, and his grey-black hair hung lank and loose around his shoulders. Apart from his clothes – mud-spattered sandals, well-worn, baggy brown trousers and a white cheesecloth shirt open to the waist – he resembled nothing so much as the pictures Church had seen of the men who helped raise the stones and build the longbarrows that were scattered across the landscape.

'Who is that?' Ruth's voice was sleepy. She rubbed her bleary eyes as she leaned close to Church to peer at the onlooker.

Laura stirred and after a few seconds she too was up, resting her elbows on the backs of their seats. She already had on her sunglasses. 'Probably just a peeping tom,' she said throatily. 'Thought we'd been having a little three-way here in the car. Let's put on a show – see if he goes blind.'

'Just some local,' Church muttered. He opened the door and climbed out. The air was chilly despite the sun, and he couldn't prevent a convulsive shiver. The only sound was that of the birds in chorus. Ruth and Laura joined him, pulling their coats tight about them, stamping their feet to start their circulation.

The old man's eyes never left them as they walked the short distance to the fencepost. Up close, the most startling quality was the colour of his eyes, which were as blue as a summer sky, and given more power by the brownness of his skin. Church couldn't tell his exact age, although he guessed from the wrinkles on the man's face that he was in his sixties.

'Morning,' Church said.

'Morning,' the man replied impassively.

'Early start,' Church noted.

'Aye. Same as you.'

Church wished he had some idea of exactly what they were trying to unearth. Although the lantern had brought them to Avebury, it didn't seem to be much help in establishing an exact location. 'Seen anything strange going on round here recently?'

'Depends what you mean,' the old man said slyly. 'I see lots of strange things in my travels. I've covered the country from Orkney to Scilly a hundred times in my life and every place I've stopped there's been something strange.'

'You're not a local?' Church gave the man a renewed examination; there were none of the slightly odd features or waxy skin that disguised what the woman in the Watchtower had called the Night Walkers, but Church felt suspicious nonetheless.

'I'm local wherever I go.'

Church was starting to feel distinctly uncomfortable in the old man's presence. There was a faintly threatening air about him and his gaze was becoming more dissecting, as if he knew exactly who Church was.

The old man glanced away across the stones and when he looked back, his eyes were cold and hard. 'You cause any trouble here and there'll be hell to pay.'

'Who are you?' Ruth asked.

'I guard the old places. Keep an eye on the hidden treasures, the undisturbed burials, the sacred spots. From the Scottish Isles to the South Downs, Land's End to the Fens.' He grabbed his staff tightly with hands that looked much stronger than his years suggested. 'Sleeping under the stars, watching out for the grave robbers and the sackers and the vandals. Tending to the land, you might say. Some call me the Stone Shepherd—'

'The Bone Inspector.' Ruth recalled Tom's account of the man who had first alerted him to the crisis. 'Tom mentioned your name.'

'And where is he?' he said gruffly.

Church and Ruth glanced at each other uncomfortably.

'He's fallen already, has he? And you are the ones he was looking for?' His expression suggested he wasn't impressed.

'Who are you exactly, and what do you know about what's going on?' Church insisted.

'And who are you to ask questions of me?' As Church began to answer, the old man waved him silent dismissively. 'There's been a Bone Inspector since these stones were put up. When one dies, there's always another ready and waiting to take over. In the old days there were lots of us. The keepers of wisdom, we were, worshipping in the groves, tutoring the people. Now there's just me.'

In his eyes, Church saw the flat, grey sky over Callanish and the green fields around the Rollrights. In his voice there were echoes of the solemn chant of ancient rituals. But there was the hardness of nature in him too, and Church knew he would be a fool to cross him. The old man held the staff more like a weapon than a walking aid, and his lean limbs were sinewy and powerful.

'How did you find out that everything had changed?' Church asked.

'I felt it in the land. In the force that sings to you if you're of a mind to listen.'

'The blue fire?'

'Aye, that's one way of seeing it.' He banged his staff gently on the turf. 'It's all changing, going back to the way it was. The cities haven't felt it yet, but out in the country they're starting to know. People are keeping clear of the quiet places, specially after dark. There've been a load of disappearances and a few deaths, all put down to accidents so far. They'll know the truth soon enough. I was up at Arbor Low in the Peaks the other day and I saw a wolf that walks like a man. Just a glimpse, mind you, away in the wild. But when I went to look I found an arm. Or what was left of it.'

'Gross!' Laura made a face.

'That's when I knew for sure, even though I'd felt the change long before. Soon they're going to have to redraw all the maps. No one will know this land, see. It will be all new, and terrible. Even some of the lost places are coming back. I saw . . .' He caught himself and looked into the middle distance. 'Well, there'll be time enough for that later.'

There was an uneasy note in his voice that made them all feel uncomfortable. They shifted from foot to foot, not really knowing what to say.

Eventually he broke his reverie and turned back to them, his face dark. 'And now you three rabbits are here. You look like troublemakers to me. Maybe I should be seeing you off.' He raised his staff menacingly. Church held up his arm in instinctive protection and instantly the staff was performing a deft, twisting manoeuvre that was so fast it was almost a blur. It flicked Church's arm to one side, then cracked him obliquely on the elbow, too gently to hurt. But in an instant fiery lances of pain ran up to his shoulder and he crumpled at the waist in agony. Ruth stepped in to help, but the Bone Inspector thrust the staff between her calves and twisted, knocking her to the floor. In one fluid movement, the staff came up to point directly at Laura's throat. 'Now you better be telling me what you're doing here,' he said in a voice like flint.

Church drew himself upright, rubbing his elbow furiously, and then took a sudden step back when the staff was levelled at him. 'Take it easy,' he said as calmly as he could muster. 'We're not here to cause any trouble for you.'

'We're looking for something,' Ruth added hastily. 'One of the four talismans.'

The Bone Inspector knew exactly what she meant. 'You'll never find them.'

'We have to,' Church said. 'Or else— Well, you tell me the *or else* bit.'

The Bone Inspector lowered the staff and looked at them slyly again. 'Who are you to think you can do something about it?'

A thought jumped in Church's mind. 'We're the Brothers and Sisters of Dragons,' he said.

It was the confirmation for which he was obviously waiting. 'So Thomas did find you,' he said thoughtfully. 'You don't look like much. How do I know you're who you say you are?'

'Wait here.' Church returned to the car and came back with the lantern. 'Would I have this if I wasn't?'

The Bone Inspector laid down his staff and approached, almost deferentially. Gently, he reached out his hands until they were on either side of the lantern, though being careful not to touch it. The flame flared brightly, painting his skin blue. 'The Wayfinder,' he said in awe. 'I'd heard it was no longer of the land.'

'It wasn't,' Church said. 'I brought it back.'

The Bone Inspector cursed under his breath. 'And you don't know what you've got, do you? Leaving it in the bloody car! Are you mad, man?' Church shifted uncomfortably. 'Keep it with you at all times,' the Bone Inspector said with irritation. 'Don't ever let it fall into the wrong hands.'

Now it was out in the open, close to the circle they could see the flame was gradually rotating. 'That must mean we're in the right place,' Ruth said. 'But where do we start looking? And what exactly are we looking *for*?' she added with exasperation.

'And why here?' Church said.

The Bone Inspector shook his head, contemptuous of their lack of knowledge. 'Stonehenge may be better known, but this is *the* place. It doesn't look much now, thanks to those Bible-obsessed fools in the last century who pulled all the stones down because they thought they were the Devil's work. But it's the most important place in the land, the source of all the power. That's why I'm here, now, to be in the most important place at the time when I'm most likely to be needed.' He knelt down and marked out a wide arc with his arm. 'Imagine it getting on for five thousand years ago – a sacred site stretching three miles. Here was the main temple, two stone circles surrounded by a circular ditch twenty-five feet deep with a bank fifteen feet high. And approaching it from either side were two gently curving avenues, a mile and a half long, each of them, marked out by ten-foot-high stones. Can you imagine the work that went into that? And they wouldn't have done it if they didn't have a reason.'

'This is the source of the blue energy?' Church asked. 'The Earth Magic?'

'This is the place where it's strongest. It's a Dracontium, a Serpent Temple, so called because of the way the avenues snaked. There were no straight lines back then – we have the bloody Romans to thank for that. But that's not the only reason – the dragon is the symbol of the Earth's power.'

'And the Fabulous Beasts are drawn to it too,' Ruth said thoughtfully as she tried to imagine the scene without any of the houses cluttering up the line of sight.

'You've heard of them, have you?' Ruth could tell from his

expression that he suddenly saw her in a different light. 'Well, that's another reason why this is the Serpent Temple.'

'What do you mean?' Ruth said.

'Sometimes,' he said with a sly smile, 'when you put your ear to the ground you can hear it roar.'

Church, Ruth and Laura looked at each other, unable to tell if he was joking. Before they could ask him further, he stiffened and turned suddenly in the direction of Windmill Hill, the ancient site which looked over the village a few miles away. His brow furrowing, he stared hard, although none of them could tell what he was seeing. After a moment, he said, 'We're being watched.'

They followed his gaze, but could see nothing across the countryside. 'Where?' Ruth asked.

'Up there. On top of the hill.'

'Right,' Laura mocked, sneering at the distance that turned the hill to a blur of green beneath the blue. 'Tell me what's happening in Birmingham while you're at it.'

The Bone Inspector ignored her, squinted, concentrated. 'I see a tight flurry of crows, swirling madly like a black cloud. And at their heart is a man. Not a man, a monster. And with him are more monsters.'

'Monsters.' The breath caught in Church's throat.

'They're here for us,' Ruth said. 'You have to help us.' He stared at her coldly. '*Please* help us.'

'How should I know what to do?' he replied sourly. 'I know as much about the resting place of the talismans as the next man, and it's something I wouldn't *want* to know.'

'But one of the talismans is here somewhere. The lantern is telling us that,' Ruth continued. 'You know the place better than anyone. Where do you *think* it would be?'

He stared at her for a long moment, weighing up her worth, then he said, 'In a hidden place.' His pause carried his doubt about revealing too much, but something in Ruth's face prompted him to continue. 'All the old sites have hidden places. It's part of my job to make sure they stay hidden, away from prying fingers that might destroy them, and by doing so destroy the land itself.'

'You have to show us,' Ruth said with passion. 'If we don't find the talismans the land will be destroyed anyway.'

'You better not be making an idiot of me.' He made a clicking sound at the back of his throat, then whirled on his heel and strode out powerfully across the grass. He came to a stop five minutes later beside a large megalith which cast an imposing shadow across the land in the dawn sunlight. 'The Devil's Chair,' he said, nodding to it. 'The villagers here say if you run around it a hundred times you'll hear the voice of the Devil. But it isn't the Devil they hear.'

'If I ran around it a hundred times I'd hear the sound of my stomach coming out through my mouth,' Laura said.

'Three times widdershins will do,' the Bone Inspector said, leading them around the stone. They felt stupid, traipsing in line like primary school children, but by the third revolution they experienced the buzz of the earth energy in the air, creating a resonance which began to creep along the meridians of their bodies from the base of their spines. 'Now, quickly, along West Kennet Avenue,' the old man said.

He hurried up a steep embankment and skidded down the other side before crossing a road and darting through a gate. Two rows of concrete markers led to the largest group of megaliths they had seen, stretching out in an avenue across the fields. As they moved forward, shimmers of blue shot out from beneath their soles and the tingling in their spines had now reached the base of their skulls. Church felt like he was hallucinating; the dappled patterns of light and shadow across the landscape seemed to move fluidly and unusual bursts of sound kept breaking through into his ears. When the ground began to open up in the centre of the avenue ahead of them, he at first thought it was a vision. But the Bone Inspector hurried them along and then they were scrambling down into the dark as the turf and soil closed behind them with a rumble.

As the Bone Inspector had seen them, the creatures on Windmill Hill had seen the strange ritual that opened the secret way to the hidden place. They were prevented from venturing into the station of light and life, but when the earth spewed out the Brothers and Sisters of Dragons, they would be waiting. Rapidly they moved towards Avebury, keeping to the hedges and ditches and whatever feeble shadows the landscape offered. But the occasional villager who glanced out of their window at that early hour would have seen only one thing: a cloud of crows churning so tightly, it was impossible to tell how they could keep aloft: a vortex of black, beak and talon, man-shaped and moving with resolute power.

'Where are we?' Church asked, blinking in the gloom. He held up the lantern, which provided enough eerie blue light to see. The air was dank and filled with the odour of loam. The hollow echo of dripping water resounded from somewhere nearby.

'The heart of the mystery,' the Bone Inspector said icily. 'Don't betray my faith in you. Or you won't be in a position to tell of this experience to anyone.' His bald threat unnerved them and they refused to meet his piercing stare. Instead, they turned their gaze ahead where a low tunnel dipped down gradually into the depths of the earth. The Bone Inspector led the way with Church at his shoulder, holding the lantern aloft, all of them maintaining an anxious silence.

They walked for about fifteen minutes, the tunnel widening almost without them noticing it; the light no longer played on the walls, merely faded into the oppressive dark, and the quality of the echoes of their footsteps became duller. It was getting brighter; the lantern's light was being dwarfed by another, more fulsome blue glow from further ahead. With a jarring mixture of wonder and apprehension, they crept forward until they stood on the lip of a ledge overlooking a lake of the blue energy, churning and roiling as if it was boiling water. Ruth began to ask what it was, but the Bone Inspector shushed her with an impatient wave of his hand. Resting his hands on his knees, he peered into the depths of the blue lake and, as they followed his gaze, they gradually saw a dark shape deep in the azure depths. It was rising; slowly at first, but then with increasing speed, churning the energy even more, until suddenly it broke the surface with its long, serpentine neck before dipping back down below. It was only the briefest glimpse, but they had a sense of something magnificent, of scales gleaming gold and green on a body filled with elegant power.

'This Fabulous Beast never left,' the Bone Inspector said. 'It merely slept.'

The others cautiously drew themselves upright, listening to the unnatural echoes that bounced around the cavern. 'Are you sure it's safe?' Ruth asked. 'It could fry us in a second here.'

'It could if it wished,' the Bone Inspector said, offering no comfort.

'It's the king of them all,' Laura said in a tone which surprised them; it was something she felt instinctively. She pushed her way past them to the edge, but the creature was lost beneath the blue waves.

'It is the oldest,' the Bone Inspector agreed. 'When all the creatures of imagination departed in the Sundering, this one stayed behind to protect the land, keeping the fire alive here in the furnace of the planet. Ready for the time when the power would flow freely again.' He looked at Church knowingly.

'Is that one of the things we're supposed to do?' Church asked. The Bone Inspector shook his head contemptuously.

'We don't know what we're supposed to be doing!' Ruth protested. 'We have no idea what a Brother or Sister of Dragons is. Why everyone thinks we're one. What's going on at all!' The stress brought a snap to the end of the sentence.

132

'Don't lose it,' Laura chided.

'I'm not your teacher.' The Bone Inspector walked to the edge and began to scan around the cavern. 'I'm giving you a helping hand here, but after this you're on your own. To be honest, I don't think you're up to the job.'

'What do you know,' Laura muttered.

When he turned she thought he was going to hit her with the staff, but instead he used it to point to the wall of the cavern nearest to them. 'There's a path that goes right round the edge of the lake to the far side. You might find what you're looking for there. Or you might not.'

Church squinted to see where he was pointing. 'It looks a bit precarious. It's only about a foot across.'

'Better not look down then,' Ruth said.

The Bone Inspector caught her arm before she could walk away. 'Just one of you.'

'Why?'

'Because the one whose home this is will only *let* one of you go.'

They stared into the blue depths for a moment, considering this, and then Church said, 'I suppose we have to trust you. But how can we be sure it won't attack even one of us?'

'It senses the dragon-spirit,' the Bone Inspector said. 'One of you will be safe.'

'What are you saying? We're family?'

'Not in any way you'd understand,' the Bone Inspector replied curtly.

Church sighed. 'Looks like—'

'Not so fast, leader-man,' Laura said. 'I admire your chivalry and all that, but I want to do this one.'

'No way!' Ruth was shaking her head forcefully. 'She's probably after the talisman for herself—'

'So you don't trust me,' Laura snapped. 'But you had better start doing so, because this is a partnership and I have an equal say. If you believe what Mystic Meg said and you believe I'm one of the five big cheeses, then you have to at least listen to me.'

'I don't know . . .' Church chewed on a knuckle.

'I say no,' Ruth said firmly.

The Bone Inspector snorted with derision. 'There isn't a hope.'

'He's right.' Church scrubbed a hand over his face, hoping he was making the right decision. 'We can't start off this way. We have to have some kind of faith in ourselves.'

'I appreciate the vote of confidence,' Laura said with a broad grin.

'I still say no,' Ruth added a little childishly.

Without a backward glance, Laura headed over to the path. She caught her breath when she saw it. Church had been right: barely a foot wide, with a precipitous drop into the roiling blue energy. Without showing her nervousness, she pressed her back against the rock wall and confidently stepped out on to the ledge.

Anxiety had turned Laura's shoulders and stomach into knots of steel cable, but she had been unable to resist the pull that had forced her to look down at the surface of the lake. The sinuous body of the Fabulous Beast occasionally broke the surface, as if it were shadowing her progress, but even the slightest glimpse filled her with excitement; she felt like a child again.

The inside of her mouth tasted metallic from the blue energy which spouted up from the surface in an effect which reminded her of a lava lamp; every tiny sound she made was strangely distorted by the cavern and the energy into something that was almost hallucinatory. She had to keep clinging on to the wall, feeling with her foot as she took each step. It was laborious and terrifying, but she was making good progress. Church and the others were lost to the blue haze and now the cavern walls had started to close in on both sides, allowing her to see things which both chilled and intrigued her. Human bones protruded from the rock, as well as the remnants of other skeletons which were not remotely human, nor animal either; they were yellowed and pitted with great age. Corroded helmets, swords and chain mail hung from ledges, next to axes and rougher tools from older times. And there was treasure, jewels beyond imagining, gold artefacts which still gleamed, mysterious objects: it was like a magpie's nest of historical plunder, all scattered on rocky outcroppings or lower ledges.

The cavern grew smaller and smaller until the walls were less than fifteen feet apart and Laura feared she would eventually become trapped. Then, as she made her way into what appeared to be a separate cavern, they widened out once more. This cave was much smaller than the other, and the ledge opened on to what Laura could only describe as a beach, where the blue energy lapped like surf.

Cautiously, she explored towards the rear wall of the cavern. As she neared, she saw the sheer face was intricately carved with symbols and shapes that were unmistakably Celtic: spirals, circles interlocking, infinite lines, faces, stylised animals, a dragon. It seemed to have some sort of meaning beyond simple design, but she had no idea what it was. Further along the wall was an alcove framed by two carved trees forming an arch with their intertwined branches. At the foot were severed heads, hollow-eyed with bared teeth; peering through the branches was a face made out of leaves.

Although the alcove appeared to be shallow, it was heavily shadowed and she couldn't tell what lay within its depths. There seemed little else of note around, so she stepped in for a better look and instantly realised her mistake.

With a deep rumble, some hitherto hidden door slammed behind her, shutting her in utter dark. A second later there was movement, a tremor of a touch at her ankle, her back, her neck. Something like bony fingers closed tightly around her wrists, yanking her arms up and to the side, caught in her hair, pinched her waist. Laura couldn't help herself, she opened her mouth and screamed.

The sound stifled in her throat as, with a brutality that surprised even her cruelly disciplined, modern, mature self, she forced calm on the frightened little girl struggling to escape. *Don't be pathetic*, she thought furiously. But it was so dark, and so claustrophobic, and she had no idea what was gripping her: things that felt like fingers, felt like bone, felt alive yet dead.

The door at her back was solid rock; no amount of pushing would budge it at all. She estimated a gap of six inches in front of her face, and if she moved from side to side her shoulders brushed the walls. It was a tomb. She choked back panic again. *Stay calm, stay calm.* Surely the Fabulous Beast wouldn't have allowed her to this secret spot just to have her sealed in a stone wall. Frantically, she tried to remember the carvings on the wall in case they had offered any instructions to escape the trap. Steel bands seemed to be closing across her chest and she was sure it was getting harder to breathe. Was the alcove airtight? She struggled against whatever was gripping her, but that only made it tighter. The panic started to come again, black waves that threatened to drown her, until she was gasping, feeling everything fall apart. And then, suddenly, a moment of lucidity that she clung to with the desperation of a drowning woman. She suddenly went limp, relaxing every muscle as she slumped forward. In response, the hands loosened their grip and, as she continued to play dead, they eventually fell away: the trap was for a threat who would fight, not for a friend who would offer themselves supinely. Or perhaps it was more than that, she thought. Perhaps it was a test of some kind.

'Abracadabra,' she said hopefully. She ran her fingers over the wall in front of her. It was uniformly smooth, except for one area where there were faint indentations. In the impenetrable dark, she could focus on her sense of touch without any distractions: a circle, and within it two smaller circles. On the left, a line snaked out and ended in a hole as big as her fingertip. On the right, another line started to snake out, but was abruptly curtailed. Laura pictured the outline in her mind, and after a moment of deliberation she realised what it was: a map of the Avebury Dracontium; except the curving right hand line should have extended, mirroring the one on the other side. She continued tracing it to where it should have ended and felt a small lump.

Suddenly she knew what she had to do. She pressed hard and the raised area sank in. A second later, there was a corresponding click and a small hatch opened at head height, flooding the alcove with a diffuse blue light. In the newly exposed area lay a shiny black stone as big as the palm of her hand. When Laura plucked it out, she was surprised, and a little disturbed, that it felt like skin, warm and soft. As she slipped it into her pocket, the doors slid back and, with a relieved gulp of dank air, she stepped back out into the cavern.

'This waiting is terrible.' Church sat with his legs dangling over the edge above the lake of blue energy; he had the disturbing feeling that if he pushed himself off he would be able to walk across its surface.

'Now you know how I felt in Salisbury.' Ruth was still annoyed he had allowed Laura to go on such an important mission; she was more angry at herself for feeling that way. The Bone Inspector had left them alone and was waiting silently in the shadows near the tunnel through which they entered.

Church stared into the blue depths, his hand unconsciously going to the Black Rose in his jacket; since they had gone underground it had felt horribly cold, like a block of ice burning his skin, and now the discomfort was starting to make him a little queasy. 'Brother of Dragons. What does that mean exactly? I wish somebody would give us a look at the script. Why are we so special?'

'Don't you feel special?' She controlled an urge to slip an arm around his shoulders and hug him. Since he had returned from the Watchtower, he seemed different; darker somehow, more intense, if that were possible. That odd conjunction of emotional fragility and strength of character moved her on some deep level so acutely, at times she wondered if she was falling ill, although she knew the truth, and that was just as bad.

'Not in the way all these weird people are intimating,' he said. 'I've always felt *different*. Even at school I knew I wasn't like other kids. She came to me, you know? When I was a boy.'

'Who?'

'The woman in the Watchtower.'

'There you are, then. You were different right from the start.'

'But I don't feel it inside me. I feel normal, like I always have done.'

'I don't know if anybody does feel different until they're called upon to—' She was interrupted by a call from Laura, who was edging her way along the last stretch of the ledge.

They ran to meet her as she stepped back on to the rock shelf. 'We'd just about given up on you,' Church said.

'Bad pennies always turn up. You should know that.' She dipped into her pocket and pulled out the stone; it seemed to glow with an inner light. 'Look what I found.'

Church and Ruth gathered round. 'Is that it? Wow! I expected a lump of rock or something,' Ruth said.

Church looked at her curiously. 'It is a lump of rock.'

'No, it's not. It's a diamond,' Ruth said incredulously.

'Are you both insane? It's a black stone, like polished obsidian.'

They looked from one to the other in disbelief until the Bone Inspector stepped up. 'Save your breath. It has no true shape in this world. It's fluid, like everything from the Other Place. Our tiny little minds can't grasp it, so we give it some kind of shape to make sense of it.'

'That's crazy,' Ruth said. 'How are we—'

'It doesn't matter what things look like,' the old man said with exasperation, 'just as long as *you* know what they are.'

Church peered at the stone in Laura's hands. 'The first of the four talismans. What does it do?'

Laura held it out to the Bone Inspector for advice, but the old man backed away hastily. 'Don't bring it near me! It's too powerful. It's your burden now.'

'But what does it do?'

'It doesn't *do* anything,' the Bone Inspector snapped. 'It's not a toy! It has a purpose which I'm sure you'll find out sooner or later. Now enough of the fool questions. Let's get back to the light. And not the way we came either. I have no doubt our friends from Windmill Hill will be waiting for us on West Kennet Avenue.'

He led them to another tunnel off to one side. As they made their way uphill by the light of the lantern, Church said to Laura, 'So did you have any trouble getting it?'

'Easy as pie,' she replied.

They emerged blinking into the warm morning light on Beckhampton Avenue, the snaking route on the other side of Avebury. After the dank passages, the air was fragrant with spring flowers and the verdant aromas of the countryside.

'You leave here quickly now and don't look back,' the Bone Inspector said gruffly. 'Dawdle too much and you'll find the Devil at your heels.'

'Where are you going now?' Ruth asked.

'I've got a country full of ancient places to tend, graves to visit, old bones to check, and in these times I think they'll need me more than ever.'

'Thanks for your help,' Church said, stretching out a hand which the old man ignored. 'We couldn't have done it without you.'

'Aye. And don't you forget it. I bloody well hope I've done the right thing. Don't go and ruin it all.'

Then he turned and was loping away, over a gate and into the fields, faster than they would have believed, almost dropping to all fours at times so that he seemed more animal than man as he disappeared into the countryside.

'We could have used his help,' Ruth said regretfully.

'We don't need any crumbly old folk.' Laura replaced her sunglasses after the dark of the cavern. 'We've got youth, good looks and sex on our side.'

'Look at this.' Church held up the lantern; the flame was now flickering towards the south-west.

They hurried through the quiet streets until they reached the car, and then they were speeding out of the village before anyone noticed.

On West Kennet Avenue, the cloud of whirling, flapping crows suddenly turned towards the south-west. A guttural voice filled with the grunts of beasts rolled out from the heart of it, and four shadows seemed to separate from the base of the hedges. The voice barked and snorted again, incomprehensible to human ears, and all the birds, and the cows lowing in the fields fell silent.

the Light that Never Goes Out

'You want to push me completely over the edge, you go ahead and play Sinatra one more time.' Laura gave the back of Church's seat a sharp kick. 'Because we've only heard "Come Fly With Me", like, what, a thousand times? Music-induced psychosis is not a pretty thing to see.'

Church ejected the tape with irritation. 'What do you want, then?'

'Somebody who's not dead would be nice.'

'I hate to say it, but I'm with her on this one,' Ruth chipped in.

'Fine. Gang up on me.'

Laura rested her arms on the back of his seat, her breath bringing a bloom to his neck. 'Have you got anything that makes your ears bleed?'

'An icepick?'

'How about some golden oldies, like, say, The Chemical Brothers?'

'No.'

'What's the matter? Don't you like music that makes your blood boil?'

His first reaction was to say *I used to*, but he realised how pathetic it sounded. If truth be told, his irritation with Laura came more from how she pointed up the parts of his character that he had lost than from her forthright manner.

'How about the radio?' he snapped, feeling the first bite of self-loathing. He switched it on and tuned across the band until he heard music.

'It'll do, I guess.' Laura slumped back into her seat, successful.

The music gave way to the syrupy voice of a local DJ who rambled aimlessly for a minute or two before another fizzy, optimistic Top Ten hit came on. Outside the car the windswept uplands had given way to sun-drenched green fields, trees on the verge of bursting with new life, sparkling streams and little stone bridges. The road behind was comfortingly empty and, despite everything, Church was feeling remarkably at ease in the light of their success at Avebury. The lantern had directed them on to the A4 towards Bath where they were able to build up some speed and put some distance between them and whatever the Bone Inspector had feared was waiting for them on West Kennet Avenue. They felt confident enough to pause briefly at Chippenham, where they bought a couple of tents, cooking equipment and other camping gear for emergencies. Laura protested she wasn't the outdoor type, but, as usual, it seemed to be more for effect.

Bath was choked with traffic, the winter season already forgotten as tourists flocked to the Roman baths or to gawp at the Georgian architecture. Ruth muttered something about the bliss of ignorance, and for a brief while a maudlin mood fell across the car as they all became acutely aware of what was at risk.

But by the time they had passed through Bath into the more sparsely populated countryside beyond, their mood had buoyed as they focused on the task ahead. They were making good time and the lantern seemed to be taking them into the deep south-west, far away from the troubled areas of the previous few days.

As they travelled through tiny, picture-postcard villages south of Bristol, with the undulating slopes of the Mendips away to their left, they were shocked by a sharp, ear-splitting burst of static on the radio. When it faded, the DJ's voice was replaced by giggling, mocking laughter fading in and out of white noise, growing louder, then softer; there was something inhuman about it. It was the same mysterious sound Ruth and Church had heard on the tape in the therapist's office when they had first discovered what they had seen under Albert Bridge. Church hastily ran the tuner across the band, but the laughter remained the same, and even when he switched the radio off, it continued to come out of the speakers for a full minute. Ruth and Church shot an uneasy glance of recognition at each other.

Five miles further on, all the electrics failed.

'I'll have a look, but there's no chance I can do anything today.' The mechanic glanced at a dusty clock above the door of the repair bay; it said 3 p.m. He was unusually tall and massive-boned, with a solid beer belly kept in check by his grease-stained blue overalls. His face was ruddy and his unruly black hair was peppered with grey. 'Everything's going bloody crazy at the moment.'

Church sat wearily on the Nissan's wing. He'd spent an hour searching for a garage with a towtruck. This one had only relented and agreed to come out after he had virtually begged.

'It's these modern cars, you see,' the mechanic continued. 'They build 'em to break down. Though this last week I've never seen anything like it. The place has been full every day, most of it electrical stuff, though I've had a fair share of busted alternators. I tell you, you need a bloody degree to sort out these electrics. This week I've worked on some all day long and then, just like that, they've been fine again. No explanation for it. Couldn't find any fault at all, yet they were dead as a dodo when they were brought in.' He shook his head at this great mystery, then added, 'Still, bloody good for business.'

Church got his assurances that the car would be looked at first thing the following day, then wandered out to Ruth and Laura who sat with the camping equipment on the dusty forecourt. The garage was well off the beaten track, a rundown affair that seemed to have been barely updated since the fifties, down to the period petrol pumps that stood dry like museum pieces at the front. Only farms lay scattered around the surrounding countryside, and there was no sound of traffic, just the song of birds in the clustering trees.

'What did he say?' Ruth asked anxiously.

'Tomorrow. I think we can risk giving it a shot before we start looking around for the local Avis.'

'Yeah, there'll really be one round here,' Laura said sarcastically.

Ruth noticed Church's concerned expression and asked him what was wrong. He repeated the mechanic's tale of mysterious breakdowns. 'I think things are starting to go wrong, just like Tom predicted. It's as if the rules of science are falling apart in the face of all these things that shouldn't exist.'

Laura looked at him curiously. 'What do you mean?'

'I mean,' he said, nodding to the computer in the bag on her arm, 'that pretty soon that will be as much use to us as it would be to some lost Amazon tribe, along with every other technological gadget. New rules are falling into place. Science is dying.'

'Unless we can do something about it,' Ruth said hopefully, but Church merely shouldered the tents and rucksack and began to trudge along the lane.

They found a good campsite in a secluded grove out of sight of the road. They didn't ask permission, preferring anonymity. The trees were thick enough to prevent the tents being seen by the casual passer-by, and there was a natural clearing shielded by a tangle of brambles where they could light a fire. Ruth seemed uncomfortable at the prospect of sharing with Laura, but they reached some kind of unspoken agreement, and Church slipped off to collect firewood.

Lost in thought as he scoured the edge of the copse, he failed to see the figure until it was upon him. He whirled in shock, ready to fight or run, and was then suffused with embarrassment when he saw it was just a girl of about ten, pretty, with long blonde hair and a creamy complexion. She was wearing a tight T-shirt with a sunburst motif and baggy, faded jeans.

'Hello,' she said in a thick West Country accent. 'Are you looking for something?'

'Just sightseeing,' he replied ridiculously.

'Not much to see round here.' She laughed disarmingly.

Relaxing his guard, Church returned her smile. 'Not really my cup of tea.'

'Where you from then?'

'London.'

'I'd love to live in London.' She looked dreamily into the middle distance. 'It'd be great to be somewhere where there's a buzz.'

'Nothing to stop you when you're older.'

Her smile became slightly more enigmatic. 'My name's Marianne. What's yours?'

'Jack.' Although he knew nothing about her, the simple matter of her name suddenly made him warm to her. 'That's a nice name,' he continued. 'I used to know someone called Marianne.'

'A girlfriend?'

'She was.'

'Did you split up?'

He thought twice, then said honestly, 'She died.'

Marianne nodded ruefully. 'It figures.' Church looked at her curiously, but she'd already danced ahead of him. Noticing the wood he'd piled nearby, she grinned and said, 'Sightseeing, eh? Looks to me like you're going to have a little fire.' She looked around. 'Where's the camp?'

Church's shoulders sagged. 'Blimey. Rumbled. Look, we're trying to keep a low profile. I'd appreciate it if you didn't tell anyone.'

Her laughter at Church's obvious dismay was innocent and infectious. 'Don't worry, I'm not going to rat on you. But if my dad finds out it'll be a different matter. He farms on this land and he's always going mad about *bloody trespassers*. Threatened to set the dogs on the last lot he caught. We're close enough to Glastonbury to get those scruffy New Age types passing through. Some of them leave the place in a right mess, but most of them seem okay to me. My dad thinks they're all scroungers and vandals, though.'

'Well, I'm neither.'

'I can see that. Come on, I'll help you collect some wood.' She walked at his side for a minute or two, then said, 'Do you miss her?'

'Marianne? Yes. A lot.'

'I thought you looked sad. I could see it in your eyes.' Church winced at the thought that it was so obvious. There was a long, thoughtful pause and then she said, 'Do you think people die for a reason?'

He shrugged. 'I don't know—'

'Yes, but do you *think*?'

'I'd like to believe that, but it's not always easy to see.' The maturity of her conversation surprised him, and made him feel a little uncomfortable. 'This is heavy stuff for someone your age.'

'Just because you're young doesn't mean you have to fill your head with rubbish,' she said tartly. 'Anyway, I do like a lot of *rubbish*. It's just I like to think about other stuff too.'

'I stand corrected.'

'Apology accepted,' she laughed, picking up a rotten tree branch and tossing it to Church. 'Why are you so bothered about dying? Don't argue – I can see you are! It's just another part of life, isn't it? The only thing worth bothering about is what we do *before* we pop our clogs.'

'It's not as simple as that—'

'Why not? I want to do exciting stuff every day, learn new things, see life. I want to pack a week into a day, a month into a week and a year into a month. Don't you think that's a good philosophy? Why doesn't everybody do that?'

Church pretended to scour the grass for wood while he attempted to think of an answer, but he couldn't summon anything that didn't sound pathetic. Her victorious grin forced him to laugh. 'I think I should be Prime Minister,' she said triumphantly, sashaying theatrically ahead of him.

When she turned back to him, she'd pulled out a locket from under her T-shirt. With a dexterous flick, she opened it and held it up to show him the tiny picture squeezed inside.

'Princess Diana,' he noted. 'Did you like her?'

'I loved her. That's why I asked you about dying. She did so much good with her life. I think *she* died for a reason.'

'Oh?'

'To make us see how bad we were all living our lives. So that we could learn from her and live more like her, you know, doing good, helping the world.'

Her tone was so adamant it would have been reprehensible to sour her views with adult cynicism. 'She seemed very decent. All that campaigning for land mines. And all that.'

Marianne looked up at him with a faintly pitying smile. 'I can see you're not a believer.'

'I'm sorry. I'm just . . . an old grouch.'

'I've got pictures of her all over my bedroom. And in one corner I've got a little table with the best photo I could find in a frame. You'd know it if you saw it. It's famous. She's looking at the camera really thoughtful, and when you look right into her eyes you can see so much goodness it almost makes you cry.' She lowered her voice conspiratorially. 'Before bed, I kneel down in front of it and pray to her.'

Church lowered his eyes, trying to remember the last time he felt such an innocent belief. 'What do you pray for?'

'For Diana to make me a better person. For me to do some good, like her, before I die.'

'Well, of all the things to pray for, that sounds like one of the best.'

'You should try it some time.'

He laughed. 'Maybe I should.'

'No, I mean it.' She undid the locket and offered it to him. 'Not to keep. Just try it tonight and I'll get it back off you tomorrow.'

'No, I couldn't—'

'Don't be silly!' She grabbed his hand and forced it into his fingers, laughing. 'She's a saint, you know. She'll listen to you.'

He felt uncomfortable taking it from her, and that made him wonder why: perhaps it *was* the cynicism – Diana, Patron Saint of Bulimics and Damaged Women Everywhere. But then maybe Marianne was right. Perhaps blind faith was what was needed. It certainly seemed to make her happy.

'Okay,' he said finally. 'Maybe you'll make a convert of me.' That seemed to please her.

They spent the next hour trailing through the trees and along the hedgerows, doing more talking than wood collecting. Church found himself enjoying Marianne's company; she was funny and passionate, filled with questions about every subject that entered the conversation, and possessed of a generosity of spirit that made him feel good to be around her, and a little humbled. She was an only child, yet quite unspoilt, with a love of music that reminded Church of his younger days. They argued about the strengths and weaknesses of a few pop icons, then listed their top ten songs, which ended in uncontrollable laughter when she made Church sing the chorus of all his selections.

Finally they'd located enough firewood and Marianne helped Church carry it back to the camp. Ruth and Laura weren't anywhere to be seen so they lit the fire together and made some tea. Oddly, Church found himself talking about his own Marianne with an openness that he hadn't managed since her death. The young girl was an easy listener and she seemed to have a handle on his emotions that belied her years. When she said goodbye, with a promise to bring them milk at breakfast, he was sorry to see her go.

Night still fell quickly at that time of year, and there was a chill to it which made a mockery of the warmth of the day. Ruth and Laura had reached an uneasy, unspoken truce; enough to follow directions from the garage to a local shop where they had bought enough provisions for the evening meal and breakfast: some vegetables for a stew, rice, bacon, eggs and bread, although Laura revealed she was a strict vegetarian. They cooked around 7.30 p.m., keeping close to the fire for warmth, speaking in voices that were subconsciously low. The conversation was muted. The darkness among the trees seemed deep and disturbing; none of them would admit how scary the quiet countryside had become.

While the food bubbled over the fire, Laura plugged her computer into her mobile. 'Thought it would be worthwhile to check up on some of those lines the old guy had been spinning you before he caught his ticket to Neverland.'

When she booted the computer up, Church noticed her desktop wallpaper was a strange design of interlinking trees. 'What does that mean?' he asked.

'It's a design. It means I like looking at it,' she sneered. 'Shit. The battery's getting low. I'll need to find somewhere to charge it soon. Anyway, earlier I found this site called the Charles Fort Institute, which is like this massive online reference library and archive for all sorts of bizarre shit. They've got lots of links to folklore sites. So why don't we start with the pooch.' The screen jumped to *The Black Dog Reporter*. 'Here we are: Black Shuck. Shuck comes from *scucca*, the Anglo-Saxon for demon.' She scrolled quickly down the page. 'There's an account of a great storm in East Anglia in 1577 when a black demon dog "or the Devil in such a likeness" appeared in Bungay Church, leaving two parishioners dead at their prayers and another "as shrunken as a piece of leather scorched in a hot fire". Loads of tales from all over the country, but he's usually described as big as a calf with saucer-sized eyes that weep green or red fire, and he only comes from his secret lair at dusk. In East Anglia when someone is dying they still say "The Black Dog is at his heels." Generally seen as a portent of something much worse, death or disaster.'

'Hang on, if it only comes out at dusk, how come you saw it in daylight in Salisbury?' Ruth asked.

'Maybe he's found a good sunscreen,' Laura said.

'The tales might simply have it wrong. Because he was only seen at night, the people thought he could only come out then,' Church suggested.

Ruth sighed. 'Some come out by day, some are nocturnal. This is all too confusing.'

'Nothing about how to drive it away?' Church asked hopelessly.

'Well, being as how this stuff is generally regarded as not *real*, there's not much of a user's guide,' she replied tartly. 'Nothing in the folklore to link him to the Wild Hunt either. But I guess we're in uncharted territory here.'

'What have you got on the Hunt?'

After she'd jumped to the next site, Church tried to read her screen, but she moved it so he couldn't see. 'Lots of conflicting stories. It comes from the Norse tradition, long before the Vikings or Christianity came to Britain.' She scanned down to the relevant section. 'Odin was supposed to race across the sky on stormy winter evenings with a pack of baying hounds. Anyone who saw the Hunt could be carried off to a distant land, while anyone who spoke to the Huntsman died. Later, Odin's place was taken by the Devil, but the Wild Huntsman has also been seen as Herne the Hunter or Sir Francis Drake, who used to ride in a black coach led by headless horses across Dartmoor. The pack is called Yeth Hounds or Wish Hounds, another bunch of demon dogs, and they say you can hear their screams on the wind as they hunt down the souls of unbaptised babies. Cute. The Wild Huntsman's also known as the Erl-King, which is some mistranslation of an old Danish legend about the King of the Elves leading the Wild Hunt.'

'We've got to remember the legends aren't the truth,' Church cautioned. 'They're just stories twisted from the few facts people recall—'

'And isn't that a relief,' Laura interrupted. 'Demon hounds whisking poor bastards off to some kind of Purgatory. Portents of death and destruction. We're still not in line for Big Fun, are we?'

'Can't you find anything useful?' Ruth said with irritation.

'Sorry, I forgot you're a completely useless waste of space. It really is all down to me.' She logged off the net and clicked off her computer.

Ruth didn't bite. 'Okay, we've suddenly been swamped with every supernatural creature known to man, but what do you think is really going on?' she said to Church. 'These Night Walkers are obviously manoeuvring in the shadows. I mean, why were they all at that depot? Are they all getting regular jobs? I don't think so.'

Church nodded in agreement. 'Exactly. If they're so powerful, why haven't they made any move yet?'

'Maybe they're planning a first strike that will wipe us off the board in one fell swoop,' Laura noted.

'Whatever they're planning, it's something so important they can't risk us messing it up.'

Ruth looked out into the encroaching dark. 'They could be all over the country, just mixing with people, and nobody any the wiser. That funny-looking bloke you always think is a bit odd at the bus stop. The weirdo staring at you in the supermarket. Everywhere.'

'That's a good recipe for paranoia.' Laura lay back so she could see the moon coming up through the trees. 'There's going to be the war to end all wars and nobody knows.'

After dinner, Laura handed out the beers she had bought and they discussed what lay ahead. Church was surprised how optimistic the other two seemed, despite everything, although he knew his view had been coloured by his vision of his own death in the Watchtower. Laura had been entrusted with the stone, although they had never discussed it; it just seemed natural as she had been the one to find it. As their conversation turned to the possible locations of the other talismans, she pulled the stone out from the small rucksack where she had decided to keep it.

'It's a weird thing,' she said. 'I still can't get over the feel of it. It's kind of creepy.'

'What do you mean?'

'You'll know if you touch it. Here, cop a feel.'

She handed it over to Church for the first time. But as his fingers brushed it, an ear-splitting shriek burst from the stone and he dropped it like a hot coal. 'What the hell was that?' he asked in shock.

They all looked at it for a moment before Laura picked it up. 'Care to try that again?' Laura held it out to him again.

Church hesitated, then gingerly brushed his fingers over the stone's surface. The shriek erupted immediately.

'Jesus, why don't you set off a flare so everyone knows where we are!' Ruth protested.

'What does it mean?' Church said curiously. 'You try it,' he said to Ruth.

She took it from Laura, passed it from hand to hand, then gave it back. 'Looks like it doesn't like men,' Laura said to Church. 'Or maybe you've just got clammy palms.'

Church felt suddenly cold. 'The woman in the Watchtower said it had the power to recognise the true king of the land.'

Laura burst out laughing. 'King Church the First! That's a good one!'

Church shook his head. 'Don't be ridiculous.'

'You can't get away from the fact it only reacts to you,' Ruth said.

'I don't want to think about that. With this kind of stuff we can spend forever guessing. Who knows what any of it means?'

Laura was still laughing like a drain. 'The king! With his royal carriage, the Nissan Bluebird!'

Her mockery was so sharp they couldn't help joining in the laughter. It eased some of the tension which had been collecting around them.

They spent the next couple of hours drinking beer, talking quietly and feeding the fire from the rapidly diminishing woodpile; a cold wind threatened a storm. The conversation never strayed far from their mission, as they called it (ironically at first, but with increasing seriousness); even Laura's attempts to keep the chat superficial failed.

Shortly after 9 p.m., Ruth felt a change come over her. It started as a simple shiver that reached from deep within her, followed by a prickling of the skin that suggested the onset of some virus; a moment or two later she heard, or thought she did, her name whispered somewhere among the trees. Church and Laura continued to talk in hushed voices, oblivious to whatever had alerted her. Yet despite their situation, she didn't feel frightened. The pull was too strong to resist; she told the others she was going to stretch her legs and slipped off into the trees.

As she walked, she realised she couldn't turn back, even though some distant part of her was warning of the dangers of straying too far from the fire; obliquely, she recognised something was in her head, dragging her on and calming her at the same time.

She had wandered barely a few yards when she regretted it. The light from the fire faded quickly, as if it were being leached by the dark which quickly enfolded her. The noises seemed unnatural and disturbing; the creak of the branches above her head too loud, out of time with the gusts of the wind, as if they had a life of their own, the arms of living tree-gods reaching down to her; crunches in the undergrowth, near then far, which could have been small animals but sounded like footsteps circling her; whispers scarcely reaching her ears, dispossessed words fading out before she could make sense of them. Within moments she felt Church, Laura and all of civilisation were lost to her; she was in a dark, elemental world that considered her an interloper.

The flap of large wings made her jump and a second later an owl swooped close to her head, its face ghostly white against the dark. The owl shrieked once, sounding more human than bird, and a second later the trees were alive with light. Tiny white flames flickered as if myriad candles had been placed among the branches and for an instant Ruth had a breathtaking vision, as if the stars had been brought down to earth.

A figure stood next to an ancient, twisted hawthorn bush, its shape distorting amongst the shadows. As Ruth drew closer, she saw it was the young girl she had seen in the park in Salisbury – although she knew in her heart it was neither young nor girl – a cloak of what appeared to be thousands of interlocking leaves billowing in the wind around her.

Ruth felt drawn to the apparition as if she were in some hypnotic state, yet at the same time she was consumed by fear and awe: the figure was so alien. She knew, on some level she couldn't understand, that the girl had some specific interest in her; she could feel the subtle strands of manipulation in her head, the sense that the girl was trying to communicate something important.

'He is missing. The night to my day, the winter to my summer.' The words came out without her mouth moving; it was the same thing she had said in the park in Salisbury.

Who is missing? Ruth thought. *And what has it got to do with me?*

As if in answer, the quality of the light changed and Ruth could see something large crashing and stumbling among the undergrowth behind the girl. It was a vision, not reality, primal and terrifying. Ruth caught a glimpse of powerful muscles, and a shape slightly larger than a man, but with antlers curving wickedly from his head. Beyond him the small grove of trees went on for ever.

Whatever moved through the trees made snorting noises and began to circle closer, but still beyond the circle of light thrown by the flames in the branches, so it was impossible to see it fully. As the vision disappeared, the girl's flowing dress seemed to fade beneath her cloak, leaving her naked. Her skin was almost translucent, milky like the moon, her breasts small, her belly rounded, hips shapely. Ruth felt an incipient sexuality in the air, as if it were electricity and the girl a generator.

'Find him and then you must join us. Become our daughter. Our champion.'

Ruth stared into her mesmerising eyes, trying to comprehend. The girl reached out to Ruth, but the thought of touching those alien hands filled her with such dread, the spell was broken. She started to back away.

The owl that had startled her earlier suddenly swept down into the space between them and stared at Ruth with eyes that were unnervingly intelligent; it made her shudder.

'A companion,' the girl continued, 'a familiar, to guide you through the dark. When you see him, remember me.'

She began to say something else, but Ruth couldn't bear to stay any longer. And then she was running wildly through the trees, terrified by the knowledge that she had been recognised by something unknowable, and filled with the awful belief that she would never be allowed to return to the life she once knew.

'Are you making any sense of this?' Laura lounged back against the twisted trunk of an old ash tree, supping on the last of the beers. In her eyes, Church saw a sharp wit, incisive, and dark things moved beneath it.

'I try not to make sense of anything any more. If you thought about all the things happening to us in any kind of rational way, you'd go mad. The only way is to just deal with it as it happens.'

She shrugged, looked away into the dark. Since Ruth had gone for her walk, she seemed to have sloughed off some of the superficiality and mocking humour; for the first time Church felt a glimmer of the real Laura. 'Sort of screws up the belief system, doesn't it?'

'Belief,' Church said with surprise. 'What do you mean?'

'You know, God and all that. Not much in the Bible about this.'

'You believe the Bible then?' Church asked cautiously.

'I've got no time for any religious dickheads,' she said brutally. In that simple sentence, Church sensed dark currents running, but she made it clear it was something she wasn't going to discuss further.

'When you get into the historical truth of that whole Bible thing, it's hard to keep any faith,' he said.

'What do you mean?'

'Well, you know, how the Bible was put together by a council of the religious establishment from all the various texts lying around. Some got put in, some got left out – the Apocrypha – so it presented a simple, uncomplicated teaching guide for the masses, and a unifying cosmology. Politics. So even if the Bible is God's word, it was edited by men. How reliable does that make it?'

She shrugged. 'Maybe it's just like all these legends you keep pontificating about – some truth, lots of crazy stories trying to explain it.' She drained her can, carefully slipping it into the rubbish sack. 'Or maybe there's nothing out there at all. The No-Point Law – the perfect justification for staying in bed every day until we finally fade out.'

'That sounds a little bleak.'

'You think there's a meaning to it all? To all this we're going through?' Church was surprised; she sounded almost desperate.

'I don't know. A few weeks back, I thought there was no meaning to anything. Now I'm not so sure. We're suddenly living in a world where anything can happen. These days it's impossible to be sure, full stop.' He paused thoughtfully. 'Maybe we just think too much.'

The hoot of an owl made them both jump and they laughed nervously. Although he knew Laura irritated the hell out of Ruth, he felt remarkably comfortable with her. He enjoyed the spikiness of her character, and there was something oddly moving about the vulnerability he sensed beneath the patina of hardness; he was surprised Ruth couldn't see it too.

Laura cracked her knuckles, then seemed to become aware of the night's cold. With a shiver she moved closer to the fire, sitting cross-legged next to Church. 'So tell me,' she said, the faint mocking smile returning once more, 'have you and Miss Goody Two-Shoes done the monkey dance yet?'

Church looked at her in bafflement at the sudden switch in conversation. 'It's not like that. We're friends.'

'Come on! Don't tell me you don't realise she's desperate to get into your Calvins?'

Church shook his head forcibly. 'She's never shown any sign—'

'What do you expect? A big, flashing neon heart? Believe me, she's yearning to get to your loins, boy. So what are you going to do about it?'

Church shifted uncomfortably. 'There are things you don't know—'

'Well, tell me then.'

It was obvious she wasn't going to back down, so he reluctantly told her about Marianne. Yet as he spoke he became aware that something had changed; the rawness he felt inside whenever he discussed Marianne was gone. He felt sad, but not devastated – for the first time since her death. His hand went to the Black Rose in his pocket, gently caressing the petals, closing around the stem. Had the rose freed him from the despair, or was it because he knew some part of Marianne still existed in whatever place the dead dwelled? A sign that the new Dark Age was not all bad.

'So you haven't had sex for two years?' Laura said insensitively when he'd finished. 'What's the matter? You've got a phobia about it now?'

He felt his cheeks redden, with irritation rather than embarrassment. 'When you've been in love you don't automatically jump to someone new once a vacancy arises.'

'Look, I'm sure she was a nice girl and all that, but she's dead. Get over it. What are you going to do? Spend the rest of your days living in the past while life passes you by? I'm sure all this moping around was touching and romantic in the first few months after she died. But let's face it, it's pretty pathetic at this stage. And not a very attractive quality for the chicks.'

He snorted in exasperation.

'Ooh. Have I touched a nerve?' Her triumphant grin made him fume, but it was instantly tempered and once again he caught a glimpse of some honest emotion moving behind. 'You don't want to cut yourself off too much. In these days, with everything falling apart, you need to have someone close to you, know what I mean?'

'Yes. I know.' He looked her in the eye. She didn't smile, but there was a faint shift of something in her face that suggested they both recognised the subtext of their conversation.

Ruth saw it too. She was standing in the shadows amongst the trees after trying to find her way back to the camp. She had been desperate to tell them of her unsettling experience, but her emotions had diffused after hearing Church speak about her in terms that suggested little more than acquaintanceship and seeing Laura's obvious – at least to her – attempt at seduction. She felt more excluded than ever as she watched them looking deep into each other's eyes, locked in their own world. She hovered, undecided, for a moment, then hugged her arms around her and turned to walk back into the night.

She halted when a distant whirring sound broke through the stillness, and when she glanced back she noticed Church and Laura had seen her as they searched the sky for the origin of the noise.

'Sounds like helicopters,' Church called to her. 'Several of them.'

They walked to the edge of the glade, where they had a better view. Four searchlights played across the fields and hills as the choppers circled, searching the landscape.

'What are they looking for?' Ruth asked.

'Some crook on the run,' Laura said.

'You won't find many forces with the resources for four 'copters,' Church noted. They watched the lights for ten minutes more until they eventually drifted away. There was no evidence, but they all felt, instinctively, that it had something to do with the growing shadow that was falling across the country.

The morning was chill and grey, with heavy clouds banked up to the horizon, and there was rain in the wind. They waited patiently for Marianne to arrive with the milk, as she had promised, but when she didn't turn up, Church rekindled the fire and cooked bacon and eggs for him and Ruth while Laura simply had some black coffee. They were keen to move on as soon as possible. Church visited the garage the moment it opened, but the mechanic had made no progress and told him to come back after lunch. The breakdowns seemed to be continuing at an unaccountable pace; cars were starting to back up on the forecourt waiting for repair and the phone in the cluttered, nicotine-smelling office rang continuously.

The rain started to fall heavily by midmorning and Church, Laura and Ruth huddled morosely in their tents, one of them continuously watching the landscape for signs of movement. The conversation was muted and at times fell to silence as they struggled with their own thoughts. Church feared the worst when he returned to the garage, but the Nissan was waiting for him. The mechanic was apologetic; all the diagnostic tests on his equipment had found nothing wrong; it had started mysteriously an hour earlier as if it had suddenly decided the time was right. Church drove quickly back to the campsite where Laura had organised a methodical clean-up, insisting nothing was left behind which would damage the environment.

As they loaded their tents and bags into the boot, they were disturbed by the sound of crying caught on the wind, fearful and despairing, lost then as the gusts twisted among the trees. Soon after they caught sight of a red-cheeked man, his face distorted by grief, running wildly along the road nearby. Church's first thought was to ignore the distraught passer-by, but some instinct had him pounding through the trees to hurdle a fence and intercept the sobbing man further along the road.

'What's wrong?' Church asked, catching at his arm.

The man, who was in his late forties, grey hair plastered over his balding head by the rain, was startled by Church's intervention and for a second he seemed to be in such a state of shock he didn't know where he was. Then he said, 'My daughter—' before he was wracked by a juddering sob that crumpled his body. He came to his senses and roughly grabbed Church's shoulders. 'Have you got a car? I need a car!' Church nodded and hurriedly led him to where the Nissan was parked. 'My daughter's sick. Dying. Bloody car won't start. Only had it serviced the other week. Too far for an ambulance to get here and back to Bristol—' Another sob engulfed him.

Ruth and Laura wanted to know what was wrong, but the man made it plain there was no time to talk. They piled in the back and Church followed the man's directions up a long, winding lane to a neatly tended farmhouse. He scrambled out of the car and ran inside and before Church could follow he was out again carrying a young girl, with his hysterical wife close behind. It was Marianne.

*

Suddenly all her questions about death made sense. For nearly three years she had been living with a blood clot in her brain after a fall at the farm. It was in a position which made it too dangerous to operate, unless it moved or spread to become life-threatening, which, the doctors had warned her parents, it could at any time, without warning. When that happened, there was so little to lose that an operation became feasible. And the clot had chosen that day to strike her down.

'Her mother found her out cold on the kitchen floor with a bottle of milk smashed beside her,' her father said.

The one she'd been on her way to bring to us, Church thought.

As her father recounted the details, her upbeat, optimistic character took on a sharp poignancy; Church marvelled at how she had managed to remain so unspoilt while living permanently in the shadow of death. And it made his own doubts and fears seem so insignificant; he felt weak and pathetic in comparison.

The drive to Bristol passed in a flash of recklessly taken corners and jumped red lights. Each time Church glanced at Marianne in the rearview mirror, his heart rattled and his stomach knotted. Her face was impossibly pale. She was still out cold and he couldn't tell if she was suffering. He couldn't believe how acutely he felt for someone he barely knew; perhaps it was just the name creating echoes in his subconscious – maybe this Marianne he could save! – but whatever it was, she had touched him on some deep level. More than anything else in the world, he didn't want this Marianne to die.

Laura warned the hospital of their approach with the last gasp of life in her mobile phone and when they arrived at Frenchay the staff were waiting for her. As Marianne was rushed on a trolley up to the operating theatre, the farmer paused briefly to offer thanks for their help before chasing after his daughter.

'Poor girl. I hope there's something they can do,' Ruth said softly. Seeing the concern on Church's face, she touched his arm gently and said, 'At least we were around to get her here quickly.'

After occasional bouts of drizzle, the gathering storm clouds finally broke in a downpour that hammered against the reception doors. Bursts of lightning crackled overhead. 'We should be hitting the road,' Laura said as she watched the fading light.

'I can't go until I know how she's going to be.' Church silenced Laura's protests with a shake of the head before wandering slowly to the lift doors through which Marianne had disappeared.

Like most hospitals, the layout of Frenchay was labyrinthine. Church thought he was following the numerous signs, but he must have missed one at some point, for he found himself in a quiet ward with no sign of any operating theatres. Looking for directions, he stepped inside. Unlike the rest of the hospital, it was so still his footsteps on the creaking, sticky linoleum sounded like he was wearing hobnailed boots. There was the unmistakable smell of antiseptic that he always associated with sickness. Small rooms lay on either side of the corridor at the start, but further on he could see double doors through which he could just glimpse a large, open ward filled with beds. The room to his right had a big viewing window like a storefront. Inside, a sickly boy lay on his bed staring blankly at a TV set which featured US cartoons that were cut so fast it made Church feel nauseous. Numerous tubes snaked from his arms and his nose and there was a bank of monitors to each side of his bed. From the intricate locking system and the red light above the door, Church guessed it was some kind of isolation unit.

The door on the room to his left was slightly ajar and as he approached it Church could hear voices whispering a mantra over and over again. Through the glass panel he could just see a middle-aged woman in the bed, her arms so thin they looked like sticks. Her eyes were closed and she had on a black wig. A man with grey hair and a face lined by grief sat on one side of her, his hand resting gently on her forearm; his fingers trembled intermittently. On the other side a younger man, in his twenties, his face flushed from crying, held her hand loosely. They were both repeating the words 'I love you' in quiet, strained voices.

'Are you a relative?' The voice made him start. A black nurse, short and dumpy with a pleasant face, was at his side.

'No. I'm sorry, I didn't mean to intrude. I just . . .' His eyes returned unbidden to the painful tableau. 'What's wrong with her?'

The nurse smiled, but she wasn't going to give much away. 'She hasn't got long. She's been in a coma for the last day. But she can still hear, we think, so they're just saying what they feel, trying to show her she's loved.'

Before the end, Church thought. He looked on to the double doors where he could now see people of all ages lying in the beds. 'Them too?'

'Leukaemia mainly. Some others. The boy in the room behind's just had a bone marrow transplant. We need to keep him isolated because he's susceptible to infection.'

'Looks like some people's worlds are ending ahead of schedule.' Laura had walked up unseen and had been watching the two men whispering to their wife and mother. Church rounded on her to berate her for her callousness until he saw her eyes were brimming with tears.

The nurse glanced at them both, then said questioningly. 'Is there someone—?'

'No,' Church apologised. 'A friend's just been rushed into an operating theatre. I got lost.'

'Easily done,' she smiled. 'This place is a rabbit warren. The next floor up.'

'Where's Ruth?' Church asked as he led the way up the stairs.

'In reception, sulking.'

Church guessed that wasn't the case, but said nothing. When they reached the next floor, he held open the door and said, 'I never thought about the repercussions.'

'What do you mean?'

'How many people rely on technology. That boy in the isolation unit, all those monitors and electronically regulated drips—' He broke off when he saw Marianne's father sitting on a chair with his head in his hands. 'How is she?' Church asked cautiously.

'They're just prepping her now. The op should take about five hours, they reckon. They think we got here in time. If all goes well—' He swallowed, grasped Church's hand again. 'Thank God you were there.' Church sat next to him, listening to the clinical sounds of the hospital, the rat-chat of swing doors, the measured step of soles on lino, the clink of trolleys, the whir of lifts. 'I've spent years preparing myself for this moment and it hasn't done one bloody bit of good,' the farmer continued. 'I should've just pretended she wasn't ill and dealt with this when it happened.' He added bleakly, 'I hope I haven't wasted the time I've had with her.'

'No point thinking about the past,' Church said calmly but forcefully.

'Do you believe in God?' The farmer's hands were shaking. He caught his wrist, then buried his hands in the folds of his jacket.

'I'd like to,' Church replied guiltily.

'And so would I. I used to pray, when we first found out about Marianne. I stopped after a while. I couldn't really see the good of it, you know? It didn't seem like the kind of thing grown-ups should be doing. The wife kept at it, though. Down the church every Sunday. I should have carried on. That was me being selfish.' Church politely disagreed, but the farmer waved him quiet. 'She's the only one we've got. We never seemed to get round to having any more, but she got lots more love because of it. You couldn't have wanted for a better child: Never been any trouble. Always done her schoolwork, passed her exams. Never been lippy to me or the wife. Helped out around the farm, even when I didn't want her to because she was going through one of her bad periods. She's a bit of a dreamer, I suppose. Used to read books all the time. Not like me. I like to be out there, bloody well doing stuff with my hands. But Marianne, she liked to think.' He paused reflectively. 'I always hoped she'd take over the farm one day.'

'She still might.'

The farmer nodded, tight-lipped, refusing to tempt fate. For a long period they sat in silence, listening to their thoughts. Laura seemed to grow uncomfortable at the inactivity and after a while muttered something about going off to find the canteen.

Through the windows at the end of the corridor Church watched the night draw in, wrapping itself around the storm that still buffeted the building. Flashes of lightning flared briefly like the distant fires in the void he had witnessed through the windows of the Watchtower.

When four hours had elapsed, a nurse emerged from the theatre, her expression closed. The farmer caught her arm as she passed and pleaded for some information.

'I can't really say. Mr Persaud will be out as soon as he knows the situation,' she began, but looking at his face, she relented a little. 'It looks like it's going well,' she said with a comforting smile. 'Barring anything unforeseen—'

As if her comment had been heard by the gods, in that instant all the lights went out. The farmer cried out in shock as the darkness swallowed them. 'Just a power cut,' the nurse said reassuringly, before muttering, 'Bloody storm.' The lack of illumination through the window suggested it had hit most of the city. 'Don't worry. We're well prepared for things like this,' she continued. 'We've got an emergency generator that will kick in any second.'

Like statues, they waited in the claustrophobic dark, their heavy breath kept tight in their lungs.

'Any moment now,' the nurse repeated. There was an edge in her voice that hadn't been there before.

It was as if the entire hospital had been held in stasis, but then the dam broke and the cries started far off, rippling towards them in a wave of despair and anxiety. Church heard the rattle of the nurse's feet as she ran from their side and then the bang of the swing door as she disappeared back towards the operating theatre. The cry that squeezed out from the farmer's throat was filled with such devastation that Church felt tears sting his eyes. A man calling out, 'They're dying! They're dying!' reverberated up the stairwell, followed by the jarring punch of a woman screaming, 'Do something!'

The movement came out of nowhere; people rushing by in the dark, what could have been a hair's breadth away, or several feet. Church tried to remember where the wall was for safety, but before he could move someone clipped him hard and he slammed against it with such force he lost consciousness.

When he recovered, the chaos had reached a crescendo. He didn't know how long he had been out, but screams and shouts punctuated the gloom, along with the sound of running feet like machine-gun fire. Church called out for the farmer, but there was no reply. He felt a sudden wave of despair when he realised there was no way the surgeons would be able to finish the operation; Marianne would be dying, if she wasn't already dead.

Before he could dwell on it, someone came hurrying along the corridor and knocked him over again.

The intense confusion and claustrophobia left his thoughts in a whirl, but he know he ought to get to the ground floor as soon as possible. He found the stairwell easily enough by scrambling along the wall. Negotiating the descent was trickier; he clung to the railing and felt for each step like a blind man.

As he reached the next floor, a burst of the purest white light suddenly flared through the glass panel in the door, so bright it lit the entire stairwell. It faded just as quickly, leaving flashes of purple dancing across his retinas. It had been far too dazzling for a torch, and without electricity nothing else could have explained the quality or the intensity of the illumination. He fumbled for the door handle and stepped out into the hall.

Oddly, the screams and cries on that ward had died away, leaving an incongruous atmosphere of tranquillity. The stillness was broken a second or two later by the sound of a man crying, only the sobbing didn't seem despairing. Then there was laughter, tinged with an obvious note of disbelief, and someone whispering, 'Thank God!' over and over again.

Another flash of the burning white light erupted through the double doors that led to the wider ward and in its glare Church caught a glimpse of a scene he would never forget. The woman the nurse had told him was in a coma and dying of leukaemia stood in the doorway of her room, tubes trailing from her arms and nose like decorations. She was staring at her hands in incomprehension, a smile of amazement drawn across her face. Her husband and son had their arms around her, burying their faces into her neck, their bodies racked with sobs of joy. And then the darkness returned again.

Desperate to understand, Church propelled himself through the double doors. As he crossed the threshold into the larger ward the power came back on. The patients, many of whom had seemed close to death, were sitting up in their beds, examining themselves with new eyes, smiling, chatting to those around them. Some were clambering out, testing legs that hadn't walked with strength for weeks, pulling out chemotherapy drips with distaste.

One tall man, his skin sun-browned but his body wasted by the illness, smiled broadly at Church. 'What ho! I feel like I could run a marathon!' He pulled back the sheets to reveal a long scar on his lower belly. 'Cancer. They said the op hadn't worked.' He held out his hands in joyous disbelief.

Moving through the wave of uplifting emotion, Church looked for some clue to what had happened. Then, when he reached the far wall, he noticed a small figure slumped on the floor like a bundle of dirty clothes. With shock, he realised it was Marianne. Before he had even knelt at her side, he could tell she was dead; she was covered in blood which had poured from the open incision on her shaved head. The wound seemed to have partly sealed itself – there was no evidence of stitching – but it was still impossible to believe she could have made it even a few feet from the operating table. Inexplicably, there was faint charring of the skin around her eyes so that it appeared she was wearing a black mask; despite that, her pale face was composed.

Church took her hand, marvelling at the softness of her skin as stinging tears sprang to his eyes.

'She did it.' A short, dumpy man with chemo-baldness stood behind him. 'At first I thought she was a ghost walking through the ward. After the lights went, I thought it was the end – I was a bit delirious, I think. And then there she was.' He raised his hands in awe. 'Suddenly she burned with the brightest white light. It was the most amazing thing. I thought, "She's an angel come for me." And when the light fell on me I suddenly felt better.' The tears were streaming down his cheeks at the memory. 'She carried on through the ward and did it again. She made everybody better. And then she just fell down here like she'd burned herself out.'

Church brushed a stray hair from her forehead, touched her cheek with his fingertips, as if the contact would in some way impart an awareness of what had truly happened. He took out the locket she had lent him – only the previous day – and considered fastening it around her neck; let Princess Diana guide her into the light. But then he hesitated, before slipping it back into his pocket. Even though their meeting had been brief, Marianne had been inspirational to him and he wanted something to remind him of her. Perhaps the new saint for the new age really would do him good too. All he could think was that in that terrible, awesome new world, belief and faith really could move mountains. Magic was alive, and it wasn't just the providence of the dark side; good people could make a difference too, lighting a beacon that would shine out in the coming night.

CHAPTER NINE

At the Heart of the Storm

Ruth and Laura were waiting anxiously for Church in reception. They were surrounded by a chaotic mass of distraught relatives, bewildered patients and hard-pressed hospital staff, their faces uniformly etched with painful disbelief. Church felt sick from the piercing noise; alarms were ringing throughout the building, mingling with the terrible sounds of grief and the barking of orders. Occasionally he caught a whiff of smoke carried on draughts from the heart of the hospital.

His journey from the cancer ward had been one of the most painful he had ever made. All the nurses had been caught up in the crisis, so he carried Marianne to a bed and drew a sheet over her before setting off in search of her father to break the news. Church found him in a state of near breakdown, running frantically around outside the operating theatre, desperately begging any passing hospital employee for information on his daughter's whereabouts. When he read Church's face he crumpled like a sick child, lost in tearing sobs that seemed to suck the breath from him. Church felt broken inside; it was even more unfair than the farmer realised: two months ago, a week ago, perhaps only a day earlier, the power cut would not have happened and Marianne might have lived.

Her father was immune to any attempts to comfort him and Church could do nothing but leave him there. As he hurried down through the floors, all his own painful thoughts about Marianne were lost as he became aware of the true devastation the power cut had wrought. On each floor the victims of failed life support systems were laid out on trolleys with sheets thrown over them. The hospital staff seemed to be wandering around dumbly. One nurse was in tears as she demanded answers from a colleague; not only had the power supply failed to a regulated drip, but the back-up battery had also ceased to work. 'How do you explain that?' she pleaded. By the time Church reached reception, he felt nauseous. He couldn't bring himself to answer Ruth and Laura's questions, and headed out to the car in silence, head bowed into the raging storm.

*

They picked up the M5 in the city and followed the lantern's flame back south. High winds buffeted the car and the rain lashed the windscreen with such force the wipers could barely function.

'Think of those cancer patients – *they*'ve survived. *Some* good has come of it,' Ruth said hopefully. 'Marianne did that. She achieved something wonderful with her life, gave hope . . . magic . . . to people lost in despair. That's more than most could ever dream of doing. It made her life mean something.'

'I can see that,' Church replied darkly, 'but it doesn't make it better.' He smiled bitterly as a flash of lightning glared off the roof of a Porsche going too fast for the weather, the driver unaware that his gleaming status symbol would soon be going the way of the dinosaurs. 'That scene at the hospital was like something out of the Middle Ages. And it's going to be like that all over the country . . . all over the world . . . before too long. I understood what was happening in an abstract way, but *that*'s the true cost of the upheaval that's being inflicted on us. It's not about TVs breaking down and cars working randomly. It's about human suffering on an unimaginable scale. It's about the end of our entire way of life.'

'So it's not about Marianne, then?' Laura chipped in pointedly from the back seat.

Church didn't respond.

The storm didn't seem to be abating. Muscles aching from being hunched over the wheel trying to peer through the driving rain, Church eventually drew off the motorway into the Taunton Deane services. He stretched out the stress knots in his back, then turned on the radio and searched for some report about the crisis at the hospital; he wanted to know how they were going to explain it. But the Radio 4 news only carried a couple of dull political stories, one about a sharp dip on the FTSE and a report about the police investigation into the horrific knife murders in the north-west; even the local stations made no mention of it.

'There's something wrong here,' he said. 'The news must have got out by now.'

'Maybe they're covering it up,' Ruth suggested.

They went to the restaurant for a drink and an attempt to plan their next step. It was empty, apart from one bored youth on the checkout, and with the storm blasting in the dark night, it felt like they had been marooned on a comfortless island.

While Ruth and Laura went to the toilet, Church brooded over his coffee. Although there were three of them, he felt the responsibility for success or failure was increasingly being heaped on his shoulders. For some reason he had been singled out – by Tom, by the woman in the Watchtower – and he really didn't know if he were up to what was expected of him. But he accepted, whatever the outcome, that he couldn't turn his back on the responsibility; he had always firmly believed in facing up to obligation.

Carefully, he drew out the Black Rose and examined it closely; it hadn't wilted in the slightest. The petals were warm and silky, almost luxurious to the touch, and the scent, if anything, was even more heady. He hadn't questioned the gift of the flower before, but if he heeded the young Marianne's advice about forgetting the past and enjoying the present, he knew he should throw it away; no good could possibly come of it. He brought it up to his lips, kissed it absently, traced it across his cheek as he weighed up his choice. Then he slipped it back into his pocket.

Church sipped his coffee, listening to the hiss of cars speeding by outside. Perhaps it was just the weather, but there seemed to be less traffic using the motorway than he would have expected for the time of year. He wondered if the change coming over the country was starting to affect people subconsciously, an unspecified unease that nagged away at them constantly. Lightning flashed, a clap of thunder rumbled loudly; the storm was directly overhead.

But as the peal died away, Church thought he heard something else, mingling with the noise, continuing for just a split second longer. It left the hairs on the back of his neck standing erect. He stood up and walked over to the window; beyond the dismal lights of the car park, the wooded hillsides clustered darkly.

He returned to his table, but couldn't settle. It bothered him that he was jumping at the slightest sound. When the rumbling thunder made the windows boom once more, he listened carefully, but there was no subsequent sound. Yet he was sure he had heard it before. And it had sounded like the howl of a dog.

'So do you think he's going to lose it?' Laura said above the whir of the hand-drier.

Ruth leaned against the wash basins, her arms folded. 'He's got his problems, but nothing he can't handle.'

'You saw him when he came out of the hospital—'

'Hardly surprising after seeing all that suffering. If you had any kind of heart you'd understand—'

'I understand all right. But it wasn't just those people dying. It was the girl. He's got her all mixed up in his head with that dead girlfriend

163

of his.' The drier died and suddenly the toilet seemed unnervingly lonely, trapped in the uncomfortable glare of the artificial lights. 'This isn't some nice jaunt to see the sights. It's life or death and a hundred other clichés. We can't afford someone tripping us up because they're too lost in their head.'

'What do you suggest? We dump him?' Ruth led the way out into the main corridor. There were a few travellers, but no one was hanging around; they all seemed eager to get back to their cars, back to their homes.

'Aren't we Frosty the Snowman? Bothered that I'm attacking your boyfriend?' Ruth flinched at the lash of Laura's mockery. 'I'm saying we keep an eye on him. Rein him in if he gets too freaky.'

'He'll be fine,' Ruth said coldly. 'You just worry about yourself. For a change.'

Lightning lit up the car park like a searchlight. Ruth had gone on several steps before she noticed she was walking alone. Behind her, Laura was peering out into the night. 'I saw something,' she said. Ruth could tell it had unnerved her.

Cautiously they approached the electronic doors, which hummed open like magic. Stepping out into the area where the overhang of the roof protected them from the rain, they searched the car park. There seemed more cars than there were travellers in the services, but the night made it impossible to see if there was anyone inside them. Parts of the car park were already flooded and water was bubbling up out of the drains. Rain gusted across the open areas in sheets and overhead a rumble of thunder barely died away before another started. It was a bleakly unfriendly scene.

'Doesn't seem to be anyone out there,' Ruth ventured.

'It was big, on all fours. Like a shadow, shifting quickly.'

'You're sure it wasn't a trick of the lightning?'

Laura stepped out into the full force of the rain. It plastered her blonde hair on to her head within seconds. 'There's something moving. Out among the cars.'

'How can you see? It's so dark.' Ruth joined her in the rain. The pounding droplets were heavy and icy, forcing their way down the back of her neck, soaking her jeans. 'I don't think we should—'

'You scurry back to be with your boyfriend if you like.'

Ruth felt like punching her. 'Oh yes. Real smart to put ourselves at risk when we could be the only ones with a chance to stop the world going to hell.'

'You do what you want. I'm not hiding away.'

An incongruous note in Laura's voice made Ruth suddenly aware there was more at play than mere bravado. 'And what are you planning to do when you discover what's out there?'

Without answering, Laura set off with Ruth close behind, regretting every step, but unable to let Laura go into the dark alone. She felt a spark of primal fear. Amidst the pounding of the rain, the wild gusting of the wind and the susurration of car wheels on the motorway, any sound of movement in the car park was drowned out; the lights seemed too dim to dispel the deeper shadows.

There were some twenty cars which could provide a hiding place for whatever Laura had seen. A few were scattered at random around the car park, but most were clustered together in the centre. By the time they reached the first one, their clinging clothes were hampering them. As they passed some of the vehicles they glimpsed an occasional pale face staring out, hands gripping steering wheels as if the drivers were afraid to move away from the oasis of light offered by the service station.

'I still don't see anything,' Ruth said, but almost as soon as her words were lost to the wind and rain they heard a low, rumbling growl, like distant thunder. Ruth clutched at Laura's arm and they both froze, unable to tell the direction of the noise. 'An animal,' Ruth said.

'You're so sharp you'll cut yourself.' Laura's mockery was drained of its usual acid.

'I think we should get back,' Ruth said. Laura hesitated, then nodded, but as they turned, a shape flashed between them and the building. Ruth caught a glimpse of something burning red, like hot coals.

Moving quickly over to one side, they tried for an elliptical route back to the light. Another growl, closer at hand this time, turned into a chilling howl.

'Shit!' Laura hissed.

Ruth thought: *It's hunting.*

And then they were running, the splashing of their feet accompanied by the thunder of powerful paws. Whatever it was crashed into a car in front with such force the side crumpled and it spun into their path. Ruth stifled a scream. They darted sideways between two other cars, no longer knowing in which direction they were running. Along the way, Laura slammed into a wing mirror and careened into the other vehicle. Ruth was already several feet away before she realised Laura had slipped to her knees.

As she turned she caught sight of the black shape, as big as a small pony; it shifted its bulk and started to run. If it hit the nearest car, Laura would be crushed between them. Without thinking, Ruth sprinted back as Laura hauled herself to her feet. At the moment Ruth yanked on

Laura's jacket, there was the sledgehammer sound of buckling metal and a crash as the windscreen exploded. The impact hurled them backwards into a deep puddle.

The beast leapt and slammed on to the bonnet where it poised over them. Their minds locked in fear at the first clear sight of it. It was the dog that had attacked Church in Salisbury. Black Shuck. The horribly intelligent eyes burned crimson as its hot breath steamed in the chill night. The rain was running in rivulets off its black velvet hide, mingling with the sizzling drool that dripped from its fangs. Unable to move, Ruth and Laura watched as its muscles bunched. Slowly, it raised its haunches to attack.

Then, from out of the swirling rain, there was a penetrating screech as an owl swooped down, claws raised at the dog's eyes. It soared away just as the beast snapped its enormous head round. But it was enough of a distraction; Ruth and Laura were already moving as the dog's jaws gnashed on empty air.

The services seemed to be at the distant end of a dark tunnel. Their lungs burned from exertion, but they closed the gap quickly as they heard the beast leap from the bonnet and start to pound the tarmac behind them. *We're not going to make it*, Ruth thought. The sound of its feet thundered closer. But then, miraculously, the doors were opening and they were slipping and sliding on the floor in the glaring lights.

Any thoughts they had reached sanctuary were dispelled a moment later. The dog was travelling with such speed the doors didn't have time to open again. They burst inwards, showering glass and twisted metal across the floor as the dog skidded, then righted itself. Two women emerging from the toilets shrieked and darted back inside. Another man chose that unfortunate moment to wander haphazardly out of the shop. The dog turned its head and in one fluid movement of its jaws, took his arm off at the shoulder. It was too quick for him to scream; he blacked out from the shock and collapsed into a growing pool of blood. Ruth and Laura scrambled away again, their eyes burning with tears of fear.

They could hear the rasping breath of the dog echoing along the corridor as they sprinted to the restaurant, a rough, traction engine sound filled with power and menace. As they burst in, Church's face registered momentary shock at their bedraggled appearance, but then he was moving without asking any questions.

'Into the kitchen,' he hissed, hauling them towards the hot food counter. They scrambled over it, burning themselves on the hot metal. When the dog entered a second later, the youth on the checkout took one look at it and slipped under his till, either in a faint or in fear. In the kitchen, two bored cooks waited patiently for orders. Their sudden flurry of protests were silenced by the roar of the dog.

'My God, what's that?' one of the women cried, eyes wide.

'Can you lock this door?' Church demanded. It was of a reinforced design to contain a fire.

The woman nodded in confusion, fumbling for a bunch of keys in her pockets. Through the door, the beast's rasping breath drew closer. There was a clang as it jumped on the hot food counter and then a dull thud as it landed on the other side. As the woman located the key, Church snatched it from her hands and secured the door. They retreated to the other side of the room and ducked down behind a stainless steel unit just as the dog thundered against it.

'What's out there?' the other woman whimpered.

Church looked to Ruth. 'Black Shuck,' she said in a small, cracking voice. She suddenly started to shake from the cold and the shock. Church slid his arms around her shoulders and pulled her close to him. 'Is it going to be like this all the way?' she said weakly. 'Never being able to rest?'

There was another crash against the door and they all jumped.

'What's going on?' one of the cooks screamed. She crawled away with the other woman, casting angry, frightened glances at Church, Ruth and Laura.

'How can we hold off something like that?' Ruth said. 'It's going to get us sooner or later.'

'The dog isn't the worst of it,' Church replied fatalistically. 'You heard what Tom said. It's a precursor, a portent.'

'For what?' Laura asked. As if in answer, there came a mighty clattering on the roof far above them, rumbling from one side of the building to the other; like hoofbeats. The dog howled, in warning or welcome.

Ruth saw the vaguest shadow pass across Laura's features; in the imposing edifice of her confidence it was as if the foundations had shattered. Cautiously, Ruth reached out a comforting hand to Laura's arm; Laura flinched, didn't look at her, but nor did she knock it away.

They stayed huddled there for the rest of the night, listening to the sounds beyond the door; the grunts and growls, snufflings and crashings that couldn't have come from any beast born on earth. On one occasion, after a forty-five-minute gulf of silence, they thought it had finally departed, but just as Church was about to turn the key in the lock it crashed against the door, almost bursting it inwards. It was a warning that they heeded.

When the faintest glimmer of dawn first brushed the clouds, Church ventured to the slatted glass windows and opened them just enough to look out. The motorway was empty, the storm blown out, although the clouds still roiled above them. And in that surging vapour he had the uneasy feeling he could glimpse dark figures on horseback, riding the clouds, lost among them; seeking refuge from the light, ready to return another night.

He turned to the others. 'Let's go,' he said.

The restaurant was empty, the dog gone, as Church knew it would be. The two cooks ran out, crying with relief, to greet the checkout youth who emerged from beneath the till looking like he'd been sedated; he hadn't come between the monstrous dog and its prey, so it had left him alone. The reinforced kitchen door was gouged and splintered.

The rest of the services seemed deserted, but Church eventually located some members of staff in the management office. In a room beyond they could see the covered body of the man who lost his arm to the dog. Phone lines had been down throughout the night, so no emergency services could have been called; even mobiles hadn't worked. Some kind of electrical disturbance caused by the storm, the staff said, but that didn't explain what had happened to those who had gone off in their cars to fetch help and had not been heard from since. No one seemed quite able to believe that what had taken place had actually happened. They talked of wild dogs, as if there had been a pack, and seemed oblivious to anything uncanny. Church, Ruth and Laura returned to the car park, leaving them trying to impose some order on an event that wouldn't accept it.

As they approached the car they noticed the interior light was on and one door was slightly ajar. They circled the Nissan cautiously, suddenly on guard, until they noticed the boot was open too, the contents of their bags strewn around the interior. A knife or screwdriver had been crudely forced into the keyhole.

'Bastards!' Laura said. 'We've really been hit with the bad luck stick.'

'I don't think it's a coincidence,' Church said as he sifted through their possessions.

'You think they were looking for the stone?' Laura asked, her hand automatically going to the rucksack.

He nodded. 'But whatever was here last night wouldn't have jimmied open the boot.'

They repacked their possessions in silence, filled up with petrol and returned to the motorway, haunted by too many unanswered questions.

After the storm, the day turned bright and clear. At that early hour the motorway was eerily devoid of even the slow caravans of lorries lumbering towards Exeter and Torbay. The scenery gradually changed as they crossed the county line, the tranquil green fields of Somerset giving way to Devon's wilder landscape of hills, rocky outcroppings and impenetrable, dark woods, filled with romance in the glimmering post-dawn light. At Exeter, the lantern, which Ruth held in her lap like a baby, began to tug westwards. The motorway died just south of the city anyway, so they picked up the A30 which ran all the way along the spine of Cornwall to the end of the world. They were only on it for a short while as the lantern suddenly flickered with irritation and guided them on to a tiny B road which spiked into the heart of Dartmoor.

'I don't like it when we get too far away from civilisation.' Ruth glanced uncomfortably out of the window at the disappearing habitation as they moved toward the looming expanse of Dartmoor on the horizon.

'You should see the map,' Laura said, poring over Church's *AA Book of the Road*. 'The roads around here look about good enough for pig-droving, and there're only a handful of villages, all with about three houses in them. Welcome to Nowhere.'

As the fields became scrubby uplands and windswept rocks, Ruth said uneasily, 'I wonder what's out there.' Then, after a moment or two when neither of them answered, 'I want tall buildings, cars, pollution—'

'I don't think that would be any safer,' Church said. 'It's just an illusion.'

Laura suddenly craned her neck to peer through the side window up into the blue sky. 'Hey! There's another one! I thought they slept during the day?'

Ruth followed her gaze. An enormous owl swooped on the air currents, dipped low, then soared again, but it seemed to have no trouble keeping up with them. Ruth squinted, trying to pluck details from the silhouette; she knew instinctively it was her *familiar*, the same one that had attacked the beast in the car park.

For some reason she didn't quite understand, Ruth still hadn't got around to telling them about her meeting with the mysterious girl in the glade. Although she had been disturbed by it, in some way it had seemed intensely private and to talk about it felt instinctively like a betrayal of trust; which was a strange way to think about it. Besides, in the cold light of day it hadn't seemed frightening at all.

'That one at the services saved our lives,' Laura continued.

'It doesn't make sense,' Church said. 'Why would a bird do something like that? They're normally smart.'

Ruth didn't answer. Now she was speculating on why the girl had particularly used that word *familiar*, with all its connotations. She followed the owl's progress carefully, and wondered.

Soon the last signs of civilisation disappeared. As if on cue, another storm blew up from nowhere. It swamped the blue sky with slate-coloured clouds that billowed and twisted in high winds like the smoke from some conflagration, and drew a line of shadow across the land. Lightning flashed on the horizon and thunder boomed out dully. Church flicked on the wipers a second after the first drops hit, but it was like someone had thrown a bucket of water at the windscreen. He pulled the car over to the side of the road in the hope that it would pass and instantly felt exhaustion overcome him. Reluctantly he suggested they find somewhere to rest.

When the rain lessened slightly, they continued slowly on their way, but there was little to see. They passed through a place called Two Bridges right in the centre of Dartmoor which seemed to consist of just one house and a sprawling, white-painted pub tucked away in a hollow. And then, as they crested the ridge beyond, they came across an ancient inn made of Devonshire stone with a half-timbered upper storey; squat and heavy, it looked as if it had been thrown up out of the ground by some force of nature. The Elizabethan windows were a mass of tiny panes, too dark to see through, although Church did catch sight of the welcoming flicker of an open fire. An old wooden sign swung in the gale featuring a hand-painted design of a vaguely human face made out of leaves and the legend The Green Man, the ancient title which offered a particular welcome to travellers. A small note in the window said *Accommodation*.

Church pulled the car on to the tiny pockmarked car park and they sprinted through the rain to the stone porch. The door was locked – it was well before opening time – but Church hammered on a brass knocker until they heard movement within. The door swung open to reveal a thin man in tight blue jeans and a white T-shirt that flapped on his bony frame. He was severely balding, with just tufts of black hair curling back over his ears. A thick moustache hung like a brush over his top lip. He had eyes like a rodent, darting and curious, and a scar curved over the right one, but his smile was pleasant enough.

'Waifs and strays from the storm?' he enquired in a fey, accentless voice.

'We could do with some rooms if you've got any spare,' Church said.

'As you can see, it's not exactly Piccadilly Circus round here at this time of year so I think you might be in luck.' He stepped back and swept his arm theatrically to invite them in. The tasteful décor of the pub reflected the building's great age: stone flags, dark wood tables, benches and stools, a few line drawings and old photographs on the stone walls. The fire Church had seen earlier burned heartily in a fireplace big enough to have two small bench seats inside the chimney breast. The landlord saw Church looking at it. 'Nice, isn't it? I have to keep it going, even in summer, though. There's a superstition in these parts that if the fire ever goes out the landlord will meet a terrible death. I don't believe it myself, naturally, being a sophisticated urbanite, but then again I'm not about to take unnecessary risks.'

There were only three guest bedrooms, none of them taken, huddled up where the sloping roof made Church stoop; the tiny windows were low down so he had to bend even further to look out. The rooms were cosy with brass beds, old-fashioned bedspreads and an open grate in every room. The landlord, who introduced himself as Simon, busied himself lighting a fire in each of them, 'to take the damp out of the air.' He seemed to enjoy the company and within minutes his non-stop chat had given them the abridged version of his life story. He used to run a bar in Leeds with his partner Stuart, but after a holiday in Devon they'd decided to buy The Green Man, which was then ramshackle and in danger of being pulled down. 'We're missionaries,' he said sardonically. 'We're here to bring wit and sophistication to a backward culture which doesn't realise the importance of good food, good wine and perfect interior design.'

'Leeds to Dartmoor is a dramatic move,' Church said.

Simon shrugged. 'It felt right, that's all I can say. Too many people expect you to follow the unwritten rules, but sometimes it's better just to go with what you feel inside. So I can't buy a good shirt or a decent pair of shoes round here – but at least I'm queen of all she surveys. Just call me a drop-out.'

There was something he wasn't telling them and when Ruth asked him about the jagged scar above his right eye he shifted uncomfortably. 'Small minds don't know much, but they know how to aim well.' It seemed he would leave it there, but the issue obviously still burned. 'We had a nice house in a nice suburb, but gradually we noticed the ambience of the area changing. Normally you expect a drug gang or some criminal layabouts to change the mood of a neighbourhood, but in this case it was the God Squad.' He sucked on his lip angrily. 'Born Agains. Fundamentalists. All those racist comments about ethnic groups colonising an area, well, no one is a patch on them. They were some particular sect based at an academy they'd had built in the area. I don't know what stripe – they're all the same to me. *He* didn't die for me.'

His eyes narrowed as he searched their faces for any anger at his comments, then he continued: 'They snapped up a house for sale in the street at well over the asking price. Then, whenever one came on the market, they were always first in the queue. It didn't take long before we were infested.' He sighed. 'You know, I'm an easy-going person – it takes a lot to rattle my cage. But it soon became obvious they didn't want people like Stuart and I in the area. Their Rule Book sees us as the spawn of Satan or something. I mean, so much for the Christian hand of fellowship. We used to know everyone in the street and we all looked out for each other. Suddenly we couldn't find anyone to talk to us. There were little things . . . constant calls to the police complaining that our car was double-parked. Then I got a call from the local paper. I used to help out at a nursery in my spare time, just organising parties, entertaining the kiddies, that sort of thing. I'd done it for years. But suddenly there'd been complaints that I wasn't a *fit and proper person*, whatever that means. It was after that that things started getting mean.'

'How awful,' Ruth said with honest concern.

He shrugged dismissively. 'Oh, it's one of our burdens in life. Anyway, one thing led to another and then one night when we were walking home some sneaky little coward threw a half-brick out of the shadows. It caught me just here.' He traced the scar, then snapped his hand into a fist. 'I wouldn't have minded, but they got blood all over my favourite shirt,' he said with a bitter smile.

'And that's why you moved?' Ruth asked.

'Actually, no. I've never run from things that threaten my way of life. But then there were so many of them they started standing for the council, elbowing their way on to school boards, anywhere where they could have influence. Once values like that get a political platform you know the apocalypse is on the horizon. Agents of the Devil, all of them. Stuart and I were on the next train out.'

He seemed filled with a terrible rage at the injustice of it all, but he moved on to enthusing with passion about his plans for the pub. It seemed obvious from his comments that he had found some kind of acceptance in the small, rural community not normally noted for an outward-looking attitude; the irony was not lost on them.

He would have talked all afternoon if they'd let him, but eventually he wandered off to let them settle in. They chose their rooms and went straight to bed, listening to the rain gust against the windows, straining to hear the howl of a dog away in the wind, afraid to close their eyes.

Church's dreams were tumultuous and disturbing. The woman from the Watchtower was there, beseeching him to do something, but he couldn't hear her words, just see her troubled expression and her outstretched arms. And then there were things circling him, drawing closer: low, bestial shapes that at times moved on four legs, then on two. Behind him he felt eyes boring into his head and an overwhelming feeling of dread, but his legs were stone and he couldn't turn to see who or what was waiting there. A sudden pain stabbed into his hand and he looked down to behold the Black Rose. A thorn had protruded mysteriously from the stem and had pierced the fleshy part of his palm. The blood fell like rain, splashing his clothes, staining the ground beneath his feet, running away in a trickle that turned into a torrent.

He woke with a start. Twilight had fallen and the fire had been reduced to a few raw embers in the grate: the faint red glow was strangely comforting. He couldn't believe he had slept so long. Remembering the fading remnants of his dream, he pulled the Black Rose from his pocket and examined it cautiously. There was no sign of any thorn. He stroked it lovingly, then glanced into the shadows in the corners of the room.

'Marianne? Can you hear me?' His voice rustled like paper in the still air. He waited hopefully for a moment and then swung his legs off the bed and rested his head in his hands.

Through the window, Dartmoor looked cold and menacing, a muddy smear of charcoal and grey and brown beneath a churning sky. At least the rain had stopped.

There was faint music coming through the floorboards, the Pet Shop Boys singing 'Being Boring' so he made his way downstairs to the bar to see Simon dancing alone in front of the roaring fire. He squealed when Church spoke.

'Lordy, you gave me a start! Do you always creep around like a thief in the night?'

Church shrugged. 'I didn't know I was creeping.'

'Well you were!' Simon flounced to the bar, then did another little dance and finished with a forgiving smile. 'Enjoy your beauty sleep?'

Church nodded. 'Any chance of something to eat?'

'You're a lucky boy. Stuart's a gourmet chef and when I say gourmet, I mean to die for. He was out all day buying some goodies in Plymouth, so we have some mouth-watering delights for tonight's menu. Salmon, John Dory, lamb in a redcurrant sauce, something very delicious with pasta and squid ink. You'll think you've died and gone to heaven. They've started to come from all over to sample his wares, so to speak.'

He disappeared behind the bar and returned with a handwritten menu. 'I hope you'll be staying around later. It's entertainment night. A little spot of glamour in a bleak landscape.'

Church smiled falsely, but his mind was elsewhere: Marianne, dead on the floor; the young Marianne, dead in his arms; his own body lying in a stream. Sometimes he wondered how he managed to keep going.

His food arrived quickly, and the pan-roasted chicken and spring onions was as good as Simon had promised. It seemed forever since he'd eaten, and as he was tucking into it hungrily Ruth emerged, her hair still wet from the shower. She looked fully refreshed, untroubled even, and flashed him a warm smile as she slipped in opposite him.

'Thinking of your stomach again,' she said, leaning over to pluck a piece of chicken from his plate.

'You seem different.' He searched her face, which seemed to glow with an inner light.

'What do you mean?'

'I don't know.' He shrugged. 'I've only noticed it since the other night when we camped out. You seem stronger somehow.'

She laughed easily and snatched up the menu. 'I didn't feel it last night with that dog chasing me.'

'At least you kept going. Most people would have keeled over faced with something like that.' He paused, averting his gaze to toy with his food. 'I'm glad you're on board.'

Ruth's eyes sparkled, but she restrained a broad smile. 'That's the closest thing to a compliment I've heard from your lips.'

'Make the most of it. That's as good as it gets.' He finished off the last of the chicken and pushed the plate away. 'I guess it would help if we knew exactly where we were going and what we were supposed to do when we got there.'

Simon lurched out from behind the bar humping a machine which he placed on a table. Sweating and cursing under his breath, he proceeded to drag tables and chairs around noisily until he had cleared a space in one corner. A young black man emerged from the bar area wearing an irritated expression. He was astonishingly attractive, with perfect cheekbones, well-defined muscles beneath his silk shirt and a faintly feminine turn to his features. They guessed he was Simon's partner. There was engine oil on his hands and he was brandishing a spanner. He was obviously about to launch into some tirade when he spotted Church and Ruth and smiled with embarrassment.

'He's tinkering with his motorbike while I'm breaking my back,' Simon said with theatrical haughtiness; it was clearly the source of their disagreement.

Ruth glanced anxiously at the windows, where a gust brought a splatter of rain as if someone had thrown it; it was too dark to see beyond the circle of light cast by the porch lamps.

'You think Black Shuck will come tonight?' Her eyes grew fearful.

'We're doing the best we can, Ruth,' he said firmly. 'We're out of our depth here. We have no defence against these things. You can't plan for it. I think we just have to face up to crises when they materialise, like anything else in life. What do you suggest?'

'I don't know.' She looked into the fire, wishing they were sitting closer together. 'Do you think we can trust Laura?' she asked incongruously.

'Don't you?'

'I don't know. Sometimes. I don't like her attitude, and I'm not convinced she always tells the truth, like she's got some secret agenda.'

'She's not going to win any good personality awards, but she seems okay so far.'

Ruth tried to read any more in his comments than there appeared. She was convinced he was attracted to Laura, whether he knew it or not, and she hoped her suspicions weren't born out of jealousy because of it. For someone who had always maintained emotional equilibrium, her latest predicament unnerved Ruth with its unpredictability. Her feelings for Church had crept up on her, forged through their harrowing experiences, yet she couldn't see a glimmer of a response in him. She didn't know if that was because he was still trapped in his feelings for Marianne, or if he simply didn't care, but she knew, deep inside, she felt like she'd finally found something for which she'd been waiting all her life.

'If you have any doubts you should say.' Church looked her in the eye. 'I'm not always the most perceptive of people.'

'Not yet. When I'm sure.' Ruth made her selection from the menu and caught Simon's eye as he pushed the makeshift sections of a stage into the recently cleared space. She didn't have to wait long for her seared salmon and grilled vegetables, which was as succulent as Church's meal.

Simon made a face at Laura when she came out of the door to the bedrooms at the foot of the stairs, her computer clutched under her arm. She glared in return and said, 'Get many guests here? Didn't think so.'

'Ooh, listen to her,' Simon said before returning to his work.

Laura glanced at Ruth and Church's plates and said grumpily, 'I hope they do vegetarian.'

'What are you in such a bad mood about?' Ruth asked.

'It's not working.' She slid the computer on the table in front of them. 'I charged up the battery fine, and then I booted it up to do some more research. The moment I got online I got some of that screeching laughter, some of the freakiest images I've ever seen, and then it just died on me.'

There was a crash as Simon dropped a microphone on the stage, which made them all jump. He smiled apologetically, then cursed under his breath as he attempted to untangle the coiling lead.

Church examined the computer briefly, then shook his head. 'I wonder if it will carry on intermittently like this – some days everything works properly, some days it doesn't – or if we'll just lose technology overnight and wake up in the stone age.'

They wrestled with their thoughts in silence for a while until Laura decided to call Simon and harangue him until Stuart could come up with a vegetarian dish that matched her unreasonably detailed recipe. When it arrived, Ruth and Laura ordered some red wine and Church had a beer. The alcohol seemed a comfort in the face of the storm lashing the building, and after Laura had finished eating they moved closer to the fire which Simon had just loaded up with cracking and sputtering logs. The warmth and the drink made them feel a little easier, although they knew it was an illusion.

Eventually Church glanced up at Simon's stage, which now had a microphone, a monitor and a strange-looking machine. 'What *is* he planning?'

'Karaoke,' Laura replied distractedly. She was stabbing her boot on to one of the new logs in the fire to make sparks shoot up the chimney. 'That man is the definition of desperate. As if all the sheep-shaggers and inter-breeders of Dartmoor are going to come to his poxy pub to lose what little dignity they have by performing a Celine Dion cover.'

'You know you'll be up there with the best of them,' Ruth gently mocked.

'Yeah, like I'm so perverse I need to debase myself before lower life forms.'

They spent the next couple of hours drinking slowly, talking little, listening to the rain patter like ghostly fingers at the window and the wind moan in the chimney. They were as close to the fire as they could get to dispel the March chill; it made them feel secure, as it had done for travellers on such a night down the long years.

Much to their surprise, the drinkers continued to arrive in dribs and drabs until the pub was full. There were bedraggled old men in beaten windcheaters with rain in their beards and cheeks flushed from the wind as though they'd walked miles across the moor, young couples holding hands and laughing at every opportunity, husbands and wives in matching Barbours and wellies, with the occasional wet Labrador, sullen teenagers, women in pearls, men in dole-cheque faded shirts and patched trousers. The moment they entered, their shoulder muscles seemed to relax and their conversation sparkled. The mood was infectious and it wasn't long before Church, Ruth and Laura found their spirits rising. In the chatter and laughter of humanity, fired by beer and wine, it seemed possible to hold the darkness at bay.

As Simon collected glasses from a nearby table, he bent down near Laura and said, 'What's it like to be wrong, Missy Sharp Tongue?'

'It's a first for me. Give me some time to assimilate the experience.'

'You seem *very* experienced already,' he said pointedly, but beneath the mock-frostiness there was a certain regard.

When he'd gone, Ruth leaned over and said with a tight grin, 'Queens always like bitches, don't they?'

'Queens are renowned for having excellent taste, which is why he didn't waste any breath on you.'

The karaoke started soon after, with Simon taking the spotlight as if he was born to it. The regulars seemed to love him, and responded to his barbs with obviously well-repeated heckles, applauding his every tart comment, forcing him to be even more outrageous. There was no shortage of people ready to take the microphone, and while their voices were rarely good, they made up for it with the gusto of their performance. The most popular was a farmer with a red face and haystack grey hair who didn't appear ever to have crossed the borders of Devon, yet who managed a rendition of *Shaft* as if he'd been born in Brooklyn South. He finished with a clenched fist salute and a shout of 'Yo!' which brought a burst of feedback.

When he'd finished, Simon took the mike once more and said, 'We've got three guests in tonight and you know The Green Man tradition for newbies.'

A chant and a clap started as Church, Ruth and Laura looked around, taking a second or two to realise they were suddenly the centre of attention.

'You have *got* to be joking,' Laura protested.

Ruth hid her head in embarrassment. 'Oh God, I can't hold a tune!'

Church took a long drink of his beer and then made up his mind. 'Come on,' he said, standing up to a loud cheer. 'We've been entertained by them.'

Laura looked away uncomfortably, muttering something under her breath, but Church took her hand and her face lightened, although her expression remained grudging; she followed him to the stage like some spoilt child. Ruth trailed behind, her cheeks stinging pink.

As Church took the spotlight, he had a sudden flashback to the first gig he had ever done. It had been at Leeds University, in the Student Union, on a similarly rain-swept November night when only a few hardened drinkers had turned out. He'd always been a quiet, introspective person, but that began to change when he bought his first guitar. And that first time on stage had been an epiphany – after he had recovered from his terrifying stage fright, his shame about the vomit; heart pounding, nerves afire with adrenalin buzz, his conscious mind slipping away as he merged with the music, a bundle of notes dressed up as a scrawny kid with a too-big leather jacket. It wasn't an ego thing; it was the sense of giving, of being a part of something bigger, of feeling the music in his arteries. It was about celebrating life. He didn't attempt to make a career of it because he knew the joy of performing wasn't backed up with any ambition, and over time the purity of the experience would have been eroded.

But there on the little makeshift stage, even though he would only be singing, he felt it as acutely as that first time, and for one fleeting instant everything else in his life fell into relief: what was right and what was wrong, the terrible mistakes he was making and the path he knew he should be taking. And even as they selected their song and the first bars eased out of the speakers, he had the awful knowledge that the insight would be lost to him the moment he walked away from the stage.

There was no doubt in his mind when he saw the song in the list, but Laura jammed her fingers in her mouth and made vomit noises while Ruth rolled her eyes heavenwards. Their protests were only for his sake, though, and the moment he took the microphone, they slipped in close to him, his two backing singers. He glanced down at the monitor, but he knew the lyrics by heart:

Fly me to the moon
And let me play among the stars . . .

When he glanced back at Laura he saw she was maintaining her expression of sullen disinterest, but her eyes were sparkling with enjoyment; she looked away when she realised he'd glimpsed behind her façade. And Ruth made up for her technical flaws with a passion that surprised him. Soon she even had Laura performing a pastiche of a backing singers' dance while Church fell to his knees and hammed up his Sinatra impression.

At any other time they probably wouldn't have been able to do it, but the anxiety and the danger drove them to seek some kind of release in an act that was simple, mindless and fun, away from thoughts of black dogs, wild hunts, and the debilitating stress of fear. The crowd loved it. Each time Church executed a few steps, or skidded across the stage on his knees while holding the microphone stand across his chest, they cheered and applauded. Laura and Ruth found their own fans among many of the men who hollered out to them in the lulls between verse and chorus. While the music was playing, for the first time in weeks, everything was right.

The storm buffeted and howled against the walls, but within, with the fire roaring and the drink flowing, everyone felt secure. The singing continued until well after last orders, with few people drifting away early. But just before midnight Simon stepped on stage to draw the proceedings to a close with a cheery thank-you and a sharp putdown to the few grumblers who wanted to keep things going. Church could understand the feeling; he didn't want the night to end either.

'We could always stay here,' Laura said bluntly, as if she could read his thoughts. She tried to pass it off as sarcasm, but there was a brief flash of brittle vulnerability in her face before she stifled it.

As the drinkers filed out to the car park or prepared for the terrible journey on foot, the storm seemed to crash even louder overhead; it felt like the very walls were rattling with the thunder. Bursts of lightning flashed through the bottle-glass windows.

'I'll never be able to sleep in this,' Ruth said quietly. Then: 'Do you think one of us should keep watch?'

'Wouldn't hurt,' Church replied.

It sounded like the storm had come down right into the car park now. The noise was unbearable and, with the wind screaming, they could barely hear themselves talk. It seemed nearer to a hurricane than a gale.

In the glare of another flash of lightning, Ruth saw one of the drinkers run past the window. She flinched; her subconscious had caught some detail which jarred. The wind crashed against the door so hard she thought it was bursting inwards.

'We should start at first light,' Church was saying. 'It seems the only way. Travel by day, find somewhere secure to shelter by night.'

Laura swigged down the last of her wine. 'Bank vaults, that's what we need. Check ourselves into safe deposit boxes every night.'

Ruth tried to peer through the nearest window, but she was too far away to see anything. She returned her attention to the conversation, only to jump again at the next flash of lightning.

'What's wrong?' Church asked.

Her heart was beating double-time. Out of the corner of her eye she thought she'd seen a white face contorted with fear pressed up against the window, hands hammering to get in. There was nothing there now, but her heartbeat didn't subside.

Another clap of thunder burst overhead, followed by the shriek of the wind, which went on and on until they realised it wasn't the wind at all. As the gale died briefly, a keening cry of fear rang out. They jumped to their feet as one, suddenly noticing other sounds that the storm was masking: a peal of thunder that had a metallic rending beneath the bass echo, a clatter of hoofbeats merging with the spatter of rain at the window, another scream, definitely not the wind this time. They ran to the window and peered out.

Intermittent flashes of lightning revealed the scene in oddly frozen tableaux. The car park was a scene of carnage. People were frantically running for cover like frightened rabbits from a group of men on horseback who were filled with the dangerous majesty of the storm. At least Church thought they were men; their faces were swathed in shadows. They wore furs and armour like barbarians from the steppes and brandished long poles with cruel sickles at the end, which they used to herd and hook the terrified, fleeing people. And at their heart was one larger and more terrifying than all the others. Church knew he would see him in his nightmares for the rest of his life: the Erl-King.

Their horses' eyes glowed red, like the eyes of Black Shuck, and the breath vented from their nostrils in gusts of steaming vapour. And around their hooves ran a pack of alien dogs with strange red and white fur, long and lean, with glittering yellow eyes, harrying the prey with snapping jaws.

There was too much blood. Church, Ruth and Laura watched in horror as the strange sickle implements tore at flesh, severed joints, sliced into muscle. In each flash they could see more bodies piling up. One horse clattered on to the roof of a car, caving it in before smashing down on to the bonnet without losing its footing. A sickle ripped open a wing, flicked out a door, like it was gutting some beast. No one could escape the hunting men. Soon there would be no one left.

An exclamation made Church, Ruth and Laura turn. Simon was behind them, watching the monstrous butchery over their shoulders. 'My God! My God!' His voice rose to a whine of shock and horror. He grabbed Church's arm in desperation. 'What's going on?'

Church's head was spinning. He'd thought they could hide away. He should have known they wouldn't be allowed, and now others were paying the awful price for his mistake.

Simon ran around shrieking until Stuart emerged to see what was wrong. When he followed Simon's pointing to the window, he suddenly bolted towards the door. Church caught the movement out of the corner of his eye and intercepted him. 'Don't go out there,' he pleaded. 'You won't stand a chance.'

'But someone's got to help them!' he said desperately.

Simon was on his knees in front of the window, sobbing uncontrollably at the horror. 'What's happening?' he whined.

Church looked from Stuart to Simon and then at the others. 'We've got to do something,' he said hollowly. 'It's our fault.'

Laura glanced out at the wild scene; it made her think of a film she'd seen of piranhas feeding on a carcass. 'If we go out there, they'll kill us.'

There was a brief instant when they all felt ice in their hearts and then Ruth said bluntly, 'He's right.' There was no fear in her face; just a blind acceptance of their fate. 'It's our responsibility.'

Church nodded in agreement, but Laura whirled, her equanimity stripped away by fear. 'You're crazy! I'm not walking out there to be butchered!' She sucked in a deep gulp of air. 'We can't sacrifice ourselves! We're the only ones who can stop all this. We're important! That's what they all say, right?'

Church snatched up her hand; time was running out. 'We can't let those people die. I wouldn't be able to live with myself. And neither would you.' There was an instant when another outburst seemed likely, but then her face, her whole body sagged, as if his words had reached the rational part of her mind closed off by terror. With a despairing acceptance that pained Church, she pulled back her hand and turned away from him, saying nothing.

'We can still make this work,' Church said, turning to Ruth, the adrenalin suddenly thumping through his system. 'We split up. You and Laura run for the car. You've got the Stone. Try to get as far away from here as you can. I'll go in the other direction. I'm betting they'll follow me. In fact, I know they will.'

'You're crazy,' Laura muttered. 'You won't get twenty feet on foot. Look at those horses, you idiot.' There were tears in her eyes.

'I've got a bike out back,' Stuart interjected. 'A scrambler. It will get you over rough ground.' You ridden one before?'

'A long time ago.' Church glanced out of the window one final time and then he was racing off with Stuart.

They hauled the bike through in seconds. Church threw Ruth the car keys before he jumped on, fired it up and positioned it in front of the door.

The desperation in their shared glance masked their emotions, and then Ruth said quietly, 'You can count on us. Take care.'

Church smiled, lowered his head and nodded to Stuart. There was a freezing gust as the storm blasted in, then Church popped the clutch. He had to fight to keep it upright in the wind and for a second he thought he'd lost control as the bike bounced down the steps of the porch. But then he righted himself on the puddled road, snatched on the accelerator and roared off without glancing back.

He didn't need to check if the Huntsmen had seen him. From his back came a roar of jubilation that rose above the noise of the storm; the hunt was on. Hooves clattered like gunshots. The horses shrieked like banshees and the dogs howled as one, ready to be loosed on the prey.

Church was shaking with terror. The only conscious thoughts that flared in his mind were images of him being torn apart by savage jaws, but his motor instinct took over, guiding the scrambler along the road at full speed.

No horse should have been able to keep up with such a powerful bike, but he could hear the thunder of the hooves and the wild whoops of the riders drawing closer. He allowed himself one glance back, but the image of the Satanic Hunt bearing down on him was so terrible he knew he would not be able to look again.

He swung the bike off the road in the futile hope that the rough ground might slow the riders, but he knew in his heart it was only a matter of time. The wheels chewed up grass and mud as he roared out into the heart of the moor. While the storm whipped him from side to side, the bike sloughed around as it countered the dips and hollows that made the going so treacherous. Even with the headlamps on full beam, Church could barely see the outcroppings of rock which he knew could be the end of him.

The hollers and whoops of the riders became almost sounds of nature, caught on the wind, soaring up to the clouds, filled with the passion of the hunt, the lust for blood. And then, from the midst of them, came a low, mournful sound that seemed to suck all other noise out of the air. Church shivered. It was the hunting horn of the Erl-King.

Church gunned the bike over a rise so fast both wheels left the ground. Somehow he kept it upright when it landed. The countryside had grown even wilder, and just as he started to wonder how many miles he had put between himself and the pub, the ground suddenly disappeared beneath his feet and he was falling in darkness. He had only a few seconds to question what was happening as the engine roared out of control, and then his head hit something and he plunged into unconsciousness.

CHAPTER TEN

the hunt

Ruth and Laura choked back their emotions as they sprinted across The Green Man's car park, which now resembled an abattoir among the burning wreckage of several cars and a minibus. The few survivors were slowly beginning to stumble out from underneath vehicles or the deep shadows where they had been hiding, transformed by the shock and horror into scurrying animals, wide-eyed and dumb.

They were relieved to find the Nissan had not been harmed during the Hunt's attack. Ruth jumped into the driver's seat and sparked the ignition, releasing the clutch before Laura had time to settle in. She was thrown back into her seat as the tyres screamed and whirled on the spot, sloughing the car around the park before it roared on to the road.

'Yee haw,' Laura said mutedly.

Heading in the opposite direction to Church and the Hunt, Ruth found the road signposted for Buckfastleigh, ten miles away. She was surprised she didn't feel more scared. Instead, she felt a cold determination to do the right thing, and an awareness for the first time that what they had to achieve was more important than everything; even her own life.

She glanced secretively at Laura who was slumped silently, half-turned to look out of the passenger window. Ruth was surprised to see she wasn't taking it well at all. Her face was white and strained, turned even ghostlier by the bleached blondeness of her hair, and her cheeks were streaked with tears. A tremor ran through her body and Ruth noticed she had her hands tucked between her thighs to stop them shaking.

'We're going to get out of this,' Ruth said supportively.

'Sorry, you must be thinking I care about your opinions,' Laura replied without turning her head.

Ruth returned her attention to the dark road ahead; if Laura felt she was better internalising her fears, there was no point wasting her breath.

Two miles further on, Laura broke her silence. 'What's going to happen now?'

'We meet up with Church—'

184

'We're not going to meet up with Church, you stupid bitch. It was a suicide run. You know that.'

Ruth did know it, but she hadn't allowed herself to think about it. Now the idea that Church might be dead made her feel like she had a cold, hard rock lying on her chest. 'There still might be a chance. He said it himself: these days we live in a world where anything can happen.'

There was a hopeful hush and then Laura said, 'Okay. But say he *doesn't* make it back. What then?'

'Then we carry on with what we have to do. Find the remaining talismans—'

'Smart plan. Except for one thing. Church took the Wayfinder with him when he left. It was stuffed in his jacket.'

Ruth dropped her head briefly in despair. She couldn't believe how stupid they'd been. Without the lantern, they'd never find the talismans. And without the talismans, everything was lost.

'So we better hope he does get back to us,' Laura said emotionlessly.

For ten minutes they drove in silence, wondering how the fate of the world had come to be placed on their shoulders, filled with despair at the mess they had made of it, when Ruth said suddenly, 'I feel strange.'

'You've only just noticed?'

Ruth focused on the unnerving sensation which seemed to be buzzing underneath her skin. A second later she saw something red glowing nearby and froze in fear, instantly thinking it was the eye of some lurking beast. When she realised it was a vehicle's rear light she laughed nervously at how the mundane was now the last thing she considered.

A large white Transit van was pulled up on to the verge. One of the rear lights was broken and it seemed to have a flat; someone was hunkering down trying to change the wheel by torchlight in the driving rain.

Ruth's heart told her to stop to help, but her head warned her it was too much of a risk. But as she drove by, the buzzing under her skin grew unbearable, as if an infestation of insects were burrowing there; she could tell from Laura's sudden jerk and expression of discomfort that she was feeling it too. Then, without warning, the lights went off. Ruth slammed on the brakes, her heart pounding.

'What's going on?' Laura hissed fearfully.

The lights came on after a long beat, but just as Ruth was about to engage the gears once more, they flashed off and on five times in quick succession.

'The electrics are going crazy,' Laura said. 'Just drive. We can't risk sitting here. Or maybe I should get out and paint red and white circles on the roof?'

Something nagged at Ruth's mind. The headlights were fine now. She glanced in the rearview mirror to see whoever had been changing the tyre was now standing in the road, silhouetted against the van's lights, staring at them. All she could tell was that it was a man. She listened to the rhythmic clack of the windscreen wipers, hit the accelerator, but the car didn't move.

'Come on,' Laura said anxiously. 'You're too young to have Alzheimer's.'

'No,' Ruth said thoughtfully. 'There are new rules now. We have to start operating by them.'

'What do you mean?' Laura glanced over her shoulder to see if the van's driver was approaching. 'He's just standing there,' she said with obvious relief.

'Instinct. Coincidence,' Ruth continued. 'We have to listen to things talking to us.'

'What kind of things?'

'*Unseen* things.' She caught her breath, hoping she was right. 'That strange sensation we both felt – that was our instinct telling us to be aware, not to miss something important. And the lights. One long flash, five short. Not an accident. A message.'

'A message,' Laura repeated with a sneer. 'The car's talking to us. Shall we give it a name?'

'Not the car. Life. The world. Whatever makes all this tick. The player behind the scenes.' Thunder rumbled ominously and lightning danced across the horizon in a breathtaking light show that beat anything created by technology. This time Laura stared at her curiously, without mocking. 'There are supposed to be five of us who make a stand,' Ruth continued. 'Five who become one, something greater than the sum of the parts.' She turned to look at the figure in the road who was stock-still despite the storm, staring at their car.

Laura followed her gaze. 'Or he might just spout hair and fangs and tear us apart the moment we get out of the car.'

Ruth shivered; Laura had instantly lanced the doubts she had tried to put to one side. Every rational thought told her not to get out of the car; it was hard to fight years of conditioning for something so intangible as a whim.

'So do you have enough faith in yourself?' Laura said. 'Or is there still some sense in your head?'

'Look at him – he feels it too,' Ruth said, trying to convince herself.

'Or else he just smells meat.'

'Stop it.' Ruth rested her hand on the gear stick, tightened her grip. *Just drive,* she told herself. *Don't be crazy. Laura's right – you can't risk everything on a notion.*

She glanced back once more, then turned quickly and flung open the door. Laura's protests were lost as she threw herself out into the wind and rain, shielding her eyes with her arm. She took a few steps to the rear of the car. The man still wasn't moving.

'Do you need any help?' she called out.

In the long moment when she thought he wasn't going to answer, the anxiety returned in force. But just as she was on the verge of leaping back in the car and driving off, he called out, 'Please.'

Ruth steeled herself and walked forward as confidently as she could manage. With the storm raging around her, it was difficult to see or hear any warning signs; she would be close enough to grab by the time she knew if she had made the right decision.

Gradually his features coalesced out of the stark shadows and light thrown by the headlights. He was Asian, about 5 ft 10 ins, with shoulder-length black hair plastered to his head by the rain. As she closed on him, Ruth guessed he was probably of Indian blood; he had the most beautiful face she had seen on any man. His bone-structure was so finely cut, his eyes so wide and dark, his lips so full, that there was a hint of androgyny. When she was near enough he unveiled a smile of perfect white teeth which was so open she instantly felt at ease.

'Thank you,' he said in a soft, tranquil voice. 'On a night like this I would not expect anyone to stop to help.' He took her hand in both of his in greeting, as if she were a long lost friend; his fingers were long, slim and warm. 'My name is Shavi.'

Ruth introduced herself and Laura, who had just climbed out of the car, casting a suspicious glance in their direction. 'Let's get this tyre changed before we all catch pneumonia.'

As they eased the wheel off the axle, Ruth asked him what he was doing driving across the bleak moor in a terrible storm at that time of night. 'Searching,' he said enigmatically. There was a glimmer in his eye that made Ruth feel he knew everything going through her head.

Laura peered over their shoulders, her arms folded. 'So are you one of us?' she said bluntly.

Shavi flashed her another smile and Ruth was surprised to see a faint warm response on Laura's face. 'Perhaps,' he said.

'You're not going to wear out that word, are you?'

'What caused the broken light and the flat?' Ruth asked.

Shavi grunted as the wheel came free and rolled to one side. 'Something came across the road in front of me, fast, just a shadow. At first it was on four legs, then two, then four again. You know?' Anyone else wouldn't have understood the meaning of the question, but Ruth nodded; they had all seen the strange shapes lurking off in the dark country night. 'I felt the van hit it, but there was no body, no blood. Perhaps it was thrown off the road.'

Ruth and Laura both glanced off into the night uncomfortably. 'We should finish up here as quickly as we can,' Ruth said redundantly.

'I'll keep watch.' Laura scanned around, but it was hopeless; the night was so dark and the rain so heavy that they wouldn't see anything until it was upon them.

Although they tried to work fast, the cold drove the feeling from their fingers and the simple act of screwing on the wheelnuts became torturous; there was repeated scrabbling in icy pools under the van for ones that had been dropped. And the more anxious Ruth got about what might be prowling in the dark, the more clumsy she became. But finally, with all of them shivering and sodden, the wheel was changed and Shavi lowered the jack.

There was such a potent inner peace about Shavi that he looked almost beatific, soaked to the skin and battered by the wind. Ruth was convinced her instinct about him was right, but what could she say – *we're trying to stop the end of the world; want to come along for the ride*?

At that moment Laura suddenly tensed. She was peering back the way they had come.

'What is it?' Ruth asked.

'Can't you see it?' Laura's voice was almost lost in the wind.

And then she could. There was something moving on the horizon, roiling and churning as if the storm clouds were folding in upon themselves; it was flickeringly illuminated by an odd, inner light as if coloured lightning were crackling within it. The billowing clouds moved towards them. Ruth felt a cold that went beyond the chill of the rain.

'What is it?' Laura asked.

A second later they heard the sound that others could have mistaken for thunder: the clattering of iron-shod hooves. And then they saw the figures among those swirling clouds, lost then revealed, distant, but bearing down on them.

Ruth whirled and made to run towards the Nissan. 'We've got to move. We might still be able to—'

Shavi caught her arm and gently but forcibly held her back. 'Take the van with me. It is fast. Turbo-charged.'

Ruth glanced at Laura who nodded; there were flashes of wild fear in her eyes. Shavi leapt into the driver's seat and the engine roared into life while Laura hauled herself through the rear doors. The bag with the stone in never left her grasp. Ruth began to follow her, but then shouted, 'Wait!' She turned and ran for the Nissan. Shavi had pulled up beside her by the time she had found what she wanted and she jumped into the passenger seat.

'The water's warped your brain,' Laura said sharply. 'What are you doing?'

Ruth held up a handful of cassettes. 'Church's music. I didn't want to leave it there.'

Laura eyed her as if she was crazy, but she said nothing; they both knew why she had done it. It might be the only thing they had to remember him by.

And then Shavi slammed the van into gear, hit the accelerator and the van hurtled forward so fast Laura was thrown across the back amidst a hail of cursing. Ruth gripped for support as she was pressed into the seat. She glanced over at Shavi who was as placid as if he were out on a Sunday drive. *Of course*, Ruth thought. *He doesn't understand what's behind us.*

'You've got to keep your foot down,' she said. 'If we're caught, we're dead. Literally.'

'I know.' He flashed her a smile. 'What is it exactly?'

Laura scrambled to the rear doors and pressed her face against the window. 'They're getting closer.'

'Something that will tear us apart if it catches us.' She glanced at him, unsure. 'Something supernatural.'

He nodded as if what she had said was the most normal thing in the world. 'The van should be fast enough.'

The engine had the throaty rumble of a big cat and the acceleration was breathtaking, although the ride was as smooth as silk. But Ruth found it impossible to put her faith in anything technological after seeing science fail so easily.

'Worry more that we should run out of road,' Shavi said. 'Do you have any direction in mind?'

'Just keep driving until the sun comes up. The Hunt seem to go at first light.'

'Definition of an optimist,' Laura chimed from the back. 'Someone who thinks they can keep ahead of the Hounds of Hell for four or five hours with just a crappy van.'

'What would you rather we do? Throw ourselves to the dogs?' Ruth snapped. She looked back anxiously. The figures in the swirling clouds were more starkly defined now, the odd lighting diminishing as they moved closer. There was a flurry of movement around the horses' legs which Ruth guessed was the pack; distantly she could hear their howling breaking through the storm.

'I'm sorry you got dragged into this,' she said to Shavi.

He shook his head dismissively. 'I was meant to be here.'

Ruth eyed him curiously. 'Meant how?'

'I was guided here by my dreams.'

A snorting noise echoed from the back, followed by some muttering which Ruth couldn't decipher.

'All my life I have had vibrant, colourful dreams,' Shavi continued. 'Sometimes they were like trips. Certainly not like the kind of dreams other people told me about. I had no idea what they meant, but I always knew in my heart they meant *something*. And then, a few weeks ago, I began to have the same dream night after night. It was about a dragon, landing on the ground, becoming part of the ground, and lines of blue light spreading out from it in all directions. And then I was following one of the lines to the place where the sun sets. To a big moor.' There was a screech of tyres as the van slid around a sharp bend, which Shavi accelerated out of like a professional rally driver. 'Somehow I found myself on the road where we met and I knew at once it was the right place.'

'How did you know?'

'I just felt it.'

Ruth couldn't concentrate on talking further; her muscles felt like steel knots and her chest hurt from breathing too hard. Looking back once more, she saw the Hunt had drawn only slightly closer. The speedo said they were doing sixty-plus on the treacherous moorland road, which was a risk in itself, but if they could maintain that speed there was a chance they could keep ahead.

In the back, Laura attempted to hold herself fast, but the cornering was so intense she was bouncing off the walls, being slammed by Shavi's holdall, narrowly avoiding a sliding tool box; she was already covered in bruises and there was blood leaking into her left eye from a cut on her temple. But the pain was the least of the things concerning her. She couldn't believe how fearful she was becoming. Each glimpse of some terrible thing that shouldn't exist made it seem her life was spinning away from her, when she really needed to keep it under tight control. The only way she could deal with it was to damp it down into the hard, cold space deep inside her where she kept every other negative experience. Only that space was full to bursting and Laura knew it was just a matter of time before everything started to eat its way out.

'Where did you learn to drive?' she vented. 'Some school for the blind?' She slammed into another wall before rolling back, her head ringing.

Shavi apologised, but Ruth said, 'Ignore her. All she does is moan. Just focus on the driving.'

Somewhere along the way the road had dropped a grade. The straight-as-a-die, well-surfaced tarmac had given way to something that was little more than a country lane, throwing twists and turns so regularly they either had to cut their speed or risk a wipe-out. Shavi shifted gear rapidly, using them to complement the brakes, but they all knew he was living on borrowed time. On one corner, the nearside rear wheel skidded on to a grass verge, churning up mud and vegetation so violently they thought the tyre was going to burst or the van roll over. Although the storm seemed to be receding with the last flicker of lightning over Rippon Tor in the north, huge pools of water still covered the road at irregular intervals, threatening to throw the van into the moorland whenever it ploughed into them at speed.

'They've got closer,' Laura said as she managed to claw her way up to look through the rear windows once more. 'These country roads are slowing us down too much.'

'Yes, but what happens when we hit an urban area?' Ruth said. 'We can't keep going at this speed.'

'We will simply have to do the best we can,' Shavi said as he hunched over the wheel, trying to concentrate on the road; Ruth marvelled that there was still no strain showing on his face. 'We should avoid the smallest country roads, the bigger roads that might be too busy, the heavily built up areas where we could be stopped by traffic lights—'

Laura began to make some sneering comment, but Ruth threw herself round and glared at her. She turned back to Shavi. 'Just do what you have to.'

He pointed to a book of maps in the pocket on the door. 'Select a route.'

Anxiously Ruth riffled through the pages until she found the correct map. It was difficult to read when she was being thrown from side to side as the van rolled around the corners, but she eventually managed to focus on the broken capillaries of roads that filled the countryside between Buckfastleigh and the motorway at Exeter. 'We've got a choice: A38 or country lanes,' she said dispiritedly. Neither were right; one prone to obstructions and police patrols, the other too small.

Buckfastleigh slowed them down; the roads were narrow and even at that time of night they had to watch out for pedestrians and other vehicles. As they picked up the dual carriageway, the Hunt closed on them. Ruth wondered how it must have looked to anyone peeking out of their windows to investigate the noise; a van roaring way over the speed limit, being pursued by a nightmarish vision of riders in furs and armour surrounded by a pack of spectral hounds howling hellishly. No one would believe it, she thought; she barely did herself. It was only the fear, sharp like a knife, that made her aware it was bitter reality; that if the engine blew a gasket or the van clipped a kerb and ran out of control she would be torn apart by dogs that had no business existing.

At least the A38 was faster. They sped through Ashburton, feeling more positive that they at least stood a chance. 'We're not pulling away from them,' Laura said in one of her regular reports, 'but at least they're not getting any closer.'

But as they passed Bickington their hearts fell as they saw a red light glowing in the distance. Major road works blocked one carriageway where the dark hulk of a steamroller loomed.

'Change,' Shavi willed the light aloud.

'You can't stop,' Ruth said redundantly. 'They'll be on us in no time.'

'What's going on?' Laura called from the back.

Shavi and Ruth focused their attention on the light. 'On a busy road like this, there's bound to be something coming if we jump it,' she said.

'We have no choice,' Shavi said grimly.

When they reached the stop light, it still hadn't changed. Shavi pulled out without braking, put the lights on full beam and accelerated. Every muscle in Ruth's body was tense. They passed the steamroller. The other carriageway had been stripped of tarmac and was a mass of broken hardcore. They travelled fifty yards in a blur, but the end of the roadworks was still hidden around a bend. A second later the trees clustering around the road lit up from as-yet-unseen headlights.

She yelled in shock as the juggernaut hauled around the bend, but Shavi was already reacting. The trees on Shavi's side were too close; if he tried to pull off it would be the end of them. The lorry's horn blared a frantic warning. Even if Shavi hit the brakes, they wouldn't stop in time. Thoughts were piling up in Ruth's mind as the lorry bore down on them. She could see the animated, terrified face of the driver in the cab, flooded sickly white in their headlights as he waved his arm at them as if he were swatting away a wasp.

This is it, Ruth thought. She threw her arms across her face.

She didn't see what happened next, but she felt the surge of forces pulling at her body as Shavi dragged the wheel to one side. There was a rhythmic rumbling and the van bounced around crazily as it ploughed through the bollards. The screaming of the juggernaut's brakes merged with the strangled sounds coming from Ruth's throat, punctuated by Laura's yells. When they hit the hardcore Ruth waited for the tyres to burst, flinging the vehicle on a wild roll into the trees. But somehow they held. The van slewed crazily as Shavi fought to regain control, tipping up on two wheels before bouncing on to the other two. Shavi managed to keep it upright, but it spun round in an arc until it was facing in the opposite direction.

Ruth could barely bring herself to look. The muscles of her neck and shoulders ached from the strain of being thrown around. As she lowered her arms, she saw with horror that Shavi was slumped across the wheel, a trickle of blood running down his cheek. But then he sucked in a huge gulp of air and raised his head, his expression as calm as it had been when they met. When he flashed her a smile she almost cried.

The juggernaut had come to a rest across both carriageways. The driver was already clambering out of the cab, an expression of fury replacing one of relief.

But their attention was drawn past him to an eerie light in the sky just beyond the silhouetted bulk of the lorry. When Shavi scrambled to start the stalled vehicle, the engine rumbled without firing.

'Flooded,' he said.

The light in the sky was growing more intense as the Hunt neared, a swirling, uncomfortable mix of greens and reds. Ruth stared wide-eyed at Shavi's hand as he turned the ignition key again.

Laura hauled herself up between their seats. Her face was streaked with blood from numerous cuts and her skin was darkening in anticipation of several bruises. 'Good driving,' she said sardonically.

As the juggernaut driver marched towards them angrily, Ruth realised she ought to call out a warning. She was too late. Transfixed, she watched the Hunt rise up above the lorry in all its awful majesty. The horses were black and sleek with sweat, but they were like no horses she had seen before: larger, more muscular, there was something almost serpentine about them; their eyes glowed as red as coals in the gloom. The riders exuded power from their large frames, but their faces were still hidden in shadow. At the head of them was the Erl-King, wearing a helmet made from the bleached bones of their prey. As they moved over the lorry, the roof of the vehicle was torn apart by their cruel weapons, showering shards of metal over a wide area as if a grenade had exploded.

The driver whirled, seeing the Hunt for the first time, and as he did so, the strange red and white dogs surged over the top of his rig. Snapping and whirling in a way that made Ruth think they were one creature, they speedily hurtled towards their target. In horror, she saw him start to run one way, then another, and then scream in fear, and then the dogs were upon him, their needle-sharp teeth rending and tearing; his frail human body was dismantled in seconds as a red mist filled the air.

Finally the engine fired and caught. Shavi popped the clutch and hauled the van back on the road, the tyres complaining loudly, but miraculously holding. As they sped past the other end of the roadworks, the silence in the van was palpable; they were jointly overcome with loathing at what had happened to the driver – another death they could mark up to their actions – and a sodden feeling that their situation was hopeless. They had lost too much time. Ruth didn't have to turn to ask Laura how they were doing; she could hear the thunder of hooves drowning out even the sound of the engine.

Shavi put his foot to the floor as often as he could, but there were too many twists and turns along the road, forcing him to brake sharply then accelerate again, and on several occasions he had to put their lives on the line to overtake cars that were already speeding. Ruth was relieved the Wild Hunt paid the other travellers no heed this time, but it was a small success as the riders spurred on their mounts to close on the van.

The villages went by in a blur: Coldeast, Heathfield, Chudleigh Knighton; when they saw the sign for the motorway just four miles away they had a brief moment of hope. It was killed in the instant it was born by a startled cry from Laura. The stink of horses, musky and oppressive, had grown stronger, even through the door and over the exhaust fumes, and it had prompted her to peer once more out of the rear windows.

The Hunt was almost within reach of the van. Laura could see the muscles rippling on the arms of the riders, the delicate ornamentation on the clasps and buckles which held their furs tight, the shining leather and metal of the bridles, and then she made the mistake of looking into their faces. They were all terrible in aspect, but the worst was the Erl-King leading the charge. His face seemed to have exposed bone breaking through on the cheeks, brow and jaw, so that when the streetlights caught him it glistened like a death-mask. And where there was skin, it had the faintest green hue and appeared to be scaled like a lizard. But it was the eyes that made her sick and terrified. Red-rimmed beneath a lowering brow, they glowed with an inner yellow light, the pupils slashed like a serpent. When he saw her frozen stare, he grinned malevolently, revealing a menacing row of stained, pointed teeth. Laura had a sudden vision of herself as a terrified rabbit before a predator and then she thrust herself backwards as the Erl-King lashed out with the spear-sickle.

There was a deafening rending as it shredded the door like paper, and then, with a tremendous heave, he tore it from its hinges. It flew up high and landed with a crash far behind them. The van was filled with the searing sound of the road and the horses. Too frightened to speak, Laura scrabbled backwards until her back pressed into Ruth's seat. Ruth's hand snaked down and caught hers, holding it firmly, squeezing for comfort; Laura squeezed back.

Framed in the hole where the door had been, the Wild Hunt drew ever closer. Ruth thought she was going to be sick when she looked at them – it was as if she was queasily drunk and everything was distorted – and she couldn't bear to look into their faces, although she was sure they were mouthing hypnotic words that hissed in the back of her head: to give herself up, to throw herself to the pack. She placed her hands on her ears and yelled.

Shavi looked at her with concern. 'We are nearly there.'

The dual carriageway gave way to the motorway outside Exeter just as the other rear door was torn free. Laura's nails were biting into Ruth's hands so hard they drew blood. With the extra lane, the traffic thinned enough for Shavi to slam his foot on to the accelerator. The turbo kicked in, propelling the van forward violently until they were hitting 85 m.p.h.

'We're doing it!' Laura gasped. The Hunt had dropped back several yards and were falling further behind as Shavi continued to accelerate. Cars swerved to avoid them as the horses pounded along the motorway, the hounds spreading out to fill all three lanes. A Lotus ploughed into the central reservation, showering sparks, glass and metal up into the air.

'God,' Ruth whispered hoarsely, looking at the vehicles driving ahead of them. 'Have we consigned all these poor bastards to death?'

'Casualties of war,' Laura said.

'I wish I could be that cold.'

'Better get used to it.' Laura tapped Shavi on the shoulder. 'Have we got enough petrol, hero?'

There was a long silence before he replied, 'Let us hope.'

'Great.' Laura's hand went limp and slipped out of Ruth's grip. 'Knock me down when I'm on a high, why don't you?'

'I am not saying we have not . . .' His voice trailed off.

'Just put some miles between us.'

The Hunt was a half-mile behind now, but they all knew the distance would be covered in no time if they had to stop. Secretly, they each checked their watch, wishing dawn upon them.

They lost sight of the Hunt somewhere past Bristol, but although his eyes were tired and burning, Shavi continued to drive. And when first light broke Ruth found herself crying uncontrollably, making no attempt to hide her tears. If Laura saw, she said nothing. They pulled off the motorway at the first junction and sat quietly watching the dark sky turn purple then gold and finally powder blue. It was going to be a fine day.

Ruth was the first one to see the owl hovering over a field nearby. When she'd finally recovered enough to talk, she convinced the others to follow it, without giving them any explanation; none of them questioned her anyway. Slowly it began to head back south at the side of the motorway. Laura took over from Shavi at the wheel, allowing him and Ruth to sleep if they wanted, although neither of them felt able. And at Junction 23 the owl veered off to the east. Half an hour later they found themselves at Glastonbury.

CHAPTER ELEVEN

Away from the Light

The first thing Church sensed as he surfaced from a world of tormented images was a miasma of aches and pains that made him agonisingly aware of what seemed like every nerve in his body. He felt like he'd been thrown down a flight of concrete stairs. Then came the odours: dank air, stale and unpleasant, mildew, straw, the musky stink of animals, and beneath it all the sickening smell of an open sewer. Dully, he forced himself to open his eyes, then realised they *were* open; the place was so dark he seemed to be drifting in space. And then the sensations came thick and fast: the sound of dripping water creating echoes that testified to some kind of confined space with bare, hard walls; nausea; a burning sensation in his arms, which were hauled up above his head. He yanked at them and heard the clang of metal on rock. Chains. Manacles around his wrists, biting into the flesh. Panic swept through him as he desperately fought to recall where he was and what was happening to him. Slowly chunks of memory floated up like wreckage bobbing to the surface of a stormy sea. The Wild Hunt. The race across the moor. That awful awareness that his life was on the brink of being snuffed out. And then . . . what? A brief sensation of falling.

The cotton wool that clogged his head gradually began to clear. He must have tumbled into some kind of shaft. He knew the moor was littered with all sorts of old mine workings, but he was sure a fall of that kind would have killed him. And then how did he end up wherever he was?

At least he was alive. With a twist of anxiety he prayed Ruth and Laura had got away too. Cautiously he stretched various muscles to try and ease some of the tension in his hanging body, but the stabbing pain that followed made him stop with a groan. The fall might not have killed him, but it felt like it had been close to it. He sucked in a deep breath and that was a mistake too; fire spread out across his ribcage. He prayed it was just bad bruising and not broken ribs.

When the agony subsided, he listened for any sign of his captors, but it was as still as the grave. Steeling himself for further pain, Church checked the chains, but they seemed solid; he wouldn't be able to pull them out of the wall, even if he were fit. Morosely he leaned back against the wall and desperately tried to think of a way out of his predicament.

The total darkness tricked his mind into hallucinating that he was floating, and in that strange state he lost all track of time as his thoughts constantly drifted in and out of daydreams. For a while he thought Marianne was there with him. He could smell her perfume, hear the soft whisper of her voice on the periphery of his senses; once he thought he saw her, pale and disturbing like the time she had come to him at Stonehenge.

'Don't worry,' he muttered. 'Soon I'm going to find out why you did it. And I'll make amends to you somehow for whatever I did. Then I can die in peace.'

She didn't reply, if she was there at all, and then his thoughts tumbled back into darkness.

Sometime later he was startled out of his deeply drifting thoughts by the noise of heavy footsteps and a muffled, hectoring voice that sounded agitated. They drew closer until a door opened, and although the light without was only a lantern, it was so blinding after the dark that Church wrenched his head away. But in that briefest instant, he got a sense of his surroundings. He was in a place which seemed to have been cut from the bedrock. A low ceiling hung only a few inches above his head and straw had been scattered across the ground. A row of rusty bars lay a few feet away; beyond them was a small passageway, before more bars for another cell which was still swathed in shadows. He heard laboured breathing and smelled the animal stink of a Night Walker. He closed his eyes so he wouldn't have to see it.

'Who's that?' The voice made him jump and for a second he did look, before screwing his eyes shut again. A man was being hauled into his cell. Church heard the jangle of the door opening and the man protesting before he was shackled to the wall. He spat noisily – obviously at his captor – and an instant later there was the sound of something heavy striking him, then silence. Church heard shuffling, sensed a disturbing presence hovering over him. It made a guttural noise deep in its throat and then moved off, pausing briefly to do something in the passageway. Church waited until he heard the main door close before looking round.

A lantern had been hung on the wall outside his cell, its flickering light casting bizarre, distorted shadows around the rough room. The man hanging from the wall nearby was around thirty, with straight, dark brown hair that fell around his slumped head. He was goodlooking, with a square jaw and sharp cheekbones, but there was a granite hardness in his features that suggested a tough upbringing. The most striking thing about him was the mass of tattoos that covered his naked, muscular torso, a swirling, iridescent panorama of odd pictures, strange images and symbols which Church had never seen before, but which affected him deeply on some subterranean level. At that distance, and in the gloom, it was impossible to make out the detail, but the more he looked, the more he felt even the pictures were speaking to his subconscious, stimulating half-remembered memories, faded dreams. In the end, he had to force himself to look away.

Church was thankful for the light, but its illumination didn't provide him with much hope. Even if he could get out of the manacles, there was no chance he would be able to break through the iron bars, and even then he would have to face whatever lurked without. But he refused to give in to despair and he steeled himself until his fellow prisoner recovered from the blow.

On awakening, his companion shook his head a few times as if being buzzed by an angry wasp and then he cursed under his breath. Looking round sullenly, he spied Church, remembering him from before the blow. 'Who the hell are you?' he asked a little suspiciously, in the hard tones of working class south-east London.

'Jack Churchill. Who the hell are you?'

Silence. Then: 'Ryan Veitch.' He continued to look around furtively. 'They pick you up too?'

Church shrugged. 'Can't remember. I was riding across the moor on a bike and fell down some kind of hole. Where is this place?'

'Some abandoned mine. The place is swarming with them.' Veitch yanked at his chain angrily, but it held fast. 'Bastards.' He took a deep breath, then said, 'What are they?'

'Our worst nightmares.' Now it was Church's turn to be suspicious. 'You seem to be taking this pretty well, being confronted by something that shouldn't exist.'

'I've had plenty of time to get used to it, haven't I? About a bleedin' week since the bastards dragged me down here. I was hitchin' across the moor. The first time I saw them I threw up, then blacked out. I tell you, it was a stomach-full, projectile. The second time wasn't so bad. Half a stomach and three hours unconscious. Now I've just about got used to them, and that's a horrible bleedin' thought in itself.'

'Even so,' Church pressed, 'you're pretty much on top of it.'

Veitch hung his head so his hair obscured his face. Church thought he was being cold-shouldered, but his companion was obviously thinking, for a moment later he looked up and said bluntly, 'I've been dreaming about these sorts of things all my life. It's like I knew they were out there. The biggest surprise was that I wasn't surprised when I saw them. It was almost like I expected to meet them.'

'Dreams?' Church felt a tingle of recognition.

'Yeah. You see these tattoos? They're my dreams. When I was a kid they used to make me miserable. I couldn't get them out of my head. I screwed up school, had trouble making friends, couldn't keep any bird on the go for too long – anti-social tendencies, they said. Attention deficit. Half a dozen other excuses. But it was the bastard dreams. I think I'd probably have topped myself by now if I hadn't found some way to get them out of my head.' He nodded to the tattoos. 'Every time one came into my head and wouldn't leave I went to this place in Greenwich and had a picture of it done somewhere or other. That night it'd be gone. I tell you, this body is a picture book of my screwed-up head.'

Church peered hard through the gloom and saw what seemed to be a tower floating in space. 'I had dreams too,' he began. 'Nothing like yours, but—'

Veitch flashed him a strange, intense look that stopped him dead. 'Dragons?' Veitch said, his eyes searching Church's face. 'Brother of Dragons?' Church nodded. 'Those words've been doin' my head in for weeks now. Just floating there. In fire, on a black background. What do they mean?'

Church shrugged.

Veitch looked truly disconcerted. 'I jacked in my job to come here. Didn't mind that too much. Renovating houses near the Dome for some tight landlord to make a mint on. I just thought I'd get some bleedin' answers—'

'But what made you come here?'

'A little bird told me.' His crooked grin was enigmatic but disarming.

'What do you mean?'

'I thought it was a dream at first, but now I'm not so sure. Some Judy turned up in my room one night and told me to head out west if I wanted to find what I'd spent all my life looking for.' He laughed sourly.

A shiver ran through Church's body. Cautiously he described the woman he had met in the Watchtower. 'Yeah, that's the one,' Veitch said. 'So she *is* real. How'd she get in my gaff then?'

Before Church could answer there came a sound like a tolling bell, echoing dully through the walls from somewhere distant. The reverberations continued for a full minute and then slowly died away, leaving a strange, tense atmosphere.

'What's that about?' Church asked.

Veitch looked uncomfortable. 'Something's going on down here. I've seen things. There's a big cave full of oil drums. Some other place that looks like a church, only not one you've ever seen before. And those things . . . what do you call them?'

'The woman in the Watchtower called them Night Walkers. God knows what they really are.'

'Right. Well, I don't know what they're eating, but I've seen bones . . .' His voice trailed off; Church didn't press him further.

They fell silent for a while, then Church asked, 'So how did you see the place? They don't let you out for a walk, I presume.'

'Every now and then they take me out for a good kicking. My exercise, I suppose. Beats walking round in circles.' He winced, then masked it with a smile. 'It's like they expect me to tell them something. They keep grunting at me in those gorilla-voices, but I can't understand a bleedin' word they're saying. Not very bloody smart, are they?' A shadow passed across his face and he added, 'There's one of them who can speak English, though. He's scary. Doesn't look like the others. He's almost . . . beautiful.' The word seemed to catch in his teeth. 'Until you look in his eyes. The others make me feel like my head's bein' pulled inside out, but he's scary in a different way.' Veitch glanced at Church curiously. 'If he talks to you, just give him what he wants, all right?'

At that moment, the lantern guttered and died.

In the dark it seemed harder to talk. But the bond Church felt with Veitch was unmistakable, even though it was operating on some deeply subconscious level; they were both Brothers of Dragons, after all.

Their distracted, mumbled conversation turned to the past. Veitch told of his childhood in south-east London, the youngest of six children struggling in a household where their mother had died when he was just a baby. His father had fallen to pieces in the aftermath and the boys had been left to keep the household running, cooking and cleaning, trying to scrape together a meagre living in any way possible. Now three of his brothers were in prison, one for drug dealing, the other two for a bungled armed raid on a building society in Kilburn. Veitch's life sounded harrowing, punctuated by brutal explosions of mindless violence, but he had a tremendous affection for his home and upbringing which Church found incongruous. The hardness of his environment had shaped his character into what seemed a mixture of knotted muscle and scar tissue, but beneath it Church sensed a basic decency with which he could connect. He could do worse than having someone like Veitch along for the ride – if they ever got out of there.

For his part, he told Veitch very little about himself – even in those extreme circumstances he couldn't bypass his overwhelming need for privacy – but he did fill him in on everything that had happened to them since that night beneath Albert Bridge.

As they began to exchange theories about what was really going on, the sound of heavy footsteps echoed loudly once again and then the door was flung roughly open. Church snapped his eyelids shut as the silhouette appeared in the doorway, his gorge rising even at that brief glimpse. The beast's voice was guttural, vibrating on bass notes so low Church could sense them in the pit of his stomach rather than hear them; the tone was insistent and grew noticeably angrier as the cell was opened. Church felt the presence approach him like a cold shadow until he caught that deep, nauseating stench. Crushing, bony fingers snapped around his jaw, digging into the soft flesh of his cheeks until they burned like hot pokers and slowly Church's head was forced round. The pressure was so great he felt his face was on the verge of disintegrating; he had no choice but to open his eyes.

He looked into deepset eyes with red slit pupils, something that could have been scales or a hideous skin deformity, monstrous bone formations, but the overwhelming terror he felt didn't come from the hellish appearance; in some uncanny way it was like he was looking deep within the creature, and what he saw there was too terrible to bear.

His mind screamed for an instant and then flickered out.

Church woke on the floor in the stinking straw, vomit splattered all around. His wrists ached as if they had been plugged with nails, but the sudden knowledge that he was no longer manacled came like a reviving draught. Although his head thundered, he sat bolt upright and glanced hastily around, ready to dart for any opening that presented itself.

'Save it.' Veitch sat in the corner, spooning something grey and watery from a rough wooden bowl. 'The cage is still locked – there's no way out.' He slurped the soup and grimaced. 'Now I know how those people in the plane crash in the Andes could eat their dead mates. You'll force down any old shit if you're hungry enough.'

Church noticed another bowl nearby. 'What is it?'

'Don't know. Don't want to know. Don't even want to think about it, so don't mention it again.'

Church slid over and picked up the spoon and bowl, his stomach contracting with hunger. Circles of translucent grease floated on the top of the grey liquid; the smell was like sour milk. Dunking the spoon in, he swirled it around, but there was no substance in it at all. He half-raised the spoon to his mouth, thought for a moment, then let it drop. 'Obviously I'm not hungry enough.'

'You will be, mate,' Veitch said ominously. He drained the bowl and threw it to one side in the straw.

'I don't intend being in here that long.'

'What's your plan?'

'I'll know it when I see it.'

Veitch laughed. 'Bleedin' hell! An optimist!'

Church hauled himself to his feet and tested the cell door. The bars were iron, solid and unshakable, the lock enormous, looking impossible to pick, even if he had the faintest idea how to go about it.

'I haven't worked out yet if this is the larder,' Veitch said darkly.

Church followed the bars along to where they were held fast in the slick, living rock. 'That might be the end of the line, but right now we're too important to be an appetiser. We're the key to stopping them and they know that. I think they're a little scared of us. Well, not of us exactly, but of what we represent, what we can do.'

'And what's that exactly?' Veitch tried to mask his incredulity, but it broke through nonetheless. Church wasn't offended; he knew exactly how Veitch felt. He lived a normal life, thought normal thoughts; there was nothing that set him apart from the ordinary. The suggestion that he was destined to become some kind of hero of mythic proportions, foretold in prophecies millennia ago, diverged from his own reality so much that it seemed laughable. But all the evidence seemed to be guiding him in that direction: the magical coincidences, the dreams, the talk of *Brothers of Dragons* which suggested some aspect of him that he hadn't seen.

'*Brothers of Dragons*,' he muttered.

'What is it? Like the Masons?'

'I think it's a catch-all for five of us who are supposed to come together *in Britain's darkest hour*. Or, more rightly, something that binds us together.' He cast his mind back to the carnage on the M4 and told Veitch about their encounter with the Fabulous Beast.

'Maybe it means we can talk to them, like Doctor bleedin' Doolittle.'

Church rested his back against the hard bars and slid to the ground. 'I think it's something more symbolic. The dragons are linked to the earth energy, the magic that we were shown at Stonehenge. They feed off it, swim in it, follow it. I can't explain it, but the energy seemed to be a part of nature. Almost a living part.'

'Its blood.'

'In a way. And dragons have always been used to represent the power in the earth, going back to the ancient Chinese. Maybe it means we're supposed to be defenders of that energy. No, of the planet itself. We're the brothers of the dragon-energy, the blood of the world.' Church surprised himself by his logical progression; even in that environment he was still capable of it.

'That's a big job,' Veitch said dismissively. 'Don't you think they'd have chosen somebody up to it?'

'I don't think choice came into it,' Church replied. 'I think this was something laid out years ago, long before any of us were born. The onus is on us to live up to that responsibility.'

'And here we are stuck in a bleedin' hole in the ground, waiting to die. I can't stand it in here!' he yelled as the repressed anger at his captivity finally bubbled to the surface. 'You bastards!'

Church was shocked to see the rage transform his face; there was so much of it within him, so close to the surface, that Church knew he was dangerous. 'Calm down,' he said. 'You don't want to bring them in here.'

But it was too late. The noise coming towards the door suggested several beasts were on their way. Church moved to a corner, bowing his head so he wouldn't have to look into their faces. When the door burst open with a crash, Veitch cursed quietly under his breath. There was something almost terrified in that small sound and Church couldn't help a brief glance up. Several of the creatures hung back in the shadows, but Church was shocked to see the one at the front was not monstrous. He presumed it was the one Veitch had mentioned before, for his face would have been beautiful if it had not been spoiled by a veneer of cruelty. Church forced himself to focus on the strange creature so he did not have to look into the terrible faces of the others: his skin was faintly golden, his face oval and delicate. The eyes were almost like a cat's, with purple irises, and his silver hair was long and lustrous; there was something about him which reminded Church vaguely of the woman in the Watchtower. And where the other beasts had bodies which were huge, misshapen and filled with an inhuman power, his was almost weak and effeminate, slim-hipped, small-waisted, with thin legs and arms that hung loosely from his joints. But although he didn't resemble them, the foul animal stink that came off him still marked him out as one of them. He wore what appeared to be a silk blouson and strange, heavily stained breeches, like some pastiche of a human. For the briefest instant, Church thought he was no threat, but then his eyes came back to the creature's face and he felt a chill run through him.

Slowly the visitor turned towards Veitch and said softly and with a faint sibilance, 'You are making too much noise again, little dear.'

Church expected Veitch to unleash some of his pent-up fury, but instead he simply looked away.

The creature turned his attention back to Church. 'My name is Calatin. Among the tribes so many tales had been told about you, Brother of Dragons, or, as you are known to us, *Arith Urkolim*.'

Church felt a sudden *frisson*. That was the same phrase the creature at Heston Services had used when it had tried to abduct Ruth.

'So many prophecies and portents delivered by our fathers' fathers' fathers, but here before me you are diminished. I see you are as weak and frail as all your kind.' He stroked his chin elegantly with a long, slim finger that ended in a dirty, broken nail. 'A cautionary tale about the validity of myths.'

Church couldn't understand the disparity in appearance nor his grasp of English when the others had only ever spoken in that incomprehensible mix of shrieks and roars.

Calatin moved forward until the reek of him was almost overpowering. 'All that energy expended in clearing you from the board. The Fabulous Beast, I must admit, was draining in the extreme to bridle. They are so independent, it takes an exhaustive ritual to direct the will necessary to control them. And the Wild Hunt demanded a price that was almost too high to pay. But pay it we did. And then you deliver yourself to our door.' He shook his head in mock disbelief. 'I still cannot decide which would have been the best outcome for you. To be cut down by the Hunt, brutal but mercifully swift. Or to end up here, with us.' He smiled coldly.

Church's head buzzed; Calatin seemed to be radiating some kind of energy field that made him uncomfortable. 'And now you have me the Hunt can go back to wherever it came from?' He hoped Calatin didn't recognise his concern for Ruth and Laura.

'Oh, there is no way to call off the Hunt until they have been sated,' Calatin replied with obvious cruelty. 'Wild magic, once unleashed, cannot be controlled.'

'But—'

'And now we have to decide what to do with you,' Calatin continued. 'There are those who feel your head will provide powerful magic if it is built into the walls of our citadel once all our plans have been achieved. Others believe a choice meal of your brains would allow your prowess, however well hidden it might be, to be passed on to the Cadrii, our greatest warriors. We can afford to take our time in deciding. In the meanwhile, there are certain matters which need to be resolved.'

He nodded, and the others moved out of the shadows to grasp Church's arms. He tried to hide from their faces, but it was impossible and within a second or two he plunged into unconsciousness once more.

The smell of some indescribable meat cooking to the point of burning filled his nose. Wherever he was, the suffocating heat was so over-powering Church almost blacked out again the moment he regained consciousness. Leather straps held him fast to some rough wooden bench, but he could lift his head enough to look around, and instantly wished he hadn't. The room had been hacked out of the bedrock like his cell, and was lit by a red glow that emanated from a furnace roaring away in one corner. One of the hideous creatures tended it with his back to Church, moving what looked like blacksmith's tools around in the blazing scarlet heart of the fire. In another corner a large black cauldron boiled away over an open fire. It was stained by thick, brown juice which slopped over the side with each viscous, bursting bubble and it was from here the heavy meat smell emanated. Next to it was a heavily discoloured bench with a variety of cleavers embedded in it, obviously where whatever food was in the cauldron had been prepared. His eyes were drawn back to the cauldron by something he hadn't first noticed. Church squinted, then looked away in disgust from the torso and head hooked over one side by a trailing arm.

Fighting back the nausea, he continued to scan the room as best he could. It quickly became apparent what its use was. Various torture instruments he had only ever seen on display in mediaeval castles hung in the half-light between the outer shadows and the furnace's ruddy glow: an iron cage, a large studded wheel, a rack of cruelly tipped tools whose uses he could only guess at, a curtain of hooked chains that hung from the ceiling, and more that he couldn't bring himself to examine.

Before his terror had chance to take root, a heavy door in front of him ground open, framing Calatin and two other beasts in the outer light. Although Church couldn't bear to look at them, he didn't feel so close to blacking out; he could only imagine he was growing numb to their horrors which upset him more than he could have believed.

Calatin glanced at him in a manner that suggested Church was almost beneath his notice before turning his attention to the creature at the furnace. They spoke briefly in that yelping, bizarre language, and from the body language and tone Church guessed Calatin was in some position of power. But as he advanced, Church saw he was shaking as if he had an ague and his face had the drawn, wearied expression of someone battling against illness. When he reached the table where Church was strapped, Calatin allowed himself one brief look which was filled with such contempt it was as if all the sourness brought on by that inner struggle had been flushed out in Church's direction.

'What now?' Church said. The two words were all he could manage without the knot of fear in his stomach breaking his voice and cracking the mask he had drawn on to protect his dignity; he had to fight to prevent his eyes being drawn to the cruel tools hanging on the wall, to prevent the images of blood and suffering flooding his mind. But deep inside him there was a place that the fear couldn't reach, where he was calmly aware of his responsibilities and of keeping his humanity intact in the face of an evil that wanted to see it broken and debased. The essence of the hero he had denied was in there too, and it startled him to recognize it, as if someone had shone a searchlight to reveal a new, pristine room in his flat.

Calatin ignored his question. He turned sharply and summoned one of the creatures who had accompanied him. The beast was carrying one of the tools he had selected from the rack, a long, sharp spike like a knitting needle which ended with a short corkscrew. Compared with the other implements on show, it was one of the mildest, but Church knew it was only the start.

'We have the Wayfinder,' Calatin began in a whining, reedy voice. 'I am astonished you would allow such a valuable and powerful tool to slip so easily from your grasp. And now you have frittered it away as if it meant no more to you than a passing fancy.'

Church stared him in the eye, but said nothing. Calatin's words were too close to the bone.

'We cannot use it, nor bear too long to be in its presence, but with it secured here your feeble compatriots should be blind to the locations of the Quadrillax,' Calatin continued. He sucked in a deep breath and said, 'We know you have the stone. Where is it?'

Church looked at him, straight through him, preparing his mind for what lay ahead.

The pain that lanced through his leg was excrutiating, and although he had hoped he could survive a while without calling out, it was impossible; his yell burned his throat. The beast removed the blood-stained corkscrew from Church's thigh and held it up so the scarlet droplets splattered his shirt. Church could feel his jeans growing wet around his wound.

'I know you're going to kill me,' he gasped, 'so there's no point me telling you anything.'

'It will be many days before we kill you, and plenty of roads of pain to explore before then.' Calatin leaned over until Church could smell the foul reek of his breath. 'But this is the beginning and all roads lead from here. I will ask you again: where is the stone?'

Church closed his eyes, muttered a prayer, and then screamed and screamed.

Calatin's voice floated to him through the waves of pain, fading in and out with the susurration of the tides.

'. . . citadels are hidden in the dark places beneath the earth. We are scattered to the four winds. No point on this island is free from us. And we wait and we wait, for we have waited for so long, until the stars are aligned, the seasons are ready, until the gates fall open for ever and we can see to eternity. The end . . .'

Fading in and fading out. Calatin standing nearby, talking as if to himself, his eyes fixed firmly on some inner horizon, painting a picture of future terror.

'. . . your land will be transformed. The eternal night will be drawn across the fields and hills, the moors and rivers, and not even the brightest light will pierce the gloom. Blood will flow through the streets of your cities like rivers and we will have fresh meat on our plates at every meal. Madness will strike you down when you look upon the face of the returned ones and know no prayer will deter them, no god will be listening. Your voice will have no authority in the face of powers you thought impossible. Your people will be herded, screaming, desperate, alone . . .'

Darkness and pain. Hiding in the hole of his head, digging down deep until he could find that spot where the hero lay sleeping, waiting to be wakened to defend the island once more. But the road to the cave was long and filled with unquiet spirits. Marianne was there, repeatedly. She blew him a kiss as she jumped off the tube on her way to her interview in Wardour Street. She paddled in the warm waters of Ganavan, splashing him with her feet before they rushed to the dunes to make love. And she stood on the deck of a boat as the rising sun painted the Thames red, offering a kiss that transformed his life. Then she was speaking the words of the young Marianne, about life and death, the two of them merging into one. Here there was meaning and that gave him the strength to continue.

He awoke on the straw of the cell once more, his body afire with agony, his clothes soaked with blood.

'I thought you were dead,' Veitch's voice floated over him. He tried to speak, but the words were strangled in his throat. Rough hands grabbed his head and levered it up so he could take some stagnant water on his tongue from a wooden bowl. Veitch's face fell in and out of focus, concerned, yet also filled with the fear of his own memories. 'You look like shit. And I thought I had it bad when that bastard got me in his little playpen.' He heaped some straw with one hand, then lowered Church's head gently on to it. 'If it's any consolation, I don't think you told them anything. He was in a foul mood when they threw you in here. You're a better man than me. I'd have given up my nan if they'd asked me.'

Church closed his eyes and felt a wave of relief settle through him like mist. He feared he might have said something and forgotten it in his pain-induced delirium, but he had come through. Ironically, the suffering had driven him so far inside himself he had found what he had been looking for all along: the sleeping hero. And now he *did* feel different: stronger, more confident, less concerned by the petty fears and mundane terrors which had been undermining him for so long. Not even the thought of more torture could bring him down. He felt reborn.

'We find strength in hardship,' he croaked deliriously. Veitch saw the smile on his face and asked him if he were going mad from the pain, but Church was already drifting off into a recuperative sleep.

He didn't know how long he had been out, but he felt much better when the sound of the door disturbed him. He managed to lever himself on to his side to see two shadowy forms dragging what appeared to be a shapeless sack before throwing it into the other cell. When they had left he watched it closer. After a while it moved, then groaned.

'Are you okay?' His voice still sounded tissue-paper thin.

There was silence for a minute, and then the new arrival pulled himself weakly across the floor and used the bars to haul himself into a half-sitting, half-leaning position. In the flickering torchlight, Church saw an old man, his face haggard from suffering, his grey hair dirty and matted. He looked about a hundred. But then, gradually, Church saw through the mask crafted by pain and a wave of horror swept over him.

'Tom?' he hissed. Nearby, Veitch stirred and looked up.

The man looked across at Church, his piercing grey eyes now dull and flat. 'I never thought they would do it.' His voice was frailer than Church's, rustling on the edge of hearing, so weak it seemed he was only a step away from death. 'The old ways do not matter to them any more. They are so sure of their power, of victory, they feel able to ignore everything that has been established. I never thought . . .'

Veitch knelt down next to Church. 'Who's that?'

Church explained briefly, then said to Tom, 'Did Calatin do this to you?'

'He wanted to know if the others still had the power without you.' Tom's Scottish brogue was stronger in his weakness. He sucked in a deep, juddering breath and seemed to find a little strength from somewhere. 'They don't want to divert their attention from whatever it is they are doing, but they know you are all a threat.'

'What are they doing?'

Tom shook his head. 'Waiting. Making preparations.'

'Can the others stop them without me?' He glanced at Veitch. 'And Ryan?'

Tom seemed to see Church's cellmate for the first time. 'I don't know. I know some things, enough to help, but not everything. The legends of the Brothers and Sisters of Dragons have always talked about them as a unit, greater than the sum of its parts. The power you represent is heightened and focused when you are all brought together. Individually, you have some particular strengths, but—'

'Not enough,' Church finished bleakly.

Somewhere far off through the rock the tolling bell started once again, striking its long dismal notes that seemed to mark the end of them all.

The blast in Salisbury had left Tom weak and disoriented. As he staggered around attempting to find Ruth, the few remaining creatures had attacked him mercilessly. And when he came around, he was in the dark and in the hands of Calatin. The tortures inflicted on him had been intense. It seemed the Night Walkers' plan was in effect, but many elements were finely balanced and the timing was crucial; they could not afford any disruption. Although their infiltration of society was overwhelming, it appeared they feared Church and the others intensely; or rather, feared what Church and the others could do if they were allowed to reach their potential.

'But did you find out anything we could use?' Church said hopelessly.

'I do not know. It is so hard to remember.' Tom seemed disoriented, older than his years. Tenderly he touched the side of his head, where Church could make out the dark smear of encrusted blood.

'Are you okay?' Church enquired; it seemed a serious wound. Tom didn't seem to want to talk about it so Church pressed him again for information. 'At Stonehenge it was obvious you knew more than you were saying. You've got to tell me everything, Tom.'

'Sometimes there's so much in my head,' he said deliriously. 'All those years of thoughts piling up . . .' Suddenly he seemed to lock on to a random memory. 'Do you want to know how it started?'

'Yes, I'd like that.'

'No, not how it really started. No one knows that. But how it started here. I can tell you that.'

'Go on.'

Tom shifted awkwardly until he found himself a relatively comfortable position. 'You're an educated man. You know about the Celtic myth cycle?'

'A little. Some reading at university—'

'That's where it began. The secret history, locked in a few stories and passed down the years so mankind would never forget the suffering and the terror.'

Church struggled to remember, but it had seemed such an insignificant part of his studies that the details had not remained. 'There was the Tuatha Dé Danann,' he began hesitantly.

'The name the Celts gave to them. The people of the Goddess Dana, the last generation of gods to rule before mankind's ascendence. When they arrived in our world, they brought with them great knowledge and magic from four marvellous cities – Falias, Gorias, Finias and Murias – as well as four talismans: the Stone of Fal, which screamed aloud when touched by the rightful king; the Sword of Nuada, their High King, which inflicted only fatal blows; the Spear of Lugh, the sun god; and above all else, the Cauldron of Dagda, the Allfather of the gods, source of life and death and healing.'

'Yes! Those are the things we're searching for—'

'People have always been searching for them. No one ever finds them.'

'But we have to. To free the . . . the Golden Ones.' He told Tom about the woman in the Watchtower.

Tom snorted. 'She is of the Danann. Of course she wants her people freed. But to find the talismans . . . They are more than they appear to be to human eyes, powerful symbols that . . .' His voice trailed off. 'Listen to me. These gods and everything they deal with are so alien they are unknowable. Their appearances, their motivations . . . the best our minds can do is give them some shape that's recognisable to us. Some are closer to us, like the woman you encountered between the worlds. Some are so incomprehensible we cannot even begin to give them form.'

'The creatures here—?'

Tom nodded. 'Too terrible for your mind to bear, but it can be taught to give them shape. The Celts called them the Fomorii.

Misshapen, violent, they were supposed to have come from the waters to invade this world. They were, to all intents and purposes, the manifestation of evil, a corruption, perhaps, or an infestation. The embodiment of negativity, constantly striving to drag the cosmos into chaos and darkness. And they were led by the most devastating, destructive force of all – the Celts called him Balor, the one-eyed god of death. The legends claimed he was so dreadful that whoever he turned his eye upon was destroyed.'

Tom's description was so desolate Church felt a blanket of hopelessness descend on him. He couldn't tell if Veitch felt it too; his head was lowered, his expression hidden by his hair.

'The Fomorii came like a tidal wave,' Tom continued. 'The Tuatha Dé Danann were unprepared. They were enslaved and the Fomorii established a reign of terror that became known as the Eternal Night.'

'But the Danann struck back.' Church recalled the woman in the Watchtower's account. 'They had the power to defeat the Fomorii.'

Tom nodded. 'The war leader Nuada led the Danann in a counter-strike, but he seemed doomed to defeat until he was joined by Lugh, the sun god, who was part Fomorii. In the stories, his grandfather was Balor. At the second battle of Magh Tuireadh, Lugh plunged his spear into Balor's eye, killing him instantly. The Fomorii were demoralised; the Danann easily regained power. But there had been too much destruction and suffering – even for gods – for things to return to the way they had been before. To preserve some kind of order, a truce was reached – the Covenant. Both the Danann and the Fomorii would leave earth to man and return for ever to the Danann homeland which the Celts called Otherworld. And they took with them almost every magical creature, everything which couldn't abide by the strict laws that would remain in their passing. That exodus was known as the Sundering and it was the end of the Age of Wonders, known also as the Age of Terror.'

'You're just talking about bleedin' stories!' Veitch said with exasperation.

Tom closed his eyes and laid his head back wearily. 'The stories can only begin to hint at the truths of those days – they are coded messages from the distant past. There have been other legends in other cultures attempting to make sense of what happened, but the Celts came the closest in their descriptions, which is why they have been the most enduring. The stories are confused – the gods were given different names by the different Celtic tribes across Europe – but in essence they were all talking about the same thing.'

'So they left us behind for good—'

'Not wholly. The boundaries between Otherworld and here were supposed to be sealed, but there were weak spots, the mounds, the lakes and rivers – the liminal zones.' Tom's voice continually faded away, then grew stronger, so Church had to strain to hear what he was saying. 'Some of the gods crossed back over for brief excursions or exerted their influence from Otherworld. Some of the magical creatures too. And sometimes people from here found their way over there.'

'I remember now,' Church interjected. 'The Celtic gods slowly metamorphosed into our faery myths and Otherworld became Faeryland. The keepers of treasure and secrets, mischiefmakers—'

'Mischief!' Church was taken aback by the venom in Tom's voice. 'They interfered with us down the years, tormenting people, tricking people. Yes, sometimes it was just lights in the sky, strange sightings of lake monsters, nocturnal manifestations. And sometimes it was slaughter.'

'That's all very interesting,' Veitch said sarcastically, 'but it doesn't exactly help us, does it?'

'Any information helps you,' Tom replied.

'It tells us the Danann have defeated the Fomorii before and they can do it again,' Church said. 'It tells us there's hope.'

'It doesn't tell us how to get out of this bleedin' cage!'

'You could have mentioned all this before,' Church said sharply.

'I could have.'

'How do you know all this? Did the Bone Inspector tell you?'

'Some of it.' There was a long silence in which he seemed to be wrestling with his thoughts, and then he said, 'I have been to Otherworld.'

Church at first wondered if it were some kind of stupid attempt at humour, but he had never heard Tom joke before. 'You're lying.'

He sighed. 'I never lie.'

'Then how?'

'Through one of those weak spots I mentioned. In Scotland, on a hillside.'

Veitch seemed excited by this turn in the conversation. He crawled to the front of the cage and gripped the bars. 'What was it like?'

'So many wonders.' Tom's voice was oddly strained. 'I was changed, immeasurably. I learned things there, wisdom, certain skills, the ability to manipulate subtle energies—'

'Magic,' Church said.

'If you like. Though I'm not adept, I achieve some little things.'

'Like getting us out of here?' Veitch said hopefully.

Tom shook his head and they all fell silent for a long minute.

'You're not lying to us?' Church stressed.

'I said, I never lie.'

Veitch hammered a fist against the bars angrily, then crawled back to the corner of the cage.

'Then you know at first hand what all these so-called gods can do,' Church continued. 'Is there hope?'

'There's always hope.'

'What about Calatin and the Fomorii?'

'The Fomorii are a race made up of tribes, some large, some small, all vying for power. Since Balor died they have been on the verge of civil war. Although Calatin is the nominal leader, his halfbreed status has not endeared him to the others. But that's by the by. Their return to our world has reunited them to a degree, but the power struggle has simply moved into the background.' He coughed fitfully, then spat through the bars. 'You and the others are a fine trophy, the symbol of everything the Fomorii wish to eradicate. Whomsoever holds you captive, or eliminates you, is advanced in the eyes of all the tribes.'

'What are you saying?' Church gripped the bars to lever himself up; although the pain had receded a little, he felt like nails were being driven into his flesh.

'Were you to escape,' Tom continued weakly, 'there would be others at your back apart from Calatin. He is dangerous . . .' He paused, moistened his lips. 'But there is one much worse. He controls dark power to a degree which Calatin can only dream of, but it has consumed him physically. Now his presence can only be contained by a murder of crows, swirling tightly together in a proscribed pattern that prevents his life energy seeping out. His name is Mollecht.'

Church remembered the description the Bone Inspector had given of their pursuers at Avebury. 'So Calatin set the Fabulous Beast and the Wild Hunt after us, but this Mollecht is hunting us too?'

'Christ, it sounds like we're wasting our time,' Veitch groaned.

'No,' Church said adamantly. 'If we can get out of here and find the four talismans by Beltane then we can free the Danann—'

'Beltane?' Veitch looked at Church in bafflement.

'May Day.'

'Shit.' He slumped down in the straw, his head in his hands.

'—and they can do all the dirty work for us,' Church finished, ignoring Veitch's despondency.

'Best be careful what you wish for,' Tom croaked. His head was nodding; he was on the verge of either sleeping or blacking out.

'Tom!' Church called. 'Stay focused. We need some answers. You've been out of this cell a lot. Did you see any chance of a way out of here?'

There was a long pause, then: 'No. No way out.'

Occasionally noises would filter through the walls, their source impossible to discern, but disturbing nonetheless; Church tried his best to ignore them. Instead, he turned his thoughts to Tom and his outrageous assertion that he had visited the home of the gods. Church had noticed a single expression that had convinced him; it was so fleeting, it had probably only been there for an instant, but it had been so stark and filled with terror Church had almost flinched.

He and Veitch spent what seemed like hours turning over every possibility that might lead to escape, but their talk only increased their sense of hopelessness. Yet as they crawled off to their separate corners to sleep, Church's mind was still turning, refusing to give up. Whatever had been released from deep within during his agonies on the torture table still fired him, refusing to allow him to drift into despair.

He awoke suddenly, aware that there was someone standing near him. With a start, he threw himself up and back against the cold, slick stone wall, ready to defend himself. But instead of a threat, there was a moment of shock while he struggled to comprehend what he was actually seeing. Before him, wrapped in a thick, dark green cloak with a hood thrown over her head, was the woman from the Watchtower. She raised a hand quickly to silence him before he could cry out. Quickly he glanced around to get his bearings; both Veitch and Tom appeared to be sleeping.

'How did you get in here?' he hissed.

Her face peered from the dark depths of her hood, pale and beautiful like the moon. 'I am here to help,' she said in that soft, musical voice that had so entranced him before. 'I am your patron, Jack. I am guiding you to a greater destiny. In the current climate, it is dangerous for me to leave the Watchtower, but you need my aid to leave this foul place. Do you know what the Night Walkers plan to do with you?'

'I can guess.'

'No,' she said darkly, 'you cannot. It was foolish of you to allow yourself to fall into their hands.' There was an edge to her voice he hadn't heard before; it suggested darker emotions lying just beneath the surface. 'It was even more foolish to let them take hold of the Way-finder. You must not leave here without it. Should they ever utilise the secrets it represents, it would be the end of everything. Do you understand?'

Church nodded dumbly.

Gold flecks flickered in the depths of her eyes. 'When next you try the cell door, it will be open. And all the doors before you this night will be open. That is my help, the rest you must do yourself. You are a Brother of Dragons, and perhaps you need to earn that title for yourself.'

'Deus ex machina,' he muttered.

She held up a hand sharply. 'Do not disappoint my faith in you again.' Her cloak seemed to shimmer and then fold in on itself. There was the strange sucking noise he had first heard outside the Salisbury depot as the air collapsed, and then she was gone.

Church stared blankly into the vacated space, trying to come to terms with what he had heard, and then he launched himself across the cell. His rough shaking woke Veitch, but Church didn't wait to explain. He was already at the cell door, almost afraid to try it, but it swung open with a loud creak at just the touch of a finger.

'How'd you manage that?' Veitch said incredulously.

'I'll tell you later.' Church propelled himself across the gap to Tom's cell; the door opened just as easily. It was a little harder to stir the exhausted man, who was mumbling and twitching in the throes of nightmare. Up close Church could see the bloody scar on Tom's temple; he wondered how much damage had been done to him.

Veitch helped Church get him to his feet, but it didn't take Tom long to fight through his daze. He seemed sharper than the last time they had spoken. 'Stop manhandling me!' he snapped. They let him go, and although he wavered slightly, he seemed able to walk unaccompanied. Cautiously they pulled open the main door.

The corridor without was shored up by rough timbers in parts. It was lit intermittently by torches, but the gloom was pervasive. As they moved out, anxiously glancing around, they became aware of vile smells awash in the air, the foetid stink of the Fomorii, the dampness of the underground atmosphere, and beneath it all the stench of cooking that Church had experienced in the torture chamber.

Their bodies were clenched, their eyes darting anxiously; Church didn't think he had ever felt so much fearful apprehension. It seemed it would only be a matter of time before they stumbled across one of the dark creatures, but the winding corridors were as silent as the grave, almost as if the Fomorii had deserted the mine.

When they reached a junction in the tunnels, Tom paused to lean against the wall. Church thought he was fading again, but Tom waved him away furiously when he went to help. Eventually he pointed along the tunnel which sloped deeper into the ground. 'That way.'

Veitch glanced in the opposite direction. 'You sure? It looks—'

'That way,' Tom snapped. 'We cannot leave until we have the Wayfinder.'

Church concurred, then led the way along the tunnel which grew steeper and steeper with each step. Soon they were almost slipping and sliding down an incline, desperately trying not to make any noise, but the sound of their shoes on the rough surface echoed crazily. The tunnel came to an abrupt halt in a cavern so large the roof was lost in shadows. After the grey and black of the corridors, Church was shocked to see the gleaming, manmade yellow of the drums he had first come across at the depot in Salisbury; they were piled across the expanse of the cavern.

Alarm bells started ringing in Church's mind. 'What's going on?' he whispered. 'I thought this chemical delivery was just a front for whatever the Fomorii were doing in Salisbury.'

'They are not chemicals,' Tom said darkly. 'Not in any sense you mean.'

Veitch prised off the lid of one of the drums and peered inside, snatching his head back suddenly as the foul stink of the contents hit him. 'Shit! That's bleedin' disgusting!' he hissed. Inside a viscous black solution like crude oil reflected their faces.

'What is it then?' Church searched Tom's face for any sign.

'A ritual potion of some kind.'

Church looked around dumbly at the stacked drums. 'What could they use all this for? And why are they transporting it?'

Veitch cocked his head and listened carefully. 'We can't hang around here gassing all day. Let's sort this out later. Where do we find that Wayfinder thing?'

Tom pointed across the cavern. 'Over there somewhere.'

Veitch shook his head. 'If you say so, mate. Lead the way.'

Their footsteps echoed hollowly off the stacks of drums as they wove their way among them; it almost seemed like they were in a maze. At any moment he expected the Fomorii to fall upon them from all directions. But though he strained to hear a sound, there was nothing, and that was just as unnerving.

It took them fifteen minutes to reach the other side, tension growing with every step. Tom led them to an upward-sloping tunnel, and five minutes later they came upon a rough-hewn door. There was a large padlock on it, but when Church touched it, it fell open in his hands and the door swung in. It led on to a small room cast in blue from the flickering flame of the Wayfinder, which stood on a bench against the far wall. Next to it, on a velvet cloth, was the Black Rose, and beside that was a handgun and some boxes of ammunition. Church stepped in ahead of the others, snatched up the rose and slipped it into his pocket.

'What was that?' Tom asked.

'Just something they took from me when I got here,' Church said dismissively. He examined the Wayfinder carefully and then hid it under his jacket.

'Is that what everybody's so worked up about?' Veitch said. 'A bleedin' lantern?' He picked up the gun and slugs.

Church eyed him suspiciously. 'Are those yours?'

Veitch shrugged. 'For self-defence.'

They hurried back into the tunnel, but Church felt increasingly uncomfortable. 'This doesn't make any sense. Surely they wouldn't leave the Wayfinder here without any guards if it's supposed to be so important to them.'

'Perhaps they didn't expect us to be wandering freely out of our cells,' Tom said sarcastically.

'Even so—' Before he could finish his sentence, the mine reverberated with the chilling sound of the tolling bell they had heard before. It seemed close at hand, but still muffled, as if behind thick walls of stone.

'Shit,' Veitch muttered. His face looked drained of blood in the flickering torchlight.

'Which way?' Church prompted. Tom was expressionless; Veitch merely shrugged. On a hunch, Church left them and sprinted back down the tunnel to the cavern. Through the gloom on the other side, he could see movement. It was hard to make out at first, just oddly shifting patterns of shadows like running water in the dark, but as his eyes focused he had the disturbing impression of insects swarming from a nest, an impossible multitude sweeping out amongst the yellow drums. The image was almost hypnotic, but it filled him with dread. He sprinted back up the tunnel, not even pausing as he reached the other two. 'This way,' he yelled as he passed.

The tunnels were low, dark and slick, and numerous times they slipped or cracked their heads against low roofs, but they were driven on by the noise growing behind them; it sounded at first like the low, deep rasp of an enormous beast, then it began to fragment into a mix of individual sounds, of rumbling, bestial voices and thundering feet.

Their breath burned in their throats and sweat stung their eyes, but they knew they couldn't slow for a moment. The tunnel rose upwards relentlessly, but Church couldn't shake the terrible feeling that it would suddenly start dipping down again, leaving them nowhere to run but round in circles. As they passed another junction, Church felt a blast of chill air. Scrambling to a halt, he herded the others up the branch tunnel. A minute later they hit a dead end.

'Shit!' Veitch's eyes blazed like a cornered animal.

The thunderous sound of pursuit was growing louder; the Fomorii couldn't be far off the tunnel junction.

'Up,' Church gasped; it was all he could force out.

Veitch and Tom raised their heads, but all they could see was darkness. Then another gust of fresh air hit them in their faces and they realised what he meant. Fastened to one wall was a rusty iron ladder. Although Church wasn't convinced it would hold, he forced Tom up first and then Veitch made him follow before taking up the rear. Tom was starting to fade, but Church egged him on insistently. The ladder was cold and wet to the touch and once or twice Church's foot slipped off it, almost hitting Veitch in the face; a flurry of cursing followed. Their muscles ached almost too much to hold on, but the threat of what lay below was enough to free any last reserves of strength they had. It wasn't long until they felt the vibrations in the ladder that signalled the Fomorii were behind them.

Church was just beginning to fear that the climb was too high for them when Tom suddenly hauled himself over the top. Church launched himself out, rolling on to scrubby grass and Dartmoor granite. It was night, cold but clear, the sky sprinkled with stars. Veitch landed on top of him, winding him.

'They're right behind,' Church gasped unnecessarily. 'We'll never get away—'

'Give me a hand.' Veitch was at the shaft entrance. For a second, Church couldn't understand what he was doing, but then it clicked. Together they gripped the top of the ladder and strained. Church thought he could see movement in the dark just below and wondered briefly if they had made the right decision. But then there was a deep rending noise as the rusty supports pulled free from the wall of the shaft. The weight of whatever was ascending continued the movement and with a loud crash the ladder tore away and plummeted into the depths.

Veitch clapped Church on the shoulder jubilantly. 'Bloody hell. We did it!'

But Tom was insisting there was no time for celebration, and soon they were stumbling across the moorland in the moonlight.

The land rose and fell, but they kept to the hollows, crawling on their bellies when they had to mount a ridge, and eventually they made their way to a windswept copse which allowed them some shelter. Church leaned against a tree and looked back, but he could see no indication of pursuit. Suddenly Church was filled with all the pain and exhaustion inflicted upon him by Calatin's torture. It had somehow been suppressed by the urgency of their flight. As he began to pitch forward, Veitch caught him and supported him to the ground.

They allowed themselves only ten minutes to rest, just in case, then Church pulled out the Wayfinder and, with Veitch's help, he wearily began to follow its flame westwards across the moor.

CHAPTER TWELVE

Mi Vida Loca

Sunlight drenched the streets of Glastonbury and the air was filled with the sweet aroma of honeysuckle and lemon. The sky overhead had been as blue as the brightest summer day since Ruth, Laura and Shavi had nursed the van into town, shattered by the rigours of their pursuit by the Wild Hunt. The temperature had remained unseasonably balmy, without the briefest hint of rain or a chill on the wind.

'It doesn't seem right,' Ruth said, trying on the cheap sunglasses she had bought after browsing in the proliferation of New Age shops. She glanced up, trying to reconcile the weather with the time of year.

'Don't knock it.' Laura was impassive behind her own sunglasses.

'It's more than just the weather,' Ruth continued. 'There's something in the air. Can't you feel it?'

'Peace,' Shavi interjected.

'For the first time since we set off from London, I feel safe. It's like there's a bubble over the place, protecting it from everything that's out there. Smell all those scents! There doesn't seem to be any pollution at all. And the air almost seems to . . . sparkle? Like there's gold dust in it.'

The mood was reflected in the open, smiling faces of the people who passed by, nodding to the three of them as if they had always lived there. The residents moved slowly, lazily, gazing into the shop windows, ambling across the road, heedless of the slow-moving traffic.

'Glastonbury has always been seen as one of the most magically powerful places in the country,' Shavi noted. 'For hundreds, perhaps thousands of years, people have been drawn here by the supposed power in the land. Celts and Christians, hippies and New Age Travellers. It is supposed to be on one of the longest ley lines in the country, running from St Michael's Mount in Cornwall, through Glastonbury, Avebury and on across the country to East Anglia.'

'You seem to know a lot about all this.'

He smiled curiously. 'When I was six years old I had a map on my wall with all the ley lines drawn on in red felt tip. When I was ten I had read every book ever written about the subject, from Alfred Watkins' *The Old Straight Track* to the latest scholarly journal. I branched out from that into reading about Buddhism, Taoism, Islam. In my head it all seemed linked.' He shrugged. 'Where does all that come from in a child?' He already seemed to know the answer to his question.

Ruth had a sudden sense of great wisdom in his eyes. 'So you think there's something in all this ley line stuff?' she ventured.

'There are plenty of people ready to pour scorn on it, as there are for anything which is difficult to categorise, compartmentalise, measure and define. But you have seen the blue fire.' Ruth nodded. She remembered the look of almost childlike wonder on his face when she described it to him as they dropped off the van at the garage for repairs. 'If only I could have seen it too,' he continued dreamily.

'You will. The visible evidence of it is all part of this new age, so it seems.'

'Did you know,' he said thoughtfully, 'that ley is an old Anglo-Saxon word, but it has an older, obsolete meaning, of *flame* or *fire*? Our ancient peoples knew more than we give them credit for. Interestingly, there is also a well-established ley linking Stonehenge and Glastonbury—'

'Yes, very interesting,' Laura interjected, 'now how about getting some food? At least with a full stomach I can sleep through all your ramblings.'

Ruth refrained from making any comment; there was plenty of time for Shavi to reach his own judgment about Laura.

They had pitched camp in a copse on the outskirts, but they needn't have worried about secrecy. They had been discovered by the farmer who owned the land within the hour, but he cheerily wished them well and continued on his way. The feel of the sun on their faces was a relief after the endless storm and the terrifying night and they had lain outside their new tents against a fallen tree, trying to come to terms with what had happened. It soon became apparent they had no idea what they were going to do next. Ruth wanted to head back to Dartmoor to search for Church, but while Laura didn't want to abandon him, she felt it was both futile and dangerous. Ruth tried to call the pub from her mobile, but the line was dead. In the end, they resolved to rest a while in Glastonbury while they recovered, hoping that some plan would present itself to them.

They wandered around until they found a café, the Excalibur, where Shavi and Laura had the vegetarian option of tomatoes on toast and Ruth opted for bacon and eggs. They felt more refreshed than they had any right to; whatever strange atmosphere now permeated

Glastonbury seemed to be healing both their psychological scars and their exhaustion.

Afterwards, they dozed for a while in the sun, catching up on the previous night's deprivation, and then they explored the town, drinking in the unique atmosphere of ancient history that seemed to permeate every street. It didn't take Ruth and Laura long to get to know Shavi. He was unguarded in a way few others were, answering every question they had for him without a hint of embarrassment or reticence; his openness seemed to make Laura particularly uneasy, and she spent the first two hours trying to catch him out, to prove he was lying to them.

He was brought up in a tight-knit family in west London, and although his father had adopted most western ways since he came to the UK to study medicine in his twenties, Shavi had still had a strict upbringing when it came to the traditions and religion of his family. Shavi's interests had soon taken him well away from his heritage, throwing him into conflict with his father almost daily. As he progressed into his teens, his father's fury at his rebellious ways had threatened the stability of the family and, once he turned sixteen, he was forced to leave home.

Ruth was aghast at the blasé way he mentioned such a period of upheaval. 'Didn't it bother you at all?' she asked.

'I shed tears for my family every day,' he replied, 'but what could I do? Remain in a life I had no empathy for, pretending to be someone else? The only option was to be true to myself, whatever price I had to pay.'

His life after leaving his family seemed to have been an odd mix of hedonism and spiritual questing. He freely acknowledged experimenting with various drugs, and, at Laura's prompting, admitted a healthy sex life fired by curiosity. Yet at the same time he had an insatiable thirst for knowledge, particularly of a spiritual and philosophical kind. 'If I indulged in self-analysis I would admit to trying to fill some kind of void,' he said, 'but it is more important to me to follow my instincts to see where they take me.'

Laura was curious about a small scar above his top lip, the only blemish on his perfect features; they were both surprised at the downcast expression her question elicited.

'It happened two years ago. I was with a boy in a club in Clapham,' he began. 'The Two Brewers. It was quite renowned in London as one of the top gay clubs—'

'You're gay?' Ruth instantly regretted her exclamation; it sounded faintly bigoted, the way she said it, although she certainly hadn't meant it that way. 'It's just, you don't seem gay.'

'I put no boundaries around my life. I have had men and I have had women.' He smiled forgivingly. 'Anyway, the Two Brewers had a reputation as the kind of place you could go without encountering any of the trouble you would find in the more unenlightened parts of the capital. The boy I was with – Lee was his name – had been a very close friend for many years. We had a good night, got a little high, plenty of dancing. When we left in the early hours we thought we'd go for a walk on Clapham Common to look at the stars. It was a beautiful night. We were walking down one of the side streets towards the common when the mood took us to stop and kiss.' He closed his eyes, remembering; at first his face was tranquil, but then a shadow flickered across it. 'Somebody hit me, hard.' He tapped the scar. 'I think it was a gun, or perhaps a piece of piping – it is very hard to remember. I think I blacked out for a while. When I came to, Lee was struggling with someone further down the street. I called out, tried to get to him, but I was so dazed.'

When he opened his eyes, they were wet, but he made no attempt to hide the emotion. 'My vision was fractured – I had concussion – but I could see the man attacking Lee. He was swinging something down on his head. The crack sounded like a piece of wood snapping in two. But even then he did not stop. He kept hitting, and hitting.' He closed his eyes once more. 'Lee died. His murderer got away. I cannot even remember what he looked like.'

'I'm so sorry.' Ruth rested a comforting hand on his forearm.

Laura was just as moved by the story. 'What a homophobic bastard! If I found out who it was, I'd cut off his dick and shove it down his throat.'

Shavi raised his hands and shrugged. 'I have done my best not to let it scar me emotionally as well as physically, but it has been difficult. I try to tell myself there is enough hatred in the world without me adding to it.'

His honesty created a bond with them both; it was impossible not to trust him completely. Ruth found herself almost hypnotised by him. His voice was so calm, it made her feel tranquil, and his eyes were both mischievous and intensely sexual. His body had a graceful power, like a ballet dancer, compact, with muscles she had not expected to see in someone so cerebral. She had watched him performing his t'ai chi after they had awoken from their nap and she had almost cried to see him so at peace with himself. She was glad he was with them.

Despite herself, Laura felt the same way. Shavi's confidence in his abilities and direction in life was reassuring to someone who felt as if her own existence had been spinning off its axis for most of her adult life. In the disparate crew so far assembled, Shavi felt like the cement that would hold them all together. It gave her secret hope that it might, after all, turn out okay.

'We need to get you some clothes,' Church noted as they rested in the wan sunlight on the lea of an outcropping of grey Dartmoor granite. He felt much better. Tom had found some foul-tasting roots and leaves which had taken the edge off much of the pain and tiredness he had felt following his ordeal in Calatin's torture chamber. Ahead of them, a large fox picked its way cautiously across the scrubland, its russet fur a splash of colour against the grubby green. Church had a sudden flashback to the one he had seen in the street near Albert Bridge on the night his life changed for ever. Oddly, he did not have the same sense of wonder.

'No hurry. It's not like it's winter.' Veitch did seem oblivious to the elements, despite his naked torso. In daylight, Church couldn't stop looking at the startling, colourful pictures tattooed on his flesh. Some were scenes of remarkable beauty, but others were almost too disturbing to consider: deformed faces that looked out at the viewer with a palpable sense of threat; odd, surreal shapes that seemed alien and unrecognisable, but touched disturbing notes in his subconscious; creatures that seemed half-animal, half-human.

Tom scanned the sky thoughtfully where a little blue was breaking through the heavy cloud. 'The weather should be fine,' he noted almost to himself before adding to the others, 'It will make travel a little easier. We may have a long way to go before we can rest.'

'We need to find Ruth and Laura.' Church fought back any thoughts suggesting they might not have survived the raid on the pub.

'Have you not learned anything yet?' Tom glared at Church through his spectacles, which, against all the odds, he had somehow managed to hang on to throughout the time in the mine. 'Time is of the essence! Your world is winding down and you want to dally searching for your friends? You are Brothers and Sisters of Dragons. You will find each other when the time is right.'

Veitch bristled at the man's tone. 'Oi. Nobody made you the gaffer. Keep a civil tongue in your head.'

Tom held his gaze for a minute, then looked to the horizon. Finally he hauled himself unsteadily to his feet and said, 'There are many miles ahead of us.'

They set off slowly across the moorland, enveloped by the moan of the wind and the plaintive cries of birds. The going was hard; the ground was uneven and marshy after the rains, while hidden hollows and boulders forced them to be cautious. The lamp was still flickering westwards, and Church wondered how far they could be expected to travel without a car. At the rate they were moving, Beltane would come and go before they left Dartmoor.

'Any idea what the date is?' he asked. 'I can't work out how long we were in that place. The lack of daylight plays havoc with your body clock.' No one had any idea.

Church noticed Tom was eyeing him strangely and asked what was wrong. 'You seem different to the last time I saw you,' he said. 'More in control of who you are. You might actually be able to live up to what's expected of you.'

'Thanks,' Church said sarcastically. He even felt different; the vision in the Watchtower, the death of the young Marianne, his terrible experiences at the hands of Calatin, all had altered him on some fundamental level. He himself was still coming to terms with who he now was.

'So, you still haven't told us what it was like in that Otherworld place,' Veitch said to Tom.

'No, and I'm not about to.'

'Why not?' Veitch said with irritation; Church was a little concerned at how close to the surface his temper lay.

'Because it would be like describing an impressionist painting to a blind man.'

'Are you saying I'm stupid?' Veitch's fists bunched subconsciously.

'No, I'm saying you're blind. But perhaps you'll see it for yourself one day, and then you'll understand.'

That thought seemed to cheer Veitch immensely. 'That would be bleedin' great! I bet it's better than this shitty little world.'

'Different,' Tom replied sourly.

Amidst regular ribald humour from Veitch, their step picked up and as the sky turned blue and the sun grew stronger, the miles fell behind them. After the disgusting food in the mine, they were all consumed with hunger and by midmorning they broke off their travelling to hunt for food. Tom did one of his tricks and returned with a couple of rabbits, and while they were cooking over a spit on the fire he pointed out various herbs for Church to collect and had Veitch grubbing for tubers and mushrooms. It was a bizarre meal, half of which Church couldn't begin to recognise, but it tasted remarkable and they finished every scrap. After a brief nap in the shade of an ancient hawthorn tree, they continued on their way and soon the grim, bleak expanse of the moor gave way to budding trees and hedgerows and, eventually, a tiny, winding lane. With sore feet and aching muscles, they moved slowly, searching for any signs of civilisation.

An hour or so later they found a small farm surrounded by a thick wall of trees. At first glance it seemed deserted; a tractor and equipment sat idle in the yard at the back of the house and there was no sound apart from the mewling of a litter of kittens underneath a broken old cart. After hammering futilely on the door, Church and Veitch searched the outbuildings until Tom's cry called them back to the farmhouse. A ruddy-faced man with wiry, grey hair was pointing a shotgun at Tom's head.

'We're just looking for a place to stay for the night,' Church protested. The farmer eyed them suspiciously, but didn't lower his weapon.

'Bloody hell, it's *Deliverance*,' Veitch hissed under his breath.

'Okay, we'll go!' Church said. 'So much for West Country hospitality.'

'Christ, a night sleeping under a hedge,' Veitch moaned as they turned away.

The farmer brought the shotgun to his side. 'You can't be staying out there at night,' he said, hesitantly. Church saw fear in his eyes. 'Don't you know what's happening?'

'What do you mean?' Church asked.

'It's changed. It's all bloody well changed.' He looked away uncomfortably.

'What's troubling you?' Tom attempted a note of concern which came across as insincere, but it didn't seem to trouble the farmer.

'Don't tell me you don't bloody see it. Everybody in the countryside knows it's different now, only nobody talks about it!' His voice rose, then cracked, on the edge of hysteria. He looked from one to the other frantically. 'You can't bloody go out at night! You take your life in your hands if you go into the wilder places! There're all sorts of things out there—'

'You've seen them?' Church asked.

The farmer's mouth clamped shut as his eyes narrowed suspiciously. 'Oh, ah, I'm not bloody mad, you know.'

'We've seen them too.' The farmer looked at Church with such sudden hope it was almost childlike. 'Things *have* changed.'

'What's gone wrong?' the farmer pleaded. 'What are they?' There were tears of relief moistening his eyes; Church thought he was going to hug them. 'You better come inside.'

The kitchen was dark despite the sunlight outside; it didn't look like it had been modernised in years. There was a large, heavily scored wooden table in the centre of the room, and a stove on the far wall over which hung a line of fading clothes drying in the dull heat. The floor was tiled and muddy and the kitchen was filled with old cooking smells and the underlying aroma of wet dogs. The farmer introduced himself as Daniel Marsh. He'd worked the land since he was a boy, as had generations of his family before him, but Church couldn't see any signs of other family members. He put a battered kettle on the stove and boiled up the water for an enormous pot of tea, which he served in chipped mugs. It soon become apparent to Church and the others that some heavy burden was lying on his shoulders beyond his obvious fear of the change in the countryside. After half an hour of small talk, he couldn't stop himself any more.

'When the sun goes down, I'm never the same,' he began cautiously. His eyes looked hollow from too little sleep and his face muscles had sagged under the weight of an array of dismal emotions. 'One of those things out there, it comes here.' He motioned to the house. 'Not every night, but enough so I can't rest.'

'What sort of thing?' Veitch eyed the farmer askance.

'A devil. A little devil, 'bout as high as this here table.' His head fell until his face was hidden and he was racked by a juddering sob. 'I don't know how I'm going to go on. I thought about taking that' – he waved towards the shotgun – 'and blowing my bloody head off, but I don't know, I don't know . . .'

'What does it do?' Church asked anxiously.

'It talks to me, pinches me. Hurts me. I know that doesn't sound much, but the things it says!' He covered his face for a moment, then seemed to catch himself. 'You can stay here tonight if you like,' he said, unable to hide his desperation.

'Sure. You've sold it to us so well,' Veitch said.

Marsh acted as if a weight had been taken off his shoulders. He promised them good food for dinner, then left them alone while he headed out to do some work in the fields.

'Do you think it's happening like this all over?' Veitch asked as they sat around the table gorging themselves on the farmer's bread and cheese.

'What do you mean?' Church was looking at deep score marks in the kitchen walls, as if they had been swiped by razor-sharp nails.

'People all around the country dealing with this weird shit, but too scared or too worried their neighbours will think them crazy to talk about it. So they just keep it all to themselves and nobody knows what's going down.'

Church shrugged. 'It can't stay bottled up for much longer. Sooner or later it's going to blow up and the Government is going to have to do something about it. It'll be on the front page of the *Sun*—'

'Unless things reach a head before then.' Tom pushed his chair away from the table and rested his hands on his belly. 'By the time anyone really realises what's happening, there might not be any Government, or newspapers. Just people running for their lives with nowhere to go.'

There was a long moment of silence and then Veitch said, 'You're a bundle of laughs, aren't you. I'm surprised the army or MI5 or some of those bastards aren't on to it already.'

Church considered the lack of media coverage about what events they had witnessed, and then thought about the stone-faced men clustered around the charred skeletons at the Salisbury depot and the helicopters they had seen scouring the landscape. 'Maybe they already are. Maybe they don't know what to do either.'

The evening was so balmy it could have been summer, and it was filled with the kind of perfumes that shouldn't have been expected for several weeks: rose, jasmine, clematis and the sweet bloom of night-scented stock. Overhead the clear sky sparkled with an array of stars that had Ruth, Laura and Shavi gazing up in awe.

'You never see that in the city.' Laura was unable to hide the wonder in her voice.

'I can't believe this place. It's almost magical.' Ruth felt a shiver run through her. 'If this is part of the New Age too then it can't all be bad.'

'A time of terrors and wonders,' Shavi agreed. 'Perhaps all the other focal points for the power in the earth are like this – a sanctuary, a place to rest and recharge your own energy where the Evil outside cannot touch you.'

'I feel like staying here for ever,' Ruth said regretfully.

'Somewhere safe.' Laura glanced from Ruth to Shavi.

His faint smile suggested he knew what they were feeling, but that it could never be. 'Let us make the most of this time,' he added, leading the way along the street to the pub. But his unspoken words lay heavy on all of them.

In the King William pub next to the Market Cross they ordered three pints of potent scrumpy. The cloudy drink had a rough quality and a powerful aroma of apples that was completely dissimilar to the mass-produced cider they had all tried before, but whether it was the invigorating, dreamlike atmosphere that pervaded the town or the sudden infusion of alcohol, within moments it felt like the best drink they had ever had.

Shavi nodded. 'This is what our ancestors used to feel. The body, mind and soul need to be in perfect balance. The trinity leading to enlightenment represented by the eye opening in the pyramid. Knowledge is fine, but the Age of Reason's focus upon it above all else threw us out of balance. Our souls became weakened. Instinctively, we all recognised it – that feeling of discontent with our lives and our jobs that has pervaded us all for the last few decades. You must have noticed it?' They nodded, entranced by his voice. 'We need to learn to feel again.'

'Well, aren't you the guru.' Laura grinned at him, but there was none of the spite that usually infused her comments; Ruth wondered if the magic was working on her character too.

'Perhaps that is part of this quest we are all on,' Shavi mused. 'Not merely to find physical objects of power to defend ourselves, but in some way to discover and unlock the truly alchemical part of our souls that will make us whole and more able to cope with the trials ahead. A quest for the spiritual rather than the physical, a search that goes inward—'

'Why don't you shut up and do a quest to the bar,' Laura jibed.

His smile warmed them both. 'I talk too much,' he apologised, 'or perhaps I think too much. Either way, now is the time for enjoyment.'

At the end of the evening they made their way back to the camp in a drunken haze of laughter and joking. But the first thing they saw when they reached the tents was clothes scattered across their sleeping bags and their possessions ransacked. Nothing seemed to have been taken.

'This is weird,' Ruth said. 'Just like the car at the service station. It feels like someone's following us.'

Even that didn't dampen their spirits, nor remove their feeling that Glastonbury was an oasis of safety for them that night. Ruth and Laura tidied up while Shavi lit a fire, and once it was roaring, they lazed around it. The atmosphere felt so relaxing and secure, Ruth only managed ten minutes before her eyes started to close. She crawled into her tent, leaving Laura and Shavi to talk dreamily into the night.

After a while he dipped into his pocket and pulled out a plastic bag filled with mushrooms. 'The sacrament,' he said with a smile. 'Care for some?'

Laura pulled out a handful and examined them in the firelight. 'Magic shrooms? Where'd you get these?'

'I brought them with me. Since the change, they have become even more powerful, almost shamanistic in effect. Taken in quantity, I find my spirit—' A smile sprang to his lips as he caught himself. 'I am talking too much again.'

'Before I hooked up with this weird crew I used to be blasted on Es and trips all the time in the clubs. Dust, even. God knows what I was doing to my body.' There was a note in her voice that suggested her experiences hadn't all been pleasurable.

'I have a feeling the lab drugs will lose their potency,' he mused. 'All part of the blight on our technological world. Natural things seem to be coming into their own.'

Laura peered into the bag. 'Been a while since I've been on mush-rooms,' she said thoughtfully. She popped a few into her mouth. 'How many do we take?'

'Not many,' he said. 'This can be a ritual of awareness and bonding, not a trip.'

'Nothing's simple with you, is it?'

'You can look at things in different ways without harming the experience. There are some who think drug-taking is inherently im-moral without considering that psychedelics have been a part of some cultures' religious experience for centuries. Other people's wine and wafer, if you will, transubstantiating into the body and blood of nature.'

Laura snorted, but didn't comment further. She chewed the rubbery mushrooms, trying to ignore the metallic taste, then swallowed with a wince. Shavi followed suit and they lay next to the fire watching the flames, waiting for the drug to kick in.

It didn't take Laura long to notice the familiar fuzziness on the edge of her vision. It was followed by the faint auditory hallucinations in the crisp crackle of the fire or the rustle of the breeze in the branches, and then the growing sense of wellbeing that made her laugh for no reason apart from the joy of being alive. They chatted amiably for a while as Laura felt the layers of her defences slowly being stripped away. *Don't make a fool of yourself*, she thought, but after so long honesty was pressing hard against her throat.

'This may sound weird,' she began, 'but despite all the shit flying around I really feel like I've found some purpose in my life. I wouldn't tell them to their faces, and I wouldn't have believed it myself if some-one had told me a few weeks ago, but I feel like I belong with Church and Ruth. For all their faults. And you. Like we're coming from the same place.' She turned her head away, suddenly aware of her words.

'You do not have to be embarrassed by your feelings,' Shavi said gently.

'Yeah, I do, because if I let my real feelings out I'll tear myself apart.'

'Is that what you believe?'

'It's what I know. Blame my parents.' Her voice trailed off morosely. She expected Shavi to question her further, but when he didn't she couldn't contain herself. 'My loving mother and father have really screwed me up and I hate them for it.'

'Talk about it if you like.'

'I don't know if I can.'

'Then ignore it.'

'I can't.' She lay on her back and watched Ruth's owl swoop and soar in the sable sky, feeling the currents beneath its wings as if she were flying alongside it. And then she closed her eyes and she was there, in the dark, nursing the welts, smelling the iron tang of blood, too sore even to move. 'You know, religion is a dangerous thing. For strong people, it's just teaching, guidance, a few rules to keep them on the path for good. But weak people let it eat them up. There's so little inside them they can trust, they allow it to control them, like some devil on their backs, following what it whispers to them even when it's obviously wrong. Which is about as ironic as it gets. For them it's a class A drug and they should be treated like addicts, put on some religious methadone treatment. Yeah, religion-lite. Wonder what that would be? The Church of the Soap Opera?' She laughed at the ridiculousness of the image. 'Anyway, guess which category my darling folks fell into.'

'Some people draw strength from it—'

'I have no problem with that,' she snapped. She sighed and added, 'Sorry. Raw nerves-a-go-go. My parents were Catholics gone mad. And like all fundamentalists, they believed absolute discipline was the only way. You know, you allow a little weakness in and suddenly the cracks are shooting up the wall. They were terrified of the chaos of life and they had to lock themselves away in their little religious fortress to stop them going mad. But of course I was in that fortress with them. A sneaky little spy who couldn't be trusted not to let the enemy past the gates, so I had to be *convinced* to be a true patriot. The slightest misdemeanour and my mum would go crazy. It started off with just the back of the hand, but as I got older it developed to a rolled-up newspaper, belts, table tennis bats, just about anything she could pick up and thrash about with. And after she'd finished and got it all out of her system she used to lock me in the airing cupboard. Pitch black. So hot I was almost choking. I cried myself out pretty young.'

'Did you tell anyone?'

'It was all I knew from when I was a tiny kid. I thought it was normal, for God's sake. Stupid bitch. Now I know my mum wasn't wired up right. Yeah, crazy as a loon.'

Shavi examined her face carefully; her words were glib, almost dismissive, but her experiences were etched harshly in her features. 'Did your father—'

'My dad never laid a finger on me. He just condoned it when *she* did. He'd crawl away like some weak little mouse and read the paper, and for that I almost hate him more.' She closed her eyes and after a while Shavi thought she had fallen asleep, but then she said, 'I killed her, you know.'

Shavi waited for her to continue.

She laughed, her hand going to her mouth like a young girl. 'Nothing fazes you, does it?'

'Go on.'

'I realised my mum was going nuts when I was in my teens. I could see it in her eyes. Whenever she looked at me, they went all starey, like she hated me. I could see the whites all around them.' Her voice had grown more serious. 'And the more funny she went in the head, the worse she got with me. Somewhere down the line it went beyond punishment. I used to get burnt, cut. Once I spent a whole weekend in the airing cupboard listening to her say her Hail Marys outside the door. What do you expect? – I rebelled. I was drinking like some rum-sodden old sailor before I was sixteen, hoovering up any drugs that came near me. I wasn't exactly an angel when it came to boys. And the worse I got, the worse my mum got. Luckily I'd an aptitude for technology. Somehow I winged it through my exams and got a place at university. She didn't want me to go, the witch, but I was old enough to do what I wanted then so I just legged it. Of course, by that time they'd decided I was the Devil himself. I was no longer part of the family, as simple as that. Which, by me, was great. It was like getting let out of jail. Just call me Papillon.'

Shavi reached over and rested his hand on the back of hers. She didn't flinch.

'A couple of years ago I must have had a brainstorm or something,' she continued. 'I had a dream about her and thought maybe it was time I made my peace with her. Yeah, right. Like some stupid, gullible idiot I turned up at the old homestead. My dad was out. She answered the door and I knew straight away she'd fallen out of the crazy tree and hit every branch on the way down. I was surprised she was still walking around. But she just smiled and invited me in like it was only yesterday she'd seen me. I had a cup of tea, tried to make small talk, but then she started spouting all that Bible crap, saying she'd been praying for my salvation. I thought, *Here we go again.* I got up to go and as I was walking through the kitchen she came up behind me and hit me with a fucking iron. Clunk. Big comedy moment, no laughs unfortunately. And when I woke up she'd done this.'

She rolled on to her side so her back was towards him and pulled her T-shirt up to her neck. In red scar tissue across her pale skin were the words *Jesus loves you*.

Shavi was overcome with such a deep pity for her he couldn't find any words to say. He reached out to trace the scars gently with his fingertips and this time she did flinch. But then she reached out behind her, caught his hand and held it against her side.

The psychedelics were swirling through her system now, releasing terrible memories, freeing the awful thoughts she had attempted to contain for so long. Under usual circumstances she would have expected the experience to induce levels of paranoia and terror that would have left her crumpled in a ball on the ground, but in that strange, charged environment all she felt was an immense sadness which she knew she had to expunge from her system.

'There's a place where you go when life's threatening to destroy you,' she continued in a small voice, without turning over to face him. 'Some kind of sanctuary in your head, and thank God it's there because right then I don't think I'd have carried on without it. She'd used one of my dad's razors. My back was in agony and I was covered in blood, vomiting from the shock. And she was still spouting Bible stuff and waving the razor around in this kind of dance. A stupid, childish dance. And at that moment I knew what a complete moron I was. I hated her and wanted her dead for everything she'd done to me in my life, but I loved her as well and I just kept asking her to hug me and make it all right. But she wouldn't listen.' A shiver ran through her, and Shavi squeezed her side supportively. 'A stupid fucking moron. Sometimes I hate myself.'

'You were just being human.'

'And then she came at me again. I tried to get out of the way, but she was crazy, thrashing around with the razor. I've got a great scar on my scalp under this perfectly styled hair. I was flailing around and somehow I grabbed this big wooden crucifix they'd always had hanging on the wall next to the fridge. I lashed out with it and it caught her on the temple. She must have hit me with something at the same time, or maybe it was just the shock of what I'd done, but I blacked out too. And when I woke up she was dead. I don't know if it was from me hitting her or where she'd gone down hard against the edge of the cooker, but whichever way you slice it, I killed her. There was blood everywhere—' The words choked in her throat.

Shavi moved in close to her, sliding his arm around her waist, pulling her into him. She went rigid at first, resisting the human contact, but then she relaxed against him, crossing her arms over his in a desperate yearning for comfort.

'My dad came back soon after and found me still sitting there. All I wanted was for him to hold me, but it was like I wasn't there. He started mumbling, "We must call the police", detached, emotionless things like that, and I was screaming, "Dad, Mum's dead" over and over. I just wanted some reaction from him. Then he turned to me and said really coldly, "If the police find you here they'll arrest you for what you've done. Get out." It was like a slap in the face. I got up, washed the blood off and walked out. Later I found out he'd told the police he'd done it. Can you believe that?'

'He was trying to save you,' Shavi suggested.

Laura laughed hollowly. 'You'd think, wouldn't you? But it wasn't about me, it was about the sacrifice. By giving himself up instead of me, he felt he'd done the right thing, the Godly thing. It was his big chance. In his eyes it made him a better person: God would smile on him and throw wide the gates of heaven. Hallelujah! There wasn't a single thought for me and I have never heard him from him since. I don't even know what happened to him – he could be rotting inside the squirrel house, or still living in the house basking in his own glory for all I know. For all I care. Whenever I go back to Salisbury to see my mates I never go anywhere near the place, and I make sure they don't tell me anything about him.'

'You could be wrong about him.'

'No, I could see it in his eyes when he walked into the kitchen and took in the situation. He was already thinking about it then.' She let out a deep breath of air that seemed to drain her. 'What a crazy life, eh? And now the world's ending. That big old Catholic God must really be despairing of everything that's been done in his name.'

Shavi hugged her tightly, nuzzling his face into her neck so he could speak softly into her ear. 'You have suffered terribly—'

'I don't want pity! That's not why—'

'And I am not giving you any. I want to show you respect for the success you have made of your life—'

'Success! I feel like a loser! Fucked in the head, washed up in drugs, lonely, bitter . . . Funny choice of words you have there, pal.'

'But you have overcome such a terrible experience. You are carrying on, and that is all we can really hope for. In the end, we have to make our own way, without our parents, without our loved ones, using our own strength. And what you are doing now shows your worth.'

'Well, that's one way of looking at it. If you're a nut.' She laughed lightly; oddly, she felt better than she had done in years. 'You're a strange dude, Shavi. I don't know why the hell I'm talking to you.'

'We are all strangers, but we have connections that go much deeper than conscious thought.'

'You could be right. Everything is insane enough now for that to be true.' She paused, suddenly aware of his hands on her skin. At the thought, a tingle ran through her groin, heightened by the drugs. 'You can't beat talking about misery for making you feel sexy,' she said.

He was silent for a long minute, as if shocked by her comment, but then he said calmly, 'Do you want to make love?'

'Sure, why not? There's nothing like gratuitous, no-strings-attached sex with a stranger to make a girl feel good. But you better have some protection, big boy.'

She could sense his smile behind her. 'I always come prepared,' he said.

Whether it was the magical atmosphere or the drugs, her nerves seemed charged. When he ran his fingertips up from her belly to the soft curve of her breast, it felt like a web of electricity crackled across her body, and when he lightly touched the end of her hard nipple she jolted with a spasm of delight. She turned her head so he could reach her mouth. The kiss was moist and supple and filled with passion. The excitement of the moment took control of her mind, and she gave herself up to it hungrily. Snaking her hand behind her, she slid it over his clothes until she felt the hard, hot mound in his trousers, which she kneaded gently. Then he was undoing her jeans, slipping his hand over her belly and under her knickers to her pubic hair and beyond, where he began to stimulate her with soft, subtle movements of his fingertips. There was something so expert in his action she had to fight to prevent herself coming in an instant. And then they were both overwhelmed, rolling over, kissing each other hard, pulling their clothes off hastily. In the heightened atmosphere, Laura could barely believe how every sensation was so charged; she felt permanently on the point of orgasm. When he flicked a tongue over her nipple, she had to clench to control herself. And when she slid her naked body up and down his before taking his erection and lowering herself on to it, she thought her senses were going to crash through the overload of excitement. She moved on top of him for a while, before they rolled over, slick with sweat, and he started to thrust into her. His body was hard muscle under her hands, his face darkly handsome in the firelight, and all she could think was he was the best lover in the world.

For a while she gave herself up to the waves of sensation, losing all sense of time, but later she did remember one moment, when she looked past him, up into the sky, and saw what seemed to be scores of golden lights swirling around in the currents from the fire. They were bigger than sparks, almost the size of fireflies, and for the briefest instant she had the oddest feeling that they were tiny, beautiful people with shimmering skin, dipping and diving around them on gossamer wings. It was a moment of pure, undefinable wonder, but later, when they rolled off each other sweat-streaked and exhausted, the night air was clear and she couldn't bring herself to mention it. The image stayed in her heart, though, adding to the feeling of transcendental joy that infused her.

The power was off and the darkness that filled the farmhouse seemed almost to have substance, refusing to retreat in the flickering light of the candles Marsh had hastily placed around the room. But the roaring fire provided some stronger illumination and warmth, although it still didn't seem to penetrate beyond their tight circle of chairs pulled close to it.

Their conversation had all but dried up long ago. Despite cooking them a fine meal which went some way to make up for the privations they had experienced underground, Marsh had been reticent for most of the evening. Church didn't get the impression he had anything to hide; more that his lonely existence had made him taciturn, and that his fear had added to his normal withdrawn state.

The grandmother clock had chimed midnight half an hour earlier, but no one seemed to want to retire; its tick was low and sonorous, like an insistent warning. Marsh had his loaded shotgun across his lap, which made Church feel nervous, but Veitch also kept reaching to the bulge of the gun in his jacket for comfort. Just as Church wondered how much longer they should sit up, the room was suddenly pervaded by a foul smell, a mix of sulphur and human excrement. When it reached Marsh's nostrils, a faint tremor ran across his face and he made an odd mewling sound in the depths of his throat.

'Is this the start of it?' Tom asked.

Marsh's terrified expression had already given away the answer. The whole room held its breath as they cast glances to the darkened corners. It began like the distant rustling of dry paper, eventually becoming something like the sound of rats' claws on wood, but it felt as if it were inside their heads. Marsh raised the shotgun and began to aim it around the room. Veitch was on tenterhooks, his eyes darting while his hand stayed firmly inside his jacket. He'd had the gun out once already, but Church had complained that he felt like he was sitting in some Wild West Saloon. 'What's coming?' he whispered redundantly.

Church watched them both warily. They were in the wrong place at the wrong time.

Overhead, there came the abrupt sound of clattering across the roof tiles and then a shower of soot billowed out from the whooshing fire. They all leapt back at once, their chairs flying. When the soot had cleared, a small figure lay huddled on the hearth. Marsh blasted both barrels of the shotgun; it sounded like a thunderclap in the room and they jumped out of their skins.

'You stupid bastard!' Veitch cursed.

But the thing had already moved like lightning into the shadowed corners before the buckshot hit. Burbling, throaty laughter floated back to them.

Church had caught the merest glimpse of the creature, but it was enough. Though as small as a child, it had the proportions of a man, with an oversized head like a baby. Black, shiny scales covered the skin and its eyes were large, red and serpent-slitted. A pointed tail snaked out behind it, seemingly with a life of its own. In mediaeval times a witness would certainly have branded it a devil, and Church wondered if he should see it that way too.

'Daniel Marsh, you are so harsh, all the things you said, soon you will end up dead.' The hideous, old man's voice ended in chittering laughter.

Tom stepped forward. 'Show yourself,' he said authoritatively, unruffled by the creature's appearance.

'Oh Daniel, you have some friends!' it replied in a sneering singsong. There was a moment when it seemed to be considering its response, and then it sashayed into the centre of the room in an odd, jerky motion which Church would have put down to poor stop-go animation if he had seen it in a film. 'What, no holy water? No crucifixes, no *in spirito sancto* or crossing hand movements and mumbled prayers? You *have* changed!' He held out his arms like some penitent Jewish tailor.

Marsh chewed on the back of his hand, moaning pathetically while Veitch stared unsurely. But Tom confronted the creature head-on. 'You are a foul thing, tormenting this poor man. And so much to do on your return. Why waste time here?'

'Why, good sport, coz!' The devil did a little flip back into the shadows as Veitch advanced on it menacingly. A second later it was back, like a tame monkey sensing food.

'Let's kill it!' Veitch snapped.

'If only you could, little brothers, but you have not grown up that much in time passing!' It moved suddenly, so fast it was almost a blur, bouncing on the sofa across the room towards Marsh before disappearing back into the shadows. The farmer howled in pain. Four streaks of red appeared on his cheek. 'First blood to me, I think!' the devil said triumphantly; the voice came from nowhere in particular.

'Why are you here?' Tom continued calmly. He seemed familiar with the creature.

'Here to fill a void,' it replied. Somehow it was back on the hearth.

'I don't deserve it! I weren't doing anything!' Marsh howled pitifully.

'Nothing apart from living!' the devil cautioned.

'My wife left me a year ago, the farm's going bust, I feel sick all the time! I've suffered enough! There's no reason for this! It's not fair!'

'But that is the reason, Daniel. I am here because you have suffered. I am making you suffer more because I can, for no other reason than that. And if you seek meaning in life, perhaps you will see it there.'

'Do not listen to him,' Tom said. 'Lies spring easily to him and his kind. His only desire is to torment.'

'You wound me!' The devil clutched his heart theatrically. 'But because I can lie does not mean that I always lie. In a field of ordure a single pearl of truth shines brighter.'

Veitch pulled out his gun and rattled off a couple of shots. 'Don't!' Church yelled too late as the bullets zinged off the stone hearth. One shattered what appeared to be an antique plate on the wall while the other burst through the window. But Veitch's attack seemed to have got closer than Marsh's shotgun blast. The devil backed up against the wall, flaring its nostrils and baring its teeth at him. Veitch moved faster than Church could ever have imagined. He launched himself forward, swinging his foot and catching the creature full in the stomach. It squealed like a pig, arcing up, head over heels, to crash against the far wall.

It bounced back like a rubber ball, ricocheting off the floor towards Veitch, a flailing mass of claws and scales. Effortlessly it clamped itself on his head and neck, then threw back its head, opening its jaw so unnaturally wide its head seemed almost to disappear. Veitch had a view of row upon row of razor sharp teeth about to tear his face from his skull.

Tom moved quickly. Snatching up the coal pincers from next to the fire, he gripped the devil firmly about the neck and hauled it off Veitch; it yelled as if it had been branded.

'You and your brethren still do not like cold iron, I see,' he said snidely.

The thing wriggled like a snake in his grasp, but Tom heaved it forward and plunged it into the depths of the fire. It howled wildly until it managed to free itself from the pincers. Then it scurried off to the shadows to compose itself. 'Not fair,' it hissed like a spoiled child. 'You know us too well.'

'Quick,' Tom said, but it was too late. It rolled itself into a ball, then fired itself out of the shadows fully into Marsh's face. The farmer went over backwards, his nose exploding in a shower of blood. As he lay on his back screaming, the devil sat on his chest, ripping and tearing at Marsh's face. It managed to get in only a couple of swipes before Church took a swing at its head with the poker. The blow sent the devil rolling across the floor. Veitch fired another shot, this time blowing the leg off an armchair. And then it was away, tearing out the stuffing of the sofa, streaking up the wall, ripping up the paper as it passed, shattering a mirror with a cry of 'Seven years' bad luck!' before settling on a sideboard where it proceeded to fire crockery at them.

Veitch and Marsh fired off random shots, while Tom and Church dived for cover. Clouds of plaster dust erupted from the walls; the light fitting came down with a crash; the sideboard burst open, showering glassware across the floor.

While they stopped to reload, Tom scurried forward and whispered, 'We will never kill it like that. Trickery is the only way.'

'Let me address you as an equal,' he said loudly to the devil. 'What should I call you?'

'You may call me "master",' the creature said slyly. 'If you wish to uncover my true naming word, you will have to do better than that. But I know your name, do I not, Long Tom? Your silver tongue seems to have forsaken its poetry for threats. And how is your Royal gift? More curse than gift, I would think.' Tom ignored him, pulling Church close to whisper in his ear. Then he turned back to the devil and said, 'Would you like me to see your future, little one?'

The creature squirmed. 'Thank you for your kind offer, Long Tom, but I prefer to live in the here and now.'

'Come, now!' Tom said with a broad grin.

The creature was so concerned at Tom's words that he failed to see Church circling round to his blind spot. Church felt a cold sweat break out on his back. The devil had shown he was terrifyingly fast and vicious; one wrong move and he could lose an arm, or worse. Tom was doing his best to distract the creature, but the things he was saying hinted at a hidden side of him which made Church feel uncomfortable.

'Perhaps I should compose an epic poem to your grandeur, little brother,' Tom continued.

'Indeed, that would be a deep honour from a bard so renowned.' The devil was not so arrogant now and he was watching Tom suspiciously, as if they were long-standing enemies who knew each other's strengths and weaknesses.

'But then what would I call it?' Tom said. 'Ode to a Nocturnal Visitor is so vague. Ode to—?' He held out his hands, suggesting the devil should give him his name.

For a second it almost worked, but then the devil caught himself and simply smiled. 'I am sure a rhymer of your great skill could imagine a fitting title. I—'

Church moved quickly, pulling out the Wayfinder from his jacket and holding it in front of him like a weapon, as Tom had instructed. The blue flame flared and licked towards the devil, who caught sight of it out of the corner of his eye and squealed. At the same time, Tom clamped the coal pincers on the devil once more. He howled as he futilely attempted to wriggle free.

'Now,' Tom said, suddenly threatening, 'we shall have some plain speaking.'

The flame sizzled like an acetylene torch as Church held the Wayfinder close. The devil tried to tug its head away, its eyes wide with fear, but it had nowhere to turn. 'Keep it away from me!' it hissed.

'The flame will consume you if we allow it – you know that,' Tom said bluntly.

'What do you require, masters?' the devil replied obsequiously.

'Just burn him!' Veitch snapped.

'No!' the devil cried. 'Anything!'

'This, then.' Tom's eyes blazed. 'You will leave Daniel Marsh alone for the rest of his days. And,' he added, 'you will do nothing to bring about that end earlier than fate decrees. Do you so swear?'

'On the warp and weft!' the devil screamed frantically. 'Now let me go!'

Tom nodded to Church, who retreated a few feet with the Wayfinder; the flame flickered back to normal and the devil bounded free to the hearth. When it turned, its face was filled with malice and it spat like a cornered cat. It turned to Church first: 'You will never find out why she died.' Then Veitch: 'There is no redemption for murder.' And finally to Tom: '*You* carry your suffering with you.'

Then it pointed a finger at the three of them. 'Thrice damned,' it said coldly before bounding back up the chimney.

Marsh stared for a moment in shock, before falling to his knees in front of the fire, tears flooding down his cheeks. He looked at them incredulously, then said simply, 'Thank you.'

Church turned to Tom. 'Is that it? Will it be back?'

'Not here. But we will have to be on our guard from now on. Word will spread quickly through the brethren, and they hate more then anything else to be humbled by mortals.'

Veitch collapsed on to the sofa. 'Blimey. What's going on?' He looked at Tom. 'What's this brethren, then? They're not Fomorii.'

'There are many things that come with the night.' Tom poked the fire, sending sparks shooting up the chimney. 'Every creature of myth and folklore has its roots in Otherworld. And they're all coming back.'

Veitch looked puzzled. 'So it's like if London Zoo opened up all its cages at once.'

Tom nodded. 'One way of looking at it.'

Church rested wearily on the mantelpiece. The room looked like it had been attacked by a wrecking crew. 'That thing thought you were someone important.'

Tom stared into the depths of the fire, saying nothing.

Marsh jumped up, trembling with relief. 'That were fine – you bloody well did it! You saved me!' He shook all their hands forcefully, unable to contain himself. 'I'll tell you what, the only thing I've ever loved in my life was the land. Then when farming went through all those rough years, I felt like I'd got nothing. But when something like this happens, it makes you think, don't it? About what's important an' all.'

Veitch watched the farmer like he'd gone insane. 'I reckon you need a bloody good sleep, mate.'

'Oh, ah, I'll tell everyone about what you bloody did,' Marsh said adamantly.

Church turned to Tom. 'And that little devil's going to be spreading the word too. Looks like we're going to get us a reputation.'

the hidden path

They ate at first light while Marsh slumbered heavily in what must have been his first good rest for weeks. After Veitch had collected eggs from some chickens roosting just off the yard, Tom plucked some new nettle shoots out of an overgrown patch that had obviously once been the garden and scrambled them all up. He claimed it had been a popular Anglo-Saxon dish, and although Veitch ate suspiciously, it tasted remarkably good. They left Marsh enjoying his sleep and were out of the house by 7 a.m.

Church suggested their first aim should be to find some transportation. With technology unreliable, Tom didn't want to risk trains, and buying another car was out of the question.

'Looks like we'll have to rely on the comfort of strangers,' Church said. 'Hope you're all good at thumbing.'

Their first ride took them into Tavistock where they convinced a farmer collecting supplies to let them travel on the back of his truck. He was just trundling west past Liskeard when Church noticed the direction of the lamp flame had turned to the north-west. Angry with himself for not paying more attention, he forced the others to jump off the truck as it slowed at a crossroads. By the time it was out of sight they were already regretting their decision. Ahead of them lay the bleak expanse of Bodmin Moor, rising up in sludgey browns and grey-greens beneath a lowering sky.

'How bad can it be?' Veitch said. 'It's half the size of Dartmoor and we're already bang in the middle of it.'

'Bad enough if the weather changes,' Church said, checking the slate clouds that were backed up over the moor. 'And the weather out here can change in a minute.'

'Oh, you're a bleedin' wilderness expert are you now?' Veitch said. 'The sooner we start, the sooner we finish.'

Church grinned at Veitch's bluntness – he had already warmed to their new companion. They chatted aimably for a while, but their conversation faded the further they got out into the moor. The higher the land, the stronger the wind, and although they were in the first burgeoning days of spring, it had a bite to it that reminded him of winter. At least there was a single-track road they could follow which made the going much easier than stumbling across the uneven turf and gorse. Half an hour after leaving the main road they might have been in a different world; there was no sound of civilisation, just the howl of the wind, no stink of car fumes, just the damp, cloying smells of nature.

'How are you doing, city boy?' Church said with a grin.

'Sorry, mate,' Veitch deadpanned, 'I'm too soft. I should live in a rough place like you to harden myself up.'

'What you need is a few archaeological digs on the North Yorkshire moors. That'd put hairs on your chest.'

They continued a little way and then a thought came to Church that he had wanted to mention the previous night. 'You handled that gun pretty well at the farm.'

'I told you I was a bit of a villain. I'm not proud of it.' There was a long pause before he added, 'There's lots I'm not proud of.'

'Last night, that devil—'

'I knew you'd ask sooner or later. He called me a murderer.'

'Are you?'

Veitch looked away. 'Bang to rights.'

'Do you want to talk about it?'

'I haven't so far, not to anyone outside the family.' He thought for a moment, then said, 'Fuck it, you might as well know what you're getting in with. You know that building society raid where my brothers got arrested? Well I was in on it too. We knew it was a bleedin' mistake before we set out, but once you start thinking about something like that, it's like it's got a weight of its own – it just carries you along. There were lots of times we could have pulled out, but we'd go to bed and when we got up in the morning it was still on. We were desperate, you know. We'd been listening to all those politicians who told us we could have anything, only we didn't have anything. We had nothing. And just like we thought, it started going wrong from the moment we went in there. But we could have got out, you know, if I hadn't screwed up. We'd all got masks on. Brendan was up there at the counter, Mitch was covering him with his shotgun. I'd got a gun too and then it was like I heard this voice in my head, or just behind me or some shit. It said, "He's going to get you" or something like that.

'Anyway, I turned round and I caught this bloke moving out of the corner of my eye. And I just let him have it. Don't ask me why. I've thought about it a million times and I can't explain it. It wasn't like me at all. But there it was. Blam. Blood, guts and some poor bastard dead. I ran like hell – Brendan and Mitch took the rap. My own brothers banged up because of me! I wanted to give myself up, but they wouldn't let me. Said it'd make it even worse for them if they knew I was inside too.' The weight of emotion in his voice made Church regret bringing the subject up. 'They didn't blame me for a minute and that just killed me! I wished they'd made me suffer for being such a fuck-up, like they should've done. So they go inside, and I'm just eaten up by what I did to that poor bloke and my own family. And I wasn't even allowed to pay my dues for it.'

Church clapped a supportive hand on his shoulder. 'It sounds like you're paying for it now.'

'But it's not enough, is it?'

'I reckon what lies ahead for us, Ryan, will give you plenty of opportunity for payback.'

'I've never done the right thing in my life, ever, even when I tried to. But I'm going to make up for that somehow.'

Church decided to turn the conversation to Tom so Veitch could have a break. He was amazed at how quickly the man had recovered; even the scars on his temple had healed. 'What about you, Tom? Are you going to break the habit of a lifetime and tell us what that devil's message meant to you?'

There was a long silence, and when Church glanced up he saw the strangest thing: Tom was trying to speak, but it was as if he couldn't control his jaw. No words would come out, and in the end he turned away in frustration.

'Are you okay?' Church asked, concerned. But Tom dismissed him with a wave of his hand, his eyes focused on the road ahead.

In the cold dark before dawn, Shavi slipped away from the camp and lost himself among the trees. He could sense the sun coming in a way that still surprised him, although he had discovered his odd sensitivity a few months earlier. It was just one of several subtle changes which, inexplicably, had been thrust upon him overnight at the same time that the change came upon the world, a transformation that was so distinct at first he thought he was suffering some sudden, debilitating brain ailment. There were the psychic flashes which he initially thought were hallucinations, but which he came to recognise as precognitive, or visions of distant events. The odd sensations he received when he handled objects were as if he could *feel* what had happened to them in the past. And he seemed to understand what animals were thinking, although he didn't know if it was an increased awareness of their rituals and routines, or if he were actually picking up what was passing through their heads. It was all still quite unfocused, but all his abilities were growing much sharper, as if his mind were learning to use them now he had them at his disposal. He accepted it without question as a gift from some higher authority, and he was determined to use it as best he could.

Shavi found a clearing in the most thickly wooded area and stripped off his clothes, shivering from the chill on his skin. For twenty minutes he worked through his t'ai chi routine to clear his mind and then followed it with twenty minutes of yoga, by which time the sun was beginning to break through the branches. His studies had showed him that ritual and drugs made his abilities considerably more effective, and he had worked hard to develop a shamanistic framework to enable them.

With his mind wiped free of thoughts, his breathing regulated, he stood and raised his arms to the coming sun; the heat from the first rays licked over him in greeting. He slipped the Mexican mushroom on to his tongue, feeling the bitter taste spread, and then chewed slowly. When he finally swallowed, he lowered himself slowly and took up the full lotus, closing his eyes so the only sensations were the sun on his feet and the gentle breeze breathing on his naked skin.

'Come to me, spirits,' he whispered. 'Show me the path.'

Ruth was already up cooking breakfast when Laura emerged from the tent, bleary-eyed and puffy-faced. 'Stay up late?' Ruth asked as she flipped the sizzling bacon in the pan.

'No,' Laura lied, slipping on her sunglasses in the bright morning light. 'I'm just not a morning person like you, Miss Perky.'

Ruth served up a mug of tea which Laura took with a nod and then proceeded to sip halfheartedly.

'Shavi must have been up early,' Ruth continued; Laura grunted noncommittally. Ruth carried on serving up her breakfast, then suddenly threw the plastic plate down in irritation. 'I don't know how much longer we can carry on doing this!'

Laura looked up in surprise at the outburst. 'What do you mean?'

'Church could be dead! Time is running out! And we're just sitting here!'

'Okay, don't blow a gasket.' Laura took another sip of her tea, then added, 'Shavi's going to try something.'

'What?'

Laura shrugged. 'He reckons he can do stuff. You know, spooky stuff. When the world changed, he got super-charged . . . seeing things, hearing things. He's trying to find a way we can carry on without Church and his little blue lamp.'

246

'You seem to know a lot about him and what he's thinking,' Ruth said suspiciously.

'That's what talking to a person gets you. You should try it sometime.'

Ruth picked up her plate and took out her frustration on her bacon and beans. She had just decided to have another go at Laura when Shavi emerged from the trees looking tired and haggard. He flopped down next to them, rolled on his back and closed his eyes.

'That's what comes of taking exercise before breakfast,' Laura said.

'There is something here, in Glastonbury,' Shavi muttered.

'What do you mean?' Ruth asked.

'One of the talismans. The energy here is so vital it acts as an ultimate defence. None of the dark creatures can enter the Isle of Avalon, so it was the perfect place to locate one of the most powerful objects.'

'Where is it?' Ruth felt a sudden surge of hope that they weren't as powerless as she'd feared.

'I do not . . . It would not . . .' Shavi's eyes suddenly rolled up until all they could see were the whites, and for an instant they thought he was going to have a fit. In his head he flashed back to the ritual in the trees, the moment of awe and terror when the air appeared to fold in on itself and the amorphous cloud which seemed to contain both eyes and teeth suddenly manifested. Somehow he dragged himself back and focused on Ruth's concerned face. 'The abbey,' he croaked. 'There is a sign in the abbey. "Where feet in ancient times walked," it said.' He closed his eyes and rested as best he could.

By midmorning Shavi had recovered enough to walk with Ruth and Laura into town. The abbey lay just off Magdalene Street, its ruined stone lying at peace amidst acres of well-tended lawns in a tranquil setting that was at odds with its location so near to the bustle of the shops. Despite the bare bones of its once powerful form, it was still easy to see how it had once been the greatest monastic foundation in all of Britain, second only in wealth and size to Westminster. Pilgrims still wandered beatifically along its winding paths as they had done since the Middle Ages, when it had been one of the most important shrines in Europe; even, some said, on a par with Rome itself.

The sun was bright and hot, but a cool breeze made their wanderings easy; the birdsong within the high walls drowned out the traffic beyond.

'It's so peaceful here,' Ruth remarked as she stood in what had been the nave and looked towards the choir. 'No, more than that,' she added thoughtfully. 'It's spiritual.'

'You notice that too?' Shavi replied. 'I wondered if it was a by-product of this new age which seems, to me, to be an age of the spirit after one of materialism. Can we now *feel* the energy of sacred sites, the cumulative outpourings of generations of the faithful? Or was it always like this?'

'Perhaps it was like this, just muted.' Ruth ignored Laura, who was faintly but obviously sneering at their intellectualising. 'You know, some of the things that have come with the change have actually been good. Perhaps this whole new age isn't as bad as it's made out to be,' she continued.

'Yeah, right,' Laura said, wandering away from them. 'Tell that to the Wild Hunt.'

While Shavi and Ruth mulled over the abbey's uncommon atmosphere, Laura picked her way amongst the stonework until she discovered a sign which made her call the others. It said:

Site of King Arthur's Tomb. In the year 1191 the bodies of King Arthur and his queen were said to have been found on the south side of the Lady Chapel. On 10th April 1278 their remains were removed in the presence of King Edward I and Queen Eleanor to a black marble tomb on this site. This tomb survived until the dissolution of the abbey in 1539.

'I thought he was just made up,' Laura said.

'He was,' Ruth agreed. 'A conglomeration of old heroes that a succession of writers have used to create this romantic myth.'

'Some say,' Shavi added, 'the monks invented this because it would bring in some funds at a time when they were particularly hard-pressed.'

'I've always said you can't trust the religious,' Laura sniffed, before turning away again.

But Ruth felt a strange *frisson* tingle along her spine. She recalled Tom talking about the sleeping king who needed to be awakened; the king who, in legend, had been Arthur.

Shavi noticed her expression. 'What is wrong?'

'It's nothing,' she said, before adding, 'Coincidences always spook me. I'm starting to see strange connections in all this, recurring themes about legends and religions, Celts and Christianity. But I can't quite fit it all together.'

'These things happen in the subconscious,' Shavi advised. 'Let it come naturally.'

Taking his own advice, he led her among the ruins, hoping inspiration would come to illuminate the cryptic hints he had received in the ritual; as they walked, they mused over the words.

'It reminds me of a line from "Jerusalem",' Ruth noted. ' "And did those feet in ancient times . . ." '

'And that, of course, is tied in to Glastonbury,' Shavi said. 'It relates to the legend of the young Jesus, who is supposed to have come here to Glastonbury with his uncle Joseph of Arimathea. The stories say they built the first Christian church out of wattle and daub, somewhere in the abbey's grounds, I think. After Jesus was crucified, Joseph gave up his tomb to house the body. It is said he took the Grail which caught some of Christ's blood at the crucifixion and brought it here where he buried it, possibly on Chalice Hill. According to legend, that is.'

' "Folklore is the secret history",' Ruth muttered distractedly.

'What is that?'

'Something Tom said. That myths, legends and folklore reflected what really happened, although not accurately, or as metaphors. And of course the Grail is part of the Arthurian tales.' She felt oddly uneasy. 'What does it mean? Anything?'

Before he could answer, Laura ambled over lazily. 'Before you two burst your brains with all that heavy thinking, you should see this.' She took them to a wooden cover in the ground in what had been the north transept. Underneath were perfectly preserved mediaeval floor tiles still in situ where they had been unearthed by archaeologists. 'This is "where feet in ancient times walked", right?'

Shavi smiled at the difference in their approach, then ducked down to examine the tiles. Although they had faded with time and the pressure of numerous soles, the intricate design was still clear and the colours shone, but there seemed nothing out of the ordinary.

Ruth knelt down next to Shavi. 'Perhaps there's something hidden in the pattern.'

'Or perhaps it's nothing to do with this at all,' Laura added. 'Why don't we talk about needles and haystacks instead.'

For the next fifteen minutes they looked at the tiles from every angle, so close their noses were almost brushing the surface, then far away, much to the irritation of the tourists who jostled to see. Eventually Laura wandered off in boredom to throw stones at the fish in the abbey pool while Shavi and Ruth lay on their backs on the grass, desperately trying to solve the conundrum.

'We must be looking in the wrong place,' Ruth said.

Shavi disagreed. 'I feel instinctively that this is it. We simply need to look at it in the correct way.'

'But can you trust the information you were given?'

'According to tradition, sometimes the spirits lie, dissemble, obscure the truth. Again, I intuitively believe that it was the correct guidance. The problem lies with us and our vision.'

'Okay,' Ruth sighed, 'lateral thinking time.'

As they lay in silence, Ruth's mind gradually turned to her surroundings. Even in ruins there was a majesty to the abbey, the cumulative power of centuries of faith and worship; she felt dwarfed in its presence, and at the same time, adrift in her inability to *feel* what generations had obviously found so comforting.

'I wish I had something to believe in,' she said, almost to herself.

'You are not alone.' Shavi's voice floated to her dreamily. 'That is the only true quest that we all find ourselves on.'

'When my father died I wished . . . I wished like a child . . . that there was a God to give some reason to his passing. And at the same time I hated myself for being so weak that I needed a crutch to help me through life. It's all so pointless.' There was a note of self-loathing in her voice. She looked over at him. 'What is your religion, anyway?'

There was a faint smile on his lips. 'My religion? Spirituality. A belief that there are foundations and walls and a roof encapsulating this life of ours. A belief in a reason. In a force for overwhelming good that all religions touch.'

'Why should there be some higher power? There's no sign when you look around. Just people fooling themselves.'

'It is important to—' He paused, then sat up suddenly and stared at the tiles. 'To ignore the noise of everyday life and focus on the signal that lies behind it.' He scrambled on his hands and knees to the tiles excitedly.

'What is it? What have you thought of?'

Ruth crawled next to him; she still couldn't see anything in the patterns. Shavi leaned forward and gently traced his finger on the glass that covered the tiles. 'Here,' he said triumphantly.

'I can't see anything,' she said in frustration.

'It is all a matter of perspective. Look past the colour and design. Look past all the noise to find the signal. It is a lesson. For life.'

Ruth followed the tracing of his finger. There was a faint indentation in the baked clay of the tile, partially obscured by the design painted over it. It was an arrow. They both looked up to follow its direction. It pointed straight at the remains of the wall in the choir and through it to the tor rising high up above the town with the remaining tower of St Michael's Chapel perched on top.

'The tor,' she said. 'Of course. With all the legends tied to it, it had to be the key.'

'Not just the tor,' Shavi corrected. 'The wall too. Both of them.'

'What do you mean?'

He wandered forward, his eyes fixed on the crumbling stonework. 'So much of this new age seems to be about duality – the light and the dark, the two forces opposing each other. And there have been dual meanings so far today. The link to "Jerusalem", Joseph and the Grail *and* to the tiles. Now this dual meaning – the wall and the tor. It makes sense.'

'What can the wall have to do with it?' Then she realised what he had said. 'You think this is about the Grail!'

'I do not know.' He turned and smiled so she wouldn't be offended by his words. 'Let me concentrate.'

She backed away and sat down; Laura joined her a moment later. After she had watched Shavi staring up at the stonework for five minutes, she said, 'He's done too many drugs, hasn't he?'

'He's a smart guy,' Ruth replied. 'I wish he'd been with us from the start.'

'Don't tell me you've got damp knickers for him as well.'

'I admire him, that's all,' Ruth said tartly. 'And what do you mean *as well*?'

Laura smiled and looked away, her sunglasses somehow adding to her supercilious expression. Ruth bit her tongue and simmered silently.

Half an hour later he called them over excitedly. 'Look! The sun is in the right position now. You can see it clearly.'

'Yeah, right,' Laura said sarcastically. 'It says, "Shavi, you are a big dickhead."'

'No, he's right,' Ruth corrected, adding in as superior manner as she could muster, 'You have to look for the signal, not the noise, Laura.'

'Do not look at the stonework,' Shavi explained. 'Look at the shadows cast by the lumps and indentations in the stone.'

And then, when they squinted and focused, they could both see exactly what he meant: the shadows spelled out words in thin, spidery writing that would not have been visible to the casual observer, nor from any other perspective. Some of it, however, seemed to be missing where the wall had crumbled.

'Aqua something,' Ruth said.

'Aqua fortis,' Laura corrected sharply. 'That's nitric acid.'

'Nitric acid?' Ruth asked.

'I know my chemistry—'

'I do not think that is the context here,' Shavi corrected gently. 'The literal translation is something like *strong water*.'

'That's right,' Ruth said.

251

'Oh, yeah, that really makes sense,' Laura huffed.

They continued to study the wall intently and eventually they decided the rest of the remaining message read *sic itur ad astra*.

'Astra is "stars",' Ruth said. 'I studied Latin before I did my law degree, but I can't remember much . . .' She paused thoughtfully. 'Something like "such is the way to the stars." That's it.'

'It doesn't make much sense without the rest of the message,' Laura complained.

'There doesn't seem to be a great deal missing,' Shavi said.

'Perhaps, then,' Ruth said quietly, 'we just have to make a leap of faith.'

The wind somehow seemed to find its way through their jackets and shirts as Church, Veitch and Tom worked their way across the moor. Although the sky regularly threatened rain, the gale managed to keep the clouds scudding along so that patches of blue and bursts of sunshine occasionally broke through. Away from the main road however, the atmosphere became almost as bleak as the landscape. Strange shapes moved ominously across the scrubland in the distance and every now and then flocks of birds would soar up into the sky, suddenly disturbed by something none of them could see. The sense of threat was palpable and growing.

'It's getting worse, isn't it?' Church said, shielding his eyes to peer at the horizon.

Tom nodded. 'These places where man has a feeble hold were always going to be the first to go. The old things can re-establish themselves without much confrontation. I think it will not be long before they move in towards the centres of population.'

'And then the shit really hits the fan,' Veitch said morosely.

In the late afternoon, they wearily mounted a ridge to look down on a wide expanse of water, grey and somehow threatening in its isolation. The wind howled around them as they moved down the slope; even when it dropped there was still the eerie sound of waves rippling across the lake, giving the uneasy sensation that something was emerging from the depths. Church felt his fear grow as they neared; he could tell from Tom's face that he felt it too.

'It's just the spooky atmosphere,' Church said hopefully.

Tom's face remained dark and troubled. 'I would have thought by now you would have learned to trust your instincts. In this new age, what you sense is as important as what you see.' He stretched out his arm, bringing them up sharply.

Veitch squinted at the murky surface of the water. 'What's that moving? Is it the shadows of clouds? Or is there something in there?'

'This is Dozmary Pool, a place of legend.' Tom said. 'Local stories claim it is the lake where Sir Bedivere threw Excalibur after Arthur's death. A hand rose from the water to pluck the sword and take it down beneath the waves.'

Church tried to read his face. 'None of that Arthurian stuff is true,' he ventured.

'Not literally, no. But all legends reflect some aspect of a greater truth. I told you before – lakes and hills are liminal zones, the boundaries between this world and the place where the old races went after they retreated from the land. There are doors in all of them. Some of them have remained closed tight down the years. But not here.'

He wouldn't venture any closer to the lakeshore, so they took a long, circuitous journey along the ridge, their eyes constantly drawn to the lapping waves. It wasn't until the lake had long disappeared from view that the sense of brooding and menace slowly started to fade.

A mile and a half further down a tiny, winding lane they reached the village of Bolventor, little more than a small group of houses huddling together for shelter. And just beyond it was Jamaica Inn, its lamps already burning in the growing gloom. It had been heavily commercialised since the days when Daphne du Maurier had used its heritage of smugglers and violence as the basis for her story, yet it still retained an atmosphere that transcended the trappings of the late twentieth century. History lived on in its aged timbers, brooding slate and heavy stone walls which kept out the harsh Bodmin weather. Exhausted, and with little sign of welcome in the surrounding moorland, they were drawn to its cheer and decided to take a room for the night. As they crossed the cobbled yard where stagecoaches once clattered and heard the inn-sign creaking in the breeze, Church felt he had been flung back hundreds of years. A few months earlier, it would have been romantic; now it seemed like a warning of what lay ahead.

They ate steak in the restaurant and drank a little too heavily in the bar before settling into their room. The wind rattled the windows and thumped against the walls and they were thankful they were secure indoors. But Church knew that however sturdy the building, it wouldn't amount to anything if the things that ranged through the night decided they wanted to break inside.

At the window he tried to pierce the darkness, but beyond the lights of the car park there was nothing but a sea of black; they could have been alone in the void, and for an instant he was disturbed by a memory of his view into the abyss from the Watchtower window.

'I hope Ruth and Laura are okay,' he said; then, to Tom, 'Do you think the Wild Hunt will be back?'

'Devon and Cornwall is their favourite hunting ground. I have tried to mask our presence as much as possible, but they will not leave until the blood of their prey has been spilled. It is only a matter of time.'

'"Mask our presence"?' Veitch repeated. 'Is that one of your little *tricks*?' Tom ignored him.

Outside, the gale clattered like iron horseshoes on stone and howled in the eaves like the baying of hounds. Church drew the curtains tightly and retired to his bed.

The stark red digits of the clock radio displayed 3 a.m. when Church woke with a start from nightmares of a pursuer that snapped relentlessly at his heels. Tom and Veitch both slept deeply, although Tom occasionally twitched and mumbled deliriously. Church stumbled out of bed and headed to the bathroom for a glass of water. On his return he had the odd sensation someone was standing outside the door, although he could hear nothing. He dismissed it as another by-product of the nightmare, but after he had slid back under the sheets it didn't diminish and he knew he wouldn't be able to sleep until he had investigated.

Sleepily cursing his own obsessive tendencies, he unlocked the door carefully so as not to wake the others, his natural caution blanked out by his half-awake state. As he had thought, there was no one without. But if anything, his uneasiness had grown stronger now the door was open. Cautiously, he leaned out and looked up and down the corridor. For the briefest instant he thought he glimpsed a figure disappearing round the corner at the far end. He weighed up his options and then closed the door behind him and hurried in pursuit.

The gale was still in full force and the creak of the inn-sign echoed ominously throughout the building; there was no other sign of life at all. But as he rounded the corner he was brought up sharply, his breath catching in his throat. Facing him twenty feet away was Marianne, as pale and dark-eyed as the last time he had seen her at Stonehenge.

This time he was more ready to confront her. 'What do you want, Marianne?' he asked softly.

There was a ripple like a sigh that seemed to run through her whole body. Church felt the shiver echo within him, filled with the terrible ache of loss that he was convinced he would never lose. He tried to look in her eyes, but couldn't; the things he glimpsed there were too awful. But her face held the same delicate combination of beauty and sensitivity with which he had fallen in love. He bit his lip to prevent the tears.

She didn't reply, although he hadn't expected it; he had come to believe speech was no longer within her power. Instead she stretched out her right arm and gently touched the wall. Where her pale fingertips brushed the plaster a spot of red bubbled out, like a thumb that had been pricked by a rose. Gradually she began to retreat, in that same unmoving, horrible way he had witnessed at Stonehenge, her fearful aspect turned upon him like the light of a beacon. And as she receded, the blood spread out from her fingertip as if it had a mind of its own, tracing words that sprang to life like a speeded-up film of flowers bursting in the sun.

Somehow Church managed to draw himself from her face to look at the message, and in that instant he felt as if he had been blasted with an arctic wind. It said:

Murder. Avenge my death.

Church thought for a moment his legs were going to buckle. Marianne had reached the far end of the corridor and was now fading into the wall as if she were slipping below waves. And in the last instant he thought he saw her expression change. The look that frightened him so much became, briefly, tender and sad and if he had had any doubt this was truly Marianne it was gone then. But it was too quick, and he was left with an aching emptiness that made him feel sick.

Back in the room he couldn't sleep. Suddenly his whole life felt like it had been turned on its head; his guilt that he had been somehow complicit in Marianne's suicide had been a part of him for so long, he could barely consider the prospect that she had been murdered. It was such an upheaval that he considered whether it had been some instance of supernatural trickery designed to destabilise him. If that were true, it had worked well. But he knew it was Marianne as well as he knew himself and instinctively he felt her message was genuine. He was shaking so much he could barely consider what that meant for him. To calm himself, he took out the locket the young Marianne had given him and rested it in the palm of his hand. Although he couldn't explain why, it seemed to do the trick.

At that moment he became aware of a strange, unearthly cold that washed out from his jacket on the chair next to him. Anxiously he pulled the Roisin Dubh from the inside pocket and examined it secretively. All of the shining black petals were spotted with droplets of blood.

Ruth, Shavi and Laura spent the next morning studying information about Glastonbury in the local bookshop *Gothic Image*. A mountain of words had been written about the town, more than any other place they had visited, and most of it formed an intricate tapestry of tradition, fact and romance, with little sign where one ended and another began. But after wading through numerous books, they stumbled across a locally printed pamphlet which gave them their breakthrough: the translation of the Latin phrase.

The Chalice Well lay at the foot of Chalice Hill, the third and gentlest of the three hills that surrounded Glastonbury; of all the many mystical sites in the Isle of Avalon, it was the most revered, and the most ancient. The well was fed by a spring rising on the slopes of the hill which provided water so iron-impregnated it flowed red. That had earned it the alternative name of Blood Spring, adding to the ancient legend that the Grail was hidden somewhere near.

Following its centuries-long veneration by pilgrims from around the world, a garden had been established to create a tranquil atmosphere for contemplation and prayer. Shavi, Ruth and Laura entered it just before noon, in the bright of the sun beneath clear blue skies. They recognised the same rare, sanctified atmosphere they had experienced at the abbey.

'In Celtic and pre-Christian cultures, springs were renowned for their magical, life-giving properties,' Shavi noted. 'They were sites of worship, the homes of fertility spirits. *Genius Locii*. Sacred groves often grew up around them. And Christianity has always followed in the footsteps of pagan worship. At all the most important sites, the old religion was there first. Who is to say,' he mused, 'that they were not worshipping the same power?'

The path to the well wound around the outskirts of the garden like a route of pilgrimage, twisting through clumps of trees and bushes where hidden seats surrounded by fragrant flowers were placed for meditation. Eventually it folded back on itself and they found themselves at the wellhead, set against mediaeval stone beneath the hanging branches of ancient trees; the light in that one spot seemed to have an unusual quality; an uncommon calm lay over everything. The well itself was covered with a lid of wood and fine wrought-iron which showed two interlocking circles revealing at their centre the ancient symbol of a fish. The pamphlet they had been given at the entrance called it the *Vesica Pisces*. The design pre-dated Christianity and represented the overlapping of the visible and invisible worlds, yin and yang, the conscious and the unconscious, masculine and feminine natures. *More duality*, Ruth thought.

Shavi noticed the troubled expression on her face. 'Are you okay?'

'That design is similar to the layouts of some of the stone circles. I think it has something to do with the earth power, the Blue Fire.' She chewed on a nail. 'Everywhere I look I see hidden knowledge, signs, portents, things that point to something unimaginably big. It makes me feel so . . . uneasy.'

'We always feel that way when we glimpse movement behind the curtain,' he replied. 'And, as you rightly point out, the signs are everywhere if you only look.'

'More signals behind the noise,' she said wearily. 'I don't think I can cope with it all.' Ruth half-expected Laura to make some sarcastic comment, but she stayed staring at the well, her face impassive behind her sunglasses.

They were about to return to the path when Ruth became aware someone was behind them. She spun round with a start. In the shadows under the trees stood a man in his late forties, his pate balding, but his greying hair bushy at the back. He was wearing the dog collar of a cleric, a black jacket and trousers, and around his neck hung a gold crucifix, glinting in the morning light.

'I'm sorry,' he said. He smiled gently; his face was honest and open. 'I didn't mean to startle you.' There was a long pause while he looked into all their faces, then he said, 'I saw you at the abbey yesterday. You discovered the message, didn't you?'

'Yes, and it said *Don't talk to strangers*,' Laura blurted defensively.

He laughed bashfully, his hands rubbing together in faint embarrassment. 'I suppose I deserved that, sneaking up on you this way.'

'Are you going to try to stop us?' Ruth asked combatively.

He shook his head, still smiling. 'The path is there for everyone who has the patience and insight to look for it. If not, do you think we would have kept those particular tiles there in that particular position? Hundreds more were unearthed and discarded. I simply wanted to be sure you were aware of the risks.' The others eyed him cautiously. 'Shall we sit?' he said, motioning towards a seat near the wellhead.

Shavi nodded and joined him on the bench, but Laura hung well back, with Ruth hovering somewhere between the two.

Once they had settled, the cleric said, 'My name is Father James, or Jim if you like. I must apologise for approaching you like this, but it seemed the best time and the surroundings are certainly conducive to contemplation.' He paused, as if to search for the correct words, then continued, 'We keep watch on the tiles in the abbey, just in case, but I don't think any of us ever expected the secret to be discovered.'

'Who's we?' Ruth asked.

'A few of us, chosen every ten years from the local parishes and abbey establishment. People who can be trusted to keep the secret. We're known as the Watchmen.' He laughed. 'I know what you're thinking: *Quis custodiet ipsos custodes!*'

'Yeah. That's just what I was thinking,' Laura said sourly.

'A vast amount of knowledge has always been stored at the abbey,' he continued. 'In the early days, the library had a collection of ancient manuscripts that was unmatched in all Christendom. Great wisdom. And much secret knowledge handed down the years. It was all supposedly destroyed in a great fire, and any manuscripts that escaped were lost during the dissolution.'

'But it was not all lost,' Shavi mused.

'Typical double-dealing Christians,' Laura said spitefully.

James didn't seem offended by her words. 'The great twelfth century historian William of Malmesbury was allowed to study some of those manuscripts before he wrote his *Antiquities of Glaston*. He quotes the story of Joseph of Arimathea's arrival at Glastonbury, and his burial here, recounted in several manuscripts. And although his reading was heavily censored, he dropped broad hints about a "sacred mystery" encrypted in the mosaic of the church floor. William had no idea what that mystery was. But we, as I'm sure you can see, had every idea and it has been passed down among a select few of us throughout the centuries. That, and another . . . prophecy? . . . legend? I'm not quite sure of the right word. Of a saviour rising in the world's darkest hour. Although the word is in the singular, in context it seems to be plural. Curious.' He eyed them thoughtfully. 'And these are certainly dark times.'

Shavi nodded. 'We are aware of these things.'

'Excellent. I am particularly interested to find out what this has to do with King Arthur. William speaks of reading a connected manuscript referring to him, but that knowledge *has* been lost to us.' Jim nodded excitedly and clapped his hands. 'This is like being at the end of history. So many different threads leading to this point. You know what you are to do next?'

Shavi stroked his chin thoughtfully. 'Take some of the water from the well—'

'Yes, yes, the *strong water*,' Jim interjected.

'—up to the top of the tor.'

'After that we get a bit vague,' Ruth added.

'Of course, part of the guidance is lost. And do you know what this all leads to?' To Ruth's surprise, Jim actually seemed pleased with their discovery. She had warmed to his pleasant, optimistic manner very quickly; and more, she trusted him, which surprised her even more.

'I would guess,' Shavi answered, 'the Grail.'

'Of course. All the legends, all the mythology, centuries of stories would suggest that is the only answer. But do you know what the Grail is?' He seemed to be enjoying the intellectual game he was playing with them.

Ruth glanced at Shavi, but he didn't respond so she said, 'Everyone knows the Grail is the cup that was supposed to have been used to catch Christ's blood at the crucifixion. It had amazing magical powers, and in the romances the Knights of the Round Table spent their time searching for it.'

'To heal the land. To bring purity to the world,' Shavi interposed.

'But we're actually looking for a Celtic artefact,' Ruth added. She turned to Shavi once again. 'I suppose, of the four, the nearest to a cup would be the cauldron?'

This time Jim laughed aloud. 'We live in a universe where the language is one of symbols. Through it, the cosmos speaks directly to our subconscious, the symbols and messages repeating across the millennia. Words written by man are only interpretations of those symbols, so it's never wise to trust them implicitly—'

'Does that include the Bible?' Laura said pointedly.

The cleric ignored her. 'Grails and cauldrons. Same thing, different names. A vessel of great power. Do you feel comfortable enough for a little instructional dialogue?'

'I suppose you're not going to let us go until you do it,' Ruth sighed.

'Officially, the Church doesn't believe that Joseph brought the Chalice of the Last Supper to Britain,' he began. 'Our scholars recognise that the myth surrounding it goes back much further than Christ's death. Back, in fact, to the pagan cup of plenty, the Graal, which had power over life and death, healing and riches. But somehow the Graal became the sangreal or the *sang real* – Holy Blood. You can see the connection. The Church has always been very good at using the religions of other cultures to further its own ends – and I don't mean that in any disrespectful way. But the Graal is one of those symbols I spoke about, representing the ultimate prize, only attainable by the most pure. Something that we constantly strive for, but can never reach. And in all the stories about it, there are always the same elements: the King, a Good Knight, a Maiden, the powers of Life and Death, a Hermit. What is the universe trying to say to us? Well, I could spend ages discussing that with you, but there's no way of truly knowing. It is simply a matter of faith.'

'So it's a big prize – how come you and your crew haven't cherry-picked it?' Laura asked.

'More than anyone, I would say, we're aware of responsibilities. It isn't meant for us.'

'For something that's so unattainable we seem to have broken into the mystery remarkably easily,' Ruth said.

'You haven't got it yet.' There was some quality to his reply that made Ruth shiver. 'Come, let us collect your water.'

He led them from the wellhead along a path to a partly walled area where the water tumbled from a lion-headed fountain. Shavi filled one of the two goblets that stood nearby and tasted it.

'Amazing!' he said. 'I can actually feel it lifting my spirits.'

'I bet you love it when the doc gives you a placebo.' Laura still refused to stand with them.

'Doubting Thomas,' Jim said with a laugh. 'Did you know the Elizabethan magician John Dee announced that he had discovered the *elixir vitae* – the water of life – at Glastonbury?'

'You seem remarkably at ease with the fact that so much of your religion is based on older beliefs,' Ruth said as Shavi filled a plastic water bottle from the spring. 'Don't you feel it undermines your faith?'

Jim shrugged. 'I can be very pragmatic. But Christianity still speaks to me more clearly than anything else; I can't ignore that. And I suppose, in my heart, I don't see a conflict between the Old Ways and the new. There are always higher levels.'

Once Shavi had taken enough water, they continued along the path past two yew trees to another decorative pool in a sun-drenched lawn area.

'I'm very happy to be here,' Jim continued. 'Glastonbury has always been somewhere special, sacred even, right back to neolithic times. The druids set up a college here to pass on their beliefs and wisdom. What is it about Glastonbury? You see, I believe the power of Christ is here, in the land itself. And I'm sure the pagans recognised the same thing, although they called it something different.'

Ruth wondered how much he knew about the Blue Fire, but she didn't raise the point. 'You said you wanted us to be aware of the risks.'

He nodded, suddenly serious. 'No one has ever followed this to its conclusion, the Grail itself. But we know enough. We know it isn't buried in any physical sense; it's in some place that lies alongside our own world. I can't really explain it any better than that. The ritual you're about to embark on will unlock the door – that has been done before, once, long ago. But after that . . . Well, we only have the stories to go on.'

'What stories?' Ruth asked. Shavi was listening intently, as if there was no one in the world apart from Jim.

The cleric wandered over to the shade beneath a tree and leaned against the trunk. 'In the third century BC the Celts established a lake village near here. In those days all the lowlands around here were underwater – there really was an Isle of Avalon. One reading has that name coming from the Celtic legend of the demi-god Avalloc or Avallach who ruled the underworld, and this was supposed to be the meeting place of the dead where they passed over to the next level of existence. Our knowledge of the Celtic tradition is limited and confusing – characters were called by different names in different parts of the Celtic world. Others said the subterranean kingdom of Annwn exists beneath the tor, ruled over by Arawn, the lord of the dead, and anyone who ventures into it encounters demons rather than the land of bliss that greeted those who were invited. Others said the place was the home of Gwynn ap Nud, Lord of the Wild Hunt, which local stories say haunts the hills around Glastonbury.'

Ruth went pale at this information, but he didn't seem to notice.

'The names don't matter. The common thread is that the place you will visit is terribly dangerous. And,' he continued darkly, 'we discovered that for ourselves when we opened the door long ago on that one occasion I mentioned. Never again. So I will ask you now to consider carefully before you continue.'

Shavi stepped forward deferentially. 'I feel we have no choice,' he said gently.

Jim nodded. 'I guessed that would be your answer. Then know this: the part of the message that is missing would have told you the timing is vital. You must take the water up on the tor at first light. And then God help you.'

CHAPTER FOURTEEN

A Murder of CROWS

Church, Veitch and Tom left Jamaica Inn after an early breakfast. The day was bright, with cloud shadows sweeping across the moor beneath the imposing background of Brown Willy, the highest point. But the light had that strained spring quality which threatened inclement weather at the drop of a hat. They could continue their trek, but there were no roads in the direction indicated by the lamp and they knew the going would be treacherous. Instead, they found a local woman who allowed them to cram into her carefully preserved Morris Minor on a shopping trip to Launceston, where they hoped they would be able to pick up another lift.

Although Tom and Veitch could both sense something was wrong, Church hadn't spoken about his encounter in the night. Marianne's revelation had tormented his sleep and on waking he wondered if he would ever sleep peacefully again. On the one hand he felt a great relief from the burden of responsibility in her death; yet the new mysteries that arose in its place were just as frightening in their implications. Who could possibly have killed her?

Despite Launceston buzzing with all the life of a healthy market town, they had to wait until midafternoon before they could find someone who could take them on the next leg of their journey. They bought some heavy Cornish pasties, which they ate in the back of a painter and decorator's van while they made their way slowly through North Cornwall villages which didn't seem to have changed since the fifties; the only sign of modernity was a huge battery of wind turbines, turning eerily in the sea breeze. 'We like the old ways round here,' the driver said between drags on a cigarette. The countryside was green and leafy after the desolation of Bodmin Moor and the closer they got to the coast the stronger the sun became, until it was beating down with all the force of a summer afternoon. Eventually they crested a ridge to see the deep blue sea ahead of them. The road wound down to the coast through an avenue of gnarled, ancient trees where the breeze smelled of salty, wet vegetation. They were dropped off in Boscastle outside the sun-drenched white walls of the Museum of Witchcraft, and although the lantern was still flickering towards the south-west, Church sensed they were near to their destination.

They set off walking along the road which clung precariously to the craggy coast, heavy with the history of smugglers and shipwreckers, and three miles later, as the sun slipped towards the horizon, they found themselves in Tintagel.

'I really should have guessed,' Church said as they rested in the village at the top of the steep track that dropped down to the ancient monument. 'Arthur again. All those references don't make sense.'

Veitch stuffed the last of his bag of chips into his mouth. 'What's this place got to do with King Arthur?'

'Just stupid legends. There was some writer in the twelfth century, Geoffrey of Monmouth, who made these outrageous claims that Tintagel was the birthplace of Arthur and that Merlin took him from here to be fostered in secret. Good for the local tourist trade, not much good for actual history.'

'There are no such things as stupid legends,' Tom interjected coldly.

'I know what you're saying, Tom, but when people believe this kind of stuff it makes an archaeologist's job so much harder.'

'*The Folie Tristan* said the castle was built by giants and that it used to vanish twice a year, at midsummer and midwinter,' Tom said with a strange smile.

'Exactly.' But Church had the uncomfortable feeling that Tom's comments weren't in support of his own argument; the man continued to smile until Church looked away.

'So was he real or not?' Veitch said looking from one to the other. 'Excalibur! Lancelot! Bleedin' great stories.'

'I don't deny they're great stories,' Church said, 'but that's all they are. Archaeologists recently dug up a piece of slate or something here with part of the name *Arthur* scrawled on it, and suddenly all the thick bastards on the national papers were saying it was proof he lived here. But Arthur and all the derivations were common names, meaning bear-like—'

'Old stories do not always tell the truth in a literal sense,' Tom said directly to Veitch, 'but sometimes they tell the truth in their hidden meaning.'

Veitch seemed quite satisfied by this, but, wearied by the travelling, Church had little patience for Tom's obfuscations. 'So what are the hidden meanings?' he snapped. 'I know this was an important place to the Celts, like all the other places we've trawled through, but I can't see what any of it has to do with a character who didn't exist, or at least not in the form everyone's talking about.'

Tom glanced up at the darkening sky, then turned to the track down to the castle. 'Come on. We must be there before nightfall.'

Church thought it was another attempt to divert his questions, but as they trudged down the steep incline, Tom said, 'When the Celts ruled Britain was the last time the land was truly alive.'

'You're talking about the Blue Fire – the earth energy?'

He nodded slowly, thoughtfully, his eyes fixed firmly on the sea in the distance. 'When the gods departed, the people were freed from the yoke of terror, but they lost something too. The people and the land are linked; like a mother and the baby in the womb, the blood that flows through one nourishes the other. But more than that, what you call the Blue Fire is also a powerful force for offence – for the defence of the land and the people. But like any weapon it needs to be nurtured to prevent it falling into disrepair. With the gods gone, there was no longer the immediate need for the people to unite and stay strong, with the force of the land at their backs. The mundane, day-to-day struggle of survival in a difficult environment took over and they forgot the importance of caring for the land through ritual at its sacred sites. The power dimmed, then grew dormant, and the people continued happily in their ignorant belief that all they needed was what their hands could grasp. But the Blue Fire is the spirit of the land *and* the people, inextricably linked for all time.'

The track grew less steep as a small valley opened beside them with a tiny stream winding among wildly overgrown nettles and brambles. To their left, the side of the valley soared up high above their heads where part of the ruined castle lay. No tourists ventured down at that time, and the only sound was that of the sea crashing against the crags.

'So now the Fomorii are back we need to awaken that power again? To help us get the strength to defend ourselves?' Church searched Tom's face for answers, but his features were unreadable.

'It's all talk with you two, isn't it.' Veitch seemed uncomfortable. He was continually scanning the thick vegetation away to their left and the growing shadows behind them.

'And Arthur?' Church continued.

'The Celts used their stories to pass vital information down the generations. Nobody can be bothered to remember facts, but if they are stitched into the fabric of an exciting tale . . .' Now *he* was distracted by the landscape. Perhaps it was the way the valley's steep slopes made them feel insignificant and trapped, or perhaps Veitch's obvious uneasiness was catching, but Tom seemed to be growing increasingly wary.

'And?' Church said with frustration.

'And all myths and legends are the same. Arthur is not a man. He is the embodiment of the spirit of man and the spirit of the land.'

Church suddenly saw what Tom was suggesting. 'The legend of Arthur sleeping under a hill to be woken in Britain's darkest hour . . . That's a coded message to awaken the power in the land.'

'Finally,' Tom said wearily.

'And all the sites linked to Arthur are ones that are important to the earth energy! But I don't understand—'

'No more talk,' Tom snapped. He stopped suddenly and glanced back up the sweeping track, as if he had heard something. Church listened intently, but the only sound was of the faint breeze rustling the bushes. 'Let us get to our destination. At least we should be safe there.'

'Safe from what?' Veitch said. Church saw his hand go unconsciously to the gun hidden in his jacket.

They speeded their step along the gravel track, falling into an uncomfortable silence. Above, the sky had turned deep blue and they could make out the diamond stars; it made Church feel very alone. The English Heritage building was locked and dark at the point where the valley opened out at the coast. The stream plunged into an impressive white waterfall cascading down on to the pebbled beach. The tide was out, the sea dark and powerful, licked with creamy surf where the waves broke powerfully.

And high up on their left were the ruins of the twelfth century castle like jagged teeth on a broken jaw. 'We go up there, I suppose,' Church said hesitantly.

'No,' Tom corrected. 'Down. To the beach.'

Church looked at him curiously, but he gave no hint of how he knew the direction.

They clambered across the culverted stream and along a path that ran over treacherous, slick rocks where signs warned of the dangers of the crumbling cliff face. In the growing gloom, it was difficult to haul their way over the jumbled boulders to the crunching pebbles, but they managed it with only a few knocked bones. The beach had the thick, fishy smell of seaweed and the thunder of the waves was almost deafening.

Tom led them across the stones to a gash of impenetrable black in the soaring cliffs beneath the castle. 'Merlin's Cave,' he noted.

Veitch laughed. 'Merlin! That's not you, is it? You've got that look about you.'

'No, it is not,' Tom said indignantly.

'We're going to do ourselves some damage in there,' Church said, trying to pierce the darkness. 'We won't be able to see our hands in front of our faces.'

Tom marched past him into the shadows. Church cursed and glanced at Veitch, who circled his finger at the side of his head. But a second later they were slipping and sliding over seaweed and rocks, splashing into pools and stubbing their toes, while desperately trying to keep up with him; in the end they were gripping on to each other's jackets so they didn't become separated. They seemed to hang suspended in the dark where the echoing sound of the sea was almost unbearable until Church cursed, irritated with himself for not thinking, and pulled out the Wayfinder. In its shimmering blue light he could see the cave actually went right through the thin promontory that joined the mainland to the bulk of the island where the oldest part of the castle stood.

'What the hell are we looking for in here?' Veitch yelled above the roar.

'A door of some kind, I suppose.' Church told him how the ground had opened magically at Avebury. Veitch shook his head in disbelief.

Tom's frustration was obvious as he stood on an enormous boulder and scanned the shadows that scurried across the walls away from the lamp's light. 'Where is it?' he muttered.

Veitch glanced back to the cave entrance nervously. 'There's something out there.' He looked back at Church for some kind of comfort. 'I must be going mad. I can't see anything, hear anything, but I feel like my heart's going to burst. I can't shake the feeling there's something bad coming for us.'

Church nodded as supportively as he could muster, then returned his attention to washing the lantern's light across the rock. 'We've all got to learn to trust our feelings,' he said distractedly.

'Thanks a bunch,' Veitch replied moodily.

And then Church did hear something, in the slight lull between the breaking of the waves. It sounded like a wild rustling or fluttering, but he couldn't think of anything that might have caused it. He looked to Tom, who was searching the walls with renewed, almost frantic energy. 'Just keep looking,' he said before Church could speak.

'There!' Veitch exclaimed suddenly. He pointed to a part of the wall that was now in darkness. 'Bring the lamp back!'

Church slowly swung the Wayfinder round until the section was illuminated. The shadows ebbed and flowed and then, for the briefest instant, a shape appeared. Church adjusted the lamp gently until the faint outline of a broadsword materialised out of a chaotic jumble of cracks that would not have been visible in any other light. Tom bounded from the boulder with a sprightliness that belied his age and slammed his palm against the symbol; blue sparks burst from his fingertips.

At that moment the pounding of the surf died again and the mysterious sound filled the cavern, throwing them all into a state of anxiety. Church looked back towards the entrance and saw some kind of whirling movement, darker even than the shadows. He thought he was going to be sick.

His attention was snapped back by a sudden rending sound from deep within the rock wall. A crevice mysteriously grew until it was wide enough for them to slip through. They hung back for just a second while the disturbing sound from the entrance seemed to rush towards them, then they dived in without a backward glance.

Although they weren't immediately aware of it, the wall closed behind them, trapping them in a tunnel in the rock barely big enough to stand upright. Their feet kicked up sand and seashells, and the deep, salty smell of the sea was everywhere.

'This place floods with the tide,' Church noted ominously.

'How can rock open up like that?' Veitch asked.

'It didn't. It simply appeared as if it did,' Tom replied obliquely.

'What was that outside, Tom?' Church asked.

'No point talking about that now. The tide is coming in. We do not have much time.' He pushed past them and led the way along the tunnel which opened up into a cave the size of Church's now burnt-out lounge. In the wall opposite were three holes set out at intervals along a line at waist-height.

'What are we supposed to do?' Veitch asked.

Tom dropped down on his haunches to peer into the holes. 'I can see something . . .' A shrug. 'I would expect the objects of power wouldn't be lying around for just anyone to pick up.'

Veitch inspected the rest of the chamber, but there were no other distinguishing marks. 'So, what? We have to find the combination?'

'Something like that.'

'Good job there's not a lot riding on it,' Veitch noted bitterly.

'You know,' Church said, 'there might be a switch in one of those holes.' He tapped his fingers gently at the entrance to the middle one.

'That's not much of a security system.'

'Here,' Tom said sharply. Church and Veitch turned to where he was pointing. A trickle of frothy sea water had washed up the tunnel to the mouth of the chamber.

'The tide must sweep in quickly through the other entrance to the cave.' Church handed Tom the Wayfinder, then turned back to the holes. 'Bloody hell. We haven't got much time. What do we do?' Steeling himself, he rammed his hand into the middle hole. It went in up to the middle of his forearm and at the far end there were two loops of metal which his fingers slipped through easily. 'I think there is a switch here!'

'Well, pull the bleedin' thing then and let's get the hell out.' Veitch eyed the advancing water nervously; it was already another six inches into the chamber.

Tom and Veitch both realised something was wrong from the sudden, bloodless expression on Church's face. 'Something's closed around my wrist. I can't get my hand out.' He tugged frantically, but his arm wouldn't retract at all.

The sea water washed around their shoes, which were sinking into the sandy floor. Veitch leapt into action. He put his arms around Church's waist, braced himself with one foot against the chamber wall and heaved. Church yelled in pain. 'You'll pull my bloody hand off!' Veitch released his grip with a curse.

'Relax your muscles,' Tom ordered. 'It might be like one of those oriental finger locks – the harder you pull, the more you are held tight.'

'I don't feel in a particularly relaxed frame of mind,' Church hissed. His socks and the bottoms of his Levis were already wet. He closed his eyes and attempted to calm himself with pleasant thoughts from his past, then felt a dismal wash of emotion when he realised they all contained Marianne. But it did the trick. Yet even when he let his hand go limp, the bond around his wrist remained as tight as ever. His shoulders slumped and he shook his head desolately.

'This water's flooding in!' Veitch barked. It was up to their calves, and when he paced anxiously it splashed dark stains up the legs of his trousers.

'That's not doing any good!' Church snapped.

'Calm down,' Tom said. 'It won't do any good to panic.'

'That's easy for you to say.' Church could feel his heart beating like a trip-hammer, his back and shoulder muscles knotting tightly. Although he tried not to think about it, images flashed through his mind of the water flooding into his mouth and nose, filling his throat, his lungs. 'You two should get out of here while you still can,' he said as calmly as he could muster.

'Don't be stupid! We can't leave you here – you're the important one!' Veitch's face was filled with the anger of frustration.

'Just get out!' Church shouted, his eyes blazing.

'He's right,' Tom said, his voice almost lost beneath the echoes of lapping water. 'Someone has to be left to try again, or everything—'

'Shut up, you coldhearted bastard,' Veitch growled. 'You're talking bollocks.' He splashed around the cave like a trapped animal, his fists bunching, then opening. 'I told you, he's the important one. We're just a couple of losers.'

'Get out,' Church repeated, gentler now he had seen the dismay in Veitch's face.

'There's got to be an answer!' Veitch exploded. 'Whoever did this wouldn't just leave it so everybody died!'

The water surged in, lapping up the walls, tugging at their legs. It appeared to be coming faster and faster. When it hit Church's waist, it seemed to flush the panic from him briefly. Suddenly, on a whim, he pushed his free hand into the left hole. There was a click and his trapped hand came free, but as he withdrew it jubilantly a bond snapped around his other wrist. He cursed loudly, waving the now-free hand to stimulate the blood supply.

'So triggering one switch frees the other one,' Tom said.

'That's a lot of use!' Church said. 'There's always got to be one hand in there.'

'But still . . .' Tom mused, wiping the splashes of water off his glasses.

'How can you be so calm?' Veitch bellowed at him. Tom replaced his glasses as if he hadn't heard a sound, and for a second Church thought Veitch was going to punch him.

'Take it easy, Ryan,' he said.

Church's calmness had an odd effect on Veitch. For a second his eyes ranged over Church's face, then he turned away as if he suddenly couldn't understand what was happening in the world.

The sea water continued to rush in, splashing up high, throwing them around. It had reached their chests in just a couple of minutes; desperation gripped them all. Tom held the Wayfinder up high, its light painting the water azure, but even when the tide splashed over the flame it didn't extinguish it. Church wondered if it would still be burning away beneath the water at the side of his drowned, bloated body.

Tom placed one hand on Veitch's shoulder. 'We need to leave,' he said quietly.

The water whooshed in, the current almost too much to bear.

Church thought it was going to tear his hand off at the wrist. He had to fight to keep his head above the swell. Now he could feel the panic surging.

There were tears in Veitch's eyes as he looked from Tom to Church, then he ducked his face in the water. When he threw his head back, the shock of the cold had sluiced off his emotion and he seemed to have a renewed purpose.

Church took a mouthful of salty water. He choked, tried to kick upwards, sucked in a huge gulp of air.

Veitch half-swam over to the holes and paused while he looked deeply into Church's eyes. Through his panic, Church could see Veitch weighing something up. Then the Londoner moved, suddenly forcing both his hands into the remaining holes.

'No!' Church yelled, but it was too late. He felt the bond around his wrist release and his hand shot free.

Before Church could vent his anger at Veitch for his sacrifice, there came a rumble from deep within the cavern wall and gradually a dark space appeared at head height above the holes. Within it Church could see blue sparks flashing, and an aged iron sword lying on a stone shelf. At the same time, Veitch's hands came free and another space opened – a doorway this time – on the other side of the chamber. Veitch whooped triumphantly as Church grabbed the sword and then they were all swimming frantically to the doorway. On the other side was a tight spiral of stairs rising steeply. They scrambled up high above the water level and crashed down on to the steps in exhaustion.

'I don't believe it,' Church gasped. 'I don't bloody believe it!'

Tom removed his glasses and rubbed a hand over his weary eyes. 'There was another dimension to the puzzle,' he said. 'The key was sacrifice. It would not give up the sword until we showed we understood *sacrifice*.'

'You're talking like it knew what we were doing.' Veitch had a satisfied, slightly amazed smile on his face. He closed his eyes and lay back on the steps until his breathing returned to normal. Then he sat up and said, 'Let's have a look at it, then.'

Church laid the sword on the steps and held the Wayfinder over it so they could examine it. Few would have given it a second glance. It was of a bare, basic design and appeared to be made of iron which had corroded badly; there were no distinguishing marks or aesthetic elements at all.

But it was obvious from Veitch's face that he was seeing something different. 'Excalibur?' he asked reverentially.

'The Sword of Nuada Airgetlámh,' Church corrected. He glanced at

Tom, who had a flicker of a knowing smile on his lips. 'Or perhaps they're different names for the same thing, for something that can't be defined.'

'That is the problem with legends,' Tom said wryly. 'They are imprecise ways of defining the indefinable.'

'You two bastards should never be allowed to talk to each other,' Veitch grumbled, pulling himself to his feet. 'Let's get out of here before the water finds us.'

As Church rose, he turned to Veitch and said awkwardly, 'Thanks. You know, for what you did—'

Veitch shifted uncomfortably. 'No problem.' Then, 'You're not going to bloody hug me, are you?'

'No, I'm not!' Church said indignantly. 'Come on. Let's climb.'

The steps ascended steeply in a spiral so tight it made them dizzy; they had to rest at regular intervals. Yet their success had left them with a strange euphoria, as if they had started living only at that moment; the sharp, salty tang in the air, the touch of the hard, cold rock, the echoes of their feet, the shimmering blue light reflected off the wet walls, all seemed heightened to such a degree they almost seemed like new experiences. The sword was strangely warm against Church's back as they scrambled up the rough-hewn steps; if he allowed himself to think about it, he would have noted it almost felt alive, like some unseen friend was resting an arm against him.

The steps ended suddenly at a stone ceiling on which was carved a stylised image of a dragon with a serpent-like body. There was another brief flurry of blue sparks when Church placed both hands on it and heaved, and then, with a loud creak, a square trapdoor eased open, revealing a patch of star-sprinkled sky. Church hauled himself out on to clipped grass and then offered a hand to Veitch and Tom.

They were on the windswept top of the island where the oldest part of the castle stood. All around, Church could see the broken foundations and rough outlines of buildings that dated back to the Celts.

'We did it!' Veitch said with a broad grin. Even Tom allowed himself a tight smile of triumph.

'If Laura and Ruth got away, we're two artefacts down and only two to go,' Church noted with a grin. 'You know, I think we're going to do it.'

'That was a buzz and a half!' Veitch continued exuberantly. 'Better than drugs. This is what life's about!'

The small island was just a high mound of rock covered by scrubby

271

grass and the ruins. From their vantage point they could look down on the surrounding coastline where the sea crashed in eruptions of white foam, and in the distance the lights of the village of Tintagel blazed like a beacon.

'You reckon we can get a room for the night? I don't fancy kipping in a ditch,' Veitch asked as they headed in the direction of the bridge over the thin neck of rock that joined the island to the mainland.

Before Church could answer, the wind died briefly and they heard the unnerving fluttering sound that had pursued them into the cave earlier. Tom's face grew taut; in the excitement he had obviously forgotten about it too.

'What *is* that?' Veitch asked anxiously. They stood stock-still, listening intently; it seemed to be coming from the direction of the bridge. As it grew louder it sounded like a sheet flapping in the wind, but there were other disturbing notes which they couldn't place.

Church looked behind him. The land fell away sharply into treacherously steep, crumbling cliffs. 'There's no other way out, is there?'

'I said, what is it?' This time Veitch gripped Tom's arm, who shook it off roughly, then started to cast around for some place to turn.

While the others held back, Church ran to the ruins of a chapel and peered down the bank to the Inner Ward, fifty yards away from where the noise seemed to be emanating. He saw several dark shapes moving cautiously through the castle and, at the head of them, a strange disturbance in the air; he could see movement, but the shadows prevented him picking out any detail. Two of the shapes waited at the top of the steps which were the only exit from the island.

'Fomorii?' Tom asked him when he ran back to them.

'I think. And something else too, but I can't make it out. There's no way past them.'

'Then we fight the bastards here.' Veitch's bravado belied the fear in his eyes. He pulled out his gun and examined it – they all knew it would do no good – before returning it to his pocket and removing a long hunting knife from a sheath he had hidden under his jacket.

'I got it while you two were buying the food in Launceston,' he said.

'I didn't think you had any cash,' Church noted.

'I don't.' He looked away uncomfortably, then pointed to a small jumble of foundations near where the land fell away on to the cliffs. 'If we make a stand there, they won't be able to come up behind us.'

As they hurried towards the spot, Church pulled out the sword; Tom shied away from it instantly. It seemed to shift slightly in Church's hand, as if it were settling into his grip. The warmth he had noted earlier flowed up his tendons into his forearm.

'That thing looks like it'll fall apart if you clout anything with it,' Veitch said.

'It's got power inside it, I can feel it. I reckon I can do a bit of damage.'

They were aware of the Fomorii approaching before the dark shapes had separated from the shadows; the attackers were preceded by an unpleasant feeling that operated beyond the five senses, churning the stomach and making their throats constrict. Tom brushed Church's and Veitch's temple briefly. 'You will keep your senses when you see them,' he said quietly.

'Magic?' Veitch grunted. 'You bloody well are Merlin.'

'Shut up,' Tom snapped.

The fluttering sound grew much louder as the hideously misshapen figures gradually took form. They crested the summit of the island and began to move forward, powerfully and relentlessly. In the centre of the approaching force was an intense, tightly constrained mass of whirling shapes.

As it drew nearer, Church picked details out of the gloom, until he said querulously, 'Birds?'

'Crows,' Tom corrected.

'Mollecht.' Church winced at the memory of Tom's description.

The crows were swirling around, wings flapping madly yet seeming never to collide with each other. Their incredibly complex pattern suggested the shape of a man at their core, but it was impossible to see any sign of him.

Veitch gasped as the birds swept across the grass towards them with an eerie, unnatural speed; it was such a terrifying sight that the other Fomorii seemed insignificant.

Tom was muttering something under his breath, prayers or protective incantations, Church couldn't tell which. Veitch kept glancing down at the hunting knife in his hand, now made pathetic and useless. He went to throw it away, then clutched it tight for security.

Church took a deep breath and cleared all thoughts from his head. Ignoring the fear, he stepped in front of the other two and held the sword up with both hands. He moved it awkwardly, but somehow it seemed to correct its balance itself. From the corner of his eye, he thought he glimpsed a crackle of blue fire along its edge.

It had an immediate effect. The crows came to a sudden halt about twenty feet away and began to shift back and forth along a wide arc. The night was suddenly torn by the monkey screeches and guttural roars of the Fomorii. Church moved the sword around, hoping it would be enough to frighten them off, but the attackers held their ground.

Before he could make another move, the crows emitted a fierce cawing and their swirling became even more frenzied. A second later a hole opened up in the heart of them. Church glimpsed an entity inside that made his eyes sting and his gorge rise, and then something dark and translucent erupted out of it and burst over their heads. The shockwave threw them to their knees and an awful sulphurous smell filled the air. Church felt his skin crawling, as if insects were swarming all over him. He glanced down to see pinpricks of blood bursting from his pores. Tom was screaming something, but Church's ears were still ringing from the explosion, and when he glanced to one side Veitch was yelling too. His face was covered with blood.

In that instant the other Fomorii surged forward. Tom grabbed Church's shirt and yanked, a signal to retreat. The three of them backed away hurriedly, but within seconds the ground was falling away beneath their feet and they were desperately trying to right themselves on the steep incline towards the cliffs. Church brandished the sword before him, but the Fomorii seemed quite content to herd the three of them where there was nowhere else to go. The buffeting wind at his back and the roaring of the sea as it crashed against the cliffs told him when they had run out of land, and time. He glanced back briefly. They were a foot away from the precipice; far beneath, the white water sucked and thrashed menacingly against the rocks. There was no way they could survive a plunge.

His skin was slick with blood from head to toe, but the only thought that dominated his mind was that he had wasted too long worrying about the Watchtower's untrue premonition of his death.

The first of the Fomorii moved forward with a roar and, despite Tom's spell, Church could still not look it full in the face. He closed his eyes and lashed out blindly with the sword. The impact made his bones ache, forcing his eyes open. He was shocked to see the sword had sliced through whatever the creature had instead of a collar bone and had imbedded itself in its skeleton. It was howling wildly and flailing its limbs as it died; Church almost vomited from the foul stench that was emanating from the wound. With an immense effort, he wrenched out the sword and swung it in an arc, cleaving off the beast's head.

He didn't have time to celebrate, for at that moment the screeching of the remaining Fomorii reached a crescendo and they moved forward as one. Out of the corner of his eye, he glimpsed Tom hunched over, muttering to himself, his hands and arms twitching as if he had an ague. Then Veitch was at his side, shouting obscenities as he waved the hunting knife so violently it no longer seemed as feeble as it had before.

The Fomorii bore down on them in a wave of deformed bodies, radiating a dark, terrifying power that made him sick to his stomach. Feeling the fear and despair surge through him, Church swung the sword back and closed his eyes. He thought, *This is*—

Something grasped the collar of his jacket and hauled him backwards. His heels kicked grass, rock and then nothing, and he was falling so fast the wind tore his breath from his mouth. There was no time to think of anything before he hit the waves hard. An instant later he blacked out as the water surged into his mouth and nose and pulled him far beneath the swell.

Shavi, Ruth and Laura sat on the cold stone bench in the tiny tower that was all that remained of St Michael's Church, perched high on top of the tor. Through the open arch where the wind blew mercilessly they could see the lights of Glastonbury spread out comfortingly in the intense dark just before dawn. On the cracked stone floor before them stood the plastic bottle which contained the water they had brought from the Chalice Well.

'I don't feel ready for this,' Ruth said. 'It would have been a little easier if Jim hadn't gone on at length about all the dangers.'

'That's God people for you,' Laura noted. 'They're never happy unless someone's worried or scared.'

Ruth watched the stars for a long moment, remembering a similar night in Stonehenge, and then said almost to herself, 'I wish Church was here.' She realised what she had said and glanced at Laura. 'I don't mean because I'm not up to it myself—'

Laura didn't look at her. 'I know what you mean.'

Shavi rose and went through a series of yoga movements to stretch the ache of the night chill from his muscles. It felt like they had been sitting in the tower for hours, although it had only been about forty-five minutes.

'So what do we do now? Do you think Mister Dog Collar could have been any more vague?' Laura asked gloomily.

'It is all about ritual,' Shavi explained, 'and part of the ritual is finding the path ourselves. He gave us *some* guidance – the time of the ritual – and I think the rest of it is pretty obvious.'

'To you, maybe, but then you're some big shaman-type.' Laura stood up and leaned in the arch, looking down at the town.

Shavi moved in beside her and pointed to the faint terraces cut into the hill centuries ago, visible by their moon-shadows even in the dark.

'You see those? What use are they? They are patently not fields, nor could they be the kind of defences thrown up on some earthworks from neolithic times. Yet it would take a tremendous amount of effort to level out those terraces, so they must be of some significance to whatever culture invested all that manpower and time hundreds or thousands of years ago.'

Ruth joined them in the archway, tracing the path of the terraces with her fingertip. 'They're like steps.'

'Exactly,' Shavi nodded. 'A path to the top, but not in the manner you suggest. A labyrinth, a three-dimensional one. You can walk a route back and forth around the tor to the summit.'

'Why do that when it's easier to go in a straight line?' Laura said.

'The labyrinth is a classical design found in rock carvings, coins, turf mazes around the world. It has more than one meaning, like everything else we have encountered, but at its heart it represents a journey to and from the land of the dead. Birth, death and rebirth.'

'I really don't like all this talk of death,' Ruth murmured.

'And what happens when we get to the end?' Laura stamped her feet to boost the blood circulation.

Shavi shrugged.

'And the water?'

'An oblation to be offered at the point where we find ourselves.'

'You call it ritual, but it sounds like magic to me,' Ruth noted.

'Perhaps.' Shavi put an arm around both their shoulders, an act that would have seemed too familiar from any other man they had just met, yet from him it simply suggested friendship and security. 'We think of magic as something from children's stories, but it may simply be a word for describing that activation of the earth force you have seen. New knowledge which we have no frame of reference to understand. Magic is as good a word as any.'

'Sometimes you sound just like that old hippie,' Laura said with an acidity that was transparent to both Shavi and Ruth.

They continued to discuss the tor and the mysteries they had uncovered for the next half hour, yet none of them touched on the matter that was most important in all their hearts; the sense that they were on the verge of something profound, a turning point which would finally reveal the truth about the events that were shaping the world, about the forgotten past and the hidden future, and, above all, about themselves.

The closer the sunrise drew, the more they seemed to feel an electric quality in the air which resonated deep within them. Barely able to contain their anticipation, they sat against a wall and watched the eastern sky for its lightening. It was a magical moment that stilled conversation, of stars, and wind and the sound of the trees at the foot of the tor, and for a while they seemed to feel the axis of the heavens turning, as they knew their ancestors would have done millennia ago.

It was during one such lull in the conversation that they were startled by the noise of something heavy hitting the ground and a strange liquid, flopping sound. It was incongruous enough to set their hearts racing, and they hurried around the tower to search for its origin.

But as they rounded the western flank of the tower, they were brought up sharp by a bizarre sight that sent their heads spinning: three figures floundered like fish on the slopes of the tor, soaked to the skin and retching up sea water.

'Oh great,' Laura said sourly. 'The old git's back.'

a Day as Still as heaven

Ruth reached Church first. 'We're on the highest spot in the area and they're drowning,' she said incredulously. Without giving it a second thought, she jumped astride him and began massaging his chest to free the water trapped in his lungs.

The others reacted slightly slower – Laura gave the kiss of life to Veitch while Shavi administered to Tom – but within five minutes the three new arrivals were sitting up, gasping and wringing out their sodden clothes.

Bafflement at the bizarre situation was washed aside in a rush of emotion. Ruth threw her arms round Church and hugged him tightly. 'God, I'm so glad you're alive!'

Although still dazed by the situation, his relief at seeing her was palpable. He kissed her affectionately on the cheek, then glanced up at Laura who was standing uncomfortably a few feet away.

'I knew you were too stupid to get yourself killed,' she said.

He smiled; the message between the lines was obvious. 'I missed you too.'

Their brief introductions dissolved into a mess of garbled comments as they struggled to understand what had happened. Church described the confrontation at Tintagel and their plunge into the ocean, while glancing at Glastonbury's lights. Then he caught Tom's eye. 'What do you know about it?'

Tom's grey, drawn face suggested the experience had affected him more than the others. 'I moved us along the lines of power.' He sucked in a deep, juddering breath.

'You *transported* us here?' Church said incredulously.

'It was always theoretically possible. A matter of shaping the energy to do your bidding, forcing a connection between two nodes. I'd been taught the ritual movements, the correct vibrational sounds to make—'

'Magic!' Shavi said, his face alight with excitement.

'—but I'd never achieved anything like this before. Desperation must have focused my mind.'

'Who taught you?' Church asked. 'You owe us a lot of explanations—'

'There is no time now,' Shavi interrupted. He explained the impending sunrise ritual and the events that had led them to it.

'Don't we get a bleedin' rest?' Veitch flopped back on the grass.

'We can rest later.' Church retrieved the sword from where it lay and made a tear in his jacket, slipping it in between the lining; the handle protruded above his right shoulder where he could reach it easily. 'Two down,' he said, 'and two to go.'

Huddled in the tower away from the wind, they made hasty introductions and exchanged fuller details of their experiences, but any excitement they may have felt at their reunion was muted by the apprehension of what lay ahead. Twenty minutes later the first faint silvering in the sky brought with it an oppressive silence. Shavi rose and led the way to the Living Rock, a standing stone that marked the entrance to the labyrinth. While the others waited uncomfortably behind him, he bowed his head silently in meditation. Then, when the first rays of dawn crept across the grass to hit the stone, it seemed to ignite with blue fire. A gasp of amazement rippled through the others, but Shavi simply rested his hand upon it for a moment before setting off along the first terrace; the others followed in a solemn procession.

The going was not easy. They weaved back and forth in horseshoe patterns around the tor, slowly rising through the terraces as the sky exploded in gold, purple and powder blue. Though none of them spoke, the dawn chorus soaring from the trees at the base of the hill provided an epic soundtrack. Whatever power lay in the ground reinvigorated Church, Veitch and Tom, but there was still a hard lump of fear in all their hearts.

It took them nearly two hours to complete the serpentine route. At the final turn, the path seemed to disappear, leaving a precipitous, near-impassable way to the summit. Veitch opened his mouth to question, but Church silenced him with a wave of his finger. At that spot, the underlying rock broke through the short grass to reveal a large boulder.

The others waited patiently while Shavi produced the plastic bottle containing the Chalice Well water and, after another moment of meditation, he poured the oblation upon the boulder. A strange dual tone emerged from deep within the tor, like falsetto singing merging with a bass rumble. Tiny threads of blue fire spread out across the boulder and then into the other exposed rock. It fizzed and licked for a moment while the noise grew in intensity and then, with a sudden roaring, the rock drew aside to reveal a dark tunnel winding down into the black depths.

They could remember nothing about that journey through the dark. Sometime later, they found themselves in a place that took their breath away; not some dingy cavern lying inside the tor, but green fields and thick woods, rustled by a slight breeze in the heat of a summer's day. Nearby they could hear the faint babbling of a brook. The air smelled sweeter than anything they had experienced before; to breathe it in was so fulfilling it was almost as if they had eaten a hearty meal. Ruth caught a fleeting glimpse of her owl soaring high above and wondered how it had got there.

'Where are we?' Veitch said in bewilderment. 'We should be underground. I can see sky.'

Tom knelt down and gently kissed the green sward. 'Tir na n'Og,' he muttered.

Ruth looked round in confusion. 'We're not in Somerset any more, Toto.'

'The Land of Youth, or Always Summer.' This Church did remember from his studies. 'The Celtic heaven. The Otherworld where all the gods were supposed to have gone to after they left Earth in the hands of man.'

'That's one aspect of it.' Tom rose and stretched; he looked revitalised. 'Like everything else, it has a dual aspect. It is also The Land of Ever Winter, or hell, by any other name, depending how you come to it.'

'I don't understand.' Veitch looked from one face to the other.

'This place is not fixed,' Tom said, 'like all the things that originate here. You are all seeing something slightly different, depending on your perception. What is within, is without.'

'Listen to the voice of Buddha,' Laura sighed.

But now he had mentioned it, they could all see it. The edges of each blade of grass, tree branches, even the horizon, seemed vaguely fluid, as if they could change at a moment's notice; they seemed to radiate a subtle, inner light, creating a distorted sense of unreality.

'But we should be underground,' Veitch protested.

'Hey, new boy, when you find your brain, let us know.' Laura kicked up a few sods of turf. 'We've crossed over. We're in Never land now.' Veitch returned a combative scowl.

'Look at it!' Shavi said. 'It is amazing. Everything is so vital.' He whirled round to take in the landscape. 'Even the quality of the air, the sounds—'

'Don't be mistaken,' Tom interjected. 'There's danger here too.'

'It looks deserted,' Ruth said.

'The Danann are missing. Everything else is in our world,' Church said.

The Wayfinder's flame pointed them down the gentle slope of the meadow to a wood that lay beyond the brook. As they walked, Church caught up with Tom. 'So this is where you stayed for all those years. Is it good to be back?'

'You misunderstand.' Tom didn't take his eyes off the path. 'I miss this place like a murderer who has spent his entire life in solitary confinement misses his cell. Familiarity forces you to love the things you hate.'

'You were a prisoner here?'

'A prisoner, a plaything, something to be tormented by the gods, torn inside out and reshaped for their enjoyment.'

Church eyed him askance. 'I hope that's a metaphor.'

'I told you – they are alien, unknowable. We cannot begin to grasp the power at their disposal. Do not be fooled because we view them in vaguely human form. They are beyond most of our emotions – love, hate—'

'Cruelty?'

He paused. 'No. Not beyond that.'

Tom was interrupted by a cry from Veitch, who had moved into lead position along the path which was skirting a thick wood. They hurried through the meadow flowers until they saw what had alerted him: an odd circular structure of timber and stone with a tower at its centre. The Wayfinder flame flickered enticingly towards it.

'Before this land was deserted you wouldn't have been able to get within an arrow's fall of this place. Even the Danann revered it and what it contained,' Tom said.

'The bloody Grail!' Veitch said enthusiastically.

They walked slowly until they were in the shadow of the building; an odd atmosphere hung heavily around it that invoked both awe and fear. Church pointed out five doors around its walls, without needing to explain what that meant. Shavi and Ruth were keen to enter, but after their experiences with the first two talismans Church, Veitch and Laura were more hesitant.

Tom wandered back into the sun and took up a position on one of the grassy slopes overlooking the building. 'You're not coming?' Church asked.

'I would be torn apart by all the power in there. This isn't for me. It's about you, all of you.'

There was something in his words that made Church feel uncomfortable, but he turned back to the others, readying himself for what lay ahead. After fifteen minutes boosting each other's confidence, they each took up a spot in front of one of the doors and on the count of three they swung them open and stepped in.

The corridor was long, pitch-black and oppressively warm. Shavi edged down it cautiously, trailing his fingertips along the rough walls for guidance. His footsteps echoed strangely, as if the size of the space were far greater than it appeared to be, and after he had been walking for ten minutes he realised that must certainly have been the case, for he could have circumnavigated the building five times in that period. By then, the faint light from the door had disappeared completely, the impenetrable darkness closing around so tightly he felt like he was floating in space. His progress slowed even further as he felt each step with his foot in case the floor fell away suddenly.

But after a short while he got a sense of diffuse illumination ahead, like candlelight. To his surprise, he found himself in what appeared to be a funfair hall of mirrors, the polished glass lined up in continuously branching avenues like a maze. After the dark it was destabilising and he had to close his eyes for a moment while he steadied himself.

It was impossible to guess where the source of the light was in the myriad subtle reflections, but it allowed him to move more freely. He chose his path at random.

For what seemed like an hour, he wandered among the images of himself, most of them normal, some grotesquely distorted. It seemed to him it was simply a trap to drive intruders insane. He could have been going round in circles for all he knew; there was nothing to distinguish the routes among the mirrors.

But as he rounded a sharp bend in the maze, he came upon a mirror which was unlike any of the others. It was larger, with a bevelled edge to the glass, and a frame of what appeared to be silver, designed with the spiral paths and interlinking patterns of Celtic art. Shavi felt drawn towards it as if it were radiating some dark power. And once he stood before it he could see it was unusual in other ways, too; at first glance, his reflection seemed perfectly normal, but the more he looked, the more he could see a difference that was so subtle it was almost a variation of mood. There was a darkness to the features, the merest tinge of cruelty around the mouth, a sense of bitter loss in the eyes, a resentment in the way the head was held.

Shavi examined it for a long moment, and then its mouth moved in no reflection of his own.

'Why do you do this to yourself, Shavi? Searching for meaning in all these silly places? All these religions that have nothing to do with you?

The meaning is here, with your family and the way you were raised. It will destroy you, Shavi.' It was his father's voice. A chill crept through him. He recalled the rest of that conversation, the anger, the terrible things that were said.

The mouth on the reflection became faintly sneering. 'You are a selfish man, Shavi.' This time it was his own voice, though harder, more contemptuous. 'You destroyed your family with your actions. Think of your father and your mother – the effort they expended raising you in the correct Muslim way. Think how they must feel to see you abandon every principle which has been the bedrock of their lives. They see themselves as failures in the thing that is most important to them. You destroyed them, Shavi.'

'I did not—'

The image spoke more forcefully to block his protestations. 'Lies. Your only motivation was your own selfish spiritual advancement, your own intellectual curiosity, and you had no concern how many people were hurt as you walked your road of excess to your own personal palace of wisdom. Life is about community, Shavi. About society. Helping others achieve their own nirvana—'

'I am helping others now.'

'Because it coincides with your own desires. You are revelling in the light these experiences shine on the dark of the greater reality.'

'True.' Shavi felt more confident after his initial shock. Once he had realised it was the test they had all expected it became easy to detach himself. The mirror was reflecting back at him his own doubts and fears about his choices in life. But there was nothing it could show him that he hadn't weighed and discarded, or had accepted in order to change himself.

The mirror suddenly took on a milky sheen and when it cleared he was looking out on a Clapham street late one night. Several yards away, Lee was being bludgeoned to death. The blood splashed high with each thunderous blow. The attacker was like a smear on the surface of the glass, but Lee's expression was in stark relief; his eyes were turned towards Shavi, pleading for help, his mouth was an O of horror and desperation of a life about to be eradicated.

'You could have saved him, Shavi. You had the strength inside you to stand up, to fight. But you were afraid for your own safety. The haziness from the blow was just as an excuse. You gave in to it easily so you would not have to risk yourself. And Lee died because of your cowardice.'

Shavi felt the emotion well up in him uncontrollably until tears sprang from his eyes like they had been pricked by needles. There was such a rush of loss and guilt he thought he was going to break down.

'You're a bitch, Laura, and you deserve everything you get.' The face in the mirror, her face, spat the words with venom. 'Let's face it, you killed your mum! On a scale of one to ten that's off the Sick Bastardometer. What do you think that did to your dad? Well, it probably wasn't what was crossing his mind when he held you in that little girlie white dress at your Christening. He probably thought you'd turn out to be a vet or a nurse. You know, something *useful*. Hell, maybe even a dutiful daughter – some stupid fantasy like that. No wonder he opted for a life of shrinks and cells instead of giving you a big soppy hug.

'So now you think you're going to find some kind of salvation with Mr Brooding-and-Soulful Churchill. Think again. You'll just screw up his life like you have everybody else's. You couldn't feel anything as selfless as love if it walked up and bit you on your bony arse. You're just sucking out of him anything you can find that will make you feel, Vampire-Girl. Get real. If you wanted to do something worthwhile you'd top yourself. Save the rest of the world any more heartache.'

Veitch felt his finger close on the trigger, felt the kick from the ejaculation of the bullet, saw it embed itself in the man's body, burst through it, spraying the bone and the blood, saw the terrible pain on his victim's face; felt the faintly perverse pleasure rise through him, like a hard porn orgasm, the kick of having ultimate power and dispensing it with the merest thought. Nothing could control him; *he* could control everything.

'That was how it was, wasn't it, Ryan?'

'No! I've been living with that every day of my life since!'

'Because you enjoyed it.'

'No—!'

'Yes. Secretly. In your quiet moments. Lying in bed when everyone else was asleep. When your other poor bastard brothers were doing time for you. You thought, "Yeah! That was what it was like to be a top man!"'

'You lying fucking bastard! I'm gonna make up for that if it's the last thing I do. That's right. Even if I have to die, I'm gonna pay it back. I learned a big lesson—'

'No, you didn't. You'd kill again at the drop of a hat.'

'You bastard! You might look like me, but you don't know me! I've never done anything right in my life and I'm sick of it! I want to be a good bloke! I want people to look at me like they do Churchill—'

'Yeah, it's all about self, isn't it, Ryan? You don't want to do good because it makes other people feel good. You want to do it because it makes *you* feel good.'

'Fuck you!'

'I loved my father!' The tears seared down Ruth's cheeks.

'You hated him. He dominated you from when you were young. He forced you into a career you didn't want to do—'

'He didn't force me! I did it because I wanted to make him happy! So it was the wrong career for me. It's not Dad's fault. He didn't—'

'What? He didn't know his own daughter? No, he was a typical working class bloke who wanted a bit of respectability for his family. A lawyer! That'd be something to tell them all down at the union meetings and in the labour club. His daughter had worked hard and made something of herself, despite starting with nothing. And he didn't care a thing about what you wanted—'

'That's not true! Dad didn't think like that!' The next few lines out of the mirror were drowned out by Ruth's racking sobs. She had not felt so raw since the day her father had dropped dead of a heart attack, in that fleeting moment when she thought time had stopped and the whole world was coming to an end. Somehow the magic surrounding the mirror had pushed all the right buttons to bring the emotions rushing out of her.

'He knew you were unhappy in your work. That's what killed him.'

'Not true! It was the shock of Uncle Jim's murder—'

The mirror went milky and when it cleared Ruth was looking on the interior of a building society. A tall man with greying hair and a pleasant face that was locked in anxiety stared out at her; he looked remarkably like her father.

'That's Uncle Jim,' she said curiously. Suddenly she realised what was coming next. 'Oh no—'

The blast of a gun made her jump with shock. Her uncle was flung back against the counter, clutching at his stomach as a large red patch began to spread across his sweater.

'Oh, Uncle Jim—'

Somebody ran forward to inspect the body. He was cursing and waving his gun at Uncle Jim, as if he had done something to provoke his own murder. Ruth was transfixed in horror. The killer had on a mask, but Ruth recognised the shape of his muscular body, the long hair that flapped around as he shook his head wildly, in anger it seemed. But most of all she recognised the garish tattoo she could see snaking out from under his sleeve.

'That's the man Church brought with him.' Even as she said it Ruth couldn't believe it; but it was true. 'That's Veitch.'

Church stared impassively at the scene of Marianne lying on the floor, her skin so pale she looked like a statue. 'You're wasting your time,' he said coldly. 'I've lived with that image for so long now I'm immune to it. When I thought I was responsible . . . when I thought I was some kind of terrible person who could live with someone yet be so self-centred they had no idea of the torment their partner was going through . . . then it might have hurt me. But now I know she was murdered.'

'You're still responsible,' his voice said as the image faded and his dark, bitter reflection returned. At first he had thought it resembled him exactly; it seemed just like the face he had seen in the mirror so many times over the last two years. But now he wasn't so sure. It didn't feel like him. He felt better than that; and that thought surprised him.

'How can that be? Someone else killed her and pretty soon, with any luck, I'm going to find out who did it. That was the promise made to me, and that's the only thing driving me forward. You see, I'm going to die soon. I've seen my own death. Can you believe that? So nothing else matters, apart from finding out what happened to Marianne and getting some kind of peace before the end. Some might call it fatalistic. But if it's going to happen it's going to happen – you've just got to make the best of it. That's a big lesson I've learned recently. It's the quality of the life up to the big peg-out that matters.' The reflection went to speak, but Church wouldn't let it. 'Shut up. And here's something that has to be said, just for the sake of getting it out in the open, really. Once I find out who killed Marianne, if I get the chance before I die myself, I'm going to take the bastard with me. That's a promise.'

The reflection opened its mouth once more, but Church had had enough. He turned his back on it and prepared to return to the maze in search of the way to the talisman. And as he did so there was a sudden shattering as shards of the big ornate mirror exploded out. Miraculously, none of them touched him. As he glanced back he noticed that behind the broken mirror there was another tunnel, this time lit by the flickering blue light of the earth energy.

Church found himself in a circular, domed room cast in sapphire by the light of four braziers burning brightly with the blue fire. There was a sense of serenity that sluiced all the negative emotions from him. In the centre was a raised marble dais bearing an object which he couldn't quite make out; the air seemed to shimmer and fold around an image which constantly changed. Church saw a construct of light with strange, unnerving angles, a robust cauldron blackened by fire, a crystal goblet, an ornate gold vase studded with jewels. As he approached, the object seemed to freeze, the air cleared and he was looking at a chipped bowl of heavily aged wood that most wouldn't have given a second glance.

He stood before it, overwhelmed by the weight of myth and symbolism; here was the dream of generations.

It was too much. Afraid to even touch it, he rested his hands on the marble top. Instantly, the bowl slid towards him of its own accord and came to a stop between his fingers, offering itself up to him. Steeling himself, he grasped it firmly, and at that moment he heard the distant sound of fracturing glass. Within minutes the other four had made their way to the chamber; Church was shocked to see their shattered expressions.

Shavi's face brightened the moment he saw what Church was holding. 'The Grail!' His voice was filled with awe and wonder.

'And the cauldron, one and the same. It—'

They were interrupted by a sudden commotion. In a fury, Ruth had propelled herself towards Veitch and slammed a fist into his face. He pitched backwards, blood spouting from his nose, and now she was raining blows upon him which Veitch batted away as best he could.

'You bastard!' she screamed. 'You killed him!'

Shavi and Laura managed to pull her off with great difficulty; she was transformed by rage, swearing and spitting. Veitch pulled himself into a sitting position, dabbing at his bloody nose. 'Stupid bitch,' he hissed, but Church could see the anger in his face was purely defensive.

Laura looked at Ruth in disbelief. 'Take a stress pill. What's wrong with you – something finally popped?'

'He killed my father.' She shook Laura and Shavi off, consumed by the coldness of her words, which brought back the terrible ache of futility and emptiness she had felt just after her father's death, and she hated Veitch as much for making her feel it again as for his original crime.

'He killed your dad?' Laura looked from Ruth to Veitch. None of them could comprehend what she was saying.

'He was some stupid, petty bigmouth with a gun trying to get rich quick by robbing a building society.' The contempt in Ruth's voice hissed acidly. 'My uncle was in there and that bastard shot him dead, then ran away. And when my father found out what had happened, it killed him.'

They stared at Veitch for some sort of denial, but he couldn't look at any of them.

'He was just an old man!' Ruth cried. 'He couldn't have done anything to you!' She swallowed noisily. 'He was going down to Brighton with my aunt to celebrate their silver wedding anniversary. We were going to have a party . . .' She swallowed again. 'What you did that day destroyed our family!'

Veitch bit his lip, said nothing.

Ruth glared at him, but her eyes were already filling with tears. She turned away and Church stepped in and put his arms around her. There was resistance at first, then she folded against him, although her body still felt rigid and cold, as if made of compacted ice.

'I didn't mean to do it,' Veitch protested. 'I know it's no fucking excuse, but I just . . . I was frightened. I knew I shouldn't have been there. And then I turned round and I thought he was coming for me . . .' He stared blankly at the ground. 'If it means anything, I've never had a minute's peace since that day.'

'It doesn't mean anything,' Ruth said coldly.

The others shifted uncomfortably in the blast of raw emotions. Eventually Church said, 'I know how you feel. Exactly how you feel. And that's why I'd never ask you to forgive him. But what's at stake in the world is more important than everything that's happening in our lives. If you break us up now—'

'I'm not going to break anything.' Ruth pulled away from Church and looked him full in the face. 'I'm not some stupid bimbo. I know what's at stake. I know what my responsibilities are. And I'll be there to the end.' She stared hard at Veitch and what Church saw in that look unnerved him. 'But don't expect me to be friends with that bastard. Don't expect me to pass the time of day with him. And if we get to the end of this alive I'm going to make sure he faces up to *his* responsibility. And see he gets put away for his crime.'

They emerged from the Temple of Mirrors to a balmy summer night alight with thousands of stars. Only the faintest breeze stirred the treetops. Church staggered up the grassy bank with the Grail held before him so Tom could see what they had achieved. Tom was already on his feet, and Church was shocked to see his face was glowing with respect.

As they walked back across the meadows, Shavi and Laura talked quietly with Ruth while Veitch trailed along behind, lonely and isolated.

Tom caught up with Church at the front and grabbed his arm. 'I'm worried we'll lose the boy.'

'I'll have a word with Ryan,' Church said wearily; the emotional distractions were a blow too much. 'I don't want us pulled apart from within. If we can't count on each other—'

'Remain focused,' Tom said. 'You've done a remarkable job so far. Better than I expected on our first meeting.'

'Is that a note of support?'

'Make the most of it. They're few and far between.'

Was that a glimmer of humour? Church wondered. He glanced surreptitiously at Tom, but his face was as implacable as ever; all his emotions were locked so tightly inside they seemed almost separate from him. Church had the impression he hadn't always been like that, that his experiences at the hands of the gods had been so terrible that emotional detachment was the only way he could have survived.

'Are you ever going to let us into all your secrets?' Church asked.

'When the time's right.'

'We're not children, you know.'

'You are children, in the ways of the gods and in the true mysteries of the universe. You're learning how to see things truly after a lifetime of being blinkered. And like any learning process, too much too soon would be detrimental.'

'And you're our teacher.' Church sighed.

'For my sins.'

'Can't you at least tell me what lies ahead?'

'That's the last thing I'd tell you.'

Church glanced back at the rag-tag bunch following and felt a sweep of pessimism. There was no one he would describe as a hero. In fact, most of them seemed damaged to the point of uselessness.

Tom seemed to sense his thoughts. 'People are forged by hardship,' he said simply.

Church shook his head, stared at the ground.

'It's a terrible fact of life that nobody has wisdom until they've tasted bereavement,' he continued. 'Of all life's experiences, that's the sole one with truly alchemical power. Knowing that, given a choice, we would all stay ignorant. Yet, ironically, we're better people for having gone through it. Bereavement is the key to meaning, and you all have that wisdom within you. The building blocks are there—'

'And you expect damaged goods to pile them into some sort of structure?'

Tom shrugged and looked away; Church couldn't tell if Tom was annoyed by his defeatism or acknowledging it.

*

289

They reached the tunnel back to the world soon after. At the entrance they all turned and looked back over the idyllic landscape, glistening in the moonlight, breathing deeply of the sweet, scented air; there was true magic in every aspect of it.

'I could stay here for ever,' Ruth said.

Tom nodded. 'Yes. That's the danger.'

When they emerged on the tor, it was the dark just before dawn, yet they all felt that only an hour or more had passed since they had first entered the tunnel. They immediately noticed a subtle difference: the night was significantly warmer.

'It's like summer,' Ruth said curiously.

They made their way down the winding path to the town as dawn broke, golden and comforting. But as they killed time on the high street waiting for the café to open for breakfast, a delivery van dropped off a bundle of papers outside the newsagents. Church wandered over to glance at the headlines.

'Look at this,' he said in an uneasy voice.

The others gathered round as he pointed out the date beneath the masthead. During their brief stay in Otherworld, two weeks had passed. It was April 1.

the harrowing

'You lot have got it all wrong. This is the key to eternal youth. You spend a couple of weeks in that place and when you get home, everyone goes, "How do you stay so young? What are your beauty secrets?" Then you go round to all your old boyfriends and point out their wrinkles.' Laura sat with her feet on the dashboard between Veitch and Shavi, who was driving. Church, Tom and Ruth sat in the back amidst the camping equipment and what clothes and supplies they could afford. The discovery of the time differential had left them feeling uncomfortable.

'You're missing the point,' Church said irritably. 'We can't afford to lose two weeks. We've still got one more of these damned talismans to recover—'

'Stop moaning.' Laura swivelled to flash him a challenging smile. 'There's nearly a month to the deadline. That's enough time to do this walking backwards.' She turned to Tom. 'Anyway, Grandad, you must have known about this before we crossed over.'

'Yes,' Ruth said. 'Why didn't you say anything? I'm sick of you not telling us things before they happen.'

Tom took off his glasses and cleaned them on his shirt. 'No point. We had to go. You would have found out sooner or later.'

'You mean you didn't want to take the chance some of us wouldn't cross over.' He didn't return Ruth's pointed stare.

'It's a good thing this mission is based on trust,' Laura said ironically before slipping off her boots and planting her feet on the windscreen.

'Bet that position feels familiar,' Ruth said sharply. Laura showed her middle finger over her shoulder.

Church rested one hand on the crate they'd picked up from the grocer's to store the stone, the sword and the cauldron; it seemed faintly sacrilegious, but the need for easy, well-disguised transport was more pressing. He could almost feel the power of the talismans through his fingertips. And sometimes it was like he could feel them talking to him, incomprehensible whispers curling like smoky tendrils around his mind. Part of it made him tremble with awe; another part of it made his skin crawl. 'I feel nervous carrying these things around with us.'

'The Fomorii can't touch them,' Tom noted.

'They'll just get somebody else to do their dirty work.' He paused. 'Now we're out of Glastonbury, does that mean we're meat for the Wild Hunt again?'

Tom nodded.

'We'd better make sure we're somewhere secure by nightfall,' Ruth said.

'How about some music?' Laura went to turn on the radio. Ruth told her to wait while she pulled a cassette out of her bag and threw it up front. Laura made a face, but put it in the machine anyway. A second later Sinatra began to sing about flying off to foreign climes for excitement and romance.

Church's face brightened with surprise. 'I thought we'd lost this!'

'Even the Wild Hunt didn't want it,' Laura said sulkily.

Ruth flashed him a grin and he smiled thankfully; he found real comfort in the way she seemed instinctively to know him. If nothing else, the previous few weeks had given him a true friend.

The Wayfinder led them back to the M5 motorway and then north in the bright, warm sunshine. The van ran as good as new after the repairs, but the cost had made them worry about their funds. They all had credit cards and made their monthly payments by phone transfer from their savings accounts, but their reserves weren't endless.

Shavi was talkative on a range of subjects and Laura kept the banter going, but Veitch hardly said a word. His confrontation with the results of his actions seemed to have had a profound effect on him; above all, it appeared to have confirmed his own worst fears about himself. Church began to worry that Tom's assessment of Veitch had been correct and he resolved to talk to him as soon as he could get him alone.

They picked up the M4 and headed west into Wales, which, as Shavi noted, was an obvious destination, with its rich Celtic history and links to Arthurian legend.

'So, we're talking themes here,' Laura noted. 'Church has got his sword, so that makes him the big, fat king. I guess the tattooed boy here is Lancelot, the old hippie would be Merlin, Miss Gallagher back there acts like Queen Bee so I suppose she's Guinevere.' She slapped a hand hard on Shavi's thigh. 'Don't know what that makes you and me, though.'

'Is that it?' Ruth said with the excitement of someone who's just seen the light. 'We're, like, some kind of reincarnation—'

'No, that's too literal,' Church said insistently. 'And I keep saying this, but those are just stories. There was no Round Table or chivalrous knights. Arthur, if he existed at all, was a Celtic warlord—'

'So the *historians* say.' Tom pronounced the word with faint contempt.

'I'm not even going to begin talking to you about it.' Church waved his hand dismissively. 'You'll keep us talking round in circles and then tell us nothing new.'

Laura grabbed the rag Shavi used to wipe the windows and threw it hard at Tom's head. 'Come on, you old git. Spill the beans or we're going to tie you up and drag you along behind the van.'

He glared at her and readjusted his glasses.

'Brothers and Sisters of Dragons,' Shavi mused. 'Could that have something to do with *Pendragon*, Arthur's family name?'

Church shook his head. 'Pendragon is a mixture of Celtic and old Welsh meaning Chief Leader. The word root has nothing to do with dragons.'

'Or perhaps,' Tom said, as if he were dealing with idiots, 'it's simply another manifestation of the duality which is at the heart of everything.'

'That means double meanings, Laura,' Ruth called out.

'Come on, Tom, you can't do this to us,' Church protested.

'Yeah, come on, *Tom*.' Laura looked around the dashboard for something else to throw.

Tom noticed her and said hastily, 'I suppose it wouldn't hurt to tell you now. You're almost there anyway. You're not reincarnations in the literal sense that you mean, but you do carry within you the essence that the legends speak of. The Pendragon Spirit. It is a subtle power, a state of mind, an ability which is gifted to some to defend the land. That's the true meaning of the legend.'

'So Arthur and the knights are also a metaphor for this Pendragon spirit?' Church said.

'So we're descendants or something?' Laura said quizzically.

Tom shook his head. 'The land gifts it to the most deserving. It chooses the ones who'll defend it the best.'

'It screwed up this time, didn't it.' Veitch continued to stare out of the passenger window.

'That is . . . a tremendous burden,' Church said.

'Yeah, if you believe this,' Laura said.

'You're still at the start of your journey.' Tom delved into his knapsack for the tin where he kept his drugs. 'The journey that the Tarot delineates. At the moment you're all the Fool. When you come out at the other end, you'll be aware of the true meaning of the Pendragon Spirit.'

'The ones who survive,' Church said. He fought to damp down a sudden flash of the portent of his death.

'The ones who survive,' Tom agreed.

'There is something happening here,' Shavi interrupted. They felt the van slow down sharply and Ruth, Church and Tom clambered forward to peer through the windscreen. The motorway ahead was blocked by a row of emergency vehicles. Police were directing traffic up the slipway at the next exit. Ominously, Church could see army trucks on the deserted road ahead and some troops with guns discreetly positioned near the central reservation and the opposite bank. 'Where are we?'

'Just past Cardiff,' Shavi said.

As they pulled off slowly, Shavi wound down the window and asked a policeman what was wrong. 'An accident,' he said with a face like stone. 'Now be on your way. And keep to the diversions.'

'I've never seen the army brought in for an accident,' Veitch said.

'They're covering it up, aren't they?' Ruth sat down behind Shavi's seat. 'They know what's going on. Or if they don't know exactly what's happening, they know something out of the ordinary has hit the country. They'd have to know. And they're trying to stop everyone finding out so there isn't a panic.'

'Like holding back the waves.' Tom's voice was quiet, but the words fell like stones.

'What do you think's happened down there, then?' Laura seemed suddenly uneasy.

'Must be something bad to close off the whole motorway,' Veitch said. 'It'll be causing chaos on all the roads around.'

'It seems like a great deal has happened during the two weeks we were away,' Shavi said darkly.

An uncomfortable silence filled the van as they joined the queues of traffic.

Although the Wayfinder continued to point west, they found it hard to follow its direction; a whole section of the country seemed to have been closed off with police and army barricades. But although they constantly checked the radio news broadcasts, there was no information about what was happening.

Just as they were considering abandoning the van and setting off on foot, they finally managed to break away from the main route and weave along deserted country roads through the soaring Welsh hills and mountains. There was an unearthly desolation to the countryside; no tractors in the fields, no pedestrians, although they could see lights in houses and smoke curling from chimneys.

Eventually they started to swing south-westwards until they hit one of the main tourist drags to the coast. Their speedy journey marked how effective the authorities had been at driving traffic away. Veitch, who was in charge of mapreading, pointed out a small town, Builth Wells, which lay ahead of a long stretch of open countryside. They all agreed it would be a good place to stop for food, rest, and to see if any of the locals had any idea what was happening nearby.

But the closer they got to the town, the more they realised something was wrong. Even on the main road in there was no traffic, while the only sign of movement was a flurry of newspaper pages caught in the wind sweeping across the huge showground where the Welsh agricultural fair was held each year. They all fell silent as they crossed the old stone bridge over the River Wye that marked the entrance to the town proper, faces held rigid as they scanned the area.

'It's a ghost town,' Veitch said in a voice that was almost a whisper.

The van swung on to the one-way system that took them up the High Street where shops which should have been bustling at that time of day stood eerily empty. Cars were parked on the right, but they could have been left there days ago for all they knew. Nothing moved anywhere. Shavi wound down the window in the hope of hearing something they were missing, but the silence was so intense it made them feel queasy.

'Do you think they've been evacuated?' Ruth asked.

Church didn't give voice to what his instincts were telling him.

They followed the one-way system round to a nearly full car park alongside the river where Shavi pulled into a bay and switched off the engine.

'What are you doing?' Veitch said. 'You could have left it anywhere.'

Shavi shrugged. 'What can I say? In situations like this, I find comfort in following old routines.'

'Head-in-the-sand dude,' Laura chided, but they were all reluctant to get out.

Eventually Church led them from the car park up a side road to the High Street, where they argued about what to do.

'Wake up,' Laura said. 'It's deserted. Looting is an option.'

'That's just what I'd expect from someone with your easy morals,' Ruth snapped. 'It's still stealing.'

Veitch emerged from a health food store chewing on a cheese and onion pastie. 'It's still fresh,' he said. 'Wherever they've gone, it's only just happened.'

Shavi looked up and down the street, noting the open doors. 'If they were evacuated, they would have locked up at least.'

Despite Ruth's initial opposition, they agreed to take some of the fresh food which would spoil quickly. Veitch and Laura picked up a couple of bags and headed into the health food store, the baker's and the butcher's with what Ruth noted as undue glee.

'Least you won't need your gun this time,' she said sourly to Veitch as he passed.

Church and Shavi left her with Tom while they explored further up the street. Church had quickly learned to value the Asian's quick insight and measured views; Shavi's obvious intelligence and ability to keep a cool head under pressure made Church feel some of the weight had been taken off his shoulders.

'What do you think, then?' Church turned and looked back down the length of the High Street and beyond to the dangerous face of nature rising up in thickly wooded hills all around.

'I think everything out there is getting braver. Villages, small towns . . . they do not seem concerned by them any more. The problem is, the enemy is not one group – it is a complete existence that is so alien to us any contact is destructive.'

'So can we hold back the new Dark Age?'

'This is a world of the subconscious, of nightmares and shadows. Those things are always more powerful than their opposites.'

'So we're wasting our time?'

'We are doing the best we can.' Shavi smiled wanly.

They were both suddenly alerted by a faint sound which seemed to emanate from a tiny cobbled alley which ran at breathtaking steepness upwards between two shops; it sounded like a firecracker in the silence.

'What was that?' Church asked.

They both moved forward to the foot of the alley. At the top they could see a parked car, a house, blue sky; no movement. Church put one foot on the cobbles, but Shavi placed a restraining hand on his arm. They stood motionless for a minute until they heard the noise again; the inhuman sound was like an insectile chittering laid over the cry of a baby. A second later a grey shape flitted across the other end of the alleyway, too quick to make out its true form.

'We should get out of here,' Church said.

Another movement; there seemed to be more than one of them.

They sprinted back down the High Street, where Ruth was leaning against the wing of a car. She caught their expressions and asked what was wrong.

'Where are the others?' Church snapped.

'The criminal fraternity are back in the health food store. Tom's gone into that clothing store.' She pointed across the street. 'Are you going to tell me what's happening? Is there something here?' She jumped off the car, glancing around anxiously.

'You two get Veitch and Laura and head back to the van. I'll find Tom.' He sprinted into the clothing store, past racks of water-proofs and outdoor wear. Tom was in the back, trying on a pair of walking boots.

'Come on,' Church said. 'We don't have time for that. Bring them with you if you want.'

Tom stood up instantly at the insistence in Church's voice. 'Fomorii?'

'I don't think so.'

Tom didn't need any more prompting. He hurried behind Church to the entrance, but as they stepped out into the street they both saw movement at the top end of the High Street: fleeting shapes that looked almost ghostly flashed back and forth across the road.

'You're the expert,' Church said. 'What are they?'

Tom stared for a second, then shook his head. 'I have no idea. The twilight lands were filled with all manner of things. I had more to do than study them all.'

As they ran across the road, movement erupted in the shops all around. The shapes seemed to be emerging from the backrooms as if they had awakened from their rest in the shadowy interiors and were now intent on seeking out the trespassers on their property. Church caught a glimpse of green eyes and gnashing teeth. A sudden wash of fear spurred him on.

With Tom close behind, he ran down the side road to where Shavi had the van warmed up and waiting. They piled in the back and the van took off with a screech of tyres, going the wrong way through the one-way system.

'Changed your mind about sticking to routine, I see,' Veitch said to Shavi. The Asian smiled tightly.

As they careered out of town, Church, Tom and Ruth glanced back through the rear windows to see the High Street now swarming with the grey shapes in a manner that reminded them of a disturbed ant hill. It was a scene that filled them all with the utmost terror.

'Where do you think the residents have gone?' Ruth asked feebly.

Church and Tom took up their seats without answering. The atmosphere had become even more dark and oppressive.

When eventually they reached Carmarthen, they were relieved to see the town buzzing as if nothing were wrong. 'It shows the size of habitation that is safe,' Shavi noted. They followed the Wayfinder along the side of the river and then on the main dual carriageway to the coast, through green fields, past caravan parks, and by 4 p.m. they had reached the palm trees that marked the entrance to the holiday resort of Tenby.

The mediaeval walled town lay perched on cliffs of brown shale and hard grey limestone, offering panoramic views along the rugged Pembrokeshire coastline. Amongst its twisty-turny streets, pastel-painted bed and breakfasts slumbered beneath a powder-blue sky in which seagulls soared and turned lazily. Looking up, Ruth also fleetingly spotted her owl companion skimming the ancient tiled rooftops, although she found it hard to believe it had followed the van from Glastonbury, or even that it had got out of Tir n'a n'Og unseen.

The streets were too small to negotiate effectively in the van, so they parked at the South Beach and returned through the five arches that formed a gateway in the soaring stone walls. Veitch and Shavi carried the talisman crate between them while Church went in front with the Wayfinder held within the fold of his jacket where it couldn't be seen by passers-by. It took them down Tudor Square, bustling despite the unseasonal time of year, and along a winding road to a picturesque harbour where rows of boats bobbed gently on the outgoing tide. At the harbour wall, Church halted, puzzled. The lantern's flame seemed to be pointing out to sea.

After a brief discussion, Veitch set off to scout the area, returning only five minutes later to herd them along a path past a tiny, white-walled museum to a bandstand on the headland overlooking the beach and the brilliant blue sea.

'There,' he said. Basking in the sun in the bay was a large island.

Caldey Island was home to an order of Cistercian monks. Regular boat trips were despatched from the mainland several times a day so tourists could experience the isolation – and contribute to the monastery's upkeep – but they had missed the last boat of the afternoon. Their only option seemed to be to find somewhere to hole up until morning and hope they could stay safe through the night.

They checked into one of the pretty bed and breakfasts in the back-streets of the old town, not too far from the front, relishing the opportunity to have a shower and sleep in a bed for a change. After an early dinner, Tom retired to his room where he agreed to oversee the talismans, although he wouldn't go near the crate. The others opted to look around the town while daylight was still with them. Church took the opportunity to steer Veitch away for a heart-to-heart, leaving Shavi, Ruth and Laura to pick their way through the streets dominated by pristine ice cream parlours and restaurants. After all they had witnessed, the place seemed uncommonly happy, untouched by the dark shadow that had fallen across the land. It both raised their spirits and made them feel uncomfortable, for they knew it couldn't last.

'I can't believe we've got this far.' Church closed his eyes so he could appreciate the early evening sun on his face as he inhaled the salty aroma of the sea caught in the cooling breeze. There on the beach, he could almost forget everything. The sensations reminded him of childhood holidays before the burdens of responsibility had been thrust on his shoulders, and happy summer days with Marianne before life had truly soured. The womb noises of the ocean and the breaking surf calmed him enough to realise how stressed he had become, his shoulders hunched, neck muscles knotted. Opening his eyes, he watched Veitch trudging beside him, oblivious to the seaside joys. 'When I went to the Watchtower and heard about the four talismans, I thought it was only a matter of time before it went pear-shaped. But finding them has been easy,' he continued, and, after a pause, 'Relatively easy.'

'That's because they were waiting for us, so Tom says,' Veitch said unenthusiastically. 'We were meant to get them, at this time, and we did. No mystery there.'

Church shook his head. 'I don't believe it works like that. Even if the stars were aligned, it wasn't fated that these things would fall into our hands. We did this and I'm not going to have it taken away from us.' Caldey Island caught his eye and he brought himself up sharp. 'But we haven't got them all yet. There's still time for things to go wrong.'

'Now you're talking my kind of language.'

Church stopped and rounded on him. 'Come on, Veitch, stop being so bloody pessimistic. You're not the only one who's had a miserable time—'

'Miserable time! I killed somebody! That's not miserable, that's a fucking catastrophe! I have to live with it every bleedin' day and now I can't forget it for a minute because I'm spending time with the poor bastard's niece, just so I can see on a regular basis how my stupidity fucked up a whole family's life!'

He made to walk on, but Church grabbed at his shoulder roughly. Instinctively Veitch's fists bunched and he adopted a threatening posture. 'So you screwed up and you're feeling guilty about it. Fine. That's how it should be. But self-pity is just you being selfish. You've got a job to do now that's more important than your feelings. If you want to tear yourself apart, you can do it after this is over.'

'Fuck off.' Veitch made another attempt to walk off and Church grabbed him roughly once more. This time Veitch's response was instant. He swung his fist hard into Church's jaw, knocking him to the sand.

For a moment, Church was dazzled by flashes of black and purple. Then he jumped up, lowered his head and rammed Veitch in the stomach. They both fell, rolling around in the sand, wrestling and punching. Eventually Church hauled himself on top and locked his arms on Veitch's shoulders so the Londoner couldn't move.

'I'm no hero,' Church said through gritted teeth. 'I didn't choose to be here. I've got my own agenda going on too. But I know I can't let all this misery and suffering happen if I can do something about it. I mean, who could?'

Veitch's eyes narrowed. 'Lots of people could.' He searched Church's face for a moment longer, then threw him off with an easy shrug. After he'd dusted himself down, he said, 'Don't worry, I'm not giving up on my bleedin' responsibilities. But I want to do something to make it up to Ruth. I know I'll never actually make amends, but I've got to try.' He paused. 'I'm not a bad bloke, you know. Just stupid.'

Church rubbed his jaw, which ached mercilessly, but he'd known what he was doing. 'Ruth's a smart person. If you've got any good in you, she'll see it eventually. You've just got to give it time.'

'Yeah, best behaviour and all that. Listen, sorry about smacking you. I've got a bleedin' awful temper.'

'Don't worry. I'll point you in the right direction before I activate you next time.' He shook sand out of his hair and added, 'Come on, let's find a pub. It's ages since I've had a pint.'

'What a great place.' Ruth sat on the steps of a statue of Prince Albert and looked out across the harbour. 'Everybody here's on holiday, so happy . . . I can't believe it might all get swept away.'

Laura crawled out to the end of the barrel of a cannon and sat back, basking in the sun. 'Talk about something important for a change. Like isn't our working class London boy a babe. I wonder how low his tattoos go?'

'If you're trying to wind me up, you've picked the wrong subject,' Ruth snapped.

'What about you, Mr Bi?' Laura said to Shavi. 'Does he get your sap rising?'

'He is not unattractive.' Shavi smiled, but continued to lie on the grass with his eyes closed.

'You know, I'm noticing a distinct pathology to your sexual obsession.' Ruth glared at Laura, who ignored her.

'That's just what I'd expect from you, Frosty. But I'm not a one-obsession woman. I like drugs, music and technology too.'

'Well, I never realised you were so deep.' Ruth stood up and wandered around the base of the statue. 'What do you think we've got to do once we get this last talisman?'

Shavi hauled himself into a sitting position. 'Perhaps everything will become obvious once we have all the pieces together.'

'Having seen just a glimpse of what's out there, it makes me feel what we're doing is so ineffectual. Do you think these other gods can really oppose the Fomorii?'

'For me, there are more profound concerns,' Shavi said. 'The Danann are supposed to look like angels. Was the Christian mythology based upon them? Are all the world's religions a reflection of the time when the Tuatha Dé Danann and the Fomorii ruled over humanity? This may be an opportunity for us all to meet our Maker.'

'*Opportunity*. I like your optimism,' Ruth said sardonically.

'That's too heavy,' Laura noted uneasily. 'It's bad enough as it is without thinking about things like that.'

'But we should think about it,' Shavi pressed. 'For millennia our lives have been based around religion. If our entire system of belief and morality rests upon a lie, we are truly adrift. It would be diffi-cult to comprehend how our society could recover from a blow like that.'

'We lose our faith in science and religion at the same time. That doesn't leave any refuge for most people,' Ruth said thoughtfully.

'Most people don't believe in anything anyway,' Laura said. 'Religion is just a place for sad bastards to go to hide, and scientists can't agree on anything, so why should anyone else believe them?'

'And I thought *I* was cynical.' Ruth looked down at the jumbled streets of the old town; from that vantage point they could almost have been in the Middle Ages. Briefly a cloud shadow swept across the rooftops and she shuddered involuntarily; unconsciously she wrapped her arms tightly around her. From nowhere the thought sprang; a portent: things were going to get worse from that moment on.

Amidst a large group of garrulous tourists, Church and Veitch spent the rest of the evening in a pub on Tudor Square finding the common ground that lay between their different backgrounds. Veitch had a dangerous edge to his character which made Church feel uneasy, but it was tempered by an encouraging sense of loyalty; and for someone who had dabbled for so long in petty crime, he seemed to have a strict moral code. Ultimately it was those contradictions which made his character so winning. Veitch showed a respect for Church which the latter hadn't experienced before.

'I can't get my head round it.' Veitch's brow furrowed as he swigged down a mouthful of lager. 'We were being set up for this from the moment we were born? Those dreams that gave me all that bleedin' misery?'

'I had the dreams too, though not as bad as you. I mean, we call them dreams, but they weren't really. It was the Otherworld contacting us – though that makes it sound like they were getting us on the phone. I think it was more like we were in some way closer to their world, so bits of it kept seeping through when we were most receptive to it.'

'Bastards. I owe them for messin' with my head, whether they did it on purpose or not. But you said that woman from the Watchtower kept visiting you when you were a kid. What was she, your sponsor?'

Church had wrestled with that thought before and he still hadn't reached a satisfactory conclusion. 'I think, maybe, because the Danann knew how important we were supposed to be, they wanted to keep an eye on us.'

'Watched over by angels, eh? You lucky bastard.' Veitch's words gave him pause, and after a moment he said, 'I wonder what they feel about us, really. I know they look like us a bit, the Danann anyway, but they're, like, God, aren't they? God and his angels. And the other lot are the Devil and his crew.'

Church felt uncomfortable at this description; old teachings had dug their way in deep and he couldn't help a shudder at the blasphemy. 'We should be getting back,' he said, draining his pint. It was already closing time and the number of drinkers in the pub had dwindled rapidly. Through the window he could see them making their way across Tudor Square to their hotels and B&Bs, quite a number for out-of-season, but still too few for him. Increasingly, he felt the desire for the security of large numbers. Wide open spaces were simply too dangerous.

They were halfway across the square when Veitch glanced up suddenly and exclaimed, 'What's that?'

Tiny sparks of light darted overhead, accompanied by a flutter of wings which reminded Church of the sound of bats on a summer evening. But as he peered up into the clear night sky he felt a tingle of wonder. Tiny, full-formed figures, neither men nor women but a little of both, flashed around high above on wings that seemed too flimsy to carry even their slight weight; the light was coming from their skin, which had the faint glow of phosphorus.

'What are they?' Veitch asked curiously.

'I would say the analogue of nature spirits. Whatever made our ancestors think the trees and rivers were alive.'

'No trouble, then?' Veitch's hand was inside his jacket where he kept his gun. Church wanted to tell him it would be worthless in what lay ahead, but he supposed if it gave Veitch comfort then it had some use. The hand didn't come out and Church could tell Veitch was weighing up whether he could get away with taking a few potshots.

'They look harmless,' Church warned. 'Leave them be. They might even be helpful to us at some time.'

'I don't want help from any of them,' Veitch said harshly. 'I want things back the way they were.'

'It's not all bad,' Church replied. 'We've got the magic back. We were missing that in all our lives.'

Veitch didn't seem convinced. 'Why are they flying around like that? Most of these things seem to stay out of the way when people are around.'

Now that he mentioned it, Church did think it was curious. He examined the fleeting trails of the creatures once again, and when one swooped low enough so he could see its face, the answer was unmistakable. 'They're frightened,' he said. 'Something has disturbed them.'

Veitch traced their path back across the sky. 'They came from over there,' he said, pointing to Castle Hill, where Shavi, Laura and Ruth had lazed earlier.

'We could go back,' Church mused. He was torn between the knowledge of what terrible things now lurked out in the night and the desire to know what might present a problem to them in the future.

Veitch was already striding down St Julian's Street. 'We'll be fine if we keep on our toes. We've got to check this out.'

The quay was awash with the reflected sodium light from the town dappling the gently lapping waves. Tranquillity lay across the area, in direct opposition to the hubbub of the day. The boat trip booth was shut, as was the ice cream shop and surf store on the ramp down to the beach. A few lights glimmered in the holiday apartments overlooking the harbour, but as they passed the old bath house and joined the path which curved around the headland, all signs of life disappeared. Away to their left, the sea rolled in calmly, the breakers crashing on the rocks under the lifeboat station. On their right the bank rose up, too steep to climb, to the top of Castle Hill.

Church and Veitch advanced along the path cautiously. Although it was a clear night, it was dark away from the town's lights and the susurration of the sea drowned out any nearby sounds.

'What do you reckon?' Veitch asked at a point where the path wound round so it was impossible to see far ahead or back.

'Doesn't seem—' The words were barely out of Church's lips when the night was disturbed by a throaty bass rumble, deep and powerful, rolling out from somewhere close by.

'What was that?' Veitch hissed.

Church felt the now-familiar shiver of fear ripple down his back. He glanced down the path behind them, then ahead, and finally up the steep bank. Another sound echoed out. 'Up there,' he whispered.

They stood stock-still, trying to peer through the gorse and willow-herb, their breath burning in their throats. Finally they caught a glimpse of a black bulk moving against the sky on the ridge above them. Veitch went to speak, but Church silenced him with a wave of his hand. The silhouette moved slowly, dangerously, and then it turned its head and Church caught the terrible glitter of red eyes, burning like embers.

'Black Shuck,' he muttered.

He thought his words had been barely more than an exhalation, but the creature suddenly froze. Another throbbing growl rolled out menacingly. Slowly, the eyes moved, searching.

The dog disappeared from view and a second later they heard crashing through the undergrowth as it thundered down the bank to the path.

'Is it in front or behind?' Veitch asked, glancing around anxiously. Church shook his head. They vacillated, desperately hoping for some sign, but they knew once they had one it would be too late.

Finally Church grabbed Veitch and forced him onwards around the corner. They breathed easily when they saw the dog wasn't there, but its growls were still reverberating loudly and seemed to be drawing closer. Church nodded to a point where the bank wasn't so steep. 'If it's down here, we should be up there.'

'Yeah, but we have to come down sooner or later.'

They launched themselves at the bank and scrambled up, digging their nails in the turf and weeds to haul themselves along. At the clipped lawn on the summit, they rolled on to their stomachs and peered back down. Church caught a glimpse of the dog prowling menacingly back and forth along the path.

'It knows we're here,' Veitch noted in a hoarse whisper. 'It can smell us.'

'Something more than that, I think.'

'Okay, but from what you've told me, if the dog's here, the Hunt can't be far behind, right?'

304

That was the one thing Church had been trying not to consider. 'We have to get back to the others,' he said.

Shavi, Ruth and Laura sat in Tom's top floor room looking out across the rooftops. Tom lay on the bed, his face pale and drawn.

'Where've they got to?' Ruth paced around anxiously. 'You're sure they're going to be all right?'

'I told you. I've done all I can. A simple direction of the energies, a masking.' The snap of anger in Tom's voice was born of exhaustion. 'If they're not in plain sight, they should be fine.'

'What if they're pissed and lying in a gutter?' Laura asked. 'You know how boys like to play once they get together.'

'You'd think they'd have thought to get back here by nightfall,' Ruth moaned.

'*They never call.*' Laura's singsong voice dripped with mockery. 'Listen to you. You sound like their mother.'

'Why don't you—'

'Listen.' Concern crossed Shavi's face. From the street without came the gentle clip-clop of horses' hooves, an everyday sound, but it made their blood run cold.

'Can you see?' Ruth knew she was whispering unnecessarily, but she couldn't bring herself to raise her voice.

Shavi pressed his face up close to the glass and attempted to look down. He shook his head. 'Only if I open the window.'

'Don't do that!' Laura snapped.

'I was not about to.'

They listened as the sound of the hooves slowly moved away and only when the sound had finally disappeared did they speak again.

'Maybe it wasn't them,' Ruth said hopefully. 'Earlier I saw a guy who takes tourists on tours of the front in a horse-drawn carriage.'

'It was the Hunt.' Tom's voice had an edge of fatalism.

'How fast does it move?' Veitch panted. They slipped and slid down the grassy bank on the other side of the hill until they reached the museum.

'Faster than you could ever run, even on a good day.' Church dropped on to a path and peered over the old castle walls. If the tide had been out, they could have taken a short cut across the beach and up the vertiginous seafront steps to the street where the B&B lay, but the waters crashed against the cliffs on which the town perched.

'Hey, I'm fit. You're the one who spends his time sitting on his arse writing about old bones.'

They hurried under the crumbling stone arches of the castle's defences and quickly arrived back at the quay. Disturbingly, the dog's growls didn't diminish. Church glanced back and thought he could see the eyes burning in the distance.

'It's got our scent,' he said. 'Or whatever. We might lose it up in the town where there are too many other distractions.'

But as they turned to run back up St Julian Street, the threatening blast of a horn echoed out across the quiet town.

Church's heart skipped a beat. 'The Hunt. They're in the old town.'

As they waited uncertainly, with the dog's growls growing louder behind them, they heard a horse approaching slowly down St Julian Street. A streetlight threw an enormous angular shadow across the front of the pastel houses in which Church could make out the cruel pike-weapon he had seen used so effectively on Dartmoor.

'Just one?' Veitch said.

'They're trying to flush us out.'

They turned and ran instead around the harbour, diving into an alley that led up to the Tudor Merchant's House tourist attraction. Church could feel the thundering of his blood in his ears. For a long time there was just the lapping of the waves. They both held their breath, listening. Church glanced at Veitch, both ready to make their move; he held up his hand for one more listen. The faint clip-clop of hooves echoed somewhere nearby.

Church cursed under his breath. 'Good job there're lots of tiny streets and back alleys to hide in.'

'And to get cornered in. Bleedin' hell. How did I get caught up in all this?'

Keeping to the shadows, they crept quietly up some old, weathered steps and headed along another alley. At the end of it Tudor Square lay deserted and brightly lit. They listened again; silence.

'We could make a run for it,' Veitch suggested.

'If they catch you out in the open, you won't stand a chance.' Church edged forward to get a better look, but just as he closed on the light, a horse and rider loomed up in the entryway. He could smell the unearthly, musky stink of the beast's sweat, see the light glint on the rider's metal buckles and arm rings, and the odd, lambent shimmer of his greenish skin.

Just as the rider started to look down the alleyway, Veitch grabbed Church's jacket and dragged him back into the shadows of a doorway. The rider stared for a moment, as if he had seen something, and then, just as Church thought he was going to investigate, he spurred the horse and it trotted away down towards St Julian's Street.

'I thought he'd marked us then,' Veitch whispered.

'There's an alley on the other side of the road next to the bookshop I saw earlier. If we can reach that, we might be able to wend our through the backstreets to base.'

Cautiously, they crept back to the end of the alley to survey the scene. The square was empty once more.

'He's probably waiting just around that corner,' Church noted.

'What we need is a diversion.' Veitch pulled out the gun and held it at his side; he seemed to carry it easily.

'What are you going to do with that?' Church asked uneasily.

Veitch moved in front of Church, raised the gun, pointed it at a shop at the top end of the square and fired, all in one fluid motion. The thunder of the retort merged with the high-pitched shatter as the window caved in and the burglar alarm started to scream. In an instant the clatter of hooves erupted as the Huntsman burst from St Julian Street and spurred his horse towards the shop, his sickle-pike glinting in the street light.

Once he'd passed by, they ran. Veitch had been cunning; the noise of the burglar alarm masked the sound of their running feet.

But just as they'd stepped into the road, a car sped up in the trail of the rider, so fast it almost ploughed into them. There were four youths inside, faces flushed from too much beer. The driver swerved at the last moment, screaming his rage through the open window, then hammered the horn. Church knew instantly that stroke of bad luck had ruined them. From the corner of his eye, he saw the Huntsman rein up his horse and turn it on the spot. Veitch must have seen it too, for he didn't slow for a moment; instead he powered up on to the car's bonnet and launched himself off to the other side.

Church was too near to the rear of the car to follow suit, but Veitch's actions were too much for the beer boys inside. They burst from the doors, their faces contorted with anger, fists bulging, mouthing post-pub threats in broad Welsh accents. One of them took a swing at Church and he had to throw himself back to avoid the blow.

'Come on!' Veitch yelled, as if it were in Church's power to respond.

The rider was almost upon him. Acting purely on instinct, Church propelled himself forward, past his assailant and behind one of the doors, surprising the beer boys with his tactics. The Huntsman's pike raised a shower of fizzing sparks as it ripped along the car's wing.

That resulted in another predictable outburst from the four youths. The driver stepped forward and hurled a near-full beer can. It bounced off the rider's shoulder, spraying cheap lager across the road.

He was already advancing, fists raised, when Church yelled, 'No! He'll kill you!' Another of the youths stepped in and kicked Church violently on the leg. More from shock than the agony that lanced up to his waist, Church pitched backwards, half-in and half-out of the car.

He tried to call out again, but it was too late. The driver rode forward, stabbing his pike and ripping suddenly upwards as he passed. A fountain of blood spurted, then showered down to mingle with the lager in the gutter.

The shouts were stifled in the other three youths' throats. But a second later, to Church's disbelief, they resumed their assault on the rider with force, hurling anything at him that came to hand, trying to kick out at the ghostly horse as it passed. Church didn't wait to see any more. He scrambled right through the car, rolled out on to the tarmac and was then up and running to join Veitch at the alleyway.

Overcome by despair and guilt, he glanced back and immediately wished he hadn't. The rider tore through the youths like a storm of knives, shredding and dismembering in a manner that suggested he had only contempt for humanity. The horse that was more than a horse jumped on to the car's roof, crumpling it, and then Veitch and Church were running as fast as they could along the alley.

They rounded into Cresswell Street, hoping to make their way along the front where they could lose themselves amongst the mediaeval streets before reaching the B&B, but the futility of their plan became immediately apparent. One rider cantered from the seafront, blocking the bottom end of the street, while another appeared at the top, their pikes raised, ready to harry them like foxes.

'Up,' Veitch croaked.

It took Church a split-second to comprehend what he was saying, and then he was running behind him and getting a leg-up on to a garage roof. He leaned over and hauled Veitch up behind him just as one of the pikes smashed into the brick with a force that belied even the formidable strength of both rider and weapon. The old buildings made it easy for them to find footholds until they could reach the bottom rungs of a fire escape, where they could scramble up to the roof. Crawling over the lip of the gutter was a terrifying experience, and once Church thought the whole frame was about to give way and plunge him to the hard pavement far below.

But eventually they were lying back on the dark slate tiles, staring at the sky as they desperately tried to catch their breath; beneath them the horses' hooves clattered insistently.

'They're not going to go away,' Veitch said redundantly.

'We could stay up here till dawn. They'll leave with the daylight.'

'You think they're just going to let us sit here? Anyway, didn't you say you'd seen them up in the *sky*?'

Church remembered viewing the eerie shapes among the clouds after Black Shuck's attack at the service station, but it was almost as if they had been in some *transitional* phase brought on by the sun's first rays. He shook his head. 'If they could, they'd have done it by now.'

He peeked over the edge. The rest of the Hunt had gathered there now, the imposing figure of the Erl-King at the heart of them. The horses snorted like traction engines as they jostled for space. A few curtains flickered in the apartments overlooking the street, but wisely, no one pursued their investigations.

'If they could rise up here in some way, I think they would have done it by now,' he said, but that didn't give him much comfort.

He had good reason to feel that way. The Erl-King raised his horn to his misshapen mouth and blew a long, aching blast. A second later it was answered by the mournful howl of a dog; not Black Shuck, Church noted – it was too thin and reedy – and then more joined in, yelping ferociously. The sound was so eerie; it almost sounded like human voices.

Within a minute, the pack arrived, surging through the alleyway that led to Tudor Square from wherever they had been sequestered, ready for the final stage of the Hunt. Church's heart froze at the sight of the demonic, red and white hounds; they were almost insect-like in the way they swarmed amongst the horses at the foot of the building.

The Erl-King gave them some silent order, and the sight that followed made Church's breath catch in his throat. The dogs were mounting the building; making inhuman leaps on to the garage roof, on to the window ledges; some even appeared to be climbing sheer faces.

'Jesus Christ!' Veitch's face was as milky-white as the dogs' hindquarters. As they advanced, their snapping needle teeth glinted menacingly.

Church and Veitch pushed their way back from the edge in shock and then stood up, frantically looking around for an escape route. The jumbled slate roofs stretched out all around them in a mix of angles and pitches that befitted the buildings' age, but there seemed only one way: further into the mediaeval quarter where the streets were narrow enough to leap across.

Veitch led the way, slipping and sliding on the tiles. Church was relieved the day had been dry, otherwise they would easily have skidded over the edge. Even so, the gutters remained unnervingly close. Church had never had a problem with heights, but he felt a tight band form across his chest as he glimpsed the street far below during their progress from house to house; and his head was spinning so much he was afraid he might black out or make a mis-step.

At ground level the Hunt was following their progress, ready to catch their prey if either of them plummeted. And behind, Church could hear the clicking of the dogs' nails as they clambered over the guttering on to the slates. He told himself not to look back, but he couldn't resist. The dogs were mounting the roofs in force, their white patches glowing in the moonlight like small spectres. They snapped and snarled venomously.

Church was amazed at how Veitch kept his attention singlemindedly on their escape. When a street opened up ahead of them, he paused, took a few steps back, then launched himself across the gulf, clattering on the tiles ahead and somehow clinging on.

He turned and beckoned to Church. 'Come on! They're almost on you!'

Church looked down at the dizzying drop and knew at once that was a mistake. The only way he could control himself was to close his eyes and jump blind. Suddenly there was a wild snapping at his heels and he threw himself across the gap. The wind whistled past his ears and his heart rammed up into his throat until he felt his feet touch down on the opposite roof. But his relief vanished when he realised he had mistimed his leap; he was toppling backwards, his arms cartwheeling.

Veitch reached out to grab his jacket and pull him forwards at the last moment and they tumbled together on to the slates.

'Try keeping your eyes open next time,' he snapped.

Out of the corner of his eye, Church saw the dogs leap the gap. He scrambled up the pitch after Veitch. The first few missed and fell howling to the street below, but others caught on to the guttering and somehow managed to pull their way up.

Church was breathless from exertion and anxiety. The dogs were relentless. He could hear the gnashing of their teeth so close behind that if he paused for a second they'd have him. At the next street, Veitch cleared the gap easily, but he still had trouble clinging on to the opposite roof's steep pitch. Church felt a brief flurry of relief when he recognised the block where their B&B was situated.

He couldn't stop to time his jump. A dog had almost sunk its teeth into his trousers, the teeth clacking so close he felt the vibration. But at the moment he launched himself, his foot skidded on the slate and he lost his momentum. He clamped his eyes shut again, and somehow his fingers clasped on to the guttering, which creaked ominously.

Veitch desperately tried to reach him, but before he could get within a foot, the guttering's supports wrenched out of the brick and Church was falling, still clinging on to the fragile metal.

That act saved his life. The guttering broke his fall enough so that he blacked out for only a second when he slammed into the road. But when he opened his eyes the Hunt had him surrounded.

The horses dragged at him roughly with their hooves, and when he saw the sharp teeth in their mouths he wondered briefly if the Huntsmen were going to allow their mounts to eat him alive. Then the Erl-King dismounted and strode over to Church, his terrible face emotionless, his red eyes gleaming. He stood astride Church and pressed the sickle end of the pike against Church's chest; the blade felt hard and icy-cold even through his jacket.

Slowly he bent forward until Church could see the scales of his skin and the bony protrusions which reminded him of the Fomorii, but were somehow very different. In his eyes, there was nothing Church could comprehend; they were alien, heartless.

Just as he had in Calatin's torture chamber, Church felt an uncanny peace come over him as he felt death near. He closed his eyes, and an instant later there was a brief flurry of movement as the pike slashed through his jacket and skin.

It took him a moment to realise he wasn't dead. When he opened his eyes he saw his jacket and shirt had been torn open and a stinging cross had been marked in the flesh of his chest. But astonishingly, that was the extent of his injuries.

Pushing himself up on his elbows, he watched in incomprehension as the Erl-King mounted his horse and led the riders to the end of the street. He gave another blast of his horn, and the dogs swarmed from the rooftops, down the side of the buildings, to gather behind the Hunt.

For one second, the Erl-King glanced at Church with a look that made his blood run cold, and then he spurred his horse and the Hunt galloped away with the hounds howling behind. A minute later, a silence fell on the deserted street as if the Hunt had never been there. With the threat gone, the shock and the pain proved too much and Church crashed back on the road in a daze.

hanging heads

Veitch clambered down from the roof, unable to grasp exactly what had happened. The moment he'd seen Church slip he'd been convinced his friend's life was over; if not the fall, then the hounds or the Huntsmen themselves would dispatch him in an instant. But there Church lay in the deserted street, dazed but alive. It made no sense.

Still half-thinking the Hunt might return, Veitch quickly checked Church for any serious injuries, then supported him back to the B&B. The owner eyed them suspiciously as they made their way up the stairs, but said nothing; he'd seen worse.

The others were waiting in Tom's room, both relieved that Church and Veitch were back safely and irritated that they hadn't returned earlier. 'Typical testosterone-addled minds,' Laura sneered. ' "Let's stay out late and show how brave we are." '

While Shavi tended to the wound on Church's chest, Veitch attempted to explain what had happened. Tom watched the scenario from his bed, saying nothing.

'Were they afraid of you?' Ruth looked exhausted, on the verge of breaking down.

'They wanted to terrify you,' Shavi suggested. 'It was a power game.'

'Partly that.' Church tried to ignore the pain lancing through his ribs. 'But more, I think it was because they couldn't *afford* to kill me.'

'What do you mean?' Ruth knelt next to him and searched his face.

'Their instinct was to hunt, which is what they were doing, but when they came to the kill they couldn't see it through because the Fomorii want us alive.' He closed his eyes and lay back in the armchair; his head was still swimming. 'The Fomorii can't touch the talismans directly. Unless they're wrapped in something. But they know how dangerous those things are—'

'—so they want us to do all the dirty work finding them, and then they're going to take them off us,' Ruth finished. 'They're just using us.'

'They let us get out of the mine for the same reason,' Church continued. 'I couldn't work out why they hadn't massed their ranks around the stone and the Wayfinder, if they're supposed to be so valuable. But we were allowed to just waltz through, pick them up, and waltz out. Thinking we'd done it ourselves, we carried on our own sweet way while they sat back, laughing.'

'That Crow guy really did try to kill us,' Veitch said, questioningly. 'He wasn't messing around.'

'Yes, but Tom said there was some kind of power struggle going on. Mollecht is probably trying to screw up Calatin's plans and get a few brownie points at the same time for wiping us out.' Church glanced at Tom for some input, but he simply rolled on his back and threw his arm across his eyes. He seemed to be shaking, as if he had a fever.

'So they're tearing themselves apart, like the Borgias or something.' Ruth blinked away a stray tear. Church reached out a hand in support, but she moved away, shaking her head defensively. Then: 'And all those times we'd thought we'd won, all the little victories – they just let us do it. We didn't win anything at all.'

'The illusion of free will.' Shavi's words sounded more sour than he had intended.

'Herded like sheep.' Ruth stared blankly out of the window, her thoughts closed off to them.

'We are still no closer to understanding their eventual aim.' Shavi finished cleaning the blood from Church's chest; the cuts weren't too deep. 'They seem well-established. They are strong. They could have moved at any time.'

'You've seen them,' Veitch said morosely. 'What chance would anyone have? The cops, the army – don't make me laugh. It'd be over in a day.'

Church winced at the pain creeping out from the wound. 'Then let's hope we can call back the Danann to do our dirty work for us.'

Laura made herself a cup of black coffee. 'So the time we really have to worry is when we pick up the last prize. Then we're fair game again.'

No one spoke. The atmosphere in the room had grown leaden with disquiet as they all turned their thoughts to the following day.

When the others crawled off to sleep, Church continued to sit up in the chair near the window, watching the dark waves roll across the surface of the sea. After a while, he took out the Black Rose, searching for some kind of comfort. In his mind, it was a direct channel to Marianne and all that she represented to him, all that she had taken away from him. 'Come on,' he whispered to it. 'You told me your name when I first found you. Tell me something else.'

It was a weak, childish thing to do and he didn't know what he really expected – Marianne hearing his voice, coming to him, making everything all right? – but he felt even more desolate in the ringing silence that followed his words. It was then he noticed a thin layer of white on the edge of one of the petals which, strangely, appeared to be frost. After he brushed it away, the cold seemed to linger unnaturally in the tip of his finger. It disturbed him so that when he fell asleep it infected his dreams with images of people he knew frozen to death in sweeping, pristine dunes of snow.

The morning broke bright and hot. They woke to the sound of cawing gulls, swooping in a clear blue sky, and the soothing sound of the tide washing against the golden sand. Still subdued, they gathered in Tom's room, where something caught Church's eye on the TV which had been playing silently in the background. He snatched the remote to boost the sound on a local news bulletin. Scenes of the police and army diverting traffic instantly placed it as the incident they had encountered on the M4.

'—cloud of toxic chemicals escaping from the Pearson Solutions plant at Barry Island has now dispersed. The massive operation by the emergency services to ensure thousands of people stayed in their homes while others in the high risk area were evacuated has been dubbed an overwhelming success by—' Church muted the TV and tossed the remote to one side.

'You believe that?' Veitch asked.

Church suddenly felt too weary to consider any of it any more. 'Who knows?'

Laura shook her head resolutely. 'How can you tell when a journalist is lying? Their lips move.'

They all jumped as a blast of insane laughter burst from the TV speaker, then the set fizzed and went blank. Shavi noticed the clock radio had gone blank too. 'Technology crash,' he said.

Ruth cursed under her breath. 'I don't get this,' Veitch said. 'Are those bastards switching everything on and off just to wind us up?'

'I think,' Shavi mused, 'it is simply the world finding its new status quo by trial and error.'

Veitch's face suggested he found this an even more disturbing prospect.

'Time to sell the computer and mobile,' Laura said. 'Beat that glut on the market.'

The power came back on in time for breakfast, which they consumed in the restaurant in near silence. Afterwards, they gathered the talismans in the crate and headed down to the quay where the first boat to Caldey Island was preparing to sail. They were the first on board, although a couple with pre-school twins joined them soon after. The sea was calm and the boat rolled smoothly. Once they were past the rocky outcropping of St Catherine's Island, topped by its Victorian fort, Caldey Island rose up, sun-drenched and green, three miles away in the bay.

When they were almost halfway there, one of the twins who had been gazing into the chopping waves suddenly called out excitedly, 'Mummy! Somebody's swimming!'

The mother laughed and rubbed his hair affectionately. 'Sometimes dolphins follow the boat, sweetie. Now sit down before you join them in there.' The boy protested until a stern look from his father quietened him.

Veitch glanced surreptitiously over the side, not wishing to show the others he was interested in seeing the wildlife, and was surprised to see the boy had been right – someone *was* swimming. Several people, in fact, their outlines distorted by the water. Veitch counted five alongside the boat, several feet beneath the waves. Yet they didn't appear to be wearing scuba gear, although they had been submerged an unnatural length of time, and they were swimming faster than anyone he had ever seen; they easily kept pace with the boat.

He thought about pointing it out to the others when a couple of the swimmers surfaced and he had another surprise. They were women, unashamedly naked to the waist, but their skin had a translucent greenish quality, almost the colour of the water, and their eyes were bigger than average and slightly slanted. And from the waist down they had scaly tails and long, gossamer fins like angel fish. As they turned and rolled in their undulating swim, their lustrous blue hair floated out behind them. Veitch saw gills slashed into the neck just below the ear.

Despite their outlandish appearance, they were stunningly beautiful. He understood how sailors of old were so transfixed by them that they plunged beneath the waves and drowned. One of the women caught him looking and swam up to just beneath the surface where she rolled on to her back and gave him a smile of such honeyed warmth, he almost felt himself melt. He smiled back, which seemed to please her. In response, she pursed her full lips and blew him a kiss before diving back to join her companions.

'What are you looking at?' Laura said accusingly. 'Thinking about jumping?'

Veitch smiled at her too, which obviously surprised her. He thought about telling the others what he had seen, then decided against it. It was his own small spot of wonder, a brief, private, transcendental moment that he would carry with him always.

After the boat docked alongside an old concrete jetty, the team followed the winding path from the small beach to the parkland that lay before the white walls and sunburnt orange tiled roof of the monastery.

'Whoever hid these talismans liked their religious spots, didn't they?' Ruth mused thoughtfully. 'Pagan. Celtic. Christian. That's quite cross-denominational.'

'You think it means something?' Veitch asked.

'Duh!' Laura mocked. Veitch flashed her a dark look.

They continued along past a roadside shrine and then the Wayfinder signalled a sudden change to the west. The paths in that direction were less well-trodden, the island more overgrown with dense trees and bushes. The heat had become almost claustrophobic and there was an abundance of midges and flies, despite the numerous birds cawing in the trees. Apprehension pressed heavily on them as they walked. The cut in Church's chest left by the Erl-King both stung and itched, while the Roisin Dubh in his inside pocket seemed to be reaching out to his heart with frosty fingers.

The dwindling path eventually brought them to a deserted beach sheltered in a small cove. Shavi stood among the blue-green and yellow banks of gorse and shielded his eyes to peer at the sparkling waves. 'Beautiful,' he said.

'Make the most of it.' Church glanced at Tom, who had stopped to wipe his forehead with a handkerchief. 'You okay?' He nodded, but still seemed uncomfortable, distracted.

Church took the lead, picking a way along the serpentine path that led down to the beach. Halfway there he realised the Wayfinder was pointing to a grove of trees on a ledge that broke the steep slope down to the sea. The thick bracken and brambles surrounding it suggested no one had been there in a long while. He nodded towards it.

'If this spear is such a big deal, how come it's left in a bunch of trees where anyone can find it?' Veitch was already on his guard, scanning the landscape for any sign of danger.

'Not just anyone can find it,' Tom said.

'Well, aren't we the lucky ones.' Church ploughed ahead through the dense fern cover.

About ten feet from the grove, he noticed a sudden change in the air pressure and temperature, as if they had slipped through the skin of an invisible bubble. He could taste metal in his mouth and there was a bizarre aroma of coffee in his nose. As he neared the trees, the hairs on the back of his neck mysteriously stood on end.

'There's something pale there,' Ruth noted apprehensively.

Church peered among the branches, but although he could make out the indistinct shapes Ruth had seen, he couldn't tell what they were.

'I advise caution,' Tom said.

'Why don't you advise us all to breathe at the same time?' Laura took a step forward.

Church crept ahead, keeping his gaze firmly on the dark shadows that clung between the trees. When they were close enough to smell the fragrance of the leaves, he finally made out the faintly luminescent orbs that seemed to be hanging like Chinese lanterns from the branches.

'Oh my God!' Ruth said before he could utter a word.

Human heads, eyes staring, mouths drooping, were draped on twisted vines, some of them as fresh and new as if they had been put there only the day before, others with skin as livid as the leaves that shaded them. Men, women, the old, the very young.

'Mondo disgusto!' Laura pinched her nose tightly.

'The Celts revered human heads. They thought they were a source of magical power. They always kept their enemies' heads on display.' Church paused, unsure whether to continue.

'We have no choice,' Shavi said, as if he could read Church's thoughts.

Church steeled himself and stepped into the shade. The smell of the heads was ripe in the hot morning sun; he coughed, tried to hold his breath. The others covered their mouths; Ruth was on the verge of vomiting.

Church felt like they were in another world; the quality of light was wrong; distorted. The shadows were too deep to see exactly where they were going.

'Marianne was having an affair.'

Church froze. The voice was rough, as if it hadn't spoken for days. He turned slowly, looked into the face of a mottled green head. Dead eyes stared back. But the lips quivered, formed new words to torment him again. 'She killed herself because she could not bear to tell you.'

'Don't listen!' Tom instructed from the back. 'Lies to divert you from the path! Thoughts plucked from your own mind!'

'How come you're never at the front?' Church snapped.

'Your uncle's guts spilled from his body,' another head said as Ruth passed. 'Ryan laughed when he saw it.' Ruth's eyes filled with tears and she turned sharply to Veitch. He shook his head forcefully, but it didn't dispel the hate in her eyes. She put her head down, kept walking.

Other words were spoken. Church heard some, but it made him sick to his stomach and the only way he could progress was to deaden his ears to it. And the heads were everywhere. The grove seemed much bigger than it had appeared from the outside, and those foul decorations looked to be hanging from every branch; he wondered if it were a crop scooped from the remnants of an enormous bloody battle. The more they moved forward, the more the trees, and the heads, pressed together until they were regularly brushing against them, feeling the dead skin, setting them swinging like Christmas tree decorations. And the words continued in hideous whispers from all sides, punctuated by the occasional shriek and howl that made their blood run cold, until it seemed like they were being suffocated by waves of noise that threatened to drown their souls.

But however many emotional blows they took, their determination kept them moving forward. Then something seemed to break, as if the heads, or whatever force controlled them, realised their tactics weren't working. The head nearest to Church moved of its own volition and clamped its jaws on the muscle of his upper arm. He howled in pain and frantically tried to knock it off, but it held fast, increasing the pressure. Just when he thought it was going to rip a chunk from his flesh, Veitch stepped forward, pulled out his gun, put the barrel to the head's temple and pulled the trigger. Bone and brain exploded over Church and the jaw dropped free to the ground.

'Jesus!' Ruth yelled. 'You've still got a fucking gun!'

But there wasn't any time for anyone to answer. As one, all the heads emitted a piercing scream and tore their jaws wide, gnashing their jagged, broken teeth as they tried to bite anything that came near them. That far into the grove they were packed so tightly there was barely any space to squeeze between them; to stand still meant the flesh would be torn from their bones in bloody chunks.

Church put his head down and ploughed forward, with the others following suit, cursing loudly and lashing out as if the heads were punchballs. Within a matter of paces, any area of bare flesh was slick with blood.

Finally, when they all doubted they would be able to get any further, they suddenly broke through to an area of hard-packed leaf mould and mud, free from any grotesque ornaments. The moment they stepped into the wide circle, the heads instantly lost all animation, as if someone had flicked a switch.

The sun broke through the verdant canopy to illuminate a small circle at the heart of the open space, like a spotlight on a stage. And in the centre of the glowing spot lay what appeared to be a long stick, intricately carved with a tiny, strange script.

'That's the spear?' Veitch said. 'Where's the business end?'

Church saw that he was right; at the end of the stick was a scored area where it obviously fitted to a blade of some kind. 'I thought it was going to be over,' he said dismally.

'The remainder of the spear will be somewhere in the surrounding area, but not in the immediate vicinity,' Tom said. He removed his glasses to wipe away the flecks of blood. 'The spear has great power as a weapon, and the two parts may have been separated to make it more secure, but they are bound on some intrinsic level and so cannot lie too far apart.'

'You have all the answers apart from the ones we really need,' Church said coolly. He picked up the spear, which seemed to sing in his hands, and inspected the odd inscription. 'Looks like Ogham script.'

'Arabic,' Shavi corrected. 'See the swirls?'

'No, I don't see that,' Church replied.

'Greek,' Laura suggested, pushing her way in next to them.

'No, that's definitely Russian,' Ruth prompted.

Church shook his head, then weighed the spear in his hands. 'What am I going to do with this? It won't fit in the crate.'

'Carry it,' Shavi suggested. 'It could easily be a staff.'

'But what if I damage it?'

Tom snorted contemptuously.

'Okay,' Church agreed, 'that was stupid. It looks like ancient wood, but it's not. It's survived millennia and I suppose it's pretty much indestructible. Let's get out of here.'

They stood on the edge of the circle looking at the gently swaying heads with trepidation, but the way they had come was the only way out; the other side of the grove was barred by an impenetrable mass of bramble and hawthorn. Finally Veitch pushed past the others and plunged among the mass of heads. Church followed swiftly behind. They were in such a state of high alert that they had travelled several paces before they realised the heads were unmoving; as dead as they looked. Nevertheless, they all continued through the stinking atmosphere as fast as they could and didn't look back until they had exited the grove and skidded down the bank, back to the beach in the tiny cove. There, they washed away the blood in the sea and dabbed at their wounds, resting on the sand until their tension eased.

Once he had recovered enough, Church took out the Wayfinder for what he hoped would be the final time. Its flame pointed across the strait to a point slightly along the coast. He checked his watch; it was just past noon. 'If we hurry, we can find it and be prepared to make our stand by nightfall,' he said.

*

Back on the mainland they hauled their few possessions to the van and set off out of town along a winding coast road that ran through beautiful, unspoilt countryside. After a few miles, the lantern pointed them down a side road which picked its way through the sleepy village of Manorbier, where they bought sandwiches, packets of crisps and Coke. At the end of a steep, tree-lined lane, they found themselves in another secluded cove. They parked in a large but nearly deserted car park near to the stony beach where the flame finally resumed its upright position.

'Where now?' Laura asked.

Shavi pointed to a ruined castle which could just be glimpsed through the trees.

They ate lunch in the van and bantered with new-found vigour, buoyed by their success on Caldey. Church and Ruth led the way to the twelfth century castle atop a red sandstone spur, still partly occupied by its current owners. Inside the gates it was quite small, a lawned area the size of a football pitch lying at the heart of the crumbling battlements. Tom bought a guidebook from the tiny castle shop for reference, which he read while smoking a joint on a wooden bench. The others wandered around looking for a sign of the way forward.

Half an hour later, having futilely scoured the castle from top to bottom, they met up in the shade of the chapel. 'I knew it was going too well.' Church checked his watch anxiously.

'What do you expect – neon signs?' Laura said. 'These things are supposed to be near-impossible to find.'

'Except for us,' Church stressed. 'We're fated to find them, remember?'

Laura bristled. 'Nice line in patronising. When was your coronation?'

'Sorry.' The tension was making them all irritable; Church could see it in their faces, their body language. Unchecked, he was afraid it might tear them apart. 'We'll start looking again—'

'Maybe we're in the wrong place,' Veitch suggested. 'It could be buried under the car park.'

Church shook his head. 'This place fits the trend. It has to be here.'

Ruth looked to Shavi. 'You could do something. Like you did in Glastonbury.'

Shavi recalled uneasily how much the exercise in Glastonbury had taken out of him; there was one point when he feared he might have been consumed by the powers he was unleashing, but he didn't let the others see his thoughts. 'I seem to have an aptitude for certain shaman-istic skills,' he agreed in response to Church's enquiring expression. 'In the right conditions, the right frame of mind, I can communicate with the invisible world.'

Veitch looked at him as if he were speaking a foreign language. 'Talk to ghosts?'

'Everything has a spirit, Ryan. People, animals, ghosts. Throughout history shamans have contacted them in search of knowledge.' Veitch sniffed derisively. 'I have always felt I had certain abilities, though unfocused, raw, but since the change that has come over the world they seem sharper.'

'I think we're all adapting,' Ruth said. There was something in her tone that made them feel uncomfortable.

'You're simply achieving your potential,' Tom said. 'That's why you've all been selected.'

'You have to survive to achieve potential,' Church said with irritation. 'Look, this isn't getting us anywhere. Shavi, if you can do something, anything, do it. If not, let's get searching.'

In the end, Shavi agreed he would find a quiet place to attempt a divination while the others continued the hunt. Accompanied by Church, they settled on an area where they were unlikely to be disturbed, in a secluded corner of the ruined hall where thistles and willowherb grew with abandon. It was a fenced-off, sheltered space under an overhanging stairway that ended in thin air.

'I normally do this alone,' Shavi said, taking a mouthful of mushrooms from a tightly wound plastic bag hidden in his jacket, 'but there is no time to recover from the trip. I fear I will be of little use to you for a while afterwards.'

'I don't care if we have to carry you round on a stretcher as long as you give us something we can use,' Church said. He sat on a lump of masonry while Shavi adopted a cross-legged position against the wall. 'This stuff really works, then?'

'Sometimes. Never quite in the way I hope, but enough to make it worthwhile. It is not scientific. If there are any rules, I have no idea what they might be.'

'That sounds like a mantra for this new age,' Church said wearily.

'It was always that way, Jack. Before, we lied to ourselves or listened to religious leaders and scientists who lied to themselves. Perhaps one of the good things that will come out of all this is that people will start searching for meaning within themselves.'

'You have a very optimistic view of human nature.' Church let his eyes rise up the cracked grey walls to the clear blue sky above. 'Sometimes I think there's no meaning in anything. Just random events impacting on one another. Chaos giving the illusion of a coherent plan.' But his words were lost; Shavi was already immersed in his inner world.

For half an hour, nothing happened. Church became increasingly agitated as Shavi sat stock-still and silent, his eyes closed. But just as Church was about to give in to the futility of the moment, Shavi began to mumble, barely audibly to begin with, but then increasingly louder; Church had the uneasy sensation that he was hearing one side of a conversation.

'Yes.'

'We are searching for something. You know what.'

'That is correct.'

'No. Everyone is to be trusted.'

'Why do you say that?'

'Everyone is to be trusted.'

'Yes, I am sure. Will you guide me to the item we need to find?'

'I will accept responsibility if things go wrong. Of course I will.'

'Yes.'

'And we will find it there?'

'Thank you for your guidance. Now I must—'

'What do you want to show me?'

'Oh.'

There was a long humming silence in which Church realised he was holding his breath waiting for the next part of the unsettling conversation. Shavi's lips seemed to quiver as if he were about to speak; Church leaned forward in anticipation.

Suddenly Shavi's eyes burst wide open and he let out a deep, strangled cry. Church leapt back in shock. 'I see it!' he gasped. Blood bubbled out of one nostril and trickled down to his lip.

Recovering quickly, Church jumped forward and grabbed Shavi by the shoulders, afraid he was about to have some kind of fit. 'Are you okay? I can get help.'

Although Shavi's eyes were open, he was not looking at anything Church could see; his pupils were fixed on a distant horizon. 'I see it!' he repeated. 'Coming across the land, like someone drawing a black sheet. They are here! They are everywhere!' He swallowed noisily. 'The city is burning! We walk over bodies heaped in the road. There is no hope anywhere. Everyone is dead. What did they do? They brought him back. Balor!' He coughed a mouthful of blood on to the stony ground. 'Balor.'

The word sent a shiver through Church. Suddenly he was back in the mine, listening to Tom's croaking voice recounting the terrible history of the Fomorii. 'Balor,' he repeated fearfully. Their long-dead leader, all-powerful, monstrously evil. The one-eyed god of death who almost destroyed the world.

Church prevented Shavi slumping sideways, then, holding him under his arms, dragged him to his feet. He was afraid to take Shavi out into the main part of the castle in case someone saw, but the fear that he might be on the verge of a coma or heart attack drove him on. As Church struggled to walk with him, though, Shavi seemed to recognise what Church was doing.

'Leave me,' he croaked. 'Fine . . . fine . . . Just need time.'

Church was torn, but when Shavi protested more insistently, Church went along with his wishes. He laid him back down against the wall, on his side in case he vomited. 'I'll get the others,' he whispered.

But as he started to walk off, Shavi grabbed his leg and hissed, 'Under the drawbridge.' He wiped away the blood with the back of his hand, but his eyes were already rolling up. Church left him there with an uncontrollable sense of impending doom.

'You reckon we're on a wild goose chase too?' Veitch caught up with Laura on top of the highest tower, where she leaned on the battlements staring out to sea.

Her ever-present sunglasses made it impossible to read her eyes, but there was the hint of an ironic smile. 'That, and other clichés.'

'We haven't had much of a chance to talk—'

'That's because you're a murderer and everybody hates you.'

Despite himself, Veitch felt his welcoming smile wash away. 'That's a sharp tongue,' he said coldly.

'I like it. I can get olives out of a jar without a fork.'

Veitch shook his head, unsure. 'You ever say anything that isn't smart?'

'Do you ever say anything that is?'

The smile remained; Veitch couldn't tell if it was playful or mocking, but his insecurities made him fear the worst. 'If you don't want to—'

'Stop being so sensitive. You shot some poor bastard. Deal with it and move on. Make amends, ignore it, just don't wallow in a big, slimy pool of guilt.' She turned back to the sea, raising her face slightly to feel the sun.

Her words gave him some comfort, but he still couldn't begin to work her out; she made him feel stupid, uncomfortable, but he couldn't deny being attracted from the first time he had heard her display her savage wit. He leaned on the masonry next to her, fumbling for the right words. 'How do you feel about giving up your life to join this nightmare expedition?'

'It's something to do.'

'What about your friends? Your folks?'

'Friends are those who're around you at the time. My parents died in a car crash.'

'Boyfriend?'

She inclined her face slightly towards him, her smile now sly. Veitch felt his cheeks colour. 'Was that your idea of subtle?'

'Dunno what you mean.' He shifted uncomfortably.

'You've got a pretty face and a good bod, but you're not my type, *comprende*? No offence and all, but I think we ought to nip this in the bud before the conversation gets clogged up with all those stupid manoeuvrings.'

Veitch looked away, unsure what to say.

'Don't get all hurt—'

'I'm not hurt.' He felt a sudden surge of irritation at that supercilious smile.

'If you're looking for a girlie, there's always Gallagher, although you could get a bad case of frostbite. Or,' she chuckled mischievously, 'Shavi.'

Veitch eyed her suspiciously. 'He's a queen?'

'Bi, actually.' His face obviously gave away his prejudices, because her smile drained away. 'You never know,' she said icily, 'it might do you the world of good.'

Before he could reply, she spotted Church walking across the green and hailed him. Veitch saw an obvious enthusiasm in her face that revealed exactly how she felt about their unelected leader; it was the first honest emotion he had seen in her, and after his rejection it made him feel cold inside. As he followed her down the steps to meet the others, his anger was already forming into an impacted lump in his chest.

Church took the others back to where Shavi lay, explaining what had happened as they ran. The bloodflow from his nose had stemmed, but he was still dazed, rambling. Ruth knelt beside him and checked his pulse.

'We should get him to a hospital.' The concern was evident on her face. 'He could have had a brain seizure. This is what happens when you mess with drugs.'

'I don't think it was the mushrooms.' Church still couldn't shake the memory of what had happened. 'It began after he had some kind of apocalyptic vision.'

'Did he tell you anything important?' Tom said anxiously.

'Come on,' Ruth protested. 'Shavi needs help!'

'I can do something for him,' Tom snapped. 'Leave him with me while you continue with the search. Now, did he tell you anything important?'

Church tried to remain calm. 'Something about them . . . the Fomorii, I suppose . . . being everywhere. About bodies in the streets and some city burning.' With a shiver, Church had a sudden flash of his own premonition in the Watchtower; he hadn't made the connection before. 'And he said they're bringing back Balor.'

Tom blanched.

Ruth saw the expressions on both their faces. 'What does that mean?'

'We can talk about it later,' Church said. 'Finding the spearhead is more pressing. Shavi also said to look under the drawbridge. That makes sense – the first three artefacts were under Avebury, under Tintagel and under Glastonbury Tor.'

He left Tom behind to care for Shavi and led Laura, Ruth and Veitch out of the castle gates. His first thought had been to leave the crate with Tom to free up their hands, but after Shavi's premonition he decided to keep the objects of power as close to him as possible. Through the gatehouse they skidded down the grassy bank into the dry moat and walked under the drawbridge. At first nothing caught their eye, but after Church had run his hands over the turf on the castle side, he discovered an odd, raised shape. It seemed to be a protruding lump of masonry, but he scrabbled the grass off with his fingernails and discovered it was in the shape of a spearhead.

After checking they weren't being watched, Church pushed, pulled and twisted the rock in a blind attempt to open it. Eventually something seemed to work, although he wasn't sure what, and there was a burst of blue sparks. An opening grew in the grassy bank, leading under the castle. As they slipped in quickly, they felt the same odd sensation of entering a bubble as they had on Caldey. The moment they were all in, the opening closed silently behind them, leaving them in the oppressive darkness of a tomb.

Church took out the Wayfinder, which gave them enough light to see they were in a tunnel in what appeared to be the bedrock. The walls were wet and shimmering, and the floor sloped slightly downwards.

'If these artefacts were hidden millennia ago, are you telling me it's pure coincidence that structures have been erected over the top of them?' Ruth's whisper was almost reverential, yet it echoed like the tide along the tunnel.

'You've felt their power,' Church replied. 'Who knows what subtle influences they exert? Maybe they drew the builders.'

The tunnel opened out into a stone chamber about the size of the one they had discovered under Tintagel.

'If you see any holes in the wall, don't put your hands in them,' Veitch deadpanned.

'There *are* holes,' Church noted, spraying the light across the chamber. 'Or niches, to be more precise.'

The four openings were of different sizes in a horizontal line on the far wall. Veitch was the first to them, and he investigated cautiously, withdrawing his hand repeatedly in case something shut down on it.

'There's an indentation at the bottom of each one,' he said. 'This one's round.' He moved on. 'Another round one.' The next. 'Long and thin. And this one, not so long and not so thin.'

They mulled over the information briefly, but Ruth was the first with the answer. 'They're for each of the talismans,' she said excitedly. 'It's impossible to solve this one unless you've already got through all the other ones.'

'Big wows. Aren't you smart?' Laura said sarcastically. 'So if we're also supposed to learn something from each of these puzzles, tell me what we've picked up from Caldey and here. Apart from never look a severed head in the eye.'

Church ignored her; he was already unloading the talismans from the packing crate. With Veitch's help, he dropped the stone and the cauldron into the first two holes; they fitted perfectly. The sword went into the fourth. The indentation in the third hole showed the full shape of the spear, including the head. Church carefully positioned the handle of the spear and the moment it lowered into place, the space for the head opened and a blue light flooded up. A second later the actual head rose into place.

'We've done it!' Church said triumphantly.

'You know, I almost expected cheers,' Ruth added with a broad grin.

Veitch didn't seem so jubilant. 'Yeah, great, we've just signed our death warrant.'

'Ah, Mr Glass-Half-Empty,' Laura said coolly. 'Just pick up the damned pieces and let's get out of here.'

They hurriedly gathered up the artefacts, and the moment the last one came out, another door opened up in the wall; they could see blazing sunlight at the end of it.

'How long to sunset?' Veitch asked anxiously.

Church checked his watch. 'Four hours. Lots of time.'

'Depends which way you look at it.' Veitch was already in the tunnel and moving as fast as he could.

Whatever Tom had done, Shavi had recovered slightly when they met up with them, but he was still loose-limbed and dazed. To the curious stares of onlookers, Church and Veitch helped walk him out of the castle and back to the van.

'He's not going to be much use to us tonight,' Church said redundantly.

'He wouldn't be much use if he was normal,' Veitch said sourly. 'So, we going to run for it or make a stand?'

'I vote we run and don't spare the horses,' Laura said hastily.

Veitch was obviously ready for a confrontation. 'And I vote we make a stand. Let's face it, they're going to catch us sooner or later. That's their whole reason for existing.'

'Well, aren't *you* the macho man. What are you doing to do – flex your biceps and hope they faint?' Laura jabbed him in the sternum with her fingertips, unbalancing him.

Church held out an arm as Veitch advanced angrily. 'He's right,' he said. 'We wouldn't get far if we ran.'

'Then what do you suggest? Wet towels at dawn?'

Church was encouraged to see some real emotion in Laura's blazing eyes; it seemed to be happening more and more. 'We've got four powerful artefacts here. Surely they've got to be some use.'

'What? Use them ourselves?' Laura said.

'It might work.'

'It might work. If we lived in cloud-cuckoo-land.'

'We are supposed to be some kind of champions,' Ruth said.

'Right.' Laura's voice dripped with sarcasm. 'A screwed-up techno head, an old hippie, a woman with a poker up her arse, a drugged-up fey romantic, a murderer and—' she nodded towards Church '—him. Some big fucking champions.'

'So we roll over and die like good little slaves?' Veitch responded angrily.

Laura pulled a face, then walked off. Church waited a moment before following and found her sitting on the grass on the other side of an ice cream van where the attendant was lazing in the back with a copy of the *Sun*.

'All this is out of our hands now, you know,' he said, sitting down next to her.

Eventually she said, 'I like to have choices.'

He nodded, watching the midges dance in the sunlight. 'I know it's a cliché, but this is bigger than anything we feel. This must be how they felt going off to the Great War. Scared, but with a great sense of responsibility, a feeling of being part of some great . . . I don't know, destiny.'

'I'm glad you feel that way, because I'm completely ruled by self-preservation here.'

'You're saying we can't count on you when the chips are down? I don't believe that.'

'You think you know me, do you?' She turned her head away so he couldn't see her expression.

'Yes. I think I know you.'

She thought for a moment, then rolled up her T-shirt so he could see the words scarred into her back.

Church caught his breath, but said nothing for a while. Then, 'Who did that?'

'It doesn't matter who.' She paused. 'Does it make you feel sick to see it?'

'My God, how could someone be so inhuman?' Church said in shocked disbelief.

'There are a lot of sick bastards out there. I said, does it make you feel sick?'

Church gently reached out to touch the scar tissue, then retracted his fingers at the last moment. Laura seemed to sense what he was doing for she leaned in towards him, only slightly, but enough to move into his personal space. Away from the pink cicatrix, her skin seemed unduly soft; he could smell her hair, the faint musk of her sweat from the morning's exertions. And suddenly he had an overwhelming need for physical contact, just to feel humanity and emotion rather than the cold, hard wind of constant threat. He reached out his hand again.

'Stop making goo-goo eyes at each other. We're running out of time.' Veitch was standing at the back of the ice cream van, his expression cold and hard.

Church jumped to his feet. 'Yeah, you're right.' He held out his hand and hauled Laura up; she held on to it for a moment longer than she needed, then withdrew her fingers so softly it was almost a caress.

Back at the van, they decided to find someplace with strong defences where they at least stood a chance of making a stand; if any of them were feeling fatalistic, it didn't show. But when Veitch went to turn the key, the engine was dead. 'We can't fucking rely on anything!' he said, hammering his fist on the steering wheel.

Time was running away. It was too dangerous to wait for everything to start working again and then find themselves caught out on the open road. Veitch hit the wheel one final time, then said, 'We'll have to hole up round here.'

'The castle would be perfect,' Ruth noted, 'but there's no way we'll be able to get in there after it's shut up for the night.'

Veitch thought briefly before pointing to a Norman church perched on the opposite side of the valley to the castle. It stood isolated amidst a sea of green fern and small bushes. 'We could do it there. Nobody's nearby to get hurt and we'll be able to see them coming from a long way off. Plus, it's got a wall round the churchyard, which may be nothing, but every little helps.'

Church was impressed by Veitch's tactical vision and at how comfortable he seemed making those sorts of decisions quickly. 'Okay. You're the boss.'

Veitch glanced at him as if he thought Church were mocking him. When he saw that wasn't the case, he looked both bewildered and a little pleased. 'Right, then. I'm the boss.'

They left the van sitting useless in the car park and walked up to the church half an hour before twilight fell so as not to draw attention to themselves. They needn't have bothered; there was no one around for as far as the eye could see, and the church noticeboard said the vicar was shared with other parishes, so there was no reason why they should be disturbed. The weather seemed to be changing to complement the approaching conflict; after the heat of the day, a chill had swept in from the sea, with slate-grey clouds which turned the waves an angry dark blue. They crashed on the stony beach with increasing violence; enormous fountains of gleaming surf cascaded high into the air, filling the valley with the deep bass rumble of angry nature.

They erected a tent in the churchyard for shelter in case it rained, and then halfheartedly chewed a few sandwiches left over from lunch. The thunder started just as the half-light of evening turned to the gloom of night. Veitch lit a handful of storm lanterns they'd bought in Glastonbury and positioned them around the tent.

'You don't think this is going to attract attention?' Ruth said as the first fat drops of rain fell. Away in the dark an owl hooted mournfully and Ruth wondered if it was the same mysterious bird which seemed to have befriended her.

'No one's going to see it, and even if they did, they wouldn't turn out on a night like this.' Church opened the packing crate and examined the three talismans inside; the spear had been lashed to it with a rope from the van and an oily rag tied to disguise the head. After a moment's thought he selected the sword, as surprised at how it felt in his hand as the first time he had touched it; sturdier than it appeared, warm, tingling.

'Let me have the spear,' Ruth said.

'You sure? I was going to give it to Ryan.'

'Why? Because he's a big tough boy and I'm a *girl*? Besides, he's got his little gun to keep him happy, for all the good it'll do him.'

Church weighed the spear in his hands, then passed it over. He wondered if it might be more effective with Veitch's strength behind it, but he had no doubts about Ruth's bravery.

'Thanks,' she said. 'I'll take that as a vote of confidence. It means a lot to me.' She took the spear and balanced it on her open palms before taking it firmly with a smile. 'Feels good.'

'Ruth Gallagher, warrior woman.'

She laughed. 'I've got so much pent-up frustration and anger I feel like I could take them all down on my own.' She brandished the spear theatrically, then her face darkened. 'What was it Shavi said that disturbed you and Tom?'

Church thought about not telling her, but decided it wasn't fair. 'Shavi discovered why the Fomorii haven't attacked. They're trying somehow to resurrect the one who used to lead them before he was destroyed by the Danann. At least, that's what he seemed to be suggesting.'

'And that's bad?'

'According to the Celtic myths, Balor was a force of ultimate evil and darkness. Virtually indestructible, terrifying to look upon, so powerful that if he turned his one eye on you, you were instantly annihilated. If the myths have captured even a fraction of the truth, it could be the end of everything.'

'Then we need to free the Danann before they bring him back.'

'But we don't know how close they are. They could be doing it tonight—'

Ruth clapped her hand on his shoulder and gave it a squeeze. 'No point tearing ourselves apart. We just have to do the best we can.'

In her face, Church saw something that brightened his spirit. 'I'm really glad we met under the bridge that night. Sorry. I just felt I had to say that.'

She smiled and gave his cheek a gentle pat. 'You're a man of excellent taste, Jack Churchill.'

He pushed the crate with the remaining talismans into the tent where Laura and Veitch sat in frosty silence, and Shavi dozed with Tom beside him. 'How's sleeping beauty?' he said.

'As well as can be expected, given the psychic shock.' Tom's Scottish brogue was more pronounced, which Church put down to the tension.

'I don't understand it,' Veitch moaned. 'We've got all the prizes together, like you said, but nothing's happened.'

Church nodded. 'I'm hoping we'll get some kind of sign.' He half-expected the woman from the Watchtower to turn up at any moment with the final piece of the jigsaw.

'I know what we've got to do,' Tom said. Everyone stared at him. 'They have to be brought together in the right place to work.'

'So when were you planning on telling us this?' Church asked with irritation.

'At the last possible moment,' Tom snapped. 'There's too much at stake to start throwing vital information around. You don't know who's listening—'

'There's only us listening!' Veitch said angrily. 'It's about time you got on the team—'

'There's no point arguing about it now,' Church said with exasperation. 'Do you all want to come out and choose your weapons, for what it's worth? We've found some pretty mean lumps of driftwood and an iron bar on the beach.'

Veitch crawled out first, and then Laura more reluctantly. 'I'll stay here,' Tom said. 'Look after Shavi and the other talismans.'

Church was disappointed, but there was no point trying to force him. 'If you've got any more tricks up your sleeve, now's the time to pull them out.'

Tom nodded, but didn't let on if there was anything he could do.

'Look at us!' Laura laughed as they gathered anxiously within the circle of light in the pouring rain. 'The Hunt will probably laugh themselves off their horses. Before they drag us off to hell, that is.'

Ruth and Veitch ignored her; they fixed their eyes on the deep gloom, their ears straining to hear any sound beneath the howl of the wind.

'Do you know how to use that sword?' Laura continued to Church, realising he was her only audience. 'It'll be about as effective as a toasting fork. Does she know what to do with that spear? And, hey, do I know what to do with this lump of driftwood? Yep, we are some defenders of the realm. Pathetic.'

The rain had plastered her hair to her head and was running in rivulets down her face. At least in the dark she had forsaken her sunglasses; Church saw the fire in her eyes.

'You'll give them hell,' he stated simply. He considered saying more, about her courage, her spirit, but the low, dolorous sound of a horn suddenly came in on the wind and he felt the blood drain from him. Laura's face, too, was white in the ghostly light of the storm lanterns; her dark eyes darted around fearfully.

As if in response to the horn a peal of thunder rolled out and then lightning streaked the sky. The gale gusted the rain at them like ice bullets.

'Okay,' Veitch said. 'Looks like we have us a situation.'

'Just what we need – a meathead raised on war movies,' Ruth muttered sourly.

Before they could utter another word, they saw the bulk of Black Shuck separate from the darkness and pad towards them. It leapt up and sat on the wall in one corner of the churchyard, where it simply watched balefully, its red eyes glowing. Its silence was eerie. It didn't threaten to attack or make any movement at all; it just stared. And there was something in that which terrified them more than at any other time they had encountered it.

They heard the baying of the hounds rising up before they heard the horses. Their white and red forms undulated like a pack of rats as they surged up the lane towards the church. A moment later the riders loomed behind them, majestic, awe-inspiring and terrible in the heart of the storm. The moment they were caught in the white flash of lightning, a primal vision in metal and fur, Church knew exactly how Laura felt; before them, he was useless, their weapons children's toys. Nevertheless, he adjusted the sword in his hands and brandished it as threateningly as he could. The others followed suit with their own weapons, as if they had read his mind.

As the Hunt galloped up the lane, it almost seemed like the storm was part of them; the wind howled from within the churning mass of horses and the thunder echoed from their hooves as they clattered on the road. The Erl-King was at the head, his monstrous face garish in the lightning.

Church prepared himself for them to come barrelling straight into the churchyard, but instead they surged around it, circling one way, then another, with the dogs before them so it was impossible to tell from which direction the attack would come.

'They're playing with us,' Church shouted above the wind.

'No, they're being careful,' Veitch replied. 'Looks like you were right about these magic things – they want them, but they're scared of them.'

Church realised Veitch was right and that gave him more confidence; perhaps they weren't as mismatched as he had thought.

'Maybe we could hold them off like this every night.' Ruth moved her weight from one leg to the other, holding the spear out before her.

'And achieve what?' Laura asked savagely.

The Hunt continued its circling for nearly an hour, by which time they were all shivering and soaked to the skin. Their constant concentration and high state of alert was exhausting them.

'I wish they'd just do something!' Ruth yelled above the wind.

As if in answer, the riders suddenly roiled around one section of the wall, then reined their mounts up before backing off slightly to leave the Erl-King standing alone. His horse reared up, its breath steaming from its nostrils, and when it brought its hooves down Church was convinced he saw a burst of sparks.

'Give up your burdens!' His voice boomed out, yet, oddly, seemed to come from somewhere all around him rather than directly from his mouth; there was a strange metallic tinge to it that set their teeth on edge.

'You're not having anything!' Church yelled defiantly.

There was a long pause and when the Erl-King spoke again, it was as if the storm had folded back to allow his words to issue with a focused power and clarity; his accent sounded different from moment to moment, as if their ears were struggling to make sense of what they heard.

'Across the worlds we dance, above the storms, beyond the wind. All barriers crumble at our command. We are like the waves, ever-changing. You can never know us. You can never cup our voices in your ear, nor touch our shells, nor smell our fragrance in the wind. Through time and space we slip and change. There are no absolutes.' His voice drifted away and for a moment there was nothing but ringing silence, as if the whole of the world had stopped.

But when his voice returned, it had the force of a hurricane and they were almost bowed before it. 'And you are feeble sacks of bone and blood and meat! Trapped in form, lost to the universe, always questioning, never knowing! Driven by lusts, chariots of wrath! You may not turn your face toward us! You may not raise your voice to speak! You may not lift a hand to challenge! For in doing so, you challenge the all and above and beyond! And your essences will be swept away and torn into a billion shreds! Hang your heads in shame! Be low before us!'

The tone of his words filled Church with trepidation. He recognised that he was dealing with something so beyond his comprehension it was almost like speaking with God. Yet however fearful he felt, he knew he couldn't back down. 'You may think we're nothing, but we'll fight to the last. And if you believed everything you said, you wouldn't be sitting there talking to us. You'd just have taken it. If you want these things, you come and get them!'

'Nice tactics,' Laura said in a fractured voice. 'Don't just stand there. Go open the gate for him.'

There was another ear-splitting peal of thunder and another blinding flash of lightning, and when it had cleared the Hunt was in motion. They galloped halfway round the churchyard wall, and then, without warning, they suddenly cleared the perimeter with a single bound, the dogs running all around. There was no time to talk or think. A hound launched itself at Church's throat, jaws snapping, needle teeth glinting, its eyes glowing with an inner light. Church swung the sword with such force he cleaved the dog in two. But instead of a shower of blood and entrails, it simply turned black and folded up on itself like a crisp autumn leaf until it disappeared in a shimmer of shadow.

Everything was happening too fast. One dog sank its teeth into Veitch's calf before he bludgeoned it to death with the iron bar. The tent was torn up and disappeared in a flurry, leaving Tom frozen in terror, hunched over Shavi's unmoving form. The hounds circled and attacked, circled and attacked, while the four of them continually lashed out to keep them at bay. But it was like holding back the tide. And out of the corner of his eye Church realised the riders were waiting, letting the hounds do all the work for them.

And then the quality of time seemed to change; images hit his brain one after the other like slides in a projector. Ruth's face, pale and frightened, but ferociously determined, in a flash of lightning. Some kind of comprehension crossing it like a shadow. Her head turning, searching, settling on one spot. The weight of her body shifting, muscles bunching, leaning forward slightly.

And then everything returned to normal like air rushing into a vacuum. Ruth erupted from the spot, holding the spear above her head. With a tremendous effort, she powered forwards, slammed her foot on a stone cross and launched herself on even faster. Church knew it was a suicide run, but there wasn't even a second to call out. She flew through the air and slammed the spear hard into the Erl-King's chest. There was an explosion of blue fire that lit up the entire churchyard. The Erl-King came free of his saddle, his face transformed by some emotion Church couldn't recognise, and the two of them went over the wall together and rolled down the steep bank into the night.

Ruth woke in the sodden bracken, her head ringing and a smell like a power generator filling the air. Every muscle ached and her skin was sore, as if she had been burned. The rain was still pouring down, pooling in her eye sockets, running into her mouth. With an effort, she lifted herself up on her elbows, and as she fought to recall what had happened, flashes came back: her attack, the impact with the Erl-King, the flash of blue fire and her last thought that she had killed herself but saved the others. With that realisation she allowed herself to focus on the outside world: she wasn't alone.

Something was thrashing around in the undergrowth, snorting like an animal, occasionally releasing a bestial bellow of anger or pain. It sounded so primal she was almost afraid to look, but in some perverse way she was drawn to it, even if it meant she might be discovered. Cautiously she peered above the level of the ferns.

Forty feet away, a dark shape crashed around, pawing the ground, stooping low, then raising its head high to the night sky. Her first instincts had been correct; there was more of the animal about it, yet also something sickeningly human. Her stomach turned at the conflicting signals. And then, in another flash of lightning, she saw what it was: the Erl-King, not wounded as she might have expected, but undergoing some bizarre metamorphosis. His entire body appeared to be fluid, the muscles and bones flowing and bulking, the posture becoming more brutish; the greenish scales and bony ridges on his face ran away as if they were melting in the rain; the nose grew broader, the eyes golden and wide-set; there seemed to be an odd mixture of fur and leaves sprouting all over his body, as if he were becoming a hybrid of flora and fauna. Yet despite its strangeness, Ruth felt the sight was oddly familiar. With each new transformation, he bellowed, and that sound also changed, conversely becoming more mellifluous. And finally twin stalks erupted from his forehead, growing and dividing until they became the proud, dangerous horns of a stag.

The vision was terrifying, yet also transcendental; Ruth felt flooded with an overpowering sense of wonder. She caught her breath; it was a slight sound, hidden by the wind, but whatever the Erl-King had become heard her. It froze, cocked its head, then lurched towards her, its hot breath bursting in twin plumes from its flared nostrils. Ruth shrieked in shock and scrabbled backwards, her heels slipping on the wet vegetation, but it was so quick it was over her before she could stand and run.

Knowing she was trapped, she turned and looked up at its huge silhouette looming over her, waiting for the wild attack that was sure to come. And then the strangest thing happened: in another flash of lightning she caught a glimpse of its expression and she was sure it was smiling.

'Frail creature,' it said in a voice like the wind through autumn trees, 'I see in you the sprouting shoots of one of my servants.'

'What's happened?' she croaked.

The creature made an odd, unnatural gesture with its left hand and then seemed to search for the right words to communicate with her. 'When the barriers collapsed, the Night Walkers were prepared. Deep in the Heart of Shadows, they had formed a Wish-Hex of immense power, forged from the dreams of lost souls. As we readied for our glorious return, it swept out in a whirlwind of vengeance, the like of which had not been seen since the first battle. None escaped its touch. Many of my kin were driven out of the Far Lands, a handful escaped to the world, or the places in-between. And some were cursed to walk the Night Walk. And I was one of them.' He made a strange noise in his throat that was part-growl, part-cry, but then seemed to regain his composure. 'But the Night Walkers' influence was always tainted with weakness. And you, a frail creature, broke its hold!'

The sound he made was not remotely human, but she guessed, in its ringing, howling rhythms, its essence was laughter. 'You have the spear, most glorious and wonderful of the Quadrillax. The eternal bane of the Night Walkers, the source of the sun's light!'

His words were strange, but she was slowly piecing it together. 'It freed you from their control?'

'I have as many faces as the day, yet I was trapped in form like you frail creatures, walking the Night Walk. Damned and tormented!'

She looked deep into his face and was almost overwhelmed by an awe, perhaps inspired by some submerged race memory. 'Who are you?' she whispered.

'Know you not my names? Has it been so long? Of all the Golden Ones, I stayed in the World the longest, dancing through even when the barriers were closed. Yet still forgotten?' His sigh was caught by the wind. 'My names are legion, changing with the season. In the first times, when the World was home, the people of the west knew me as Gwynn ap Nudd, White Son of Night, Lord of the Underworld, leader of the Wild Hunt, master of the Cwm Annwn, a Lord of Faery, a King of Annwn. In the great land, across the waves, I was Cernunnos, the Horned One, Lord of the Dance, Giver of Gifts. In the cold lands I was Woden, leader of the Herlethingus; heroism, victory and spiritual life were my domain. Each new frail creature saw me differently, yet knew my heart. Green Man. Herne the Hunter. Serpent Son. Wish Huntsman. Robin Hood. My home is the Green, my time the dark half of the year. Do you know me now?'

Ruth nodded, terrified yet entranced. Images tumbled across her mind, scenes from childhood stories, ancient myths, all pieces of an archetype that walked the world before history began. Whatever stood before her, it was impossible to grasp him in totality; he had as many aspects as nature, his form depending on the viewer and the occasion. The Erl-King, the dark side in which he had been locked and controlled, was now gone. 'What do I call you?' she whispered.

She trembled as he bent down, but when he brushed her forehead with the side of his thumb, the touch was gentle. 'Call me whichever name comes to your heart.'

She plucked a name from the long list. 'Cernunnos,' she said. His description made it seem a gentler aspect. And then she realised why he had seemed familiar: he was in the vision the mysterious young girl had shown her at the camp outside Bristol; the one for whom the girl had been searching. *The night to my day, the winter to my summer*, the girl had said. Twin aspects of the same powerful force.

He rose to his full height, still looking down on her. 'One face of the Green lives within you, another in one of your companions – their eyes, and yours, will open in time. As a Sister of Dragons, your path will be difficult, but my guidance will be with you until your blossoming. And in the harshest times, you may call for my aid. By this mark will you be known.'

He reached down and took her hand. She shuddered at his touch; his fingers didn't feel like fingers at all. A second later a bolt of searing pain scorched her palm. She screamed, but the agony subsided in an instant. Turning over her hand, she saw burned into it a circle which contained a design of what seemed to be interlocking leaves.

He was already turning away as he said, 'Seek me out in my Green Home.' He smiled and pointed to the owl which was circling majestically over their heads.

'What are you going to do now?' Ruth enquired reverentially.

'Once the Hunt has been summoned, it cannot retire without a soul.'

Ruth shivered at the awful meaning in his words. She began to protest, but his glance was so terrible the words caught in her throat.

He raised his head and sniffed the wind, and then, swifter than she could have imagined for his size, he loped off into the night; she was already forgotten, insignificant. A moment later the rain stopped and the wind fell, and when she looked up in the sky she saw the storm clouds sweeping away unnaturally to reveal a clear, star-speckled sky. She hung her head low, desperately trying to cope with the shock of an encounter with something so awesome it had transformed her entire existence. But when she closed her eyes, she could still see his face, and when she covered her ears, she could still hear his voice, and she feared she would never be the same again.

the Shark has pretty teeth

The moment Ruth disappeared with the Erl-King, Church thought all their lives were about to end. He was hacking blindly with the sword, watching the hounds crisp and fade, but seeing another replace each one he killed, realising Laura and Veitch were within an instant of being overwhelmed. Yet in that instant that the spear pierced the Erl-King, the Hunt seemed to freeze in its attack, and a second later the dogs were milling round in confusion, while the remaining riders were reining their horses back and retreating beyond the churchyard wall.

'She's done it,' he gasped, barely able to believe it.

Laura's eyes were filled with tears of fear and strain and blood was dripping from a score of wounds. 'I thought we were dead,' she moaned.

Veitch, who was just as injured, still held the iron bar high. 'Don't relax! They might just be gearing up for a new attack!' he barked.

Church knew he was right and returned to the alert, but he couldn't help calling out Ruth's name. When there was no reply, his heart sank.

They remained watching the Hunt for what seemed like hours, fighting against the exhaustion that racked them all. And then, as if in answer to a silent call, the riders simply turned their mounts and galloped away, the hounds baying behind them. Church looked to the wall in the corner of the graveyard; the glowering presence of Black Shuck was gone too.

Soon after, they heard a noise in the bracken and Ruth emerged from the shadows, pale and shaking. As she clambered over the wall awkwardly, Church ran forward and grabbed her.

'You did it!' he said, unable to contain his relief. 'I could kiss you!'

'Well do it now, before I faint,' she gasped. And then she did.

After retrieving the battered tent, they lit a fire on the edge of the beach and enjoyed the calm which had followed the departure of the storm. Though not fully recovered, Shavi seemed well enough to talk, which raised their already high spirits. With the van's minimal medical kit, they tended to their wounds, and by the time the warmth had started to penetrate their bones, Ruth was ready to tell them what she had experienced.

Afterwards, they stared into the heart of the fire, trying to assimilate all the new information. 'So,' Ruth said, summing up, 'the way I see it is this: for some reason we don't yet know, the doors between Otherworld and here were opened. The Danann were preparing to return when the Fomorii launched something called the Wish-Hex, which I imagine as a kind of nuclear bomb in their terms. When the blast swept out, it took the majority of the Danann to some place from where they can't return on their own. But some of the Danann were corrupted by this Wish-Hex radiation and, against their basic nature, fell under the control of the Fomorii. The Erl-King . . . Cernunnos . . . was one of them. And some of the other creatures of Otherworld must have been affected too. I think this explains the Fabulous Beast that attacked Church and I near Stonehenge. Obviously they're linked to the earth spirit, power, whatever, so they wouldn't have done the Fomorii's bidding against us unless they were forced.'

'And a few of the Danann escaped entirely,' Church added. 'Like the woman in the Watchtower. But she didn't tell me the doors between the two worlds were already open and the Danann were planning on coming through. She implied everything happened because the Fomorii broke the *Covenant*.'

'Maybe she was spinning you a line,' Veitch said.

Church shifted uncomfortably. Could they really trust a race that was so far beyond them that their motivations were almost incomprehensible? And what did that mean for the woman in the Watchtower's promise that his prize for success in freeing her people would be knowledge of Marianne's fate? He had a sudden image of cynical, educated western explorers conning indigenous people out of land and resources for a few paltry beads.

'So it was like a first strike,' Veitch continued. 'The Fomorii tried to wipe out all the opposition in one swoop, leaving them free to do whatever horrible stuff they wanted once they got over here.'

'But what was he *like*?' Shavi asked shakily. He was in a sleeping bag, propped up by a pile of rucksacks. 'Did you get a sense of something divine?'

Ruth saw the excitement in his eyes, but it was an issue she didn't really want to face. 'I don't believe in God,' she replied, but her voice wavered enough that she knew he wouldn't let her leave it there. 'Yes, I have tailored my beliefs a little. I couldn't be a humanist in the face of something like that. There is an existence beyond our own, and he was certainly unknowable. But divine? You might consider him a god.

Others might call him an alien, or a higher being.' She couldn't tell if it was Shavi's smile or her own unsureness after a lifetime of disbelief that irritated her the most.

'But do you not see? *This* is the question. The thing we spend all our lives searching for—'

'Oh, I don't know,' she snapped.

Church stepped in quickly. 'This isn't the time for intense theological debate—'

'No, it's the time for a party!' Veitch held out his arms in jubilation. 'We won!'

'That's poultry you're calculating,' Laura snorted. She finally seemed to be coming out of the fearful mood that had gripped her since the encounter in the graveyard.

'What do you mean?' Veitch threw a box of Elastoplast at her with a little more force than was necessary. 'We've found all the talismans. The Hunt has gone for good. And we're all alive!'

'As much as we ever were,' Laura said coolly.

'But we still don't know what to do with the talismans.' Ruth turned to Tom. 'When are you going to spill the beans?'

'When we're nearly where we need to be and there's no chance of anything going wrong,' he replied gruffly.

'At least we're well under the wire on the deadline,' Church said. 'More than three weeks to go. I never thought we'd do it so quickly.'

Despite their certain knowledge that their trials were not over, they slept more easily than they had done in weeks. When they awoke to the sound of seagulls, the sun was already up and the fire had burned out. They all laughed when a man out walking his dog avoided them by a wide margin, realising they must look like dirty itinerants with their matted hair and crumpled clothes.

The sea air was invigorating and by 8 a.m. they felt fully rested and ravenously hungry. Their supplies were low, so Veitch volunteered to walk up to the village to see if he could find something for breakfast. Church, Shavi and Tom said they wanted to come too, to stretch their legs, and once Ruth saw she would be left alone with Laura she opted to join them.

'You lot are freaks,' Laura gibed. 'Choosing physical exercise when you can lounge around and chill?' Tom convinced her she should sit in the van to guard the talismans so she could drive away at the first sign of trouble. Church borrowed Laura's small knapsack and tucked the Wayfinder inside it. 'I'm never letting this out of my sight again, whether we need it or not,' he said with a grin.

They strode up the leafy lane to the village with a lively step, despite the exertions of the night before.

'You know what?' Veitch said to Church ahead of the others. 'I never felt as alive as I do now.'

Church knew what he meant. 'It's like you don't fully appreciate life until you've faced up to death. I know that's a real cliché – all those adrenalin junkies doing dangerous sports say it all the time. But I never thought for a moment it might be true.'

'Makes you think how bad we're leading our lives, with awful office jobs and poxy suburban houses.' Veitch thought for a moment, then glanced at Church. 'Maybe we're on the wrong side.'

'What do you mean?'

'We're fighting to keep the things the way they always have been, right? What happens if that's not the best way? What if all this magic and shit is the way it really should be?'

Church recalled a conversation he had with Ruth soon after they first met about his dismay at the way magic seemed to have drained out of life. 'But what about all the death and suffering? People getting slaughtered, medical technology failing?'

'Maybe that's all part and parcel of having a richer life. What's better – big highs and deep lows or a flatline?'

Church smiled. 'I never took you for a philosopher, Ryan. But it all sounds a little Nietzchean to me.'

'You what?'

At that point Tom and Shavi caught up with them and introduced a vociferous religious debate. Veitch listened for a moment, then dropped back until he was walking just in front of Ruth. She eyed him contemptuously. 'Don't even think of talking to me.'

'I just wanted to say that was a really brave thing you did last night. You saved us all.'

'Do you really think I need your validation?'

Veitch went to reply, but her face was filled with such cold fury he knew it was pointless. He dropped back further and trailed behind them all.

The village shop was just opening up for the morning. Church and Shavi both picked up wire baskets and loaded them up with essentials. Just before they reached the checkout, a short, ruddy-faced man in his fifties with white hair and a checked flat cap rushed in, leaving the door wide open.

'Born in a barn, Rhys?' the woman behind the counter said.

Ruth, who was nearest, saw that he wasn't in the mood to banter. His face was flushed and he was breathless, as if he'd run all the way there. 'Did you hear about Dermott?' he gasped. The woman shook her head, suddenly intrigued. 'Missing, he is. They found his bike and a shoe up near the old Pirate's Lantern. Edith is in a right old state. She expected to find him in bed after the night shift and when he wasn't there she called the police.'

The woman and the man launched into a lurid conversation about what might have happened to their friend, but Ruth was no longer listening. She *knew* what had happened to him. The Hunt had found their sacrificial soul. Feeling suddenly sick, she dashed out of the shop and sat on the pavement, her head in her hands. How many people who had crossed their path had suffered? she wondered.

The others emerged soon after, laughing and joking, but she found it impossible to join in. Even when they won, there was a price to pay.

The knock at the passenger door window came just as Laura had settled out in the back, mulling over whether or not she had fallen for Church, hating herself for it. It was brief, friendly; not at all insistent. Deciding it was kids playing or the part-time car park attendant wanting to check their ticket, she decided she couldn't be bothered to answer it. But when it came again thirty seconds later, she sighed irritably and then scrambled over the back of the passenger seat. She was surprised to see a man who looked like a tramp in his shabby black suit. Yet his red brocade waistcoat added a note of flamboyance, as did his swept-back silver hair and sparkling eyes, which suggested a rich, deep humour. His skin had that weathered, suntanned appearance that only came from a life on the road, but his smile was pleasant enough.

Laura wound down the window. 'I haven't got any spare change. I like to sharpen it to throw at authority figures.'

'An admirable pursuit, my dear,' he said in a rich, theatrical voice. 'But I am not seeking financial remuneration. Although I must say I am a little down on my luck at the moment. Travelling great distances can be an expensive business. But that is by-the-by. In actual fact, I am seeking young Mr Churchill. Is he around, by any chance?'

Laura laughed in surprise. 'You know Church?'

'We had a wonderful evening of great humour, fantastic storytelling and, frankly, serious inebriation at a Salisbury hostel. Why, your generous friend even allowed me to drink his health into the night on his hotel tab. A wonderful fellow, and no mistaking.' Laura laughed at his *faux* dramatic persona, which seemed to have been culled from old films and older books, but his charm was unmistakable. 'And, as is his genial nature, he asked me to look him up the next time I was in the vicinity. And here I am!' He suddenly clapped his hands into a praying posture and half buried his face between them. 'Oh, forgive me! I have forgotten the very basis of good manners – the introduction. My name, my dear, is Callow.'

He held out his hand. Laura hesitated for a moment, then took it. 'Laura DuSantiago,' she said, aping his theatrical style.

'And will you allow me to rest a while in your vehicle until young Mr Churchill's return? I fear my legs are weary.'

Laura began to open the door, but then a thought jarred: Church didn't have the van when Callow would have met him, and there was no way he could have known they'd be there in an obscure Welsh village. She looked into his face suspiciously.

Callow smiled, said nothing. He was still holding on to her hand and his grip was growing tighter. 'Let go.' Her voice was suddenly hard and frosty.

She tried to drag her hand free, but Callow's strength belied his appearance. His smile now seemed grotesque. He forced his head through the open window and she was hit by a blast of foul breath. She realised he was trying to prevent anyone seeing what was happening. 'You bastard—'

Before she could say any more, Callow gently brushed his free hand across the back of her arm. She couldn't understand his action, until she saw a thin red line blossom where his fingers had passed. It seemed almost magical. She watched it in bemusement, trying to work out how he had done it. But the stinging shocked her alert and she caught hold of his wrist, forcing his hand up; a razor blade was surreptitiously lodged between his tightly held fingers. She had only a second to take it in when he suddenly let go of her hand and smashed his fist hard into her face. Laura saw stars, felt the explosion of pain, then pitched backwards across the seats in a daze. When she came around, Callow had the door open and was clambering in over her.

She savagely kicked a foot towards his groin, but instead it slammed into his thigh. He winced, but the smile never left his lips. His eyes, no longer sparkling, were fixed on her face.

Laura began to yell and struggle, but Callow made another pass with his hand, slashing the soft underside of her forearm, dangerously near to the exposed veins at her wrist. Before she could respond, he started sweeping his hand back and forth across her face. She threw her arms up to protect herself, feeling her flesh split and the wet warmth trickle down to her T-shirt. She yelled out, the agony of the moment multiplied by a sudden image of her mother showing her the bloodstained razor blade two years earlier. *Not again*, her mind roared.

The seriousness of her predicament hit her like a train; no one was going to save her; Callow had forced her into a position where she couldn't fight back; and just as she decided her only hope was to scream until someone came running, he hit her in the face again, grabbed her by the hair and bundled her over the back of the seats.

In her daze, she was vaguely aware of him dropping down beside her like a giant spider, and then he had gripped the razor blade between knuckle and thumb and was cutting into her in a frenzy. The last thing Laura saw before she blacked out was so horrible she couldn't tell if it was a hallucination brought on by the pain and the shock of her approaching death: his eyes seemed to be flooded with blood, as if every capillary in them had burst at once, and there was a subsequent movement under the skin around his orbits. As if something was crawling there.

Church was the first to notice the rear doors of the van hanging raggedly open. There was nothing inherently sinister in the image – Laura might simply have opened them to get some air to the suffocating interior – but his intuition sent a flood of icewater through his system. And then he was running, leaving the others chatting obliviously behind him. Bloody footprints led away from the van. Anxiety spurred him on, driving all rational thought from his mind. When he reached the doors and glanced in, his stomach turned.

The inside of the van looked like an abattoir. Blood was splattered up the walls and across the floor where Laura's pale, unmoving form lay. Her T-shirt was in tatters, the taunting legend *Jesus Saves* looming out at him, now appearing as if someone had attempted to scribble it out.

And the crate containing the talismans was gone.

The journey back to Tenby passed in a high-speed blur of madly overtaken vehicles, blaring horns and heart-stoppingly dangerous turns. They screamed into Accident & Emergency at the hospital on Trafalgar Road and Church ran in with Laura in his arms, her blood soaking through his shirt, leaving sickening spatter marks behind them like the spoor of some giant beast; despite his first impression, she was still alive, but in shock. If they had tried to deny it until then, the moment they saw the faces of the team of young doctors and nurses, they were left in no doubt as to the seriousness of her condition. She was whisked off behind flapping curtains, leaving them alone in an empty waiting room.

'But we'd won!' Veitch pleaded, his staring expression revealing the shock that played across all their minds. 'It's not fair.' It sounded pathetic and spoilt, but it was all he could think to say.

Ruth chewed her thumb knuckle. 'God, I hope she's going to be okay.' Church watched the regret and guilt play out on her face.

'But we'd won!' Veitch repeated, as if saying it enough times would make it come true.

'They selected the right time to attack,' Shavi noted, 'when our defences were down. Perfect, really.'

'She was attacked with a knife or a razor – you saw the cuts. That doesn't seem like the Fomorii,' Church said. 'Maybe it's just a random disaster – just some nut who crossed paths with us. The kind of thing that happens in life all the fucking time,' he added bitterly.

'Who specifically took the talismans?' Tom seemed more upset than Church would have expected. His eyes had been filled with tears from the moment they had discovered her; sometimes he could barely talk; at other times he shook with the ague which increasingly seemed to be afflicting him.

'All that bleedin' struggle. For nothing!' Veitch buried his head in his hands.

'This is probably not the best time to discuss it,' Tom began, 'but we need to get on the trail of the talismans. There's much more at stake here than—'

'No!' Church stared at him angrily, but all he could see was Marianne. 'Nothing is bigger than people! Individuals. People you love. They deserve your time and attention and passion. Not a world that couldn't care less if it went to hell in a handcart!'

Tom made as if to argue, then looked away.

'I don't care about anything else right now. I just want to see my friend pull through. If you haven't got friends, if you haven't got people you love, you've got nothing.'

Veitch stared at Church as if he was seeing him in a new light, then nodded thoughtfully.

Just then Tom put his head in his hands and started to sob silently. The others stared at him in surprise. Ruth slid up next to him and put a comforting arm around his shoulders, but he seemed inconsolable.

Veitch's shoulders were weighted with desolation. 'What the hell are we going to do now?'

They were allowed to see her at noon. Against the crisp white sheets of the bed she looked uncommonly frail, like a sickly child; they barely recognised her. Her dyed-blonde hair was matted and unkempt, her skin like frost, her body somehow thinner and more angular than they remembered. Pads had been taped to the left side of her face. A couple of tubes snaked into her; she was dead to the world.

'We sedated her,' the doctor explained. 'It was for the best, after the shock.'

'Is she going to be okay?' Church asked.

The doctor didn't look too sure of his answer. 'Physically, I suppose. We gave her some blood, stitched the deepest wounds, bound the others. But . . .' – he shrugged – 'you know, a razor attack. It's sick, disgusting. When I see the mess it leaves, I can't understand how anybody could be so twisted as to carry it out.' He paused, swallowed. 'And her face . . . she's going to have some bad scarring on that left side. You saw her back, her arms. She looks like a jigsaw. The psychological scars will be the hardest to heal. I noticed the old scar tissue . . .' He looked from one face to the other, hoping for an explanation.

'She's suffered before,' Church said simply.

The doctor nodded as if that was answer enough. 'That makes it worse. She's been bitten twice, as it were.'

'When can we take her with us?' Tom asked tentatively. He succeeded in ignoring the others' annoyed stares.

'Oh, well, a few days. She needs lots of rest, nothing too strenuous. I can put you in touch with the counselling service.'

They thanked him for what he had done, but said nothing further until he had left the room. Then Church turned on Tom. 'Christ, if she were dead you'd have us dumping her at the side of the road!' When Tom didn't seem too shocked by this allegation, Church became even more angry.

'You may not be so outraged when you see the way things will be in a few short months.' He seemed to be struggling with the conversation, dragging up each word individually, but some of his old frostiness had returned. 'If you do not pursue the talismans now, you'll be making the decision to give up the world, civilisation, everything. Is that what you are prepared to do?'

Church looked away, angry that Tom was making him face up to it, when all he wanted to think about was Laura.

'She's going to be fine,' Tom continued. 'You heard the doctor. But we can't afford to leave it another day. The trail could be lost by then.'

The room was filled by a long, hanging silence and then Veitch said, 'I'd really like to find who did this to her.'

'You heard the doctor. She's in no state to be moved,' Church protested. 'What happens if she gets an infection in the wounds? Tears one of them open? We could be putting her life at risk.'

'A decision needs to be taken now,' Tom said insistently.

Church saw all eyes were on him. 'Why are you looking at me?' he raged. They looked away uncomfortably, but the answer to his question was obvious; no one else was going to speak out.

Tom stepped in front of him and rested a hand on his shoulder; there was an honest paternalism in his face. 'It's your call,' he said softly.

Church had the sudden, terrible feeling that he would be damned whatever he decided.

Veitch managed to find a wheelchair and they lifted Laura into it after a heated discussion about the status of the drips and whether they should remove them; one appeared to be a rehydrating solution, while the other was a painkiller with some kind of electronically timed dose. In the end, they decided to wheel both of the drips out behind her, still attached. A blanket was hastily thrown over her legs to try to hide the fact she obviously wasn't in any condition to be moved. If they were stopped, they would never be allowed to take her out, and would probably pay a heavy price for trying to kidnap a patient, so they hurried through the corridors, desperately following a roundabout route that took them away from the busiest areas. The alarm was raised only at the last minute by a furious nurse, when they were forced to pass through reception to where they had abandoned the van.

They made a makeshift bed of sleeping bags on the floor of the van for Laura and tried to secure the drip trolleys with clothes, but every time Shavi went round a corner they fell over with a clatter.

After the euphoria of the morning, the mood in the van was dismal. Suddenly it seemed like everything was turning sour and whatever they did would not be able to make it right. Church sat on the floor next to Laura, watching her face for any sign of awakening, or of her condition deteriorating. He hated himself for the decision he had had to make, and for the fact that he had no choice. And he wanted to yell at them all that he wasn't up to the job of being leader and making enormous choices that people's lives depended on; he had been so unperceptive that he had allowed his own girlfriend to die, hadn't even realised she had been murdered. Sometimes he wondered if it would be better for all of them if he simply walked away and left them to it.

The Wayfinder pointed them north-east out of Tenby. Shavi kept just within the speed limit in any area where it was likely there might be traffic police and floored the accelerator at all other times. Although the lantern suggested a route which took them across country, after their experience in Builth Wells they agreed it would be best to avoid the open Welsh countryside and instead keep to the main roads. They picked up the busy A40 just outside Carmarthen and followed it all the way to Ross-on-Wye, then cut across to the motorway. There the Wayfinder resumed its northwards pointing.

'Whoever has the talismans is travelling fast,' Shavi noted. 'And they obviously have a definite direction in mind.'

'Here, why don't you do that thing you do? You know, with the mushrooms and the trance and everything? We could find out where they're going and try and head them off at the pass,' Veitch suggested.

Shavi fixed his gaze on the road ahead, his face suddenly emotionless. 'No,' he replied simply.

The sky grew an angry red, then shifted through various shades of purple as they trundled north through the West Midlands conurbation, the flat countryside of Staffordshire and Cheshire and then over the Manchester Ship Canal, where the traffic seemed as busy as if nothing were wrong. By the time they had passed Lancaster and the proliferation of signs for the Lakes, darkness had fallen.

In the back, Church, Ruth and Tom sat quietly around Laura's unmoving form while Veitch and Shavi found security in a rambling discourse on the mundane, punctuated by long, introspective silences.

'I've never seen this much of the country,' Veitch mused. 'Barely been out of London before. The odd trip to Southend to see me nan. Never north of Watford.'

'Beautiful, is it not?' Shavi noted thoughtfully. 'Every part of it. And not just the parts you expect to be beautiful, like the downs and the heaths. Cooling towers seen in the right light are golden. Once I was on a train coming out of Derby and we passed through a terrible industrial wasteland that they were in the process of turning into some civic site. There were heaps of dirt and weeds and huge pools of polluted water. And then, just for one moment, the quality of the light reflected the grey clouds off the pools and the whole landscape turned silver. It was so wonderful it took my breath away. We have lost sight of that wonder in the every day.'

'Yeah, I suppose. But have you ever been to Becton?' Veitch thought for a moment, then looked at him suspiciously. 'You don't look like a queen.'

Shavi returned his gaze, a faint smile on his lips. 'I do not like labels.'

'Well, you are, aren't you? A shirtlifter?'

'I prefer to consider myself polymorphously perverse.'

'What's that bollocks?'

'It means I take my pleasure from wherever and whatever I please.

349

We have a limited time to indulge ourselves. Why limit yourself to just one sex?'

Veitch snorted, stared out the passenger window.

Shavi stifled a laugh at his Victorian values. 'What is wrong?'

'Makes me sick what you people do.'

'Do not think about it, then. I will not force you.'

'You better not try it on with me.'

'You are not my type.'

Veitch snapped round indignantly. 'Why not?'

'You are just not.'

Veitch turned back to the passenger window, muttering under his breath.

At that moment, Laura stirred in the back. Church leaned forward anxiously and for a moment the tense silence in the van was unbearable. Gradually, her eyes flickered open, burst with momentary panic as they tried to establish her situation, then calmed when they saw Church leaning over her.

'Shit, this hurts,' she said in a fragile voice.

'Take it easy,' Church whispered, 'you've been through a lot.'

His heart ached when he saw the terrible memories suddenly play out across her features. Her hand jerked up to the pads that covered her left side. 'My face,' she said desolately. Her eyes filled with tears that brimmed over on to her cheeks. She clamped her lids shut so they wouldn't see her weakness.

Church took her hand, thinking she would shake it off, but she held on tightly. 'We're here with you,' he said gently.

'God, nobody's going to want to look at me.' Her voice was filled with such awful pain that he felt queasy. In her despair he could see through all her defences and the honesty was almost too much to bear, like someone had opened a door on to a searchlight from a pitch black room.

'Don't be silly. You're with friends here.'

She snorted a bitter laugh. 'Friends? You all hate me.' Church could hear the irrational, overly despairing ring of the drugs in her words.

'We'd stand by you through thick and thin.' Church looked round in surprise as Ruth leaned in next to him.

'Hey. Miss Frosty,' Laura said weakly. 'Do I smell the stink of pity?'

'No. That's Tom.'

Laura lifted her head as much as she could then let it drop once she had seen his indignant expression. She let out a wheezy laugh. 'Old git. Nice to see you. Bet you thought there was someone actually going to die before you.'

'You need to get some rest,' Tom replied acidly. 'A week or two, maybe. We could turn up the drip—'

'How do you feel?' Church asked. When he looked into her face he felt something flash between them; a brief light in her eyes, the faintest hint of a smile; it sang through the air and he felt a shiver run down his spine.

He could see she felt it too; she smiled at him, then it slipped away uncomfortably, as if she couldn't understand the emotions sweeping through her. 'Like I've been on the bacon slicer,' she said.

'They did quite a number on you. Do you know who it was?'

Her brow furrowed as she struggled to remember. 'Some tramp. He said you knew him.' A long pause as the name surfaced. 'Callow.'

'Callow?' Church and Ruth said in simultaneous surprise.

'He's just a scrounging no-mark!' Church looked at Ruth for some explanation. 'He was in Salisbury. What's he doing here?'

'He knew where we were,' Laura said. 'There's no way he could have found us by accident.'

'Shit! What the hell's going on?' Church felt an impotent rage sweep through him. 'When we find the bastard, I'll kill him.'

'There was something else . . .' Laura's voice almost broke from the strain. 'I remember . . . His eyes turned red, like they were filling with blood. And there was something moving under his skin. He wasn't human . . .'

Her voice trailed away and the van filled with silence until Veitch called back, 'We've got to pull in at the next services for some petrol.'

They swung into the sweeping drive of Tebay Services, past clustering trees that seemed too dense and frightening, but the cafeteria was a welcoming oasis of light blazing in the night. Enormous picture windows looked out over the bleak high country of the northern Lakes, the stark interior lamps casting illumination over a cold duck pond and wind-blasted scrub. Church noticed the breathtaking view and thought briefly how pleasant it must have been in summers past; now it seemed too close to the dangerous, deserted countryside.

'I've got to stretch my legs,' he said. 'Get some tea. We should take ten-minute breaks in twos. Who's with me?' Ruth volunteered, but Tom, who had been poring over the book of maps with a pocket torch, overruled her rudely.

They found a seat in the cafeteria next to the windows looking out over the impenetrably dark landscape. There were a few other travellers, scattered around, as if they didn't dare sit near to anyone else, just in case.

'It's changing quickly now, isn't it?' Church stared out into the night morosely. 'I wonder how long we've got before everything falls apart.'

'Not long.' Tom sipped his hot chocolate thoughtfully. 'But there's still time for you to make a difference.'

'Is that irony? We've lost everything we've fought for, and Laura . . . Christ, I can't believe that.'

Tom looked away for a long moment. When Church glanced up to see why he was so quiet, he saw sweat standing out on Tom's brow and shivers rippling though him, as if someone were shaking his shoulders.

'What is wrong with you?' Church said with a lack of sympathy he instantly regretted. 'Have you got some kind of illness you're not telling us about?'

Tom took a moment to compose himself, then said hoarsely, 'None of your business.' He took another drink of his chocolate and continued as if nothing had happened. 'Callow is obviously working for one or the other of the Fomorii tribes – as a backup to the Wild Hunt for Calatin in case of their failure, or as a chancer for Mollecht, hoping to snatch the talismans during the confusion of any of our conflicts with Calatin's agents.'

'He seemed fine when we met him in Salisbury.'

Tom shrugged. 'Perhaps they got to him after then. That's immaterial. The point is to reach him before he hands over the talismans to whomever controls him. And I believe I know how to do that.'

'How?'

'In the current climate, the Lake District will be one of the most dangerous areas in the country. Lakes are liminal zones, as I told you, doorways between here and there, and with so many lakes the place will be overpopulated with all the misbegotten creatures of Otherworld. Certainly a place where it's too threatening to travel at night.'

Church sipped his tea, wincing at the bitterness. 'Go on.'

'That would also make it a prime spot for the Fomorii. Callow *must* be travelling there. If we knew where he was going we could intercept him.'

'But we don't know where he's going.'

'There's a place called Loadpot Hill overlooking Ullswater. It has always held a peculiar attraction for the Fomorii. They'll make the handover somewhere near there.'

'How do you know that?'

'I just do.'

Church searched his face; as usual, there was something Tom was not telling him, but he had learned to trust Tom's silences, if not to appreciate them.

'There are plenty of other things out there beyond the Fomorii, so it will still be dangerous for Callow to travel over the fells at night. I would guess he will probably take the best-lit route rather than the most obvious. We might be able to beat him to the road to the hill where we can cut him off.'

'By the dangerous, direct route? You expect me to sell that to the others?'

'At this stage we have to take risks.'

Tom headed off to the toilet, leaving Church alone to finish his coffee. For some reason he hadn't been able to get warm for the last couple of days, even though he was wearing a T-shirt, shirt, sweater and jacket buttoned tightly. He hoped he wasn't coming down with something.

Despite Tom's claims, the first mile or so from the motorway into the heart of the Lake District was uneventful. Although they saw no other traffic, they passed houses with lights gleaming through chinks in drawn curtains and caught the occasional whiff of smoke from their hearths. But then it was as if they had passed an invisible boundary. Odd, lambent lights moved across the fells that provided the district with its magnificent backdrop, and as they travelled down from the heights, will o' the wisps danced deep in the thick forests that crowded the road. Things were caught in the corner of their eyes which they never saw full on, but could tell instinctively were inhuman. And at one point something flying that seemed half-bat, half-human baby was caught briefly in the headlights before slamming into the side of the van with a hefty clang and a sickeningly childish shriek.

'Don't stop for anything,' Tom said as if any of them had entertained the idea. 'Keep your foot to the floor.'

They all remained silent, eyes fixed on the scenery flashing past, apart from Laura, who was drifting in and out of consciousness; at times she seemed so delirious Church feared seriously for her wellbeing.

But the short cut Tom suggested seemed to work; when Church next checked the Wayfinder, it was clearly indicating the talismans were behind them. Finally Tom ordered Shavi to pull over on a shadowy layby beside the lonely road which wound its way around a hillside halfway up the slope. 'You sure?' Veitch said, peering into the thick woods on both sides. 'Why is this place any safer than anywhere else we've just driven through?'

Tom shrugged. 'I never said it was. But this will be the best place to wait to intercept him.' He motioned away to the west. 'Loadpot Hill is over there. This is the nearest road to it and it ends a little further up the way.'

Veitch didn't seem convinced. 'We can't see anybody sneaking up on us here.'

'If we keep the doors locked, we can drive off if anything comes near,' Ruth suggested hopefully.

Tom shook his head. 'We need to keep watch at the bend in the road. We can pull the van out to block the road at the last minute before he sees us.'

'And you think somebody's going to volunteer to go out there on look-out?' Veitch said.

'We should all go,' Church said. 'Safety in numbers.'

'I should stay here, ready to pull out when the car comes,' Shavi said.

'There will be plenty of time to get back and behind the wheel when we see the headlights,' Tom replied.

'What about Laura?' Ruth stroked a couple of stray hairs from her forehead.

'She'll be fine here with the doors locked.' Church turned to Tom. 'How will we know his vehicle?'

'It'll be the only one on the road in this place at this time.'

'You have all the answers.' Church became even more aware of the chill once the engine was switched off. He wished he had the sword with him. As he opened the rear doors and jumped out, he felt as defenceless as if he had both hands tied together.

The others followed him silently, with Veitch on his guard at the rear, his eyes constantly searching. They took up position at the bend in the road, although it was impossible to stand still for too long; wherever they were, their backs were to the dark, brooding trees, which made them all feel uncomfortable. Several times they turned with the unmistakable feeling that someone was just behind them.

Tom had been correct; the vantage point allowed them a clear view of anyone approaching. Veitch repeatedly complained they were too far from the van until Ruth threatened to shove him in front of Callow's vehicle if he didn't shut up.

Despite the danger, Church felt a tingle of wonder when he opened himself up to their surroundings. He had never experienced a night so silent – no drone of cars or distant rumble of planes, and the air had the clear, fresh tang of the pine trees, as if all the pollution had been drained from it. It was so intoxicating it seemed unnatural – an irony that was not lost on him – and he wondered if it was another by-product of the change.

Their conversation dried up quickly, until the only sound that punctuated the silence was the stamping of their feet to keep warm. They never lowered their guard for a second, even though they kept watch for the better part of an hour. But instead of getting used to their situation, the atmosphere of menace increased gradually until it became so claustrophobic Ruth complained that she felt like being sick.

'Tell you what, I could shoot his windscreen out,' Veitch suggested. Church could tell from the timbre of his voice that he was only speaking because he couldn't bear the now-unpleasant silence any longer.

'Guns are so symptomatic of the worst of what went before,' Shavi said. 'They do not have a place in this new age. I feel the more we rely on the old ways, the more likely we are to bring something terrible down on our heads.'

'What, *more* terrible?' Church said.

'I'm sick of people moaning about how bad guns are,' Veitch said. 'What, you think we should go back to swords? Have you seen what damage they can do?'

'Have you?' Ruth snapped.

After a pause, Veitch replied, 'No, but I can guess.'

Ruth was about to attack this line of reasoning when she suddenly did a double take at Tom. 'You're bleeding,' she said.

Blood was trickling from both his nostrils. Tom dabbed at it with his fingertips and then examined them curiously.

'Hang on, can you hear something?' Veitch began to look around anxiously, but the night seemed as silent as ever.

Church became aware of the unpleasant expression on Tom's face. It didn't seem to be a reaction to his nosebleed; more as if he were struggling with some terribly disconcerting thoughts. 'Are you okay?' he asked. 'Is it the illness again?'

Tom looked at him with an inexplicable expression of such horror Church fell instantly silent.

'There is something,' Veitch said insistently. 'Listen!'

'Will you shut up!' Ruth snapped. 'There's nothing! You're just winding everybody up!'

Tom choked, raised his hand to his mouth. Church noticed with alarm there were now trickles of blood at the corners of his eyes, and another seeping out of his left ear. 'Jesus!' he said. 'What's wrong with you?'

'Wait!' Shavi said. 'Ryan is right. There is something.' The two of them were looking with concern all around.

Ruth glared at both of them, then looked to Church for support. 'Is everybody going mad?'

Church turned to the van, thinking of Laura. It did seem too far away. 'Maybe we should move back that way a little,' he suggested.

Tom pitched forward, clutching his head. Blood spattered on to the road surface. Kneeling like a dog, he retched and hawked as if something was stuck in his throat.

Anxiety transfixed Veitch's face. Ignoring Tom, he gripped Church's shoulders. 'Let's get out of here. Something bad is going to happen.'

'I agree,' Shavi said.

But Church was already crouching down next to Tom, one arm around his shoulders. 'We have to get help for him. This looks serious.'

'Church?'

Ruth's quizzical, faintly unnerved voice caught Church's attention more than anything the others could have done. He looked up into her face, now pale and troubled.

'I *can* hear it,' she said edgily.

And then he could too. It was reedy, high-pitched, almost beyond the audible range, jarring in its intensity. A queasy sensation bubbled in his stomach. It reminded him of the cry of sea birds, yet continuous, and with a vague, uneasy human quality that was intensely disturbing.

'What *is* that?' he said, rising to his feet, Tom now forgotten.

'Look.' Shavi had walked ahead of them a few paces to peer into the trees on the upward slope. 'Is there something in there?'

'I said let's get out of here!' Veitch snapped.

Shavi was correct; shadows seemed to be flitting amongst the trees, oddly lighter in quality than the surrounding gloom.

Tom made another stomach-churning retching sound deep in his throat. Droplets of blood were flying everywhere.

'Why won't he shut up?' Ruth cried uncharitably. Her fearful thoughts played out on her face.

We should run, Church thought, but the shadows' strange movements and the shrieking sound that was emanating from them were so hypnotic he was rooted to the spot.

The shapes were sweeping down the slope towards them across a wide arc. And as they drew closer they appeared grey and oddly translucent, as if they were filled with smoke, finding consistency only in their proximity to whomever was viewing them. Church caught his breath when he realised there were scores of them. Their movements were strange and jarring, almost a dance amongst the trees, twisting and fluttering like paper in a breeze. Church couldn't understand how they could have substance and no substance at the same time.

And then as they drew closer still, Church could make out their grey faces; they were women, quite beautiful in their way, but with hollow cheeks, eyes staring, unblinking, mouths frozen wide to make that terrible scream. They were wearing billowing shrouds and their wild hair streamed behind them. Church, Ruth, Shavi and Veitch were frozen in horror.

'What are they?' Ruth asked hoarsely.

'The Baobhan Sith.'

Church was shocked to hear the croaking words come from Tom's mouth. He had rolled on to his back and was staring crazily at the sky.

'The Baobhan Sith?' Church recalled the sharp pang of fear he felt as he lay under the quilt in the Salisbury hotel room while the unseen thing prowled around the room. Then he realised Tom had uttered the name without seeing. Terrible understanding gelled in his mind. 'You knew this was going to happen! You led us here on purpose!' he shouted at Tom with dismay.

Tom made to reply, but all that came from his mouth was a gout of blood.

It seemed to break the spell, just as the Baobhan Sith were on the verge of emerging from the trees. As one, Church, Veitch and Shavi turned and bolted towards the van.

Still caught in the horror of the moment, Ruth simply backed across the road. For an instant reality seemed to hang in the air, and then suddenly everything erupted in too-fast speed. The Baobhan Sith burst from the trees, now a monstrous hunting pack. The sharp retort of Veitch's gun came and went ridiculously. Most of the shades swarmed round and descended on the fleeing figures of Church, Shavi and Veitch, screeching with an animal ferocity. Although their forms still seemed insubstantial, Ruth saw them latch on to her friends with hideously cruel fingers. And then they seemed to sweep up, as if they were lighter than air, and their mouths seemed to open wider than was possible, revealing rows of needle-sharp teeth. The last thing she saw before she tore her gaze away were the heads swooping down, jaws about to snap shut on her friends' exposed necks.

The remaining Baobhan Sith were coming for her. They bypassed Tom as if he were not there and danced across the road. Ruth continued to back away hurriedly until she was moving into the trees on the downward slope; she had to escape so she could find some way to save the others. The ground fell away sharply. Her heels kicked, didn't find any purchase. And then, as the shriek of the Baobhan Sith seemed to fill everything, she was falling, turning over and over as she plummeted down the slope, feeling the branches and brambles tear at her skin, rolling faster and faster until everything became a blur of fear and pain.

flight

Ruth came to a rough halt against a drystone wall, knocking the air from her lungs and stunning her for the briefest moment. She had leaf mould in her nostrils and mouth and myriad scratches across her face and hands. Coughing and spluttering, she scrambled to her feet, the terror rising within her as images of the Baobhan Sith burst like fireworks in her mind. Desperately, she glanced back up the slope. There was no sign of them in pursuit, but she could hear the haunted shrieks floating down through the budding branches. It wouldn't be long before they found her.

The thought of having to flee through the wild countryside filled her with dread. Her best option would be to find somewhere secure to hide, but how easy would that be? Glancing round, she discovered she was resting against the garden wall of a tiny cottage. It appeared ancient; the thatch came down to just above the ground floor windows, which were barely larger than portholes. What walls were visible appeared as thick as the length of her arm, to keep out the bitter winter winds. It was surrounded by a neat garden containing a handful of fruit trees that were so gnarled and twisted with age they looked like old men gossiping on a street corner. But Ruth was warmed to see a golden light glowing behind the curtains and the air was scented with the aroma of woodsmoke rising from the large stone chimney.

The shriek of the Baobhan Sith seemed unpleasantly near – she didn't have time to weigh her options. Cursing as she cracked her knees and shins, she clambered over the wall, dropped into a bed of herbs and ran round the side of the house to the front door. It was oak and so weathered it probably hadn't been replaced since the cottage was built. A cast-iron bootscraper stood next to it, alongside a broom made of a branch with twigs bound for bristles.

Although she felt frantic, Ruth knocked on the door as calmly as she could, so as not to frighten whoever lived there. The inhabitant must have heard her run round the house, for the curtain at the window next to the door twitched in an instant; Ruth caught a glimpse of glittering eyes in a woman's face before the curtains fell back.

But still no one came to the door. The nerve-jangling cry of the

Baobhan Sith sounded just beyond the garden wall on the other side of the cottage now. There wasn't time to flee anywhere else.

Ruth hammered on the door with all her strength and this time it did swing open. The woman was in her late fifties, her hair long and silver and tied at the back with a black ribbon. Her cheeks bloomed with the broken capillaries of life in the cold Lake District gales. She stood several inches shorter than Ruth, but she was just as slim and elegant. For a split-second she searched Ruth's face, and what she found there must have been agreeable, for she grabbed Ruth's wrist tightly to drag her inside, slamming the door behind her. Three iron bolts shot across an instant later.

Ruth sucked in a lungful of air. 'There's something out there—'

'I know what's out there,' the woman barked. 'Come away from the door!'

They were inside the woman's sitting room, which was spartanly decorated. It was lusciously warm from a log fire banked up in the wide stone hearth. A cracked and aged dresser stood against one wall and a similarly ancient dining table against the other, on which were arrayed a collection of corked pot containers; the contents of a few – seeds and dried herbs – were scattered around. Other herbs hung in bunches from the rafters creating a heady, perfumed atmosphere. A rush mat lay on the flags near the fire, but the only other item of furniture was a heavy wooden armchair with a floral cushion right next to the hearth. A sandy cat was curled up next to it.

'We could barricade ourselves upstairs. Try to keep them out till dawn—' Ruth began.

'They won't even know we're here if we don't draw attention to ourselves.' The woman watched Ruth suspiciously, her eyes still glittering in the light of the fire. 'What are you doing around these parts at this time? It's no longer safe to travel by night – nor even by day, really.'

'I didn't have any choice,' Ruth replied. The full force of what had happened hit her and she rested against the back of the armchair, placing one hand over her eyes to try to clear the image of the Baobhan Sith attacking Church, Shavi and Veitch. When she'd blinked away the tears a moment later, she brought her hand down and noticed the woman was staring at it intently.

She suddenly lurched forward and grabbed Ruth's wrist, turning her arm over so the palm was uppermost. The mark Cernunnos had scorched into her flesh was revealed in the firelight.

'Goddess!' The suspicion drained from the woman's face and was replaced by awe. When she looked up into Ruth's face, her features were now open and smiling. 'These are very strange times. Sit! I'll brew up a pot.'

'There's no time!' Ruth protested.

'There's always time. I've cast a spell of protection on this place. It's invisible to any of those hideous things crawling around out there these days. But we can't go out until the ones after you have gone or they'll have us in a moment. Times when you can relax are few – grab hold of them!'

Ruth reluctantly allowed herself to be pressed into the armchair, but her thoughts were in chaos and she felt a desperate urge to run away, even though there was nowhere she could go. The heat from the fire was comforting after the attack, but still she felt like crying after the strain of it all; everything seemed to be going wrong; Tom betraying them was one blow too much.

'It's all a bloody awful mess!' she said, her voice breaking. 'No. I've got to help them!' She jumped up and ran to the window. Outside, the Baobhan Sith roamed, their wild eyes ranging over the vicinity. Ruth knew she wouldn't get five yards from the door. Dejectedly, she trudged back to the fireside.

'Cheer up, lovie. It's always darkest.' The woman hung a blackened kettle over the fire, then placed two mugs, a strainer, a tin of tea leaves and some milk and sugar on a tray with the pot. 'I'm Nina, by the way.'

'Ruth.' She rested her head on the back of the chair and closed her eyes. 'What's all this about a *spell of protection*?' she added wearily. 'It seems like everybody can do something they shouldn't these days.'

Nina laughed. 'You're right there. I spent ten years studying the Craft, working on spells and rituals. Sometimes they worked, or seemed to work, in a halfhearted way, but very rarely. It always seemed more like wishful thinking on my part. And then just after Christmas it was like I'd had an electric charge! I could do things I never dreamed of! It was . . .' – she laughed again – '. . . magic!'

'Everything's changed,' Ruth said morosely.

'Oh, indeed. At first I thought it was just me, like after all this time I'd suddenly chanced on the knack. But then I saw what was happening all around and I knew it wasn't me at all. It was the world.' She noticed the gloom in Ruth's face. 'It's not all bad – just different. The magic is back. How it probably was centuries ago. That's a cause for celebration.'

'You really can do stuff?'

'Not great, world-changing things. Just the skills we were always reputed to have. Controlling the weather, communing with the birds and animals, making potions that work. It's the link, you see. With nature. It's solid now.' She pointed at Ruth's hand. 'But you should know. You're one of us. Greater than me, certainly. That's the mark of the Horned Hunter, consort of the Mother Goddess.'

Ruth shook her head. 'I don't know what you're talking about. I've never been into all this.'

There was an unmistakably dismissive note in Ruth's voice, but Nina wasn't offended. 'Your brain may not know, but it's there inside you. Or you wouldn't have received the mark. You're a wisewoman, no mistake. You just need to learn and apply yourself.'

'With all due respect, I can't see myself doing, you know, whatever it is you do. I'm a lawyer.'

Nina laughed. 'What, you think only embittered old crones like me get to learn the Craft?'

'I didn't mean—'

Nina silenced her with a goodnatured wave of her hand. 'The only qualification is being a woman. And probably having a natural aptitude for the necessary skills. Take me – I wasn't always how you see me. I just happened to like the traditional lifestyle.' She motioned around the room. 'I used to be in medical supplies. Worked all the hours given to build up the business. Then my Ralph was taken suddenly. Brain tumour. He didn't suffer long.' She fell silent for a moment, the weight of memories adding age to her face. 'After that, work didn't seem important. There wasn't much of my life that did.' She smiled sadly. 'It's terrible, isn't it, that it takes a tragedy to point out that all the things we trick ourselves into relying on in our lives have no substance? We have to have something to believe in – it's the way we're made. But once work and the family disappear, you start to wonder what there *really* is to have faith in. I fell into the old religion. At first it just made me feel good. Then it started to feel right. Now I can't imagine being without it.'

Ruth watched her as she used a teacloth to lift the hissing kettle from the fire. She warmed the pot, then put in the tea leaves, adding a pinch of spice from a dish on the side. 'My own special recipe,' she said conspiratorially. 'Gives it a little kick. It's how they drink it in the Middle East.'

'What's it like to be able to make things happen?' Ruth asked as she took her mug. 'It's the kind of thing you always dream about as a child.'

'Well, it's not like any of that fairybook stuff,' Nina replied a little brusquely. 'You can't just wish and make things happen. It's all about controlling energy – the invisible energy of the world. I always saw it as a science that the physicists haven't got round to explaining yet.' She smiled at the curiosity in Ruth's face.

As the fire blazed and as they sipped their spiced tea, Nina explained about the Craft while Ruth attempted to batten down her anxiety and desperation; she wanted to be doing something, not listening to old stories. When Nina mentioned the triple deity of mother, maiden, crone, though, Ruth's heart quickened as she connected with her visions of the mysterious girl.

She related her experience to Nina who smiled and said, 'See. You were called long before you realised. And probably a long time before that.'

'There was an owl—'

Nina nodded towards the cat on the hearth. 'We all have our friends.'

Ruth stared into her tea, trying to divine her feelings about what she was hearing. The stubborn streak of scepticism her father had instilled in her as a girl was still there, but her instinct was beginning to shout louder.

'Look, this is all too much to get my head round right now. I can't stay here talking. There's got to be something—'

She made to rise, but Nina stopped her with a hand on her thigh. 'I might be able to help you.'

'How?'

She thought for a moment, then said, 'We can fly up, see what has happened to your friends, get the lie of the land. Then, once you have the knowledge, you'll be able to decide on your course of action.'

'Fly?' Ruth said incredulously. 'What? On broomsticks?'

'No, no!' Nina said sharply. 'Stop falling for the old propaganda, please! I'm showing you how it really is.' She paused, and added with a smile, 'But actually yes, on broomsticks, only not the way you think!'

Ruth sat back down. She covered her eyes for a moment, suddenly aware she might break down in tears if she allowed herself to think about her situation too closely. 'So you're probably the only person in the area who can help me and I ended up here by chance. I don't like coincidences.'

'There are no coincidences. Once you understand there's an invisible world, you can see that.' Nina took her hand and pulled her to her feet again. 'If you really want this, you will have to do exactly what I say.'

'I'll do anything to save my friends.'

Nina nodded understandingly. 'Come, then. Take off your clothes.'

When Ruth hesitated, Nina made hurrying gestures, then turned to the table and went along the rows of jars until she found the one she wanted. Ruth undressed a little unsurely, but Nina just pulled her dress over her head. She was naked beneath it. Her breasts had long lost their firmness and she had shaved off her pubic hair, but she walked around completely unselfconsciously. She opened a cupboard in one corner and pulled out a broom like the one Ruth had seen outside the front door.

As Ruth stepped out of her knickers, she was shocked to see what appeared to be a tiny little man slowly lowering himself upside down from the chimney to peer at her curiously. Ruth pointed and yelled out, 'What's that?' at which point a look of dismay crossed its face and it disappeared from where it had come.

Nina seemed as unconcerned as if it were the cat who had entered. 'One of the brownies,' she said distractedly. 'They seem to have settled in here. They help me out quite a lot with the cleaning at night.'

While Ruth stared at the chimney unsurely, Nina gently pushed her back into the chair, then sat down before her on the rush mat, the broom and jar beside her.

'As with all these things, you must place your trust in me and always do as I say,' Nina stressed.

Ruth nodded.

Nina opened the jar and dipped in two fingers. When she removed them they were covered in a greenish cream, which she proceeded to smear over the end of the broom handle. 'A little hemlock, some monkshood – sacred to Hecate – a little thornapple and a touch of belladonna.' Then she lay back, opened her legs wide and placed the handle against her vagina. 'It would be easier if you could help me,' she said, 'if you can overcome your embarrassment.'

'I'm not putting *that* inside me!' Ruth said in horror.

Nina sighed and sat up. 'The salve has an antiseptic quality, if that's what you're worried about.'

'That's not all I'm worried about! It's disgusting!'

'Let's not be prudish,' Nina cautioned like a school ma'am. 'This is the way it's been done traditionally. When those who weren't practising heard about us riding our brooms, they got the wrong end of the stick, as it were. The vaginal walls absorb the active drug much more effectively. I could insert it in your anus if that suits you better,' she added acidly.

'I don't need a drug trip! I need help!'

'That's what I'm doing!' Nina said with irritation. 'It's not just a drug trip. The mind and body are separate entities. The drug in the salve enables our brain to free our spirit-selves so we can fly over the countryside, see things, hear things, gain knowledge, then return with it to our bodies. All the shamans and the magicmen and women in the old cultures use it.' She laughed dismissively. 'The scientists said their experiences were just hallucinations because there was no way they could *really happen*. I wish I could take a few of them along with me!'

Ruth shook her head, still horrified. *I can't do it,* she thought.

Nina seemed to read her mind. 'Do you want to save your friends or not?' she snapped.

Ruth stared at the broom handle with distaste for a long moment. Then she asked, 'Are you sure this will do any good?'

'A few months back I would have said no. Now . . . of course!'

Ruth grimaced. 'Okay. I suppose. What do I have to do?'

'Hold the handle.' She opened herself up. 'Now insert it gently.' Ruth steeled herself, but Nina didn't seem concerned. She relaxed on to it, then closed her eyes. After a moment she motioned to Ruth to remove it. 'Now it's your turn.'

Nina reapplied the salve to the handle, then positioned herself between Ruth's legs. Ruth's muscles were so tense she couldn't get the stick to penetrate, but whatever powerful drug was on it seemed to begin to affect her from even a cursory application. She gradually relaxed, allowing Nina to insert the handle. At first she felt a not-unpleasant burning sensation, but then it changed, so that she felt like warm syrup was slowly rising up her body from her groin. There was a definite sexual element to it; her clitoris engorged and she had a sudden, nearly overwhelming desire to bring herself to orgasm. But when Nina removed the handle, the edge was taken off her desire and she was able to look up and around. The quality of light in the room had changed; it was more diffuse and golden, as if it were being refracted through crystal. The edges of the furniture sparkled and shimmered and the crackling of the fire shushed and boomed like the sound of the sea.

Then there was the odd sensation of her retreating into her body, as if she were looking out at the world from the end of a long tunnel.

'Hold on,' she heard Nina say distantly. 'It's beginning.'

And then she was rushing out of herself, as if she had been fired from a cannon. She rocketed up to the ceiling, where she briefly looked down at her naked body staring with glassy eyes up at her; Nina was slumped next to her, one hand draped across her thigh. And then she felt as if someone had yanked a rope attached to her neck and she was dragged wildly into the fire, which fizzed coldly around her, and then up into the yawning black hole of the chimney.

A second later she burst out into the night sky, swooping and swirling as if she were smoke caught in the wind. It took her a second to get her bearings and then she discovered that, with the right mental effort, she could begin to control her movements. Ruth twisted in practice and caught sight of Nina floating over the thatch waiting for her. She looked beautiful, years younger, with a firm, full body. She smiled and beckoned.

'Where are we going?' Ruth said, but no sound came out of her mouth. Nina seemed to understand nonetheless. She pointed along the valley, away from where the Baobhan Sith had attacked. Ruth looked at her curiously, but she acted as if she wanted to show her something important.

And then she was away, rushing on the night winds. Ruth launched herself behind her, lost in the wild, exciting sensation of flying. She could feel the breeze on her skin, feel her hair flow behind her, but although she was still naked, she didn't feel the cold. It was a wonderfully exhilarating feeling as she swooped and soared, remembering a score of similar dreams, wishing she could never come down; it was so powerful it almost made her want to cry.

The trees passed beneath her in a black carpet, the sweet scent of the pine floating up to fill her nostrils. With care, she could dive down and skim their gossamer-frail uppermost branches, leaving them waving in her passage. From her vantage point, she could see the landscape in its true form: alive; the sweep and swirl of the hillsides, the subtle gradation of colours in the grasses, the snake-twist of rivers, the mirror-glimmer of lakes, all linked into one awesome organism, each part affecting its neighbour. From there, it all made sense.

A long, low hoot made Ruth look round to see her owl-companion flying in circles nearby. She waved to him, but he continued spiralling on the thermals without any sign that he had any connection with her.

Nina's mad aerial dash slowed near Loadpot Hill. Ruth could read caution in her body language as she took advantage of the occasional treetop for cover. Eventually she came to a halt and pointed to something ahead, her face drained of the good nature Ruth had seen before; now she was fearful.

Ruth followed her guide and could instantly see why. Rising up out of the isolated green hillside was something that reminded Ruth of pictures of enormous African termites' nests. It was the first part of a tower that was still under construction, covering an area the size of ten football pitches. Although it was fundamentally black, she could make out crushed cars and trucks, washing machines, fridges, plastic, girders and broken masonry embedded in its walls as if the makers had plundered the local communities for the material. Above it, the stars were obscured by smoke from a hundred fires burning a dull red, visible through ragged openings all over the tower. And as she watched, Ruth could see movement around the base of the construction, up its walls, on its growing summit; the termites were swarming.

In her uneasy curiosity, Ruth flew a little closer, only to be disturbed by roars, shrieks and insane monkey chattering. She felt as if a terrible power had been turned on her, like a black ray projected from the tower; she suddenly became so cold her entire body shook, and an unbearable sense of despair began to gnaw at the pit of her stomach.

It was numbing, but then she felt Nina frantically tugging at her arm. Her terrified face left no doubt that they had been seen. The fear was infectious, and as Nina pirouetted in the air and sped away faster than Ruth could imagine, she felt instinctively that whatever was being built there would be too terrible to even imagine.

Nina's panic lessened only once they had put several miles between them and the black tower. They followed the landmarks back to the cottage, and then Nina took the route Ruth had first expected, up the hillside to the road above. As they neared where the van had been parked, they dipped down beneath the treetops and made their way cautiously among the upper branches until they found an eyrie where they could peer down on the stretch of road like two ghostly birds.

The van was still there, glowing white in the moonlight, but weaving in and out of the trees in a wide circle around it were the Baobhan Sith, no longer shrieking or as wild and predatory as they had been earlier. Tom was sitting a distance away, his head between his knees. Church, Shavi and Veitch were on the ground, slumped against the van. They weren't moving and blood stained their clothes and skin; Veitch, in particular, had a ragged wound in his neck where Ruth had seen the spectral creature prepare to bite. Her first thought was that they were dead. Her stomach knotted and she felt like bursting into tears; another part of her told her that wasn't the case. With an effort, she calmed herself and watched.

Not long after, the silence was broken by the drone of a car engine as twin beams splayed light over the trees. A nearly new BMW, but with deep, fresh scratches on its wing, screeched to a halt near the van. Callow's grinning skullface was behind the wheel; in the back seat an ominous form was sprawled with a car blanket pulled roughly over it. Ruth could tell from its shape that a man lay beneath it; she guessed it was the car's former owner.

Callow stepped out with a flamboyant flourish, leaving the headlights switched on so they spotlit Church and the others. 'Mister Churchill! So pleased to see you again!' he said, grinning superciliously.

At his voice, Church stirred and looked around. When he saw Callow, rage crossed his face and he forced himself to his feet. A second later the Baobhan Sith were around him, shrieking and gnashing their teeth, and they didn't retreat until he had fallen again.

'Nice little doggies!' Callow said after them.

'You bastard!' Church yelled.

Callow waved his finger and tut-tutted, but he didn't seem interested in engaging in conversation. Instead, he walked to the rear of the car and opened the boot. The Baobhan Sith looked towards it and hissed as one, moving away from it before resuming their weird circling dance.

As if in answer to the boot opening, Ruth realised she could just make out an odd, distant noise, like metal being dragged across gravel, and the kind of hideous animal sounds she had heard at the black tower. Callow turned in its direction and peered into the gloom. Slowly, his grin melted away.

Ruth could feel whatever was coming on some instinctual level. Her skin, however insubstantial, was crawling, and she felt like snakes were slithering through her intestines. The Baobhan Sith seemed to sense it too; for the first time she saw them motionless, facing in the same direction as Callow. The air seemed to swell with feverish anticipation.

Tensely, she watched the shadows that clustered around the bend in the road and within minutes the night seemed to come alive with a greater darkness. An insectile swarming broke free from the gloom and headed towards the van. Although her eyes told her there were individual shapes, she felt there was just one hideous, dark creature, radiating an evil power that made her feel sick. And in the mass, the shapes themselves were difficult to distinguish, although she knew they were Fomorii. They continued until they were teeming around the van, the car, Callow, Church and the others, so that the road now resembled a churning black river.

My God! Ruth thought. *I never realised there were so many of them!*

One of the forms separated from the others and walked into the glaring circle of light thrown by Callow's car headlamps. It was a man with golden skin, long hair and a frail, spindly body; there was an air of sickness and decay about him, and however stylishly he had dressed, his long, white silk tunic appeared dirty. Ruth recognised him as Fomorii, although he was closer to how she had imagined the Tuatha Dé Danann. She guessed, from Church's description of his captor in the mine, that it was Calatin.

Veitch and Shavi were also conscious now, and Church was muttering something to them, although Ruth couldn't hear what it was.

'Little rabbits!' Calatin said in a voice like breaking glass. 'You ran the course I mapped for you so perfectly. How you slipped from your cell remains a mystery, but it was only a matter of time before the doors were left ajar. And from that point you did everything I hoped.

Reclaimed the Quadrillax – a remarkable achievement. Even as Brothers and Sisters of Dragons, I thought it beyond you. And turned back the Wild Hunt too, though there was more of chance in that. But then this frail creature . . .' – he motioned to Callow – '. . . served his purpose well. And now, for the first time, the Quadrillax are in Fomorii hands. We thought you too weak for the responsibilities laid upon you and we have been proven correct.'

Ruth winced at that and she could see it hit Church too.

'Tom—' Church began weakly.

Calatin's smile was so cold it froze the words in Church's throat. He turned and summoned something from the seething mass of Fomorii; a second later something glinting silver, small and scurrying like a spider ran out, up his legs and into his hands, where it formed itself into a dagger. Ruth recognised it: she had seen something like it before, at Heston Services when the Fomor had first tried to kidnap her.

'The Caraprix,' Calatin said, examining it. In his hand the dagger shifted its shape, became something indistinct but disgusting, then returned to its dagger form. Calatin showed it to Church as if it was explanation in itself, but when he saw Church's blank look, he continued, 'Their fluidity and versatility makes them useful to us.'

'They are alive?' Shavi asked.

Calatin looked at him as if he didn't understand. 'They do our bidding in many different ways. Sometimes,' he mused to himself, 'they are almost companions.'

'What's this got to do with Tom?' Church looked at him, still slumped on the roadside nearby.

Calatin eyed him slyly. 'Oh, the pain of betrayal.'

Church winced, looked away.

'When the wanderer fell into my hands, I saw the opportunity to have a subtle hand on your wheel.' He held up the Caraprix, which wriggled in the light from the headlamps. 'One deep incision is all it takes. Painful, but he remained conscious until the last. The Caraprix slipped in through the wound, attached itself in here.' He tapped his temple. 'It sits there still, tormenting him, doing our will.'

At first Church couldn't grasp what Calatin was saying, but then he remembered the wounds on Tom's forehead when they first met him in the mine and he felt horror grow within him. 'He's got one of those in his head?' he said with disgust.

'Oh, it's not all bad.' Callow sidled up until he was near Calatin.

'You've got one too?'

'Mine was by choice, dear boy. I have a remarkable aptitude for seizing opportunities.'

'You call that an opportunity?' Church was disgusted. 'It's probably eating away at your brain.'

'It can be removed at any time, or I can simply live with it. If you think that's bad, you should try to get rid of lice.'

'Why did you do it?' Church asked.

'I told you, an opportunity. By declaring my allegiance early in the game, it gave me access to all the miracles and wonders that will rain down on us.'

'You sold us all out.' The intensity of hatred in Veitch's voice made Church feel almost uncomfortable.

'Now, now,' Callow cautioned. 'You must accept some responsibility. If young Mr Churchill had not been so indiscreet about what was happening to the world that night in the tavern, I would not have been prepared when I did encounter my good allies here.' He sighed theatrically. 'Oh, how strange fate is. I knew sooner or later you would involve yourself in something that would favour me, so after our evening's wassailing I resolved to follow you. I must admit, after the devastation you wreaked at the depot in Salisbury I thought things might be a little too hot even for me. But then I met my good friends!' Callow seemed about to clap Calatin on the shoulders, then thought twice about it. 'They made it easier for me to shadow you. But at a distance it was so hard to discern exactly what you had achieved; it required a little, shall we say, investigative skill on my behalf. Did you ever wonder who had gained access to your car? Your tents?'

'I'm going to kill you.' Veitch's voice was low and understated, but the words contained power.

'I don't think so,' Callow replied sneeringly, but Church could see a flicker of unease in his eyes.

Calatin lurched forward unsteadily, knocking Callow out of the way; he looked even sicker than he had in the mine. 'You still do not seem to understand exactly what has occurred. Your loss of the Quadrillax has destroyed more than merely your own feeble attempt to stop our advance. Through all time and all space, their significance has radiated: objects of such power that we never dared achieve our ultimate dream – the eradication of all light from the universe. Our victories were always tempered. We settled for control, in the certain knowledge that a step too far would rebound on us tenfold. Now, anything is possible.'

As he neared, Church's gorge rose at the hideous stink coming off him. Calatin bent down and lowered the living dagger until its tip was only an inch from Church's right eye. Church tried not to blink, nor even to think about what Calatin was going to do next; the Fomor had revealed his sadism quite plainly in the mine's torture chamber. He thought for a moment, then lowered it to Church's cheek, where he pressed its razored edge into the soft flesh and made a slight downward cut. Church winced as the blood flowed.

'With the Quadrillax in our hands, everything has been lost. And you are responsible.' He showed a row of blackened teeth and released a blast of foul breath into Church's face.

'You're going to destroy them?' Church asked once he had recovered.

Calatin peered at him as if he were insane, then rose and limped away. 'They will be taken from here to our nearest retreat, where they will be encased in molten iron, then buried in the furthest reaches of the earth, never to be recovered—'

'What about Balor?' Shavi interrupted.

Calatin whirled, his eyes blazing, but slowly the insipid smile returned to his face. 'The Highfather will soon be back,' he said in a manner that made Church shiver, 'and the glory will be mine.'

Then he turned and yelled out something in the guttural Fomorii language before limping away. A second later Church, Shavi and Veitch were wrenched up in the black mass of bodies and swept away.

Ruth watched the scene in horror from the treetop branch, then turned to Nina, who motioned that they should return. The brief journey back to the cottage contained none of the awe and wonder Ruth had felt during her first flight, just a sense of impending doom and a feeling of utter futility. Nina led the way back down the chimney and as they emerged into the main room, Ruth had the same sensation of being fired from a cannon as she rushed back into her prone body. A second later, she stirred, feeling leaden and stupid, her thoughts no longer quicksilver; her mouth felt as if she had awoken after a night on the tiles; all her muscles were aching. The loss seemed so great her eyes filled with tears.

'I could have stayed like that for ever,' she said.

'And there lies the danger.' Nina levered herself to her feet, stumbling awkwardly. 'Spend too long in that form and your essence begins to break down, dissipate like smoke, until you return to the universe.'

Ruth rose and dressed dismally, trying to tell herself it was simply the effects of coming down off the drug. But as the initial edge of her experience began to fade, the threat facing them returned in force.

'I can't let them take Church and the others to that awful black tower. I can't let them take the talismans. But what can I do?'

Nina nodded sympathetically. 'There were so many of them—'

'They've got a way to go to reach the tower. We could head them off!'

'You're starting to sound like John Wayne.' Nina's faint humour underlined the futility of what Ruth was saying, but she wasn't going to be deterred.

'Will you come with me?'

Nina shook her head. 'I love my life too much. If there was a chance—'

'Then I'll have to try it alone. I can't give up.' She fastened her jacket and strode defiantly to the door.

'Wait.' Nina hurried to the dresser and returned with what appeared to be a piece of root with grass and vines wrapped around it. 'I laboured hard over that. Slip it in your pocket. It won't make you invisible to the things out there, but it should mask your presence enough to make it easier for you to travel through the countryside at night.'

Ruth thanked her, but her mind was already on what lay ahead. As she opened the door and slipped out, Nina called behind her, 'Be true to your destiny. Blessed be.' And then the door slammed shut and Ruth was alone in the night.

It was a real effort to scramble up the steep hillside amongst the trees, but soon she was at the road. It was deserted, with no sign that the Fomorii had ever been there. Callow's car had gone too, and Ruth presumed they were using it to transport the talismans because the Fomorii were unable to touch them.

She ran to the van, then swore angrily; she didn't have the keys. 'Laura!' she called out. 'It's Ruth.' At first there was no answer and Ruth feared the worst, then she heard what seemed to be a stream of abuse in a frail voice. 'Never mind that. Open the doors.'

It took an agonisingly long time, but finally the doors swung open. Laura hung on the handle, obviously in great pain, barely able to hold herself up. 'It's freezing,' she said hoarsely. 'I thought I was going to die in here.'

'There's still a chance for that.' Ruth clambered past her. 'God, I hope your shady past taught you how to hotwire an ignition system.'

'Yes, but if you think I'm going to crawl under a steering wheel—'

'Just tell me!' Ruth heaved herself over the back of the seats. 'I never thought I'd say this, but I'm glad it's you here and not someone who's law-abiding.' She paused. 'How come they left you here?'

'I guess they thought I was dead after what that bastard did. No one figured to look in the van.'

Laura guided Ruth through the process, laughing at Ruth's scream as she almost burned her fingers in the flash as the spark jumped between the two wires. Once the engine roared into life, Ruth slammed the van into first and pulled on to the road. While she powered through the gears, Laura told how she had listened to the attack of the Baobhan Sith and everything that happened after, while keeping as quiet as she could to avoid detection.

'How do you feel?' Ruth asked.

'Like I've been slashed into bloody chunks with a razor. How do you think I feel?'

'Just asking.'

There was a long pause and then Laura said, 'I could do with some more painkillers.'

'Hurts?'

'Like hell. I think some of the wounds have opened up.' Ruth heard Laura shift around under the pile of sleeping bags that were supposed to be keeping her warm. 'Sorry I'm not going to be much use.'

'Even if you were fighting fit, there wouldn't be much you could do.'

'No big plan, then?'

Ruth didn't answer. She didn't even know what she was doing. The thought of that mass of Fomorii filled her with dread. The only way she could avoid paralysis was to keep moving on instinct, ignoring the ringing alarms in her head that were saying her futile act was going to be the death of her.

She took the treacherous bends at breakneck speed, peering over the wheel for some sign of the Fomorii. She knew they couldn't have travelled far in the time since she had left the cottage, so she killed the lights and cruised by the light of the moon, using the central white lines for guidance. She had the window wound down a little, listening for the cacophony of grunts and shrieks, but the night was eerily still, just the rustling of the trees and the singing of the tyres on the road.

Then, as she rounded the next bend, she saw the seething mass ahead of her, moving in complete silence – which was somehow even more disturbing than the hideous sound they normally made. She slammed on the brakes and slewed to a halt, switching off the engine as quickly as she could and praying the Fomorii were singleminded enough to ignore the sound of her approach. Away up front she could make out the headlamps of Callow's car, moving slowly.

She turned to Laura, whose shock of blonde hair glowed like the moon where it stuck out of the sleeping bags. 'Hold tight,' she said softly.

Although Church could feel rough hands on him, he seemed to be floating in and out of consciousness. It was all he could do to maintain any rational thought among the overwhelming sense of evil which seemed to wrap around him in thick, black swathes. But he could feel movement as he was dragged or carried, smell the sickening stink that clouded all around, hear the rasp of inhuman breath. He had no idea where they were being taken, but he knew their lives wouldn't last long after their arrival, and he feared, in a way he didn't think possible, what tortures Calatin would inflict before his death.

Then, through all the turmoil, he became aware of a distant sound, slowly rippling closer like the rumbling of an approaching tidal wave. As it neared, he tried to clutch at his ears to keep it out; his stomach bucked and flipped, his gorge rose, his mind threatened to switch off completely. And only then did he guess what it was: the sound of the Fomorii in fear.

Suddenly there was chaos. The night was torn apart by ferocious cries as the Fomorii broke up in disarray. Church was dropped roughly to the ground, where he bounced around like a pinball as the beasts surged in all directions, tearing and bruising his flesh. But with the claustrophobic atmosphere of evil disrupted by the confusion, he found it easier to think. Somehow he got to his feet and looked around frantically for Veitch and Shavi. Instead, he saw what appeared to be a whirlpool in the dark sea of Fomorii ahead of him as they circled crazily in one spot. At first he watched in confusion, until he realised there was something at the heart of the maelstrom. Slashing sounds began to cut through the frenzied gibberings, and then the black wave parted and he saw what lay at the heart of the churning area. There was a group of creatures about five feet high, their skin a sickening green, scaled in part, with long black hair and monstrous features. They were moving through the Fomorii with some kind of weapons that Church couldn't quite make out, but he saw the aftermath: disembowellings, severed limbs, hacked heads. A slurry of blood and bone was beginning to mire the green grass. There was something about the creatures' heads that didn't appear right, but it was only when they drew closer that he could see what it was; they wore head-dresses made out of bloody human body parts – torsos, scalps, faces – and the grue from them matted the creatures' hair and bodies.

Church was transfixed by the sheer savagery of their attack. The manner in which they cut a swathe through the Fomorii was almost hypnotic in its brutality.

The spell was broken when someone grabbed his arm. Church whirled, ready to lash out. He caught himself when he saw it was Tom, then roughly pushed him away in disgust.

'They don't control me all the time!' Tom protested.

'I can't believe you!' Church began searching for Veitch and Shavi.

'Then don't. But heed me – don't let the Redcaps see you! They're being controlled to attack the Fomorii, but their natural enemy is man!'

Just as Tom spoke, one of the creatures broke off his dismemberment of a Fomor and stared in Church's direction. A second later it had broken away from the pack and was running towards him, its face contorted with rage.

Church moved at once, sprinting painfully off to one side, but the Redcap followed him unerringly. There were still Fomorii everywhere, though most of them had turned on the attacking Redcaps and were attempting to repel the intruders. He tried to weave among the Fomorii, who were too distracted to pay him any attention, but still the Redcap dogged his heels. And now he could hear the noise it was making – a roar like a big cat that set the hairs on the back of his neck rising.

Then, through the turmoil, he spotted Shavi curiously up high, waving to him frantically. He turned and ran in his direction.

Emerging through a pack of Fomorii, Church saw Shavi standing on the top of Callow's car while the battle raged all about. Veitch was at the rear with the boot open, repeatedly smashing his fist into Callow's face, which had dissolved into a bloody pulp. But it was Veitch's expression that concerned him the most: he was lost to the violence and rage. Church barged past him, almost stumbling into the boot, and flicked open the crate. A shimmer of blue fire crackled through the talismans. As Church reached in to grab the sword, he was taken aback to feel it leap into his hand. He whirled round with the sword raised just as the Redcap thundered towards him, roaring like the wind, a strangely shaped, heavily chipped axe raised above its head.

As the axe came down, Church parried the blow, half-expecting his sword to shatter. But it held firm, although the force of the clash jarred every bone in his body. He stumbled backwards against the car, fighting to regain his equilibrium. Then, as the Redcap raised the axe for another blow, Church lashed out madly. The sword hacked into the creature's face like a knife slicing through butter. Greenish blood showered all over him, burning his skin where it landed, and the Redcap slumped to its knees, dead.

Church yanked the sword out with an effort, then turned and caught Veitch's arm mid-punch. 'Leave him. We've got to get out of here.'

Without waiting for an answer, he clambered atop the car alongside Shavi, to get a better view. 'Any way out?'

'I cannot see one,' Shavi replied.

Oddly, Church found himself unable to focus on the Fomorii fighting the battle. He could see movement, flying blood and limbs, could hear the terrible sounds they were making, but beyond that it was almost as if they had merged into one lake of darkness which was roiling in the grip of a furious storm.

But he could see what remained of the Redcaps hacking a path directly to the car. 'They want the talismans too,' he said with sudden certainty. And then it came to him. Scanning the vicinity, he soon spotted the unmistakable flurry of movement in a field picked out in silver by the moon's light. Mollecht and a small group of Fomorii waited patiently.

'Whoever wins the talismans, gains the power,' he muttered to himself. He turned to Shavi. 'Infighting. Suits me fine. Now how—'

He was cut off by a high-pitched, shrieking cry in the nerve-jarring Fomorii dialect. Calatin had spotted them and was trying to divert his troops from the Redcaps to a defence of the talismans. Church felt a gush of icy fear drench him as the entire ranks of Fomorii and Redcaps turned as one to face him.

Ruth watched the chaos break out from further up the road, but from that distance it was impossible to tell exactly what was happening. She watched anxiously, wishing she were confident enough to make a decision, batting away Laura's increasingly irritated calls for information. But then her attention was caught by the briefest shimmer of blue fire and she picked out Church and Shavi standing on the car roof.

'Hold tight,' she said as she spun the van around in the road.

'You can't leave them!' Laura yelled angrily.

'I'm not. I'm . . .' – she took a deep breath and slammed the van into reverse – '. . . ramraiding.' Then she popped the clutch and the van shot backwards with such force Laura screamed. 'I said hold tight!' Ruth shouted above the roar of the engine.

They thundered into the middle of the Fomorii as if they were crashing into a forest. Every time they hit one, something buckled; the nearside was so badly dented Ruth was sure it was going to cave in. The rear windows shattered, showering Laura with glass, then the doors burst open and the one that had been replaced at Glastonbury was torn off. Ruth kept her foot on the accelerator and her gaze on the wing mirror, although she was shaking from head to toe. Even if they made it to Church, she wondered if the van would be in any condition to get them out.

But then she saw the car's headlamps loom up and she popped the brakes, stopping an inch or so from its bumper. Before she had thrust the gear stick into first, Veitch had launched himself into the back, with the crate under one arm and the spear in the other hand. Church and Shavi dived in after.

The Fomorii were already regrouping. Ruth revved the engine and prepared to drive.

'Wait!' Church called out. She saw him scramble to the back of the van and drag in a bedraggled figure. It was Tom.

'Leave him!' Veitch yelled. 'He's a fucking traitor!'

Church bundled the man towards the front of the van, then called for Ruth to go. The van shot forward just as a Fomor punched a hole through the offside. Others were ready to clamber through the open doors. Ruth swung the van from side to side to throw off any that might be clinging on, then ploughed through whatever was in her path. The van was tossed and turned as if it were in an earthquake; she lost the wing mirror; one headlamp exploded; a terrible whine started to come from the engine.

But somehow she managed to keep going. And when they rumbled over the last body and hit the open road, she was so overcome with relief her eyes filled with tears. She wiped them away before any of the others could see, then moved through the gears rapidly. Soon the dark, turbulent countryside was whizzing by and they were heading back in the direction of the motorway.

CHAPTER TWENTY

Revelations

'I still say we should have dumped him.' Veitch was squatting danger-ously near the missing door, trying to tend to his neck wound with the van's depleted first aid kit.

'He had his flaws, but he was okay before those bastards stuck that parasite in his head.' Church watched Tom surreptitiously as he sat quietly with his back to the driver's seat, bound with the tow rope. He looked about a hundred years old; his skin was sallow, his grey hair matted, and there was a crack across one of the lenses of his wire-rimmed spectacles.

'I tried to fight it,' Tom said. 'Every time it attempted to make me do something against my will, I tried.'

Church recalled the blood that had been streaming from his nose, ears and eyes at the roadside before the Baobhan Sith attacked, and realised just how hard he had fought.

'It doesn't matter,' Veitch continued. 'He's still a liability. However much he *wants* to help us, that thing in his head means he could turn against us any time. If you don't want to just throw him out the back, we should at least leave him at the side of the road somewhere.'

'If you leave me, you'll never discover what you have to do with the talismans to summon the Tuatha Dé Danann,' Tom said pointedly.

Veitch bristled, and made to advance on him. 'You trying to blackmail us now?'

'Leave it, Ryan.' Church turned to Tom. 'Is this another of your great deceits, or can we get a kernel of truth out of you this time?'

'I know,' Tom stressed. 'You need me.'

'Perhaps that creature in his head could be removed,' Shavi suggested.

'What? We should kidnap a brain surgeon next?' Veitch said sarcastically.

'There might be a way,' Tom said.

Church eyed him suspiciously. 'Who could do a thing like that?'

'No one on this earth.' Tom gave a sickly cough. 'Just take me home.'

They debated the matter as they limped through the remaining hours of night towards the motorway. Veitch was adamant he didn't want to follow any advice from Tom in case they were led into another trap, but Church felt Tom was telling the truth. He finally extracted a promise from him that he would tell them everything if they helped him, and that was enough of a spur to convince the others; without his information they were lost anyway.

Home for Tom was near Melrose on the Scottish borders, not far in terms of distance, but it might as well have been a million miles. The engine's insistent whine told them the van wouldn't last much longer, and even if they managed to get it fixed, the damage to the body was so bad the police would pull them over the moment they got on to the motorway.

When dawn finally broke and the landscape was transformed into a place they all recognised, they stopped at a small farm not far from the M6. The farmer was pleasant enough to suggest the nightmares they had experienced at the heart of the Lake District hadn't yet touched his borders. Even at that time of day he was a canny negotiator though, and he offered to give up his own battered Transit – a second vehicle that was at least ten years old and looked like it barely moved – only for Laura's portable PC. But at least his Transit was whole, and although the exhaust rattled noisily, it allowed them to continue on their way.

The day was already turning fine, with just a few streaky clouds on the horizon to mar the blue sky, but the atmosphere in the van was depressive. Although they had regained the talismans, they had paid a huge price. Laura looked sicker than ever, and they were worried she had developed an infection in some of the wounds; Church was concerned that if they didn't get her to a doctor soon she could become fatally ill. Veitch, Shavi and Church himself were all weakened from their experience and bore numerous wounds inflicted by the Baobhan Sith, with Veitch's neck the worst. Church was convinced the Baobhan Sith had wanted to kill them, but whatever control Calatin exerted had somehow restrained them at the last. Only Ruth seemed to have the strength to continue, and Church could sense she had changed in some way he couldn't quite understand; she seemed far removed from the woman he had first encountered under Albert Bridge.

The journey up the M6 was uneventful, but their vigilance didn't waver; they knew either Calatin or Mollecht would be on their trail soon enough; however, their own little difficulties had been resolved, and with the Fomorii's shapeshifting abilities, everyone they encountered would have to be studied carefully.

Tom began to speak more freely as soon as he saw the others were behind him, even though Veitch appeared to be unable to forgive him. As they dissected their experiences in the Lake District, Tom chipped in with occasional pieces of information, about the Baobhan Sith, and about the Redcaps, whom he claimed used to stalk the Border counties in the days when man was first beginning to get a foothold on the island. The battles between the two were bloody, but the Redcaps were eventually driven back into the wildernesses, their numbers dwindling until they eventually retreated to Otherworld. He declined to answer any questions about how he came by the information.

They took the M6 past Carlisle and then crossed the border into Scotland and headed up to Galashiels. Heavy traffic on the motorway and the arterial road suggested an unshakable normality, which jarred with what they had witnessed in the Lakes. Tom told them to make the most of the façade; it would soon all change.

Melrose was a compact town below the Eildon Hills on the south bank of the Tweed, dominated by a twelfth century Cistercian abbey. They parked the van near the golf course and wearily stretched their legs; it seemed like weeks since they had slept. Tom claimed his original home had been in the nearby village of Earlston, but after his wanderings began he found a new and unspecified home in the hills.

Church surveyed the three volcanic peaks which seemed to rise to at least a thousand feet. 'You're expecting us to climb up there?' he said incredulously. 'Look at us – we're on our last legs. Laura can barely stand.'

'You could always carry me in your big, strong masculine arms, Church-dude,' Laura said ironically.

'Two of us could accompany Tom,' Shavi suggested, but Church instantly vetoed the idea.

'After what happened in the Lake District, nobody should be isolated. We ought to stay together, and carry the talismans with us at all times until we get a chance to use them.'

Laura levered herself into a sitting position. Her skin was so pale it was almost translucent and her hair was matted to her forehead. 'There's a real stink of testosterone round here. Listen, don't wrap me in cotton wool – I'm not some fragile girlie. You might have to take baby steps, but I'll keep up with you.' Church began to protest, but she pulled a tape measure from the tool box and threw it at his head. He ducked at the last moment, and when he saw her searching for more ammunition, he knew he would have to relent.

They took a path beside the golf course. Although the day was sunny, the air had a definite crispness. They passed slowly through gently inclining fields where cows grazed lazily before reaching the wooded lower slopes of the rounded hills. True to her word, Laura kept pace, but Church could see the effort and pain played out on her face; she never complained, nor asked for help. Yet the weakness that occasionally consumed her when they broke for rests gave him cause for concern; he could almost see her health deteriorating before his eyes.

As the afternoon drew on, grey clouds swept in from the north-east and the chill in the air took on a sharp edge. They became increasingly worried about being caught out in the hills in a storm, or not making it back before night fell.

'There's not a house in sight,' Ruth said with breathless irritation as the steepness of the climb increased sharply. 'If you're not having us on, where the hell do you expect to get any help?'

'Nearly there,' Tom said without meeting her eye. He scanned the landscape before pointing to a hawthorn sapling thirty feet away. 'The old tree died,' he said cryptically, 'but hawthorn always marks the spot.'

When they got within ten feet, Tom broke into a run and dropped to his knees before the hawthorn, where he delicately bent forward and kissed the ground.

'It's eaten his brain,' Veitch said.

'Wait, he's saying something under his breath,' Ruth said anxiously. 'He could be tricking us again.'

Before they could move, there was a deep judder that reverberated deep within the hill and then the ground next to the hawthorn began to tear apart. They fell to their knees from the tremors and when next they looked there was a ragged slit in the earth big enough for them to walk through.

'Just like the tor!' Shavi said with wonder. 'A passage to Otherworld!'

'I don't like this.' Ruth plucked up the spear and held it ready for defence. 'Who knows where that leads?'

'Wait. Look at Tom.' Church ran to his side; he had fallen over backwards and was trying to crawl away from the doorway. Strain was etched on his face as he fought the urging of his body and there was blood once more around his nose and ears. 'It's trying to stop him going in there!'

'Could be a double bluff,' Veitch pointed out.

'Remember what happened at the tor,' Ruth cautioned. 'Time moves differently over there. We might come back and find we've missed the deadline.'

Church ran back to the crate and took out the sword; it rang with inner vibrations as it touched his flesh. 'I don't reckon we've got any choice. Let's get him inside.'

Church grabbed one of Tom's arms while Veitch hooked the other and together they hauled him towards the rift. A wind howled out of it, carrying with it alien scents that made the hairs on their neck stand upright. For an instant they glanced at each other for support and then, without saying a word, they marched into the dark.

Church had expected a balmy summer landscape like the one they had encountered beneath the tor. Instead the passage brought them out on to a rocky mountainside shadowed by night, strewn with craggy boulders, thorny, windswept trees and bunches of gorse. A harsh wind howled around them and lightning flashed across the great arc of the sky, although there was no rain. They bunched together for security, searching for any sign of where they were supposed to be going.

'Blimey. This is a bit different,' Veitch said unsurely.

'Otherworld has as many different aspects as there are views.' Tom raised himself up to his full height and looked around, a faint smile on his lips. He seemed transformed, at ease. 'It's fluid. A world behind every doorway.'

'How are you?' Church asked.

'As well as can be expected. The Caraprix isn't comfortable in this particular part of Otherworld – that's why it attempted to prevent me entering. It will hibernate until we leave.'

'Where do we go?' Ruth asked. The mountainside disappeared down into darkness and it was impossible to make out anything of the landscape beyond.

Tom searched the night, then pointed just above the edge of a massive boulder which was keeping the worst of the wind off them. In the distance they could make out a flickering light.

'I hoped there would be someone here who escaped the Wish-Hex,' Tom said. 'If it were to happen anywhere, it would have been in this place. Come.' He set off down the mountainside, keeping a surefooted control as he slipped and slid on the pebbles and exposed rock.

Before they could follow, Laura suddenly keeled over; Church lunged for her before she hit the hard ground, swinging her round into his arms. Her breathing was shallow and he could see the whites of her rolled eyes beneath her half-closed lids.

Shavi took Laura's pulse at her neck. 'We need to get her to a doctor very quickly,' he said grimly.

Church looked round frantically, wishing someone else could take responsibility, hating his own ineptitude at leadership. 'We've got to get her back – find a doctor in Melrose!'

'It's a long way down that hill,' Veitch said doubtfully.

Tom stepped forward with an expression of surprising concern. 'Our only hope is to go on. Otherwise she'll die.'

'No!' Church tried to get a grip on her to carry her back to the doorway.

Tom placed a gentle hand on his forearm. 'Believe me, I *know* she'll die if you try to take her back.' There was an unnervingly confident insistence in his voice.

Church felt a sudden hopelessness sweep through him. 'If you're lying and she dies, I'll kill you myself,' he said quietly.

Veitch helped Church carry her, all of them hoping the light wasn't as far away as it looked, praying that Church had made the right decision; wondering whether Tom really was leading them into a trap. And all the while the strange electrical storm seemed to grow in intensity over their heads.

The light was coming from a torch in the front porch of an imposing building which resembled a mediaeval stone monastery, although one constructed into, and part of, the mountainside. Above the porch was a squat, three-storey tower topped by a weathervane in the shape of a dragon and a lightning rod. Behind it, the slate roof and the walls with the tall, arched, leaded windows went straight into the bedrock, almost as if the mountain had formed around it. Three steps led up to the porch, where they were confronted by a large oaken door, studded with black nails.

'Where is this place?' Church asked suspiciously.

Tom traced his fingers down one of the porch's stone columns. 'Using the name you would understand, it is the Library of Ogma, wisest of all the Old Ones.'

Church searched his memory for the dimly recollected reference. 'In the myths he was supposed to have invented Ogham.'

'That's the writing you thought was on the spear,' Ruth said.

'A runic writing system. There's not much of it about, but it's the earliest form discovered in Ireland.' Church looked at Tom, who was lost in thought. 'One of the Danann?'

'His store of knowledge is vast. Chamber upon chamber, filling the entire mountain. If he were at the heart of it when the Wish-Hex struck, it should have afforded him some protection.' Tom climbed the steps cautiously and hammered on the door.

'So he's good with words. How's he going to help us?' Veitch asked.

'Have respect,' Tom cautioned; his tone suggested it was an imperative. 'He bonded with Etain, daughter of the great healer Dian

Cécht. In his constant search for great wisdom, he has archived all the knowledge they possess.'

'That's not all.' Church suddenly began to make connections. 'He was also supposed to ferry the souls of the dead to Otherworld for a period of rest before they were reborn in our world.' There was almost a prayer woven into his words. 'Are there souls here?'

'So they say.'

'Don't you *know*?' Church wanted to shake Tom, to stop his obfuscation; there was only one lost soul that mattered to him.

'I'm just human like you, Jack,' Tom replied with some exasperation. 'I'm not privy to the great scheme. I observe, I consider, but I'm not always correct in my assumptions. And the gods don't give up their wisdom freely, and certainly not any wisdom that matters.'

'Typical bosses,' Veitch muttered. 'Keep the menials in the dark.'

'Actually,' Tom said tartly, 'they presume, rightly, that we wouldn't be able to handle the truth.'

'How very patrician of them,' Ruth replied, just as acidly.

They were interrupted by the sound of heavy footsteps approaching the door. When it finally swung open silently, they all caught their breath at the figure revealed: for a second, different faces seemed to flicker across him, some almost too terrible to behold, before one settled that was kind and thoughtful. It reminded Church of Oscar Wilde; Ruth of Einstein; Veitch of the only teacher who ever tried to help him. He was wearing long flowing robes that were grey and almost metallic in the way they caught the light.

His gaze took them all in in a second, but a broad smile formed when it fell upon Tom. 'Thomas!' he said warmly, in a voice that didn't seem to come from his mouth.

Tom bowed his head deferentially. 'Wise One. We come to ask your help in these difficult times.'

'Difficult times indeed. You have heard my brothers and sisters are scattered to the wind?' Tom nodded gravely. 'The Night Walkers, you know.' A rumble of what seemed like hate formed deep in his throat. 'Only a few of us evaded the Wish-Hex. I have since heard murmurings of an attempt to locate my brethren and return them to me.'

Tom motioned to the others. 'And here are the searchers, Wise One. They need to be restored if they are to complete their task.'

'And you, Thomas. I see you too need my ministrations.'

Tom nodded, looked away uncomfortably.

Ogma turned to Laura, who was cold and still in Church's arms, her breathing barely noticeable. Gently, he ran his fingers over her face. His expression grew a little darker. 'Her light is weak. I do not know if there is aught I can do for her.'

'Please try,' Church pleaded.

'It was always said Dian Cécht could bring even the dead to life,' Tom interceded.

'But I am not Dian Cécht. And healing is not simply knowledge.' There was a brief pause while Ogma seemed to consider the matter. Then: 'Come, bring her. I will see what I can do.'

The place smelled of candle wax and limes. They trailed behind Ogma as he led them through an endless maze of chambers filled from floor to ceiling with leatherbound books, some half as big as Church and as thick as his thigh, manuscripts and papyri tied with red ribbon as if they were legal briefs. But when Shavi held back to sneak a peek at one of the books, they appeared to contain only a brilliant white light.

Finally, after what seemed to them like an hour, they reached a series of chambers that were filled with rough wooden furniture, which Church guessed were Ogma's personal rooms. He laid Laura on a low bed and stroked the hair from her forehead.

As his fingers touched her flesh, her eyes flickered open and focused on him briefly. 'I don't want to die,' she said weakly. There was a sheen of panic in her eyes.

'Do something,' Church implored Ogma.

If the god heeded, it didn't register on his face. He opened a large cabinet in one corner which was filled with jars and phials of powders, liquids and dried herbs. He selected a few, then began to mix them with a mortar and pestle on a heavy oak table. After a few moments of introspection, he seemed satisfied with a thick, reddish-brown salve, which he smeared on Laura's lips. It remained there for only a second before it was rapidly absorbed.

'Will that work?' Church asked anxiously.

Ogma fixed his curious eyes on Church, like an adult looking at a child. 'We wait. If she has it within her, her light will shine again.'

Church had to turn away from her then, barely able to cope with the painful emotions flooding him after so many months of numbness.

Ogma seemed to comprehend what was going through his head, and after cursorily examining Veitch and Shavi from a distance, he said, 'Your own light wavers. You must all rest. Use my chambers as your own. There is food and drink—' Tom started, but said nothing. Ogma noted his concern and added, 'It is given freely, without obligation.'

This seemed to satisfy Tom. After Ogma left them to explore his rooms, Veitch asked, 'What was that all about?'

'Never take food or drink in Otherworld, from anyone, unless you have their promise that it is given freely and without obligation. Otherwise, when the first drop or crumb touches your lips, you fall under the control of whomever has given it.'

Veitch looked to the other three, puzzled. 'Is that right? Or is he bullshitting again?'

'In the old tales,' Shavi began, 'anyone who crossed over to Faeryland had to avoid eating the faery food or they'd fall under the spell of the Faerie Queen.'

'So is that where we are? Faeryland?' Veitch said incredulously.

'Get a grip, Ryan,' Church replied wearily. 'Let's find somewhere to crash.'

In a nearby chamber, they found a room filled with sumptuous cushions, the harsh stone walls disguised by intricate tapestries. On a low table in the centre was an array of bowls filled with apples and oranges, some berries, tomatoes, and a selection of dried, spiced meats. A jug of wine and four goblets stood nearby.

Relishing the chance to rest their exhausted bodies, they fell on to the cushions, which were so soft and warm it was like they were floating on air. It was a difficult choice between sleeping or assuaging their pangs of hunger, but in the end the subtle aromas of the food won out. Yet as they ate and drank, they discovered their tiredness sloughing off them, and by the time they had finished their meal they felt as fully rested as if they had slept for hours. It provoked an animated conversation for a while, but Church had other things on his mind.

'We got you here,' he said to Tom. 'Now you owe us some answers.'

'What do you want to know?'

'For a start, how you know everything you do. Why you called this place home. Why Ogma seems to know you so well.'

'And no lies,' Veitch said.

Tom turned to him, eyes ablaze. 'I have never lied. I may not have given all the facts, but no untruths have ever passed my lips. I cannot lie.'

'What do you mean?' Church asked.

'What I say, as always. It is physically impossible for me to lie. One of the *gifts* bestowed upon me for my time in Otherworld.' There was a note of bitterness in his voice.

Church's eyes narrowed. 'Who are you?'

'I told you my name. Thomas Learmont. But you may also know me as Thomas the Rhymer.'

Veitch looked from the confusion on Church's face to the others. 'You bastards better keep me in the loop.'

'Thomas the Rhymer,' Church began cautiously, 'was a real person who managed to cross over into mythology. He was a Scottish Nationalist during the war with England. In a way, he's like Scotland's answer to King Arthur – a mythical hero who was supposed to sleep under a hill—'

'Under this hill,' Tom interrupted.

'—until there was a time of great need, when he would return. That's what the old prophecies said. But he lived in the thirteenth century.'

Veitch looked at Tom. 'Blimey, you've aged well.'

'I lived at Earlston, a short ride from Melrose,' Tom said. 'We were an old family, quite wealthy, with land hereabouts, although my estate was eventually gifted to the Church by my son.' The faint sadness in his face at the memory was amplified by the shadows cast by the flickering torches. 'Unlike my father, who worked hard, I was always too much of a dreamer. I was an elegant singer and I spent many an hour lazing in the countryside composing new works, usually just ditties about the people I knew and the women I loved. There was one girl in particular. To seek true inspiration for a song about her I rode up into the Hills of Eildon, where I settled myself beneath a hawthorn tree with a view of what seemed like, at that time, the entire world. I chose to ignore the old wives' tales linked to the hawthorn, that it signified death, that its blossom represented rebirth.' He sighed. 'That it was the chosen tree of the Faerie Queen. But I had no idea that an entire world existed under the hill, like all the fools used to say about the faery mounds. But I was the true fool, wasn't I? They were simply misremembering old wisdom. I was ignoring it.'

He took off his cracked glasses to clean them. Church searched his face for any sign that this was more dissembling, but he could only see honesty there.

'So the Faerie Queen got you?' Veitch asked; he was still having trouble grasping the truth of everything they had experienced. In numerous conversations he had exasperated Shavi with his apparent inability to see beneath the surface of the myths and legends.

'The Faerie Queen. The Great Goddess. Just names we give to attempt to understand something unknowable. She was terrible to behold. Terrible. When I looked at her I swore I was looking into the face of God. I loved her and hated her, couldn't begin to understand her. I let her take me apart and put me back together, let her put me through the most unimaginable torments, to sample the wonder that came off her. It was a time of the most incredible experiences, of pain and pleasure, of being given a vista deep into the mystery of existence.' He blinked away tears and, for a second, Church thought he saw in his eyes something that looked disturbingly like madness. 'I was like a dog looking up at his mistress,' he added wistfully. 'And I was a hostage who came to depend upon his captor.'

'It sounds awful.' Ruth placed a sympathetic hand on the back of his. 'Is that how they see us – as playthings?'

Tom nodded. 'In the main. Some are close to us and have grown closer through contact down the ages. Others could strip the meat from our bones and leave the remains in a pile without giving it a second thought. They see themselves as fluid, as a true part of the universe. We are just some kind of bacteria, with no significant abilities, no wisdom.'

'Then how did you get out?' Ruth said.

He smiled coldly. 'She took a liking to her pet. At times I felt like I was in Otherworld for just a night, at other times all that I experienced made it feel like centuries. In truth, seven years had passed when I was allowed to return. I wandered down from the hill, crazed and gibbering, and was eventually returned to my home to recuperate. It was only later I discovered how much she had changed me.'

'What did she do?' Ruth's voice was hushed; the others watched Tom intently.

'During one of my torments I was given the power of prophecy and The Tongue That Cannot Lie.' His laugh made them all uncomfortable. 'In a world built on lies, that was bad enough. But being able to see into the future . . .' He shook his head, looked away.

'You know everything that's going to happen?' Church asked.

'Not at all. I see glimpses, images frozen as if they were seen from the window of a speeding car. That's how *they* see it. They know time isn't fixed.'

'It must have been impossible for you to adjust,' Ruth said.

He smiled sadly at her insight. 'After all I'd been through, how could I begin to associate with my old friends and neighbours, my family? I tried. I married, and my wife bore me my son, Thomas. But I no longer felt a part of humanity. No one could begin to understand the thoughts in my head. I looked around me and saw simple people living simple lives, people ignorant of the universe. Savages. I'd moved beyond them, but I could never be a part of Otherworld. I'd lost everything. And I knew, in one terrible moment, that I was always meant to be alone.'

There was power in the emotion of Tom's words. Church had never truly liked the man, certainly had never trusted him, but now he was overcome with respect; how many people could have survived all he had experienced?

'True Thomas, they called me!' Tom laughed; the others could barely look at him. 'Still, I did my best. I became involved in politics, as an agent for the Scots against the English, but politics isn't a place for a man who cannot lie. I wasn't successful, to say the least, and as my failures mounted I discovered the Earl Of March was plotting to have me murdered.'

Tom rummaged in his haversack for the tin containing his hash and made a joint with such laborious attention to detail that Church could tell it was merely to distract him from the full force of his memories. The others waited patiently until he had sucked in the fragrant smoke, then he continued.

'I fled into the Highlands briefly, eventually ending up at Callanish, and it was there I met one of the guardians of the old places and the old wisdom that stretched back to the days of the Celts.'

'The people of the Bone Inspector?' Church asked.

Tom nodded. 'It seemed we had much in common. *He* knew the true meaning of the hawthorn. After much pleading, and due in the main to my particular circumstances, he agreed to initiate me in the ancient natural knowledge that his people had practised in the sacred groves until the Romans had driven them out to become wanderers, hidden from the eyes of those who needed them.'

He sighed and took another long, deep drag. 'But it still didn't give me that sense of belonging which I so desperately needed. I was adrift in this world and eventually, as I knew in my heart I would, I wandered back to Otherworld. By then, of course, my patron had lost interest in me, but I was accorded some respect for my shaping at her hands, and for my singing voice and poetry, by many of the others in this place.'

'But you still couldn't feel a part of it,' Ruth said.

He nodded. 'For nearly four hundred years in the world's time I attempted to find a place for myself, although it only seemed a handful of years here. But eventually I grew homesick and I realised that all my suffering had brought me one thing – my freedom. I could come and go as I pleased. Every now and then I would spend some time in our world, and when I got bored I would wander back.'

'The best of all possible worlds,' Church said.

'No. The worst.'

'Is that how you got stuck in all that sixties stuff?' Veitch nodded disrespectfully at Tom's hair and clothes.

'That period marked my longest time away from Otherworld. It was closest in thought and deed to how I felt inside me and I thoroughly enjoyed every moment of it.'

Ruth put an arm around his shoulders. 'Tom, you really are an old hippie. Peace, love and self-indulgence!'

'You could have told us all this before,' Church said.

'I had to be sure I could trust you implicitly before I told you anything of significance. If I learned anything from my time as a spy, it was that knowledge is power, and I didn't want to have my true nature exposed and used against me too early in the game.'

'And you're sure now?' Veitch said tartly. 'That's a relief.'

'What about the Fomorii and Balor?' Church asked. 'Did they let you in on what was happening?'

Tom shook his head; a spasm of pain crossed his face. 'It still will not let me talk about that.' He rubbed at his nose furiously. 'After Ogma has done what he can, perhaps.'

With the final barrier of deceit removed, they felt they had been brought closer together. Perhaps it was the special qualities of the food and drink, or the sense of security offered by Ogma's library, but despite the pressures and secrets amongst them, they felt ready to face up to what lay ahead; their failures didn't seem so bad, their successes great in the face of monstrous odds. Church even ventured to say they had a chance.

While Tom smoked another joint and Veitch finished off the wine, Shavi decided to investigate the bookshelves again, although he seemed disturbed at what he had discovered before. Church slipped out quietly, and though he didn't say where he was going, they all knew he was checking on Laura. Ruth was sure in her heart she had more in common with him than Laura; that, if they allowed themselves, they could have the kind of relationship about which they both had dreamed.

These thoughts were preying on her as she wandered disconsolately through the chambers until, by chance, she entered a room where Ogma sat at a table, hunched over an enormous book. She was so deep inside herself she was halfway across the room before she saw him and by then it was too late to retreat. He raised his head and levelled his undecipherable gaze at her.

'You have the mark of one of the Golden Ones upon you,' he said, although she was sure he hadn't glimpsed the design scorched into her palm.

She described her experiences with Cernunnos and he nodded thoughtfully as he listened. 'The Wish-Hex caused great hardship for us all.'

'Do you hate them?' she asked. 'The Fomorii, I mean.'

He raised his eyebrows curiously, as if he couldn't grasp her question. 'The Fomorii are an infection to be eradicated.' He seemed to think it was answer enough.

'If you don't mind me saying,' Ruth continued, 'you seem very different to Cernunnos or whatever his true name is. More approachable.' *But not much,* she thought.

He thought about this for a moment, then said, 'We are not of a kind. Some of us are very close to you, barely a shimmer of difference. Others are so far removed that they are like distant suns burning in the vast reaches of space. We have our own mythologies, our own codes, our own hierarchies. There are those we look up to and those we look down upon.'

'You have a structured society like ours? But you're supposed to be gods, at least that's what the ancient people of my world thought.'

He smiled. 'Even the gods have gods. There is always something higher.'

'Are you gods?'

He raised his open hands, but gave nothing away.

Church watched Laura for a while, but could tell nothing from her face. The only relief he felt was that at last he had some time alone to deal with the mess he felt inside. It was as if the moment he had reached out to touch Laura's back at Manorbier, his emotions had split open like a ripe peach. He didn't know how to deal with any of them; every single thought and sensation was almost unbearable. He fumbled anxiously with Marianne's locket, but it seemed to have lost its magic; nothing could calm him.

Worse, he still couldn't shake off the sensation of cold which seemed to be eating into his marrow. There was a thin coating of frost on the Black Rose which he constantly dusted away, only to see it replaced every time he secretly inspected it. He wondered if the rose itself were actually the cause of the iciness, but he didn't seem able to let himself consider that too deeply. He certainly couldn't bring himself to throw the flower away,

About an hour later, Ogma was ready to deal with Tom. They gathered in a room that was bare, apart from a sturdy oaken table and a small desk on which lay a range of shining silver instruments of indefinable use; Church was instantly reminded of Calatin's torture rack. While Tom climbed on to the table, apparently unafraid of what lay ahead, the others gathered in one corner to watch the proceedings.

'How's Laura?' Ruth whispered to Church.

His weary head shake told her all she needed to know. She didn't probe further, but deep down she wondered how the five Brothers and Sisters of Dragons would fare if one of them were missing.

Ogma applied some thick, white salve to Tom's lips and while it didn't knock him out, it must have anaesthetised his nerve endings, for a second later the god began to slice into Tom's temple with a long, cruel knife; Tom didn't flinch at all, but Ruth closed her eyes.

The salve must have done something to the blood flow too, for despite the depth of the incision, there was little bleeding. Ogma followed in with a hand-powered drill which ground slowly into Tom's skull as the god rotated the handle; all the time Tom's eyes flickered as he stared implacably at the vaulted ceiling.

But then, as the judder of Ogma's hand showed the drill had broken through, a transformation came over Tom: his eyes appeared to fill with blood and his face contorted into an expression of such primal rage it made him unrecognisable. The salve had worked its power on his body too, for it was obvious he couldn't move his arms and legs, but he opened his mouth to yell and scream in the hideous Fomorii language. Ogma ignored him, but it was so disturbing to see that the others had to look away and even Veitch blanched.

Then, as they looked back, they saw the strangest thing. The drill hole must only have been a pencil-width, but somehow Ogma seemed to work the tips of two fingers in there, then three, then four, and then his entire hand was sliding into the side of Tom's forehead. Tom shrieked and raged impotently, but Ogma simply laid his other hand on his head to hold it still. Finally his hand was immersed right up to his forearm before he began to withdraw it.

Church winced; Ruth gagged and covered her mouth with her hand; Veitch and Shavi were transfixed.

And then, with a twist of his wrist, Ogma's hand came free. Clutched in his now-stained fingers was a wriggling thing which looked like a human organ, slick with blood and pulsating. But worst of all was that the shriek that had been coming from Tom's mouth was now emanating from the Caraprix. The cry soared higher and higher and they had to cover their ears to protect themselves. When it reached its climax, the thing began to mutate. At first it started taking on the hard form of a weapon, then something furry with needle teeth, but before it could fix its shape, Ogma dropped it on to the table and brought his enormous fist down on it hard. It burst like a balloon filled with blood.

In the silence that followed the insane shrieking, the room seemed to hang still; then Ruth turned away, coughing, and the others muttered various epithets of disgust.

Ogma turned to them. 'It is done,' he said redundantly. 'True Thomas will recover apace. The Caraprix is a parasite, but it causes no permanent damage to its victim.'

'They're hideous!' Ruth said, still refusing to look at the splattered mess on the table.

Ogma seemed uncomfortable at this. 'The Danann have their own Caraprix,' Tom interjected. He levered himself up from the table with remarkable sprightliness after what he had just been through; the hole in his head had already healed.

Ogma removed a clasp from his robes, which transformed itself into a shape like an egg with tendrils, glowing bright white. 'Tools, weapons, faithful companions,' he said.

Church eyed it suspiciously for a second, then helped Tom to his feet, although he didn't appear to need it. 'We have much to do,' Tom said with a vigour Church recognised from the first time they had met. 'A brief rest, a talk about what lies ahead, and then we must be away, for Beltane is now too close for any more delays.'

After the operation, Ogma had lost himself among the chambers, leaving them free to talk and plan. They gathered in a dark, echoing room which resembled a baronial hall. At one end a log fire blazed in a fireplace so big Church could easily have walked into it, and collected before it were several sturdy wooden chairs with studded leather seats and backs. For some reason, no torches burnt in that room so they pulled the chairs up closer to the fire.

Tom had centre stage, his newly repaired glasses glinting in the firelight, his eyes merely pits of shadow. 'I'll answer all your questions as best I can,' he said, 'but I caution you that I don't know all.' He took a sip of wine from a goblet rescued from the dining room.

'Tell us what you know about the Bastards,' Veitch said; it was how he had taken to describing the Fomorii.

Tom nodded. 'Some said their forefather was Ham, who was cursed by Noah, and that curse transformed every descendant into a misshapen monster. Others claimed they were born in the all-encompassing darkness before the universe began.' The fire cracked, spurting a shower of sparks up the chimney, and they all jumped. The shadows at their backs seemed uncomfortable and claustrophobic. 'They were led by Balor, the one-eyed god of death,' Tom continued, and for a second his voice wavered. Church looked round suddenly; he had the unnerving feeling someone was standing just behind his chair.

'Balor.' Shavi shifted uncomfortably. 'That is the name I heard in my trance.'

'The embodiment of evil,' Tom continued. 'Born of filth and corruption. So terrible that whoever he turned his one eye upon was destroyed.'

The room grew still; even the crackling of the fire seemed to retreat.

'In the first times, Balor led the Night Walkers across the land and all fell before them. After that we have only the myths to enable us to understand what happened. Before the Fomorii invasion, the Tuatha Dé Danann were led by Nuada, known as Nudd, known as Nuada Airgetlámh – Nuada of the Silver Arm – for the replacement created by Dian Cécht he wore for the hand he lost in the first battle of Magh Tuireadh. But because of his disability, the Danann deemed him not fit to lead them against the Fomorii and he was replaced by Breas, who was renowned for his great beauty.

'Except Breas was half-Fomorian and he allowed the Night Walkers to terrorise the land and enslave the Danann. Dian Cécht grew Nuada a new hand and he regained his position, but by then it was too late – he couldn't break the grip of the Fomorii.

'All seemed lost until Lugh presented himself to Nuada at Tara. Lugh, the god of the Sun, known as Lleu, or Lug, or Lugos, was a young, handsome warrior, but he, too, was part-Fomorii. Indeed, his grandfather was Balor. Lugh rallied the Danann and they rose against the Fomorii. All hung in the balance until the two sides faced each other at the second battle of Magh Tuireadh. It seemed that once again the battle would go the way of the Fomorii. But then Lugh, with the spear you recovered in Wales, fought his way through the lines and plunged it into Balor's eye. The Dark God was slain instantly and the Fomorii fell apart.' He sipped at the wine thoughtfully. 'Yes, Balor is a terrible threat. But the Danann who helped defeat him still exist, locked in the place where the Wish-Hex banished them.'

'Then there is hope,' Church said.

'Is that how their original war really happened?' Ruth asked.

Tom shrugged. 'The Danann will no longer discuss that time. It was a period of great upheaval for them. At least now we know what the Fomorii are trying to do.' Veitch looked at him blankly. 'The truth was there in Shavi's vision, and Calatin confirmed it. They are attempting to bring back Balor.'

'How can they do that if he was destroyed?' Ruth asked apprehensively.

'The yellow drums you saw at the depot in Salisbury and which we found in vast quantities in the mine in Cornwall are the key.'

Ruth cast her mind back. 'That black gunge inside them—'

'A foul concoction distilled at one of the Fomorii warrens like the tower you saw being constructed in the Lake District. It will be the medium for the Dark God's rebirth.'

'Then that's why they haven't moved on the cities yet. They're waiting for Balor to lead them,' Veitch said.

The logs cracked and sputtered, but their thoughts were so leaden they barely registered it.

'Only the Tuatha Dé Danann could stand up to something like Balor,' Church said eventually.

'But take heed too. The Danann are not overtly predatory, nor do they act with malice unless provoked. But they have their own agenda and if we get in their way we will be destroyed without a second thought,' Tom warned.

'I thought they were angels,' Ruth said sadly.

'At times they *look* like angels. Perhaps they were responsible for our myths of angels. But they are so complex in thought and deed, so unknowable in every aspect, good is too simplistic a concept.'

They were suddenly disturbed by a movement in the dark behind them. Veitch jumped to his feet, bristling alert, but the others watched cautiously as two figures emerged from the shadows.

'You never get treatment like this on the NHS.' Laura was walking with only the faintest sign of weakness, smiling apprehensively; everything about her body language suggested defensiveness, and the reason was plain to see. The patch of bandages had been removed from her face, revealing the mess Callow had made. Although the wounds appeared to have miraculously healed, the pink scars were still evident against her pale skin.

Ogma laid a heavy hand on her shoulder. 'She is strong of spirit. My attempts at healing merely gave her respite to fight back herself.'

She raised a hand to her face. 'Just let me know when you're opening the cosmetic surgery ward.'

She seemed afraid to come into the circle of light, so the others went to her. Shavi hugged her warmly and Veitch attempted to do the same, but she kept his show of emotion at arm's length. Tom's nod of support was restrained, but left her in no doubt of his feelings, while Ruth circled her before she gave in to her feelings as much as she could and clapped her on the arm.

And then Laura turned to Church, searching his face for any response to her scarring. She seemed pleased by what she saw.

'We were worried you might not be along for the last leg of this great road trip,' Church said, smiling.

'Somebody's got to keep an eye on you. Make sure you don't slip back into your moody, maudlin ways.'

They held each other's eyes for a moment, then shifted uncomfortably and moved away without any physical contact.

Ogma led them to a series of interconnecting chambers where he offered them beds for the night. After their conversation with Tom, they were all convinced they wouldn't sleep a wink, but within ten minutes most of them were resting peacefully.

For Church the thoughts and emotions were crashing around his head too turbulently and he lay with his hands behind his head, staring at the ceiling, trying to put them in order. When he heard Laura's whisper at the open door soon after, everything else was swept away in an instant.

'I couldn't sleep.' She snorted contemptuously. 'I'm getting good with the clichés. It's like some cheap romance novel.' The analogy seemed to surprise her, and then made her feel uneasy, but she sat on the edge of his bed nonetheless. She thought for a moment, then put a hand on his chest. He slid his own on the top of hers and she instantly folded against him, nestling into the undulations of his body, resting her face against his neck. 'Don't worry,' she said. 'I'm not going to say anything pathetic.'

'Then that's up to me.' His words seemed to float in the dark. 'I'm glad you're here.'

They held each other for a moment longer and then they turned to each other and kissed; there were so many complex emotions tied up in that simple act – affection and passion, guilt and loss, loneliness and fear – that they were both afraid it would swallow them up. Then the desperation that knotted them up faded for the first time in years, leaving a sense of simple contentment they had both convinced themselves they would never feel again.

They awoke wrapped together several hours later, although in Ogma's library it was almost impossible to mark any passage of time. Laura hurried back to her room before the others discovered them, but the glance she gave him at the door was enough to show a bond had been forged.

They gathered for a breakfast of bread, fruit and milk in the dining chamber where they were all, once more, astonished by how rested they felt.

'You promised to tell us what we need to do next,' Church said to Tom as they finished up the last of the food.

Tom wiped the milk from his mouth and replied, 'The power of the talismans will act as a beacon for the Danann once they have been brought into contact with another sacred item which has been used as an article of communication with the gods for generations.'

'What, there's a big searchlight somewhere that shines the shape of a sword on the clouds?' Laura sniggered. 'Or is there a god-phone with a direct link—'

'In Dunvegan Castle on the Isle of Skye is the Fairy Flag, the Bratach Sith,' Tom said. 'It has the power we need.'

'If we drive hard we could reach it in a day,' Shavi said.

Veitch clapped his hands. 'Then we can wrap it up and be down the boozer for last orders!'

'You think the Fomorii aren't going to try to stop us?' Ruth asked caustically. 'It would be a big mistake to think it's all going to be plain sailing from here. They'll probably throw everything but the kitchen sink at us to stop us.'

'Ruth's right,' Church said. 'It's been tough so far, but this could be the worst part.'

They gathered up their things and Ogma led them through the maze of chambers to the entrance. They thanked him profusely for his hospitality and his aid for Tom and Laura, but it was so hard to read his emotions they felt uneasy and headed hastily back to the path up the mountainside.

Tom hung back on the steps of the porch to offer his private thanks to Ogma. Together they watched the others walking away, chatting and bickering.

Ruth's owl appeared suddenly from somewhere above their heads and swooped down until it was hovering a few feet away. Ogma spoke to it in a strange, keening voice.

'What is that?' Tom asked.

'A friend. An aide on your mission.'

The bird soared once over their heads, then shot up into the sky. Ogma watched it disappear into the clouds, then turned his attention back to the others as they made their way up the mountainside.

'You see clearly, True Thomas?' Ogma asked.

Tom nodded, his face suddenly dark and sad. 'We're going to hell and we won't all be coming back. How do I tell them that?'

'You offer the truth selectively, Thomas, as you always have.' For a second his eyes seemed to burn with fire, then he turned and went back to his books without another word.

Tom stood on the steps a moment longer, struggling to damp down the simmering emotions that threatened to consume him. Once he had regained his equilibrium, he hurried after the others, fervently wishing he had died the day before he had fallen asleep under that hawthorn tree.

CHAPTER TWENTY-ONE

Last Stand

The sun was only just rising as they passed through the rift back into the world and by the time they had trekked into Melrose, it was apparent it was going to be a fine spring day. The sky was blue and cloudless; in the sun it was beautifully warm, but with an exhilarating crispness from that faint underlying chill that was always present at that time of year that far north. But not even the fair weather could mitigate the desperate anticipation they all felt.

They picked up the van and drove to a 24-hour garage. 'Everything looks normal,' Church said. 'But here's the moment of truth.'

They all watched anxiously as Ruth darted inside to buy a paper. She picked one up, scanned the date, but her face gave nothing away. By the time she had clambered back into the van, the others couldn't contain themselves. 'Well?' Veitch almost shouted.

Ruth held out the paper. 'It's Mayday. Today's the day.'

There was a long moment of silence until Church said, 'Do we still have time to reach Dunvegan?'

'It is less than a day's drive,' Shavi replied. 'Unless we encounter any obstacles.'

His words hung in the air for a second or two, and then they launched themselves into frantic activity. Veitch ran back into the garage to load up with sandwiches and crisps while Church selected a cheap portable radio to replace the one they had lost with their old van.

Once they were on the road, he swept through the bands, but the radio could only tune into a disappointing handful of stations. There was one playing classical music, another with easy listening tracks and one which concentrated on old pop and rock back-to-back, punctuated by the occasional jingle, but with no DJ in evidence. The jaunty sound of The Turtles' 'So Happy Together' rang out.

'Spare us the sickening optimism,' Laura moaned. 'I could do with some jungle or techno or anything with a beat to clear my head out.'

'At least it's not Sinatra,' Ruth said.

'Bit of a coincidence that we emerged with just enough time to spare,' Church noted. He caught Tom's eye and mouthed, 'There are no coincidences,' just as Tom started to spout his mantra. The others laughed; Tom looked irritable.

'So what's this Beltane?' Veitch asked.

'The great festival of light in the Celtic world,' Tom replied moodily. 'It's the midpoint of the Celtic year. In the old days, the people used to offer tributes to Belenus, the god of sun, light and warmth, to mark the onset of summer, the return of the sun's heat and the fertility of the land.'

'But why's today so important as a deadline? It's just a day like any other one.'

Tom opened a bag of cheese and onion crisps and began to munch on them with irritating slowness. Out of the corner of his eye, Church could see Laura glancing around for something to throw at him. 'Imbolg, Beltane, Lughnasad and Samhain – the four great Celtic festivals – weren't just chosen at random,' he said with his mouth full. 'They were of vital importance to the gods, when all of reality was so aligned that power flowed back and forth between Otherworld and here. On those days it was like the whole of the universe was filled with a charge. Days when anything could happen.'

'So if we miss out today we've got to wait until the next festival?' Veitch asked.

Tom nodded. 'And by then it will be too late.'

Despite the momentous events that lay ahead, Church found himself feeling surprisingly bright. It wasn't hard to guess why: in just a few short hours he would finally get the answers he had prayed for during the bitter months when his life had seemed to be over, although the *why* had now been replaced by *who*. He could barely contain his anticipation, yet behind it he felt the cold, hard core which he knew was a desire for retribution just waiting to be unleashed. Closing his eyes, he drifted along with The Beach Boys singing 'Wouldn't it be Nice'. If only he could get warm.

They took the A72 out of Galashiels, then swung north to Edinburgh, crossing the Firth of Forth to pick up the M90. They selected the major routes, both for speed and to keep away from the more desolate areas, but as they hit Perth, where the map showed fewer and fewer signs of population, they knew they were drawing into dangerous territory.

After passing Dalwhinnie, they steeled themselves and set off across country. Up in the hills the air was crystal clear and filled with the scent of pines. They passed barely a car and any traffic they did see appeared to be local; farmers in beat-up old bangers splattered with primer, or old ladies taking the air, driving excruciatingly slow. An eerie stillness lay over the whole landscape.

As they progressed further into the Highlands, Church felt the biting coldness in his chest begin to grow more intense, as if someone were driving an icicle into his heart. A corresponding sweat sprang out on his forehead. Slipping his hand into his pocket and touching the Roisin Dubh, he felt as if he had plunged his hand into snow. When he drew it partly out, away from the eyes of the others, he saw its delicate petals were now obscured by hoar frost that sparkled when it caught the light; it was almost too cold to touch. And the iciness seemed to be spreading from the rose deep into his body; it felt like it was consuming him. He knew he should tell the others, but the cold seemed to have numbed his brain. He fumbled with Marianne's locket, vaguely hoping it would make him feel better. Then he slipped the flower back into his pocket and tried to ignore the alarm bell that was starting to toll sonorously, deep in his mind.

They crossed the country without incident, and after following the placid, picturesque waters of Loch Lochy for a short spell, they picked up the A87 which would take them directly to Kyle of Lochalsh, the crossing point for Skye.

But as they trundled along the edge of Loch Cluanie, Shavi noticed a column of black smoke rising from an area beyond a steep bank just off the road. Although wary of stopping, once the acrid stink permeated the van it brought with it such an overwhelming sense of unease that they felt an obligation to pull over to investigate. While Veitch scrambled up the bank, the others watched from the van. They knew their worst fears had been confirmed when they saw him grow rigid at the summit. For several moments he stared at what lay beyond and then, without turning, he waved a hand for them to follow. Outside, the smell of oily smoke was choking and the air was filled with the screeching of birds. Cautiously they climbed the bank.

Stretched out in a large field was a scene of utter carnage. Scattered as far as the eye could see were the dead bodies of hundreds of soldiers, some of them mutilated beyond recognition, the churned turf of the field dyed red with their blood. It was like some horrific mediaeval battlefield. The carrion birds were already feeding on the remains with greedy shrieks and frenzied pecking. The smoke was billowing up from the remains of a burnt-out truck or troop carrier.

'They didn't stand a chance.' Veitch's voice trembled with emotion.

As they returned to the van in silence, Veitch pulled out his gun, examined it for a second, then tossed it away.

It was several miles before they could bring themselves to discuss what they had seen.

'At least we can be sure the Government knows. There's some kind of resistance,' Ruth ventured.

'For what it's worth.' Church hugged himself for warmth. 'All those modern weapons, all those experts in the art of warfare, they didn't mean a thing. There wasn't one enemy body there.'

'So what chance do we have if a bunch of professional killers can't cut the mustard?' Laura was wearing her sunglasses once again, hiding her true emotions from them all.

'You want to know what's worse?' Veitch said quietly. 'That they're obviously somewhere between us and where we're supposed to be going, settled in to a nice defensive position.'

'We have to keep going,' Ruth said. 'What else can we do?'

They fell silent once more.

They saw the smoke from fifteen miles away. They had probably noticed it earlier and mistaken it for a storm cloud, so large was the black column; it rose up thickly and rolled out to obscure the sun. At ten miles Shavi had to use the windscreen wipers and spray continuously to clear away the charred flakes caught in the wind.

'Black snow,' Laura said absently. 'Trippy.'

The atmosphere became unbearable as they neared the coast; even in the confines of the van they were coughing and covering their mouths. Then, as they crested a ridge and looked out over the sea, they saw the source. Kyle of Lochalsh, the tiny historic town that guarded the crossing to Skye, was burning. From their vantage point, they could see almost every building was ablaze, painting the lapping waves burnt orange and smoky red. It was almost deafening: the roaring of the flames caught by the wind, the sound of dropped milk crates as superheated windows erupted out, the thunder of crashing walls, every now and then punctuated by an explosion as a car petrol tank went up. There was no sign of life.

They stumbled from the van like drunks, intoxicated by the sheer horror of their vision. At least they could breathe a little easier as the wind took the worst of the smoke inland, but every breath was still filled with the stink of charcoal, rubber and plastic.

'God,' Ruth said in a voice so small it was almost lost beneath the noise of the inferno. 'Is this how the world is going to look?'

Through their daze, harsh truths began to seep; eventually Laura gave voice to them. 'Nobody's forcing us to do this. We could turn back, make the most of whatever time we've got left . . .' Her voice trailed off hopefully.

'How could we live with ourselves?' Church glanced at her briefly before staring back into the flickering light. 'Nobody wants to be here, but some responsibilities are too big to ignore. This is what we were *meant* to do—'

'Perhaps it is the only reason we are alive,' Shavi noted.

'We have to see it through to the end.' Laura nodded reluctantly at the resolution in Church's voice; in her heart she had known there was no other option.

'Should we search for any survivors?' Shavi suggested.

Church shook his head. 'I don't think there's any point. It looks like they went through the place systematically.'

'Look.' Veitch pointed beyond the flames to the short stretch of water that separated Skye from the mainland. The bridge that had been built at a cost of millions of pounds was shattered. The first section ended suddenly, as if it had been lopped off by an axe, and chunks of concrete and steel protruded from the swirling water. Nearby they could see the old ferries that had prospered before the bridge were burning or half-submerged in the tiny harbour.

'What are we going to do now?' Veitch continued. 'Swim?'

'I do not think so.' Shavi stood beside him and directed his gaze away from the harbour to the deep water in the middle of the channel. At first it just seemed to be a mass of chopping waves and odd little eddies and whirlpools, but then Veitch noticed a strange sinuous motion that was at odds with the movement of the water; it was like a black pipe rolling gently as it moved between the mainland and the island.

He was about to ask what Shavi was suggesting when there was a sudden churning of the water and something large rose up in a gush of white foam and sleek black skin cast ruddy in the light of the fire. Its head reached as high as a double-decker bus for just an instant before it ducked back beneath the waves.

'What the hell was that?' Veitch looked dumbfounded.

'The sea serpents have always been close to the Fomorii. They don't need to be coerced like the Fabulous Beasts.' Tom shuffled up beside them to watch the swirling water. 'Even when the doorways were supposed to be closed, the serpents swam back and forth, prefering neither here nor there, but somewhere in between.'

'Are they dangerous?' Veitch's eyes narrowed thoughtfully as he considered ways to reach the island.

'They have the teeth of sharks and their coils can crush bones and boats.'

'A watchdog,' Ruth said.

'Then how the hell are we going to get over there?' Veitch's frustration boiled over into impotent rage.

While the others threw ideas around, Laura watched from a distance, and she was the only one who saw the faint shadow cross Shavi's face. Quietly she tugged at his sleeve and drew him away from the rest.

'Spit it out,' she whispered.

When he looked at her she realised the expression had been one of fear. 'I cannot control these changes that are coming over me—'

'You should try being a twelve-year-old girl.'

'—the things I can do . . .' He struggled to find the correct words.

'I know it's scary. But everything's spinning out of control.'

He sighed and lowered his dark brown eyes. 'At first it seemed so wonderful, all these amazing new possibilities opening up to me. The trances, the dreams. But when I had that vision at Manorbier, it took nothing at all to get it started and it was so powerful it was almost as if I was really there. I could *smell* the blood on the wind . . .' He raised the back of his hand to his mouth in distaste. 'Now I am afraid. I wonder where it will all end.'

Surreptitiously, Laura took his hand; his fingers were cool and supple against her hot palm.

That subtlest of connections brought a smile to his lips. 'One should never shy away from new experiences, I suppose.'

'So what can you do?'

'When the change first came over me it was like I could almost understand what the birds were saying in their song. Then, as time progressed, I discovered it was more than that . . . it was as if I were in their heads, listening to their thoughts. And not just birds, but all animals.' He paused for a long time as he weighed his words. 'It is possible I could get into *that* creature's head, enough to subtly direct it. Perhaps enough to keep it away from a boat.'

'But?'

'But I am afraid if I truly try to enter its mind, I may never be able to get out again.' He watched her face closely for her reaction. When none was noticeable, he said, 'I am waiting for you to tell me not to be so ridiculous and to do my duty.'

'You're talking like I'm the responsible one. It's your call – I won't think any differently of you one way or the other.'

He smiled broadly. 'You are very mature. Why do you act like you are not?'

'We all know what happens to cheese when it gets mature.'

Veitch suddenly spotted them huddled together. 'Oi! What are you two plotting?'

Shavi lost himself in thought for a moment, then confidently strode over.

They headed back a couple of miles until they found a road which skirted the town; the fires were burning too hard to drive through it. On the north side there were plenty of little coves and they eventually chanced on one where a boat was moored at a private jetty. If the owner had survived the Fomorii attack, he was nowhere to be seen. Reluctantly they abandoned the van and transferred the talismans and what provisions they thought absolutely essential to the boat.

'This may seem a stupid question,' Church said once they were all aboard, 'but has anyone here sailed before?'

Veitch made a face. 'Been on the Thames Ferry. Didn't like it very much. And that boat in Wales.'

'I owned a small boat for fishing on the loch in my heyday,' Tom said. 'And I have even fished at sea, so I have enough knowledge to get us out there. But the currents between the mainland and island are rumoured to be strong and if the serpent gets angry, his backwash will capsize us. I presume we can all swim?'

They all nodded, apart from Veitch, who began to look a little wary.

'That's not an option,' Church said. 'How are we going to do anything if the talismans are at the bottom of the deep blue? You've got to get us out there and keep us steady so Shavi can do his bit.'

'*Try* to,' Shavi stressed.

They cast off and Tom steered the boat away from the shore. Although the water had appeared calm from dry land, they were soon bouncing across the waves in a queasy chopping motion. The wind had changed direction and now the thick, acrid smoke was being blown out across the bay; it was as if a thick fog had rolled between them and Skye.

'If we get past the serpent, we can take the boat around the north of the island to Dunvegan. It is built on a sea loch, so we can go right up to its walls.'

Church stood in the prow, tasting the salt as the spray stung his face, trying to ignore the icy cold that now permeated his entire body. Shavi rested on the wooden rail next to him to stare into the blue-green depths.

'How are you holding up?' Church asked.

'I think we are all holding up remarkably well, seeing that we are a mass of neuroses and contradictions wrapped up in skin and bone – in short, very human – being expected to do the job of heroes.'

Church shrugged. 'What's a hero? Some big muscular guy with a sword? Or some normal person who takes a swing for the greater good, despite everything?'

Shavi looked at him curiously.

'I'm just saying we're trying to do the best we can under the circumstances. Maybe the historians will come in with their whitewash brushes in a few years' time to turn us into heroes.'

'You are only a hero if you win.' Shavi looked up, his smile taking the edge off the bitter words. 'There is no place in Valhalla for those who simply tried hard.'

The smoke rolled in around them, choking, stinging their eyes. They all sat down in the bottom of the boat where the air was freshest, listening to the eerie echoes as the smoke muffled the lapping of the water and the sound of the town burning. They could have been hundreds of miles away, lost in the centre of the Atlantic.

Then Shavi's clear, sharp voice made them all start. 'It is coming.'

At first they could hear nothing. A few seconds later, from out of the smoke, came the almost mechanical sound of something breaking the water at regular intervals, growing louder as it drew closer. Church watched anxiously as Shavi closed his eyes, his face growing taut with concentration. The splashing, stitching sound came on relentlessly. Shavi's brow furrowed, his lips pulled back from his teeth.

At the last moment Church realised it wasn't going to work and he called out to the others to hold on. The serpent surged just past the prow and the boat lifted up at forty-five degrees. Church ground his eyes shut and gritted his teeth: someone cried out; he was convinced they were going under, dragged to the bottom in the backwash; a horrible way to die. But the boat poised on the cusp of tragedy like some terrible fairground ride and then went prow down just as steeply into the trough left by the serpent's passing. Waves crashed over them. Church sucked in a mouthful of seawater, but somehow held on. The boat righted itself jarringly, as if it were skidding across sand dunes. Church looked round; amazingly, everyone was still clinging on.

'If it hits us astern it'll shatter the boat,' he yelled to Shavi.

Shavi screwed up his face in anger at his failure before flinging himself upright and gripping on to the rail. 'Here!' he shouted. 'To me!'

'Get down!' Church cried. 'If it comes by again you'll be over the side!'

Shavi ignored him. A second or two later a shiver ran down Church's spine as he heard the serpent stitching water towards them. It was like a goods train; his breath grew as hard as stone in his chest. He braced himself for the impact. And waited, and waited.

There was a sound like a boulder being pitched into the water and then the drizzle of falling droplets as a shadow fell across him. The serpent had risen up out of the waves, as high as a lamppost, its flattened head swaying from side to side like a cobra. It had skin that was as shiny black and slick as a seal and eyes that seemed to glow a dull yellow; odd whiskers tufted out around its mouth like a catfish. And it seemed to be staring at Shavi.

Church was about to call out to his friend when he noticed the rigid posture and ghosted expression on Shavi's face, as if he were in a coma with his eyes open. They stayed that way for a long moment, two drunks staring each other out in a bar, and then, slowly, the serpent melted into the waves and swam languorously away.

Church heard Laura whisper, 'Good doggy.'

A spontaneous cheer arose from the others, just as Shavi pitched backwards alongside Church. His face was still locked tight. Church felt a sudden surge of panic when he looked into those glassy eyes; there was not even the slightest sign of Shavi within them. He scrambled forward and began to shake his shoulders.

The others' jubilation died away when they saw the edge of panic in his actions. 'Shavi,' he said. 'Come back!'

'Leave him!' Tom barked. 'If you disturb him now he could be lost for ever!'

'But what if he can't get back?' Church said. He stared again into those glassy eyes and couldn't control his desperation; the price they were paying was increasing constantly and he despaired at where it would end.

'Leave him!' Tom shouted again.

Reluctantly, Church stood back in the prow – then suddenly all thought of Shavi was gone. A gust of wind cleared the billowing smoke like a theatre curtain being rolled back, presenting a view of Skye that chilled him to the bone. At first details along the coast were blurred and he blinked twice to clear his vision. Then he realised the loss of distinction to the sharp edges of the green and grey coastline was caused by constant movement. Along the seafront, Skye was swarming; there was a sickening infestation of darkness as far as the eye could see, like ants on a dead rat.

'My God! How many are there?' Ruth was beside him, one hand on his shoulder.

They were mesmerised by the sheer enormity of what they were seeing, the malevolence that seemed to wash out across the water towards them. In that one moment, they knew: the world was ending and there was nothing they could do about it.

Church turned to Veitch, Laura and Tom, who were bickering at the rear of the boat, oblivious to the brief vision of hell that had been presented. 'Come on,' he ordered. 'We need to get a move on if we want to be there before sundown.'

It was a long, arduous journey up the Sound of Raasay, where the currents were as powerful as they had feared. Tom fought to keep the boat under control and eventually they rounded the north of the island as the afternoon began to draw on. They were all desperately aware of the hours running away from them, but no one gave voice to fears that there was not enough time left. At least they had left the massed ranks of the Fomorii behind, which gave Church a little more hope. Shavi's sacrifice had at least bought them that.

As the wild hills rose up grey and purple, brooding and mist-shrouded, away to their left, Tom steered the boat around to the west and eventually into the loch that led to Dunvegan Castle. The more they progressed inland, the more the choppy seas subsided, until they were sailing on water as smooth as polished black glass. Everywhere was still; no birds sang, the wind had dropped and the only sound was the gentle lapping of the water against the boat. Eventually the castle loomed up, a squat, forbidding presence perched on a rocky outcropping overlooking the loch. There were no signs of life around it.

Church and Veitch scanned the steep banks where gnarled, rugged trees clustered together in the face of the biting Atlantic winds. 'Do you think they're lying in wait?' Veitch asked.

'Could be.' But Church's instinct told him otherwise. 'We might be lucky. I don't think they expected us to get this far.'

'After all the hassle we've been through, wouldn't it be a laugh if we just waltzed into the castle, got the flag and did our business?' He snapped his fingers. 'Over. Just like that.'

'You love tempting fate, don't you, Ryan?'

They pulled the boat up on to the rocks at the foot of the castle where there was an easy path among the boulders round to the front. Veitch and Church shouldered the talismans between them, every muscle taut, eyes never still. They hated having to leave Shavi behind, but he was too much of a burden and time was short; the sun was already slipping down the sky and Church was afraid the castle would be sealed and they would have to find some way to break in.

But they had gone barely twenty paces from the boat when they heard Shavi cry out. They ran back to find him near-delirious, foam flecking his mouth, his eyes roving, unseeing. 'The Fairy Bridge!' he called out to someone they couldn't see. 'They come across the Fairy Bridge!'

'What's he talking about?' Veitch said dismissively. He had half-turned away when Tom caught his arm.

'The Fairy Bridge lies not far from here. It's over a stream, near to one of the liminal zones. Some of the Fomorii may pass through Otherworld to appear there quicker than if they'd travelled over the land.'

Veitch looked puzzled. 'Yeah, but doesn't everything move slower over there?'

'Time is fluid. Slower, faster, there are no rules. If there is a chance, the Fomorii will take it.'

Church chewed on a nail for a moment. 'Ryan and I can go down there and do what we can to delay them while the rest of you get into the castle.' He hoped it didn't sound as futile as it did in his head. Veitch nodded his agreement; in one glance they both recognised that it was probably a suicide mission.

Leaving Shavi raving in the boat, they all hurried up the path to the front of the castle. It was open, but there was no one in the ticket booth, nor could they hear any sound coming from anywhere within.

While Veitch searched for some weapons, Church opened the crate to examine the sword one final time; it seemed comfortingly familiar, radiating strength and security, and he wished he could take it with him, but it was needed for the summoning ritual. As he reached in to caress the worn handle, a blue spark jumped out from it with such force it threw him across the floor. His fingers ached painfully and there was a dim burning sensation; it felt so powerful because his entire body was numb with cold.

'What was that?' Ruth said. 'It was like it didn't want you to touch it.'

Church shook his head, puzzled, but he had a nagging feeling he knew why. The Roisin Dubh continued to pulse coldly against his heart.

Veitch returned soon after with two swords which he had stolen from a display at the end of the entrance hall. Church examined them apprehensively. They would be as much use against the Fomorii as a pair of dinner knives, but there was no point stating the obvious.

They took directions for the bridge from Tom and had just set off when Ruth called Church back. She ran forward and gave him a hug of surprising warmth. 'Don't be stupid,' she said. 'I don't want to lose my best friend.'

'Don't I get a hug and a kiss?' Veitch called to Laura, who seemed to be avoiding Church's gaze.

She blew him one theatrically. 'Throw yourself at them. It might buy us a minute.'

He mumbled something, then they turned and hurried across the moat to the winding road that led away from the castle.

'Where's this flag, then?' Laura asked as they began to trawl through the castle's many rooms. Their footsteps echoed dismally in the empty chambers.

'It has always been kept in the drawing room,' Tom replied. 'Wherever that might be.'

'What I don't understand is why beings as terrifying as the Danann provided the basis for faery tales,' Ruth said. 'You know, cuddly, mischievous little men and women with wings sitting on toadstools.'

'In the old days faeries *were* frightening. Their reputation has been watered down over the years.' Tom paused at a junction in a corridor, irritated by the maze of rooms. 'People would not venture near sidh – the fairy mounds – at night and would not take their name in vain for fear of their reputation. Their memories of when the Danann walked the earth were too strong.' He chose the lefthand path at random and strode away without checking that they were behind him. 'When the Age of Reason came around, the fear generated by the gods was too much to bear in the brave new world, and so the people set about diminishing them – not only in stature – to make them less of a threat to their way of life.'

Ruth wondered if the others recognised that they were making small talk to avoid thinking about what might be happening to Church. 'And the Fairy Bridge has that name because the locals dimly recollected there was some doorway to Otherworld nearby?' she continued.

'Not so dimly recollected. The Danann had connections with the Celts long after they left other parts of the country alone. In Scotland, Wales, Cornwall and Ireland they are always felt strongly nearby. They may be unknowable in their actions, but they seem to feel loyalty for the people who first accepted them.' He cursed as they came to another dead end, then swung on his heel and carried on marching forcibly. 'The Fairy Bridge is so called because of an old tale about a MacLeod clan chieftain who married a woman of the Danann—'

'What? Inter-species romance?' Ruth exclaimed.

Tom sighed. 'You know very well some of the Danann are not so far removed from us. And those nearest seem to feel a kinship which isn't evident in the higher gods. May I continue?' She nodded. 'After twenty years of marriage, the Danann wife felt driven to return to Otherworld – she couldn't bear to be separated from her people any longer. The

husband was heartbroken, but as a gift to show her love for their long –
in human terms – romance, she gave him the Bratach Sith, the Fairy
Flag, so he could call on her people for help if the MacLeods ever faced
defeat in battle. And the Fairy Bridge was the place of the giving and the
place of the parting.'

'What a sad story.'

'Over here.' Laura was standing near an open doorway, motioning to
them.

Once they entered, Ruth could tell it was the drawing room, but
there was no sign of a flag. 'Where is it?'

Tom pointed to a picture on the wall. 'That's all that's left of it.'
Behind the glass was the remnant of what once had been a proud flag of
brown silk, intricately darned in red.

'It looks like it will fall apart if we touch it,' Ruth said, not knowing
what she had expected.

'It isn't how it appears.' Tom dropped the crate on the floor and
Laura carefully removed the talismans while he took the flag down.
With trembling hands, he cracked the back from the frame, then laid
the glass on one side. Once the flag was freed, he took a step back and
bowed before it. Then, with an obsessive attention to angles and
distances, he laid out the artefacts around the flag so they made the
four points of a star.

From his breathing and his body language, Ruth could tell he was
gripped with a curious anxiety, but it didn't seem the time to ask what
was on his mind.

'Now,' he said tremulously, 'it is time for the ritual of summoning.'

Tom stood before the artefacts, head bowed, and muttered something under his breath. There was an instant change in the quality of
the atmosphere in the room; Ruth and Laura backed anxiously to the
wall.

Above the talismans, light appeared to be folding out of nowhere,
like white cloth being forced through a hole. There was a sucking
sound, a smell like cardamom, and then the air tore apart and they
saw something terrible rushing towards them.

Ruth felt her head start to spin. 'Oh Lord,' she whispered.

The road from the castle was bleak, the trees disappearing the further
they got from the loch to leave a heartless landscape of rock and sheep-
clipped grass. They were thankful for the faint, late-afternoon sun
which at least provided a vague patina of colour to the desolation.

Church and Veitch rarely spoke; the oppressive weight of what lay
ahead made any conversation seem too trivial. And for Church, the

cold had become almost more than he could bear. There was a part of him demanding that he throw away the flower, tell Veitch that he was far from his peak, but a stronger and more worrying part suppressed it easily. Worse, the cold now seemed to be affecting his vision; he could see what appeared to be little dustings of frost appearing round the edges of his sight, sparkling in the sunlight.

But the rose was a gift from Marianne, the suppressing part of him said. *How could it be anything but good?*

They heard the babbling of water before they saw the bridge, but once they crested a slight incline it was before them: just a single arch in a mediaeval construction of stone. Yet the moment Church took in its style and setting in the rocks and grassy banks, he felt like his heart was being crushed. It was exactly the image he had seen in the Watchtower when he had received the premonition of his death.

His sudden terror must have played out on his face, for Veitch turned to him with concern. 'What's wrong?'

'Nothing.' But he was transfixed by the sight and he couldn't have moved if he had wanted to.

The spell was broken when Veitch clapped a supportive hand on his shoulder. 'Yeah, I'm scared too. But we've just got to do our best. No point worrying about what's going to happen.'

Church sucked in a juddering breath to calm himself. 'You're right.' Before he drove all fatalistic thoughts from his head, he had one fleeting wish that he had properly said goodbye to Laura, and then it was replaced with the unsettling certainty that soon he would be with Marianne again.

They took up position on their side of the bridge, ready for their last stand. The sword felt awkward in Church's hand; more than useless after wielding the Otherworld weapon. He wondered how long they would last. A minute? Two?

For a long time there was nothing but the tinkling of the brook and the smell of damp grass, constants that made the subtle changes which came next seem like the blaring of an alarm. First there was a stink like a hot generator and burnt diesel, then a sound that reminded Church of a long-closed door being wrenched open. Then, some time between his eye blinking shut and opening again, the entire world slipped into horror.

They seemed to rise from the grass and heather like twisted black-thorn in time-lapse photography, filling the banks and road ahead of them, bristling with hatred, eyes burning in faces too terrible to consider, dark skin that seemed to suck up the sunlight and corrupt it.

Eerily silent, motionless, a tidal wave poised at the moment before it suddenly crashed forward.

Veitch stifled some faint noise in his throat. Church was so frozen he had barely been able to feel anything, but even the iciness could not contain the hot blast of fear that roared through him.

'Is it like staring into the face of death?' The voice floated out from the serried ranks. Church recognised it instantly. A second later Calatin limped from the mass, a fey, malignant smile on his lips. He held a rusty sword with darkly stained teeth along one edge like a saw.

Church gripped his own sword tightly, though he could barely feel it in his grasp. Veitch was saying something to him, but the words seemed to be breaking up like a badly tuned radio. He turned, saw Veitch's concerned face through a haze of hoar frost. He realised the iciness was starting to reach his brain.

Calatin was facing him across the bridge now, smiling maliciously as though he knew exactly what was going through Church's mind. Behind him there seemed to be just a black wall. Strangely, when he spoke, his voice rang as clear as a bell.

'Do you feel the thorns in your heart?' He laughed like glass breaking. 'We have her, you know, at least that pitiful part of her that remains after the body withers. I love to hear her screams.'

Marianne, Church thought. His heart began to pound, the heat dispelling some of the cold.

'If you had not allowed death and the past to taint you so, there might have been the slimmest of chances that you might have snatched victory here.'

'The sword—' Church croaked.

'The power is not in the sword, Dragon Brother, it is in you. You are the host of the Pendragon Spirit. And you have proven yourself a betrayer of that tradition. Too weak, too trapped by guilt and doubt. We could not have given you the Kiss of Frost if you had not allowed us into your life.'

Slowly, the truth stirred in the depths of his frozen mind. The Fomorii had left nothing to chance, attacking with the Fabulous Beast and the Hunt, using Callow as backup; but most subtly of all, invading him from within, driving into his heart and soul. The Roisin Dubh – the Kiss of Frost – had been seeded into his presence right at the very start, lying dormant until releasing its cold bloom when most needed, when everything else had failed. And the worst thing was that Calatin was right: he had done it to himself; he had known in his heart he should have thrown the rose away, but he had been trapped in his obsession with Marianne and her death and that had driven him to his fate. He *had* been weak, pathetic; and he had doomed them all.

'Oh, the pain,' Calatin mocked. 'It hurts so to see oneself truly in the mirror of life. Sick little boy. Weak little boy.'

Church raised his sword, but the heat he was generating from his emotions was not yet enough; the weapon shook violently in his hand. Veitch seemed to sense Church's inability to act and, with a growl of obscenities, he launched himself forward. It was an attack born more out of desperation than expertise, and as he swung his sword, Calatin parried easily and lashed out with a backhanded stroke. It caught Veitch a glancing blow across the forehead and he fell to the bridge, unconscious.

Calatin gave a sickly, supercilious grin at Church. 'We come with the night,' he hissed, 'and all fall before us. Our ways are the truth of existence. Everything you see is decaying, winding its way down into the dark. Why fight the natural order? Welcome it into your lives. Drink up the shadows, still the ticking of the clock, open your heart to the void.'

Church shook his head weakly.

'Now,' Calatin said sarcastically, 'let us see how well you fight.'

Ironically, by focusing on Marianne and her torment, Church found he could move a little easier, although it was still not enough. Calatin came at him lazily, swinging his sword like a father fencing with a child. Church blocked and almost dropped his sword. Calatin nipped in and brought the serrated edge of his weapon across Church's arm; the blood burned on his frozen skin.

And then the strangest thing happened. Church felt as if a bright, white light had suddenly burst through his body; just a flash, and then gone in an instant. And somehow he knew it had emanated from Marianne's locket, which he kept hidden in the same pocket as the Black Rose.

Whatever had caused it, it was enough to give him a burst of energy. With a skill that seemed to come from somewhere else, he brought his sword up sharply. The tip caught Calatin's cheek, raising a line of insipid blood. The Fomor whipped his head back in shock, and when he next levelled his gaze at Church, another eyelid appeared to have opened vertically in the eyeball itself, revealing a piercing yellow slit-iris. There was no mistaking the fury in his face. In a frenzy of chopping and hacking, he moved forward. One blow raked open Church's chest. The next bit deeply into his neck. Blood flowed freely.

Church staggered sideways from the bridge and fell on to the bank. The hoar frost in his vision was turning black. Calatin jumped beside him, still wielding the sword venomously. Another blow, more blood.

413

Church fell on to his back and slithered down to the water's edge. He knew he was dying. As Calatin bore down on him, his sword wet with Church's blood, Church thought of Marianne as a painful swell of bitter emotions washed the ice from him, then Laura, then Ruth and all the others.

Calatin brought the sword down hard and Church had the fleeting impression of floating above himself, looking down on the vision he had had in the Watchtower. And then all became black.

Everything was golden and shimmering, like a river of sunlight, and Ruth felt herself drifting along at the heart of it. It was a far cry from the rush of terror she had felt when the doorway first opened and she had been presented with a vista on the terrible place where the Danann had been banished. But then they had burst out of it, like dawn breaking on a desolate world, and she had been swept up with them, along with Tom and Laura; quite how, she did not know, although she had images of stallions and mares and chariots. Everything was a blur of wonder and awe. Some of them seemed almost human, with beautiful faces, golden skin and flowing hair, but others seemed to be changing their shape constantly as they moved; a few appeared just as light and one or two made her eyes hurt so much she couldn't bear to look at them or attempt to give them any real shape.

We did it! she thought with a sweeping feeling of such relief and ecstatic joy it brought tears to her eyes. *We brought the angels down to earth.*

Within seconds they were out of the castle and on the road to the Fairy Bridge. Ruth caught glimpses of sky bluer than she had ever imagined, and grass so green and succulent she wanted to roll in it laughing. And there was music, although she had no idea where it was coming from, like strings and brass and voices mingling in one instrument. She closed her eyes and basked in the glory.

It didn't last long. Another sound, discordant and somehow stomach-turning, broke through the golden cocoon and she snapped her eyes open. She saw a wall of black, of monstrous eyes, and deformed features, and she recognised the sound of the Fomorii shrieking in anger. As the Danann swept down the hillside towards them, they seemed to roll up, fold in on themselves and melt into the grass.

And then in the stillness that followed there was another sound, smaller and reedier, and she discovered Veitch kneeling on the bridge, yelling something at them. His face was filled with despair so acute it broke through her trance. With a terrible wrench she pulled herself from the golden mass and ran towards him.

There was blood on his temple, but that wasn't the cause of his dismay. He motioned over the side of the bridge, then looked away. She already knew what she would see. She told herself to turn away before she saw so the image would not be with her for ever, but she knew she couldn't be a coward. Her eyes brimming with tears, she looked down on Church's body half-submerged in the brook, his blood seeping away with the water. She didn't cry or shout or scream; it was as if all emotion had been torn out of her by a sucking vacuum.

By the time she skidded down the bank her tears were flowing freely and her throat burned from sobbing. She knelt next to the body and took his hand. Why should she feel so bad when it was someone she had met only a few weeks before?

A shadow fell across her and she looked up to see Laura silhouetted against the setting sun. She shifted her position to see Laura's face and it was as she had guessed: cold, dispassionate. 'Don't you feel anything?' she said in a fractured voice.

But Laura didn't even seem to recognise she was there. She stared blankly at Church's staring eyes, cocking her head slightly to one side like she was examining a work of art. 'I knew you'd do this to me, you bastard,' she said softly.

Veitch slumped down on the edge of the bridge. 'At least we won,' he said wearily. 'We drove them off. Despite, you know . . . Despite us being a bunch of losers. We did it.'

They remained there for a painful moment, not knowing what bound them together any more, barely able even to recognise themselves. And then they heard a crunch of gravel and turned to see Tom and one of the Danann walking towards them. The god exuded power from every pore of his golden skin, and when they looked into his almond eyes they saw nothing they knew.

He stopped before them and rested his gaze on each one of them in turn, a faintly disturbing smile playing on his lips.

'Who are you?' Ruth asked faintly.

The smile grew even more enigmatic. 'Once my names were known to everyone in the land. So soon forgotten? It will change, it will change. Who am I? I am Nuada, known as Nuada Airgetlámh, known as Nudd, known as Lludd, known as Lud, founder of Londinium, wielder of Caledfwlch.' There was an unpleasant arrogance in the turn of his head. 'The Tuatha Dé Danann give you thanks for freeing us from our place of banishment. In return, the Allfather has given permission for the use of his cauldron.'

Tom held out the bowl they had found under Glastonbury Tor. Ruth looked at him blankly. 'The Cauldron of Dagda is the cornucopia, the

Horn of Plenty,' he said softly. 'It is the Grail, the source of spiritual renewal. The taker of life and the giver of life. The crucible of rebirth.' He smiled. 'Take it.'

Ruth's hands trembled as she took it, barely able to believe what he was saying. The moment her fingers closed around it, she felt a subtle heat deep in her stomach, rising up through her arms to her hands. The moment it hit the bowl, it seemed to weep droplets of gold, which collected in the bottom. When it had partially filled, Tom motioned to Church.

Though uncomprehending, Veitch jumped from the bridge and dragged Church from the water, resting the body in his lap and the head in the crook of his arm. He looked up at Ruth with the simple belief of a child.

Ruth glanced at the golden liquid, which moved almost with a life of its own. A part of her could not bring herself to accept what was being suggested: the dead were dead, a machine switched off never to be restarted; there was no subtle spirit, no *beyond* or Happy Home fairy-tale for the religiously naive; everything she had seen could not shake that part of her. But still there was another part of her that accepted wonder and hope, that believed in the World Where Anything Can Happen. There was a time for cynicism and the restraining lessons of adulthood, but this was a time to be a child. She knelt down and placed the bowl to Church's lips, while Veitch manipulated his mouth so the liquid would flow in. And then the world seemed to hang in space.

There was darkness and warmth and a vertiginous, queasy plummet into something unpleasant. And then Church opened his eyes. Briefly, Veitch and Tom had to restrain him as he was overcome with convulsions; images of Calatin's attack, the agony of the serrated sword biting into his flesh, the smell of his own fear, passed through his uncomprehending mind in an instant. But the sensations of the changes coming over his body drove the disturbing thoughts from him; the golden liquid seemed to be seeping into every part of him, transforming him as it passed, although he had no idea what he was becoming; yet beneath it there was the numb antagonism of the Fomorii Kiss of Frost still within him; heat and cold, light and dark, battling for supremacy.

'You have been reborn.'

Church looked up into the face of Nuada. It took a second or two to recognise who he was and what he was doing there. Slowly he looked round at the vision of gold and silver, faces almost too beautiful, presences too divine, and the transcendental wonder he felt brought a shiver of deep emotion. Tears sprang to his eyes in relief at the miracle. 'The Danann!' His voice sounded like it was being ground out. 'The others freed you . . . you drove away the Fomorii . . .'

'The Night Walkers departed rather than face our anger at their betrayal of the Covenant.'

Church closed his eyes in relief, resting back against Veitch's arm. 'But you came. We won. Now you can face up to them . . . drag them back . . .'

In the long silence that followed, Church knew there was something wrong. He opened his eyes to see Nuada smiling dangerously. 'Now we are back,' he said, 'we will not be leaving.'

'What do you mean?' Church levered himself upright, suddenly afraid.

'We always coveted a return to this place. We staked our claim upon it in the time before your race. But the pact prevented it and the doors remained closed. Now the Night Walkers have broken the pact. And the doors are open.'

'But the Fomorii are your enemy!' Church protested.

'The fruits of this land are too succulent to ignore for unnecessary confrontation. We have co-existed before. Uneasily, certainly, but the pursuit of our will overrides all other concerns.'

'But they are going to bring back Balor!' There were tears of frustration in Ruth's eyes.

'Perhaps they will succeed,' he mused superciliously.

Tom knelt before Nuada and bowed his head in supplication. 'The Brothers and Sisters of Dragons sacrificed a great deal to free you from your place of banishment, my Lord.'

'And they have our thanks, True Thomas. But their work was not all as it seemed.' Tom looked up at him quizzically. 'We are not without foresight. The Fomorii betrayal was anticipated – after all, it was in their nature. We had our preparations. The Brothers and Sisters of Dragons were guided to this moment from the beginning.'

'How?' Church thought he was going to be sick; suddenly he could see all the answers, but he was afraid to examine them.

'The alchemy of death was necessary to change you, to spark the Pendragon Spirit, to start you down the road that would lead to this moment.'

They all looked blank. Tom turned to them, troubled, disorientated. 'In all your lives, someone had to die—'

'You killed Marianne!' Church raged suddenly.

Nuada fixed such a dark expression on him Church was shocked into silence. 'Our own hands were never raised. We set events in motion.

We removed checks, moved balances.' He pointed at Veitch. 'He turned and used his weapon at the perfect moment, against his will. Other fragile creatures followed our guidance—'

'Then who killed her?' Church asked dismally.

Nuada turned from him; his smile was both patronising and frightening. 'There are many games we can play with this world.' Tom blanched at his words. 'The prize has been well worth the rigours.'

He began to walk back to the shimmering golden horde massed beyond the bridge. Church tried to scramble to his feet, but had to be helped up by Veitch. He choked back his emotion and said, as forcefully as he could muster, 'At least help us remove the Fomorii. We need you.'

Nuada turned coldly. 'Your voice might have carried more weight if it were not polluted by the taint of the Night Walkers. In times before, the Pendragon Spirit would not have occupied such a weak host.'

And then he had joined the rest of the Tuatha Dé Danann, and Church, Veitch, Tom and Ruth could only watch as the shining host swept out across the countryside like a tidal wave of terrifying, alien force.

CHAPTER TWENTY-TWO

Beltane

Night fell quickly. Perhaps it was their mood, or the events of the day, but it seemed more preternatural than any they had so far experienced, alive with ancient terrors. They built a fire in the shelter of a grove on the top of a hill where they could see Skye spread out beneath the arc of stars. Ruth remarked they could easily have gone back in time to the Neolithic era. Church replied that in a way they had.

Before the sun set they had fetched Shavi from the boat. He had regained some of his equilibrium, but although he attempted to put on a brave face, they could all see that when his smile dropped, he had a look about him like something had been damaged inside; he was haunted, detached. He refused to talk about what had happened when he had linked with the serpent, but he was no longer the man he had been.

Since their individual journeys began, they had all gained new scars, some within, some external, but as their conversation slowly emerged from the atmosphere of desolation they were all secretly surprised to discover bonds of friendship had been forged among them which would not have been there in other circumstances. As Church looked at their faces around the fire, he found a surprising burst of hope at that revelation; it was such a tiny thing in the face of all that had happened, but somehow it seemed important.

Without it, he mused, the realisation that their lives had been manipulated and ruined by higher powers could have destroyed them. Even so, each of them, in their own way, felt broken. Veitch, who had been ruined by the guilt of the murder he had committed; Ruth, who had lost her uncle and father; Shavi, who had lost his boyfriend; and Laura, whose mother had died while she lay unconscious. And there he was, two years of his life wasted by a suffering that need never have happened, the one thing he valued most destroyed, his entire existence spoiled; Marianne had been so important to him, life itself, and she had been treated as if she mattered less than a weed in the garden. All of that misery had been carried out purely on a whim, by a race of beings who thought so little about humanity they couldn't even bring themselves to act with contempt. He would have felt rage if it hadn't been so terrible; instead there was just despair at the senselessness of it all.

He sat in silence with Laura for the first hour after twilight, both of them lost to their thoughts. 'Still, it could have been worse, right?' she said eventually. 'If the Danann hadn't returned, we wouldn't have been sitting here now. The Fomorii would have wiped the world clean. You did that.'

'*We* did it,' he corrected.

'So we live to fight another day. We don't give up, right? Right?' She wasn't going to back down until he agreed, and when he did, she smiled and kissed him gently on the cheek. 'Sinatra would be proud of you, boy.' She slipped away, trailing her hand across his shoulders and the back of his neck. It was a simple touch, but it filled him with strength.

The Danann's involvement in their tragedies had at least helped Ruth begin to come to terms with Veitch's murder of her uncle. The kind of person he had been prevented her absolving him of all guilt, but they were talking. As the fire began to die down, the two of them, together with Laura and Shavi, went in search of more wood while Tom and Church sat watching the glowing embers.

'We were supposed to be some kind of heroes,' Church began disconsolately. 'The defenders of humanity, of the world itself. What a laugh! Talk about fooling ourselves. We were so insignificant to the Danann they ran us like mice through a maze. We did all their dirty work for them *and* we suffered for it. And what did we get in return? Nothing.'

'You're blinding yourself to your achievements.' Tom rolled a joint and lit it. 'The Danann may still help us. They simply need to be won over. If you'd failed to release them by Beltane, everything truly would be lost. The Fomorii would have had no opposition.' He echoed Laura's words and Church wondered why he was the only one who failed to see anything positive. He began to protest, but Tom silenced him with a hand. 'No. This has been a setback, but your victory in freeing the Danann has bought us more time. And the recovery of the talismans was a remarkable thing – something that has never been achieved since the Danann hid them away.'

Church shook his head, unconvinced. 'You know the worst thing? We've brought about exactly what we were trying to stop. If the Danann are as dangerously unpredictable . . . as alien . . . as you described, if they can devastate our lives without a second thought in the way that they did, I'm afraid of what they're going to do now they're here.'

In Tom's silence, Church heard his worst fears confirmed.

'That's something to tell the grandchildren I'll probably never have,' he said with a bitter laugh. 'I was the man who helped bring about the end of the world.'

A shooting star rocketed breathtakingly across a sky unspoiled by light pollution. Tom followed its arc while taking the smoke deep into his lungs. 'When all this began I thought we were without hope,' he began quietly. 'You'll forgive me when I say, but when I looked at all of you I saw failure writ large. But you've torn the scales from my eyes. Through hardship you persevered and the Pendragon Spirit has truly awoken in you, in all of you. You carry within you the manifestation of all that is good in humanity, the strength, the true power, perhaps, of the highest force.' He nodded to himself thoughtfully. 'We must have faith.'

'Faith, right. I tell you what I've got faith in: that I'm going to find out who or what the Danann used to kill Marianne and the others and I'm going to make them pay. And if I had the power within me, I'd make the Danann pay too.'

Tom said nothing.

Church watched the others approaching through the gloom, laughing amongst themselves, despite everything. Slowly, deep within him, he began to feel the stirrings of that affirmation to which Tom had given voice. He was the one who had ruined everything; his weakness; but he could change. It would have been easy to give in to it, but that wasn't the kind of person he was. Somehow he had to dig down deep, learn from his terrible failure and move on. And hope that redemption lay somewhere in the future.

'What have you done with the Roisin Dubh?' Tom asked.

Church dipped in his pocket and pulled out the rose; it was withered and desiccated. Wrapped around the stem was Marianne's locket. 'We're living in strange times,' he began. 'Look at this – a little girl's piece of cheap jewellery. And now it's a thing of wonder.' As he carefully untangled the chain, he explained about the white light that had infused him during his battle with Calatin. 'We've seen a lot of terrible things, but this . . . this fills me with hope. I still don't know what it means, but I know what I'd *like* it to mean.' He flicked open the locket and glanced at the photo inside. 'A time of miracles,' he said under his breath. As his words disappeared in the wind, the rose finally crumbled into dust and was whisked away from his palm.

'Gone,' Tom said.

'But not completely. I can still feel some of its taint inside me. I don't know what that will mean.'

'The Danann will not heed you while it remains.'

They fell silent for a long minute, and then Tom said, 'I think you need to make some explanations to the others.'

'I know. I owe them that, certainly. And I hope I'll be able to make amends. I'll tell them later, after we've eaten.' He sighed.

'Just a few weeks ago I thought I was incapable of feeling anything again,' he went on, thoughtfully. 'Now I could be convinced I'm feeling too much.' He laughed ironically. 'In this new Dark Age, it's easy to think we've lost so much – a way of life, technology that works, logic. But is that true? We've still got all the things that truly matter. It might sound twee, but maybe the importance of life comes down to just a few simple things – friendship, love, trust, a belief in something better. Faith. And in the face of all this inhumanity, maybe those human things are all we really need.'

Tom laughed, a sound Church couldn't recall hearing before. 'And you call me the hippie.'

Church scanned his face, saw the suffering and the strengths that had overcome it. 'It's not over, you know.'

'I know.'

'You're right, we've done great things. Amazing things. We may not be much to look at, but . . .' He looked round at the others. 'Look at them. I wouldn't want anybody else by my side. We're going to fight back. Find some way to make a difference. And we'll do it, you know?'

'I know.'

'So what do we do now?'

'That,' Tom said, 'is a question for tomorrow.'

They stoked up the fire and dined on the last of the sandwiches and crisps they had brought from the van. Later, while the others sat quietly thinking, Laura took the radio Church had bought in Melrose and wandered off, trying to find some music. Not long after she came hurrying back with it.

'You'd better listen to this,' she said. 'I went right across the bands trying to find some music that wasn't from another century. But every station was playing the same recorded message – that there's about to be some kind of Government statement.'

They put the radio down and huddled round it. Soon after there was a burst of sombre music, and then the clipped, precise tones of a BBC newsreader.

'This is the BBC, calling the country from London. We have a statement from the Prime Minister which will be repeated at intervals of thirty minutes.'

A recording of the Prime Minister rang out, the voice clear, unwavering, drained of any emotion at all. 'As of 10 p.m. on May 1, martial law has been declared throughout the United Kingdom. The activities of Parliament have been suspended until further notice. This difficult decision has been taken in the light of the crisis facing the country. I can give no further details at this moment. In the meantime, once the situation has been clarified, official announcements will made through the BBC radio and television channels. In this troubling time, I would urge you all to remain calm. This action has been forced upon us, and it has been adopted reluctantly, but it is for the protection of all. A curfew will be instigated during the hours of darkness. The Government offers the strongest advice to congregate in areas of human habitation. Stay away from open countryside. Avoid lakes and rivers. The National Parks are restricted areas until further notice. Do not venture into any area considered lonely or secluded. Remain in well-lit localities at all times. Do not travel alone. In rural areas our stringent gun laws are being relaxed for the protection of the populace.

'On a more personal note, I must say I am well aware of the strength of character that lies at the heart of this proud nation. In the days and weeks that lie ahead, we must all reach deep into that well of courage that we have exhibited so many times before in our glorious history. By standing together, we shall prevail.'

There was a brief pause and then the announcer said, 'That is all. This is the BBC, calling—'

Laura flicked off the radio. They remained silent for a long moment and then Veitch said, 'It's started, then.'

As if in response, a fire erupted magically on the hilltop close by; there was no fuel anyone could see, and though it blazed powerfully, it didn't seem to scorch the surrounding grass. Then others burst like tiny fireflies on nearby hilltops, spreading out across the land as far as the eye could see.

'The Beltane fires,' Tom said quietly. 'The season has turned.'

They stood together looking out at the flickering beacons, feeling lonely and insignificant in the vast chamber of night. The world was no longer their own. The Age of Reason had died, and a new Dark Age had dawned.

darkest hour

book two of the age of misrule

MARK

CHADBOURN

Life during wartime

May 2, 8 a.m.; above the English Channel:
'Somebody must have some idea what's going on.' Justin Fallow fiddled uncomfortably with the miniature spirit bottles on his tray as he watched the dismal expressions sported by the air stewardesses. It was amazing how little fluctuations in the smooth-running of life were more disturbing than the big shocks. Those looks were enough to tell him something fundamental had changed; he had never seen any of them without those perfectly balanced smiles of pearly teeth contained by glossy red lipstick.

'I wouldn't lose any sleep over it. Everything will be back to normal in a few days.' Colin Irvine stared vacuously out of the window at the fluffy white clouds. The reflection showed a craggy face and hollow cheeks that seemed older than his years. The trip to Paris had been better than expected; the business side tied up quickly, then two days of good food and fine wine, and one brisk night at a brothel. His head still felt fuzzy from the over-indulgence and he would be happier if Justin shut up at least once before the plane landed.

'Well, I wish I had your optimism.' Fallow's public school accent was blurred by the alcohol and he was talking too loudly. He flicked back the fringe that kept falling over his eyes and snapped his chubby fingers to attract the attention of one of the stewardesses. 'Over here, please. Another vodka.'

'I like a drink as much as the next man, but I don't know how you can get through that lot at breakfast,' Irvine said, without taking his gaze away from the clouds.

Fallow slapped his belly. 'Constitution of a horse, old chap.' When the vodka arrived, he brushed the plastic glass to one side and gulped it straight from the bottle.

'Steady on, eh?' Irvine allowed himself a glance of distaste.

'But what if it isn't going to be sorted out in a few days?' Fallow drummed his fingers anxiously on the tray. 'You know, we have no idea what's going on, so how can we say? A sudden announcement that all air traffic is going to be grounded indefinitely doesn't exactly fill one with confidence, if you know what I mean. Now *that* sounds serious.'

'We were lucky to get the last flight out.'

'I mean, the country could be on its knees in days! How will business survive?' His startled expression suggested he had only just grasped the implications of his train of thought. 'Never mind your bog-standard business traveller who has to get around for meetings – they can muddle through with a few netcasts and conference calls in the short term. But what about import–export? The whole of the global economy relies on—'

'You don't have to tell me, Justin.'

'You can sit there being sniffy about it, but have you thought about what it means—?'

'It means we won't be able to get any bananas in the shops for a while and international mail will be a bastard. Thank God for the Internet.'

'I still think there's more to it than you think. To take such a drastic step . . . Trouble is, you can't trust those bastards in the Government to tell you anything important, whatever political stripe they are. Look at the mad cow thing. It's a wonder we're not all running around goggle-eyed, slavering at the mouth.'

'You obviously didn't look in the mirror last night—'

'This isn't funny. Go on, tell me why you're so calm. What could cause something like this?'

'Let me see, Justin.' Irvine began counting off his fingers. 'An impending strike by all international air traffic control which we haven't been told about for fear it causes a panic. You know how much pressure they've been under recently with the increase in the volume of flights. Or some virus has been loaded into the ATC system software. Or the Global Positioning Satellite has been hit by a meteorite so all the pilots are flying blind. Or all those intermittent power failures we've had recently have made it too risky until they find the cause. Or they've finally discovered that design glitch that's had planes dropping out of the skies like flies over the last few years.'

'I'd rather we didn't talk about this now, Colin.'

'Well, you started it.'

Justin sucked on his lower lip like a petulant schoolboy and then began to line up the miniature bottles in opposing forces. 'I suppose all the trolley dollies are worried they might be out of work,' he mused.

A crackle over the Tannoy heralded an announcement. 'This is your captain speaking. We anticipate arrival in Gatwick on schedule in twenty minutes. There may be a slight delay on the—' There was a sudden pause, a muffled voice in the background, and then the Tannoy snapped off.

Fallow looked up suspiciously. 'Now what's going on?'

'Will you calm down? Just because you're afraid of the worst happening doesn't mean it's going to.'

'And just because you're not afraid doesn't mean it isn't.' Fallow shifted in his seat uncomfortably, then glanced up and down the aisle.

What he saw baffled him at first. It was as if a ripple was moving down the plane towards him. The faces of the passengers looking out of the starboard side were changing, the blank expressions of people watching nothing in particular shedding one after the other as if choreographed. In that first fleeting instant of confusion, Fallow tried to read those countenances: was it shock, dismay, wonder? Was it horror?

And then he abruptly thought he should be searching for the source of whatever emotion it was, but before he had time to look, the plane banked wildly and dropped; his stomach was left behind and for one moment he thought he was going to vomit. But then the fear took over and it was as if his body were locked in stasis as he gripped the armrests until his knuckles were white. He forced his head into his lap. Screams filled the air, but they were distant, as though coming at him through water, and then he was obliquely aware he was screaming himself.

The plane was plummeting down so sharply vibrations were juddering through the whole fuselage; when it banked again at the last minute, the evasive action was so extreme Fallow feared the wings would be torn off. Then, bizarrely, the plane was soaring up at an angle that was just as acute. Fallow was pressed back into his seat until he felt he was on the verge of blacking out.

'It can't take much more of this punishment,' he choked.

Just as he was about to prepare himself for the whole plane coming apart in mid-air, it levelled off. Fallow burst out laughing in hysterical relief, then raged, 'What the *fuck* was that all about?'

Irvine pitched forward and threw up over the back of the seat in front; he tried to get his hand up to his mouth, but that only splattered the vomit over a wider area. Fallow cursed in disgust, but the trembling that racked his body didn't allow him to say any more.

One of the stewardesses bolted from the cabin, leaving the door swinging so Fallow could see the array of instrumentation blinking away. She pushed her way up to a window, then exclaimed, 'My God! He was right!'

The whole planeload turned as one. Fallow looked passed Irvine's white, shaking face into the vast expanse of blue sky. The snowy clouds rolled and fluffed like meringue, but beyond that he could see nothing. Then, out of the corner of his eye, he noticed a shadow moving across the field of white. At first he wondered if they had narrowly avoided a collision with another plane, but the shadow seemed too long and thin; it appeared to have a life of its own. There was a sound like a jet taking off and then the colour of the clouds transformed to red and gold. A belch of black smoke was driven past the window.

Fallow rammed Irvine back in his seat and craned his neck to search the sky. Beside and slightly below the plane, flying fast enough to pass it with apparent ease, was something which conjured images from books he had read in the nursery. Part of it resembed a bird and part a serpent: scales glinted like metal in the morning sun on a body that rippled with both power and sinuous agility, while enormous wings lazily stroked the air. Colours shimmered across its surface as the light danced: reds, golds and greens, so that it resembled some vast, brass robot imagined by a Victorian fantasist. Boned ridges and horns rimmed its skull above red eyes; one swivelled and fixed on Fallow. A second later the creature roared, its mouth wide, and belched fire; it seemed more a natural display, like a peacock's plumage, than an attack, but all the passengers drew back from the window as one. Then, with a twist that defied its size, it snaked up and over the top of the fuselage and down the other side.

Shock and fear swept through the plane, but it dissipated at speed. Instead, everyone seemed to be holding their breath. Fallow looked around and was astonished to see that faces that had earlier been scarred with cynicism or bland with dull routine were suddenly alight; to a man or woman, they all looked like children. Even the stewardesses were smiling.

Then the atmosphere was broken by a cry from the aft: 'Look! There's another one!'

In the distance, Fallow saw a second creature dipping in and out of the clouds as if it were skimming the surface of the sea.

Fallow slumped back in his seat and looked at Irvine coldly. 'Everything will be back to normal in a few days,' he mocked in a singsong, playground voice.

May 2, 11 a.m.; Dounreay Nuclear Power Station, Scotland:
'I just don't know what they expect of us!' Dick McShay said frustratedly. He threw his pen at the desk, then realised how pathetic that was. At 41, he had expected a nice, easy career with BNFL, overseeing the decommissioning of the plant that would stretch long beyond his life span; a holding job, no pressures apart from preventing the media discovering information about the decades of contamination, leaks and near-disasters. Definitely no crises. He fixed his grey eyes on his 2-I-C,

Nelson, who looked distinctly uncomfortable. 'I have no desire to shoot the messenger, William, but really, give me an answer.'

Nelson, who was four years McShay's junior, a little more stylish, but without any of his charisma, sucked on his bottom lip for a second; an irritating habit. 'What they want to do,' he began cautiously, 'is make sure most of Scotland isn't irradiated in the next few weeks. I don't mean to sound glib,' he added hastily, 'but that's the bottom line. It's these power failures—'

McShay sighed, shook his head. 'Not just power, William, technology. There's no point denying it. Mechanical processes have been hit just as much. I mean, who can explain something like that? If I were superstitious . . .' He paused. '. . . I'd still have a hard time explaining it. The near-misses we've had over the last few weeks . . .' He didn't need to go into detail; Nelson had been there too during the crazed panics when they all thought they were going to die, the cooling system shut-downs, the fail-safe failures that were beyond anyone's comprehension; yet every time it had stopped just before the whole place had gone sky-high. He couldn't tell if they were jinxed or lucky, but it was making an old man of him.

'So we shut down—'

'Yes, but don't they realise it's not like flicking off a switch? That schedule is just crazy. Even cutting corners, we couldn't do it.'

'They're desperate.'

'And I don't like *them* being around either.' He glanced aggressively through the glass walls that surrounded his office. Positioned around the room beyond were Special Forces operatives, faces masked by smoked Plexiglas visors, guns held at the ready across their chests; their immobility and impersonality made them seem inhuman, mystical statues waiting to be brought to life by sorcery. They had arrived with the dawn, slipping into the vital areas as if they knew the station intimately – which, of course, they did, although they had never been there before. *For support*, they said. Not, *To guard*. Not, *To enforce*.

'All vital installations are under guard, Dick. So they say. It's all supposed to be hush-hush—'

'Then how do you know?'

Nelson smirked in reply. Then: 'We might as well just ignore them. It's their job, all that Defence of the Realm stuff.'

'What are they going to do if we don't meet the deadline? Shoot us?'

Nelson's expression suggested he thought this wasn't beyond the bounds of possibility.

'I just never expected to be doing my job at gunpoint. If the powers that be don't trust us, why should we trust them?'

'Desperate times, Dick.'

McShay looked at Nelson suspiciously. 'I hope you're on our side, William.'

'There aren't any sides, are there?'

A rotating red light suddenly began whirling in the room outside, intermittently bathing them in a hellish glow. A droning alarm pitched at an irritating level filled the complex. The Special Forces troops were instantly on the move.

'Shit!' McShay closed his eyes in irritation; it was a breach of a security zone. 'What the fuck is it now?'

Nelson was already on the phone. As he listened, McShay watched incomprehension flicker across his face.

'Give me the damage,' McShay said wearily when Nelson replaced the phone.

Nelson stared at him blankly for a moment before he said, 'There's an intruder—'

'I know! It's the fucking intruder alarm!'

'—in the reactor core.'

McShay returned the blank stare and then replied, 'You're insane.' He picked up the phone and listened to the stuttering report before running out of the room, Nelson close behind him.

The inherent farcical nature of a group of over-armed troops pointing their guns at the door to an area where no human could possibly survive wasn't lost on McShay, but the techies remained convinced someone was inside. He pushed his way past the troops on the perimeter to the control array where Rex Moulding looked about as uncomfortable as any man could get.

Moulding motioned to the soldiers as McShay approached. 'What are this lot doing here? This isn't a military establishment.'

McShay brushed his question aside with an irritated flap of his hand. 'You're a month late for practical jokes, Rex.'

'It's no joke. Look here.' Moulding pointed to the bank of monitors.

McShay examined each screen in turn. They showed various views of the most secure and dangerous areas around the reactor. 'There's nothing there,' he said eventually.

'Keep watching.'

McShay sighed and attempted to maintain his vigilance. A second later a blur flashed across one of the screens. 'What's that?'

The fogginess flickered on one of the other screens. 'It's almost like the cameras can't get a lock on it,' Moulding noted.

'What do you mean?'

There was a long pause. 'I don't know what I mean.'

'Is it a glitch?'

'No, there's definitely someone in there. You can hear the noises it makes through the walls.'

McShay's expression dared Moulding not to say the wrong thing. 'It?'

Moulding winced. 'Bob Pruett claims to have seen it before it went in there—'

'Where is he?' McShay snapped.

As he glanced around, a thickset man in his fifties wearing a sheepish expression pushed his way through the military.

'Well?' McShay said uncompromisingly.

'I saw it,' Pruett replied in a thick Scots drawl. He looked at Moulding for support.

'You better tell him,' Moulding said.

'Look, I know this sounds bloody ridiculous, but it's what I saw. It had antlers coming out like this.' He spread his fingers on either side of his head; McShay looked at him as if he had gone insane. 'But it was a man. I mean, it walked like a man. It looked like a man – two arms, two legs. But its face didn't look human, know what I mean? It had red eyes. And fur, or leaves—'

'Which one?'

'What do you mean?'

'Fur, or leaves. Which one?'

'Well, both. They looked like they were growing out of each other, all over its body.'

McShay searched Pruett's face, feeling uncomfortable when he saw no sign of contrition; in fact, there was shock and disbelief there, and that made him feel worse. Moulding suddenly grew tense, his gaze fixed on the monitors. 'It's coming this way,' he said quietly.

Unconsciously, McShay turned towards the security door. Through it he could hear a distant sound, growing louder, like the roaring of a beast, like a wind in the high trees.

'The temperature's rising in the reactor core,' Nelson called out from the other side of the room. The second tonal emergency warning began, intermingling discordantly with the intruder alarm; McShay's head began to hurt. 'The fail-safes haven't kicked in,' Nelson continued. He pulled out his mobile phone and punched in a number; McShay wondered obliquely who he could be calling.

'It's nearly here,' Moulding said. McShay couldn't take his eyes off the security door; he was paralysed by incomprehension. That horrible noise was louder now, reverberating even through the shielding. He couldn't understand how the troops could remain immobile with all the confusion raging around them; their guns were still raised to the door, barrels unwavering.

The one in charge glanced briefly at McShay, then said, 'If it comes through, fire the moment you see it.'

What's the point? McShay thought. *It's been in the reactor core and it's still alive!* He was overcome with a terrible feeling of foreboding.

There was a sudden thundering at the door and it began to buckle like tinfoil; McShay thought he could see the imprints of hands in it. Despite their training, some of the troops took a step back. The roaring which sounded like nothing he had ever heard before was now drowning out the alarms.

'I don't wish to state the obvious, but if that door comes down, it will take more than a shower to decontaminate us,' Moulding said in a quiet voice that crackled with tension.

McShay came out of his stupor in a flash; the thought that a security door designed to survive a direct nuclear strike might ever be breached was so impossible, his mind hadn't leapt to consider the consequences of what was happening.

'Everybody fall back!' he yelled. 'We need to seal this area off—'

The next second the door exploded outwards. McShay had one brief instant when he glimpsed the shape that surged through and then the gunfire erupted in a storm of light and noise, and a second after that a wave of soft white light came rushing from the reactor core towards them all.

The first person to see what had happened to Dounreay Nuclear Power Station was a farmer trundling along the coast road in his tractor. The sight was so bizarre he had to pull over to the side to check it wasn't some illusion caused by the sea haze. The familiar modernist buildings had been lost behind an impenetrable wall of vegetation; mature trees sprouted through the concrete and tarmac, ivy swathed the perimeter fences and buildings, dog roses and clematis clambered up the side of the administration block, cars were lost beneath creepers; all around squirrels, rabbits and birds skittered through the greenery. And if anyone had decided, for whatever reason, to check for radiation, they would have found none, not even in what had been the reactor core. Nor would they have found any sign of human life.

May 2, 8 p.m.; News International: Wapping, London:
'There's no point in us being here.' The accent was pure Mockney, hiding something from the Home Counties. Lucy Manning repeatedly

punched the lift button, then shifted from foot to foot with irritation as she watched the lighted numbers' soporific descent. She was in her twenties, dyed-blonde hair framing a face that had the cold hardness of a frontline soldier.

Beside her, Kay Bliss could have been a mirror image or a copycat sister, but the look and the accent were all part of the office politics; a game they both knew how to play. 'Oh, fuck it, Lucy, we're getting paid, aren't we? It's nice not to be out doorstepping some twat until the early hours for a change.' Her voice had the hard vowels of a Geordie, though she could hide it when she had to.

'There's some idiot from Downing Street permanently in the newsroom,' Lucy continued, 'going over every piece of copy with a fine-tooth comb. D-Notice on this, D-Notice on that. We'll be like some fucking cheap local rag soon. Golden wedding stories and photos from the Rotary lunch.' Lucy strode into the lift the second the doors opened, then rattled her nails anxiously on the metal wall. 'Come on. Why are these things so fucking slow? All the technology we've got in this place, you'd think they'd be able to get lifts that worked quickly.'

'We're not even supposed to be using them. All those technology crashes—'

'Like we've got time to walk up and down flights of stairs all day.'

Kay held her breath until the doors opened on the newsroom floor. She'd spent an hour stuck in it with three monkeys from the loading bay and it wasn't an episode she wanted to repeat.

Lucy was still talking as she dodged out between the opening doors, 'It started with that terrorist strike on the M4—'

'Damon covered that.' Kay looked puzzled for a second. 'Terrorists?'

'It had to be terrorists. It wasn't that long before the Martial Law announcement.'

'Someone said a Yank plane had gone down carrying nukes.'

Lucy shrugged. 'And there were all those phone calls from the great unwashed claiming they'd seen some fire-breathing monster.' She flung open the swing doors. 'Sometimes I wish I worked for the *FT*.'

The newsroom was quiet now that all the dayshift had departed. The night news editor stared at the slowly scrolling Press Association newsfeed on his computer while lazily chewing on a cheese roll. One of the sports reporters whistled loudly.

''ello, darlin',' Kay shouted back with a cheery wave.

'It's all right for them,' Lucy muttered moodily, 'their Ludo tournaments never get censored.'

'You're in a right mood, aren't you?'

They'd walked on a few paces before Lucy said, 'I had the splash today and they pulled it.'

'Oh, that explains it. Bitter and twisted at not getting any front page glory. What was the story?'

'A whole unit of Royal Marines slaughtered up in the Highlands. A hot tip from my man at Command Headquarters.' She stuck out her bottom lip like a sulky child.

'Wow. A *proper* story. No *EastEnders* stud getting bladdered in that one,' Kay said with what Lucy thought was an unreasonable amount of glee. 'But you didn't really expect to get it through, did you?' Lucy shrugged. Kay's expression gradually became troubled. 'Slaughtered? In Scotland?'

'Hey, it's the Barbie twins!' Kevin Smith, one of the sales managers, had been lurking around the news desk. The hacks hated him for his retro-yuppie look and his aftershave stink, but he insisted on pretending he was one of the boys.

'Fuck off, Kevin,' Kay said with a mock-sweet smile.

'Careful you don't cut yourself with that.' He patted the desk so they could both sit next to him, but they studiously went round to the other side where they could talk to the handful of freelancers doing the night shift.

'What's up?' Lucy perched on the edge of the desk so she could tease the newbies with a flash of her thigh.

'Don't bother the fresh meat!' the news editor barked. 'Get over here!'

Kay was first over. 'What is it, chief?'

He tapped the screen as he spoke through a mouthful of cheese roll. 'PA says the PM's making an announcement at nine. Half the cabinet is getting the boot and they're setting up a coalition with the other parties. Government of National Unity or something.'

'Good policy. Get all the losers in one place. It'll probably be as successful as their Martial Law that they haven't got enough manpower to enforce.' Kevin had wandered over and was reading the newsfeed over the night news editor's shoulder.

'I'll take that one,' Lucy called out.

'You're both working on it.' The night news editor rammed his chair backwards into the sales manager's groin. Kevin exhaled sharply, but continued to force a smile.

Kay tore off a sheet of printer paper to make notes. 'Blimey. Two proper stories in one day. It's a sign – the world really is coming to an end!'

They all stopped what they were doing as the night news editor leaned forward to peer at the screen, swearing under his breath. 'Somebody must have rattled Downing Street's cage. There's a whole load of stuff coming up here. Flights grounded earlier, now we get "train services limited . . . No international calls . . . maybe extended disruption of the phone network . . . orders to shoot looters on sight . . ." What the fuck is going on?'

A middle-aged man in a smart dark suit moved slowly from the editor's office towards the news desk. He had a nondescript haircut and bland features and he carried himself with the stiff demeanour of a civil servant.

'When are you going to tell us what the fuck's going on?' the night news editor bellowed. 'It's a fucking outrage! The people have a right to know—'

The dark-suited man dropped a sheet of paper on the desk. 'This is tomorrow's page one story. "PM Launches Battle of Britain".'

They all looked at it, dumbfounded. 'You can't do that!' Lucy could see another byline disappearing before her eyes.

The night news editor scanned the paper, then hammered it beneath the flat of his hand. 'We can't print this! It doesn't fucking say anything! Just fucking PR guff! Nobody has any idea what's going on, they don't know who the fucking enemy is! It could be a fucking coup for all anyone knows! There'll be panic in the streets—'

'This has been carefully designed to *prevent* panic,' the man said calmly. 'The problem is internal, but not a coup. That is for your information only. The Government needs to act quickly and efficiently and that means the public must not get in the way—'

'It's like *1984*!' The night news editor's face was flushed bright red.

The civil servant held up a hand to quieten him, which served only to irritate him more. 'This is being done with the full approval of your editor—'

'Does *he* know what's happening?'

'He's been briefed by the PM personally, as have all media editors—'

'What's it got to do with all the technology blackouts?' Kevin interjected. 'There's stuff happening there that makes no sense at all. And all those freak calls we've been flooded with . . . people claiming they've seen UFOs and God knows what. I mean, someone said their dead uncle had come back to haunt them. And some farmer said his cows were giving up vinegar instead of milk. I mean, what's that all about?' He looked from face to face; everyone was staring back at him as if they had a bad smell under their nose. 'The switchboard keep putting them through to my office.'

'I wonder who arranged that?' Kay eyed the night news editor, who gave nothing away.

'We will be making a full and clear statement as soon as the situation demands it,' the civil servant said blandly. 'We have no intention of a cover-up. There is a state of emergency for a very good reason and our primary directive has to be to deal with that. It is taking all our resources. You have to believe me on this. Keeping everyone informed comes a very distant second.'

The night news editor read the replacement story one more time, then lounged back in his chair with his hands over his face. 'I don't know why I'm even bothering. We might as well all go down the pub—'

'You can't go out,' the civil servant said. 'There's a curfew once the sun goes down.'

'And you're going to stop me personally, are you, you cunt?' The night news editor glared at him venomously. Kay noticed a strange note in her boss's voice, something that was a little afraid; a suspicion of how bad things really were.

She glanced back to the civil servant who sported a curious expression; it reminded Kay of the look some older people, burdened by life's problems, gave to teenagers acting stupid and frivolous; a *one day you're going to have a rude awakening* look. He masked it quickly with expert precision, shrugged as if everything were beneath his notice, then sauntered slowly back to the editor's office.

Kay shrugged too. What did he know? Boring, jumped-up twat.

Once the office door had been closed the night news editor said, 'I think I might have to kill the bastard.'

'I'm getting a bit worried about this.' Kevin chewed his lip, his gaze still fixed on the office door. 'It seems really bad.'

'If it's a war I could be a war correspondent.' Lucy made a paper aeroplane, but it died mid-flight.

'Aren't you worried?' Kevin asked.

She eyed him contemptuously. 'What's to worry about? You want to try getting a drink up the road when all the circulation twats are in trying to pinch your arse. That's dangerous.'

'Hang on.' The night news editor was staring intently at his terminal.

'Not more bad news,' Kevin said.

The PA newsfeed seemed to be melting, the letters sliding down the screen into a mass at the bottom. Eventually the whole screen was clear. A second later a single word appeared in the top lefthand corner: WARE.

'What does that mean?' Kay asked. 'Software?'

The word began to repeat until it filled the whole screen.

'It might mean Be-WARE,' Kevin said. 'Some kind of warn—'

'Lucy, get on to Systems.' The night news editor threw the phone across the desk. 'This fucking thing isn't much use to us at the moment, but at least I can see what PA are doing.'

Lucy picked up the phone and instantly dropped it as ear-piercing laughter shrieked from the receiver. 'Fuck! What was that!' She stared at the phone as if it were alive.

'Interference,' Kay said wearily. 'Try the other one.'

The same inhuman laughter burst from that one too. They had an instant to look at each other in puzzlement and then all the lights and the computer screens winked out, plunging the entire windowless office into total darkness.

There was a long period of deep, worrying silence until everyone heard Kay say, 'Fuck off, Kevin.'

May 2, 11 p.m.; Balsall Heath, Birmingham:

'What did your dad say?' Sunita chewed on a strand of her long, black hair while she watched Lee's face. The night was uncomfortably muggy against the background stink of traffic fumes drifting in from the city centre.

Lee shifted uncomfortably as he scrubbed a hand across his skinhead crop. 'What do you think he said?'

The glare from the streetlamp over their heads seemed to draw out the sadness in her delicate features; her large eyes became dark, reflecting pools. 'That he doesn't want his son going out with some Paki.'

'He's not my dad anyway,' Lee said defensively. 'Stepdad.'

They both subconsciously bowed their heads as across the road a crowd of youths making their way back from the pub made loud kissing noises. Once they'd passed, Lee slipped his arms around her back; she felt so fragile against the hardness of his worked-out muscles that he just wanted to protect her.

'Why do we get all this shit?' She rested her head on his chest. 'I'm not even twenty yet! We should be having a good time, enjoying it all. Sometimes I feel like an old woman.'

He knew how she felt. When they'd first started seeing each other a year ago he had been almost overwhelmed by the *frisson* of doing something wrong, at turns both exciting and deeply disconcerting. And the fact that he did feel that way made him queasy because he knew how much his stepfather had corrupted his thought processes. There *was* nothing wrong with their relationship, but he'd had to keep it secret from his stepfather through what seemed like a million minor deceptions and big lies. It had cast a shadow over everything, when they should have been revelling in the feeling of falling in love; that pure sensation had been lost to them and he hated his stepfather for that loss. There was relief when he finally discovered who Lee was seeing after spotting them holding hands on New Street, but that had brought with it a whole different set of problems, the most worrying of which was that Sunita might no longer be safe. His stepfather's *associates* from his weekly meetings were brutal men with a harsh view of life that didn't allow such weak concepts as love the slightest foothold, and they were relentlessly unforgiving.

Sunita knew all this, and she knew it would be safer for her to leave Lee well alone, but how could she? The choices had been made and imprinted on their souls; they had to live with the consequences. 'What are we going to do? Carry on as normal, just . . . going to different places?'

'You know we can't do that. They know where you live.' He took a deep breath. 'We're getting out of Birmingham.' He paused while he watched her expression. 'Least, that's what I think. I know it'll be hard with your family—'

'It'll be a nightmare! My dad'll go crazy, my mum . . . all that wailing!'

'You're old enough—'

'That's not the point.'

He winced at being so insensitive, but he found it hard to see anything from the perspective of a loving, caring family. 'I'm sorry, Sunny, but, you know, we've got to do something—'

'Where were you thinking of going?'

'Down south somewhere. Just hit the motorway and see where we end up. They'll never be able to track us.'

She sighed. 'It's not just your dad. It'll be good to get out of this city. Sometimes it seems like it's choking the life out of me. There's something . . . a meanness . . . it just gets me down.'

'I know what you mean.' He listened to the drone of city centre traffic drifting over the wasteland and abandoned houses waiting for demolition. 'It'll be good, a fresh start.'

'Do you think it will work out?'

'I know it will.' He wondered if he could tell her why he was so sure; saying it out loud made even him feel like he was crazy; and he'd been through it. 'Come on, let's walk.' He took her hand and began to lead her in the direction of the house.

She looked uncomfortable. 'Your dad—'

'He's at one of his meetings, wishing we still had an empire.'

The familiar streets were thankfully empty, adding to the wonderful illusion that they were the only people left in the world. Away from the wasteland the air was a little fresher. They turned down the hill from the imposing big houses towards the line of pokey semis where Lee had lived all his life. It felt odd to think he might not walk down there again. He'd miss his mum, and Kelly, but not Mick; he'd be happy if he never heard Mick's voice again.

'When are you thinking of going?' Sunita asked.

'Now. Tonight.'

'Oh.'

He couldn't tell her that his stepdad's beetle-browed cronies might act after they'd finished their rebel-rousing for the night. They had to be as far away as possible from Brum before everything blew up. But even though he didn't say anything, he could tell from Sunita's response to the tight deadline that she understood the dangers.

'Mum and Dad will understand,' she said confidently. 'I'll call them once we're on the road. They'll be asleep when I get back to pack. Though you know, things aren't so different between us. They both wish I was with a boy who knew the Koran back to front.'

He shrugged, said nothing. There were always too many people wanting to interfere in everybody's life.

Sunita slipped her arm through his and gave it a squeeze. 'We'll never be able to agree on the music for the car, you know. There'll be me with my Groove Armada and Basement Jaxx and you with some ancient old toss like The Redskins or one of those other old fogey bands you like. I don't know how you got into all that stuff. Most of them were playing before you were born.'

'You've got to appreciate the past to know where you're going.'

'You've been reading books again, haven't you? I told you it was bad for you.' She smiled, but it drained away once she realised they were standing outside his home. Over the year her imagination had turned it into some kind of nightmarish haunted house, the place where all bad things originated. Even on the few times she'd been into the empty place there'd been an unpleasant atmosphere mingled in with the cheap cigarette smoke and smell of fried food. 'Are you sure he's not in?'

'He never misses a meeting.' Lee led her round the side of the house. The small back garden was in darkness; a few items of clothing still fluttered on the washing line.

'What about your mum and Kelly?'

'They'll have stopped off for a drink after the bingo.'

'Lee, why are you bringing me here?'

'There's something I want to show you. To put your mind at rest.'

'About what?'

'That everything'll be all right.' She still seemed unsure, so he took her hand and tugged her towards the shed in the shadows near the rear fence. It was much larger than average. Mick had put it up when he was thinking about breeding racing pigeons, but he'd never got round to that, like so many other things in his life.

'You don't want to get down to it here one more time, do you?' she said with a sly smile.

'Wait and see.' They stepped into the darkness of the shed and its familiar smell of turps and engine oil. He took her hand and waited a couple of seconds before saying in a clear voice, 'Come out. It's me.'

In the dark Sunita looked at him in puzzlement; she could feel his hand growing clammy. 'Who are you talking to?'

He hushed her anxiously. He kept his gaze fixed firmly on the back of the shed and when he didn't get whatever response he had been expecting, he tried again, a little more insistently. Still nothing. 'Please,' he said finally. 'This is Sunita. I told you about her. She's okay, you know that.'

He waited for another moment and then sighed. 'We better go,' he said reluctantly.

Outside, she gave him a peck on the cheek. 'It's a good job I love mad people. Now are you going to tell me—'

'You better not laugh!'

'Of course not.'

'Promise?'

'I promise, idiot. Now get on with it.'

He bowed his head with the odd, wincing expression which she knew signalled deep embarrassment. 'It started a couple of weeks ago. I kept hearing noises in the shed.'

'Noises?'

'Yes, you know . . . voices. They kept chattering in there. I thought some smackheads had broken in, but every time I went to check there was no one in there.'

'Ooh, spooky!'

'Yeah, that's what I thought. But then last week there *was* someone there.'

Sunita eyed him askance, trying to predict the punchline. 'Who was it?'

He rubbed his chin, obviously not wanting to continue. Finally he said, 'Do you believe in fairies?'

'Fairies?' She burst out laughing.

'You said you weren't going to laugh!'

'Sorry, but . . . You can't be serious!'

He looked away grumpily.

'Okay, go on!' she said, tugging at his sleeve. 'What did they look like?'

'They looked like fairies! Well, *a* fairy. Small, pointed ears, green clothes. It was just like one I'd seen on a book I had when I was a lad.'

It took him another ten minutes to get her to take him seriously, but eventually she accepted it. 'Okay, there's been a lot of strange stuff going on all over. If you say fairies, I believe fairies,' she said, bemused. 'So there are, really and truly, fairies at the bottom of the garden.'

'I don't know why I even bother with you,' he sighed. 'Just listen then, if you're not going to believe me. I tell you, I thought I was going loopy to start with, but every time I went in, there he was, so I *had* to accept it. And we started talking.' He snorted with laughter at the ridiculousness of the idea. 'I told him all about you, about my dad, about . . . well, everything.'

'I bet he had a good fairy laugh at all that,' she said bitterly.

'No, actually. He said his people always looked after young lovers. "Simpletons and those in love", that's what he said.' He laughed. 'Same thing, I suppose. Anyway, I told him I was going to leave town and he said not to worry, everything was going to be all right for us.'

'So where was he just?'

Lee looked troubled. 'I don't know. He's been in there every time I've been in recently. Maybe he doesn't appear if there's more than one person . . .' His voice faded away as he recognised how stupid he sounded. 'Or maybe all the stuff with Mick really has turned my brain to jelly.'

'Jelly boy!' She danced a few steps ahead before he could pinch her; instead he swore forcefully. 'Okay, okay!' she laughed. 'But there's one thing I never could quite work out as a girl. Can you really trust fairies?'

From the darkened lounge Mick Jonas watched his stepson and the Paki bitch step into the shed, obviously for a quick touch-up, and he was still watching when they headed back towards the road. He quickly switched on his mobile phone and hit the speed dial. 'They're on their way now,' he said in his thick Birmingham accent. 'Follow 'em till they're outside Brum then get 'em off the road. You can do what you like to the cunt, but just give our Lee a good fucking hiding. Teach him a lesson.' He listened to the voice on the other end for a second, then added, 'If you want to use a can of fucking petrol on her, pal, you do it.

Just make sure Lee doesn't get burned up. The old woman would kill me.'

He switched off the phone and lit a cigarette before lowering his overweight frame into the frayed armchair he had made his own. He felt a triumphant burst, that he'd got one over on his lefty, Paki-loving stepson who thought he was so fucking superior. But Mick had seen him sneak the suitcase out and store it in the boot of his old banger. He knew what the little shit was planning.

He closed his eyes and sucked deeply on the cigarette, enjoying the moment and the certain knowledge that a blow had been struck against the fucking multi-cultural society. But when he opened his eyes a moment later he was almost paralysed by shock. Through the window he could see something moving rapidly across the lawn from the bottom of the garden. He couldn't tell what it was – its shape seemed to be changing continuously and his eyes hurt from trying to pin it down – but it was horrible. The scream started deep in his throat, but it hadn't reached his mouth before the window had imploded, showering glass all around him. And then it was on him.

Maureen and Kelly returned from the local five minutes later. They tiptoed through the front door, just in case Mick was dozing after a few pints. They'd both pay the price if they woke him. But the moment she was across the threshold, Maureen had the odd feeling something was wrong. There was a strained atmosphere, like just before a storm, and an odd smell was drifting in the air. While Kelly went to the bathroom she crept into the lounge to investigate.

The first thing she saw was the broken window and felt the glass crunching underfoot. Her mind started to roll: burglars; some of those shabby youths who didn't like Mick's little club.

And then she looked into Mick's armchair and at first didn't recognise what she was seeing. It was black and smoking and resembled nothing more than a sculpture made out of charcoal. A sculpture of a man. And then she looked closer and saw what it really was, and wondered why the armchair hadn't burst into flames as well, and wondered a million and one other things all at once.

And then she screamed.

'I don't believe we did it!' Lee was bouncing up and down with excitement in his seat as the car pulled on to the M6 heading south.

'Well, your fairy told us, didn't he?' Sunita said with a giggle.

He gave her thigh a tight squeeze. 'This is about us now. We can do anything we want. We can really enjoy ourselves, just the two of us. God, I love you!'

She smiled and blew him a kiss. 'Things are strange right now, aren't they?' she said dreamily as she stared out of the passenger window into the night. 'People seeing all those weird things. You and the fairies. Uncle Mohammed having those dreams that came true.'

'Maybe it's a sign.'

'Of what?'

'I don't know. Of hope. That things are going to get better.'

She shook her head, her smile not even touching on the endless happiness she felt. 'You're a hopeless romantic.'

And the road opened up before them.

CHAPTER ONE

What now My Love

Smoke still billowed up from the ruins of the Kyle of Lochalsh across the water, sweeping a curtain of grey across the bright moon. Here and there small fires continued to burn like Will-o'-the-Wisps. The night was thick with the reek of devastation and despair, the smell of a world winding down.

Jack Churchill, known to his friends as Church, sat on the sea wall at Kyleakin next to Laura DuSantiago, and together they surveyed what little of the carnage they could make out on the mainland. It provided an odd counterpoint to the tranquillity that came from the gently lapping waves and the wind which blew through the deserted village. They were both exhausted after the nerve-racking journey across Skye in an abandoned car they had found in Kilmuir. The oppressively claustrophobic atmosphere was brought down by their fears of an ambush at every bend in the road, and magnified by the eerie stillness of the surrounding countryside, devoid of any sign of human life; it had been eradicated as easily and completely as a germ culture on a microscope slide. Nor were there any bodies; whatever the Fomorii had done with the former inhabitants did not bear considering. By the time they reached Kyleakin they had to accept that the Fomorii had deemed them too small a threat to pursue them any longer, and somehow that was even more jarring than the constant fear of attack. They were worthless.

'Well, it could be worse.' Laura brushed a stray strand of dyed-blonde hair out of her eyes as she shuffled into a more comfortable position on the wall.

Church, his dark hair emphasising the paleness of his wearied face, looked at her askance. 'How could it possibly be worse?'

'We could be going to work tomorrow.'

She kept her gaze fixed firmly across the water, but Church had learned to read the humour in her deadpan expression. Their relationship, if that was what it was, still surprised him. He wasn't quite sure how he felt about her. On the surface they had nothing in common, but deep down it seemed that something had clicked; after so long in the emotional ice-field following Marianne's death it felt good to reconnect with another human being, and the sex had been

446

great. He hoped it was more than a simple alliance forged through the desperation of terrifying times, but there was no point losing sleep analysing it; it would find its own level soon enough, he was sure of it. Cautiously he reached out and took her hand. She was so unpredictable he half-expected her to snatch it away and accuse him of being a romantic idiot, but her fingers closed around his, cool and comforting.

'Do you think the others have forgiven me for screwing up so badly?' he asked. The notion drove a pang of guilt through him.

'They didn't give it a second thought. They might look like morons, but they can see you're all right. For a dickhead. And let's face it, you only acted like a human being. One who doesn't tell his friends anything, but a human being nonetheless. Who's going to fault you for that?'

Despite her words, Church couldn't stop the guilt growing stronger. The Tuatha Dé Danann had been right in their brutal assessment of his worth; it was his own weaknesses that had dragged them down. If he had told the others about the visitations of Marianne's spirit, about the Kiss of Frost that had corrupted him and brought about the Danann's contempt, the world might have been saved.

'Did you ever hear *Beyond the Sea*?' he asked, staring into the chopping black waves.

'Is that by one of those dead, old white guys you enjoy so much? Some Sinatra shit?'

'Bobby Darin.' He didn't rise to the bait. 'It's the best metaphor for death I've ever heard. Just a simple little song, but when you think about it in those terms it becomes almost profound.' He sang a few bars: '*Somewhere beyond the sea, somewhere waiting for me, my lover stands on golden sands.* So sad, but so optimistic. I'd never really thought about it like that until just now, you know, about it talking about what lies beyond death—'

'Or it could just be a simple little song.' The comment would normally have been concluded with some note of mockery or contempt, but when none came he turned to look at her. Laura's face was still and thoughtful, and when she spoke again her voice was uncommonly hesitant. 'How do you feel?'

'What do you mean?'

'All that stuff floating around inside . . .' She was skating around the edge of an issue that was so monumental it was almost impossible to put it into perspective.

'I feel okay, under the circumstances. Different, though I'm not sure how. Sometimes I get a wave of cold when the Fomorii corruption seems to get the upper hand. Sometimes I feel like I've got liquid gold in my veins, thanks to whatever the Danann did to me. The rest of the time I just feel like me.'

'Must be a real head-fuck to die and get reborn.'

'Yes.' In his darker moments he wondered if it meant he was still human, still alive, even, in any sense that people understood. How could you die and then come back? What scars did that leave on the soul, if such a thing existed? And what did it mean for the rules that were supposed to give a structure to existence? He combatted such black thoughts by trying to consider his rebirth an opportunity to leave the past and all his weaknesses behind, to become something much more valuable. It was the only way to stop himself cracking up.

'When you died, you know, what was it like? Inside?' It was obvious Laura wasn't about to let the subject drop. Though her face remained impassive, there was a deep gravitas at the back of her eyes that showed how much the issue meant to her.

He threw his mind back to when he was lying half in the stream, his blood mingling with the water, his body racked with pain. 'Like slipping into a hot bath and just carrying on down and down.'

She nodded thoughtfully. 'And after that?'

He winced. 'I don't remember.'

'Nothing at all?'

His sigh was uncomfortable. 'Just fragments . . . nothing that makes sense. And it's all breaking up like a dream after you wake.'

'But you remember something?'

'Just something that looked like a big church.' There was a sharpness to his voice that he regretted, but couldn't control. 'Or a cathedral. Massive, going right up past the clouds. That's it.'

'Okay, I won't bug you about it any more.' She made to leave, but he caught her arm and pulled her back. She gave a wry smile. 'Getting frisky?' Before he could answer, she pushed him back off the wall and followed him down.

'You ever wonder why there aren't any bodies?' Ryan Veitch put his street-hard shoulder muscles to the rear door of the grocery shop and heaved one final time; it burst open with a crack.

'I don't want to think about that.' Ruth Gallagher looked around uncomfortably. Even though she knew they were the only ones in the area and that the laws of the land probably didn't hold much sway any longer, she still didn't feel right breaking and entering.

Veitch didn't have any such qualms. His increasingly long hair hid his expression from her as he headed through the doorway, but she could have sworn he was actually enjoying it. Inside the store her fears were confirmed when the makeshift torch illuminated his hard, handsome features; he was grinning. 'I'll be happier when the power comes back on,' he said.

'Maybe it's gone for good this time,' Ruth said morosely, as she reluctantly followed him in. Cartons of tins and breakfast cereals were piled around and it smelled warmly of fruit and bread. 'Enough of the talk. Just get the provisions we need and let's get out of here.'

'I like to talk. Anyway, who's going to rumble us here?'

Ruth pushed past him with a flick of her head that sent her long, brown hair flying. She began to fill a dustbin bag with packets of muesli. 'Perhaps we should leave a note for the owner. Tell him why we took the stuff. Offer to pay him back—'

Veitch gave a derisory snort. 'You're living in cloud cuckoo land, you. Get real. He's not coming back. None of the poor bastards are. The Fomorii have hauled them off to their larder.'

Ruth glared at him, but his words made her feel numb and she quickly returned to her petty pilfering.

Veitch helped her halfheartedly and then said out of the blue, 'Are we going to start getting on?'

'We're stuck in this together. We don't have any option.'

'That's not good enough.'

Her eyes flashed. 'Well—'

'No, listen to me. I know I've done some bad things in my life, but you can't keep on blaming me for what happened to your old man—'

'How can you say that! You shot my uncle!' As she turned to face him her elbow clipped a box of *Special K* and sent it flying across the storeroom; all the emotions which she had bottled up for so long rumbled to the surface. She fought to hold back tears that seemed to come too easily, then said, 'I'm sorry. I heard what the Danann said—'

'That's right! It wasn't my fault. They made me do it, like they made all of us suffer.'

Ruth remembered the horror she felt when the Danann explained how all five of them had been forced to experience death as some sort of preparation for the destiny that had been mapped out for them.

'I might be a stupid little two-bit crook, but I've never killed anybody in my life before!' Veitch continued. 'I'm not that kind of bloke. I wish you could know how much it screwed me up when I saw I'd shot your uncle . . .' He winced at the memory. 'Listen, all I want to do, all I've *ever* wanted to do in my life, is do something that's right, you know what I mean? Be a good guy for a change. But even when I try, it seems to go wrong. I just want a chance to show what I can do.'

His pleading was so heartfelt, Ruth couldn't help feeling sympathy.

'Because I like you,' he continued. 'I like all of you. You're all trying to do the right thing, whatever it might mean to you, and I've never been around people like that before. I don't want you all thinking bad of me all the time.'

Ruth read the emotions on his face for a long moment, then returned to her packing. 'Okay,' she said. 'I forgive you. But it's not going to be forgotten just like that—'

'I know. I just want a chance.'

'You've got it.'

She could feel him staring at her like he couldn't believe what she had said, and then he started loading up his bag with gusto. Once they'd got everything they might need for a few days, they headed back out. As they slipped away from the shadows at the back of the shop, a dark shape flashed out of the sky and circled them, drawing closer. Veitch was instantly alert, ready for defence.

'It's okay,' Ruth said. The owl, her gifted companion, glided down and landed on her shoulder; she winced as its talons bit into her flesh, then pushed her head to one side for fear it would start flapping its wings. It was the first time it had come close enough for her to touch. The owl turned its eerie, blinking eyes on Veitch, who was grinning broadly.

'What's his name?' He reached out a hand, but the owl snapped its beak in the direction of his fingers and he withdrew sharply.

'Who says it's a he?'

'Well what's *its* fucking name then?'

'It hasn't got a name.' She paused. 'Not one that I know, anyway.'

'Well, don't you think you should give him one? Or her. It. If it's going to be on the team—'

'Maybe I'll ask it later.' Her eyes sparkled.

Veitch looked at her for a second or two, but he couldn't tell if she was serious or teasing him. He decided to opt for the latter and responded in kind with a faint smirk. 'Witch.'

'Fuckhead.'

Their eyes locked for a long moment, then they burst out laughing. Turning, they threw the bags over their shoulders and marched towards the seafront.

'So what exactly can you do?' Veitch said.

Ruth shrugged. 'I don't know yet. It's like spending all your life as a man and then someone coming up to you and telling you you're actually a woman. How do you get your head round something as monumental as that? How can you comprehend you've been chosen by the gods for some task?'

'Sounds pretty cool to me. I wouldn't mind.'

'You might think differently if it actually happened to you. It's hard enough understanding that the world's changed. That different rules operate now, fundamental rules, about the way everything works. The woman I met in the Lake District—'

'The old magic-biddy?'

'The Wiccan. She'd spent years practising certain rites and not getting anywhere. Then, earlier this year, she woke up and suddenly found out things *happened*. At her command.'

'What kind of things?'

'Altering the weather. Controlling animals . . .' Ruth had a sudden flashback to the spirit-flight she experienced and was surprised at the depth of her yearning to savour it again. 'I don't think it's a matter of having any kind of power. It's just an aptitude for controlling things. Like physicists bending nuclear power to their will. You have to learn how to access it.'

'Any luck so far?'

'I haven't really tried. I'm a little nervous.'

'I read sex helps with magic.' He didn't look at her, but she could sense his grin.

'Don't go down that road. You're still on probation.'

'Okay. Just offering my services if you need me.'

'Thanks, but I'd rather put my eyes out.'

For a brief moment the wind shifted and the omnipresent stink of burning was replaced by the salty aroma of the sea and the heady tang of green hills. They both stopped and breathed deeply.

The fire roared as Tom threw on another broken dining chair, the glow painting a dull red over his wire-rimmed spectacles. Shavi sat crosslegged in front of his tent, staring deep into the flames. His long hair hung limp around his face, his perfect Asian features so still he could have been a mannequin. Wiping the sweat from his brow, Tom eyed him surreptitiously as he turned from the blaze.

'It was a terrible experience, but you gained wisdom from it.' He adjusted the elastic band holding his grey ponytail in place.

Shavi's eyes flickered, as if he were waking from a dream. 'At the moment that seems little consolation.'

'There's always a price to pay for knowledge. What you did was a great leap forward in your abilities.' Tom sat next to him, but far enough away so as not to encroach on the invisible barrier Shavi had placed around himself.

'I feel something has broken inside, deep in my head. Only I cannot tell exactly what. I simply feel different, damaged.'

'You projected your consciousness, your very self, out of your body and into an unthinking beast. It was a triumph of your shamanistic abilities. Unfortunately there will be short-term repercussions—'

'I have no wish to talk about it further.' Shavi fell silent for a few minutes, then said, 'I am sorry. I am being very insensitive. What I have experienced is nothing compared to your suffering over the centuries in Otherworld.'

'It wasn't centuries when I was there.' Tom paused. 'Although it felt like it.'

'And was the wisdom you gained from your experience worthwhile?'

Tom looked away into the night.

'What does your power of prophecy say for us, True Thomas?' Shavi lay back so he could watch the stars twinkling through the gaps in the smoke. He felt a twinge of deep regret that his experience with the serpent on the crossing to Skye had left him with such a black depression that he could no longer truly appreciate them.

'There are hard times ahead.'

'Even Ryan could have predicted that.'

'It's not as if I see the future rolled out before me like a map. There are flashes, glimpses through different windows on a winding staircase. I prefer not to say too much. Guessing at the meaning of a future image can alter the way one would react in the present.'

'Do you know who will live and who will die?' Shavi's voice floated up hollowly.

Tom remained silent.

A second later they heard the sound of the others approaching up the road from Kyleakin. Church had his arm around Laura's shoulders, while Ruth and Veitch carried the bags of provisions. They were all laughing at a joke.

'Come on, you old git. It won't ruin your image if you smile. It's not as if you're going to get any more wrinkles,' Laura shouted to Tom. He looked away haughtily.

Shavi forced a smile. 'Any fine food for dinner?'

Ruth upended her bin bag. 'Beans, fruit salad, muesli, pasta or any combination of the above.'

'Better get your cauldron on then,' Laura said to her tartly.

'There's meat for those who eat it.' Tom motioned to a brace of pheasants that lay on the outskirts of the camp.

'How the hell did you get those?' Veitch asked in amazement. He picked up one by the claws and searched for any kind of injury.

'Don't ask him that,' Church said. 'It'll just give him a chance to put on his mysterious-but-wise Yoda routine.'

'Well, meat for me.' Veitch threw the bird down. Laura wrinkled her nose in distaste.

While Tom set about preparing the birds, Ruth got out the cooking utensils they had picked up from the camping shop where they'd also, in Laura's words, *liberated* the tents. Tom jointed the pheasants with his Swiss Army Knife and they cooked quickly over the campfire, while Veitch prepared pasta and beans to accompany them.

After they'd eaten, they all sat back listening to the crackle of the fire. It was Church who spoke first, and from the way they turned to him as one he realised they had been waiting for him. 'I think,' he began, 'it's time to decide what we're going to do next.'

'Let's weigh up the options.' Church watched Ruth's face grow serious as she turned her sharp lawyer's mind to the mountainous problems that faced them.

'Rolling over and doing nothing, always a popular favourite. That's my number one.' Laura began to count off on her fingers. 'Driving off until we find a nice, secluded beach somewhere. Taking a boat and getting away across the Channel. Taking a shedload of drugs and spending whatever time we've got left blissed out.' She paused thoughtfully. 'Um. Burying our heads in the sand—'

'Or,' Veitch interrupted, 'we could do the right thing.'

'And what's that?' Laura sneered. 'Rob a building society?'

Shavi leaned forward, his eyes pools of darkness despite the firelight. 'We are Brothers and Sisters of Dragons. After all that has happened, there is no denying it. For better or worse, we, of all the people in the world, have had responsibility thrust upon us. We can no more turn our back on what is expected of us than we could on life itself.'

'Speak for yourself,' Laura sulked.

'And what *is* expected of us?' Church said, although the answer was obvious.

Shavi moistened his lips. 'To oppose the powers that threaten to drive humanity into the shadows. To shine a beacon of hope in the night. Whatever the cost.'

'Plain English,' Veitch interjected. 'To overthrow the bastards or die trying.'

Ruth raised her eyes and muttered, 'Thank you, John Wayne.'

They all fell silent for a long moment, and it was Laura who gave voice to the thought on all their minds. 'Look at us. What can *we* do?'

'I can give you all the clichés,' Church began. 'David and Goliath. The ant that moved several times its own weight—'

453

'Okay.' Laura smiled falsely. 'Now let's talk about the real world.'

'There's some way out there,' Veitch said adamantly. 'We don't have to go out in a blaze of glory like the Wild Bunch. There's guerrilla warfare. There's—'

'—different rules now,' Church said. 'Powers out there we can use. Like the artefacts we uncovered.' He still felt troubled that objects of such great power were in the hands of such an unpredictable race as the Tuatha Dé Danann.

'Guerrilla warfare,' Ruth said. 'I like that. We turn our weakness into a strength. Move fast, strike hard and be away before they can respond.'

'Excuse me? Are we living in the same world?' Laura said. 'These are things that can crush us faster than you can get on a high horse.'

'Get a spine.' Ruth turned to the others. 'We all know what's going to happen next.'

Every head dropped as one.

'Somebody's got to say it—'

'Let's not, and say we did.' Laura tried to make out it was more sour humour, but they all heard the faint undertone in her voice: fear.

Ruth looked around the circle slowly. 'They're going to try to bring Balor back. If we don't try to stop them—'

'Why us?' Laura no longer made any pretence of humour.

'But that is why we have been brought together,' Shavi said quietly. 'That is the reason why we contain this nebulous thing called the Pendragon Spirit, this thing that none of us truly understands. But it has been gifted to us so we can defend the land against this overwhelming threat.'

Laura winced. 'If you can believe all that—'

'You don't believe it?' Veitch asked sharply.

'You know what? I don't feel any different to before I met all you. You're just fooling yourselves, playing at being heroes. We're normal. Some of us, worse than normal. Weak, pathetic little shits. And the only time you're going to realise what a fantasy it is, is that second before you die in a gutter.' Her features were flinty; it was obvious she wasn't going to back down.

There was a long period of silence filled only with the crackle of the fire. Then Tom began slowly, 'It is all right to be scared of Balor. This is not some Fomorii like Calatin or Mollecht, who are frightening, but within our power to beat. As the Fomorii are to us, so Balor is to the Fomorii. He is their god, the embodiment of darkness, evil, death, chaos . . .' He shook his head slowly. 'He is more than a force of nature, he is an abstract given form: destruction. You only have my word for this, but I can see from your faces your fear goes beyond what I say. Because you know. In the furthest reaches of your worst nightmare, in the dimmest purview of your race memory, in your primal fear of the night, he lives. If Balor returns, it truly will be the end of everything.'

No one spoke. They listened to the wind whistling across the hills of Skye and somehow it seemed harsher, colder, the night too dark.

'Then we really do have no choice,' Church said.

Laura turned away so the fire didn't light her face.

'How are they going to bring him back?' Ruth asked finally.

'None of those ancient races truly die,' Tom said. 'They flitter out of this existence for a while. Time is meaningless, space insignificant. They simply need to be anchored and dragged back.' He shrugged. 'How? I have no idea. Some ritual using the powerful distillation they have been amassing which we saw in Salisbury and under Dartmoor.'

'Then we've got to stop the bastards before they start the ritual.' There was an innocent optimism in Veitch's voice that raised all their spirits slightly.

'But where will they be doing it? And when?' Ruth asked.

'The when I can answer,' Tom said. 'The ritual of birthing will not be conducted until the next auspicious date when there is a conjunction of power and intent. What the Celts named the feast of Lughnasadh, the Harvest Festival. August 1.'

'Three months.' Church mulled over this for a second or two. 'Doesn't seem very long. But we managed the unthinkable by our last deadline—'

'With no time to spare,' Tom cautioned. 'This task is far, far harder. The essence of Balor will already be contained in the birthing medium, ready for the ritual, and the Fomorii will have it hidden in their deepest, most inaccessible stronghold. To them, this thing is more valuable than anything in existence. Imagine if you held the spirit of your God? How much would you fight to protect it?'

'Do you think they've got it at that fortress we saw them building in the Lake District?' Ruth asked.

Tom shook his head. 'It will be somewhere none of their enemies will have seen, beneath ground, certainly, and protected against all eventuality.'

The wind came howling down from Sgurr Alasdair high in the Cuillin Hills, whipping up the fire so the sparks roared skywards like shooting stars. Looking up into the vast arc of the heavens, they felt suddenly insignificant, all their plans hopeless.

'Then how are we going to find it?' Ruth asked. 'If they've gone to such great pains to make it safe for them, we're not just going to stumble across it.'

Tom nodded in agreement; slowly, thoughtfully. 'We need guidance. There is a place we could go, a ritual I could conduct—'

'Then let's do it as soon as possible.' Church looked around at their faces; they were watching him with such intensity it made him feel uncomfortable. He didn't want the responsibility they were forcing on his shoulders.

'So you've decided, then.' Laura's expression hid whatever she was thinking. 'We've been lucky so far.' Her hand went unconsciously to the scars on her face. 'If you can call barely surviving luck. But sooner or later someone's going to die, and I don't intend it to be me.'

'No one wants—' But she had risen and marched off into the night before Church had a chance to finish. He sighed and waved his hand dismissively. 'We better get some sleep. We can start at first light.'

Veitch and Shavi headed off to their tents while Tom lit a joint from his rapidly diminishing block of hash and wandered off beyond the light of the campfire.

Ruth sat down next to Church, slipping a tentative arm around his shoulders to give him a comforting squeeze. 'No rest for the wicked.'

'No rest for anyone.' Church sighed. 'I wish I had some Sinatra to play. He always makes me feel good at a time like this.' Overhead a meteor shower set pinpricks of light flashing in the black gulf. 'You remember when we sat in that café after we first got dragged into all this under Albert Bridge? You asked me if I was scared. I didn't even know what the word meant then. Now every morning when I wake up, it hits me from a hundred different directions: fear of screwing up again, fear of dying, fear that the world doesn't make sense any more, that there's no secure place anywhere.' He paused a second before continuing, 'Fear of what this nightmare means on some kind of spiritual level. That there is no meaning. That we're just here as prey for whatever things are higher up the food chain than us. Fear that the whole mess doesn't even end with death.'

'You think too much.' Ruth gave him another squeeze before removing her arm. 'That morning in the café? It seems like a lifetime ago, doesn't it? I barely knew you then.'

Church looked up, unable to pinpoint the tone in her voice. She was smiling, her eyes bright in the dying firelight.

'I think you should look for meaning in the small picture, not the big one,' she continued. 'It seems stupid with all the upset and suffering, but on that micro level my life is better now than it ever was before. I was in a job I hated, just going through the motions because I knew it would have made my dad happy, not really having any idea who I was at all. Now everything in my life seems heightened, somehow. Even the smallest thing has passion in it. You know I'm not one to get poetic, but compared to how I live my life now, I was dead before. Maybe that's where the meaning lies.'

'Maybe,' he answered noncommittally, but he knew what she meant.

'And I feel like my life's been enriched for knowing you and the others. I feel closer even to the ones I don't particularly like than anyone I knew before. Maybe when the rulebook was redrawn, the dictionary was too.' She laughed at her metaphor.

'What do you mean?'

'I know what friendship means now.' Her smile slowly faded until her features were sadly introspective. 'I don't know how to say this, but at this point, with all that shit lying ahead, it seems important.'

'So what does friendship mean?' He tried to raise the mood with a smile.

'It means being prepared to lay down your life for someone.'

'If we're careful, that's something we won't even have to think—'

'Church, be realistic. If we go into this, we're not all, maybe not any of us, going to come out of it alive. You know that. Don't insult me by pretending it's not true.'

He was hypnotised by what he saw in her eyes.

'You've changed too,' she continued. 'You've grown in a lot of ways, in just a few short weeks.'

'Yeah, well, you know how it is. Pressure is the catalyst for change.'

'It's a shame we have to lose our innocence.' Although she said *we*, Church felt she was talking about him.

'You can't stay innocent and face up to sacrifice and death and war. Those bastards killed my innocence when they arranged for Marianne to die. *To forge my character*,' he added with a sneer.

'You mustn't let it eat you up.'

'I won't. I let that happen before, when I thought I was somehow complicit in Marianne's *suicide*. It's not going to happen again. I'm going to find whoever killed Marianne and I'm going to get my revenge, but I won't be *consumed* by it. This is different. It's colder, harder.' He could tell she wasn't happy about what his words implied about the change in his character, but on this subject he didn't care. 'I'm not stupid. I've read the classics and I know how revenge destroys people. But for the kind of suffering that's been caused to all of us, there has to be some kind of payback.'

The fire was starting to die down and a chill crept across the campsite, belying the summer that was just around the corner.

'What's to become of us all?' Ruth said with a troubled smile.

It was a rhetorical question, but Church felt the need to answer it nonetheless. 'We'll do the best we can and damn the consequences.'

The morning was clear and fresh. The fires on the mainland had mostly burned themselves out, but there was still the occasional tendril of smoke snaking up into the blue sky. Shavi was the first to rise and he immediately went to the sea wall to survey the stretch of water that separated Skye from the blackened ruins that remained of the Kyle of Lochalsh. Returning to the camp as the others prepared breakfast, he announced that the serpent which had patrolled the waters seemed to have departed with the Fomorii presence. Only Ruth caught the glimmer of relief in his face.

After they had eaten an unappetising breakfast of muesli and water, they found a boat on the sea front and Tom steered it across the strait to where they had abandoned their van the previous day. By 10 a.m., they were on their way north along deserted main roads. Ten miles outside of the Kyle of Lochalsh, they saw a farmer attending to hedges away on a hillside, and the further they progressed the more signs of life they encountered, until it seemed the devastation they had encountered was just an aberration.

When they stopped at a pub in Achnasheen for lunch, they were chased away by the landlord and some irate locals. The explanation came at an old-fashioned garage further along the road. When the owner shuffled out to fill their tank, checked cap raised over a ruddy face, he told them of a rumour circulating in the area that the Government's imposition of martial law and the censorship of the media was to prevent panic because a plague was loose in the country; what kind of plague, no one was quite sure. He didn't believe it himself. The view among his own particular group was that the 'bastard politicians' had finally been overcome by their innate corruption and were using a manufactured crisis as a smokescreen to get rid of the democratic process. It had all started with the gun laws, he said. The tragedy at Dunblane was the excuse, but the weapons had really been controlled to prevent an armed uprising. But, he said conspiratorially, a few landowners had held on to their shotguns and were stockpiling them for use 'when the soldiers come'. At this, he decided he had said too much and took their money in silence before retreating to his dusty shack.

The further north they travelled, the more the people seemed to be untroubled by everything that was happening. They stopped at one farm for supplies of milk, bacon and eggs, only to discover the farmer's wife who served them knew nothing of the martial law. 'We don't have a telly,' she said in her thick Highlands accent, 'and we're too busy to listen to the radio.'

The final leg of the journey took them on a road that was straight as a die through the Beinn Eighe nature reserve, where pine trees and gorse clustered hard against the road. The wildness of this no man's land made them all uncomfortable; they felt as if humanity had been driven out by an angry, hateful nature for all the crimes it had committed; the new occupants were more respectful of nature's rules, and unforgiving of anyone who dared venture back into that dark, green domain. Sometimes strange movements could be glimpsed among the shadows beneath the trees; occasionally the quietness was disturbed by cries that came from no bird or animal they could recognise.

The oppressiveness eased slightly when the road took them along the banks of Loch Maree, which was so clear and still it looked like the sky had been brought down to earth. The scenery all around was breathtaking. Across the loch, the banks rose up sharply to soaring, rocky hillsides which were dappled by purple cloud shadows interspersed with brilliant patches of sunlight. From the top, white waterfalls cascaded down gloriously.

Soon after they arrived at Gairloch, a small fishing village perched on the edge of a sheltered sea loch. It was a balmy late afternoon with the seagulls screeching overhead and the smell of the day's catch mingling with the salty aroma of seaweed all along the harbour front. Boats sat up on trailers everywhere, but only the gentle lapping of the waves disturbed the lazy atmosphere.

After parking the van overlooking a tiny jetty, Veitch clambered out and stretched his muscles before turning to survey the thickly wooded slopes all around. 'I thought we were driving up to the bloody top of the world. Who the hell are we supposed to be seeing up here?'

Ruth turned her face to the warmth of the sun. 'Come on, Tom. You've kept us in suspense all day.'

'You know, the old git only does it because he knows if he tells us everything we'll dump him in the nearest rest home.' Laura adjusted her sunglasses, studiously avoiding Tom's fierce glare.

'You'll wait until the time's right,' he said icily. 'If you had a little patience and started listening a little more, you might actually gain a little wisdom. We won't be doing anything until sunset so you may as well make yourself busy.'

They unloaded the camping equipment and split it between them before setting off on foot along a valley that ran up into the hills. They walked for two hours until they were exhausted, continually scanning among the trees for any sign of danger. When they broke above the treeline they pitched camp on the sunlit, grassy slopes, admiring the amazing views across the wildly beautiful countryside. After lighting a fire Shavi cooked the bacon and eggs and prepared beans on toast for Laura, which they devoured hungrily after their exertion.

Tom avoided all their questions in his usual irritatingly brusque manner until the sun started to ease towards the horizon, and then he marshalled them and led them across the slopes and around rocky outcroppings where the only sound was the whistle of the wind. Finally they mounted a bank and looked down on the remnants of a stone circle.

It was only identifiable as a henge at close inspection; to the cursory observer the arrangement of rocks looked almost natural, an illusion that was added to by the few recumbent stones which had not survived the passing of the centuries. Set on the grassy plain, with a vista across the forested landscape towards the setting sun, they could fully under-stand why their ancestors had located it in that spot; there was a sense of awe from simply being there with only nature all around. A respect-ful silence came over them the instant they laid eyes on it and, auto-matically, they all bowed their heads in respect. When they were just a few feet away, Church dipped down and stretched out his fingers to the short grass. A blue spark leapt up from the earth to his fingertips and disappeared up his arm.

'It's true,' Ruth said. 'Can you feel it?'

Shavi closed his eyes and put his head back beatifically. 'Yes. The earth power.'

'A few weeks ago I didn't feel a thing in any of these old sites. Now I've got a tingling in my legs, my hands.' Ruth looked round curiously. 'A feeling of—'

'Well-being,' Tom interrupted. 'The Pendragon Spirit within you has grown stronger through your experiences. The spirit and the earth power come from the same source. Naturally, you sense an affinity.'

'If the spirit inside us grows stronger, where will it end?' Shavi asked with an expression of wonder.

Tom smiled enigmatically. 'Millennia ago, when the blue fire pulsed through the arteries of the earth, all men experienced what you feel now. And perhaps they will again. Once you have awakened the sleeping king.'

They processed into the centre of the circle and looked around. All was silent apart from the breeze humming in their ears. The sun was fat and scarlet on the horizon, about to tip below the distant hills, the sky red at the lowest point, merging through purple to dark blue.

'There's no one anywhere near here,' Veitch protested. 'We just going to sit around till somebody turns up?'

'No,' Tom replied. 'We are going to summon the *Gruagaich* and petition them for aid.'

There was suspicion in all their faces, to which Church gave voice. 'We've had enough of being manipulated by any supernatural force that happens to cross our path—'

'Don't worry,' Tom interjected sharply. 'This time we turn to our own.'

'What do you mean?'

Tom motioned to the stones. 'This has been a place of summoning for as long as people have settled in the area. You see that stone over there? It is the *clach na Gruagaich*, one of several by that name scattered around Scotland. This site is hardly known by anyone outside the locals, who would leave an offering in its hollow for the spirits they knew could be contacted here – mainly milk, for protection of the cattle. They believed the spirits were brownies or some other *daoine-sith*.' He smiled contemptuously. 'The *good neighbours*, their euphemistic term for the beings of Otherworld, or Elfame as they called it. Faerie.'

'But they weren't?'

'No. The clue is in the name. *Gruagaich. Long-haired ones.*' He watched the sun for a long moment. Only a thin arc was visible now above the silhouetted hills. 'The first among the old tribes. The people who took up the mantle of the power discovered by the ones who put up these stones. The Celts.'

After a long pause, Veitch said doubtfully, 'You're going to talk to ghosts?'

'We will summon the Celtic dead,' Tom stated emphatically.

Ruth's brow knit. 'What can they know that could help us?'

'In the spirit world, all vistas are open. And these are not just any spirits. They are linked to you through time, the first Brothers and Sisters of Dragons.'

Tom's words sent a shiver running through all of them just as the sun slipped completely below the horizon and darkness swept across the land. But a second later, a cloud drifted away and the moon cast its silver light on the circle, limning every stone, throwing long shadows across the grass.

'It's time,' Tom said.

From his left pocket, he took a plastic bag which appeared to contain

461

pieces of twig and dried vegetable matter. 'The sacred mushroom,' he said.

'You're a regular drugstore.' Laura's normally confident tones were softened by apprehension. 'I know where to come when I want to get blasted.'

Tom ignored her. He took a handful of the psychoactive mushrooms from the bag and moved among them, placing small quantities in their mouths. They chewed the rubbery, metallic-tasting pieces and swallowed with distaste.

Tom ingested several himself, then took out the battered tin in which he kept his hash and meticulously constructed a joint. When he was done, he lit it and inhaled before walking over to the altar stone. There, he blew out the smoke gently. It rose like a ghost in the moonlight. Using his lighter, he charred the edge of the remaining hash and crumbled some of it into the hollow on the stone. Then, head bowed, he took a few paces back and sat cross-legged, drawing the pungent smoke deep inside him.

Veitch and Laura shifted uneasily, but Shavi, Church and Ruth were overcome by an atmosphere of sanctity. On some level they couldn't quite comprehend, they sensed a change begin to take place around them, as if the air itself were growing heavier, filled with the weight of what was to come. Church swallowed and tasted iron filings in his mouth; his heart began to beat faster as a tingling sensation ran from his groin along his spine to his head. He wondered how much was the drugs and how much was actually happening.

It felt like they waited for an age, feeling the wind gently brush their skin, filled with the summery scent of the warm pine forests. But then they noticed a distant movement away in the night. Initially it seemed to be only moonshadows on the rolling terrain, except it became too insistent; the blurred edges of the shadows hardened, the undulating movement became more defined into smaller units. Slowly, Church scanned the area, squinting to draw form from the gloom. Another shiver ran through him when the images finally took shape.

Figures were separating themselves from the landscape in a wide arc, advancing slowly on the stone; he estimated there must have been about a hundred of them, mostly men, but some women. At first they were just silhouettes against a lighter dark, but in their eerie, silent advance, details began to emerge. Long, dark hair; skin that was swarthy where visible but in the main covered by what appeared to be mud, as if they had camouflaged themselves for guerrilla warfare; with the furs and hides that kept them warm and the way they moved, in a low, loping way, they resembled some odd half-beast creatures.

Finally they came to a halt thirty feet from the stone. The breeze blew among them, rustling hair and furs, but they were so unmoving in the gloom they merged with the stones and the outcropping rocks. It was impossible to discern their faces; pools of shadows filled their eye sockets, leaving Church and the others with the horrible sensation that if the shadows cleared, there would be no eyes there at all. The night was suddenly alive with anxiety and danger; Church knew in some instinctive way that however insubstantial the revenants appeared, they were not passive creatures; he couldn't shake the feeling that, with the wrong word or movement, they would attack. From the corner of his eye he could see the others staring at Tom, silently urging him to break the oppressive mood.

After what felt like an age, Tom rose to address the dark assembly; he held out his hands in the universal sign of friendly greeting.

'What do you want, teacher?'

The voice seemed to be in Church's head. The words rumbled with a strange accent, but they were clearly modern English, although he couldn't begin to understand how the communication was taking place. One of the figures moved out of the mass. He didn't appear to walk; it was almost as if, in the blink of Church's eyelid, the figure had shifted forwards several feet. There was nothing about him that signified he was a leader or spokesman.

'We come in this time of crisis to call upon your great wisdom, revered ancestor.' Tom's head was slightly bowed in respect.

'It must be a matter of import to summon us back from the Grim Lands.' There was a worrying note in the words, but then the speaker inclined his head slightly towards Church and the others and his tone became more respectful. 'I sense in these the shimmering blue fire of the Great Mother Bridgit.'

'They are Brothers and Sisters of Dragons.'

The Celt bowed his head. 'The fire of life has found a good home.'

Church felt a sudden surge in his heart. In the Celt's words was a regard and acceptance that cut through his own fears about his abilities.

'In our hearts and spirits, we make our offerings,' Tom continued. 'Will you hear me?'

'We know you too, brother. Your kind administered to us from the sacred groves. It is good to know the lore survives the years. We will hear you.'

Church saw the tension go out of Tom's shoulders. 'You will be aware, as in the first days, that there is darkness on the land and blood in the wind. The Fomorii have returned.' A tremor seemed to run through the throng; Church's heightened senses felt a wave of threat.

'They wish to trap the people in the Eternal Night. That must never happen again. We can no longer rely on the comfort of the Children of Danu. But, as in your days, though the arm is weak, the heart is strong. Yet, still, we need something more to aid us in our struggle. Guide us with your wisdom.'

There was a moment of hanging tension when Church thought the spirits weren't going to answer. Then: 'You must find the Luck of the Land if you are ever to unleash the true power of the people.'

'What is the Luck of the Land?'

Silence; just the soughing of the wind. Tom chewed on his lip. 'Then tell me this, I beseech you: in the Grim Lands, all existence is laid out before you. Where is the Fomorii nest where Balor will be reborn?'

'The Heart of Shadows will rejoin this world betwixt here and there, but he will find his home where the Luck of the Land is kept.'

Church could sense Tom fighting with his normally irritable nature at their opaque answers, but the Rhymer knew a word out of line would not only ruin their opportunity to discover more information, it could prove fatal to them. The spirits may once have been kin, Church thought, but their time in what they called the Grim Lands had changed them immeasureably; he didn't want to antagonise them at all. Cautiously scanning the massed ranks for any sign of attack, he saw a shape that seemed familiar. It was only a fleeting glimpse of a profile against the starlit sky, but it struck a chord with him. He lost it almost instantly and before he had chance to seek it out again, Tom's measured tones distracted him.

'Revered ancestors, is there any guidance you can give us which will aid us in our great task? Anything at all?'

'Wise teacher, in my words lies your salvation. You require more? Then heed this: for the source of threat, look within as well as without. For direction, follow your hearts south to the city of the Well of Fire. For success in battle, cleanse the darkness from the spirit of your chieftain. And remember this: an ally already stands tall among the Children of Danu. Treat him with respect to keep his comfort close. Now, your offering was gratefully received, but it will buy no more of my patience. If you require anything else, you must pay for it with a life. Do you wish to proceed?'

Suddenly, the arc of Celts seemed too close, ready to cut off any retreat. As Church looked round, they seemed to waver like an image in a heat haze and for a moment he sensed something very like hunger; anxiety began to turn to fear deep in the pit of his stomach.

'Revered ancestor, we have been enlightened by your wisdom,' Tom began. 'And we offer our gracious thanks for your time. We shall delay you no more. We wish you well on your return to the Grim Lands.'

The Celt who had addressed them lowered his head slightly in parting and, for the briefest instant, the shadows that covered his eyes seemed to clear; what Church glimpsed there made his mind squirm and he had to stop himself fleeing back to the campfire.

It was several minutes after the Celts had melted back into the landscape before anyone spoke. It was as if they were coming out of a dream, one tinged with incipient menace where strange truths had been made known, so strange that they could barely be comprehended upon awakening. The feeling was heightened when they realised they could only hazily remember what they had seen, although the words still rang out in their minds.

'Did we actually experience that, or was it the mushrooms?' Ruth asked. Church saw she was gripping her hands together to prevent them shaking.

'A little of both,' Tom replied.

Shavi nodded in agreement. 'The mushrooms are the key to opening the doors of perception.'

Tom smiled suddenly. 'I remember seeing Jim Morrison perform in Florida—'

'Most old gits talk about the war,' Laura interrupted. 'We get reminiscences of the happy hippie trail. Now can we get back to the fire – it's freezing out here.'

Veitch pulled out a bottle of single malt he'd found in the grocery store on Kyleakin and they drank it from plastic cups around the fire.

'So, correct me if I'm wrong, but that was just a load of cryptic bollocks that wasted our time, right?' Although Laura sat next to Church, she was careful not to make the others feel uncomfortable by showing any sign of her affection for him, though Church had sensed an obvious proprietary instinct in the way she had taken her seat just as Ruth was walking up.

Tom shook his head. 'They didn't make it easy for us, but all the information they offered is vital.'

'Except we probably won't crack the code until it's too late,' Church noted. 'What's the Luck of the Land?'

'I have no idea. The Celts believed it was dangerous to name a sacred thing by its true name, which is why these exercises end up in irritating circumlocution.' Tom took a deep swig of the whisky and then said tartly, 'But we can pull some pearls from the verbal ordure. The city of the Well of Fire is Edinburgh. There's an extinct volcanic feature in the city called Arthur's Seat.'

'More Arthurian code for a site linked to the earth power?' Church mused.

'It's a very powerful source, the most powerful in Scotland. The Well lies under Arthur's Seat.'

'Then that's where we've got to go. Shouldn't take too long from here.' Veitch lay back with his hands behind his head.

'The ally is obviously Cernunnos.' Ruth examined the mark that had been burned into the flesh of her hand by the nature god. She had a sudden flashback to the rainswept night in Manorbier, the terrifying power she had seen in the being as its body melted and changed like oil on water.

'Your ally,' Veitch noted. 'You're his big pal.'

'As long as I'm with you, he's with you. But how are we supposed to show him *respect*?'

'These beings,' Shavi mused, 'seem to expect deference from those beneath them in the hierarchy of power.'

'I'll just tug my forelock in front of the toffs,' Veitch sneered. 'Blimey, talk about things being the same all over.'

'The Celts rightly believed islands were prime places for carrying out rituals,' Tom stated. 'Not far from here, in Loch Maree, there's an island called Eilean Maree, with a sacred grove dedicated to the Tuatha Dé Danann, where we can make an offering to—'

'How do you know all these things, *wise teacher*?' Laura asked pointedly.

Shavi eyed Tom incisively. 'Tom knows all of the lore of the Celts, is that not right? You told us you were tutored by the people of the Bone Inspector—'

'And so the knowledge of being a freak is passed down,' Laura sniffed.

'And the Bone Inspector spoke of his people, an unbroken line of guardians of the *old places* stretching back through history,' Shavi continued.

Church threw another branch on the fire. 'Well, we all know what cleansing the darkness from the chieftain means,' he added sombrely, 'though a little guidance on how to go about it wouldn't have gone amiss.'

'There was one other thing,' Ruth said. 'What did *for the source of the threat, look within as well as without* mean?'

'As if you don't know.' Laura stared deep into the heart of the fire. 'It means one of us is looking to earn thirty pieces of silver.'

After the others had retired to their tents, Church and Laura sat warming themselves by the dying embers. In the midst of all the chaos and tension, Church felt remarkably comforted to have Laura curled up next to him. With his arm around her and her head on his shoulder, the emotional closeness to another human filled him with a sense of well-being.

'This is what it's all about,' he muttered to himself.

'You're talking to yourself again.'

Although they were entwined, Laura still seemed a little stiff and distant. He had started to strip away the many defences she had erected to protect herself, but he knew it would be a long time before she gave her inner self up freely. In fact, the more he got to know her, the more he felt the acid-tongued, confident, aggressive Laura was a character that had been completely constructed, and whatever lay within was something he might not recognise at all. But that sense of protecting the vulnerable heart of their being was something they shared, and possibly what had attracted them in the first place.

'So this Marianne must have been a big thing in your life,' she said after a long period of introspection.

'We'd been together a long time. We were going to get married. So, yes, she was a big thing.'

'I suppose that explains why you were knocked so out of whack when she died. Do you think you'll ever get over it?'

'I don't think anybody ever gets over something like that. You just learn to accommodate it.'

She thought about this for a moment, then said, 'What was she like?'

'Oh, I don't know—'

'Go on, I want to know. Was she a good person?'

'I suppose. I never really thought of her like that. She was pretty much a malice-free zone. But she had her bad qualities – who doesn't?'

'Yeah, right. But it's a balancing act, isn't it? There aren't any real goodies or baddies. Most people manage to keep that scale just right, a little bit up, a little bit down, over the course of a life. And just a few go up one side or the other.' She dug him sharply in the ribs with her elbow. 'Christ, it's like getting blood out of a stone with you.'

'I think that's a black kettle and pot situation.' He sighed. 'She was smart. She read a lot. She liked to talk about ideas, about things that mattered. She made me laugh. She took the piss out of me when I was being pompous. She didn't take the piss out of me when I was talking about a list of dreary finds from some boring dig in Somerset. She could argue the case for northern soul when I was banging on about guitar music. She'd watch *Star Wars* with me and wouldn't beg me to watch *Jean de Florette* with her. And she allowed me to be weak.' He paused, feeling the rawness of some of the emotions that were surfacing. '*Life's good as long as you don't weaken* – that's a pretty good rule of thumb. We all have to keep up a resilient front, but you know you've found someone good when you can let the barriers down to show that weak, pathetic, character-destroying side of you, that part that you have to let out every now and then or go mad, but you normally have to do in the privacy of your room.' He took a deep breath and let it out slowly. 'Is that good enough for you?'

'It'll do. For now.'

'Why did you want to know? For the sake of comparison?'

'No. What's gone is gone. That doesn't bother me. But you can find out a lot about someone from the way they view the love of their life.'

Her words made him give pause. 'Very lateral thinking. So what did you find out?'

'You don't think I'm going to tell you, do you?'

'Okay. Tell me about the love of your life.'

She laughed. 'You must think I'm a real sucker. Sorry, pal, my past is a closed book.'

He pulled her in tight and gave her scalp a monkey scrub.

'Ow! Just because you can't compete with my intellect.' She pinched him hard until Veitch hollered from the depths of his tent for them to be quiet. Then they giggled like schoolchildren and continued their conversation in hushed tones.

'So,' Church said eventually, 'do you and I get a happy ending, do you think?'

There was a long pause that surprised him, and when he looked up at her face he saw the humour had drained from it. 'Come on, Church, you're a big boy now. Look around you. There aren't going to be any happy endings.'

Church sighed. 'Why's everyone so pessimistic? Ruth said something similar.'

'Yeah, I knew she'd been talking to you. Well . . . maybe it's a chick thing. You boys have no perception. No happy endings. We just have to make the most of what we've got for as long as we've got it.' There was a note of deep sadness in her voice, but a second later she had forced herself to brighten and was tugging him towards the tent. 'Come on. I want my brains removing and you've got just the tool to do it.'

CHAPTER TWO

turn Off Your mind, Relax, and float downstream

'It's beautiful.' Pressing her face against the window, Ruth looked out at the tranquil expanse of Loch Maree. The water was as glassy as it had been the previous day, reflecting the overcast sky punctured by bursts of blue and the hillsides that soared up steeply in a breathtaking wall of brown, purple and green. In the centre of the water lay Eilean Maree, serene and secret among its thick trees.

It had taken them only twenty-five minutes from Gairloch after a hearty breakfast of farmhouse bacon and eggs. They were all eager to continue on to Edinburgh and civilisation, but Tom had convinced them that a brief pause to make an offering to Cernunnos would pay dividends in the long run.

'I've got some reservations about this,' Church said as they parked up on the water's edge. 'Making an offering is a tacit admission that we accept they're our gods rather than simply beings that are more powerful than us. I have no intention of doffing my cap and being fawning—'

'Even if it means saving your life?' Tom interrupted.

Church radiated defiance. 'Even then. I'm not bowing down. I'm not folding up and showing my throat—'

'Then don't see it as an offering. See it as a bribe.' Tom marched off across the pebbles to a small boat that had been pulled up on the bank.

Veitch rowed Laura, Ruth and Tom over first, then came back for Shavi and Church. The island was small and rocky along the shoreline, but heavily wooded with a thick undergrowth. They moved cautiously away from the light at the banks to the shadows that lay beneath the leafy covering. There was a tangible atmosphere of peace which put them at ease; it reminded Shavi of the aura of calm that hung over the grounds of Glastonbury Abbey. Yet despite the idyllic setting, no birds sang at all.

Tom led them through the trees to the tip of the island. In a grove, out of sight of the road, an obvious altar had been created from a tree stump. Wild flowers lay on it, along with a cup of milk and the remnants of a loaf of bread. The air of sanctity was at its most concentrated in the altar's vicinity.

'Looks like someone's been here before us,' Church noted.

'The power that Cernunnos represents didn't die away when the old gods left,' Tom replied. 'In places away from the cities there's been an unbroken chain of worship. Some people are still close to the land. Some refuse to forget.'

'Fuckin' nutters,' Veitch muttered.

'And there's the arrogance of the urban dweller.' Tom pressed his spectacles back on to the bridge of his nose, a mannerism which Church recognised as a sign of irritation. 'I thought you would have learned by now not to judge by surface. Whales move in deep water and leave no mark of their passing.'

'Whales?' Veitch said distractedly. 'What the fuck are you talking about?'

They stood in front of the altar for a moment, deep in thought. Then Ruth said, 'I want to make an offering too.'

Church looked at her in surprise, but Tom said, 'As you choose. You must respond to your feelings.'

High in the branches above them echoed a long, mournful hoot which seemed to come in response. Church picked out Ruth's owl looking down at them. 'Your familiar seems to be happy about that.' He had a sudden twinge of uneasiness when he glanced back at Ruth; he couldn't shake the feeling she was being sucked into something she couldn't control.

'What would make a good oblation, I wonder?' Shavi asked.

'Something important to us,' Tom replied.

Shavi searched in his pocket for the few remaining magic mushrooms which he used to induce his shamanistic trances. Church thought he laid them on the altar with undue gratitude.

While the others discussed the offering, Laura drifted away. She had little interest in what they were doing, certainly little belief, and sometimes she was overcome by an abiding need to be on her own, alone with her thoughts; since they had joined forces there had been little opportunity for that.

She leaned on one of the trunks and looked through the trees, watching the rippling waves sparkle in the scant sunlight. The place made her feel good in a way she hadn't really experienced before; it was so peaceful she wouldn't have complained if they'd decided to pitch camp there for a few days, maybe even longer.

It was only when the tranquility blanketed her that she realised how anxious she always felt, a constant buzz that set her teeth on edge and locked her shoulder muscles. Gradually, though, the stress began to ease away, and the droning voices of the others slipped into dim awareness.

It stayed that way for long enough that she felt a wash of damp emotion when she realised something had changed. It took her a second or two to grasp what it was: no one was speaking in the background. An unsettling tingle started at the base of her spine. Her first thought was that they had all stopped talking to stare at her. She prepared an acid response and turned to confront them.

She was surprised and unsettled to see they were still standing in the same position, unmoving; a deep unnatural silence lay over them. They weren't holding their breath, or listening for something. Everyone was frozen, hands mid-gesture, mouths poised in question or response, as if time had stopped in that one small spot.

Laura felt a chill creep over her. A change had come to the soothing atmosphere on the island too; it was now heavy with anticipation.

Something's coming, she thought, without quite knowing how she had recognised that.

Her eyes darted among the trees. The island wasn't so big that someone could creep up on them unannounced; they would have heard *something*. As if in answer to her thought, she *did* hear a sound. Branches cracked, leaves rustled suddenly. She spun round quickly, her heart hammering.

Light and shadow changed on the periphery of her vision. It could have been an illusion caused by her blinking, but, coupled with the sound, she was sure: something big was lumbering around in the trees. But whenever she tried to pin it down among the undergrowth it had already moved on to somewhere else. She caught a flicker of a silhouette, then gone. A heavy footstep that sounded only feet away, then another one near the water's edge.

She backed up hastily to the others, tugged at Church's arm in the hope of somehow waking him, but when her fingers brushed his skin, it felt as cold as marble. Something like a stone seemed to grow in her throat. She crouched down to lower herself below the line of sight, then moved forward through the vegetation. If she could get to the boat, she could row out on to the water and reassess the situation, possibly go around the island until she could get a good view of what she was up against. Either that, or she could just run back to the van and drive off.

But the moment she was away from the tiny clearing surrounding the altar, things became even more confusing. Sounds were distorted by the undergrowth, the shape began to move faster, its thrashing becoming more animal-like. Anxiety knotted in her chest. She put her head down and dashed, but she hadn't gone far when her foot caught on a branch which she was convinced hadn't been there before. She went sprawling; the impact knocked the wind out of her. As she attempted to scramble back to her feet, a dark shape loomed above her like a cloud moving across the sun. Cold, unforgiving. She glanced up into a face which registered for only the merest instant before her consciousness winked out under the protest of an incomprehensible, alien sight.

When she came round, Church was crouching next to her. The others had gathered a few feet away, watching her with concern.

'Stop looking at me,' she snapped.

'What happened?' Church asked.

'There was something here, in the trees.' As her thoughts whizzed, she became aware of a dull ache on the back of her right hand. She raised it slowly, turning it until she located the right spot. Burned into the flesh was a familiar design: interlocking leaves in a circle.

Laura's attention snapped on to Ruth who was staring in shock at the tattoo. It matched the one she carried: the mark of Cernunnos delivered to her after the confrontation in Wales.

'Get a grip. It doesn't make us sisters.' Laura rubbed her hand, obscuring the sign.

'It looks as if our great nature god has decided to honour two of our number,' Shavi said thoughtfully.

'He told me there were two of us.' Ruth looked at Laura curiously.

'What's the matter? Can't believe you're not *special* any more?' Laura let Church haul her to her feet, then quickly thrust her hand into her trouser pocket. 'So does this mean I'm going to be a witch-bitch too?'

'It simply means,' Tom said, 'that Cernunnos has some plan for you.'

'That's a relief,' Laura said sourly. 'I thought it was something bad.'

They rowed back across the water in silence. Laura seemed even more locked-off than normal, ignoring all their attempts to get her to talk about her experience, but they could see it lay on her shoulders like a rock. Church, who probably understood her the best – and even then, not very well at all – saw something in her eyes that made him want to take her on one side and hold her; it was a look that suggested she was ready to run from something with which she could no longer cope.

As they gathered at the water's edge, mulling over what the encounter meant, Shavi glanced towards the van and raised the alarm. They all scrambled over the rocks as one, but Church was the first one to reach it, not quite believing what he was seeing. On the bonnet was a dead rabbit, its blood trickling down towards the radiator grille. It had been gutted, the stomach cavity splayed to the air, its internal organs carefully laid out beside it.

'What the fuck's this?' Veitch said in disgust.

Shavi stepped forward and examined the carcass without touching it. 'It was left for us particularly,' he said after a brief moment. 'You can see the precise nature of the cuts. Someone took the time to do this.'

'Is it linked to what happened on the island?' Ruth asked.

Tom shook his head. 'I wouldn't think—'

'Wait!' Shavi leaned forward to peer into the stomach cavity. 'There is something in here.'

'Don't touch it,' Ruth pleaded.

Church watched her from the corner of his eye; she seemed unnaturally fearful, as if she were sensing something without being aware of it. 'Be careful,' he cautioned.

Shavi looked around until he located two twigs which he held like chopsticks. Cautiously he used them to investigate the rabbit's interior. A second later he retracted what at first appeared to be a small pink slug smeared in blood.

'That is gross!' Laura screwed up her face, but couldn't tear her eyes away.

It was a finger, severed at the knuckle.

Shavi laid it on the bonnet and they all gathered round, as if they expected it to move. 'Who could it belong to?' Shavi mused. 'And why was it left here for us?'

Veitch scanned the deserted hillsides, which were suddenly unwelcoming and lonely. 'We should be getting out of here.'

The grisly discovery cast a pall over their journey south. For the first few miles they travelled without speaking, struggling to make sense of it all, feeling a deep dread creeping out of the mystery. There was something about the image that was inherently evil, ritualistic, beyond mere threat. Yet it made no sense, and it was that which wormed its way into their subconscious and lay there, gnawing silently.

They picked up the A9 just north of Inverness and followed it south through the rugged, desolate landscape of the Cairngorms. Two technology crashes slowed them up and it soon became apparent they would be searching for somewhere to stay in Edinburgh by the time the curfew came around. The best option seemed to be to break their journey and set off for the city fresh and early the next day. So, hungry and bored with the road, they arrived in the small town of Callander at the foot of the Highlands in the late afternoon.

The jumbled collection of stone buildings nestled so hard against the thickly wooded foothills that, with the mountains soaring up in the background all around, they felt instantly enveloped and protected; it was a pleasant sensation after all the wide open spaces. The town smelled of fish and chips and pine, but that too was oddly soothing. A lot more people were wandering around than they had seen for days, their faces free of the taint of fear. It gave hope that the major centres of population still hadn't been too affected.

It was a long time since they had experienced the comfort of a soft bed so they opted to spend the night in a hotel. The Excelsior lay at the end of the main street, a Gothic-styled pile of stone that resembled a fortress with its turrets on four corners and enormous windows looking out on all sides. The thick, wild forest swept down almost to the very back of it, but it still seemed a place that could be secure.

While the others rested or abluted, Church and Veitch went down to the hotel bar. It was comfortingly cool and dark away from the bright afternoon sun and had the cosy feel of a place which had grown organically rather than been designed to fit the frenzied drive for increased profits. Veitch had a Stella, Church a Guinness, and they took their drinks to a table in a window bay where they could look out on to the sun-drenched main street.

'It's the little things I'm going to miss,' Veitch said introspectively.

'What do you mean?'

'Like this.' He held up the pint so it glowed golden in a sunbeam. 'If things carry on falling apart, we're not going to keep getting things like this, are we? It won't be important. All the bigshots will be making sure everyone just has enough food, trying to keep the riots to a minimum.'

Church laughed quietly. 'So that's your motivation, is it? Fight for the pint?'

'No,' Veitch replied indignantly, missing the humour. 'It's just the little things that bring all this shit home. You look out there and you can almost believe everything's the same as it always was. But it's right on the brink of going belly-up. How long do you think it's got?'

Church shrugged. 'Depends how soon the Fomorii and the Tuatha Dé Danann start flexing their muscles and really screwing things up. Maybe they'll leave us alone enough to carry on with some kind of normality.' Even to himself, he didn't sound very convincing.

There was a long pause while they both sipped their beer and then Veitch said, 'You know what those spooks said. About one of us being a snake in the grass. It isn't me, you know.' He looked at Church uncomfortably. 'Because with my past record, I know that's what everyone's going to be thinking.'

'I don't think that's true, Ryan.'

'Don't get me wrong, I don't blame them. Everything I've ever done points in that direction. I'm just saying. It's not me.' His gaze shifted away as he asked, 'Do you believe me? It's important that you believe me. The others, I don't—' He held back from whatever he was about to say.

Church thought for a moment, then replied, 'I believe you.'

Veitch's shoulders relaxed and he couldn't restrain a small, relieved smile which crept around the lip of his glass. He finished the lager with a long draught. 'All right, then. Who do you think it is?'

'It's hard to believe any of us could be some kind of traitor. I think I'm a pretty good judge of human nature and I don't see anything that makes me even slightly suspicious.'

'The old hippie sold us down the river once.'

'But that wasn't his doing. Anyway, that's been sorted out. Once the parasite was removed from his head he was back to normal.'

Veitch leaned back in his seat and rested one foot on a stool. 'You reckon they were making it up then?'

'Not making it up exactly. It seems to me that whenever any information comes over from some supernatural source, it's never quite how you think it is. They're saying one thing, you hear another. I think they do it on purpose, another power thing,' he added with weary exasperation.

'Well, I'm going to be watching everyone very carefully.'

'That's what I'm worried about. I don't want paranoia screwing things up from within. There's enough of a threat outside.'

An old man with a spine curved by the years and a face that was little more than skin on bone shuffled in and cast a curious glance in their direction before making his way to the bar. He was wearing a checked, flat cap and a long brown overcoat, despite the warmth of the day. Pint in hand, he headed towards a seat in a shadowy corner, then seemed to think twice and moved over to the table next to them.

'Mind if I sit here?' His accent had the gentle, lilting quality of the Highlands, his voice steady, despite his appearance. Once he'd settled, he glanced at them with jovial slyness. 'Out-of-towners?'

'We're travelling down to Edinburgh,' Church said noncommittally.

'On holiday?'

'Something like that.'

The old man sipped his beer thoughtfully. 'You wouldn't happen to know what's going on in the world, would you?'

'What do you mean?'

'With the papers all printing junk and the TV and the radio playing the same old rubbish from the Government, you can't get any news worth hearing. It's got to be something bad to shut down the TV. We

475

always get lots of tourists travelling through here from the cities, but there's been nary a soul over the last few days. So what have you seen?'

Church wondered how he could begin to explain to the man what was happening; wondered if he should. Veitch interjected before he could reply, 'All seems pretty normal to me, mate.'

'Aye, that's what everyone round here is saying. Oh, there was a bit of panic when those Government messages started repeating, but once the police went round calming everyone down and we all saw it wasn't the end of the world, everyone carried on as normal.' He chuckled. 'What are we going to do with us, eh?'

'So what do you think's happening?' Church asked.

'Aye, well,' the old man rubbed his chin, 'that's the question. Like I say, at the moment it doesn't seem too bad. Oh, there's a few things you can't seem to get in the shops, but there's talk they might be rationing petrol—'

'Oh?' Church glanced at Veitch, both aware of the problems that might arise if their ability to travel was hampered.

'Aye. So they say. Could be shortages. And the phone's off more than it's on. It's awful hard trying to find out what's happening in the next village, never mind in the cities.' He looked at Church and Veitch with a tight smile. 'Reminds me of the war.'

Church glanced out into the main street at a boy cycling by lazily. 'I bet you get a lot of your income round here from tourism. What's going to happen if that dries up?'

'People will find a way to get by.' The old man took out a pipe that looked as ancient as he appeared and began to feed it with tobacco from a leather pouch. 'They always do, don't they? The Blitz spirit. People find a way.'

They all gathered in the bar at 6 p.m. to eat. The food was plain but filling and it was even more comforting to feed on something they hadn't prepared themselves on a Calor Gaz stove. The atmosphere in the place seemed so secure and easy-going after their nights on the road that even Laura's usual complaining seemed half-hearted.

After they ordered drinks, they assessed their situation and considered their plans for the future. Ruth and Shavi were bank-rolling them as the others had all run out of funds, but the two of them still had enough savings to keep them going. They discussed the possibility of fuel rationing and agreed to top up the tank first thing and, if possible, get some large diesel containers they could keep in the back. None of them discussed their prospects for success, nor did they mention Balor by name, although his presence hung oppressively on the edge of the conversation.

Apart from a few minor points, it was the severed finger that concerned them the most. During the day its obscure symbolism had set unpleasant resonances deep in their minds, triggering images which they couldn't recognise; the lack of obvious meaning made them feel hunted and insecure.

'The Fomorii wouldn't have resorted to such a subtle tactic,' Tom noted. 'They would have been upon us in an instant. But they don't care about us any longer. We're no longer a threat. In their eyes, we have failed in our primary mission.'

'Losers,' Veitch said with obvious irritation. 'At least if they're not watching us we can come up on their blind side.'

Church was heartened to see the fatalism which had infected them ever since they came together was slowly dissipating; now there seemed no doubt that they could do *something*, however little that might be. Against the all-powerful forces lined against them, that was a great victory in itself.

'It has the hallmark of someone working alone,' Shavi noted. 'In this new world, perhaps we inadvertently antagonised something. Trespassed on land it presumed was its own.'

'But who did the finger belong to?' Ruth asked.

'Some poor bastard,' Church muttered.

'Let us hope it was a warning not to go back there,' Shavi said, 'and that it has not decided to pursue us for recompense.'

The hotel was holding its weekly ceilidh that night and by 7.30 p.m. the regulars began to drift in to the large lounge next to the bar. The band had already started to set up; it was the fiddle player's intense warm-up which had attracted Church and the others. They wandered in with their drinks and were welcomed with surprising warmth. The old man Church and Veitch had met in the bar earlier was there and gave them a wink as they took a beer from the barrels lined up on a table at one end of the room.

At 8 p.m. the dancing began. The moment the fiddle player launched into his reel the lounge turned into a maelstrom of whirling men and women of all ages, skirts flying, heels flicking, grins firmly set on faces. A girl of around seventeen grabbed Shavi's arm and dragged him into the throng. He took to the dance with gusto.

Veitch backed off in case anyone pulled him in. 'Bleedin' Scottish dancing. Not my scene, mate,' he muttered.

The drink was flowing as fast as the music, with every glass of beer followed by a chaser of malt. In that atmosphere of wild abandon and life celebration it was impossible not to become involved, and soon Church and the others had lost all thought of the stresses and tensions that assailed them.

As the night drew on, they made new friends and drifted from conversation to conversation. Shavi seemed particularly popular with the young women and Ruth with the men; she surprised herself by revelling in the attention she was getting, a liberating experience after the oppression of the previous few weeks.

Sweating after a vigorous dance, she adjourned to the bar area where she found Laura lounging against the wall, sipping on a glass of neat vodka.

'Keeping all the boys happy,' Laura said coolly.

Over the weeks, Ruth had learned to ignore Laura's baiting, but with the drink rushing round her system, she found herself bristling. 'I can understand how you'd be jealous of someone who's popular.'

'Jealous? Look in the mirror, Frosty.'

'What do you mean?'

'You know what I mean.'

Ruth did, and that irritated her even more. 'If you think I'm bothered about you and Church—'

'It's pretty obvious you've been trying to wrestle him to the ground since you met him. But he's got about as much in common with you as he has with Shavi. Face it, the best woman won.' Laura smiled tightly, but her eyes were cold and hard.

Ruth could feel her anger growing, which made her even more angry. She hated to lose control, but somehow Laura knew how to punch all the right buttons. 'Do I hear desperation in your voice? Now you've got him, you're afraid of losing him, aren't you?'

Laura thought about this for a moment. 'We're right for each other.'

'What you mean is, he's right for you. You've finally found someone strong enough to carry the weight of all your emotional baggage.' Ruth caught herself before she said anything more hurtful.

'What do you know about emotions? You're an ice queen.' Laura tried to maintain her cool, but she knocked back her vodka in one go.

'That shows how much you know.'

'All I'm saying is, stay away from him. I saw you talking to him the other night, trying to wheedle your way into his affections—'

'I wouldn't dream—' Ruth caught herself as her defiance suddenly surfaced. In the background the music was raging and she had to raise her voice. 'And what would you do if I did?'

Laura turned and stared at her for a long moment with eyes impossible to read and then walked away through the crowd.

Veitch and Shavi had got into a drinking competition, knocking down shots while they were egged on by a cheering crowd. But all paused as Tom stepped onto the small, makeshift stage and whispered something to the fiddle player. A second later the musician handed over his instrument which Tom shouldered before beginning to tap out a rhythm with his right foot. And then he started to play, a low, mournful sound that made everyone in the room stop what they were doing and stare. The tune was mediaeval in construction, the melody filled with the ache of loneliness, of love never-to-be-found, of yearning and failed desire; Church felt a cold knot develop in his chest, but Tom's face was impassive, his eyes icy. And then, as if he had suddenly awoken to the fact that he had dampened the mood, Tom began to pick up the beat, slowly at first, but then quicker and quicker, until he had developed the melody into a rampant jig. A couple down the front began to clap, and the sound ripped back through the crowd until everyone was joining in, physically driving the mood back up. Within a couple of minutes, everyone was dancing again and Tom seemed to be having the time of his life.

As Church sipped on his glass of malt, his head woozy from drink, feeling uncommonly happy for the first time in days, he felt a strange sensation prickling along his spine, as if someone was watching him. In the days since he had first encountered the unknown under Albert Bridge he had learned to be attentive to his instincts. He turned quickly. There was no one behind him, but the door to the corridor which ran down to the hotel entrance was open. For a second or two, he weighed his options, then crept over to the doorway and peered out. The corridor was empty.

He had just about convinced himself it was nothing but his imagination at work when the door out on to the street swung open slightly, as if it had been buffeted by a breeze; as it did, he thought he heard a faint, melodic voice calling his name.

His heart picked up a beat, but after all he had been through, he still didn't feel wary. There was something . . . a feeling, perhaps . . . which seemed to be floating in the air from the direction of the door and it was overwhelmingly comforting. His first reaction was that he was being summoned by the spirit of Marianne, as he had been twice before, but it felt different this time. He finished his whisky, left his glass on an ornamental table in the corridor and walked towards the door.

The main street was completely still, although it wasn't late in the

479

evening. The streetlights were bright, but not so much that they obscured the glittering array of stars in the clear sky. The night itself was balmy with the promise of summer just around the corner. He looked up and down the deserted street until he saw something which caught his eye.

Across the road was the park that rolled down to the river. During the day it had been filled with the whoops of children racing around the adventure playground and the jeers of teenagers hanging out next to the log cabin where the refreshments were served, but at that time it was deserted and unnervingly quiet. He crossed the road and leant on the wall, searching the paths that wound among the waving, fluffy-tipped pampas grass. Something moved. His rational mind told him it would be ridiculous to venture down into those wide open spaces, but his instincts didn't register anything that worried him. He steeled himself, then opened the gate.

Away from the streetlights, he was uncomfortably aware of the wild presence of nature looming away in the dark, but the splashing of the river prevented the silence becoming too oppressive. Whatever had brought him down there seemed to be leading him. Every now and then he would catch sight of a movement ahead, steering him down the paths until he was following the course of the river back towards the heart of the town. Eventually he came up to a brick bridge with an old churchyard next to it. It was an odd, triangular shape, the jumbled mass of markers mildewed, with some so timeworn they resembled the ancient standing stones of Gairloch. The grass among them was thick and along the walls age-old trees were so gnarled and wind-blasted they looked like menacing figures daring him to enter. It was so eerily atmospheric in the quiet that he almost did turn back, but after another movement on the far side, he took a deep breath and swung open the green, iron gate that hung ajar.

Cautiously, he moved among the white and grey stones muttering, 'Stupid, stupid, stupid,' under his breath, but the truth was, he still didn't feel any sense of threat. And then he reached the far side and the shape that had been luring him was no longer insubstantial.

Before him stood the woman he had encountered in the Watchtower floating between the worlds, the one who had visited him on the edge of dreams as a child, and freed him from the Fomorii cells, claiming to be his patron. She was one of the Tuatha Dé Danann, infused with the beauty which permeated that race. It was almost as if her skin was glowing with a faint golden light. Her eyes, too, were flecked with gold, and her hair tumbled lustrously about her shoulders. She was wearing the same dress of dark green he remembered from before; its material was indeterminate, but it clung to her form in a way that was powerfully appealing.

She was smiling seductively, her eyes sparkling. At first Church felt as entranced as he had the first time they met as adults, but gradually a mix of other emotions surfaced: suspicion, sadness and then anger.

'You tricked me,' he said. The anger took shape, hardened. 'You and all your people. You had Marianne killed. So I could be shaped into your slave to set your people free in your hour of need. You discarded a human life—' he snapped his fingers '—just like that.'

There was no sign in her face that she had been offended by his words. 'There is little I can say to put right the hurt you feel.' Her voice remained gentle. 'There is tragedy stitched into the fabric of the lives of all fragile Creatures and sometimes my people, in their endless, timeless existence, forget the suffering that comes from a simple passing.' For a surprising second, he thought he saw real tenderness in her eyes. 'I have been close to you all your life, Jack Churchill. I watched when you were born, when you played and learned. And when you were old enough, I came to you on the edge of sleep to see if you were the one who fitted the eternal pattern. The true hero infused with the glorious essence of this land. I saw in you . . .' She paused and, for the first time, seemed to have trouble finding the correct words. '. . . a nobility and passion which transcended the nature of most Frail Creatures. The Filid will one day sing tales of the great Jack Churchill.'

'That's not—'

She held up her hand to silence him. 'My part in this was small. I guided the destinies of the Brothers and Sisters of Dragons, but the decision to shape you in the crucible of death was taken elsewhere. It was never my intention to see you hurt, Jack.'

There was something in her words, in the turn of her head and the shimmer of emotion across her features, that made him think she was saying something else beyond the obvious. Her eyes were so deep and numinous he felt swallowed up by them; he couldn't maintain his anger towards her.

'If not you, then someone else is responsible. They'll have to pay. I can't forgive and forget what's been done to me, to all of us.'

'Nor would I expect you to.'

'Then who arranged it? And who carried out the act? Who killed Marianne and the others?'

'I cannot say.'

'You can't or you won't?' He tried to keep his voice stable in case he offended her. Despite her demeanour, he sensed great power and unpredictability just beneath the surface.

481

She pressed her hands together, almost as if she was praying. 'From your perspective, we may seem untrammelled by responsibility, as fluid in our actions as our natures. But we are bound by laws in the same way that you are, in the same way as the mountains, the seas and the wind. No one is truly free. I cannot tell you what you wish to know.'

'I'll find out.'

She nodded, said nothing.

Once he had got that out of his system, he became more aware of the situation. 'Why've you come to me?'

'To renew our acquaintance. To show you that I have no desire to abandon you, even though my people have achieved their desire.'

Church was troubled by the complexity of the emotions running through him. He felt drawn to the woman, but he couldn't tell if that was an honest feeling or simply a by-product of her manipulation of him over the years. 'What are you saying? That you want to be an ally?'

'That, and more.'

'How, more? A friend, then?'

She didn't reply. Her smile remained seductive.

Church felt a shiver of attraction run through him, fought it. 'If we're going to be friends, then you ought to tell me your name.'

'I have many names, like all my brethren.'

He waited, refusing to be drawn by her game-playing.

Her smile grew wider. 'I have been known as the Queen of the Waste Lands.'

This raised a spark of recognition in Church, but he couldn't remember where he had heard it before.

'Of the many names I have been called when I last freely walked your world, the one most used by your people was Niamh.'

'Niamh,' he repeated softly. A gentle dreaminess seemed to encircle them both; when he looked away from her, the surroundings shimmered and sparkled. 'So you're royalty?'

'In the hierarchy of the Golden Ones, I hold a position of privilege.' She held out a hand to him, and he didn't think he could resist it even if he had wanted to.

Her fingers were long and cool. They closed around his and gently pulled him towards her. As he moved in, the scent of her filled his nostrils, like lime and mint. For a moment they seemed to hang in stasis, their eyes locked; Church felt he was being pulled beneath green waves, deep, deep down to the darkness where miracles and wonders lived. And then, slowly, she moved her face closer. He felt the bloom of her breath on his lips; a tremor of anticipation ran through him down to his groin. When her lips touched his, he almost jolted from a burst of energy that could have been physical, emotional or psychological, but it left his head spinning. Her lips were as soft as peach-skin and tasted of some fruit he couldn't quite place. Her tongue flicked out and delicately caressed the tip of his own. And then the passion rushed through him, driving out all conscious thought, filling him up with insanity, and he was kissing her harder and feeling his hands slide around her slim waist to her back. And the sensation was so beyond anything he had experienced before he was suddenly tumbling through a haze into blackness.

There was darkness and then awareness that someone was summoning him. Church thought instantly: *I'm dreaming*, although he knew in the same instant that it wasn't a dream. From his vantage point at the centre of an inky cloud he saw Ruth's owl circling and at first he wondered obliquely if it was hunting. Then he realised its movements were frantic, as if it was disturbed by something attacking it.

'What's wrong,' he called out; his voice sounded like it had come from the bottom of a well.

The owl drew nearer, and then, suddenly, it was not an owl, although he wasn't quite sure what it was. It had the shape of a man, yet certain characteristics of an owl around its face, and batlike wings sprouting from its back which flapped powerfully. There was something so terrible about it that he couldn't bring himself to look it full in the face.

You must go to her. The creature's voice sounded like a metal crate being dragged over concrete. *She is in great danger. I can do nothing.*

'Who?' Church asked.

Blood. Its voice was almost threatening. *Blood everywhere.*

Church woke on the ground so disturbed he instantly jumped to his feet, as if he were under attack. An overwhelming sense of dread flooded his system. At first he couldn't fathom what was happening to him, but as he frantically looked around the deserted churchyard it started to come back. There was no sign of Niamh. And with his next thought he recalled the odd dream of the owl-thing and suddenly he understood his feelings.

'Ruth,' he murmured fearfully.

Shavi, Veitch and Tom were gathered together around a table in the hotel lounge. Church had no idea how much time had passed, but everyone else in the room had gone. They all looked up in surprise as he burst in.

'Where's Ruth?' he barked.

'Went upstairs,' Veitch slurred. 'Ages ago. Couldn't stand the—'

But Church was already sprinting back out into the corridor to the stairs. As he reached the foot, he was brought up sharp by Laura, who was just making her way down. She was staring at her hands in a daze, leaning heavily against the bannister. In horror Church saw she was splattered with blood.

'My God.' His voice seemed to be coming from somewhere else. Desperately, his eyes ranged from Laura's hands, to her face, to the blood. 'What's happened to her?'

Laura shook her head blankly, struggled to find any words that made sense. But all the backed-up tension had suddenly burst out and Church was taking the steps two at a time, pushing past her. At the top he bolted down the landing until he came to Ruth's room. The door was ominously open. He kicked it wide and barged in.

There was blood splattered across the quilt, droplets thrown up the wall like a Jackson Pollock painting, a small pool already soaking into the thick carpet. Church glanced around frantically. Ruth was nowhere to be seen.

He was halfway back to the door when his eyes lighted on the small table under the window and he was brought up sharp. Laura appeared in the door, still looking like she was somewhere else. But when her gaze followed Church's it was like she had been slapped across the face.

'Jesus!' Her hand involuntarily went to her mouth.

On the table was another finger in a little puddle of blood with other droplets spattered around. And from its long delicate shape they could tell it was Ruth's.

A few seconds later the others shambled in. Although they were worse for wear from the alcohol they soon sobered up when they glanced from Laura's tear-streaked face to Church's bloodless expression of horror and despair.

Before any of them could speak, Church shrugged off the paralysis and ran out onto the landing. For the first time he noticed tiny splatters of blood leading away from Ruth's room down the stairs. Frantically he threw himself down them, following the stains out to the street. But there the trail ended and he found himself running backwards and forwards along the deserted road searching futilely for any sign of what had happened to her.

Back in the bedroom, the others could read what he had found in his dejected face.

Veitch suddenly noticed Laura standing apart, still in shock. 'What did you do?' His voice rumbled out infused with so much threat, Church felt his blood run cold.

Laura shook her head dumbly. 'I don't know—'

Veitch moved quickly. He was already gripping Laura's shoulders roughly before the others realised. 'You better tell us, you bitch. You're the one! Look at all the blood—'

'Ryan!' Church and Shavi grabbed him by the arms and hauled him off her roughly. His face was filled with rage.

'Look at the blood!' Veitch spat accusingly.

Laura held out her hands which were stained red. 'It's not like that—'

'What is it, then?' Veitch struggled briefly, than allowed the others to restrain him.

'I was asleep on my bed,' Laura began hesitantly. 'I woke up . . . some kind of noise. My head was fuzzy . . . you know, the drink.' She looked around the room, didn't seem to see any of them. 'I got up to find out what it was . . . thought it might have been Church. When I was out on the landing there was another noise. I saw Ruth's door was open.'

'Who was there, Laura?' Shavi asked calmly.

Her eyes widened and filled with tears as she looked past him into the shadows in the corners of the room. 'I don't know . . . I can't remember!'

Veitch searched her face. 'You're lying,' he said coldly.

She shook her head, held out her hands pleadingly, but all anyone could see was the blood.

'You don't remember anything?' Church asked.

There was a flicker of pain in her eyes. 'Don't *you* believe me?' She started to back towards the corner.

'Stay calm, Laura.' Shavi's voice was warm and reassuring. 'We are simply trying to find out what has happened to Ruth—'

'We haven't got time for this!' Veitch snapped. His clipped movements and roving eyes reminded Church of an animal; he was surprised how concerned Veitch seemed to be for someone who had hated him only a few days before; it suggested feelings beyond friendship. Church laid a calming hand on Veitch's upper arm. He half-expected Veitch to throw it off instantly, but the Londoner responded almost deferentially.

Laura slumped on to a chair in the corner and rested her head in her hands before realising she was smearing the blood over her face. She jumped up in a fury and stormed into the bathroom to wash herself.

Her departure seemed to break the dam of disbelief that constrained the others. 'Why weren't we more careful? Christ, we should have known by now.' Church's voice hummed with repressed emotion.

Veitch glanced from one to the other. 'Do you think she did it?' he whispered, jerking his head towards the bathroom. 'All that blood on her—'

Church gnawed on a knuckle. The others looked away, unsure what to say.

Veitch scrubbed his face, suddenly sober, then walked over to the window and threw back the curtains. 'Where is she?' Then, fearfully: 'Do you think she's dead?'

'They'd have left a body,' Church replied. 'Wouldn't they?'

'Unless they needed it for ritual purposes,' Tom noted. Church glared at him for his unfeeling bluntness.

Veitch finally found it within himself to look at the finger on the table. 'What kind of a sick bastard would do a thing like that? Christ, what must she have felt—' His voice choked off.

Shavi dropped to his haunches to scrutinise the stains on the carpet. 'The amount of blood is commensurate with the removal of a finger. There is a chance—'

'Don't touch it!' Tom yelled as Veitch stretched out a trembling hand towards the finger. Veitch snatched his arm back as if he'd been burned.

Tom marched over and bent down to examine the finger at table height. 'I think it's a sign.' He removed his cracked glasses and said, 'Which direction do you think it's pointing?'

Shavi glanced out of the window. 'The sun set over there,' he said with a chopping motion of his hand, 'so I would say, maybe, south-east.'

Tom replaced his glasses and stood up. 'Exactly south-east, I would guess. Towards Edinburgh.'

Church broke the long silence that followed Tom's comment. 'What does it mean?'

'Whoever did it is showing us the way. They want us to follow.' He stared out to the shrouded countryside that lay beyond the feeble lights of the town. 'In all this there is the pathology of evil, of ritual. Somebody is trying to bend the power that is loose in the land towards darkness.'

'Calatin?' Church suggested. 'Mollecht? Some other Fomor?'

Tom shook his head. 'This is not their way. It is the first play in a new game.'

CHAPTER THREE

New Words for an Auld Sang

The night dragged on interminably. They sat in a state of near-paralysis, fearing the worst, afraid to discuss what had happened, unable to decide what they should do next. The finger remained on the small table, the blood rapidly congealing. Their gaze kept returning to it, as if its unchanging pointing were a Poe-esque accusation.

Laura sat apart, staring out of the window blankly. Church found it impossible to read her; the impassive expression could have been hiding a sense of deep betrayal, or something he didn't want to consider, but which was nonetheless licking at the back of his mind. He hated himself for thinking it, though when he looked around he could tell the others felt the same. The thing he had dreaded had come to pass: a cancerous suspicion was eating away at them all.

Beyond that he found it almost impossible to cope with the raw emotion searing his heart. At times, if he allowed himself to inspect it too closely, it reminded him of those terrible feelings that had consumed him after Marianne had died, and that surprised him; had he grown so close to Ruth so quickly? So much had changed over the past few weeks, bonds materialising on a spiritual level, others being forged through hardship: he hadn't even begun to get a handle on what was happening inside him.

As the first rays of dawn licked the rooftops across the street, the intermittent, stuttering conversation told him what he feared: that the others were looking to him to make a decision. Before Beltane, he would have wanted to tell them he wasn't up to it, he didn't have the resilience or tenacity of leadership within him. But his failure had made him face his responsibilities, and he would take the difficult decisions however much they might corrupt his essential character and beliefs. *That*, he told himself, *is what it's all about*. He had to make sacrifices for the greater good. He just hoped the sacrifices wouldn't be so great that there would be nothing left of him by the end of it.

'We need to move on to Edinburgh rapidly,' he said eventually.

'We are going to look for Ruth, right?' Veitch asked.

'Of course.'

Veitch eyed him suspiciously. 'What would you have done if she'd been taken in the opposite direction?'

Church didn't answer.

None of them could decide how they should dispose of the finger so they wrapped it in a handkerchief and buried it in the depths of Church's bag. They packed quickly and checked out, despite the obvious concern of the hotel manager who wondered why they were leaving so early, without breakfast and one travelling companion short.

The last building of the town was barely behind them when a police car came screaming by, lights flashing, forcing them to pull over. The driver was a man in his mid-forties with greying hair and the wearied expression of someone who had been pushed to the limit, while his eyes suggested he'd been dragged out of bed to catch them. Veitch wound down the driver's window as he approached.

'You're going to have to accompany me back into town, sir.' His eyes were piercing, but Veitch didn't flinch from the stare.

'No can do, mate. We've got business down south.'

'I don't want to have to ask you again, lad. Since the martial law was brought in, I've been run ragged. They don't think it's the rural areas that need the help, so we have to fend for ourselves. So don't push me around because I'll push back harder if it makes my life easier.'

As Veitch bristled, Church hastily leaned across him. 'What's the problem, officer? We were driving okay—'

'You know what the problem is.' There was a snap of irritation in his voice. 'A certain matter of blood on the carpet.'

'Oh, that. A bit of horseplay that got out of control. If the manager wants us to pay for cleaning—'

'Get out of the van. Now.' The policeman's body grew rigid with tension.

Shavi tugged at Church's jacket from the back. 'He thinks we killed Ruth,' he whispered, too low for the policeman to hear. There was something in his voice that suggested he wasn't simply reading the policeman's mannerisms.

Everything seemed to hang for a second. Church saw Veitch's eyes narrow, his forearm muscles tense, and an instant later he had snapped on the ignition and popped the clutch. The van roared away, leaving the policeman yelling furiously behind them. Veitch drove wildly until the police car was out of sight, then he slammed on the brakes and reversed up a rough foresters' track which wound through ranks of pine. When the trees obscured the road he killed the engine.

'Big macho idiot,' Laura said coldly from the back. 'Now we'll be on everyone's most wanted list. We won't be able to travel anywhere.'

Veitch glared at her. 'You haven't got any right to talk. We wouldn't be here if not for—'

'Leave it out,' Church ordered.

Veitch grew sullen. 'The moment he got a look at my record we wouldn't stand a chance of getting out of the area for days,' he continued. 'We can't afford to waste that time.'

'You did the right thing, Ryan.' Church put his head back and closed his eyes wearily. 'If things are as bad as they seem . . . if things are going to get as bad as we expect . . . the cops will have too much on their plate to worry about us. It might make things a little more difficult, but if they're not putting a dragnet out, I reckon we'll be okay.'

'You better be right,' Laura said gloomily.

Church recalled Shavi's apparent knowledge of the policeman's thoughts and turned to him. 'You can read minds now?'

Shavi shrugged. 'It was empathic.'

'But you can get into heads, you've shown us that.' Shavi wouldn't meet Church's gaze.

'What are you getting at?' Laura asked.

'I think Shavi should try peeling back the layers of your memory so we can find out what you really did see last night.'

Even Laura's sunglasses couldn't mask her concern. 'Not in my head.'

'What have you got to hide?' Veitch asked coldly.

Laura's face froze.

'Ruth and I went through something similar when all this mess started.' Church tried to be as reassuring as he could, for Shavi's sake as much as Laura's. 'It wasn't so bad. And it really helped us to get all those trapped thoughts out in the open.'

Laura moved her head slightly and Church guessed that behind her sunglasses she was looking at Veitch, weighing up his words and her options; his barely veiled accusations made it impossible for her to back out.

'Okay, Mister Shaman. You get to venture where no man has been before.' Her voice was emotionless.

Church clapped a hand on Shavi's shoulder. 'It'll be okay.'

Shavi smiled at him tightly.

They locked up the van and ventured into the pines until they found a spot where the sun broke through the canopy of vegetation, casting a circle of light. Laura and Shavi sat cross-legged in the centre, facing each other, while Church, Veitch and Tom leaned on tree trunks and watched quietly. Shavi had already eaten some of Tom's hash to attune his mood. He spent a few moments whispering gently to Laura; after a while her eyes were half-lidded, her movements lazy.

The atmosphere changed perceptibly the moment Shavi leaned forward to take Laura's hands; the birdsong died as if a switch had been thrown, even the breeze seemed to drop. There was a stillness like glass over everything.

When Shavi spoke, the world held its breath. 'We are going back to last night, Laura. To the hotel, after the dance. You and Ruth had gone to bed early.'

'I wasn't in the mood. I'd had enough of Miss Prissy. And too many people were looking at my scars.'

'You both went into your rooms. And went to sleep?'

'I lay down on the top of the bed. I was tired, the booze was knocking me out.' Her voice was soporific. 'I don't know how long I was asleep. Couldn't have been long. I heard a noise—'

'What was it?'

'I can't remember.'

'Try.'

She thought for a moment. 'It was Ruth. She cried out.'

'What did you do then? Tell me, step by step.'

'I got up. I felt like someone had beaten me around the head with a baseball bat. I walked to the door . . . Actually, it was more of a stagger. I thought, "I'm glad Church isn't here to see this. I'd never live it down." There was another noise. Sounded like a lamp going over. I thought I could hear voices through the wall. I stepped out on to the landing . . .' Her breath caught suddenly in her throat.

'What was it?'

Tears sprang to her eyes and trickled down her cheeks. 'I . . .' She shook her head, screwed her eyes up as if that would prevent the images forming.

Shavi's reassuring voice grew so low the others could barely hear it. 'Concentrate, Laura. Focus on the interloper.'

'It was . . .' A shiver ran through her. 'No, no. I see a large wolf. It reaches right up to the ceiling. Bigger. Passing through. It's growing to fill the whole hotel. It has sickly yellow eyes and it turns them on me. And it smiles . . . it smiles like a man.'

She started to hyperventilate. Shavi let go of her hands and put his arms around her shoulders, gently pulling her towards him until she was resting against his chest, where her breathing gradually subsided.

'A giant wolf? She's making it up,' Veitch hissed.

They moved into the circle of light and squatted down, waiting for Laura to recover. She wouldn't meet any of their eyes. 'That's what you get delving around in the depths of my mind. I told you I'd done too many drugs.'

'What do you think? A shapeshifter?' Shavi seemed to have gained renewed confidence from the success of the exercise; the faint, enigmatic smile Church remembered from the first time they met had returned to his face.

'I don't think so.' Tom's expression was troubled. 'The wolf could be representational of whatever she saw. She might be converting her memory into symbols to help her deal with it.'

Church remembered his own experience of regression therapy to try to unlock the memories of the terrible sight beneath Albert Bridge, images so horrible his mind had locked them away. Although what eventually surfaced had proved to be the truth, the therapist had talked about false *screen* memories designed to protect the mind's integrity from something too awful to bear.

'This is doing my head in,' Veitch said. 'It's like you can't believe anything you see or remember or think!'

'That's how it always was,' Tom replied curtly.

'So how do we break through the symbolism to get to what Laura really saw?' Church asked.

Shavi rubbed his chin uncomfortably. 'I would not like to try again so soon after this attempt. I think Laura . . . both of us . . . need time to recover. The mind is too sensitive.'

'Yeah, and it's the only one I've got.' With an expression of faint distaste, Laura rubbed her hands together as if wiping away the stain of the memory.

'At least we know Laura saw something . . . someone,' Shavi continued.

'So do you believe me now, musclehead?' With her sunglasses on, Church couldn't tell if she was talking to him or Veitch.

'I still think she could be making it up,' Veitch said suspiciously. 'None of you know what's going on here, what her mind can do, what's real and what's not. She might have dreamed it up this way. Some kind of self-hypnosis, I don't know.' He turned to Laura. 'You didn't say anything about how you got the blood on you.'

'I remember that now. Whatever I saw turned my head upside down. I wandered into Ruth's room like some kind of mental patient and I just, sort of, touched the blood because I couldn't believe what I was seeing.'

'Fits together perfectly, don't it?' Veitch sneered.

As Laura bristled Church jumped in to prevent further confrontation. 'We can't stay here any longer with that cop driving around.' He glanced among the trees. 'Who knows what's in these woods anyway? We need to get to Edinburgh.'

'That cop will at least have put out the van's description and number,' Laura said. 'Face it, we're not going to get far in that.'

'Then we dump it, find another form of transport,' Church said. 'Time to use our initiative.'

Before they left, they took Ruth's finger and buried it in the leaf mould. It made them sick to leave it there, but there was nothing else for it. Then they took the A84 to Stirling where they found a dealer who took the van off their hands for two hundred pounds. It was an effort to lug their bags, camping equipment and remaining provisions to the station, but they didn't have long to wait to pick up a train to Edinburgh Waverley. There were only two carriages but apart from a trio of people at the far end of their carriage, the train was empty.

'I thought they would have shut the trains down by now,' Church said to the conductor as they boarded.

'Make the most of it,' he replied gruffly. 'The last service is tonight. Indefinite suspension of the entire network.' He shrugged. 'I still get kept on at full pay, at least for the moment. Not many people travelling anyways.'

They settled into their seats, lulled by the sun-heated, dusty interior, and once the train gently rocked out of the station they found themselves drifting off after their night without sleep. The journey to Edinburgh would be under an hour, but they had barely got out into open countryside when they were disturbed by the loud voices of two of their fellow travellers. It appeared to be a father and daughter conversing in a heated manner. His greying hair was slicked back in a manner popular during the war, and he had on an old-fashioned suit that seemed brand-new. A cracked briefcase was tucked under one arm. The daughter, who was in her early thirties, wore clothes that were smart, if unstylish. She was quite plain, with a complexion tempered by an outdoor life.

Drifting in and out of half-sleep, Church made out they had a farm somewhere outside Stirling which was experiencing financial problems and they were heading into Edinburgh to attempt to secure some kind of grant. But there was an edgy undercurrent to their talk which suggested some other issue was concerning them and they couldn't agree about how to deal with it.

Veitch shifted irritably in his seat and plumped up his jacket as a pillow. 'Just shut up,' he said under his breath as their voices rose again.

They all managed to get some sleep for the next ten minutes, but then they were jolted sharply awake by the farmer snarling, 'There's no bloody fairies in the fields! No bloody God either! It's not about luck! It's about those bastards in the Government, and in Europe!'

Church glanced around the edge of the seat ahead. The woman was pink with embarrassment at her father's outburst and trying to calm him with frantic hand movements. But there was something else concerning her too.

'What are you talking about, girl? Words can't hurt anyone! Who's listening?' The farmer's face was flushed with anger. 'This is what's important: the farm's going broke and we'll all be in the poorhouse by the end of summer if something's not done!'

His rage was born of desperation and tension bottled up for too long, and he probably would have carried on for several more minutes if the woman hadn't suddenly jumped to her feet and marched to the toilet.

The strained atmosphere ebbed over the next few minutes as Church drifted again. In that dreamy state, he found himself faced with an image of Ruth pleading with him for help in a scene disturbingly reminiscent of when the spirit of Marianne had begged him to avenge her death. His anxiety knotted: so much pressure being heaped on his shoulders, so much expectation he was afraid he couldn't live up to. And then he looked into Ruth's face and all the emotions he had tried to repress came rushing to the surface. He had tried to pretend she hadn't suffered, wasn't dead, but—

A piercing scream echoed through the carriage. All five of them jumped to their feet as one, ready for any threat, hearts pounding, bodies poised for fight or flight. The woman had returned from the toilets and was standing opposite her father, who had his back to them; her face was frozen in an expression of extreme shock.

Shavi was the first to her, grabbing her shoulders to calm her. She was shaking her head from side-to-side, oblivious to him, her eyes fixed so firmly on her father Shavi was forced to turn to follow her gaze. The old man was no longer there; or rather, his clothes and his briefcase were there, but his body had been replaced by straw; it tufted from the sleeves, dropped from the trouser legs to fill the shoes, and sprouted from his collar into a hideous parody of a human head, like an enormous corn dolly.

'Dad!' the woman croaked.

Veitch reached out to prod the shoulder curiously and the mannequin crumpled into a pile of clothes and a heap of straw. This set the
woman off in another bout of screaming.

'What happened?' Laura asked with a horrible fascination.

While Shavi led the woman to the other end of the carriage where he
attempted to calm her, Tom knelt down to examine the remains. 'You
heard the things he was saying,' he said.

'I don't get it,' Laura replied. 'So he was a crotchety old git like
you—'

'In the old days, the people who worked the land were terrified of
saying anything which might offend the *fairies*, the nature spirits,
whatever,' Tom snapped. 'They even had a host of euphemisms like
the Little Folk or the Fair Folk in case the powers took offence at their
name.'

'And now they're back . . .' Veitch began without continuing.

'They always were a prideful race,' Tom said. 'They demanded
respect from all those they considered as lesser.'

'But all he said was . . .' Laura caught herself before she repeated the
farmer's words. She glanced back at the sobbing daughter. 'Poor bitch.
At least the old man will be able to keep the crows off the fields.'

'Oh, stop it!' Church said sharply. He looked at the broken expression on the daughter's face and read her future in an instant; he felt a
deep pang of pity.

'It simply shows the contempt in which they hold us,' Tom noted.
'We need to be kept in our place.'

Veitch looked round suddenly. 'Wasn't there someone else in here?'

'That's right. There were three other passengers.' Church looked to
the seats where the third traveller had been. 'I don't remember him
getting up. No one got off.'

'That might have been one of them.' Tom hurried to the adjoining
door to peer into the next carriage. It was empty. 'Now they are back, I
presume they will be moving among us, seeing how things have
changed.'

As if in answer to his words they heard a sudden scrabbling on the
roof of the carriage, then a sound like laughter and footsteps disappearing to the far end. Veitch ran after it and pressed his face up close
to the window in an attempt to peer behind, but all he saw was a large,
oddly shaped shadow cast on the cutting. It separated from the train,
rose up and, a second later, was gone.

Soon after, the train trundled slowly through the regimented green
lawns and blooming flowers of Princes Street Gardens into Waverley

Station, the volcanic ridge topped by the imposing stone bulk of Edinburgh Castle rising high above them. The daughter was bordering on hysteria by the time Shavi led her out on to the platform in search of a guard, who promptly took her off to the medical centre for treatment. There were few travellers around for such a large station, but that only made the small pockets of police more obvious; at the furthest reaches of the platforms where they would be unobtrusive to the majority of travellers, armed troops patrolled.

'This is creepy,' Laura hissed. 'It's like Istanbul or something.'

Paranoia crept over them when some of the police started looking intently in their direction, and they hastily collected up their bags and moved off. 'Do you think that bastard in Callander radioed through our descriptions?' Veitch said under his breath.

'Just another worry to add to the list,' Church replied darkly.

They argued briefly about conserving their cash – a policy favoured by Church and Shavi – but eventually agreed credit cards would probably be useless within a short time and so opted to live in style while they stayed in the city. It was Laura who won the argument when she said, 'Might as well make the most of it. We may not get the chance again.'

For accommodation, they selected the Balmoral, an opulent Edwardian pile that loomed over Waverley Station at the eastern end of the bustling main drag of Princes Street. They all laughed at the comically shocked expression on Veitch's face when he first walked into the palatial marble reception, but although he slipped to the back, where he furtively eyed the smartly uniformed staff as if they were about to throw him out, he was soon making the most of the luxurious surroundings when they were shown to their rooms with views of the castle and the Old Town.

Despite all that was happening, at first glance the city seemed virtually unaffected; cars still chugged bumper-to-bumper through the centre, people took their lunch in the sun in Princes Street Gardens and the shops and bars of the New Town seemed to be doing a brisk trade.

But as they took a stroll towards the Old Town, they could see it was different. It was almost as if the people had taken a conscious decision to avoid its long shadows and gloomy stone buildings, driven out by an oppressive sense of old times. The pubs, restaurants and shops still remained open, but the crowds that moved among them were thin; they always kept to the sunny side of the street, expressions furtive, shoulders bowed by invisible weights.

It was Shavi who characterised it the best as he stood on the Esplanade and looked from the jumbled rooftops of the Old Town to the clean lines and Georgian crescents of the new: it was a city split in two, Jekyll and Hyde, light and dark, night and day.

'Another sign of the duality that seems to be infusing everything in this new age of metaphor and symbolism.' The wind whipped Shavi's long hair around his face as he scanned the area.

Laura pressed her sunglasses up the bridge of her nose. 'At least we know which side we'll be drinking in tonight.'

Tom shook his head. 'Look at the New Town – it hasn't been affected yet. This seems to be the centre of change. If we want to learn anything, we have to come here.'

Laura scowled at him. 'You always know how to bring things down, you old git.'

They ate dinner in the hotel's elegant dining room at a table far from the few other residents. But despite the high quality of the food, they only picked at their meal; after Ruth's disappearance, an air of hopelessness had started to congeal around them, growing stronger with each passing hour.

It was Veitch who finally gave voice to the questions that troubled them all. 'What's the plan? Try to find Ruth or work out why we're supposed to be here?'

All eyes turned to Church, but he kept his gaze fixed on the remnants of his venison. 'We can't waste time looking for Ruth.' His words sounded harsher than he intended, but it was impossible to soften them. 'We don't know if she's still alive. And if she is, we can't even be sure she's here in the city. A hunch about the direction of the city just isn't enough.'

'What are you saying? That we just forget about her?' Veitch's face grew colder.

'Of course I don't want to forget about her, but we've only got a few short weeks to prevent the Fomorii bringing Balor back and that time will go quickly, believe me. Christ, we've got no idea how we're going to start. The way I see it, it's our responsibility. We're the only people who might stand a chance of succeeding, and a slim one at that. If we get distracted, the whole of the world goes to hell. Could you live with that?'

'You know what? Right now I don't really care about that.' For a second Veitch looked like he was going to cry.

'It's heartless, but those are the kind of choices we're being forced to make.' Church kept his face impassive because he knew if he allowed vent to even the slightest fraction of the emotion he was feeling, he wouldn't be able to maintain the strength they expected of him. Ever since Ruth had disappeared he'd been tearing himself apart about what they should do, but on cold reflection he knew where his responsibilities lay, whatever that did to him, however much the others grew to hate him for it.

'So that's it? She's gone? Just like that?' Veitch looked around the others for support. They said nothing, but the conflicting emotions struggled just behind their features. Veitch shook his head slowly. 'Fuck it.'

'Ryan—' Church began.

'What is it? She means nothing—'

'Of course she doesn't mean nothing.' The steel in Church's voice brought Veitch up sharp. 'And I don't believe this is the end of it. Whatever got to her isn't going to leave us alone. And when he or it or whatever it is comes back we're going to find out what happened to her before we gut the bastard.'

The unrestrained venom took the others aback. Laura pushed the vegetables around her plate with her fork while Tom tapped out a beat with his spoon.

Shavi leaned forward and broke the silence diplomatically. 'Then what is our next step?'

Tom answered. 'The guidance offered to us specifically mentioned the Well of Fire. Historically it was the most abundant and powerful source of the earth energy. Some say it even provides a direct channel with the source of the energy, whatever or wherever that might be. But with the gradual break between land and people it has lain dormant for a long time.'

Church nodded. 'We're supposed to be waking the sleeping king . . . arousing the wounded land . . . whichever metaphor you want. This fits the pattern. How do we get to it?'

Tom shrugged. 'The entrance lies somewhere on Arthur's Seat, that big pile of rock at the bottom of the Royal Mile, in the middle of Holyrood Park—'

'But the guidebook says the name has nothing to do with Arthur,' Church interjected. 'Not like all the other places where the blue fire is strong. Historians think it's just a corruption of Archer's Seat.'

'Which shows how much they know.' Tom removed his spectacles and polished them with the tablecloth.

'Then we head up there.' Church glanced through the window at the late afternoon sun. 'Tomorrow, now. And tonight—'

'Tonight,' Tom continued, 'we visit the Old Town.'

The warm evening was filled with the oddly comforting aromas of the modern age: heated traffic fumes, food cooking in restaurants downwind, burnt iron and hot grease rising from the train tracks that cut through the city. Girls in skimpy summer clothes and young men in T-shirts and jeans lounged in the late sunlight outside the Royal Scottish Academy on the Mound. There was an air of spring optimism that made it almost impossible to believe that anything had changed.

But as the companions wound their way up Ramsay Lane into the Old Town, the shadows grew longer and an unseasonal chill hung in the air despite the heat of the day. The area centred on the Royal Mile was the oldest part of the city. In the Middle Ages it had been hemmed in by city walls, forcing the housing to be built higher and higher; they were crammed too close together, blocking out the sky, so that a claustrophobic anxiety seemed to gather among them. Tom, who had obviously been in the city before, led them down Lawnmarket to one of the numerous, shadowy closes that lined the Royal Mile. At the end was an eighteenth-century courtyard and the Jolly Judge pub. They decided it was as good a place as any to discuss their plans.

It was small and cellar-like, with a low, beamed ceiling painted with flowers and fruit. A fire glowed nicely in the grate and the comfortable atmosphere was complemented by the hubbub of conversation coming from numerous drinkers gathered at the tables or leaning on the bar.

As they bought their drinks, Veitch said, 'It doesn't seem right sitting here getting pissed.'

'We could be roaming the streets like some moron tourists.' Laura took a gulp of her vodka as if she hadn't drunk for weeks.

'She's right,' Tom said as he led them over to the only free table. 'Inns are still the centres of community, even as they were in my day. Sooner or later all information passes through them. We simply have to keep our ears and eyes open.'

'That's good,' Church said, recalling all the pubs he'd passed through with Ruth, 'because I don't feel much like drinking.'

He changed his mind quickly. There was a desperation to all their drinking, as if they wanted to forget, or pretend the blight that was infecting reality was not really happening. The rounds came quickly, their mood lifted as they settled into the homely ambience of the pub. And once again Tom was proven right. They overheard snippets of conversation which added to their knowledge of the situation in the city, and Laura and Shavi engaged in brief chats with people they met on their way to the bar or the toilet.

As they had found elsewhere, after the announcement of martial law there had been an initial flurry of panic, but when no hard evidence of anything presented itself, people slipped back into old routines, cynically blaming the Government for some kind of cover-up or coming up with numerous wild hypotheses in the manner of old-fashioned campfire storytellers. It quickly became apparent to everyone that martial law wasn't enforced anyway; the police and armed forces appeared to have more important things on their minds, so everyone quietly ignored it. That resilience gave Church some encouragement, but he wondered how they would fare once the true situation become known.

Certainly everyone seemed to accept that some kind of change had come over the Old Town, although this was a topic few were prepared to discuss. When Church raised the matter, conversations were quickly changed or eyes averted. All that could be discerned was that the ancient part of the city had somehow become more dangerous and that after the pub closed the drinkers would 'hurry home to wifey'. But Church could tell from their faces that some of them had seen or experienced things which they couldn't bring themselves to discuss with their fellows.

Sometime after 10.30 p.m. another technology failure took out all the lights, but the drinkers dealt with it as they did any of the other minor changes which had come into their lives. A loud cheer went up, a few shouted comments about raiding the pumps while the landlord couldn't see, and then lots of laughter. The blazing fire provided enough light while the bar staff scrambled round for candles which they quickly stuffed into empty wine bottles and placed on every table and the bar.

'Nice ambience.'

Church started at the voice which came from the previously empty seat beside him. A large-boned man carrying a little too much weight inside an expensive, but tie-less, suit was smiling knowingly, a pint of bitter half-raised to his mouth. His hair was collar-length and he had a badly trimmed beard, but the heaviness of his jowls took away any of the rakishness he was attempting. Church placed him in his early to mid-thirties and from the perfectly formed English vowels of his public school accent it was obvious he wasn't a local.

'Pleasant enough,' Church replied noncommittally.

'And how are you finding this new world you're in? A little destabilising, I would think.' He smiled slyly.

Church eyed him suspiciously. There was an awareness about the stranger that instantly set him apart. 'Who are you?'

'A cop,' Veitch said threateningly.

'Good Lord, no,' he replied, bemused. 'How insulting.'

Church inspected the cut of his suit, the arrogance in his posture. 'Security services.'

The stranger made an odd, vaguely affirmative expression, one eyebrow half-raised. 'Once, not so long ago. Decided to head out on my own. Not much point having a career structure in this day and age.' He took a long draught of his bitter and smacked his lips.

'What are you doing here?' Church wondered if it had anything to do with the encounter with the police in Callander; he was ready to leave immediately if the situation called for it, and he tried to convey this surreptitiously to the others, but all their attention was on the spy.

'Why, to see all of you, dear boy.' He chuckled at their uncomfortable expressions. 'That would be a little bit of a lie, actually. Stumbled across you by accident in town earlier. Thought I'd drop in on you . . . see how you're getting on.' The chuckles subsided into a smile that made them even more uneasy.

Shavi leaned across the table curiously. 'And the security services know who we are?'

'Well, of course. They know everything that's worth knowing. That's their job, isn't it?' He looked around at their faces, still smiling in a manner that might have seemed jovial until it was examined closely; it was a social pretence. 'You really don't know what's happening, do you?'

'We have a good idea,' Church replied.

'No, you don't. You just think you do.' He took another sip of beer, playing with them. His eyes narrowed thoughtfully. 'Let me cast my mind back, remember all those reports and discussions. So much said and written, it's hard to believe it's only been going on for three months, give or take. Right, I have it. The M4, back in March. Terrible pile-up, cars and lorries and buses all mangled. A conflagration that blocked the entire motorway, caused traffic chaos for days. You remember it, don't you?'

Church gave nothing away.

'And what caused all that carnage?'

Church's eyes flickered towards the others; no one spoke.

The spy chuckled again. 'I understand your reticence. Really. It's not the kind of thing one talks about, is it? Well, let me answer the question for you. You believe the disaster was caused by some kind of flying creature out of a fairy book, blasting gouts of flame from its mouth.'

'And you're saying it wasn't?' Church made an attempt to pierce that jovial mask, but all he could see beneath it was more lies and deceit.

'Perception is such a funny thing,' the spy mused. Their uneasiness had started to turn to irritation at his undisguised patronising manner. 'We have all these faculties which paint a picture of the world for our mind.' He made a fey, airy gesture. 'Something we can make sense of. But can any of them really be trusted, that's the question? If there is one fact known by all security agencies around the globe, it is that there are no absolutes. Sight, sound, smell, touch, taste, all can be manipulated to present a view of the world as real as the *real* one.'

'What are you saying?' Church bristled. 'That we didn't see what we thought we saw?'

'Come on, old chap! It was a creature from a fairy book!' The spy aped disbelief. 'It all depends how you see things. Fire streamed down from the sky and blew up a chunk of motorway and some poor commuters. Well, of course, it *could* be some kind of mythical beastie. But, really, come on now, we are all intelligent people here, are we not? What would you say is the most rational explanation? The flames of a dragon's breath? Or a missile fired from a plane or a helicopter?'

His words struck them all sharply, prising open the doubt and dislocation they had felt in the early days. 'We saw—'

The spy silenced Church with a furious shake of his head. 'No, no, no, that's not good enough. Can't be trusted. After you witnessed the murder under Albert Bridge, you and the young lady went to see a therapist, did you not? And he attempted to recover the hidden memory of the incident—'

'How do you know about that?' Church's angry indignation masked a growing concern; how long had he been spied upon?

'He told you about screen memories,' the spy continued. 'False memories created by the mind to hide a truth which is unbearable. Or false memories created by an outside source to hide a truth which they do not want to come out.'

'You make it sound as simple as flicking a light switch,' Laura said.

'It is. Drugs, mind-control techniques, subliminal programming, targeted microwave radiation, post-hypnotic signals. The mind is a very susceptible organ.'

Veitch snorted derisively. 'Bollocks. That's what it is, mate, whoever the fuck you are. You're saying we can't trust anything we see or hear. Or think—'

'Exactly.' The spy settled back in his chair and smiled triumphantly.

'You speak as if you are saying something new.' Tom surveyed the spy with a face as cold and hard as marble; the spy looked away. 'But that is exactly how it has always been in life. You simply have more ways of manipulation now.'

Church shook his head. 'Everything we've experienced – everything supernatural – is just a big lie created by a lot of jumped-up public schoolboys with too much free time? I don't believe you.'

'That's your prerogative. But you know the old adage about big lies working the best. And it's not just a few jumped-up public schoolboys. It's . . .' The words dried up, and he waved his hand dismissively. 'Occam's Razor. The most likely explanation is the correct explanation. Dragons or attack helicopters? Shape-shifting demons or special forces assassins? Wizards juggling occult forces or very clever scientists? Demon torturers in underground dens or a few rough lads who've lost their natural calling in Ulster, making the most of the peace and quiet in high-security converted mines? Listen to me again: drugs, post-hypnotic programming, screen memories. Lies heaped on lies.'

'And this is the biggest one of all.' Church went for his drink to give him a moment to think. Wasn't this the kind of thing he first feared in the aftermath of that night beneath Albert Bridge? Suddenly he wanted to smash the glass and turn the table over. All that suffering, and they still couldn't trust what was happening.

'Tell me,' the spy continued, 'when you look at one of these shape-shifting demons, do you feel queasy? Does your mind protest that it's not seeing the right thing? When you look at one of those glorious god-like beings, do you occasionally think you see the truth behind it? The bottom line is: do you want to carry on living a lie because it's easy and comforting to believe? Lots of lovely magic and heroic derring-do, just the kind of way you dreamed the world really was when you were children. Or do you want to face up to the harsh facts about how life *really* is? No magic at all. Just lots of cynical, powerful people manipulating you on a daily basis for their own ends?'

'That's a difficult choice,' Laura said acidly. 'And not in the way you think.'

'There have been too many facts which uphold—'

'Don't argue with him, Shavi,' Church snapped. 'He's enjoying screwing with your mind.'

'I admit it is a very carefully constructed scenario,' the spy mused. 'In fact, it would even fool someone who knew how these things were done.'

Shavi, however, seemed to be enjoying the intellectual game. 'If what you are saying is true, then why is so much effort being expended?'

'Power. Control.' The spy smiled. 'You should never raise to high office, either democratically or through promotion, people who *want* high office. That desire is a signifier of some very unpleasant character traits.' He paused while he finished his beer. 'We have martial law now. The democratic process has been suspended. For how long? Until the crisis is over. Oh dear. Let me posit a scenario: there has been a coup. Those sick old aristocrats couldn't take losing their seats in the Lords . . . Friends in the military, the security services, the judiciary, all those Chief Constables . . . Late-night chats in the Lodge—'

Church shook his head vehemently; he realised vaguely that he looked like a sullen schoolboy.

'Think about it for a minute. Doesn't it make a certain kind of sense? Can anything that you've experienced be perceived in another way? Think *deeply* about every incident you've experienced. Could it have happened in a different way, from another perspective?' He raised his hands, prompting their introspection.

'Interesting,' Shavi said with what the others thought was undue excitement. 'But that would imply that we five have been specifically targeted for mind control. That begs the question, why us? We are nobody special.'

'Perhaps the powers behind the curtain believe you *are* somebody special. But no, more people than you five have been influenced. Just to keep the grand illusion growing. A big lie is the best lie, and this is the best lie of all.'

Church could see from the faces of the others that the spy's words were disturbing them, destabilising a world view which had already been fragile in its unreality; he had to admit, he felt the world was moving under his own feet. Only Tom seemed unaffected.

'Give me one reason why we should believe you,' he said.

'Oh, God, you shouldn't. That's the subtext of what I'm saying, isn't it? Don't believe anyone, don't believe anything. Not even yourselves. This is my reality. We all make our own. Perhaps it's yours, perhaps not.'

'You're a victim of your own disinformation,' Church said harshly. 'There's no point us questioning you at all. You're either lying to us or lying to yourself.'

The spy rattled his empty glass on the table, as if he were expecting one of them to buy him another. 'Do you know people can die of sadness? We find them all over the place, just sitting, slumped, a blank expression, no evident sign of death. They stopped believing in their reality. Switched themselves off—'

Veitch's growing confusion triggered the anger that was always just beneath the surface. When he leaned across the table there was such repressed violence in his movement that the spy was taken aback. 'This is just bollocks. You're screwing with our heads just to knock us off course. You're working for the Bastards, aren't you?'

'Believe what you want—'

'Shut up.' Veitch jabbed a finger in the spy's face. 'Get out of here before I break something.'

The spy shrugged, rose, still smiling, but there was now an obvious wariness behind his patina of chumminess; he glanced once more at Veitch, almost relieved to be moving away. 'Think about what I said—'

'Get out,' Veitch said coldly.

The spy made a gesture of reluctance and moved off, but when he was far enough beyond their arc to feel safe once more, he turned back and flashed the same arrogant smile. 'Be seeing you.' And then he was swallowed up by a crowd of drinkers heading towards the bar.

They played with their drinks in silence for a moment and then Shavi said, 'What do you think?'

'You know what I think,' Veitch replied. 'He's a liar. How can you believe any of that bollocks?'

'You know how it is with these gods and mystical items and all that stuff that's supposedly crossed over. We all see them in different ways.' Laura gently rubbed the scar tissue on her face, a mannerism she had developed whenever she was feeling particularly uncomfortable. She rapped her head. 'All this stupid grey matter up here can't begin to grasp what they really are.'

Tom adjusted his spectacles thoughtfully. 'I've had more occasions of altered perception than most people so I have little fondness for some over-arching view of reality. He was right – everyone has their own reality, none more valid than any other. Personally, I find it hard to believe that all my memories have been implanted, but it's certainly possible. I could be a carpenter from Wigan or a used-car salesman from Weymouth who only *believes* he's the mythical Thomas the Rhymer. Who's to say? But I do believe this – you can chase your tail round in circles for the rest of your life trying to find out what the *truth* really is, or you can just deal with it the way you think it is. Paralysis or action. And does it really matter what the higher power truly is – some incomprehensible power seen as dark gods by ancient man or corrupt humans? Surely the aim is to defeat it, whatever it is.'

'It matters to me,' Laura said. 'If I can't put a head in the target sights, I can't pull the trigger.'

The confusion had brought an air of despondency to the table. Church knew he had to take some action to prevent the paralysis Tom had mentioned. 'Tom's right. There's no point sitting here like a bunch of pathetic losers. We've operated in a state of permanent confusion for the last few months, so this isn't going to make any difference.' He turned to Laura, although his words were meant for all of them. 'Okay, if you want to believe somebody who turns up out of the blue and frankly admits his life is based on telling lies, then that's your prerogative. But at least keep it at the back of your mind until you find some evidence to back it up. I don't believe we should mention it again. What do you say?'

Laura shrugged. 'You're the boss, boss.' A ripple of agreement ran through the others.

As the clock neared midnight, the bar began to thin out. Church watched the drinkers hovering near the door as if they were reluctant to venture out into the night, making jokes about watching out for the 'bogles' waiting to chase them home.

'It's as if they all secretly know there's something frightening out there, but won't admit it to themselves or anyone else,' he mused aloud.

'Normal human nature,' Shavi said. 'Who would *want* to believe the world is how it is?'

Laura finished her drink and slammed the glass down theatrically. 'So are you really trying to fool yourself this was anything other than a night's serious drinking?'

'We have actually learned a great deal with this reconnaissance,' Tom said indignantly. 'Would you rather rush into danger blindly? We know that in the New Town Edinburgh seems untouched by what is happening. Yet the Old Town is transformed, corrupted. That tells me the Fomorii are here as we suspected, and here in this particular quarter of the city.'

'You better not be saying we need to get out on the streets at this time of night.' Although Laura was as combative as normal, Church could hear the uneasiness in her voice.

'I don't think it would be wise after midnight,' Church said.

'So far the Fomorii have confined themselves to the out-of-the-way places, the lonely places,' Shavi began. 'Why do you think they are here, at this time?'

'Because,' Tom replied, 'the Well of Fire makes this one of the most significant places in the land. In times past the Fomorii would not have been able to come within miles of this site, but now the Earth-blood is dormant. So, I presume, there is a certain frisson in colonising a place that was so important to everything they despise.'

'The dark overcoming the light,' Shavi noted.

They finished their drinks and left, their heads swimming with too much alcohol and all the doubts implanted by the spy. Outside, the unseasonal chill had grown even colder. Laura shivered. 'Jesus, it's like winter.'

The Royal Mile was deserted. Church had visited the city with Marianne for the Festival and he knew it was never so dead. An eerie stillness lay oppressively over everything; no lights burned in any windows, the late-night coffee shop was closed, even the street lights seemed dim.

They didn't need any prompting to move hastily back to the hotel. But as they made their way up Lawnmarket towards the spotlit bulk of the castle, the night dropped several more degrees and their breath bloomed all around them. A dim blue light seeped out of Ramsay Lane, although they couldn't tell if it was some optical illusion caused by the stark illumination of the castle. As they drew closer, however, there was no doubt. The sapphire glow emanated from somewhere along the road they had travelled earlier that evening, casting long shadows across their path; the shadows moved slightly, as if the light was not fixed.

'Police?' Shavi suggested.

Tom was unusually reticent. 'I don't think so.'

A deep hoar frost sparkled on the road and gleamed on the windows near where Ramsay Lane turned sharply. They marvelled at the display of cold in the first thrust of summer, but then a dark shape suddenly lurched into view and they all jumped back a step. Veitch quickly moved in front of them, lowering his centre of gravity ready to fight. The shape moved slowly, awkwardly, in a stiff-limbed manner; they saw it was a man with long black hair and a bushy beard they had seen drinking in the pub – except now his hair and beard was white with frost and his skin had a faint blue sheen that shimmered in the street light. He slumped against a wall, saw Church and the others and reached out a pleading hand. A faint strangled sound escaped his throat which they presumed was a cry for help.

As they ran forward, he crumpled to the pavement, still.

Laura went to turn him over, then snatched back her hand. 'Ow! Too cold to touch.'

Shavi blew on his hands, then quickly pressed two fingers against the man's neck. 'No pulse.'

'What do you think, Tom?' Church said.

It was only when the Rhymer didn't answer that they realised he wasn't with them. They looked up to see him standing at the top of Ramsay Lane, staring towards the source of the blue light. His expression had grown even more troubled.

As the others ran back to his side they were shocked to see the whole of Ramsay Lane was covered in ice, as if it had been transported to the middle of the Antarctic. At the bottom of the winding street the blue light glowed brightly. It was bobbing gently in their direction and at the heart of it they thought they could make out a dark figure. As it moved, the ice on the surrounding buildings grew noticeably thicker.

'What is it?' Church asked in hushed amazement.

Tom's voice was choked so low Church could barely hear the reply. 'The Cailleach Bheur.'

'In English,' Laura snapped.

He looked at her with eyes shocked and wide. 'The Blue Hag, spirit of winter. Quickly, now!' He roughly pushed them until they were moving hurriedly back down the Royal Mile, the way they had come. Tom kept them to the middle of the road and only calmed once they had turned off the High Street on to the broad thoroughfare of the North Bridge. Once they were firmly over Waverley Station he slumped against a wall, one hand on his face.

'What was that?' Church asked forcefully.

It was a moment or two before Tom answered, 'One of the most primal forces of this land.'

Church couldn't help glancing over his shoulder towards the shadow-shrouded Old Town. 'Fomorii?'

'No, nor of the Tuatha Dé Danann. Like the Fabulous Beasts, the Blue Hag and her sisters are a higher power, almost impossible to control. Yet the Fomorii have somehow bent her to their will, like they did with the first Fabulous Beast you encountered. They have her patrolling the Old Town like some guard dog, leaving them free to carry on their business.'

'She's some kind of evil witch?' Veitch said hesitantly.

Tom turned a cold gaze on him. 'If the deepest, coldest, darkest, harshest winter is evil. The Cailleach Bheur is a force of nature. Nothing can survive her touch.'

'You know, *hag* doesn't sound too frightening when you think about it. It makes you think of bath chairs and whist drives that never end—'

Tom's glare stopped Laura in her tracks. 'The Cailleach Bheur controls the fimbulwinter. If she unleashes it the entire planet will freeze and all life will be destroyed.'

'That sounds like a tremendous power for the Fomorii to influence,' Church said.

'It's a mark of their confidence. Or their arrogance.' Tom put his head back and took a deep breath. Some of the strength returned to his face. 'It will have taken a tremendous ritual, an appalling sacrifice, for them to control her, and even then it will undoubtedly be for only a short while. They really are playing with fire this time.'

'Bad joke, old man.' Laura rattled a stone across the road with her boot. 'And this thing has sisters?'

'Black Annis, the devourer of children, who makes her home in the Dane Hills of Leicestershire. And Gentle Annie, who controls the storms.'

'I think I prefer that last one,' she said.

'The name is ironic,' Tom said, 'and designed to placate her. You wouldn't want to be caught in one of her storms.'

Church recalled Black Annis from his university studies. 'But the scholars believe the myth of Black Annis grew out of the Celtic worship of Danu or Anu, the Mother of the Danann.'

'The same provenance,' Tom snapped, 'but very different.'

The night in the New Town was summery and relaxing, but a blast of wind filled with icy fingers rushed down from the hill, as if to remind them what lay only a short distance away.

'Then to get to the Fomorii, wherever they might be, we have to go past the Blue Hag,' Church said.

Tom nodded. 'And in the minds of the old people, the Cailleach Bheur was another name for Death.'

His voice drifted out on the chill wind that spread out across the city.

the Perilous Bridge

In daylight the Old Town seemed less oppressive, but there was still an uneasy undercurrent which made them keen to move through it quickly. Veitch wondered if the authorities had any idea what was happening among the jumbled clutter of ancient buildings; although it hadn't been sealed off, the tourist office was closed and the crowds that moved in the historic sector were even thinner than on the previous day. The body of the frozen man had been removed.

From the Royal Mile they stopped to survey their destination. The extinct volcano of Arthur's Seat presented them with the curve of Salisbury Crags, dark and formidable.

'At least 350 million years since it last erupted,' Laura said, consulting the tourist guide she had shoplifted earlier; Church had been forced to return to the bookshop to pay for it. 'But with our luck . . .'

'This is an ancient landscape,' Tom mused. 'There were people hunting here nine thousand years ago.'

'Wow, that's even older than you,' Laura jibed.

He harrumphed under his breath. The others couldn't understand how he always fell for Laura's jibes. 'You know, the Celts recognised the importance of this place,' he continued with his back to Laura. 'The Castle Rock was a stronghold for the Gododdin tribe, who named it *Dunedin*, the hill fort. But they weren't here because the high ground was easily defendable. It was that.' He pointed to the soaring heights of Arthur's Seat. 'The sacred place of power.'

With the help of Laura's guide book, they ignored the steepest paths to the top. Hiring a car for quick passage along the winding route of Queen's Drive, they drove up through the increasingly rough country-side towards the 823-foot summit. At the start of their journey they passed an odd grille set into a wall before being drawn by the placid waters of St Margaret's Loch, overseen by the grim ruins of St Anthony's Chapel. Not long after they arrived at Dunsapie Loch, where they found a path with a gentle gradient. The summit presented them with an astonishing view across the city and beyond, to the Borders and Fife. When he saw it, Tom grew still as he quietly studied the homeland he had left so many hundreds of years before, and after a moment or two he wandered off to be alone with his thoughts. Veitch and Shavi set off in a different direction to explore the surroundings.

'This is amazing.' Church was surprised to hear wonder had driven the cynicism out of Laura's voice. 'We're right in the middle of the city!'

'I didn't expect you to be bowled over by lyrical views,' Church said.

She glanced at him from behind her sunglasses. 'Shows how much you know. Nature is the only thing worth believing in in this shitty life.'

She slumped down on a rock in her usual couldn't-care-less manner, but Church knew she wanted him to join her. He sat close, feeling her body slowly come to rest against him. 'Nature girl, eh?' He mentioned the unusual desktop wallpaper of interlinking trees he had seen on her portable computer not long after they met. 'You nearly took my head off when I asked you about that before, but it was an environmental thing, wasn't it?'

'Oh, you're so sharp. It's an Earth First design.'

'What's that?'

'A radical environmental group. I'm a member. We believe in taking action where it's called for, like when some developer is ripping up ancient woodland or some farmer's trying to make a fast buck growing GM foods.'

This surprised him. 'You're good at keeping secrets, aren't you? I didn't think you believed in anything.'

'Everybody has to have something to believe in. And that's mine.' She adjusted her sunglasses slightly, then let her fingers stray to her scar tissue. 'So do you still think I have something to do with Little Miss . . .' She caught herself. '. . . with Ruth disappearing?'

'I never said I thought that.'

'No. You never say much of anything that's important.' There was a sharp edge of bitterness in her voice.

'It was just seeing you with all that blood. I knew you weren't getting on—'

'So naturally I'd go and slit her throat and hide the body. That makes a lot of sense. For the leader of this sorry little clan, you really are a moron.' She sighed. 'I just want a little trust, you know. Is that too much to ask? I know I've not gone out of my way to endear myself like some perky, eager-to-please tele-sales girl, but that's my way. You should be able to see through that.'

'I'm sorry. I—'

'Everybody else can act like a moron, but I have high expectations for you.'

Her words contained a weight of emotion that was in conflict with the blandness of the surface meaning; so much, it was almost too charged for him to deal with. He felt attracted to her, cared for her, certainly, but beyond that he had no idea what she meant to him. The pressure of events made his own deep feelings seem like a foreign language to him.

He searched deep in himself for some kind of comfort to give her, but all he could do was put his arm around her shoulders and pull her closer. That simple act appeared enough to satisfy her, and that made him feel even more guilty.

'So what do you reckon our chances are?' Veitch clambered on to an outcropping of rock, his muscular body compensating for the buffeting of the wind; he was fearless despite the precariousness of his position. 'You know, of finding her alive?'

'I can tell you care for her a great deal.' Shavi smiled mischievously; he knew his words would plunge Veitch into a clumsy attempt to talk about his emotions.

'She's a good kid.' Veitch kept his gaze fixed on the landscape spread out before them.

'And you feel that way even though she treated you so harshly for killing her uncle?'

'I deserved it. I did kill him. Are you going to answer the bleedin' question or not?'

Shavi squatted down on his haunches and absently began to trace the cracks in the rock. 'I have hope.'

'You know, I'm going to kill the bastard who did that to her.'

'Revenge never does much good, Ryan.'

'It makes me feel good. Do you reckon Blondie had anything to do with it?' He glanced over to where Church and Laura were sitting.

'I do not know. My instinct says probably not.'

'I just want to be doing something. All this sitting around is driving me crazy.' He found a pebble and hurled it with venom far out across the landscape. After he had watched the descent of its arc, he said, 'After we find her . . . if we find her . . . do you think, you know, me and her could ever get together? I know we're chalk and cheese and all that, but you never know, do you?'

'No, you never know.' Shavi watched Veitch fondly; for all his rage and barely repressed violence, at times he seemed like a child; inside him Shavi could sense a good heart beating, filled with values that were almost old-fashioned.

Veitch laughed. 'I don't know why I'm talking about stuff like this to a queen.'

For the first time Shavi sensed there was no edge to the slur; in fact, it was almost good-natured. 'I don't—'

'Yeah, yeah, I know what you're going to say. Men, women, they're all the same to you.'

'And emotions are all the same as well, whoever you care for.'

Veitch eyed him thoughtfully for a second, said nothing.

Shavi came over and sat next to him on the rock. 'There is a belief in many cultures that we create who we are through will alone.'

'What do you mean?'

'That we are not a product of breeding or environment. That if we wish ourselves to be a hero or a great lover, and wish hard enough, than we will transform ourselves into our heart's desire.'

Veitch thought about this for a second. 'And if we mope around thinking we're a nothing, loser, stupid, small-time crook, then that's what we end up as well.'

'Exactly.'

'So why are you telling me this?'

Shavi shrugged. 'I just want to help.'

Veitch looked at him curiously, but before he could speak, Tom wandered up to them along a muddy path worn into the scrub. Shavi and Veitch made no attempt to read his mood; at times his thought processes were as alien as those of the Tuatha Dé Danann or the Fomorii.

''s up?' Veitch asked.

'I can't find any sign of the gate to the Well.' Tom stood next to them, as detached as ever.

'You didn't have any problem down in Cornwall,' Veitch noted.

'The power here has been dormant for a long time. There are no structures or standing stones to keep it focused. It may even be extinct.'

'So, what? We're wasting our time? Those haunts wouldn't have bothered mentioning the place if that was the case.'

'The Aborigines have a similar view of an earth energy. In fact, it is an extremely widespread cultural belief around the world.' Shavi brushed his wind-whipped hair from his eyes. 'The Aborigines call it *djang*, the creative energy from which the world was formed. In their stories of the Dreamtime, *djang* spirit beings transformed into things in the landscape – rocks and trees, bushes and pools. That residue was always there so the people could tap into their spiritual well at any moment. And like the ley lines we have discussed before, there were *dreaming tracks* and *song lines* linking sacred sites. But the *djang* could also be conjured up with correct, traditional dances and rituals.'

Tom's eyes narrowed thoughtfully. 'Your shamanic abilities are very potent. Do you think you could find the *dreaming tracks* that would lead us to the source?'

'If I have that ability I do not know how to access it. Yet.'

Veitch noticed Shavi's faint smile and tapped him firmly on the chestbone. 'But you could learn!'

'Possibly. Given time—'

Tom shook his head. 'We have little time for you to fritter away meditating. You'll need to do what shamans have done throughout history when they were searching for information or guidance.'

Shavi looked at him, puzzled.

'Ask the spirits of the dead.'

They made their way down from Arthur's Seat in the early afternoon. The day had grown cloudy and thunderheads backing up in the east suggested a storm was approaching. Just off the comforting modernity of Princes Street they located a small café where they discussed Tom's suggestion.

'Why are you asking Shavi to do it?' Church asked Tom between sips of a steaming espresso. 'You seemed to have a good-enough handle on it when you called up the spirits at Gairloch.'

'To continually contact the dead allows them to learn to notice you. And then they will never leave you alone.' Tom's tone suggested this was not a good thing.

'So it's all right for the Shav-ster to set himself up for a lifetime's haunting, but you have to protect yourself,' Laura said sharply. 'You sound like one of those First World War generals sending the boys off to die.'

'I may be remarkably talented,' Tom replied acidly, 'but Shavi is the one with true shamanistic abilities. He is more able to cope with the repercussions.'

Laura began to protest, but Shavi held up his hand to silence her. 'Tom is correct. I fully understand my responsibilities. It is the role of the best able to do all they can for the collective, whatever the outcome.'

'You sure you're all right with this?' Veitch said with a note of concern. 'Nobody ought to be bleedin' bullied into doing something they don't want.'

'I will not deny that the prospect is unnerving, but then everything about life at the moment is very frightening. There are no longer any certainties.' Shavi smiled to himself. 'Perhaps there never were. I have had difficulty adjusting to my new-found abilities.' His face darkened. 'On the way to Skye, when I gained control of the sea serpent, I felt like my mind had been spiked. That sense of losing control, of finding yourself in something so alien, it was like waking entombed beneath the earth, of giving up your body and never knowing if you could ever get back . . .' His voice drifted away, but after a moment his smile returned. 'It was a little like dying. But now I am resurrected.'

Laura snorted derisively. 'You're saying something like that isn't going to screw you up for ever? Yeah, right.'

'Only if I let it. The shadow is still there, the fears. But not to do something because of fear is even worse.'

Laura's expression suggested she didn't understand a word he was saying. She focused on her cappuccino.

'Okay, it's agreed,' Church said. 'But where's all this going to take place?'

'Somewhere suitable,' Tom replied. 'Somewhere regularly frequented by the dead.'

Laura threw the guide book across the table. 'It's all in there,' she said with an odd note to her voice. 'God help you, you poor bastard.'

Early evening sunlight streamed into the hotel bedroom, catching dust motes in languid flight. Through the open window came the gritty sounds of the city, rumbling and honking with optimism and stability; the normality was powerfully soothing. Church and Laura lounged in the tangled sheets, listening to their subsiding heartbeats, daydreaming of the way the world used to be. The sweat dried slowly on their skin as they held each other silently. For a long while nothing moved.

Even then Church couldn't find complete peace. The thoughts that had been creeping up on him since that evening on the quayside at Kyleakin had gathered pace; of Niamh and the kiss that had filled his entire being, almost forgotten in the upheaval of Ruth's disappearance; of Laura and her slowly revealing deep affection for him; of his own strained ambivalence. For too long it had seemed like events were uncontrollable and now he was beginning to feel his personal life was going the same way. After so many months trapped in the sphere of his grief and guilt over Marianne's death, his emotional landscape was an uncharted territory. He knew he felt an attraction to Niamh, but whether it was physical or emotional, or even pure curiosity, he wasn't entirely sure. And the same with Laura – why couldn't he read what he felt about her? The only time he was truly in tune with her was during that moment in sex when his conscious mind switched off and the shadow person at the heart of him took over.

'What are you thinking about?'

He glanced down to see her eyes ranging over his face. 'Life, death, and all things in between.'

She nodded thoughtfully.

He slid down and threw one arm across his eyes; the darkness was comforting. 'What did you think I was thinking about?'

'It would have been nice if you'd said, me.'

'Sorry.' There was a stress-induced unnecessary sharpness in his voice which he instantly regretted.

He felt Laura's muscles tense next to him and a second later she had levered herself up on her elbow to fix an incisive eye on him. 'What's on your mind?'

'What isn't? The weight of the responsibility on our shoulders. All that bullshit the spy told us last night – I can't get it out of my head, even though I know I should. The fact that I'm eaten up with vengeance for whoever it was killed Marianne and your mum.' He caught himself. 'You've never told me how you feel about that.'

'I don't feel anything. I'm not even numb. Don't get me wrong, I'm glad it wasn't me who did it to the old bitch – at least I can still look at myself in the mirror – but it's not as if I'm tearing myself apart that she's dead. After all she did.' She shifted selfconsciously to hide the original set of scars on her back.

The tone of her words made him feel uncomfortable. 'That sounds a little—'

'What? Cold? Psychotic? Don't criticise me. You don't know anything about my life.'

'I'm trying—'

'Not hard enough.'

He suddenly felt angry that he constantly had to pussyfoot around her; it was more strain that he didn't need. He knew she had her own problems – the rumbling trauma from the scars Callow had inflicted on her face, the doubts over why Cernunnos had marked her – but all of them had problems and no one else acted like a spoiled brat.

They sat in silence for five minutes watching the dust motes dance in a sunbeam, and when she spoke again she sounded calmer. 'Anything else on your mind?'

He paused for a long time, then admitted it aloud, to himself as much as to her. 'That I should be sending us all to look for Ruth instead of—'

'What? Trying to save the world and everyone in it? That makes sense.' Another whiplash in her voice; he felt the irritation rise again.

'I'm on your side. Why do you always give me such a bad time?'

'I'm having a bad life.'

'It's not all about you, you know,' he snapped. 'I sit here with my thoughts and I can't even tell who I am any more. Thanks to that stuff I drank from the Danann cauldron, sometimes I think I can hear alien voices chattering at the back of my head, saying things I can't understand but I know they're terrible. Then everything flips on its head and I feel the rumblings of whatever the Fomorii did to me with the *Roisin Dubh*, deep in the same place—'

'Well, boo-hoo for you.'

Unable to contain the building rage any longer, he hammered his fist into the mattress. 'Shit, why am I here?'

'Yes, why are you here?' She gave him a harsh shove to the other side of the bed. By the time he'd turned back, angrily, she was out and starting to get dressed. He wanted to shout at her, that *she* was the one destroying the relationship, but then her mask of cold aloofness dropped slightly and he saw the hurt burning away underneath. He had never seen such emotion in her face before.

The shock of it calmed him instantly. 'Look, I'm sorry. We're all under a tremendous strain.'

She muttered something under her breath as she marched to the door, then turned and said, 'Go fuck yourself,' before slamming it behind her.

Laura hated the way she had to blink away tears of anger and hurt as she marched out of the hotel. For years she'd been good at battening down any emotion so that even those closest to her had no idea what she was thinking. But now it seemed as if the stopper had come out of the bottle and wouldn't go back in again. And Church seemed to have a particular talent for painfully extracting feelings, even when he wasn't trying; and somehow that made the process hurt even more.

However much she tried to pretend to herself she didn't like him, she realised she felt something closer to a childish ideal of love than anything else she had experienced in her life. At first she had hoped it was purely sexual, like so many of her previous relationships. Then she wished it was born of circumstances; of fear; of desperation. But it wasn't. Emotionally she'd suffered enough at the hands of her parents. And now everything was happening just as she'd feared.

She headed directly towards Princes Street, hoping to lose herself in some of the trendy bars which were still doing a roaring trade. Shavi and Tom, who had been in search of psychoactive substances for their respective rituals, hailed her as they returned to the hotel. She pretended she hadn't seen them.

She opted for the noisiest, most crowded bar and forced her way to the front to buy a Red Stripe. Although her attitude never wavered, it wasn't long before the locals were trying to pick her up. She fended a few off with acid comments, but as the drink took hold a little company that was interested in her seemed increasingly attractive.

For the next two hours she found herself at the centre of a group of young men and women whose only concern in life appeared to be having a good time. The conversation was sharp and witty, the jokes raucous, the flirtation charged. There was no talk of darkness or death. Laura found herself gravitating increasingly towards two of the most powerful characters in the group: Will had short brown hair and blue eyes that were gently mocking, a supremely confident demeanour and a certain sexual charisma; Andy was more openly loud and humorous, taller and bigger-boned, with corkscrew hair and a wispy goatee.

After a long, sparring conversation, Will grinned at Andy knowingly before turning to Laura. 'So, you up for going on somewhere else?'

'Subtle. Wouldn't happen to be your sweaty, beery bedroom, would it?' Laura sipped on her beer, enjoying the game.

'You've got me all wrong.' Will's grin suggested she hadn't got him as wrong as he'd like her to think. 'We're going on to a club. Great fucking place. Different venue every week. Cool fucking crowd. Good beats. You'll like it.'

'Ah, I don't know . . . I'm getting a bit old for clubs. I'm usually tucked up long before now with something hot and comforting.'

'You can't pull out on us now. Or we'll have to call you a big, blonde, soft, southern saddo.' Andy pushed his face into hers in a mock challenge.

'There might be another way we can convince you,' Will interjected. 'Come to the toilet with us.'

'Like I haven't heard that one before.'

He took her by the hand and led her through the crowded bar to the toilets at the back. Laura whistled at the men at the urinals before they herded her into a cubicle. Once the door was locked Will surreptitiously pulled out a small plastic bag from his Levi's pocket. Inside were five or six yellow capsules.

'Es?' Laura said.

'Like none you've ever tasted before. The best MDMA cut with a little something extra. Same loved-up strength with a little more trips. Straight off the boat from the States.' Will waved the bag in front of her face. 'Our gift to you, just to show you how much we want you along.'

The sight of the Ecstasy made her suddenly uneasy. Too many unpleasant memories surfaced of the months she'd spent in Salisbury and Bristol blasted out of her head, driving herself to the brink with a wilful disregard for her own health, both mental and physical, before she'd finally cleaned herself up. Drugs weren't good for her; or rather, she wasn't good for drugs; and she didn't want to go down that road again. But she'd had enough of all the repression and fear of the last few months. She wanted to celebrate life with abandon, forget Church and the stupid mission that was ruining her life, forget who she really was. She just wanted to have fun.

She dipped her hand in the bag and then, fighting back the nagging doubts, she popped one of the capsules on to her tongue. 'Let the good times roll,' she said with a grin.

The grim shadows that gripped the Old Town by day had merged seamlessly into the oppressive darkness of night as Shavi made his way cautiously along the Royal Mile. He had attempted to put on a brave face for the sake of the others, but he felt a nugget of dread heavy within him. Each new experience since he had discovered his aptitude for the mystical and the spiritual seemed to have taken him another step away from the light of humanity into a tenebrous zone from where he feared he would never be able to return. All he had to see him through was an outsider resilience honed through the disenfranchised days of his youth. He hoped it was enough.

He started as the slam of a door echoed along the length of the near-deserted street. Someone emerged from one of the pubs further down the way, glanced around uneasily at the gloom, as if surprised by the lateness of the hour, then broke into a jog towards the bright lights of North Bridge.

Shavi sucked in a deep breath to calm himself. He had read and reread the guide book entry for his destination, but its terrible story had done little to ease his anxieties. The handful of mushrooms taken to enhance the shamanic experience hadn't helped either. At the cobblestoned Heart of Midlothian at Parliament Square he paused briefly and spat, as custom dictated, to ward off the spirits of those executed at the old Tolbooth Prison. It might have been ineffective – the customs of the Unseen World were unknowable – but he thought it wise to proceed with caution; he had no desire to be confronted by the spectral severed heads of those dispatched and later exhibited in the area.

Across the road loomed the Georgian façade of the City Chambers. It spoke of elegance and cultured discourse, the best humanity had to offer; like all of the modern world it hid a multitude of sins. Beneath the chambers was what remained of an entire city street, Mary King's Close, locked away in darkness. The guide book described it as the most haunted place in all Scotland, which was hardly surprising. The City Chambers had been built there to seal off for ever a part of Edinburgh history the people hoped to forget, couldn't bring themselves to face, with all its shame, guilt and suffering. But like all bad memories it refused to stay buried.

In 1645, when Edinburgh was in the grip of the Black Death, the filthy, overflowing tenements of the Old Town were filled with the diseased and the dying, and Mary King's Close was worse than most. *A sickening plague pit*, the city fathers had said. The rich, cultured, upstanding Great Men of the City had a view of the poverty-stricken that was less than human, and in an act of brutality that reverberated down the years they ordered the entire close blocked up. They called it quarantine. The truth was not so clean: every resident was left to die without food or water in the hope that the disease could be contained. And if that was not enough of a monstrosity, when the moans of the inhabitants had finally drifted away, two butchers were sent in to dismember the corpses.

Shavi shivered at the extent of the cold-hearted cruelty. No wonder the spirits of those who had suffered couldn't depart the prison of their misery. For hundreds of years, visitors to the hidden street had reported the most awful, shrieking spectres, accusing revenants, a little girl, her china doll face filled with such overwhelming sadness it caused physical pain in those who saw it, watchers from the shadows whispering threats and prophecies of suffering and pain; an oppressive atmosphere of despair hung over all, and even the sceptical left the place changed on some fundamental level.

Shavi surveyed the City Chambers carefully, then let his gaze slowly drop to ground level. If even normal, rational people experienced such dread, what would he find, with his super-charged perceptions? With apprehension tightening a band around his chest, he set off across the street.

The entrance to the buried close was a nondescript, rickety wooden door off Cockburn Street. He flicked on his torch the moment it opened, listening to the echoes disappear into the depths. Spraying the light around inside, he was confronted by a path that rose steeply to another entrance. To his left, about halfway up, was an ancient front door almost lost in the gloom. Dust was everywhere, in thick layers on the floor and hanging in choking clouds in the air, so that he continually had to stifle coughs; the resultant noise, twisted by the echoes, was like the bark of a beast prowling nearby.

Slowly he moved through a maze of bare rooms, claustrophobic in the dark, where an oppressive atmosphere gathered among the creaking timbers that propped up the ceilings. He tried to shake off the knowledge that he was alone there, far beneath the road where no one would ever hear him if he yelled, but the thought kept creeping back.

The mushrooms turned the echoes of his footsteps into percussive bursts rattling off the confining walls in a syncopated rhythm that rose and fell, grew and receded; there was something about the quality of the reverberations that didn't seem quite right and in the brief snatches of silence that lay inbetween them he was sure he could hear other disturbing, muffled sounds. He didn't pause to listen too closely. The air grew dank as he moved deeper into the heart of the Close's system of ancient bedrooms, living rooms and kitchens, where families of ten or more were forced to live together in abject poverty.

After a while he stopped to try to get his bearings; the last thing he wanted to do was get lost down there. In the darkness that lay beyond the beam of his torch he thought he could see sparks of light swirling like fireflies; he dismissed it as a trick of his eyes, although it continued to nag at him. The atmosphere was even worse than he had anticipated, alive with dismal emotion and sour memory, brooding for centuries, ready to lash out with bitterness.

Shavi attempted to maintain his equilibrium. His gradual understanding of the Invisible World told him that whatever power lurked there away from the light would see anything less as a sign of weakness; and that could, very possibly, be a fatal mistake.

He sprayed the beam around. He was in a small room next to an old fireplace. The plaster on the walls was cracked and flaking. There was nothing out of the ordinary until something caught his eye in a flash of the torch beam: one corner was filled with an incongruous collection of dolls, teddy bears, photos, dollar bills, Tamagotchis: a pile of offerings left by those who had been there before him. It was just rubbish, but there was a strange, eerie atmosphere that surrounded it.

The place was starting to affect him; his breathing had grown shallow. A compulsive desire to flee came in waves, forcing him to grip the torch tightly as he fought it back. Briefly he stared at the torch, trying to clear his mind; despite years of meditation, in that spot, it was almost impossible. His heart was pounding so wildly, the throb of his blood made his head ache. But somewhere he managed to find the reserves of strength for which he was searching. He switched off the torch.

The darkness was all-encompassing.

His breathing stopped suddenly, until his head spun and he thought his lungs would burst. And when the ragged inhalation did come, it sounded so loud he wanted to tear the air from his throat for fear it would mark him out. Cautiously, he lowered himself to the ground and sat cross-legged, and through an effort of pure will he managed to calm himself a little; at least enough to remain in that awful place.

The dark gave him the destabilising sensation that he was floating in space. There was no up or down, no here or there, just a sea of nothing, with him at the centre of it. Gradually his other senses became more charged to make up for his lack of sight: distant, barely perceptible echoes bounced off the walls which seemed, unnervingly, to have no particular point of origin, but which he attributed to changes in the temperature of the building fabric; the floor was dusty and icily cold beneath his fingertips; his nostrils pierced the cloying mist of damp to pick up subtler smells which intrigued him – tobacco smoke, perfume, leather – which he confidently told himself were the fading memories of visiting tourists.

But he knew what he was really sensing: the smells and sounds and textures of the resting body of that place, which was, in a very real sense, alive, more than an amalgamation of bricks and mortar, a creature bound together with the bones of pain and the blood of suffering, guts of despair and the seething, sentient mind of hatred. He knew. And he knew he was there at its mercy.

For nearly half an hour, he sat in the deep dark, listening to the sound of his own breathing. He had just started to wonder if the place would keep him there in torment without presenting itself to him when his nerves began to tingle; his heightened senses had picked up a subtle change in the atmosphere. The temperature had dropped by a degree or two and a strange taste like milky coffee had materialised beneath his tongue.

There was no sound or movement, but he suddenly felt an overwhelming presence looming behind him. His mind demanded that he turn round, defend himself; somehow he managed to hold still. He could feel it, he was sure; it wasn't his imagination. Whatever was there seemed to rise up over him, poised to strike, still silent but radiating a terrible force. It hung there, his hair prickling at faint movements in the air currents. The effort to turn round almost drove him insane, but he continued to resist. And in that instant he knew, although he didn't know how, that if he had turned, he would have been struck dead immediately.

Although it was dark, he closed his eyes and concentrated. He could feel it above him, frozen, waiting for him to make any move that would allow it to attack. Shavi sensed oppressive, primal emotions, but not what it truly was.

And then, when he thought he could bear it no longer, it receded like

521

a shadow melting in the dawn sun, slipping back and back until Shavi felt alone once more. He released a tight breath of relief, although he knew it was not the end.

He didn't have long to wait. At first he couldn't tell if the odd movement his eyes registered were the purple flashes of random nerves sparking on his retina or if it was some external phenomenon. White dots sparkled in one spot, like dust motes in a sunbeam, but moving with a life of their own, coming together almost imperceptibly, coalescing into a shape. His heart began to beat faster.

The shape glowed with an inner light, took on a pale substance, until he realised he was looking at the form of a small girl. Her blonde hair was fastened in pigtails, her face as big and white as the moon, from which stared the darkest, most limpid eyes he had ever seen. She wore a plain shift dress and had her hands clasped behind her back. More than her presence, it was what she brought with her that truly disturbed Shavi: an atmosphere of suffocating despair. It didn't simply make him sad; he felt as if it was being curled into a fist and used to assail him.

'Hello,' he said in as calm a voice as he could muster.

Her eyes didn't blink. The more he looked into them, the more he felt they were not human at all: alien, demonic, too dark and deep by far.

'I hope you will help me,' he continued.

'Ye shouldnae have come here.' It was not friendly advice.

Knowing what was at stake, Shavi arranged his thoughts carefully. 'I understand your pain. I recognise the wrong that has been done to you. But I come to you with open arms, seeking aid. Would you turn your back on another who walks the long, hard road?'

Shavi's heart seemed to hang steady in the long, ringing silence that followed. He couldn't tell if the girl was ignoring him or if her dark, luminous eyes were coldly weighing his presence.

Eventually the glass sliver of her voice echoed once again. 'You're a wee hank of gristle and bone. There's no a handful of meat on ye.'

There was something about her words that made him shiver.

The little girl looked away from him into the sucking dark. 'I can hear Mama calling. Always the same. "Will ye no come here? Marie. Marie!" ' Her voice rose to a sharp scream that almost made Shavi's heart stop. 'But I've no had any food for days and my poor belly hurts! And then the night closes in and still Mama calls!' Her face filled with a terrifying fury. 'And now the men with the choppers are coming, with the sound of squealing pigs in their ears and dirty old rags tied across their faces!' She turned the full force of her regard on him and his head snapped back involuntarily. 'Are ye sure ye wish tae lay your heart afore us?'

Her question was weighted with some kind of meaning he couldn't discern, but he felt he had no choice. 'I am.'

There was another unnerving period of silence and then she suddenly cocked her head on one side, as if she had heard something. A few seconds later Shavi heard it too: a sound like chains rattling. It was accompanied by the overpowering, sickly-sweet stink of animal blood.

The little girl looked back at him. 'They're coming. Ye better run now. Ye better run.'

And then she took a slow step back and the darkness folded around her until she was gone.

The appalling claustrophobic atmosphere of pain and threat grew even more intense. Shavi realised he was holding his breath, every muscle in his body rigid. Then, in the blink of an eye, he was abruptly aware he was no longer alone. He couldn't see who was out there in the dark, but he felt that if he did perceive their forms, he would go instantly insane. He swallowed, unable to ignore the feeling that his life hung by a thread.

'Welcome,' he began.

'Ye come with death at your heels and darkness like a cloak.' The hollow voice cut Shavi off sharply; there wasn't a hint of warmth or humanity in the sepulchral tones.

'We hate all life.' Another voice, even colder. 'Here, in the deep dark, we are imprisoned. Abandoned tae shadows, forgotten by almost all. We have nothing tae believe in but revenge. So we wait. And we remember. And we seethe.'

Shavi steeled himself. 'I know your story. You were the innocent victims of abject cruelty.' Somewhere distant came the dim sound of chopping, growing louder, becoming distorted before disappearing; bitter memories, trapped but continuously recurring. 'There is nothing I can say to assuage your suffering, but my heart goes out to you.'

'And ye think that is enough?'

Shavi swallowed again; his throat was too dry. 'It is all that I can do, apart from offer my prayers that you will soon be freed from this Purgatory to find the rest you deserve.'

A heartrending shrieking erupted all around. Shavi's heart leapt and he wanted to clutch at his ears to shut out that terrible sound. After a few seconds it died away and then there was just the tinkling of nonexistent chains and faint movement in the dark. He hoped what he had said was enough.

Then: 'Ye have fair eyes and ears tae sense us. Most only feel us like a shiver on the skin.'

'What d'ye want?' Another voice, gruffer, more uneducated; a hint of threat.

'Knowledge,' Shavi replied. 'I can see some, but not all. From your dark place, you can see everything. You have great power. I bow to you and ask for your aid.' Shavi smelled woodsmoke and that disturbing stink of animal blood once more.

'Speak.'

'The world is plunging into darkness—'

'Why should we care?'

'Not everyone is like your persecutors. Somewhere, descendants of your friends and family still live. Do not forget the good—'

'Dinnae preach tae us!' The voice cracked like a gunshot.

The atmosphere of menace grew stronger; Shavi knew he was losing control. 'Then I will not argue my case at all. I will simply say, we need you. And the world needs you.' In the absence of a reply, he continued talking, hoping that at least the sound of his voice would keep them at bay. 'The old gods have returned and they are already wreaking havoc across the land. But now some of them are attempting to bring back the embodiment of all evil. Balor.' The dark susurrated with their whispers. 'You must have sensed all this?'

'Aye.'

'And if *he* returns, it will truly mean the end of everything. He will draw the darkness of the abyss across all existence. Somehow we have to stop the Fomorii. Whatever they are planning is beginning here, in this city. But where? And how *can* we stop them? They are so powerful, we are so weak. But there must be a way. We will never give up while we breathe.' Shavi tried to order his thoughts. There were so many questions he wanted to ask, but he had to be selective; the dead would have only limited patience, if they told him anything at all. Yet there was only one other question that truly mattered. 'And I would beseech you to answer one more thing. One of our number is missing, presumed dead. Ruth Gallagher, a good, decent woman. We hope in our hearts she is still alive. Perhaps you could guide me towards the truth.'

As his words drifted out into the dark, he was sure that whatever was out there had drawn closer while he spoke. Every sense told him if he reached out a hand he would touch . . . what? He shook the thought from his head.

'There is a price tae pay for anything gleaned from the other side.'

'I will pay it.'

'Do ye not want tae know what it will be?' The words were laced with stifled triumph and sharp contempt, which unnerved him greatly, but it was too late to back out.

'It does not matter. I have my responsibilities. This information has to be uncovered. I will have to bear the burden of whatever you demand, however great.'

'So be it.'

Shavi felt a wash of cold. He couldn't shake the feeling he had agreed to something he would come to regret, but what he had said was correct: he had no choice. Whatever the price, he would have to find the strength to pay it.

'The woman lives, but only just. And her future looks very dark. Hold out little hope.' Shavi had not heard the voice before. It was clearer, younger and had an intelligence that wasn't present in the others.

Shavi didn't know whether to feel joyous or disheartened by the answer. 'If there is anything we can do to save her we will do it,' he said. Odd, muffled noises which sounded like mocking laughter echoed away in the gloom.

'Seek out the stones from the place that gave succour tae the plague victims if ye wish to find the path beneath the seat.' A woman's voice this time. The words were cryptic, but Shavi had expected no less; the dead were helping and hoping to torment at the same time.

'But the Well of Fire will not be enough tae help ye. The worms have burrowed deep in their nest and the Cailleach Bheur is tae powerful for even the blue flames.'

'Then, what?' Shavi asked.

More mocking whispers rustled around the edge of his perception. When the woman spoke again, her voice was tinged with a dark glee. 'Why, call for the Guid Son, Long Jack. Only he can help ye now.'

Shavi hoped Tom could make some sense of their cryptic words. 'I thank you for all the aid you have given me. But one thing still puzzles me—'

'The where,' the educated voice interrupted. 'Know this: the girl and the worms keep their counsel together, deep beneath Castle Rock.'

Shavi felt the tension ease slightly; he had all he came for. But his muscles still knotted at the prospect that the dead had merely been toying with him and, having given up their secrets, would not let him leave alive. Tentatively, he said, 'You have been most gracious in your aid.' He took a deep breath and steeled himself. 'I am ready to pay the price you requested.'

'That has already been put intae effect. Your time here is done. Get thee gone before we rip the life from ye.'

Shavi bowed slightly, then made his way in the direction of the exit as hastily as he could muster without breaking into a run. The hatred of the jealous spirits was heavy at his back and for a few steps it felt like they were surging in pursuit of him, unable to contain themselves any longer. Anxiously he flicked on the torch, which appeared to make them hold back beyond the boundary of the light. But he didn't breathe easily until he was up in the empty street, sucking in the soothing night air, his body slick with cold sweat. The intensity of the experience had left him shaken, even after everything else he had been through over the past few months; he had never believed he could suffer such mortal dread.

But he had come through it and that alone gave him strength. Knowing it wasn't wise to tarry in the Old Town any longer than necessary, he hurried back towards the hotel, desperate to tell the others everything he had learned; but most of all that Ruth was still alive.

As he marched back towards the lights of the New Town, he didn't notice a dark shape separate from the shadows clustering the entrance of an alley. It began to follow him, shimmering in the light, insubstantial, as it dogged his every step. If he had thought to glance behind him, curious at what price the spirits had asked of him, he would have recognised it instantly: his friend and lover, murdered in a South London street two years before.

There were no longer songs, just drum and bass suffusing her brain and body, mixing with the drug, driving reality away on waves of sound. Laura couldn't even recollect a conscious thought for the past hour; she had given herself up to the trip of flashing lights she could hear and noise she could see, dancing, sweating, not even an individual, just a cell in the body of the crowd-beast.

Will and Andy had led her to an old building on the eastern edge of the Old Town. From the outside it didn't appear to have been used for years, but inside it had been transformed by vast batteries of lights, stacks of speakers fifteen feet tall and machines pumping out clouds of dry ice and occasional frothing spurts of bubbles. The place was big enough to cram in several hundred people, yet managed to avoid feeling impersonal. By the time they arrived, the trip had already started and the two young Scots were growing animated.

Will leaned forward to whisper in her ear, 'This drug always makes me feel horny. Come on, let's away to the toilet for a bit of slap and tickle.'

He was right; her pleasure centres were already being caressed by the warm waves that washed through her and she felt herself grow wet at the thought of him between her legs. It wasn't as if she hadn't had numerous other episodes of seedy, horny, loveless sex while off her face in some club or other. She wasn't a prude; it was fun, like taking the drug in the first place; nothing more. At least that's what she had always told herself, but although it would have been the easiest thing in the world to give in to, she suddenly realised she felt strangely reluctant. Part of her was telling her to do it to punish Church, but even then, she couldn't bring herself. It didn't make sense to her at all, and the more she thought about what it meant, the more uneasy she felt.

In the end she grabbed hold of his right hand and raised it in front of his face. 'This is more your scene.'

She flashed a fake smile and left hurriedly to get a drink of water.

On her way back she got drawn into the heart of the dance floor where she lost herself in the music. It was the relief of nothingness, but as the trip reached one of its plateaus, she was irritated to discover occasional thoughts leaking through to her foremind. Most of them concerned Church, but she didn't want anything to bring her down. Angrily, she looked for something to distract her, losing the rhythm of the music in the process. Stomping off the dance floor she leaned against a pillar with her arms folded, where she waited for the trip to pick up again. A goodlooking young man with an annoyingly untroubled face came up to talk to her, but she couldn't hear a word he was saying over the unceasing thunder of the music. She waved him away furiously.

After a few moments, she was relieved to feel the drug begin to take her to the next level and her mood calmed. A smile sprang to her face; she was surprised at how good it felt. The closeness of all the other clubbers cheered her, made her feel part of something. She surveyed the moving crowd warmly, then found her gaze drawn to the flashing lights which a moment ago had seemed dissonant, but now, with the music, made perfect sense: red, green, blue, purple. A white flash. Red again. A strobe. The meaning of life. Slowly she raised her eyes heavenwards, revelling in the growing sense of bliss. And there, as if in answer to her feelings, was an astonishing sight. The entire ceiling was sparkling like a vast canopy of stars in a night sky. She caught her breath as a revolving light splashed upwards, adding to the coruscation. 'That's amazing,' she whispered in wonder.

In the throes of the trip she suddenly became obsessed with sharing her breathtaking vision with Will and Andy. The crowd was so densely packed she felt a moment of panic that she wouldn't be able to find them, but after pushing her way back and forth through the dancers for a few minutes, she spied Andy sitting at a table near the door with a glass of water before him and a cigarette smouldering between his fingers.

'You've got to see this!' she called out. He didn't respond, even glance her way. She guessed her voice had been dragged away by the rumble of the music. She waved excitedly to catch his eye. Still nothing.

The trip started to roll with force and she was almost distracted by the music and the lights, but one thing stuck in her mind and wouldn't shake itself free: the sparkling that had glimmered across the ceiling had now transferred itself to Andy. His corkscrew hair glistened in the occasional beam of light, stars gleamed in his goatee.

'Amazing,' she whispered once more.

But the thing was still niggling at the back of her head, like fingernails scratching on a window pane. It was something more than the spangly effect; something discordant. *What was it?* she mused. She tried to take a step back through the effects of the drug. His skin, too, had that faint twinkling quality. It wasn't that he had been dusted with the gold make-up some of the women dancers used, nor was it the drug. She *was* seeing it. Wasn't she? Her inability to distinguish reality from mild hallucination began to irritate her, throwing the drug off-kilter.

Be careful, she warned herself. *You don't want this trip to go bad.*

She concentrated, focused. The effort twisted the trip a little more.

And there it was. The water before him had risen a full half-inch above the level of the glass. And there it hung, suspended in time.

First the scratching at the back of her head turned to an insistent hammering. Then the trip turned, sucking up the anxiety from the pit of her stomach. She knew. If only she hadn't been drugged she would have seen it long before. She wouldn't have gone there at all. She would have known better.

The water hung, suspended. *Frozen.*

She took a step back, desperately trying to stop herself falling into full-scale panic. Her heart was thundering like it was going to burst out of her chest. She was finding it difficult to breathe.

Andy's stare was locked on the dancefloor. It didn't waver, he didn't blink. There was no movement in him at all.

Frozen, she thought.

Behind him, the walls, too, glistened. It was spreading out gradually from the doorway like an invisible field, creeping across surfaces, leaving its tell-tale sign.

Poor Andy, she thought obliquely. Then, a drug-induced twist: *My God! He's dead!*

And now that she knew, she could feel the bloom of it on her skin; the temperature had dropped several degrees and was still falling fast.

She's coming. The notion drove her into action. She ran for the door, but as she neared it the cold was almost unbearable; her skin appeared to sear from its presence. It was more than winter, more than Arctic; it seemed to Laura to represent the depths of space. She took another few paces and then gave up as the hoar frost thickened on the door. She began to shake as cracks developed in the wood. She was already backing away rapidly when it was torn apart by the freezing moisture and burst inwards with a resounding crack.

The Cailleach Bheur was framed in the doorway, painted red, then blue, then green, then purple by the club's lights, like some hideous MTV video effect. Laura's breath caught in her throat. At first she couldn't quite make out the creature's appearance as the shape shimmered and danced, becoming briefly this and then that. But then her mind settled on a form which it found acceptable and Laura saw an old crone hunched over, dressed in tattered, shapeless rags, her face a mass of wrinkles, her hair as wild as the wind across the tundra. She supported herself on a gnarled wooden staff that was bigger than she. And all around her the air appeared to shift with gusts from unknown origin, suffused with an icy blue illumination that seemed immune to the club's lights; in the glow were flurries of snowflakes that came and went eerily without leaving any trace on the floor behind her.

She moved forward spectrally, almost as if her feet weren't touching the ground. And then she slowly turned her terrible gaze on everyone in the room. In the depths of those swirling eyes, Laura saw nothing remotely human; they contained the desolation of the ice-fields, of the depths of frozen seas. And the sight triggered the trip to bring up a fear so powerful and primal it wiped out all conscious thought. Laura turned and drove herself wildly through the crowd, knocking people over, punching and gouging to get away, oblivious to the angry shouts directed at her.

She was on the other side of the club, huddled behind a table on the beer-puddled floor, when some semblance of sense returned to her, and even then the panic was coming and going in waves. She cursed the drug, but knew she had no option but to ride it out; and that could last for several more hours.

The lights were still flashing, the music still pounding, but through it she became aware of sudden frenzied activity. The dancers had recognised the threat of the Cailleach Bheur. They were surging around crazily, searching for an exit, trampling anyone who fell before them in their panic. Raw screams were punching through the beats like some hellish mix. Laura tipped over the table in front of her to offer her some kind of protection and then desperately tried to order her thoughts enough to get out of there. An emergency exit. Surely there must be one somewhere. But it wasn't a regular club, probably wasn't even legal. What if there was only one way out?

That brought another wave of panic which almost sent her fleeing into the tumult, but she'd used enough drugs in her shady past to know how to calm herself a little. She focused on one of the flashing lights and did deep breathing to clear her mind. When the wave had passed, she peeked above the lip of the table to get her bearings.

What she saw filled her with dread. The walls, floor and ceiling shimmered with ice, reflecting the flashing lights in a breathtaking manner that was amplified by the drugs coursing through her system: it was the ultimate light show. But the wonder was corrupted by the grisly piles of frozen bodies heaped across the floor, faces locked in final expressions of terror, hands clawed, legs bent ready to thrust forward, taken by the cold in seconds. Laura instantly flashed back to sickening images of World War I battlefields she had seen in a history lesson.

And moving through the scene slowly was the Cailleach Bheur, her face as dark as nature. The cold came off her in waves, metamorphosing at the tips into snaky tendrils which reached out to anything not yet touched by the icy blast of eternal winter. The speakers fizzed and sparks flew off the decks. A second later the ear-splitting music ended in a shriek of feedback. That only revealed the awful screams of the surviving clubbers huddled in one corner of the room. Laura covered her ears, but couldn't drive out the sound. She couldn't even tear her eyes away as one of the tendrils wound its way along the floor like autumn mist before wrapping itself around the ankle of a young man who was futilely trying to kick it away. It was followed instantly by an odd effect which, in her state, she found both fascinating and horrible: ice crystals danced in the air before forming around his leg, moving rapidly up to his waist. Yelling, he tore at it, but it simply transferred to his hands where he touched the crystals, turning the skin blue, then forming a film of ice over it. A second later he fell to the floor with the same rictus, catching the light like a gruesome ice sculpture.

Laura was convinced she was going insane from the magnified panic and terror. Irrationally, and with desperation, she threw herself over the table and ran to the men's toilets. The door slammed behind her just as a rapidly pursuing wave of cold crashed against it. She heard the familiar cracking sound as the wood froze, but when it didn't burst in she guessed the Cailleach Bheur had turned her attention back to the remaining clubbers.

Frantically she tore around the small room and was overjoyed when she discovered a tiny window over one of the cubicles. She wrenched it open gleefully, oblivious to the breaking of a fingernail and the spurt of blood as it ripped into her skin. When she saw the solid bars that lay on the other side she burst into a bout of uncontrollable sobs.

'I can't think straight!' she yelled at herself between the tears. 'Why was I so stupid? I'm a loser! A fucking loser!'

The screams echoing dimly through the walls were bad enough, but when they finally faded away, the silence that followed was infinitely worse. Laura collapsed into a corner of the cubicle and hugged her knees, realising how pathetic her whimpers sounded, unable to do anything about it.

The silence didn't last long. The telltale sounds of forming ice and cracking wood gradually made their way towards the toilet door. Laura pressed her back hard into the wall as if, just by wishing, it would open up and swallow her. Her cheeks stung from the tears which had soaked her top. She was already making desperate deals with God: no more drugs, no more stupidity, if He whisked her out of there to safety, turned the Hag away from the door, did anything, anything – when she suddenly noticed a curious sight which broke through the panic. The blood which dripped from her cut finger was green. It wasn't a trick of the light or a vague visual hallucination; an emerald stain had formed on her top. Cautiously she touched the tip of her tongue to it; it didn't even taste like blood. It reminded her, oddly, of lettuce.

'Jesus Christ, what's going on?' It seemed like the final straw of madness. And an instant later she heard the toilet door begin to break open. Her breath clouded around her; the temperature was plummeting.

Clarity crept back into her mind as the drug entered one of its cyclical recessions, and with it came a decision not to die screwed up on the floor of a toilet like some pathetic junkie. She jumped up on to the toilet seat and began to wrench at the bars on the window in the hope that they were looser than they appeared.

By now she was shivering uncontrollably. The door groaned and began to give way.

'Come on,' she pleaded, but the bars held fast. Then another strange thing happened. Where her blood splashed on to the bars it appeared to move with a life of its own, spreading over the metal, changing into something which, in the gloom, she couldn't quite make out; all she could see through the shadows was movement and growth. Instantly the bars began to protest and a few seconds later they burst out of the brick.

The sound of the toilet door bursting inwards and the wave of intense cold that followed drove all questions from her mind. She pulled herself through the opening and fell awkwardly into a dark, litter-strewn alley that smelled of urine. Pain drove through her shoulder where she hit the ground. Ignoring it, she forced herself to her feet and hurried away just as a white bizzard erupted out of the window above her.

The relief that hit her was so overwhelming she burst into tears again, but by the time she stumbled out on to a main road her head was spinning; there was no point trying to make sense of what had happened until the trip was over. Yet she couldn't resist one last look at the green smears across her hands. An involuntary shudder ran through her that did not come from the cold.

CHAPTER FIVE

Storm Warning

There was neverending darkness, and pain, more than she thought she could bear. How long had it gone on for now? Months? Ruth's head swam, every fibre of her body infused with agony. At least the sharp lances that had been stabbing through her hand where her finger had been severed had subsided, a little. She didn't dare think how the wound had healed in the dirty confines of her tiny cell.

Since she had been snatched from the hotel in Callander she had cried so many tears of pain and anger and frustration she didn't feel she had any more left in her. Through all the hours of meaningless torture, it was the hope that kept her going: that she would find a way out, however futile that seemed; that the others would rescue her. But it had been so long— She drove the thought from her mind. *Stay strong*, she told herself. *Be resilient.*

It would have helped if all the suffering had been for a reason, something she could have drawn strength from by resisting, but the Fomorii holding her captive seemed merely to want to impose hurt on her in their grimly equipped torture chambers. They had held back from inflicting serious damage – they always stopped when Ruth blacked out – but she felt it was only a matter of time before they lost interest in their sport.

Feeling like an old woman, she shuffled into a sitting position. Her straw bedding dug into the bare flesh of her legs. She'd mapped the cell out in her mind long ago: a bare cube carved out of the bedrock, not big enough to allow her to lie fully out, smelling of damp, scattered with dirty straw, a roughly made wooden door that had resisted all attempts to kick it open.

There's still hope. It was her mantra now, repeated every time the despair threatened to close in.

She couldn't remember anything about her capture, who did it, how it happened, where she had been brought. Her recent memory began with the shock and dismay when she discovered her missing finger and she wondered if it was the upheaval of that discovery which had driven out all the other thoughts.

Somewhere distant the deep, funereal tolling of a bell began. Soon they would come for her again. Tears sprang to her eyes unbidden and she hastily wiped them away with the back of her hand. She wasn't weak, she would survive.

There's still hope.

Afterwards, with the pain still fresh in her mind and her limbs, she enjoyed the cool, anonymous embrace of the darkness, where thoughts were all; this was the place she could live the life she wanted to live. But, as had happened so many times, the balm was soon disrupted by the familiar voice which made her think of the serrated teeth of a saw being drawn across a window pane.

'Does the light still burn?'

'It burns,' she replied. 'Not brightly, but it's there. You're a good teacher.' She caught herself. 'Teacher. I still haven't worked out what our relationship is. Are you a teacher, aide, confidant—?' She wanted to add *master*, but a frightened part of her made her hold back.

'All of those, and more. I have been entrusted with your well-being.' The sound of his words made her think he was smiling darkly, wherever it was in the gloom he existed. Though he had been helpful and supportive, she had an abiding sense that buried within him was a contempt for her powerlessness.

'What are you?' she asked, as she always did in their conversations.

And he replied as he always did: 'I am who you want me to be.' It had almost become their little joke.

But she didn't know, and that unnerved her. She remembered all she had read throughout her life about *familiars* being demons or sprites doing the Devil's bidding, and however much she had grown to realise that was propaganda put out by the early Church, she still couldn't shake the irrational fears it had set in her. Whatever, she knew she would have to stay measured and protective in her dealings with him.

'I think I prefer you as an owl,' she noted. When the Goddess had gifted her the familiar in the dark countryside outside Bristol, she hadn't realised what she was taking on; certainly with regard to what the Goddess had planned for her, but she had grown into it, reluctantly. And after her meeting with the woman who practised the Craft in the Lake District, she had seen its benefits. But still, she was scared. There was so much she didn't know, so many repercussions she couldn't begin to grasp. And she was afraid that when they did happen they would be terrible; and it would be too late to go back. 'So what's the lesson for today?' she continued hesitantly.

The voice began, telling her dark, troubling secrets: about the way the world worked, about nature, some things she didn't feel comfortable

534

hearing at all, for they hinted at greater, darker mysteries which under-pinned every aspect of existence. But her body of knowledge about the Craft was growing. There in the dark she had learned how to use thorn apples and white waterlilies to make flying ointments, how Christmas roses could convey invisibility, how periwinkles could spark passion in the right potion and how henbane could be used to conjure spirits and intensify clairvoyance. She had discovered which plants could be used for healing and which for protection. And she knew the release of sexual energy was the core of all magick, linked directly to the blue fire that bound together the spirit of the world. Amazingly, she seemed to understand it all on first hearing and forgot none of it.

Time passed. There was a brief discussion about the raising of storms and communication with animals, enough to pique her interest and to make her realise how much there still was to learn.

'And all of this works as you say?' she asked.

'All works if applied in the correct manner by the right strength of will.'

'If I don't get out of here all this information is going to be a complete waste, isn't it?'

He ignored her question. 'This secret knowledge exists to be put into practice and it will be meaningless to you until you do so. Do you understand the message that underpins this gift I give you?'

She thought for a moment. 'No, I don't. I don't understand anything.'

'Listen, well. There is no reality. There is no shape to anything, except the shape you give it. In these matters, your will is all-powerful. If you learn to apply it—'

'I can do anything.' She weighed his words carefully. 'If you're to be believed . . .' Her voice faded. Then: 'There's always hope. That's what it means. It's down to me.'

In the dark, he concurred. 'There is always hope.'

Church paced around the hotel room before coming to rest at the window, as he had done repeatedly over the last three hours. The sun was just beginning to tint the sky pink and pale purple away to the east.

'You are worried about her,' Shavi stated.

'She can look after herself.' The words sounded hollow the moment he uttered them. He knew Laura was resilient enough to cope in almost any situation, but the danger she always carried with her was the dark, self-destructive demon buried in her heart. And after their argument he feared she had been prepared to give full vent to that side of her nature, to punish both herself and him.

He turned back to Shavi, whose face was still bloodless an hour after he had returned to the hotel. Church knew that there was much more to his experiences in St Mary's Close than the bare bones of information he had told them. But Shavi was defined by his decency and he wouldn't tell them anything that might burden them; his suffering was his own. Church couldn't resist clapping a supportive hand on his shoulder as he passed. When everything else seemed to be falling apart, he was glad for the people he had around him. It was more than he could have hoped for; he was surprised by the warmth of the feeling.

'Look, forget all the bollocks the spooks spouted,' Veitch said with a grin. 'Ruth's alive and kicking. That's the good thing, right? That's the important thing.' He grew irritated when he looked around the room to see only gloomy expressions. 'What's wrong with the lot of you?'

'The spirits implied her situation was dire,' Shavi began. 'We should not get our hopes—'

'Why should we believe them? All they do is talk in bleedin' riddles anyway—'

'She's with the Fomorii, Ryan,' Church cautioned. 'We've both been there.'

Veitch fell silent.

Shavi ran his fingers through his long hair. 'What could they possibly want with her? I was under the impression we were beneath their notice since we failed to win over the Tuatha Dé Danann.'

Tom waved a hand dismissively. 'Her situation is not paramount—'

Church stepped in before Veitch could jump to his feet angrily. The South Londoner's eyes were blazing with the barely controllable rage he always carried close to the surface. 'What's wrong with you? She's a friend, you bastard.'

'This is about more than any of us. We're all dispensable.' The coldness in Tom's eyes made Church shiver; the emotional detachment was so great he wondered how apart from them Tom really was.

'I thought you were supposed to be the big mythic hero,' Veitch sneered. 'Turning your back on a girl in trouble isn't very heroic, is it? You weasel.'

Tom turned to Church. 'Tell him. You understand.'

Of course he understood, but he could barely put it into words because it was the antithesis of everything he felt: they *were* all disposable, their petty little human concerns, hopes and fears meaningless against the end of everything. He felt like he was trading off his humanity little by little. If they succeeded, would it be worth it if there was nothing of him left to appreciate it?

Before Church could open his mouth, Veitch saw in his face what he was about to say. With a contemptuous shake of his head, Veitch stalked over to the other side of the room where he stood with his back to them.

Tom pushed his glasses back up the bridge of his nose. 'Now that's out of the way—'

'Have a little heart, for God's sake,' Church snapped. 'Just because you're right doesn't mean you have to stamp all over people's feelings.'

Tom eyed him coolly. 'Keep a level head,' he cautioned.

'Let us examine the evidence,' Shavi said diplomatically; his smile was calm and assured. 'Do we have enough to move forward?'

Church sighed wearily. 'Every time we try to get some information from anything supernatural it always ends up as mysteries wrapped in smoke and mirrors, so vague you can never be sure you've deciphered it correctly.'

'They do it on purpose,' Tom said. 'They want to see us misinterpret their words and fail or suffer. It's a power thing. Good sport. But they have given us enough.' He nodded to Shavi. 'You did well.' Coming from Tom, it was like a cheer.

Shavi looked down shyly. ' "Seek out the stone from the place that gave succour to the plague victims." Do you have any idea what that means?'

'Something particularly relevant to the residents of St Mary's Close. A little research should turn it up.'

'Then that will lead us to the Well of Fire,' Church said. 'And if we can find some way to bring that back to life, then we stand a chance of disrupting the Fomorii stronghold which we now know is somewhere beneath the castle.'

'Destroy that,' Tom said, 'and we will prevent Balor returning. They would not have guarded the place with something as terrifying as the Cailleach Bheur if this was not the location for the ritual of rebirth.'

Since they had been in Edinburgh they had all felt a darkness pressing heavily at their backs. It was something more than a premonition, almost as if the threat of Balor were reaching out from whatever terrible place his essence inhabited; as if he were aware of them. It left them desperate to win the struggle ahead, and dreading what would happen if they failed.

'And then we get Ruth,' Veitch chipped in pointedly without turning from his investigation of the mini-bar. He pulled out a bottle of lager.

'But the spirits said the blue fire was not enough,' Shavi noted. He stretched out his legs and rested his head on the back of the chair. 'They said we should call for the Good Son, whatever that means.'

Out of the corner of his eye Church saw a flicker cross Tom's face; it was like a cloud obscuring the sun. 'What is it?' he said to Tom.

'Nothing.' Tom looked at his feet. 'A story I heard once long ago.'

'Oi. Spit it out then. You were the one who said all those old tales were important,' Veitch said irritatedly.

Tom walked over to the window where he seemed to be eyeing the rising sun suspiciously. 'The Good Son was the name given by the ancient worshippers to one of the most important of the Tuatha Dé Danann. The Celts knew him as Maponus or Mabon – which simply means *Son* – or Oenghus. He was, in their stories, the son of Dagda, the Allfather, and the Great Mother. The Son of Light. When the Romans came into the Celtic lands he became associated with Apollo. When the Christians came, he was the Christ. He was linked to the sun, the giver of life. More double meanings, you see. The Good Sun.'

'What, you're saying Jesus didn't exist?' Church asked.

'Of course not,' Tom snapped. 'I'm simply saying Maponus was an archetype. An original imprint that other cultures drew on for their own myths.'

'Well, I'm glad you answered that one, then,' Veitch said sarcastically.

'He was widely worshipped throughout the world,' Tom continued. 'The Divine Youth who would lead the world back into the light; he was a great musician, *the player of the lyre*, a great lover, a patron of the arts, worshipped at the sacred springs and seen as a direct line to the powers of creation. Beautiful, witty and charming. But there was another side to him.' He paused. 'The Irish used to call him the Lord of Love and Death.'

The sun broke through the window, casting his distorted shadow across the wall; Church had a sudden vision of something monstrous moving across the room. 'What happened?' he asked quietly.

'I have no idea. After the great sundering, when all the old gods and creatures of myth left here for Otherworld, some of them, the ones with the greatest bond to our world, returned. Maponus was one of those. His links were possibly the strongest of all. There was a reason he, of all the Tuatha Dé Danann, was seen as a saviour by mortals. And then, suddenly, he disappeared.'

The others waited for him to continue. 'What happened?' Church prompted.

'The Tuatha Dé Danann would never speak of it,' he said hesitantly. 'In all my time in Otherworld it was the one question I dared not ask.'

538

A shadow crossed his face. 'That's wrong. I did ask it once. But never again.' Church caught a glimpse of the same terrible expression Tom had worn when he had first told them about the suffering he underwent during the gods' *games*. 'The Tuatha Dé Danann indulged me. I was an amusement, a curiosity, but certainly not an equal. They considered me so far beneath them they would never discuss something they considered important. And this, whatever it was, was obviously of vital importance.'

'If he disappeared, how the hell are we supposed to find him?' Veitch asked.

'When I returned to this world and was inducted into the secret knowledge of the land by the Culture . . .' He looked at them sharply as if he had given something away. '. . . the people of the Bone Inspector, I learned another strange story which perhaps shed a little light on it. One of the great old gods had been bound by the Culture in a place just south of Edinburgh, sealed in the earth for all time.'

'I don't fucking understand.' Veitch's irritation was growing. 'If this geezer was so loved, why was he banged up?' He glared at Tom as if the hippie was personally setting out to confuse him.

'I never learned why. That information was kept by the highest adepts within the Culture. I never stayed with them long enough to rise that high.'

'The Culture . . . the people of the Bone Inspector . . . they seemed to have a lot of influence. Power,' Church noted.

Tom nodded. 'Supposedly eradicated by the Roman forces, they simply went underground, for centuries. But in the time when they bound the old god, they were at their strongest, worshipping in their groves, tending to the people, turning to face the sun at the solstice, standing proud, no longer stooped in hiding.'

Veitch drained his lager and tossed the bottle into the waste bin with a crash. 'I don't get it. I've seen these things in action. You can't just stand up and wave a sword at them.'

'At that time, the keepers of the knowledge had unprecedented control of the lifeblood of the Earth. They used the blue fire to shackle a god.'

'Then he is imprisoned still,' Shavi noted, 'waiting to be released?'

Tom merely looked out of the window towards the sun, closing his eyes when the light caught his face.

'Sounds a bit dodgy to me,' Veitch said suspiciously. 'He's not exactly going to be of a mind to help us after being underground all that time.'

'I thought you were the one prepared to risk anything for your lady-love?' Tom said curtly.

'*Can* we control him?' Church asked. 'How do we know the dead weren't lying to us, playing another of their games so we'd actually get into an even bigger mess? Like having an angry god giving us a good kicking for his unjust treatment.'

'We don't know.' Tom sighed. 'But it makes a queer kind of sense. If the Fomorii are preparing for the rebirth of Balor in their fortress beneath the castle, it will have been deemed impregnable. They will not risk losing their sole reason for existing. The Cailleach Bheur . . .' He swallowed hard; his mouth had grown unfeasibly dry. 'She is a power of nature, greater even than many of the powers you have already witnessed. Of all the gods, Maponus is possibly the only one who could hold her at bay, contain her so she didn't unleash the fimbulwinter. And if, at the same time, we could awaken the Well of Fire then the shadows might finally be turned back.'

'Alternatively, everything could go to hell in a handcart,' Church said acidly.

Tom shrugged. 'Did you expect easy choices?'

'No, but I don't expect you to be glib, either,' Church replied. He knew the decision would ultimately rest with him and he didn't feel up to making it. So much seemed to lie on every choice. He wished he could just return to the pathetic little life he had before.

'Do you know where Maponus is imprisoned?' Shavi asked.

'Not exactly. Not to the foot. But I know the place.' He took off his glasses and rubbed a hand over his tired eyes. 'A place called Rosslyn Chapel.'

'I have heard of it,' Shavi mused. 'A place of many mysteries. But it was founded many years after the time of which you speak.'

'And the Good Son was there long before the first stone of Rosslyn Chapel was laid. The building was devised as a resting place.'

'I remember now.' Shavi took the bottled water Veitch handed him from the mini-bar. 'The chapel is famous for its blend of Celtic, Christian and Masonic iconography in its structure. For a supposedly Christian place of worship there are pagan symbols everywhere, more representations of the Green Man than anywhere else in the land.'

'And The Green Man,' Church said, 'is another way of saying Cernunnos—'

'Cernunnos was an important element in the ritual of binding. He is, to be glib—' he glanced at Church '—the flip side of Maponus. The thick, dark forests to the sunlit plains. Winter to summer. Night to day.'

'His brother,' Church ventured.

'As if that term means anything to them.'

'I am impressed that the memory of Maponus survived the centuries strong enough to prompt the erection of such a magnificent, codified building,' Shavi said.

Tom nodded thoughtfully. 'A good point. Of those few who held the knowledge, a separate group was established in perpetuity. The members were called, in our parlance, Watchmen. Their aim was not only to keep the knowledge of the old god's imprisonment, but that a line of civil defence would be established to prepare for any further incursions from Otherworld. They were of their own creed to begin with, but as the role was essentially spiritual, when Christianity began to become established, representatives were chosen from the new Church. And from all the other faiths that eventually set up roots in this land. Over time, each faith's Watchmen became almost separate entities, unaware of those groups formed by their rivals. But they all kept the same knowledge and the same mission.'

'It was one of the Watchmen who pointed us in the right direction at Glastonbury.' Shavi moistened his throat with the water. Some of the blood seemed to have returned to his features, much to Church's relief. 'And it was another group which built Rosslyn Chapel?'

Tom nodded. 'Under the direction of Sir William St Clair, a prince of Orkney. In the increasingly Godless twentieth century most of the groups have withered. I have no idea if one still exists at Rosslyn—'

The faint knock at the door made him tense, as if he had heard a gun being cocked. Before anyone could speak, Veitch was already moving on perfectly balanced limbs until he was poised at the door jamb, ready to act. He looked to Church for guidance.

Church waited a moment then called out, 'Who's there?'

'Laura.' Her voice sounded like paper in the wind.

Veitch wrenched open the door and she almost collapsed in. Church moved forward quickly to catch her.

She looked into his face before her eyelids flickered and a faint smile spread across her lips. 'You know, I always saw it like this.'

It was midmorning before she had recovered. Faintly contrite but determined not to show it, Laura sat in a sunbeam on the bed, wrapped in a blanket, her skin like snow, her pupils still dilated so much her eyes seemed black. She had attempted to tell them the full horror of what had happened at the club, but so much had been tied into her trip she couldn't separate reality from hallucination herself. 'Maybe that spy was right,' she said. 'Maybe it is all how we see it in our heads. Who knows what's really happening?'

'Exactly!' Shavi began excitedly. 'Liquid nitrogen would cause—'

Veitch pushed forward, barely able to contain his irritation. 'What's wrong with you? Look at the state of you – off your face, talking bollocks. This isn't a holiday. You can't just carry on having a good time—'

Church clapped a hand on his shoulder. 'Not now, Ryan.'

Veitch glared. 'Jumping to her protection just because you're shagging her, even though you know I'm right?'

'It's not like that. We all know she could have made some better choices, but this isn't the time.'

Veitch shook his head angrily. 'This is war. We've got to have some strict rules. Because if one person fucks up, it could drag the rest of us down.'

'He's right,' Tom said. 'We have to have discipline—'

'And that's one thing I haven't got, right?' Laura said sharply. 'You lot are such *blokes*.'

She desperately wanted to talk about her fears, about what was happening to her body, but everyone seemed more ready to criticise than to listen. She didn't feel any different, but the shock of seeing what happened to her blood lay heavy on her. Part of her wondered if she had contracted some hideous new virus which had crossed over from Otherworld; there were so many new rules, so many things still hidden, it was impossible to put any event into any kind of context. Perhaps it had lain in her, dormant, but was now beginning to ravage her body. But with all their talk of discipline and missions and responsibility to the cause, how could she even bring it up? It was something she had to deal with herself.

Veitch leaned against one of the lobby's marble columns, adopting a look of cool detachment while secretly believing the attendants were all sneering at him, whispering behind their hands that he shouldn't be there, that someone ought to throw him out. It made him feel angry and hunted and at any other time he wouldn't have subjected himself to it, but those feelings paled in comparison to the betrayal he felt at Church's dismissal of Ruth's plight. He understood in an oblique way what Church said about obligation and responsibility, but loyalty to friends overrode it all; and love was even more important than that.

He was suddenly aware of an old man moving across the lobby towards him. His gait was lazily elegant, although he looked in his seventies. The sharp cut of his expensive suit, the delicate way he held his silver-topped cane, the perfect grooming of his swept-back white hair and old-style handlebar moustache, all suggested a man of breeding.

Here we go, Veitch thought. *Somebody who wants the riff-raff thrown out.*

But as the elderly gentleman neared, Veitch saw he was smiling warmly. 'I am an excellent judge of a man's face,' he said in the well-formed vowels of a privileged Edinburgh brogue, 'and I can see we've both been touched by magic.' His eyes twinkled as he took Veitch's left hand in both of his; Veitch was so shocked he didn't snatch it back as he normally would have. 'I can see troubles too,' the gentleman continued. 'And if it is any comfort, hear the words of someone who has grown wise in his long life: never give up believing.' He tapped Veitch once on his forearm and then, with a polite nod, turned and moved gracefully back across the lobby.

'What was that all about?' Church had come up on Veitch while he curiously surveyed the gentleman's retreat.

'Dunno. Some old duffer who's had too much sun.'

As they wandered in the morning sunlight towards the sandwich shop to pick up lunch, Veitch put on the cheap sunglasses he had picked up at one of the department stores on Princes Street. He couldn't contain himself any longer. 'I don't know how you can dump her, mate.'

Church nodded, relieved it was finally out. 'I know how you feel, Ryan. More than you might think. But after how I almost screwed things up before Beltane because I was so wrapped up in my own problems, I've got to keep my eye on the big picture. I learned the hard way that we all come second.'

Veitch shook his head; the sunglasses masked his emotions from Church. 'I hear what you're saying, but it's not right.' His feelings were heavy in his voice, but he was managing to control himself. 'She's one of us. We should look after our own.'

'And maybe we can. There might be a way we can do what we have to do and save Ruth at the same time. I just haven't thought of it.'

'Well, you better get thinking. It's your job.'

'Why *is* it my job?' Church bristled. 'Did I miss the election? How come I ended up leading this pathetic bunch?'

Veitch looked surprised, as if Church had asked the most stupid question in the world. 'Course it had to be you. Who else could do it?'

'Shavi.'

'He's got his own responsibilites. Listen, you know your strengths. Thinking, planning. Seeing the *big picture*.'

Church grunted, looked away. 'Well, I don't like it.'

'You're good at it. Accept it.'

'Okay,' Church said. 'Well, you accept this. The Pendragon Spirit, or whatever it is, is pushing all our strengths out into the open and yours are obvious too. You're not just the fighter, the warrior, you're the strategist. I've seen it in you – you're a natural at choosing the right path whenever we're in a tight spot. So here's your job: sort out how we can save Ruth *and* do everything else we need to do.'

Veitch looked even more surprised at this, but after a moment's thought he said seriously, 'All right, I'll take you up on that. But if I do it, you've got to give me a good hearing.'

'Deal.'

The relief on Veitch's face was palpable. As they crossed Princes Street, he said, out of the blue, 'So what's happening with you and the big-mouthed blonde?'

Church shrugged. 'We get on well. We've got a lot in common.'

'I don't trust her.'

'I know you don't. But I do. Is that what you want to hear?'

'Yes.' He paused outside the sandwich shop and turned to Church. 'She's got it bad for you, you know.'

'So you're an expert on affairs of the heart now, are you?'

'I know what I see. Do you feel the same about her?'

Church shifted uncomfortably, then made to go into the shop, but Veitch stood his ground. 'Everything is a mess these days,' Church said irritably. 'All I can do is get through each day acting and reacting, not thinking at all.' He missed Ruth much more than he might have shown, but he kept quiet because he didn't want to give Veitch any more fuel for his argument; but Ruth was the only one to whom he could truly talk. Her listening and gentle guidance had helped him unburden numerous problems. 'Is that the end of the inquisition?' he asked sharply.

'One more thing. Something that's been on my mind. That dead girlfriend of yours. How you coping with that?'

Church winced at Veitch's bluntness. 'You have got this strategy thing, haven't you? Checking up I'm not a liability?'

'No—'

'Yes, you are. You just don't realise it. Marianne's death doesn't haunt me any more. Neither does she, if that's what you mean. Since the Fomorii stopped bothering with us they've not sent her spirit out to make me suffer. But that doesn't mean I've forgotten they've still got her.' He tapped his chest and then his head. 'It's in here and it's in here. And one day soon I'm going to set her free *and* get my own back.'

This seemed to satisfy him. 'I just wanted to be sure.'

Church watched him disappear into the shop with an increasing sense of regard. His skills as a warrior were growing stronger with each passing day, as if ancient history were shouting through his genes. The Pendragon Spirit had chosen well, each of them maturing into a different role, the resources most needed for the task at hand. Perhaps there was a chance after all.

As they made their way back to the hotel they noticed signs of activity on The Mound just beyond the National Gallery. Two police cars were parked across the road, lights flashing, and armed soldiers had been discreetly positioned near walls and in shadows in the vicinity. A crowd had gathered near the cars with a mood that seemed at once irritated and dumbfounded.

'Looks like trouble,' Veitch said. 'We should stay away.'

'I want to find out what's happening.'

He grabbed the arm of a man at the back of the crowd to ask for information. 'They're closing off the Old Town,' he replied, obviously troubled by an event which seemed to shake the natural order. 'Public safety, they say. If the Old Town isn't safe, what about the rest of us?'

'I hear there was some kind of Government laboratory up there doing top secret experiments and they had an accident,' a middle-aged woman whispered conspiratorially.

'Now why would they do experiments where people live and all the tourists go?' another woman said with a dismissive snort.

A young man with a shaved head and a pierced nose butted in. 'No, it's a serial killer. A pal o' mine went to a club up there last night and he dinnae return home. The word is a whole load of people were murdered.'

Church listened to the theories bouncing back and forth until he was dragged away by Veitch tugging insistently on his arm. 'One of the cops spotted us and went for his radio,' he said. 'Looks like we're still on the Most Wanted list.'

Church was back soon after, this time with Laura. After discussion, they had decided that, despite the risks, they had to get to the Central Library in the heart of the Old Town to search for the information they needed. At least in the daylight the supernatural threat was minimised, but it increased the danger of them getting picked up by the police.

'Why couldn't they have closed the place off tomorrow?' Church grumbled as they surveyed one of the road blocks.

Laura fixed a relentless, icy glare on a woman who had been staring at her scars; the woman withered and hurried away.

'Don't pick on the locals. They don't have your power,' Church said drily.

'I always use my powers wisely.' Laura looked around surreptitiously, then fixed her sunglasses. The blockade at the foot of Cockburn Street was manned by one young policeman who kept glancing uneasily up the steeply inclining road behind him.

'God knows why I chose you. That blonde hair stands out like a beacon. It's not the best thing for subterfuge.'

'Actually, I chose you, dickhead. And it's my beauty that attracts all the looks, not my hair.' She scanned the street briefly before picking up an abandoned beer bottle at the foot of a wall. 'What we need is a diversion.'

Before Church had time to protest she hurled the bottle in an arc high over the policeman's head while he was glancing round. It exploded against the plate-glass window of a record shop, which shattered in turn. The policeman started as if he had been shot. Once the shock had eased, a couple of seconds later, he ran to investigate the shop, still obviously disorientated.

'There we go.' Laura ran for the shadows of Advocate's Close, which disappeared up among the buildings.

'You like taking risks, don't you?' Church said breathlessly when he finally caught up with her at the top of the steep flight of stairs.

'Life would be boring without them.' They both came up short against the eerie stillness which hung over the normally tourist-thronged Royal Mile. 'Spooky,' she added.

'The Fomorii are getting stronger. They're slowly spreading their influence out from the castle to secure their boundaries. That's what you saw last night at the club.' Church suddenly glanced back into the shadows clustered at the foot of the steps.

'What is it?'

'I don't know . . . thought I saw something. I'm just jumpy.'

'If the copper was after us we'd know by now.' She strode out across the street. 'So you've forgiven me, then?'

'There's nothing to forgive.'

'What, apart from my stupidity?' She didn't meet his eye.

'Come on, anybody could have done what you did. It's hard to adjust to all the new dangers that are out there.'

'Veitch doesn't think so. The Cockney bastard wants me dead.'

'You're overreacting. He's our tactician and warrior. It's his job to be cautious.'

'*Tactician and warrior?*' she sneered. 'That's a strange euphemism for wanker.'

As they made their way up to George IV Bridge Church couldn't help looking behind him again. The apprehension he felt from the moment they entered the Old Town was increasing rapidly.

'Stop being so jumpy,' Laura cautioned sharply. 'No one's behind us.'

Church found himself involuntarily grasping for the locket the young Marianne had given him before she died; it felt uncommonly hot in his hand, as if it, too, was responding to something that couldn't be defined by the five senses. Despite its cheapness, with its crudely snipped photo of Princess Diana, it gave him some comfort. Infused with the power of faith, it represented to him the tremendous power of good that had come from the terrible changes in the world, a counter-balance to everything else they experienced. Instinctively he felt it had even stronger powers than the inspirational ones he attributed to it.

They walked quickly to the Central Library. The evacuation had obviously taken place hurriedly that morning after the discovery of the carnage at the club, for the swing doors at the front were unlocked. They slipped in and ducked beneath the electronic barriers to reach the stacks in the sunlit room at the back. It didn't take them long to find the section dedicated to Edinburgh history.

'It's like technology never happened,' Laura said with distaste as she glanced at the rows of books.

Church ignored her; she was only trying to get a reaction, as usual. He pulled out a pile of general history books and heaved them over to one of the reading tables. They spent the next hour wading through the tales of murder, intrigue and suffering which seemed to characterise Edinburgh, reading beyond just the plague years in case the spirits had been less than direct in their guidance.

While Church quietly immersed himself, Laura attempted new levels of irritation by announcing every time she came across something of interest. 'Listen to this,' she said, ignoring his muttered curse. 'This used to be the most crowded city in Europe. There're six thousand living in the Old Town now. Back then there were nearly *sixty* thousand. That's like Bombay or something. No wonder the plague went through here like wildfire. They were all crammed inside the city walls so instead of spreading out, they just built the houses up and up. Eight, nine, ten storeys. Sometimes just shacks of wood on top. They were collapsing all the time or catching fire, killing—'

'Fascinating.'

'Hey, there's another great fact here.'

'Really.'

'Yes. It says all people with the surname Churchill are pompous windbags.'

It took a second or two to register and before he could say anything she'd grabbed him and pulled him halfway across the table to plant a kiss on his lips. 'Get the poker out of your arse, dull-boy. Just because it's the end of the world doesn't mean we can't have fun.' There was almost a desperation in her comment. She glanced around, then leered at him. 'A good place for sex. How many people can say they've done it on a reading table at the public library?'

'You're only saying that to get out of doing boring work.'

'You reckon.'

He gave her a long kiss, but as he pulled away his gaze fell on a passage in an open book next to them. 'There it is!'

'That's it. Change the subject—'

'No, listen.' He levered her to one side so he could read: 'Down where Princes Street Gardens are now there used to be a lake, the Nor' Loch, which was the main source of drinking water for the city. It was also where all Edinburgh's sewage used to flow—'

'Very tasty.'

'—so everyone's immune system was low, particularly those who were close to the Nor' Loch, like the residents of Mary King's Close – which is why they suffered particularly badly when the plague came.' Church traced his finger along the tiny print of the book. 'There was a nearby village called Restalrig, which has been swallowed up by the city now. Next to Restalrig's church was a natural spring which was a major source of clean water during the plague years.'

'So that's *the place that gave succour to the plague victims.*'

'Sounds like it.'

'Now there was a stone surround to the spring and when they decided to build a railway depot on the site in 1860 they moved it to another natural spring. At the foot of Arthur's Seat.'

'We saw it!' Laura exclaimed. 'When we drove past on our way to the top. There was a grille and a big pile of stone shit set in the hillside—'

Church grinned triumphantly. 'That's the way in. A natural spring which was always seen as somewhere sacred, probably because it was a potent source of the earth energy—' They were distracted by a faint sound.

Laura looked round anxiously. 'What was that?'

Church silenced her. Nothing moved in his field of vision across the library. No sound came through the windows from the normally

548

bustling Old Town. Cautiously he moved forward, motioning to Laura to investigate one side of the library while he looked down the other.

He soon lost sight of Laura among the stacks. Although he could *feel* on some instinctive level they were not alone, there was no sign of anyone else in the building with them.

He'd got to the edge of the stack dedicated to religion when he heard Laura cry out. He sprinted across the library to find her slumped against the wall in a daze, her eyes flickering with fear as they focused on some inner landscape.

'The black wolf,' she said, as if she were drugged. 'He looked at me. And his eyes were yellow.'

Once Church was sure she was physically unharmed he quickly turned his attention back to the room. It was still empty, but there was an increasing air of tension; someone was definitely nearby.

'Don't worry,' he whispered distractedly, 'it'll be okay.'

'No,' Laura said forcefully. 'It's the Black Wolf.' The fear surged up in her; she covered her face with her hands.

Church moved on. The stacks rose on all sides; the interloper could be round any corner. His attention was drawn to a door away to his right which seemed to be moving gently; it might have been simply the result of an air current. Holding his breath almost involuntarily, he approached. The movement of the door stilled. Apprehensively, he reached out for the handle.

The door crashed against him, forcing a yell of surprise. Before he could recover, boney fingers were clamped around his wrist, wrenching him towards the gap. Through the shock Church registered the bizarre sight of what appeared to be tracings of black veins against parchment-white skin. By the time he reacted, his hand was already through the gap and the door had been yanked back sharply against his forearm. He cursed loudly and struggled to drag his hand back, but it was held tight.

'One for the unified force of my anger. And one for revenge.' Church's blood ran cold. The voice was barely human; it was like hot tar bubbling in a pit. 'And five is the number of my despair. Each digit a catechism in the ritual of salvation. A symbolic death to be followed by a real one.'

A new pain, harsh and focused, erupted in Church's hand. With horror, he felt the skin of his middle finger break open, the blood start to trickle down into his palm.

He's trying to cut it off! The terrible thought burst in his mind, and with it came the certain knowledge that this was the one who had mutilated and abducted Ruth.

He wrenched at his hand with increasing desperation, but it was pinned with an inhuman strength. And the blade bit deeper. Red hot needles danced across his skin. His forehead felt like it was on fire, his vision fracturing around the edges as he started to black out.

No, he pleaded with himself.

It felt like the blade was down to the bone now. His head started to spin, his knees grew weak.

Somehow he found an extra reserve of strength to give one last pull, but it was not enough. Just as he started to lose consciousness, arms folded around him, adding to his strength. Laura set her heels and heaved and somehow he found the will to join in. His wrist felt like it was going to snap, his arm like it was popping from its socket.

But then something gave and he found himself flying backwards. He landed on the floor several feet back, with Laura pinned beneath him.

'You big bastard,' she gasped.

Desperately he rolled off her and pulled out his handkerchief to stem the flow of blood. The cloth was soaked crimson within seconds, but the blood slowed enough for him to tie it tight.

Laura was anxiously watching the door which had swung shut. 'I think they've gone,' she ventured. Then: 'What *was* that?'

'I don't know.' Church still felt nauseous at the memory of the voice. It had sounded like something from *The Exorcist*. Fighting off the rolling waves of pain that were rising up his arm, he moved forward cautiously and pulled open the door. There was no one on the other side. Splatters of his own blood, that had run off his attacker, marked a trail out of the building.

'Whatever it was, it's not going to be satisfied until it's had us all,' he said.

'I need my fingers. They're a lonely girl's best friend.' Although she was trying to make light, there was no humour in her words. 'Come on, we've got to get some stitches in that.'

In spite of having found their next step forward, their confidence had ebbed as they made their way up the street from the library. Apprehension almost prevented them crossing the Royal Mile, with its clear vista from the imposing bulk of the castle at the top, but they pulled themselves together enough to continue towards the worrying darkness of Advocate's Close.

Halfway across the road Laura caught at Church's sleeve and whispered, 'Look at that.'

Above the castle, grey clouds were roiling unnaturally, unfolding from the very stone of the place, rolling out across the Old Town.

Within seconds the hot summer sun was obscured. The temperature dropped rapidly and Church felt the sting of snow in the cold wind.

They raised their faces up to stare at the dark skies, suddenly shivering in the heart of winter.

CHAPTER SIX

Only Sleeping

Dawn came up over Calton Hill like gold and brass. Summer heat quickly dispelled the cool of the night, and the air was soon filled with the chorus of waking songbirds and the aroma of wild flowers. Amongst the treetops that clustered to the south-west side of the hill, tiny figures danced and swooped on the warm currents, their gossamer wings sparkling in the sun's first rays.

For Veitch, it was a transcendent moment that pointed up the hollowness of the world before the change. His hard face softened as he followed the winged creatures' magical trail; the tension eased from his muscles. His smile transformed him into the kind of man he might have been if he hadn't grown up at a certain time in a certain place, trapped by destiny, punished by reality for no crime apart from existing.

And Shavi watched Veitch, and he too smiled. And the others looked to Shavi and felt the genuine warmth and hope he exuded, even in the darkest moments. It was he who had suggested the ritual to greet the sun as a way of marking the next phase of their life, and as a memory of something good to carry with them into dark places. Tom had helped out with the details of the ancient rite which had been carried out at the stone circles in the long-forgotten days, and they had chosen Calton Hill, where every year Edinburgh residents gathered for a pagan rite of seasonal renewal on Beltane. It was the place, it was the time.

And there, in the aftermath, they all felt stronger and they could turn their eyes away from the still-sleeping, geometrical streets of the New Town to the clouded, chaotic and thunderous bulk of the Old. Above it, the winter clouds still churned.

'We will always remember this moment.' Shavi's voice was a whisper but it carried through the still air with a strength and clarity that sent a shiver down their spines. 'This is not just an age of darkness and anarchy. It is a time of wonder and miracles too. Never forget. Light in dark—'

'The best of times, the worst of times.' Church smiled.

'Sweet and sour,' Laura chipped in. 'Cabbage and chocolate—'

'All right!' Shavi laughed. 'You have no sense of occasion!'

'And you'd get on a pretentious spiral up your own arse if we'd let you.' Laura rolled on to her back, chuckling playfully.

For that brief time, Church forgot his brooding nature and turned to look through the twelve Doric columns of the National Monument towards the sun, pretending it was Athens, dreaming of Marianne – but no longer in a bad way.

Tom, stoned and grinning, looked more like a Woodstock refugee than he had done in weeks. When he smiled, the lines of suffering and despair turned to crinkles of good humour and his piercing eyes sparkled with a blissed-out hippie's playfulness. 'Shavi's right.' His voice, too, became less sombre, and more of its original Scottish brogue was evident. 'Make the most of it.'

'Okay,' Church said. 'Pop quiz. Favourite golden oldie. I'll start: *Fly—*'

'—*Me to the Moon*, you predictable Sinatra dickhead,' Laura chided. 'You hadn't mentioned the *great man* for a while. I thought you'd grown out of that.'

'We haven't had much time to kick back and listen to music.'

'*Scooby Snacks*.' Veitch's voice surprised them all, floating out dreamily and distracted while he watched the sprites in the trees. 'Fun Lovin' Criminals.'

'*Strange Brew* by Cream,' Tom grinned.

Laura stared at him as if he was insane. 'No, wasn't that Beethoven?' she said sarcastically.

'Stop criticising and chip in so we can criticise your musical taste,' Church said.

She wrinkled her nose. 'Oh God, I don't know. *Hey Boy Hey Girl* by the Chemical Brothers. Or maybe something by Celine Dion,' she added with a sneer. 'What's yours then, Shav-ster?' Laura raised her sunglasses slightly to get a clearer view of his expression. 'Some Andean pan pipe music? Kashmiri drum and bass? Tibetan chants? Aboriginal didgeridoo solos?'

'*Move On Up* by Curtis Mayfield, if you must know,' he said with mock playfulness. 'The ultimate positivity in music.'

'Oh God, can't you just say you like the beat?' She pulled off her boot and threw it at him. He ducked with a laugh and crawled behind Tom, who suddenly looked very perturbed.

Church didn't want to break the mood, but it had to happen sooner or later. 'We need to talk about divvying up,' he began. Nobody looked at him as if he had only thought the words, but he sensed a change in the atmosphere, as if everything was suddenly hanging in stasis.

'I think it's up to me to go into Arthur's Seat—'

'And you said that with a completely straight face, Church-dude.' Laura's voice was suddenly weary. 'I always said you had no comic timing.'

'—and I think Tom should go to Rosslyn Chapel—'

'No,' Tom said firmly.

'But you know the history of what happened there. You've been taught some of the knowledge of the people who did the binding. It's obviously yours,' Church protested.

'No,' Tom said again.

Laura scanned his face for a moment. 'He's scared.'

Tom glared at her. 'Yes, I am, and I don't mind admitting it, as any wise man would do. But that's not the reason. We've all got a part to play here and mine is as teacher, as guide to the ways of the land, the earth energy. I need to go with Jack to show him, tell him, teach him. I may not be the embodiment of the Pendragon Spirit like you, but I am bound to it for all time. It lights my way. And I, in turn, help it in any way I can.'

'So it's not about you being scared at all, then,' Laura said, with a false smile. Tom looked away.

'Veitch, Laura and I can go to Rosslyn Chapel,' Shavi began, but this time it was Veitch's turn to refuse.

'I'm staying here.' He turned towards them, his face set.

'Why?' The fresh stitches in Church's finger began to ache.

'Someone has to get Ruth out.'

'On your own!' Church exclaimed. 'I know I asked you for a plan, but I expected it to be one you'd thought about for more than five minutes.'

'I know what I'm doing—'

'Right. So you're going to waltz into a stronghold filled with Fomorii out to tear you limb from limb, go directly to Ruth and carry her out like at the end of *An Officer and a Gentleman*.'

'Something like that.'

'And, of course, it'll be no problem that when the Well of Fire is ignited or redirected or whatever I'm doing, you'll be right at ground zero.'

Veitch shrugged. He obviously wasn't going to be deterred.

'Muscle boy's in love,' Laura mocked in a singsong voice. Veitch flashed her a cold, hateful stare, but said nothing.

'Ryan—' Church began.

'I'm going to find a way in to that place and I'm going to do my best to get her out. Because it's the right thing. Just like you're trying to do

554

the right thing for everybody else. If I can get in just before the shit hits the fan, there's a chance—'

'How will you know the right time?'

'I'll know. I feel things. You know, the right way to act. The right thing to do at the right time. I don't know where it's coming from, but it's getting stronger. You said it yourself.' He stared into the middle distance, faintly uncomprehending. 'I'm different now. Better. I'm not going to let it go to waste.'

Church searched his face for a moment, then nodded. 'It's decided, then. I go to the Well with Tom. Laura and Shavi head south to Rosslyn Chapel. And Veitch—'

'Attempts *Mission: Impossible.* I don't fancy your chances, even for a big, tough, street boy.' Church heard a surprising note of concern in Laura's voice. 'A nest of Fomorii. Their biggest stronghold, protecting the thing most valuable to them. And you.' She paused. 'Shall I order the pine box?'

'I'll take my chances. Let's face it, I'm the only bastard who actually has a chance among you bleedin' lot. If I kick the bucket, well, you know, it was for the right reason. That's what this is all about, right?' He turned to Church. 'That's what you keep saying, innit? Do it for the right reason. This is *my* right reason.' He seemed surprised to see admiration in their stares and grew uncomfortable.

Laura attempted to break the mood with some glib, mocking comment, but for once the words escaped her. Church watched her face sag as she bit her lip; he wondered what lay behind her sunglasses.

'Where are we gonna meet up afterwards?' Veitch asked optimistically.

'Greyfriars Churchyard.' Church had spent most of the previous afternoon planning, armed with a map of the city and the guidebook, while fighting back nausea from the pain in his finger.

'Why there?'

'Because I always wanted to see that statue of the little dog that sat by his master's grave. Greyfriars Bobby – what a great tourist attraction that is.' He tried to make light of the conversation, but he couldn't shake the feeling that Veitch wouldn't be meeting them. 'I think we can pick a quick route out of town from there. And it's an easy place to find if the shit really is hitting the fan.'

They all thought about this for a moment.

Nobody wanted to be the first to go, but eventually Shavi shouldered the responsibility. He knelt beside Veitch and gave his shoulder a brief squeeze before setting off down the hill. Tom followed, resting one hand on Veitch's head in passing, a restrained show of respect that was surprisingly voluble in a man normally so emotionally detached. Laura paused, but couldn't bridge the gap and hurried uncomfortably after the others.

It was only then Church realised how truly strong were forged the bonds that joined them. Their communication was silent, but deeply expressed; powerful emotions united them, of respect and trust, friendship and faith, even love. It was even harder to believe the Celtic spirits' accusation that one of them was a traitor.

'Are you going to be okay here on your own?' he said.

Veitch grinned with fake confidence. 'No, but fuck it.' He stripped off his shirt to feel the sun on his skin, his tattoos gleaming across his torso. 'See this?' He pointed to a pentacle picked out in an intertwining Celtic design. 'I always wondered what that was. But it's us, innit? See, five points, all separate, but all joined together, and stronger for it.'

Church gave him a friendly clap on the shoulder. 'You're a smart bloke, Ryan. You shouldn't hide it so much.'

'Yeah, smart like shit.' He fumbled for Church's hand and shook it awkwardly. 'You know, I never thought I'd ever be a part of something like this . . . fuck it!' He shook his head, embarrassed. 'You better get going. It's time to go to work.'

Church set off down the hill. Halfway down, where the trees began to close in around the path, he glanced back to see a figure silhouetted against the dawn sky, framed by the soaring Athenian columns. It was such a sad, lonely sight he quickly turned and hurried after the others.

It was already early afternoon as Shavi and Laura made their way south. The sun had started to give way to the sea mist the locals called the haar. It swept in from the north-east, obscuring Arthur's Seat and the castle, rolling out across the rooftops and clinging hard to the streets. They had considered hiring a car, but Church had cautioned them about keeping a low profile, so Shavi had convinced Laura to walk the six and a half miles towards the misty, purple bulk of the Pentland Hills. She refused, however, to carry any of the camping gear which was mounted on a framed rucksack on his back. As they set out through Tollcross the Old Town seemed uncomfortably close; Laura was convinced she could feel a wintry chill radiating out from the streets that emptied on to Lothian Road. They kept to the other side, near to the comforting modernity of the new financial district, until the blackened, ancient buildings of the Old Town were far behind.

Although it was not raining, the haar infused the air with so much moisture their clothes soon became damp and Laura's spikey hair sagged on to her forehead.

'You can probably remove your sunglasses now,' Shavi said wryly.

'When you get the pomposity out of your arse.' She looked around. 'Not much traffic for a capital city.'

'People are only making journeys when they feel it is absolutely important. They subconsciously sense the danger that is all around.'

'And it hasn't got so bad yet.'

The street rode the rolling hills, past rows of smart shops where a few people seemed at ease enough to hover outside the windows, up towards the ring road. Laura leaned over the barrier, still curious to see such little transport.

'Well, the airport is shut now all the flights have been grounded,' Shavi pointed out. 'And with the Old Town closed off I suppose they have lost the parliament, the newspaper offices, many businesses—'

'Don't they realise they can't carry on with their lives?'

'I think they probably do. But it is human nature to carry on with routines in an attempt to maintain normalcy, often in the face of all reason.'

A little further on Laura began to complain of aching feet, and from then on, as they left the city behind and wound out into the country-side, they had to take numerous long breaks while she nursed her burgeoning blisters.

'I've never walked this far in my life,' she moaned.

'I once walked the entire length of Kashmir—'

'Oh, shut up.' She was limping away before she had to listen to any more of his tale. 'It hurts enough already,' she muttered.

It was late afternoon before they reached the Rosslyn Chapel sign which pointed down a lane off the main road. Between wet fields and under a slate-grey sky, it took them in to the village of Roslin.

'Did you know,' Shavi began, 'that the Roslin Institute is nearby, where they cloned Dolly the sheep. A place of mysteries both old and new.'

'Whoop de doo.'

They were barely in the village when another tiny lane led them off to the right. A little way down it they reached the chapel car park; they could tell they were nearing their destination from the stark change in atmosphere: it grew oppressive and brooding, as if the mystery that lurked there was potent enough to affect the air itself. The chapel was completely obscured by trees, a visitor centre and high fences which made it difficult for anyone to get inside. The custodians had already locked up for the day.

Shavi checked the sky and rubbed his chin thoughtfully, but before he could speak, Laura said, 'Pull yourself together. We're not going in there today. I'm not going to be caught anywhere near the place after night has fallen.'

Shavi smiled. 'Then we make camp.'

They needed to find somewhere where they wouldn't be stumbled across or reported to the authorities. Picking their way down a steep path, they came to the graveyard, with its neatly tended plots, ancient and new stones mingling together. Another footpath led off to one side where the trees grew thickest. The whole area was still. No traffic rumbled, no birds sang.

'Maybe it's just the weather, but I can feel something like . . . despair.' Laura glanced into the thick vegetation beneath the tree cover where the water dripped from the leaves in a steady rhythm.

Shavi nodded, said nothing.

The path wound around until the graveyard was lost behind them and the branches closed over their heads, sealing them in a gloomy, verdant world. A rabbit started at their approach and dived into the undergrowth. Eventually they could hear the splashing water of a stream or falls, and then they were out of the trees again, suddenly confronted by the breathtaking view of a tree-clustered glen far beneath them. The haar drifted eerily in white tendrils among the treetops. Everywhere was still, waiting.

'It's beautiful,' Laura said. 'But there's something not natural about the place. Which is a pretty stupid thing to say about the countryside.'

The path wound round until it crossed a tiny stone bridge which soared high above the glen. On the other side, hanging over the steep sides of the valley like some fairy-tale fortress, were the majestic stone ruins of Rosslyn Castle. Just beyond the broken turrets and fallen walls they could see lights; part of the building was still in use. They picked up a rough track just before the bridge which led them scrambling down into the glen and then the trees were closing over them again. Oak, ash and elm mingled all around, hinting at the great age of the woodland, and this was reflected in the diversity of the undergrowth that prospered beneath the tree cover: wood sorrel, ransoms, golden saxifrage, dog's mercury and wood-rush.

The place was so lonely Laura couldn't help but feel unnerved and when she glanced at Shavi she could see it reflected on his normally stolid face too; it was in the air, in every tree and rock. They trekked along the floor of the glen by the banks of the white-foamed North Esk until they found an isolated clearing where the smoke from any fire would not be seen from the castle.

'Are you sure we shouldn't go back and find a B&B?' Laura ventured. She was even more disturbed when she saw Shavi almost considered it.

They pitched the tent with its rear end in an impenetrable cluster of undergrowth to prevent anyone approaching them from behind. To Laura's growing anxiety, the flora all around was so dense, the noise from the swishing leaves and the thundering river so great, it would have been impossible to discern strangers until they were almost upon them.

'If this was a movie,' Laura began, 'I'd say, "I can't shake the feeling there's somebody watching us." ' Shavi nodded. 'You're supposed to say, "Don't be so stupid, it's just the trees," ' she added irritably.

'I think we should take a chance and light the fire now.' He looked up at the streaks of drifting white in the gloomy treetops. 'It will get dark here much quicker than if we were out in the open.'

'You can build a beacon they could see in Holland for me.'

Shavi spent the next half hour collecting enough wood to last them all night while Laura sat morosely in the mouth of the tent. Her anxiety eased a little when he finally had a small fire glowing in the clearing a few feet away from them. They boiled up a little rice while Shavi roasted kebabs of peppers, onions and tomatoes, which they ate while listening to the crack, drip and shiver of the living wood around them.

Shavi was correct about the dark, which swept in unnervingly quickly until it was sitting just beyond the glimmer of the campfire, breathing in and out oppressively.

After a while Laura found herself leaning against Shavi; she had shuffled up to him almost unconsciously, for comfort. He slipped an arm around her shoulders, out of friendship; there wasn't a hint of any of the passion they had shared in Glastonbury. And she leaned her head gently against his shoulder, glad he was there, for so many reasons she could barely count them.

'You seem unhappy,' he ventured.

'And you look like a dickhead, but do I take it out on you?'

He smiled and waited for a few moments while the rushing of the river took over. 'Romance is by necessity difficult.'

'Everything is difficult.' Then: 'Why "by necessity"?'

'The value of anything is defined by the effort it takes us to get it. And romance is the most valuable thing of all.'

'That's one opinion. Me, I'd go for an iced bottle of Stolichnaya, an ounce of Red Leb and some peace and quiet.'

'Jack is going through a difficult time. He has suffered an extreme emotional blow—'

'We've all got our problems.'

'—and a great deal is expected of him, more than he thinks he can possibly give. He is torn between the things he wants to do, the things his heart is telling him, and what he feels is the right thing to do.'

'He's too wrapped up in this whole "heroes have to sacrifice" thing.'

'Yes, he is.' Shavi gave her a faint, comforting squeeze. 'But he is a good, decent man. The best of all of us.'

'I know that.'

'Everyone knows it. Except Jack.'

'And you're about to say I should cut him some slack.'

'No. I am just saying this by way of explanation.'

'You think I've done the wrong thing by getting in with him, don't you?' She looked round at him, but his gaze was fixed firmly away in the trees.

'I think your romance would have a better chance at a different time. There are so many obstacles being placed before it by external events.'

She looked away so he couldn't see her face.

'But you know your heart better than I.' He turned and stared at the back of her head, hoping she would look at him, but she kept the barriers up. 'And if there is any lesson from all this hardship we are experiencing, it is that things are worth fighting for and fighting to the last, and tremendous things *do* happen.'

'Who do you think he should be with?'

'I—' He struggled to find words that would not hurt her. 'My opinion does not matter.'

'It matters to me.' When he didn't answer, she said in a barely audible voice, 'He's my last chance.'

'What do you mean?' he asked curiously.

'Nothing.'

Shavi thought about what she said for a moment. 'You are a good person,' he stated firmly.

'No, I'm not. I'm a bad girl. And I've got coming to me what all bad girls get.'

'No—'

Her face flared with long-repressed emotion. 'Don't give me all that redemption shit! Don't even begin to tell me everything will turn out bright and sunny. That's not how it works!'

'It does in my world.'

That brought her up sharp. She eyed him askance, then looked away, her expression so desolate with the flood of uncontrollable feelings and ideas that Shavi wanted to pull her tightly to him to comfort her.

But before he could act he caught a movement away in the trees. It was barely anything, a shift of a shadow among shadows in the gloom, and it could easily have been some small animal investigating the fire, but his instincts told him otherwise.

Laura felt his body stiffen. 'What is it?' she asked, sensing his urgency.

'I do not know.' He rose and advanced to the fire.

'Didn't you ever see *Halloween*?' she cautioned. 'Don't go any further, dickhead.'

'I am simply trying to see—' The words strangled in his throat in such an awful manner Laura didn't have to see his face to know he had glimpsed something terrible.

'What is it, for God's sake?' she hissed.

The fear surged into a hard lump in her chest, but it melted into burning ice when she saw him moving quickly away from the firelight into the dark.

'Don't go!' Her yell trailed away in dismay and disbelief. How could he be so stupid?

And then she was alone in that dismal place with the dark pressing tight around her, feeling small and weak in the face of all the awful things loose in the world. She couldn't bring herself to move even a finger. Instead, she strained to hear the sound of his returning footsteps, any sound from him that proved he was still alive. But there was nothing. Just the constant rustle of the leaves, the creak of branches under the wings of the wind, the rumble of the river; the lyrical sounds oppressed her. It was too noisy, too alive with nothing.

'Shavi,' she whispered, more to comfort herself with the sound of a voice than in the hope he might hear. *Don't do this to me*, she wanted to say. *I'm not strong enough to deal with this on my own.*

She sat there for an age while she grew old and wizened. Her rigid muscles ached, her stomach was clenched so tightly she thought she was going to vomit or pass out. And still there was no sign of him. He could have been swallowed up, torn apart; there could be things feeding silently on his remains right then, waiting to finish their meal before moving on to her.

And then he suddenly lurched into the circle of light and all of it erupted out of her in a piercing scream.

'Don't worry,' he croaked.

'You stupid bastard!' she shouted in a mixture of embarrassment and angry relief.

But then, as he clambered down next to her, she saw his normally dark, handsome features were grey and there was a strained expression which made him look fifteen years older. 'What was out there?' she said, suddenly afraid once more.

He couldn't seem to find any words. Then: 'Nothing.'

It was such a pathetically inadequate response she hit him hard on the arm. 'Don't treat me like an idiot. Don't try to protect me like some stupid little girlie. That's the worst thing you can do to me.' She swallowed, glanced fearfully beyond the firelight.

'It is nothing. Nothing for you to worry about.'

'Then, what?' She searched his face and saw things in his eyes which unnerved her on some deep plane. With his philosophical outlook, Shavi had always seemed immune to the terrors that plagued the rest of them; he was an anchor for her, a sign that it was possible to cope better. And suddenly all that fell away. 'What is it, Shavi?' She reached tentative fingers to his cheek. 'What did you see out there?'

'What did I see?' His voice sounded hollow. 'I saw Lee. My boyfriend. Two years dead now, two years dead. His head smashed out in the street. And he spoke to me. The things he said . . .' His voice was dragged away by the wind.

Laura recalled how Shavi had told them of the murder arranged by the Tuatha Dé Danann, one of the deaths that had prepared them all for their destiny. 'He was really there?' Her concern for Shavi was suddenly overtaken by the sudden fear that if Lee was there, her dead mother could be too. And that really would be more than she could bear.

Shavi seemed to sense what she was thinking, for his face softened a little. 'It is my burden. The price I had to pay for getting the information from the spirits in Mary King's Close.'

'But that's terrible! That's not a price, it's a sentence! It's not fair!'

'It is my burden. I will cope with it.' It was obvious he couldn't bring himself to speak any more, and however much she wanted to ask him what the spectre had said, she knew it was something he would never tell. But she could see from the expression on his face that it must have been something awful indeed. How much longer would he have to put up with it, she thought? The rest of his life? The thought filled her with such pity that all she could do was hug him tightly and bury his face in her shoulder.

When she awoke in the dead of the night, she was surprised she had actually managed to fall asleep. Shavi's haunted face had hung in her mind, feeding every deep, mortal fear she had about death and what lay beyond it. She remembered stroking his head as it lay on her breast, desperately trying to comfort him, although he gave no voice to his fears; but then she looked in his eyes and she knew there was nothing she could do that would ever make him feel better.

The thoughts faded with the realisation she was awake, and the knowledge that she had woken for a reason. At first, in her sleep-befuddled state, she had no idea why. Shavi slept soundly beside her. Outside the tent the wind moaned gently among the trees and the leaves and branches sighed, but no more nor less than at any other time during the night.

As she went to lower her head back to the pile of clothes she was using as a pillow she realised . . . it was there on the edge of her senses, barely audible, almost a hallucination. Her fingers felt the gentle yet insistent throb of it from deep within the ground. When she lowered her ear towards the groundsheet, she could hear it. *Lub-dub, lub-dub.* So distant, which made her realise how powerful it must be; never ceasing. She tried to tell herself she was mis-sensing it on the edge of a dream, that it was a water pump, that it was the reverberation of the river through the soil and the rock.

Lub-dub, lub-dub.

It seemed to be calling out to her and issuing a warning at the same time. And then she knew what it really sounded like. The beating of a heart that would never know death, buried far beneath the ancient landscape. The image spawned a wave of terror. Laura screwed up her eyes and covered her ears, but it was there inside her head and there was nothing she could do to get it out, and she knew she would not sleep again that night. *Lub-dub, lub-dub.* The relentless rhythm of death and madness.

While Laura and Shavi were just winding their way out of the city centre, Church and Tom skirted the edge of the Old Town before cutting across its easternmost edge to break into the green expanse of Holyrood Park. The sedate mass of the Royal household loomed up silently through the haar which obscured all of Arthur's Seat apart from the lowest twenty feet. The area, normally a haven for joggers and dog-walkers, was deserted. In its desolation it seemed unbearably lonely and ancient.

No words passed between them until they were standing before the well-head, feeling unseasonably cold.

'Here we are then,' Church said banally.

Now they were there, they could see how out of place the well-head looked, surrounded by the wild grass and bare rock of the wilderness that soared up above the city: a defiant statement that man would not be bowed by nature. Iron bars ran on both sides of the forecourt before the well and up the hillside over the top of it. The well-head itself was dark stone stained with the residue of years; the water trickled out into a small pool just out of reach beyond more vandal-proof bars.

It smelled of cold iron and dark tombs. Above it was a plaque which said:

> St Margaret's Well
> This unique Well House dates from the late 15th century. It originally stood at Restalrig, close to the church, and its design is a miniature of St Triduana's Aisle there. In 1860 it was removed from its first site, which was then encroached upon by a railway depot, and was reconstructed in its present position near a natural spring.

Church read it carefully then said, 'When they moved it, did whoever was in charge know this was the entrance to the path beneath Arthur's Seat? Or was it coincidence?'

'There is no coincidence.' Tom surveyed the well-head carefully, as if he were looking for a lock.

'So someone did know?'

'Perhaps. A great deal of secret knowledge has been maintained down the years. There are numerous societies which keep their version of the truth close to them, many secret believers passing words down from mother to daughter, father to son. Or perhaps the people who moved the well-head were simply guided by an unseen hand.'

A few weeks earlier Church would have met such a comment with derision, but now he was more than aware of what lay behind the visible. 'So how do we get in? Can you see the switch like you did at Tintagel?'

'I can, but I'd be remiss in my job if I didn't start teaching you.'

'I can't see anything!'

'That's because you are not looking correctly,' Tom replied with exasperation.

Church squinted in the feeble hope it would reveal some hitherto obscured detail, but it only brought an irritated snort from Tom. 'Haven't you learned anything yet?'

'I've learned you're an annoying bastard,' Church snapped.

'The mistake you people constantly make is that you see the five senses as separate, and as the only tools at your disposal. Haven't I told you to trust your intuition? Sense where the switch is. Feel the power of the earth energy in this spot, its arteries and veins, where it pulses the strongest. Then let it inform each sense in turn, until they are all working together. Smell the switch, taste it in the air. Hear it calling to you.'

Church attempted to do what Tom said. After a few seconds he said, 'It's not working.'

Tom cuffed his shoulder so that Church spun round in irritation.

'You're not trying hard enough. Concentrate. Open your mind and your heart to it. If you don't *believe*, you won't do it.'

'Why should I be able to do it?'

'Why? Because you're special, though God knows why. You are a manifestation of the Pendragon Spirit. Its force moves through you. You're closer to the land and the energy than I am. In an ideal world, you should be teaching me!'

Church sighed and turned back to the well-head. 'It's not easy to believe in something like that.'

'Stop whining. Get on with it.'

Church concentrated. After a while he gave up trying to look at the detail in the stone and closed his eyes; that seemed to help. In the dark behind his eyelids he imagined he could see blue tracings like the trails left by firework sparklers. But then he realised it wasn't his imagination, and if he concentrated, he could make the paths stronger, see the faint web they made. A little more concentration and he could hear them fizzing, as if he were standing near a high-tension power line; they smelled and tasted like burnt iron.

And then he opened his eyes and he could still see the blue trails glowing beneath the surface of the stone and the surrounding grass. 'It's there.' His awed voice was hushed. He let his gaze slip slightly to the side and he could see the blue arteries continuing out and up into Arthur's Seat, across the ground behind him towards the city. 'It's in everything. Everywhere.'

He noticed that some of the arteries and veins glowed with a paler blue and others appeared oddly truncated, as if they had withered and died. With this realisation and the conscious stream of thoughts it generated, he began to lose control of the vision. It flickered as his senses fragmented, became individual units again. Desperately he launched himself forward and hammered the palm of his hand on to the point on the well-head where the blue fire had appeared to converge. There was a surge of needle-pain in his fingertips and blue sparks flew. With a deep rumble, the well-head split open, flooding water out, but giving access to a dark tunnel which lay beyond the spout of the spring.

Tom grabbed his elbow and propelled him in. The moment they set foot in the tunnel the well-head ground shut behind them. Church had expected stifling darkness, but there was a faint phosphorescent glow to the slick rock walls which gave the passage the gloomy appearance of the last minutes of twilight. But it was enough to see by, and Tom was already marching ahead.

Church caught up with him with a double-step, breathing in the dank air and shivering slightly. His footsteps echoed off the walls. 'That was amazing.' Although there was no reason for it, he spoke in a whisper. 'Is that how you see things?'

'Sometimes. When I allow myself.'

'It's—' He searched for the right word, but couldn't find one to match the immensity of what he felt. He settled for, 'Tremendous. I can understand how people could get all religious about that. It showed the interconnectedness of everything. That blue, spiritual fire, in the land, in the rocks.' He gazed at the back of his hand. 'In us.'

'It's the neolithic mindset. Once everybody could see things that way.'

'Then what happened? Why did we lose it?'

Tom shrugged. 'The more we developed the rational side of the brain, the more we lost touch with the intuitive. We simply forgot the skill to combine the senses, to be holistic in feeling. It's one of the great arrogances of man that we consider we are constantly evolving, that to dwell wholly on reason and science and logic is somehow *better*. But what would you think of a man who chopped off his left arm to make his right arm stronger? That ability to combine the senses, to *feel*, that was the most amazing skill of all. Man hasn't been whole for a long time, yet everyone in this century thinks they're some kind of super-man, the pinnacle of existence. If it wasn't so bitter, the irony would make me laugh.'

Church thought about this. The passage began to slope down, but just as he thought they were going to head into the bowels of the earth it rose up sharply, then descended again. Soon he'd lost all sense of direction.

'I've got a question,' he said eventually.

'Go ahead.'

'In all the stories there's a myth that the fairies are scared of iron. The Fomorii and Tuatha Dé Danann don't seem to have any problem with it.'

'Correct.'

'But I noticed the earth energy seems to smell and taste of iron—' Tom's sudden grin brought him up sharp.

'Very perceptive! You've found the source of the myth! It's the blue fire and everything it represents that fills them with fear. That's what can bind them. And in its most potent form, that's what can destroy them.'

Church surprised himself with the awe he felt. 'I didn't realise the power of it. Then if we can control it—'

'The Brothers and Sisters of Dragons truly can be the defenders of the land.'

'We have to awaken it,' Church said firmly, almost to himself.

'That's your destiny,' Tom added.

Ahead of them the tunnel dipped down into the darkness again. Church found himself subconsciously going for the locket given him by the young Marianne; it filled him with strength in a way he still couldn't quite understand.

'What lies ahead, then?' he said uneasily.

Tom shrugged. 'It won't be an easy journey. This close to such a powerful source of the earth energy, time and space will warp. It will be disorientating. We will have to keep our wits about us.'

'And when we get to where we're going, how are we supposed to get the blue fire moving again?'

'Do I look like the fount of all knowledge?' Tom said irritably. 'We'll find out when we get there. Hopefully.'

And with that he set off into the darkness.

The hotel seemed empty without the others around. Veitch ate dinner early, steak and potatoes with a good red wine, but the high life he could never have afforded before did little to raise his spirits. With everything in such a state of flux, so many pressures and so much at risk, there was too much even to think about. And it wasn't just that the world was changing, it was the deep things shifting within him. Here, finally, was a chance to change; he could leave behind the Ryan Veitch he had despised all his life and become the person he always dreamed he would be: good, decent, unselfish, caring. Until chaos had descended on the world, he had dismissed the idea with the certain knowledge that he was who he was – he would never change. But now he had a chance, he was determined not to let it slip through his fingers.

When the sun started to go down he took his brooding with him to the bar. The room was near-deserted. It would have been wiser to stick with wine, but he couldn't resist ordering a pint of lager, which he took to a table where he could see the door; an old habit.

He'd got halfway down his drink when he noticed the elderly gentleman who'd come up to him in the lobby the previous day. He was smiling at Veitch from a nearby table, as elegant as ever with his smart suit and his swept-back white hair. He sat with his hands crossed on top of his cane.

'You know, this old place used to be thronging at this time of year,' the man said. Veitch smiled politely, but he had never been one for small talk, particularly with a higher class. Toffs always made him feel insignificant, stupid and uncultured, whatever his better judgement. But this man seemed pleasant enough; his smile was warm and open, and there didn't seem any judgment in the way he looked at Veitch. 'Do you mind if I join you?' He smiled at Veitch's reticence. 'Oh, don't worry. I'm not some predatory shirtlifter. I merely wish to share your company and, well, and perhaps my thoughts.' His smile changed key, but Veitch couldn't read what it signified.

'Okay,' Veitch said, recognising his own loneliness. 'I'll have a drink with you.' He took his lager over to the man's table and sat opposite him. Up close, he could see the man's eyes sparkled with a youthfulness that belied his age. He smelled of expensive aftershave and pipe tobacco.

'Gordon Reynolds,' the old man said holding out a well-tended hand. Veitch shook it and introduced himself.

For the next hour they exchanged small talk: about how Veitch was finding Edinburgh, about the weather, the best tourist sites, the malts that really ought to be sampled and a host of other minor issues. Reynolds broke off to sip at his whisky and when he replaced his glass there was a gleam in his eye. 'You look like a bright young man,' he said. 'You are aware, of course, that something very strange is going on in the world.'

'I've seen some funny things.' Veitch sipped at his lager.

'They closed off the Old Town today.'

Veitch nodded.

'You're very reticent.' Reynolds smiled. 'I suspect you know much more than you're saying.'

'I know a bit. Don't like to talk about it.'

'It's bad, then. No, don't bother telling me otherwise. I've some friends in Wick who used to keep in touch before the telephones went down. They were keen hill-walkers, used to go off into the wilderness. Well, rather them than me. Give me a warm fire and an old malt by it any day. But one day, not so long ago, they went off into the wilds and saw some . . . quite terrible things. Quite terrible. Now they never leave the town. No one does. The wilderness is off-limits.' He scanned Veitch with a dissecting gaze, taking in every minute movement of the Londoner's face. 'But you know all this, I can see. Then you know it's not just happening up in Wick. There's word coming from all over. Here in Auld Reekie, with our sophisticated ways, we could laugh at the superstitions of our country cousins. And now they've closed off the Old Town.'

'It's going to get worse before it gets better.'

'I'm sure it is, I'm sure it is. And there's the Government with the hints and whispers and "it's a crisis, we can't give you too much information", trying to make us think it's the Russkies or the Iraqis or God knows who while they desperately flounder around for an answer that will constantly evade them. Never trust the Establishment, my boy. They're in-bred with arrogance. They think we're too stupid to be told anything as radical as the truth.'

'I'll drink to that.' Veitch drained his pint and glanced towards the bar, hoping for a lull in the conversation so he could get a refill.

'The ironic thing is that most of the people are starting to know better than they. The Establishment is too inflexible and this new age needs people who are prepared to take great leaps forward. They'll be left behind. Only the fleet of mind will survive. What do you think of that?'

'I think—' Veitch raised his glass '—I need another lager.'

Reynolds looked up and motioned to the barman. A minute later another round of drinks arrived at their table.

'How did you manage that?' Veitch asked. 'They don't do table service.'

'Oh, I've been a resident here for many years, my boy. They grant me my little indulgences out of respect for my great age and my deep wallet.'

Veitch laughed. 'You're all right, Gordon.'

'That's very decent of you to say, my boy. But tell me, you're troubled, aren't you? I could see it written all over your face whenever I saw you around the hotel. Share your burden. I may, *may*, I stress, be able to help.'

Veitch sighed, looked away. 'No, best not.' But when he caught Reynolds' eye, the elderly man seemed so supportive he said, 'Oh, bollocks, what's the harm.'

He wasn't sure it was completely wise of him, but over the next hour he proceeded to tell Reynolds everything that had happened since he had encountered Church in the old mine beneath Dartmoor. He was sure some of it made no sense – he could barely grasp the intricacies himself – but Reynolds kept smiling and nodding.

'So that's the way it is, Gordon,' he said after he had related the latest impending crisis. 'Sometimes I wonder, what's the fucking point.' He caught himself and smiled sheepishly. 'Sorry. Bad habit.'

Reynolds dismissed his apology with a flourish of his hand. 'So, you feel it's hopeless. Hopeless in that you feel there's only five, or six, or whatever, ineffectual people facing down the hordes of hell. And hopeless because the girl you love is locked away in some dismal place with no chance of a rescue.'

'I never said I loved her!' Veitch said indignantly.

Reynolds waved him away again. 'Of course you do! It's obvious!'

Veitch coloured and shook his head. 'And I'm not saying it's hope-less. I mean, I'm going in there to get her, you know. I'm giving it my best bleedin' shot.'

'But you don't hold out much hope of getting out again.'

'Ah, who knows?'

Reynolds sat back in his chair and thought for a moment, sipped at his whisky, then thought again. Veitch watched him with growing impatience. Eventually, tweaking his moustache, Reynolds said, 'Are you in the mood for a story, my boy?'

'A story?'

'Yes. A true-life story. Like they have in the women's magazines. It's about a young man of style and elegance, dashing and debonair, not really one for books, but a whizz with the girls—' He laughed richly. 'Now I can't fool you, can I? Yes, it's my story. Still interested?'

Veitch nodded. He had warmed to Reynolds; his old prejudices had been forgotten for the moment.

'Let me tell you then. I was twenty-four, from a very good family with a little money in my pocket and a lot of confidence. A dangerous combination. My mother and father had always considered me for a career in the law. Edinburgh is the lawyers' city, after all. But, you know, that thing with the books . . .' He shook his head. 'No, not for me. I wanted something a little more colourful. Why should I consign myself to a prison of dusty old books when I could run off to sea or enlist in some war in an exotic clime? And that's just what I did. I set off on foot for Leith with a head full of Robert Louis Stevenson and dreams of hiring aboard some tramp steamer to the Orient.'

'Nothing wrong with that,' Veitch mused. 'Better than getting stuck in a rut at home.'

'Exactly! But then the strangest thing happened to me. As I walked towards Leith with the sun climbing in the sky, I came across a vision of such beauty it made me stop in my tracks. Now this wasn't film star beauty, do you understand? But she was beautiful to me.' Veitch nodded. 'Even to this day I don't know why I did it. Perhaps it was because I was filled with the kind of joy you can only experience when you embark on something new, or perhaps it was the quality of light, or the fresh tang on the wind, or all those things aligned in an unrepeat-able harmonious conjunction. But that moment was so special it felt like my skin was singing.'

He caressed the ornately styled head of his cane for a long moment, so deep in thought he appeared oblivious to the people around him.

But when he spoke again, his voice was so infused with happiness Veitch felt warmed simply to hear it. 'Her name was Maureen. She had red hair that fell in gorgeous ringlets and skin so pale it made her eyes seem uncommonly dark. She was walking into town on the other side of the street. What did I do? Why, I threw all my plans in the air and ran across the road to talk to her.'

'You're an old romantic, Gordon.'

'Oh, indeed,' he chuckled. 'I thought perhaps I'd pick up my plans later in the day, or the next day, or the next week. But as we walked and talked, and as she laughed, and as we recognised, in our looks and our gentle touches, that we were carved from the same clay, I realised I would never set sail from Leith. It takes someone very, very special for you to give up all your dreams in a single moment. But it was there, love at first sight, like all the poets say. Do you believe in that?'

Veitch sat back in his chair and looked up into the dark sky through the window. 'I'm not sure, Gordon. I think I'd like to, but it's not the kind of thing you get to think about too much in Greenwich, know what I mean?'

'I think you're not being very honest with yourself,' Reynolds said with a knowing smile. 'Maureen and I quickly became inseparable. On the surface we had very little in common. She came from a good, upstanding family, but they had little money, little of any material possessions. She had been forced to leave school at thirteen to help earn the family's keep. But those things don't matter, do they?'

'S'pose not.'

He pressed his fist against his heart. 'These are where the real bonds are made.' Then he touched his temple. 'Not here. But there was one difference even we could not overcome.' He paused; the muscles around his mouth grew taut with an old anger. 'I was a Protestant and Maureen was a Catholic, you see. That means nothing to you, I can see, and that's good. You're a modern man – you're not burdened with centuries of stupidity. Everybody thinks of that kind of prejudice as the Irish problem, but it's always been here in Scotland, even to this day. You told me you'd heard the stories in the city about Mary King's Close, the street boarded up to let the Black Death sufferers die.'

Veitch flinched at the coincidence. He nodded.

'The people of Mary King's Close were Catholics. Demonised, made less than human. Mothers of the time would frighten their children by saying the terrible people of Mary King's Close would get them if they weren't good. Would the horrors inflicted on them have happened if they were Protestants in this most Protestant of cities? I think not.'

'But Protestants might have got it in a Catholic city.'

'Of course, and I've damned them both to hell many times.'

Veitch tried to read his face. There was a seam of ancient emotion fossilised just beneath the surface. But he kept smiling, his eyes kept sparkling. 'What happened to her?' Veitch asked.

'Ah, you see which way the story is going. We kept our romance a secret from my family and friends for as long as we could, but in a city as watchful and atrociously gossipy as Edinburgh it was bound to come out sooner or later. To say it was a scandal would be to overstate the case. In the wider sense, no one cared about a thing like that, and that is to the general population's merit. The people of Edinburgh *are* good people. But in my own particular circle . . .' He sighed.

'You got a hard time from the folks,' Veitch said with understanding.

'My father was apoplectic. My mother took to her bed for days. The rest of my family treated me as if I'd developed some severe, debilitating mental illness. My close friends, who came from the same social circle, were acidic in their comments, but they directed most of their vitriol towards Maureen, who must, quite obviously, have led me astray.'

'And there was trouble.' Veitch took a long swig of his lager, trying to delay what he knew was coming.

Reynolds's face crumpled, but only for an instant before he brought the smile back; in that tiny window Veitch saw something that made him flinch. 'There was blood. They found her with her head stoved in on the edge of Holyrood Park. She'd been raped, several times, they said, not just murdered, but humiliated. Taught a lesson, in the good old-fashioned way.' His words were bitter, but his tone was as gentle and measured as ever.

'God Almighty!' Veitch went to take another drink, then had to put his glass down. He was overwhelmed by a terrible sense of injustice against a man he was sure, in the short time he had known him, was better than most. He felt a surge of anger, a desire to rush out and gain retribution in the most violent way possible, forgetting the crime had happened decades earlier. 'Who did it? Who fucking did it?'

'Oh, no one was caught. Understandably. The rich and well-to-do are always protected by the law. There was an outcry in the city, but it blew over when the next scandal came along, as these things do. Who did it?' He raised his eyebrows thoughtfully. 'One of my friends, several of my friends, all of them, my family. I would suppose they are the prime suspects. They were all guilty, whatever the detail.'

'Didn't you try to find out who it was? Didn't you try to get them?' Veitch felt the heat rising up his neck to his face.

Reynolds shook his head dismissively. 'No, of course not. It didn't matter, you see. Nothing mattered. Maureen was gone. My life was over.'

The baldness of the statement made Veitch bring himself up sharp.

'I loved her, you see. I loved her in all the clichéd ways – more than life itself, more than myself. We'd devoted ourselves to each other in a way that, I think, people find hard to understand these days. The night before her death we'd spent six hours talking about our life, about what we meant to each other, about the here and now and the sweet hereafter. In all the world she was the only person that mattered. And a few hours later I was more alone than anyone could be.'

There was a long silence which Veitch couldn't bear to fill. After a while the emotions between them became unbearable too, so he said in a quiet voice, 'How did you carry on, mate? I don't know what I'd have done . . . Blimey . . .' His words failed him.

'Why, I carried on. As Maureen would have wanted me to do. But I carried on a different person, as you would have expected. I went into the law, which made my family very happy. And I never married, which was better than they feared, but not what they hoped. I never kissed another woman. I never smelled another woman's perfumed hair. I never touched a woman's skin.'

Veitch felt a lump rise in his throat. He thought he might have to go to the toilet before he made a fool of himself.

But then Reynolds said, 'Come up to my room for one last drink. I have a bottle of malt that is quite heavenly. I retire early these days. It gets lonely when the night falls.'

They moved slowly through the quiet, deserted hotel, their thoughts heavy around them. 'You're a better man than me,' Veitch said as they reached the lifts.

'No,' Reynolds said assuredly. 'I lived a life without hope and thus wasted it. In what you told me I can tell you have hope, or at least the potential for hope. And perhaps I can help you.' They entered the lift and he punched the floor number. 'I lived a life with nothing to believe in,' he continued. 'How could I believe in anything? Family? Friends? Religion? What kind of God would let a thing like that happen? What kind of God was worshipped by the people closest to me?'

The thick carpet muffled their footsteps. It was comfortingly bright in the corridor.

'There is a gun in the drawer of my bedside table.' It seemed like a non sequitur, but Veitch was suddenly alert, Reynolds was going somewhere. 'An old service revolver. A family heirloom.' He laughed. 'Fitting, really.'

Veitch looked at him, but he kept his pleasant gaze fixed firmly ahead. 'I'd made my plans, composed my mind and a few nights ago I was ready to kill myself.' His smile made it sound as if he was discussing attending a picnic. 'I'd had enough of the drudgery of days. The emptiness of thoughts. The coldness of life. It seemed time for a Full Stop. Wrap things up neatly. The end of my story.'

'So why didn't you do it?'

Reynolds looked at him in surprise. 'My, you are a blunt man. I like that. You wouldn't get that in my family. They'd just pass the brandy and someone would see fit to mention it a few days down the line. Why didn't I kill myself? Why *didn't* I?' he mused, as if he had no idea himself. 'Because of my very last conversation with Maureen, that's why.'

Reynolds unlocked the door and they stepped into his suite. It was spacious and well turned-out, but still a hotel room; there were no personal touches to show it had been his home for so long. It spoke of an empty life lived for the sake of it.

'Nice place,' Veitch said uncomfortably.

Reynolds poured two large glasses of twenty-year-old malt and handed one to Veitch. 'It's a place to rest my head.'

Veitch perched on the edge of a desk. 'So, are you going to tell me, or punish me for a bit longer?'

Reynolds laughed heartily. 'I wanted you to hear my story before I got to the crux of the matter. Stories are important. They provide a framework so we can't easily dismiss the vital messages buried at the heart of them.' He pulled open a bedside drawer and took out the service revolver, which he tossed to Veitch so he could examine the archaic weapon.

'Blimey, that's a museum piece. You're just as likely to have blown your bleedin' hand off as your head.'

Reynolds gave a gentle laugh. 'The last conversation with Maureen has never left me.' He lowered himself into a chair on the other side of the desk, put his head back and closed his eyes. 'All those years and I can still smell her hair, feel exactly how her hand used to lie in mine. And I can remember every word we said. Most of it, I'm sure, would seem nauseatingly cloying out of the context of our lives, but it held meaning for us. But there was one point . . .' He drifted for a moment, so that Veitch thought he had fallen asleep, but then his voice came back with renewed force. 'The only thing left to discuss was what would happen should one of us die. We knew our situation, that anything could happen. And we made a pact that whoever went first would send a sign back to the other that love survived, that there was hope beyond hope, a chance, at the end of the long haul, of being reunited. Love crosses boundaries, that's what we felt. Our feelings were so strong, you see. So strong. How stupid you must think we were.'

'No—' Veitch began to protest, but Reynolds held up a silencing hand.

'After her death I waited every day for that sign. Weeks passed, months. Of course, there was no sign. Two people in love create a fantasy world where anything can happen, one that has no connection with reality. In reality there is no hope. Love does not cross boundaries.'

Veitch stared into the golden depths of his drink, his mood dipping rapidly. Gradually he became aware that Reynolds was staring at him and when he looked up he saw the elderly man was beaming.

'And then the other afternoon, when I woke from my nap, I found this on my pillow in a slight indentation.' He dipped in his pocket and held up something almost invisible in the light.

'What is it?' Veitch said squinting.

Reynolds summoned him closer. Between the elderly man's fingers was a long, curly red hair. Reynolds brought it gently to his nose, closed his eyes, inhaled. 'And here I am, all those years ago.' When he opened his eyes they were rimmed with tears. 'Her scent was on the pillow, and again this morning.'

'You're sure—?' Veitch began, but he saw the answer in Reynolds's face.

Reynolds traced away one of the tears with a fingertip. 'I wasted my life believing in nothing when there was everything to believe in. I wasted my life by not holding hope close to my heart. Don't make the same mistake, my boy. Don't wait until you're too old and wrinkled to appreciate what life has to offer, and don't wait until you're nearly on your deathbed before you gain some kind of salvation. There really is a bigger picture. We might have no idea what it is. It might not fit any of our past preconceptions. But knowing it's there changes the way we look at the world, the way we deal with each other, the way we face up to hardship. It changes everything.' He smiled as another tear trickled gently down his cheek.

Veitch took a hasty swig of his whisky as another lump rose in his throat.

'In the last few weeks nothing has changed, really, truly, apart from a way of seeing the world. An old way, made new again. We forgot it for so long, settled for a new reality that seemed better, but was much, much worse,' Reynolds said quietly. 'There may be a lot of trouble that has been introduced into the world in recent times. But everything is defined by its opposite, and with the fear and terror have come hope and wonder. These times are not all bad, my boy. There are a lot of wonderful things out there. And perhaps, for all the suffering, this new world is better than what existed before: all its machines that made our lives so easy, yet no wonder, no magic. This is what we need as humans, my boy. Hope, faith, mystery, a sense of something greater. *This* is what we need. Not DNA analysis, faster cars, quicker computers, more consumer disposables, more scientific reductionism. *This* is what we need.'

'I've been thinking,' Veitch began; he struggled to find the right words. 'Maybe it's not all as bad as people have been making out. You know, for me, personally, I think it might be better.'

'Then go into your big quest with a strong heart,' Reynolds said, 'but don't try to make things back the way they were, for all our sakes.'

Veitch drained his malt slowly, thinking about Ruth, about the terrors they were facing. 'Something to believe in,' he said quietly, almost to himself. 'That's all we need.'

CHAPTER SEVEN

Good Son

In her deepest, darkest, most testing time, Ruth plumbed the depths of her character for reserves she never knew existed. Every hour seemed torturous, trapped in a minute world that encompassed only the claustrophobic confines of her cell, the ever-present darkness, the chill that left her bones aching to the marrow, the foul odours that occasionally drifted through from beyond the door. Part of her resilience, she knew, came from her ability to view her crucible of pain as a chrysalis. She would store up as much learning from her invisible companion as she could and when she emerged she would be wiser, more confident, stronger; no longer the weak-willed Ruth Gallagher who was living her life for the sake of other people. When she emerged.

She had grown numb to the regular periods of suffering inflicted on her by the Fomorii. Her body bore numerous wounds which would scar over into a mural of pain that would never leave her. The stump of her missing finger ached constantly and sometimes she almost imagined it was still there. But in a way the routine was almost comforting: the dull sounds of bodies moving towards her door, the insane shrieks and grunts growing louder, the feeling of nausea as the door was thrown open to reveal the almost unbearable visage of a Fomor. And then the long drag to the chamber where the instruments were kept, where the furnace burned in one corner, the atmosphere sticky and foul.

This time it was different. When the door burst open, the first face she saw was the corrupt beauty of the hybrid Fomorii priest Calatin, his expression contemptuous and cruel. He wore a filthy white shift top and leather breeches; his long hair was greasy and infested, a parody of a sophisticated aristocrat.

'*Serith Urkolim,*' he said in his guttural dialect as he nodded to Ruth. 'I thought I had seen the last of you. You proved a minor irritation until your grand failure exposed how truly pathetic you were. An insult to the very essence of the Pendragon Spirit. Oh, how your world must have mourned and wailed and cursed your name into the cold void. In that most important hour, you proved yourself as insignificant as the rest of your kind – we needed waste no more time on you.

'But then there you were, delivered to our door, at a turning point in our plans.' He chewed on a fingernail and giggled. 'And a notion came to me of great irony. Oh, to strike a blow against the feeble order of nature! To throw up an abomination! To show our contempt for all existence!'

'Just get it over with,' Ruth spat.

This time they dragged her to a different room. No furnace, no torture instruments; it was almost stately by Fomorii standards. Rough wood and stone, a tapestry hanging on the wall depicting scenes Ruth couldn't bring herself to examine, and, in the centre, a strange curved bench which appeared to be made of polished obsidian. Flickering torches cast a sickly, ruddy glare over the room.

Ruth was so weak she could barely stand. The Fomorii strapped her to the bench with harsh leather straps that bit into her flesh. Her head was spinning so much from her fragility she couldn't begin to under-stand what was happening. Instead she focused on the small joy that came from the knowledge there would be no torture that day.

Through watery eyes she watched Calatin pacing the room, suddenly intense and serious. He examined the bench, the straps, and then gently stroked a long, thin finger down her cheek and smiled cruelly. 'You have proved you are ready.'

He stepped to one side and motioned to the rear of the chamber. Two Fomorii emerged from the gloom carrying an ornate wooden chest which they placed somewhere below her feet. Through the thick stone walls Ruth heard a deep, slow rhythm, as if an enormous cere-monial drum was being hit. Every few beats it was followed by the grim tolling of the distant bell she had heard before; there was something about the relentless sound that made her very frightened.

'What are you going to do?' she croaked.

Calatin merely smiled. He motioned to the other Fomorii, who bent down to open the chest. A second later they rose with a purple velvet cushion on which lay an enormous black pearl, the size of a child's bowling ball. When Ruth saw it, she was overcome by an irrational wave of terror. Unable to control her feelings, she tried to drive herself backwards and off the bench, but the straps held fast.

Two more Fomorii moved in on either side of her and held her head fast. 'No,' she gasped.

One of the Fomorii forced some kind of metal implement between her lips and then ground it between her teeth. With a snap he forced her mouth open so sharply pain stabbed through the tendons at the back of her jaw.

Almost tenderly, one of the other Fomorii lifted the pearl and brought it towards her.

Ruth had a sudden flash of what Calatin intended. Her eyes widened as panic flooded through her system, but she couldn't move, couldn't even scream; the only sound that emerged from her throat was a desperate, keening whine.

'If it will not go in, break her jaw,' Calatin said curtly.

Ruth watched in terror as the pearl came towards her. It was so big it would choke her instantly. She thrashed from side to side, but the Fomorii held her fast.

And then the pearl was so close it was all she could see; the darkness engulfed her every sense. Her lips touched it and it felt as cold as ice, but it tasted of nothing. It pressed hard into her mouth, grinding against her teeth. Her muffled gasps grew more laboured. Her panic obscured all rational thought. There was simply the constantly increasing pressure, the pain as they forced her mouth wider and wider still, the thought that it would never fit, the horror if it did.

And then somehow her mouth was around it and just as she waited for them to retreat, they increased the pressure and began to ram it further, trying to force it down her throat.

She choked, felt her lungs protest at the lack of oxygen. And still they pressed and rammed and forced.

And then a strange thing happened. Through her overwhelming anxiety, she felt an odd sensation deep in her throat; it seemed like cotton wool at first, and then as if her throat was coming apart in gossamer strands.

And then the black pearl began to go down.

The last thing Ruth felt was an enormous pressure and a terrible coldness filling her neck. And the last thing she saw was Calatin's face swamping her vision, grinning triumphantly.

Shavi and Laura woke at first light, entwined together as if they were desperate lovers afraid to face the world. No words were exchanged as they crawled out into a land of drifting white mists and thick greenery. The morning was chill, despite the season, and an eerie stillness hung over all, punctuated only by the occasional mournful cry of a bird and the regular drip of moisture from the leaves. The nagging atmosphere of lament and loneliness had not dissipated in the slightest.

They ate a breakfast of beans and bread in silence against the dull rumble of the river which was so unceasing they no longer heard it. Laura kept a surreptitious eye on Shavi, who still appeared pale and drawn, but whenever he saw her looking he flashed his open, honest smile; even so, she could tell the weight of the night and what was to follow lay heavy on him.

After breakfast they washed the pots in the river and packed up the tent with a meticulousness that suggested they were both playing for time. Eventually they had no choice but to pick their trail back along the glen until they reached the steep path up to the bridge.

Ten minutes later they stood outside the chapel compound trying to get a glimpse of the building, but it was obscured by trees and high walls as the current custodians intended. The mist collected even more tightly around them, so it was impossible to see beyond the perimeter of the small, stoney car park outside the visitors' centre. It had the odd effect of distorting sounds so that at times they felt someone was approaching, only for the noise – whatever it was – to materialise yards away. They waited and listened, but after a while they had to accept there was no one else in the vicinity.

'I guess we climb over the wall,' Laura said tentatively.

Shavi nodded, rubbing his chin introspectively.

'But what then? Where do we even begin to start looking for . . .' She glanced over her shoulder uncomfortably, as if she had sensed someone standing there '. . . that thing we're looking for?'

'The chapel is consistently described as an arcanum, a book in stone. The carvings that cover the building are a code designed to be pondered upon. They may offer religious guidance, or fables—'

'Or they may tell us where the prison cell is.' Laura hugged her arms around her. 'Okay. Now don't get me wrong – you're a mustard-sharp guy, Shav-ster. But if people have been trying to decipher this place for centuries, what makes you think you can waltz in and do it in a few minutes?'

Shavi wagged a finger at her, smiling. 'I never said I could decipher it in minutes. But we have two things denied the searchers who came before us.'

'Yeah? And what's that?'

'Firstly, we know what we are looking for.' He took the wagging finger and tapped the side of his nose. 'And secondly, intuition.'

'A shaman's intuition, you mean. You going to be doing some more of your funny stuff?'

His smile grew enigmatic as he looked towards where the chapel was hidden. 'I intend to allow the building to speak to me.'

'Well, give it my regards.' She turned and walked towards the compound wall. Shavi heard her mutter, but obviously loud enough for his benefit, 'You nutter.'

She gave him a leg up on to the wall and he pulled her up behind him. A second later they had dropped into the chapel grounds. The building lay just a few feet away across the wet grass, a grim, Gothic pile that looked like it had been designed for some thirties Expressionist movie; it was breathtaking, despite the ugly, silver scaffolding that clung to it. An oppressive, brooding aura rolled off the building, dampening their spirits, almost physically forcing them to bow their heads. It was both threatening and frightening, Laura decided.

'You know that supercharged feeling we got at all the other sacred sites, whatever the religion? I don't get it here.' She could see Shavi felt the same.

Slowly they advanced on the chapel, as if it were sleeping, as if it could turn on them and bite. Despite his growing anxiety, Shavi marvelled at its intricate design. Rows of spired columns ranged around three sides like sentinels, or missiles waiting to be launched: the last defence against an uncaring higher power? Towards the west end, a towering wall separated the baptistry from the rest of the chapel. It seemed oddly out of place, like a shield to repel invaders from the west; Shavi could tell from its design that from above, each end of the wall was shaped like a cross.

'A bit over the top, isn't it?' Laura ventured. 'I know these old piles were thrown up to show the glory of God and all that bollocks, but this is even more ornate than York Minister. And it's just a tiny chapel in the middle of nowhere.'

'It is special,' Shavi replied distractedly. 'But the architecture itself is a message, or many different messages. Everything has been included for a reason, every stone, every tiny carving.'

'Well? Is it talking to you yet? Because I'd really like to get out of here as soon as possible.'

'What are you doing?' The stern voice made them both start. They whirled to see a man standing near the door into the visitors' centre. He was in his sixties with a pale, wrinkled face and thinning silver hair, and he was wearing a dog collar beneath an unsightly purple anorak.

'Shit. Rumbled.' Laura hissed to Shavi, 'You better do the talking. He'll probably think I'm Satan incarnate.'

Shavi walked forward, smiling, proffering an open hand. The cleric eyed it suspiciously. 'We apologise for the illicit entrance, but time is of the essence,' Shavi said.

'The chapel doesn't open until ten a.m.,' the cleric said in his mild Borders accent. 'I'll have to ask you to leave until then. And to be honest, you're lucky I don't summon the police.'

'We are not tourists,' Shavi continued. 'We are on a mission of vital importance—'

'We get a lot of strange types round here,' the cleric interrupted, 'and they all say they're on some kind of mission or other. The legends that surround the place seem to attract all sorts of unsavoury types and, frankly, many of them are distinctly unbalanced.' Despite his words he seemed to be eyeing Shavi a little more thoughtfully; he made no further attempt to move them on, as if he was waiting to hear what Shavi had to say.

'We would like to meet with a Watchman.' Laura could tell Shavi was shooting in the dark, but his words seemed to have an effect.

'What do you know of the Watchmen?'

'I know they are the secret guardians of places like this. We met one of their number in Glastonbury. He helped us in our mission.' Shavi paused. 'Are you a Watchman?'

'I may be. What would you be wanting?'

'You know of the change that has come over the world?' The cleric nodded. 'Your traditions talk of five people who will fight to save mankind. At least that is what the Watchman in Glastonbury told us. We are two of the five.'

The cleric's gaze flickered briefly towards Laura. 'You don't look like much.'

Shavi held up his hand to silence Laura before she let forth a stream of bile. 'Nevertheless, we are a Brother and Sister of Dragons, and we are here at a time of great peril.'

'A Brother and Sister of Dragons, eh?' The cleric smiled disbelievingly, although they could see the name resonated deeply with him. Shavi spent a further ten minutes convincing him of their credentials until they saw his expression become confused, then troubled. 'Perhaps you are who you say. Then what has brought you here to Rosslyn?'

'You know why this place is?' Shavi turned to face the building. 'You know what it hides?'

'I know some of it. Stories, traditions. It is hard to pick truth from myth sometimes. And every tale has a different meaning, depending which mouth tells it.' The cleric walked over and peered deeply into Shavi's eyes. 'You know,' he began with a new seriousness, 'I believe you actually might be who you say you are.' He suddenly appeared flustered. 'Then this is an important time. I've been remiss. To be honest, I never really expected this to happen in my lifetime.' He caught Shavi watching him intently. 'I never expected it to happen at all,' he backtracked. 'When you get as old as I am and you don't see any sign of all the things you've been taught, you start to lose your . . .' He made a gesture with his hand to fill in the missing word. 'But how would you know the traditions of the Watchmen, if there was no substance to all I've been taught?'

He was obviously finding the psychological and philosophical repercussions of the sudden revelation troubling. Shavi recognised his growing anxiety and held out his hand once more to deflect the cleric's thoughts. 'My name is Shavi. This is my companion Laura. We would appreciate any help you can give us.'

This time the cleric took the hand. 'Seaton Marshall. Of course I will give you any help I can. But what can Rosslyn offer you?'

'There is trouble in Edinburgh. We are doing what we can, but we are not strong enough. We were told there was power here that could help us, if only we could locate it.'

'Power?' Marshall looked puzzled. 'Really? Well, I always wondered . . . You know, I've been coming here on my rounds at this time every day since I took on the responsibility of the Watchman thirty years ago, and never once have I encountered a soul. It was such a surprise to see you, such a surprise.' He was clearly overjoyed at this exciting break in routine. 'Then the stories *are* true? That's amazing, that truly is. Come.' He took Shavi's arm and led him towards the North Door. 'Let me show you one of the most puzzling and marvellous buildings on God's earth.'

The interior of the chapel was illuminated only by subdued lighting which had obviously been installed for the benefit of the tourists; it smelled of damp, stone and candles. It was also small, which added to the sense of claustrophobia; gloom collected in the roof and corners like bats. It took a second or two for Shavi's and Laura's eyes to adjust to the shadows, but then they were instantly hit by the true wonder of the place. Everywhere they looked there were intricate carvings in the stone: grinning devils, beatific angels, Green Men peering from the foliage, daisies, lilies, roses and stars, too much to take in. As Shavi slowly surveyed the amazing detail, though, he began to get a sense of the allegories and messages coded in the stone. Books get lost, parchments turn yellow and crumble, but here was something that would carry its meaning for centuries; and how important was that meaning if such a place had to be constructed at such great cost and effort to preserve it?

He felt a *frisson* that could have been excitement or unease when he realised how many of the carvings translated to their own experience: the Green Men that were everywhere, peering down with the terrifying beneficence of Cernunnos, the angels and devils that bore a disturbing resemblance to the Tuatha Dé Danann and the Fomorii. He stopped and caught his breath. There, at the foot of a pillar, was the image with the greatest resonance: a dragon, so out of place in any church, yet at the foundation of the great edifice, as the blue fire and the dragons that represented it were at the root of everything. 'Amazing,' he whispered. It was all there. Stories and legends, teaching and warnings. It was nominally a Christian place, but here it was speaking of things that were potent long before Christ walked the earth. What did it mean; for them; for all the great religions that sprang from that time?

'Ask me any question you want,' Marshall said. 'I know the history of this place back to front. I've mulled over every carving until my head hurt, trying to understand what Sir William St Clair meant when he had the place built. Sometimes I think I've got it. I see God in the great scheme of it all, but—'

'But the Devil is in the detail,' Laura said coldly. Shavi was surprised; she was normally at best silent and at worst openly virulent in the face of religious authority.

Marshall coughed uncomfortably. 'Not quite what I meant to say, but, yes, I do get a sense of great unpleasantness in certain areas.'

'And that's not what I meant,' Laura replied, but her attention had already been drawn by the disturbing iconography.

'Why did Sir William decide to build it?' Shavi asked. 'There must be some records.'

'Many of them went missing in 1700 after a cleric drew on them to write a history of the St Clair family,' Marshall said. 'Just one of the mysteries that surround the place.'

'Perhaps he uncovered something that others wanted to remain hidden.'

'Perhaps. But it may have been that the St Clairs remained Roman Catholics instead of giving in to the Reformation. The religious divide has always remained strong in Scotland and many Catholics have suffered persecution down the centuries. The desire to remain secure in such a volatile atmosphere has led both the truth and the history to be obscured.' His eyes were bright and intelligent; he seemed to have been transformed by boyish enthusiasm at the hope that some of the mysteries might finally be unveiled. 'But the St Clairs also had very strong links to the Freemasons, who guard their secrets jealously. And, some say, to the Knights Templar. And the Rosicrucians. It has been said that the true history of the world is the history of secret societies and if that is true, then all history converges here at Rosslyn.'

'Are you going to keep me in the loop or carry on speaking in this foreign language?' Laura asked tartly. 'In which case I'm going off to find an icon to kick.'

'In the Middle Ages there were many stories about the existence of

Enlightened Ones,' Shavi explained patiently, 'the Rosicrucians, an intensely secret society whose leaders were only known to an innermost circle of adepts and the great and good leaders of society who protected them. They were supposedly highly advanced alchemists who were former members of the Knights Templar.' Laura gave a weary sigh and made a hand motion for him to continue.

But it was Marshall who carried on: 'The Knights Templar were the warrior priests of Christianity, established to protect pilgrims travelling to the Holy Land. Experts at fighting, but also intellectually superior. As well as armourers and knights, their number contained cartographers, navigators, doctors and learned clerics. But the Church became jealous of their growing power and turned on them in 1307. They were accused of taking part in blasphemous rituals—'

'That sounds interesting.' Laura's smile was a challenge Marshall chose to ignore.

'The penalty for helping them was excommunication. That is an example of how seriously the Church attempted to eradicate them. It is rumoured that an entire fleet of Templars fled to Scotland, where they went into hiding. There is a village near here called Temple which owes its name to their presence.'

'There was much more to it than that, though, was there not?' Shavi said.

Marshall nodded. 'It was rumoured the Templars had learned great secret knowledge in the Holy Land which terrified the Church, which threatened belief in the entire religion. And they were supposed to have brought that knowledge back here to Rosslyn and secreted it somewhere within the chapel.' He paused. 'And some even say what they brought back was the preserved head of Jesus Christ himself.'

'Oh, gross!' Laura made a face.

'And the Templars were linked to the Rosicrucians *and* the Masons. And the St Clair family had close links with the Masons,' Shavi noted.

'This is all rumour and hearsay,' Marshall stressed. 'Writers have built an edifice of *proof* by linking disparate and fragmentary evidence.'

'We have learned there is truth in all legends, and the constant truth here is that the chapel hides something of great importance. I feel we have come to the right place,' Shavi said.

'Is there any way I can help?' Marshall asked excitedly.

'Yeah, a coffee would be nice.' Laura nodded towards the door.

Marshall's brow furrowed for a moment, but if he felt her antagonism, he suppressed it. He nodded and slipped out.

'You should not treat people so harshly,' Shavi cautioned. 'There is no malice in him.'

'The way I see it, anybody who stands up for the Church is some kind of hypocritical bastard, so that makes them fair game.'

She wandered away from him, not wishing to discuss it further. When he caught up with her she was staring at the stained-glass windows above the altar which depicted the Resurrection. The one on the left showed three women arriving at the sepulchre; in the right window two angels sat, one holding a scroll which read: 'He is not here but is risen.' She shivered.

'It's true what he said about secret societies,' she noted thoughtfully. 'Not just the ones that you said, but the Watchmen, that freakish geek the Bone Inspector's people, all this shit going on behind the scenes. You can't get anything straight any more. They teach you one history at school like that's all there is and then you find out there's a whole 'nother load of crap going on.' She shook her head, the thoughts suddenly coming fast and furious. 'You know, you can't even trust your eyes any more. Everybody sees the so-called gods differently, all those magical items we found – it's like nothing is real. So what can you believe in?' She turned to him. 'How can you go on when you can't trust anything at face value? When you don't have any idea what's real or not? What's important or not?'

He shrugged. 'Faith.'

'In what?'

'That is the question, is it not?' He slipped an arm around her shoulders and she rested against him briefly before pulling away.

Marshall walked in with two steaming cups of coffee. 'There's a little café section in the visitors' centre,' he said. 'But there's no fresh milk at the moment, unfortunately.'

Laura thanked him, a little curtly, but with no real sharpness.

'Can you show us some of the things of interest?' Shavi asked the cleric.

'Certainly.' He took them over to the south door and pointed to the top of a pillar. 'See there. A lion and what appears to be a unicorn. The lion's often linked to the Resurrection. The unicorn is symbolic of Christ. Yet the two are fighting. What do you think that means?'

'I do not know,' Shavi replied thoughtfully.

'It seems like a warning,' Laura noted. 'Fighting, you know. Not a good thing. Christ fighting against the Resurrection.'

'That doesn't make any sense,' Marshall said.

He led them around to the north aisle and pointed out the burial stone of William St Clair, which contained both a Templar insignia and the carved outline of the Grail; Laura glanced at Shavi, but he gave no

586

sign that it was important. Two more dragons; an angel with a scroll. 'There are carved images of open books everywhere,' Marshall explained. 'One line of thought is this is supposed to refer to the Book of Revelation and the Day of Judgment. *I could see the dead, great and small, standing before the throne: and books were opened.*'

'So, you have an ambiguous reference to the Resurrection and constant reference to the Apocalypse.'

'Christians of that time were obsessed with these issues,' Marshall said.

Laura snorted. 'They still are.'

'Up here.' Shavi pointed to a carving of angels rolling away the stone from Christ's tomb. And on the pillar to the right, three figures, one without a head, observing the crucifixion scene.

'No one knows who the three figures are,' Marshall said. 'Here's one I've always admired.' He indicated sixteen figures dancing up and down a ribbed arch; next to each one was a skeleton. 'It's the danse macabre, the dance of death, showing death's supremacy over mankind.'

'Hey, Happy Jack.' Laura wandered away, wishing she was with Church, the two of them on some beach miles away from everyone else. Suddenly she felt a cold flood wash over her, pinpricks dancing up and down her spine. It was as if her subconscious had seen something she wasn't aware of, something exciting, stimulating or important. She looked around, saw nothing. Then, slowly she raised her head and there it was; but there was no way she could even have glimpsed it.

Looking down at her was the biggest, finest example of the Green Man she had yet seen in the chapel. Branches protruded from his mouth like tusks, curling back in an abundance of leaves across his head. The face was darkly grinning, the eyes black slits beneath plunging eyebrows. She couldn't tell if it was supposed to be evil, mischievous or threatening.

Something about the eyes, she thought. Almost as if it were looking directly at her, communicating with her.

'Y'know, maybe this isn't such a good idea,' she called out. But Shavi and Marshall were immersed in examining two unusual pillars. The doubts suddenly began ringing through her. The carvings all seemed to suggest something bad, some warning not to disturb what had been sealed there. To release it could bring about the Apocalypse, that was the message, wasn't it? she thought. Why couldn't Shavi and Marshall see it? It seemed so obvious to her. But maybe she was just being stupid. They were both smarter than her, more perceptive. She glanced back up at the face of the Green Man and shivered once more.

'Explain to me about the two pillars,' Shavi was saying as she approached. The one on the left stood tall and straight, with intricate carvings rising in tiers from the base. But the one on the right was even more elaborate and sophisticated in its design. Instead of rising in straight lines, the detailed carvings twisted around the column in what must have been a display of the prowess of a master mason.

Yet Marshall indicated differently. 'The one on the left is called the Mason's Pillar, the one on the right the Apprentice Pillar. There's a story that goes along with them: in the absence of the Master Mason, his apprentice set about working on the pillar, creating this perfect marvel of workmanship. On the Master Mason's return, instead of being delighted at the success of his pupil, he was so overcome with envy he flew into a rage and killed the apprentice with one blow of his mallet. And of course he paid the penalty for his actions.'

'The sacrifice of something good. An act of betrayal sealed in blood,' Shavi said. He ran his fingers through his long hair as he tried to read more meaning in the story.

But Laura's attention was drawn by the dragons and vines wrapped around the base of the Apprentice Pillar, binding it with the symbols of the Green and the Earth Spirit. Now her doubts were starting to make her feel queasy.

'This is where we need to look.' Shavi indicated the Apprentice Pillar.

'Are you sure?' Marshall said. 'People have pondered over the meaning of this place for centuries. You've drawn your conclusions rather quickly, if you don't mind my saying.'

'Perhaps. I am simply making an intuitive leap. But here is my reasoning: this pillar cries out that it is unique in its very design – twisted, while all the other pillars remain straight and true. It even has its own legend, which sets it apart as something formed under special circumstances. And myths and legends, as a friend of mine repeats incessantly, are the secret history of the land.'

'Then what do you suggest? Digging beneath it?' Marshall looked uneasy at this act both of sacrilege and the destruction of an ancient monument.

Shavi nodded. Laura and Marshall both winced for different reasons.

'This floor is stone. The pillar . . . Lord! You might bring the whole roof down! As if we haven't had enough structural problems with this place over the last few years.'

'Nevertheless. Our need is great. We must find a way.'

'And I have no power here,' Marshall continued. 'I am, I suppose, at best tolerated. Someone will try to stop you. The police will be here in minutes.'

Laura glanced at her watch. 'The place doesn't open till ten. We've got hours yet.'

Shavi looked beyond the Apprentice Pillar to a flight of stairs leading down into the gloom. 'Where does that lead?'

'The sacristy. It's believed to be even older than the chapel,' Marshall said.

'So the chapel was built around it,' Shavi mused.

'It's not so important. I mean, it's completely bare of ornament, unlike this place. It's just a rough rectangle of stone some thirty-six feet long. Records say there are three Princes of Orkney and nine Barons of Rosslyn buried down there.'

Shavi went to the top of the stairs and peered down. 'Buried where, exactly?'

'Why, no one knows exactly.' Marshall gestured as if it was such an unimportant fact it was barely worth discussing.

Shavi rested his cheek against the cold stone of the door frame and weighed the place and dimensions of the room below before glancing back at the Apprentice Pillar. 'So,' he began with a faint smile, 'the burial chamber could be a walled-off extension from the back of the sacristy.'

'Possibly.'

'Which would put it somewhere beneath the Apprentice Pillar.'

Marshall thought about this for a moment, then nodded fulsomely. 'You could be right. And of course that would make it a little more accessible from the sacristy.'

'Well, I wish we could hang around to hear you explain the big pile of rubble and the hole in the wall,' Laura said snidely.

'There are tools available. Near the graveyard there's a store for those who've been working on the repair of the building,' Marshall said. He slipped out and returned soon after with two pick-axes and a shovel.

Cautiously Marshall led the way down the treacherously worn steps into the dank, bare sacristy. Shavi followed while Laura took up the rear with a feeling of growing apprehension. 'Are you sure about this?' she hissed to Shavi once Marshall was far enough ahead to be out of earshot.

'I am not sure about anything. All I know is we have no alternative. We do not have the power to oppose the Fomorii directly, certainly none that could deflect the Blue Hag.'

'Yeah. You're right, I suppose. I just have a feeling this is going to be a frying pan/fire scenario.'

Shavi searched her face. She was surprised to see he was taking her views seriously. 'Would you like to turn back?' he asked genuinely.

That surprised her even more. 'Let's see how we go. We can always pull out if things get too hairy.'

They identified the spot on the sacristy wall that corresponded with where Shavi guessed the burial chamber lay. The wall was old stone, sturdy enough, but the cement between the blocks was ancient and would crumble easily. They stood in silence for a long moment, attempting to come to terms with what they were about to do. Then Shavi raised the pick-axe above his head and swung it at the wall.

The moment it struck an echo ran through the building that sounded like an unearthly moan filled with anguish. It was surely a bizarre effect of the chapel's acoustics, they told themselves, but it had sounded so vocal it made them all grow cold. Shavi and Marshall glanced at each other, saying nothing. Laura backed a few paces away, wrapping her arms around her.

Shavi swung the pick again. This time the moan seemed to be outside, all around the chapel, caught in the wind. It grew palpably darker in the already gloomy sacristy.

'There's a storm coming,' Marshall noted, but it didn't ease them. Almost at his words, the wind picked up and began to buffet the outside of the building.

The stone wasn't as resilient as it had first appeared. Large chunks had fallen to the ground and the cement had all crumbled away; they would soon be able to remove an entire block and from then on the job would be relatively easy.

Shavi raised the pick for the third time.

A tremendous boom resounded through the main body of the chapel above them. They realised at the same time it was the sound of the chapel door being thrown open. Shavi threw down the pick and hurried up the steps with the others close behind.

Framed in the doorway was a man of indeterminate age, although Shavi guessed he must have been in his sixties. His greasy, grey-black hair was long and hung in an unkempt mess around his shoulders, framing a skull-like face that was sun-browned and weatherbeaten from an outdoor life. He was thin but wiry and exuded a deep strength that belied his age. Shavi would not have liked to have been on the receiving end of a blow from the six-foot, gnarled staff that the man clutched menacingly. At first sight Shavi guessed he was some kind of itinerant; his well-worn baggy trousers had long lost their original colour to become a dirty brown; he wore tired sandals and a dingy cheesecloth shirt open to the waist. But then Shavi noticed the warning issued by his dark, piercing eyes; the power within showed he was a man with a mission.

'I've come to stop you two doing something you probably won't live to regret,' he said with a rural accent Shavi couldn't place.

Laura tugged at Shavi's arm. 'Here's a word of advice: stay out of the way of that staff.'

'You know him?'

'We met in Avebury before you came on board,' she said.

And then Shavi recognised him. 'The Bone Inspector.' He smiled and held out his hand in greeting.

The Bone Inspector didn't take his eyes off Shavi's face.

'Who is he?' Marshall asked.

'The custodian of the land's old places, the stone circles, the long-barrows and burial mounds. The last in a long line of wise men who kept the knowledge of nature's ways.' Shavi tried to read him, sensed a threat, though he didn't know why.

'Do you know what you're doing here?' the Bone Inspector asked.

'Trying to save the world,' Laura said from the back. 'You should try it some time.'

'I couldn't believe it.' His voice was low, trembling with repressed emotion. 'When I felt it in the land, like a shiver running through the soil, I came as quick as I could to stop you, you damn fools. I'll ask you again: do you know what you're doing?'

'We have been guided here to free the hidden power—'

The Bone Inspector snorted derisively. 'Hidden power! Then you don't have any idea what's beneath your feet. Or why this place was built to keep it there.'

'Then tell us,' Shavi said firmly.

The Bone Inspector laughed contemptuously. 'It's beyond you, boy. It's bigger and darker and more dangerous than you could ever im-agine, and if you had any idea what it was, you wouldn't even be within ten miles of this place. All of you, you're like mice, getting into things you shouldn't, causing trouble. I knew you weren't up to the job.'

'We're up to it,' Laura said adamantly, 'so you can take your staff and shove it—'

Shavi silenced her with a cut of his hand. 'I mean to find what is here and take it with me. Everything turns on this. If we return without it, all is lost.'

The Bone Inspector's face grew harder. 'And I mean to stop you. I could sit quietly and explain why what you're doing is a mistake of nightmarish proportions, or I could beat the shit out of you. Either way you'll get the message – and I know which one will be more effective. So let's see who's up to the job, eh? Boy.' There was arrogance in his voice; he was not used to being opposed. He raised his staff aggressively and in a liquid movement rolled on to the balls of his feet, primed and ready to attack. Shavi could see he knew how to use the staff; there was something in the way he held his body which suggested the rigid discipline of the martial arts, although Shavi guessed the fighting style was uniquely British, and very ancient. 'How do you plan to fight, then, boy?' the Bone Inspector asked.

Shavi stood calmly with his arms by his side. He registered no fear, no sense of urgency at all. He knew he would be no match physically for the Bone Inspector. Instead of tensing, he let his muscles relax, pushed his head back slightly and closed his eyes.

'You do that,' the Bone Inspector said. 'Pretend I'm not here.'

Shavi had never tried it before, but the fact that his abilities were improving each day was unmistakable. It was difficult to attempt something untried in the crucible of conflict, but he was growing increasingly confident. He knew in his heart what he *should* be able to do. It was only a matter of seeing if he could.

At first nothing seemed to be happening. Then, gradually, the Bone Inspector's sneering voice seemed to fade until it sounded as if it were coming from the depths of a long tunnel. At the same time Shavi's vision skewed like it was being twisted through a kaleidoscope. Dimensions stretched like toffee, turned on an angle. Once the distortion took over, different, deeper senses took over. Time appeared to be running slowly. He could hear sounds, whispers, that had not been there before, although he had no idea who was talking; and he suddenly seemed to be able to see *through* the dense stone of the wall and out across the land for what appeared to be miles. In that dream-like state he was beyond himself, beyond the chapel; although he had touched on it with his experiments he had never achieved such clarity before. And then he was ready: he put out the call with a voice that was not a voice.

'Shavi! This is no time to zone out on me!' Laura shook his arm but he didn't even seem to feel it.

'What's going on?' Marshall said. Then, to the Bone Inspector, 'Why are you threatening these people?'

The Bone Inspector grinned, his staff still levelled at Shavi's throat. 'Hold your voice, church-man. Your kind act like you know everything about everything when you know nothing about nothing. Don't go sticking your nose in where it doesn't belong.'

'This is sanctified ground!' Marshall said irately. 'I will not have fighting here!'

'No, but you'll let these two take a pick-axe and shovel to the place. Hypocrites, your kind, always have been.'

Laura was distracted from the confrontation by a movement outside the door: a shadow flitting against the background of clipped grass and mist. Another one, too quick to pin down the shape. There was something outside, several things, and they were drawing closer.

'Shavi?' she muttered.

'Playing dead won't help, lad,' the Bone Inspector mocked. 'You'll have to learn your lesson soon enough.'

'What lesson's that?' Laura's eyes darted back to the door. *Closer.* 'That sooner or later everyone turns into a bitter old git?'

The Bone Inspector's grin soured. He opened his mouth to speak. And in that instant something flashed through the door and hit him, and then he was howling in pain. Everything moved so fast it took a few seconds for Laura to register what was happening. A large russet fox was scrabbling wildly at the Bone Inspector's torso, its teeth sunk deeply into his forearm. Blood trickled down his brown skin. He flailed around with the staff, trying to thrash it off, but it was holding on too tight and the pain was throwing him off-balance. Before he could toss away the staff and grapple it with his free hand, a large mongrel and a Great Dane still trailing its owner's lead burst through the door and set about him with snapping jaws. Laura could tell they were not really trying to hurt him, but they kept him reeling and gave him enough nips to make his skin slick with blood and saliva. More shapes were moving towards the chapel; she glimpsed another fox, a badger, bizarrely, several rabbits, all heading towards the Bone Inspector. In the whirlwind of fur and fang, snapping and snarling, he was driven backwards by sheer weight of numbers until he was on the threshold. Laura picked up his stick and ran forward to jab him with it so he went spinning out on to the grass.

'Quick!' Shavi gasped. 'The doors!' He pitched forward, spraying spittle, his eyes rolling, and grabbed the back of a pew for support.

Laura and Marshall ran together and slammed the doors shut, then helped each other to drag pews in front of them. When they had finished it would have taken a bulldozer to plough the doors open.

And then, eerily, the crescendo of awful animal noises ended suddenly, to be replaced by the dim sound of paws padding quickly away. There was a choking moan, quickly stifled, as the Bone Inspector started to feel the full pain of his wounds.

Laura whirled. Shavi still clung to the pew, pale and weak. 'You did that!' she said incredulously.

He nodded, tried to force a smile. 'I never realised I had it in me.'

'Good Lord!' Marshall muttered. He slumped down on to a pew blankly.

Laura and Shavi hurried round and piled pews against the west and south doors too. 'He's going to find a way to get in as soon as he recovers,' she said.

Shavi nodded. 'Then we better get moving.'

Back in the sacristy, Laura felt cold, queasy, barely able to continue. Shavi, though, seemed oblivious to the growing anxiety which hung over the chapel like a suffocating fog. He swung the pick-axe at the wall with force; the reverberations exploded to the very foundations. Up in the choir Marshall still sat in a daze, staring at the floor, his arms hugged tightly round him. And at the door the Bone Inspector hammered and hollered, his voice growing increasingly fractured. It was a terrible sound, filled with a growing sense of fear. Laura covered her ears, but even that couldn't block it out.

'What's in there, Shavi?' she asked, but he didn't seem to hear. His face was fixed, almost transcendent.

And the pick-axe rose and fell, rose and fell. Shards of stone flew off like bomb fragments and clouds of dust filled the air. He coughed and choked and smeared his forehead with sweaty dirt. 'Nearly there,' he hacked.

Laura wanted to say *Don't go any further*, but with that thought there was a sudden crash and several stones collapsed into a dark void beyond. Laura jumped back in shock, not quite knowing what to expect. Shavi paused in mid-swing. Slowly the dust settled.

As their eyes adjusted to the gloom beyond, Laura saw Shavi had been correct in his assumptions. He had uncovered a large tomb filled with dusty stone sarcophagi; on several were carved the sign of the sword which Marshall had attributed to the Knights Templar. The atmosphere that swept out was so unpleasantly stale it forced Laura to clutch her hand to her mouth. But it was more than just the odour that choked her; there was a wave of oppression and threat which came on its heels. She couldn't bear to stay any longer. She hurried back up the steps; Shavi didn't even notice. His gaze was fixed on an intricately carved column of death's heads, Green Men and dragons which he guessed from its siting was a continuation of the Apprentice's Pillar above. Halfway up the column was an area where nothing was carved at all. Gently he touched it. It appeared to vibrate coldly beneath his fingertips.

'Here we are, then,' he whispered.

*

594

Marshall still sat with his head in his hands, didn't even look up when Laura walked by. She wanted to be out in the open air, where she could breathe, but the Bone Inspector didn't show any sign of giving up. If anything, his hammering against the wooden door had grown even more frenzied, his yells hoarse and broken.

'Give it a rest,' she said angrily. 'This is supposed to be a place of peace and serenity. We can't hear ourselves think in here.'

At her voice he subsided. It was so sudden Laura felt a brief moment of panic that he had something planned, but then he spoke in a voice that was full of such desperation she was shocked. 'You musn't go through with this. You have to stop now. I'm begging you.'

'If you hadn't acted so up your own arse and told us exactly what was wrong we might have listened.' She chewed on her lip. 'So what's the big deal?'

'Listen, then.' His voice echoed tremulously through the wood. 'It is not *what* lies here, but *who*: The Good Son.' He laughed bitterly. 'A name of respect given to placate, to keep something terrible at bay.'

'He was supposed to be a good guy,' Laura noted.

'You should know by now,' the Bone Inspector said with thin contempt, 'that when it comes to the old gods there is no *good* or *evil*. They are beyond that.'

'You know what I mean,' Laura replied sourly.

'If you could trust any of the Tuatha Dé Danann, then he was the one,' he conceded. 'He *was* loved. As I said, it would be wrong to attribute human emotions to these gods. They're alien in the true sense of the word, unknowable—'

'But you're going to,' Laura noted slyly.

'The Fomorii loathed Maponus—'

'Jealous of his good looks and way with women, I'd guess,' she said humourlessly.

'In their bitterness at their overwhelming defeat at the second battle of Magh Tuireadh, the Fomorii were determined to launch one last desperate strike at the Tuatha Dé Danann,' the Bone Inspector continued. 'And Maponus as the favourite son of the Tuatha Dé Danann was the perfect target. They attacked as he attempted to cross over from Otherworld to visit his worshippers here.'

'Attacked how?'

'All that's known is that Maponus was struck down as he crossed the void between there and here—'

'If he was killed—' Laura interrupted.

'Not killed. These gods never truly die anyway. What the Fomorii planned was much worse. Whatever they did to him in the void, when he arrived here, he had been driven completely, utterly insane. That's the ultimate punishment: eternal imprisonment in a state of suffering. The world never knew what had hit it. The first sign of what had happened was a small village in the Borders. Every inhabitant was slaughtered, torn apart in so vile a manner it was impossible to identify the dead, even to estimate how many had died. In his dementia Maponus roamed the wild places and in the long nights people spoke of hearing his anguished howls echoing among the hills. Every attribute he had was inverted. He was not the giver of light and life, but the bringer of darkness and death. No love, only mad animal frenzy, no culture, only slaughter. It is impossible to guess how many died during his reign of terror. Tales passed down through the generations told how the fields ran red with blood. And the Good Son, once a name to be revered, became a source of fear.'

'What happened to him?' Laura's voice sounded oddly hollow, as if the room had mysteriously developed other dimensions which allowed it to echo.

'He couldn't be allowed to continue in this way,' the Bone Inspector replied darkly. 'He may have been seen as saviour once, but now he was cast in the role of destroyer, and if humankind wanted to survive, it had to destroy him. Or the next best thing.'

'We're a fickle bunch, aren't we?' Marshall was suddenly next to her, his voice painfully sour. 'If salvation doesn't arrive just how we expect, we bite that outstretched hand.'

'My people gathered in their college, first at Anglesey, then at Glastonbury,' the Bone Inspector continued. 'It was their time, you see. After so long in the dark, the Sundering had allowed them to grow in strength and hope. Their sun-powered cosmology, their worship of that bright side of Maponus, allowed them to turn their backs on the night and the moon and hope for a greater role for mankind in the mysteries of existence. They weren't going to see all that swept away, especially by a god whose time had passed, even one so close to their hearts.

'In a ritual which took seven nights to prepare, they eventually drew up enough power to bind Maponus in one spot. Even so, it cost the lives of two hundred good men, so the legends tell, reduced in Maponus's frenzy to a shower of blood, bone and gristle. But the others held fast, and Maponus was caught.'

Laura glanced over her shoulder towards the steps to the Sacristy. The flinty clink of pick-axe on stone echoed up. 'Jesus.' Her voice sounded pathetically small.

'You have to stop him!' Marshall hissed. 'For the love of God! Before it's too late!'

'But we don't have a choice.' Laura repeated the mantra, her head spinning. 'If we don't do this here, everything goes fucking pear-shaped.' And then she was running towards the steps, yelling, 'Shavi!'

Shavi couldn't hear anything, not even the sound of his own frenzied attack on the pillar. His concentration was drawn into the stone and nothing beyond existed. He coughed through the clouds of dust he was raising, scrubbed at the sweat that was dripping from his brow, and swung, and swung. And then finally, with a crack that seemed to tear through the very foundations of the chapel, a sound almost like a human roar, the pillar burst apart. Shavi staggered backwards and fell. And as the dust gradually cleared he saw what lay inside.

'They cut off his head!' the Bone Inspector was bellowing. 'They cut it off while he was still alive and sealed it in a pillar. And it was still alive even then! Still screaming! And they buried his body nearby—'

Laura reached the top of the steps, still shouting Shavi's name, just as the first tremor rattled through the building. A shower of dust fell from the roof as a large crack opened up in the stone floor, pitching her to one side. She hit the flags hard, knocking the wind out of her.

Marshall was already moving past her, his arthritic joints cracking under the strain. Laura caught a glimpse of wild emotions in his face as he headed down the stairs. Another tremor hit and he fell from halfway down, banging his head against the stone. Blood spattered from a deep gash as he slammed into the sacristy floor.

The tremors came faster, building in intensity. As she hauled herself to her feet, Laura had a sudden image of the chapel crashing down on top of her, crushing every bone beneath the enormous weight of stone.

Shavi's head was spinning and for a brief moment it felt like he was surfacing from a dream until reality suddenly jolted him alert. The clouds of dust that swept through the chamber were almost choking, and the intense vibrations running up through the floor made him nauseous. But it was the sound that disturbed him the most; it moved effortlessly from a barely audible bass rumble to a high-pitched keening. There was something in the quality that filled him with an overwhelming despair, while making his gorge rise; he could hardly bear it.

And then the dust cleared and he saw the origin of that awful noise. Where he had smashed away the stone of the pillar lay a dusty space, and within it was a severed head. It took him a second or two to make any sense of the features, but gradually they fell into relief: full lips, perfect cheekbones, large eyes, a straight nose. There was something about the face that was incredibly beautiful, yet at the same time sickeningly corrupt. The skin seemed to glow with an inner golden light, but near the jagged skin of the severed neck the hue was queasily green. And the eyes, though dark and attractive, moved from an angry red to purple. The rear and sides of the head were still trapped in the stone, so only the face peered out, as if the owner was comically peering through some curtains. Long hair turned white and matted with stone dust poked out on either side.

Shavi could barely tear his eyes away from those full lips, which moved sensually to make that foul sound. He could feel it rumbling in his stomach cavity, vibrating through his teeth, deep into his skull. He pressed his hands against his ears, but it made no difference.

Although the spectacle was hideously mesmerising, Shavi realised instinctively he ought to get out of there. Before he could move, the largest tremor of all opened a massive fissure in the floor. Chunks of stone dropped from the ceiling and Shavi threw up his arms to protect himself. When he next dared look, he realised a golden light was rising up slowly out of the fissure. The apprehension held him fast; he *had* to see what was coming.

Within seconds a hand protruded from the dark, and then slowly Maponus's headless body hauled itself out of the hole. For a brief moment it staggered around as if it were learning to walk and then it moved to clamp its hands on the pillar. The remaining stone that held the head crumbled away. Its eyes ranged wildly; there seemed to be no intelligence there at all.

The thin, delicate fingers clutched until they caught on to the head. A second later it was placed firmly on the shoulders, the eyes still rolling. A sickly light eked out from between the head and the body as the two knitted together. And then Maponus stood erect and whole for the first time in centuries, slim and beautiful and golden and filled with all the terror of the void.

Shavi thought his eyes were about to be burned from his head at the wonder of what he saw. 'Please,' he whispered. 'Hear me.'

Maponus fixed his monstrous gaze upon Shavi. The eyes flickered coldly; Shavi saw nothing human in them at all. Slowly the god began to advance.

'In Edinburgh, the Fomorii await,' Shavi continued. His voice sounded like sandpaper. 'We call on you to help us defeat the Cailleach Bheur. Defeat the Fomorii.'

Maponus listened, and then he smiled darkly.

Shavi sighed, relieved his message had been understood. But when he raised his eyes back to the glowing figure he saw Maponus was still advancing, his features frozen and murderous. The god stretched out his arms and golden sparks spattered between his hands. Shavi could taste the ozone on the back of his throat. One more step and he began to feel the temperature rise, the pressure build in his head. Deep inside, a part of him was trying to drive him out of there, but he was held in the stress of that dazzling regard. The hairs in his nostrils began to sizzle.

'No! If you have to take anyone, take me!' Somehow Marshall was there, trying to interpose himself between Shavi and the god. His face was scarlet with the blood from his wound, and with his staring, terrified eyes, in other circumstances, he would have cut a comical pantomime figure. But there, in the light coming off the creature, he looked like some tormented soul from a painting by Bosch. Despite his fear, he managed to raise his frail, trembling body until he could look Maponus in the eye. 'Take me.' His voice was quiet, gentle. He stretched out his arms in a posture of sacrifice, not supplication.

Maponus clamped his hands on either side of Marshall's head. In an instant Shavi could smell the sickening odour of cooking flesh. Marshall howled as the blood began to boil in his veins. Those sparks danced and sparkled all over the cleric's twitching body, raising plumes of grey smoke.

The horrific sight broke the spell. Shavi rolled over and scrambled out of the chamber, throwing himself up the steps from the sacristy two at a time. Laura was waiting for him at the top, her face streaked with tears.

'That smell,' she choked.

He grabbed her and drove her towards the door. As they madly threw the pews away from the exit, the chapel began to shake wildly. Enormous chunks of masonry fell from somewhere above, and rifts opened in the walls and floor.

Laura glanced over her shoulder just once at the light gradually rising from the sacristy. 'He's coming!' she moaned.

The last pew was thrown aside just in time and then they were hurtling out into the chill, misty morning air. The Bone Inspector was waiting for them, his face showing all the horror that they felt in their hearts. With a deafening rumble, the chapel fell in on itself, shaking the ground like an earthquake.

The three of them were already at the perimeter wall, pulling themselves over to safety. Shavi paused on the summit to look back at the devastation, hoping against hope that the monstrous thing they had unleashed would be trapped under the rubble.

He was overcome by an awful sickness when all he saw was a golden light fading into the mist, moving out across the countryside.

the Deep Shadows

The first sign that all was not as it should be hit Church twenty minutes after they had entered through the well-head. No longer stale, the air in the tunnel smelled of cinnamon and mint. And it almost seemed to be singing, harmonious melodies bouncing back and forth off the walls. 'Is this the start of it?' he asked.

' "This is the best part of the trip".' Tom's voice echoed curiously behind him.

'What?'

'Nothing. Just remembering the sixties.'

'This is no time to be getting nostalgic.' Church was tense with apprehension.

'If you'd enjoyed the sixties to the full you'd be a little mellower in dealing with everything life has to throw at you now.'

'Sorry. I was born too late for the summer of love.' There was a *shush-boom* effect deep in the stone walls, like a giant heart beating.

'You missed a great time. That smell, it reminds me of Californian nights, hanging out at Kesey's parties when he and the Merry Pranksters set up shop after they did the Magic Bus ride. Jerry Garcia doing the music. Two kinds of punch – normal and *electric*. That was before the Hell's Angels moved in and ruined it.'

'What are you talking about?' Church said distractedly. 'You *have* done too many drugs, haven't you.' He reached out to touch the tunnel wall; strange vibrations rippled up his fingers.

'You know, Kesey, Leary, all those psychonauts, they set things in motion that could have changed the world before the Establishment stamped it down. They believed the psychedelics could help them see God, did you know that? And by doing that they were just like all those people who threw up the great monolithic structures around the world where the earth energy is at its strongest. Before our feeble *modern* culture, psychedelics fired civilisation.'

'Are you saying all those hippies were right?' Church said distractedly.

'We all need to be neo-hippies if we're going to cope with this new world that's being presented to us, Jack.'

The note of tenderness in Tom's voice surprised Church so much he looked around and was instantly disoriented. He appeared to be viewing Tom through a wall of oily water, the image stretched, skewed, distorted.

'Tom?' He reached out a hand, but his friend seemed to recede with the action until he appeared to be floating backwards along a dark corridor, growing smaller yet glowing brighter.

'It will be all right, Jack.' Tom's voice grew hollow, deep and loud, then faint, as if it were cycling between two speakers. Church blinked and Tom was gone.

Unable to understand what was happening, he was overcome by a sudden wave of panic. They had been walking along quite normally, and now he was alone; it made no sense.

Desperately, he clamped his eyes shut, focusing on Tom's advice to be *mellow*, and then he remembered how Tom had warned him that space and time could warp that close to such a potent source of the earth energy. He composed himself with a deep breath, accepted that he was on his own, and forged on down the tunnel.

After following its undulating path for about fifteen minutes, lulled by the background harmonics of the air, he suddenly rounded a corner into a large cavern. He could tell it was enormous from the change in the quality of the sound of his breathing and footsteps, although the roof disappeared into the deep shadows above him. The danger of getting lost in such a place was a distinct possibility. He could follow the walls with their faint phosphorescent glow around the perimeter, but he instinctively felt the correct path was directly across the floor of the cavern, through the darkness that could hide treacherous fissures, sinkholes and pits. His fears were confirmed when he glanced down and noticed a carved rock set in the floor by his feet. It was well-made, polished and indented. It showed a dragon, its tail curling to form an arrowhead which pointed the way into the centre of the cavern. He hesitated for just a moment, then strode off into the shadows.

It seemed like he had been walking for hours, although he guessed it was only about fifteen minutes. In the enveloping dark the going was laboriously slow, feeling with each foot before taking another step. At times the visual deprivation was so hallucinatory he felt his head spinning and he had to fight to stop himself from pitching to the ground; in that warped atmosphere he was having trouble discerning what was happening in his head and what was external.

Without eyes, sound took on added meaning and he was alert to any aural change in his surroundings. When he first heard the distant, reverberating *ching-ching-ching* of metal on metal he froze instantly.

Listening intently, he held his breath as the noise grew louder until it was accompanied by the trudge of heavy footsteps. A faint light began to draw closer, which he at first thought was just his eyes playing tricks on him. Gradually, though, an enormous figure presented itself to him, but it seemed unreal, like an obvious movie effect, with the light buried deep within it and seeping out through its surface. As it came into focus he felt a sudden pang of fear. From the sickening waves that rolled off it, it was undoubtedly a Fomor, but it was encased in black, shiny armour; the chainmail that glinted darkly beneath the plates was making the metallic sound that had alerted him to its presence. The oddly shaped armour with its gnarls and ridges was like a carapace, making the figure resemble a giant insect; on the head was a helmet which concealed most of the hideous face, two curved horns reaching out from the temple with a row of six smaller ones beneath. It was gripping in both hands an unusual but cruel weapon with on one side a nicked and sickly smeared axe-head and on the other a line of sharp tines of irregular length. Church heard its breath rumbling like a traction engine, the vibrations churning in the pit of his stomach.

The figure was terrifying to see. Church had the sense it was more powerful than any of the Fomorii he had encountered before. And as it advanced, the threat around it grew until he felt queasy from the potency of the danger.

His shock at what he was witnessing finally broke and he took a couple of staggering backwards steps before turning and running. He hadn't gone far when he stumbled over an outcropping rock and crashed down, winding himself. But as he glanced back to see how close the Fomor warrior was behind him, he saw the figure begin to break up into tiny particles, as if it were made out of flies. There was no sound, and a second later it had completely disappeared.

Church rolled on to his back, breathing heavily, trying to make sense of what had happened. He had felt the Fomor was definitely there, yet it didn't seem to have been aware of him. Was it simply a hallucination or a by-product of the strange atmosphere that existed in that place?

As he climbed to his feet a more important concern pushed all those questions from his mind. In his attempt to get away he had done just as he had feared – lost his sense of direction. It was impossible to tell where he had been going. There was nothing for it. Despondently, he selected a path at random and set off.

*

The mesmerising darkness became claustrophobic. He was flying, he was falling. He was hearing voices singing from the void, fading, rising again in anger or despair. There was Marianne, his Marianne, saying, 'So the real Dale is still in the Black Lodge?' He scrubbed at his ears and it went away.

To his right he saw a dim golden glow pulsating with the beat of the blood in his brain. As he drew near, figures separated from the light, all shining, all beautiful. He recognised faces he had seen when the Tuatha Dé Danann had swept to his rescue at the Fairy Bridge on Skye. Lugh stood, tall and proud, reunited with his spear, which he held at his side. And behind him was the Dagda, a starburst from which features coalesced, alternately ferocious and paternal, always different; his own father appeared there briefly. And there were others who seemed both benign and cruel at the same time; some were so alien to his vision it made his stomach churn. They were talking, but their communication was so high-pitched and incomprehensible it might as well have been the language of angels.

He almost stumbled among them, but they were oblivious to his presence. He had the sudden urge to lash out, a childish desire born of his own powerlessness, but he knew it would be futile, and so restrained himself; if he admitted it to himself, there was some fear there too.

But were they hallucinations? Or was the potent energy drawing him towards real moments plucked from the flow of time? As if to answer his unspoken question, Lugh pointed to an image which coalesced among them. It was Veitch, obvious despite the mask that covered his face, clutching a shotgun, his nervousness masked by anger. Church knew instantly what he was seeing: the moment when his friend had his life torn from him. Veitch waved the gun back and forth. In the background the building society was still, tense.

One of the Tuatha Dé Danann Church didn't recognise leaned forward and said something in the angel-tongue. On cue, Veitch whirled and fired the gun. An elderly man was thrown back as if he'd been hit by a car, trailing droplets of blood through the air.

Ruth's uncle, Church thought. *The act that brought on her father's heart attack.* Two lives ruined by the arrogance of power.

He watched the faces of the Tuatha Dé Danann expecting, hoping almost, to see cruel glee or contempt there, but there was nothing. It was an act inflicted on beings so far beneath them that there was no call for any response; it was nothing more than a brushing away of a dust mote.

Sickened, he turned and hurried away.

He hadn't gone far when an idea struck him. If what he was viewing was random, such a turning point in all their lives would have been too much of a coincidence. In some way the events were arriving before him like lightning leaping to the rod on a church steeple, summoned by his subconscious, or some other vital part of his being.

Maybe we're operating on the quantum level, he thought, *where everything is linked.* But if that was true, what did the first terrifying image mean? *Maybe I can make this work for me.*

He concentrated until he dredged up images from his subconscious, some so painful they brought tears to his eyes. He remembered how Tom had used the blue fire to warp space before, drawing them along lines of power from the stormy sea off Tintagel to the top of Glastonbury Tor in the wink of an eye.

Do it for me now, he wished, feeling like a boy, not caring.

For long moments nothing happened. And then, suddenly, he was falling. When the descent stopped he was standing in his old flat. But it didn't have the familiar look of bachelorhood, the secret layers of dust, the scatter of magazines, piles of videos and CDs, and odours that wouldn't shift. It was before. When Marianne lived there.

His heart leapt, but that was just the start of a complex flood of emotions that overwhelmed him. He breathed in deeply. He could smell her! That brought a fugitive tear, which he hastily rubbed away.

Stay focused. This is where you find the truth, he thought. *If you can bear it. If you can feel your heart ripped out, see things that will scar your mind for the rest of your life.*

He wished he could let it go, move on, but Marianne's death had destroyed him and not even a saint could turn the other cheek to that. Here was something he *could* believe in: revenge. Cold and hard.

The flat appeared empty. One of her acid jazz CDs played innocuously in the background. And then he could hear her moving around, humming to the music, at peace with herself and the life they had.

Don't cry, he told himself futilely.

He remembered where he had been at that moment: in the pub two streets away, drunk on booze, drunk on life, singing old Pogues songs with Dale and thinking what it would be like to be married.

Don't cry, he told himself futilely.

He wiped his face, forced himself to stay calm in the centre of a room a lifetime away, when he had been whole; listened intently. Soon. Soon.

Marianne singing now, in perfect harmony with the track. Leaving the kitchen where she had been washing up. Crossing to the bathroom. He strained to see, then averted his eyes at the last moment. Then regretted it a second later.

The bathroom cabinet opening. She was taking out something. Bath oil? No taps yet. There had been no water in the bath.

There it was: the bare, brief click of the door. Nausea clutched his stomach.

'Church? Is that you?' Her voice; he couldn't bear it.

Take me away. His eyes were flooded, blurring everything.

He took a step forward. A dark shape flitted across the hall towards the bathroom. The damp ebb of his emotion was replaced by a cold hatred that surprised him; but it was better, definitely. It allowed him to act.

He moved quickly. He was going to find out who the bastard was who had destroyed everything. It didn't matter that he was a puppet. He was a killer of dreams and he was going to pay the price.

Don't scream, he prayed.

Marianne screamed. And then he was running, and running, but the bathroom was a million miles away, and he knew if he reached it, what he wanted most in the world would destroy him. Every sight, every experience stays with you forever; that one would ruin him for all time.

I have to see, I have to see, he pleaded with himself. And still he ran, but he knew he couldn't bring himself to do it. And then the bathroom, the flat, everything that had ever mattered to him was receding, and he was falling, upwards this time, yelling and crying, like some drunken fool, brutalised by the pain of his emotions.

And then he was back in the dark once again.

He wandered for what seemed like hours. If that were the case, the cavern would have been enormous, but he had the unnerving feeling he was no longer walking through that place; his meanderings had taken him much, much further afield. He didn't dare think too hard about that; the chance that he might be lost and walking for all time hovered constantly at the back of his head.

Sometimes he thought he was about to break through into another solid place; shadowy figures moved in the distance, lighter than the surrounding dark, but he never seemed to draw near enough to reach them. Sounds continued to burst through the void, fading, then growing louder, as if they were being controlled by a mixing desk: psychedelic aural hallucinations. Briefly, he heard Ruth calling for his help, but it was lost the moment he thought he recognised her voice.

And still he walked, until he heard something enormous moving away in the dark, circling him. A chill insinuated itself into his veins. There was a sound like the rough breathing of a wild animal and when he turned suddenly, he glimpsed a giant wolf. He knew instinctively this was the thing that had taken Ruth and attacked him in the library. But he also knew, although he did not know how, that it was not really a wolf, nor any kind of supernatural creature; it was mortal, and more, it was someone he knew.

For the briefest instant a yellow eye glinted in the dark and he was filled with an immeasurable dread. He turned and ran in the opposite direction until he was sure he had left it far behind him.

'Jack!'

The voice came as a shock because he had seen no sign of any other figure after fleeing the wolf that was not a wolf. It was crystal clear, unlike the other hallucinations, and when he spun round there was Niamh, arms outstretched towards him, her normally placid face filled with concern; it made him fearful to see it.

'It is a maze,' she was saying. 'If you do not pick your way through, you will be lost.'

Unlike the other visions of the Tuatha Dé Danann, she was able to see him. In fact, he felt she had come looking for him, to lead him out of there, back to safety.

'Your own thoughts are trapping you,' she continued.

'How do I get out of here?' he called.

But before she could answer, her face grew scared and she was pulled apart, as if she were nothing more than smoke caught in the wind. Even she did not have power over that place.

After a long while he came to the conclusion that he was not making his way through a maze. It was a whirlpool. The blocked earth energy was causing eddies in the very fabric of reality, sucking him back and forth. How *was* he ever going to get out of it?

He finally realised the futility of walking and getting nowhere, so he simply sat on the cold, stone floor and tried to think his way out. No further scenarios presented themselves to him, nor did doors open, but during a meditation on the nature of the blue fire, a possible solution presented itself.

Gently he closed his eyes, which seemed a bit unecessary in the uncompromising dark, but it was the only way he could do it. Then, with as much willpower as he could muster, he tried to focus on the earth energy as he had done at the well-head. It was a long shot, but Tom had told him the energy was in everything. Perhaps there was some kind of pattern he could see that would show him the way out.

He thought it would be hard, but it took much longer in coming than it had before; the anxiety gnawing away at him seemed to be a barrier. Eventually he saw the first familiar blue streaks, just flashes against the blackness, like tracer bullets in a night-time air-raid. Slowly, though, his perception came into focus and he recognised that the earth energy was as prevalent there as it had been out on the land.

It seemed that his analogy of a whirlpool had been correct. The tracks of light were sucked into different eddies that formed complex patterns, reminding him of Mandelbrot set illustrations he had seen: chaos everywhere, yet, paradoxically, an overriding pattern to it; a blueprint for existence. The marvel of it was mesmerising; he could certainly see how the ancients had been in awe of its power and majesty. The lifeblood of everything.

Even so, in places the traces of light fragmented or seemed to dry up completely. There was none of the pulsating vitality he had seen when Tom had first introduced him to the blue fire at Stonehenge. Was this what had been happening all over the land, all over the globe: the gradual break-down of the fundamental essence of the world, driven to extinction by people with an increasing morbidity of spirit?

His dreamy musings came to an abrupt end. There was one area where the light was brighter and more forceful; it seemed to be driving in to the confluence of tiny whirlpools that made up the bigger maelstrom. He hurried towards it and was pleased to see that beyond that area there was a definite flow, although it was more of a trickle than a torrent.

He moved as quickly as he could, not knowing how long he could maintain his altered perception. Occasionally it flickered and threatened to fade and he had to fight to bring it back, but he was buoyed by his progress.

The visual and aural hallucinations appeared to have been left behind in the whirlpool area, so he was surprised when an insistent voice came echoing through the darkness to him. Its familiarity was more of a shock: it was his own. As he turned suddenly, the view of the earth energy fizzed out. And there he was, coming towards himself through the void. His ghost-image was subtly changed: longer hair, a goatee, the drawn, pale face of a man who had seen too many terrible things; it was the same Church he had seen watching a burning city in his vision in the Watchtower.

'Is this it? Is this the right time?' his future-self was saying to him passionately; Church couldn't decide if it was fear or anger or a mixture of both he was hearing in the voice. 'You have to listen to me! This is a warning!' He looked around, confused, as if trying to work out where he was. '*Is* this the right place? Am I too late?'

His words fell into relief and Church said quickly, 'Tell me what you have to say.'

The future-Church shook himself, regained his focus. 'When you're in Otherworld and they call, heed it right away! They're going to bring him back! They're—'

'Calm down! You're babbling!' Church yelled. '*Who* is going to bring *who* back?'

The other Church suddenly looked terrified, glanced over his shoulder. 'Too late!' he yelled.

And then he was gone.

The encounter disturbed Church immensely. The message was garbled, disorienting, but he felt he had missed a vital opportunity to discover something important, perhaps something that would be a life-or-death matter. He vowed to keep the message in his head so that if any fitting situation arose, he would be able to act instantly.

When they call, heed it right away.

At least he had managed to maintain his sense of direction. He continued walking along the path he had been following and soon he saw the gently glowing cavern walls approaching from either side. They met at a rough opening where the tunnel continued. And on a boulder near the entrance sat Tom, quietly sucking on a joint.

'How the hell did you get here?' Church asked in disbelief.

'I walked.'

'You know what I mean!'

Tom shrugged, giving nothing away. Then he couldn't seem to resist, and said with a faint smile, 'You were the one who had to go through it. It was a test.'

'It was a natural obstacle caused by the backed-up earth energy. Wasn't it?'

'It was. But you were drawn into it for a reason. I told you, it was a test.'

'Why was I being tested?'

'You know,' Tom snapped.

Church tried to make sense of it. 'The things I saw out there! It was—'

'I know. I've experienced that kind of thing before. We can carry on now. We've been allowed access.'

'You're talking like the blue fire's got some kind of intelligence,' Church laughed mockingly.

'It has. Of a kind. Everything thinks, everything feels, everything hurts.'

'More hippie bullshit!' Church snorted with derision, but the concept stayed with him. They set off along the new tunnel and after a moment or two, he said, 'So tell me, is it God?'

'Call it that if you want,' Tom said dismissively. 'If you want to reduce something so enormous and complex to such pathetically, childishly simplistic terms.'

Church chopped the air with his hand and cursed under his breath, picking up his step so he didn't have to walk in irritation at the older man's side.

And then, suddenly, they were at a blockage in the tunnel. Boulders of varying size were piled up to the tunnel roof.

'Is this what we have to clear to get things flowing again?' Church said.

'Don't be an idiot,' Tom replied. 'Did you think it would be that easy?'

Through the rock, Church perceived a sound like an engine running. In a moment of *frisson* he realised it was the sound of breathing.

'Change is the important thing,' Tom continued. 'You have to bring things out into the open, for good or bad.'

Church tried to read his face, but he knew how futile an exercise that was. 'I don't like the way you said that,' he noted.

The walk back from the strange, ritualistic room had been a blur to Ruth. The pain and shock of her experience had, for a brief while, almost wiped her mind clear. Only one thing had struck her through the haze: a sound from behind a heavily padlocked door, like a flock of birds crazily flying around the confined space.

She barely noticed they had taken her to a new cell, as depressing as her old one, but almost palatial in size; although it was pitch dark she could tell how large it was from the bouncing echoes of her footsteps. After the cramped confines of her last prison, it should have been cause enough for joy, but her every thought was taken up with the struggle to accept she was still alive. When the black pearl was being forced into her mouth, she had so convinced herself she was going to die her survival had left her disoriented, shocked and, in an odd way, depressed.

She could still feel the awful weight of the pearl deep in her stomach; it was radiating cold into every fibre of her being. She turned to one side and vomited on the flags, sickened by the pressure and the changes taking place in her body. The nausea never left her. What did it all mean? They'd be coming for her again soon and she really didn't know how much more she could bear.

She crawled away to the other side of the cell, trying to avoid the smell of vomit, but the stench was too strong. She retched again. Shaking, she lowered her head on to the cold floor and hoped sleep would come soon to save her from the nightmare.

Veitch's instincts had been sending sharp prompts throughout the morning, and by late afternoon he had already made up his mind to move by sundown. Scarcely had he accepted the decision than he heard a tumult echoing across the city from the Old Town. From his window he could see nothing but scattered groups of people looking up to the old, grey buildings that crested the great ridge which ran down from the castle, so he quickly made his way outside.

Dark storm clouds hung oddly over the Old Town, while the rest of the city was bathed in the reddish light of the setting sun. Further down the Royal Mile towards Holyrood those clouds seemed to be churning and there were flashes of light that were not lightning erupting among them; each flash was accompanied by a rumble like distant gunfire.

The crowds were uneasy and apprehensive. It was a manifestation of all their deepest fears that had grown since the Old Town had been so mysteriously sealed off. 'What's going on up there?' one man asked darkly, of no one in particular. Those nearest looked at him fearfully, looked back at the disturbance, said nothing.

Veitch watched it for a moment or two longer, until he decided it might well be the diversion for which he had been waiting. He didn't know if it was the doing of Shavi and Laura or Church and Tom, but he should move fast to seize the moment. He broke away from the crowd and hurried in the direction of the Old Town.

He realised how much had changed the moment he began to climb the steep steps of Advocate's Close. Within the space of a few feet the temperature had changed from summer balm to deepest winter; his breath clouded and the steps shimmered with hoar frost. When he reached the summit he was startled to see thick, fresh snow drifting across the Royal Mile, unspoilt by footprints or tyre tracks. The mist had quickly descended, casting a spectral pall over the entire area.

Shivering, he zipped his leather jacket to the neck and waded out into the street. The covering of snow was crisp; it was several degrees below zero.

Another flash and rumble startled him. The battle, or whatever it was, was still raging at the foot of the Royal Mile, obscured by the haar. His first instinct was to head straight to the castle, but he knew he had to be sure the Cailleach Bheur was being distracted. He made his way out into the middle of the road where the snow wasn't so deep and set off towards the disruption.

About halfway down the Royal Mile the mist had thinned out enough for him to see what was happening. The Cailleach Bheur stood with her back to him, both hands grasping her gnarled staff, which was planted firmly in front of her. Bubbles of blue energy were forming around her, increasing in size rapidly, then rushing out in waves. Whenever they burst, the deep rumble rolled out, making Veitch's ears hurt. That close to her, it was almost unbearably cold; Veitch convulsed with shivers.

The object of her attack was a gloriously beautiful young man floating several feet above the road, his long hair whipped by the force of the energy. He seemed to glow with an inner golden light, but there was some unpleasant quality in his face which disturbed Veitch immensely. The flashes of light appeared to be generated somewhere within him; they were diffuse, like a heat haze on a summer day. Veitch occasionally felt their warmth breaking through the cold. He guessed this was the power Shavi and Laura had been despatched to find and was pleased by their speedy success. The first strike went to the underdogs, he thought; perhaps things weren't so bad after all.

Although the two forces were obviously in battle, Veitch saw no anger, no emotion of any kind that he recognised. But he was relieved to see the new arrival was more than a match for the wintry ferocity of the Cailleach Bheur. With renewed vigour, he left them to their fight and hurried back up the steep road.

Edinburgh Castle stood at the very summit of the Royal Mile on a mound of volcanic rock created three hundred and forty million years before. The Fomorii had chosen their location well. Surrounded on three sides by sheer cliffs, its position was impregnable. And if the Fomorii had somehow burrowed into the very rock beneath the castle, Veitch knew they would be almost untouchable. His comfort came from the knowledge that he didn't have to defeat them – that would be up to the others – he must merely get Ruth out.

To that end he had spent his time well since the departure of the others, reading up on the fortress's history and studying its layout in intricate detail until he had his strategy well mapped out in his mind. Subterfuge was the only way forward. In the times when the garrison had fallen into English hands, the Scots had only been able to retake it through stealth, once by scaling the cliffs and taking the defending troops by surprise, once by disguising themselves as merchants and using their supplies to block open the castle gates so a larger force could sweep in. Deception went against his nature – a direct assault always made him feel much better – but he was learning rapidly.

The approach to the castle was across the wide-open forecourt where the Tattoo was held every year. In normal weather Veitch would not have been able to cross it unseen, but the drifting thick mist provided reasonable cover. He sneaked into an entryway near the Camera Obscura for a few minutes while the sun set completely. Then, with the night providing added protection, he crept around the perimeter wall.

It was an eerie scene. The castle was ablaze with light reflecting off the thick snow, a Christmas confection designed to lure tourists from across the city, but there wasn't a sound in the vicinity. The drifting mist that resembled smoke on a battlefield muffled any sound from the New Town and obscured any view of the modern city. Veitch felt like he had been transported back in time.

The castle gates were open – the Fomorii obviously feared no direct assault. Veitch ducked below the level of the low stone wall and crept beneath the dark arch of the gatehouse. Adrenalin was coursing around his body; he felt revitalised, ready for anything. In the Lower Ward he paused and glanced through a window back into the gatehouse. A guard in military uniform stared blankly across a bare table. Veitch couldn't reconcile the army presence with the Fomorii until he recognised the waxy sheen to the guard's face; on close inspection, it resembled a mask: it was a shape-shifted Fomor. This was obviously how the Fomorii had managed to take the castle in the first place, quietly, unnoticed, while the Old Town bustled around them. Somewhere, he guessed, there lay a charnel house filled with the bodies of all the soldiers who had been replaced.

He kept to the shadows as he climbed the stairs towards the Middle Ward, trying to muffle his footsteps as much as he could. If he allowed himself to recognise it, he would have had to admit he was terrified, but every sense was fixed on the here and now, smelling the wind for the familiar reek of the Fomorii, listening for even the slightest sound, constantly scanning for any movement in the shadows. He had no idea if the Fomorii had established any kind of secret defence which would alert them to his presence, but he put his faith in moving fast, so he didn't stay in one place too long.

As he rounded the corner into the Middle Ward he was brought up sharp by a patrol moving in step across the windswept expanse. Quickly, he pulled himself back against the wall, praying he had not been seen. With foreknowledge, it was obvious the patrol did not consist of human soldiers; there was a brooding presence to it which set his nerves on edge.

He held his breath, let the darkness settle on him; the cold bit sharply and he could no longer feel his feet where they were covered by the blanket of snow. As he scanned the battlements, towers and building, it was clear the Fomorii were everywhere. It would take all his skill and a large dose of luck to slip by them unseen; if he were spotted at this early stage he wouldn't stand a chance.

His task was to find where the Fomorii had established their entrance to whatever lay beneath the castle; his only chance of discovery was to follow some of the Bastards to the location. He guessed, though, that entrance could lie in the Castle Vaults, which were on the closest level to the base rock. But his progress wasn't going to be easy – the Fomorii patrol was marching back and forth across the Middle Ward, barring his advance. At least his detailed preparation had left him with a fairly comprehensive knowledge of the castle's labyrinthine byways. Slowly, he edged backwards through the shadows until he found the Lang Stairs, seventy mediaeval steps that led up into the mist. Cautiously he advanced up them; if a Fomor was coming in the opposite direction, the haar would prevent him knowing until they were on top of each other.

By the time he reached the top he was covered in a cold sweat. Somewhere ahead he could hear the crunch of footsteps in the snow. Quickly he dashed past the rows of cannon lining the battlements until he found another hiding place. At that point he was off the beaten track and the chance of another Fomorii patrol passing by was slim. He squatted down and caught his breath, wondering what Church would have done in the same situation. The tension was so high it would have been easy to turn back, but his evening of conversation with Reynolds had filled him with an uncommon, fiery hope; he really believed he could reach Ruth, get her out, even. And then, perhaps, she would recognise him for who he truly was.

It was too cold to remain in one spot for long. Crown Square, with its clustering, towering buildings, was his best chance for cover as he made his way towards the Castle Vaults. At the square's east entrance he paused to survey the scene. It was quiet and deserted, the snow deep and unbroken across the broad expanse. The mist drifted hazily along the rooftops. To his right, the Scottish National War Memorial loomed up, dark and foreboding; there would be no one in there at least, among the silent monuments to those who had died in defence of the realm. The other buildings around the square could well be occupied, but they were all dark too.

Warily, he stepped out; the snow crunched unnervingly loudly under his feet. The exit to the vaults was directly opposite him, just a stone's throw across the way. He had made it halfway across when he came up sharp. The lights from the Upper Ward that filtered into the square were suddenly throwing a large, distorted shadow on to one of the walls ahead of him. Veitch had only an instant to think before launching himself to his left and his only possible hiding place: the Great Halls, where the door hung open.

The shadow was across almost the entire square as he threw himself through the opening. He prayed he had been quick enough, but as he scurried into the gloom his foot clipped the door and it swung shut. It must have been seen by whoever was approaching, for it was followed by the insistent, nauseating barks and shrieks of the Fomorii dialect. Veitch propelled himself into the main hall and searched for a hiding place. If he could lie low, the Fomorii guard might simply think the door had been blown shut by the wind.

The darkness in the hall was magnified by the oppressive wooden panelling beneath the deep red walls and heavy beams which supported the vaulted roof. Stained-glass windows along one wall allowed dull beams of light to filter through. The hall was a museum to armoury: swords, pikes, spears, shields, breastplates and helmets were everywhere. Two heavy wooden chairs stood in front of an enormous stone fireplace at one end. Veitch dived behind them into the shadowy hearth and waited there.

A second after he'd settled, footsteps echoed across the room. He peered under the chairs to see a Fomor disguised as a Royal Scots Dragoon march into the centre of the hall and slowly survey it. Veitch held his breath, every muscle of his body tense. The moment was suspended for what felt like hours until the creature turned and began to walk back towards the door. Just as Veitch was about to breathe again, the guard stopped, threw one more glance around, then began to fumble for a radio at its belt. Veitch knew instantly from the body language what was intended: a warning of a potential intruder, or just a call to be more vigilant; either way, it was bad news.

The thought had barely registered when he was stealthily slipping out from behind the chairs. As the guard brought the radio up, Veitch pulled a stout short sword silently from a baize-covered display table and began to creep across the floor. He could catch it unawares, drive the sword into the base of its skull before it had a chance to raise the alarm. He'd seen how powerful the things were; he didn't want to risk a face-to-face confrontation.

He slid quickly across the room, raising the sword as he moved. He was almost ready to put his shoulder behind the plunge when the radio suddenly let out an ear-piercing shriek. In a split second it had changed form, like mercury being dropped on to the floor. A silver sheen flooded over it as it sprouted legs like a spider before scurrying up the guard's arm, where it proceeded to shriek.

Veitch only had the barest instant to realise the thing was a Caraprix – one of the symbiotic shape-shifting creatures which both the Tuatha Dé Danann and Fomorii carried with them – before the guard was whirling. In the same fluid motion his human face began to melt away like candle-wax, rolling, pluming, becoming something so hideous it made Veitch's gorge rise. He tried not to look as he continued with his sword stroke, driving it towards the creature's head. But the Fomor had shifted enough for the blade to glance off its shoulderbone or whatever the unpleasant ridge was that was materialising under the guard's shirt, splitting it open.

The creature swung something that had been an arm but now resembled a scorpion's tail, still changing, catching him hard on the side of the head. He flew sideways, hitting the floor hard as purple stars burst in his brain.

He rolled on to his back as the Fomor advanced like a reptile, indistinct and dark and sickening, smelling of raw meat. Veitch gave himself wholly over to instinct, that strange fighting prowess that had gradually emerged from deep within him. He propelled himself forward, tangling himself in the creature's legs. Its momentum carried it forward and over him. As it fell, he held up the sword, then rolled out of the way at the last moment. The Fomor's own weight drove the sword through its neck and into its skull. It lay on the floor twitching and shrieking, leaking a substance that smelled so bad Veitch had to fight back the nausea.

The Caraprix, too, was wailing. It leapt from the fallen guard and scuttled across the floor. Veitch reacted instantly. He jumped forward and stamped down hard with one heavy boot, splattering it in a burst of grey ichor; its wail of alarm was cut off mid-note.

Veitch allowed himself one moment of relief, scarcely able to believe he had killed one of the creatures, though he still didn't fancy his chances in a direct fight. Then he hurried over to the wall display, selected another short sword and a dagger which he tucked into his jacket, then a crossbow and some bolts, which he hung on a strap over his shoulder. And then he headed hastily to the door to see if anything had responded to the creature's dying cries.

The square was as quiet and deserted as when he had first seen it. The only tracks were the guard's and his own. Quickly he ran to the west exit from the square. He could hear the patrol still moving around the Middle Ward, but there was nothing between him and the Castle Vaults.

He kept close to the walls until he reached the entrance, still amazed he had made it so far. The vaults were dark and dank and smelled of wet stone and earth. The first section consisted of a long arched corridor; there were two rooms leading off it. After the wide open spaces, the place felt claustrophobic. Water was dripping from the ceiling in a constant rhythm and echoes bounced wildly off the stone.

His teeth went on edge when he heard the Fomorii dialect reverberating from the furthest room. Guardedly, he crept to the corner and peered round. Two more Royal Scots Dragoon guards stood talking next to an enormous cannon, which he knew from his reading was the mediaeval siege gun, Mons Meg. Beyond it was a ragged hole in the stone floor from which cold air currents drifted. He had been right. Here was the entrance to the Fomorii's subterranean lair. But how was he going to get past the guards?

He noticed the room had a door near the far wall, which he guessed connected with the other chamber that led off the corridor. He returned to the first room, where there was a tourist display detailing the vault's history as a prison, a bakehouse and barracks. Steeling himself, he used the haft of the sword to smash the glass, then hurried back to his original position outside the second room. As he had guessed, the guards took the back route to investigate the disturbance, allowing him a free run to the hole in the floor. Rough steps led down into the dark.

There was no time to deliberate. It had been a gamble to do anything which might alert the Fomorii to his presence, but it had been the only option; he would deal with the consequences later. Fighting back his anxiety, he put his foot on the top step.

Seconds later he was in dark, freezing tunnels only occasionally lit by a barely flickering torch. Branches broke off on either side from which drifted foul smells like the cooking of rotted meat; from the distance he could hear odd sounds of indiscernible origin which made him strangely fearful. It was a maze. The chances of finding Ruth were slim, of returning alive even slimmer.

CHAPTER NINE

the Well

Night had fallen by the time Shavi and Laura made it back to Edinburgh on the back of a lorry delivering builders' supplies to Leith. The Bone Inspector had long since abandoned them, loping across the fields in the direction of the city, one backward glance of contempt and horror showing them what he felt of their actions.

From more than five miles from the city centre it was obvious something terrible was happening in the Old Town. The sky was filled with flashes and rumbles and as they drew closer they could see the wintry clouds that obscured the area were churning as if violent winds were gusting in that one spot.

'What do you reckon?'. Laura said as they stood on the pavement where the driver had dropped them off.

Shavi could tell from her voice she feared the worst. 'We will see when we get closer.'

'We're going in there, then?' She didn't wait for an answer. 'Do you think the others will be all right?'

'I do not know.'

'That's him, isn't it? That freak?'

Shavi said nothing. He felt complicit in the awful things that were happening, were bound to happen. If he had listened to Laura's doubts, if he had not been so driven in his desire to accomplish their mission, the mad god might not now be loose. Perhaps Maponus had been subtly influencing him, drawing him in until his free will was compromised, but that was not enough of an excuse. His mind was strong; he could have resisted.

'Come on.' He walked away from Lothian Road into Bread Street. Shivering in their light summer clothes, they hadn't gone far through the shadowed, twisty-turny streets before they noticed a building which had crumbled into a pile of rubble, as if it had been hit by a bomb.

Shavi ran forward to inspect the wreckage, then noticed a curious sight. It took a second or two before it dawned on him what he was seeing. 'Look here,' he said as Laura joined him.

She followed his pointing finger over the debris and saw another crumpled building beyond it, and more beyond that. A swathe had been cut through the city to the outskirts. She turned a hundred and eighty degrees and realised the path continued in the opposite direction to the heart of the Old Town. They looked at each other, but couldn't think of any way to express the thoughts that were colliding in their heads. After a moment of silent contemplation they scrambled across the bricks, stone and tiles towards the Royal Mile.

In the next street they found the body of an old man who had obviously refused to abandon his home during the great evacuation. It wasn't simply crushed by the housefall; it had been lovingly rendered into its component parts. The head was missing, but there was a fine red dew across an arc of virginal snow. Shavi and Laura both blanched.

'We're going to burn for this,' she said.

They could see the battle raging through the gap in the buildings long before they clambered up on to the Royal Mile. It was furious in its intensity: a clattering of light and dark, summer and winter, two different aspects of hell; Shavi and Laura could barely look at it. Maponus' beautiful face was contorted by an expression of such overwhelming hatred it made their blood run cold. His eyes were ranging wild, his fingers flexing, unflexing, as the energy or whatever it was rolled off him. Sometimes his attention wavered and he would let off a venomous blast at one of the abandoned buildings nearby, as if his pent-up hatred was for everything in existence. But then the Cailleach Bheur would strike again in her coldly emotionless way and his skittering attention would return to her.

At that moment the crone seemed less human than ever; her features had dissolved into the sucking darkness of the void, her limbs were black and angular like the branches of a wind-blasted tree on a wintry heath. Her power was awesome to experience; even at a distance they could feel the cold like knives in their skin. The way the blue illumination shimmered drove Laura's mind back to the club, as the flashing lights had been refracted then obscured by the hag's relentless ice. For the first time she truly realised how close to death she had come. Before the power of these old gods, they were nothing. She wiped a stray tear away hurriedly before Shavi had a chance to see it.

They scurried for cover behind a tumbled-down wall, their breath clouding in the cold air. 'What's going to happen if he gets by her?' she asked.

'At the moment they seem fairly well matched—'

'But sooner or later—'

'We put our faith in the others. In Church and the blue fire.' It was the first time she had heard an edge to his voice.

'What about Veitch?' They both looked into the depths of the thick mist that shrouded the castle.

'We should head to the rendezvous point. Just in case.'

Laura snorted derisively. 'Is it me, or is this a head in the sand situation? You know, I hope one of us bastards has a Plan B. Otherwise I'd say, in our fine tradition, we've made things even worse.' Shavi was already departing. 'Don't walk away, you bastard! If that thing we set free gets away from here, we're going to be knee-deep in killing fields.'

He turned slowly; his eyes were brimming. 'I know,' he said quietly. And then he was moving away into the night once more and she had no option but to follow him.

Veitch could barely control his shivering as he progressed along the freezing, gloomy tunnels. The torches on the walls were too far apart to give him any comfort, but at least he didn't encounter any Fomorii guards. That unnerved him even more, because he knew it was only a matter of time – he would have expected the place to be swarming with them. Were they all hiding to lure him in there so they could sweep down to tear him apart? He drove that thought out quickly.

The entire place was a maze. All the tunnels looked the same, all were filled with the foul stench of spoiled meat cooking. Roughly constructed wooden doors were occasionally spaced on both sides. He had tried some of them tentatively, but they had all been locked. In the end he had been forced to hiss Ruth's name, expecting to be answered by a Fomorii roar, but there had been no response from any.

In a way he almost wished he *would* be confronted by something; that would be better than the unbearable tension of expecting an encounter around every corner, of constantly straining to hear footsteps approaching from behind.

When the side tunnel loomed out of the dark it came as a shock. Its surround was ornately carved with writhing things and disturbing twisted shapes; over the top there was a stone face so unbearably hideous Veitch had to look away. The cold air currents which swept from its depths suggested it opened on to a large space. As he took a few steps in, trailing one hand along the wall for support, he picked up a strange, deep bass rumble like heavy trucks rolling; it made his stomach curdle. A few paces later and he recognised voices, scores, perhaps hundreds of Fomorii, but instead of the chaotic jumble of their usual dialect, it was controlled, two conflicted notes repeated over and over again. They were singing.

In a strange way, that was worse than anything he could have anticipated. There was something about that sound that made him want to flee back to the lights of the New Town, but he forced himself to press on. By the time he emerged from the tunnel, he was shaking uncontrollably, his body once again covered in sweat. He was at the top of a flight of rudely carved stairs leading down into a large chamber. And the room was filled with Fomorii. He had been right: hundreds of them. The sum of their presence was so terrible the bile surged into his mouth and he had to shuffle back to retch where he would not be seen. When he looked down into the chamber again, his vision became liquid; he couldn't fix on their forms and for an instant he was convinced there was just one beast down there, enormous and black and filthy with all the evil of existence.

He averted his gaze as his eyes swam, then they fell on what appeared to be a raised dais at the far end, flanked by two flaming braziers. On the centre was Calatin; the corrupt half-breed had his arms raised in some act of worship. When he dropped them, the intolerable singing stopped on one drawn-out note which slowly faded into the dark. Then he began to speak animatedly in the barks and shrieks of the Fomorii dialect. Veitch couldn't bear any more, but just as he began to retreat he glimpsed something in the shadows beyond Calatin: an enormous Fomorii dressed in black battle armour and resembling some giant insect.

Back in the main tunnel, he fought to control his nausea and spinning head. He couldn't work out what he had witnessed – a rallying of the troops? A prayer session? – but it had left him thoroughly disquieted. There was no point wasting time considering it. He returned to his mission with a renewed vigour born of dread.

Lost in his thoughts, he almost walked straight into a Fomorii guard as he rounded a corner. At the last minute he threw himself back, praying he hadn't been seen. The guard had been at the end of a tunnel which was reached down a short flight of steps. Veitch had only glimpsed him, but he had been alerted by a buzzing in his head and the now-familiar sickening in his stomach; it could have been instinct, but it was more as if the Fomorii existed on some level beyond the corporeal, as if they were a foul gas he could smell or a discordant sound constantly reverberating. But it was more than both those things; the creatures offended some fundamental, instinctive part of him.

Peeking round the corner as much as he could dare, he watched the dense area of blackness and the suggestion of a shape at the heart of it. The creature was so big and threatening, its position in the tunnel was almost impregnable; a full-frontal attack would undoubtedly be suicide. He could sneak by, continue exploring the tunnels, but a guard suggested the first site of importance he had come across. He gnawed on a fingernail, desperately urging himself to make the right decision, at the same time aware that he had never made the right decision in his life.

Church and Tom scrabbled away at the rocks that blocked the tunnel until their fingers and knuckles bled, but eventually they had cleared a large enough path to crawl through. It was warmer on the other side and the air smelled of lemon and iron. The breathing sound that had first alerted Church was now so loud it made their ears ring.

Tentatively, he advanced down the tunnel. More rubble crunched underfoot and the walls were cracked and broken open; there were holes so big he could put his hand through them.

'We must be right in the heart of Arthur's Seat now,' he said, suddenly claustrophobic at the weight of rock lying above his head.

'You would think,' Tom replied.

'You have a remarkable knack of sounding superficially like you agree with me while at the same time suggesting I'm completely wrong and an idiot into the bargain.'

'It's a skill. I've had centuries to perfect it.'

Church suddenly noticed an unusual texture on the rock that lay at the end of one of the fissures in the wall. Squinting, he could just make out a strange diamond pattern. 'That's odd.' Cautiously he reached in and ran his fingers over the surface; it was rough and cool to the touch, but the pattern was certainly regular.

'Jesus!' he exclaimed, snatching his hand back.

Tom was instantly at his side. 'What is it?'

'It moved! No, the rock didn't move, but something just beneath the surface of it did. It was like . . . It was like . . .' He blanched.

'What?' Tom stressed.

Church leaned forward and peered into the fissure, shaking his head.

'Like what?' Tom repeated. There was an irritated edge to his voice.

'Like . . . Like muscles moving beneath skin.' He swallowed, moved to another fissure further along the wall. Bending down, he peered into it, then hesitantly held his hand over the opening, wondering if he dared. Slowly he reached in, all the time watching where his fingers were going.

'Oh my God!' This time he threw himself back, shaking his hand in the air in disgust. The movement had been greater, something seemed to roll up. In the dark of the fissure he could see something red glinting. He crept forward. 'Oh my God' – a whisper this time. The red glowed brighter, shifted slightly.

'What is it?' Tom hissed.

'An eye.' Church swallowed, repulsed. 'I touched an eye and it opened.'

Suddenly there was a tremendous rumbling deep in the rock and the tremors rippled out so powerfully it threw them off their feet. Showers of dust fell from the ceiling, choking them, blinding them, as the wall cracked and finally crumbled.

'Get down!' Church threw himself over Tom to protect him. But the ceiling held steady and only a few tiny rocks from the wall bounced across his back. When he eventually felt safe enough to look up, coughing and spluttering, he instantly realised what the unnerving sound had been.

On the other side of where the wall had been lay a long, sinuous figure, its muscles and tendons shifting under the scaled skin that reflected the faint light in bronze and verdigris with a touch of gold. The Fabulous Beast breathed in and out, regularly, peacefully, moving gently in its deep sleep, but its bulk was so big even the slightest tremble of its lithe body sent tremors through the rock. Church couldn't even get a sense of its true size, for much of it was hidden under the fallen rock; even that had not disturbed it.

He took a step forward, overcome by the sudden wonder of what he was seeing.

'You feel it?' Tom was watching him curiously.

'What?'

'An affinity. You may not be of the same blood, but you are of the same spirit.'

And he did feel it, tingling in his fingers, up his spine, singing in the chambers of his head; he felt like a tuning fork ringing in harmony with the sleeping beast. 'A Brother of Dragons,' he muttered.

'Your heritage.' Tom moved in next to him, clapped a grounding hand on his shoulder. 'You are learning, growing. It's been a slow process, but you're getting there.'

'Why hasn't it woken?'

'It hasn't woken for a long, long time. It is kin to the old one that lies beneath Avebury, younger, but only just. This place was once almost as potent a source of the blue fire as Avebury, but for some reason the energy dried up quicker here once the people turned away from the spirit.'

'And the Fabulous Beast went into hibernation?'

'Hibernation? I suppose that's one way of looking at it. It is detached from the world and everything in it.'

Church dropped to his haunches to examine the creature's flank. 'It's magnificent . . . beautiful—'

'And dangerous. Make no mistake, the Fabulous Beasts are not pets. They are wild and untamed, a force of nature.'

Church stood up, sighing. 'Where did they come from? They don't fit in with how we thought the world operated.'

'They fit in with the way the world should be, and once was.'

'What are we supposed to do now?' Church asked, looking down the steep slope of tunnel where it disappeared into the gloom. 'I don't know how the hell I'm supposed to get the earth energy moving again. And to be honest, even if we could find a way, I still don't see how it's supposed to help us.'

Tom set off walking, his voice floating back ethereally. 'Perhaps it won't help us. But healing the wounded land, perhaps, is a mission that exceeds opposition to the Fomorii. Your prime mission.'

'If Balor returns, there won't be a land left to heal,' Church said sourly, trying to keep up.

The tunnel pitched downwards steeply until there were points when Church had to grab hold of the walls to stop himself slipping out of control. The air grew colder and dustier and at times he felt the blast of strong air currents, although he couldn't begin to guess where they were coming from. As they descended they seemed to move into an oppressive doom-filled atmosphere; their sporadic conversation dried up accordingly, so the only sound was the soft tramp of their feet.

The air currents grew worryingly stronger until gusts surged up the tunnel, knocking them against the walls. It was almost as if they were coming to the edge of a cliff. Church had a sudden vision of the vast underground sea in *Journey to the Centre of the Earth*. And then the tunnel ended abruptly and the the source of the wind became clear.

They were standing on a small ledge which ran around a yawning hole so big they couldn't see the other side. It plunged away from their feet in a dizzying drop into darkness, but the rush of air and odd, disturbing echoes suggested it was very deep indeed. It may well have gone down for ever. Church closed his eyes and threw himself backwards into the tunnel mouth as a rush of vertigo made his head spin.

'Here we are,' Tom said. 'The well of fire.'

Church eventually found the strength to creep forward on his hands and knees to peer over the edge into the abyss. The wind rushed up, buffeting his face, tugging at his hair. His head reeled as he fought the sensation that he was being sucked over the lip.

'There are spirit wells like this all over the country, all across the world.' Tom's voice floated distantly behind him; Church felt like the darkness was swallowing him whole. 'Few as mighty as this, however,' Tom continued. 'And fewer still that are actually alight.'

Church sat back, pressing himself firmly against the rock wall. 'What am I doing here? It's a dirty, big hole in the ground. This is hopeless.'

'Hopeless?' Tom said. 'Haven't you learned anything yet?'

'You're great at tossing out cryptic advice. Why don't you say something useful for a change – tell me what I'm supposed to do.'

'Sort it out yourself,' Tom snapped. 'You're the one who's supposed to be learning.'

Church cursed under his breath and returned his attention to the abyss. He peered into it for inspiration, but nothing came. Slowly his mood dipped. Was he going to fail again? Then thoughts surfaced like bubbles on that black, oily pool. This was a source of the blue fire. It wasn't truly a hole in the earth; they weren't really under Arthur's Seat. It was a place between worlds, beyond reality, like Otherworld. Perhaps it was Otherworld, but somehow he doubted it; it was more likely the well was a channel through to wherever the blue fire originated. He looked up at Tom who was standing with his hands behind his back, as if on a stroll through the park. 'Where does that go?' he said, pointing into the well.

Tom smiled like a teacher whose favoured pupil had just made a great leap of logic. 'Where do you think it goes?'

Church cursed again and waved him away; answering questions with questions was Tom's favourite type of conversation and over the months it had not diminished in irritation factor.

Church pondered some more; gradually his thoughts seemed to come together. What was the nature of the blue fire? That was obvious, if everything Tom had said was true: it was the essence of the spirit. And the blue fire had dried up here and stagnated across the land, once the people had turned away from believing.

'Can we ignite it again . . . can we draw back the blue fire . . . by doing . . .' The words failed him and he held up his hands in irritation. Then: 'An act that touches the spirit, that resonates in that plane.'

Tom nodded thoughtfully. 'Perhaps. In this new world a leap of faith can have as far-reaching an effect as a leap of logic. Will it work? Perhaps, if you want it enough.'

The strain of the responsibility began to seep into Church's shoulders. He wanted out of it, back to the life he once knew, but there was no hope of that, ever again. He closed his eyes, feeling his emotions and thoughts wash over him, then he dipped into his pocket and pulled out the locket given to him by the young Marianne.

'This saved my life.' He held it up so it spun gently. 'A cheap piece of jewellery with a cut-out magazine photo of Princess Diana stuffed inside. Meaningless, really. And then suddenly infused with meaning and power. Why? Because a little girl put her heart and soul and dreams into it? It's like some stupid fairy story.'

'We now live in a time of myth,' Tom began quietly, 'where archetypes live and speak with a power that can bend reality, where thoughts take shape. If something is wished to have meaning, then it will have power. Things were like that before the change, but the power was muted. Myth has always shaped us, you know that. You can see it in Diana's life – the years of suffering, the sacrificial death, the mourning that became almost worship. The resonances and coincidences shout out loudly, so much so that you would not believe them. Diana, the name of the moon goddess, the goddess of hunting and woodlands and fertility, worshipped by women. Which Diana are we talking about?' He shrugged. 'There have always been powers moving behind the scenes, ordering our lives. We call them by different names, trying to make sense of them, but we never will. The only way to proceed with any equanimity is to accept that we exist at the heart of magic and mystery and nothing will be revealed, certainly not before death, and perhaps not even after. Enjoy the moment, go with the flow—'

'And all the other hippie values.' Church shook his head. 'I should make this locket my offering in the hope that somehow its power, its spirit, can set things in motion. But that girl, she changed my life in just one meeting. She was a kid, but she was everything I wasn't. Brave in the face of death, positive, filled with some kind of faith. It was magical to see.'

'And the name connection reminds you of your girlfriend,' Tom said pointedly.

Church nodded slowly. 'Yes, they're both tied up in my mind. I can't see where one ends and the other begins. With Marianne's spirit still trapped, I don't know if I can give this up. It feels like my only connection with her. Maybe I'm supposed to have it to free her.'

He looked at Tom for some kind of support and guidance, but the face he saw was impassive and unreadable.

'I know what you're thinking,' Church continued. 'That I screwed everything up before Beltane because I was so wrapped up in my own problems and Marianne. I promised myself I'd shake all that, but some things run too deep.' He looked back at the locket, spinning gently, catching the light like a tiny star. 'I wish I was better at this.'

A noise echoed along the tunnel behind them, just a tiny sound, but in the acoustics of the well chamber it sounded like thunder; they both snapped alert immediately. Breath held tightly, eyes staring unblinkingly up the tunnel, they waited. For a moment there was nothing. And then another sound, a crunch of a foot on the grimy tunnel floor, but so faint it suggested whoever was there was walking cautiously, so as not to be discovered. That alone sent uneasy signals running through them.

'Someone's coming,' Church whispered redundantly. 'Who else could be in here?'

'No one,' Tom replied. 'Unless we were followed.'

Church looked around hastily; the tunnel was the only way out. 'This isn't the best place to get caught. I wish Veitch was here.'

Tom surveyed the thin ledge. 'We could edge around to the shadows on the other side.' His voice was barely audible.

Church glanced into the deep dark of the well and felt his head spin again. 'Or we could greet them here with open arms. It might be nothing . . . it might be somebody . . .' His voice faded; he was being stupid. The chances were, in that place, at that time, whatever was coming was a threat. He looked at the ledge and winced. 'I don't know if I can do it.'

'And the alternative is?' Tom said, irritatedly. He grabbed Church's arm to try to drag him, but Church shook him off so violently they both almost fell into the well.

'Jesus!' Church hissed. 'Leave me alone! You're going to kill us both!'

'*You* are if you make us stay here.' Tom forced himself to stay calm. 'Face the wall. Feel with your feet and don't look down.'

'That's easy for you to say!' But Tom was already inching his way along the ledge. Church froze. The path seemed unbearably thin; the tip of Tom's heels hung over the drop. Sweat grew chill down his back and on his forehead.

Then he glanced up the tunnel and saw something which cut through his fear with a greater terror. A glint of yellow, gone, then yellow again, something small and insignificant, but he knew instinctively what it was. The thing he had glimpsed earlier in the cavern that had the shape of a great wolf, but was not a wolf; the terrible cutter of fingers that had taken Ruth. He had thought it another hallucination, or a glimpse across time and space caused by the bizarre rules of the whirlpool cavern, but it had really been there. And now it was coming for them.

And still he hesitated. The magnetic pull of the well's vertiginous depths was almost unbearable. The more visceral danger of what was approaching down the tunnel stabbed him with sharp knives. But if he could find his rational mind somewhere among his primal fears, he knew what the only route could be.

Feeling he was saying goodbye to his life, he put his first foot on the ledge.

Slowly he edged round the lip of the immense hole, feeling his heart beat so loudly in his ears he thought he was going to go deaf. His view alternated between the backs of his eyelids and the cold, dark rock of the cavern wall which repeatedly brushed the tip of his nose. Every sensation was heightened, almost too painful to bear. He felt sick. Every few seconds his mind told him he was going to die; he couldn't shake the feeling he was going to flip over backwards.

More than anything he wanted to glance back to the tunnel mouth; he could hear the rough breathing of the thing approaching, the scraping of its feet on the rock; it was making no attempt to hide itself now. But he couldn't bring himself to look, so all he was left with was the approaching noise and the feeling that he wasn't moving fast enough, that it would follow him on to the ledge, and then he truly would be trapped.

Suddenly his left shoulder hit a body. It was Tom, who had stopped, but the shock of it when he was lost in his thoughts broke his concentration and he made a startled sound. And then he was moving slowly away from the rock wall, and although he held his muscles rigid, it was not enough to drive him back. He strained to grip the wall, but it was moving away. He was going over.

Tom's arm came from nowhere and slammed between his shoulder blades, propelling him back upright. The strangled gasp that rushed from his throat was a mixture of relief and terror.

'Hush.' Tom's voice was so low it was almost a faint exhalation, which Church had to strain to hear.

'Why did you stop?' he responded in kind.

'If you could tear your eyes away from the rock you'd realise we can't see the tunnel any more. Which means it can't see us. Did you see what it was?'

Church swallowed, composed himself, repeated the mantra in his head: *Don't look down!* But there they were, hanging over an abyss, trying to have a normal conversation; it was madness. 'I got a glimpse . . . the eyes . . .' His mouth was too dry; he swallowed again. 'It's whatever took Ruth, what Laura thought was a giant wolf. And I saw it that way too, in the big cavern. But it's not. I know . . . somehow, I know . . . that it's human.'

'Sometimes, when the old gods have *tampered* with someone, it's hard to get a handle on them,' Tom mused. 'It screws up the mind's perceptions. It's like they've changed in some fundamental way and the mind is struggling to make sense of all the confusing signals so it imposes an image on it. The closest one that seems to fit. But it's a lie, a desperate lie, to preserve sanity.'

'Then what does it really look like?' Tom's use of the word *tampered* made Church shiver. He remembered the age-old man's account of his suffering at the hands of the Tuatha Dé Danann Queen, when he had been taken apart and put back together again, for little more than sport. *Fragile Creatures* the Danann called them. Frail. Easily broken. Never put back quite right again.

The conversation died in the face of the threat. And so they listened to sounds that really did seem to issue from an animal, but then, eerily, intermingled with a guttural, warped human voice. It was muttering to itself. For a second they thought it might retreat up the tunnel, but after a moment's lull the breathing began to draw closer and they heard the scrape of a foot on the ledge, the click of nails on the cavern wall.

And then Church did tear his eyes away from the wall to stare wide-eyed into Tom's face. Tom moved off with the fast, supple movements of a man who had already experienced things worse than death. Church tried to keep up, but every muscle ached from forcing to keep himself close to the wall, and with movement his head had started spinning again. His throat seemed pencil-thin; he couldn't suck in enough air. And behind them the pursuer was drawing closer. He wondered if they could travel all around the well and head back up the tunnel to lose their pursuer in the cavern.

His foot slipped off the ledge and he had to grip on to the wall so tightly he was sure the delicate skin under the tips of his nails was bleeding. He was moving too fast, making stupid mistakes. But whatever was behind was relentless. He moved on.

And the well sucked at him again, sucked and inhaled and wished him off the ledge. And only a gossamer-thin wish was holding him on.

How much further? he wondered. It was impossible to tell how far around the arc they had travelled.

And then he heard the sound behind him, just a heavy breath, but in it a dark, malevolent triumph. He glanced to his right and saw, suspended in the black, the cold, yellow eyes, staring at him.

Their awful pull was destabilising. He tried to move away faster, but his foot slipped again and this time he went down on one knee. Off-balance, he was scrambling at the wall, shifting his weight wildly, trying to throw himself forward, shifting to the side, having to over-compensate, and then his knee was slipping off the ledge too, and the weight of the well was dragging him down.

For an instant time seemed to hang, pictures dropped from a hand, caught in midair. He looked up, saw Tom's face ahead of him frozen in horror. Realised some noise was coming from his mouth that made no sense. Felt his weight go completely over the edge. Looked down, saw nothing but dark, dark, dark, pulling him in. Falling.

At the last moment he reached out and slammed both hands on the ledge; his body swung hard against the wall, winding him. Tendons strained. His shoulders felt like they were going to explode. His fingers blazed with fire, seemed to be snapping. And his heels kicked wildly over nothing at all.

'Tom,' he croaked.

Tom looked at him, then slowly up at their pursuer. The ragged breath was so close now, Church swore it was almost above him.

'Tom,' he said again. Then: 'Go on. You can't help me.'

There was a look in Tom's eye as if all the repressed emotion in his body had come rushing to the surface, of more than tears, more than despair. But he remained, caught.

Church closed his eyes, knew he didn't have long. If the drop didn't get him, the Big Bad Wolf would. This was it. The end. He thought of Marianne and Marianne and Laura and Ruth and Niamh and all his new friends and his old ones and his family, and then he removed one hand from the ledge and somehow, through force of will, managed to keep hanging. *For just an instant longer*, his mind sparked.

The free hand swept into his pocket and pulled out the locket.

'I wish, I wish . . .' he whispered, but there were too many tears in his eyes.

And then he let it go, and it went spiralling down, the last star disappearing into the inky void.

A second later he joined it. His stomach shot up to his neck, his brain felt like it was twisting in his skull, and the air was rushing around him and somewhere Tom was yelling and . . .

Ruth had tried not to weep throughout all her ordeal and she had survived until that moment when she remembered the meal she had had with Church at Wodka in London before the whole mess had truly started. For some reason that triggered the tears and she hadn't been able to stop for a good quarter of an hour.

At least she had been provided with a rough bed of sacking and straw. Things seemed to be moving within it, but after the cold floor it seemed like paradise. That small piece of special treatment from creatures without even the slightest shred of humanity disturbed her more than anything; it was as if they were giving her a brief respite to build up her strength before something even more terrible. That brought another flood of tears. The black pearl had almost destroyed her. What could be worse than that? How much more could she take? Sometimes, although she dreaded to consider it, suicide almost seemed an option.

As if in answer to her thoughts, she heard a noise beyond the distant cell door, lost in the overpowering gloom. It was a Fomorii voice, insane and bestial. There were notes in it she had never heard before, so terrifying she clutched at her ears to drive it out, but the tumult continued until it ended in sudden silence. They were coming for her again.

'No more,' she pleaded in a broken voice. 'There's nothing left in me. I can't take anything else.'

She blinked away the tears, felt her head spin with the nauseating noises, waited, waited. There was a sound of metal on stone, some terrible torture instrument being dragged in. Blades, growing slicker, cogs turning, sparking pain that would consume her. The sounds grew closer, right outside the door now.

'Please,' she whimpered.

The lock turning. Click; a note of finality. Then slowly, slowly, swinging open. The light flooding in from outside, burning her eyes. And then the unbearable wait. She battened down her emotions, tried to think and feel nothing.

A figure was silhouetted in the flickering torchlight at the top of the flight of stone steps that led from her cell. It didn't make sense. Her head spun, her heart leapt with the rush of a hope she hardly dared accept.

The figure shifted, the torchlight sweeping over its torso, illuminating its face; a disbelieving grin of triumph. Words coming to her across the void between them.

'And the crowd went wild.'

Tears, no longer despairing, burned her cheeks. It was Veitch.

'Jesus Christ!' The jubilation on Veitch's face turned to horror when his eyes finally adjusted to the gloom enough to see Ruth huddled on the other side of the cell. It took a second for him to take in her filthy, matted hair, the dirt smeared across her skin, the unclean rag tied around her hand across the stump of her finger, but it was her face that affected him the most; it carried the weight of punishment and suffering to a degree that was painful to see. Yet despite that, at its core there was the defiance and strength he had recognised the first time he met her; diminished certainly, restrained, but still there. She had not been broken.

'Thank you.' Her voice sounded delirious.

Veitch threw himself down the stairs and sprinted across the cell, scrubbing at the spots of foul black ichor on his bare skin that burned like nettle sting.

'What's that?' Ruth said weakly, watching his actions; she seemed so detached she was barely conscious.

'Shit that came out of one of the Bastards. Blood, I suppose. Burns like fuck.' He knelt down and gripped her shoulders. 'Look, I know it's been a nightmare for you, but you've got to pull yourself together till we get out of here. I got in, but I don't know if I can get out again, and we're going to have every Bastard in here on our heels soon.'

'You came for me?' She couldn't seem to make sense of what he was saying.

'Couldn't leave you down here, could we?' The way she held her face up to him, slightly puzzled, slightly relieved, filled him with emotions he had never experienced in such an acute form before; there was a sharpness to them that almost made him wince, but a warmth too, and he knew at that moment that this was what he had been searching for all his life. He couldn't bear it if those feelings slipped away from him. 'Come on, girl,' he said softly. 'You and me against the world.'

At first he was afraid she wouldn't be able to walk and he'd have to carry her, but after he helped her to her feet she quickly grew steadier and soon she was moving across the cell without any aid. Outside the door she wrinkled her nose at the gruesome mess that smeared the corridor. Black and green slime was everywhere, along with chunks of matter and what looked like the horned, twisted remains of a Fomor; it appeared to have been hacked to pieces. Three crossbow bolts protruded from one part of it she couldn't recognise. Veitch retrieved them quickly and held them in the flame of one of the wall torches to burn the ichor off them.

'You did that?' she said.

Veitch couldn't tell if it was astonishment or horror he heard in her voice. 'You can't go in halfhearted. They'll tear you apart.' He paused, then added almost apologetically, 'I had to disable it with the bolts before I could move in. Probably wouldn't have stood a chance otherwise. You know, wouldn't fancy one of them in a fair fight . . .' He realised he was starting to ramble and caught himself. 'Come on.'

He attempted to lead them back the way he had come, but the tunnel system was a maze and every turn looked alike. He had the horrible feeling they were going deeper into the heart of the complex. 'There was some big hall where they were all praying or something. If I could find that I'd know we were on the right track.'

'So we're lost?'

'Blimey, it's not Oxford Street down here!'

'It's okay. I wasn't criticising.' Her voice sounded weary; a wave of pain crossed her face.

He instantly felt guilty at bristling. 'I just need to get my bearings.'

They headed down the tunnel a little further and stopped outside a heavily sealed door. From behind it, they heard the unmistakable sound of birds; it was as if a whole flock had been imprisoned within.

'I've heard that before,' Ruth said.

'Want to check it out?'

'Best not.'

They both felt oddly uneasy in proximity to the door, even more than the heightened sense of tension they had experienced in their journey from the cell. But before they could decipher the clues presented to them, the very walls of the tunnel reverberated with the crazed sound of a tolling bell. It wasn't how Ruth had heard it before; it was relentless, jarring, and she wanted to clutch at her ears to drive the sound out.

'Shit, we've been rumbled.' Veitch recalled the first time he had heard the noise in the abandoned mines under Dartmoor, just before the Fomorii swarmed in pursuit. 'Come on!' he said insistently, grabbing her wrist. 'We haven't got any time now!'

They hurried onwards, Ruth desperately attempting to keep up, but they hadn't gone far when they heard a rising tide of Fomorii grunts and shrieks approaching them. Veitch cursed under his breath and pivoted, heading back the way they had come. He took the first side tunnel he came to, sighing with relief when the faint slope appeared to go upwards. Yet as they rounded a bend to the right they came up against a stream of fast-approaching Fomorii at the end of a long stretch of tunnel. The sudden roar that erupted from the mass as it surged like oil along the corridor was terrifying.

Veitch spun round again, putting his arm across Ruth's shoulders to propel her forward. 'It's like a fucking ant hill.' He took another branching tunnel and tried to batten down the cold weight of fear rising in his chest so Ruth wouldn't see it, but he knew they were rapidly running out of options.

This tunnel was sloping up too, but the clamour behind them was increasing in intensity, drawing closer. Even if they made it out of the tunnel, they had to get through the castle before they were safe.

Suddenly Ruth grabbed his arm and hauled him to a halt. 'We can't stop!' he snapped.

She was pointing to a trapdoor in the wall they had just passed. It was about four feet off the floor, the size of a domestic oven. Seemingly oblivious to the approaching noise, she pulled herself away from him and wrenched the door open. A cold blast of air surged out of a dark tunnel. 'We could hide in there,' she said exhaustedly. 'We're not getting anywhere running around.'

He could tell from her face she was aware of all the thoughts he had been trying to hide from her, but she seemed more determined than scared. He nodded. 'Let me go first, though. Just in case . . .'

He collapsed the arms of the crossbow and boosted himself. Ruth followed immediately behind his boot heels. She pulled the trapdoor shut behind them, plunging them into an all-encompassing darkness. It was freezing cold in the tunnel, and intensely claustrophobic. Veitch had to wriggle to get his shoulders forward; he was uncomfortably aware of the weight of rock pressing down upon his back.

Shivering, they lay as still as they could, until they heard the awful sound of the pursuing Fomorii rushing up the tunnel. Their blood ran cold; it was like the screech of demons surging out of hell, hungry for souls. As the creatures approached the trapdoor, Veitch screwed his eyes tight, listening to the noise, wishing he couldn't hear it, waiting for the flood of light as the trapdoor was pulled open. And then they would be torn from their hiding place, ripped apart in a blood-frenzy of tearing claws and rending jaws. Any second now. He winced, waited.

But the sound carried on, up to the door, past it, and along the tunnel until it dwindled into the distance. 'They'll realise they missed us in a minute or two and they'll be back. We have to get out of here,' he hissed.

'We can't go out there.' Ruth's disembodied voice floated on the air. 'They'll be looking everywhere. We don't stand a chance. You'll have to crawl on to see where this tunnel goes.'

Veitch's heart suddenly went up into his mouth. He inched forward slightly as a test and his shoulders rubbed painfully on the walls. 'We'll get stuck,' he protested.

'The alternative's going out there and getting eaten alive.'

'I prefer that to getting trapped in here and dying slowly.' He had a sudden vision of how it would feel, the rock pressing in at him from every side, unable to move backwards or forwards, the rising panic, the sudden clutching insanity at the certain knowledge of one of the worst deaths imaginable. 'Anyway,' he choked, 'it's so small it won't go anywhere.'

'Of course it goes somewhere.' Ruth's voice had a school teacher snap. 'There's a trapdoor on it, for God's sake! They wouldn't put a door on a tunnel that went nowhere.'

He couldn't argue with her logic, however much he wanted to, and it was a certainty that there was no refuge for them back in the tunnels. 'You better be bleedin' right,' he said.

'Just get on with it and stop whingeing.'

'Oi, can't you control that tongue even at death's door?'

'Shut up.' She gave his calf a gentle punch; despite her words there was something reassuring and supportive in her manner. Veitch recognised a growing bond, or thought he did, and that was enough to drive him on.

With an effort, he dragged himself forward, shifting the muscles in his back and shoulders until they ached. There wasn't even the faintest glow of ambient light ahead of them, which made him wonder how far the tunnel actually went. And the more they progressed, the more he became aware of the tiny space embedded in the rock, the size of a coffin, barely enough air to breathe. His chest began to burn; he was working himself up to a panic attack.

'How ya doin'?' he called out to deflect his mind. But all that came back was a gasp of assent that suggested Ruth was having as hard a time as he was.

Don't panic, he told himself. *There's no way you can back out of this place in a hurry. You'll go fucking mad if you lose it.*

And just when he thought he couldn't bear it any more, it got worse. It was the width of the tunnel that had been causing him the most problems, but at least he had been able to crawl on his hands and knees. Now the ceiling was getting lower. He tried to tell himself it was just a by-product of the panic he was holding in stasis, but soon it was impossible to crawl, and it seemed to be getting tighter and tighter.

He sucked in a deep breath, then another, then another, trying to calm himself enough to speak; he couldn't let Ruth see how weak he was. 'Bit of a problem here.'

'What?' The word was barely a gasp.

'The roof's coming down. I think it just comes together, a dead end. We're going to have to back up.'

'That doesn't make any sense!'

He heard tears in her voice; she was running on empty and a failure at this point would destroy her. He couldn't bear to hear that sound again. 'Look, I'll give it a bit longer, right? It's not closed up all together.' The words felt like pebbles in his throat.

Slowly, on shaking arms, he lowered himself down until he was slithering like a snake. There was a brief moment of relief at the few spare inches above his head, until the ceiling came down so sharply there was only a gap of about seven inches. If he turned his head on its side he could just about keep going. His panic was on the verge of raging out of control; a band of steel was crushing his chest so tightly he was sure he was having a heart attack. He knew if he allowed himself to speak it would turn into a scream, and then he would be scrabbling at the rock until his fingers bled, and kicking and yelling, and then the last bit of thin air that seemed to be in the tunnel would finally go and he would be left choking and dying.

He felt Ruth's hand on the back of his leg, so supportive he almost cried. 'You can do it.' It was as if she could read his thoughts. There was such belief in her words it snapped him out of the panic. Focusing his mind, he pressed his cheek firmly against the floor and pushed with his toes. He moved forward an inch or two. He tried again, but this time the going was more painful. And then, suddenly, he was wedged. He tried to wrench his head back, but the rough rock of the ceiling only dug into his flesh like the barbs of a harpoon. He couldn't go back.

In the flash of terror he was immobilised.

'Stay calm,' Ruth whispered behind him. 'You can do it.'

Couldn't she see? He started to writhe as he fought for some way to free himself, but any movement backwards only made the situation worse. There was no air at all; however much he sucked in, it felt like only a thin rasp reached his lungs. The rock pressed down on him, crushing harder and harder. Sparks of light started to flash in front of his eyes. He was blacking out; dying.

He didn't know if it was a spasm or some last rational thought crashing through the chaos, but suddenly he gave one final push forward with his toes. It drove him an inch or so. Through the haze he discovered he could move his head a little. He pushed again, and after a tough moment when he thought his shoulders were going to jam, he slipped forward even further. He could barely believe it; the ceiling had started to rise again.

'It's all right!' he yelled with barely concealed relief. 'It's getting higher again!'

Scrambling forward, he was soon back on his hands and knees, and although he couldn't turn to help Ruth through, he gave her enough verbal encouragement to bring her past the scariest part.

The blast of cold air was stronger there, and a faint light glowed. 'Why's it so cold?' Ruth asked.

'Trust me on this – it's winter up top, summer everywhere else. The whole world's gone crazy. Situation normal.'

Veitch moved forward as fast as he could until the tunnel came to a sudden end. He smelled the clear, cold night air, heard distant sounds. 'We're through,' he said.

'Where are we?' Ruth whispered.

Cautiously, he leaned out of the tunnel. It opened into some tubular, stone structure. There was a drop beneath them into what appeared to be water; he could see the black surface reflecting light from above. Twisting, he looked up into a circle that framed the drifting, white haar, lit by the castle's lights.

'It's a well,' he said, retreating back into the tunnel. 'Least, I think it is. Right, there are two wells at the castle. One's too small, more like a cistern really. So this must be the other.' After the strain of the tunnel crawl, it took a second or two for the details to surface. 'The Fore Well. The main water supply a few hundred years ago, but it's out of use now so there shouldn't be too much water in the bottom. Just in case we slip, like. Now if only we can climb out of the bastard—'

'How do you know all this?'

'Did my research, didn't I? I wasn't going to come waltzing into this place without knowing what I'm doing.'

'I'm impressed.'

He shrugged, but inside he was enjoying her praise. 'It opens out on the Upper Ward. When I was up there a while back there weren't any guards in that area, so we could be on to a winner. If we can get past the cover.'

'Cover?'

'There's a grille fastened on top to stop all the tourists falling in—'

'Oh, shit,' she said, dismal again.

'Hang on, don't start getting negative already. We've come this bleedin' far. Just give me a chance, all right?'

Without waiting for an answer, he dropped in to the water. The icy shock almost made him call out. He was saved only by the fact that he had misjudged the depth. He plunged down beneath the surface and had to kick back up, spluttering and shaking from the cold.

'Are you okay?' Ruth asked worriedly. Her pale face was framed in the dark of the tunnel opening.

'Yeah, but it's like fucking ice.' He blew the water out of his nose, treading hard to prevent the weight of the sword and the crossbow pulling him down.

'You need to get out quick before you get hypothermia.'

'Thanks for the advice.' He dug his numb fingers into the grooves between the stones, braced his back against one side of the well and set his feet against the other. Then, with a tremendous effort, he began to edge himself up. Twice he fell back into the freezing water with a loud splash and a foul curse, but no one came to investigate. The newly discovered steel inside him pulled him through and finally he had made his way to the top. Gripping the grille with his left hand to give him some support, he slid the sword under the area next to the fastening and heaved. It was hard to get leverage from his precarious position and he was afraid that either the sword would snap or the lock would hold fast, but after a moment or two he heard the sound of protesting metal. A second later he was heaving the grille off the well-head and climbing out into the freezing night.

He didn't bother to rest from his exertions. Checking there were no guards in the vicinity, he rushed over to the Great Hall where he remembered seeing some netting in the armoury display. The corpse of the Fomor guard had still not been discovered.

Back at the Fore Well, he lowered the netting so Ruth could tie it round her. Then, bracing himself, he hauled her to the surface. Weakly, she rested against the battlements, looking round anxiously.

'Are you sure it's safe?'

'Not for long.'

She brushed a frail hand across her eyes. Veitch winced when he saw the space where her finger should be. 'Thank God,' she said. 'I thought I was going to die in there. I thought I was going mad. How I didn't panic, I don't know.' She gulped in a mouthful of air. 'I'm babbling now.'

He slipped an arm round her shoulder; she didn't flinch. 'It's okay,' he said.

Her eyes sparkled when she looked up at him; was that a connection he saw? He felt warmth rise up into his cheeks. 'You were great,' she said. 'You were like a rock. I wouldn't have got through it without you.'

The irony made him wince, but he couldn't break the illusion. For the first time she thought he was somebody who was worth something, who was capable, decent. But the conflict made him feel like a cheat. Even when he was getting what he wanted, his guilt and self-loathing got in the way. 'We've still got a way to go yet. That was the easy bit,' he said flippantly.

Before she could answer, her attention was distracted by something in the sky towards the bottom of the Royal Mile. The haar had started to drift away from that area and the black, star-sprinkled sky was clear.

'What is it?' Veitch asked.

'I don't know. I thought I saw something.' She scanned the sky uneasily. 'There it is again!' she said, pointing. The heavens were fleetingly lit by a strange, blue glow. In it, dark shapes seemed to be moving. 'What do you think?'

'I don't know.' Veitch had a sudden *frisson* which he couldn't explain. 'But I reckon we need to get to the rendezvous site pronto.'

The air was rushing so fast it ripped the breath from Church's mouth; his stomach flipped and twisted. The initial shock and terror was wiped away in a second by the helter-skelter sensations and the adrenalin that surged through him; the whole world seemed to be moving so fast he didn't have a chance to think. Beneath him, above him, all around him was darkness so intense he could have been plunging through space. Some hidden, rational part of him was scanning the shadows for any sign that could prepare him for the terrible moment of impact and it was that which caught the faint glimmer of blue light far, far away in the acheronian tunnel. It resembled a slight rip in black silk and it was growing wider, as if the fabric were rending.

The sight mesmerised him, driving out all other sensations, and his mind suddenly began to churn out notions to fill the vaccuum. *It's the blue fire,* he thought. *Is that the bottom?*

But it didn't look like the bottom; the well appeared to carry on past the growing speck of light. It grew wider still, the rate of tear increasing rapidly. *The locket did it!* he realised.

And at that moment the blue fire suddenly burst through. It was like a geyser rushing up towards him. He had only a split second to marvel at the wonder of it and then he was hit full-force by the eruption of splendour. It knocked all sense from him for a while, and when he finally came round he was hurtling back up the well even faster than he had dropped down; the velocity tore at the muscles of his face, pulled his lips back from his teeth, stole even more of his breath until he thought he was going to black out again. The coruscating energy licked all around him, yet astonishingly it hadn't burned him as he had feared in the instant before it had hit him. Instead he experienced an almost transcendental sense of wellbeing; it felt cool and like honey at the same time.

He couldn't tell if he was hallucinating from the wild sensations, but there seemed to be things moving in the fire all around him, large, dark shapes that twisted and turned sinuously. He almost felt he could hear their alien thoughts whispering in his head, accompanied by an over-whelming sense of freedom and jubilation.

He caught the briefest glimpse of Tom's dazzled face as the energy exploded out of the well and then it rocketed up and curled around the roof, the waves protecting him. He tried to suck in some air, but all he could get were a few gasps. And then he was hurtling along the tunnel, through the cavern, which seemed smaller when lit with the burning blue light, up to where the Fabulous Beast was sleeping. Only it wasn't asleep any longer. Fleetingly he saw its blazing eyes, its mouth roaring, spitting fire, in a tremendous display of exultation, and then it unfolded its wings just as it was caught in the flood.

And then he did black out. When he came to he had the briefest sensation of flying through cold night air and landing in a bone-jarring impact on the mist-damp grass, the wind smashed from his lungs. Finally he sucked in a lungful of air, his head swimming as he stared up at the vast, sparkling arc of the sky, waiting for his thoughts to catch up with the rush of sensation.

When he could, he rolled over and jumped to his feet. Tom was lying in a tangled heap nearby. Church ran over, worried, but the old man stirred and shook himself, muttering some curse under his breath. Smoke was rising from their skin, as if they had been singed by the fire, but they felt no pain. The disorientation was still swamping Church's head as he looked around and recognised they were once more at the foot of Arthur's Seat near the spring.

Tom pulled himself to his feet and instantly grew still. 'Look,' he said in a voice filled with awe.

Church followed his glance. At first he didn't see it, but when the peculiar perception came on him it was unmissable. Streams of blue fire were running from Arthur's Seat into the Old Town, where they were growing stronger, until they became a burning river heading towards the castle. And all along, tributaries were breaking off, flowing into Edinburgh, out across the country into the dark distance: a magnificent tapestry of blue fire. The land was coming alive.

And overhead, swooping and diving in the currents that followed the energy lines, was the Fabulous Beast. It let forth an enormous blast of fire which showered down among the buildings and in the red glare Church saw it was not alone. Three other, smaller beasts twisted and turned in complex but unmistakably jubilant patterns. And they were all heading towards the castle.

CHAPTER TEN

the Substance of things
hoped for

The night was filled with awe and fire. The Fabulous Beasts rose up from Arthur's Seat like a bell tolling the passing of an age now out of time, subsumed with righteous wrath and primal fury. And all across the city people threw open their windows or pulled over their cars to watch the end of it all.

The first column of fire came from the oldest of the creatures, sizzling through the air like a missile strike. It hit the centre of the Palace of Holyroodhouse, which ended its long life in an explosion that was heard twenty miles away, ballooning debris as far away as the New Town; it spiralled down in flaming arcs like celebratory fireworks, crashing into the streets, demolishing cars and roofs. The fire itself was almost liquid as it cascaded through the ruins, swamping those who tried to flee.

And high overhead the beasts swooped and soared in a display of freedom, occasionally pausing to roar another blast at the corrupted zone beneath. Their intricate flight patterns almost looked like a form of communication as they slowly worked their way up the Royal Mile. Tron Church became a needle of flame. The City Chambers, which buried the spirits of Mary King's Close, rose up in a bonfire of past hatred. St Giles's Cathedral exploded in a shower of rock and slate and superheated stained-glass. And among them the smart shops and houses of the regal street dissolved in fire. The remnants of the haar burned off, to be replaced by a thick, black pall of smoke which glowed red and gold on the underside.

A few very privileged souls were astonished to see what appeared to be a river of blue fire surging up the Royal Mile to the castle, as if it were seeking out its destination with sentience; and where it passed, the shadows that had clung to the Old Town in recent times seemed to leap back in horror from the burning light.

All of it was converging on the castle with a rapidity that left onlookers breathless and disoriented.

At the foot of Arthur's Seat, Church and Tom watched the growing conflagration with an odd mixture of dismay and relief.

'It all depends on the others doing their job now,' Church said, coughing as the wind gusted charred, sooty air into his face. 'I hope Veitch got out.'

'If he did, he had God on his side. If he didn't, there's nothing we can do for him now. Nor for the girl.'

Church bit his lip, said nothing. Then he covered his mouth with his handkerchief and set off in the direction of the rendezvous point, praying silently that someone would be there to meet them.

Shavi and Laura were sitting morosely on South Bridge when the attack began, still trying to make head or tail of what had happened at Rosslyn. Laura was concerned at how badly Shavi had been affected by the experience, which lay heavily on the already deep scars of his encounter with his dead friend. Neither thing would go away easily; during their short walk she had seen him continually glance into empty doorways or down shadowed alleys, as if someone were standing there. But the moment Holyroodhouse exploded, all that was forgotten. They ran back through the deserted, snowy streets to see what was happening, only to be knocked flat on their backs by a blast of heated air as another house went up in flames.

'This is too dangerous,' Shavi said. 'We need to be away from here.'

'He did it!' Laura could barely hide the jubilation in her voice. 'I knew the old bastard would pull through!' She watched the Fabulous Beasts for a moment, tracing their flight path back to Arthur's Seat. 'Church-dude – a hero, not a zero.' She brushed hair away from her eyes, grinning broadly. 'At least one of us isn't a fuck-up.'

Her pleasure was sharply interrupted by a terrible sound of pain and anguish that left them both clutching their ears. 'What the fuck was that?' she said when it had died away. But Shavi was already slipping and sliding through the snow closer to the Royal Mile.

Laura caught up with him at the vantage point they had occupied before. The source of the sound was two Fabulous Beasts, circling, blasting the spot where Maponus and the Cailleach Bheur had been involved in their titanic struggle. At ground zero was an enormous smoking crater, so hot at the core the stone was turning to molten lava. To one side lay what Laura guessed was the Blue Hag, but her shape seemed to be shifting constantly, desperately trying to hold on to the appearance Laura knew. A blizzard whirled frantically around the tight core of her being where a blue light glowed brightly; the awful sound came off her intermittently, like an alarm threatening imminent meltdown.

Of Maponus she could see nothing at first. But then the smoke cleared to reveal a terrible sight: the beautiful god was also in semi-fluid form, but whether it was because of his own madness or the ferocious heat of the blasts, he had been transformed into a twisted, grotesque shape from which three faces and several limbs protruded obscenely. His mouths opened and closed noiselessly, the silent screaming even more disturbing than the Blue Hag's shriek. Laura wondered why his writhing was so constrained until she saw he was half-fused into the wall of a house.

'He has fallen!' Shavi said triumphantly.

But the words had barely left his lips when a smell like frying onions filled the air and the dim golden light that always suffused Maponus' skin began to grow slowly more intense. The god's skin began to melt from his bones, then the bones themselves, and the odd things that vaguely resembled organs, all of them dissolving into one pure white light. The shapeless radiance pulled itself into a tight orb as it released itself from the wall and then began to move away across the debris.

Another blast from one of the Fabulous Beasts blinded them with a shower of dust and choking smoke for a moment, and when it had cleared they saw the Bone Inspector loping more like a beast than a man across the rubble in pursuit of the diminishing white light.

'Do you realise what this means?' Shavi said, aghast. 'He cannot be destroyed. None of them can.' His face was drained of all blood.

Laura grabbed his arm and began to pull him away; the heat was so intense she could smell her hair singeing. 'There's nothing we can do now.' She had to shake him hard to stop his protests. 'Mister Freak is on his tail. He can carry the can for a while.'

'We have a responsibility—'

'That's all we do have! Later, before I hit you with a rock. You've gone all *Apocalypse Now* combat crazy, and if you start mumbling like Marlon I really will be forced to cause pain.'

Shavi fell silent, but his eyes remained troubled.

'This isn't over,' she continued. 'Think of it as a brief retreat, right?'

'It is not over,' he agreed firmly.

Veitch and Ruth had barely moved several yards along the ramparts before they had once again become transfixed by the Fabulous Beasts.

'Shit, they're blowing the whole place up!' Veitch wrapped his arms around himself to stop shivering; the water from the well freezing on his clothes and hair made him resemble a walking snowman.

Ruth watched carefully for a moment, then said, 'They're coming this way.'

Veitch grabbed her arm and dragged her to the Lang Stairs, and although they were lethal with ice and snow, he took them three at a time. At the bottom he paused briefly to scan the Middle Ward. The Fomorii patrol were rooted near the Cartshed, their waxy human faces turned to the approaching threat. Their statue-like appearance was emphasised by their lack of emotion, but in one second they began to change, the flesh and clothes falling away as horns and carapaces and bones began to emerge amidst a sudden cacophony of monkey-shrieks. Mid-transformation, they scattered like a disturbed ants' nest.

Their stomachs were turning, but Ruth and Veitch were already moving down to the Lower Ward before the change was complete.

'I'll never get used to that,' Ruth said queasily.

Veitch paused near the Gatehouse and Old Guardhouse. 'Maybe we can sneak—'

The words caught in his throat as the Fomor guard emerged from the doorway and barked, 'Arith Urkolim!' the moment he caught sight of Veitch. The Londoner tensed, torn between going for the crossbow or the sword, knowing either would be useless as the Fomor advanced relentlessly.

But before he could move, the glaring, reflected light from the snow suddenly darkened and a deep shadow fell over them. It was accompanied by what sounded like giant sails unfurling in a heavy gale.

Ruth dragged him back just as the oldest of the Fabulous Beasts swooped down in a blaze of glittering bronze and green scales. The Fomor and the Gatehouse were caught up in a furious firestorm that left Veitch and Ruth huddled in the snow, choking for breath as liquid fire and rubble rained down all around them. The crashing of mighty wings grew even more intense above them. Ruth rolled on to her back and peered through the billowing smoke. Four Fabulous Beasts were circling the castle.

'Let's move,' she choked.

They clambered to their feet, shielding their faces from the blazing ruins of the Gatehouse. 'We'll just have to put our heads down and run,' Veitch gasped.

The flames closed around them for a second, the heat searing their lungs, but then they were out in the bleak, snow-swept Esplanade, slipping and sliding down the slope towards Lawnmarket.

Behind them they heard the terrible sound of the Fomorii raising the alarm. Ruth glanced back briefly and saw Calatin standing on the battlements of the Upper Ward, shrieking at the darkness that surged around him, pointing in fury at the circling Beasts.

'I hope those monsters don't hurt the Beasts,' Ruth said.

Her fears were unfounded. A second later the purifying fire rained down from the heavens. The entire castle was engulfed in an inferno of living flame. Stone which had stood firm for centuries flowed like water or exploded in the instant heat. The lights popped out and windows crashed in.

Ruth and Veitch scrambled down the Royal Mile, trying to put distance between them and what they knew was to come. Ruth guessed the Scots Guards must have had an ammunition store in the castle, for a moment later there was an explosion that felt like the city was being levelled. They were knocked flat on their faces by the pressure wave, which also drove them momentarily deaf. In a world of eerie silence, Ruth rolled over to see a column of fire reaching up to the heavens where the castle had once stood. It shimmered red and gold as the Fabulous Beasts did soundless rolls and turns around it.

At the base there was an odd sight. The flames there were blue and they reached deep into the core of the rock on which the castle had stood.

'It's over.' The tears of relief came with the words. She scrubbed them away with the back of her hand, then turned to Veitch, smiling and crying at the same time. 'It's over,' she repeated, even though she knew he couldn't hear her.

The temperature rose dramatically within minutes as the summer rushed back in to replace the fleeing winter. The near-instantaneous thaw sent water gushing into the drains and pouring in torrents from the rooftops. As their hearing returned, Veitch and Ruth were enveloped in the thunderous sound of the castle and the Royal Mile burning, filling the air with choking particles, obscuring the stars with thick, oily smoke.

They hurried down George IV Bridge as fast as they could, but in the aftermath of their victory the adrenalin retreated rapidly and Ruth, in particular, was overcome with a powerful exhaustion. Eventually she was clinging on to Veitch as he almost carried her the last few yards into Greyfriars Kirkyard.

The graveyard sprawled away from the overpowering presence of the kirk, surrounded by high stone houses that made it a peaceful backwater untouched by the city. Ancient trees clustered all around, their thick cover blocking out the glare from the inferno. The choking fumes hadn't reached it either. There was only the sweet scent of the rose garden that lay before the main jumble of stones, mausoleums, obelisks and boxes that glowed eerily white, like bones, in the gloom.

None of the others had arrived, so Veitch and Ruth collapsed on to a stone box; he slid his arm around her and she rested her head on his shoulder.

After a second or two, he said, 'I know what you went through. Back at Dartmoor, when those bastards were dragging me through their torture mill . . .' He exhaled loudly. 'You did fine.'

'It doesn't feel fine. It was like, hanging on, you know?'

'You'll put it behind you soon.'

'Is that right?'

A pause. 'No.'

She retched and dipped her head between her knees.

'Are you okay?'

'No, I feel terrible.'

He laid her down on the box and put his jacket over her. Her skin was so pale it was almost the colour of the stone her cheek was touching. She huddled up into a foetal position and a second later she was asleep.

Veitch kept watch over her, his eyes flickering from the gentle rise and fall of her chest to the dark shadows that clustered all around. He wished the others would hurry up. Despite the destruction of the castle, he couldn't believe that was the end of it. With Ruth asleep, the kirkyard seemed too quiet and exposed; an attack could come from any direction. The rustling of the leaves and the shifting of the branches in the faint breeze made him think there was something moving around in the gloom. And the more he sat in silence, the more he thought he could hear faint noises on the other side of the kirkyard.

Another sound nearby warned him that it wasn't all in his mind. It could have been a squirrel or a cat, but over the last few weeks he had learned to expect the worse.

At first there was nothing. Then he glimpsed movement around the kirkyard, shapes flitting among the trees, appearing and disappearing behind the grave markers. He started to count, then gave up, although there was nothing to suggest they were Fomorii. But whatever was out there seemed to be moving closer. His grip grew tighter on his sword.

'Unclean.'

The word was just a rustle caught on the wind. He looked around suddenly in the direction it had come from, but the area was deserted.

'Who's there?' he called firmly.

No answer. The nerves along his spine were tingling; he had the uneasy sensation that he was being watched. More movement. He couldn't put it down to imagination; there was definitely someone out there.

'You better come out,' he said forcefully.

'What's going on?'

Veitch started at the voice. Church had just marched through the kirkyard gates, beaming broadly, Laura hanging on his arm, looking honestly happy for once. Behind them was Tom, as impossible to read as ever, and then Shavi, who seemed uncommonly downcast. 'Did you see it? Did you see what we did?' Church continued. 'All those screw-ups and bad luck and this time we got it right!'

Church suddenly noticed Ruth asleep under Veitch's coat and threw off Laura's arm to run to her side. Laura's expression changed to one of irritation before she managed to mask it.

'Is she okay?' Church gently touched her wrist where it poked out from beneath the coat.

'She's had a bad time.' Veitch kept one eye on the kirkyard; all the movement had ceased. 'The Bastards really put her through it, but she's tough. She'll be okay.'

Church grinned. 'Then we're celebrating! Everything worked out fine. I don't believe it!'

'Unclean.'

This time the voice was clear and unmistakable. Church looked round, puzzled. 'What was that?'

'There's somebody out there.' Veitch pulled out the sword where it could be seen. 'I don't think it's the Bastards, but I don't have a good feeling about it.'

The others gathered around. 'I sense something—' Shavi began.

'Can't you see them?' Tom snapped. 'Amongst the trees?'

And then they could all see them: grey figures moving slowly, some of them raising their arms to the heavens as if they were in some kind of distress. They moved forward, silently at first, but as they drew closer faint whispers sprang up like echoes in their wake, growing louder until their voices were clear. They were protesting about something, frightened, outraged.

'What are they?' Church asked.

'The dead,' Tom said. 'The spirits of the kirkyard.'

'Eighty thousand of us.' The voice came from behind a mausoleum. Gradually a figure emerged, hollow-cheeked and staring, with eyes that made their blood run cold. He was as grey as the stone, wearing clothes which dated his time to the turn of the century. 'That's how many of us are buried here. Eighty thousand.'

The spirit of a woman rushed up to them, wailing so loudly they all flinched, but at the last minute she turned away and fled among the stones.

'What's wrong with them?' Laura's voice was hushed, frightened.

The spirits were in a semi-circle before them now, tearing at their ghostly hair, beating their breasts; their anguish was palpable.

647

'Leave now.' The man near the mausoleum was pointing at them accusingly. 'You are damned!'

'They are coming for you! They are not departed!' a woman shrieked, her hair as wild as snakes. 'They will not let you go!'

'Coming into this place, so unclean!' the man continued. 'Foul! Besmirched! And the Night Walkers will follow in your wake, hunting you. You will bring them here!'

'What's wrong?' Veitch yelled at them. 'We've actually done some bleedin' good for a change—'

He was cut off by more shrieking.

'Come on,' Church said, 'let's go.' He shook Ruth, who struggled to stand, barely able to keep her eyes open.

The spirits followed closely as the six of them started to back away to the kirkyard gates; the voices became more shrill and intense, wailing like sirens, enough to set teeth on edge.

'Unclean!' the man yelled so loudly Laura jumped back a step. 'You corrupt this sacred ground! Your black trail scars our home!'

The dead crowded in suddenly, and although they appeared insubstantial, their clawed fingers caught at the group's clothes, tore at their hair. Church and the others broke into a run, pursued by the shrieking spirits, which were dipping and rising across the kirkyard like reflected light on mist. It was as if the spirits were being tortured by unimaginable pain.

Only when the group was resting against the foot of the bridge outside the kirkyard gates did the sound subside; and even then the spirits could be glimpsed flitting around the kirk in a state of distress.

'That freaked me out,' Laura said. A flicker crossed her face and she glanced to Church, hoping perhaps that he would deny her thoughts. 'They were saying the Fomorii were going to hunt us down.'

But he seemed more concerned by something else. 'What made them act like that?' He looked to Tom for an answer.

'It doesn't matter about any of that,' Veitch said animatedly. 'We did it.'

They all turned to him.

'There was some ritual going on under the castle—'

'Ritual?' Church's eyes gleamed.

Veitch nodded, smiling tightly. 'Something big. I reckon it was *the* big one. And we stopped the Bastards doing it.'

A ripple of relief ran through the group; they could hardly believe it. Church turned to Tom, questioning silently.

'You saw the place.' He was almost smiling. 'All that's there now is a big crater.'

'We stopped them,' Church said quietly, as if the words would break the spell. After all the weeks of failure, disbelief hung at the back of his voice. But it was true. 'We burned out the nest. They won't be able to bring Balor back.' He dropped to his haunches, one hand over his face while he assimilated the words. The moment hung in the air, and then Laura draped a tentative hand on to his shoulder. It was as if that was the signal; suddenly they were hugging each other, slapping backs, laughing and gabbling inanely as the tension rushed out of them. Veitch let out an ear-piercing yell of triumph that bounced among the buildings.

'But those spooks—' Church hugged Laura off her feet and crushed the rest of the sentence inside her. She tried to look aloof, but she couldn't keep the smile in.

'The Fomorii are still here,' he explained. 'You saw the nest in the Lake District – they're all over the damn place. We've just stopped them getting the upper hand, that's all. That's all!' He let out a whoop. 'We've kicked them so hard it's going to take them a while to get back on their feet! Now *we*'ve got the upper hand! All we've got to do now is find a way to get the Tuatha Dé Danann on our side and kick the Bastards out for good.'

'Oh well, it's almost over then,' Laura said with a smile that dripped irony.

'Ah, shaddup, you miserable git.' He kissed her and that surprised both of them.

'We owe ourselves a bleedin' big piss-up,' Veitch said, his arm tight around Ruth's shoulders. She was smiling wanly, still scarcely able to believe what she was hearing.

But they all agreed Veitch was right. Swept up in their jubilation and relief, they turned towards the south and began to move out of the city.

They had travelled barely a quarter of a mile when it became apparent they wouldn't get far on foot. Church and Veitch had been supporting Ruth, but with each step they were doing more dragging than carrying.

They eventually halted on a corner while Veitch and Laura disappeared down a side street. Forty-five minutes later they pulled up in a pristine Transit.

'Who'd you kill for that?' Ruth croaked.

'God, even half-dead she's Mother Superior.' Laura raised her eyes in an exaggerated response.

They loaded Ruth in the back and made her as comfortable as possible, then Church joined Laura and Veitch in the front. 'Just like old times,' she said, without a hint of sarcasm.

Beyond the reach of the Old Town, the streets gave way to well-heeled neighbourhoods where the houses were rambling and set well back from the road, and beyond that were the plain, structured streets of suburbia. By two-fifteen a.m., they were crossing the ring road, enjoying the balminess of a warm summer night after the chill environment of the Cailleach Bheur.

Unlike most English cities, the built-up area ended abruptly and they were plunged immediately into rolling green fields punctuated by peaceful woods. The tyres sang on dry roads through tiny villages. Away to the east, the remnants of the haar still clouded the horizon, but overhead the skies were clear and iced with stars.

At the sign for Roslin Village, Laura glanced over her shoulder to see Shavi's chin droop on to his chest. He was normally so bright and optimistic, it pained her to see the dismay etched into his features. More than anything, she wanted to clamber over the seat and give him a hug, but there was no way she could in front of the others.

After a long journey through thick woods, they entered a desolate valley plain where sheep wandered morosely over the clipped, yellow grass. In the distance the hills rose up steeply while, nearer to hand, train lines cut a swathe through the heart of the valley. At 4 a.m. they broke off to make camp for the night. Veitch and Church had been determined to keep going until dawn, but the decision was made for them by another technology failure which left the van drifting aimlessly on to the verge. They pushed it for a little way until they found a lane which led behind a small copse of trees where they could hide; even after their success, paranoia still hissed in the background. They'd abandoned all their clothes, camping equipment and provisions at the hotel, so they made themselves as comfortable as they could in the confines of the van. Tom was particularly concerned about Ruth, but she appeared to be sleeping easily enough. After their exertions, they drifted off within an instant of resting.

By the time they rose the sun was high in a clear blue sky and the interior of the van was beginning to bake. Although still weak and exhausted, Ruth was much brighter. They helped her outside where she propped herself up against a wheel and before too long she was exchanging banter with Shavi and Church and baiting Laura and Veitch. On the surface it was like old times, but something had changed; where there had been malice, now there was affection, however well-hidden.

They were eager to exchange details of their experiences. Veitch was reticent in his description of his assault on the castle, and when Ruth emphasised the extent of his bravery his ears turned red. They all did their best to boost Shavi, but his account of Maponus and the thought that he was still at large cast a chill over them all.

Tom listened carefully, then said, 'He is beyond our remit now. If anyone can find a way to restrain him, then it would be the Bone Inspector. He has knowledge denied to you and I, and it was his people who imprisoned Maponus initially.' He paused. 'But he is just one man.'

'But Maponus cannot be killed – we saw,' Shavi stressed. 'None of the gods can.'

'No,' Tom agreed, 'not in the way you mean. Although the lowest of the Fomorii, the troops, if you will, *can* be eradicated, as Ryan found out at the castle.'

'How can we be guerrillas if we can't hurt the ones that really matter?' Laura protested. 'We're just an irritation—'

'Situation normal for you, then,' Veitch muttered.

'We've done what we can,' Laura continued, 'done a good job. Can't we leave it up to somebody else, now? We've earned a rest, haven't we?'

Nobody seemed comfortable debating this line and the conversation drifted on to Church and Tom's encounter beneath Arthur's Seat.

'It was the weirdest experience,' Church said. 'The way reality, time, space, everything, seemed to be fluid in proximity to such a powerful source of the blue fire.'

'Maybe that's how reality really is,' Ruth mused. 'God knows, we've had enough proof we can't trust our senses to perceive anything correctly. When you think about it, it's scary. We're prisoners in our heads, completely at the mercy of our brain functions, and beyond that little bit of bone, the universe might be completely different to how we imagine it.'

'There is a line of scientific thought, currently growing in popularity,' Shavi mused, 'that suggests time does not exist. We perceive it as flowing constantly because that is the way our brains have been structured to understand it. But we are really living in all times at once. That would explain precognition—'

'But how does it work?' Ruth said.

'I wish you lot would shut up – you're making my head hurt,' Veitch said irritably. 'Talk, talk, talk, like a bunch of bleedin' students. Things are how they are, that's all. We've got more important things to think about.'

A hawk hunted for prey over an area of scrubby undergrowth in the middle distance. The image triggered a succession of disturbing thoughts in Church.

'Tom and I weren't alone beneath the Seat,' he said.

'Yeah, the old git took along the chip on his shoulder,' Laura said tartly.

'The one who took Ruth was there.' Church flashed a glance at Ruth, not quite knowing how she was going to react.

Veitch bristled. 'What did he look like?'

Church exhaled through the gap in his teeth. 'You know what he looked like. A bloody big wolf, just like Laura said. With yellow eyes and everything.'

'You should never have left the path, little girl,' Laura said to Ruth with a faint smile. From the corner of his eye, Church caught Veitch watching the two of them intently, coldly.

Church nodded to Tom. 'You tell them what you told me.'

Tom took off his spectacles and cleaned them on his shirt. Without the glasses he looked less like the sixties burn-out case and more like the erudite, thoughtful aristocrat he was. 'When the old gods have . . .' There was a long, jarring pause while he searched for the right word. '. . . *adjusted* someone, it is often difficult for the mind to fully fix their shape. It's as if something fundamental has been altered on a molecular level, something so in opposition to nature it seems to set up interference patterns for the senses. The first few times you see something like this, unless you're prepared, it's like a punch in the stomach. To make sense of it, the mind gives it a shape which is closest to the essence of its being—'

'So it's a wolf at heart?' Ruth asked. There seemed to be a stone pressing at the back of her throat.

'Is this the origin of werewolves?' Shavi interjected.

Tom shook his head. 'The *Lupinari* are different. This creature was mortal once. And the ones who have been altered sometimes seem so enamoured of this inner self, they grow into it. Physically.'

'I've met a few guys like that,' Laura said. 'They don't need a full moon. Just seven pints.'

'You don't remember anything?' Church asked Ruth.

She shook her head. 'Just Laura—'

'Laura?' Veitch's voice was a whipcrack.

'Laura was around somewhere. That's all I remember.'

They sat in silence for a few moments, weighing the evidence. And then, once they had exhausted all possibilities, they were forced to turn to Ruth again, although none of them wanted to hear what she had to say.

'How was it in there?' Church asked tenderly.

She smiled weakly. 'Oh, you know . . . You can guess.'

He nodded. 'Do you want to talk about it?'

She shook her head. 'I just want to get back on my feet.'

'I might be able to help there.' Tom gave her a faint smile, but it was warm and honest, a rare sight. He headed off into the countryside. They watched him for a while, dipping down occasionally to pluck something from the ground.

'Hmmm, grass and weeds. You're in for a treat,' Laura said. 'What is it with the old git? He knows all about these herbs and shit like he's some old witch.' Ruth flinched, but no one noticed.

'He's had a long time to learn.' Church continued to watch Tom. Their relationship had always been abrasive, but he had respect for the Rhymer's wisdom.

'He learned it from the Culture, the people of the Bone Inspector,' Shavi said. 'It is age-old knowledge, from the time when people were close to the land.'

'We need to sort out the way forward.' Veitch cut through the small-talk sharply.

'What's to sort out? I'm so hungry I could eat you.' Laura let the double-entendre hang in the air teasingly, her sunglasses obscuring her true meaning. 'Calm down, big boy. That wasn't meant in a nice way.'

'Laura is right,' Shavi said. 'Hot food first, then provisions, camping equipment, clothes. We need to replace everything we left at the hotel.'

'Yeah, because that city is not going to look very pretty after the air-raid,' Veitch said sharply. 'We need to find a place to lie low while we work out what we're going to do. Somewhere the Bastards can't find us.'

Church nodded in agreement. 'We should head south.'

'Yeah, I'm sick of heather and tartan,' Veitch said. 'And all the bleedin' Jocks hate us anyway.'

Tom returned half an hour later with two handfuls of vegetation while Ruth was vainly searching the sky for her owl. He used the wheel brace in the van to pound them into two piles of pulp. One he applied as a poultice to Ruth's finger, the other he made her eat, despite her protests.

'Stop whining,' Laura said. 'As soon as you get past the gag reflex it'll be fine.'

Eventually she ate it, and she did retch noisily for a while, but nothing came back up. They helped her back into the van and she fell asleep as soon as they set off.

*

The journey was not easy going. They stopped at a roadside café for a large meal that doubled as breakfast and lunch, before they were hit by two technology failures, lasting two hours and forty-five minutes respectively. In Peebles they used their credit cards to stock up on everything they needed, but the shop assistants were wary of taking the plastic; with the failure of the phone system it was impossible to check their validity, and everyone seemed to suspect the whole system was collapsing anyway. To recognise that fact was a blow too far so the cards were swiped in the old-fashioned way, with an unspoken prayer that everything would sort itself out soon. But it was obvious to Church and the others that the balloon was on the point of going up.

As they passed through Melrose, Tom waxed lyrical about his home area until Laura yawned so loudly and repeatedly it brought him to cursing. Jedburgh passed in a blur and they crossed the border in late afternoon.

There was a heated debate about which route to pursue after that, but everyone bowed to Veitch's strategic decison to head into the wide open spaces of high hills and bleak moorland that comprised the Northumberland National Park. They swept from the rolling fields of the Scottish Lowlands into a majestic landscape of purples, browns and greens, brooding beneath a perfect blue sky. It was a place of rock and scrub, wind-torn trees standing lonely on the horizon, and a howling gale that rushed from the high places as if it had a life of its own.

The hardiness gave way to the pleasant shade of the Border Forest Park, where the play of light and dark through the leaf cover on to the windscreen made them all feel less hunted. There was a deep peace among the thick woods that was a pleasure after the omnipresent threat of Edinburgh.

While Shavi drove, Veitch took charge of the map book. He made them follow a circuitous route through the quiet villages that must have added fifty miles to their journey, but he insisted if there was any pursuit it would make their destination less apparent. Laura noted tartly that he'd already baffled the rest of them about where they were going.

They eventually came to a halt at an abandoned railway station at High Staward, eight miles south-west of Hexham. They loaded all their possessions into four rucksacks which Church, Veitch, Tom and Shavi shouldered with much protesting. Laura taunted their lack of manliness, and even Ruth tossed out a few quips, and eventually they were marching along a footpath northwards through the deserted countryside.

Veitch had selected the location after careful study of the maps, and they all had to agree it was so off the beaten track it was as good a hiding place as any. They plunged down into thick woodland where the dark lay heavy and cool and the only sound was the eerie soughing of the wind, like distant voices urging them to stray from the path. A mile later they emerged to a breathtaking sight: the Allen Gorge. Four miles long, its precipitously steep sides soared up two hundred and fifty feet, covered with so many trees it looked like an Alpine landscape. Secluded pathways wound along the riverside and away into the trees.

'We could hide here for weeks if we wanted.' Veitch's voice held a note of pride that the reality matched up to his expectations.

They followed a path into the area with the thickest tree cover and then ploughed off into the wild. They finally halted when they couldn't see the path clearly any longer. The tents went up quickly in a circle, and at the heart of it Veitch dug a pit for a fire.

In the early evening sun, Church and Shavi went exploring. They found an outcropping rock in a clearing on the side of the gorge where they had majestic views over the entire area. They were both instantly struck by the immaculate beauty of the place.

'You know, if we lose all the technology, maybe it won't be so bad,' Church mused. 'We'll still have all this.'

Before Shavi could reply, the tranquillity was shattered by the roar of two jets burning through the sky in the direction of Newcastle. 'I bet they're not test flights,' Church said. 'Looks like trouble.'

Fifteen minutes later another one followed, but before it had crossed the arc of the sky, the technology chose that moment to fail once more. They saw the jet plummet from the sky like a boulder, hitting the ground with an explosion that made their ears ring despite their distance from ground zero. They stood in silence for a long time, watching the black pall of smoke merge with the clouds. Wrapped up in that incident was the failure of everything they knew; Church found himself questioning his earlier statement. They couldn't put it into any kind of perspective, and in the end, they didn't even try. They wandered back to the camp, thinking about the poor pilot, wondering what was happening in Newcastle, glad they were hidden in their perfect isolation.

Dinner was beans and bread, and sausages for all except Laura and Shavi. They ate around the campfire in the balmy summer evening atmosphere, enjoying the fading light as it filtered down through the canopy. The crack and pop of the fire was relaxing as the night drew in. It was the first time in weeks they had been able to eat peacefully without a very real fear of pursuit or some other pervasive threat hanging over their heads; they found it hard to adjust.

After the meal, they sat drinking coffee for a while, listening to the sounds of the owls coming alive in the trees and then they broke up for some time to be alone with their thoughts. They agreed to meet up later in the evening to celebrate with the good supply of beer and whisky they'd brought with them.

Church was the first back to the camp after a quiet stroll among the trees, where he had forced himself not to think about anything too troubling. Ruth was still resting where they had left her, staring into the flames. She looked up and smiled when he approached.

'How are you feeling?' he asked.

'Much better. My stump's stopped aching and I feel quite rested – my energy's coming back. Whatever Tom puts in those foul concoctions he makes up, he should sell it in bulk to the NHS.' She paused thoughtfully. 'If there still is an NHS. Apart from that I've just got a queasy feeling in the pit of my stomach, like I've eaten sour apples. That's the least I expected, to be honest. I could be up and about like normal in a couple of days.'

He dropped down next to her and slipped an arm around her shoulders. They had grown easy in their friendship since the night they had met under Albert Bridge, drawing comfort from the many similarities between them, enjoying the differences. They both felt that when the situation was at its worst, they could always turn to each other for support.

'I'm glad you're back,' Church said matter-of-factly.

Ruth dropped her head on to his shoulder, remembering a similar scenario on Skye, not so long ago, but a world away in experience. 'There was a time I thought I wasn't going to make it back. I thought they were going to torture me and torture me until I died just because I couldn't take it any more.'

'Ryan's right, Ruth. You came through it. You've shown what huge reserves you've got inside you. It may seem like a nightmare now, but in the long term, that's a good thing.'

One thing still troubled her, but she didn't see any point in telling Church; it seemed so minor after everything else. Since she had left her cell there had been no sign of her owl, or whatever creature it was that took that form. She was surprised at how distressed that made her feel. It wasn't just that it hadn't found her yet; she felt instinctively that some deep bond had been broken.

What could have happened to cause that? The education she had been receiving in her cell still sang in her mind, so powerfully had it been learned. She had been rapidly growing closer to the way the familiar had wanted her to be.

One thought did worry her: that there had been no familiar; it was all a hallucination caused by her suffering, and the owl that had followed her for the last few weeks was simply a bird and nothing more.

Church lounged back on his elbows. 'It feels good to know we've done something right for a change.' He glanced down at her hand and winced. 'Even though we paid a big price for it.'

'What are we going to do now? We can't call ourselves losers any more.' Ruth butted him gently with her head; their easy familiarity soothed her almost as much as Tom's herbal remedies. 'Don't tell me you've finally shaken that miserabilist streak.'

'What, and change the habits of a lifetime? It's just taking a few days off.' He laughed quietly. 'And I'm certainly not going to let anything ruin the celebration tonight. After all the shit we've waded through over the last few weeks, this is going to be the party to end all parties.'

Laura had found a boulder near to the river where she could sit and think. The sound of rushing water always calmed her. As a girl she'd dreamed of living near the coast and taken every opportunity to let her parents know how she felt. Her father had even agreed once, and they'd sat together looking at his *AA Book of the Road*, searching for the perfect home. If she remembered rightly, they'd decided on somewhere in South Devon. But that was before her mother had truly let God move her in mysterious ways – all the way from sanity to the other end of the scale. The failure to uproot, despite her father's promises, was just the first and most minor of a lifetime of disappointments. Since then there had been so many she'd become inured to them; any happiness was an aberration to be questioned.

She'd never really thought her cynical outlook actually brought about her disappointments, but if it was the case, it was too late to change. After she'd met Church, it had seemed her life's route had taken a sudden detour to the sunny side of the street and things really could work out as she hoped. But perhaps that had just been the desperation influencing her. She'd long ago learned wishing and hoping didn't make things real, and now it all seemed to be slipping back to the old ways. Church didn't love her, not the way she loved him. The others, she was sure, secretly hated her; she certainly hadn't done anything to make them think otherwise, however much she secretly admired them. She was always screwing up, dragging them into bad situations.

And now there was the thing with her blood. What was happening to her? It terrified her to the core of her being and she desperately wished there was someone she could talk to about it. But there wasn't, not even Church. Her thoughts and emotions had to stay locked up, same as they always had; it was the only true way to protect herself.

She would have expected a degree of bitterness, but now that she examined her state of mind she realised there was only a damp, grey acceptance. And wasn't that the most pathetic thing?

A vague movement among the trees caused her to turn suddenly. It was only Veitch, his face a curious mask that hinted at emotions but gave nothing away.

'I thought you were supposed to be the big warrior-strategist-whatever,' she sneered. 'You couldn't creep up on a deaf, blind person.'

'I wasn't creeping.'

Now she thought she did see emotions: anger, suspicion, hatred, although that was perhaps too strong. Suddenly, inexplicably, she felt frightened. 'Yeah, well, don't try coming a-wooing. I've already told you where I stand on that front.'

'I wouldn't dirty myself.'

'Ooh, bitchy. Well, you're not exactly the catch of the century, believe me.'

He grabbed her arm so roughly she let out a sharp squeal.

'What the fuck do you think you're doing?' She shook him off angrily.

His eyes blazed coldly and suddenly she was aware of the hardness of his body, the tendons like steel wire. She jumped off the rock and began to march back in the direction of the camp. He made another lunge at her, but she anticipated it and dodged beyond his fingers.

'Don't fucking walk away from me.'

'What's the matter? Can't get laid the normal way so you have to take it like some Neanderthal?' She fought to keep the tremor from her voice.

Her words, though, seemed to shock him. A puzzled expression crossed his features, as if he was struggling to understand her meaning. Then the anger returned harder than ever. 'I'd never do anything like that!' The words hissed between his teeth like steam from a fractured pipe. 'Is that what you think of me?'

'You're not exactly acting like Prince Charming.' She couldn't resist turning to face him, knowing she had a clear path to the camp if she needed to make a run for it.

'You've got a smart mouth.' He took a step forward, but he restrained himself from making another lunge for her.

'Come on then!' Suddenly it was impossible to control herself and all the pent-up rage, all the self-loathing and despair erupted. 'Give it to me! What's rubbing you up the wrong way?'

'You!' He jabbed a finger at her face. 'You wander around throwing out smart comments, acting so cool and aloof like you're better than everybody! But I've got you sussed! I know you had something to do with what happened to Ruth—'

She threw up her arms in amazement. 'You are so off the fucking mark you're on another planet!' She turned and set off through the trees, her head spinning from the rush of emotion.

The roar of breath expelled from Veitch's mouth was animalistic, the sound of someone who couldn't cope. And then she heard the crash of his feet on the ground as he set off after her. She didn't wait any longer. She put her head down and ran, glad she was wearing boots and jeans, weaving through the trees as fast as she could go. But it was too dark. She slammed against a tree, winded herself, smashed a shin against an outcropping rock. Behind she could hear the grunts and yells of Veitch's angry pursuit; he was moving swiftly, avoiding all obstacles like some night-hunting panther. He'd be on her in a minute.

The fear sluiced all the hot emotions from her in a cold wash. And what would he do when he caught her? Her heart hammered as she leapt a fallen tree, ducked beneath a low branch.

'Bitch!' The word was low and hard.

In her rising panic, her thoughts flatlined. She made a move to jump a hollow, twisted her ankle, and then she was falling off-balance. She hit the ground hard, saw stars, slid through the undergrowth that tore at her face and hair, and came to a halt against a pile of rocks. Pain flared through her side and involuntary tears sprang to her eyes.

Veitch was over her a second later, rising up dark and empowered like some monstrous creature from a forties horror movie. His fists were bunched, raised to hit her. 'I know you did Ruth somehow! Did it yourself, or fucking sold her down the river! You're the traitor they told us about! But I'm fucking on to you!'

Something seemed to explode in his face and then the fist was swinging. Laura cried out, closed her eyes, threw her head to one side.

When the blow didn't come, the chaotic jumble of her thoughts fell quickly into place and she looked up. Veitch was sitting down, his head in his hands and when he looked up a few seconds later, his eyes shone with tears. 'Fucking bitch! You've brought me to this!' His voice was a croak of repressed emotion. 'I'd never hurt a woman. Never!'

'You have a good way of showing—' For the first time she managed to bite off her comment. 'I didn't have anything to do with what happened to Ruth. And I'm not a traitor.' She tried to keep her voice measured.

'I don't believe you.' By the time he'd stood up and walked a few paces through the trees he'd composed himself. 'I don't believe you,' he repeated; the threat in his voice made her blood run cold. 'I've been watching you. I'll keep watching you. I'm not going to let the others get hurt. I'm going to make sure someone pays for Ruth. One sign, that's all I need. One sign. And you're dead.'

He disappeared into the gloom among the trees, silently, dangerously.

Once he was out of sight, Laura crumpled and all the tears she had held in for a lifetime came flooding out.

After she had managed to collect herself, the golden glow of the fire drew her back to the camp. But as the trees thinned towards the clearing her heart caught in her throat. There was Church, his arm around Ruth, her head on his shoulder. It wasn't jealousy she felt; she could see there was nothing furtive about their body language. Instead she was hit by the aching revelation that she could never attain the depth of Church and Ruth's relationship: the easy familiarity, the emotional honesty, the warmth were all apparent, even at a casual glance. And she could see there was love there, a kind she would have given anything to experience, so subtle Church and Ruth seemed oblivious to it themselves.

She couldn't blame Church. The fault was within herself. Something had been broken during those lean years of childhood and early teens; however much she tried, she couldn't give up her emotions honestly, and so she had consigned herself to a life of being shut in the prison of her body, feeling something keenly, hearing a corrupted version emerge from her lips; an emotional synaesthesia.

As she watched them, she hurt so profoundly she felt there was a physical pain deep inside; the hopelessness for herself was even more overwhelming than when she had realised she could never attain the loving family life of her school friends, so deep there was no point fighting it; acceptance was the only option.

She rubbed her face muscles, as if that would break up the desperate expression, fixed an ironic smile and stepped out from the shadows.

'Well, Siamese twins,' she said sharply. 'You should get on the waiting list for the operation.'

Within the hour they were all sitting around the heartily blazing campfire. The night was balmy, dreamlike, alive with the crackle of the burning wood, the calls of hunting owls, the flitter of moths and crane-flies. It felt like a time of peace, a time when anything could happen.

Church lounged on his side and threw twigs into the flames. Next to him was Ruth, who seemed to be getting brighter with each passing moment, except for the occasional queasy expression. Laura and Veitch sat on opposite sides of the fire, never making eye contact, yet acutely aware of an atmosphere of suspicion and threat hanging over them like a poisonous cloud. They both knew, whatever happened, they would never overcome it.

Tom sat cross-legged, rolling a joint, alone with his thoughts. Shavi was beside him, handing out the cans of beer when needed, ensuring the bottle of whisky never stayed in one place too long. When he had first returned to the camp, his face was grey and haggard, as if he was suffering from some debilitating illness, but Laura recognised the truth instantly. She knew in the dark woods he had encountered the thing that would never leave him alone, and she knew how deeply it had affected him, yet he never complained to any of the others about his private burden. She wished she had some of the inner strength that saw him through it. When the others weren't looking she gave his hand a secret squeeze; his smile made her night.

The drink flowed freely, the conversation ranged across a variety of subjects: archaeology, drugs, music, films, sex, football, but nothing dark or threatening; it was a celebration of all the things that made their lives worth living.

Shavi became animated when the talk drifted on to some of the places they had seen in their travels: the wonders of Stonehenge and Avebury, infused with history, meaning and mystery, the rugged beauty of Cornwall, the joys of little seaside towns, the majesty of the Lake District and the Scottish Highlands.

'There is nowhere in the world that is richer in natural beauty than Britain,' he said. 'Stories of the people live on in the shape of the hedgerows, in the cut of fields, in the landscape itself. The place is a living mythology, constantly changing with the weather. The fens in a storm, Oxfordshire in winter, London on a summer night. Mountains and marches, beaches and flood plains, rivers and gorges and chalk downs. Where else can you find all those in a short drive of each other?' He sighed, tracing his fingers along the soil. 'There is magic infused in the very fabric of the place.'

'The history adds to it for me,' Church noted. 'It's not just about the beauty of the landscape. It's the places where humanity and nature have interacted.'

'Exactly,' Shavi said passionately. 'Which is why an industrial landscape can be as exciting as a natural one. It all comes down to single images, frozen in time. Step back, look at them, and you can see the magic instantly. Power stations gushing white clouds at sunset. Wildfowl skimming the glassy surface of the Norfolk Broads. People trooping home from the tube after work on a cold winter night, smelling cooking food, hearing music and TV noise coming from a hundred windows. Tractors rolling down a snow-covered lane.' They drifted with his lyrical words, conjuring up the pictures he described. 'And that,' he said firmly, 'is what the blue fire represents.'

The conversation came to an abrupt halt when Veitch saw the light. It floated among the trees like a golden globe, slowly and silently, almost hypnotic in their drunkeness. But they had seen too much to accept any phenomenon at face value; threats lurked in even the most mundane sight. Veitch leapt to his feet instantly, his sword gripped firmly. Church and Shavi joined him a second later.

'What is it?' Ruth whispered, but Veitch waved her silent.

The globe bobbed and weaved directly towards them, and as it drew closer they realised it wasn't alone. They could hear a faint, melodious singing, and although they couldn't understand the words, the music made them feel like they were filled with honey. The sword gradually fell to Veitch's side. Only Tom remained alert.

A second later they spied the outline of two figures approaching through the shadows. The globe was a lantern one of them was holding to light the way. The singing grew louder as they neared, and it seemed like it was a song of joy with the world, of great experiences savoured, of drinking in all life had to offer.

Veitch's languor disappeared the moment the two arrivals stepped into the light from the campfire. They were both of the Tuatha Dé Danann, their skin faintly golden, their features breathtakingly beautiful. They were obviously of the caste closest to humans, for none of them felt the squirming alien thoughts in their heads or experienced the warping perception caused by the more powerful of the gods.

One of the visitors had long, flowing fair hair and a face which seemed to permanently beam. The other looked more sensitive and thoughtful; his hair was tied in a ponytail. They both wore loose-fitting blousons open to the waist, tight breeches and boots like movie buccaneers.

'What have we here? Fragile Creatures? Alone in the woods at night?' The smiling one turned his open face from one to the other and they all found themselves smiling in return. 'Do you not realise the seasons have changed? The dark is no longer a time for Fragile Creatures to walk abroad.'

'We are not as fragile as you think.' Tom stepped from behind Shavi to present himself to the visitors.

'True Thomas!' His smile grew broader, if that were possible. 'We have missed your rhymes in the Far Country. How have you fared, good Thomas?'

'As well as could be expected, Cormorel, under the circumstances.' Tom gestured to the others. 'You have heard of the Brothers and Sisters of Dragons?'

Cormorel looked surprised for an instant, but then the smile returned and he bowed his head, politely and formally. 'It is indeed a great honour to meet the blood-champions of the Fixed Lands. The fame of the Pendragon Spirit's vessels has extended even unto our home. Hail, Quincunx. The faithi have spoke proudly of the five who are one hero.'

Veitch surveyed the two new arrivals suspiciously, poised to move at the slightest sign of danger. Church was afraid Veitch's barely contained rage would force an unnecessary confrontation, until he realised his friend was surreptitiously watching Tom for his lead.

'This is my good friend and fellow traveller, Baccharus,' Cormorel continued. The other golden one's bow was more clipped than that of his colleague.

Church and the others introduced themselves hesitantly. Tom motioned to the campfire. 'Will you join us?'

'Gladly, True Thomas. It has been too long since we enjoyed the company of *people*.' Cormorel pronounced the last word as if it were alien to him.

Cormorel and Baccharus sat together next to the fire, seemingly revelling in the event. Church took a position next to them with Tom on the other side, while the others gathered around the rest of the fire with varying degrees of discomfort; only Shavi seemed truly at ease.

Church picked up his beer to take a sip, then noticed Cormorel's eyes following his hand. 'Would you like a drink?' Church said. 'Can you drink?'

'We can eat, drink, make merry in many ways.' Cormorel eyed Ruth and Laura slyly. 'Of course, we may not appreciate the sensations in quite the same way as you Fragile Creatures. But it is the experience we seek, the keys to existence.' Church opened two cans for him and Baccharus, which they took gratefully. They sniffed the drink, sipped at it cautiously, then nodded to each other. 'When we were last here there was something made of honey,' Cormorel noted thoughtfully. 'This is more to my palate.'

'What brings you here, Cormorel?' Tom asked.

'We are reacquainting ourselves with the Fixed Lands, True Thomas. It always held a special place in our hearts. We have been denied its pleasures for too long.'

Baccharus leaned forward and said quietly, 'Here, with your truncated existence, lives burn brightly. Experience is savoured. There is a potency which we find invigorating.'

'And you are all so much fun!' Cormorel added with a flourish.

'Glad we entertain you,' Veitch muttered coldly. If Cormorel and Baccharus noticed the offence in his voice, they didn't show it.

'We are revisiting the places we knew before the Sundering,' Baccharus said, 'but so much has changed. The air is filled with unpleasant particles. The water in the rivers is sour. Even the trees are in pain. I can hear the dryads whispering their distress as I pass. You have not fared well without us.'

'Things haven't gone well on a lot of fronts,' Church agreed. Baccharus' words touched a nerve with him that made him uncomfortable. Was humanity really better off when the gods ruled over them?

Cormorel suddenly noticed Ruth staring at him curiously. 'What is it?' he asked.

'We don't know anything about you,' she replied. 'The only ones of your kind we've met before weren't exactly easy to talk to.'

'And as you can see,' Cormorel said, raising his hands, 'we are not all cut from the same cloth.'

'Tell us about you, then. About your people. Where you come from, what excites you.' Church recognised the incisive gleam in her eye; she was using her lawyerly skills to extract information which might be of use to them later.

'You are trying to define us in your terms and we cannot be defined. We simply *are*. A part of the universe and outside the universe, outside of time and all reality. We move among the stars, slipping between moments. As great as the fabric of existence, as fluid as thought.' He winked at Tom. 'It is hard to know us, eh, True Thomas? However long you spend at our side.'

'But you seem comfortable with the way we perceive reality,' Ruth continued, undeterred. 'Try to express it in terms which make sense to us.'

Cormorel nodded thoughtfully. 'Then I will try to tell you of the glory and the wonder and the anguish and the pain. Of a race cut adrift from its home, condemned to wander existence for all time.' His voice took on a mournful quality which made their hearts ache; there was something in the way the Tuatha Dé Danann manipulated sound which had a dramatic effect on human emotions; Church wondered if this explained his confused feelings for Niamh. 'We have always been, the Golden Ones. There when the universe winked into life. And we will be there when it finally whispers out. Our storytellers spin vast accounts of our days when all was well with Creation and we resided in four cities of wonder. It is the arch-memory, the homeland, to which we all dream of returning. We have never found it in our wanderings.' His voice grew sadder still. 'And I for one would say we probably never will. But the Far Lands, with their ebb and flow, and, strangely, the Fixed Lands too, are the closest in our hearts. And so we move between one and the other, and we stay and go, and we yearn. And though we remember our home and see the connections, we are always an echo away. That is our curse. Never to be at peace. We exist in the great turn of the universe. Our lives are lived at the heart of everything. And so our joys are great, and our sorrows too.' He fixed a sad eye on Ruth. 'Can you understand what it is never to have the only thing that makes you whole? Without our home, we cannot understand our place in the scheme of things. We are bereft. That is our character.'

'That is everybody's character,' Shavi said.

Baccharus began to sing in their lyrical, alien tongue; there was so much sadness in every syllable they felt as if their chests were being crushed by despair. Their heads bowed as one, and in that song they finally felt the true pain of the Tuatha Dé Danann.

When the last note of Baccharus' magical singing finally faded away, there was a brief moment of ringing silence, and then Cormorel brightened instantly. 'Come. We have driven the sadness from our being for a time and now we are free to drink deep!' He raised his beer and emptied the can, letting forth an enormous belch. Church handed him another one, which he glugged eagerly.

'Now let me tell you of joy and wonder!' he continued. 'Would you like to hear how our greatest warriors crushed the Night Walkers beneath their heel at the second battle of Magh Tuireadh? Or perhaps a personal tale of my great wassailing? Or perhaps something of the Fragile Creatures who preceded you?' He gave a strange, weighted smile that none of them could quite understand. 'Not so fragile, some of them. For your breed at least. They did not accept us with kindness in the early days.'

'I heard they resisted you quite forcefully,' Tom noted.

Cormorel mused on this for a moment. 'They were slow to

appreciate the true order of things. They were, I think, quite brutal in spirit. There was something of the Night Walkers about them.'

'A matter of perception, I would say,' Tom persisted.

Cormorel didn't seem offended by his tone. 'We crushed them in the end, you know.'

Tom nodded. 'Yet they still exert an influence. Knowledge encoded in the landscape for future generations to decipher. Information to be used to resist you.' Church and the others all looked at Tom, but he wouldn't meet their eyes. 'Their bravery is beyond question, but perhaps you have underestimated their intelligence. They were playing a very long game.' Tom let the words hang, but it was obvious he was not going to elucidate.

Cormorel maintained a curious expression for a moment, then shrugged as if it were nothing, but Church could tell Tom's comments were still playing in his mind.

'Tell me why some of you are almost like us and some are just . . . unknowable,' Ruth said.

Cormorel smiled condescendingly. 'None of us are truly like you.'

Baccharus held up his hand to silence his partner. 'No, that is a good question. Some of us are very like the Fragile Creatures, if only in our joys and sorrows. How many of our brethren would take pleasure in this, here, tonight, around this fire? Yet to me this is a moment of great pleasure, to be savoured and discussed at length once we are back in the Far Lands.' He smiled sweetly. 'We love our stories. They are the glue that holds the universe together.'

Tom bent forward to intrude in the conversation once again. 'There is a hierarchy among the Tuatha Dé Danann. They have a very complex society which is layered depending upon the power they wield. At the top is the First Family. At the bottom . . .' He motioned towards Cormorel and Baccharus.

Church flinched; it sounded distinctly like an insult. Cormorel seemed to feel the same way, for he eyed Tom askance as he sipped his beer.

'Do you hold no grudges, True Thomas, for the time you spent with us?' he asked pointedly.

'I have learned to be at peace with my situation.'

Cormorel nodded. 'That is not quite an answer to my question, but I will accept it nonetheless.' His smile grew tight. 'Did you know, True Thomas, your Queen has returned to her court under Tom-na-hurich, the Hill of Yews? Your white charger still resides there, as vital as the last day you saw him.' His eyes never left Tom's face.

Tom's face remained as emotionless as ever, but Church recognised a faint hardening. 'The point I was making,' he continued, turning to the others, 'is that power seems to come with the extent of time they have existed, and some of the Tuatha Dé Danann are much more powerful and alien than us. Although they say they have all existed since the dawn of time, it would appear that some are much older than the others. Dagda, the Allfather, was there at the beginning, and he has no connection to us at all. These two, I believe, came later.'

'Then perhaps there is an evolution, even among the gods,' Shavi mused.

Church was struck with a moment of clarity. 'And perhaps one day we will evolve to be like the Danann.'

Cormorel laughed faintly, patronisingly. 'And perhaps the arc of sky will rain diamonds.'

'It is unwise to be so arrogant, Cormorel,' Baccharus said. 'Though it is easy to accept our place in the universe, we of all races should know there is a cycle to everything. Powers rise and fall, influences ebb and flow. And the Fragile Creatures have shown their resilience in the face of the uncaring hand of existence. You see these here, you know the power they represent.'

Cormorel shrugged dismissively. 'You are a dreamer, Baccharus.'

In the brief lull that followed, Church saw his opportunity. 'How are you dealing with the Fomorii?'

Cormorel took the whisky and sipped it, smacking his lips. 'They leave us alone. We do not bother them,' he said as he passed the bottle on.

'They won't leave you alone for long. They were trying to bring Balor back. Now we've stopped them they'll just turn to something else. And you could be the target next time.'

'Oh, most certainly. And when they dare raise their hands against us, we shall strike them down.'

Church couldn't believe Cormorel's arrogance. 'Surely it would be better to attack first, before they can—'

'There are too many things to do, too many places to visit here in this world that has been denied us. We need to be making merry, drinking this fine . . .' He held up the can, then shook his head when he couldn't summon a word to describe it.

'They beat you once before. When they first emerged into this world.'

Cormorel's gaze lay on Church coldly. 'We did not fully realise the extent of their treachery. Now we are prepared.' He sighed, his annoyance dissipating quickly. 'However much I meet *people*, I find it hard to understand your inner workings. You have so little time and indulge in so little enjoyment. But you are entertaining, for all your foibles. We will continue to try to understand you.'

'Have you heard what the Fomorii are doing now?' Shavi asked.

Cormorel smiled and shook his head. 'They may burrow into the deep, dark earth and wrap themselves in shadows until the stars fall, for all I am concerned. The Night Walkers are a poisonous brood, given to plotting and hating, but they are wise and would not seek to challenge us unnecessarily. We can afford to leave them alone.' He peered at Church, his brow furrowed. 'Strangely, I see you have the taint of the Fomorii about you.'

Church explained how the Fomorii had infected him with the Kiss of Frost and how, although the *Roisin Dubh* had been destroyed, some of its dark power still lay within him.

Cormorel shook his head sadly. 'Very unwise, Brother of Dragons. You will not find any of the Golden Ones aiding you until you have expunged that taint.' He wrinkled his nose as if there were a bad smell.

'And how do I do that?' Church asked.

Cormorel shrugged. 'Perhaps if you travelled to the Western Isles, immersed yourself in the Pool of Wishes . . .' His voice trailed off; the question was obviously of no interest to him. 'Now,' he said animatedly, 'have we more drink? This is a celebration, not a conference!'

They drank deep into the night, with Cormorel and Baccharus taking it in turns to entertain with wild songs and great stories which carried with them the vast movement of the depths of the ocean or the shifting of tectonic plates. Church and the others were entranced with stories of the four lost cities of wonders, of the many, deep, mysterious mythologies which the Tuatha Dé Danann kept close to their heart, of puzzles and tricks, great battles and terrible failures, of passion and love, cruelty and hatred. The Tuatha Dé Danann, for all their alienness, were a race of powerful emotions and Church and the others could not help but be awed by the things they heard. Even Veitch gave in to a broad grin during one song, while Laura had to hide the tears that came to her eyes during another particularly sad lay. Only Tom remained impassive throughout.

And when the birdsong rose in earnest and the shadows receded at the first lick of dawn, Cormorel and Baccharus stood up and bowed, thanking the others profusely and politely for their hospitality.

'The next time you are in the Far Lands we will return the favour,' Cormorel said.

'I fear not,' Tom interjected.

Cormorel eyed him cunningly and nodded, but said nothing. And then the two of them turned and set off through the woods, their melodious singing eventually fading into the sounds of nature awakening.

'They were very charming,' Ruth said. 'The stories they told were wonderful. You could yearn for everything they've experienced, the sights they've seen. Otherworld could be such a magical place to live.'

Tom turned his back on them and headed towards the tents. 'Yes, and that is the greatest danger of all.'

CHAPTER ELEVEN

Along Darker Roads

Their dreams were filled with spires of silver and gold, of giants who cupped spinning suns in their palms, of wonders so bright and startling they could not bring them back to the world of waking. When they did finally emerge from their tents, dry-mouthed and thick-headed, the day seemed more vital than even the blazing sun and clear blue sky promised. They bathed in the cool, rushing river, ate a lazy lunch of beans on toast and drank tea while gently reminding each other of the stories they had been told, like old friends remembering favoured times.

By one p.m., Veitch was starting to get anxious. He scanned the trees continuously, and while the others laughingly told him to unwind, he refused to rest. 'We've been here too long,' he said, packing his bag. Using belts and rope and a few other items they'd picked up in town the previous day, he made a makeshift harness to hold his sword and crossbow. His jacket hung over it awkwardly – he looked like a hunchback, Laura gibed from afar – but he could reach the weapons easily.

Eventually he'd dampened the mood enough that everyone reluctantly packed up and returned to the van. 'I *liked* it here,' Ruth said with irritation. 'There was some peace and quiet for a change. And lots of nature.'

'There'll be other places.' Veitch spoke without looking at her directly, but he'd been watching her all day, surreptitiously. Her health seemed to have improved immeasurably, thanks to Tom's potions. She'd still vomited among the trees on emerging from the tent, but she was sure that was the alcohol she'd downed. He felt good to see her so well, especially knowing he'd contributed to it. He still wished she'd look at him sometimes, talk to him in the close, confiding way she'd done when they first emerged from the castle. But there was time. And he actually felt like there was hope.

They picked up the A68 heading south. Traffic normally streamed along the route, but vehicles were sparse; fewer and fewer people seemed to be travelling any great distance from their homes. The landscape was green and rolling, with a fresh breeze blowing in from the coast. Yet despite the wind, Tyneside was obscured by unnaturally dark clouds which looked suspiciously like smoke.

Veitch had studied the maps intently before they set off, weighing strategies, discarding options. He eventually decided they should head to the Peak District, where they could find enough of a wilderness to lose themselves but would be close enough to several major conurbations if they needed the security of people.

With Shavi driving they sped past Consett, which was still reeling from the terrible deprivations of the eighties, and through the open countryside west of Durham. As they passed the branch road to Bishop Auckland the traffic began to back up.

'Probably an accident,' Church mumbled, leaning forward in his seat so he could peer over the roofs of the cars ahead. A few hundred yards away a blue light flashed relentlessly. The van crept forward a few feet. Shavi wound down the window; exhaust fumes and the stink of petrol wafted in. Above the sound of idling engines, voices carried. 'Is it an accident?' Church asked.

Shavi strained to hear, then shook his head. 'I cannot make out what they are saying.'

The van moved forward again, jerked to a halt as Shavi pulled on the handbrake. Church could see blue uniforms moving around; a few standing in a huddle. There didn't seem any sense of urgency.

'No ambulances. No fire engine.' He wound down his window and hung right out for a moment. 'Can't see any wreckage,' he called back.

Eventually the van had crept forward enough for him to get a clear view. He slammed into his seat, his face concerned. 'It's a police roadblock.'

'They're not going to be doing a traffic census with the country falling apart around them.' Ruth leaned over from the back to see. They were only a few cars away from the checkpoint now.

'I've got a bad feeling about this.' Church glanced in the side mirror. There was a solid queue of cars behind them.

'Why should it be anything to do with us?' Laura said. 'No one even knows we're coming this way.'

'For all we know, there could be blocks on every road south.' Church turned to Shavi. 'When they wave the next car through, don't pull up any further. We'll play it by ear.'

Everyone's attention was focused on two policemen with clipboards who were peering into the cars to check the passengers. Church watched them for a moment; a skittering at the back of his head told him his subconscious had glimpsed something else more important. Slowly he surveyed the scene. At first he saw nothing, but a second sweep picked out a subtle detail that sent ice water running down his spine.

Three policemen stood in a tight group away from the others, watching the proceedings carefully. There seemed nothing untoward about them at first glance until one became aware of the odd way the bright sunlight was striking their skin. It created an odd sheen on the flesh that made it appear like a wax mask.

'Fomorii!' Church hissed. Without drawing attention to himself he carefully indicated the bogus police. 'They've arranged this for us, like the trap they set at Heston services. They're using the report from the Callander cop as a pretence to pull us over.'

One of the policemen with the clipboards was marching towards them, irritated that they hadn't pulled the van forward. He started to gesticulate angrily, then paused as his gaze flickered across the faces framed in the windscreen. He glanced down briefly at his clipboard, then spoke hurriedly in the radio pinned to his breast pocket.

'Shit,' Church muttered.

Shavi didn't wait for instructions. He pounded his foot on the accelerator and thrust the van into gear. There was a screech of tyres and the stink of burning rubber as he threw the wheel to one side. The van squealed out of its starting position and hurtled forward. Church braced himself on the dashboard, but everyone in the back was thrown across the floor amidst yells and curses.

Bollards went flying in all directions as the van rattled from side to side. Church had a glimpse of the fake policemen's curiously dispassionate faces as the van whirled by. Voices rose up above the whine of the engine.

'Don't hang about, Shav. Put your foot down,' Laura called out sourly from a heap somewhere in the back.

They sped down the road at ninety, but the sirens which had risen up in the background were growing louder.

'We're not going to outrun them,' Veitch said, glancing over his shoulder.

'I know.' Shavi took one look in his side mirror, then threw the van across the opposite lane in the path of a lorry. Its horn blared. Church and Veitch both swore as they instinctively threw their heads down.

The van missed the lorry by a few inches, bounced over a kerb and careened down a B road leading into the heart of the fells. Shavi gunned the engine along the deserted road and didn't let up until they had put a few miles between them and the main road. A village called Eggleston flashed by and the road branched in several directions. Shavi chose the southern route; the police would have to be lucky to follow them immediately. By then the others had just about recovered from the chase.

'You mad fucking bastard!' Veitch looked angry, but there was a note of respect in his voice.

The others in the back were fine, if bruised, but they were all aware their predicament had taken a turn for the worst.

'We're going to have to abandon the van,' Veitch said. 'After that stunt they're going to be looking out for it on every road.'

Laura peered through the rear windows at the landscape, a wind-swept smudge of greens and browns, patches of firs, areas of dark scrub beyond the fields that lined the road, leading up to the high country in the north. 'Great. We're back in *Deliverance* country. Where are we going to find another van round here?'

'We aren't.' Veitch motioned for Shavi to pull up a rough side lane which led behind a thick copse. 'We're going to keep well off the roads. All roads.' Aghast, Laura dreaded what was coming. 'We've got plenty of supplies, tents, we can live rough. If we lose ourselves out there, with all the shit that's going down they're not going to have the time or equipment to find us.'

Church nodded thoughtfully. 'It's a good plan.'

'It's *a* plan,' Laura said in disgust. 'So's lying in the middle of the road until something runs us over! Listen, I'm not a camping kind of girl. What we've done so far, fine. At least there was, you know, civilisation nearby.' She looked back out the windows. 'All I can see are blisters, no bathrooms, cold wind and rain.'

'You'll live,' Veitch said dismissively. He grabbed the books of maps. 'We'll have to use this to navigate. The way I see it, we can pick a good route south from here to the Pennines. They'd have to really want us to come after us.'

'They really want us,' Church said.

They removed all their rucksacks, tents and provisions, shared them out, then drove the van as deep into the copse as it would go. The leaf cover was thick enough to ensure it would take a while for it to be discovered. Sirens wailed across the open landscape as they moved hurriedly south away from the road. They crested a ridge where the wind gusted mercilessly, and then they were in open countryside.

The going was slow. Although Ruth was much recovered, she flagged easily and had to take many long rests, even over the first five miles. The A66, the main east-west route across the north country, appeared in the late afternoon. They waited in the thick vegetation by the roadside for nearly ten minutes until they were sure there was no traffic nearby, and then scurried across, ploughing straight into the fields beyond.

According to the map there were only four villages between them and the next main road ten miles away. The rest of the area was eerily deserted: just fields and trees and the occasional scattered farm. Although they needed to be away from the main thoroughfares, the isolation unnerved them. They knew the old gods were not the only things that had returned with the change that had come over the world; other things best consigned to the realms of myth were loose on the land; some of them frightening, if harmless, others sharp of tooth and claw, with a wild alien intelligence. None of them relished a night in the open countryside. That thought stayed with them as they marched in silence, trying to enjoy the pleasant birdsong that rang out from the hedgerows and the aroma of wild flowers gently swaying in the field boundaries.

As twilight began to fall they neared the first of the villages marked on the map. Ruth suggested they pitch camp somewhere within the village boundaries, for safety. If they were going to risk a night in the wild, there were plenty of opportunities ahead. She looked ghostly white in the fading light and she had twice headed over to the hedgerow to be sick; the whole journey was taking its toll.

Her voice sounded so exhausted they all agreed instantly, whatever their private doubts.

Darkness had fallen completely by the time they reached the village and the golden lights were gleaming welcomingly across the night-sea of the fields. They hurried down from the high ground with an exuberance born of the potent desolation that emanated from the deep gloom shrouding the rest of the landscape; sounds which they could not explain by bird or foraging mammal pressed heavy against their backs; movements of shadows against the deeper shadow seemed to be tracking them in adjoining fields.

Laura cried out at one point when a figure loomed out of the night. It was only a scarecrow; even so, there was something about it that was profoundly unnerving. The clothes seemed too new, the shape of the limbs beneath oddly realistic; as she passed she had the strangest sensation it was turning to watch her. She could sense its disturbing presence behind her as she continued down the field and suddenly she was thinking of the man on the train turned into a figure of straw. When she felt a safe distance from the scarecrow she glanced behind her, and instantly wished she hadn't. Although it could have been her troubled imagination, she was sure there were two red pinpricks staring out of the shadows beneath the pulled-down hat. Watching her.

The village was an odd mix of country money and rural decline: a handful of run-down sixties council houses cheek-by-jowl with sprawling ancient dwellings, overlooked by an Elizabethan manor house. There was only one main street, not blessed by street lights, and a couple of brief offshoots. Somehow a small pub and a tiny shop had survived the decline that had afflicted many similarly sized villages. There warm night air was thick with the aroma of clematis and roses which festooned the houses on both sides of the road. Everywhere was still and silent; although lights shone from the occasional undrawn curtains or crept out from slivers between drapes, there was no movement anywhere.

'We ought to ask if it would be all right for us to pitch our tents within the village boundaries,' Shavi said with his usual thoughtfulness. He selected a house at random and wandered up the front path among the lupins and sunflowers. His rap on the door was shocking in the stillness. A second later the curtains at the nearest window were snatched back with what seemed undue ferocity to reveal the face of a middle-aged woman. She bore an expression not of surprise or irritation at being disturbed, but of unadulterated fright. When her searching gaze fell on Shavi she waved him away furiously and drew the curtains with a similar, and very final, force. He returned to the others, looking puzzled.

'I told you,' Laura said, '*Deliverance* country. Don't bend over to tie your shoe laces. You'll be squealing like a little piggy.'

'There's always one miserable battleaxe in every village,' Ruth said. 'Knock somebody else up.'

'You don't have a trace of innuendo in your body, do you?' Laura noted.

Shavi tried the next house, then one a few doors up the street and one across the road; the response was the same in all of those that deigned to peek through the curtains: fear.

'Look, this is bleedin' crazy,' Veitch said with irritation. 'Let's try the boozer. I could do with a pint. At least they won't turn us away.'

As they moved down the main street towards the creaking sign and bright lights of the pub, Church slipped in next to Tom. 'Looks like they've been having some trouble here.'

'Hardly surprising, an isolated place like this. They should count themselves lucky they're still hanging on. Remember Builth Wells?'

Church recalled the deserted town, the preying things lurking in the shadows waiting for new blood. 'From their reactions I don't think it's the kind of place we should be out sleeping under canvas.'

'I think you're right. Let's hope the inn has some rooms.'

The pub was The Green Man, echoing the name of the tavern on Dartmoor devastated by the Wild Hunt; another strange, disturbing connection in a world now filled with them.

Church led the way in to the smoky bar; flagged floor, stone fireplace with cold ashes in the grate, dark wood tables, chairs and bar, an old drinking den, a hint of establishment. Small wall lamps provided focused pools of light which threw the rest of the place into comforting shadow.

Drinkers, mainly men, were scattered at tables and along the bar, a surprising number for a small village pub at that time of night. They heard the hubbub of hushed voice as they swung the door open, but the moment they were all inside every conversation stopped and the drinkers, as one, turned and stared, their expression shifting through the same emotions: fear, relief, suspicion, surprise.

'*Deliverance*,' Laura repeated in a singsong voice as she marched over to the bar.

Veitch leaned over to whisper to Church. 'Nah, it's like that other film. *American Werewolf.* The Slaughtered Lamb. Rik Mayall. And that bloke who did the tea adverts.'

'Brian Glover.'

'Yeah, him.'

Church glanced round, not sure whether to smile at the ludicrousness of the response or feel disturbed at whatever lay behind it.

'You know,' Ruth broke into the conversation, 'sooner or later someone's going to say *Folk don't come round here much* in a hick accent.'

Laura fixed a cold stare on the barman, who appeared to have frozen midway through pouring a pint of bitter. 'You see these scars?' she said pointing to her face. 'The last landlord who didn't get me a drink quick came off much worse.'

'Sorry.' The barman was a side of beef in his fifties with curly ginger hair and rock 'n' roll sideburns. 'We don't get many new faces in here these days.'

Ruth exchanged a secret smile with Church.

The barman checked his watch. 'Just stopping off for a quick one on your way to . . . ?' He waited for her to finish off his enquiry.

She ignored him, glanced along the optics. 'Better get me a big vodka. Ice, no mixer. Make it a treble. I've had a day of hard labour and I'm a wilting flower who's not used to that kind of treatment. Oh, and whatever this lot want.'

The barman didn't make any other attempt at conversation; he seemed thrown by Laura's demeanour, as if she were speaking to him in a foreign language. They took their drinks to a gloomy corner and the only two free tables, which they pulled together.

'It certainly has character,' Shavi noted as he scanned the room while sipping on his mineral water.

'If you like wall-to-wall crazy and forties horror movie cliché.' Laura swigged her drink gloomily. 'I don't know why we couldn't have stayed in the city.'

'What do you think's going on?' Church asked.

Tom wiped the cider from his drooping, grey moustache. 'Just a local problem. Otherworld was filled with the detritus of a million nightmares, little ones and big ones, and I presume most of them have found their way back here.'

There was something comforting about the age-old atmosphere of the pub after the fearful atmosphere out in the night. They settled back in their chairs to enjoy their drinks, appreciating the half-light which gave them a measure of cover from the suspicious glances. While Laura amused herself by staring out the few locals who dared to look their way, the others discussed their apparent success in evading the Fomorii. 'They're obviously determined to catch us,' Church noted. 'But it was interesting they used subterfuge. We must have set them back so much in Edinburgh they're afraid of taking an over-the-top approach.'

'When have you known them not to be over-the-top?' Veitch noted.

'He's right,' Ruth said. 'There was something about this that reeked of desperation, not revenge. You'd think they'd have gone for the nuclear option.'

Tom pressed his glasses back against the bridge of his nose. 'I think their true motivations will become apparent very quickly.'

'So in the meantime let's make the most of this lull and enjoy ourselves,' Laura said sharply. 'You lot, you're like, *Let's look for some big, heavy stuff to depress us.* You know, fun is an option.'

Church smiled, gave her leg a squeeze under the table. He was surprised to see the palpable relief on her face.

Before they could say any more a man sauntered over, holding a half-drunk pint. He was in his late twenties, with a soft, rounded face and a conventional, side-parted haircut. Unlike many of the others in the bar, he seemed relaxed and easy-going. 'Hello,' he said, 'I'm the official welcome wagon. Max Michaels. My parents had a thing about alliteration,' he added half-apologetically. 'You probably think it's all a bit

strange in here. Which it is, make no mistake. Mind if I sit down?'
Once they'd agreed he pulled up a chair; there was an old-fashioned
politeness about him.

'Look, can I be blunt?' he said. 'You all look like intelligent people.
You obviously know there are some very strange things going on all
over.' He warmed when he saw the recognition in their faces, then
asked them further questions until he was sure they understood the
change that had come over the world. 'That's a relief. There's nothing
worse than having to tell some unbelieving idiot the world has become
a fairybook. So I can talk plainly, that's good. Now I haven't quite
figured out what's happening, but the way I see it, for some reason
reality has skewed away from science to the supernatural. The way
appliances, cars, everything, fails suddenly for no apparent reason. The
sudden rise in coincidences, premonitions, prophetic dreams. Do you
get where I'm coming from?'

Church nodded. 'We've experienced all that. And more.'

'Good, good. If that was the end of it, it would have been bearable.' A
shadow crossed Max's face. 'A few weeks ago a local farmer came in
here raving about this strange sighting he'd had in one of his fields. It
was a great laugh for everybody. We all thought he'd been inhaling too
many organophosphates. Then some of the other farmers claimed
they'd seen something. So then we decided we'd got our very own
Beast of Bodmin. You know, some escaped panther living in the wild.
Only it didn't really fit with the descriptions . . .' He chewed on a
knuckle briefly, his thoughts wandering. 'And then things just went
crazy. People went crazy. You can't just adapt overnight to having the
whole world turned upside down. There were . . . a lot of casualties.
Psychologically speaking. Depression, wouldn't leave their houses—'

'We saw that on our way here,' Veitch said.

'No, that's because it's dark. You don't move round much after dark,
not if you can help it. A few of us meet up here mob-handed, to plan. I
suppose, really, just to keep some kind of normality ticking over. We
see each other home.' He took a deep draught of his beer, then grew
animated. 'The problem's been the isolation. When all the phone
systems went off-line and the postal system was suspended, and all
the media, we were just left to stew in our own juices. It would have
helped if we could have found out if other people were suffering too.
Misery isn't so bad if you know it's been spread around.' He laughed
humourlessly.

'Believe me, it's been spread around,' Ruth said. There was something about Max that she was warming to; a geniality, perhaps, or a lack
of cynicism.

'Yeah, so I gather. I'm a reporter by trade, a stringer for the nationals. 'Course, when the phone lines went down, that put paid to that career. Thank God for the food-sharing system we've got going. Anyway, journalism, you know, it's in your blood. I *wanted* to know what was happening, and I wanted to let everybody else know. So we set up a jungle drums news service, passing information to the next village along, and they would pass it along to the next, and so on.' He shrugged in embarrassment. 'It was the best we could do. We *had* to know.'

'I admire your ingenuity,' Ruth said. 'Getting it set up so quickly. Most people wouldn't have bothered.'

'Information is power. I've had that drummed into me ever since I started on a local rag.' He seemed warmed by the praise. 'We've managed to stretch from Appleby to Durham so far. And you wouldn't believe how much trouble we had setting that up. Some bloody civil servant or council twat stumbled across it at some point and tried to stop it. Can you believe it? He was ranting on about D Notices and not causing a panic. Then he set out to the next village in his car at twilight and we never heard from him again.' There was a long pause while he sipped his beer. 'You've got to adapt, haven't you? Nothing makes sense, but if you don't get your head round it you're just . . .' He searched for the right words. 'Driving in a car to the next village, thinking it's a normal trip.'

'You've done a good job here,' Ruth said. He seemed to need the comfort; when he relaxed the strain was evident on his face.

'So tell me what you know,' he said, suddenly excited. 'Anything will help. Any little thing.'

'Any little thing,' Church repeated with an amused expression.

They didn't see anything wrong with filling Max in on many of the things they'd experienced since they'd got together. A hour and a half had passed before they'd finished and Max looked shellshocked. 'That's amazing. Stupendous.' He eyed them suspiciously for a moment, but it was obvious from their expressions that they weren't spinning him a yarn. 'So you're some kind of heroes. Basic, day-to-day people standing up against unimaginable odds. This is just what people have been waiting to hear!'

'You've got it all wrong,' Church said with a dismissive laugh. 'From our perspective it looks very different.'

'You're right there,' Laura added grumpily.

'No, don't you see! This is something I can do! Tell the world about what you're doing – or at least the world as far as I can reach. Give people hope. You know, war reporting. Because that's what it is.'

Veitch shook his head with irritation. 'We don't need that. A bloody spotlight shining on us all the time! No way. Anyway, we wouldn't even recognise ourselves once you've finished. I know what bleedin' reporters are like.'

'You owe this to the people. It's part of your job—'

'We don't owe anybody anything.' There was an unpleasant harshness to Veitch's voice.

'We were thinking about camping in the village somewhere,' Ruth said to change the subject.

'You can't do that.'

'No, you're probably right there. How about getting some rooms here?'

Max glanced over at the barman. 'I'll have to ask Geordie. I don't know . . . In the current climate I'm not sure how keen he'll be to have strangers in the place.' He sighed. 'But we can't send you out into the night either, so he'll have to.'

Tom leaned across the table to catch his attention. 'You haven't told us what's going on here.'

'Yes, of course.' He scrubbed the hair at the nape of his neck, suddenly uneasy. 'Well, it's not like we *really* know. We've all glimpsed things out there in the fields, but what they truly are—'

'What do they look like?' Ruth asked.

'We've only seen flashes, but we pieced things together from different accounts. When they move they're like sheets blowing in the wind. They seem to change and twist all the time, so they look, you know, not really solid, like they're not quite there. But they are.' He took another swig of beer to moisten his drying mouth. 'They've got teeth. One of the farmers saw them go through a sheep like it was a threshing machine. Turned the poor beast into chunks. That was the start of it.'

'But not the end,' Church said.

Max shook his head. 'While they were out in the fields they were terrifying, but we could deal with it. They weren't *here*, you know? We were safe in our castles.'

'But once they'd found their footing they began to come into the village.' Tom nodded at the familiar pattern. 'More prey, and easier to catch.'

'They came into town one night like a storm blowing in, sweeping up the High Street, swirling around all the houses. Everyone knew what was out there in the fields, so they didn't really venture out that much at night. Anyway, they found their victim. Mrs Ransom. She lived on her own in the big house at the top of the High Street. Quite well-to-do, but everyone got on with her, I suppose. There was a lot of blood, and . . .' His words dried up. As he stared blankly into the dregs of his pint, the awful strain was apparent on his face. 'After that the place just shut down. It was hard to go anywhere during the day. A farm hand, Eric Rogers, went missing in the fields. They found him. Part of him. Some people thought they'd try to drive away to the city . . . some did, but most were afraid even to go anywhere in their cars. We were virtually prisoners in our houses. Every night we barricaded ourselves in, and every morning we'd run out to meet here.'

'It's a wonder you managed to carry on living your lives,' Veitch said.

'We didn't, at first. But we began to get an idea of their patterns. They'd be in the village every night after dark, but we didn't actually see them in the environs during the day. Just on the outskirts, in the fields and the roads. Then we realised something. After Mrs Ransom, they hadn't taken anybody else from their house, even though a lot of the barricades were pretty flimsy things. But one night Jimmy Oldfield, who was this old lush from Recton Close, he got a bit funny in the head from all the pressure. He'd been in here drinking all day, telling everybody he'd had enough, that he was going to make a stand. Everybody thought it was just the booze talking.' A guilty expression crossed his face.

'Anyway, that night they seemed to know Jimmy had the least defences because they hovered all around his door for ages, but they couldn't get in, didn't even try, really. That's what the people holed up across the road said. But Jimmy . . .' Max shook his head slowly. 'I reckon he'd pickled his brain with all the whisky he'd drunk. He came to the door with his shotgun. All those awful things were gathered on his front garden, poised, like. Ready to attack. Jimmy opened the door just a crack to shove the shotgun out and that was it. They were in. There wasn't anything left of him the next day.' He sighed, finished his beer. 'So the upshot is, they only come into the village at night, and however dangerous they are, they can't get into your place if the door's shut tight.'

Veitch shrugged. 'It's a bit of a bastard not to be able to go out at night, but it shouldn't be too much trouble to keep everyone safe.'

'You'd think, wouldn't you?' Max waved his glass for the barman to pour him another pint. 'Anyway, after somebody got killed they never bothered us for a while so we could pretty much go about our lives as normal. We used the time to tell everybody in the village what we knew and to make sure all the old folk had good defences. They all got the rule: nobody opens their door after sunset.'

They could all see what was coming. 'But somebody else died,' Church said.

'Not just one, three people. It doesn't make any sense! The things can't get inside if the house is shut up. And everybody knows they have to keep their doors locked at all times. So tell me how people are dying?' He took his drink from the barman and drained half of it too quickly.

'People do silly, dangerous things even when they know they shouldn't,' Ruth suggested.

Max shook his head. 'One of them, Dave Garson, I was only speaking to him the afternoon he died. He was terrified. There was no way he was going to open his door. But he was gone the next day. His wife and kids were hysterical. They said the things came bursting in after they'd gone to bed and Dave was finishing off his beer in the kitchen—'

'Maybe you're wrong about them getting into locked houses,' Church began.

Max shook his head furiously. 'That's not it. We're as sure as sure about that. We've been watching them. They can't get in.' He turned around to call over an aristocratic-looking man who was drinking a short at the bar. He was tall and thin, probably in his late sixties, with white hair and a handlebar moustache. He reminded Church of an ex-army type.

'This is Sir Richard,' Max said as he made the introductions. 'He lives in the Manor House on the green. We decided to form an action group to gather information on these things.'

'Surveillance is one thing I am *very* good at,' Sir Richard stressed. 'We set up a good team around the village, keeping watch all night long. We tracked the movements of these things. Took a few pot-shots at them to see if we could do them any damage. No luck, unfortunately. Like shooting fog.'

'And they definitely can't get into shut-up houses, right, Sir Richard?' Max said.

'Absolutely. They'll gather at the door, but never go inside. The most damnable thing. We honestly have no idea what to do next.'

Having made his point, he retreated to the bar. Max leaned forward and whispered, 'Ex-Tory MP for his sins, but he's a pillar of the community, great at organising things and getting people involved. In fact, I'm surprised how much this nightmare has brought everyone together. I used to think this was a right stuffy place, but since all this started I've seen a different side of all sorts of people. It seems to have brought out the best in everyone. Ironic, isn't it?'

For the rest of the evening they mulled over this point. They had all seen the good that had come out of hardship and suffering, but however much they argued, they couldn't agree if what they had lost was a fair price for what they had gained.

Geordie the barman had some spare rooms he used to let out to foreign tourists touring the area, but he agreed to give them up reluctantly. He was a little warmer when they promised to pay handsomely if he could arrange some food. He disappeared into the kitchen and forty-five minutes later came back with some cold ham, mashed potatoes and peas. Laura moaned about the meat 'infecting' her vegetables, but after their hard day's walking the others polished off their dinner and washed it down with more beer.

Max left them alone while they ate, returning to the other drinkers to pass on what he had learned. Church watched their expressions move through disbelief to a dumbfounded acceptance and then something approaching awe. It made him feel uncomfortable.

At eleven p.m., all the drinkers gathered together at the door. Church could see the apprehension jumping from one to the other like electric sparks, lighting their faces for just a fleeting moment. Max maintained his cheeriness somehow and threw a bright wave before wrenching open the door and peering out into the oppressive darkness of the street. They all hovered for a moment, and then some kind of circuit was thrown in their minds and they surged out. Church could almost hear the unified exhalation of fear. Then, with a rustle and a bang, they were gone and the door was shut.

'Will they be all right?' Ruth asked.

Geordie leaned his heavy frame across the bar. 'With a prayer. They've done it enough times, got it down to a fine art. They don't take any risks.'

'It would be easier to stay at home.' Church was surprised how concerned Ruth appeared.

'That'd be a bit like giving up, now wouldn't it?'

'I suppose so.'

After he'd finished wiping up, Geordie led them through the back and up a twisting staircase to a roomy first floor. Several bedrooms lay off a dog-leg corridor. They were all Spartan – a double bed, chair, dresser, wash basin – but they were clean and the beds were all made up with crisp linen.

'What time's breakfast?' Veitch asked.

'You're paying, you decide,' Geordie said grumpily. 'Gi' me a knock when you're ready.'

Church and Laura took the first room. Veitch angled to share with Ruth, but she opted for Shavi.

'Looks like it's you and me, son,' Tom said wryly.

'Whoop de doo.' Veitch kicked the door shut. 'He's definitely a queen, right?'

Laura made love to Church voraciously, pinning him to the mattress and riding him so roughly the clatter of the bedframe against the wall left no one in the building in any doubt what was happening. After ten minutes, Veitch hammered on the wall and shouted something indecipherable but obviously angry and obscene.

'Just 'cause you aren't getting any!' Laura yelled back. 'One-hand boy!'

Her passion brought Church to an early climax, but she didn't seem to want anything in return. She collapsed next to him, flushed and laughing at her exertion. 'Just call me Rodeo Girl.'

Their breathing subsided slowly as they stared at the ceiling until all they could hear were the creaks of the old house settling in the night. During the sex, Church's doubts had drifted to the back of his head, but there in the silence they returned in force. More than anything he didn't want to hurt Laura. He knew her better than all the others, her well of insecurity, her secret fears and lack of confidence, the kind of things she would be horrified if he said he recognised in her. Yet he seemed incapable of getting any handle on his emotions as far as she was concerned.

She seemed to sense what he was thinking, for she smiled and put a hand firmly across his mouth. 'Less is more. Don't ruin things with intellect.'

He took her hand away gently. 'I just want to be honest with you. You know . . . no false pretences. I—'

She clamped the hand down even more firmly. 'Churchill, this is me you're talking to. Do you think I'm going to be led up the garden path like some dreamy-eyed girlie? I'm a mature adult. Without wishing to define mature. I'm able to make choices. I know what I'm getting into. I know the inside of your head looks like something out of *Saving Private Ryan*. Back in Edinburgh I let the pathetic . . . yes, even desperate . . . side get out of control. But if it happens again, I'm going to put my own eyes out.'

She took her hand away. He went to speak and she clamped it down again, laughing in enjoyment at the small power.

'So the bottom line is, don't worry. No strings. If things work out, that's fine. If not, well, at least we tried. So let's just enjoy the moment.'

He wriggled free and buried his face half in the pillow so she couldn't get at him again. Laughing, he said, 'You're sure.'

'Sure as shit, big boy.'

They play-fought briefly, unable to represent their feelings any other way, before falling back side by side, giggling. Once they'd quietened again, Laura said thoughtfully, 'You know what, I don't take anything for granted any more.'

'What do you mean?'

'I used to drift through life accepting everything that came my way. Didn't get too excited because that was the way it was. It was just . . . nice. You know that tingly feeling you get in the pit of the stomach? I get that all the time these days. Sometimes just looking at shit, like the way the sun hits the fields. Like the smell of really good food. Or woodsmoke? Have you noticed how good that smells? I get excited when we all have a good conversation, you know how it is when the ideas are bouncing around and I'm bitching like hell and people are batting it back at me. The world's falling apart and people are dying out there, and I'm sitting thinking these are the best days of my life. What does that say about me?'

'It's not just you.'

'What?'

'I feel it too. I think we all do. What does it say? Something about the way life should be lived, I guess.'

'Urrp. Heaviness alarm. Why can't you just say it means I'm fucked in the head and leave it at that?'

'Because you're not.' He felt a sudden wave of affection for her. 'You don't do yourself any favours, you know. Why do you keep acting out this, shall we say, *difficult* persona?'

'It's a natural selection process. I know anybody who fights their way through that crap has got to be all right. Anybody who gets turned away by it isn't worth the time or effort.'

'There are easier ways—'

'No, there aren't. You can't trust anybody at face value. They might be smiling and pleasant and say nice things, but what's going on inside? It's a life lesson, idiot-brain. I'd have thought you would have learned that by now. This is the only way I can work out who's all right.'

The thought stayed with him as he floated in the warm peace of the room. The complexities of her character intrigued him, but there was something deep in her words that kept nagging at him, hinting at something important. He wrestled with it for a while, but it was stubbornly resistant and before he knew it he was drifting off into sleep.

Veitch relaxed once the sound of Church and Laura's love-making faded, but it had obviously left him with a surfeit of irritation. He prowled the room like an animal, stripped to the waist, the brilliant colours of his tattoos rippling with the movement of his muscles.

'Will you sit down! You're making me feel uncomfortable,' Tom snapped.

Veitch glared at him, said nothing at first. He slumped in the chair and removed the crossbow from the harness hanging on the end of the bed. From a little leather bag he took an oily rag and proceeded to carry out his nightly ritual of cleaning the weapon and ensuring it was in full working order. The routine seemed to give him some comfort.

'Your skills as a fighter seem to be coming on apace,' Tom noted. 'Do you think you're up to it?'

Veitch grunted, but didn't rise to the obvious bait. 'You're supposed to be the hero of a country – or so the stories say. Why don't you do something fucking heroic?'

Now it was Tom's turn to grow cold. 'You don't believe stories. They're there to *make* heroes so weak people have something to look up to. Try the real world some time. You'll see people making difficult choices, compromises, trying to do the best they can, despite everything.'

'So you're not a hero? You've got a rep based on a pack of lies.'

'Don't stick your ignorance on a flag. You'll regret it. Believe me.'

'You're dead weight, if you ask me.'

Tom took out the tin in which he kept his drugs and began to roll himself a joint. 'You have too much anger.'

'Life makes me angry.'

'You make yourself angry.'

Veitch focused on the crossbow.

'You wish you were something else,' Tom continued. 'You're angry with yourself that you're not.'

'You sound like a fucking social worker.'

Tom lit the joint and inhaled. 'You know that old story about the scorpion being given a ride across a rushing river by some other animal . . . I can't remember which one now.'

'Yeah, I know it. The scorpion promises not to sting, but halfway across he does because he can't help himself so they both die.'

'People always reel out these trite little stories as if they're supposed to be some great, unshakeable wisdom. There is no great, unshakeable wisdom, not that anyone on this planet can see, anyway. Everything is open to debate. That story was supposed to show people are prisoners of their nature. It's a sad story really. It says there is no hope for redemption. You will keep repeating your mistakes until you die. Don't you think that's sad?'

686

Veitch said nothing.

'I happen to believe people can change. That they can grow wise with the years, slough off the skin they were presented with as children. If they really want to.'

Veitch continued working on the crossbow as if he hadn't heard Tom at all. The room slowly filled with the fragrant hash smoke. When he did finally speak, Veitch's voice was miraculously drained of all the rage that had fractured it before. 'I think that Laura tart is the one who's trying to sell us down the river.'

'Why do you say that?'

'It's obvious, innit?' A pause. 'Don't you reckon?'

'I don't know. I think it might be you.'

Veitch looked up in shock. 'What are you talking about?'

Tom shrugged. 'Just an instinct.'

Veitch searched his face for a moment to see if it was another wind-up, but as usual couldn't tell a thing from Tom's impassive features. 'Listen, I'm doing the right thing here.' His voice trembled again from the repressed emotion. 'I know everybody thinks it must be me because I never played it straight before. These people mean more to me than anything. What we're doing . . . for the country, you know . . . for everybody . . . I'd give up my life for that.' His stare challenged Tom to argue.

'I stand corrected,' Tom replied in such a way that Veitch couldn't tell whether he meant it or not. 'But it's not wise to go pointing the finger without evidence.'

'Aren't you worried about the fact that one of us might be fucking everybody up?'

'I'm aware of it, certainly. But you can't take everything the dead say at face value. You've seen evidence of that. Be patient. As long as we remain on our guard then we will be better placed to protect ourselves. But a constant and high level of suspicion for those we are relying on is not helpful.'

'Is this some kind of pep talk?'

'See it how you want.'

Veitch finished the crossbow and returned it to the harness. 'I'll take your advice. Fair enough?'

Pain, terrible pain. Torture instruments that flared in the dark with the glow of heat. The animal stink, and those voices that were not voices, like the jungle at twilight. And Ruth thinking, *I can't take any more hurt. It would be easier to be dead.*

But they wouldn't relent. Another cruel blade, another corkscrew attachment, and hammers. Tears burning her eyes, throat constricting so tightly there was no air for her lungs. And then the scream, raw and bloody.

The scream.

'It is okay. You are having a bad dream.'

Thrashing wildly, still screaming, still torn between the hell of the torture chamber and the darkness of the room. And then, gradually, reality intruding, Shavi's face forming out of the pale shape that appeared before her eyes.

'It is okay,' he repeated. Gently, he pulled her towards him. Her tense muscles slowly relented and she laid her head against his chest, her mind spinning, her heart thundering, the tears still rolling down her cheek.

'I'll never forget,' she whispered. 'Never.'

It might have been Ruth's scream that woke them all, but within minutes in their separate rooms they all became aware of something going on in the street beneath their windows. At first it was hard to see anything in the deep dark, but they could pick out movement swirling up and down the street in shallow gusts. It took a second or two to realise what they were seeing until Max's description came back to them: *like sheets blowing in the wind.*

The motion itself was eerie in its unworldliness, but occasionally they picked out tiny sparks of red light they all knew must be eyes. Laura felt the *frisson* most acutely when she remembered the scarecrow they had passed on the way in.

Whatever the creatures were, they were like a force of nature in the way they howled along the streets, sending gates crashing open and shut. But Sir Richard had been right: they did not enter any houses.

That was almost enough to calm the group's jangling nerves, until ten minutes later they all heard an unmistakable sound, high pitched and insistent like the wind in the trees, yet somehow strangely unnatural; it made them all feel queasy. A second later the creatures began to sweep back towards the fields. But as they passed the pub, another noise rose up, briefly, along with a flash of something pale caught among the flurry of movement. It sounded very much like a child crying.

a heap of Broken Images

Despite the danger, Veitch and Church were out of the pub and racing up the High Street within seconds, but there was no sign of where the creatures could have gone. The night was too dark, the countryside too empty. It didn't take them long to locate the victim's home; the shrieks could be heard across the village.

A woman in her late twenties clutched at the door jamb of one of the council houses, her face ruptured by grief. She was trying to propel herself out into the street while a man and another woman fought to restrain her, their expressions of deep dread revealing their motivation. Her dyed black hair flailed all around as she howled like an animal: sometimes Veitch and Church picked out the name Ellie among the incomprehensible wailings of a ruined life.

Lights were coming on all around and soon other neighbours were at the scene. One of them forced some tablets into her mouth and shortly after they managed to calm her enough to get her inside. Veitch and Church waited patiently until the man who had been holding the mother back ventured out, hollow eyes staring out of a chalk face. He was barefoot, still wearing grey pyjama bottoms and a Metallica T-shirt.

'What happened?' Church asked quietly.

It took a second or two for him to register their presence and even then he seemed unable to focus on them. Tears leaked out of the corner of his eyes. He furiously scrubbed them away, saying, 'Sorry, mate, sorry. Fuck.' He leaned on the gatepost, shaking. 'She said it was locked! Fuck.' He turned round to look at the open front door. It had once been painted white, but now it was a dirty cream, scuffed with old bootprints near the bottom, some of them very small. Inside the hall the light was stark and unpleasant. The man turned back, stared at them for a long moment as if he were about to say something and then he staggered towards the house next door.

Once he was inside, Veitch slipped down the path to examine the door. 'Look at this,' he said pointing to the jamb. The wood was splintered. 'They forced it open. That Max was wrong.'

Church ran his fingertip over the damaged jamb. 'Maybe those things are learning new tricks.'

The smell of frying bacon, eggs and sausages filled the pub. As the group sat around the tables in the bar, they felt convinced that even aromas were more vibrant in the new world. But even that simple joy couldn't dispel the dismal air that had grown after the night's events. Talk turned quickly to whether the village should be evacuated en masse if the safety of the occupants could no longer be guaranteed.

'That's up to the villagers,' Tom pointed out, 'but I would say they would be loath to leave their homes, even in the face of such a trial. In this time of crisis, stability is vitally important.'

'That poor woman. Her only child.' Ruth's face still looked a little grey; since her ordeal she rarely gained her colour until after breakfast. 'We have to do something to help.'

'As if we haven't got enough on our hands,' Laura said sourly.

'No, I agree with Ruth,' Church said, to Laura's obvious annoyance. 'We can't leave these people high and dry if there's anything at all we can do.'

'Max said the creatures leave the village alone for a while after they have secured a victim,' Shavi reiterated. 'That gives us a little time.'

'Then we should start straight away.' Church broke open his egg with his fork. 'Talk to everyone we can. There must be something we can use, some kind of defence that will keep these things out—'

'I don't believe you lot,' Laura snapped. 'One minute you're talking about this big mission to save the world, the next you're taking time out to save the waifs and strays. Anything could happen here. You saw what was going on last night. There's no guarantee one of us won't get hurt or worse, and then we won't be able to do what's expected of us. I say we save ourselves.'

Veitch eyed her coldly. 'It's all about doing the right thing too.'

'What must it be like to be you?' Laura sneered. 'All those echoes from that one thought rolling around your head—'

'Least it's a good thought.'

'Okay, okay!' Church held up his hands to calm the bickering. 'Let's see what we can do.'

As they filed out into the sunlit street, Shavi hung back until he caught Church's eye. They stood behind in the pub doorway while the others went off to explore the village. The air was already hot and filled with clouds of butterflies drawn by the heavy perfume of the roses. Bees buzzed lazily from bloom to bloom.

Church could see from Shavi's expression it wasn't going to be good news. 'What's wrong?' he asked.

'I find this very hard to say,' Shavi began hesitantly, 'but as soon as we have finished our duties here I am afraid I will have to leave.'

Church's heart sank. 'You can't leave, Shavi! For God's sake . . .' He floundered around for the correct words. 'We're relying on you. You're the backbone of the whole team. The only stable one among us!'

'I fear you are not doing yourself or any of the others justice. Please do not make this difficult for me. I understand my responsibilities to you and all, and to the mission destiny has delivered to us. It is just—'

'What?' There was an unnecessary hardness to Church's voice.

'It was I who freed Maponus. And every life that is cut down by his hand is on my conscience.'

'Look, we asked you to seek him out and free him. You couldn't have—'

Shavi held up a hand to silence his friend. 'Whether I knew what I was unleashing or not is immaterial. I certainly exhibited arrogance in my approach which allowed me to be manipulated. Even without apportioning blame, any deaths are my deaths. I have to do something to make amends—'

'Like what?'

'Help to imprison him again.'

'Shavi, with all due respect, what can you do? It took a collection of the most powerful people in the land to bind him originally. And not all of them survived.'

'I do not know what I can do. But if there is a chance that I can do anything I have to seize it. I will seek out the Bone Inspector and offer my help. Perhaps the two of us can find some way—'

'Shavi, I'm not having any of this.'

Shavi smiled. 'This goes far beyond our friendship and your leadership, Jack. I am burdened by this responsibility.'

Church tried to dredge up some relevant argument. He felt massive failure for all of them staring him in the face. 'The Pendragon Spirit called us together to complement each other with our abilities. Losing you would be like losing an arm – there's no way we'd be able to carry on.'

'I am not leaving for ever, Jack. Just until I have found a solution. Then I will return to help in—'

'Okay, stay a little longer. Take some time to weigh things up—'

'I have—'

'No, listen. The woman in the Watchtower who set us on this path originally. Her name's Niamh. There's some kind of bond between us. Before you make any move, let me contact her. She might have a

691

solution. For God's sake, Maponus is one of their own. They have to help!'

Shavi looked unsure.

'I'm not asking you to change your mind. Just defer it until I've tried this path.'

Shavi nodded politely. 'All right. I will do that.'

As Church watched Shavi wander down the summery street towards the others, he couldn't escape the feeling that the burdens which had been placed on him as leader were growing with each day. Sooner or later he knew he would be found lacking.

'We should question all the information we've been given. Go back to first principles.' Ruth checked the list of victims Max had given her. She was enjoying the opportunity to use her naturally incisive abilities on a problem rather than dwelling on the queasiness and weakness that afflicted her too often now.

Tom sighed in a manner which suggested he could barely find the energy for the task at hand.

Ruth knew him too well to rise to the bait. 'I think I've found out your special ability, Tom,' she said without raising her eyes from the list.

'Oh?'

'Directional irritation. You turn it on, pick out a target, boom.' He snorted in such a comically affronted way Ruth couldn't help a smile. 'Look,' she continued, 'we know nothing about these things. If the information is flawed, any response we decide on could be flawed too. And that might be the *fatal* flaw.'

He shrugged dismissively. 'There are more important things—'

'Don't start that again. We've made the decision. Let's stick to it.'

He snatched the list from her and compared the addresses to the village around him. 'At least the last three are in the same area. We can turn this around quickly.'

With Laura and Veitch talking to some of the villagers who had seen the creatures and Shavi already at the house of the first victim, Mrs Ransom, they headed off to the cluster of other victims. The addresses were all in the vicinity of Recton Close, where the drunk Jimmy Old-field had lived and died. His council house stood empty, the garden gate wide open, one window shattered from what was probably a randomly thrown stone; one of the local kids, Ruth guessed.

Not too far away they could see the house of the previous night's victim. The curtains were tightly drawn. They thought it best not to trouble the recently bereaved mother and instead concentrated on the neigbours of Oldfield and the other two people who had died.

There was little to distinguish those who had been taken. Oldfield might have been an alcoholic, but he was fondly regarded by those who lived in the small pocket of sixties housing. Of the other two, a young milkman who had been laid off by the local dairy just before the troubles and a middle-aged cleaning woman who worked at some of the more well-to-do houses, there was little to suggest they would have been foolish enough to allow access to their houses after dark.

Ruth and Tom pored over the information they had gathered on a bench overlooking the village green. 'It's too much of a coincidence to think all these people could have mistakenly let those things in,' Ruth said. 'And that poor woman last night . . . She'd seen at first hand what could happen with her neighbours—'

'Unless the child opened the door,' Tom ventured.

'Maybe these things are some sort of sirens,' Ruth mused. 'Something about them hypnotises people into letting them in.'

'Possibly. But Ryan said the door he inspected last night had been broken open.'

Ruth chewed on her knuckle, watching the ducks waddle down to the pond in the centre of the green. It was quiet and lazy in the late-morning sun and there was no sign anywhere across the picture-postcard village of any of the suffering that descended on it with nightfall. 'Then everyone *must* be mistaken,' she said. 'These creatures have to be able to get in when they want.' Even as she said it something didn't seem quite right, but whatever it was stayed hidden in her subconscious.

'No, I cannot stress strongly enough that these creatures cannot get into any property that is shut off. Even a closed but not locked door seems to deter them.' Sir Richard stood erect and still, as if he were on parade outside the sprawling, detached house of Mrs Ransom at the far end of the High Street. The residence was cool beneath the shade of several mature trees around the low-walled front garden, while the building itself was covered in a sweet-smelling mass of clematis.

Shavi nodded politely. 'I hope you do not mind me going over this again—'

'No, no, old chap, not at all.' Sir Richard adjusted the Panama hat that shaded his eyes. 'I know you're only trying to help. But, really, we have got a very efficient defence force here. We've done everything in our power to protect the village. As to those creatures, well, I've watched them with my own eyes, and I am a very well-trained observer. I am in no doubt of their limitations.'

'Then how can—'

'No idea at all. People make mistakes, leave a door ajar at twilight. It's easily done.' There was a note of sadness in his voice.

Shavi looked up at the dark face of the large, old house. 'A lovely property.'

'It certainly is. Been in the Ransom family for generations. Sadly Alma was the last of the line. I come down here every now and again to keep an eye on the old place, make sure the local yobs don't start tearing it apart. It's a very, very sad situation.'

'She was the first?'

He nodded. 'An awful wake-up call to all of us.' He motioned to the rambling, well-heeled properties that lay all around. 'You think you're impregnable here, in this beautiful countryside, and this historic village. It was such a safe haven away from the rigours of modern society. I retired here after I lost my seat at the last election. Somewhere to tend the roses, enjoy a relaxing life for a change. And now . . .' His words dried up.

'Everyone has suffered,' Shavi agreed, 'all across the country, but people are finding ways to survive.'

'True. Very true. It has been an extraordinarily testing time, but I cannot stress enough how much my faith in human nature has been restored. The way everyone in the village pulled together once we understood the nature of the threat facing us. It's been the Blitz spirit all over again.' His eyes grew moist as he looked around the quiet street. 'I fear for the future, though. If things carry on as they are, all of this could be swept away. It's not fair at all, is it? What's to become of us?'

After the surprising kiss in Callander, Church had been wary of having any further contact with Niamh, but he couldn't see any alternative. Shavi was the backbone of the team: resilient, dependable in every circumstance, fully aware of all his obligations; they couldn't afford to lose him. The real problem was how he should contact her. He had no idea how the system of transfer worked between Otherworld and what he laughingly called the *real* world, nor what the abilities of the Tuatha Dé Danann were in hearing communication between the two places. Were they as omnipotent as some of them sometimes appeared? Would it be enough just to call her name? She had, after all, stressed the bond between them; perhaps that was enough.

In the end he decided at least to make things a little easier. He asked around the village for any site that carried folk tales of fairies or supernatural activity. An old woman directed him to a small, overgrown mound on the outskirts where she had seen 'the wee folk' playing one night when she was a girl.

He sat on the summit and closed his eyes, feeling the sun hot on the back of his neck. His instinct told him he needed to be in tune with the spiritual power of the blue fire, although he was unsure of attempting it without Tom around to guide him. But after a few minutes trying to clear his mind, he found it surprisingly easy. Perhaps it was a skill that grew commonplace with repetition, or perhaps it was simply that the blue fire was stronger in the land since his success at Edinburgh, but as soon as he could concentrate he was aware of the tracings of power shimmering across the countryside, casting a sapphire tinge across the golden corn, adding new depth to the rich, green grass. When he finally felt he had tapped into it, he whispered her name. At first there was nothing; and not for the first twenty minutes. But just when he was about to give up, a strange vibration hummed in the air, like the sound around an electricity sub-station. An instant later she was standing before him, her smile as mysterious and deep as the ocean.

'You called, Jack. I came.'

Before her, he was suddenly aware he felt awkward and faintly embarrassed, his emotions and thoughts stumbling over each other like a schoolboy before his secret sweetheart. 'I need help.'

She nodded, her eyes heavy-lidded. She took his hand and led him down to the warm grass. As he sat, she leaned near to him, not quite touching, but close enough so that he was constantly aware of her presence; close enough for him easily to breathe in that pleasing aroma of lime and mint. 'Why are you interested in me?' He hadn't meant to ask the question, but it had appeared on his lips almost magically.

She gave a soothing, melodious laugh, as if it were the most ridiculous question in the world. He enjoyed the way her eyes crinkled, her face innocently lit up. In that moment it was hard to see her as one of a race so alien they treated people with oblique contempt. 'I have seen you grow, Jack. I was there, in the half-light, the moment you were born. I saw your potential take shape, your good heart grow stronger. I stood a whisper away the first time you cried from hurt emotion. I saw you develop decency and honesty and love for your fellow man. I saw you suffer broken hearts, and persevere even at that terrible point when you felt your world was coming to an end. And you came through, Jack. You became the best you could be. So few Fragile Creatures can say that. And I was there in every moment, so much a part of your life in the highs and the lows that I knew every secret thought, every half-wish and barely remembered dream. I was a part of you, Jack. No one knows you better. No one.' There was almost a pleading quality to her voice.

'But I don't know *you*.'

'No. No, you do not.' And now sadness, so fragilely potent he almost felt it. She looked away briefly, too much going on behind her eyes for him to see.

'What is it you are saying, Niamh?'

'There is nothing I can say. I merely reveal to you the slightest fragment of the minutest strand of my feelings. Our races are as far apart as Otherworld and here. And as close. No good has ever come of any bond forged between the two. One passes so quickly, the other goes on for ever, both are bound in tears.'

Her voice filled him with a deep melancholy. For the first time, in her eyes, in her body language, the way she held her mouth, he could see how deeply she felt for him and it was monumentally shocking. To be loved so much and not know it was astounding, and truly moving, to such a degree he felt he should seek deep within him to see if there was any way he could repay such a profound investment. But all he found inside was confusion. He thought of Laura and the desperate scramble of emotions he felt around her. And, oddly, Ruth, whom he thought he considered a friend, but when he attempted to examine his emotional response he found it was too complex and deep-seated. And now this woman, who was so open and honest, she was like a cool desert oasis he wanted to dive into and slough off all the corruption that had mired him over the weeks and years.

'I don't know how I feel,' he said honestly.

'You are fortunate.' More sadness. 'To know and not to have is the hardest thing.'

He tried to find something comforting to say, but nothing came.

She looked around, at the rolling summer fields, and some of the sadness eked away. 'This world is changing. Soon it will be a land of myth once more, where magic lives in every turn.' She turned back to him, her smile sweet once again. 'A land where anything can happen.'

He nodded thoughtfully. 'When you put it like that, it doesn't seem such a bad thing.'

'How can I help you, Jack?'

He felt almost guilty asking for something when she had bared her soul to him. But once he had told her about Maponus, and seen her face register surprise, then darken, all other thoughts were wiped away.

'The search for the Good Son has never ended,' she explained. 'The Golden Ones were riven by despair when he was lost, the brightest of all our bright stars, our very hope for the future. There was no knowledge of his disappearance – he was simply there, then not. Of course we must bring him back to us. There will be much rejoicing, scenes of wonder not witnessed since the victory celebrations after the second battle of

Magh Tuireadh.' The notion excited her greatly, but gradually her face darkened as the implications of Church's information wormed their way through. 'If he has been so severely damaged by the Night Walkers, there may be little even the Golden Ones can do to restore the Good Son to his former glory. The Night Walkers' revenge is swift, cruel and usually irreversible.'

'But you will attempt to get him back to Otherworld?'

'Of course. He is the jewel of the Golden Ones.' She was positive, yet Church could see she was troubled. 'Yet he is so powerful.' Her voice faded into the wind.

'You're saying even your people might not be able to restrain him?'

'He could cause great destruction to this world. Your people will fall before him like—' she looked around '—like the ripe corn.' She turned to Church with fleeting panic in her eyes. 'You must not go anywhere near the Good Son. Do you understand?'

'At the moment I'm going where I'm called. We have an obligation—'

'You have an obligation to defend this world. You cannot do that if you are no more.'

'I'm asking you for help.' He looked her directly in the eye; her irises seemed to swirl with golden fire.

'Then I will help. But I ask something of you in return.'

'All right.'

'A chance to show you my heart, to prove that universes can be crossed. To show that the love of a Golden One and a Frail Creature can surmount all obstacles.'

Church searched her face; suddenly events seemed to be running away from him.

'I know you have a dalliance with another Frail Creature. You must end it. You must give your love solely to me for a period. A chance, that is all I ask. And if our romance does not rise up to the heavens, then we will go our separate ways.'

Dismally, Church thought of Laura, how much it would hurt her. Could he do that when there was still a chance they were right for each other? Could he hurt her, knowing how much she would suffer? And once more he thought of Ruth, and wondered what she would think of him. Niamh was watching the play of his thoughts with innocent, sensitive eyes.

He wondered why he was even bothering to deliberate; there was no real choice. He couldn't afford to let Shavi leave. And if he could do anything to stop Maponus's rampage, he had to try. He had learned through bitter experience over the last three months that he couldn't

697

put his own feelings first; that was the burden of his leadership. Sacrifices had to be made. Always. 'Okay,' he said. 'I'll do what you say.'

The sudden swell of emotion in her face surprised him, and in that instant he wondered if he really could feel something for her. She took his hand, an act that to her was obviously filled with meaning; it was as if she was some Victorian heroine whose every gesture was infused with import to make up for her stifled emotion. 'Much deliberation will need to take place if we are to bring Maponus back with us,' she said. 'I will need to devote myself to the planning and to attending my brethren in this. You will not see me for a while. But then . . .' Her cool fingers grew tighter around his hand and her smile deepened. She nodded politely, stood up and walked slowly away. Briefly she turned and flashed him a smile weighted with emotion, and then she was gone in the blink of an eye, as if the sky had folded around her.

Laura and Veitch didn't quite know how they ended up interviewing villagers together, but they managed to do it with as little communication between the two of them as they could manage. If anything, Veitch seemed to Laura a little contrite in his body language and whatever gruff comments he made, but after his rage in the gorge, she wasn't taking any chances. She was thankful for her sunglasses which hid the fear she knew was flickering in her eyes.

Eventually, though, they found themselves walking alone down the sun-drenched High Street and there was nothing for it but to make conversation. 'Nothing new there, then.' Laura broke the silence, stating the obvious because she couldn't think of anything else to say that wasn't heavy with all sorts of difficulties. 'Another morning of my life wasted.'

Veitch grunted. His own cheap sunglasses gave nothing away.

Laura was suddenly struck by the absurdity of the image. 'Look at us. It's like Tarantino meets *Emmerdale*.' That brought a smile to him. It was only a chink, but she felt she had to give it a shot. 'About the other day—'

'I'm sorry, all right.' It was as if someone had pulled the blinds down on his face. 'I've got a bleedin' awful temper and half the time I can't control it. I don't know where it came from. I never used to have it.'

'Stress, probably. But that wasn't what I wanted to say. You're right for worrying about one of us selling the others down the river. Nobody else seems to worry about it too much, but it's there – can't ignore it. But it's not me, all right? That's what I wanted to say. It's not me. I don't care if you believe me or not, but I've got to say it out loud. I'm a big fuck-up – and I'll deny I said that if you ever bring it up – but I wouldn't screw over any of us in this group.'

Her normal reticence made the honesty in her words palpable. Veitch was taken aback for a moment, but he didn't show it. 'Who do you think it is, then?'

She paused, unsure whether to continue, but it wasn't worth turning back at that point. 'Are you going to bite my head off?'

'No.'

'Okay. I know you've got the hots for Ruth, I know she's been through the worst fucking shit imaginable, but I think it's her.'

'Bollocks.'

'Thank you for that measured response.' She bit her tongue; she could feel the power in his hard body at her side. 'I'm not just being a jealous bitch, which I am, but not right now. Here's what I think. She's been waking up with nightmares about what those bastards did to her—'

'Wouldn't you?' He was already starting to bristle. She had to get to the point.

'I think those nightmares are caused by something real. You remember what the Bastards did to Tom under Dartmoor? They stuck one of those creepy little bugs in his head so he'd do everything they wanted.'

Veitch's head snapped round. For a second Laura's blood ran cold until she saw the troubled expression on his face. 'You think they did that to her?'

'Makes sense.'

He considered it for a moment, then shook his head vehemently. 'Bollocks.'

'Just think about it, that's all. It could've happened. Someone needs to keep an eye on her, and seeing as you've appointed yourself official judge, jury and executioner—' She caught herself. She'd done enough. She could tell from Veitch's expression that the notion was already burrowing its way into his head.

'Come on, I need you.' Ruth caught Veitch's arm when they all met up outside the pub. She pulled him over to one side where the others couldn't hear them, oblivious to the odd way he was looking at her.

'What's wrong?'

'I want us to have sex.'

Veitch's expression was so comical she had to stifle a giggle and that wouldn't have helped at all; he was sensitive enough as it was. His mouth moved, no words came out; his whole, stumbling thought process was played out fleetingly on his face. 'You're taking the piss now.'

That was the first response she expected. 'No, I'm not. I'm deadly serious.'

Veitch shook his head. There was a pink flush to his cheeks. He was eyeing her askance, still trying to read her motives.

'When we started out on this whole nightmare I was just a normal girl, but I've changed, like we've all changed. I've learned some things. Powerful things. How to change the world around us, things . . . things I don't want to talk about because I can hardly believe it myself. You know the owl that followed me around?'

His eyes ranged across her face; he seemed to be trying to peer into her head. He nodded.

'That wasn't just an owl. It was . . . Well, I don't really know what it was. I'm not making much sense, am I? I wish I could understand it all better myself.' She became lost in her own confusion of thoughts briefly. 'Look, the owl's some kind of familiar. You know what that is? A demon . . . I don't know . . . Some kind of supernatural creature, anyway. That took the form of an owl to be with me. But when the Fomorii had me under the castle I found out what it was really like. Not what it looked like. I mean, I couldn't see it. But . . . it taught me things—'

'What kind of things?'

Her mind sparked and fizzed with wild current when she considered the answer to the question; it was suddenly as if she could look into the infinite. 'Things that could help us. Only the trouble is, now the familiar has gone away and I don't know why, but there are still so many things I need to know.'

'Well this is all very fucking nice, but what's it got to do with us shagging?'

She sighed. 'I'm sorry, Ryan. I really am making a mess of this, aren't I? Let me try again. Sex is at the heart of all magic. Throughout history it's been used in all sorts of rituals. The earth energy, the blue fire in the land is the same energy we have inside us. In our spirits, our souls. It runs in grids over our bodies the same way it does in the land. Like the stone circles are areas where it's at its most powerful, there are places on our bodies where the power is strong. In eastern religion they're called chakras—' She watched him start to glaze over and quickly picked up the pace of the conversation. 'Normal sex fills us with this energy which we can use. But a particular kind of sex – it's called tantric sex – supercharges these chakras and—'

'And you know how to do this?'

'The familiar told me. I mean, I've never tried it, but—'

'There has to be a first time.'

'Right. Look, I don't want to take advantage of you. This isn't an emotional thing. But you get a good screw out of it and all the experiences you could want. And I get—'

'What?' His brow furrowed. 'If you don't want it to be anything serious, what do you get out of it? You're not some slapper—'

'You're so sweet,' she said with a mock-smile. 'I get knowledge, hopefully. Power I can bend to my will.'

The incomprehension was chiselled into his face. He felt uncomfortable. It wasn't what he wanted, in the slightest, but it seemed important to Ruth.

'Look, don't waste time thinking about it now. If you're up for it, I'll fill you in as we go along. Are you?' He nodded, unsurely. 'Right. Then let's do it.'

Back in the pub bedroom she drew the curtains and locked the door. None of the others would even think of disturbing them at that time of day. They were downstairs in the bar, picking over the remainder of their lunch, having a quiet drink, chewing over the village's problem. Her breath was ragged from apprehension and, if she admitted it to herself, a sexual charge.

'You're sure about this?' She could hear faint nervousness in Veitch's voice. She sensed that if she called it off he would be more than happy.

'I am. Are you?'

'Yes.'

Not exactly a ringing endorsement, but what did she expect. 'I know this isn't how you expected, Ryan. It's not exactly every maiden's dream either. Not that I'm a maiden.' She blushed, looked away. 'But it's the only way I can think of—'

'It's okay. You don't have to explain any more.' She smiled; underneath it all he was quite sweet. 'So how do we start?' he continued.

'Take our clothes off first, I suppose.'

It felt unduly uncomfortable, so artificial in the way it was drained of all passion, but she knew she couldn't afford to be selfconscious, for Veitch's sake. If he saw her being embarrassed, the atmosphere would completely fall apart and he probably wouldn't be able to perform. She set her mind and tried to act as brazen as possible. She pulled her T-shirt over her head and threw it on the bed, then unhooked her bra. Her nipples were already hard; her breasts almost ached. She tried to fool herself that her instant and powerful arousal was because it had been so long, but she knew in her heart she was physically attracted to

Veitch. As he pulled his own T-shirt off she let her gaze run over his lean, muscled torso, watching the flex and ripple of the tattoos, like cartoons in animation. There was a hardness to his body she hadn't experienced in any of her previous lovers; it wasn't even the kind of hardness that came from working out in a gym. It was the kind of compacted yet supple muscle that came only from a life lived at street level, in onerous situations that tested the body on a daily basis in a way the fitness trainers couldn't even imagine. His own nipples were hard; that excited her even more. Briefly, his clear, powerful eyes caught hers and there was no embarrassment there at all. Energy crackled between them. She saw his own passion laid bare as his gaze dropped to her breasts.

She undid her loose belt, unpopped the buttons and dropped her jeans to her ankles. In the same motion she slipped down her briefs and stepped out of them. She felt the chill of the wetness between her legs send a tingling fire into her belly.

Veitch removed his trousers and his shorts. He was very hard, aching for her. A shiver ran through her. He seemed filled with vitality, as if the blue fire burned in every cell, nuclear fission raging out of control, ready to consume her.

She took his hand and pressed him towards the floor. When he was sitting with his legs out in front of him and his hands behind, she climbed astride him and gently lowered herself on her taut leg muscles, gripping his erection in her fist and feeding it into her. His hardness was shocking; it seemed to go in so deep she felt it was almost in her chest. She wrapped her legs around him and supported herself on her hands behind her. Her heart was thundering, the passion crackling through every fibre of her.

'Don't move,' she said. 'This is the hard part. The aim is to achieve orgasm without moving, through meditation, directing the energy. I've had some guidance how to do it. Normally it takes a long period of training and discipline. Do you think you can do it?'

'I can try.' He closed his eyes, his body rigid, still.

Ruth took the opportunity to scan his features; in relaxed mode there was a surprising tenderness to his expression, almost an innocence. In that moment she could imagine how he would have turned out if not for the privations of his early life. And then she lowered her gaze to the startling colours of his torso: the Watchtower was there, swimming in a sea of stars, some kind of sword, a bulky creature in an insectile armour that made her feel so uncomfortable she moved on quickly, a strange ship skimming blue waves, a burning city and, most disturbingly, a single, staring eye which she knew represented Balor.

She put all thoughts out of her mind, leaned forward and kissed his clavicle. A slight shiver ran through him. She moved up, kissed the curve of his throat. Then up further to gently brush his lips. She felt his erection throb inside her.

Leaning back, closing her own eyes, she focused her sharp mind in the way the familiar had told her, the way she had practised during those long, terrible hours of imprisonment. It came to her with surprising ease. She felt the world moving beneath her, the shifting of subtle energies deep in the rock and soil. Whatever Church had done in Edinburgh had worked. The Fiery Network was slowly coming to life, breaking through the dormant areas, joining up the centres that had remained powerful, like blood filling a vascular system. She saw in the darkness in her head the flicker and surge of the blue fire as it ran in the earth, came up through the ground, through the walls of the building, along the floor, burst in coruscating sapphire into the base of her spine. And gradually it started its serpentine coiling up towards her skull.

Time was suspended; they had no idea how long they were there. Their very existence was infused with the dark, shifting landscapes in their heads, the feeling of the engorged blood vessels in their groins. Veitch fought the urge to thrust, although every fibre of his being was telling him to drive hard into her. Her vaginal muscles seemed so tight around him, massaging him gently. Even with his eyes closed he was aware of her body as if he was staring at it: the flatness of her belly, the heaviness of her breasts, the hardness of her nipples, electric sexual signals driving into the depths of his mind.

And then everything came in a rush, the blue fire suddenly crackling up the final inches of their spines, erupting in their heads like the birth of stars; every nerve bursting with fire, rushing back down to their joined groins. Veitch ejaculated in such a fierce manner he felt as if his life was being sucked out of him. The sudden crackling current inside Ruth's vagina danced jaggedly to the tips of her fingers and then to the front of her brain. Their orgasm brought a fleeting moment of blackness that felt like the end of everything.

And in the following instant, Ruth was consumed with a power she had never experienced before. It felt like she was flying high above the earth, deep into the depths of space. And there she saw the thing that had the face of a man and the face of an owl simultaneously, and it was frantically tracing a strange sigil in the air with its hands, desperate to keep her at bay.

'I cannot come near you,' it said in its half-shrieking voice. 'You are tainted. Seek help now. Seek help or die.'

She fell into Veitch's arms and he held her tightly while their thundering hearts subsided. But Ruth couldn't enjoy the warm honey glow that infused them both in the aftermath of their passionate experience. She pulled herself back and looked Veitch deep in the eye; he was horrified to see the fear shining brightly within her.

'Something's gone badly wrong,' she said in a fractured voice. 'What the Fomorii did to me under the castle . . . it isn't over. It's still going on inside me.'

They dressed hurriedly and found the others sunning themselves on the steps in front of the pub while Tom finished his cider.

'Where did you two scuttle off to?' Laura asked suspiciously.

Ruth turned straight to Tom and Church and began to explain her fears, and for the first time told them about the black pearl. Her heart sank as she saw Tom's face at first darken and then blanch.

'Why didn't you tell us this before?' Tom hissed.

'It was too traumatic!' she protested. 'I could barely get my head round it myself!' She tried to look him in the eye. 'What's going on?'

'I don't know. But it was a ritual the Fomorii carried out. They wouldn't have done it without a reason.'

'You have your suspicions,' Ruth pressed.

'I have ideas, but it's best not to say them right now. Not until I'm sure.'

Tears stung Ruth's eyes. 'It's going to get worse, isn't it? I thought the sickness was just a natural result of all that trauma. I thought it'd pass.'

Church stepped in and put a comforting arm round her shoulder. Both Laura and Veitch flinched. 'What are we going to do?' he said to Tom.

Tom took off his glasses and cleaned them while he thought. 'She needs to be examined by one of the Tuatha Dé Danann. They are the only ones who might reasonably be able to tell us what the Fomorii have done.'

'And they might be able to help,' Ruth said hopefully, 'like Ogma helped you when you had the Caraprix in your head.' Veitch's gaze grew sharp.

'Will they help us?' There was an edge to Church's voice.

'They might.' Tom rubbed his chin, his gaze fixed firmly on the ground. 'If I asked them.'

'But what if they don't help?' Church continued. 'What's Plan B?'

Tom said nothing. After a long moment he wandered off down the road to weigh his thoughts.

The shadows were growing longer when he eventually returned to them. Ruth had been away to throw up twice in the meantime; Church guessed the stress was already contributing to what was wrong with her. The others waited anxiously around the pub table.

Tom looked around their concerned faces, then said, 'One of the Prime Courts of the Tuatha Dé Danann can be reached through a door not far from here. The Court of the Final Word is the closest translation of its name. Unlike the usual Tuatha Dé Danann courts, it is a place of quiet reflection, of study. If there is anyone who can provide an insight into Ruth's condition we will find them there.'

'Where is it?' The concern in Veitch's voice was palpable.

'Beneath Richmond Castle.' Tom glanced at the clock over the bar. 'If we move quickly we can be there before nightfall.'

'Is it that serious?' Church asked.

Tom's silence was the only answer he needed.

CHAPTER THIRTEEN

Where the Devil Is

'I'd been keeping the full tank of petrol for emergencies,' Max said ruefully. 'The way things are going, I think it's going to become a priceless commodity.' He cast a worried glance at Ruth's drawn face. 'But if this isn't an emergency, what is?' He smiled, trying to bolster the atmosphere.

The car was a red Fiesta, peppered with rust on the wings and sills. The inside was a mess. He opened the doors with some embarrassment, then swept the crumpled maps and fast food wrappers out on to the pavement. 'Sorry. You can always tell a hack's car.'

Tom climbed into the passenger seat while Church took the back seat with Ruth. He slipped an arm across the top of the seat; her head fell naturally on to his shoulder. The others stood on the pavement; Veitch and Shavi were grim-faced, but Laura was impossible to read.

They eventually picked up the B6270 through the ragged, romantic countryside of Swaledale, heading south-east. During the journey Church and Tom tried to explain to Max about Tir n'a n'Og, the Otherworld, and the alien ways of the Tuatha Dé Danann to prepare him for what lay ahead. In other circumstances his dumbfounded expression would have been comical, but it soon fell away as he assimilated every detail with a speed that surprised them both. It wasn't long before he was babbling excitedly about a new way of seeing the world.

The scenery flashed by in a blur of rolling fields and green hedges; seeming normality. While Max and Tom passed the time in sporadic conversation, enthusiastic on Max's part, barely tolerable on Tom's, Church and Ruth slid down in the back seat and spoke in hushed voices.

'I can't believe this is happening,' she said, staring out of the window at the blue sky.

'You're right. You've suffered enough,' Church said.

'No, the people out there have suffered enough. I've had a little pain, but at least I know what's happening in the world. What's a few aches and pains compared to having your life turned on its head? I mean, I want to get back to doing something that matters and there's all this—' she gestured irritatedly '—holding me back.'

The weariness was evident on her face. Slowly she lowered her head back on to his shoulder, but Church continued to watch her while she rested, feeling a sense of deep respect that almost overwhelmed him.

They'd just moved on to the A6108 when Tom exclaimed loudly.

'What's wrong?' Church threw himself forward between the seats. He quickly saw it wasn't the right thing to do. Tom was already sliding down as low as he could go. On the side of the road, three policemen stood stiffly around a patrol car. They were gone so quickly Church had no way of telling if they were Fomorii, nor if they had seen him. He ducked down, turned and crawled up the seat just enough to peer out of the back window. The police all appeared to have got into the car, but it wasn't in pursuit. He held his breath and watched until it was out of sight.

'Close shave,' he said, still not wholly sure.

Shavi had spent an hour doing his best to boost Veitch's spirits, but the Londoner still wore the broken expression of someone who had seen ultimate victory snatched from his fingertips. 'We have to believe Ruth will be all right.' Shavi's voice rolled out softly across the quiet bar. His arm rested comfortingly around Veitch's shoulders, and Veitch made no attempt to shake it off. Laura watched them both carefully from behind her sunglasses, but added nothing to the conversation.

'You saw the old man's face. He looked like it was already over.' Veitch gently massaged his temples. There was an intensity about him that made the atmosphere uneasy.

'We have to have hope, Ryan. That is the message of this whole era.'

Veitch looked up suddenly and curiously into Shavi's face. He seemed surprised at what he saw there. After a moment's contemplation, he said, 'Okay, you're right. Course you are.' In the centre of the table where they had been abandoned earlier, he noticed the sheaf of notes Ruth had prepared. 'We've got to sort this out. Help these poor bastards.'

Shavi could see it was merely a displacement activity for the futility Veitch was feeling at his inability to do anything to help Ruth, but if it kept his mind focused on something positive, it was worthwhile. Veitch examined the notes with gusto, making observations as he read before handing each paper he finished to Shavi or Laura. No obvious conclusion presented itself to them, but they continued to turn it over while they ate the dinner Geordie had prepared for them.

'There's nothing new here,' Laura protested. 'Unless you're thinking of tracking them out to their lair, and then we wouldn't know how to kill them.'

'We don't even know where the *lair* is,' Veitch said. He shovelled a forkful of mashed potato into his mouth.

'It must be somewhere in the vicinity of the route we came in.' Laura told them about the scarecrow and the glowing red eyes.

'That's something,' Veitch said, 'but you're right, we don't know how to wipe them out yet. No point looking for them until we get a handle on that. It didn't look like we'd get much of a result with the sword or the crossbow.'

Laura re-examined one of the pages of notes. 'At least we know where the feeding ground is.'

Veitch perked up at this. 'What do you mean?'

Laura pointed out the rough sketch of the village lay-out with the victims' houses highlighted.

'That's a bit of a coincidence, isn't it?' he said.

'I don't know what you're talking about.'

'All those poor bastards in one place.'

'The old biddy wasn't anywhere near them. It's probably just that they've settled on this area because it's near to where they come in to the village. Or something.' She stared at the map intently, turning it this way and that.

Veitch chewed on a jagged nail thoughtfully. 'I'm getting a very fucking unpleasant idea,' he said.

The evening was warm and still as they moved through the village. The chorus of birdsong filled the air, but there was no sound of cars or human voices. Even though it was still light, everyone had retreated to their homes.

Veitch first took them to the large, detached house of Mrs Ransom, quiet beneath its canopy of old trees. They slipped through the creaking iron gate and up the brick path to the front door. Instead of knocking, Veitch simply inspected the door jamb before growing suddenly excited. He ran back down the path and vaulted the low brick wall on to the pavement. Shavi and Laura hurried to keep up with him as he ran the two streets to the collection of council houses which had provided all the other victims.

Oldfield's house was the first to be inspected. Veitch ran from there to the other two. He didn't bother checking the door of the young mother who had lost her child. Finally he rested breathlessly against the wall of one of the houses. He'd obviously figured something out that everyone had missed, but there was no jubilation in his face; instead, he seemed intensely troubled, and when he looked up Laura saw the familiar glint of cold, hard anger in his eyes.

'Fucking hell,' he said.

Max gunned the Fiesta into Richmond just as dusk was falling. The town was dominated by the ruins of the Norman castle which over-looked the River Swale, the keep towers soaring up a hundred feet into the darkening sky. Beneath it, the cobbled market was filled with people enjoying the warm summer evening as they made their way to the pubs.

Max scrutinised the scene. 'People carry on trying to be normal even when they realise something is badly wrong,' he mused.

'Nothing there to write about,' Tom muttered.

A tight, knowing grin crept across Max's face. 'That's where you're wrong. That is something to write about. That's something that speaks loudly.'

'Yes. And it says "Sheep to the slaughter",' Tom noted sourly.

Max laughed easily in disagreement. 'And that's just what I'm going to do. Write about it. About all this. This is something I can do, let the people know the truth. It's a kind of—'

'Calling?' Church knew just how he felt. Max nodded, still smiling.

They left the car in the centre and headed towards the castle on foot, Ruth trailing apprehensively between Church and Tom. Church surveyed the broken stone silhouetted against the blackening sky.

Tom followed his gaze. 'Do you feel it?'

Church nodded. 'The blue fire.'

'All the clues are there in the legends. The secret history. The story goes that a potter by the name of Thompson found a secret tunnel under the castle. He followed it and found a large cavern where King Arthur and his knights lay asleep. Sound familiar?'

'What are you talking about?' Max asked.

'All the legends have truths stitched up inside them. Important information, vital lessons.' Church could see the reporter was soaking up all the information. 'The King Arthur legend is a metaphor for the power in the land, what we call the blue fire. The legends surround all the places where this earth energy is most potent, many of them with links direct to Otherworld.'

'Like here,' Tom said.

'So when the legends say the king needs to be woken to save the country in the bleakest of times, they're really talking about waking the power in the land?' Max looked up at the castle in a new light.

'Thompson found a horn and a sword near to the sleeping knights,'

Tom continued, obviously irritated that his story had been interrupted. 'When he picked up the horn, the knights began to wake. Naturally, he was scared to death. He dropped the horn and ran back down the tunnel, and as he did so a voice came after him. It said, "Potter Thompson, Potter Thompson, If thou hadst drawn the sword or blown the horn, Thou hadst been the luckiest man e'er born".'

'Good story,' Max said warmly.

They wound their way up for a while until they looked back and saw the lights of the town coming on before them. They all found it uncannily comforting; Richmond looked bright and at peace in an inky sea.

Tom followed the lines of blue fire as Church had done at Arthur's Seat until he located their confluence on an open spot on the hillside. The sparks flew like molten metal as he pressed his hand down hard. Within seconds, to Max's obvious amazement, the grass, soil and rock tore apart with a groan, revealing a dark path deep into the hillside.

Max peered in nervously. 'Are you sure it's okay?'

'No,' Tom said, and gave Max a shove between the shoulder blades that propelled him into the shadows.

Otherworld was bathed in the crisp, creamy light of an autumnal morning just after sunrise. Swathes of mist rolled across the wet grass at calf-height. The air was rich with the perfume of turning leaves, fallen apples and overripe blackberries. Melodic birdsong floated out from a nearby copse that was painted gold, red and brown in the dawn light.

Max looked around, disoriented. 'I don't get it.'

'Time moves differently here.' Church strode out towards gleaming white Doric columns he could just make out through another thick copse. 'Sometimes faster, sometimes slower. It's not fixed.'

Max's face showed his difficulty in grasping the concept of this new reality.

'Here are the rules,' Tom said curtly. 'Eat and drink nothing. If you are offered anything, politely refuse. Treat everyone you meet with respect. Never, ever raise your voice in anger. It would be best if you said nothing at all. Try to stay in the background.'

'I'm getting a little nervous now,' Max admitted.

'Just pretend you're in a different country with a culture you don't know,' Church said. 'You have to be cautious until you know the rules of the society, right?'

They moved quickly through the trees, the curling leaves crunching underfoot. Beyond, they had to shield their eyes from the glare of the sun reflecting off the polished white stone of their destination which rested in majesterial splendour among intricately laid-out gardens. The Doric columns supported a portico carved with an astonishingly detailed tableau showing aspects of the history of the Tuatha Dé Danann. Behind it, the Court of the Final Word spread out as far as the eye could see, like some Greek temple reflected in infinite mirrors.

'It's enormous.' Max's voice was laden with awe.

'It would seem.' The door was made of polished stone. Tom was there first and hammered on it. His fist barely seemed to make a sound, but they could hear the echoes rumbling through the structure into the distance.

When dim footsteps approached Church and Ruth both caught their breath. Despite all they had seen, they were not inured to the wonders and terrors of Otherworld. The life forms were myriad and astonishing in their complexity; even with the Tuatha Dé Danann, one could never quite be sure what would present itself.

The door swung open silently, as if it weighed no more than a feather. It framed two figures standing in a cool, enormous hall dominated by a large, tinkling fountain and tall trees which oddly seemed to be part of the structure. The young man and woman looked barely in their twenties and were dressed in what appeared to be gleaming white togas, edged with gold braid. Church and the others' eyes had no trouble accustomising to their appearance, which meant the Golden Ones were of low level and low power.

'Frail Creatures?' the young man said curiously, his beautiful face like marble, his heavy-lidded eyes moving slowly, like a lizard in the sun.

'I am True Thomas,' Tom began. 'You may have heard of me. I have been granted the freedom of your realm.'

The woman bowed courteously but a little stiffly, her long, black hair shimmering as she moved. 'Greetings, True Thomas. We are aware of your prestigious position.'

Tom winced at this, although there was no irony in the woman's words. 'My companions and I seek the aid of the Council of the Final Word. Are any of them present this day?'

'All the council members are concerned with the business of study, True Thomas,' the man said. 'A great deal was lost in the storm that followed the Wish-Hex and now so much has been opened up to them once more. The Fixed Lands for one. I am sure you understand.'

Tom nodded slowly; Church was puzzled to see a grey cast fall across his face. 'They are not involved in any dissections?' The young man said nothing. Tom composed himself and continued, 'With the freedom granted to me, I would wish to wait.'

'It may be some time. In your perception.'

'If you would inform the council of my attendance I am sure one of the Venerated Ones would eventually find a way to greet me.'

The man nodded and stepped aside so they could enter. They were led to a room off a long, lofty atrium. It was filled with marble benches and sumptuous cushions piled alongside rushing crystal streams cut into the gleaming stone floor.

'I wish I'd brought Laura's sunglasses,' Ruth said feebly.

'How are you feeling?' Church gave her a hug.

'Still sick.'

They arranged some of the cushions in a circle and lounged. 'They're like the worst kind of arrogant aristocrats,' Max whispered. Tom made a silencing move with his hand. Max nodded and continued, 'How long are they going to keep us waiting?'

'Hours. Perhaps days. Maybe even weeks.'

'Weeks!' Ruth said dismally.

Yet it was only twenty minutes before they heard movement in the corridor without. 'Looks like you've still got some clout,' Church whispered.

A deep, unfocused light glimmered across the white walls, as if whoever was approaching held a lantern, but when the figure emerged he carried nothing. And this time Church did experience the unnerving shift of perception; faces seemed to float across the figure's head, some of them sickeningly alien and incomprehensible, others cultured and sophisticated. Eventually he settled on a set of educated, aristocratic features that centred on a Roman nose and a high forehead with piercing grey eyes and full lips; his hair was long and grey and tied at the back in a ponytail. There was a sense of tremendous authority about him that made Church almost want to bow, although he was loath to debase himself before any of the invaders.

Tom, however, was already down on one knee. 'You honour me, master.'

'True Thomas. It pleases me to see you so hale and hearty after everything.' His smile was broad and warm; Church felt instantly at ease. 'And these companions, are they as resilient as you, True Thomas?'

'Oh, more so by far.' Tom stood up and gestured to Church and Ruth. 'A Brother of Dragons, a Sister of Dragons.' Tom introduced them by name, studiously avoiding bringing any attention to Max. Then he motioned to the gentle, kindly figure while keeping one eye on Ruth. 'You are honoured. This is Dian Cecht, High Lord of the Court of the Final Word, seeker of mystery, master healer, supreme smith, builder of the silver hand of Nuada—'

Dian Cecht waved him silent with a pleasant laugh. 'There is no need to trumpet my successes unless you also tell of my many failures, True Thomas, and those I would rather leave to the shadows. I would thank you, Brother and Sister of Dragons, for the part you played in freeing us from the privations of the Wish-Hex.' Church winced at the memory of how the Tuatha Dé Danann had manipulated them, made them suffer in the extreme, just for such an occasion. Dian Cecht gestured magniloquently. 'Now, tell me your request.'

Tom laid a hand on Ruth's shoulder and pressed her forward. 'The Night Walkers have inflicted their corruption on this Sister of Dragons, Good Lord. We ask your favour in helping to remove it.'

Dian Cecht nodded thoughtfully. 'I sensed the whiff of the Night Walkers' presence. Their vile trail is too distinctive to hide. I would not have thought a Sister of Dragons would have allowed herself to be so tainted.'

Ruth felt as if she had failed in his eyes.

'There is nothing ignoble in this suffering,' Tom said in her defence. 'This Sister of Dragons has proved the most hardy of her companions. She succumbed only in the face of overwhelming force.' He paused, then added, 'Much in the way the Tuatha Dé Danann succumbed to the first onslaught of the Fomorii.'

There was a flicker of coldness in Dian Cecht's eye as he cast it suddenly in Tom's direction. 'Ah, True Thomas, one would have thought you would have learned diplomacy during your time among us. Still, I am sure there was no offence intended, and I understand your point.' He turned back to Ruth, now smiling warmly. 'The Filid I am sure will sing loudly of your courageous struggle. I will do for you what I can.'

As he turned to go, he spied Max hovering behind the others. 'I see you have left this Fragile Creature out of your accounts, True Thomas.'

Tom had the expression of a schoolboy who had been caught out. 'He is here to keep a record of these great things transpiring in this world of ours.'

'Ah,' Dian Cecht nodded thoughtfully. 'Then you maintain the traditions of the Filid. Good, good. Wisdom and knowledge needs to be recorded and disseminated.'

Once he had glided out of the room to make his preparations, Ruth turned to Tom. 'Who is he? Can he do the job?'

'I was speaking correctly when I said you were honoured. Dian Cecht is one of the greatest of the Tuatha Dé Danann.' Tom flopped down on to a cushion as if his conversation with the god had wearied him.

'He seemed . . . wise,' Max ventured.

'Wisdom is the essence of him. He has a vista into the very workings of existence. He sees the building blocks that make up everything, the spirit that runs through them. That is why he is the greatest of physicians, the deepest of thinkers, the best maker of all things.' Although his words seemed on the surface to be filled with awe, there was a sour note buried somewhere among them.

'All of the Tuatha Dé Danann seem very different from each other,' Church noted.

Tom nodded. 'While obviously a race, they are all set apart as individuals—'

'So he's a top doctor?' Ruth interjected.

Tom sighed at her phraseology. 'He is the god of healing in the Tuatha Dé Danann pantheon. He was renowned for guarding the sacred spring of health, along with his daughter, Airmid. It is believed it has its source here, within this temple complex, though no one knows for sure. Its miraculous waters can cure the sick and bring the dead back to life.' Church stirred at this, but he didn't dwell on the thoughts that surfaced. 'It can, so they say, even restore the gods.'

Ruth could barely contain her relief. 'So he shouldn't have any problem with whatever those dirty bastards did to me.'

'Then he's one of the good guys,' Max said.

'You could say that,' Tom replied contemptuously. 'The truth is buried in the old stories. When Nuada lost his hand in the first battle of Magh Tuireadh, Dian Cecht made him a new one out of silver. The Tuatha Dé Danann were impressed by his handiwork, but it was not enough. Because he was not truly whole, Nuada was no longer allowed to lead them into battle. He coped as best he could with the shame, but eventually he turned to Dian Cecht's son, Miach, who was believed to be an even greater physician. And it was true. Miach knew the workings of existence even better than Dian Cecht. He grew Nuada a new hand, a real one, and fixed it on to him. A remarkable feat, even for the Tuatha Dé Danann. Nuada was whole again and once more took up the leadership of the race. A time of celebration, you would think? Instead, Dian Cecht promptly murdered Miach for upstaging him. So, yes, a good guy. That's a fair description, isn't it?'

They all fell silent while they considered this information. Then Church said, 'If he's such a big shot, why did he come so quickly when you called instead of sending out some menial?'

'Perhaps,' Tom replied, 'he was stricken with guilt.' But he would not elaborate on his comment any further.

The young man and woman who had greeted them at the door were sent to fetch them an hour later. With Church supporting Ruth, who had been overcome by another bout of nausea, they were led into a massive precinct with a ceiling so lofty they could barely see it through the glare that streamed in through massive glass skylights. Vines crawled around the columns which supported the roof, while some seemed to have trees growing through them as if the stone had formed around the wood.

Dian Cecht stood in a shaft of sunlight in the centre of the room, next to a spring which bubbled up out of the ground. The water was crystal clear and caught the light in a continually changing manner. Although it had no odour, the air near it seemed more fragrant, clearer. They found their gaze was continuously drawn to its sparkle and shimmer, as if it were calling them on some level they didn't understand.

Dian Cecht was wearing robes of the deepest scarlet, which made Ruth instinctively uneasy; he was like a pool of blood in the whiteness of the room. A scarf of red was tied around his head, hiding his hair. He motioned to Ruth to come forward. She glanced briefly at Church for support, then moved in front of the tall, thin god. His eyes were piercing as he silently surveyed her face; she felt he was looking deep into the heart of her, and that made it even more worrying when a troubled expression crossed his face.

'What is it?' she asked.

He shook his head, said nothing. Beside him, a strange object lay on a brass plate that rested atop a short marble column. Ruth tried to see what it was, but her eyes strangely blurred every time she came close to focusing.

He bent over the object and muttered something that sounded like the keening of the wind across a bleak moor. It seemed to respond to the sound, changing, twisting, folding inside out, until it settled on the shape of a bright, white egg with waving tendrils. Ruth instantly recalled the creature she had seen in Ogma's library immediately after the operation to remove the Fomorii equivalent from Tom's brain. 'A Caraprix,' she said.

Dian Cecht smiled when he looked on it. 'My own faithful companion.' He said something else in that strange keening voice and the creature glowed even brighter.

'What are you going to do with it?' Ruth asked, suddenly wary.

'Do not worry. You will not be harmed.' He took her hand to comfort her, but the moment they touched a shudder ran through him. 'The Fomorii have weaved the darkness tightly inside you. I cannot see through it.' He retracted his hand a little too quickly. 'But my friend here should be able to penetrate to the periphery of the shadows and return with the information we need.'

Church's heart leapt when he saw the pang of fear in Ruth's face. 'What is inside me? What have they done?' Her voice sounded as if it was about to shatter.

Dian Cecht smiled a little sadly, then gentle brushed her forehead with his fingertips; she went out in an instant, as she had when Tom had utilised the same technique at Stonehenge. Church started forward, but Dian Cecht caught her easily in his deceptively strong arms and carried her to a pristine marble bench nearby. Church was shocked to see her skin was almost the same colour as the stone on which she lay.

The atmosphere grew more tense and Church had the uncomfortable feeling that a cloud had passed across the sun, although the light in the room remained as bright as ever. Dian Cecht knelt down beside Ruth's head and held the gently throbbing Caraprix in his palm. Church glanced to Tom for support, but the Rhymer would not meet his eyes; Max's face was still with queasy concentration.

The Caraprix was brought slowly towards Ruth's right ear. When it was almost touching, the creature burst into life, snapping like elastic in a wild blur before becoming something like a tapeworm that darted into the waiting orifice. Even unconscious, a spasm crossed Ruth's face.

Dian Cecht stood up and took a step back, fingering his chin as he watched Ruth with resolute thoughtfulness. Church fought to contain his disgust. He imagined the Caraprix wriggling through the byways of Ruth's body, probing into the nooks and crannies as it sought out the Fomorii corruption. But he guessed it wasn't like that at all. Instinctively he knew that if a surgeon cut Ruth open he would find no sign of anything unusual in her body at all; the shadow Dian Cecht sensed was lodged in the invisible shell of her spirit.

The moments went by agonisingly slowly. Neither Dian Cecht nor Tom moved, which made Church realise how very alike they were, although he would never have told Tom that. Max, it was obvious, was forcing himself to watch the proceedings: a trained observer, lodging every incident for posterity.

The tableau seemed frozen in time and space; and then everything happened at once. There was a sound like a meteorite shrieking through the atmosphere to the ground. Ruth's face flickered, then grimaced; finally she convulsed, jackknifing her knees up as if she had been punched in the belly. There was a blur in the air erupting from Ruth's ear and then a *shush-boom* as the shrieking sound crashed into the room with them; Church clutched at his aching ears.

The Caraprix, once more in its egg shape, lay on the floor, surrounded by a pool of gelatinous liquid, throbbing in a manner that Church could only describe as distress. Dian Cecht's face contorted, ran like oil on water until Church found it unrecognisable; it settled only when he was on his knees beside the Caraprix, scooping it up into his hands like a broken-winged sparrow, and then he was hurrying out of the room, the air filled with the terrible keening of the wind.

Ruth came round soon after with the sluggish awareness of someone waking from a deep anaesthetic. She made no sense at first, talking about a ship skimming across the sea, and then her wide eyes focused and locked on Church. He held her hand tightly, brushed a strand of hair from her forehead. Beads of sweat dappled the pale skin.

'What did he find?' Her voice was a croak. Church maintained his demeanour; she looked past him, at Tom, and then Max, and a single tear crept on to her cheek.

They wondered if Dian Cecht was ever going to return. He kept them waiting for more than two hours in the cathedral silence of the precinct. When he did finally arrive, he was not alone. On either side were the young man and woman who were obviously his attendants, and behind them at least twenty others, some with the stern, shifting faces that signified high power. A grim atmosphere wrapped tightly around them.

Dian Cecht spoke in moderate tones; the others remained silent, but it felt as if they were on the verge of screaming. 'We cannot help you or your companions, True Thomas.'

Tom stepped forward and bowed slightly. 'Thank you for the assistance you have given, High Lord of the Court of the Final Word.'

Church couldn't believe what he was hearing. 'Hang on a minute,' he said incredulously, 'you can't just brush us off like that!'

Dian Cecht surveyed him with aristocratic coldness, his warm nature suddenly departed. 'It would do well to maintain respect—'

'No,' Church said firmly. 'You respect me. I represent this world, these people. I'm a Brother of Dragons.'

Tom stepped in quickly. 'He has not learned the ways of—'

Dian Cecht silenced him with an upraised hand. 'For all your power, Brother of Dragons, you are powerless. You are a Frail Creature. Your voice may crow louder than your stature prevails, but in essence that is what you are and that is what you will always be. And even by your own meagre horizons you have failed so dramatically that you are not worthy of whatever position to which you so feebly aspire.' His freezing gaze washed over Church's face. 'You have no notion what has happened?'

'What did you find?' Church tried to maintain equilibrium in his voice. His contempt for the Tuatha Dé Danann was growing; he wanted to drive them all from the land at that moment, Niamh included.

Ruth's hand closed tightly on his forearm. 'Church. Don't.' He ignored her.

'The Sister of Dragons has been corrupted beyond all meaning of the word.' Dian Cecht's stare fell on Ruth, but he seemed unable to keep it there. 'She is the medium for the return of the Heart of Shadows.'

His words fell like stones in the tense atmosphere. There was a sharp intake of breath which Church guessed came from Tom. Church watched the Rhymer's hand go involuntarily to his mouth, but slowly, as if it were only confirmation of an idea he had not dared consider.

'What do you mean?' Church didn't want to hear an answer.

'The black pearl—' Ruth began.

'Was the essence of Balor, the one-eyed god of death, Lord of Evil, Heart of Shadows.' Dian Cecht's face filled with thunder.

Church's head was spinning; he looked from Dian Cecht to Ruth to Tom, who seemed to have tears in his eyes, then back to Ruth.

'The black pearl, the Gravidura, was distilled over time by the Night Walkers to maintain the consistency of whatever essence remained from the Heart of Shadows,' Dian Cecht continued. Church recalled the drums of the foul black concoction they had come across in Salisbury and under Dartmoor. 'It is the seed. He will be reborn into the world at the next festival of the cycles.'

Ruth turned to him, her face filled with a terrible dawning realisation. Tears of shock rimmed her eyes. 'What are you saying? That I'm pregnant?' Her hands went to her belly; she watched them as if they belonged to someone else, with a look of growing horror. 'Inside me?' She started to scratch at her stomach, gently at first, but with growing manic force until Church caught her wrists and held them tight. The look in her eyes was almost unbearable to see. 'What will happen?' she asked dismally.

'When the time comes, the Heart of Shadows will burst from your belly fully formed.' Church wanted to run over and hit Dian Cecht until he removed the coldness from his voice. 'No Fragile Creature could survive that abomination.'

Ruth looked dazed, like she was going to faint. Church slipped an arm around her shoulder for support. 'Why are you treating her this way? She's a victim, not a—'

'She allowed it to happen.'

'Don't be ridiculous—!' Church caught himself, tried a different tack. 'Look, you've got him here, your arch-enemy. If you can get the essence . . . the seed . . . out of her—'

'We will have nothing to do with the corruption. Even to be in the same presence fills us with . . .' He made a gesture as if there was a foul smell under his nose.

'But it makes no sense! If Balor is reborn he's not going to leave the Tuatha Dé Danann alone for long. He'll wipe you out like he's going to wipe out everything—'

The words dried in Church's throat when he saw Dian Cecht's face flare with rage, become insubstantial, shift through a range of alien visages. He suddenly acted as if Church were no longer in the room. 'We will deal with the Heart of Shadows and the Night Walkers if they become a problem, True Thomas—'

'If!' Church raged.

Tom moved quickly to push him and Ruth towards the door. 'Quiet, you idiot!' he hissed. 'You're close to having your blood boiled in your veins!'

'Leave now, True Thomas, and do not bring this foul thing to this place again.' Dian Cecht turned sharply and led the others from the precinct.

The silence that lay in their wake was all-encompassing. Ruth dropped her head heavily on to Church's shoulder. 'God . . .'

'Are you going to tell us your blinding revelation or what?' Laura tried to keep apace with Veitch as he marched back towards The Green Man. His face was flushed with anger and there was determination in every fibre of his being.

'I'll do more than tell you.'

Laura glanced back at Shavi, who shook his head dumbfoundedly.

Veitch burst into the pub like he was looking for a fight. Most of the action group had already gathered there, hunkering in serious conversation at the bar. They looked up in shock as Veitch marched up. He muttered something to one of the group which Laura and Shavi couldn't hear and then he spun round and was heading out of the door again. Laura thought about catching his arm to slow him until she glimpsed his expression. She dropped back several feet and let Shavi move ahead to keep up with the Londoner.

Night had almost fallen by the time they had reached the area of large, old houses at the top of the High Street. Only a thin band of pale blue and gold lay on the horizon and that was disappearing fast. Veitch ranged back and forth along one of the streets, his fists bunching then opening, his breathing ragged. Eventually he found the house he was looking for. One boot burst the wooden gate from its hinges and then he was racing up the path.

The door was locked. He hammered on it so loudly the glass in the front windows rattled. 'Open up!'

A hollow voice echoed somewhere inside.

'I said open up or I'll kick the fucking thing down and then you'll have nothing to protect you!' he raged.

Footsteps approached quickly and they heard the sounds of bolts being drawn. The door had opened only a crack when Veitch kicked it sharply, smashing it into the face of whoever was behind it. There was a groan as someone crashed back against the wall of the hall. Veitch pushed his way in with Laura and Shavi close behind. They didn't recognise the man who was desperately trying to staunch the blood pumping from his nose; it had streamed down over his mouth so that he resembled a vampire from some cheap horror movie. He was in his fifties, balding and overweight, with large, unsightly jowls.

But instead of berating him, Veitch marched past, glancing into the first room he came to before moving on to the next. He stopped at a large drawing room at the rear of the house. French windows looked out over a garden so big they couldn't see the bottom in the dark. The room was decorated with an abundance of antiques on a deep carpet; large, gilt-framed paintings hung on the walls and a log fire crackled in the grate, despite the warmth of the day. A piano stood in one corner.

Several people were gathered in the room, their apprehensive, pale faces turned towards Veitch, Shavi and Laura. There were four women, one in her forties with blonde hair so lacquered it resembled a helmet, the others in their sixties or older, but still well turned-out. The rest were men of different ages and shapes, but they had one thing in common which only Veitch could see: the vague air that the world belonged to them.

'I say, what do you think you're doing?' Sir Richard stepped forward from the back of the group, a glass of brandy nestled in his palm. His cheeks were slightly flushed; Laura couldn't tell if it was from the fire, the brandy or the interruption.

Veitch stepped forward and smashed the glass from his grip with the back of his hand. It shattered on the floor.

'Good Lord, are you mad?'

'I fucking hate toffs and rich bastards,' Veitch spat. There was a note in his voice which made Laura's blood run cold.

Shavi stepped forward. 'Ryan, are you sure—'

He whirled. 'Yes, I am fucking sure! You two wouldn't even have thought of this because you've got a good outlook on life. You were brought up right in a modern world where everybody treats each other at face value, and that's how it should be. But there are still people out there, even in this fucking day and age, who think they're better than others, because they were born that way or because they earned a bundle of fucking cash.' He turned back to Sir Richard. 'Am I right?'

Sir Richard flustered indignantly. 'If you're implying that I—'

'Shut the fuck up.'

Laura watched the scene with a terrible fascination. The sense of irrational, uncontrollable threat that Veitch was radiating scared even her, so God knows how frightened the great and good of the village felt. She looked round and saw the dismay and worry marked in their faces; they looked as if Veitch was about to shoot them, then rob them; and with her hand on her heart, Laura couldn't say that he wouldn't.

Veitch turned to Shavi, but he was obviously talking to the whole room. 'Let me tell you what happened. When the rich old lady was the first to catch it, this lot were horrified. They thought they were fucking untouchable here in their little sanctuary. But that was a big alarm: anybody could get it now the whole world had been turned on its head, and they had no special fucking privileges to protect them. And then when the drunk got it the little lightbulbs started popping over their heads. He was a fucking undesirable, a piss-head and a burden on fucking society. Maybe it wasn't even so *bad* that he got it. The village would look a lot prettier without his piles of puke in the gutter. And then they thought, it didn't *have* to be them who ended up as dead meat. There were a few more that the village could do without. Lazy layabouts without a job for a start.' He put on a mock high-class voice, but it was still laced with venom. 'Wasn't there a little pocket of them down in that part of the village we never went to, where those cheap, dirty little houses were?'

'Now hang on a minute! Those were our neighbours!' a tall, thin man in a dark suit said sharply. 'We always got on well with them.'

'You tolerated them because you were on top,' Veitch snapped. 'But when your backs were against the wall, you didn't have far to look for sacrifices. You knew those fucking creatures left you alone for a bit after they'd eaten. But you knew they couldn't get into a house without the door open. So what did you do? One or two of you fucking cowards went down after dark and jimmied a door open.'

Laura suddenly realised why Veitch had been examining the door frames; he'd been looking for splinters where the locks had been forced.

And she guessed from his past experience he had a perfectly good idea what a jimmied door looked like.

'So you consigned those poor bastards to be meat for another scavenging class we've all had dumped on us.'

Shavi was looking from Veitch to the faces of the assembled group and then back; the truth of Veitch's account was in the guilt that was heavy in every feature. But Shavi was still puzzled. 'I do not understand. If all the doors were locked, the creatures would not have been able to get to anyone—'

Veitch shook his head. 'You're too much of a good bloke, Shav. You've got to think like these bastards. They like cash. They'll do anything for cash. It's their fucking god. They hated being prisoners in their own homes. Couldn't make any lucre. But if those creatures laid low for a few days they had a chance to see if they could get their businesses going. Working their fucking big farms or trying to keep their fucking wine-importing business going or whatever the fuck it was.' He turned slowly around to them. 'That was it, wasn't it?'

Sir Richard began to protest. Veitch stepped forward and hit him sharply in the mouth; his lip burst open and blood splattered on his clean, white shirt. A gasp rippled round the room, and Laura realised she had joined in, so shocking was the image.

One of the old women started to cry. 'I'm sorry—'

'Bit fucking late for that. Thought you'd get rid of a single mum last time, didn't you? Instead you got a poor kid.'

'We didn't mean—'

'Shut up. Whose idea was it?'

There was a long silence while everyone in the room tried to read what his next actions would be. Finally Sir Richard stopped dabbing at his lip. 'It was all of us. We discussed it together.' There was an unpleasant defiance in his face that gave the truth to everything Veitch had said.

'Yeah? Fair enough.' Veitch nodded reasonably. Then he slowly drew the crossbow out of the harness, loaded it and pointed it at the thin man in the dark suit; his face turned instantly grey. 'We'll start here then.'

'No, Ryan,' Shavi cautioned. Veitch ignored him. He slowly tightened his finger on the trigger.

'No!' The thin man pointed a shaking finger at Sir Richard. 'It was his idea! Yes, we all went along with it! But it was his idea!'

'You know what? I fucking thought as much. I'm a good judge of character like that. I know scum when I see it. And I knew you slimy fuckers would all be jumping to save your own skin when the shit hit the fan.' He motioned to Sir Richard with the crossbow. 'You're coming with me, matey.'

'I certainly am not!' Sir Richard's eyes darted round like a hunted animal. Before he could move Veitch had loosed the bolt into the floor and had clubbed him on the side of the head with the crossbow. Sir Richard slumped to the floor unconscious.

Veitch coolly reclaimed the bolt and slipped it back into the harness with the crossbow. Then he bent down and effortlessly slung Sir Richard over his shoulder. He turned to Shavi and Laura as he marched towards the door. 'I'll see you at the pub later.'

'Where are you going, Ryan?' Shavi asked darkly.

'I said, I'll see you later.' He tried to mask what was in his face with a tight smile, but Laura and Shavi both saw, and wished they hadn't.

The journey through the temple, across the autumnal fields, and out into the wide world, resembled a funeral procession. Ruth's face was like jagged shards of glass, her eyes constantly fixed on an inner landscape. She leaned on Church, for emotional rather than physical support, but his tread was heavy. Tom followed behind, unusually disoriented, with Max looking poleaxed at the rear.

In Richmond it was midmorning, the air heavy with an unpleasant heat. Insects buzzed in from the surrounding dales, and traffic fumes choked the market place. They had no idea if it was the next day or several weeks hence; although it remained unspoken, they all knew the date was now mightily significant.

In the back seat of the car, Ruth could no longer contain herself. She undid her jeans and pulled them down over her belly; there was an unmistakable swelling there.

'It doesn't make any sense!' Church protested to Tom. 'There's nothing actually, physically inside her! Is there?'

Tom looked away, shaking his head; it could have meant anything. Ruth broke down in sobs of shock.

After they had subsided, she slumped on the back seat in desperate silence. Tom caught Church's eye and the two of them slipped out, leaving Max to keep an eye on her.

'There must be something we can do,' Church said when they were far enough away from the car not to be overheard.

'Perhaps. But there is a more immediate problem. The Fomorii will never leave us alone until they have Balor back. Inside her is their entire reason for existence, the Heart of Shadows. They *must* have regrouped after the devastation in Edinburgh. Once they locate us their pursuit will be relentless.' He paused. 'They can't take the risk that you'll kill her to prevent Balor being born.'

'Kill her?' The thought hadn't even entered Church's head.

Tom nodded gravely. 'At the moment it's the only option.'

Church cursed Tom furiously for his cold-heartedness, but his reaction was so extreme because he knew, if he could bear to examine his thoughts rationally, that the Rhymer was right. The rebirth of Balor meant the End of Everything. To prevent that, Ruth's life was a small price to pay. Rationally, objectively, from a distance. But from his close perspective she was so dear to him her life was more important than everything. How could he kill her? And he knew, with a terrible, hollow ache, that ultimately the decision would come down to him; one of the burdens of leadership. And whatever his choice, he also knew it would destroy him for ever.

The atmosphere on the way back was thick with unspoken thoughts. Church could see Max was seething with questions, but he didn't feel like answering anything; it was too big to consider even in the privacy of his head. Ruth had dried her eyes and was coping with the shock remarkably well; somehow, that made Church feel even worse.

'That's why my familiar has disappeared,' she muttered, almost to herself. 'It won't come anywhere near me while that thing's inside me.'

They drove with all the windows down, but even that couldn't disperse the oppressive heat in the car. They were sleeked in sweat, sticking uncomfortably to the seats, flushed and irritable. There wasn't even a breath of wind across the lush landscape; the trees remained upright, the crops and hedgerow flowers unmoving.

Max drove speedily along the empty roads, leaning forward to peer through the windscreen that was streaked yellow and orange with the remains of a hundred bugs. But as he rounded a corner, he cursed loudly and slammed on the brakes, the Fiesta fishtailing to a sudden halt. A stream of cars filtered past the turning they needed for the route home: ahead were the unmissable signs of another police roadblock.

'They did see us on the way here.' Church grabbed Max's shoulder. 'You need to back up and get out of here. Find a different route.'

The words were barely out of his mouth when a spurt of blue activity broke out at the road junction; someone had already spotted them. Officers wearing body armour and helmets were tumbling out of the back of a van parked on the edge of the road; Church thought he glimpsed guns.

Max slammed the car into reverse and stepped on the accelerator.

With a screech of tyres, they shot backwards, but they'd only travelled a few yards when he hit the brakes. Church and Ruth crashed into the seats in front. Roaring out of a field behind them where it had been hidden was another police van, lights flashing.

'What now?' Max shouted. Before Church could answer he engaged gears, threw the car to the right and shot through an open gate into another field. The going was easy on the sun-baked ground, but they were still thrown about wildly as the car propelled itself over ridges and furrows.

Church gripped on to the ridge of the back seat so he could watch through the back window. The police were drawing closer. 'I hope you watched *The Cannonball Run*,' Church said.

Max grunted something unintelligible. All four wheels left the ground as the car crested a rise. They came down with a bone-jarring crunch and careered sideways on the dusty soil for a short way. 'It always looked easier in the movies,' Max said.

The police were only yards away when Max swore fitfully and suddenly drove directly at the barbed wire fence ahead. They ploughed through it with a rending and scratching and slid down a steep bank, bouncing over a small ditch on to the road with a shower of sparks.

The police vehicle followed suit, but when it hit the ditch its higher centre of gravity flipped it over. It smashed upside down and slid along the tarmac. Max gave a brief cheer as he watched the scene in the rearview mirror.

'Don't celebrate too soon,' Tom said gruffly. They followed his gaze to the bottleneck of traffic at the police checkpoint. ·

A shadow had risen up ten feet off the ground beyond the vehicles. Its outline shifted ominously in a manner Church had seen too many times before. Max started to retch loudly.

'Don't look at it!' Church snapped. 'Whatever you do. Keep your eyes on the road. Drive!'

Max couldn't resist one last look and vomited on to the floor between his feet. It deflected his attention from driving. The engine idled while he wiped his mouth, shook his dazed head.

The shadow moved, began to take on a sharper form. It was enormous, powerful, dense, seeming to suck in all light from the vicinity. It accelerated towards them, oblivious to the vehicles lined up in its path. A Renault flipped up end over end with a sound like a bomb going off, then a Peugeot and a Mondeo. A Jag folded up like paper in an explosion of glass and a rending of metal.

Church was transfixed; it was like a shark ploughing through water, leaving carnage in its wake. Cars flew like sea spray as it surged onwards. 'Drive, Max.' Church's voice was almost lost beneath the orchestral crashing of metal on tarmac.

It was relentless; as it built up speed it began to change, parts of the dense shadow detaching themselves and folding out, unfurling then reclamping themselves around the figure. It was like the horny carapace of an insect slowly building before their eyes, impenetrable plates, then something that looked like a helmet, but with horns or claws, and all of it in shimmering black. And still it moved.

Finally Church recognised his vision of the monstrous Fomorii warrior in the distorting cavern beneath Arthur's Seat; the same creature Veitch had seen at the ritual under the castle.

A People Carrier went over as if it weighed no more than paper. *How powerful is it?* Church thought. 'Come on, Max!' he yelled again.

The urgency in his voice finally shocked Max into activity. The car shot forward, throwing them all around once more.

'Don't look in the mirror,' Church cautioned; he knew Max, who was not inured to the terrible sight of the Fomorii, would black out instantly. 'Give it all you've got.'

The car began to race just as the Fomorii smashed through the last of the cars and started on the open road between them. Church could feel the thunderous vibrations from its pounding feet through the frame of the car.

'Is it gaining?' Ruth asked. She was clinging on to a corner of the seat to stop herself being thrown around.

'It's making the car jump around!' Max shouted over the racing engine. 'I'm having trouble controlling it!'

Agonisingly slowly, the car began to move faster. It didn't appear to be fast enough, but Max kept his foot to the floor, bouncing up and down in his seat as if trying to add to the momentum. And then, although they hardly dared believe it, the bone-jarring vibrations began to subside a little. Church glanced back once more at the nightmarish image of the beast and saw it had started to fall back; but it was still driving on, and he knew that even if they escaped this time, it would always be somewhere at their backs until it had completed its frightful mission.

'We're doing it,' he said. 'Just pray we don't have another technology failure. And be thankful we've got an open road ahead of us.'

Eventually the twists and turns of the road took them out of sight of the pursuing creature, although they could still hear it for several minutes after. Gradually, Church's heart stopped racing and he rested his face on the back of the seat.

'That's it,' he said. 'That's what they've sent after us.'

'One of the things,' Tom corrected. 'Every resource will be marshalled—'

'Oh, God!' There was a note of hysteria in Ruth's voice.

Church took her hand gently. 'Once we get back to the village we need to get moving again,' he said. 'We can't stay in one place too long.'

'Why? We've only got to kill time until Lughnasadh. Then it will all be over,' Ruth replied bitterly.

He didn't know how to answer that.

'We thought you lot were never coming back,' Veitch said when the car pulled up in the dusty High Street. He tried to hide his concern behind an irritated façade.

'How long have we been gone?' Church helped Ruth out, wondering how he was going to break the news to the others, in particular to Veitch.

'Three days.' Veitch couldn't contain himself any longer. He stepped up so he could look Ruth in the eye and said tenderly, 'How are you?'

She forced a smile. 'Pregnant.' Veitch looked shocked, then worried, and that made her laugh. They retired to The Green Man where Church, Tom and Max had a steadying drink and Ruth attempted to put a brave face on the end of her life.

Veitch's face never flickered when they told him what they had learned, but Church knew he would never forget the look buried deep in the Londoner's eyes; it was the mark of someone who had discovered there wasn't a God. Veitch took a drink, put his arm round Ruth, cracked a joke and said they'd find a solution – they always did; all the right noises. But that deep look never went away. Church wondered how Veitch would cope the closer it got to Lughnasadh; and what his response would be if that terrible decision had to be taken.

The mood remained sombre while they caught up over drinks. Shavi's account of what had taken place in the village left the returnees horrified. Max looked dazed, then queasy. 'I've known Sir Richard since I've been here. All those others too. I can't say I ever really got on with them, but I thought we were all coming from the same place. And I'm supposed to be a trained observer and a good judge of character.' Despite the shock, his spirits soon raised as they always seemed to, and it wasn't long before he was feverishly scribbling everything down in his notebook.

Their attention turned to Veitch's success in uncovering the deception. His ears coloured when Church congratulated him effusively; he looked genuinely touched by the praise.

'And I always thought he'd been clouted with the stupid stick,' Laura said. 'Looks like I'll have to find some other insults. Good job there's a long list.' She was getting braver once more; and Veitch, for his part, seemed to take her words in good humour.

'But you haven't told us what happened to Sir Richard,' Church said. 'You couldn't really take him to the cops, could you?'

Shavi and Laura watched Veitch intently. 'I convinced the bastard to leave town,' Veitch replied coldly.

Finally it was time to go. Max offered them his car, an act of generosity that brought a warm hug from Ruth and a back-slap from Veitch, but Church knew the police would be watching for it. After a heated discussion they decided to make their way on foot across the deserted countryside far away from the roads, cities and towns, despite the dangers that might lie away from the centres of population; it would give them a better chance of evading the Fomorii while they decided what to do next.

It was midafternoon and still unbearably hot when they left the cool confines of the pub. There was still plenty of the day left to put them deep into the heart of the wild upland country. They shook Max's hand, waved to Geordie, who grunted gruffly, and then they wound their way wearily towards the horizon.

Max stood with Geordie in the middle of the street until they had disappeared from view. 'Bloody rum bunch,' Geordie muttered.

'No, mate, heroes,' Max said. 'They might not know it, but they are. They just need writing up. Some of the rough edges taken off them so people can see the wood for the trees.'

Geordie grunted dismissively. 'Not my kind of heroes.'

'You're not seeing it right, Geordie. We're at war now. Under siege. In times like this the people need someone to look up to, someone who'll give them courage to keep fighting.' He smiled tightly. 'I reckon that lot fit the bill – if their story is told in the right way. And I'm just the man to tell it.'

As they passed the outskirts of the village, Laura glanced up at the scarecrow which had unnerved her so much on her way in. She was surprised to see it looked different, although she at first wondered if it was a trick of the glaring sun. Squinting, she tried to pick out what had changed; gradually details emerged. It was no longer just a scarecrow. Something had been tied to it. She squinted again. Another scarecrow appeared to be hanging at the front of the original in the same crucified position, only the bottom two thirds of it was missing. And the head of the second one didn't look very good either.

But something was still jarring. Curious, she took a few steps forward so the sun was away from it. And then, in a moment of pure horror, she realised what it was. It wore a white shirt splattered with something dark near the collar. Instead of straw, something gleamed in the sun; bone that had been picked clean by the creatures in the fields.

Unable to mask her queasy thoughts, she snapped round at Veitch, suddenly aware of the dark, hidden depths of his character. She knew from his body language he realised she was watching him, but he never turned to meet her gaze. His eyes were fixed on the horizon, his expression cold and aloof.

CHAPTER FOURTEEN

Wretched Times

The clear blue sky was so near they felt like they were in heaven, the air so clean and fresh it burned their throats, which were more used to the particles and fumes of city living. There, high up on the dinosaur-backed ridge of the Pennines, they felt like they had been sucked into the thunderous heart of nature, or into the past where no chimney belched, no meaningless machine disturbed the stillness. Amidst out-cropping rock turned bronze by the unflinching sun they picked their way through swaying seas of fern, down sheep-clipped grassy slopes, across bleak upland moors where the wind cut like talons.

Tom navigated by the sun and the stars, leading them on into the remotest parts of the land where the sodium glare had never touched. At night the vast spray of stars looked like a milky river leading them back to the source. They made their camps in hidden corners, dips below the eyeline, behind boulders and in low-hanging caves; all except Ruth took turns keeping watch over the dying campfires.

At times they saw things moving away in the dark or heard sounds that had little to do with any animals they knew; one night Shavi had a conversation with someone unseen whose voice switched between the mewling tones of an infant and the phlegmy crackle of an old man. When the sun began to rise, Shavi heard the mysterious stranger scurry away on many legs, an insectile chittering bouncing among the rocks.

Their decision to steer clear of any centre of population meant finding food was a constant problem, though they were thankful that Tom had an encyclopaedic knowledge of the roots, plants and herbs which grew in secret places where no one would have thought to look. He taught Veitch his many skills at catching rabbits and the occasional game bird, and how to snatch fish from the sparkling streams and rivers they crossed. When cooked on the campfire, the fare was mouth-watering; even so, they soon yearned for a richer and more varied diet.

'This feels like *Lord of the Flies*,' Shavi remarked one calm morning as he watched Veitch carve a spear with his knife; he refused to use his crossbow for hunting.

'Let's hope it doesn't end the same way,' Church replied; he attempted to take the edge off his words with a smile.

'Say, why don't you focus on the black side?' Ruth chipped in with cheerful sarcasm. After the initial shock she had put them all to shame with her bright mood, refusing to be bowed by what had been inflicted on her. Church kept waiting for her to crack as the black despair he was sure lurked within came rushing to the surface, but it never did, and as time passed he came to think it wasn't there at all.

'Look around,' she continued. 'This is the best there is in life. Stars you can see, food and water you can taste, air you can breathe. I've never felt as much at peace. You know, despite everything. Back in London, with work and all that, life had a constant background buzz, like some irritating noise that you force yourself to get used to because it's always around. Now . . .' She held out her arms. 'Nothing. It's not there.'

'It always takes a disaster to show you what you're missing in life.' Laura's voice dripped with irony, but they all knew she was speaking the truth.

Ruth's health continued to be up and down: morning sickness as if she had a normal pregnancy, which always made her laugh darkly, aches and pains in a belly that continued to grow by the day, then times when she felt as robust as she usually did.

Despite the urgency they all felt with Lughnasadh approaching rapidly, they hadn't been able to reach any decision on what to do next. It was almost as if they were paralysed by the enormity of the task before them, and the certain knowledge that the repercussions of one wrong step would be more than any of them could bear. Instead, most of the days and nights passed in the denial of reality that was small-talk, as if they were on a pleasant summer hike. If they could have brought themselves to examine what was in their hearts they would all know they felt there was only going to be one awful, unbearable option.

It was always Tom who was expected to find a solution; he was, after all, the one with the most knowledge of the new rules that underpinned reality. After five days of brooding and weighing of options, of trying to read the stars and muttering away in the thick groves, he thought he had a plan, but the others could tell from his face that he didn't give it much weight. He refused to discuss it there in the open, dangerous high country.

'Talk of such dark matters needs somewhere secure and comforting, where energies can be recharged and preparations made for what lies ahead,' he said. Any questions were simply met with a finger pointing towards the horizon.

That night they made their camp in a sheltered spot on the southern slopes of Pen-y-Ghent not far down from the summit. It was a clear evening and after they had eaten they sat looking at the brilliant lights of the West Yorkshire conurbation spread out to the south-east.

After a long period of thought, Ruth said, 'It's too big, isn't it?'

'What are you on about?' Veitch put the finishing touches to another spear; he was becoming expert in the construction of weapons.

'Look at it.' She outlined the extremes of the lights with a finger. 'They used to be just a few settlements. Then they became villages, then towns and cities, and now they're all merging into one. They're driving nature out completely. There's no human scale at all. People need to feel close to nature to be healthy, psychologically and physically.'

'I thought you were a city girl,' Veitch said.

'I was.' Ruth closed her eyes for a moment. 'I've changed.'

'Perhaps this whole disaster happened for a reason,' Shavi mused.

Ruth eyed him, her eyes bright, waiting for him to say what she was beginning to think herself.

'We have had Government after Government concreting over huge swathes of the countryside,' he continued. 'How many acres have been lost since the Second World War? How much of the ancient woodlands have been cut down? How many hedgerows torn up by greedy farmers? How much moorland destroyed by Army firing ranges? How many rivers polluted, chalklands debased, coastal floodplains disrupted? There was a relentless advance of urbanisation, of what was laughingly called *progress*—'

'And now it's stopped,' Church said thoughtfully.

'Perhaps something drastic had to happen to redress the balance. To save the land.' Shavi lay back with his hands behind his head to stare at the stars.

'What are you saying?' Veitch looked confused and a little irritated. 'That the Bastards invaded us and slaughtered all those people just to save a few bunny rabbits?'

'Oh, *they* do not know about it,' Shavi mused. 'Perhaps they are just part of the plan.'

'Plan?' Veitch looked to Ruth for guidance.

'The great scheme of things,' she said.

Laura slapped her forehead theatrically. 'Tell me you're not going to start talking about God!'

'*There is always something higher,*' Ruth mused. 'That's what Ogma said in Otherworld.'

Shavi leaned up on his elbows to laugh gently at Veitch's expression. 'We are only throwing ideas around, Ryan. Do not let it trouble you.'

'Well, it does,' Veitch said moodily. 'I get worried when people start talking about God. There's enough to worry about down here.'

'Exactly!' Shavi said. 'We are all crabs living in an enclosed rock pool. Occasionally water rushes in, changes things around, adds something new. We do not know it is the sea. Because the rock pool is all we see, we think it is all there is. We are puzzled by the mystery, but comforted by the regularity of our existence. We could never see that an infinite variety of wonder lies just feet away, that intelligent beings roam that place doing miraculous things. We are stuck in the rock pool and we can never see the big picture. So why try to make sense of something we cannot grasp? Why not just enjoy the wonders the next tide brings in?'

There was a long pause and then Laura said, 'You're getting up your own arse again, Shav-ster.'

'What I don't get,' Veitch said, 'is how any of this magic shit really works. I mean, somebody does something, then miles away something else happens with no connection between the two. What's that all about?'

'Look at it this way.' Shavi was growing excited that the conversation was moving away from mundane matters. 'You play computer games, no? The same as Laura. You both know about cheat codes. You type the code in and it cuts through the reality of the game. You can do anything you want – walk through walls, get all the weapons or secrets. Be a god in that fantasy world. There is a writer by the name of Warren Ellis who described magic as the cheat code for reality, which, I think, is a perfect analogy.'

Realisation dawned on Veitch's face. 'I get it! Blimey, why didn't you put it like that before?'

Even Laura seemed intrigued by this line. 'Now those are the kind of cheat codes I could do with.'

'This whole world now, it's all about mystery and discovery. It's like being a kid all over again,' Church said. He thought for a moment, then added, 'When I fell into the pit under Arthur's Seat, feeling like my life was going to be over in an instant, I saw the blue fire come out of thin air. Not thin air, that's wrong. From somewhere else, like Otherworld, but not there.' He looked from Ruth to Tom to Shavi. 'Where do you think that was?'

'The source of it all?' Tom shrugged, the ashes of his dwindling joint glowing red in the dark. 'Is it really worth asking that question? Do you think we'll find out the truth? Not in this life.'

'It *is* worth asking,' Church insisted, 'even if we can't find the answer. The asking is important. It—'

'Look at that.' They followed Ruth's pointing finger into the sky. A serpentine silhouette curled among the stars, riding the night currents on leathery wings. Although they could pick out no detail of the jewelled scales, the Fabulous Beast still filled them with an inspiring sense of wonder; it was a sign of a connection with the infinite that always surrounded them. 'You look at that,' she continued dreamily, 'and then all those city lights destroying the night . . . there's no comparison, is there.'

Instantly the entire landscape was plunged into darkness; it was just another technology failure, but they all audibly caught their breath, the coincidence with Ruth's words seeming unnervingly meaningful.

'Spooky,' Laura said. 'Now make them come on again.'

The brief tension punctured, they all burst out laughing, then lay back to watch the Fabulous Beast gently tracking across the arc of the sky.

Exhausted by their daytime exertions, Ruth, Tom, Veitch and Shavi drifted off to the tents long before midnight. Once they were alone, Laura slumped next to Church, her head resting on his thigh. She had trouble making any first move which might lead to affection, so her actions always followed the same pattern of casual contact. Church tried not to flinch or give any sign things had changed, but he felt guilty he hadn't yet brought the relationship to a close as he had promised Niamh. It was odd; once Niamh had left his side he felt less of an attraction, more inclined to stay with Laura. He was sure Niamh hadn't been consciously manipulating his feelings; it had simply happened, in the same way they had all been subtly influenced by the musical tones of Cormorel and Baccharus. Perhaps there was something in the nature of the Tuatha Dé Danann that made humans fall under their spell. The old fairy stories that had been based on the ancient memories of the Tuatha Dé Danann often told how hapless night-time wanderers were bewitched by the soft voices of the Fair Folk. Even so, he had given Niamh his word. Could he break it? Did he want to risk offending someone so powerful?

'You're starting to become a cliché, Churchill. Sitting there brooding while you've got the world's most glamorous woman lying next to you.' He realised she had been staring up at him while he had been lost in his thoughts.

'Sorry. You know . . . so much to think about . . .' It sounded feeble, almost insulting. She laughed, but he suddenly realised he could see something squirming deep in her eyes. 'What's wrong?'

'We never really talk, do we?'

'You don't like talking.'

'No.' That look again, even though she was trying to hide it.

'Tell me what's wrong.'

Her eyes flickered away from him; she pretended she was watching the dying embers of the campfire away near the tents. Then: 'I'm scared.' A pause. 'And that was about as easy to say as swallowing nails.'

'We're all scared.'

'Do you think you can be any more glib?'

He sighed. 'Don't try to pick another fight. There are easier kinds of sport.'

'I'm not. You are being glib.' Her voice sounded hurt, the first time he had heard that tone. 'I'm scared something's happening to me. Inside.'

'What, you're ill?'

'I guess.' She flinched, looked unsure. 'When that winter witch came after me in the club in Edinburgh something happened that I didn't tell anybody about—'

'Why not?'

'Because I was scared, you dickhead. Are you going to hear me out or talk bollocks for the rest of the night? I was trying to get out, thinking I was dead, regretting being a stupid bitch like usual, and I cut myself. Nothing much.' She held up her finger and drew a faint line on her skin where the scratch had been. 'Only the blood wasn't red, it was green.'

'Some kind of poisoning?'

She shook her head forcefully. 'When it splashed, it seemed to have a life of its own. It moved all over some bars on a window, broke them open.' She stared at her hand as if it belonged to somebody else. In a quiet voice, she added, 'I think I'm jinxed for life.'

Church took her hand and examined it closely. Slowly, he turned it over; there was the tattoo of interlocking leaves that had been burned into her flesh on the island in Loch Maree, the mark of Cernunnos.

Gradually realisation crossed her face. 'The bastard did something to me! I was so worried I didn't even think of that.'

'Maybe. Seems like too much of a coincidence.'

'And there are no coincidences,' she added bitterly. 'So what's happened to me? God . . .' She slammed her fist against the ground angrily.

'I don't know, but I'm betting we'll find out sooner or later. The way Cernunnos acted, he must have something in mind for you.' He felt a surge of anger at how the gods continued to manipulate them all. 'Look, you're obviously still healthy, still walking about, try not to worry about it—'

'That's easy for you to say! How would you feel if you'd suddenly got anti-freeze for blood?' She brushed at her eye before he saw the stray tear, the only honest admission of all the churning emotions in her.

Suddenly he was aware of how fragile she felt, alone and worrying, trying to do her best for everyone else while keeping her personal fears deep inside. She was more of a mess than all of them and that was saying something: filled with self-loathing, unable to see even the slightest good in her character. Yet still trying to do her best. He brushed the hair from her forehead; she wouldn't look at him. He had responsibilities here too; no one else was looking out for her and she wasn't up to doing it herself. Once again he was trapped by doing what was right and damning the consequences. He couldn't abandon her; that would be inhuman. So what if Niamh found out? He could explain the situation. How bad could it be? Certainly not as bad as leaving Laura to fend for herself when she was at her lowest ebb.

'Come on,' he whispered. 'Let's go to bed.'

Morning came bright and hard. Tom was up before everyone else, lighting the fire and boiling up the remnants of the rabbit stew they'd eaten the night before; it met with uniform disapproval, but there was no alternative so they forced it down despite their protesting stomachs.

By seven a.m. they were on their way. Using Veitch's book of maps in conjunction with the sun, Tom strode out confidently. He still refused to give them even a hint as to their destination.

'I don't get it,' Laura said. 'Yesterday my feet were two big, fat blisters. Today they're fine.'

Tom snorted derisively from the front of the column. 'Don't you *ever* pay attention? Why do you think your esteemed leader healed so quickly after the Fomorii masters of torture were loose on him under Dartmoor? Do you think they simply didn't do a proper job? Why do you think Ruth has regained her—'

'What's your point, you old git?'

'It's the Pendragon Spirit,' Church said. 'It helps us heal.'

'Pity Tom Bombadil up front hasn't got it, then. He could grow himself a new head when I rip this one off.'

Tom replied, but it was deliberately muffled so Laura couldn't hear.

'Keep walking, old man,' she shouted. 'And watch out for those sudden crevices.'

Not long after, Veitch and Shavi broke off from the others to see if they could catch something for lunch. They were wary of getting lost, so they arranged a meeting place they could easily pick out on the landscape. After an hour of futile tracking for rabbit pellets and scanning the landscape for any sign of game birds, they gave up and rested against a young tree which had been so battered by the wind it resembled a hunched old man.

Veitch cracked his knuckles, then progressed through a series of movements to drive the kinks from his muscles. Shavi watched him languidly.

'Do you want to talk about what has happened to Ruth?' he asked eventually.

'No.'

'You should. It is better to get these things out in the open.'

'You sound like the counsellor my mum and dad dragged me to when I was a kid.'

Shavi laughed gently. 'I am talking as a friend.'

This seemed to bring Veitch up sharp for a second, but then he carried on as before. 'I never thought I'd have a queen for a friend.'

'These times have changed us all.'

Veitch sighed. 'You better not say any of this to the others, all right?'

'Of course not.'

' 'cause you're the only one I could talk to about it. Yeah, it's doing my head in, course it is. I thought after going through hell to get her back from the Bastards that would be the end of it. And now this. It cuts me up thinking what she's going through. She doesn't deserve that. She deserves . . .'

He seemed to have trouble saying what he was thinking so Shavi gently prompted him: 'What?'

'The best. Whatever makes her happy.'

'Even if that is not you?'

Veitch looked away. 'Yeah. I just want her to be happy.' He was lost in thought for a moment, but then his brow furrowed. 'What do you think's going to happen to her?'

'I do not know. I do know we will do our best.'

'I know it looks black, but I just can't believe she's going to die. Everyone thought she was a goner when the Bastards had her. They didn't say it, but I know they did. But I never doubted we'd get her out for a minute. And I reckon we'll do it this time.'

Shavi smiled; there was something heartwarmingly childlike about Veitch beneath his steely exterior. 'You believe in happy endings.'

'Never used to. I do now, yeah.'

A sound like the roar of some unidentified animal thundered across the landscape. They both started, the hairs standing on the back of their necks. Something in the noise made them instantly terrified, as if some buried race memory had been triggered.

'What the fuck was that?' Veitch dropped low to peer all around.

They could see nothing in the immediate vicinity, so they crawled to the top of a slight rise for a broader vista. At first that area too seemed empty, but as their eyes became used to the patterns of light and shade on the landscape they simultaneously picked out a black shape moving slowly several miles away. The jarring sensation in their heads the moment their eyes locked on it told them instantly what it was.

They squinted, trying to pick out details from the shadow, but all they got were brief glimpses of something that seemed occasionally insectile, occasionally like a man. Yet there was no mistaking the dangerous power washing off it.

Veitch, who had seen it more clearly before, realised what it was. 'It's that big Bastard, the warrior, that almost got the others on their way back from Richmond.'

'It is hunting,' Shavi said instinctively.

'Do you think it knows we're here?'

Shavi chewed his lip as he weighed up the evidence. 'It seems to have an idea in which direction we are going, but it does not seem to be able to pinpoint us exactly.'

'They've sent it after Ruth, the biggest and baddest they've got to offer. What the fuck are we going to do now?' He answered his own question a moment later. 'Keep moving. We can't hang around.'

They retreated down the rise, then hurried back to tell the others.

There was no further sighting of whatever was hunting them, its path had appeared to be taking it away to the west while they were moving south-east. Even so, they were now even more on their guard.

As the day drew on, dark clouds swept in from the west and by midafternoon the landscape had taken on a silver sheen beneath the lowering sky. There, on the high ground, the wind had the bite of winter despite the time of year; they all wished they had some warmer clothes, but they had only brought a few changes of underwear and T-shirts.

Dusk came early with the clouds blackening and they knew it was better to find shelter and make camp rather than risk a lightning strike in the open ground. The rain fell in sheets, rippling back and forth across the grass and rocks; the clouds came down even lower and soon visibility was down to a few yards.

Not even Tom's outdoor skills could find any wood dry enough to make a fire. They sat shivering in their tents, observing the storm through the open flaps. Eventually the rain died off and the clouds lifted, the storm drifting away to the east. They watched its progress, the lightning sparking out in jagged explosions of passion, the world thrown into negative, the martial drumroll.

Laura's voice drifted out across the camp site. 'We need a band. You can't beat a light show like that with any technology.' The wonder in her words raised all their spirits.

It took two more days to reach their destination. The first was dismal with occasional downpours. The going was hard in the face of the gale and the landscape was treacherous in the intermittent mists. They made camp early and slept long.

The second day was much brighter from the onset and by midmorning even the smallest cloud had blown away. Veitch, Shavi and Church stripped to the waist in the growing heat, prompting them to tease the women to follow suit. A mouthful of abuse from Laura brought their jeering to a quick end.

For the first time in days they had to cross major roads and avoid centres of population. They wound their way by Shipton and Ilkley, and whenever the moorland gave way to lanes they ducked behind stone walls every time they heard the sound of a car. After their enforced isolation they felt oddly unnerved when they realised the most populous areas of Yorkshire were close. Tom even claimed to smell Bradford and Leeds on the wind.

Ilkley Moor was almost mystical in the way it responded to the weather conditions and the shifting of light and shade across its robust skin. The green fields on the edge gave way to romantic bleakness the higher they rose, where gorse and scrubland looked copper in the midafternoon sun. There, in the midst of it, the sense of isolation returned, potent yet oddly comforting.

They knew the spot the moment it came into view. The standing stones glowed brightly, their shadows like pointing fingers. But it wasn't the sight of them; after only a few days away from the trappings of the modern age their senses were attuned to changes in the world around them, the crackling energy in the atmosphere that instantly seemed to recharge their flagging vitality, the feel of a powerful force throbbing in the ground as if mighty machines turned just beneath their feet; a sudden overwhelming sense of wellbeing.

Church closed his eyes and had an instant vision of the blue fire flowing powerfully in mighty arteries away from the circle. 'There's nothing dormant about this spot.'

Although he tried to hide his emotions as usual, Tom seemed pleased by Church's sensitivity. 'This has always been a vital spot. Welcome to the Twelve Apostles of Ilkley Moor.'

*

The twelve standing stones which Tom called the Apostles were roughly four feet high and hacked from the local millstone grit. 'There were originally twenty,' Tom said. 'In the nineteenth century they thought it was a calendar and christened it the Druidical Dial.'

Amongst the stones they felt instantly secure and relaxed, as if they instinctively knew nothing could harm them there.

'It feels like Stonehenge on a smaller scale.' Ruth felt comforted and hugged her arms around herself.

'All the sacred sites used to be like this,' Tom said. 'Places of sanctuary. Linked to the Fiery Network. So many have been torn down now.'

Shavi stood in the centre of the circle, closed his eyes and raised his arms. 'The magic is vibrant.'

'It's one of the places that remained potent, even during the Age of Reason,' Tom continued. 'In 1976 three of the Royal Observer Corps were up here. They saw a white globe of light hovering above the stones. Throughout the eighties there were many other accounts of strange, flashing lights and balls of light descending. That helped the circle regain some of its standing in the local community and every summer solstice there used to be a fine collection of people up here for celebration.'

Church drifted away from the others to press his hand on one of the stones; he could feel the power humming within as if there were electronic circuitry just beneath the surface. It seemed so long since Tom had introduced him to the blue fire at Stonehenge, although it was only a matter of weeks, yet now it felt such a part of his life he couldn't imagine living without it. The image of Tom manipulating the blue flames that first night had haunted him and he had begun to realise it was something he desperately wanted to be able to do himself. Cautiously he removed his hand an inch from the stone and concentrated in an effort to produce that leaping blue spark.

Nothing came. Yet he felt no disappointment. He was sure it was only a matter of time.

They set up camp within the tight confines of the circle. In no time at all the earth energy had infused them, recharging them, healing their aches and pains, and Ruth felt better than she had done since Callander; the nausea had almost completely gone. Yet the moor stretched out so bleakly all around and the camp was so exposed they couldn't shake their sense of unease and the feeling they were constantly being watched.

For long periods, Veitch sat half-perched on one of the stones scanning the landscape. 'See anything?' Church asked him while the others were preparing dinner.

He shook his head without taking his eyes off the scenery. 'Look at it out there. There could be somebody ten feet away lying in the scrub and we'd have trouble seeing them.'

'At least if that big Fomor comes up we won't miss seeing him.'

'Yeah,' Veitch said darkly, 'but then where do we run, eh?'

When darkness fell, the sense of isolation became even more disturbing. There was no light, no sign at all of human habitation; they might as well have been Neolithic tribesmen praying to their gods for the coming of the dawn.

Their small-talk was more mundane than ever, with none of the usual gibes or abrasiveness, as they all mentally prepared themselves for the discussion to come. Eventually Tom took out his hash tin and rolled himself a joint, which they all recognised as the signal that they were about to begin. Ruth suddenly looked like she was about to be sick.

'Over the last few days we have all done a remarkable job in avoiding the severity of the problem that faces us,' Tom began. 'That's understandable. It's almost too monumental to consider. But let's speak plainly now so we know exactly where we stand. Here in this circle we have the chance for ultimate victory in the enormous conflict that has enveloped us. And we face a personal, shattering defeat that will devastate us.' Church was surprised to hear the raw emotion in Tom's words; the Rhymer had always pretended he cared little about any of them.

'What you're saying,' Ruth said, her face pale but strong, 'is that if I die, Balor dies, the Fomorii lose, we . . . humanity . . . wins. But if you're overcome by sentimentalism and you can't bring yourself to kill me, Balor will be reborn and everybody loses. And I get to die anyway, in the birth. That last point pretty much makes any debate unnecessary. Either way I die. So . . . we should get on with it as soon as possible.'

'Hang on a minute—' Veitch protested.

'Yes,' Church said. 'I know you'd just love to be a martyr, but maybe we should see if there are any other options before we rush to slit your throat and bury you out on the moors.'

'I'm just letting you know I'm prepared,' Ruth said.

Shavi leaned forward. 'The Tuatha Dé Danann, certainly at their highest level, seem almost omnipotent. Can we ask them to help us?'

'You didn't see Dian Cecht.' The contempt in Church's voice was clear. 'The Fomorii are corrupting in their eyes, and Balor is the ultimate corruption. They're not prepared to get their pristine hands dirty, even if they *could* do something.'

'They're like a bunch of toffs telling the labourers what to do,' Veitch said venomously.

Laura had been watching Tom closely while the others spoke. He had been drawing on his joint, inspecting the hot ashes at the end, as if he wasn't really listening. 'You've got something in mind, haven't you?'

Tom seemed not to hear her, either, but the others all turned to him. 'The Tuatha Dé Danann will not be able to destroy Balor's essence in its current form unless the medium for the rebirth is destroyed,' he began. 'But, as Shavi said, their abilities are wide-ranging. It is possible they may be able to do something to help. I've seen some of the wonders they can perform . . .' His voice faded; he bit his bottom lip.

'How are we going to get them to help us?' Church said. 'They don't want anything to do with anyone who's been touched by the Fomorii.'

'I may be able to help.' Tom drew on the joint insistently; it was obviously no longer about enjoying the effect or using it for some kind of consciousness-raising – he was trying to anaesthetise himself. 'You recall around the campfire in the Allen Gorge, Cormorel told me my *Queen* had returned to her court?'

'She was the one who first took you into Otherworld,' Church said. Whose immense power had taken Tom's body and consciousness apart and reassembled it, who had treated Tom like a toy in the hands of a spoilt but curious brat, his torment so great his mind had almost shattered. And the woman he had grown to love in his captivity and suffering. Church shivered.

'The Faerie Queen, humans called her. She was also known as the Great Goddess by the older races, and a legion of other names.'

'So, she's, like, a bigshot?' Veitch said. 'The Queen.'

'There are many queens among the Tuatha Dé Danann, all with their own courts, although that term is about as relevant as any other when discussing them. But, yes, she is higher than most.'

'And you think she will help?' Church asked, watching Tom carefully for the truth behind his words.

The Rhymer smiled tightly. 'How could she not when her pet returns, rolls over and asks so nicely?'

The bitterness in his voice stung them all. Church knew what a sacrifice Tom would be making; after both the agonies and the crushing blow to his ego, to put himself at risk of facing it all again was more than anyone should be expected to do.

Ruth recognised it too, for there were tears rimming her eyes. She wiped them away, stared at the ground desolately.

'There is no guarantee that she can help, though?' Shavi asked.

Tom raised his hands. 'There are never any guarantees.'

'Then we should have an alternative plan.' Shavi rested a comforting hand on Ruth's back; she shivered, seemed to draw strength from it. 'We already have patrons among the Tuatha Dé Danann. Niamh—'

'I don't think I can ask her for any more help. She's trying to sort out Maponus,' Church said; but he had a pang of guilt knowing that he was afraid to approach her after failing to end his relationship with Laura.

'More importantly,' Shavi continued unfazed, 'there is Cernunnos. Ruth saved him from the control of the Fomorii. Now she is in difficulty, perhaps he will return the favour.'

'Yes.' Ruth's eyes grew wide. 'He said *the Green* was inside me.' She struggled to remember his exact words. 'He said *in the harshest times, you may call for my aid. Seek me out in my Green Home.*'

'That's it, then!' Veitch said excitedly. 'Plan A and Plan B. One of 'em's got to work!'

'We have to be wary not to get too in debt to any of the Tuatha Dé Danann.' The weight in Tom's words gave them all pause.

'This is a desperate situation,' Church said. 'We have to take risks.'

'I know,' Tom said. 'But you have to be aware there is always a price to pay, and that price may be very high indeed. Do not go into this blindly.'

'Then what's the plan? How do we get to these freaks?' Veitch had latched on to the suggestions with the simple hope of a child; the brightness of relief lit his face.

Tom cursed under his breath. 'I think a good starting point would be for you to learn how to treat them with respect. If you open your mouth like that you won't have a second chance to speak.'

'Right.' Veitch looked suitably chastened.

'The Queen's court is accessed under Tom-na-hurich, the Hill of Yews, in Inverness,' Tom said. 'It will be a long, difficult journey, so I propose to set off at sunrise—'

'You're not going alone.' Church didn't leave any room for debate in his tone, but he was still surprised when Tom didn't argue. Church quickly looked round the others, then stopped at Veitch. 'Ryan, you had better go with him. We can't risk the Queen hanging on to him. There needs to be someone to bring back the goods in an emergency.' He hated speaking so baldly, but he could see Tom knew exactly what the potential risks were.

'Not back up to Scotland,' Veitch moaned. 'We've only just scarpered from there.'

'What about Cernunnos?' Ruth asked. 'Where's this Green Home?'

'Cernunnos has been most closely linked with the site of the Great Oak in Windsor Park,' Tom said. 'The oak is no longer there, but the god is rumoured to appear at the spot which was the prime centre of his worship in antiquity. They say,' Tom added, 'he appears there most at times of national crisis.'

'I remember,' Church mused, 'another legend linked to that site. About Herne the Hunter.'

Ruth nodded. 'Cernunnos said that was one of the names by which he was known.'

'The legends say Herne was a Royal huntsman who saved a king's life by throwing himself in front of a wounded stag that was threatening to kill his master,' Tom said. 'As Herne lay dying, a magician appeared who told the king the only way he could save his huntsman's life was to cut off the stag's antlers and tie them to Herne's head. He recovered and became the best huntsman in the land. But he was so favoured by the king, the other huntsmen, overcome by jealousy, eventually persuaded the king to dismiss him. Herne was so broken by this he went out and hanged himself. And the king never had the same kind of success in his Royal hunts.'

Shavi mused over this story for a moment, then said, 'I feel that legend is more metaphor than fact.'

Tom agreed. 'There is secret information in all these stories that has the power to survive down the years. That one tells of how the people turned their back on the resurrective and empowering force of nature, how they suffered for it, and how nature suffered too. It was a warning, albeit a gentle one, compared with some of the legends.

'You see,' he continued, as if the information buried under centuries of experience in his mind was starting to come out in a rush, 'Cernunnos and his bright, other half are, if you will, the bridge between the Tuatha Dé Danann and the natural power of this world. In many ways, they are closer to us than they are to their own. It was a joining that happened in the earliest times, when the two gods pledged themselves to this world and, in doing so, the best interests of the people.'

'You'd be good for this one, Shavi,' Church said. 'You're the shaman. You've developed all those links to nature. You should be able to communicate with Cernunnos.'

Church felt Laura shift next to him and he knew exactly what she was thinking: Cernunnos had put his mark on her too; Ruth obviously wasn't in any condition to undertake the journey, but as a favoured of Cernunnos, Laura would have been a natural choice. Church hadn't chosen her because he felt she wasn't up to the task, couldn't be trusted with something so important; and she knew exactly what his reasons were. He felt a pang of guilt at hurting her, but he had to focus on the best interests of the group.

'When I get to the park, how do I contact Cernunnos?' Shavi asked.

'There is a story I recall from my long walk around the world in the sixties,' Tom replied. 'In 1962 a group of teenagers found a hunting horn in the forest on the edge of a clearing. They blew it and were instantly answered by another horn and the baying of hounds. It was Cernunnos and the Wild Hunt, with the wish-hounds. The boys fled in fear.'

'And the Hunt, I presume, did not depart until they claimed a life,' Shavi noted darkly. 'A price to pay indeed.'

'Perhaps he won't appear in that form,' Ruth suggested hopefully.

Shavi shrugged. 'Then I seek out the horn.'

Laura avoided Church's gaze when he looked from her to Ruth. 'That leaves just the three of us,' he said.

'You're sure we're up to protecting the Queen Bee,' Laura said acidly.

'We'll do our best, as always.' It wasn't a question he really wanted to consider too deeply.

Thunder rolled across the moor; a flash of lightning lit up the northern sky. 'Looks like we're in for a storm.' Veitch seemed happier now he felt he was doing something positive.

They watched the sky for a while, but the bad weather was skirting the edge of the moor, moving eastwards. Another flash of lightning threw the landscape into stark relief.

'What's that?' Ruth said suddenly. But the night had already swallowed up whatever she had seen.

'What did it look like?' Church asked.

'I don't know.' Her voice sounded like she had an idea. She moved to the edge of the circle to get a better look.

'Don't go beyond the stones!' Tom said sharply. 'The earth energy gives a modicum of invisibility here if there's anything supernatural in the vicinity. They'd have to stumble right across us to see us.'

'I don't know . . .' Ruth peered into the dark, but it was too deep.

Another flash of lightning, moving away now, so the illumination was not so stark. Even so, Ruth caught her breath; this time it was unmistakable. A large black shape like a sucking void was moving rapidly across the bleak moorland.

'It's here.' Her voice barely more than a whisper. She turned, eyes wide; the others could read all they needed in her face.

Tom rushed over and kicked out the campfire. 'Stay down, stay quiet! It may pass us by.'

At that moment twin beams of light cut through the night, rising high up into the sky like searchlights. A second later they lowered sharply as a car came over a rise and started to head towards them. The headlights briefly washed over the stones as the car came on to the road that ran within sight of the circle.

'Shit,' Veitch said under his breath.

Across the quiet landscape music rolled from the car's open windows. Church unconsciously noted it was New Radicals singing *You Get What You Give*, but that thought was just a buzz beneath a wash of rising panic. The car's engine droned. Young voices sang along loudly, male and female, four, maybe five of them.

'Shut up,' Laura hissed to herself.

'Turn off the headlights,' Veitch said.

As if anything will do any good, Church thought.

The car continued its progress, a firefly in the night.

Veitch spun round, his face contorted with anxiety. 'We've got to get out there and do something! The Bastard will be on them in a minute and those poor fuckers won't stand a chance!'

Church hesitated; he was right, they ought to try.

Tom seemed to read his mind. 'No! No one leaves the circle! If you go out there you will surely die. Even here, your chances are slim—'

'Fuck! We have to do something!' Veitch protested. Church thought he was going to cry.

'You go out there and die in vain, everybody else dies with you!' Tom's voice was a snarl that would brook no dissent. 'You're too important now! You have to think of the big picture!'

Veitch was starting to move. Tom gripped his shoulder and Veitch tried to shake it off furiously, but Tom held on so effortlessly it seemed incongruous. Veitch half-turned, eyes blazing, but he didn't move any further.

Another diminishing flash, an instant's tableau: the dark hulk of the Fomorii warrior had risen up, started to change as its insectile armour clanked and slid into place, preparing to attack. The car trundled along, the occupants oblivious.

Ruth's eyes were tear-stained. She stared at Church, aghast. He winced, looked away.

'Maybe we could . . .' Laura stopped, shook her head, walked away until she was out of the others' line of sight.

Shavi was like an iron staff, his face locked, his eyes fixed on the feeble beams of light.

Suddenly there was a sound like aluminium sheeting being torn in two. Several stars were blotted out. And then the ground trembled. There was an instant when they all had their eyes shut, praying. But they had to see, so they would never forget. The darkness swept down like a pouncing lion. There was a crunching of metal. The headlight beams shot up in the sky. Singing voices suddenly became screams that must have torn throats. New Radicals were still singing, just for an instant longer, then snapped off at the same time as the screams. A second later the lights blinked out. More crunching. Silence. And then an explosion which rocketed flames and shards of metal high into the sky as the petrol tank went up.

Everyone in the circle was holding their breath. The universal exhalation came slowly, filled with despair.

'Get down!' Tom hissed.

They dropped flat so they could feel the vibrations in the ground, fast, growing slower. They didn't stir until they had died away completely. When they eventually sat up, everyone looked shell-shocked; faces pale, eyes downcast.

'We did that,' Veitch said bluntly. He walked over and leaned on one of the stones, staring out across the moor. The crackling fire cast a hellish glare across the scrub, the smoke rising to obscure the stars.

Ruth leaned in to Shavi who put his arms around her. Church looked over to Laura, but she had her back to him, wrapped in her own isolation.

'You were right,' Church said to Tom, 'but I don't know how you can be so cold.'

All Tom would say as he slumped down at the foot of a stone was, 'Life's much more simple when you're young.'

It was over an hour before they felt able to talk some more. Veitch still looked broken, the others merely serious.

It was Ruth who voiced the thought that was upmost in all their minds. 'If that thing is hunting us, what chance do Church, Laura and I stand? Do you think we can possibly keep ahead of it until one or the other of you gets back?'

'No,' Tom said baldly. 'But I have a plan—'

'Well, yippee,' Laura said flatly.

'There is a place not too far away that has the potency of this circle. Another blindspot. It is big, very big, and if you choose your hiding place carefully you should be able to avoid detection for . . .' He chewed on a knuckle for a second or two. '. . . Quite a while.'

'That's not the wholehearted answer I was hoping for,' Ruth said irritatedly.

'Where is it?' Church asked.

'In the High Peaks. It's a magical hill, more a mountain really, called

747

Mam Tor, the *Heights of the Mother*, rising up 1,700 feet. The most sacred prehistoric spot in the entire area.'

'A mountain to hide in!' Veitch said in astonishment.

'Great. We can play at being the Waltons,' Laura said.

'The ancients recognised it as a powerful spot. Nearby there is a hill dedicated to Lugh, now known as Lose Hill. All around there are standing stones and other ceremonial sites, all looking up to the hill of the Mother Goddess. At the foot is the Blue John Cavern, where the semi-precious stone originates. A landscape filled with magic and mystery. The perfect hiding place.'

'Great,' Church said. 'Now all we have to do is get there.'

Church woke in the middle of the night with a familiar, uneasy feeling, but one he hadn't felt for a few weeks. He crawled out of the tent, feeling his stomach churn. Laura was on watch, but she was dozing near the dying embers of the fire; he would have to have a word with her in the morning.

Slowly he looked around the darkness that pressed in tightly against the stones. Nothing. The wind blew eerily across the moor, making an odd sighing noise in the scrub. He prayed he was wrong, but in his heart he knew.

'Where are you?' he said softly.

A second later a figure separated from the dark: indistinct, almost blurred, as if he were looking at it through a curling sheet of smoke. He thought after all his brooding, all the weighing of emotions, the logical acceptance, he would feel nothing, but the pang in his heart was as sharp as ever.

'How are you, Marianne?' He held the tears back successfully.

The smoke appeared to clear and there she was, as beautiful as when they had shared a home; when she was alive. She didn't speak, she never did, but he felt he could almost read her thoughts. Her face was so pale, by turns frightening and filled with despair.

'I should have known when they'd failed to find anyone with the big beast, they'd send you to hunt me out,' he said softly. 'Do they have a message for me, Marianne? Anything? Or have they just sent you here to break my spirit?'

A sighing. Was it still the wind, or was it her?

He smiled sadly, wishing he could leave the circle to try to touch her hand one final time, although he knew that was impossible; he had learned his lesson. He wouldn't break the protection of the stones and put himself under the malign Fomorii influence that inevitably surrounded her. 'Did they think I'd fall for it all again?' His voice was low and calm; he didn't even know if she could hear it, anyway. 'Tell them it won't work any more – I'm not as weak as I was. If anything, seeing you here, knowing what they've done to you, gives me more strength to carry on. I'm going to set you free, Marianne. And then I'm going to make them pay. If you can take anything back to them, tell them that.'

He couldn't be sure, but he hoped, and he hoped: her face seemed to register the faintest smile.

And then she was gone.

the Ravening

Beneath the soaring vault of a gold-and-blue dawn sky they said their goodbyes. Less than a month remained until Lughnasadh. Conflicting emotions darted among them like electricity between conducting rods, but although the currents ran far beneath the surface, they all recognised the secret signs. Few words were said, but hands were shaken and backs slapped forcefully.

Church surprised himself by the depth of his affection for Shavi, Veitch and even Tom; there was the mutual respect of the survivors of desperate times, certainly, but also a recognition of qualities of decency and bravery which often lay hidden in modern life. It was uplifting to realise even damaged goods carried with them the blueprints for rectitude. He feared for their safety, but he had no doubt that if anyone could overcome such adversity, it was them.

Ruth hugged them all, although Tom looked uncomfortable at the contact; he walked away a few paces so the unpleasant experience would not be repeated. Laura too tried to appear aloof, but her repressed nods to each of them shouted as loudly as if she had thrown her arms round their necks. Then Shavi turned to Veitch with a broad grin.

Veitch brandished his hunting knife threateningly. 'If you try to hug me I'm going to kill you. I'm not joking.'

Shavi laughed as he pushed the knife to one side. He put his arms around Veitch and pulled him tight. Veitch was like a rod for a second, then relaxed and hugged Shavi just as warmly. It was an act of deep friendship, yet no one was surprised; they had all watched each boundary fall over the weeks until only Veitch had been left to recognise it.

'Fuckin' queen,' he muttered as they broke off.

'Thug,' Shavi responded.

Despite the gravity of the situation, there was more hope around than they truly deserved to feel.

When they finally felt ready, Veitch and Tom turned to the north and set off across the uneven terrain, carefully avoiding the blackened, still-smouldering wreckage of the car. Shavi, who was to accompany the others to Mam Tor before continuing to Windsor, led the way south.

*

Away across the moor a lone figure watched the two parties, as they had been watched for so long. The choice was difficult, but eventually the selection was made. As the figure set off across the scrub anyone could have been forgiven for thinking they were seeing an unfeasibly large wolf loping after its prey.

Mam Tor rose up majestically from the stone-walled, patchwork green of the surrounding countryside, a slab of imposing rock, brown and grey against the brilliant blue sky. None of them could believe how tall it was, how sheer were the cliff faces. Far beneath its imposing summit the two valleys of the Hope and Edale rivers stretched out, cool and verdant in the heat of the day.

'I can see what the old git meant.' Laura's sunglasses protected her eyes as she peered upwards. 'Nobody's going to scramble up there on a whim.'

'Bronze Age people forged a settlement there because it was impregnable as long as food supplies lasted,' Church said, harking back to his archaeological studies. 'An excavation up there in the sixties found a stone ceremonial axe and other bronze axes. It was a ritual place for the Great Mother that protected them all.'

'Let's hope it protects us as well,' Ruth said.

Their journey to Mam Tor had been without incident, but they all felt exhausted from helping Ruth along the rugged route which wound like a clear, rushing river between the overpopulated, overbuilt sprawl of Greater Manchester and the industrial zone of West Yorkshire. As the days passed, her stomach had started to swell rapidly, straining at her clothes. With it had come a sapping of energy, as if her very life force were being leached from her; but somehow she still managed to keep going. Her nausea, particularly in the morning, had become debilitating, and they had to find regular supplies of clean water to keep her from dehydrating. By night she shook as if she had an ague, her face ghostly white, her skin almost too hot to touch, sweat soaking through even her jeans.

There, looking up at Mam Tor, she had somehow found the strength to stand unaided. It seemed right, important. The place was sacred to her ancestors. And the Mother Goddess, or one of them at least, was her patron now. She prayed this was the place she was supposed to be to survive her ordeal.

'Are you going to be all right from here?' Shavi brushed his long hair from his face where the wind whipped it continuously. He looked remarkably fit despite the exertions of the journey, standing straight and tall, his body lithe, his limbs loose. The others felt calm just being near him.

Church nodded. 'We'll be fine.'

'Speak for yourself.' Laura surveyed the steep, precarious path that rose up to the summit.

'Watch how you go,' Church said. 'I'm sorry you've got to go on your own.'

Shavi smiled. 'I am comfortable with my own company. And I can travel faster alone.' He hugged Church tightly before giving both the women a warm kiss. Then he turned and continued his journey south.

The wind became more merciless the higher up Mam Tor they ascended. 'Well, it's going to be a lot of fun living up here,' Laura said sourly. 'There's nothing like the harsh elements to give a complexion that wonderful ruddy bloom.'

'Just be thankful it's not winter,' Church said as he strode off ahead. The truth was, he didn't know how well they would do. None of them had the trapping skills of Tom or Veitch and the environment was truly bleak and exposed. His only plan was to find a sheltered spot to pitch the tent, one which couldn't be seen from any great distance. Beyond that, it would be a matter of taking things a day at a time, which didn't seem the best strategy in the world when so much was at stake.

With Church and Laura virtually having to drag Ruth with each step, it took them nearly two hours to get a significant way up the tor, and by that time the sun had started to set. They turned and looked back over the breathtaking vista as the huge sweep of the country slowly turned golden in the fading light. It was an instant so beautiful they felt a brief *frisson* of transcendence that pushed their troubles to one side.

But then the high peak called again and they continued on their way. 'We need to find a good site by dark.' Church scanned the rugged, unforgiving slopes.

'Why don't you just go ahead and state the obvious?' Laura muttered.

'And why don't you just keep on sniping until I get *really* irritable?' Church snapped. 'What's wrong with you?'

'Please don't argue,' Ruth said weakly. 'Let's just try to get somewhere quickly.'

They bit their tongues for her sake, although the tension between them had not been given vent since Church had selected Shavi for the mission to Cernunnos. Church knew Laura had been hurt by the decision, but he couldn't understand why she didn't see it as a tactical choice instead of the personal blow she obviously considered it.

The night seemed to come in uncannily quickly, pooling like an inky sea across the countryside, rising rapidly up the tor. They were all too exhausted to look around much more and their calves felt like they were being burnt by hot pokers after the steepness of the climb.

Church was just about to select a campsite at random when he spotted a series of regular dark shapes among the gloom, hidden in a fold in the mountainside. They were too stark to be natural. He led them over to the place amidst Laura's protestations and was surprised to see an abandoned house hidden in the shadows. It looked like an old hill farmer's home, just three stark rooms on a single level. It had obviously been empty for some time; the door sagged on its hinges, the windows had been put out and the inside was strewn with the detritus of the years: a few slates from the roof, Coke cans, plastic bags, old newspapers, a couple of shrivelled condoms.

'Home, sweet home,' Church said, slapping his hand cheerily on the door jamb. 'Hey, I *can* believe in serendipity.'

'I don't like it.' Ruth stood a few feet back from the shadow the house threw, her arms wrapped around her. She looked it over like it was going to jump out and bite her. 'It's spooky.'

Laura marched past them both. 'Well, I'm sick of tents and if it'll keep the rain and wind off, it's good enough for me.'

'It's a good hiding place.' Church could see he wasn't going to convince Ruth easily. 'Nobody will be able to see us unless they're right on top of us.'

'Look at this.' Laura's voice floated out from the dim interior.

Ruth followed Church in with some trepidation, unsure if it was worse to be outside in the open night. Laura was pointing to a wall lit by the last meagre rays of the sun. It was covered in a mass of writing, some in huge letters, but vast swathes in an almost microscopic scrawl; most of it seemed unintelligible.

'Kids,' Church said.

Laura leaned forward to try to read the tiny print. 'They really don't have much to do round here, do they?'

Ruth stood in the corner, her arms still wrapped around her. From the corner of his eye, Church could see her gaze jumping back and forth, as if she was expecting something to come out of the corners of the room. 'I feel like something bad has happened here,' she said.

And at that moment the sun set and darkness claimed the land.

*

The rain started as Tom and Veitch reached the lowland slopes with twilight drawing in. By the time they had arrived at a main road, their clothes were soaked through and their hair was plastered to their heads; it was a hard, unforgiving downpour, uncommonly chill for that time of year. The cars hissed by, steaming in the spray, their headlights blazing paths through the night. Most of them were driving too fast for the conditions, desperate to get to the safety of their destinations before the deep night encroached.

After long deliberation during their walk, Tom and Veitch had decided to eschew the established policy of tramping through the wilderness. With only two of them, they felt they could move quicker and with a greater chance of being unseen by picking up a vehicle and following the main roads north, at least up to the Scottish Highlands.

But after forty-five minutes standing on the roadside in the splash zone they began to question their choice. No one was prepared to stop to pick up a hard-faced, muscular young man and his older companion who looked like he'd done too many drugs.

'We're going to be here all bleedin' night.' Veitch's voice was thin with repressed anger as a Volvo hurtled by in a white glare and a backwash that showered him from the waist down. 'This was a stupid idea.'

Tom removed his glasses to wipe the droplets off them for the third time in as many minutes. He kept his attention fixed on the stream of traffic.

'It's hardly bleedin' surprising, though, is it? We could be anything here. Everyone must know by now you can't trust stuff at face value. Once we were in the car we could tear their faces off.' He took a perfectly timed step back to avoid the splash from a Golf. 'I haven't seen this much traffic for ages. Probably 'cause it's a main route. Safety in numbers and all that. I bet the back roads are deserted—'

'You're talking too much.'

'Nerves, all right? I'm worried about Ruth.'

Tom stuck out his thumb once more with undiminished optimism.

'We don't stand much chance of winning now, do we?' Veitch continued. 'I mean, I'm still staying hopeful we can help Ruth, but what's inside her . . .' He looked into the middle distance. 'If it finds its way back, what's it going to be like?'

Tom didn't seem to hear him at first. Then he said, 'When Balor led the Fomorii across the land in the first times, it was said daylight was driven from the land. In the eternal night there was only the stink of burning flesh and the rivers ran red with blood. Humanity was driven to the fringes of existence.' His pause was filled with the rushing of the wind and the rain. 'If he returns once more, there is no hope for anything.'

Veitch chewed this over while the cars sped past, and when he spoke again it was as if it hadn't even been mentioned. 'How long are you planning on sticking it out here before you realise nobody's going to help us? Come on. We better find some shelter.'

'People haven't changed. There are still some who'll help out a fellow in need.'

'Yeah—' Veitch began cynically, just as a 2CV indicated and pulled over sharply.

The passenger door opened on to a man in his early thirties, his face surprisingly open and smiling. His cheeks were a little chubby, his eyes heavy-lidded beneath badly cut jet-black hair which made him look more like a boy.

'Where are you going?' he said loudly over the white noise and rumble of the road sounds.

Tom leaned in. 'As far north as you can take us.'

'Okay. Hop in.'

Veitch clambered into the back, scrubbing the excess moisture out of his hair, while Tom took the front. It was only when they were both settled that they saw their driver was wearing a dog collar.

'You must be mad hitching at this time, in this weather,' the driver said as he pulled away.

'Needs must.' Tom glanced at him askance. 'We were counting on a Good Samaritan,' he added wryly.

'There're still a few of us around.' The driver laughed. 'Actually, I had selfish motivations too. I wanted some company.' He stuck a hand out sideways. 'I'm Will.'

Tom and Veitch introduced themselves, then fell silent, but Will was keen to talk. 'I've been down to London. Came down yesterday and stayed overnight. I've got a parish in Newcastle. Rough area, good people though. I'd be the first to admit it's been a struggle. Still, the last few months have been a struggle for all of us, haven't they?'

'There's been some trouble up there, hasn't there?'

A rawness sprang to Will's face and he shifted uncomfortably; he didn't appear to want to talk about that. 'They've closed off part of the city. Terrible business. Terrible. But that's nothing new today, is it? Have you heard any news about what's happening?'

'Only what we've seen with our own eyes.' Tom was enjoying the warmth of the heater on his feet.

'They say the Government is on the verge of giving up the ghost.

Apparently they've set up a coalition, a Government of National Purpose. As if that will do any good. They're all politicians, aren't they?'

'Anybody who seeks out power should never be allowed to have it,' Tom agreed.

'I don't think they've any idea what's going on at all.'

'Does anybody? Do you?' Tom watched him curiously. He seemed a little naïve and idealistic, like many younger clerics.

'Nobody knows the details, but we have all seen what we've seen. We know science is on the back foot. What should we call it – the super-natural, the strange, the wondrous? Those who believed in that kind of thing always struggled to identify it on the periphery of life. Now it's right there at the heart.'

'I would suppose,' Tom noted, 'that you were one of those believers. Being a clergyman and all.'

Will grew quiet, his face lost in the shadows between street lights. After a moment's contemplation he said, 'Actually, that's not true. I considered myself one of the new breed. You know, trendy, the papers called us, because we had raves, flashing lights and dry ice instead of hymns. No time for the miracles and magic of the Bible. There was no truth in it, just a true way of living, little stories to teach decency.'

In the back, Veitch began to doze. After the exertion of the last few weeks, the warmth, the rhythm of the wipers and the hiss of the wheels created a soothing atmosphere that made his limbs leaden. Will's voice was calming too; he began to drift in and out of the conversation.

'And now you think differently?'

'You're damned right.' He paused. 'Must watch my cursing these days. My basic belief before was: God is a supernatural entity. If there's no evidence of the supernatural – and I've never seen any – how could there be a God, a virgin birth, even an Ascension? But I carried on because the Church still did good, important work. And then the miracles happened. All over the country – lame people walking, blind people seeing, the dead reviving. All the clichéd stuff. But this time there was evidence.' He hammered the steering wheel passionately to emphasise his words. 'There was a meeting in London. The General Synod was discussing all the monumental events that have been happening all over. I was still quite cynical until I heard all the personal testimonies, from every single part of the country.'

'And you think these are some signs from your God?' Tom did little to hide the faint contempt in his voice.

'I honestly don't know. I'd like to think that. Some of my colleagues think the opposite. They say everything they've seen in the world proves there *can't* be a God – not our God, anyway. How can miracles be special . . . be miracles . . . if they're happening randomly every day? It's magic, they say, not God's work. And the reports presented at the meeting of—' he eyed Tom unsurely '—powerful beings—'

'Not God's creatures,' Tom said.

'So *they* say.'

'And you think differently?'

'Until I've seen them with my own eyes . . . If you believe God created the universe and everything in it, then he could have created the most bizarre, alien beings. Who are we to begin to wonder at His reason for putting them here? The scheme is too big, our perspective too small.' He glanced at Tom. 'I take it from your words you don't believe in God.'

Tom grunted. 'I believe in a higher power. Call it God if you will. The common belief is that people who have seen great suffering cannot believe in God, for how could God allow such things to exist? That is shallow and misguided. Only people who *have* seen great suffering can know without a doubt that God truly exists.'

The vicar's brow furrowed. 'How can you say that?'

'Work it out for yourself. That's the only way true wisdom comes.' Tom watched the dark hedges and closed-off villages flash by.

Will didn't seem offended by Tom's brusque manner. 'All I can tell you is what this means for me. Two days ago science told me there was no place for miracles. Now we live in this world where wonders are commonplace. And they may not be caused by *my* God, as you put it, but the fact that they are happening means that for me miracles are now truly possible. Anything is possible. And once I realised that, I just had to rush back to my church to tell everyone about it.'

'Well, isn't that a conversion on the Road to Damascus,' Tom said drily.

'I can understand your cynicism, I really can,' Will stressed. 'But despite all the misery that's been caused – and I accept there's been a lot – on a spiritual level, there's also so much more hope. All the things the Bible teaches aren't abstract concepts any more. Life has just become so much more, I don't know, vital. How can you worry about making more money or seeking out power when all this is happening? It focuses the mind on the truly important things.'

They continued northwards, the rain finally drifting away to leave a cloudy, warm night. The conversation was punctuated by long periods of silence when they each wrestled with their own thoughts, but that was often too uncomfortable and they would be forced to return to discussing the state of the country and how much life had changed.

757

Veitch was oblivious to it all as he slept soundly, stretched out across the back seat.

As the midnight hour passed and Newcastle drew nearer, the air being sucked in by the heater gained an unpleasant tang of chemicals and burning, Tom glanced over at Will; the vicar's face, oddly, seemed to have lost some of its youthfulness and his expression had grown darker.

'How bad is it back at home?' Tom asked.

A pause. 'Very bad.'

'You're aiming to pass on some of that hope you feel.'

He nodded. 'Something magical. The Church lost touch with that, with the reason why people needed it. There's been too much looking inward, too much rationalising and reasoning and not enough heart. Not enough magic.'

The sky overhead was briefly lit up, as if it were daylight.

'Good Lord.' Will leaned over the wheel to peer up into the sky. 'Was that a flare?'

They travelled on for another five minutes without any further disturbance, but then something else caught Will's eye and he slowed the car down. 'Look at that.' There was awe in his hushed voice.

Lights were moving in complex patterns across the sky. Some were balls, glowing red or white, others cylinders that seemed to have all the colours of the rainbow on them as they rotated slowly.

'UFOs,' Will noted.

'That's what they used to call them. Keep going, they won't disturb you.'

Will glanced sharply at Tom. 'You're saying they're alive? They're just lights.'

'Just lights? There is no *just* anything in this world.'

'Then what?' He looked back up to the heavens, slowing the car even further.

'Spirit forms, I suppose you would call them. Sentient beings that reflect what is taking place in our heads.'

'How do you know this?'

'I've seen them before.'

'They look like cherubs. Or angels.' Will chewed on a knuckle excitedly. 'Perhaps that's what they are. If they were seen in ancient times . . .' He paused, holding his head to one side. 'I can feel something. Can you feel something?' Will didn't seem to notice Tom's lack of a reply. 'It fills me with a sense of wellbeing. Almost of transcendence.'

'That's part of their nature too.'

758

A tear trickled from the corner of Will's eye. 'You say they're, what, spirit forms? But if I say they're angels, who's to say which of us is right?'

Tom shrugged disinterestedly.

'It's all a matter of perspective.' He pulled the car over to the side of the road, transfixed. The lights continued to bob and weave across the sky, their flares lighting the clouds like fireworks. Then, as Will watched intently, their movement ground to a halt. There was a brief period when they hung suspended in the heavens, and then gradually they shifted in unison towards some kind of alignment. A few seconds later they formed a blazing cross of many colours, hanging in the eastern sky.

Will caught a sob in his throat, but the tears streamed down his cheeks. 'I've been so wrong.'

The lights stayed that way for a long moment, and then the cross slowly broke up and they. drifted away to lose themselves among the billowing clouds. Will chewed on the back of his hand; he appeared to be shaking all over.

Tom winced, then sighed, unsure quite how to say what he felt. 'It might—'

'I know what you're going to say. It might not be what I think. I might be putting my own interpretation on it. But can't you see – that doesn't matter! It's a sign of something bigger. That's all we really need.'

He sat for a while with his head resting on the steering wheel. When he did finally look up, he was transformed, beaming and optimistic. Seeing him, Tom couldn't help but think that perhaps he was right.

Will left them on the outskirts of Newcastle, where Tom caught up on his sleep in a back garden shed. The next morning they picked up a succession of lifts that took them north. They crossed Hadrian's Wall without incident and made better going across the Scottish Lowlands, with several other lifts taking them north of Stirling. They were dogged by repeated technology failures on the outskirts of Perth and, in frustration, decided to proceed on foot. Although it was rough going as they moved into the foothills of the Cairngorms, they knew it was also the best option for safety. With only the A9 as the main route northwards, their chance of discovery would increase tenfold in a vehicle.

The pines in the Forest of Atholl were cool and fragrant and filled with game birds. Veitch even brought down a deer with his crossbow and that night they enjoyed a royal feast, with enough meat left over to last them days. Beyond the trees they headed across the deserted countryside towards Ben Macdui, which dominated the skyline, rugged and brown against the blue sky. Crystal-clear springs plummeting down from the peaks provided them with a plentiful supply of refreshing water and away from the pollution the clear air was invigorating; they both felt much better for it.

Their relationship passed through raucous humour, anger and mild bickering, often in the course of a single hour. Veitch couldn't work Tom out at all; he got lost in the hidden depths of his companion, found himself unable to navigate the subtleties of his intellect and moods. But he couldn't shake the feeling that the stone-faced, grey-haired man was a fraud, trading on his reputation as some hero of myth. Tom seemed to have a great deal of knowledge about every subject, but he rarely volunteered it when it was needed, which was anathema to Veitch, who believed at all times in acting quickly and decisively.

With only twelve days remaining, they had been through a period of uncomfortable silence brought on by an argument over which was the quickest route to take across the hills. The uneasy atmosphere dissipated sharply when Veitch caught sight of a swathe of constant motion, passing across the lower reaches of the mountain range far below them. At first glance it appeared as if the land itself were fluid, rippling and changing in a dark green wave moving slowly across the landscape.

'What is that?' He tried to pick out detail from the glorious sweep of the countryside.

'Look.' Tom pointed to what appeared to be a tiny figure moving ahead of the wave.

Veitch continued to stare until he realised what was happening: the wave was actually vegetation; trees were sprouting from the ground and shooting up to full maturity in a matter of minutes, and the uncanny effect seemed to be following the tiny figure.

'The Welsh knew her as Ceridwen,' Tom said.

Veitch glanced at him disbelievingly. 'How can you tell that from here?'

'My vision is better than yours.' Tom made no effort to convince Veitch. 'Better than any human's.'

'Okay, what's she doing then?'

'She's one of the Golden Ones – she comes from the family of Cernunnos. What is she doing? It looks to me like she's returning the primaeval forest to the Highlands, the way it used to be before all the trees were cleared for agriculture and industry.'

'What for?'

760

'To her branch of the Golden Ones, nature is very special, and the trees and their living spirits are the best representation of that. She's bringing magic back to the land in a way that people will truly be able to appreciate. For wherever trees grow, magic thrives.'

Veitch dropped to his haunches, balancing himself with the tips of his fingers. He caught a glimpse of black hair, flowing like oil, and what appeared to be a cape swirling behind Ceridwen, sometimes the colour of sapphires, then emeralds. 'I don't get it. If they're supposed to be the enemy, how come they're looking after the land? I thought that was our job.'

Tom shrugged. 'On most levels they're higher beings. They understand the things we take for granted.'

The Rhymer wandered off, but Veitch stayed watching the verdant band spread back and forth across the desolate landscape. It filled him with a tremendous sense of wellbeing that he couldn't quite explain, and when he took his leave five minutes later, he did so reluctantly.

They spent half an hour looking for a place sheltered enough to make camp in the bleak uplands and by that time twilight had turned to near dark. Despite the season, the wind had turned bitter again and there was a hint of icy rain in the air.

'I don't like this,' Veitch said as he tramped breathlessly up an incline.

Tom grunted; he was in one of his moods where conversation was a burden.

'The dark, out here in the country.' Veitch knew he was talking as much for himself, but it made him feel a little more easy. 'I'm a city boy. It never gets dark in the city, even when it's night. You've got other things to worry about there, but at least they're always easy to see.' He looked up. 'The moon's full. It'd give us more light if not for the bleedin' clouds.'

'You're not afraid of a few shadows, are you?' Tom snapped. His brogue had grown a little thicker now he was back in his homeland again.

'Ah, fuck off.'

'City boys. You think you're so hard,' Tom taunted.

Veitch's anger flared white and hot for an instant; sometimes he was afraid of it and the way it seemed to take him over completely. He wondered, when he was in its grip, what he was really capable of. Before he could respond with a comment that would bring about another raging argument, he glimpsed a light high and away to his right that was quickly lost behind an outcropping. He pulled back until he saw it again.

'There's a place up there.' The light seemed more than welcoming in the sea of darkness. 'Maybe they'll let us bunk down for the night.'

Tom wavered for a moment, but the prospect of a night with a roof over his head seemed too attractive. He pushed past Veitch and marched briskly towards the white glow.

It was a crofter's cottage, built out of stone, but still looking as if it had been hammered by the elements almost to the point of submission. Smoke curled out of the chimney to hang briefly and fragrantly in the air; it smelled of peat or some wood they couldn't quite identify. The ghostly outlines of prone sheep glowed faintly on the hillside all around. They both watched the place for a few moments while they weighed up any potential dangers, then, finding none apparent, Tom strode up to knock on the door.

There was a brief period of quiet during which they guessed the occupant was shocked that someone had come calling to such an out-of-the-way place. Then heavy footsteps approached. 'Who is it?' a deep voice said in a hesitant Highlands accent.

'We were out walking. There looks to be a storm blowing up,' Tom said politely. 'Do you think you could give us shelter for the night? We—'

'No. Be off with you.' There was a sharp snap in the voice that could have been anger or fear.

'Miserable bastard,' Veitch muttered. 'Come on, I thought I saw somewhere to make camp just over there. He's probably in-bred anyway.'

Before they could move away another, unidentifiable, voice rose up from somewhere at the back of the house. They heard the man move a few steps away from the door and a brief, barely audible argument ensued. A few seconds later the door was jerked open so sharply they both started.

A man in his late forties with dark, unwelcoming eyes barked, 'Get in. Quickly now!'

They jumped at his order and he slammed the door behind them, throwing a couple of bolts as if to emphasise his order. He was wearing a faded *Miami* T-shirt with old blue braces over the top holding up a pair of dirty grey, pin-striped suit trousers. His hair was curly black and grey, but his three-day stubble made him appear harsher than he might otherwise have been. He sized them up suspiciously, then beckoned them over to the fireside with a seemingly approving grunt. 'Better get y'sen warmed up. It gets cold up here at night, even in summer.'

He disappeared into another room and came back with a woman in her early twenties who had obviously been the source of the argument. Her face was bright and confident, as welcoming as the man was suspicious. Her hair was long and shiny-black, her eyes dark, and she was slim, in a clean white T-shirt and faded Levi's. There was something about her that reminded Veitch of Ruth, although her features had more of country stock in them.

'You'll have to forgive my dad. He doesn't know the meaning of hospitality.' The father began to speak, but she silenced him with a flashing glare; a fiery temper clearly lay just beneath the surface. 'I'm Anna. Dad here, he's James. Jim.'

'Mr McKendrick,' the father mumbled in the background.

Tom and Veitch introduced themselves. 'You've been having some trouble,' Tom noted, slipping off his rucksack.

'Something's been worrying the sheep.' Looking uncomfortable, McKendrick wiped his mouth with the back of his hand. 'Worrying? Savaging more like. Six dead in the last two nights. Eight gone last month.'

'A wild dog,' Tom suggested, not believing it for a minute.

'Sat up with my gun last night. Never saw a damn thing. Found what was left of the carcasses at first light.'

Tom nodded. 'I can see that would be a problem. And you thought the culprit had come knocking at the door?'

McKendrick ignored him. Anna stepped in. 'Have you eaten? I could do you some bacon sandwiches?'

They both agreed this would be a good idea. While McKendrick pulled back the curtains to peer outside, Tom disappeared to use the toilet. Once Veitch heard the spattle of hot oil and smelled the first singe of the bacon he followed Anna into the small kitchen, which was barely big enough for the two of them.

She smiled when he entered and asked him to slice the bread. 'You'll have to excuse Dad. He's been under a lot of pressure. You don't make any money with a croft at the best of times, and the last few years certainly haven't been the best of times. He cannae afford to lose sheep at this rate.'

'You help him out here?'

'Don't look so surprised!' She slapped him playfully on the shoulder. 'My mum died earlier this year. It was a shock to us all, but Dad took it really hard. Went to pieces, really. I was living down in Glasgow, having the time of my life, but I jacked it all in to come back here and get him back on his feet.'

Veitch took the spatula from her hand and turned the bacon, but he couldn't take his eyes from her face. Her own eyes matched his, move for move. 'That was good of you.'

'Don't make me out to be a saint. Anybody would have done it for family. But no good deed goes unpunished, right? Now he doesn't want me stuck in a miserable life like crofting miles away from anything anybody could call society, and he doesn't want to lose me and be on his own either. So we sit here every night stewing in our juices.'

'Must be pretty hard.'

She shrugged. 'So what about you? You don't look the kind to be hill-walking in these times.' She looked him in the eye. 'Nobody would be up here alone at night in the Troubles. Unless they had a very good reason.'

'I have a very good reason.'

'Tell me about it, then.'

'I'm a big bleedin' hero trying to save the world from disaster.'

Her eyes ranged over his deadpan face as she tried to pick the truth from his comment. Eventually she held his gaze, while a smile crept across her lips, and then she turned back to the cooker. But she never told him what she thought.

They ate the sandwiches in front of the fire. McKendrick thawed a little and even offered around a shot of malt which looked, from its unlabelled bottle, as if it had been distilled locally. Veitch still couldn't take his eyes off Anna. He didn't know if it was because she reminded him of Ruth or because of some other attraction, and that thought filled him with guilt about how fickle he really was. For her part, Anna seemed truly taken by him. While Tom and her father talked in quiet, serious tones by the fire, the two of them sat in creaking, threadbare armchairs in one corner, their lighthearted conversation punctuated with humour.

But at one point Veitch looked up and found McKendrick watching him with a cold annoyance bordering on anger. Veitch knew why, didn't care; life was too short.

They were disturbed shortly after midnight by a wild commotion outside: the undeniable sound of sheep in torment, deep rumbling from some unrecognisable animal throat that turned into a guttural roar. Veitch was the first to the window, but the light inside made it impossible to see more than a few feet. McKendrick had his gun and hovered hesitantly at the door, but Veitch was by his side before he had his fingers on the handle.

'Let me go first, all right?' The crossbow was in his hand as he slipped out into the chill night. He regretted it instantly. Even outside it was impossible to see much beyond the small circle of illumination from the croft's windows; he could almost feel the darkness pressing hard against him. He had advanced to the edge of the light before McKendrick came out with a powerful torch. He had never heard the noise the sheep were making before; it was frenzied and high-pitched and at times almost sounded like the shriek of a woman.

'Quick! Over there!' He pointed redundantly in the direction of the noise.

The determination in McKendrick's face didn't quite mask the underlying fear as he swung the torch round wildly. It flashed over undulating grass, the ghostly grey shapes of fleeing sheep, past something that was just a glimmer, but a splash of colour and a jarring shape that shouldn't be caught Veitch's eye. 'Back! Back!' he yelled.

McKendrick retraced the arc. They caught a glimpse of a low shadow that moved away like lightning. Left behind was the carcass of a sheep, gleaming slickly, the white bones protruding like enormous teeth. It had been so torn to pieces they had trouble recognising which part was which.

'Holy Mary, Mother of God!' McKendrick hissed. 'It *is* a dog!' He nestled the barrel of his gun over his forearm while still trying to manipulate the torch.

'Careful,' Veitch said. 'It might be rabid.'

The white light washed over more grass, its movement jerky with McKendrick's anxiety, so at times it looked like they were glimpsing images illuminated by a strobe: a rock that made them all start; a sheep running in their direction. The carcass again. The wind had whipped up and was moaning across the high land, scudding the clouds across the moon and stars so it became darker than ever. And against it all was the sound of the sheep's hooves constantly driving across the grass, disorienting them so it was impossible to tell where the dog was.

McKendrick gritted his teeth in frustration. 'Stay behind me. If I see it I'm just going to let rip with both barrels. Might scare it—'

They had heard tell of animal sounds that could chill the blood; McKendrick had thought it poetic license, but when the howling rose up, at first low and mournful but then higher and more intense, they felt ice-water wash through them. The primal sound triggered some long-dormant race warning that was so overpowering that their instinct rose to the fore and instantly drove them towards the house.

Just as their backs were at the door, McKendrick's final sweep with the torch locked on to a prowling shape, so fleeting they caught only a glimpse of golden eyes glowing spectrally in the light. McKendrick fired instantly, but they didn't wait to see the result. They slipped through the door and locked it firmly behind them.

'I think I got it,' McKendrick said breathlessly with his back pressed hard against the door. 'Winged it, at least.'

Veitch wasn't so sure. Anna and Tom waited anxiously in the centre of the room; it was apparent from their faces they had been as disturbed by the howling. McKendrick and Veitch looked at each other, but it was the older man who finally gave voice to what they were both thinking.

'It was a wolf, I'm sure of it.'

Anna shook her head furiously. 'You're joking! There haven't been wolves here for centuries.'

'But this was once their homeland,' Tom mused. 'Perhaps they've returned.'

'With the forests,' Veitch added.

'How?' Anna asked. 'That's crazy!'

McKendrick went to the window and peered out cautiously. 'Crazy things are happening all the time these days,' he mumbled.

'Are you sure it was a wolf?' Tom said pointedly. 'Not a man?'

Veitch knew what he was implying. 'Bit bigger than normal, but nothing out of the ordinary.'

Anna looked at them both curiously, but said nothing.

'If you did hit it, we might be able to track it at first light. Follow the blood,' Veitch said confidently. 'It would be easier if we could see the bleedin' thing. We don't stand a chance out there in the dark.'

This seemed like the most sensible course of action, so while Anna retired to the kitchen to make a pot of tea, the men sat by the fire, slowly feeling their heartbeats return to normal.

McKendrick retired an hour later, and while Tom dozed fitfully in a chair in front of the fire, Veitch attempted to make up a bed on the floor in one corner. Anna helped him, talking animatedly in a hushed voice.

'Sorry if I'm rattling on,' she said with a giggle. 'It seems like ages since I've had a body to talk to. Apart from my da', that is.'

Veitch lay back on the collection of cushions with his arms behind his head. 'He seems like he's got it pretty much together now. He's a tough bloke. Bit of a no-nonsense life he's got going up here. Maybe it's time to get back to your life.'

She looked wistful. 'I don't know. I can't be selfish—'

'You've got to be, sometimes. Otherwise you can just give up your life to all these responsibilities everyone throws at you. They'll never stop.'

She stifled a yawn, then lay down next to him, staring up at the ceiling. 'That sounds like a lot of sense. Right now. But then I'll catch him looking at Mum's photo and crying when he doesn't think I'm around—'

'Don't you get lonely?'

She turned to look at him with her deep, dark eyes. 'Sometimes.'

He rolled on to his side and propped his head with his arm. 'You look like you like big fun. You're gonna go stir crazy in this place after a while.'

'Sometimes I think I already have.' She shrugged. 'You know how everybody needs something in their lives they believe in? Well, this croft is Dad's thing. For all the blood and sweat that goes into it and the poverty that comes out, he loves it. He'd die if he moved away. It looks boring, bleak, hard. But then you get up on an autumn morning to see the dawn slowly moving across the mountains in orange and brown. And you hear the wind across the hillsides on a winter's night, almost like it's a real person.'

'So what do you believe in?'

'Right now, looking after a man who raised a bairn while managing to keep body and soul together in a place like this. He's sacrificed for me. It's the least I can do in return. The very least.'

Veitch rolled back, his expression faintly puzzled, vaguely troubled. 'And what do you believe in?'

That question troubled him even more. 'Still looking for it, I reckon.'

She leaned over and gently touched the tattoo on his forearm; her fingers were cool, the contact hot. 'Tell me about these.' She smiled with mock lasciviousness. 'Do they go all the way down?'

Before he could reply, the door to the bedroom swung open and McKendrick glared out. 'Anna! To bed. Now,' he hissed.

She smiled at Veitch a little sadly, but there was nothing else to say.

The gale picked up during the night, whistling in the chimney and clattering around the eaves. Veitch woke repeatedly, reminded of Anna's description of the wind as a real person; at times he was convinced he could hear an insistent voice, warning or challenging. Over near the dying embers of the fire, Tom grumbled and twitched in his sleep. Veitch checked his watch: three a.m. Shouldn't be too long until dawn.

A rattling ran along the length of the roof. He sat bolt upright in shock an instant before he realised it was still the wind. He wouldn't be surprised if half the tiles were off come morning. He lay back down, but the rattling sound came back in the opposite direction.

His instincts jangled. Slowly he raised himself on his elbows and listened. It didn't sound like the wind at all. It sounded like there was someone on the roof.

A shower of soot fell down the chimney and the fire flared. His attention snapped to it, but his mind was already racing ahead. The resounding crash against the front door had him to his feet in an instant; it was so hard he thought it was going to burst the door from its hinges.

Tom staggered to his feet, still half asleep. 'What . . . what in heaven's name . . . ?'

Veitch ran to the window and peeked out. A large grey wolf which looked, in his state of heightened tension, as big as a Shetland pony, was hurling itself at the door. With each impact, the hinges strained a little more. Veitch struggled briefly to make sense of the wolf's unnatural actions before jumping back and yelling, 'McKendrick! Bring your gun!'

But the crofter was already half out of the bedroom with his shotgun, looking dazed. 'You better see this,' he said.

Veitch ran into the bedroom. Anna was sitting up in a Z-bed, trying to make sense of what was happening. The curtains had been dragged back and outside Veitch could see several sleek wolves circling, all as big as the one battering the front door. The rattling on the roof echoed again; at least one of them was up there too.

'There must be eight or nine of them!' McKendrick said in disbelief.

'Have you got another gun?' Veitch snapped. The crofter shook his head.

Cursing, Veitch ran back to the living room and scrambled for his crossbow, suddenly aware of how feeble it really was. He barely had time to load a bolt when the door burst open and the wind howled in; the curtains flew wildly. The wolf struck him full in the chest with the force of a sledgehammer. He went down, winded, and then it was on top of him, jaws snapping barely an inch from his face. Its meaty breath blasted into his nostrils, its saliva dripped hot on his chin. He could barely breathe from the weight of it.

He forced his face to one side in desperate, futile evasion, anticipating the enormous power of the jaws stripping the meat from his skull. And then the strangest thing happened: deep in his head he felt an uncomfortable tickling sensation, like a dim radio signal on the end of a band. Slowly he found his face drawn back round until he was looking deep into the wolf's eyes, golden with the cold circle of black floating at the centre; they drew him in until he was lost in a gleaming intelligent soup, at once alien, yet a part of him.

The terrible spell was broken with the sound of smashing glass. Another wolf burst through the window and sprawled in the centre of the floor before righting itself. And then the rest of the pack was inside, circling low and fast. Tom tried to fend one off with a wooden chair. The wolf played the game for a second, then suddenly unleashed its jaws in a frenzied snapping that turned the chair to splinters in an instant.

From the corner of his eye Veitch could see his crossbow where it had fallen. Slowly he crept his hand spider-like along the floor towards it; it was already loaded, so he could put a bolt through the wolf's head with just one hand.

He was halfway to it when the wolf noticed what he was doing. A low, bass rumble started somewhere deep in its throat then rolled upwards into a bloodchilling snarl. Its movement was so swift Veitch barely saw it. Those golden eyes were shining before him, and then suddenly he was encompassed in darkness and the foul stink of the beast's breath. He felt its fangs sink into the flesh at the top of either cheekbone; fiery pain ran deep into his temple. It had his entire head in its mouth; it had to exert only slightly more pressure and his skull would shatter.

It held him like that for a few seconds while every desperate thought he had ever had rattled through his mind, and then, mysteriously, it released its grip. Before he could begin to fathom what was happening, it had released the crushing pressure on his chest and was padding away and out of the door.

All the other wolves had gone too, but the room looked as if it had been torn apart by a tornado. Shattered furniture lay all around, covered with shards of glass and torn material. Tom was slumped in a daze in one corner, but as he struggled to sit up it became apparent he wasn't badly hurt.

McKendrick, however, lay on his back half in, half out of the bedroom. His face was covered in blood and his gun was nowhere to be seen. Veitch scrambled over to him and raised his head so he could dab at the wounds with a remnant of curtain. After the shock of his appearance, the cuts seemed mainly superficial and it wasn't long before his eyes flickered open. Veitch began to speak, but the panic that flared in McKendrick's face silenced him instantly.

'They've taken Anna,' he croaked.

The winds had moved off across the mountains with the first light of dawn as they picked their way across the chill, dew-laden hillsides in search of Anna. Veitch took pole position with Tom at the rear; between them was McKendrick, who looked like a spectre, his skin grey, his eyes filled with a painful desolation; it was the face of a man who had seen his entire world destroyed in an instant.

They hadn't been able to bring themselves to discuss Anna or what was likely to have happened to her after the wolves took her. Instead they had attempted to understand why the pack had acted so unnaturally, and there were no easy answers there either. And so, silently and unanimously, they had agreed to pursue the creatures to bring back Anna, or what was left of her.

Veitch felt numb. His emotions about Anna and Ruth had been so confused, although even his usually superficial self-analysis admitted that Anna's minor problems were a psychological substitute for Ruth's more intractable ones; solving the former had been his unrecognised key to achieving his heart's desire. And he had been thwarted again.

The track was easy to pick up, even for the untrained eye: flattened grass and too many splatters of blood, which they tried to convince themselves belonged to the wolf McKendrick had wounded. They made quick progress downhill, but there was no sign of the wolves ahead of them. The pack had moved away from the croft with alarming speed.

They soon found themselves on the perimeter of the new-grown forest, which already seemed to have attained its own ecosystem: thick forest floor vegetation, woodland flowers and a wide array of birds. Mist had settled in the depths of the valley and among the trees like candyfloss. The more they penetrated the shade beneath the verdant canopy, the thicker it became, blanketing all sound, obscuring what lay on every side.

After they had moved through it a little way, Tom pulled Veitch on one side. 'This is insanity. If the pack attacks here we don't stand a chance. They could be circling five feet away from us now and we wouldn't know.'

Veitch agreed, but he couldn't turn back. 'If we retreat now we'll lose the trail.'

'You can't help saving damsels in distress, can you?' Tom said sourly. 'It's a pathological obsession.'

'I might listen to what you're saying if you weren't so fucked up yourself.' Veitch marched back into the lead with an irritation that came from knowing Tom was right. He had to save Anna because that was what heroes did. And if he couldn't be a hero, he had to be the person he always had been, and who could live with that?

They'd progressed about half a mile into the thickest part of the forest when they first heard movement, all around. McKendrick's finger jumped to the trigger and Veitch had to rest his hand on the barrel to calm the crofter; he looked like he was about to have a breakdown.

'Take it easy, mate,' he whispered in a strong, calm voice. 'You'll end up blowing one of us away.'

McKendrick's bottom lip was trembling. He plunged his teeth into it and a trickle of blood ran down on to his chin.

The mist continued to distort the forest sounds; the birdsong seemed to come and go, and when they heard the vegetation crushed beneath loping paws it was impossible to pinpoint the location. But the pack was undoubtedly nearby, possibly surrounding them, as Tom had feared. Twigs cracked from somewhere behind them, grass or a bush swished just ahead. Yet despite the muffled nature of the sounds, something about them didn't sound right to Veitch's heightened awareness; the weight burden was wrong, the movements not as sleekly lupine as he would have expected.

'They're moving closer,' he hissed.

'How can you tell?' McKendrick's gun was wavering so much Veitch thought there was more danger there.

'I can hear things clearly.' *These days*, he mentally added. He truly did feel a different person to the woolly-minded, sluggish old Ryan Veitch. The Pendragon Spirit had given him the chance to rise above himself.

Tom moved in close so only Veitch could hear him. 'So what's the big strategy now, warrior-boy?'

A large figure shimmered in and out of the tendrils. 'There!' McKendrick cried and raised his gun.

Another shape erupted out of the mist and knocked McKendrick flying; the gun disappeared into the undergrowth. Veitch lashed out instinctively and caught the attacker a glancing blow. It howled sharply before it was gone.

He dropped low, whirling around. 'That wasn't a wolf!'

As if in response to his words, another figure dropped out of the air in front of him, obviously from a tree branch above. It was a man, but oddly different to any man Veitch had seen before. His long, matted hair was a deep black and his skin swarthy, with an excess of body hair. His bone structure was clearly defined above his sharp jaw, forming handsome features which suggested both pride and an incisive intelligence. He was naked, his body lithely muscled, filled with power. But it was his hands and feet that caught Veitch's attention; they were over-sized, the fingers long and gnarled, with sharp, jagged nails that more resembled talons. He was sweating profusely from his exertions and there was a sheen of forest dirt across his skin. Gradually Veitch's attention was drawn to his thick, dark eyebrows which menacingly overhung glowing golden eyes; Veitch knew instantly he had seen those eyes before.

Veitch went to lift his crossbow in warning, but the man raised his arm quickly with a strange hand gesture that had the little finger and index finger extended while the others were folded back; oddly, it was filled with a threat Veitch didn't feel comfortable opposing, and he let the crossbow drop.

'Who is this?' McKendrick said in a broken, uncomprehending voice. Tom helped him to his feet.

'The *Lupinari* have returned to the deep forests,' the man said in a deep, almost growling voice which rang with an unplaceable accent.

Recognition suddenly dawned on Tom's face and he took a step towards the strange, beast-like man to communicate, but he was halted in his tracks by the same threatening hand gesture.

Tom held his open hands up, palms outwards; a primal gesture. 'I never encountered your people in the Far Lands.'

The man eyed him coldly. 'Then you never ventured into the forests of the night.'

'No, I never did.'

The man let his hand drop slightly and used it to gesture around. 'The Far Lands, for all their twilight appeal, were uncommon grounds to us. These are our homelands. This is our world, where we have hunted since time began.'

Other figures began to appear out of the mists, both men and women, all naked, dark-haired and swarthy-skinned; they moved low and sinuously, like animals; occasionally their eyes gleamed like cats'.

'In the days of our ancestors, we lived side-by-side with humankind. The wild men of the woods, you called us, and in the dark wintertime you even came to look upon us fondly, as you yet feared us. For sometimes we would bring gifts to your door, and keep away the privations of the long, dark nights. For it is in our nature to help fellow creatures of intellect.' There was a hint of anger in this last sentence. 'Your people knew us, and our powers, and never hunted us, for they knew we never ate human flesh. For if we did, the taste of it would consume us and we would desire it ever more and there would be nothing but war between our races.'

The other members of the pack circled round, filtering in and out of the mists. Veitch kept a wary eye on them; the mention of human flesh had unnerved him.

'And if one of our people turned rogue, and ate mortal meat, we would hunt him down and destroy him ourselves,' the leader continued. There was a long pause while he looked into each of their faces, and then he said, 'But this night gone you did attack us.'

Veitch suddenly noticed the splatter of dried blood across his left ribcage. 'You attacked his sheep.'

The leader fixed his cold eyes on Veitch. 'But we never ate human flesh.'

Tom took a cautious step forward to attract the leader's attention away from Veitch's lack of diplomacy. 'We had no idea the *Lupinari* had returned to these lands,' he said in as conciliatory a tone as he could muster. 'We would never wish to offend you. We would hope to live in peace, as we always did in times past.'

Golden eyes blinked slowly, implacably. 'Nevertheless, a blow has been struck. There must be some retribution before we agree a pact.' His face contained no emotions they could understand, and they all feared the worst.

McKendrick had seemed in a daze to this point, but in that moment he appeared to grasp what was happening. 'Not Anna,' he whimpered.

'His sheep, given freely,' Tom suggested hastily.

The leader shook his head slowly. 'We had no knowledge they were his beasts or we would not have taken them. We can easily find other prey. For that is what we do.'

'Not Anna,' McKendrick said again.

'You better not have killed her,' Veitch snapped.

The leader's eyes flashed towards him, filled with such bestial rage Veitch instinctively went to protect his throat. 'I held your head in my jaws,' the leader growled. 'You are nothing to me.'

'You don't eat human flesh,' Tom noted. 'You said.'

As if on cue, another figure advanced from the mists; it was Anna. At first she moved with the sluggish pace of someone who had been hypnotised, but when she neared them, recognition dawned in her eyes and she ran to her father. They held each other, crying silently.

'What do you require?' Tom asked quietly.

The leader fixed his unflinching stare on the Rhymer. 'For one night, every year, she will leave her father to be with us.'

McKendrick's eyes grew wider. 'What will happen to her?'

'She will learn to hunt with the *Lupinari.*'

'To hunt?' McKendrick brought the back of his hand to his mouth. 'My wee girl?'

Veitch saw something else. 'She isn't going to stay around here for ever.'

The leader's eyes narrowed. 'If the pact is broken the *Lupinari* will seek retribution through the hunt.'

'It is agreed,' Tom said.

'No!' McKendrick was blazing with righteous anger now. 'I won't leave my daughter with these things!'

Tom placed a firm hand on his shoulder. 'There isn't another way. If you want to save her life, and yours, then you'll do this.' He turned back to the leader and repeated, 'It is agreed.'

The leader nodded slowly. 'Then perhaps in times to come our peoples can live closely and wisely once more.'

There was a note of conciliation in his voice. Veitch herded McKendrick away before he could put up any opposition, relieved that it hadn't come down to a fight, knowing they wouldn't have stood a chance if it had.

After a few paces he glanced back, just to be sure they were not being followed. But all he saw were vague impressions as the *Lupinari* melted back into the mist, and not a single footfall was heard to mark their passing.

Back at the croft McKendrick was in a state of shock, but Anna seemed to have accepted her tribulation with equanimity. When she saw Veitch watching her intently, she left her father sitting on the floor next to the hearth and pulled him to one side.

'No grim faces now,' she cautioned with a gentle finger on his cheek. 'It's not the end of the world.'

'You don't know what they'll be expecting of you on your nights with them.'

'I'll deal with it when it happens.'

'And it's going to be hard for you ever to get away from here now.'

'What's to stop me coming back just for the night?' But they both knew it wasn't going to happen. 'I just wanted to say, thanks for helping us.' She seemed to read every troubled thought passing through his head. Then she took his face in her hands, stood on tiptoes and gave him a long, deep kiss. Afterwards she said, 'It's a shame you have to go—'

'I have to.'

'I know. But it's a shame.' And then she smiled once and turned to her father. Veitch watched her for a while, kneeling next to

McKendrick, one hand round his shoulder, whispering comforting words that only the two of them could hear. But then Tom caught his eye and nodded towards the door.

They made their goodbyes as best they could, and then when they were out walking over the sun-drenched hillsides, Veitch asked, 'Is this always how it is?'

'What do you mean?'

'When you're trying to do the right thing in the world. When you've got all these responsibilities. Like a big fucking rock on your shoulder.'

Oddly, Tom appeared pleasantly surprised by the comment. He clapped Veitch warmly on the shoulder. 'That's how it is. You get your reward later.'

'How much later?'

Tom's tight smile seemed filled with meaning, but Veitch couldn't understand it at all. 'Much, much later,' the Rhymer said before turning his attention to the path ahead.

They walked nonstop for the next day across the exhausting mountainous landscape and made camp in a gorge as night fell. They hadn't seen or heard anyone since they had left the croft; in the desolation, humanity could have been stripped from the face of the planet and they would never have known.

Since he had left Anna, Veitch hadn't been able to settle. He had found his thoughts turning to the others he had spent so long with over the past months. Why did they act the way they did? Why did they say one thing while believing another? His own thoughts had always moved swiftly and directly into words, and in the past he had judged others by the same standard, although he had known subconsciously that was rarely the case. And finally his attention had turned to Tom; he had spent the day secretly watching the way he moved, the subtleties of his facial expressions, his strange choice of words, and by the evening he knew that he didn't know the man at all.

As they sat around the fire finishing up the last of the provisions McKendrick had given them, the questions were plaguing Veitch so much he couldn't keep them in any longer. 'You said yesterday your eyes were better than mine.' Tom nodded. 'How much else has changed?'

The Rhymer prodded the fire, sending the sparks soaring. 'A great deal.'

'Like what?'

'I can hear better. Smell things more acutely. Can't really taste very much any more, though.'

Veitch gnawed on a crust while he thought. 'If a doc cut you open,' he began, 'what would he find inside?'

Tom stared into the fire, said nothing.

'If you don't want to talk about it—'

'I don't think I'm quite human any more.'

'Don't think?' Veitch watched Tom's face in the firelight, wondering why it was always so hard to tell what he was thinking or feeling.

'I don't know. I don't know if I should be here with people, or back in Otherworld with the rest of the strange things. I don't know if I can trust my feelings, if I really have any feelings, or if I just pretend to myself I have feelings. I don't know if I cut myself open if I'll find straw inside, or diamonds, or fishes, or if all the component parts are there, just in the wrong order.' He continued to watch the flames.

Veitch had a sudden, sweeping awareness of Tom's tragedy. He had lost everything; not just his family and friends, who were separated from him by centuries, but his kinship with humanity, his sense of who or what he was. He was more alone than anyone ever could be. Yet he still wished and hoped and felt and yearned; and he still tried to do his best for everyone, despite his own suffering.

'I think you're just a bloke, like me and the others,' Veitch said.

Tom looked at him curiously.

'And I think you'll find what you're looking for.'

Tom returned his attention to the fire. 'Thank you for that.'

'It must be hard to go back to that bitch who wrecked your life.'

Tom remained silent, but Veitch noticed the faint tremor of a nerve near his mouth.

'You know when I said I couldn't understand why everybody thought you were a hero. I'm sorry about that.'

Tom threw some more wood on the fire and it crackled like gunfire. 'We need to get some sleep.'

'Okay, I'll take first watch.' He stood up and stretched, breathing deeply of the night air. 'What are we going to find when we get where we're going?'

'Everything we ever dreamed of.' Tom wandered towards the tent. 'And everything we ever feared.'

Tom had been in the tent barely five minutes when an awful sound echoed between the steep walls of the gorge. All the hairs on the back of Veitch's neck stood erect instantly and a queasy sensation burrowed deep in the pit of his stomach. Veitch hoped it was just an unusual effect of the wind rushing down from the mountains, but then Tom came scrambling out of the tent, his face unnaturally pale, and Veitch knew his first instincts were correct: it was the crying of a woman burdened by an unbearable grief.

At first he wondered if it was Anna, who had followed them, but Tom caught at his sleeve as he made to investigate. 'Don't. You won't find anyone.'

'What do you mean?' Veitch felt strangely cold; his left hand was trembling.

'You can always hear the Caoineag's lament, but you will never see her.'

Veitch peered into the dark. The wailing set his teeth on edge, dragged out a wave of despair from deep within him. He wanted to crawl into the tent and never come out again. 'What is it?'

'She is one of the sisters of the Washer at the Ford.' Tom's voice was so low Veitch could barely hear it. 'A grim spirit.'

'Is this her place, up here in the mountains?'

Tom shook his head. 'She is here for us.'

'For us?' Veitch dreaded what Tom was to say next.

'Those who hear the sound of the Caoineag's mourning are doomed to face death or great sorrow.' And with that he turned and dismally retreated to the tent.

CHAPTER SIXTEEN

On the Night Road

The light from the fire glowed through the trees like a beacon in the darkness of the night. Another technology failure had left Shavi breathless as the sea of illumination that spread out across the Midlands winked out in an instant; even after all this time it still chilled him deeply to see it.

He had just been coming down the final, gentle slopes of the Pennines after Ashbourne when it happened. He never travelled at night, particularly in the wild country, but he wanted to complete the last leg of that difficult part of the journey before he reached the more comforting built-up areas that lay towards the south. Now he wondered if he had made the wrong decision.

More than anything, he was aware of time running away from him; Lughnasadh was only eleven days away, little enough time to put everything right. He still found it hard to believe their great victory in Edinburgh had turned to such a potentially huge failure. His mind kept flashing back to Ruth and the suffering she must be feeling. But more, he was aware of the looming presence of Balor, in the shadows beneath the trees, or the chill in the wind, or the deep dark of a cloudy night. There had been no sign of the Fomorii, but he knew they were out there, searching for him. He could palpably sense the god of death and evil close to their reality. He felt it like a queasiness in the pit of his stomach and in the many dreams that had increasingly afflicted his sleep. An overpowering atmosphere of dread was beginning to fall over everything he saw and heard.

Although the night was warm and there were plenty of stars, a smattering of clouds kept obscuring the moon. That made the darkness almost impenetrable and he was sure he could hear something moving nearby. On several occasions he had been convinced someone was following; not too close, but tracking him from afar, sometimes off to one side, sometimes the other, always out of sight. He tried to pretend it was paranoia, but he had learned to trust his sharpened senses.

His main comfort was that if it were some kind of stalking beast, it had had plenty of opportunity to attack him while he slept. Yet it kept its distance, almost as if it were sizing him up. A twig snapped, too loud in the still of the night. He looked round briefly, then hurried towards the fire.

Almost forty people were seated around a blazing campfire next to a copse on the edge of a field. In the gloom beyond were parked a motley collection of vehicles: a black, single-decker bus of fifties vintage, a beat-up Luton van · spray-painted in Day-Glo colours, other coaches, obsolete and heavily modified, minibuses stocked high with effects. The gathered crowd were obviously travellers, camouflaged by old army fatigues, leather and denim, hair long, spikey or shorn, piercings glinting everywhere, tattoos glowing darkly in the flickering light. They were all ages: children playing on the edge of the firelight, a few babes in arms, several pensioners, and a good selection of those in their twenties, thirties, forties and fifties. The hubbub of conversation that drowned out the cracking, spitting wood dried up the moment Shavi stepped into the circle of light.

Shavi scanned their faces, expecting the suspicion and anger that came when a tight-knit group was disrupted, but there was nothing. He looked for anyone who might be a leader or spokesman.

A thickset man with long black hair and a bushy beard waved Shavi over with a lazy motion of an arm as thick as Shavi's thigh. He wore a cut-off denim jacket over a bare chest and had a gold band straining around his tattooed bicep; a matching gold gypsy earring shone amidst the black curls. He was grinning broadly; one of his front teeth was chipped.

'The last brave man of England!' His voice had the rich, deep resonance of a drum. 'Come over here and tell us what it takes to walk alone in the countryside at night!'

Shavi squatted down next to him, perfectly balanced with the tips of his fingers on the ground. 'I did not intend to be out so late—'

The man's bellowed laugh cut Shavi short. 'Now how many times have we heard that before?'

The others laughed in response, but it wasn't directed at Shavi. 'Come on, pull up a pew.' The man slapped the dry ground next to him. 'You don't want to be going back out there in a hurry, do you?'

Shavi accepted his hospitality with a smile. The easy conversation resumed immediately, as if he were an old friend who had just returned to the fold. A second later a cup of warm cider was pressed into his hands. He could smell hash on the wind and soon someone switched on an eighties beat-box. It pumped out music which seemed to switch without rhyme or reason from upbeat to ambient, jungle to folk. There

779

was a strange, relaxed mood that was oddly timeless. He felt quite at home.

Shavi's host introduced himself as Breaker Gibson. He'd been with the convoy for six years. As a group, the travellers had followed the road for most of the nineties, their number ebbing and flowing as people tagged along at different sites or drifted away without explanation; an extended family that owed as much to a gaggle of mediaeval itinerants as it did to any concept of modern grouping. Their neverending journey was seasonal, taking in most of the festivals: Glastonbury and Reading, some of the counter-culture get-togethers in Cornwall and Somerset, the summer solstice at Stonehenge, Beltane in Scotland. They had their own code of conduct, their own stories and traditions that were related and embellished around the campfire most nights, their own myths and belief systems: a society within a society.

Breaker didn't want to talk about his life before he joined the collective; Shavi got the sense it was an unhappy time that he was trying to leave far behind, and the constant motion of his new existence appeared to be working. But of his time with the group he was robustly happy to discuss, and had a plethora of stories to tell, most of which he wildly exaggerated like a storyteller of old, all of which seemed to involve some kind of run-in with the law. After an hour Shavi liked him immensely.

For his part, Shavi was completely open about what had happened to him over the long weeks since he had hooked up with Church and the others, but he said nothing about the reasons for his mission south, nor his destination; it was too important to trust to someone he had only just met.

Breaker peered into the night beyond the light of the campfire. 'Aye, we've seen some rum things over the last few weeks. We stopped to pick up a guy hitch-hiking near Bromsgrove. Dressed all in green, he was. But each to his own – I'm not a fashion cop.' He chuckled throatily. 'We got to the point where we'd promised to drop him off. Looked around – he wasn't anywhere on the bus! And we hadn't stopped anywhere he could have jumped off. Next thing, someone discovered all the pound coins had turned to chocolate! The kids had a feast that night, I tell you!' His chuckle turned to a deep laugh. 'Could have been worse, I suppose.' A shadow suddenly crossed his face. ''Course, we've seen some rotten things at night.' Now a tight smile; Shavi knew what he meant.

'Still,' he said, raising his mug of cider, 'it's wonderful to be alive.'

*

As they drank and chatted, two women came over. One was in her late twenties, with a pleasant, open manner and sharp, intelligent eyes. She had a short sandy bob and wore a thick, hand-knitted cardigan over a long hippie skirt. Her name was Meg. With her was a Gothy woman about ten years older with a hardened face and distinctly predatory eyes, but a smile that was welcoming enough. She said her name was Carolina. They both seemed eager to talk to Breaker, who obviously had some standing within their community.

'Mikey doesn't want to do the late watch,' Meg said, drawing out a list of names and quickly running her eyes down it.

'The little git says we keep picking on him to do it,' Carolina interjected sharply.

'But I've·checked the rota and it's been divided up fairly,' Meg added.

Breaker sipped on his cider, suddenly serious. 'I'll have a quiet word with him. We can't afford to have too much dissent in the ranks.' He turned to Shavi. 'We had to instigate the watches a few weeks back after some bad shit happened.'

Shavi could feel the eyes of the women sizing him up. 'What was it?' he asked.

'Woke up one morning, hell of a commotion. Penny over there—' he motioned to a thin, pale woman whose eyes bulged as if she had a thyroid problem '—she was in a right state, understandably. Her baby, Jack, he'd gone missing. Taken in the night. And in the cot where he'd been lying was a little figure made out of twigs tied up with strands of corn.' Breaker's cheerful face sagged for a second. 'Naturally we told the cops, went through all their rigmarole, getting the usual treatment that it was partly our fault for the way we lived. It was just going through the motions. Everyone knew what had really happened. Since then we've had the watches going through the night. No more trouble, so I suppose you can say it's worked. But some of our . . . less-committed . . . friends don't like having their sleep disturbed.' This was obviously a source of great irritation for him, but he maintained his composure.

'So what's your deal?' Carolina said to Shavi bluntly. 'Why are you walking the land?'

'A friend of mine is very ill. I need to find some way of helping her.'

'Medicine?' Meg asked.

'Something like that.'

'So where are you going? Maybe we could give you a lift.' Carolina glanced at Breaker, who nodded in agreement.

Shavi weighed up whether to tell them. 'South,' he said. 'To Windsor.'

Breaker tugged at his beard thoughtfully. 'We could do south.'

'Yeah, haven't been that way for a while.' Carolina winked at Shavi. 'We tend to steer clear of some of the posher areas. The residents used to run us out with pitchforks in case we robbed them blind.'

The two women were called over by a teenager who looked as if he hadn't bathed for days; thick mud coated his face and arms like some Pictish warrior. Once they were out of earshot, Breaker said, 'They just about run this place, those two. We couldn't do without them, though I wouldn't say it to their faces. Give 'em bigger heads than they've got.' He looked Shavi in the eye. 'So, are you with us?'

'I would be honoured.'

'Good. One more for the watch rota!'

The camp was already alive when Shavi awoke from the best night's sleep he'd had in days. In the light it was easier to get a better handle on the people roaming around, and to see the vehicles, which looked like they would have trouble travelling a mile, let alone thousands. He ate a breakfast of poached eggs on toast with Meg, who had an insatiable desire for information about what was happening in the country; she was bright and sparky and he warmed to her. Afterwards he had his first mug of tea since The Green Man; it made his morning complete.

Once everyone had started preparing for departure, Breaker hailed him to invite him to sit up front in his sixties vintage bus, which had been painted white and vermilion like an ice cream van. The back was jammed with an enormous sound system and what appeared to be the cooking and camping equipment for the entire community.

'Hell-bent or heaven-sent,' Breaker said with a grin as he clicked the ignition. He pulled in behind the black fifties bus and the convoy set out across the country.

The open road rolled out clearly ahead of them, with no traffic to spoil the view of overhanging trees and overgrown hedges.

'You have experienced the technology failures,' Shavi said with a teasing smile, his gaze fixed ahead.

Breaker eyed him askance, then laughed at the game that was being played. 'Oh yes, we've had our fair share of problems with that.' He winked. 'Some of us were even kinda happy to see it. Bunch of Luddites, I ask you! Travelling around on the Devil's Machines!'

'And what happens if the technology fails completely?'

'Well, that's why God invented horses, matey! If it's good enough for the old ancestors, it's good enough for me and mine. I can see it now: a big, old, yellow caravan . . .' He burst out laughing. 'Bloody hell! Mr

Toad! Poot, poot!' He was laughing so much tears streamed down his cheeks and he rested his head on the steering wheel to calm himself. Shavi had a sudden pang of anxiety and considered grabbing the wheel, but Breaker pulled his head up a second later and righted the bus as it drifted towards the hedge.

Shavi noticed an ornate Celtic cross hanging from the rearview mirror. 'For safety on the road?'

Breaker nodded. 'Though not in the way you think. That symbol was around long before the Christians got hold of it.' He muttered something under his breath. 'Bloody Christians stamping all over any other religion. Some of 'em are the worst advert there is for Christianity. On paper it's not a bad religion. Love thy neighbour, and all that. But once they start mangling the words, anything can happen. Having said that, we've got a few Christians here, but they're not the kind where you can see the whites of their eyes, if you know what I mean. The rest of us are a mixed bag of Pagans and Wiccans, an Odinist, a few Buddhists, some I don't even bloody well know what they're called, and I don't reckon they know themselves either!'

'In these times faith has come into its own. It really can move mountains.'

'What do you believe in, then?'

Shavi rubbed his chin thoughtfully. 'Everything.'

Breaker guffawed. 'Good answer! I tell you, the people you have to watch are those bastards who don't believe in anything. You can see them all around. Scientists who reckon they know how the universe works 'cause they know how one molecule bumps into another. Bloody businessmen who think they can screw anyone over in this life to get what they want because there's no afterlife so no comeuppance. Property developers flattening the land . . .' He chewed on his lip. 'Making a fast buck, that's too many people's faith.' He raised a hopeful eyebrow in Shavi's direction. 'Looks like they could have a few problems in this new world.'

'Oh, let us hope.'

They laughed together.

The convoy avoided the motorways and kept to the quiet backroads. It was a slow route that involved much doubling back, but Breaker explained it meant they could more easily avoid undue police attention. As they cruised down the A444 towards Nuneaton they passed another convoy coming in the opposite direction, but these were the army. Grim-faced soldiers peered out from behind dusty windscreens; they looked exhausted and threatened.

'We live in a time of constant danger,' Shavi said.

'Something big's been happening, but we never get to hear about it. They go bringing in martial law, then they haven't got the resources to police it because everybody's off fighting somewhere. At least that's what the rumours say.' He glanced at Shavi. 'You hear anything?'

'I have seen signs . . . a little, here and there. The authorities have no idea what they are doing. They are trying to fight with old thinking.'

'They don't stand a chance, do they?' He mused for a second. 'We always wanted the Establishment to leave us alone. I wonder what the world's gonna be like without them?'

As they rounded a corner they were hit by a moment of pure irony: a police roadblock barred their way.

They were held there for half an hour. Everyone was forced out of their vehicles on to the side of the road while they and all their possessions were searched. Nothing untoward was found; those who did carry drugs had found much better hiding places, after years of bitter experience. Even so, the indignities were ladled on: verbal abuse, women pushed around, homes turned upside down and left in chaos. All the travellers remained calm. They had obviously learned any opposition would result in a rapid escalation into a confrontation they could never win.

Shavi expected the police to pounce on him in a second, but they seemed to have no idea who he was. Eventually, once the police had had their sport, the convoy was turned around for no good reason that anyone could see; other cars and lorries were waved right through.

Breaker's face was stony as he headed back north and looked for a side road. 'Just like the bleeding miners' strike. And they call this a free country.'

They eventually made their way around the blocked area and pitched camp for the night in the deserted countryside to the east of Stratford-on-Avon. The area was thickly wooded enough for their vehicles not to be seen from any of the roads in the area.

'One of the good things about all this – we never get hassled at night any more,' Breaker said. 'Everybody's too afraid to leave their homes once the sun goes down.'

Once they were all parked up, they assembled for the tasks to be handed out. Three went off to dig the latrines while others scouted the area for wood for the fire; no one was allowed to touch any living tree. The cooking range was erected from Breaker's bus and several volunteers set about preparing a vat of vegetarian chilli. The mouth-watering aromas drifted over the campsite.

After everyone had eaten their fill, Shavi sat with Breaker, Meg and Carolina next to the fire, watching the gloom gather. He had spent the day mulling over the story Breaker had told him about the abducted child and he had grown increasingly disturbed that so little had been done.

'What could be done?' Carolina said dismally.

Meg agreed. 'We've seen the things away in the field. Enough of us have come across all the strange, freaky shit that hovers around the camp at night. We're not stupid.'

'I am not suggesting you are,' Shavi said. 'But if you believe in the reality of the things you talk about, then you should not be surprised when I tell you I have certain abilities which may be of use to you.' He explained the gradual development of his shamanic skills over the weeks since the world had changed. It was a difficult task – he knew most people were still mired in the old way of thinking – but after all he had seen of the travellers' nonconformist lifestyle, he guessed they would not be so blinkered.

'So what do you suggest?' Carolina suggested. 'A shamanic ritual?'

'That might be effective. It is a matter of trying to peel back the layers to achieve contact with the invisible world, where all knowledge lies.'

'And you think you've got what it takes?' Carolina gave a wry smile.

'Bloody hell, Carolina! Give the bloke a chance!' Breaker berated loudly. 'He's right – we've done bugger-all so far. It wouldn't hurt to take a shot at this.'

Meg nodded. 'I'm in agreement. We can do it tonight, if you like. What do you need?'

'A quiet place among the trees, a handful of us to provide the focus of energies, some mushrooms or hash preferably, natural highs to alter consciousness. If not, we will have to make do with alcohol.'

The others looked from one to the other and laughed. 'Yeah, I think that's doable,' Carolina said with a smirk.

Penny broke down in a sobbing fit once Meg told her what was planned. She pushed her way past the others to clutch at Shavi's clothes, her tearful face contorted by all the emotions she had not been able to vent. 'Please God, help me find Jack!' she wailed.

Meg led her away to calm her down with a cup of tea while Breaker rounded up a few people to help with the ritual. By the end there were eight of them: Shavi, Breaker, Meg and Carolina, a woman in her sixties with long white hair tied in a ponytail, the mud-covered eighteen-year-old, who was known as Spink, a ratty-faced man with curly ginger hair and his partner, a heavyset woman who smiled a lot.

They found a clearing in the woods where they couldn't see the camp or hear any voices. Breaker had been wary of straying so far from the safety of the fire, but Shavi had convinced him the ritual would protect them as much as any physical defence.

The evening was warm. They sat in a circle, breathing in the woody, verdant aroma of the trees, listening to the soothing rustle of the leaves in the cooling breeze. It wasn't as dark as they had feared under the trees. The night was clear and the near-full moon provided beams of silver luminescence that broke through spaces in the canopy like spotlights picking out circles on the wood floor. The patterns of light and shade it created provided an attractive, stimulating backdrop to what they were about to do.

Breaker had rustled up a plastic bag of dried mushrooms and a block of hash, which they shared out equally. They didn't have to wait long for it to take effect. Shavi had primed them to begin a regular, low chant. He knew, instinctively, that the insistent vibrations coupled with the psychoactive drugs stimulated the particular region of his brain he needed to achieve the higher level. He didn't know how he knew that, but it was there in the same way that he knew it was the technique employed by their ancestors in the stone circles and chambered tombs millennia ago.

The chant moved among the trees until it became a solid, living thing, circling back and forth, then inserting probing fingers deep into his mind. He closed his eyes and raised his face so the breeze caressed his skin. The blood was singing in his veins as a tremendous sense of wellbeing consumed him; he felt roots going down from his body into the soil, moving underground until they joined with the trees and the shrubs. He felt a part of it all.

The next step was the hardest. There was a deep anxiety locked inside him from the time his mind had been almost lost to the sea serpent just off Skye, and he had to fight to ensure the drugs didn't amplify it to the point where it overwhelmed him. He regulated his breathing and focused, riding the waves with mastery. And then it was just a matter of falling back into his head, and back and back, as if he were plummeting into a deep well. Paradoxically, that journey deep within saw him suddenly out of his body. He was in the air over the clearing, looking down at himself and the others, still chanting. The view was strange, fractured; colours seemed oddly out of sorts and the dark was almost a living, breathing thing. He had only the warped perspective for an instant before his mind was jumping like lightning through the woods.

There was a sensation like pinpricks all over his body, and then he was blinking, seeing the world at ground level; a wrinkle of his nose and a bound; he was a rabbit investigating the strange scene. Another lightning leap and suddenly he was up in the treetops, seeing with astonishing precision. There was the rabbit, white cotton-tail twitching. He was consumed by raptor-lust; his big owl eyes blinked twice and then he was on the wing. The lightning leap plucked him away again, to a badger snuffling in the undergrowth further afield, to a fox probing the outer reaches of the campsite for any food to steal, to a moth battering against the windscreen of a bus, trying to reach the light inside.

And then, suddenly, he was jolted back into his own body, only this time he was seeing with different eyes, feeling and hearing and smelling with completely new senses. The invisible world was opening to him.

'Come to us,' he said loudly. There was a ripple in the chanting, but he felt Breaker glance round the others to maintain the rhythm.

Above him, in the centre of the clearing, the air seemed to be folding back on itself. What looked like liquid metal bubbled out and lapped around the edges of the disturbance. There was an odour like burned iron. Shavi could feel the nascent fear of those sitting near him, but to their credit they all held firm in their trust in him. A hand thrust out of the seething rift with the white colour and texture of blind fish that spent their lives in lightless caverns. Then another hand, followed by arms, elbows wedged, heaving itself out into the night. A head and shoulders protruded between them, featureless, apart from slight indentations where the eyes, nose and mouth should have been. Shavi knew from experience it was one of the human-form constructs shaped out of the aether that the residents of the Invisible World often used to communicate.

'Who calls?' It was suspended half out of the rift, as if it were hanging from a window.

'I call.' Shavi knew better than to give his true name. 'I seek knowledge. The whereabouts of a mortal child.'

The white head moved from side to side in a strange pastiche of thinking. 'Know you there is a price to pay for information.'

Shavi held up his hand and slit the fleshy pad of his thumb with a hunting knife he had brought from the camp. Several droplets of blood splashed on to the ground.

'Good,' the construct said. 'A tasty morsel of soul. How is Lee?'

Shavi winced at the mention of his dead boyfriend's name. 'No games. Now, information. The mortal child was stolen from this group several weeks ago. A twig doll was left in its place.'

'The child is in the Far Lands.'

'Alive and well?'

'As well as can be expected.'

'Who took him?'

'The Golden Ones enjoy the company of mortals.' There was a faint hint of irony in its voice. 'They pretend they like to play with their pets, which they do, but that is not the true reason.'

This sounded like it could be dissembling, but he pressed on anyhow. 'What is the true reason?'

'That answer is too large and important for one such as I to give.' This gave Shavi pause; he made a mental note to consider it at a later date. 'Rather you should ask me if there is hope the child will be returned,' the construct continued.

'Is there?'

'No hope.'

'None?'

'Unless the Golden Ones can be made to bow to your will. Or you can provide them with something they need in exchange.' There was none of the mockery Shavi had expected in these comments. What was the construct really saying?

'Where is the child?'

'In the Court of the Final Word.'

Where Church and Tom had encountered Dian Cecht. Where the Tuatha Dé Danann carried out their hideous experiments on humans.

'I thank you for your aid. I wish you well on your return to the Invisible World.'

'One more thing.' There was a note of caution in the construct's voice. 'Turn quickly when the howling begins or the world will fall beneath your feet.'

Before Shavi could ask about this unsolicited, oblique advice, the construct had wriggled back into the rift and it had folded around him. The warning, if that was what it was, turned slowly in his mind, but he didn't have a second to consider it. Carolina yelled sharply; Shavi followed her wide-eyed, frightened stare.

He was shocked to see Meg, who had been sitting cross-legged at the foot of a mighty oak, was now being swallowed up by the tree. The wood appeared to be fluid and was sucking her into it like quicksand. Her eyes were wide with horror, but she couldn't scream for what looked to be a hand made out of the wood of the trunk had folded across her mouth. It dragged her further in; soon she would be lost completely.

Breaker leapt to his feet and grabbed her right arm, but to no avail.

Then all the others joined in, but however much they tugged, they couldn't halt Meg's inexorable progress.

'Wait!' Shavi yelled. He pushed past them and placed his hand on the rough bark. It slid like oil beneath his fingers, attempting to pull him in too. The others fell back, waiting to see what he would do. 'Be at peace, Man of Oak. We summoned the Invisible World for information. There is no harm intended to you.'

For a moment the repellent sucking at Shavi's hand continued, but then gradually it subsided. The trunk appeared to ripple and an unmistakable face grew out of the ridged bark, overhanging brow shadowing deepset eyes, a protruding nose and a gash for a mouth.

'We know of you, Brother of Dragons.' The voice sounded like wood splintering.

There was a gasp of surprise from the others. 'I know of your kith and kin too, Man of Oak, though I have never spoken with any of you before,' Shavi said.

'We remain silent when mortals walk beneath our leaves. They have never treated the Wood-born with respect.' A sound like the sighing of wind in branches escaped the mouth. 'But we know you are a friend of the Green and the people of the trees and the people of the lakes, Brother of Dragons. Do you vouch for these others?'

'I do.'

There was a moment's pause, and then Meg was slowly ejected from the tree trunk. She fell gasping on to the ground, where Breaker and Carolina ran to help her to her feet. She looked unhurt, but Shavi asked gently, 'Are you all right?' She nodded, bewildered; her eyes were still rimmed with tears. Shavi felt a wave of relief that she was safe. He'd read of the dryads and naiads, the tree and water spirits, and he had sensed them at times during his previous explorations of his abilities, but it was the first time they had manifested. This time he had responded instinctively and it seemed to have worked.

'Those who move within the Invisible World are dangerous to call, Brother of Dragons,' the tree-spirit said.

'I proceed with caution, as always, Man of Oak. How do your people fare?'

'In our groves, our woods and deep forests we are as strong as we ever were in our prime. Strong enough to repel any who try to fell us. Already blood has been spilled in the north country and in the west, and after nightfall the people have learned to avoid the coppices where our fallen bodies lie.'

The grim note in the creaking voice was so powerful the others blanched and took a step away. But Shavi sensed an opportunity and persevered. 'Our stories say there was not always such enmity between man and tree.'

'In the days before your people turned away from the wisdom of the land we were treated with respect and we, in turn, respected the men who moved among us.'

'It could be that way again.'

'It may still be too early, Brother of Dragons. The new season has not been long in the—'

'No.' Meg stepped up to Shavi's side. The tree creaked in protest at being interrupted. 'I'm sorry for speaking out of turn,' Meg continued hurriedly, 'but not all people are the same. We've always respected trees, nature. It's part of our belief. We never cut green wood. We don't pollute the land.' Shavi saw the wild intelligence bright in her eyes; she knew, as he did, that the Oak Men would be strong allies.

A whispering like the crackling of dry leaves seemed to run through the ground to nearby trees, then out through the wood. 'They're talking,' Carolina said, a little too loudly.

Soon after lights appeared in the deep dark, far among the trees, flickering will-o'-the-wisps that, oddly, put them all at ease. 'Spirit lights,' Shavi said in awe. 'The spirits of the trees moving out from the wood.'

'It has not been seen by mortals for many lives, even by how the Wood-born measure time,' the oak said. 'We accept your words. We call you to come to us as friends. Embrace the wood. Move through our home, listen to the whisper of our hearts. Show respect for us, men and women of flesh and bone, and we in turn shall forever grant you the good fortune that comes from our protection. Let this be the first act of a new age.'

'I thank you, Men of Oak, for your good grace in forgiving the sins of the past.' Shavi rested his hand on the bark once more; it was warm and comforting to the touch.

'Seasons come and go. A fresh start will be to the benefit of both our people.'

Shavi turned to face the others. They were watching the lights floating gently among the trees, their faces almost beatific. Race memories, long buried echoes of wonder and awe had been released in them. In one moment they had become their ancestors.

Gradually, one by one, they drifted off lazily among the trees. Shavi watched their transcendental expressions as they reached out to the lights, touched the wood, caressed the leaves, lost to the mystery. The Oak Man had been right: this was a moment of vital importance for the new age, the reforming of a bond that had been so powerful in times long gone.

Shavi followed a little way behind, observing the change that had come over the travellers as they wandered in and out of the circles of moonlight; they were more at peace than he would have believed. Deep in the woods some of them came across a glassy, moonlit pool where water trickled melodically over mildewed rocks from a tiny spring, a green and silver world that smelled as clear and fresh as a wilderness mountaintop.

Carolina sat on a rock at the edge and trailed her hand dreamily in the water. She retracted it suddenly when she saw a face floating just beneath the surface, big eyes blinking curiously. The figure was not solid; in fact it seemed to be continuously flowing and reforming. But no sense of threat came off it. Cautiously, Carolina reached out her hand and paused a few inches above the surface. The water rose up in a gentle crystal spiral to touch her fingertips briefly before rushing away. There was a sound like gently bubbling laughter. Carolina looked up and smiled, her face as innocent as the moon.

Hours later, back at the camp site, the eight of them tried to express to the others what had happened. Amidst the gushing enthusiasm it wasn't hard to communicate the overwhelming sense of wonder that possessed them, and by the time midnight turned they all felt they had been part of an epochal shift.

Penny was overjoyed that her son was still alive, but the thought that he wasn't even in the world left her dismal. 'You've got to help me,' she said to Shavi, clutching at his sleeve like he was the Saviour; her face was pitiful, broken.

'I will do what I can,' he replied, and it wasn't quite a lie. He didn't tell her what was likely to be her son's fate in the Court of the Final Word, that even if he could find some way to bring the boy back, his mother might not recognise him.

Still, his brief words seemed to cheer her. She left the fireside hurriedly to wander among the trees in the hope that the Wood-born's promise of good fortune would find its way to her.

Shavi retired to his tent early, exhausted by his experience. As the firelight began to die he had also seen a grey shape flickering like reflected light among the vehicles, and he did not feel strong enough to deal with Lee that night. His guilt at his boyfriend's death had not been assuaged by the knowledge that it had been part of some over-arching scheme by the Tuatha Dé Danann; he still could have done something to save Lee, he was sure of it, but fear for his own safety had paralysed him. If being taunted and berated by his dead lover on a nightly basis was the price he had to pay to purge the emotions that were eating away at him, then that was how it would have to be; even if the words he heard were driving him insane.

There was a faint scratching on the canvas. A silhouette he would never forget. He buried his face in his bag and tried to sleep.

And then the whispering began.

At some point he must finally have dozed off for he woke with a start to a rustling at the entrance to the tent. His first befuddled thought was that it was Lee until Carolina pushed her way in past the flaps. Behind her was Spink, now miraculously cleaned of the mud that had grimed him from head to toe. He was handsome, dark-eyed and black-haired beneath his disguise. Shavi switched on his torch and positioned it so it illuminated the tent.

'Do you mind if we come in?' Carolina said when she was already inside.

Shavi gestured magnanimously; if truth be told, he was keen for company. 'How can I help you?'

Spink seemed awestruck in his presence, so it was Carolina who did all the talking. 'The people out there are talking about you like you're some kind of Messiah.' Her eyes sparkled in the torchlight.

'I am no Messiah.'

'They saw what you did in the wood. You've got powers of some kind. You do things that no ordinary person can do.'

Shavi nodded. 'But inside I am just a man. Flawed, frightened, unable to know what is the right decision.'

She shook her head; her black hair shifted languorously. 'You're not convincing me. You told us yourself, you're a man with a mission. You're here to deliver us all from evil.'

'Not like that.'

'Not a Messiah, then. But a mystic, a wise man. Shaman. You used the word yourself.' This he had to concede. 'Then you could teach us all things—'

'I am not a teacher.'

'Look at us all here!' she protested. 'Why do you think we've opted for this kind of life when we could be living in warm homes where there's always plenty of food on the table, where there's always some nice loving husband or boyfriend there to make sure everything's all right?' There was a sliver of bitterness in her voice; she swallowed it with difficulty and continued. 'We're all searching for something, something better. It was a spiritual choice. You must understand that?' He nodded. 'We've been failed by society, failed by the Church, all the religions. But there's a deep hole inside us that we want filled.' She hit her chest hard. 'You can help fill that.'

Shavi was humbled by her passion and eloquence. 'So you are saying that you want to be my disciples?'

She glanced at Spink, whose eyes brightened. 'That's exactly what we're saying.'

'Let me tell you something,' he began slowly. 'I grew up in West London in a family of brothers and sisters and aunts and uncles and nieces and nephews and . . . too many even to count. As a child, it was quite idyllic. I never wanted for love. I studied hard at school to make my father proud of me, and he *was* proud, and I was happier than any boy had any right to be. My father . . . The thing I remember about him sometimes when I am drifting off to sleep is the way his eyes would light up when I would bring him my school books to show him my work. They would crinkle round the edge, and then he would smile and pull me over to him. There was such integrity and honesty in his face, all I wanted was to be like him.'

He closed his eyes, the memories flashed across his mind almost too painful to bear. 'My family was very strictly Muslim. It was the glue that held everything together. The mosque was as much a part of our life as the kitchen. And for my father and mother, for all my relatives, it was the thing that gave them strength to face all the privations the world brought to their door. But it was not right for me. I tried. I tried so hard I could not sleep, I could not eat, because I knew it would make my mother and father proud. But it did not speak to me, here . . .' he touched his chest, then his forehead '. . . and here. It did not feel right, or comforting, or secure, or even begin to explain the way the world works. For me. For I still believe, of all the religions, it is one of the strongest. But it did not speak *to me*. And so, in all good faith, I could not continue with it.'

Carolina and Spink watched every flicker of his face, his deathly seriousness reflected in their own.

'I told my father. The shock I saw in his features destroyed me. It was as if, for one brief instant, I was a stranger who had washed into his room. And I never saw his eyes light up again. At first he tried to force me to be a good Muslim. And then, when that did not work, at sixteen he drove me out of the house for good. I stood crying on the doorstep, the same good son who had pleased him all his life. And he would not look me in the face. And he would not speak a word. And when the door closed it was plain it would be for ever.'

'What a bastard,' Carolina said.

'No. I could never blame my father. He was who he was and always had been. And there is not a night goes by that I do not think of him warmly.'

'Why are you telling us this?'

'Because I have spent all my life since then searching for something which would give me the same feeling of warmth and security I felt as a child, and which would fill that void inside.'

'But you've found—'

'No. I have not. Once you set off along that path to enlightenment it is a very dark road indeed, and I have not seen even the slightest glimmer of light at the end. It is a journey we must all make, alone. What worked for my father did not work for me. What will be right for me, will not be so for you. Do not seek out masters. Look into yourself.'

There was a long pause. Then she said, 'Can't you see? That's just the kind of guidance I was looking for—'

He sighed.

'Okay, okay, I hear what you're saying. But I tell you now, we are going to be your disciples. We'll just do it from a distance.' Her smile was facetious, teasing; he smiled in response.

He could see in her face there was something else. 'What do you want?'

'We want to be with you.'

It took him a second or two to realise what she was truly saying. 'That may not be a good idea.'

'Why? Because you think we're being manipulated somehow? We know what we're doing. This isn't an emotional thing, it's a . . . it's a . . .' She searched for the right words.

'A ritual thing,' Spink said suddenly.

Shavi nodded. He understood the transfer of power through the sexual act and he certainly understood the power of directed hedonism. But he was uncomfortable with how they were elevating him to the position of some potent seer and hoping that some of whatever he had would rub off on them during intimacy.

Before he had a chance to order his thoughts, Carolina had stripped off her T-shirt. Her breasts were small and pale in the torchlight. Spink followed suit; his chest was hard and bony, the ribs casting strips of shadow across his skin.

'Spink's bi,' Carolina said. 'Or maybe gay, I don't think he's decided yet.'

She leaned forward and kissed Shavi, her mouth open and wet. Spink moved in and began to nuzzle at Shavi's neck. There was too much sensory stimulation for Shavi to keep his thoughts ordered and eventually he gave in to the pleasures of the moment.

794

The torch was switched off. His fingers slid over warm flesh. Hands caressed his body, stripping him naked. Their bodies moved over his, both of them hard, at times impossible to tell who was whom. The atmosphere became heightened with energy and for that brief moment he felt renewed.

The scream cut through the early morning stillness, snapping Shavi out of a deep sleep. He untangled himself from draping limbs, only just stirring, before pulling on his clothes and scrambling out on to the dewy ground. The air was chill; it couldn't have been long after dawn.

The first thing he saw brought that cold deep into his veins. There, in the tufted grass by the tent opening, was a slim, pale, severed finger.

All over the campsite people were falling out of camper vans, buses and cars, staggering bleary-eyed into the light. Shavi lurched past the finger, barely able to take his eyes off it, then tried to estimate the direction from which the scream had come. He didn't have to look far. In the no-man's land between the vehicles and the wood, a woman silently dipped down, then rose up, dipped down, rose up, a surreal image until Shavi saw her face was contorted with such grief she couldn't give voice to it. A shapeless mass lay at her feet.

Shavi ran as fast as he could, but several people reached the site before him. He pushed through them a little too roughly. Lying at the centre of the shocked circle of travellers was Penny, the ground stained in a wide arc around where her finger should have been. She was white with death.

Shavi felt his stomach knot, his mind fizz and spark with the awful realisation that he had brought this horror to the gentle, peaceful travellers. The ground seemed to shift beneath his feet and he had to stagger away where he could no longer see the body.

CHAPTER SEVENTEEN

Ꝺust oꝼ Creeꝺs Outworn

What do you mean, it's all your fault?' Breaker's face was shattered, his cheeks still stinging red from tears. Carolina stood beside him like a ghost while Meg squatted nearby, her hands pressed against her eyes, as if she were trying to stop the image from entering her brain.

Shavi explained everything, from when it had all begun on the banks of Loch Maree. The others listened intently, their faces impassive; Shavi couldn't tell if they were judging him. Afterwards Carolina asked in a breaking voice, 'So why is it hunting you?'

'I have no idea.' He swallowed, composed himself. 'I thought we had seen the last of it in Edinburgh. I had no idea it was following me or I would not have brought it to your door. You must believe me—'

'We do.' Meg came forward and hugged him tightly. 'We can all see you're all right. You wouldn't have put us at risk if you'd known.' She glanced over to where the body lay covered by a sheet. 'Poor Penny. Just after she'd found out what'd happened to Jack.'

'That is why it happened,' Shavi said morosely.

'What do you mean?' Breaker asked.

'The attack was meant to show there is no hope. Penny was snuffed out just as she achieved it.' Shavi chewed his lip until he tasted blood. 'It was a message for me. The finger was left outside the tent, a sign that the killer could have come for me while I slept.'

'But why?' Carolina looked like she was about to vomit.

'To make me suffer, I would think. To make me frightened, always looking over my shoulder, so never knowing when the attack will come.'

'What's the obsession with fingers?' Breaker asked.

'I have no idea. Are you going to report this to the police?'

Breaker toyed with his beard, but it was Meg who gave voice to the thoughts in all their minds. 'There's no point. With all the shit going down, the cops haven't got time to look into this. They'll probably just use it as another excuse to harass us.'

'Then I would suggest we bury her among the trees. The Wood-born will watch over her,' Shavi suggested.

The grave party ensured the hole was six feet deep, carefully avoiding all the roots that criss-crossed the area. There were enough of them to ensure the work was done quickly, then everyone in the camp gathered for the ceremony; their faces were disbelieving, angry, distraught. Their lives had been disrupted so suddenly and completely no one had quite been able to assimilate what had happened. Breaker and Meg said a few words in a ritual which echoed the cycles of the seasons and spoke to the overwhelming force of nature.

Once the grave was filled, everyone was surprised to see a spontaneous shower of leaves from all the surrounding trees, until the overturned soil was covered by a crisp blanket of green; it was an act of such respect several people wept at the sight. Shavi felt, in a grimly ironic way, that the bond between the two groups had been strengthened further.

They decided to postpone any wake until everyone had had time to come to terms with what had happened. Instead, Breaker, Carolina, Meg and Shavi gathered around a makeshift table in the back of Breaker's bus.

'Of course, I will be leaving shortly,' Shavi announced once they were seated.

'Why?' Meg's eyes blazed.

'This sickening thing is pursuing me. When I leave he will follow me and you will be left to return to your lives.'

'No,' Meg said forcefully.

'I agree,' Carolina added. 'You're one of us now. We're not going to desert you.'

'They're right,' Breaker said. 'They're always right about everything, that's why we love them.' His words seemed honest rather than patronising. 'There's safety in numbers, Shavi. You go off on your own across that deserted countryside, well, that bastard could pick you off at any time. We're organised here. We can do more, better, watches. We'll get you where you need to go.'

'But—'

'Don't fucking argue,' Carolina said wearily. She wiped her eyes with the back of her hand. 'Think of your friend. Think of the big picture, all you're trying to do. Here's where we do our bit too.'

Shavi sagged back against the window and slowly rubbed a hand across his eyes. 'Thank you. You are true friends.'

'Just do one thing for us,' Breaker said.

'What is that?'

'If you get a chance, any time, ever, bring Jack back. For Penny.'

Shavi put one hand on his heart and held the other up, palm out. 'For Penny.'

Church perched on a rocky outcropping over a precipitous drop, contemplating how quickly the remaining nine days would pass. Before him the Derbyshire countryside rolled out in the hazy, late morning sunshine, a patchwork of green fields, shimmering water, ribbon roads and small, peaceful villages. But it wasn't the great beauty of the scene that caught his attention.

Nearby, houses were burning. The tangled wreckage of vehicles glinted in the sunlight. Things he couldn't quite comprehend moved along the hedgerows or kept to the dark at the edge of copses. Occasionally one would be forced to cross a field, like a cloud-shadow moving across the land. It always made him shiver to see it.

The Fomorii appeared to be growing in force, more daring in their desperation as Lughnasadh neared. They sensed Ruth and what she contained were somewhere in the area, but the magic Tom had identified at Mam Tor was, so far, enough to blind them to the exact location. But if he allowed himself to admit it, he knew it was only a question of time. For once, he could do nothing; it was a matter of placing his faith in Shavi, Veitch and Tom.

Sometimes he saw the Fomorii hunter-warrior circling the area, more intense and threatening than the other shifting shapes, like a localised storm filled with lightning fury. It left him feeling fearful and nauseous. And something more than that: he was starting to feel the bitter taint of hopelessness. Only days to go. What could they do? They were going to fail again, and it would be the end of everything.

Cautiously he crept back from the edge. What would he do when the black tide did begin to surge up the mountain? Fight them off with sticks and stones like schoolboy war games? Or sit back and pray there really, truly was a God in His heaven?

Ruth lay in her sleeping bag on a bed made of flattened fern in a corner of the room. Her skin was ashen, her hair matted from the bouts of sweating and delirium that were coming with increasing regularity. Her eyes flickered, her features trembled; terrible thoughts that did not seem to come from her own mind stumbled through her head.

They had cleaned up the place as best they could. Church and Laura had spent a morning sweeping out the rubbish and depositing it in the shadows at the back of the house. Church had patched up the roof with dead wood and vegetation, but the wind still whipped through the broken windows and sometimes it was uncommonly cold for that time of year; perhaps it was the altitude. Food was a problem. There was little to trap on the mountain and none of them were any good at it anyway. Church had made several forays into a nearby village and had stocked up the larder as best he could. The increasing Fomorii activity in the area made it too risky to go foraging any more. They all prayed the provisions would hold out.

Laura squatted in the corner, occasionally casting a subdued glance to Ruth's restlessly sleeping form. The sunglasses rarely came off these days, even at night. Her brooding consumed her. She hated the way Church cared for Ruth; there was real tenderness in his touch, an honesty in his words that made her yearn; the feeling between the two ran so deep it was as if it had formed when the earth was just cooling. She knew it was jealousy, pure and simple; it was the kind of relationship she had always dreamed about, had expected once she had hooked up with Church, yet even though all the facets seemed in place, it had never materialised, and that was the bitterest blow of all. If she couldn't find it with Church, who could she plumb those depths with?

And she could see Ruth was dying; they all knew it, though no one spoke it aloud. Yet there she was, being petty and jealous and bitter. That filled her with guilt and self-loathing, which once more fed all those negative emotions; a terrible, dark spiral that had no end.

'What are you thinking?'

Laura started; she hadn't realised Ruth was awake. 'I'm thinking, "Boy, I hope she doesn't start whining any time soon".'

Ruth managed a weak laugh; her voice sounded like autumn leaves. 'You'll never change, will you?'

'Count on it.'

Ruth tried to lever herself into a sitting position. Her arms were feeble and her belly was enormous; she seemed to have gone almost full-term of a natural pregnancy in a matter of days. Eventually she gave up and settled for half-sitting, half-lying. She snorted with laughter at her own pathetic attempt.

'How do you keep so up? You've had the bum deal to end all bum deals. Some psycho slicing off your finger. Getting tortured by the Bastards. Now this—'

'Now I'm pregnant with the one-eyed God of Death and he's going to burst out of my stomach in a few days and tear me apart. Well, when you put it like that . . .' She laughed again, before breaking into a coughing fit.

'What is it with you? When I first met you, you were such a

poker-up-the-arse kind of girl. Some spoilt little middle-class moron. I thought you'd fall apart at the first sign of trouble.'

'What's the matter? Jealous?'

Her words were lighthearted but they stung Laura as if she'd been slapped. 'You have a real sense of the absurd, don't you?'

'I'm dying. You're supposed to be nice to me.'

Laura watched her impassively.

'That was the point where you were supposed to say, "Course you're not dying. Everything will work out in the end".' Ruth threw an arm across her eyes. Laura couldn't tell if she was trying to hide her emotions, but she felt bad anyway.

But not bad enough she could bring herself to be nice. Nice was for losers. 'What do you expect me to say?'

'I don't know. Nothing to say, is there? I'm dying. I know I'm dying. And any chance I have is the longest of long shots.' She removed her arm and Laura was surprised to see a remarkable peace in her face.

That twisted the knife in her gut even more and suddenly she felt like crying; the words just bubbled out. 'What is it? Church, you can see he's a hero. It's stitched right into the heart of him, always beating himself up about responsibilities and obligations and doing the right thing. Shavi's just Mister Decency. You know he'd give up his life if the cause was right. Even Veitch, the Testosterone Kid, a fucking murderer by his own admission! Even he's fighting against type to be good, to be a hero. And despite all his very obvious limitations, you know he's going to come through, when the chips are down and all those other clichés. And then there's you, kicked around and tortured from pillar to post, taking all this shit that *nobody* should have to take. And dying with dignity. I don't fit in here. You give me a choice between saving my own skin and doing the right thing and you watch my dust!' The self-pity was sickening, but she seemed unable to control herself.

'You're not being fair on yourself—'

'Don't start analysing me. I don't need it. And for God's sake, don't start being *nice* to me.'

'I won't—'

'Just don't.'

'Look, can't we just be friends? Even now?' Ruth's eyes filled with tears; despite her calm, her emotions were on a knife-edge.

Laura remained silent, staring at the wall. The mass of scrawled writing disturbed her immensely and in all their time there none of them had felt up to making any effort to decipher it. It was just part of the oppressive mood that lurked in the corners of the house. She was sure Ruth sensed things there that she wasn't talking about, and there were times when she felt it acutely herself, and she was less sensitive than anyone she knew. *Something bad had happened*, Ruth had said, and something bad was *going* to happen. Perhaps that was it: not an echo of the past, but a premonition. She felt it so strongly she could almost touch it.

'You've always hidden yourself away from all of us.' Ruth's voice was hazy and Laura could tell she was on the verge of drifting into one of her intermittent periods of delirium. 'Hiding behind your sunglasses, trying to be smart and glib all the time so no one knew what you were really thinking. Even that name – Laura DuSantiago. That's got to be an alias, a new persona to hide in.' She swallowed; her mouth sounded sticky with mucus. 'Tell you what,' she continued weakly. 'You tell me your real name now. I won't tell a soul. A dying woman's last wish.' She laughed hollowly.

Laura sat quietly for a moment, then moved to the bedside and knelt so her mouth was close to Ruth's ear. Ruth strained to hear.

'Go fuck yourself,' Laura said softly.

Then she rose and calmly walked out of the room in search of Church.

Breaker cursed under his breath as the lead bus began another difficult three-point turn in the middle of the road. About half a mile ahead they could see the tailback leading up to the police checkpoint. It looked like the police were barring every road they tried; Shavi had lost count of the times they had turned around and sought an alternative route. But that wasn't what was troubling him. It was the things he increasingly caught glimpses of from the corner of his eye, moving as fast as foxes, or slipping back into shadows when he half-turned his head. He hadn't mentioned them to Breaker or the others, but he knew what they were: the Fomorii were abroad.

He took some relief from the fact that they were still wary enough to stay out of plain sight; just. They must be terrified about having let the essence of their god slip through their fingers, if it were possible for such creatures to feel fear. But he was concerned about how widespread they were and how their number appeared to be increasing. If they were this close to the surface now, what would happen when desperation set in as Lughnasadh neared?

He knew they were searching for any sign of Balor, but was it possible they could *sniff out* the Pendragon Spirit too?

'You look worried.' Breaker cast a sideways glance as he pulled up behind the bumper of the bus in front.

'I was merely trying to second-guess the obstacles which might lie between us and my destination.'

'You reckon the Finger Hunter is somewhere nearby? I don't see how he could be keeping up with us unless he's smelling us on the wind.'

Shavi thought that was a distinct possibility, but said nothing.

'The biggest problem is the cops. We need to stay out of their way. I don't know what's happened to them. They were always bugging us, but now they seem to be hassling *everyone*. All these checkpoints. What the hell do they think they're trying to do?'

Some of the police at every checkpoint had waxy faces, Shavi had noticed; it was obvious to him what they were trying to do. And it appeared that there was some link between what Breaker called the Finger Hunter and the Fomorii too. Shavi had an overpowering image of a net closing around him. Perhaps he would never reach Windsor at all.

After leaving the camp where Penny had been buried, they had taken a couple of days to pick a relatively short route past Banbury before cutting through the lanes between Oxford and Bicester to reach their current position just north of the M40. On the map Windsor looked to be only forty minutes' drive away. Two rapidly successive technology failures slowed them down even more, but every attempt to cross the motorway failed and they were continually pushed east towards London. With only a week remaining before Lughnasadh Shavi could ill afford any more delays.

'We can't get too close to the Smoke,' Breaker said, concerned. 'A convoy this size'll draw too much attention. We'll get snarled up and they'll have us off the road in a minute. Plus, some of our valued members get very uneasy whenever they're near any built-up area. All that pollution.'

Shavi barely spoke any more; his attention was directed at the apparently empty countryside. Thoughts were piling up inside his head, forcing him down a very worrying path. The one who killed Penny was obviously not Fomorii, but possibly had some kind of link with the Night Walkers. The killer knew who Shavi was travelling with, probably knew exactly where he was. What if the killer decided to point the Fomorii in his direction? Shavi scanned the fields cautiously. He had not seen any sign of the Fomorii for some time. Perhaps they too were wary of getting too close to the Capital. Still, he would be on his guard.

They paused in a lay-by on the A40 east of Postcombe to weigh up their options. Most people stayed in their vehicles, taking the opportunity to have a quick snack or a drink, but the ones who had naturally gravitated towards the leading group gathered on the roadside for a conference. There were Breaker, Meg, Carolina, and four others whom Shavi didn't know by name. While they spoke heatedly, Shavi circled the group, focusing his attention on the fields that swept out to the north and east.

It was late afternoon and the sweltering temperature of the day had been made worse by thick cloud-cover rolling in to trap the heat. They would have to consider making camp soon, and that was a prospect Shavi did not relish.

Exhausted by the day's driving, still shattered by what had happened to Penny, the travellers' nerves were fraying, their voices growing harsh. Shavi tried to ignore them to concentrate on the darkening landscape, but their debate grew louder and more hectoring until he turned and snapped, 'Quiet!'

They all looked at him. A car roared by and then the road grew still. 'What is it?' Carolina said. 'There's nothing—'

He waved her quiet with a chopping motion of his hand. Something was jarring on his nerves, but he couldn't quite put his finger on what it was. There was the wind in the trees. Distant traffic noise from the motorway. Nothing, nothing . . . And then he had it. The field birds were cawing harshly; on the surface it was not unusual, but instinctively he seemed to know what they were saying. He could hear the tonal differences, the faint nuances, almost as if it was speech. They were frightened.

He spun round to the others. 'Back to the vehicles. Quickly. It is not safe here.'

The words had barely left his mouth when there was movement along all the hedgerows of the fields: darkness separating from the shadows near the hedge bottoms, rising out of ditches; the Fomorii were moving.

Most of the travellers obeyed him instantly and ran towards their vehicles. One of the men whom Shavi didn't know turned to look at the fields curiously; his eyes started to roll and nausea passed across his face. Shavi gave him a violent shove in the direction of his camper van before he could see any more.

'Do not look at the fields!' Shavi yelled. 'Get on the road and keep driving! Follow Breaker's lead!'

He threw himself in beside Breaker and the bus lurched out on to the road. A horn blared furiously as a Porsche overtook at high speed. 'What's going on?' Breaker asked.

'The Fomorii are attacking,' Shavi said darkly, one eye fixed on the wing mirror. 'They want me. And they will destroy you all to get at me.'

The vehicles surged on to the road in a wave of creaking, protesting metal. But age lay heavy on some of them and their response was poor. Shavi held himself tense as he watched the trail pull out of the lay-by as the fields turned black with movement; it was as if a termites' nest had suddenly been vacated.

'Are they all with us?' Breaker asked anxiously.

Shavi counted the vehicles out. 'Nearly there.' A bus. Another. A mini-van. 'One more.' The straggler was the camper van belonging to the traveller Shavi had forced into action. It was slow, weaving unnecessarily, and Shavi knew the driver was trying to see what was in the fields through his mirror. 'Do not look,' he prayed under his breath.

The camper van slewed suddenly to one side and came to a halt. Shavi pictured the driver vomiting, then passing out. He slammed a hand against the side window as if it would jolt the driver awake.

In the mirror Shavi watched the darkness sweep over the hedgerow into the lay-by. He had an impression of teeth and body armour, wings and too many legs, all shimmering sable, and although he had grown almost immune to the appearance of the Night Walkers, he still felt his stomach churn.

The Fomorii hit the camper van like a tidal wave. It crumpled as if it were made of paper, then shredded into a million pieces. Shavi looked away quickly.

Breaker glanced at him, but didn't have to ask. After a long silence, the traveller said, 'Do you think they'll follow us into London?'

'They will not be able to keep up with the vehicles if you travel at speed. But now they know I am with you they will continue to hunt you down. If we go into London there is a danger we will be obstructed, slowed down.'

'Then what?' Breaker's thumb was banging on the wheel in an anxious rhythm.

Shavi thought for a moment. 'We must speed up, but not go completely out of sight. They must see you drop me off—'

'We can't abandon you to them!' Breaker flashed him a dismayed glance.

'I will have a better chance of hiding from them alone. There must be somewhere near here where I can attempt to lose them.' He snatched up Breaker's dog-eared book of maps and hastily riffled through the pages. When he found the page they were on, he pored over it for a minute, then stabbed his finger down. 'Here.'

*

When Breaker was convinced the convoy was going to go straight into the centre of High Wycombe, Shavi indicated a turning. They came to a stop at West Wycombe and waited anxiously, with constant reference to the mirror. Meg and Carolina could contain themselves no longer, and ran from their respective vehicles to see what was planned. They pleaded with him not to go, but he would not be deterred; his leaving was the only chance they had.

When he spied movement in the countryside on either side, he kissed them both, shook Breaker's hand forcefully, then sent them on their way. His last view of the travellers was a series of pale, frightened faces trying to comprehend what was happening in their lives.

He waited alone in the road for as long as he could. It quickly became obvious the dark stream of Fomorii had realised he had left the convoy, for they hurtled towards him relentlessly, without heeding the disappearing vehicles.

Once he was sure of that, he dashed through a gate and ran as fast as his legs would carry him.

The lowering clouds made the late afternoon into twilight. The very air around him seemed to have a gun-metal sheen and he could taste iron on the back of his tongue; a storm was brewing, which he hoped would be to his advantage, although he had the unnerving feeling the Fomorii could see in the gloomiest weather conditions.

But at least he was sure he could make the location work for him. Once he saw the name on the map, the information about myths, legends and history that he had amassed over a lifetime instantly came into play.

He was sprinting through the classically designed grounds of West Wycombe Park in full view of the gleaming Palladian mansion where the Dashwood family had made their home for hundreds of years. It was one of their ancestors who had earned the place such notoriety. In the mid-eighteenth century Sir Francis Dashwood founded a private brotherhood of the upper crust, which he ironically named the Knights of St Francis. There was little of the chivalrous about a secret society dedicated to orgies and blasphemous religious ceremonies, acts which earned it the nickname the Hellfire Club and a motto *Do what thou wilt.* The truth had turned into legend, which had haunted the family and the area ever since, but somewhere in the grounds was another part of Sir Francis' grim legacy which Shavi thought might save his life; if only he could find it.

He headed for the unmistakable landmark of St Lawrence's Church, built by Dashwood, with a meeting place for ten of his Hellfire Knights in a gleaming, golden ball on the top of the tower. Shavi had half-expected to be met by security guards or someone trying to make him buy a ticket, but things were falling apart quickly all over; what was the point of maintaining tourist locations when everyone was trying to live on a day-to-day basis in a climate of increasing fear?

At the church he stopped and glanced back. The shadowy shapes were closer now, massing as they flowed down the sweeping green slopes of the garden. Quickly he scanned the area.

Eventually he found what he was looking for: an entrance cut into the hillside overlooking the park. Within lay a network of artificial caves going deep underground where the Hellfire Club had held its magic rituals and orgies. It was tucked away at just such an angle that the approaching Fomorii would not see him take the detour and would presume he had continued on through the grounds; and it was discreet enough that unless they knew it was there, they would not see it. He hoped.

He skidded inside, his chest aching from his ragged breathing; even fit as he now was, he hadn't moved at such a clip for a long time. The catacombs were filled with an inky darkness. Lights had been installed for the tourists, but he didn't dare attempt to put them on, even if he could have located the light switch. He moved as swiftly as he could while feeling his way along the chill, dank walls. When he rounded a corner and the ambient light was extinguished, the gloom was complete. He had a sudden flashback to the grim ruins of Mary King's Close and felt his heart begin to pound. He had attempted to bend the supernatural to his will, but the more he had learned about the Invisible World, the more he realised how much there was that terrified him. He wondered if any remnant of the monstrous rituals carried out by the Hellfire Club had been imprinted in the rock walls; if Sir Francis Dashwood's spirit still walked the place, trying to expunge his lifetime's sins; if there were other, worse, things there that had been called up by the Club's desire to be an affront to natural law.

But more than the otherworldly threat was the certain knowledge that if the Fomorii did enter the catacombs he would not be aware of them until they were upon him.

When he felt he had progressed deep enough into the heart of the tunnels, he slumped down against the foot of the wall and took a deep breath. His whole body was shaking from the strain and the fear, his blood pumping so loudly he didn't think he would hear if a column of hobnailed soldiers were marching towards him; he forced himself to do a series of breathing exercises to calm himself. Once he had relaxed as much as he could he tried to concentrate all his energies on his hearing.

In his mind's eye he pictured the scene above ground: the oppressive force of Fomorii smashing down small trees, tearing through shrubs and flowers, sweeping up and around the church. By now they should have reached the entrance to the catacombs.

He listened intently. Nothing.

Perhaps they had already passed, thundering through the rest of the grounds, not stopping for miles, like robot drones pointed in one direction and turned on. Of the Fomorii he had encountered, there appeared little of independent thought and cunning; that rested in large quantities with their leader Calatin; and Mollecht, the Fomor who appeared as a swirling mass of crows, whom Shavi had not seen since that night in the Lake District when they thought they had snatched victory.

Time passed in deep silence. How long should he wait there, he wondered? In the dark he found he was losing track of the hours. If the Fomorii had not already found him, it would be logical, he supposed, to wait until morning before attempting to leave. They would be scouring the countryside for him and the night was not the best time to be trying to evade them. But even if he did make it through the night undiscovered, what chance would he have of reaching Windsor Park? It was not far on the map, but if there were an army of Fomorii between him and his destination, it might as well have been a million miles away.

At some point he fell asleep, and he must have been out for a while, for on awakening suddenly his mouth and throat were uncommonly dry and every muscle ached. When he opened his eyes he was completely disorientated by the dark and had to struggle to recall where he was. But as soon as his memory clicked into action he became alert; he knew something had woken him.

His first thought was that the Fomorii had finally tracked him down, but the dark caves around him seemed as empty as they ever had been. His next thought was of some supernatural presence; his instincts were as attuned to the Invisible as the visible world. But he didn't have that queasy sensation which always materialised in the pit of his stomach whenever something uncanny was nearby.

He held his breath and listened. At first, nothing; then a sound, just the slightest scuffle of dust from a footstep that many would have missed, but his own hearing had grown hyper-sensitive in the dark. There was someone else in the caves, and they were creeping, so as not to be discovered.

The construction of the caves meant all sound was distorted, so it was impossible to tell from which direction the footfall had come. In the all-consuming darkness Shavi was loath to move one way or the other in case he bumped into the intruder. But then neither could he sit there and wait to be discovered.

Weighing the odds, he decided to attempt to make his way back to the door; at least then he would have the option of fleeing if necessary. He stood up and rested his left hand on the wall before moving forward a few paces. He paused and listened. Another few paces and he stopped again.

The unmistakable scrape of a foot on the gritty floor. A tingle ran down his spine. It seemed to come from somewhere over to his right. Cautiously he continued ahead, placing each foot down slowly and carefully, so as not to make even the slightest noise.

His breath was held tightly in his chest. He half-expected to come face to face with something terrible; the dark was so deep he wouldn't have known if there were someone standing motionless even six inches in front of him. With an effort he drove those thoughts from his head; it would do him no good; he had to stay calm.

Another noise, this time in front of him. The echoes were mesmerising. He couldn't tell if the intruder was circling or if he was misreading the direction of the sounds. He moved back a few paces and waited again.

In the claustrophobic space of the caves, Shavi knew it was only a matter of time before his pursuer caught him. Yet there was a slim chance to weight the odds a little more in his favour. He closed his eyes and took a deep, calming breath, focusing far within himself. He still couldn't turn his nascent shamanistic abilities on and off like a light switch, but with concentration there were little tricks he had practised. He felt the force rising within him like a billowing sheet, filling him, moving out through his mouth, to wrap itself around him. The first time he had attempted this he had been standing within a few feet of Veitch, yet the Londoner had not even noticed him, at least for a moment or two. He didn't know *how* it worked, but he perceived it as a cloak which made him merge in with the surroundings. It was a subtle trick and easily punctured, yet in the gloom of the cavern it might have more force. He hoped it would be enough.

His throat had grown painfully dry. After several minutes without a sound, he moved off again. This time he progressed a long way through the caves, but somewhere in the dark he must have taken a wrong turning, for he knew he should have come across the door by then. There was no point retracing his steps – he wouldn't have any idea when he arrived back at where he had slept anyway. His only option was to keep going left, in the hope that it would lead him to an outside wall which would eventually take him around the perimeter of the catacombs to the exit.

As he moved he listened as intently as he could, but there was no sign of anyone; at the same time he had an overwhelming and unpleasant sense of *presence*. And then he froze as every nerve seemed to fire at once. Was someone standing right behind him? His mind screamed at him to run, but somehow he held his ground. In that heightened moment his senses started playing tricks on him. Was that the bloom of a breath on his neck? An involuntary spasm ran through him; he didn't even dare swallow. The most natural thing in the world would have been to run away, but he was as sure as anything in his life that that would be the end of him.

And so he waited, and after several minutes the feeling slowly ebbed away. He didn't know if the intruder had been there, just inches away, listening, unable to see him, or if it was all in his mind. But the nausea he felt at the strain was certainly real.

He began moving again, hugging the wall, straining not to be heard.

His journey seemed to take hours, punctuated by long pauses brought on by dim echoes, the faintest footfalls, that might very well have been all in his mind.

And then, just as he was about to dismiss the entire experience as a flight of fancy, he happened to glance behind him, though his eyes were useless. The intensity of the darkness was almost hallucinatory and for a while his mind had been conjuring up flashes of colours, streaks of light, that were just brief electrical bursts on his retina. He could have dismissed it as another mind-flash, but what he saw made him stop and stare. No flash, no streak. Two tiny points of yellow away in the dark.

But then they disappeared and reappeared and he knew what they were: eyes, glinting with an awful inner light.

In his shock, he turned back and there was a thin grey band of dim light. It was seeping through the entrance. He moved towards it as quickly but as quietly as he could.

Steeling himself, his hand hovered over the handle. Then he wrenched it open and hurled himself out into a world just coming to life. On the threshold, he couldn't resist making the most of that pre-dawn light and threw one glance over his shoulder before sprinting across the park as fast as he could go.

And then he ran and he ran, that briefest glimpse staying with him as he put as much distance between him and his pursuer as he could.

What he half-saw in the gloom was a shape that looked like a giant wolf, its eyes growing with a malignant fire. But an instant later his mind had started to rearrange it into something else: a human figure. The killer was still close behind him, as relentless in its pursuit as the wolf his mind presumed it to be.

But what troubled him more than the knowledge that he had escaped death only by a hair's breadth was that in that instant when the shape had started to change he was almost convinced he knew the person it was becoming. In the gloom and the fear, he hadn't been able to harden up the vision, and the connection remained disturbingly elusive.

To his infinite relief, there was no pursuit; nor were there any Fomorii in the immediate vicinity. But what he had half-seen continued to haunt him long after the sun had driven the greyness out of the landscape.

the Court of the Queen
of Elfland

Inverness appeared out of the dark Highlands landscape like a small island of light in a vast sea of shadows. Veitch and Tom walked down from the hills with leaden legs, burdened with the crushing weight of exhaustion. They had spent the last few days endlessly dodging the Fomorii, who were swarming across the purple moorland in increasing numbers. Tom had utilised some of his tricks – a ritual, some foul-tasting brew made from herbs and roots – which made the two of them oblivious to the Night Walkers unless they were in direct line of sight. But that still entailed endless hours of creeping along rocky gullies, taking the hard route over peaks or skulking in woods until the danger had passed.

It was a far cry from the first leg of their Scottish journey, when they had dined out on wholesome provisions from the villages they dropped in on. Now Veitch was heartily sick of wild game, roots and herbs, however well Tom cooked it. He had an almost unbearable craving for pizza or a curry, washed down with a beer.

'You reckon we'll get time to stop off for a ruby?' he said wearily as they trudged into the outskirts of town.

Tom looked at him blankly.

'Ruby Murray. Curry. It rhymes.'

Tom shook his head contemptuously. 'Eight days left. Why don't we go on a pub crawl while we're at it? We could have a few drinks for Ruth. That should make her well.'

'All right. No need to act so bleedin' crabby.' He took a few steps, then muttered, 'Twat,' under his breath. That made him feel better.

The truth was, their nerves were growing frayed. Time was running away from them. Lughnasadh was close, and the presence of Balor was almost tangible. They had both dreamed of a single eye watching them malignantly from the dark, and had woken sweaty and sick, with the feeling that the monstrous god of the Fomorii was *aware* of them. Even when they walked, they could feel his attention sweeping over them, the air thick with dread; with it came an overpowering sense of black despair that conjured thoughts of suicide, which they had to fight constantly to repel.

The weariness shucked off their shoulders the more they progressed into town. It felt good to see sodium lights after the oppression of a country night, to smell motor oil and the aroma of home cooking. But the closer they got into the centre, the more they began to realise something was wrong. No cars had passed them at all. Nobody walked the streets, even though it was only just past ten. The pubs were all locked, the curtains drawn, although Veitch could hear people drinking within; when he hammered on the doors a deep silence fell, but no one ever came to answer.

Eventually an old man swung open an upstairs window and hung out, his face filled with such fear Veitch gaped for a second.

'For God's sake, man, get yourself to your hearth!' The old man glanced up and down the street; he hadn't noticed Veitch wasn't alone. 'Can you not see it's after dark!' He slammed the window shut and drew the curtains before Veitch could question him; Veitch shouted to him several times, but there was no further response.

'What's up?' Veitch asked Tom with disquiet.

Tom continued to walk briskly, seemingly oblivious to the sense of threat. '*What's up?* Old friends have come to visit Inverness and they won't leave until they've expressed their infinite kindness.' Sarcasm dripped from his words.

'You're talking about the ones we're going to see?'

'The Queen of Elfland—'

A curiously amused expression jumped on Veitch's face. 'You're kidding me.'

'The Queen of Elfland. That's what they used to call her in the old stories. As if to pretend she was some kind of nice, acceptable *fairy*—' the word was filled with bitterness '—would somehow deflect her attentions.'

'So what would you call her?'

'Nothing she could hear.' He looked away so Veitch could not see his face. 'The moment we cross over, we must be on our guard.'

'You make her sound like some witch ready to tear our bleedin' heads off.'

'She will be filled with charisma, magnetic and alluring. That is her danger.'

'Okay. No problem.'

'No, you do not understand. The slightest wrong move could be the end of you. Every court of the Tuatha Dé Danann is different. The Court of the Yearning Heart embraces chaos and madness, which is why it is given over to pleasure. It is very easy to be seduced by it.' The deep tone of personal experience was unmissable. 'Listen carefully. You know the rules of Otherworld, and they go doubly here. You must accept no food nor drink from anyone or you will instantly fall under the power of the Queen. And she will find it greatly entertaining to trick you into doing so. You have to be sharp, Ryan. You have to be sharp.'

Veitch was shocked by the familiarity of Tom's use of his Christian name. For the first time, he felt the Rhymer was truly concerned about his safety. 'What'll happen, you know, if I do—?'

'Don't.'

'But if I do?'

Tom sighed. 'You will not be allowed to leave the Court of the Yearning Heart, at least not until the Queen has taken you apart down to your very molecules and has rebuilt you in whatever way her whims take her at the time. Until you have suffered every pain and pleasure imaginable, until it has become such a way of life that you *want* such suffering. And when she has finished, you will no longer be the man you are. You will no longer be a man.'

If Tom had tried to scare him, he'd succeeded.

'There isn't a man alive who couldn't love her,' Tom continued. 'But she dishes out joy and cruelty in equal measure; sometimes she isn't even aware that's what she's doing. The gates at Tom-na-hurich remained intermittently open long after the Sundering. There is a story of two itinerant fiddlers who crossed over. The Queen paid them to entertain the Court and allowed them to eat one of the sumptuous meals that are always laid out there. The fiddlers played their hearts out for the rest of the night. But when they were taken back to the Hill of Yews come the morning, they crumbled into dust. Two hundred years had passed without them knowing, and the Queen had taken great pleasure in hiding this from them.'

Veitch was silent for a moment. 'So how come you didn't turn to dust?'

Tom laughed hollowly. 'Why, only humans suffer such fates! The Queen has seen that I can never fit that bill.' He stopped in the middle of the road and looked out across the city to beyond the River Ness; Veitch guessed their destination lay in that direction. 'The legends say I lie under Tom-na-hurich with my men and white horse, ready to save Scotland in her hour of need.'

'Well, that's what you're doing, ain't it?'

Tom snorted. 'Heroes only exist in stories. There's no nobility in what people do. We're all driven by a complex stew of emotions and it's down to fate whether people see us as good or bad.'

'You're a cynical git,' Veitch said dismissively. 'And you're wrong.'

They continued in silence for the next fifteen minutes until Veitch noticed a golden glow washing over the shops of the High Street. It was moving gradually towards them, casting strange shadows up the grim brick walls of Eastgate Centre. 'What's that?' His hand went to his sword under his coat.

'The welcoming committee.'

As the glow drew nearer, Veitch saw it was coming off a small group of people wandering along the road, although there was no sign of any light source. The moment he looked at the figures he experienced the now-familiar disorientating effect.

Tom drew himself up; the faintest tremor ran through his body, but his face was a mask of calmness. Veitch moved in next to him, tight with apprehension.

Five figures were approaching, all of them wearing outlandish clothes which mixed golden armour and red silk, topped by unusual helmets like enormous sea shells.

'The Queen's guard,' Tom noted. 'Out hunting for entertainment.'

Veitch took his lead from Tom, although his instinct was to hide. He watched as the guard progressed down the street, glancing into alleyways and side streets, shining their terrible regard into windows.

When they first clapped eyes on Tom and Veitch, sly smiles spread across their faces and they picked up their step as if they expected their quarry to flee for their lives. As they neared, their expressions became even more triumphal with recognition.

'True Thomas!' the leader of the guard exclaimed; there was a dark glee in his words, a contemptuous sneer shaping his mouth.

'Melliflor,' Tom said in greeting, giving nothing away.

'Why, we thought you had gone from our doors for all time, True Thomas!' Melliflor smiled with barely disguised mockery. 'The many wonders of the Court of the Yearning Heart are hard to resist, are they not? It calls to you always, even when you do not want to hear. Or,' he mused, 'is it your mistress who has brought you back? Our Lady of Light would be overjoyed to see you, True Thomas.'

Two of the guards had moved behind Veitch and Tom, to prevent any retreat. Veitch watched them suspiciously from the corner of his eye.

'Then take me to her, Melliflor,' Tom said. 'It will be good to see my Queen again after so long.'

Melliflor made an exaggerated sweeping gesture with his right hand to allow Tom to lead the way. After a few steps he arrived by Tom's side; Veitch might as well not have been there.

'May I enquire why you have returned to our doorstep?' Melliflor asked artfully.

'To renew acquaintances, Melliflor.'

'I hear you played a significant part in our return to the solid lands. I am sure our Queen will wish to offer her gratitude in her usual way.'

'Lead on, Melliflor. I have come far these last few days and I am too weary for conversation.'

Melliflor's sneering smile suggested he knew the meaning behind Tom's words; Veitch could quite easily have loosed the crossbow at him there and then.

They moved silently at a fast pace through the deserted streets, crossing Ness Bridge with the water rolling silently beneath, then along Glenurquhart Road, past suburban houses all deserted; some were merely burnt-out shells. Tomnahurich Cemetery loomed up suddenly, the white ghosts of stones gleaming. Melliflor led them past the neatly tended plots to a road running up a hill which looked strangely unnatural on the flat valley bottom. It soared steeply, cloaked in a thick swathe of trees: yews, oaks, holly, pine, sycamore, all interspersed with thick clumps of spiny gorse; the air was heady with the summery aromas of the wood. Hundreds of graves were hidden among the trees right up the hillside, as if they too had grown there. The road curved in a spiral dance around the hill to the summit, modern in construction but hinting at an ancient processional route. 'Welcome to the Hill of Yews,' Melliflor said respectfully, 'known by the local people as Tom-na-hurich.'

They followed the road round until they were swallowed by the trees and the lights of Inverness were lost. It was a strange, mysterious place, eerily still, yet their footfalls echoed in an unusual and unnerving manner; no one felt like talking until they had reached the summit. Here a large area had been cleared at the centre and filled with the jarringly regimented rows of a Victorian cemetery. The fringes were thickly treed with the oldest yews and oaks. At the highest point a cross had been raised to mark Remembrance Day.

They stopped at a nondescript spot among the crumbling, brown gravestones. Melliflor took a step forward and bowed his head before muttering something under his breath. A second later the ground vibrated with a deep bass rumble, as if enormous machinery had come to life, then the grass and soil prised itself apart. From within the long, dark tunnel which had materialised Veitch could hear faint music that immediately made him want to dance; the tang of rich spices wafted out into the balmy night and he was suddenly ravenously hungry. But then he glanced up at Tom and all his desires were wiped clean; the Rhymer's face was as white as a sheet and taut with the effort of keeping in his fear; a faint tick was pulsing near his mouth which, in the emotionless dish of his face, made him look like he was screaming.

At the other end of the tunnel were a pair of long, scarlet curtains. Melliflor held them aside for Veitch and Tom to pass into a great hall which appeared to be the venue for a riotous party. The music was almost deafening; Veitch heard fiddles, drums, a flute, other instruments he couldn't quite place, although he could see no sign of a band. A roaring fire in one corner made the air very warm, but not as uncomfortable as he would have expected at the height of summer. It was filled with an amazing range of scents, with each fresh waft bringing a new one: lime, pepper, roast beef, strawberries, cardamom, hops – so many it made his head spin.

So much was happening in the hall, he couldn't concentrate on one sense for too long. Long tables ranged around the outside of the room on which were heaped every food imaginable, though many he couldn't recognise and some made him turn away, although he couldn't explain why. In the centre of the room the Tuatha Dé Danann were dancing. Scores of them whirled round and round with wild abandon to the odd music, which occasionally flew off the register of Veitch's hearing. It was like a turbulent sea of gold waves crashing against the tables and the walls; it made him queasy to watch.

The assault on Veitch's senses was so great he felt his knees go weak and for a moment he was afraid he was going to faint. But then the rush hit him powerfully and he was swept up in it all. His body was reacting as if he had taken a cocktail of drugs, some mild hallucinogen and an amphetamine; he wanted to fling himself into the seething mass.

He was vaguely aware of someone on his right proffering a goblet of deep, red wine. Unconsciously he reached out to take it, his gaze still fixed on the dance floor.

He was jolted alert by the weight of Tom's hand on his forearm. The Rhymer was already thanking the young girl who had offered the wine with the studied politeness which seemed necessary to prevent any retribution. The girl looked disappointed and her face darkened as she turned away.

Veitch bowed his head sheepishly as Tom glared at him; he couldn't believe how quickly he had almost gone against all of Tom's deeply stressed cautions. He would not forget again.

His attention was drawn back to the dancing, and beyond it to the shadows that clustered along the edges. There he could just spy writing bodies; the gods looked to be in coitus. He could just make out bobbing heads, violent thrusting, sensuous movements, and occasionally the sounds of passion broke through the music; but there was something about it which did not seem quite right, as if the bodies were not penetrating and enveloping, but flowing in and out of each other like mercury; merging. He looked away.

Melliflor was at Tom's side, hands cupped, falsely oleaginous. 'The Queen was overjoyed to know you had returned, True Thomas. She will see you shortly. In the meantime, you and your companion be accepted as our guests. There is food and wine aplenty, the finest music in all of the Far Lands. Make merry, True Thomas, and be a perfect son of the Court of the Yearning Heart.'

'And is it all given freely and without obligation?' Tom asked dispassionately.

'Ah, True Thomas,' Melliflor said cunningly, 'you know we can make no promises here.'

Veitch and Tom found a pile of luxurious cushions in one corner from where they could watch the dancing. Veitch felt so comfortable after the exhaustions of the previous weeks he could have fallen asleep in an instant, but he was sure that was not wise. He was afraid to do anything in case he committed himself to something unpleasant and he wished he had listened more carefully to Tom's instructions during the long walk to Inverness.

Several times revellers walked up to offer jugs of wine or plates lavishly filled with juicy fruit or spiced meat, but always Tom politely refused. It was like a game the Tuatha Dé Danann were playing to see if they could catch their guests out; Veitch could see them talking excitedly and pointing at him before an even more tasty offering was brought up. By the end Veitch's mouth was watering and his stomach rumbling, and all he could do was think how long ago his last meal had been.

Eventually Melliflor glided up. He bowed deeply. 'The Queen will see you and your companion now, True Thomas.'

The two of them were led out of the great hall along stone corridors hung with intricately embroidered tapestries and rich brocaded cloth. Braziers burned with scented wood so the atmosphere was constantly heady. They passed many closed doors and from behind them came strange, unnerving sounds; some sounded like yelps of pain, others like moans of pleasure; some it was impossible to distinguish.

They were eventually presented to a chamber draped throughout its length and breadth with gossamer ivory silk which filtered the flickering light of the torches on the walls so that the room was infused with a dreamy white glow. The material was almost transparent, but hung in so many places it was impossible to see what lay at the centre. Melliflor bowed and retreated, silently urging them to continue. They pushed their way through the gently swaying silk, which felt like the wings of butterflies when it brushed their skin. As each layer was passed they could see shapes more clearly. Veitch's heart began to beat hard in anticipation.

Finally they were through to the middle of the room. The Queen lay on a bed made of luxuriant cushions, so deep they looked as if they would swallow her. Her face was more beautiful than anything Veitch had seen in his life; there was a cruelty there which counterpointed the beauty in such a way it made her even more desirable. Her black hair was long and lustrous, her lips full and red; her eyes sparkled with an inner green light. And she was naked, her golden skin shimmering in the filtered light. Her breasts were large, her nipples tautly erect, her waist slim, her hips shapely, her belly flat; the epitome of what many would consider a male fantasy, truly the Queen of Desire. Veitch wondered if that was how she really looked, or if it was a form she thought could manipulate him; he tried to tell himself that with the Tuatha Dé Danann nothing could be trusted.

But then his eyes were drawn to her sleek, black pubic hair. She lay with her legs curled round so he could see her vagina. She made no attempt to hide herself; indeed, she seemed to be presenting herself to them. Veitch could see how Tom had been so entranced by her.

'It is wonderful to see you again, True Thomas.' Her voice was lazy and filled with strange, enticing notes.

'My Queen.' Tom bowed.

'Come.' She waved them nearer. 'Who is your companion, True Thomas?'

They stood so close Veitch could smell the warm perfume of her skin. She looked at his face intently, her eyes dark beneath half-lids; Veitch felt sucked in by them.

'This is Ryan Veitch, my Queen. He is a Brother of Dragons.'

'Ah, one of the champions of the solid lands.' There was none of the mockery or contempt in her voice that Veitch had heard in so many of the other Tuatha Dé Danann. She sounded honestly interested, even impressed. He attempted an awkward bow, which seemed to please her. 'You did us a great service by freeing us from the Night Walkers' place of exile,' she said directly to Veitch. 'You are in our gratitude. If there is anything you require here in my court, you only have to ask.'

'Thank you.' Veitch was embarrassed his voice sounded so strained.

The Queen suddenly noticed the colourful tattoos only half-covered by the sleeve of his jacket. Her brow furrowed in curiosity. 'What have we here? Is that the Staff of Heart's Desire?' She looked up brightly into Veitch's face. 'Please. Remove your shirt. I must see.'

Veitch glanced at Tom who nodded curtly. Selfconsciously he slipped off his jacket and shirt; on his naked skin, the tattoos gleamed vibrantly. The Queen leaned forward until her face was close to his hard stomach muscles; Veitch could feel her breath. 'The Watchtower,' she mused. 'And here, the sword, Caledfwlch. Amazing. You are a walking picture book.'

She smiled seductively. Then, while her eyes were fixed firmly on his, she reached out gently until her fingers touched his skin just above his belt. A deep, uncontrollable shiver ran through him. Within an instant he had an erection so hard it was painful. The Queen kept her fingertips there a moment longer, then withdrew them just before he came. Veitch took an involuntary step back and sucked in a juddering breath.

Her little game won, the Queen turned from Veitch as though he were no longer there and spoke directly to Tom. 'You were always my favourite, True Thomas.'

He bowed. 'You are gracious, my Queen.'

'Why have you returned to me? I thought it likely I would never see you again. I presume you are not here to seek my affection?'

'We request your aid in a matter of great importance, my Queen.'

'*We*, True Thomas?' Her gaze was incisive.

'*I* request your aid, my Queen. And I will be forever in your debt if you will help *me*.'

'That is indeed a gift worth having, True Thomas.'

Veitch had the impression of an owner curbing her dog. Suddenly he could see the huge edifice of power and malice that lay behind her eyes, but that did not stop him desiring her.

'One of the Sisters of Dragons has been infected with the taint of the Night Walkers,' Tom began. He paused while he formed his argument, knowing that everything depended on it. 'That understates the situation. It is not a taint, it is the ultimate corruption. The essence of the Heart of Shadows grows within her. The Night Walkers seek to bring back the End of Everything.'

'That is indeed a serious development.' Her gaze never wavered from Tom's face; she didn't seem even slightly troubled by the news. She shifted her position, raising her behind slightly so Veitch once again had a perfect view of her sex. 'What is your primary wish?'

Tom collected himself before he said, 'To destroy the End of Everything.'

Veitch started. 'To save Ruth's life,' he corrected sharply.

The Queen's smile grew as she looked from one to the other. 'A disagreement?'

'No disagreement.' Tom fixed a cold eye on Veitch.

'There is no need to argue.' Her voice was like honey. 'There is a possibility I may be able to help you achieve both your aims.'

Tom bowed again. 'Anything you can do to help us would be gratefully received, my Queen.' She glanced at Veitch and he realised he was supposed to prostrate himself too. He bowed awkwardly once more and muttered something that approximated Tom's statement.

It appeared to please her; she nodded and smiled. 'There are many secrets here in the Court of the Yearning Heart, some which are hidden even from my brethren; even from the Court of the Final Word. Here, all things are given up eventually.' She sucked on her index finger as she thought deeply for a moment. 'The Eddy-Ball,' she said with a certain nod. 'A gift of great value to me.' A smile; the game had begun. 'The orb opens out into the void between worlds. It has the ability to suck the essence from the solid.'

'And this could be done without harming the Sister of Dragons?'

'Of course. And the Heart of Shadows will find itself in a place where no shadows are cast.' This amused her.

Veitch could barely contain his relief. Although Tom maintained his plain expression, Veitch could see the signs in the Rhymer's face too.

'Thank you, my Queen,' Tom said.

'And you will do something for me. True Thomas?'

His face grew taut. 'Of course, my Queen.' Tom waited for her to demand he stay behind.

She pretended to think, toying with him. 'No, True Thomas, not you. This Brother of Dragons.' She glanced seductively at Veitch. 'I will give the Eddy-Ball to him and him alone, and in return he will carry out a simple request for me.'

'Anything,' Veitch replied before Tom could stop him.

There was a triumphant note in her smile that made Veitch uneasy. 'The Questing Beast has again escaped from the pits beneath us. It is loose in the solid world. It is my heart's desire that this Brother of Dragons seek it out and destroy it, or at least lead it back here to the Court of the Yearning Heart.'

Veitch could hear her words, but all he could see was Tom's face, which had grown eerily bloodless. 'The Questing Beast—' he began.

The Queen silenced him with an upraised hand, her eyes watching Veitch's face intently. 'Will you do this for me?'

Whatever doubts Tom felt, Veitch knew he didn't have an option. 'All right.'

'Then I will make the arrangements. Go with Melliflor and he will provide you with all you require.'

They moved slowly away until the gently stirring sheets of silk had swallowed up the Queen once more. As they walked, Veitch brushed against Tom and felt the trembling that was running through the Rhymer's body.

They were provided with two connecting chambers far from the noise of the Great Hall where they could rest and prepare themselves. They were both ravenously hungry, made worse by the plates of food left for them on tables in the corners of the room. Tom plucked from his ever-present haversack two bags of roasted peanuts he had been saving as a last resort, and they munched on them hungrily.

Veitch was filled with questions, but at first Tom wouldn't speak to him; it was almost as if he couldn't bring himself to do it. He retreated to his chamber for an hour where he smoked a joint quietly on the deep, comforting bed.

Veitch couldn't begin to rest. His mind turned over all that he had experienced, but kept returning to the image of the naked Queen; it was beginning to torment him. And when he forced himself not to think about her, his eyes drifted to the food.

When Tom finally walked in, he sat bolt upright with relief and said, 'Come on. Spill the fucking beans. What am I up against?'

Tom pulled up a chair and sat on it backwards, folding his arms on top of the backrest. 'You and your big mouth, agreeing to anything she said.'

'We didn't have any choice.'

'Of course we had a choice. They play games, barter, throw things back and forth. You don't take the first thing offered. You were too hypnotised by the sight of her cunt.'

'And you weren't? You were almost down on your knees with your tongue hanging out!'

Tom cursed under his breath and put a hand on his eyes. 'There's no point arguing about it. It's done. We have to find a way to make sure you survive.'

Veitch kicked the other chair so hard it flew across the room. 'Come on, then. Talk. What's this thing I've got to hunt?'

'The Questing Beast. It's a living nightmare, something that even the Tuatha Dé Danann are wary of facing head-on. Their own legends say it was there in Otherworld long before they arrived, one of the first creatures to exist after the universe was formed. They call it a Rough Creature. A prototype for what was to come, if you will. Not fully formed.'

Veitch sat carefully on the edge of the bed. 'If it's in *their* legends—'

'Exactly.'

'So they're sending me out there because they don't want to have a go themselves. That's par for the course, isn't it? Those Bastards don't like getting their hands dirty. So if they're so wary of it, what was it doing here? And how the fuck am I going to kill it?'

'The Queen keeps many dangerous things here at the Court. It's a mark of prestige. How are you going to kill it?' He shrugged wearily. 'I don't know enough about it. Neither do the Tuatha Dé Danann. But their distaste for it isn't because of its power, it's because of its imperfect form, which they find abhorrent in the same way they react to the Fomorii. Us, they can just about tolerate. Anything less is to be despised.'

'So how dangerous is it?'

'Very. Make no mistake about that. It escaped into our world several centuries ago, before my time, and many people died before it was driven back to Otherworld. The general belief of the time was that a mortal girl gave birth to it after having sex with the Devil. The legends that grew up around it described it as having the head of a snake, the body of a big cat and the hindquarters of a lion, which is just another way of saying the people of the time couldn't describe it. It was said to give off a sound like forty hounds baying, or questing, in its stomach, and that's how it got its name.'

'So we don't know what it looks like, just that it's very fucking bad.' Veitch jumped to his feet and started pacing round the room; his eyes repeatedly strayed to the appetising food. 'Well, it was driven off, so it can be done. It sounds like a big deal, but I'll be hunting it, not the other way round. Anyway, it's got to be, for Ruth, for Church and everything. Can't fuck up now.'

Tom realised he was talking to himself, planning, bolstering; it was like the ritual of a boxer preparing for a fight.

After another moment's pacing, he turned to Tom and said, 'Okay, I've got my head round it. I'm going to get some Zs in now. We'll do it when I wake.'

As he left the room, Tom hid the fact that he was secretly impressed; once a conflict situation had been established Veitch's developing abilities made him like a machine. Fear or overconfidence didn't burden him; he simply weighed up all the available evidence and decided what needed to be done. Tom hoped that would be enough.

In the court it was impossible to know if it was night or day. But when Veitch woke his body told him he had had a good rest; the exhaustion had seeped from his muscles and he felt ready for anything. He was still hungry, but he knew he could find something to eat back in the real world.

Tom joined him soon after, as if he had been waiting for the sounds of stirring. Together they stepped out into the corridor where Melliflor was waiting.

Veitch had hoped the Queen would have come to see him off, but she was nowhere around. Instead, Melliflor led them to the armoury, a long, low-ceilinged chamber where the walls were covered with a variety of bizarre weapons and strangely shaped body armour. Veitch picked up one of the weapons which looked like an axe with a spiked ball hanging from it, but in his hands it felt a different shape completely to how it appeared and he replaced it quickly.

While Melliflor oversaw, three other members of the guard brought Veitch different pieces of armour. They strapped across his chest a breastplate which shone like silver, but which was covered with an intricate filigree. Shoulder plates were fastened on, and he was given a helmet which vaguely resembled a Roman centurion's, but was much more ornate. After mulling over the weapons for fifteen minutes he eschewed them all for his own sword and crossbow.

He had no idea of what the armour was constructed, but it was surprisingly lightweight; he could have walked for miles in it. He didn't have to, though, for as soon as he was ready Melliflor took him through to an adjoining stable which contained enough horses for a small army.

'Stolen from our world,' Tom muttered. 'It allows the lesser members of the Tuatha Dé Danann to travel quickly when they cross over.'

'This is no bleedin' good, I've never ridden before,' Veitch moaned.

'The steed will respond to your every movement. We have adapted it,' Melliflor said ominously.

Melliflor offered Veitch a handsome white charger, but he didn't feel comfortable with it. 'Too flash,' he grumbled. Instead he chose a nut-brown stallion indistinguishable from many of the others.

Once he had mounted the steed, Melliflor led it by its reins to a blank stone wall at one end of the stable. He made a strange hand gesture and the wall opened with a deep, rumbling judder. They were high up on a hillside with a vista over Loch Ness. Mist drifted across the water in the post-dawn light. From all around came the sweet aroma of pine trees. Everywhere was still and quiet.

Veitch turned to view the scene in the stables, but he couldn't think of anything to say to Tom. Instead, he merely waved; Tom nodded curtly in reply, but there was much hidden in the two gestures. Then Veitch spurred his horse and galloped off into the world.

The darkness licked at the foot of Mam Tor, an angry sea crashing on the rocks. From his vantage point beneath a burning sun and a brilliant blue sky, Church watched as hopelessness washed over him.

'They'll be coming up soon.' Laura's voice made him start.

'Best not to think about that.'

'Sure. Do you want me to help bury your head or can you do it yourself?'

Church managed a tight smile; he didn't have much humour left in him. With Ruth's condition worsening by the day, the strain of their isolation and the constant fear that their hiding place would be discovered at any moment, it was surprising he hadn't lapsed into permanent silence.

'No sign of the others yet?' Laura rested on his shoulder and peered out to the horizon. It was a running joke; she asked the same thing every day, knowing the answer.

'Not yet. Maybe tomorrow.' He tried, but he couldn't help believing that they wouldn't be coming back at all. He knew they had long distances to travel, with huge obstacles along the way, but they still seemed to have been gone a long time. Even if they did return, how would they be able to slip past the mass of Fomorii? He had been right the first time: best not to think about it.

'She's asking for you.' Laura continued to scan the horizon, as if by doing it everything in the foreground could be forgotten.

'How is she?'

'Not talking like she's pissed up for a change.' Ruth's lucid moments were increasingly few and far between; at times she ranted and raged in the throes of her delirium so much they thought they would have to restrain her. It always happened at night, in the small hours, snapping them out of sleep and filling them with fear that they were being attacked. Sometimes she would hold conversations with someone neither of them could see; on those occasions they didn't go to sleep again.

Church turned despondently to wander back to the house, but he hadn't gone more than a few steps when Laura grabbed him and gave him a long, romantic kiss. It was an astonishing show of emotion for someone who seemed ever more locked up with each passing day.

'What was that for?' he asked, pleasantly surprised.

'What's the matter? Can't I show you I love you?' She had turned and was walking away before he had a chance to grasp what she had said.

He mulled over it until he was in the house, but the moment he saw Ruth it was driven from his mind. Her skin was like snow, emphasised by the darkness of her hair, which was plastered with sweat to her head. There were purple rings under her eyes and her cheeks had grown increasingly hollow. Beneath the sleeping bag, her belly was hugely swollen. Her appearance was so shocking he had a horrible feeling she was going to die before Balor's rebirth. A part of himself that he never faced hoped that was the case; then he would be saved from having to make the awful decision to kill her.

Although he was creeping quietly, she looked up before he had crossed the threshold. 'Hi. You're starting to get a tan.' Her voice was just a rustle.

'You know how it is. Nothing to do apart from lie by the pool with a good book.' He knelt down next to her to brush a strand of hair from her forehead. When he rested his hand against her cheek, her skin felt like it was burning up.

She put her hand on top of his and gave it a squeeze. 'I'm glad you're here.'

'Sure. I'm doing so much—'

'I just feel better having you around.' He smiled; her eyes brightened briefly before she was forced to close them; a tear squeezed out and trickled down her cheek.

'I'm sorry you've had to go through all this,' he said gently. 'You've had the worst of all of us. One bad thing after another.'

'You know, bad things happen.' She pulled his hand round so she could softly kiss his fingers; her lips were too dry.

'You don't have any right to take it so well. You're giving us all too much to live up to. You git.'

They laughed together, and the sound of it in that dismal room made Church's own eyes burn. He blinked them dry. 'Sometimes I feel like I've known you for ever. I know it's only been a few months since that night under Albert Bridge, but it seems like a lifetime ago.'

'Maybe we have known each other for ever. Maybe it's that old Pendragon Spirit speaking. Telling you we've stood side by side across the centuries.'

'You're an old romantic.'

She tried to laugh again, but it broke up into a hacking cough. When the attack had subsided, her mood had grown forlorn. 'I just wish it wasn't happening here. This house feels bad, sour. I don't know what happened here, but sometimes I can hear voices whispering to me. The things they say . . . that Ryan's going to die . . . that other terrible things are going to happen—'

'Hush.'

'That writing on the wall . . . Sometimes words seem to leap out at me—'

He put two fingers on her lips to silence her. Gradually the delirium returned to her eyes as they started to roll upwards. After a moment or two she began to rave, occasionally speaking in tongues, thrashing from side to side. Church sat patiently beside her during the worst of it, then stroked her head until she eventually drifted off to sleep.

Sometimes Church thought he had never seen a night sky like the one above Mam Tor. Unencumbered by light pollution, benefiting in some indescribable way from the sheer height above sea level, they seemed to be enveloped by the sparkling heavens. If not for their circumstances, it would have been a sublime experience.

He stood with Laura in his arms, looking up at the celestial vault; for once she had removed her sunglasses. 'We've come a long way, despite everything. Pity if it had to end here.'

'No fat lady singing yet, boy.'

'No, not yet.' He watched a meteor burn up over their heads, wondering if it were some kind of sign. 'Sometimes it's hard to take a step back and appreciate exactly what we're doing here. You know, I look at myself, look at you and the others, and all I see is normal people with all the stupid kinds of problems everybody has. And that's who we are, but at the same time we're something else as well – the champions of a race, a planet. The living embodiment of the Pendragon Spirit, whatever that might be—'

'Maybe we're not special.'

'What do you mean?'

'Maybe this thing the old git calls the Pendragon Spirit is in everybody. Maybe it's the spirit of man, or some shit. Listen to me, I sound like some wet-brained New Age idiot. What I'm trying to say is, what if he's just calling us special to keep us on board. So we think sorting out this whole mess is just down to us.'

'Or so we dig deep to find the best in us to get the job done.'

'That too.' She rested her forehead on his shoulder. 'That would explain why we all seem like such a bunch of losers. We *are* a bunch of losers.'

'Doing the best we can. And doing a damn good job—'

'So far. But if we've not got any special dispensation, the chances of us fucking up are even greater. We've got through on a wing and a prayer and too much confidence. But sooner or later the blind, stupid luck is going to run out.'

Church thought about this while he continued to watch the stars. Then: 'I might have agreed with you a few weeks back, when we first met each other. But in all the shit we've waded through, everybody has shown a real goodness at the heart of them. There isn't anybody else I'd want around me at this time and there isn't anybody else I think could do a better job—'

'You don't know the thoughts in my head—'

'I can guess at them.'

'No, you can't. There are sick, twisted things crawling around up there. Take Little Miss Goody-Shoes back there. Sometimes I wish she'd hurry up and die so she wouldn't carry on getting between me and you. I know it's a nasty, evil little part of me and I hate myself for it. But I still do it.'

'She doesn't get between us.'

'You're too stupid to see it. She loves you and I think you love her, and if there wasn't a constant state of crisis you'd recognise that.'

Her words sparked rampant, brilliant bursts in his mind, but they were all too fleeting to get a handle on. He pulled back slightly so he could try to read her; she half-turned her head away. 'You're a good person, Laura.'

'You're a good liar.'

'You've got an answer for everything.'

'If I had, I wouldn't be feeling like my brains were leaking out of my ears. Too much thinking isn't good for anyone.'

'Look—'

She slammed her hand on his mouth. 'Don't say anything. It'll sort itself out one way or the other.' He didn't like the look that crossed her face when she said that.

He hated to think anything unpleasant of her, so instead he kissed her. At first she seemed to be resisting him, but then she gave in, and for the briefest instant everything seemed in perfect harmony.

But then an unseasonally cold wind came whipping across the tor and buffeted them. Church broke off the kiss, shivering. Away in the west, billowing clouds were sweeping towards them at an unnatural rate. Lightning flashed within them, illuminating the underside of the roiling mass; one bolt burst out in a jagged streak to the ground. But they were not storm clouds, and there was no thunder.

The wind grew stronger as the clouds neared until it was lashing their hair, then threatening to throw them to the ground.

'What's going on?' Laura said. 'Is this it?'

The clouds came down until they were rolling across the ground, and at that point Church realised there was a figure among them. At first it was just a silhouette almost lost beneath the shrouding mist, but then it came closer to the fore and Church realised who it was, and what was happening.

'Get back to the house.' The snap in his voice stifled any questions instantly. Laura took one more glance at the clouds, then ran for the cottage. Halfway across the turf she realised Church wasn't behind her, but when she looked back he waved frantically for her to continue.

Then the wind did knock him to his knees and as he tried to scramble to his feet again, it hit him with all the force of a rampaging bull. He rolled over and it kept him rolling, driving him towards the jagged cliff edge and the precipitous drop to the rocks far below. Desperately he tried to dig his fingers in the grass, but they were torn out immediately; his bones cracked on stones, his face was dragged across the rough ground until it burned and bled.

The cliff rushed towards him. He had a fleeting vision of his broken, bloody body smashed at the foot of the tor and then the wind eased off just as he was half-hanging over the edge. He sucked in a deep breath, shaking with shock, tried to scramble back using his heels for purchase, but another gust came and pinned him on the cusp between life and death.

He had to calm himself, order his thoughts; it was his only chance. The gulf beneath him tugged at his hair, made his head spin.

Niamh hovered in front of him a foot above the ground, wrapped in the clouds of her discontent. He barely recognised her. The beautiful face was lost; instead, it rippled and twisted, unable to settle in a vision his mind could comprehend; her fury and dismay had reduced her to her primal form.

'*Betrayal!*' The word seemed to come from all around them, not spoken by any human voice, filled with strange vibrations that reverberated in the pit of his stomach.

'I didn't—'

'*You gave me your word! You promised me your love solely! You lied! Untrustworthy, like all Frail Creatures!*' A gust pushed him another inch over the drop. His fingers ached from clinging on to the rock lip.

'I'm sorry!' He had to raise his voice to be heard above the wind that was rushing all around the tor.

'*No more lies!*' Her voice exploded with the fury of a breaking storm, but at the centre of it Church could hear her heartache.

'I'm sorry!' he shouted again. This time she seemed to hear him, for there was a faint lull. He seized the opportunity. 'I was stupid . . . confused—'

The wind hit him hard; he moved another inch. One more and he wouldn't be able to stop himself falling. His fingers felt like they were breaking from clutching on; the panic in his throat made it difficult to catch his breath.

'*Lies.*' Her voice sounded less frenzied, more openly emotional, more humanity creeping into it. Church forced his head up so he could see. Her face had settled back into the features he knew, but they were broken with hurt. At that moment his heart went out to her and he was consumed with guilt at how he had disregarded her feelings. 'We Golden Ones live our lives in the extremes of passion. We feel too strongly. You cannot even begin to understand the slightest working of our hearts and minds!'

The clouds continued to churn behind her, occasionally lifting her a few more inches higher before she settled down at the same level. Church wanted to say something to calm her, but he didn't have any grounds to defend himself and he was afraid he would only make it worse.

She floated closer to him, almost to the lip of the edge, so he could see her face without straining. Her pain had now turned to a cold, hard anger; he feared for his life once again. 'My people always said nothing good could ever come of an affair with a Fragile Creature, and it appears they were correct. I have watched you too long from afar, Jack Churchill, and I have allowed my judgement to be swayed by what I saw.'

The gale began to press on his chest; he could feel himself sliding. In that moment, thoughts went rushing through Church's head and he was surprised to realise he was less scared for himself than angry that he had once again allowed his emotions to ruin everything; if he died, every hope would die with him.

Before he could say anything the wind retracted and Niamh began to drift away, her face still cold and hard. 'Our agreement is broken.' Church followed her pointing finger towards the dark horizon; there, golden light flashed ominously. 'The Good Son will soon be paying you a visit.'

And with that, the clouds folded around her so she was completely lost to him, and the whole mass moved quickly back over the landscape until it disappeared beyond the summit of the tor.

Church scrambled back. When he was lying on solid ground, he gulped in mouthfuls of air and felt his pumping heart slowly return to normal. As he dragged himself to his feet, Laura ran from the house.

'You really know how to fuck women up, don't you?' she said breathlessly.

He could barely hear her. His attention was drawn to the occasional bursts of light in the distance and the engulfing darkness closer to home.

'I've done it again,' he said quietly.

'What?'

'Screwed everything up.' He couldn't even bring himself to tell her that a near-hopeless situation had suddenly become much worse. With his head bowed, he turned and trudged back to the house.

Veitch spent the first two days roaming through the heavily wooded slopes which enclosed the loch. It was a place like none he had experienced before, enveloped in its own strange, eerie atmosphere; purple hillsides cloaked in mist just beyond the tree boundary, outcroppings of orange, brown and black rocks, ancient trees, gnarled and twisted and scarred with green lichen that showed their great age, and over all the constant, soothing sound of the waves lapping against the pink shale and pebbles at the water's edge. The way the pines clustered so deeply to the shore on the south bank made him feel penned in, and there was an unshakeable sense that he was being watched from somewhere in their depths. But there was also a deep serenity, almost mystical in its intensity, with the birdsong hanging melodically in the air. At times the water was as still as glass, reflecting the verdant landscape and clear blue skies so perfectly he felt he could dive in and walk among the cool glades. At other times storms sprang from nowhere, sweeping up odd, eddying waves that crashed against the steep banks. Fog came and went among the trees, like ghosts, and at night, beneath a shimmering moon and diamond stars the valley was filled with the pregnant hush that came before a conversation.

He saw no traffic at all along the sinuous road that ran along the banks of the loch, and he didn't know if that was down to the Questing Beast or if everyone had simply fled to the cities. In Drumnadrochit, the quiet village that lay where Glen Urquhart intersected the Great Glen, the houses were still and locked, although a wisp of smoke rose from the occasional chimney. At the loch's southern tip, Fort Augustus was near-empty too, and the occasional resident who saw him coming quickly ran for cover.

He made camp on both nights in a tree-lined gorge not far from Fort Augustus. Without even the slightest sign of the Questing Beast, he had started to wonder if it was another of the Queen's incomprehensible machinations, perhaps to separate him from Tom.

On the third day, he realised his hunt was true. In the early morning, he travelled alongside the tumbling river at the bottom of Glen Urquhart. The valley was blanketed beneath the drifting white mist that seemed to come and go with a mind of its own, muffling and distorting the splashing of the water and the clipped echoes of the horse's hooves. In a lonely spot surrounded by acres of sheep-clipped grass he came across an old stone cairn. There was a fading majesty to it, and even he, who was usually insensitive to the blue fire, felt a hint of its power there. But among the standing stones beyond the cairn he came across the remains of a man, half-strung over a barbed-wire fence. From his clothes, he looked like a farmer or an agricultural labourer. He was partially disembowelled as if he had been gored by a bull or a boar, but he had been out there long enough for the carrion birds to have been at his eyes and genitals, so it was impossible to tell if the Beast had consumed any of him as well. Veitch inspected the corpse and the surrounding area for anything that might help him, but there was no spoor or other discernible sign. The only thing that troubled him was that the poor man's blood had splattered randomly on the ground in a shape that resembled a screaming face. After spending time with Shavi he had grown reasonably adept at reading meaning in things that appeared to have none, and that image began to eat away at his subconscious. As he moved away his mind's eye had already begun to paint a picture of the true appearance of the Questing Beast.

That night he made camp among the trees high up on the hillside where he had a clear view of the loch and the bleak southern slopes. The setting sun painted the water red and purple; it was once again so still the water gave the illusion of glass. The air was sweet with the aroma of pine and wild flowers, and an abiding peace lay over the landscape. Yet it was hard for him to rest knowing that the thing could come at him from any direction at any time; he had even started to think of it as invisible or as something that flew on silent wings. All he wanted was something solid to latch on to, something he could stab or shoot or hack at, and then he would be fine.

As he had done the other nights, he dined on chocolate, biscuits and crisps he'd taken from a mysteriously deserted garage in Fort Augustus; the sugar and the processed taste sickened him, but he would have felt ridiculous striding into a supermarket for something more sustaining in the armour bequeathed him by the Tuatha Dé Danann. He was almost too distracted to think of food. Whenever he rested, Ruth loomed heavy in his thoughts, her face, darkened by fear after her discovery of what she carried with her, a frequent, troubling image he never seemed able to shake. Spurred by Church's right-thinking motivations, he had set out to help in the fight, but he knew his own motivation had been a quest for redemption for his past crimes. The chance to become a better person still weighed on him, but now, more than anything, he was doing it for *her*; to find some solution to heal her in the short term, to save her in the long term, whatever the cost to himself. Being driven by love was a strange experience for him and he was surprised how much he liked it.

As darkness fell, he stoked up the campfire for warmth during the cold night ahead, before taking time to groom the horse of which he had grown increasingly fond. When he had asked Melliflor for its name, the reply had been something indecipherable, so he had secretly decided to call it Thunder after the horse of some cowboy hero in an American comic he had read as a child. He would never tell the others something like that, but it gave him a deep, personal comfort. He got pleasure from treating it with affection, although he privately wished it were a little more responsive. It seemed unduly wary of him, almost as if it were scared, which he guessed must have come from whatever treatment had been meted out in the strange stables of the Court of the Yearning Heart. *I can't even get a horse to like me*, he thought as he stroked its flank; the notion was so ridiculous it made him laugh out loud.

It was Thunder who alerted him to danger as he settled down to sleep next to the fire under the fragrant canopy of a pine. It whinnied and stamped its hooves long before Veitch heard any sign, and he was up on his feet with the sword in his hands as the howl of fear came from somewhere near the road on his side of the loch. The cry was suddenly infused with pain, before being snapped off.

Veitch jumped on to Thunder and spurred him through the trees on the steep slopes down to the road. The horse was uneasy, but it responded to his heels and it didn't take him long to find the mangled remains of a motorbike. There was a pool of blood on the tarmac, but no sign of any body. He dismounted and examined the road surface. It was difficult to tell in the dark, but the splatters of blood appeared to point in the direction of the inlet overlooked by the ruins of Castle Urquhart. Briefly, he stopped and listened, but the night was as quiet as ever. He wondered how swiftly the Beast could move; perhaps it was already miles away. Cautiously he climbed back on Thunder and headed in the direction indicated by the blood.

The clatter of the hooves echoed loudly in the quiet. It still surprised him to be riding down the middle of a road without seeing any sign of headlights in the deep night that hung over the water.

Ten minutes later he passed the still ruins of Urquhart Castle. There was no anxiety within him, just a quiet, intense concentration that took over his mind and permeated his being. His instinct told him his quarry was somewhere in the vicinity; there was a constant resonance vibrating inside him that he had come to trust: a warning to be as alert as he could be.

Around the bend in the road that led to Drumnadrochit he came across a few shreds of bloodied clothing. He jumped down to investigate without once lessening the sharp focus of his attention. He could hear nothing, smell nothing. The Beast left no sign in its passing, but Thunder seemed to sense something; its eyes rolled and it stamped its hooves again.

From the shape of the clump of clothing he could at least discern the direction in which the Beast had been travelling when the remnants were dropped. It was moving towards the area where the road was darkest and the trees clustered claustrophobically close. Back on Thunder, he gently urged it on; slowly, slowly, eyes constantly searching the surroundings. He rounded the small bay; ahead, the road moved off towards Inverness.

From the corner of his eye he caught a sudden movement in the trees away to his left. It was a darkness deeper than the surrounding shadows, moving so quickly it disturbed him.

He spurred Thunder into the trees, his crossbow held over the crook of his arm, his finger poised on the trigger. At that point there was little opportunity to manoeuvre among the trees. The movement of the branches in the faint breeze made odd shifts in the ambient light that at times made him feel something was creeping up on him. His heart pounding, he kept glancing all around to reassure himself.

Another movement, again away to his left. Was it trying to circle him, come up from behind? He suddenly realised it was a mistake to be in such a constricted space and he quickly sent Thunder back on to the road. From somewhere came the sound which Tom had described as forty hounds baying. That didn't even begin to capture the bone-chilling noise which now drifted out across the deserted countryside: high-pitched and filled with an abiding hunger, it didn't sound like anything earthly at all.

Something shifted back up the road. This time he was ready. In an instant his mind weighed up all the evidence, projected the path of the Beast; he aimed the crossbow, loosed the bolt. It shot into the shadows, bringing what could have been a squeal of pain. His teeth went on edge.

He spurred Thunder on while managing to use the crank to draw the crossbow for another shot.

There was no sign of the Beast at the point where he had hit it, but he hadn't expected to bring it down with just one bolt. But there were dark splatters on the tarmac which smelled like charred batteries. So it could bleed, he thought. It could be hurt. That was all he needed to know.

It was heading back towards the castle ruins which rose up like bleached bones in the cold moonlight. Once it got on to the rugged, irregular promontory jutting into the icy waters, he would have it cornered. Could he take it out with just a crossbow and a sword? His blood thundered with the thrill of the hunt. He thought he probably could.

The car park for the castle was lit for tourists who would probably never come again. Across the shadowed edge of it the deeper darkness moved. Veitch got another impression of something big and dangerous. He loosed another bolt. It rattled across the car park, slammed into the fleeing rear of the creature. Another squeal of pain. It was proving easier than he thought.

His horse trotted down the steep path from the car park that eventually ran across an open stretch of grassland up to the castle's defensive ditch. At the drawbridge he dismounted and left Thunder next to a light. He had more freedom to move and react quickly on foot.

The castle was ruined, but still robust enough to glimpse the majesty of the fortress that had looked out over the loch, in one form or another, since the Pictish kings ruled the land in the Dark Ages. The grey stone of the impenetrable walls stretched out on either side, while the still-standing tower loomed like a sentinel away to his left.

There was more ichor splashed across the path that ran under the gatehouse; it looked like the Beast had been seriously injured. Veitch reclaimed the two bolts that had been knocked loose and prepared for another shot.

He could hear movement within the castle compound. He entered through the gatehouse slowly, aware that the enclosed space, with its dips and hillocks and many ruined buildings, could be a dangerous maze. Cautiously he scanned the area. There were too many places in which the Beast could hide.

Another sound sent him sprinting up the steps across the grass to the Upper Bailey. From this vantage point he had a view across the castle and the loch beyond. Nothing moved. Sooner or later it would give itself away, especially if it was badly injured, he told himself; but it was possible, if he was clever enough, to herd it to the area around the tower where it would have no escape.

He spent a few minutes convincing himself it was nowhere in the Upper Bailey and then he advanced slowly towards the hulking ruins of the chapel, Great Hall and kitchens. A brief wind swept up from the black water, singing in his ears.

But as he crossed into the Nether Bailey a figure erupted out of the periphery of his vision. He had only the briefest instant to register what was happening and then he was flying through the air. The landing stunned him for a second, but his sense of self-preservation took over and he shook himself awake. He lay on the grass in the shadow of the North Lodge; nothing moved near him. There was a chill wetness across his chest. When he looked down he saw his jacket and shirt lay in ribbons and there were three deep gashes cut into his flesh. The blood was pumping out through his ruptured armour. Desperately he tried to staunch it with a torn-off piece of his shirt, but as he tended to himself there was another blur of movement. His head snapped round so sharply he thought his neck had broken. Stars flashed across his vision; then the pain came, thundering out in a wave across his temples. By the time he had caught himself, his eyes were filling with liquid. He wiped them clear with the back of his hand, glanced down, saw the dark smear, dripping on his trousers.

The blow had dazed him; everything seemed to be moving too slowly, fractured, as if a strobe had been activated. The terrible hunting cry rose up all around him, different this time, triumphant.

No, he thought. *I had it.*

A shimmer of activity, so quick he barely saw it. Somehow he managed to fire off a bolt. The Questing Beast avoided it with ease.

As it could have done before, he realised. How stupid was he? He searched for a path back to Thunder, the images coming in broken, stinging form; he had to get away, recover. But the blur of movement was going around too fast, circling, forcing him back. It had cut off all escape routes. He was trapped, his back coming up against a stone wall. Then he stumbled through the gap of the Water Gate and rolled over and over down a steep bank, coming up hard against more stone blocks beyond which was a small, pebbled beach and the dark, lapping water.

As his thoughts started to come free from his daze, he realised: the Questing Beast had shown a ferocious intelligence and cunning, recognising the danger from him, probably over the days he thought he had been stalking it. He had been treating it like a stupid beast; it had been waiting for the opportunity to neutralise him.

It lashed forward from the dark and retreated in the blink of an eye. A gout of blood erupted from his forearm.

The pain was lost in the wild reel of his thoughts. He tumbled over the stone blocks on to the beach; now there was only water at his back.

The Questing Beast knew he was wounded; fatally, he realised, the same time the word entered his head. He could feel his clothes heavy with blood. How much longer did he have? The fragility of his thoughts gave him an answer. He'd failed: himself, Ruth, all the others. His stupidity had come through as it always did.

The Beast no longer seemed to be hiding from him. Through the haze he could pick it out more clearly than he had before. Its shape was not fixed and did not settle down like the Tuatha Dé Danann did once his mind had formed an analog; it was as if it preceded form, shouting across the aeons from a time when there was only intelligence and emotion. He glimpsed writhing, serpentine coils, something hard and bony, something that moved like gelatin and lashed with the spike of a scorpion's tail; felt, in one terrible moment, the cold, hard fury of its mind, as if it could reach out physically and strike him. This was bigger than him, better than him.

And then he realised, with some primal instinct, that it was gearing up for the final blow. He had little sense left through the pain; most of it was leaking out with his life's blood. But he asked himself this question: how cunning was he?

How cunning?

Blackness formed a tunnel around the periphery of his vision. He dropped the crossbow, went down to his knees, blood pooling in his eyes; he only had his instinct to go on. He bowed his head, prepared himself for the final blow.

The Questing Beast came forward in a wave of night; it was as if the wind had teeth and was roaring at him.

Veitch threw himself down on his stomach. At the same time he somehow managed to pull the sword free and raised it above his head. He held it firm when he felt it bite deep, and even when the sheer force of the Questing Beast's attack threatened to knock it from his grasp, he dug in and angled. The stink of charred batteries filled the air. The liquid swamped him in one awful deluge. The Questing Beast's momentum carried it over his head, screaming so loudly his eardrums burst.

And then he was in a syrupy world of silence, didn't hear the splash as the creature plummeted into the water. He turned on his back, saw stars and the moon; knew, in a damp, sad way, it would be the last time he would see them. He'd lost feeling in every part of his body. There were just his thoughts now, bursting like fireworks, slowly winding down.

The play of light on the lapping water was hypnotic. It was a good sight to see as the last sight. But it wasn't the end, it wasn't the end. The Beast wasn't dead; not yet. The black shape was moving through the water like a stalking shark. Thoughts triggered, stumbled into each other and then ran away obliquely; and he wondered how many times in the past it had broken through before Otherworld sucked it back, slinking through the waves, creating ripples of mythology on flickering black and white frames.

And as he thought this, it suddenly spurred into life, sending a V-shaped ripple breaking out on either side as it hurtled towards him. He had only a second to force himself up on his elbows before it erupted out of the water in front of him. He had a brief impression of a blackness as deep as space, of sharp, clacking teeth, and things that could have been tendrils or tentacles or arms, and then he closed his eyes and waited for pain that never came.

Somehow his lids flickered open again, and this time he wondered if he was already dead, for the scene around him had changed dramatically. There was a flurry of activity. Melliflor was there with the rest of the Queen's guard, oddly twisted spears catching the moonlight, and nets that billowed like the sails of a ship. And there was Tom looming over him, looking like Veitch had never seen him before; not stern nor angry, but caring and frightened, and in that instant he knew he was dead; or dreaming; or both.

The tunnel around his vision closed in tightly. And as everything faded into oblivion, his mind flashed back to that brief contact with the alien mind of the Questing Beast. It was a moment of sublime mystery, but there were some human reference points he could grasp: loneliness, a terrible yearning for another of its kind, long, long gone, lost in those early days when the world was new. That was why it was questing. Pain and hurt as brittle as glass; not a beast at all.

How awful, he thought. To be hunting it in that way. For it to be imprisoned by the Tuatha Dé Danann in the stinking bowels of their court. How awful and stupid and meaningless.

'You'll be okay now.'

The voice: in his head, or somewhere outside? Then, like treacle flowing into his mind, the realisation that he was *hearing*; how could that be? When Veitch's eyes finally responded he saw through a haze the stables in the Court of the Yearning Heart. His blood stained the dirty straw. Thunder stood nearby, stamping its hooves.

With the return of consciousness, agony exploded throughout his body. He was slumped against the wall in the mangled remnants of his armour, now coloured browny-purple with his dried blood. The deep gash across his chest was still ragged, but it didn't look quite as deep; even so, Veitch couldn't understand how he was still alive. From the way he had started to shiver, his death still seemed a definite possibility. But he could hear again, although he knew his drums had burst at the lochside.

Tom hove into view, dropping down on to his haunches; it was his familiar Scottish brogue Veitch had heard earlier. 'What happened?' Veitch's voice a feeble croak.

'The Queen saw—'

'I saw your tremendous victory.' Tom stood up and walked over to the other side of the stables as the Queen knelt down next to Veitch. She was wearing flowing, diaphanous white robes that were startlingly out of place in the bloody grime of the stables. 'You proved yourself a great champion. My champion.' There was great pride in her voice. 'I had you brought here, for in my court nothing truly dies if I so wish it. Here your wounds will have time to heal. You will be well again, Ryan Veitch.' Melliflor laid a crystal bowl of water next to her. She took a white cloth from him, dipped it in the water and began to dab gently at his forehead, slowly wiping away the splatters of his blood.

'I can't believe it,' he muttered deliriously. 'A Queen . . . tending to me . . .'

'Even Queens must recognise great bravery. Your name will be exalted, even among the Tuatha Dé Danann. And that bravery was carried out in my name, a fitting tribute to the Queen of the Yearning Heart. The Questing Beast is back in its chamber—'

'It survived?'

'It exists, as always.'

Veitch had the sudden feeling the Beast had been released merely for him to hunt it down, a perverse sport for the Tuatha Dé Danann so they could see what depths existed within him; and on that front he had even surprised himself. 'Will you help Ruth?'

The Queen continued to dab at his forehead. Some of the water ran into his eyes and she wiped it away softly. A drop trickled down the bridge of his nose. 'I will be as good as my word, Ryan Veitch.' A smile he couldn't quite read.

Veitch could feel himself starting to black out again. The Queen's ministrations were so soothing, her touch so gentle; the coolness of her fingers seemed to ease his pain wherever they touched.

She wiped down his cheeks, brushed the drips from his chin. He had lost so much liquid his body felt like sand inside.

She dabbed at his brow, smiled enigmatically. Then she held the cloth before his face and squeezed tightly. A single droplet eked out of the bottom, hung for a second, then dropped. He stuck out the tip of his tongue.

'No!' Tom's voice, filled with the most indescribable anguish.

From the corner of his eye, he saw the Rhymer rushing forward. Melliflor and another guard restraining him harshly. The droplet hitting his tongue, so cool and refreshing, belying its size. Slowly seeing the Queen's expression change, from gentle care to something much darker, like a shadow falling across the face of the moon. Still not grasping what had happened. Hearing Tom shouting his pain to the heavens.

The Queen put the bowl to one side sharply, stood up and swirled her robes around her as she strode to the door; there she turned and flashed a smile that was both triumphant and proud, the expression of someone who always gets her way. Veitch, in his befuddled state, still tried to grasp why the ministrations had stopped. The break had been so harsh; he wanted to feel that cool touch of her fingers.

And hearing Tom's words for the first time and feeling instantly cold and hopeless: 'You took a drink, you fool! You took a drink and you're in her power now! She'll never you let go!'

Then she was gone, and Melliflor and the guards trailed out behind her, each of them smirking in turn at Veitch and Tom, knowing there was no longer any need to guard them.

Veitch's thoughts turned instantly to Ruth and the three days she had left. An awful emptiness opened up within him at the knowledge that he had failed her; he might as well have killed her himself. His part in everything was over. He was scum; when it all came down to it, that was all he was and all he could ever be.

'I can't leave you here,' Tom croaked. 'Not on your own. I'm going to stay with you.'

'The others need you.'

'You need me more.' Tom's face was filled with the all the terror and suffering that lay ahead for Veitch; that stretched out for years and decades and centuries.

Veitch looked through him, two thoughts turning over and over in his mind: that he wouldn't have the resilience that Tom had exhibited to survive the relentless tearing apart of his body and mind; and that he would never see the world, and Church, and Ruth, ever again.

Tom dropped to his knees and took Veitch in his arms. Veitch could feel vibration running through him, felt moisture splash on his face, and realised Tom was sobbing. And somehow that was more terrifying than everything, for all it said about what the future held for him there, in the Queen's incisive power.

CHAPTER NINETEEN

Gifts freely Given

It was a perfect summer's day, echoing warm memories of half-remembered childhoods, infused with the scent of grass and trees and heated tarmac; and it was only two days before Lughnasadh. Church sat on his favourite rock with the sun hot on the back of his neck and thought of how he would kill his closest, dearest friend. He'd weighed up the problem, on and off, for three hours, between checks on Ruth's condition, and he could still barely comprehend it.

'You going to sit out here until you turn into a crispy piece of bacon?' Laura had come up behind him quietly and had spent almost a full minute watching him silently, wishing more than anything she could connect with him on a level deep enough to help.

When he looked up at her, her heart went out to him at the desolation that lay in his eyes. Her first reaction was some asinine comment just to get a cheap laugh, but the weight on him was too great. 'What's the big deal?' she said, pretending to look distracted.

He shook his head, barely able to bring himself to talk to her, but when he started it all came flooding out. 'How do people deal with these kinds of decisions? You know, the big-shots, the leaders of countries, the people who make the world turn? You reckon they've got some kind of equation to make everything square in their minds? Because otherwise how can they live with themselves? On paper it looks great. You sacrifice this nameless, faceless person here and save this many lives. Simple maths. Any kid can do it. But when it's someone you know and care for, it doesn't balance out the same any more. The rational side of your brain tells you one thing. The other side says this person is too valuable to sacrifice, whatever the outcome.' A long pause. 'And that's the truth, isn't it? *Everybody* is too valuable. Life is too important. This isn't a decision for people. It's for God.'

Her sunglasses stripped the emotion from her stare. 'So what are you going to do?'

He cursed loudly, looked round as if searching for something to lash out at. 'I'm going to kill her. Of course I am, and I'm going to damn myself for all eternity and I'm probably going to kill myself straight after.'

Laura snorted derisively. 'You know, I'm appalled you're even considering that.' She grasped for the words to express the unfocused dismay she was feeling.

'Can't you get real? We're talking the End of Everything. The life of one person—' he made an overstated weighing act with his hands '—it doesn't balance. Any idiot can see it doesn't balance.'

'I thought this New Age was supposed to be a good time for women more than anything else. Feminine values and all that shit after hundreds of years of testosterone stupidity. Look at her, in that house, what she's been through. You could at least have hoped it would be Veitch or the old git—'

'We've all suffered.' He knew he was only arguing as a distraction; it wasn't even relevant. 'I was tortured—'

'Yeah? How bad? That bad?'

'All right. What do *you* think we do? Wish upon a star? She's going to die anyway, when Balor comes through.'

'Oh, fuck off. I don't know. But I know she's one of the good guys and it shouldn't be her.' She walked off a few paces angrily, then turned and said, 'Don't ever, *ever* tell her I said that, even when she's acting like she's got a bug in her head.'

He had a sudden vision of when he and Ruth first met, when everything had seemed confounding, but the choices simpler. 'What the hell am I supposed to be doing?' he muttered.

'You're the leader, Church-dude. Why are you asking me?' She picked up a handful of stones and began to hurl them out into the void without a thought for where they might land. 'I'm just along for sarcastic comments and pithy asides. Go with your instinct or whatever you leaders do.'

She threw the last pebble then turned and sauntered back to the house as if she didn't have a care in the world.

The dawn of the final day broke through the ragged cottage window in pink and gold, but when Church went to get a little sun on his face he saw the sky was painted red along the horizon; the folklore warning of bad weather ahead wasn't wasted on him.

At least the faint warmth refreshed him after the dismal night. He hadn't slept at all. Ruth had spent the long, dark hours in the grip of a delusion that had left her screaming and clawing at her face and belly until blood flowed. It had been almost unbearable to see, the cracking screech of her voice so dismaying he'd wanted to cover his ears and run from the place rather than listen to the magnitude of her pain or face the extent of her decline. But he'd stayed by her side for all that harrowing time, caring for her, doing his best to prevent her harming herself, and now he felt drained of every last emotion. Laura was huddled in a corner like a child, sleeping the sleep of the exhausted now that Ruth's ravings had subsided with the coming of the light. Several times during the night she'd had to leave the room, crying, unable to cope with what she was seeing. Church had pretended he hadn't noticed.

The faint breeze that came with the dawn stirred the stagnant air with a hint of freshness. He stretched the kinks out, then walked back to look over Ruth. Her sleeping face gave no signs of the terrible things he had seen during the night. Her chest rose and fell with an incongruous peace. She was beautiful, he thought, inside and out; it wasn't fair that she was suffering. For a moment he drank in that innocence and then a jarring thought crept into his mind: he could do it there and then. Smother her with the sleeping bag. Strangle her, gently at first so she didn't wake. It would be perfect; he wouldn't have to look into her eyes; he could remember her this way instead of twisted by the torments that were sure to come. It wouldn't really seem like murder at all, would it?

The thought hovered for a second and then he felt a twist in his gut so sharp he thought he was going to vomit. He couldn't do it now – he was too tired. But later, certainly; he had, at last, accepted it was an inevitability.

As he turned away so he wouldn't have to look at her, his eyes fell on the insane scribbling that covered the wall. From a distance the minute writing resembled some intricate pattern; swirls and waves like a Middle Eastern carpet. Only up close were the hidden messages revealed, incomprehensible, but with some sort of intelligence behind them. There was something in this observation which tugged at him, but he didn't have the energy to start getting philosophical. Instead he blanked his mind and allowed himself to be drawn in by the mesmerising scrawl, a Zen meditation where obvious meaning was discarded for an overall *sense*. He stayed in that state where all the words blurred into one mass for what must have been minutes, feeling the stresses of the night begin to slough off him, until he gradually realised he was becoming aware of certain words rising out of the morass. It was almost as if the wall was speaking to him. And what was it saying?

I love you.

A nice sentiment, he thought ironically. Perhaps Ruth had been wrong about something bad happening there. The house may have been a place where forbidden lovers trysted, or was that his stupid, sentimental, romantic side coming out? He thought he'd finally eradicated that on the hilltop overlooking Skye.

Church.

His breath stung the back of his throat, hung there, suspended. The word seemed to glow, then fade, so that he couldn't quite be sure it was his name he'd seen.

Marianne.

This time he felt sick. His head began to whirl and he thought he might pitch forward. Marianne, speaking to him. A tingle ran along his spine, warning him not to analyse what he was seeing too much or the spell might be broken. Just wait, he told himself. Be open to it.

For a moment or two he saw nothing else. His eyes started to burn from the effort of not concentrating on what was before him. He had that queasy feeling he always got when he looked at Magic Eye pictures.

Then: *Be brave.*

Be wary.

The end is

coming soon.

There was a cold sweat stinging the back of his neck. He wanted to ask questions, make some kind of direct contact, but he was afraid it would break the moment.

You have it

within

you, I always knew

that.

Don't fear for me. Don't

hold on to me.

Face the future.

Go forward.

Church wondered how long the words had been there, hidden in the garbled, idiot pattern, and he had never seen them till now; by accident. At the moment he needed them most. He knew what Tom would say: no accidents, no coincidences; there was meaning in every little thing. But if only he had seen it before, how much strength he might have drawn from it during the long, painful days they had waited there.

I

can see you even

when you

can't see me. We all

can.

There's a

reason

for everything, Church.

You just

have to see
it.

In that moment he wanted to break down and sob, all the repressed feelings of the years since she died, all the strangled emotions of the last few months, ready to burst out in one rush. But all he managed were a few, brief tears that burned his eyes and were easily blinked away.

I may be
trapped,
but they can't
hurt me.
And I'm happy now
they can't
use me to control
you.
Don't worry, Church.
I love you.

The message began to repeat like one of those tickertape electronic messages that run around buildings in New York. He stayed a few minutes longer, just to be sure, and then walked out into the pale sunlight, his cheeks still wet.

Her words had been few, but there was so much to take in; an entire worldview. He was overjoyed that she wasn't suffering, that the resilience he had admired was still there, but more than anything that she was still *around*, like an old friend, keeping an eye on him. And not just her; she had said.

We all can.

What did *we all* mean? He walked towards the edge and looked down at the flickering shadows moving across the landscape. For him, right there, at that particular moment, it meant the world. Never give up.

There's meaning in everything.

There's a reason for everything.

He only had to see it.

Church skidded over the grass and rock down the tor. He felt consumed by a renewed sense of purpose, almost courage, although he had never considered himself brave. Risking your life meant nothing when everything was meaningless; but now there was meaning. The clues had been around him from the start – even before – but he had never pieced them all together to accept the sublime patterns. Even the Fomorii, the antithesis of it, proved its existence. Tom had subtly attempted to guide him towards that illumination, Church realised, and now he had it, he realised why: the world looked different.

Now they couldn't afford to lose; not just for humanity, or life as they knew it, but for something so big it made even that seem insignificant. An awareness of that responsibility would have crushed most people; Church felt enlivened by a new sense of direction.

Halfway down the tor he paused at a huge boulder and slowly crawled out on top of it so he could survey the countryside beneath. To most eyes, the rolling fields would have looked a little darker than usual. Strange shadows flickered on the edge of vision, but beyond that everything appeared normal. Church's heightened perception, however, picked out the Fomorii's half-seen shapes for almost as far as the eye could see. It was as if an army had massed at the foot of the tor, ready for a siege on some mediaeval castle. For a moment he blanched at the prospect of what lay ahead; then he drove all thoughts from his mind and hurried down the tor.

His target was relatively easy to find in the stillness of the countryside where no cars moved, no birds sang. Waves of golden light washed upwards like some strange aurora borealis, gilding the surrounding trees; occasionally strange booming noises echoed among the hillsides as if a jet had passed over. Church kept beneath the level of the hedgerows as he progressed along the lanes towards the epicentre. He had judged rightly that there would be little or no Fomorii activity in that area. The fact that even they were scared should have given him pause, but he kept driving forward, working at the plan that had started to form in the back of his head. The risks were great – even being there was ridiculously dangerous – but at that stage bold action was the only thing that could work.

Close to the golden light the air was filled with an unpleasant charred taste. He dropped to his belly and wriggled forward until he could peer through a break in the hedge, every muscle tensed to flee in case he was seen.

Maponus roamed around the field, his path apparently random, but, on closer inspection, forming strange geometric shapes. A scattering of bloody bones radiated out from him in what looked like a blast zone. Church guessed when Niamh had plucked up the Good Son and deposited him here she had brought some of his victims in the backwash. Church watched intently. Sometimes Maponus dropped to his knees and scrabbled wildly at the turf. Other times he stopped to throw his head back and howl soundlessly. The chaotic rhythms of his madness were eerie to see: oblivious to the outside world, trapped in a repeating loop of thoughts. Occasionally they became so intense his face would dissolve into a swirl of wild activity in which Church saw snapping jaws, writhing things, razor-sharp blades glinting in the sunlight, then just a globule of unbearable light.

He looked away, suddenly queasy. Maponus' insanity was destabilising; it sucked at him, threatening to drag him in.

Cautiously he began to move around the perimeter of the field. How long would he have to search before he found what he was looking for? Could he have guessed wrongly?

He needn't have worried. Something hit him with the force of a wild animal, knocking him painfully across the road, pinning him beneath its weight. Stars flashed across his vision, but when he looked he felt a wave of relief. Yet the Bone Inspector's features spoke of a madness waiting to break out: he looked anxious, hunted, a man driven to the edge of survival.

Despite his age, his strength was almost superhuman. Church couldn't begin to wriggle out from beneath the wiry arms that held him tight. The Bone Inspector's eyes ranged crazily, his lips pulling back from his teeth in a feral grimace. For one moment, Church thought the custodian of the old places was going to dip down and tear out his throat.

'It's me!' Church gasped. 'A Brother of Dragons!'

The Bone Inspector's eyes cleared gradually. A long drool of spittle dripped on to Church's cheek. 'I know who you are, you bloody idiot!' he hissed. Cursing beneath his breath, he rolled off Church, instantly adopting the posture of a cornered animal, ready to fight or run. 'What are you doing here, you fool? Do you want to throw your life away?' His voice was strained with tension, but it barely rose above the sound of the wind rustling the leaves of the hedgerow.

He gave a sharp nod with his head, directing Church to a field on the other side of the lane. They scurried through an open gate and rested against a metal trough filled with stagnant water. The Bone Inspector closed his eyes for a moment, his lined face suddenly looking a hundred years old. His shirt was in tatters and a filthy, bloodstained rag had been tied roughly around his left hand. There were numerous gashes across his lithe, suntanned torso. A brief shiver ran through him and then his eyes filled with his old clarity. 'I've followed him up mountains and across rivers. I've waded through a swamp of blood, seen whole villages burning. I've lived on raw squirrel meat and drunk stagnant ditchwater. I've seen the kind of pain and suffering you can only imagine.' His voice was filled with a passion that bowed Church. 'And why? Because your idiot brethren dabbled with something they shouldn't! What did they think they were doing?'

'It had to be done—'

'Had to be done?' The Bone Inspector's eyes blazed furiously; Church thought the old man was going to hit him. 'All that death and grief was a decent price to pay?'

'That's not what I meant.' His anger grew hard. He thought of Ruth and the decision he had to make, of the world he used to inhabit where there was a clear distinction between right and wrong, and then came a sudden rush and tumble of regrets and bitterness. 'You can't criticise me.'

The Bone Inspector seemed taken aback by what he saw in Church's face.

'We're all wading through shit trying to put this nightmare right. Nobody has the higher ground. Nobody,' Church said coldly.

The Bone Inspector looked away at the waves of golden light. 'Pretty, ain't it? I can't see how we're going to put it right. When he was first bound under Rosslyn there was a whole load of my people carrying out the ritual. There's no way I can do it myself. I thought it was all sorted when those golden bastards came for him—'

'What happened?'

'There were six of them. Some of the big-shots, all light and thunder and faces you couldn't see. You could tell they were desperate to get him back. "Finally," I thought, "they're going to start sorting out their own shit." They'd got him cornered up near Aberdeen in what was left of a village. I was down among the ruins, trying to pull out some kid, but the poor bastard was already dead. And he'd seen me, and he was coming for me.' The Bone Inspector looked down at his hands; they were trembling. 'They'd opened up some kind of doorway in the air and they were going to drive him through. And then that bitch came out of nowhere. Crazy. As mad as he is.' He jerked a thumb towards the wash of light. 'There was a big flash, felt like I'd been hit by a shovel, next thing I knew I'm here.'

Church felt a pang of guilt; he wondered if the Tuatha Dé Danann would punish Niamh for her actions.

The Bone Inspector looked up at him piercingly. 'So what are you doing here?'

'Looking for you.' The Bone Inspector's brow furrowed; Church smiled. 'Listen, this is what's going to happen.'

As Church moved speedily along the lanes back to the tor he was gripped with fear that in his absence the Fomorii would have swept up the mountain and taken Ruth and Laura. But as he neared he could see the slopes were still clear.

The hardest part of the return journey was a wide-open space at the foot of the tor and the lower reaches of the climb. Even though the power in the mountain kept them hidden from the Fomorii senses, plain sight was still a problem. He couldn't believe he had made it to the Bone Inspector and back without discovery; it left him wondering how powerful those Fomorii senses truly were. Perhaps they didn't need to hide on the mountain at all. Was it possible that they could creep away under cover of darkness and find another hiding place far away?

The blow came from somewhere behind him, lifting him high into the air. His body exploded in excruciating pain; there didn't seem to be any oxygen left in his lungs. He slammed down on to the grass verge and bounced into a barbed wire fence. The twisted talons snagged his flesh and tore. For a second he hung there suspended like a scarecrow, thought processes fragmented, aware only of the agony that fried through him. His awareness came back in jerking fragments. A deep, dark shadow was moving across the road. He looked up for the cloud, the low-flying plane.

It hit him so hard the barbed wire burst as it yanked out of his flesh. He skidded into a cornfield. The sharp stalks stabbed his back, the dust clouded round him. Next to his face on the ground a large black beetle scurried away from the disturbance.

Full realisation only came when he rolled on his back, trying to scrabble to his feet. The Fomorii warrior loomed over him. At first there was no sense of solidity, just an impression of an immense, sucking void about to enclose him. A perception shift came as if someone had grabbed his mind and twisted it through forty-five degrees. Suddenly there was bulk, the sound of armour plates clanking into place as if they were a part of it, that familiar, sickening zoo-cage smell. Still couldn't quite get a full fix on it. It was an enormous insect with dripping mandibles and multiple legs, something that was covered with fur, with glaring red eyes, talons poised. And at times chillingly human-shaped, though as big as a tank, with the blackest armour.

Church jumped to his feet, started to run. What could have been a powerful arm lashed out, catching him full in the stomach. The pain was so great it felt like his internal organs were rupturing. He came down hard again, deep in the swaying corn. He had been so arrogant, thinking he had escaped detection. It must have been stalking him, checking he was defenceless.

His thoughts fizzed out as he suddenly found the energy to roll and run. The beast thundered like a bull, missing him by an inch. And then he was away, leaping wildly through the corn, knowing that he couldn't outrun it for an instant. The vibrations from its pounding feet felt like a mini-earthquake beneath him, but at least it allowed him to tell when it was almost on him. He threw himself to the side, and it crashed past; its size and momentum prevented it turning easily.

Anxiously, he glanced up at Mam Tor. It was close enough for him to sprint towards it. The beast was so big he might be able to lose it on the slopes where a sure foot was more necessary than strength. But if the Fomorii hadn't already established where they had been hiding, he couldn't lead the creatures back to Ruth and Laura.

He leapt out of the way again. This time he cut it too fine and the beast clipped his foot, spinning him round like a top. Dazed, he glanced across the field. If he didn't go to the tor he didn't stand any chance at all. He only had a second to make up his mind; it was no choice. He headed for the centre of the field, accepting his sacrifice with an equanimity that surprised him, gloomy that his great plan would never come to fruition, afraid of what the future held for the others. But all this was wiped from his mind in an instant when the beast smashed into his back.

He went down, blacked out for the merest instant, and then came to with the sensation of being lifted into the air. The beast's grasp was biting into his flesh; he felt the skin around his waist burst and blood trickle down his legs.

Where's Ryan when you need him? he thought ridiculously.

And then a strange thing happened. It was suddenly as if he could look directly into the creature's mind, understand fleeting thoughts and emotions that were so alien they could barely be described as such. He knew as surely as he was aware of his own name that the creature hadn't alerted the other Fomorii, that it had no idea where Ruth and Laura were. The sensation both sickened him and fascinated him. But he knew what caused it: the reviving essence of the Tuatha Dé Danann and the corruption of the Fomorii mingling within him *had* made him something more, something closer to them.

The creature seemed to be surveying his face; perhaps it was reading his thoughts too. Slowly it raised what at that time seemed an enormous gauntleted fist and took his left hand. Then with a sudden flick of its wrist it snapped back all his fingers at right angles, a sign of strength to show how frail he was in comparison. The cracking vibrated through Church's body and he cried out in agony. It threw him to one side just as he blacked out again.

When he came round a few seconds later it was advancing towards him for what he knew would be the killing blow. It stopped a foot away and he waited, almost relieved that the pain that racked his body would finally be over.

At that moment there was a smell like burning oil. The creature threw its arms in the air and let out a howl that sounded like rending metal. Church covered his ears from the shockwave. Desperately he tried to understand. Was it some kind of bestial roar of triumph? It sounded like pain.

The Fomor's body was more insubstantial than those of its brethren, suggesting, he guessed, its particular power. But at that moment it seemed to harden into the armoured shape, now seen more clearly than he had done before. Its black helmet gleamed in the sun. In the eyelets, white staring orbs ranged with such an expression he was left in no doubt that it was in the throes of some terrible torment. Pustules erupted all over it, even on the armour, and began to burst and release a foul-smelling ichor that sizzled where it hit the ground. The warrior's hands went to the side of its head and for a second it stayed in that position, its eyes still rolling madly. And then, like an overinflated balloon, it burst open. Globules of black flesh streaming with ichor shot across the field in all directions; somehow most of them missed Church. He had a glimpse of a twisted skeleton that bore no relation to the creature's outward shape. Then the bones became like candle wax, melting and flowing until there were just indescribable heaps scattered across flattened patches of corn.

Church didn't have to guess what had happened. A few feet away, previously hidden by the warrior, a flock of birds whirled madly. Gradually they flew tighter and tighter, reclaiming their true pattern. They fluttered in a formation so concentrated it was unnatural that they didn't crash into one another. And finally they settled into something that resembled the shape of a man, still flying round wildly like a whirlpool of feathers, beaks and talons.

'Mollecht,' he muttered through the haze of his pain.

The powerful Fomorii tribal leader stood silently; Church didn't even know if he could speak. Whatever hideous experiment had transformed him into primal energy that could only be contained by the continuous ritual flightpaths of a murder of crows had pushed him even further beyond the boundaries of his already unknowable race. The Fomor had destroyed the warrior by opening it up to release his essence, the terrible power that seemed to mimic the effects of contagion. Church recalled their confrontation at Tintagel and his blood seeping through his pores; the only escape had been to plunge into the sea.

But why had Mollecht destroyed the warrior? They were of the same people; Mollecht had the same contempt for humanity as the rest of the

Fomorii. The pain from his broken fingers was washing in waves up his arms. He leaned forward and vomited. All that had happened was that he'd swapped one form of death for another, and he guessed Mollecht would be infinitely more cruel than the brutish warrior. On the verge of blacking out again, he glanced around for other Fomorii coming to help capture him, but the surrounding fields were empty.

And when he looked back at Mollecht, the dark cloud of birds was already moving off through the corn. Where the creature had stood, a large, black sword stood embedded in the earth.

Church's head swam; he blinked away the tears of pain. Mollecht was setting him free? He limped forward to examine the sword, without actually touching it. It was definitely Fomorii; one edge featured the cruel serrated teeth that would inflict maximum damage in a fight. There was also an intricate pattern on the blade, scored so finely it was hard to make out unless the light was in the right place, but it appeared to be a pattern of magical symbols of some kind.

Mollecht was now just a black smudge following the hedge line. There was no doubt Church was being allowed to escape and that the sword had been left for his use. What did it mean? After the Kiss of Frost he was no longer so naïve that he would take an obvious Fomorii gift. But this time his instincts were telling him the sword was not a threat to him, although he had no idea what the ulterior motive was. A weapon would certainly be useful. He weighed up his options, and decided to go with his instincts after all. Tom would have been proud of him, he thought.

Fighting against encroaching unconsciousness, he tried to blot out the pain by using the sword as a staff to help him limp back towards the tor.

Shavi stood on the edge of the parkland that rolled up to Windsor Castle filled with a relief that pulled him back from the brink of exhaustion. For days he had played a cat-and-mouse game with the Fomorii, who knew he was in the vicinity, but hadn't quite been able to pinpoint him. It had meant advancing, retreating, doubling back, searching for each tiny break in their lines; on one day he had advanced a mile, only to find himself five miles back by evening. He had slept under hedges, curled in the branches of trees, once even dozed on a pile of Sunbrite at the back of a coal shed. There were times when he thought he would never reach his destination at all.

The Fomorii were everywhere, but only to his advanced perception. Most people seemed to be continuing with their lives, oblivious to the unusual shadows, the bushes and trees that were there one day, not the next, with only a vague feeling of unease to warn them things were different.

As Lughnasadh approached the Fomorii were growing more desperate. Shavi had noticed a light in the sky over Reading to the west which had the ruddy glow of an enormous conflagration. Strange, worrying sounds were occasionally carried on the wind, but they were too brief for him to recognise their source. But where were the army, the air force, the civil defences? He had seen no sign of any opposition. Perhaps they had already crumbled, or else there was a vacuum at the top, the Government paralysed or fallen apart at its inability to confront anything so alien and powerful.

But finally he had seen the tower of Windsor Castle in the distance, the flag waving in the summer breeze, and he had skipped into the back of a lorry which had brought him directly to the park. Even so, time was short. Already the heat of the day was starting to fade. But if he acted quickly and Cernunnos could help, he could still commandeer a car that would get him back to the others before midnight.

Halfway across the parkland he was aware of a rejuvenating atmosphere that seemed profoundly magical. Clouds of butterflies danced across the grass and the air was clear of any stink of pollution, despite the proximity to the Capital; it smelled and tasted as fresh as a mountain-top. The sun had blazed from a clear blue sky all day, but there was no sign of parching on the ground, which was lush and verdant. A languid quality eased his troubled thoughts; he felt something wonderful could happen at any moment. He found himself smiling.

When he moved beneath the cool shade of the trees everything seemed to take on an emerald tinge. There was a fluttering among the branches high above his head which he at first thought were more butterflies, but when he looked up he caught sight of a group of gossamer-winged people, minute but perfectly formed, their skin dusted green and gold. They weaved backwards and forwards, some-times merging with the leaves until they were completely invisible. One stopped to watch him curiously, then laughed silently before rushing away. He moved on, wishing the whole of the country was like this.

He had no idea where the Great Oak had been, but he was trusting his instinct to lead him there. Yet as he progressed he suddenly heard the sound of faint laughter and happy voices. He ducked down and moved through the undergrowth until he came to a sundrenched clearing. On one edge a teenage Asian woman lay in the arms of a young man with a skinhead haircut. From the disarray of their clothes it appeared that they had been making love. The woman rested her head on her boyfriend's chest and traced circles with a long nail on his bare, muscular stomach.

'No one can ever take this away from us,' she said.

He chuckled throatily. 'Who'da thought it, eh? You and me, no worries.'

'I can't believe we got out of Birmingham. Your dad—'

'He's not my dad.'

'You know what I mean.' She tapped him sharply on the chest. 'When that van came crashing into us on the motorway, I thought—'

'We had a guardian angel. I told you that.'

She rolled on her back and shielded her eyes from the sun, her fragile features framed by her long, black hair. 'I reckon things are going to get good from here on in.'

'There's a lot of strange stuff around.'

'Doesn't matter. This is about you and me. All that shit's behind us now.' She gave him a tight hug. 'There's no one to tell us what to do any more. We stand by each other, we can face up to anything. We've proved that.'

He started singing *Stand By Me* then burst out laughing at his feeble attempt. She gave him a short punch in the ribs for teasing. 'So,' he laughed, 'we going to get married?'

'Could do. Sooner or later. We've got plenty of time for that. We've got a lot to see, lots to do.'

She rolled over and kissed him passionately. Shavi felt suddenly like a voyeur and crept away quickly. But the tableau stayed with him. Strangely, it filled him with so much hope, and it wasn't just because they were at the start of their lives, on the cusp of the great adventure and a great love. After a moment's thought, he realised what it was. The woman had been right. The terrible upheaval, the failure of an entire way of life, none of it mattered. The truly important things were still continuing as they always had. Those things could never be beaten down. It was a simple thing, but at that time, in that magical place, it seemed like a great revelation to him and he was fired to tell the others when he got back to them.

For the next hour he searched among the woods. Every now and then he felt a strange sensation at the base of his spine, as if he were crossing some invisible electric barrier. Eventually he became sensitive enough to it to follow the waves which progressed in a spiral pattern, growing tighter and tighter, until he arrived at the epicentre.

He was in a grove among the wider wood. The trees rose up on either side to form an arched roof high above his head, and that deep, emerald light infused everything. A cathedral stillness lay all around. No wind touched that place, no blade of grass stirred. Even the calls of the birds sounded miles away, as if they had been muted by a dense wall. This was the Green Home, the place where the Great Oak altar had once stood, where men had worshipped the all-consuming power of nature for millennia. Unconsciously he bowed his head.

Almost by accident his eyes fell on a chipped, dirt-engrained horn lying in the grass; he was convinced it hadn't been there before. His palms were sweating with anticipation; he wiped them on his shirt before picking it up. It felt uncommonly light, too normal to be what he expected. He had at least anticipated some sense of great power or crackling energy that burned his fingers when he touched it.

He weighed it in his hands, knew it was only a delaying tactic, then slowly raised it to his lips. When he blew, the sound that emanated was strangely hopeful. It washed out through the woods in a cleansing wave.

For long minutes everything remained exactly as it was. Just as he was about to blow one more time, another horn answered, from far, far away. This one had a regal ring to it, but there was also something that sent a shiver through him. A few seconds later the wind began. It howled mournfully into the grove, forcing him to take a step back; it was chill, as if it had rushed hundreds of miles from a desolate mountaintop just to be there.

Shavi shuddered as he slowly turned, searching among the swaying trees, his hair lashing around his face. Something was coming; he could feel it deep in his chest; a heaviness. The branches moving back and forth, the noise; distracting. And then movement. Out of the corner of his eye, the merest flicker that could have been just a shadow. He turned sharply, but it was already gone. It was his other senses that picked up the true signs: the musky odour of horses on the wind, a muffled but unmistakable whinny, the thud of hooves on the wood floor. Dark shapes flitted in and out of the boles. They were drawing closer, circling him, but still not enough of the world to be easily seen.

Then they did break through. There was an effect like a heathaze over a road on a hot summer day; shapes shimmered, fell into relief, and suddenly he was aware of horses among the trees. The Wild Hunt had arrived.

He had been sure they could only materialise in that form at night, but in that place their power appeared much stronger. Another blast of the horn close at hand; all the hairs on his neck instantly stood to attention. Away beyond the horses in the deep shadows of the wood was the terrible baying of hounds yearning to be unleashed.

Shavi stood his ground as the horses came stamping and whinnying just beyond the edge of the grove, their eyes glowing fiery red. The riders still wore the furs and armour and carried the long poles topped with sickles he recalled from the grim pursuit across Dartmoor; he looked away from their shrouded faces. The ranks parted and a larger horse moved through, its nostrils steaming despite the heat. And on its back was the Erl-King and his face was not hidden; Shavi saw bare bone, scales like a lizard instead of skin, and eyes that glowed with an inner yellow light, the pupils just a serpent slit. His stomach tumbled in response.

As the Erl-King dismounted, he was already changing. His body grew bigger, hunched over like an animal prowling, an odd mix of fur and leaves spreading across his form. His eyes moved further apart, his nose wider, and then stags' antlers sprouted from his head. Finally Cernunnos stood revealed, the awe and terror of nature beating like a heart. He made a strange hand gesture and the other riders fell back into the trees.

'Who summons the Wild Hunt?' His voice was like the sound of the winds on a mountaintop, his presence radiating such power Shavi felt like bowing before him.

'I, Shavi, Brother of Dragons.' He lowered his head in deference.

'I know of you, Brother of Dragons.'

'I come on behalf of my sister, Ruth. Her situation is dire. Once, you said she could call to you in the harshest times. I am here before you now to ask for that assistance.'

Cernunnos hunched down over his massive thighs and scrabbled at the soft loam. Gently, he sniffed the breeze. 'A face of the Green lives within her, and she has carried out the Green's True Word to the best of her abilities, even at times of great trial. The Sister of Dragon's heart is strong.'

'Will you aid her?'

'I will.' He snorted; Shavi could smell his thick animal musk, even stronger than the horses'. 'What ails her?'

Slowly Shavi explained her capture by the Fomorii, the implanting of the black pearl, the suffering she was enduring as the medium for the rebirth of Balor; and as he spoke Shavi had the strangest feeling that Cernunnos already knew everything that was being said. After he had finished Cernunnos nodded slowly, grunting and snuffling. 'It was only to be expected that the Night Walkers would seek to bring the Heart of Shadows back to form, but the Sister of Dragons deserves better than to suffer their corruption.'

'What can be done?' Shavi asked. 'Other Golden Ones have refused to have anything to do with it. Some have said there is nothing that can be done.'

'Little can be done, it is true. The Heart of Shadows is a vile canker. Once established, it grows without respite. It is too hard in its corruption to be eradicated.'

'Then what?' Shavi stared deep into Cernunnos' gleaming eyes, trying to make sense of what he was saying. 'Is it hopeless?'

'Nothing is hopeless. We Golden Ones guard our secrets with pride, and this is mine: the Heart of Shadows can be removed without harming the Good Sister.' Shavi's mood brightened at once. 'The ritual must be carried out tonight, before the turn of the day when the moon is clear. And a sacrifice is called for.'

'Anything,' Shavi said without a moment's thought. 'I will do it.'

'Anything?'

Shavi nodded. 'She is a good person. She deserves more.'

'And you do not?'

'If there is anything I can do to help, I must.'

Cernunnos watched Shavi's face like an animal surveying something which could be prey or predator. Then he turned slowly, making strange, unnatural gestures with his left hand, and when he was facing Shavi again he was holding a small, smoky-coloured bottle with a wax stopper. 'Here is the radiance that will burn out the Heart of Shadows.'

He held out the bottle. Shavi took it gingerly. 'What will happen?'

Cernunnos' eyes narrowed until the light within them seemed like distant stars, but he said nothing.

The bottle felt odd in Shavi's hand, not like glass at all. He slipped it quickly into his pocket. 'On behalf of Ruth, I offer my great thanks for your aid. On behalf of all the Brothers and Sisters of Dragons.'

'Go with speed, Twilight Dancer. I have always entertained your forebears well.'

Shavi turned to leave, then paused, wondering if he dare give voice to what was lying heavy on his mind. 'When the Wild Hunt has been summoned, someone must die. Is that correct?'

Cernunnos said nothing; in the background the Hunt was growing restless.

'There are a young man and woman nearby. Do not take them.'

Cernunnos eyed him curiously for a moment, then nodded slowly in agreement. He looked towards the sun, now moving towards the horizon. 'When night comes, the Wild Hunt will ride.'

Though he had saved the young couple, Shavi felt the weight of his guilt: there would be yet another death on his conscience. Even the friendly powers that had colonised the world had no real respect for humanity; they agreed to whims with the gentle weariness of patrons who could turn suddenly if the mood took them. There would be no freedom until they were all driven out.

He bowed slightly, although it was a little curter than his greeting. Cernunnos made some strange animal noise, then moved back towards the riders, his shape slowly metamorphosing back into that of the Erl-King. After a few paces, he turned back towards Shavi, an enigmatic expression on his face. 'I hail your sacrifice, Twilight Dancer, and I wish you well in the Grey Lands.' And then he was gone, twisting and changing like sunlight on water. The horses moved away into the trees, the baying of the hounds more insistent; terrifying.

Shavi's shoulders sagged briefly, but then he pulled the bottle from his pocket. Here was confirmation that things were not all bad; that there were miracles among the nightmares. All he had to do was to reach Ruth before midnight. He checked the angle of the sun, then started to run across the parkland towards the nearest road. He would ride like the Devil was at his heels.

CHAPTER TWENTY

Venceremos

Church didn't know how he made it back to the house. The sword was his support over the rough ground, levering him up over rocks which were too much for his battered body to surmount. There was so much pain in every inch of him that he no longer focused on it; he simply floated in a cloud untouched by his senses. The most sensible thing would be to black out and rest where he fell, let his body heal a little. But night was not far away, and Lughnasadh was rising after that. Everything depended on the next few hours; a moment's weakness would doom them all.

Laura was waiting for him as he crested the last ridge, a look of such contempt on her face he thought she was going to punch him. 'Suicide boy,' she sneered. 'Looks like you got unlucky.' Then she saw the pain that was racking him. 'A close thing, though. Maybe next time, eh?'

He expected a supportive hand, but she marched back to the house, leaving him to make his own way.

By the time he reached the house he was feeling much better than when he had started his journey; the Pendragon Spirit was helping, coupled with whatever earth energies were focused within the tor, but he knew it would take many days to get back to full form; longer for his hand to heal properly. He had attempted to bind it with his hand-kerchief – the agony had almost made him black out. He would need Laura's help to fasten it up tightly enough for the bones to start to knit without any disfigurement.

But the moment he stepped into the house all thought of his own pain disappeared. Ruth was huddled in one corner, her belly distended and mottled grey, green and purple, as if it had been beaten with a stick. Her skin was drained of blood, the crescents under her eyes and the hollows of her cheeks so dark she looked as if she were close to death by starvation. There was no longer any ranting or delirium; her eye-lids barely flickered and her breath was so shallow it was almost imperceptible. It was obvious the end was near.

Laura refused to look at her; she kept staring out of the windows or at the walls, as if there was something more interesting to see. 'So when are you going to put her out of her misery?' she said bitterly. 'I see you've found something for the execution.'

'There's still time,' he replied wearily; he didn't have the energy to deal with her baiting.

He knelt down and brushed the hair from Ruth's forehead; her skin was clammily unpleasant to the touch. Hesitantly he moved his hand down, hovering over her belly for an instant before he laid it on her skin. The instant he touched it something moved beneath. He snatched his hand away, stifling a cry of disgust. It had felt like a dog had snapped at him.

Laura must have seen something too, for there were tears in her eyes born of incomprehension and horror. 'How can that happen?' Her voice was a small child's. 'It can't really be inside her. Nothing's inside her, is it?'

Church rubbed a hand across his face, composed himself, then stood up and walked to the door. 'We'll give it till nearly midnight,' he said without looking at her. He had to find some place to rest so he could find the reserves he prayed were buried deep within him. 'We've got to have hope. There's still a chance one of the others could make it back.'

He felt her eyes heavy on his back, urging him to go back to her, comfort her. He paused briefly, then walked out into the afternoon sun, mentally preparing himself for what the night would bring.

The sun was uncomfortably close to the horizon when Shavi made it across the park to the nearest road. He was slick with sweat, his throat burned and his stomach was in knots, but none of it mattered; he knew instinctively he was the last hope for Ruth, for all of them. There was still time to make it back with Cernunnos' mysterious potion, just as long as he found a vehicle quickly.

Desperately he scanned the road in both directions. Normally there would have been a constant flow of traffic in both directions, but in the twilight of society's dissolution there was no sign of anything.

'Please,' he whispered. 'Whatever gods are listening—'

A white Renault Clio appeared from around the bend. Stifling a wave of exaltation, he took a step out into the road, furiously trying to think how he would convince the driver to hand over his vehicle, knowing he would take it by force if he had to.

As he neared he saw the troubled face of a white-haired old woman leaning over the wheel, peering ahead anxiously as if she expected a sudden rush of juggernauts. Suddenly she glanced in his direction and her expression froze in horror, her mouth a growing O.

What is wrong with her? Shavi thought.

He took another step into the road. She put a foot on the accelerator. 'No!' Shavi shouted. 'I need—!'

From somewhere nearby there came the strangest sound. It could have been the wind blowing across the park, but it sounded very much like howling. Sirens went off in his mind; there was something important he hadn't remembered. A second passed. And then he had it: the ritual in the woods with the travellers. The spirit construct hanging in the air, warning him, something about howling. Then he had it: *turn quickly.*

The pain in his back felt like a red-hot poker had been rammed through his skin. His thoughts fractured. He hung on to the image of the woman's face, her mouth growing wider and wider until he thought it was going to swallow her head; the car speeding up, rushing by, taking hope with it.

No, he tried to call, but his voice had gone with the car.

The howling, like a wolf.

And then suddenly he felt an arm round his chest, dragging him back, across the road, into the park, into the trees. He tried to fight, but in his shock his limbs felt like jelly, his thoughts in disarray.

Roughly he was thrust backwards, hitting the ground hard. His shirt felt wet near his shoulder blade. He could smell the meaty odour of the blood. Quickly his fingers slipped behind him. When he withdrew them, they were dark and wet.

The shock of the image kickstarted his thoughts into life and he threw himself on to his elbows, ready to drive up to his feet.

A boot cracked sharply on his right elbow and he fell back to the ground in pain. Before he could move again a figure was over him, brandishing a knife at his face. Shavi's immediate impression was of an enormous wolf and he knew at once that this was the creature that had stalked them from the Highlands. But gradually his perception fought back, struggling for the truth, and it was as if a mist was shifting from before his eyes.

The wolf began to grow smaller, the yellow eyes becoming less and less intense, until it coalesced into the shape of a man. At first, details were hazy, but as the veil was drawn back a feeling of revulsion slowly engulfed Shavi. The veins of his attacker stood out in deep black on his pale skin, as if they were filled with ink instead of blood. His eyes were lidless, the unchanging stare charged with a mix of insane fury and crazed despair. His teeth were rotting and blackened too, which made his mouth look like the gaping maw of an alien beast; although he couldn't possibly survive in that form, whatever the Fomorii had done to him kept him going.

It was almost impossible to consider him a man; yet in the straggly mane of silver hair and the shabby, dark suit, Shavi recognised him.

'Callow,' he hissed. Ice water washed through him at the thought of what monstrous things must have been perpetrated on the itinerant to transform him into such a thing.

But once the initial shock had dissipated, Shavi was overcome with a deep loathing. Normally he tried to maintain an equilibrium for all living things, but here was the man who had slashed Laura's face, sliced off Ruth's finger and delivered her into the hands of the Fomorii to be tortured; who had tried to sell humanity to the beasts for his own gain.

Shavi clapped his hand on his wound to staunch the blood flow; it didn't seem too bad. 'What have they done to you, Callow?' he asked, biding his time while he looked for a way out.

'What have they done?' Callow rolled his eyes insanely. 'Look at me! They've ruined me! Calatin's punishment for my involvement in the farrago which you and your pathetic colleagues brought about in the Lake District. Punishing me more for his own failures. The indescribable bastard!' He made a strange noise in the corner of his mouth which could have been a laugh or a curse; the insanity brought on by his suffering was writ large in every movement he made. 'And once he had tormented me, he didn't even keep me around. He threw me out into the world to make my own way.'

'You paid a terrible price—'

'Not fair!' He wiped his mouth feverishly with the back of his hand. 'It was your fault! All of you! You are the ones who should have suffered! That was why I sought you out. To make you pay.' He waggled his filthy fingers in front of Shavi's face. One was missing; the first severed finger they had found next to Loch Maree had been his own. 'Each one of you, a little pinkie!' He chuckled. 'The five fingers that held my fate in their grasp. I will sever each of you until I am free. And any other one who dares to hold me back.'

Cautiously, Shavi dug his heels in the ground and shifted his weight, ready to throw himself at his attacker if Callow dropped his guard. 'If all you wanted was revenge, why then did you deliver Ruth to the Fomorii?' Desperately he tried to keep the conversation going.

Callow's expression grew rueful. 'I thought she might buy my way back into the Midnight Court. She is the most powerful of all of you, you see. More powerful even than you. I explained to Calatin that this would make her the perfect vehicle for the return of their Dark Lord. The delicious irony! The champion of this world bringing about its demise! Calatin had no sense of irony, but he realised her strength would make her more likely to withstand the rigours of the pregnancy.'

He chuckled crazily to himself. 'Pregnant! A virgin birth! They were going to use one of their own up to that point. So he took her, and then he threw me out again! But once I have eliminated the rest of you, he will take me back. I know he will.'

'Why do you *want* to return when they have done this to you?' Shavi could not keep the disgust out of his voice.

Callow did not seem to notice. 'He loves me. He shaped me with his own hands. I hate him and I love him too. There is nowhere else in this world for me now, unless it's by his side.'

In his words Shavi heard echoes of Tom's twisted relationship with the Tuatha Dé Danann. What was it in the psyche of humankind that made them complicit in the actions of their tormentors, he wondered?

Callow wiped his knife on Shavi's trousers, leaving a thin trail of blood. 'You have to give in to them, you see,' he continued, almost to himself. 'They're our gods. They control our lives.'

Shavi eyed the sinking sun nervously. He had to break free from Callow soon or all would be lost. 'We give in to no one. If humanity is to rise again, it will not come from kowtowing to any earthly power. We must seize control—'

Callow's painful laugh cut him short. 'You think they can be beaten?'

'Not easily. Not without a great struggle. But I believe it is man's destiny to rise, not to kneel in servitude.' The pain and the wetness in Shavi's back was starting to spread. The wound might not have been deep, but it still needed treatment or he'd bleed to death there, in conversation with a lunatic.

'You'll be the first to die. Then I'll take your finger. Or perhaps I'll take the finger first.' Callow watched him slyly with those permanently uncovered orbs like twin moons, glowing unnaturally white. He started to turn the knife slowly in his filthy fingers. Shavi watched his muscles tense, preparing to strike.

'We may be able to help you,' Shavi said with a comforting smile. 'The Tuatha Dé Danann have remarkable abilities and their opposition to the Fomorii may induce them to find a cure for you.'

'Really?' Callow's muscles untensed.

Shavi felt the relief creep into his chest. Now was the time to act. 'Yes. We can—'

Callow lunged forward like a cobra. The knife plunged into Shavi's chest with the force of a hammer, knocking him back on the ground. And again. And again. For an instant his thoughts flashed out and he was left in infinite darkness. When he came down he seemed to be buried deep in his head with only a tiny window to look out on to the world. There was an unbearable pain in his left hand, but he couldn't move to drag his arm away, couldn't even move to see what was happening. A receding part of him knew, but what remained of his conscious mind wouldn't accept the knowledge. It couldn't make sense of anything; there were just random impressions: the comforting feel of the grass against his cheek, the summery aroma of woodland, the feel of the heat slowly fading as the sun slipped down the sky, an overwhelming but fleeting grief that he had failed everybody, a snapshot of Ruth, Church, Laura, Veitch, Tom, Lee, his mother and father.

And then he heard Callow's voice as if from across a desolate pain: 'There is no cure. This is all there is – pain and suffering.'

The sounds of Callow shuffling away. Silence. Another face moving in towards him, familiar, but insubstantial; and it wasn't even dark. The guilt and regret. The voice that tormented him on a nightly basis, softly, so softly. *'You'll be with me soon, Shavi.'* Lee bending closer to tell him terrible things that would stay with him in the Grey Lands for ever.

And then there was nothing.

The sun was low on the horizon and long shadows ran across the Windsor parkland. Darkness had started to gather among the trees. From somewhere nearby came the forlorn baying of hounds. One shadow separated from the others and moved across the grass until it found Shavi lying in a pool of his blood. There was a brief snuffling around the recumbent form and then Cernunnos raised his antlered head and howled at the sky. It merged with the questing of the dogs into a sound that would have broken the heart of anyone who heard it.

Complete silence followed; no bird called, no insect chirruped; it was as if a blanket had been lain across the parkland, and that was somehow as unbearable as the noise that preceded it. Finally, Cernunnos groped inside Shavi's jacket and removed the smoky bottle he had handed over earlier. The god held it delicately for a moment, his head moving slowly from side to side, and then he loped back into the undergrowth.

Church sat on his favourite rock, watching the sunset. The sky had turned an angry red, almost apocalyptic in its intensity. His body felt like it belonged to someone else, a mass of aches and bruises highlighted by the throbbing in his hand, which had receded from its initial agony to a dull pain that made him feel sick. He had passed out briefly as Laura bound it tightly for him and she had chided him for that, although there wasn't much heart in her mockery.

The sword felt uncomfortable in his good hand, the strange, cold, metal more like the skin of a snake; sometimes he was even convinced it

864

moved beneath his palm. The way he felt, though, he doubted if he would have the strength to use it.

He couldn't help continually checking his watch as he counted off the minutes until midnight. More than anything, he thought of Ruth. He recalled when they first met how he had the overwhelming feeling they were kindred spirits. Lying together beneath the sheets in her Salisbury hotel room when one of the Baobhan Sith was stalking only feet away. Sitting beside the campfire on Skye when she told him, 'We're not all going to come out of it alive.'

He bolstered himself with the thought that until Lughnasadh rose there was still a chance of the cavalry riding in to save all of them from damnation. Yet in his heart he knew a little piece of hope went with each glimmer of light that ebbed out of the sky.

Could he kill the woman he felt closer to than anyone, even though she was going to die anyway? Could he drive that last piece of life out of her, and watch as her face returned to innocence? For the first time in many years, he covered his eyes and prayed.

Laura sat in the corner of the room where Ruth slept, hugging her knees, watching the tremors that ran through the sleeping form. Seeing Ruth's suffering played out before her had been agonising, as much for what it made her think about herself as the effect it had on the woman she had professed to dislike. For so long she hadn't even been able to look at Ruth; now she could do little else. She didn't know if she was punishing herself, some subconscious reflex instilled by her parents' religious education, or if she was merely waiting for something to happen.

And she could sense they were on the cusp of something monumental. There was a feeling in the stale atmosphere of the room of unpleasant tension, as if a storm were about to break.

'Don't die,' she whispered. She told herself it wasn't a prayer, but then added, 'Bring Ryan or Shavi back with good news.'

She felt useless sitting around doing nothing, while heroic events were being played out around her. Was that why she'd been pulled into the whole damn mess – to act as little more than a cheerleader for others who had greater depths and more significant abilities? In fact, if she admitted it to herself, she had no skills, nothing to contribute at all; not even any homely wisdom to guide them out of a sticky situation. She'd been a coward, a fuck-up, jealous, divisive, manipulative, while secretly hoping some of the others' strengths would rub off on her. But all she'd got was some hideous blood disorder that was doing God knows what to her insides.

Why *had* she been marked as a Sister of Dragons? What did she have to offer?

She covered her eyes, then regretted it when Church walked in because it made her look weak. He was too distracted to notice. His face was pale and drawn from the pain of the day; in the queasy, fading light he looked ten years older.

The deep currents of affection she felt for him began moving, as they always did when he was around, and her biggest regret was that she had never let him know how she really felt. Now it was too late. She could barely believe how, only a few weeks earlier, it had seemed perfect. She'd finally found someone she felt in tune with after a lifetime of searching; someone who was decent, hopeful, everything she wasn't. And, true to form, it had fallen apart almost the moment it had started.

''s up?' she said blandly.

His features grew dark and she knew the answer even before he spoke. 'I think it's starting.'

They crawled out on to the overhanging boulder and looked down at the pooling blackness far below. It took Laura a second or two to realise it was moving.

'They know where we are,' Church said. 'They're coming up.'

Laura shrugged. 'So, it's Alamo time. Well, it's not like it's a surprise or anything.'

Church looked at that fat, red sun hanging on the horizon. 'It's too soon.'

Laura followed his gaze, couldn't see anything. 'What do you mean?'

'I didn't expect them to make their move till after dark.' He gnawed on a knuckle, even more worried than he had been a few moments earlier. 'I've got to try to hold them off for a bit.'

Laura snorted with mocking laughter. 'Throw stones at them! That'll do some good.'

He rounded on her bitterly. 'I'm sick of your carping. Couldn't you say anything useful, even here at the end?'

'Sorry to be such an irritant, shithead.' She looked away so he couldn't see her face.

The black tide was rising quickly. Church was transfixed as it swallowed grass and stone, lapping ever upwards. At that distance Church couldn't make out any shapes within the greater mass, adding to the illusion of an ocean stretching out around the island of the tor; and with the sun so low it was impossible to guess how far it did reach, the night and the Fomorii merged into one. He guessed, from the average size of them, there must have been thousands gathered round the tor, ready to celebrate the rebirth of their own dark god and bear him back to whatever burrow they had made their own. And there he sat with a sword, nearly crippled by his injuries. If the situation wasn't so tragic it would be laughable.

The bitterness had drained out of him by the time he turned back to Laura. 'I want you to go back and sit with Ruth,' he said tenderly.

'Well, aren't you the big macho bastard. Send the womenfolk back to the homestead while you do men things.'

'It's not like that. Ruth deserves to have someone sitting with her, you know—'

'Up to the end?' She seemed to understand this. She stared back at the house impassively, and after a long pause, she said, 'You're not expecting me to do it, are you?'

'No. Don't do anything. That's my job.'

'But what happens if . . .' She struggled to find words that wouldn't hurt too much to say them.

'I'll find some way to get back in there to do what needs to be done before it's all over.'

She nodded slowly. 'This is it then. The fuck-ups fuck up big time.' Still nodding, she began to walk back to the house. She hadn't gone far when she turned and came striding back to him. The last rays of the sun highlighted the glimmering wetness in her eyes. She wiped them with the back of her hand, then threw her arms round his neck and hugged him tightly. 'I'd like to say it was fun, Church-dude. Bits of it even were. But I can say this – I'll never forget it until my dying day.' She kissed him passionately on the lips and then she was gone.

Church's thoughts turned to what lay ahead. He desperately tried to think of some delaying strategy to give him the added time he needed, but there were so many, whatever he did, they'd keep going right over the top of him towards the house. The building wasn't even protected enough for him to make any kind of stand. A pass in the mountains, that's where he needed to be, or at a bridge. Instead he was on a flattened ridge on a bleak mountaintop where they could come at him from every direction at once. Clever.

'Shavi. Tom. Ryan,' he said out loud. 'If you're going to make a move, now's the time to do it.' His words were picked up by the evening breeze and flung out over the countryside.

He sat on the boulder, his stomach muscles knotting, his heart beating faster and faster until he thought it would explode with anxiety. They were moving slowly, staying together in one tight corpus. It allowed him time to consider their nature. The times he had seen them en masse they had moved almost like one creature. He remembered the Lake District and how he felt like he was being borne along on a river of darkness. Perhaps that was the way to perceive them, as the embodiment of evil, one mind, one form, which could break itself down into smaller parts when called for. That line of thinking made his head spin. The Fomorii, and the Tuatha Dé Danann too, were so alien the only yardsticks he could apply to measure them were human ones which made no sense. There was a whole new set of rules and regulations out there which mapped the existence inhabited by those two races.

He wondered, with a note of dark humour, how the scientists were coping right then. Madly trying to apply their laboratory conditions to something which could not be measured or categorised? Going crazy trying to force all those square pegs into the round holes which comprised their intellectual life?

Yet, strangely, there were some parts of the Fomorii that were parallel to human experience, as if people had learned the baser part of their existence from the Night Walkers long ago. Or perhaps, he mused, everyone was cut from the same cloth. That thought was so depressing he wiped it from his mind immediately.

They certainly had a hierarchical structure, tribal in nature, with the different factions constantly rivalling. He guessed only the iron rule of Balor could keep them united, in fear and in the promise of ultimate victory over all existence. But while the Fomorii were like the barbarians in the outer darkness, the Tuatha Dé Danann reminded him of some emperor's court structure, but one that had passed its peak and was winding down into decadence and decay. How could they be gods when aspects of them were so human?

And so he waited. Halfway up the tor he began to hear those horrible animal cries and grunts that tormented his sleep. Then came the zoo smell, thick and stomach-turning. And then, finally, he could see them, no longer as one dark mass, but as swarming black insects, thousands upon thousands of bodies, scrambling upwards, clambering over each other, their shapes flickering in and out of his perception so that sometimes they seemed to have bony shells and wings, other times gleaming black armour, sometimes wielding twisted limbs with scorpion stings and lobster claws, other times brandishing cruelly deformed battle axes and those terrifying swords with the serrated edge along one side. It was too much. He had to withdraw from the edge as he felt the nausea rise to the point where he was almost blacking out.

He retreated until he was a few yards from the house door and then he took his stand again.

Laura watched the impending confrontation from the house with a mounting sense of desolation. All the suffering and heartache had come down to this: more failure. Behind her, Ruth had started to buck and writhe once more. *Getting ready to give birth*, Laura thought.

She wondered what it would be like to die, almost welcomed it in a way. But in contrast the thought of Church or Ruth passing filled her with an overwhelming sickness; it brought tears to her eyes.

As she blinked them away, she caught sight of a movement close to the house. Her stomach turned. The Fomorii had outflanked Church and were coming. It was an obvious ploy; they wouldn't leave their god in the hands of others for longer than they had to, she thought. She glanced round frantically for some kind of weapon. She'd go down fighting if she had to, protecting Ruth to the last. If only she could have had time to say sorry for all the terrible things she had done; for being so weak and pathetic and twisted when confronted by someone so unselfish.

Before the thought had barely formed, the door burst open and it was in there with her. Terror bloomed in her face and in that instant she knew it was over.

An age seemed to pass while the atmosphere grew charged with the overpowering force of an electrical storm; he tasted burnt metal in his mouth, felt disturbing vibrations run through the ground and into his legs. Although he tried to find that place deep within him where all his aspirations to heroism and bravery lay, when the Fomorii rose into view the cold fear that washed through him almost drove him to his knees.

The black tide came over the edge relentlessly. Images were caught briefly in his mind, disconnected: limbs that became tentacles before turning into articulated legs like a spider's, staring eyes that occasionally became multifaceted like an insect's, body parts that looked like knives, wings that weren't, other shapes he couldn't decipher but which would haunt him for ever. There was one brief moment when everything just hung. Before him stretched the glistening blackness, the upper surface tinted deep red by the rays of the dying sun, swaddled in a stifling atmosphere of heat and tension. The acute impression of decay and corruption was almost beautiful in its intensity.

The sheer speed of their approach was terrifying; how pathetically naïve he'd been even to think he could do something to delay them. They swept across the turf and then rose up until they blocked out the sun. He waited for the black wave to crash down on him, pounding him into grains, but then it separated and flowed on either side until the serried ranks of the Fomorii formed a crescent around the house. And he was suddenly smothered in the stink of them, the sound of them.

Somehow he found the reserves to steady himself. He focused on some dim spot deep in his head so he didn't have to look at them, forced himself not to think about what the next minute would bring, hoped he didn't look like some weak, frightened *Fragile Creature*.

And then, in an instant, everything grew still. Wherever his eye flickered, nothing moved; the Fomorii may as well have been obsidian. The only sound was the plaintive whispering of the wind as it began to growing in intensity with the dying of the day.

What are they waiting for? he wondered.

And then he knew. A shiver of anticipation ran through the assembled throng and a second later the last glimmering of the sun winked out and darkness fell across the land. A sound rose up into the night like the rending of metal as the Fomorii gave voice to their feelings; Church gave an involuntary shudder. A second later silence fell once again, heavy with a different kind of anticipation.

Away near the edge Church noticed the darkness start to part, then reform, moving slowly towards him like a stingray slipping through the waves. He held his breath. The ripple broke at the front of the ranks and Calatin stepped out to face him. He was wearing a filthy white silk shift beneath unsettling black Fomorii armour and he was lightly holding the rusty sword that had killed Church at their last face-to-face confrontation.

'Here we are again, on the eve of another festival.' Calatin's fey voice was rich with contempt and triumph. 'Is one death not enough?'

Church said nothing, but his mind was whirling. The sun had set; perhaps there was still time.

'You chose well, Dragon Brother,' Calatin continued mockingly, 'hiding here in the blur of blue light rather than confronting us. Still betraying the tradition of the Pendragon Spirit. You recognise your abiding weakness in the face of a greater power—'

'We caused you enough problems in Edinburgh. Destroyed your base. Stole your . . .' Church paused for emphasis '. . . *prize*.'

A shadow crossed Calatin's face; his smile grew darker. 'And you discovered high-born Night Walkers are not easily despatched.' He limped forward a few paces, the sword almost too heavy for him to carry. The effort allowed him to compose himself after Church's gibe. He gestured up to the dark arc of the sky. 'This is a night filled with power and wonder. Soon, all of existence will align harmoniously, the cycles will turn further away from the light, and the Heart of Shadows will return once again to the centre of all there is. And you and your brethren will have played a part in that glory, Dragon Brother.' Another ripple ran through the Fomorii.

Church knew he would have to do anything to buy time. 'Why Ruth?' he asked.

'She is a powerful and resilient vessel, Dragon Brother. Stronger even than you.' Calatin smiled, as if this were the ultimate insult. 'The birthing cauldron must be able to contain the significant forces at play. She had that strength. It was not my initial belief, but when she was delivered to me the thought of a Sister of Dragons bringing about the return of the Heart of Shadows was so richly imbued with meaning, it had to be.'

Church tried not to let himself become angered by Calatin's words. 'You've been planning this—'

'This has always been our design. In the Far Lands, we were bereft – that was part of the pact agreed with the Golden Ones after the Sundering. But that could never have been our state in perpetuity. Without the Heart of Shadows, the Night Walkers are . . .' he made a strange floating movement with his hand '. . . insubstantial. And so we built the Wish-Hex to break the barriers and propel us out into this world once the cycles turned. And once here, we simply had to wait for the right alignment to set events in motion.' The light of someone seeking glory began to burn in Calatin's eyes. 'And it will always be remembered that I was the one who brought the Heart of Shadows back into existence. My tribe will hold the highest place. None of the others. Mine.'

'Balor isn't in your hands yet.'

Calatin stifled his tinkling laughter with the back of his hand before it broke into a hacking cough. Then he rested on the sword, one hand drooping over the handle, his chin almost hanging on top of it, while he surveyed Church with languid eyes. 'What goes through your mind now, Dragon Brother? Regret? Self-loathing at your inability to meet your responsibilities? What?'

'I'm not the person you met three months ago, Calatin. Now all my emotions are focused outwards. I feel contempt, for you and your kind, for all you outsiders who think you can come here and tell us how to live our lives. I feel a cold, focused anger for the pain you've inflicted on our lives. And for what you've done to Marianne—'

'Ah, yes!' Calatin made a flourishing gesture. 'Another failure on your behalf. I expected you to seek me out for vengeance, at the least. But you chose to abandon the one who occupied your heart while you entertained yourself with brief dalliances with others.' He punctuated his sneer with a sly smile.

Church knew it was designed to hurt, but it drove home nonetheless. 'Not *chose*, Calatin. I have learned to accept my responsibilities, whatever the cost to myself.'

. Calatin laughed.

'You don't believe me?' He motioned towards the house. 'She's dead. I killed her earlier. And your god has died with her.'

A shiver ran through the breadth of the Fomorii, accompanied by a sound like knives being sharpened; there was a timbre to it that sent a corresponding shiver through Church. An incandescent fear alighted briefly on Calatin's face before he brought it under control. 'No! The resonance would have torn through us!' A tremor ran through his body; it looked like it wasn't going to stop. He couldn't prevent himself glancing towards the house. Then he half turned towards the wall of darkness at his back. 'If the Heart of Shadows was gone, we all would know.'

Now it was Church's turn to laugh.

Calatin rounded on him angrily. 'Besides, you do not have it within you. I have looked inside you, Dragon Brother, and you truly are too much of a Fragile Creature.'

'The only way you're going to find out is by going in there.'

The expression which rose on Calatin's face showed this was a prospect he relished; his smile froze cruelly. He raised one hand to bring the razored might of the Fomorii down on Church.

'What? You're not going to do this one-on-one again?' Church glanced towards the distant sky; still nothing.

'You remember—'

'Last time you'd hampered me with the Kiss of Frost. It wasn't a fair fight, it was a big cheat. You knew you'd win. Without that, I could beat you easily.'

Calatin's gaze wavered; Church could almost see every thought passing across his face: the reputation of the Brothers and Sisters of Dragons had sifted into Fomorii myth in the same way the Night Walkers and Golden Ones had entered human mythology; he couldn't quite be sure there wasn't some weight to it, that Church really could destroy him in an instant.

Church's palms were sweating as he gripped the handle of the sword. Things had reached a head. Every part of his rational mind told him it was time to throw in the cards, to run into the house and slay Ruth with one swing of his sword. But whenever he thought about it, his legs felt like lead.

And there was still time, he thought, still hope.

He raised his sword and prepared to face Calatin. And as he did, the strangest thing happened. Confusion, disbelief, then shock crossed Calatin's face, he took a shaky step back. Another unnerving sound reverberated among the Fomorii, almost querulous this time.

'That sword . . .' Calatin pointed a tremulous finger.

Church eyed it curiously, then shrugged. 'Come on,' he said with a confidence that belied his thoughts. His hand was afire with pain and his body was racked with aches. 'Or are you going to back out now you know I'm ready to take you?'

Calatin raised his chin nobly, but his eyes flickered from side to side as if he were searching for a way out. There was an instant of brief despair that was so profound Church was taken aback, and then Calatin raised his own sword and advanced.

They circled each other warily; if either of them had expected an echo of their previous confrontation, they both soon realised the dynamic had changed. Calatin was cautious, his step unsure, afraid to come within Church's circle; that in turn gave Church confidence, although he couldn't grasp quite why things had altered.

Church knew his only hope was to eliminate all the negative impressions bearing down on him: the pain he felt from his many injuries, the physical and spiritual accumulation from weeks of striving, suffering and numerous set-backs. The upsetting wash of threat and evil that came off the Fomorii had to be put on one side, however much it felt like pins stabbing his flesh; but he had trouble shaking the rumbling paranoia that they were moving in to strike every time he turned his back to them. He fixed his attention on Calatin's face, a cauldron of conflicting emotions the Fomorii leader would have done better burying deep. In there, for the first time, Church saw hope.

The tension rose as they continued to move, feinting but never quite striking. And with each *faux* beginning to the battle Church could see Calatin's anxiety rising; he was *afraid* to attack, and just as afraid to continue dodging the battle for fear of losing face.

Eventually his twisting emotions proved too much for him. He lashed out, but even in his unfocused blow his remarkable skill came to the fore. All Church saw was the rusty, stained blade suddenly become a blur, whirling in circles before licking out. He ducked at the last minute, but the serrated edge still took a jagged slice out of the meat of his cheek; an instant's hesitation and he would have lost his head. He cried out in pain and a brief cruel smile leapt to Calatin's lips. The Fomor felt a surge of confidence from first blood, and pressed his attack with a rapid scything motion.

Church barely saw it, but his sword leapt up to block and Calatin's blade slid off with a bone-jarring clang. A coldness washed through Church's limbs; his sword had blocked it *of its own accord*. By rights he should be dead; in his pain-dulled state he hadn't seen enough of the attack to make any move himself.

He took his eye off Calatin to survey the grim, black sword. Calatin saw this opening and attacked again, lunging in an attempt to disembowel Church. The sword forced Church's arm to parry and then came up sharply, ready to attack if Church gave it the lead.

Church felt sick from the sensation; it was as if there was something alive in his hand. It no longer really felt like a sword at all; it was almost slimy and resilient in his grip.

When Calatin attacked again, this time swinging low in a bid to take off a kneecap or two, Church blocked it with ease. And at the same time he allowed the sword to guide him, putting his weight behind the attack. It passed through Calatin's defences easily and ripped open his forearm. Calatin howled wildly in pain. When it had passed Church saw the hesitancy of true fear in his flickering eyes. Church expected the ranks of Fomorii to show some sign of emotion at this weakness, but there was only utter silence; and that was more damning.

Church took a step back to inhale deeply; sweat was soaking through his clothes. He was ready for Calatin to seize the opportunity, but now his opponent was even more wary than when they had started.

Calatin moistened his dry lips, couldn't take his eyes off the sword. 'He gave it to you, did he not?'

Church ignored him, still breathing deeply. He was surprised to notice the perception of the blue fire Tom had taught him was now almost operating independently. Across the landscape he could see the thin azure lines growing brightly in the deep darkness. Some were broken, others intermittent; the land still needed to be truly awoken. But they were growing stronger. And there on the tor the earth force was strongest of all. He had a sense of being engulfed in a brilliant blue light shining up out of the ground; it was awesome and transcendent, and he could feel it seeping into every fibre of his being, refreshing him, starting to heal him. Above all, it gave him a deep sense of connectedness that added meaning to his existence, and from that he drew a deep, abiding strength. He was ready.

'I should have destroyed him,' Calatin said bitterly.

In desperation Calatin drove himself forward, hacking and slashing like a wild man. There was no sign of the decaying, fey persona he normally exhibited, just a driven, cruel ferocity.

But it was not enough. Infused with the blue fire, with the black sword dancing like a beast in his hands, Church moved sleekly to block every blow, returning each with a harder strike that drove Calatin back and back. A lunge came through and ripped open the Fomor's breastplate. Another sliced across the bridge of Calatin's nose; he howled again, flicking black droplets from the wound as he shook his head.

And still Church moved forward. A blow came down so hard that Calatin went to his knees to block it. He wriggled out and danced away as Church's next attack missed him by a whisker. But Calatin had nowhere to turn. The Fomorii forces were pressing too close, as if they were refusing to allow him to retreat; nor were they giving him any aid. And that was just how Church expected them to see it: in a race without any compassion, the weak should be allowed to perish so that the collective would grow stronger.

Although Calatin knew his end was coming, to his credit, he never gave in to his fear. It was only visible in his eyes, but to Church it shone out like a beacon.

Church bore down on him with the last reserves of his energy, all his joints aching from the explosive vibrations of sword on sword. A flurry of thrusting and slashing smashed through Calatin's defences, knocking his sword hand to one side. His chest was wide open for the killing strike, but Church knew there would be only a second before Calatin brought the sword back to block the blow. It was his moment of victory, yet he couldn't take it. Although Calatin was a god, there was too much humanity in his eyes.

Not a god at all, Church thought.

But the sword would not be deflected. With cruel efficiency it attacked, almost leaping from his fingers as it propelled itself into Calatin's chest, burrowing deeper like a worm in sand. There was too much black blood; Church had to cover his face with his free arm. Calatin bucked and writhed like there were thousands of volts going through him. As Church looked back he was struck by the expression on the Fomor's face: utter desolation that was almost painful to see. Calatin knew he was dying, finally and irrevocably, and for a being that thought he was an inexorable part of existence it was an ultimate terror that Church couldn't begin to grasp.

Sickeningly, the sword continued to vibrate in Calatin's chest, seeming to suck the life out of him, everything out of him. His cheeks grew hollow, his clothes and then his flesh began to fall in drapes on his bones, and then even the skeleton itself was pulled out of him. Church let go of the handle, but still the sword continued until there was nothing left of Calatin but a smear on the ground, and soon even that was gone.

But that wasn't the end of it. As the sword clattered on to the stone and turf, it began to change shape, growing smaller, sprouting legs like a scorpion, until it scurried off rapidly across the ground to disappear in the enclosing dark. And Church knew then that it was not a sword, but Mollecht's own Caraprix, the strange, symbiotic creature that all the gods carried. But the vampiric qualities it had displayed in its final attack gave Church pause; he wondered whether the odd little creatures really did act at the behest of the gods, or if the gods were their puppets.

He didn't have time to consider the notion any more. The moment Calatin passed on, the Fomorii had begun to move warily, but now they had seen the Caraprix depart they were advancing on him menacingly. He wanted to fight them too, but all he could do was drop feebly to his knees, every last reserve of energy drained out of him.

This is it, he thought, more with weariness than despair. He'd done his best, more than he thought he ever could do. If he had failed, that was all he could truly ask of himself.

The Fomorii rose up in front of him, an enormous wall that must surely have been death. And up and up it went, his perception giving up as it tried to comprehend the eternal permutations of form. It hovered over him, like a tidal wave waiting to smash down on a coastal village, and he was cast in the coldest shadow he had ever experienced.

Church bowed his head, waiting for the strike. But the wave seemed to hang there interminably. In hesitant disbelief, he looked up just as it trembled, then twisted and finally broke apart in a wild thrashing. Dark, frantic motion erupted all around him, and he suddenly felt he had instead been sucked into a sable whirlpool. There was that strange rending metal noise he had heard earlier, faces that were alien, yet still filled with a recognisable fear, the rapid movement of fleeing forms.

And suddenly the whole night was lit in gold.

'Finally,' Church said, barely able to believe what was happening. 'The cavalry.'

The still-thrashing, dismembered body of a Fomor crashed into the ground in front of him, spraying foul gunk all around.

Another Fomor sent him flying several feet, and for a few seconds he blacked out. When he came round, chaos had erupted everywhere. The Fomorii were scrambling back and forth and the air was suffused with a high-pitched squealing like pigs in an abattoir. Church had to keep on the move to dodge the rampaging beasts, now oblivious to him. The ground had grown slick with the ichor that served as the creatures' blood and he was slipping and sliding, feeling his skin burn where it splashed up on him. Body parts rained from the sky, bouncing off him as he ran. In disarray and shock he had the awful impression he was looking at a vista from hell.

And then the blackness of the Fomorii parted and suddenly every-where there was golden light, and before him was Maponus, moving through the scurrying forms like the righteous wrath of God, dealing out death and punishment on either side. Bodies burst into flames or just fell apart. Others were crushed by his powerful hands. His face was beautiful and serene, as if he were doling out salvation instead of carnage, but his clothes and his golden skin were covered in the black muck that sprayed out of his victims. As he advanced, his wide, innocent eyes staring out of a now-black dripping face, Church knew it truly was Hell. He fell to his knees in the face of such power, not strong enough to run any more. Maponus bore down on him relentlessly.

Before the Good Son reached him, a blur shot out of the corner of Church's vision, yanked at his shirt and dragged him across the grass out of the insane god's path. Church crashed, gasping, on to the ground and rolled over to look up into the face of the Bone Inspector.

'Nearly didn't make it.' The old man's eyes rolled with a hint of madness at the terrors he had experienced. 'Trying to drive him up here . . . get him to follow me . . .'

'You did good.' Church gripped the old man's forearm in gratitude. 'To be honest, I'd started to give up hope.'

'Never do that.' The Bone Inspector slumped down wearily, clutch-ing his staff for support.

No longer able to talk, they both turned to watch the retreating darkness as the Fomorii swept down the tor like oil running off glass. Behind them the Good Son followed, wreaking his crazed vengeance for a spoiled existence; light flashed off him, wondrous and terrifying to see.

But when Maponus reached the foot of the tor, Church was surprised to see an odd effect in the sky, as if it were folding back on itself. And through it came riding members of the Tuatha Dé Danann, swathed in a diffuse golden light. At their head Church recognised Nuada Air-gitlámh, who had helped bring him back from the dead on Skye. He was wielding the sword of power, Caledfwlch, which they had liberated from its hiding place. The five or six gods behind him were not known to Church, until he saw the final rider on a white horse with glaring red eyes. It was Niamh.

She couldn't shirk her responsibilities either, Church thought.

The Tuatha Dé Danann rounded on Maponus, herding him towards the rift in the air. At first he was reluctant, but then it seemed as if a small acorn of sanity in his mind recognised his brethren and he moved speedily and willingly towards the rift. A second later it closed behind them and the Golden Ones were gone.

Despite all the suffering he had caused, Church hoped the Tuatha Dé Danann would be able to find some kind of peace for Maponus after all his centuries in Purgatory. The Fomorii didn't appear to notice that their harrower had departed, or if they did, they were consumed with too much fear to give up their fleeing. The streams of shadows disappeared into the greater darkness of the night.

And then they were alone on the tor, a small island in a sea of carnage, as a sudden stillness descended over everything.

It was a moment that should have been savoured, but Church could no longer turn away from the horrors of his responsibility; there was nothing to distract him any more. He stood up, looking back and forth. Tears sprang from nowhere to brim his eyes.

'I wish I'd died,' he said honestly.

The Bone Inspector stared at him, uncomprehending. 'Where are you going?'

'To face up to my responsibilities.' Church looked along the bleak, million-mile walk to the house.

He flexed his fingers, wondering if he had it in him, knowing he had no choice. He sighed, brushed the tears from his eyes. He took the first step.

He was halfway across the distance, feeling his legs grow more leaden with each yard, when the door of the house swung open.

Oh God, not Laura now. He couldn't help a sweep of dismay at having to deal with her acid tone and cheap mockery.

But the figure that lurched out in a daze had a pale, beautiful face and long, dark hair. Church felt a swell in his chest that he thought would tear him apart.

And then he was running crazily, not knowing where the reserve of energy had come from, and he swept Ruth up in his arms and crushed her to him like some fool in a stupid romantic film. But it was honest, raw emotion: relief, and joy, and most of all, love. It filled every fibre of him to such a degree it was as if he were feeling the emotions for the first time.

He looked up into her face, afraid the features would change in some last, cruel blow, but it was definitely her. When he began to speak she silenced him with her fingers on his lips.

'No,' she cautioned. A panic seemed to be growing deep in her eyes. 'No. It's not like that. It's still bad.'

'What do you mean?'

She shook her head, unable to find the right words. Instead she made him put her down, then took his hand and led him back into the house. He looked round for Laura to join in the celebrations, but the place was empty.

'I'm so sorry,' Ruth said in a small voice.

CHAPTER TWENTY-ONE
Lughnasadh

'It was like I was floating above myself. I could see and hear everything that was going on around me, and some things that were happening even further afield.' Ruth stared bleakly at the makeshift bed where she had lain for so long.

Church slumped in the corner, eyes fixed on the middle distance, too weary to attempt to rationalise anything. There was no sound apart from Ruth's voice and the occasional gust of wind battering against the aged walls.

'It was near the end . . . I know it was near the end because my consciousness was starting to break up like some radio station on the edge of its frequency. I could see what was happening to my . . . my shell.' She looked down at her belly, now returned to its normal size and shape. There was no sign of the disfiguring blemishes, and her skin had regained its usual colour. In fact, apart from the intense weariness that afflicted her spiritually as well as physically, there was no way of telling she had been through anything.

'You know, she wasn't as bad as we all thought,' she said, glancing up at Church.

'I never thought she was bad.'

'You didn't think she was good. I didn't. Especially me. And the worst thing was, she didn't even think it herself.'

Church let the exhaustion pull his head down. He could feel each breath going in and out of his lungs. 'What happened to her?'

'But she was good, you see. She deserved to be one of us.'

Church looked up sharply. 'What happened?'

'While you were out there facing up to the Fomorii there was a sound like an animal snuffling and scrabbling around the house. Laura got frightened by it. She looked round for anything that might make a weapon to defend me. You know, she was pretty close to the edge by then, and not just because of what was going on outside.'

'You're pretty good with that perception.' It sounded a little more sour than he had intended.

Ruth ignored him. 'I think she was about to barricade the door when it suddenly burst in. It was Cernunnos.'

Church's brow furrowed. 'He came here? What about Shavi?'

Ruth shook her head. 'It wasn't his Wild Hunt persona. It was the pleasing side of him . . . the Green side. He had a bottle.' She was staring blankly at the wall of unintelligible writing as if the images were playing out like a movie. 'Small, smoky-coloured. He spoke to Laura—'

'What did he say?' Church snapped. His inability to understand her was grating on him; he could sense some mystery behind it all that he didn't want revealed.

'I didn't hear it all. But the bottle held some kind of . . . potion, I suppose . . . something that Shavi had been after—'

'And he didn't say anything about Shavi?'

'No, I told you. The potion was supposed to save me. It wouldn't destroy Balor. It would . . .' She struggled for the correct words.

'What?' Church said in exasperation.

Ruth took a deep breath to compose herself. 'He explained it all to Laura so she could make the right choice. He kept saying it was important she knew what she was doing. She didn't have to, there was no pressure, she could walk away – I remember him saying that, not quite in those words. But it was there if she wanted to use it. He wanted to help us, Church. He'd marked Laura and me—'

'A sacrifice. There always has to be a sacrifice.'

'With magic, yes.' She paused. 'I suppose there's a price to pay for everything.'

He put a hand over his eyes. 'What was it?'

'It wouldn't destroy Balor, but it could transfer him—'

'What?' He felt something cold and hard start to grow inside him.

'Cernunnos left the bottle on the floor and went. Laura stared at it for a while. I could see her face, all the emotions so raw on it . . . I wish I'd been nicer to her. I was a bitch.'

'She was a bitch. Don't start eulogising her.' What did he feel? Anger? Bitterness? He was surprised he felt anything.

'She took the bottle. I don't think she knew whether she was supposed to drink it or pour it on me or what. But when she pulled out the stopper this smoke licked up, and it moved like it had a life of its own. And suddenly I was in agony, I mean real pain, worse than anything the Fomorii did to me. It was like wrenching, like . . .' She covered her eyes briefly. 'And the next thing I knew, Laura was face-down on the floor. Out of it. Completely. Mercifully. And Balor was inside her, or wherever he—'

'Christ!' Church chewed on a knuckle, staring at the floor, picturing the scene, wishing he couldn't.

'She transferred it from me to inside herself.'

881

'Christ.'

'She did it for me, Church. For all of us.'

'Christ.'

Ruth wandered over to the window. The Bone Inspector sat forlornly on the lip of the ridge, exhausted, but she didn't seem to see him.

Church looked round. 'Where is she, then?'

Ruth turned to him and her expression said it all. 'The Fomorii took her. While you were out there fighting Calatin, a few of them came in here. One of them was—'

'Mollecht.'

She nodded.

'He gave me what I needed to kill Calatin so he could seize control. And he took her?'

She nodded again. Then she came over and squatted next to him. He rested his head on her shoulder, acceptance crushing him down.

'So they have Balor. They've won.'

They drifted outside in silence. From their vantage point they could see civilisation lit clearly in sodium, the cities glowing orange in the distance, the village oases, the ribbons of lights connecting them, mapping out humanity's hegemony. Church checked his watch, waited. A moment later every light winked out as one.

'It's time,' he said bleakly.

From the south came a distant howling, growing louder. A wind tore across the countryside, bending the trees, ripping at the hedgerows, screaming up to them like lost souls en route to hell. The clouds tumbled before it, spreading out across the sky, obscuring the stars one by one until there wasn't even the light of the heavens to see by: only complete darkness, impenetrable, claustrophobic, too terrible for life. And in that awful howling wind Church could almost hear Laura's death-scream. It was all over. Balor had been reborn. The End of Everything had begun.

So this is the way the world ends, he thought.

Except it didn't. Things carried on the same, though sapped of hope, and everything he could pick out in the dark was dismally grey. There was the wind, quieter now, and Ruth beside him, unmoving. Or perhaps it was just an illusion, random flashes on his mind's eye. But it smelled the same, and it sounded the same, and that was worse than a sudden ending.

'I can't believe she's dead.' Church stared into the heart of the blazing fire, remembering Skye at Beltane when they thought they had suffered a terrible defeat; not really knowing what the word meant. Behind him, Mam Tor loomed up against the sky; he couldn't bear to stay on it any longer. But at least the initial shock and dissolution had finally subsided. Now there was only a sickening numbness as he tried to come to terms with what the future held.

'We all knew there was a chance we were going to get it at some point.' Ruth threw more wood on the blaze, enjoying the feel of the heat on her skin; despite everything, enjoying just being alive. 'I'm sorry, Church, that sounded really harsh and I didn't mean it like that—'

'I know, I know. We were all aware our lives were hanging by a thread. But however much you think about people dying, it never really prepares you.'

'It's a shock at the moment, more than anything because she was the last one you would have thought would have put her neck on the line. She never gave any sign—'

'That's because it was all going on inside.'

Ruth eyed him incisively. 'Did you know what she was really like?'

He shook his head. 'I knew she had depths, but I don't think anybody in the world really knew what was going on inside her head.'

'Did you love her?'

There was a long pause. 'I don't know. I don't think so. I *cared* for her. This sounds like some stupid sixth-form conversation!' He stood up and paced angrily around the perimeter of the firelight.

Ruth waited till he'd calmed a little before continuing, 'I wonder what's happened to the others.'

'I can't believe they're dead. I'm not even going to think it until I see the evidence in front of me.'

'You have changed, you know.'

He nodded. 'We both have. We've been to the lowest, darkest points of our lives and we've come out the other side. And I think we're both better for it.'

Ruth let his words sink in, then asked, 'Would you have killed me?'

He looked at her suspiciously across the fire, the dancing flames throwing curious shadows across his face. 'I don't know. I knew I ought to.'

'You were right. Of course you were. I would have done it to you. We have to think of the big picture—'

His look stopped her in her tracks; there was too much emotion in it, the backed-up excess of weeks of agonising deliberation. 'There is no big picture. The only one that counts is this one here.' He drew a small rectangle in the air in front of his eyes. 'Reality exists inside us, not out here.' He gestured towards the dark countryside. 'And sometimes one life is more important than millions.'

They stared at each other for a long moment, neither of them sure what to say next. They were saved from having to say anything in the too-charged atmosphere by the Bone Inspector, who strode out of the night with an armful of food. 'There are some houses down the ways. Nobody left alive in them.' He threw the provisions next to the fire and leaned on his staff for support; he looked hundreds of years old in the firelight.

'Are you sticking around?' Church asked him.

'No.'

'What are you going to do now?'

'None of your business.' He paused, then relented. 'There's a lot to do.'

'What's to do? We lost. It's over.'

The Bone Inspector snorted derisively. 'I was right. You are a pathetic little runt.' He was swaying backwards and forwards on his staff, obviously on the verge of collapse.

'What do you mean?' Ruth asked curiously. 'Balor's back. You saw the sky. You could feel it. At least I could, here, in the pit of my belly, like vibrations from a drill going off just under my feet.'

Church nodded. 'I felt it too, only for me it was a queasy feeling as if I'd eaten something rotten.'

'Everybody felt it, even the animals,' the Bone Inspector snapped. 'Something that big shakes the foundation of life.' He gave a hacking cough. 'Look around you,' he continued with watering eyes. 'Is it over? Has the world folded up and been put away? Are we dead and not realising it?' He dropped to his haunches, still holding the staff between his legs as if it were a rudder steering the world. 'Never give up hope. That's the message of life.'

Church noted how like Tom he sounded. He was surprised by how much he suddenly missed his old companion; he wanted the benefit of Tom's wisdom, and his incisive overview of any situation, however bad-tempered he always was.

'We could still do something,' Church suggested hopefully.

'You, not me. Of course you can still do something. That's what you're here for. *In England's darkest hour—*'

'I know, I know, *a hero shall arise.*'

'And if this isn't the darkest of all darkest hours, what is?'

Sighing, Church stared pensively into the fire. 'I wonder how long we've got before he starts wiping everything out.'

'He'll start straight away,' the Bone Inspector said. 'At least once he's recovered from getting dragged back into this God-forsaken world. He can't be in tip-top shape after being locked up on the other side of death for God knows how long. Then there's getting established in his new little nest,' he sneered, 'and motivating his troops, listening to all their whiny little pleas after all that time they've been separated from him.'

Church looked at him curiously.

'And of course he won't be at full strength till he's drained every last drop of power at the next festival, the big one on their calendar, when the gates really do open and all the worst nightmares in the universe come scurrying back to this place to be here for the end of it all.' The Bone Inspector fixed a cold eye on Church, almost daring him to continue.

Church glanced at Ruth. 'You're right, I have changed. Not so long ago I'd have rolled over and died at odds like that. But, you know—'

She nodded in agreement '—maybe there's a chance we *can* do something.'

'Don't get me wrong,' the Bone Inspector continued, 'the End of Everything *has* started. But it's still gathering pace. Maybe you can jam a stick in the spokes, maybe not.'

Church continued to look into Ruth's eyes and he was pleased at what he saw. 'Of all of us, I certainly don't think we were the most deserving. Veitch, maybe, Shavi, they were better than us in many ways. But we've learned a lot from all we've been through and maybe this is our chance to put it to good use.'

'Maybe we can finally prove our worth.'

'Rather you than me,' the Bone Inspector snorted; but Church glimpsed a faint smile before he wiped it away.

'This is our chance, then,' Church said. 'The last one. Rearguard action while the world's going to hell around us.'

Ruth pulled her knees up under her chin. 'It's amazing how brave you can feel when you've got nothing left to lose.'

Church realised she was right; surprisingly, he didn't feel any fear, nor any of the worries nor indecision that had dogged him before. There was a clarity to his emotions that gave him hope. 'What do we have to do?'

The Bone Inspector sucked in a weary breath of air. 'Are you expecting me to do it all for you?'

'I'm expecting you to use some of that knowledge that's been sitting around in your head gathering dust,' Church said sharply. 'We might not have got in this mess if you'd told us more before.'

'Don't get snippy with me. It's secret knowledge for a reason, you idiot. It's not there to be told to any little runt who comes asking—'

'Just give us some guidance,' Ruth pleaded. 'Where do we go from here? We've lost two-thirds of the people helping us – we don't know if they're alive or dead. We've got no idea what the next step is!'

The passion in her voice seemed to strike a chord with him. 'It's a good job you're here. I wouldn't have told that little bastard anything.' He pulled himself up on his staff and walked slowly to the twilight zone beyond the firelight; he appeared to be weighing up his responsibilities. 'All right,' he said eventually. 'But don't go asking me for anything else. The only way you're going to get anywhere is with the sword, the spear, the cauldron and the stone.'

'The Quadrillax,' Ruth said. 'But the Tuatha Dé Danann have them now.'

'And they're not going to help us while I've got the Fomorii taint in my system,' Church said despondently.

'Well you better do something about it, then, hadn't you?' the Bone Inspector said bluntly. 'Remember, it was the spear that killed the Great Beast last time. The sword, the spear, the cauldron and the stone are the only things in the whole of existence with enough power to do him in.'

Deep in thought, Church threw more wood on the fire so it roared away wildly. It seemed to him, at that moment, that the light was more important than anything and he had to do everything in his power to preserve it. 'When we came across two members of the Tuatha Dé Danann one night a few weeks back, I asked them how I could clear the Fomorii corruption out of my system. They said I should travel to the Western Isles to find something called the Pool of Wishes.'

The Bone Inspector shrugged. 'I wouldn't know about that. The Western Isles are somewhere in Otherworld, so the stories say. But I'll tell you this, there's another old story that says if you go down to Mousehole in Cornwall and stand at the quay and look across to Merlin's Rock, you can catch a fairy ship that will take you wherever you want to go.'

Church nodded thoughtfully. 'It isn't a lot, but we've gone a long way on much less.' The Bone Inspector dipped into his pocket and pulled out a half-bottle of whisky. 'Found it in one of the houses.' He took a long slug, then threw it to Church. 'You're at a turning point in your life. The mechanics of the mind are rituals. They tell that ancient bit at the back of your head to clear out the last cycle and prepare to move on to the next. This is your ritual, now – the best we can do under the circumstances. Make a toast.'

Church didn't have to think long. He held up the bottle and said, 'To absent friends. Let's hope they're all well. And to Laura, for being the best of all of us.' He took a drink and tossed the bottle to Ruth.

'I'll drink to that,' she said, 'and I'll say this. It's just the two of us now, like it was when we started. But that'll be enough. And we'll win.' There was so much fire and defiance in her voice Church almost believed her.

After that they sat drinking quietly, talking about their friends, trying to keep them alive with words; and at some point, they looked up from their discussion and found the Bone Inspector had gone, back to his age-old round of the sacred sites of their ancestors.

They moved as close to the fire as they could without burning themselves and kept it well-stoked against the oppression of the night. 'Do you really think we can do it?' Church asked above the crackling of the wood.

'Look what we've achieved so far.' Ruth slid next to him and rested her head on his shoulder; he put his arm around her. 'You killed Calatin—'

'With Mollecht's help.'

'But *you* killed him. And it was your planning that brought Maponus here to devastate the Fomorii forces. You pulled out a great victory when it didn't look like we had a chance.'

'There was a lot of luck—'

'And that's a quality a good leader needs.' She looked up into his dark eyes and smiled. 'But don't try lording it over me, all right?'

They rested silently, half-dozing, but too uneasy to sleep fully. Although they never discussed it with each other, they both knew the world had changed: a faint smell of cinders drifted in the chill wind and there was an unpleasant feeling of a great weight pressing in all around them. And though they waited and waited for the streetlights to come back on, they never did.

Somewhere away in the dark, the Heart of Shadows had started to pulse, a beat that was growing stronger with every passing minute; relentless, like the pounding of war drums signalling the End of Everything.

always forever

book three of the age of misrule

MARK

CHADBOURN

CHAPTER ONE

the End

Icy rain blasted across the deserted seafront like stones thrown by a petulant child. Jack Churchill and Ruth Gallagher kept their heads down, the hoods of their windcheaters up, as they spurred their horses out of the dark countryside. Despite the storm, the ever-present smell of burning was acrid on the back of their throats. Twilight lay heavy on the Cornish landscape, adding to the abiding atmosphere of failure; of a world winding down to die. The heavy clouds rolling across the sea where the lightning flashed in white sheets told them the storm would only grow worse as the night closed in.

Dead street-lamps lined the road, markers for the abandoned vehicles that were rusting monuments to the death of the twenty-first century. Occasionally they caught a glimpse of candles in windows or smelled smoke from fires in the houses that had hearths; beyond that, there was only the oppression of the growing gloom.

As they rounded a bend, a light burned brightly in the middle of the road. Surprised, they slowed their horses until they saw the illumination came from an old-fashioned lantern held aloft by a man wrapped in a sou'wester, struggling to keep himself upright in the face of the gale.

'Who goes there?' he said in a thick Cornish accent.

'Friends,' Church replied, 'who don't want to stay out in the night a moment longer than we have to.'

The lantern was raised higher to bring them into its glare. It illuminated the face buried deep in the shadows of the hood: suntanned; grey, bushy beard. He eyed them suspiciously. 'Where've you come from?' he yelled above the wind.

'A long way.' Ruth fought to keep her lank hair from her face. 'We started off in the Peak District. It's taken us days—'

'Aye, well, it would.' He looked from one to the other, still unsure.

As the lantern shifted again, Church noticed a shotgun in the crook of his arm. 'You haven't got anything to worry about—'

'You can't trust anyone these days.' He nodded towards a pub that glimmered with candlelight a few yards away. 'In there.'

Church and Ruth dismounted and led their horses towards the inn.

The man followed a few paces behind; Church could feel the shotgun pointed in his direction. But as they tied up their steeds in a makeshift shelter adjoining the pub, the guard relented a little. 'Any news?' A pause. 'What's the world like out there?'

Ruth shook the worst of the moisture off her hair. 'As bad as you'd expect.'

The guard's shoulders slumped. 'Without the telly or the radio it's hard to tell. We hoped—'

'No,' Ruth said bluntly.

It sounded unduly harsh. Church added sympathetically, 'We followed the M5, then the main roads down here. We never ventured into any of the big towns or cities, but—'

'Nothing's working,' the guard finished.

Church nodded.

'You better get in the pub,' the man said with a sigh. 'We haven't had any trouble here in town, but you never know. We've seen what's out there,' – he peered into the night – 'and sooner or later they're going to get brave enough to come in.'

'You're on watch all night?' Ruth asked.

'We do shifts. Everybody's involved. We're trying to keep things going. They'll tell you more in the pub.'

Heads down, they ran from the shelter, but before they reached the door a crack of lightning burst over the sea. Church stopped to stare down the street.

'What is it?' Ruth blinked away the rain, following his eyes.

'I thought I saw something in the light.'

'Probably another guard.'

'It was on the rooftops, moving quickly. Looked like . . .' He paused. 'Let's get inside.'

A blazing log fire in the grate was the most welcoming sight they had seen in days. With the candles flickering in old wine bottles all around the room, it created a dreamy impression of another time. About thirty people were gathered around. A young mother with a baby watched some children playing near the hearth. Four old men played cribbage in one corner with the grim determination of a life-or-death struggle. Everyone looked up when they entered. In one instant Church took in curiosity, suspicion and fear.

He was distracted by a glimpse of himself in a mirror as he passed. His dark hair was now almost down to his shoulders, and his close-cropped goatee was a sign he'd given up fighting against predestination; he resembled the future-vision he'd had of himself in the Watchtower between the worlds, watching a city burn. His features fell into a naturally troubled expression that served to make him look older. But Ruth didn't look any different. Her long brown hair tumbled in ringlets around her shoulders while her face still looked as pretty and serene as the first time he had seen it. There was something new there, though: an enduring confidence that gave her bearing.

A burly man in his fifties hurried over, one large hand outstretched. His skin had the ruddiness of someone who spent a lot of time outdoors in all weathers. 'Welcoming committee,' he said in a loud, deep voice. They each shook his hand in turn. He was Malcolm, a local businessman. 'What brings you to Mousehole? Don't get many tourists these days.' Although he was friendly enough, the steely scent of fear was palpable in the atmosphere.

What's happening to us all? Church wondered.

'We're looking for a safe haven.' Ruth's calmness was the perfect antidote; Church could see everyone warm to her instantly. 'It's not very pleasant out there.' Her understatement made them smile.

'Any idea what's happened?' Malcolm's eyes showed he was both hopeful and afraid of what her answer might be. 'We thought . . . some kind of nuclear exchange . . . ?'

'No,' Church said adamantly. 'There's no sign of anything like that. Whatever's happened, it's not anything nuclear, chemical or biological—'

'Face up to it, Malcolm, it's the End of the World.' A long-haired man in his thirties hung over his pint morosely. 'You can't keep fooling yourself it's something *normal*. For Christ's sake, we've all seen the signs!'

Malcolm grimaced in a manner that suggested he didn't want to hear. 'We're muddling on as best we can,' he continued blithely. 'Set up a local network of farms to keep the food supply going. With no communications, it's proving difficult. But we're pulling through.'

'Boiling water,' the morose man said to his beer. 'Every day. Boil, boil, boil.'

Malcolm glared at him. 'Don't mind Richard. He's still working on his attitude.'

'You're not alone,' Ruth said. 'We've travelled a long way over the last few days. Everywhere people are trying to keep things going.'

That seemed to cheer him. 'I've got to get back to the meeting – a lot of planning needs doing. You must be hungry – I'll get some food for you. We can't offer you much, but—'

'Thank you,' Ruth said. 'We appreciate your generosity.'

'If this isn't a time to be generous, I don't know when is.'

Malcolm left them to dry off at a table in one corner where the candlelight barely reached. 'I feel guilty not telling them everything we know,' Ruth whispered once they were sitting.

'They don't need to know how hopeless it all is.'

Ruth's eyes narrowed. 'You don't think it's hopeless. I can tell.'

Church shrugged. 'We're still walking.'

'That's what I like about you.' Ruth gave his hand a squeeze. 'You're such a moron.'

The exhausting journey from Mam Tor in the High Peaks had been conducted against a background of constant threat; although they saw nothing out of the ordinary, they were convinced they were about to be struck dead at any moment. Somewhere, Evil in its most concentrated form had been born back into the world: Balor, the one-eyed god of death, a force of unimaginable power dragging all of existence into chaos. Whatever it truly was, the Tuatha Dé Danann called it the End of Everything. They had expected fire in the sky and rivers of blood flowing across the land, but the reality had been more prosaic. At first there was simply a vague *feeling* that something was not quite right, then an *impression* of imminent disaster that kept them scanning the lonely landscape. There was a sour taste in the wind and occasional violent storms. The only true sign that the world had slipped further from the light was the complete failure of all things technological. No vehicles moved. Pylons no longer hummed. The night was darker than it had been for more than a hundred years.

The Bone Inspector had suggested Balor would not be at its peak until Samhain, one of the Celtic feast-days marking an occasion when the great cycle of existence unleashed powerful forces. From a Christian perspective it was chillingly fitting: the Church had made Samhain into Hallowe'en, when the forces of evil were loosed on the earth. And there was no doubt the threat was gathering pace. The progression was like the darkness eating away at the edges of the vision of a dying man: each day was a little gloomier. Soon all hell *would* break loose.

There appeared little they could do; and just three months before the doors of Samhain opened: no time at all. But Church's experiences over the preceding months had left him with the belief that there was a meaning to everything; he refused to give in to fatalism, however dark things appeared. If the Tuatha Dé Danann could be convinced to help them, they stood the slimmest of chances.

To win over the Golden Ones, he had to expunge the Fomorii corruption from his body, an act he had been told could be achieved only in the mysterious Western Isles, the home of the gods somewhere in T'ir n'a n'Og. The journey to that place began at Mousehole on the Cornish coast, and a landmark called Merlin's Rock where legend said it was possible to spy a fairy ship that travelled between this world and the next. But one thing in the myths disturbed him greatly: his destination had another name – the Islands of the Dead.

More than anything, Church was glad he had Ruth along with him. Her suffering at the hands of the Fomorii had been terrible, but she had survived to become a much stronger person, free from the fear and doubts that had consumed her before. Now when he looked into her eyes it was like looking into a dark river where deep waters moved silently. She maintained she had died in the last few minutes before Lughnasadh, when she had been close to giving birth to Balor; only Laura's monumental sacrifice had brought her spirit back to her body. Whether that was simply a hallucination on the verge of death or the truth of the matter, it had forged something strong inside her.

As their journey to the South-west progressed, she had been relieved by the reappearance of her owl familiar. But when Church saw it dipping and diving in the grey sky, all he could think of was its manifestation as a strange bird-man hybrid when it had warned him of Ruth's capture in Callender. Could something so alien be trusted, he wondered?

Yet the abilities it had bequeathed to Ruth were extraordinary. She had told him how it had whispered knowledge to her that wormed its way into her mind as if she had known it all her life. When Church fell ill with a stomach bug after drinking from a dirty stream, she knew just the plant for him to chew to restore his health within hours. When they were beaten down by an electrical storm with nowhere to shelter, she had wandered a few yards away from his gaze and minutes later the storm abated. It was amazing, yet also strangely worrying.

Across the roiling, grey sea, lightning twisted and turned in a maniac dance. There was too much of it to be natural: nature's last stab of defiance. Resting against the edge of the window in the bedroom that had been prepared for Ruth, Church let his thoughts drift in the fury of the storm, considering their options, praying the power of hope carried some kind of weight.

'I hope you've got a strong stomach for sailing.'

Ruth's words pulled him from his reverie and he turned back to the pleasant, old room with its wooden floorboards and walls draped with nets and lanterns and other sailing memorabilia. He felt secure in its warm aroma of candle smoke, dust and fresh linen.

Ruth sat on the edge of the bed, finishing the cold lamb, mashed potatoes and gravy the locals had prepared for them. 'I wish we could pay them back for this.' She speared the last piece of meat. 'They must be worried about maintaining their supplies, yet they offered to take us in without a moment's thought.'

'Doing what we hope to do will be payment enough.'

She made a face.

'I'm not giving in to hopelessness. Not any more. You know the band Prefab Sprout? They had a song which went, *If the dead could speak, I know what they would say – don't waste another day.* That's how I want to live my life. Whatever's left of it.'

The candlelight cast a strange expression on Ruth's face, both curious and concerned. 'You really think there's a chance?'

'Don't you?'

She shrugged. 'I try not to think beyond the end of each day.'

The window rattled noisily, emphasising the frailness of their shelter. 'I think about the others. A lot.'

Ruth drew a pattern in the gravy: two interlocking circles. It hypnotised both of them for a second. 'They might still be alive,' she said after a moment or two.

'I feel bad that they might be back at Mam Tor now, wondering where we've gone.'

'If they're alive, I think they'll find us. That bond brought us all together in the first place. It could do it again.'

'That's another thing.' Church sat on the bed next to her, then flopped backwards, bouncing on the sagging mattress. 'Everything we've heard spoke about the five Brothers and Sisters of Dragons being one. The five who are one. One spirit, one force. And now—'

'Laura's dead. No doubt about that one.' Ruth shifted uncomfortably. 'Where does that leave us?' The question hung in the air for a moment and then Ruth pushed away the rickety table and sat back. 'No point thinking about it now.'

'There's something else that strikes me.'

His voice sounded odd enough for her to turn and look at him; one arm was thrown across his face, obscuring his eyes.

'Three months ago when Tom called back the spirits of the Celtic dead, they said one of us would be a traitor—'

'You know any help the dead give is always wrapped up in mischief.' She waited for him to move his arm so she could read his mood, but he lay as still as if he were asleep. 'It's not me, if that's what you're saying.'

'I'm not saying anything. I was just mentioning—'

'Well, don't.'

He mused quietly for a moment. 'I hope I'm up to it.'

'What?'

He gestured vaguely. 'Everything. I do my best, like anyone would, but—'

'Not anyone. That's the difference.'

'—I wonder sometimes how much is expected of me.'

'I've never really been one to believe in Fate, but the more I've been through this, the more I've come to understand it's just a name for something else. We've been chosen, there's no denying it—'

'By God?' he said incredulously.

'By existence. Whatever. We have a part to play, that's all I'm saying.'

He sighed. 'I feel weary. Not physically. Spiritually. I don't know how much longer I can go on.'

'You go on as long as you have to. This is all about a higher calling. It's about doing something important that's bigger than you and me. We can both rest when we're dead.'

There was a long, uncomfortable silence until he said, 'First light, then.' He sat up and kissed her gently on the cheek. It was an act of friendship, but Ruth couldn't help the conflicting emotions she felt for him. *'The two of us together, just like it was right at the start.'*

'You and me against the world, kid.'

Voices echoed up from the bar as Church made his way along the dark landing to his own room: the locals, still trying to make head or tail of a life turned suddenly senseless. There was a twinge of sadness when he listened to their planning and rationalisations. Whatever they did, it would all amount to nothing.

He lay on his own bed for a while, staring into the shadows that clustered across the ceiling as his mind wound down towards sleep. A song by The Doors drifted in and out of his consciousness. Despite everything, he felt a deep peace at the very core of his being. He was focused in his intentions, ready to live or die as Fate decreed. Some of the debilitating emotions he had felt over the last few months were now alien to him: his despair after Marianne's suicide; the cold, bitter desire for revenge when he discovered she had really been killed. The knowledge that her spirit had survived death was a source of transcendental wonder that had lifted him from the shadows. He had known it from the first time her spirit had materialised to him outside his London flat, but in his misery, he had not realised what it truly meant. It was such an obvious thing, he still couldn't believe it had taken him so long to fully understand the monumental, life-shaking repercussions, but life was full of noise and the signal often got lost. The message that made sense of their suffering was plain, at least to him: live or die, there is always hope.

Gradually his thoughts turned to Laura. Amidst the sadness there was a twinge of guilt that he had misjudged her so badly. She had been selfish, cynical, bitter, cowardly, yet in the end she had sacrificed her own life to save another. He missed her. He had never come close to matching the intensity of her feelings for him, a love driven by desperation, loneliness and fear that burned too brightly, but he had certainly felt a deep affection for her. Given other circumstances, perhaps he could have loved her more; he wished he had been able to give her what she wanted.

Somewhere above him there was a loud clattering. The storm had plucked some slates from the roof, or torn down a chimney pot. The gale buffeted the building, wrapping itself around the frail structure, yet deep within the wind's raging he was sure he could hear other sounds. The slates sliding down into the gutter, he guessed. He strained to listen. Despite its violence, the storm was soothing, like womb-sounds. Slowly, his eyelids started to close.

And then he was suddenly overcome with the strangest sensation: that he wasn't in a room in a pub on a storm-tossed coast in a world turned insane by ancient powers. That he was in a stark white laboratory with lights blazing into his eyes, strapped to some kind of bench, with shadowy figures moving all around. Somebody had a syringe waiting to inject into him.

And there was a voice echoing in his head, saying, 'It all depends how we see the world.'

Uneasiness started to knot his stomach. He wanted to shout out, but he couldn't move his lips. *You're daydreaming,* he told himself. Sleep came up on this image suddenly, but the words remained.

'It all depends how we see the world.'

Of late Ruth didn't find sleep easy. Whenever she was on the cusp, her mind flashed back to lying in the cottage on Mam Tor on the brink of death, with the obscene sensations of Balor growing inside her: snakes writhing in her gut, slithering along her arteries and veins, her head resounding with the sensation of a thousand cockroaches nesting in her brain. But the worst was when the final date drew near and the thing had matured. One day she had become aware of alien thoughts crawling through her mind; then the awful feeling of another intelligence nestling at the back of her head, listening to her every secret, knowing her heart, slowly consuming her. It was like she was in a dark room with something monstrous standing permanently behind her shoulder.

She always woke with a start when she reached that point. It had been the ultimate violation, the scars so deep she was terrified she would never forget. And in her darkest moments, she feared much worse than that: that it hadn't gone away at all; that a permanent connection had been made.

Sleep finally came.

Ruth was dreaming, but some part of her sleeping mind recognised that it was not really a dream at all. Few details made sense, only abstract impressions adding shape to her thoughts. First was suspicion, until that gradually coloured into a growing apprehension. Then came the unmistakable sensation that something was *aware* of her. It was not simply unpleasant; she was overwhelmed with an all-consuming mortal dread; she felt she was going to choke and die on the spot.

Somewhere an eye was opening. Before she could drag herself away, the awful weight of its attention was turned fully on her, like a burning white light that made her brain fizz. And crackling through that contact was the intelligence she feared: a familiar, ugly hand reaching out to grip her. Her entire being recoiled. She wanted to flee, screaming, but it held her fast, probing continually, peeling back the layers of who she was.

She dreamed of a black cloud, as big as the world, and in the centre of it, the unflinching eye that watched her alone. It was the source of insanity and hatred and despair. It was the worst of existence. The End of Everything.

He had noticed her.

Balor, she thought, and snapped awake as the word burned through her mind.

Her eyes ranged around the room without seeing. Aspects of the contact still seared her mind. She remembered . . . Black forces moving up around the edge of existence, starting to skin the world, pecking away at humanity, preparing to strip the carrion from the bones of all life.

She shivered at the thought of what lay ahead, but before she could begin to consider the depth of her fears, she half-caught a movement that snapped her out of her introspection.

Something was outside her window.

Church awoke, irritable and out-of-sorts, with a nagging in his subconscious. The storm still rampaged across the seafront, but there was another sound he knew had been the cause of his waking: an owl's shriek mingling with a high-pitched mewling that set his teeth on edge. He was out of bed in an instant, pounding along the landing towards Ruth, his mind flashing back to all the blood in her room in Callander.

At her door the mewling was so intense it made his stomach turn. Without a second's hesitation, he put his shoulder to the door.

Wind and rain gusted into his face through the windows hanging jaggedly in their frame. Shattered glass crunched underfoot. Outside, Ruth's owl emitted a hunting shriek. An impression of a grey wolf at bay formed in one corner, but then the image coalesced into something smaller, but just as frightening: a dark figure like a black spider. Even the quickest glance increased Church's queasiness. It was obviously a man, yet there was something sickeningly alien about it too.

When he turned to look at Ruth he saw her face was so cold and hard with brittle rage she was a different person. She was hunched back near the bed, her hair flailing around in the wind, one hand moving slowly before her as if she were waving to the intruder. Inches from her palm the air was gelatinous, moving out in a slow wave to batter her assailant with increasing pressure. Whatever she was doing, the creature's mewling turned into howls of agony. It clutched a hunting knife and looked torn between throwing itself forward to stab her and fleeing.

Ruth's concentration shifted slightly and her power flagged. The eyes of the creature took on a murderous glow as it attacked, screeching. Church was rooted in horror; Ruth didn't stand a chance.

Her brow knitted slightly, her hand made one insistent cutting action and the intruder collapsed in an unconscious heap.

Filled with questions, Church moved towards her, but when her head snapped in his direction a chill ran through him. She was still caught up in the intensity of the moment, fury locked in her face, so much that she barely recognised him. Her hand lifted, ready to strike out.

'Ruth!'

It took an uneasy second or two for recognition to seep into her coldly glittering eyes. 'The bastard thought he could take me unawares again.' Her voice was drained of energy.

Cautiously, Church approached until he was sure the Ruth he had seen earlier had departed. It wasn't the time to voice his doubts. Instead he asked, 'What is it?'

She levered herself off the bed and crossed the room. 'What is it?' she repeated bitterly. To Church's discomfort she launched a sharp kick at the prone figure. 'He's the bastard that cut off my finger.' She held up her hand to show him the mass of scar tissue that marked the missing digit. 'The bastard that delivered me to the Fomorii and put me through weeks of hell.' She used her foot to roll the intruder on to his back. 'Callow.'

Church started when he saw the figure's face for the first time. It was indeed Callow, but so transformed he was almost unrecognisable. The wild silver hair and dark, shabby suit were still there, but his skin was as dry and white as parchment across which the veins stood out in stark black. Although he was unconscious, his lidless eyes continued to stare; in his gaping mouth they could glimpse the dark of rotting teeth.

'My God, what have they done to him?' Church knelt down to inspect him, but the sour stench that came off the once-man made him pull back.

'Careful. He'll be awake soon.'

They bound him tightly in the old fishing net that had hung on one wall, then waited for him to come to his senses. It was unnerving to watch his constantly staring eyes, not knowing if he was still unconscious or slyly watching them, but a slight tremor in his facial muscles gave away his waking.

'I ought to kill you,' Ruth said.

'Do it. Put me out of my misery.' He looked away. Tears had formed in the corner of his eyes, but unable to blink them away, he had to wait for them to break.

'Don't try to make us feel sympathy,' Ruth sneered. 'You drained the well dry a long time ago.'

'I don't want sympathy, or pity, or any other pathetic emotion.' It was the voice of a spoiled child. 'I want you dead.'

The curtains flew up like a flock of birds as another gust of wind and rain surged in. 'We were very generous to you when we first met,' Church said.

'I wouldn't look like this if not for you. I wouldn't be on my own, neither fish nor fowl. I can't move amongst people any more, and Calatin will no longer—'

'Calatin's been wiped from all existence by one of his own kind.' Church watched the confused emotions range across Callow's face.

After a moment he began to cry again, slow, silent, juddering sobs that racked his body. 'Then there's nowhere for me!'

Unmoved, Ruth turned to Church in irritation. 'What are we going to do with him?'

The sobbing stopped suddenly. Callow was watching them intently. 'Little pinkies!' He started to giggle at this. 'Five fingers, and I'm taking them one at a time, to pay you back for raising your hand against me! I took your finger, did I not, girlie? Your life should have followed, but I can rectify that, given half a chance. And I have another finger in my collection, too.'

It took a second or two for his meaning to register, and then Ruth flew across the room in fury. 'What do you mean?'

The black veins tattooing his face shifted as his sly smile grew wider. 'One little pinkie, one little life—'

Ruth cut his words short with a hefty blow to the side of his head. Church caught her wrist before she could repeat the assault.

'Temper, temper.' Callow's overly theatrical voice was incongruous against his hideous appearance. Yet when he looked into Ruth's face his arrogance ebbed from him. He muttered something to himself, then stated, 'The long-haired Asian boy, the one as pretty as a girl—'

'Shavi.' The word became trapped in Ruth's throat.

Callow nodded soberly. 'He's dead. Most definitely. I took his life, and his finger, in Windsor Park.'

That last detail was the awful confirmation; Windsor Park had been Shavi's destination in his search for the solution to Ruth's predicament.

Ruth walked to the shattered window where she stood in the full force of the gale, looking out into the night, hugging her arms around her as if to protect her from her sadness. She was such a desolate figure Church wanted to take her in his own arms to comfort her. Instead, he turned his attention to Callow.

The twisted figure giggled again like a guilty schoolboy. Church's overwhelming sorrow began to transmute into a hardened rage. It would have been the easiest thing in the world to ease his emotions by striking out, but he controlled himself.

'I feel sorry for you,' he said to the hunched figure.

That seemed to surprise Callow, who looked upset and then angry. 'The first of five!' he raged. 'You'll all follow!'

Church slipped his arm round Ruth's shoulders; she was as cold and rigid as a statue. The rain was just as icy and stung his eyes shut, but he remained there with her until she slowly moved closer to him.

'Poor Shavi,' she said quietly.

Church recalled his friend's deep, spiritual calmness, his humour and love of life. Shavi had been a guiding light to all of them. 'We mustn't let it drag us down,' he whispered.

Ruth dropped her head on to his shoulder, but said nothing.

They rose at first light after a night in Church's bed, trying to come to terms with Shavi's death. Although they had known him for only a few months, he had affected them both deeply. They felt they had lost much more than a friend.

The seafront was awash with puddles and scattered with the debris deposited by the gales, but it was brighter and clearer than any morning they had experienced since Lughnasadh, with the sun rising in a powder-blue sky and not a cloud in sight. It felt strangely hopeful, despite everything.

Ruth's room, where they had bound and gagged Callow, was reassuringly silent as they passed. No one else was up at that time so they ventured hesitantly to the kitchen for breakfast. Aware of the shortage of food, they toasted a couple of slices of home-made bread each to take the edge off their hunger. While they ate around a heavily scarred wooden table, Church surveyed the jars of tea and coffee on the shelves.

'I wonder what's happening in the rest of the world,' he mused.

'I thought about this.' Ruth eyed the butter, but resisted the urge. 'We get the analogues of Celtic gods because it's part of our heritage, our own mythology. Do you think they got Zeus in Greece, Jupiter in Italy, some Native American gods in America, Vishnu and Shiva or whatever in India? The same beings perceived through different cultural eyes?'

Church shrugged. 'Possibly. What I can't figure out is why Britain is the battleground.'

'With communication down, anything could be happening. The rest of the world might be devastated for all we know.'

Church couldn't take his eyes off the coffee and tea, things taken for granted for centuries. 'The global economy will have crashed. There'll be death on a massive scale – famine, disease. No international trade at all. Even here in the UK we've forgotten how to feed ourselves locally. What about in less-privileged areas?'

'Let's look on the bright side: at least all the bankers and money-lenders will be out of a job.'

His laugh was polite and humourless.

'Best not to think about it.' Ruth watched him from the corner of her eye while she chewed on her dry toast, trying to see any signs of the melancholy that had debilitated him too many times in the past. 'Creeping death is the last thing we need to worry about. Everything could be over in the blink of an eye.'

'You're right.' He stood up and stretched.

'I always am. You should know that by now. It's my hobby.' She finished her toast and tried to ignore the rumblings that still came from her belly. 'We need to decide what we're going to do with Callow.'

Church cursed under his breath. 'I'd forgotten about that bastard.'

'We could execute him.' She appeared to be only half-joking.

Church forced a smile that faded quickly. 'We can't leave him here. These people have enough problems without a psycho like that around. And if Ryan and Tom are still alive he'll just go after them—'

'We can't take him with us!'

'We don't know we're going anywhere yet. If we do find the ship, we might be able to do some good for him. I'm going to try to get the Fomorii shit cleaned out of my system. Maybe we can do the same for him—'

'Do some good!' she said incredulously. 'The bastard murdered Shavi! Almost killed Laura.' She showed him the gap between her fingers.

'I know, I know.' He waved her protestations away. 'But still. Keep your friends close and your enemies closer, they say.'

Ruth grunted in grudging agreement, but as she rose from the table she muttered, 'I still think we should execute him.'

'You sound more like Laura every day.'

The morning was brittle, but filled with the warmth of a good summer. The air had the salty tang of seaweed and fish. In the daylight, Mouse-hole was quaint and comforting, hunkered up against the rugged Cornish coastline. Church and Ruth herded Callow along the deserted seafront, the half-man keeping his peeled-egg eyes away from the brilliant light of the sun. Church was disturbed how the creature had begun to grow into his new form; his manner of walking had become almost insectile in the way he skittered in and out of the gutter, a little too fast, a tad too angular.

'You make a bolt for it, I'll boil those freaky eyes out of your head,' Ruth said calmly. 'You know I can do it.'

Church eyed her, not sure if it *was* within her new powers, which were as mysterious to him as the sea, a feeling she did nothing to dispel. Callow flashed her a brief glance that suggested he would kill her, given half a chance.

'What do we do when we get there?' Ruth asked.

'We call out for the ship to come to us.' It sounded so stupid, he winced. He wished Tom were there. Despite the Rhymer's brusque and generally unpleasant manner, Church missed his wisdom and his knowledge about all the new, strange things that had found a place in the world.

The information they had found in the pub pointed them in the direction of Merlin's Rock. As Callow scuttled ahead of them, Church couldn't shake the ludicrous image of the world's most bizarre couple out walking their dog.

Ruth glanced at the white-rimmed waves before flashing a teasing smile at Church. 'Better get calling, then.'

'Your trouble, Ruth, is you're too strait-laced to let yourself go,' he said wryly. 'You should unbutton a little.'

'I'll take that on board, Mr Black Pot.'

Callow started to edge away, sure the others couldn't see his subtle movements. Church grabbed the collar of his jacket and hauled him forward so he teetered on the edge over the choppy waves. 'Enjoy the view. You might never see it again.'

'You can't make me go!' Callow protested.

'I can't make you swim, either, but I can put you in a position where you have no choice.'

'You don't understand! Those wretched golden-skinned creatures will detest everything about me. They'll make *me* pay for what the Night Walkers did to me, and it's not *my* fault!'

'They don't care too much for me either,' Church replied. 'Thankfully I don't give a toss what those in-bred aristocrats think. They might believe they're better than us, but they're not, and given half a chance I'll bring that home to them.'

'They'll hurt me!'

'Not while I'm there. You deserve some justice for what you've done, Callow, but not at their hands. You're one of us and if anyone's going to make you pay—'

Callow struggled frantically. He calmed instantly when Ruth rested a hand on his shoulder.

Church moved away from them and faced the horizon. The wind rustled his long hair with soothing fingers; a tingle ran down his spine. He thought of Frank Sinatra singing 'Fly Me To The Moon', remembering the great times he'd had with that music playing in his head: kissing Marianne in the lounge of their flat in the early hours of New Year's Day, staggering through Covent Garden, drunk with all his friends, watching the dawn come up on a boat on the Thames. They were at the start of something big, a great journey, and there was still hope; he could feel it in every fibre of his being. The moment felt right.

'Come to us.' The wind whipped the words from his mouth. He coughed; then spoke with greater firmness and clarity: 'Come to us. Take us to the Western Isles.' Once again his voice was caught by the wind, but this time it rolled out across the waves. The tingling in his spine increased a notch.

Cautiously he scanned the horizon. The weather was so clear he would see any ship miles away. He glanced back at Ruth, unsure.

'Be patient,' she said firmly.

Once more he spoke loudly. 'I beseech the Golden Ones to carry us, their humble servants, away to the wonders of the Western Isles.' Behind him, Callow sniggered.

For several long minutes he waited, sure he was making a fool of himself, but gradually he began to sense slight changes in the atmosphere. The air grew more charged, until he could taste iron in his mouth, as if he were standing next to a generator. He looked back at Callow and Ruth and saw they could sense it too; Ruth was smiling, but Callow had an expression of growing anxiety. Church couldn't stop himself smiling either – almost laughing, in fact: a ball of gold had formed in his gut and was slowly unfolding along his arteries and veins. Everything around became more intense. The sea shimmered as if the waves were rimmed with diamonds, emeralds and sapphires and the sun's golden light suffused every molecule of the air. The scent of the ocean was powerfully evocative, summoning a thousand childhood memories. The wind caressed his skin until every nerve tingled.

This is the way to see the world, he thought.

Despite the glorious morning, a misty luminescence had gathered along the horizon like a heat haze over a summer road, igniting in him a feeling of delighted anticipation that he could barely contain.

'It's coming,' he whispered.

It felt like the air itself was singing. Church realised he was kneading his hands in expectation and had to hold them tightly behind his back to control himself.

The white, misty light curled back on itself, suggesting a life of its own. There was a billow, another, and then something could be glimpsed forcing its way through the intangible barrier. His heart leapt.

A second later the ship was visible, ploughing through the waves towards him. It gleamed brilliantly in the sunlight, a water-borne star of gold, silver and ivory. At first it looked like a Phoenician galley he had seen during his university studies. Then it looked Greek, and then Roman, then like nothing he had ever come across before, its shape changing with each crash of white surf on its prow, although he knew it was his own perception that was altering. A white sail marked with a black rune on a red circle soared above it, but the ship didn't appear to be driven by the wind, nor were there any oars visible. Every aspect of it was finely, almost oppressively, detailed. Fantastic golden carvings rolled in undulating patterns along each side, culminating in an enormous splash of silver and white like streamlined swans' wings at the aft. The prow curled round into a statue with an awesome visage made of what appeared to be thousands of tiny, interlocking figures; the eyes glowed ruby-red. There was something about the design of the face that spoke to Church on a deep level; it was as if it were an analogy for the ultimate secret made plain for all to see.

Ruth appeared at his side, eyes fixed on the approaching ship. Her arm brushed his and goosebumps rushed across his skin.

'It's magnificent,' she said in a hushed voice.

Church turned, expecting Callow to be galloping away now Ruth had abandoned his side, but he remained just as fixated, although the wonder in his face was tempered by a steely streak of terror.

It took five minutes for the ship to reach them. Church attempted to scan the deck on its approach, but whatever was there remained hidden; his eyes couldn't focus on it at all and he was repeatedly forced to look away.

When it was only feet away, a jewelled anchor lowered into the water. Church was beginning to feel a touch of apprehension.

Once the ship was secure, they waited and waited. Ten minutes passed without a sign or sound. Before Church could decide on a course of action, there was a shimmer of movement on the deck, like light striking a mirror. A second later a booming voice rolled out over the water, the quality of it constantly changing across a wide scale so it sounded like it was rising from the deepest depths.

'Who calls?'

Electricity spiked Church's spine and he suddenly wished he were a thousand miles away.

CHAPTER TWO

Beyond the Sea

The gangplank unfurled towards them as mysteriously as the ship had been propelled through the water. It was made of brass, and though there was a mechanical clattering, the motion was as smooth as if it were a carpet. Church released his breath only when it clicked perfectly into place. Everywhere was tranquil; waiting. It was still impossible to see what lay on deck.

When no one summoned them aboard, he put one tentative foot on the gangplank, although it didn't feel strong enough to take his weight. He threw out his arms to steady himself when it gave slightly, but it held firm. He glanced back at the others. Callow was shying away in fear, but Ruth placed her hand between his shoulder blades to propel him forward. He squealed and Church had to grab hold of his collar to prevent him plummeting into the waves; from his expression that would have been the better option.

Cautiously Church led the way. Beneath them, the water slopped against the sea wall in a straightforward wave pattern, as though the ship wasn't even there. Callow's whimpering grew more insistent the closer they got to the deck.

'Any last words?' Ruth said ironically.

'You wouldn't want to hear them.' He took a deep breath and stepped on to the deck.

The moment his foot landed on board, everything became instantly visible. He caught his breath at the sight of numerous figures all around, watching him silently. The taste of iron filings filled his mouth.

'Ho, Brother of Dragons!' The voice made him start, but he recognised its rich, faintly mocking tones instantly.

'I didn't expect to find you here.'

Cormorel was beaming in the same warm, welcoming way Church recalled from their talk around the campfire in the north country, but the darkness behind his expression was a little more obvious. In the sunlight his skin almost gleamed; his hair flowed like molten metal. 'Our brief discussion of the Western Isles gave me a desire to see them again.' Cormorel's smile grew tight as he looked to the shore. 'Besides, the Fixed Lands have lost much of their appeal.'

Church felt irritated at Cormorel's easy dismissal of a place he had professed to enjoy, but he knew by now the Tuatha Dé Danann cared for little. 'You don't have the appetite to face up to Balor,' he said, pointedly.

Cormorel answered dismissively, 'There will come a time, perhaps. But for now the Night Walkers leave us alone, and we, in turn, have more enjoyable things to occupy us.' Brightening, he made a theatrical sweep with his hand. 'But I am forgetting myself! You are an honoured guest, Brother of Dragons. Welcome to Wave Sweeper.'

Church followed his gesture, expecting to see only the Tuatha Dé Danann standing around the deck, but there were many who were obviously not of the Golden Ones, their forms strange and disturbing. Cormorel saw Church's confusion play out on his face. 'Wave Sweeper has always accepted many travellers. The journey to the Western Isles is one of significance to many races, not just the Golden Ones.'

'A pilgrimage?'

Cormorel didn't appear to understand the term. Church was also concerned that the god was talking about the ship as if it were alive. He looked more closely at the wooden deck and the unnervingly detailed fittings flourishing on every part of the structure.

Cormorel noticed Ruth for the first time. 'Sister of Dragons, I greet you.' But then his eyes fell on Callow and a tremor ran across his face. 'What is this? Night Walker corruption, here on Wave Sweeper?' His gaze flickered accusingly to Church.

'He's a danger to others. We can't afford to leave him behind.'

Cormorel weighed this, then reluctantly nodded. He motioned to two gods with the youthful, plastic, emotionless faces of male models. Callow shied away from them until they were herding him in the direction of an open oak door that led beneath deck.

'What are you going to do with him?' Church asked.

'We cannot allow something so tainted by the Night Walkers to move freely about Wave Sweeper. He will be constrained for the remainder of the journey.'

'You won't hurt him?'

'He is beneath our notice.' Cormorel turned, the matter already forgotten. 'Come, let me show you the wonder that is Wave Sweeper before we set sail.'

He led them from the gangplank across the deck, gritty with salt and damp from the spray. The crew and passengers watched them impassively for a moment before returning to their business, as strange and unnerving a group as Church could have expected. He felt over-whelmed at the presence of so many of the Tuatha Dé Danann in one place. The whole array were represented, from those like Cormorel, who appeared barely indistinguishable from humans, to what were little more than blazes of unfocused light he could barely bring himself to examine. Although he could tell Ruth was also disturbed, she maintained an air of confidence that kept Church at ease.

Cormorel was enjoying the attention the other Tuatha Dé Danann lavished on him. *Exhibiting his pets,* Church thought sourly.

'Firstly, we must introduce you to the Master of this ship.' Cormorel directed them to a raised area bearing a wooden steering wheel with ivory and gold handles. Next to it stood a god whose presence took Church's breath away once the shifting perception had settled into a stable form. He stood more than seven feet tall, his long hair and beard a wild mane of silver and brown. His naked torso was heavily muscled and burnished. Gold jewellery wound around his arms from wrist to bicep, but beyond that all he wore was a broad belt and a brown leather kilt. Even from a distance Church could see his eyes were a piercing blue-grey like the sea before a storm. With no sign of emotion, the god watched Cormorel, Church and Ruth approach, standing as still as a statue.

For once, Cormorel appeared humbled. 'Here is the Master of Wave Sweeper, known to you in the ages of the tribes as Manannan Mac Lir, also known as Manawydan, son of Llyr, Barinthus, ferryman to the Fortunate Island, Lord of the Stars, Treader of the Waves, Nodons, Son of the Sea, known as Neptune by the journeyman, Lord of Emain Abhlach, the Island of Apple Trees, known also as the King Leir.'

Church felt little respect for the Tuatha Dé Danann's wilful disregard for humanity, but he feared their power and he knew, although he hated it, that they were needed if the day was to be won. He bowed politely. 'Jack Churchill, Brother of Dragons. I am honoured to be in your presence.' Ruth echoed his words.

Manannan nodded without taking his stern regard off them. 'I welcome you to Wave Sweeper.' His voice sounded like the surf break-ing on a stony beach.

'It is auspicious that the Master greets you at the beginning of your journey,' Cormorel said. 'Who knows? Perhaps it bodes well for you achieving your stated aims.'

'Which are what, Brother of Dragons?' Manannan showed slight curiosity.

'To travel to the Western Isles to cleanse myself of the corruption of the Night Walkers,' Church began, 'and then to beseech the Golden Ones for aid in driving the Night Walkers from the Fixed Lands.'

Manannan was plainly intrigued by the suggestion. 'Then I wish you well, Brother of Dragons, for that is an honourable aim.' Manannan's attention crawled over them uncomfortably for a moment longer before Cormorel ushered them away.

Church and Ruth were gripped with the overwhelming strangeness of their situation, but they were distracted from discussing it by a tall, thin figure looming ahead of them. It appeared to be comprised of black rugs fluttering in the breeze beneath a tattered wide-brimmed hat. In the shadows that obscured the face, Church saw eyes gleaming like hot coals. It stretched out an arm towards Ruth, revealing a bony hand covered with papery white skin. 'Watch your step,' the figure said in a whispery voice like the wind over dry leaves. 'There are things here that would drain your life-blood—'

Before the dark figure could continue, Cormorel stepped between it and Ruth, brushing the arm aside. With one hand in the small of Ruth's back, Cormorel steered her away.

'What was it?' Ruth looked back, but the presence had already melted away amongst the busy crew. She felt as if a shadow lay across her, although the effect diminished within seconds of leaving the figure behind.

'The Walpurgis,' Cormorel replied coldly.

'Yes, but what *was* it?'

'A memory of the world's darkest night. A disease of life. An unfortunate byproduct of the Master's policy of admitting all-comers is that occasionally we must play host to . . . unpleasant travellers.' He eyed Ruth suspiciously. 'You would do well to avoid the Walpurgis at all costs,' he warned.

'Did you hear me calling?' Church asked when they stood in the shadow of the mast.

'We hear all who speak of us.' Cormorel had sloughed off the mood that had gripped him after the encounter with the Walpurgis and his eyes were sparkling once again. 'A muttered word, an unguarded aside – they shout out to us across the void.' He surveyed them both as if he were weighing his thoughts, and then decided to speak. 'You did not call the ship, the ship called you – as it did everyone who travels on board, myself included. Wave Sweeper offers up to us our destiny, revealed here in signs and whispers, symbols that crackle across the void. It is a great honour. For many who travel on Wave Sweeper, the journey *is* the destination.'

The concept wasn't something Church wished to consider; he yearned for the old days of cause and effect, linear time, space that could be measured; when everything made sense.

Irritated by the salty sea breeze, Ruth took an elastic band from her pocket and fastened her hair back. It made her fine features even more fragile, and beautiful. 'You don't mind us coming?'

'We accept all travellers on Wave Sweeper. They are a source of constant amusement to us.'

'That's nice,' Ruth said sourly. She looked out to the hazy horizon, aware of the shortening time. 'How long will it take?'

Cormorel laughed at the ridiculousness of the question. 'We will pass through the Far Lands, Sister of Dragons.'

'We have to be back before Samhain. A long time before.' She fixed him with a stare that would brook no dissent.

'You will be in place to face your destiny.' There was something in Cormorel's smile that unnerved them both.

Before they could ask any further questions, they were hailed from the other end of the deck. Cormorel's companion Baccharus hurried to meet them, his ponytail flapping. Where Cormorel was over-confident, proud and arrogant, Baccharus was humble and almost shy, traits they had never seen in any of the gods before. If they could trust any of them, he was the one.

Ruth greeted him with a smile, Church with a bow, but if anything he was more pleased to see them. 'We are honoured to have a Brother and Sister of Dragons on board the ship that sails the Night Seas,' he said quietly; he even sounded as if he meant it.

Cormorel laid a hand on his friend's shoulder. 'Baccharus will show you to your quarters. They have already been prepared for you—'

'You were expecting us?' Church asked.

Cormorel smiled in his irritatingly enigmatic way. 'Food and drink will be sent to your rooms—' He caught the look in Church's eye and added, 'It is given freely and without obligation. Wave Sweeper is a place that defies the rules that govern our existence. It is the Master's wish.' He gave an exaggerated bow.

Baccharus led them to the door through which Callow had been herded. Behind it, creaking, irregular steps went down into the bowels of the ship. The torches that lit their path were set a little too far apart, so uncomfortable shadows were always clustering. Despite the flickering flames, there was little smoke and no charring on the wooden walls. Ruth steadied herself on the boards at one point, but the surface felt so much like skin she never tried again.

They came on to a corridor that twisted and turned so much it was impossible to see more than fifteen feet ahead or behind. It was oppressively claustrophobic, barely wide enough for one person, with the ceiling mere inches above Church's head; doors were on either side, each with a strange symbol burned into the wood that was not wood. Baccharus stopped outside two doors marked with the sign of a serpent eating its tail.

Or a dragon, Church thought. He let his fingers trace the symbol. It felt as if it had been branded into the wood years before. Not wanting to consider what that meant, he stepped into the room sharply once Baccharus opened the door.

The room unnervingly echoed their bedrooms in the pub, as if they were still on land, dreaming their encounters on Wave Sweeper. A fishing net hung on one side, while lanterns, billhooks and other implements of a sea-faring life covered the walls. The bed was barely more than a bench covered with rough blankets beneath a window with bottle-glass panes that diffused the light in a dazzling display across the chamber; even so, shadows still clung to the corners. A connecting door gave access to Ruth's room, an exact replica of Church's.

Ruth summoned up the courage to touch the wooden walls once more. Something pulsed just beneath the surface, while her feet picked up faint vibrations, as if somewhere in the core of the vessel a mighty heart was beating. The notion left her feeling queasy and disorientated.

Baccharus watched her curiously, as if he could read her thoughts, and then warned, 'The ship is large, with many wonders, but many dangers too. You are free to roam as you see fit, but take care in your investigations.'

Once he had left, Church threw open the window and looked out across the waves. 'This isn't going to be easy.'

'Did you expect it any other way? From the moment we started on this road we've had trouble at every turn.' Ruth examined the cupboards. They were generally empty and smelled of damp and dust.

'You can't trust any of the Tuatha Dé Danann, any of the other creatures. They've all got their own agendas, their own secret little rules and regulations—'

'Then we don't trust them. We trust each other.' Ruth joined him at the window; the sea air was refreshingly tangy, but her face was troubled. 'Last night I had a dream . . .' She chewed on a nail apprehensively. 'No, it wasn't a dream at all. I felt Balor in my head.' The gulls over the sea suddenly erupted in a crazed bout of squawking. 'It knows what we're doing, Church.'

A chill brushed slowly across his skin.

'It was so powerful.' Her eyes were fixed on the horizon. 'And it's growing stronger by the minute. I'm afraid of what the world's going to be like when we get back. And I'm afraid that Balor will be waiting for us.'

The food was delivered about an hour later by one of the blank-faced gods: bread, dried meat, dried fruits, and a liquid that tasted like mead. They ate hungrily and then returned to the deck. Manannan was at the wheel, surveying the horizon, while the crew prepared the ship for departure.

'If we're going to back out, now's the time,' Ruth said. 'Once it sets sail, we'll be trapped with this collection of freaks until the bitter end.' She thought for a moment, then revised her words. 'Until we reach our destination.'

They moved over to the rail to take one last look at Mousehole. People moved quietly along the front, oblivious to Wave Sweeper's presence. The sky was still blue, the sun bright on the rooftops, the wind fresh. Church scanned the length of the coastline, then closed his eyes and breathed deeply.

'I love it,' he said.

'What?'

'Britain. The world. There's so much—' He broke off. 'I never thought about it before. It was just there.'

Ruth said nothing, caught in a moment of admiration for the untroubled innocence that still lay at the heart of him, despite all that was happening.

Twenty minutes later everything appeared to be in place. Manannan looked at various crew members scattered around the ship waiting for a nod of approval before raising his hand and slowly letting it drop. A wind appeared from nowhere, filling the sail with a creaking of canvas and a straining of rope. Almost imperceptibly at first, the ship began to move, turning slowly until it was facing the open sea in a tight manoeuvre that would have been impossible for any normal vessel.

Church allowed himself one last, yearning look back at the Cornish coast and then they were moving towards the horizon, picking up speed as they went.

Wave Sweeper skimmed the sea at an impressive rate. The activity continued on deck, but Church couldn't work out exactly what it was the crew were doing; at times their actions looked nonsensical, yet they were obviously affecting the ship's speed and direction. Overhead, the gulls screeched as they swooped around the sails. Manannan faced the horizon, eyes narrowed against the wind that whisked his mane of hair out behind him.

'Can you feel it?' Ruth asked.

Until then he hadn't, but her perceptions had become much sharper than his. It manifested as a burnt metal taste at the back of his mouth, a heat to his forehead that caused palpitations and faint nausea. A drifting sea haze appeared from nowhere and was gone just as quickly, and suddenly the world was a much better place: the sun brighter, the sky bluer, the sea so many shades of sapphire and emerald it dazzled the eyes. Even the scent of the air was richer.

The gods relaxed perceptibly and an aura of calm fell across the ship. Church went to the rail and watched the creamy wake spread out behind. 'I wish I could understand how all this worked.'

'I shouldn't trouble yourself.' Ruth held her head back to feel the sun on her face. 'For years all the rationalists and reductionists have been fooling themselves, building up this great edifice on best guesses and possibilities and maybes while ignoring anything that threatened the totality of the vision. It was a belief system like any religion. Fundamentalist. And now the foundations have been kicked away and it's all coming crashing down. Nobody knows anything. Nobody will ever know anything – we're never going to find out the big picture. Our perceptions just aren't big enough to take it all in.'

Church agreed thoughtfully. 'That doesn't mean we shouldn't keep trying to understand it, though.'

'No, of course not. There are too many wonders in the universe, too much information. The best we can hope to do is build up our own, individual view of how it all fits together. Though most people can't be bothered to look beyond their lives—'

'That's not fair. When they're not held in check by authority, people can do—'

Ruth burst out laughing.

Church looked at her sharply. 'What is it?'

'You sound like my dad! He was such a believer in the strength of the people.'

'Everybody has to believe in something.'

Their eyes held each other for a long moment while curious thoughts came to the surface, both surprising and a little unnerving. It was Ruth who broke away to look wistfully across the waves. 'I miss him.'

Church slipped a comforting arm around her waist. It was such a slight movement, but a big gesture; boundaries built up during the months they had known each other crumbled instantly. Ruth shifted slightly until she was leaning against him.

'Jack.'

The voice made the hairs on the back of his neck stand alert. He snatched his arm away from Ruth like a guilty schoolboy. Niamh was standing a few feet away, her hands clasped behind her back. Her classical beauty still brought a skip to his heart, her features so fine, her hair a lustrous brown, her skin glowing with the inner golden light of the Tuatha Dé Danann. Church didn't know what to expect. Only days ago she had been dangling him off a cliff for his refusal to return her love in the manner she expected. The fury within her at that moment had terrified him.

'Hello, Niamh.' He tried to see some sign in her face, but anything of note was locked far away.

Her eyes ranged across his features as if she were memorising them. He steeled himself as he felt a sudden surge of attraction for her. Proximity to the Tuatha Dé Danann set human emotions tumbling out of control. It wasn't manipulation, as he had at first thought, just a natural reaction to contact between two different species.

Ruth glanced from one to the other, then said diplomatically, 'I'm heading back to my room for a rest. I'll see you later.' She smiled at Niamh as she passed, but the god gave no sign that she was even there; Church was the only thing in her sphere that mattered. He couldn't begin to understand the depth of her feeling. They had shared barely more than a few moments, exchanged a smattering of words, the sketchiest of emotions, though Niamh had been with him all his life, watching him constantly from his birth, a whisper away during every great happiness and every moment of despair; even that couldn't explain the depth of her love, so pure and overwhelming it took his breath away.

'How are you, Jack?'

'As well as can be expected, given that my world is on the brink of being torn apart.' He tried not to sound bitter; it wouldn't do any good. But he wanted to say: *considering you tried to murder me with a lunatic god who could boil the blood in my veins at a gesture.* Even as he thought it, contrition lit her face. 'How is Maponus?' he asked.

'The Good Son is . . . as well as can be expected.'

'Will he recover?'

She looked down. 'We do what we can.'

'I'm sorry.'

'May we talk?' As she gently touched his hand, a spark of some indescribable energy crackled into his arm. She led him across the deck to the highest level beyond Manannan's vantage point. A table placed

916

where one could admire the view was laid out with crystal goblets and a jug of water.

'The Master will not mind us sitting awhile. He knows I love the sea as much as he.' Niamh filled two goblets, then watched the waves for several moments, a faint smile on her face.

'The Far Lands fill me with such joy,' she said eventually. 'In my worst times I feared them lost to me forever.' She turned to him and added sadly, 'As I fear I have lost you.'

'What happened—'

'Fills me with the deepest regret. I was cruel and foolish in my hurt. I sought to punish you so you would feel some of my anguish.'

'You tried to kill me—'

'No.' She shook her head forcefully. 'I would never harm you. Once I reflected on my actions, I sought to make amends. It was I who alerted my people to bring the Good Son back to the Far Lands. Yet I knew I could never take back what I had done, however much I desired to make things well between us again. And that was almost more than I could bear.' She sipped at her water, the sun glinting off the glass in golden shards.

'I can't understand it. You're all so far beyond us, yet emotionally you're just as screwed up.'

'Those of us who are close to Fragile Creatures still feel deeply. We have great passions. Yet it tears through us like fire in the mighty forest. It leaves us bereft. That is our curse until we move on to the next stage.'

Church looked down at Manannan, who had his back to them, wondering what rules governed the evolution of the gods.

'My heart was torn apart at the thought that I had driven you away, Jack, the only thing I ever truly wanted. And so I came here, to Wave Sweeper, in the hope that I could wash away the pain with a visit to the Western Isles, where all balm lies, if one looks carefully enough.'

'You've watched over me since I was a child—'

The note of sadness in her smile had a curious tone; almost too intense for what they were discussing. 'I have known you for a very long time, Jack Churchill.'

'All my life. That may be a long time for you. But I've only known you for a few months and then we've only been together for – what? – an hour or more? That's not enough time for me to fall in love with anyone. I don't believe in love at first—'

She turned her face from him so he couldn't see what lay there.

He hadn't the heart to finish. 'I don't hold it against you, Niamh. What you did was wrong, but I wasn't fair to you either. I shouldn't have promised something I couldn't live up to.'

She turned back to him in surprise, quickly checking that it was not a cruel joke before smiling shyly. 'It seems that for all I know you, I do not know you.'

'We've both got a lot to learn about each other.'

'May we try to be friends?'

'Of course. But don't think about anything more than that. I don't know you, I don't really know myself any more, everything's in such upheaval. It would be wrong to expect anything to happen.'

'I understand,' she said seriously. 'But to be friends—' Her smile lit up her face.

'*It's all right to lose your heart, but never lose your head.*' The words popped into his head, from a lifetime away, a happier time, but oddly, he didn't feel despondent. Niamh looked at him curiously. 'Just a line from an old song,' he explained. 'I'm glad we're going to get on fine. This could be a difficult journey for all of us.' He took a long draught of the water, which tasted like no water he had ever had before: vibrant, refreshing, infused with complex tastes. He savoured it for a moment, then said, 'Tell me, the Golden Ones have a strange relationship with time. The past, the future . . . You don't see it how we see it. How are things going to work out? Not for me – I don't want to know that – but for the world, my world? Is all this for nothing?'

'Nothing is ever for nothing.' The words had an odd resonance in her mouth. 'There is meaning in even the most mundane act.'

'The fall of a sparrow.'

'Yes. The slightest act. A pebble dropped in water. Ripples run out, bounce back, and then out again. You might not be able to see the results from your perspective, but if your actions are taken with good heart, they will be magnified.'

'I'm getting the feeling you're not going to answer my question.'

'You Fragile Creatures have a limited view of the turning of the Great Plan. Until your abilities advance it would be unwise to provide you with a glimpse of our vista.'

'That's patronising. You're saying we're not up to it.'

'That is correct. You are not ready. It is the arrogance of all emerging species that they have an understanding of everything. True wisdom comes from accepting that nothing can be understood. All existence has a framework, but it is not clockwork, although at first glance it may look so. Consider this: from the clouds the coastline is a simple unbroken line. As you fall, you see the twists and turns, the tiny inlets, the craggy outcroppings that comprise its complex shape. You fall to the beach and you see a billion, billion grains of sand, and suddenly there is no shape at all, simply chaos making an illusion of a complex pattern.'

'And so it continues. Yes, I understand that—'

'But the chaos is ordered.' She smiled enigmatically. 'You Fragile Creatures think you see the way everything works. You can measure the height and length and breadth of it, and in your arrogance—'

'Okay, okay, I get your point. We're just kids who haven't learnt how to draw pictures with perspective. So we have to learn to see before we can be shown the view. But—'

She shook her head.

He sighed. 'I can see where Tom got it all from. Everything's just *too* complex to sum up with words.'

'Yes,' she said. 'It is.'

'So I just do my best, and be damned.'

'Or not.' She took his hand briefly, then pulled away, as if she had overstepped some invisible boundary. 'Everything we need to know is encoded within. Everything. But you have to be strong to trust yourself. It is easier to be a child and let others tell you this and that. That is the key to all wisdom: listen to no one. Trust what your heart tells you.'

For the next ten minutes they sat in silence while Church mulled over her words. She had made exactly the same point as Ruth. It might have been coincidence, but Tom had told him so many times that what he thought was coincidence was the universe contacting him. But what was he supposed to take from it?

High overhead the owl soared on the thermals rising from the waves. It had moved along effortlessly when the ship had slipped between the worlds, though now it looked bigger than Ruth recalled, and she was sure she could see its eyes glinting golden in the sun; more than an owl. But then it always had been. In Otherworld it was simply one step closer to its true nature, Ruth imagined. She shivered, despite the heat, recalling all the things it had whispered to her in the miserable dark when she had been a prisoner of the Fomorii: secret knowledge that had transformed her into something else, while at the same time terrifying her. She was afraid she was losing part of herself in the process; her innocence, certainly. Sometimes she even feared for her sanity.

As she crossed the deck, the whispering began in the back of her head, the secret code words that shaped existence bursting continuously in her mind like bubbles on a stagnant pond: the price she had to pay for her secret knowledge.

She ignored the sly glances from the crew that followed her and slipped through the door beneath deck. As she progressed along the oppressive corridor system she became convinced the layout had changed, although it was impossible to tell for sure. Confusion reigned everywhere on that vessel. Eventually she reached her room, but the moment with Church before Niamh had arrived had left her out-of-sorts and she didn't really feel like resting. Exploring was a good way to take her mind off things, so she ploughed on past her door into the heart of the ship.

She walked for what felt like an hour or more, until her legs ached and her throat was dry. From the seafront, the ship looked like it could have been traversed in ten minutes, but she had gone at least two or three miles and there was no sign of the boat ending.

The maze of claustrophobic corridors had soon changed in form. There were passages where the roof was lost to shadows high overhead and where a jumble of beams protruded at incongruous angles like an Escher sketch, or which were as wide as a Parisian boulevard, with carved stone columns and arches where gargoyles peered down ominously. Chambers led off, some as vast as banqueting halls, while others were as cramped as her own cabin. At one point she found what appeared to be a tree growing upwards through the floor and ceiling, its roots lost somewhere in the bowels of the ship. Strange scents floated everywhere, whisked on by phantom breezes: cinnamon and onions, candle smoke, something that had the tangy bite of fresh blood, the acrid odour of hot coals, fresh lemon and cooking fish. Disconcerting symbols appeared intermittently on the walls, as if they were sigils to ward off unquiet spirits; Ruth found she couldn't look at some of them.

The immensity of the vessel made no sense to her. After a while she became convinced that however much she walked, she would never reach the end of it. The surroundings, too, were growing more chaotic and unnerving and she was afraid of what she would find if she carried on. It felt like a good time to head back.

But when she turned, the corridor wasn't how she remembered. A brief spark of panic flared within her. She glanced back the way she had been going and saw faint lights dancing in the gloom. They dipped and dived in complex patterns, reminding Ruth of the tiny, gossamer-winged figures that could occasionally be glimpsed amongst the trees of an evening. Those creatures, which had inspired the dreams of generations in times past, represented much of the good that had swept in with the chaos that had descended on the land. The corridor behind had changed layout once again. She considered her options, then headed towards the phantom lights.

However fast she walked, she never managed to catch up with them, although she couldn't tell if they were fluttering beyond her reach, or if it were some trick of the warped perspectives in Wave Sweeper. After a while the dancing lights became almost hypnotic and she had the odd sensation she was being dragged along instead of pursuing of her own will.

It might have been minutes or an hour later when she became aware she was in an area devoid of torches; the gloom was so intense she was overwhelmed by the feeling of floating in space. Uneasily, she clutched on to a wall before her troubled senses made her pitch forward. She cursed herself for following the lights, unable to recall what had prompted her to do so in the first place.

When she had calmed, she noticed an odd animal smell, thick and musky; it rankled. She leaned against a wall, trying to decide what to do next, afraid she could be wandering for days, perhaps forever. Hoping for a sound to guide her, she listened intently. At first, she could make out only the distant womb-echoes of the waves against the ship, but then another noise drifted up to her like a stranger on padded feet. Sounding dimly like an anxious rumble a cat makes deep in its throat, it filled her with inexplicable dread. She pressed her back hard against the wall and began to slide away from the approaching noise. It could be nothing, she knew, but every fibre of her being told her it was a threat.

What's down there? she wondered.

If she ran, it was so dark she would either injure herself or stumble, so whatever was there would be on her in a second. The throaty growl grew louder, the shuffling of feet echoing along behind. There was more than one, she was sure of it: they were coming from different directions. Then: a ruby glint of an eye opening and closing, the smell growing stronger until she felt like choking.

The malignancy was palpable. *Be strong*, she thought.

Cautiously she crept away from the approaching figures, moving as fast as she could without making a sound. In motion, she couldn't hear what was behind, so after a while she stopped and listened again. Nothing. The gloom was undisturbed by movement, although the smell remained.

Satisfied whatever was there had taken an unseen branching corridor, she began to edge along the wall.

The growl was so close every hair on her neck stood erect at once. It brought up a primal fear of being hunted at night, so strong that, despite herself, she launched herself down the corridor. Now she *could* hear whatever was behind: low growls, padding feet, rough breathing filled with a hungry anticipation. Terror began to lick at her; the growls sounded so bestial, so predatory. She was blind, but instinctively she knew they could see. Unable to control herself, she ran faster.

It was madness. She clipped one wall, careered over to the other, stumbled, smashing her elbows and knees, so scared she scrambled to her feet in a second and was away again.

She hit another wall head-on, dazed herself. The pursuit was growing louder, closer, more eager.

Stumbling into a side corridor, she began to run again, this time trailing one hand against the wall in a feeble attempt to guide herself. It worked reasonably well; at least she didn't knock herself out, although she picked up several more bruises. Anxiety pain spread across her chest. And then, suddenly, she realised she could no longer hear anything behind. Gradually, she came to a halt. Had she lost them?

Out of the corner of her eye she glimpsed rapid motion and jerked herself to one side. Something that resembled a battle-axe, although oddly organic, crunched into the wall where her head had been. Splinters of wood showered over her. A roar nearby made her ears ache, and then shapes moved towards her, at first serpentine, then like a pig, and then covered in fur. The intensity of the stink made her retch. Her hypersensitive senses picked up more motion. This time she didn't wait for the jarring impact. She turned and ran as fast as she could, bouncing off the walls, somehow managing to keep her balance, her heart thundering wildly.

The sounds of pursuit were now deafening; there was a pack at her heels. The corridor turned sharply and in the distance she saw a flickering torch that provided enough light for her to increase her pace. She found a split-second to look back, but all she could make out were leaping shadows, heavy and low, the burning sparks of eyes and the glimmer of weaponry.

She took another sharp turn into an area of more concentrated torchlight and then, mid-step, a door to her left opened suddenly, arms reached out and she was dragged inside.

Behind the closed door, she dropped into a defensive posture, ready to claw at anything that came near her. But the only occupant of the tiny chamber was Baccharus, who pressed one finger to his lips, demanding silence. She calmed instantly, her breath folding into her throat as the frenzied pack approached, then passed without pausing. Once silence had returned, she relaxed her muscles and turned to her rescuer. 'Thank you.'

Baccharus nodded shyly. 'You should not venture into this part of

Wave Sweeper. The dangers down here are many and Fragile Creatures are easy prey.'

'What were they?'

'The Malignos.'

She stared at him blankly.

'Misshapen dwellers in the dark places, beneath the earth, or under bridges or within the barrows. The natural predator for Fragile Creatures. In your North Country one became known as Hedley Kow, another as Picktree Brag. On the Isle at the Hub off your west coast, another is still known in whispers as the Buggane. They haunt your race memory.'

'I couldn't work out what they looked like.'

'They are shapeshifters. In the old times they taunted their victims by appearing as gold or silver before adopting a form that could induce nightmares.'

'They're like the Fomorii—'

Baccharus shook his head. 'They share many qualities with the Night Walkers, but they are lowborn. They cannot transcend the Fixed Lands. Your world is their home.'

Ruth slumped against the door, sucking in a deep breath as the adrenalin wore off. 'I was following some lights—'

'The *Ignis Fatuus*.'

Ruth started at the strange, tiny voice that was certainly not Baccharus's. She scanned the room twice before her eyes alighted on a figure barely half an inch high seated cross-legged on the floor next to the wall. She knelt down to get a closer look. It was a man, but although his body was young and lithe, his face was so wrinkled it looked ancient. His eyes gleamed with a bright energy that put Ruth instantly at ease.

'The Foolish Flame, your people used to call it, though it also went by the names of Spinkie, Pinket, Joan o' the Wad, Jack o' Lantern—'

'A Will o' the Wisp,' Ruth added.

He nodded. 'Very dangerous indeed. Another shapeshifter that used the form of gold to lure you avaricious creatures to your doom. It never allied itself with the Malignos, but here—'

'Here there are many strange bedfellows.' Baccharus was still listening at the door. 'Shared interests draw together. Races that would be at odds beyond these walls are forced to co-exist in the confines; new alliances are drawn.'

'It's not much of a luxury cruise,' Ruth noted.

'All things dwell aboard Wave Sweeper. At one time, just two of each species, but now . . . There are many things long-forgotten in these depths, some that have not seen the light of day since your world was new-formed.'

The tone in Baccharus's voice made Ruth grow cold. She turned quickly to the tiny figure and asked, 'And what are you?'

'*What* is not a pleasant way of asking. *Who* would be more polite. And even then naming words should be proffered, not demanded.' His eyes narrowed; Ruth thought she glimpsed sharp teeth as his mouth set.

'I'm sorry—'

'I will vouch for her, Marik Bocat,' Baccharus interjected. 'She is a Sister of Dragons.'

'And thus above reproach,' the little man said. 'Then, to you I am Marik Bocat. To others my name is neither here nor there. And to answer the *what*, my people are the oldest species of the Fixed Lands, distant relatives to the People of Peace.' He motioned towards Baccharus. 'Though the Golden Ones have more wit and sophistication, we can stand our own in conversation.' He smiled so pleasantly Ruth couldn't help smiling in turn. 'Your people used to call us Portunes, thanks to one of your educated folk who first wrote of us and our *diet of roast frog.*' He wrinkled his nose in irritation. 'Damn his eyes. See how he likes roast frog.'

Baccharus opened the door a crack to peer out into the shadowy corridor. 'We should move back to the lighter areas before the Malignos return. They will be even hungrier after their exertions.'

'Won't we meet them on the way back?' Ruth asked.

'Wave Sweeper's configuration will have altered many times by now. They should be a distance away.'

'Or a room,' Marik Bocat noted. 'Speed is of the essence.'

'Do you want me to carry you?' Ruth asked.

Marik Bocat looked insulted once again. 'Perhaps my legs are invisible to you?' He motioned to what appeared to be a mousehole in the wainscot. 'We have our own routes about the ship.'

'I'm sorry.' Ruth's head was spinning from everyone she had encountered, each with their own peculiar rules and regulations. 'I seem to be saying that a lot.'

'Never mind. You will have time to make up for your appalling manners.' He smiled sweetly again, then bowed with a flourish before disappearing into the hole.

'A strange race,' Ruth noted as she slipped out of the door behind Baccharus.

His voice floated back to her, strangely detached. 'We are all strange. That is the wonder of existence.'

She found Church watching the waves with Niamh at his side. There was an easiness to them, in their body language and the way they stood a little too close, that made her feel an outsider. She considered leaving them alone, but the tenacious part of her nature drove her forward.

Niamh smiled politely when she saw Ruth, but she didn't appear too happy with the intrusion. 'I will leave the two of you alone,' she said a little stiffly. 'I am sure you have much planning to do if you are to achieve your aims.'

Once she was out of earshot, Ruth said, 'You seem like you're getting on.'

Church's eyes narrowed; he knew her too well. 'What does that mean?'

'Nothing. Just what I said.'

'There's nothing going on.' He turned his eyes back to the cream-topped surf. The sun was slipping towards the horizon, painting the waves golden and orange. 'When it comes to romance I've been an idiot in the past. I was just trying to fill the gap left when Marianne died, and it was a big, big gap. But I couldn't see what I was doing. I can now. I'm not going to make any stupid mistakes again.'

'Still, it's obvious she wants to get in your trousers.'

'I don't think it's a physical thing. I don't know, maybe I'm wrong, but the Tuatha Dé Danann value emotions more than anything. Don't worry, I'm going to be careful, not lead her on. Especially after the last time.' He flinched. 'It's hard, though. The way they unconsciously manipulate emotions. It's overpowering.'

'I can't understand why she's so full-on.'

'What, you don't think I'm worth it?' He laughed as he leant on the rail to peer down the side of the boat.

'On second thoughts, go for it. You should take what you can get.'

'Steady on, acid-tongue.'

She slipped an arm around his shoulders; it was something a friend would do, but, as earlier, the warmth was unmistakably stronger and they both drew comfort from it.

'I know lots of terrible things have happened, but when I think about everything that's been lost so far it's all the normal things I feel acutely about,' he continued. 'Never being able to go to a movie. No more *Big Sleep* or *Some Like It Hot*. No more electric guitars at some seedy gig. Sometimes I'm so shallow.'

'What do you miss the most? The one thing above all else?'

He thought about this for a second, then gave an embarrassed laugh. 'Never being able to hear a Sinatra song again. Stupid, isn't it?'

'No.'

'It's not even about the music, it's what it means to me.' He tried to pick apart the tangled emotions. 'It means a love of life, abandon, not worrying – just enjoying.'

'Does it remind you of Marianne?'

'No, it reminds me of what life used to be like before responsibility.'

In the distance sea creatures resembling dolphins frolicked in the pluming water, their shiny skin reflecting the late afternoon light. There was a certain poetry to the image that wasn't lost on either of them.

'The quicker we get there, the quicker we can get back and do something positive,' Ruth said.

'Maybe we shouldn't be in such a hurry to arrive.'

'Why?'

'In all the old stories, the Western Isles are a metaphor. They're where the dead live.'

'Heaven?'

'Or Purgatory, in some cases. So we're leaving life behind us and moving into death.'

'Trust you to put a damper on things.'

He forced a smile. 'Let's hope we can make the return journey.'

CHAPTER THREE

On the Wings of Golden Moths

After Ruth had related to Church her encounter with the Malignos, the Portune and Baccharus, they retired to their rooms for a brief rest. When the red sun was bisected by the horizon, Cormorel disturbed them with a sharp rap on the door.

'The Master requests your presence at his table for dinner,' he said with his usual ironic smile.

They weren't about to argue; their stomachs were rumbling and the cooking aromas floating through the ship were mouth-watering. Spices, herbs and roast meat were prominent, but there were other, subtler scents they couldn't quite place. Cormorel led them across the deck to the raised section at the aft where Manannan's quarters obviously lay. A winding, wood-panelled staircase took them down to another corridor. Here torches roared furiously, as if fired by gas burners. At the end, Cormorel swung open two double doors to reveal a scene that took their breath away. Spread out before them was a banqueting hall so large it could have filled eight or nine ships the size of the Wave Sweeper they had seen from the seafront. They could barely think with the noise that echoed amongst the lofty rafters. Oak tables ranged in lines, around which sat a mesmerising array of strange creatures of all shapes and sizes, interspersed with the more sedate figures of the Tuatha Dé Danann. There was babbled, incomprehensible conversation, shouts and screeches; in a few places brawls rolled amongst the aisles.

'Do not worry,' Cormorel said wearily, 'you will get used to it.'

The walls were an odd mix of stone and wood, hung with luxuriant drapes of the deepest scarlet. Log fires roared in enormous stone hearths at strategic points around the perimeter, yet the temperature remained pleasant; the flames cast dancing shadows over the army of diners, making them even more bizarre and terrifying. Some of them looked towards Ruth and Church with unpleasant stares that made the blood run cold.

'Is everyone here?' Ruth asked. 'The Malignos?'

Cormorel raised an eyebrow. 'Ah, you have met some of your fellow travellers, I see. No, not all dine here. Some have very, shall we say, individual tastes.'

'Where do you find the food?' Church said.

Cormorel smiled. 'Our kitchens are particularly well-stocked.'

He led them amongst the diners where the smell of sweat and animal musk was almost overpowering. The tables were laid out with what appeared to be pewter plates, knives and goblets, each section with an intricate centrepiece of feathers, flowers and crystal. Nothing had yet been served. Something reached out and tugged at Ruth's arm, but she shook it off without daring to turn around.

At the far end of the room was the long table of the Master, piled high with the most magnificent gold and silver plates and dishes. Manannan sat in the centre on a large chair carved with intertwining dolphins, fish and rolling waves, his face still a mask, his eyes unfathomable. On either side sat members of the Tuatha Dé Danann, obviously the more highborn members of the race; there were two whose forms were so alien they hurt Church's eyes and forced him to look away, but Niamh was there, at Manannan's right hand. Three spaces remained at the far end, next to where Baccharus sat patiently.

Manannan let his eyes wander over them when Cormorel presented them to him; they were unable to decipher his emotions. 'Welcome to my table,' he said in a voice like the cold depths. 'It is good to dine once again with a Brother of Dragons.'

Church gave a curt bow. 'We are honoured.'

'This sustenance is given freely and without obligation,' Manannan continued. 'Enjoy this repast, Fragile Creatures.'

Cormorel led them to the empty chairs. 'Good evening, Baccharus,' he said a little tartly as he took the seat next to his friend. 'I hope you have been passing your time well while I was engaged in the business of the Master.'

'Well, indeed. I have met many of our travelling companions and investigated some of the wonders hidden in Wave Sweeper.'

'You always were a sociable and inquisitive fellow,' Cormorel noted dismissively. Church and Ruth sensed some kind of tension between the two. Cormorel clapped his hands once. Instantly some of the bland-featured Tuatha Dé Danann emerged from side rooms carrying platters of food and goblets of wine. Their perfect features, so devoid of even the hint of emotion, made Church and Ruth uncomfortable.

'Why are these young ones always servants?' Ruth asked.

'They are new. They must exist in servitude until they have learnt what it truly means to be a Golden One.' Cormorel virtually ignored them.

'New?' Ruth persisted.

'Barely Golden Ones at all, but still not of the race of Adam. They have not settled into their greatness or understanding of the fluidity of it all. Fixed, if you will, like you and your world.'

'So, the lowest of the low,' Church noted acidly. 'You can't escape hierarchy whichever way you turn.'

'There is a structure to everything, Brother of Dragons. You should know that by now.' Cormorel eyed him sardonically.

'Yes, that's always the argument. It must be nice to have such a full understanding of the rules and regulations of the Maker.'

They were interrupted by the servants, who laid out the food and drink before them: roasted, spiced meat, a few vegetables, bread, and other things so strange they made their stomach turn. One platter contained something like a living squid, though it had fifteen legs, all of them writhing madly in the air. The food they could enjoy, however, tasted more sensational than anything they had experienced before; every complex flavour burst like a firework on their tongue. The wine was finer than the most celebrated earthly vintage and made them instantly heady.

Despite the wonders of the meal, it was hard to keep their attention on the food when so many strange sights were on view all around. The array of creatures and their confusing, chaotic mannerisms as they devoured the food was like staring into a grotesque parody of a child's fairybook. There were things Church half-knew from the vague descriptions of folk tales, others that ignited recognition from some deeply submerged race memory; a few were completely unrecognisable. He was sure the echoing of archetypes dredged up from the corners of his mind would give him nightmares for the rest of his life.

Ruth recognised his thoughts from his expression. 'The whole of our psychology was based on this,' she said. 'Our fears, our dreams. We're stripping back layers that shouldn't really be uncovered.'

A half-man, half-sea creature moved down one of the aisles. It had fins and scales and bestial features, but it moved like a human being. Church leaned over to Cormorel. 'What's that?'

Cormorel mused for a moment, then said, 'I believe your race would know it as an *Afanc*. They once roamed the lakes and shores of your western lands, invoking terror with the fury of their attacks. Your people could not kill them by any means at the employ of Fragile Creatures.'

The Afanc reared up, then rushed out of sight, but there were plenty more things to pique Church and Ruth's curiosity. Cormorel followed their gaze, smiling at the questions he saw in their faces. 'If we had all night I would not be able to introduce you to the many, many races passing time on Wave Sweeper. But let me indicate some of the highlights.' He appeared to enjoy the idea of playing host. With a theatrical gesture, he motioned towards a large, lumbering figure like an exaggerated circus strongman. He had his back to them, but when he half-turned they saw a horn like a rhinoceros's protruding from his forehead. 'The Baiste-na-scoghaigh. He stalks the mountains looking for prey in the island where you lost your life to the Night Walker Calatin.' He smiled at Church; point-scoring. On the far side of the room, large, misty shapes faded in and out of the light, occasionally appearing like mountain mist, at other times as solid as the other creatures in the room. When they became material their features were grotesque. 'In the western land of moors, they were known as Spriggans, believed to be the ghosts of giants, a description that arose from their shapeshifting abilities, like many of our guests. The people of the Far Lands are always removed from the perception of those from the Fixed Lands. They could be found around the standing stones where the soul-fire comforted their violent nature. They are the Guardians of Secrets.'

'What kind of secrets?' Ruth asked curiously.

'The kind that can never be told.' Cormorel was enjoying his games.

Church saw something that resembled mediaeval woodcarvings of a griffin, another that resembled accounts of a manticore.

Ruth stood up, suddenly spying something so hideous in the shadows on the edge of the room she could barely believe her eyes. 'Is that a giant toad?' she asked disbelievingly. 'With wings? And a tail?'

Cormorel laughed. 'Ah, the Water-Leaper. The Llamhigyn Y Dwr. Feared by your fishermen, many of whom were dragged to their deaths after it seized their lines. The Water-Leaper rarely ventures up from the bilge-tanks. I wonder why it is here tonight?'

Ruth shook her head in amazement. 'God, I don't believe it. This place is insane.'

'Oh, this is indeed a Ship of Fools, Dragon Sister. So many searching, looking for guidance, meaning, in their short, unhappy lives.'

'But you don't need to search, Cormorel?' Church said.

'I am happy with my place in the great, unfolding scheme.' Baccharus muttered something under his breath, eliciting a stony glare from Cormorel.

Before any further comment could be made, a group emerged from a door hidden behind curtains away to one side. There were five of them, all Tuatha Dé Danann, but of a branch on a par with Cormorel and Baccharus, carrying musical instruments: a pair of fiddles, a flute, something percussive that Church didn't recognise and another thing that looked completely unplayable. A muttering rippled through the diners; it appeared generally appreciative, though it was hard to be sure.

'Hey, they got a band,' Ruth said in a bored, *faux*-Brooklyn accent.

But once the musicians began playing, both Church and Ruth were instantly entranced. Their music soared to the rafters, taking on a life of its own so it was impossible to tell which instrument was playing which section. Every bar evoked deep emotions within them: joy, sadness, wonder, passing in the blink of an eye, to be replaced by a new feeling. They could both understand the old stories of hapless mortals entranced by the fairy music, only to discover a hundred years had passed.

There were wild reels that set half the room dancing, a sight that was as terrifying as it was amazing; the crowd moved in perfect unison as if choreographed for some Busby Berkeley movie, yet they were as silent as the grave; it was eerie yet hypnotic. And then there were sad songs that made Ruth want to weep on the spot, yearning ballads that reminded her of her father, others that forced her to probe the feelings she had for Church. She fought the urge to hug him, though it brought tears to her eyes.

And Church was lost in thoughts of Marianne, of times frittered in the belief they could be picked up in the future, in thoughts of guilt at what he had done to Laura and Niamh; and then, once they had dissipated, at Ruth beside him. But before he had a chance to turn to her, the tempo increased and another emotion washed everything else away.

The food and drink came in a neverending stream. Once they had eaten their fill, another dish materialised to tempt them, and when they certainly could eat no more, there was still wine, and more wine.

During a lull while the band members refreshed themselves with a drink, Ruth rose from her chair and hurried over to them. They drew in close around her as she spoke in low tones, their faces at first curious, then intrigued. When she retook her seat, Church asked, 'What was that all about?', but she dismissed him with a wave.

He got his answer once the band started up again. Although the tone was oddly distorted, the song was unmistakable: 'Fly Me To The Moon'. Each note was filled with meaning, of his old life, certainly, but more importantly, and surprisingly, of the time at the pub on Dartmoor when he had performed karaoke with Ruth and Laura in a few moments of pure, unadulterated fun. He looked over to her, felt a surge of warmth at what he saw in her smile: she had remembered what he had said about never hearing Sinatra again.

'I hummed it to them,' she whispered. 'They picked it up straight away.'

What he felt in that instant, he tried to blame on the drink or the music, but he knew he would not be able to deny it, even in the light of the next morning. He put his hand on the back of hers, but it didn't begin to express what he was feeling.

'You know,' he said, mesmerised by the moment that felt like a lifetime, 'these days everything is so much more vital.' He was rambling, drunk. 'This is what life should be. Meaning in everything. Importance in everything.'

She smiled, said nothing; so much more assured. How could he not feel for her? He leaned forward, closed his eyes, savoured the anticipated moment as if he had already tasted it.

This is the time. This is everything. The words burst in his head unbidden, meaningless, yet filled with meaning. 'It's like I'm on drugs.' He could feel the bloom of her breath on his lips.

'I am the Messenger. The Message here is very clear.' The voice was a blast of cold wind, freezing the moment. Church looked up at the tattered rag-figure Cormorel had called the Walpurgis, a sucking core of darkness, too much for one space. There was something so alien about it, Church's skin crawled; in the back of his head a worm of terror began to wriggle.

Cormorel had been involved in an intense, whispered conversation with Baccharus and the Walpurgis's arrival had taken him by surprise. He turned sharply, his face hard. Church hadn't seen that expression on any of the Tuatha Dé Danann before; he had the face of someone with something to hide.

'Away with you, Dark One.' Cormorel waved his hand dismissively. 'We have no time for your shadowy discourses.'

The Walpurgis began to back away, until Church said, 'Wait. Who are you?'

'I am the Messenger.' The voice came from everywhere and nowhere.

'He is a dismal leech,' Cormorel said. 'Nothing more.'

'A leech?' Ruth's brow had knitted; Church could tell she was sensing something too.

'The Walpurgis reaches into heads and pulls out dreams.' Cormorel made a snapping motion with his fingers. 'A distasteful trait, even by the low standards of his fellow travellers.'

'You have a very contemptuous view of your fellow sentient beings, Cormorel,' Church noted sardonically.

Cormorel eyed him, aloof. 'All are beneath us.' It was announced as a statement of fact, with no obvious arrogance.

Church was unable to pierce the gloom falling from the brim of the Walpurgis's hat; there were only those hot-coal eyes, unpleasant in their intensity. 'You said you have a message?'

The Walpurgis nodded his head slowly. 'But first there is something within you which should be examined.'

'Within me?'

'A dream.' A bony finger snaked towards Church's forehead. Instinctively Church drew back, his skin starting to crawl.

'You want to pull out my dream?'

'Did you know,' Cormorel said icily, 'the Walpurgis eats the souls of the dying?'

Church ignored him. There was something about the Walpurgis that made him feel queasy; it was so alien he couldn't begin to judge its trustworthiness. Perhaps this was how it preyed on its victims.

'All have dreams hidden away that could change the way they live their lives,' the Walpurgis said in its rustling voice. 'It is the nature of existence to obscure the important. A game it plays with us. The finding is often part of the lesson.'

Church weighed this for a second. There was something repugnant about admitting so alien a being into his head, but he could see Cormorel did not want him to continue, and that was enough.

'Will it hurt?'

The Walpurgis said nothing.

'Okay. Do it.'

Cormorel moved to stop him, then his pride made him turn back to his conversation with Baccharus, as if Church, Ruth and The Walpurgis no longer existed.

'You're sure?' Ruth asked.

Church presented his forehead to the Walpurgis. The creature reached out again with its skeletal hand. The fingertips brushed his skin like the touch of winter, but their advance did not stop there. Church was shocked to feel the coldness continuing into his skull. It had not been a metaphor: the fingers were literally moving through his head as if it were mist, reaching inside him. He gagged, shuddered involuntarily; a spasm made his fingers snap open and closed.

What's it doing to me? The thought fizzed like static on a TV; he was losing control of himself.

Panic rose within him, but just as he began to believe he had made a dreadfully wrong decision, the sickening sensations faded and he was suddenly jolted alert by a stream of intensely evocative images. The Walpurgis had tapped into the cable wire from his subconscious.

His mother and father, seen from the perspective of his cot. Niamh appearing at the end of his bed, strangely happy, yet tinged with sadness. Coming faster now: school, university, knee-deep in mud at an archaeological dig in North Yorkshire. And then Marianne. The shock of her face was like a punch; so clear, like she was really there, like he could reach out to touch her. His emotions welled up and threatened to overflow his body; everything felt so acute.

And then it was like the images were playing on a screen just in front of his eyes and he could see through them to the Walpurgis. His red eyes were growing brighter. 'Near. So near.' The words echoed so deep in his head he didn't know if the Walpurgis had spoken them aloud.

A rapid flicker of memories, the speed making him feel queasy. Making love to Marianne, slicked with sweat. Out drinking with Dean and his other buddies. Kissing Marianne under the stars. Watching a band. Drinking. Writing something. Eating . . . somewhere. A restaurant. Already gone, and two more as well. Brighton. And . . . and America. And back to South London. The pub with all the bric-a-brac in Clapham. Faster, and faster still. And then . . .

Oh God. No. Not that.

The images were slowing down as if the Walpurgis had been fast-forwarding through a video and was now getting closer to the point he was after. Flicker, flicker, click, click, click. The flat, the night he had been out drinking. The night Marianne died.

No. Please, no.

But how could he be remembering that? He hadn't been there. And then he realised he wasn't exactly remembering the night, he was recalling his experience in the vast cave beneath Arthur's Seat in Edinburgh, when time bent and he had been thrust into that awful moment.

The Walpurgis's eyes cut through the familiar image of his flat. 'Here. Now.'

'No!' Church said aloud.

The image coalesced. The empty flat, removed of the clutter of his maudlin bachelor years. And it was no longer just an image: he could hear and smell, feel the texture of the carpet through the soles of his shoes. In the background one of Marianne's acid jazz CDs played quietly, and she, just out of sight, was humming along. There was no sorrow, only cold, hard fear; he knew what was coming.

'Please.' The Walpurgis ignored him, draining every sensation out of his head.

Marianne crossed to the bathroom. The sound of the cabinet opening, just as he recalled it from Arthur's Seat. But then he had broken the spell before the final, sickening moment, so what was the point of the

Walpurgis's actions? He loosened up a little; of course he wouldn't see the worst thing.

And there it was: the faint click of the front door opening. Nearly there now. Through the moment, Church could feel his fingernails biting into the flesh of his hand. 'Church? Is that you?' Her voice, almost unbearable. The shape, like a ghost, flitting across the hall. He hadn't concentrated before; it had all been too painful.

And then, oddly, the image rewound a few seconds and played again. Church's head spun. *What was going on?*

It reached the same point, then rewound again. And again. And again. And then Church realised: the Walpurgis was trying to show him something. This time he concentrated.

The shape, flitting across the hall. No, not the shape; that wasn't it at all. He was looking at the wrong thing. What was it? The image rewound and played again. And then he saw something: the shadow the shape cast on the wall as it passed. So brief, a fraction of a second, but Church knew he had seen its outline before. That wasn't all, though: a smell, wafting briefly in the air. A familiar smell. Vague, unsettling thoughts began to ripple up from the hidden depths of his mind. What were they? Piece them all together.

And then he had the first part of it. The realisation swept through him like the harshest winter. The shadow of the intruder, the one who had murdered Marianne, had been one of his recent companions: a Brother *or* Sister of Dragons. Every subtle indicator told him his instincts were right. At that stage he couldn't pin it down any more, but he knew if he watched the image a few more times he would have it.

His stomach was turning loops. Surely it couldn't be true. One of the people who had been closest to him over the last few months, someone he trusted more than life itself? Not Laura. Or Veitch. Surely not Shavi. Not Ruth. His stomach flipped again and he felt like he was going to vomit. It was so close, he could almost see the face. So close, so close.

'Here it is,' the Walpurgis said sickeningly.

Church wanted to snap himself away. He didn't think he could bear the revelation, like discovering a loved member of your family had committed the ultimate perversion. It would destroy him, he was sure.

But he had to see. It was his responsibility. He concentrated and waited for the dismal tableau to begin once more.

But within seconds of it beginning again, the whole world went sideways. Electric fracturing lines lanced across his vision; pain crackled deep within his head. The Walpurgis was breaking contact. His stomach did another flip. When the bizarre TV screen effect disappeared and he saw the Walpurgis's fingers withdrawing from his forehead, he knew the revelation wasn't going to come.

'No!' he yelled. He reached out to drag the Walpurgis's arm back to him, but it was like a cartoon nightmare: though he stretched and stretched, the Walpurgis was receding in slow-time. Church's stomach was continuing to move of its own accord. A sudden bout of vertigo made him reach for the table that was no longer there.

'Church!'

His thoughts rolled in a daze. The world was turning turtle.

'Church!' His shoulders were roughly dragged round. It was Ruth yelling at him, concern etched on her pale face. 'We're going down!'

It took another second for her words to register and then he snapped completely back into the real world. The room was engulfed in chaos. Platters and cutlery were floating through the air, along with the occasional traveller. The floor was at an impossible angle.

'We're going down!' she screamed at him again, so close to his ears it made them ring. She pulled him to his feet, they clung for an instant before pitching across the floor.

Everywhere were screams and yells and clanging metal and splintering wood. Church was rolling as the floor rose to forty-five degrees. Violent vibrations thundered back and forth, at odds with the sucking, downward motion; it felt like Wave Sweeper was being shaken apart. Some enormous creature that smelled of burned rubber crashed against his back with such force he thought he had broken it. He had barely recovered when the gigantic top table began to slide, picking up speed until it was rushing towards his head. When it was inches from turning his skull to jelly, he propelled himself a few inches to one side so he passed between the hefty, carved legs.

He too started to slide backwards towards the mêlée of bodies thrashing near the far wall. He'd moved a few feet, spread-eagling his arms and legs as far as they would go to slow his fall, when his fingers found purchase in a crevice between two floorboards. Clutching on tightly, he searched for Ruth, but she was nowhere to be seen.

Something cut through the madness and left him feeling like he was floating in a soundless, slow-motion vacuum: Manannan moved eerily across the floor, perpendicular to it, oblivious to the force of gravity dragging everything else downwards. Bodies flashed past him, but he continued his gradual progress in such a languid manner it looked like he was actually floating an inch or two above the boards. And then, when he was halfway across the room, his head turned almost mechanically and his attention fixed on Church. It was only a second or two, but it made Church's blood run cold.

The ship tipped a degree more and Manannan was lost behind more flying bodies as he made his way to the main exit at the rear of the banqueting hall. Just as Church feared he couldn't hold on any longer, the boat pitched forward. The moment the keel hit the waves, Church was thrown six feet into the air before landing hard on the boards.

Instantly the ship began pitching from side to side. Creatures careered wildly around the room, throwing him to his knees every time he tried to stand upright. Finally he was attempting to run with them towards the exit, but the rippling floor made him stagger as if he were gallon-drunk. In the end he clubbed aside anyone or thing which got in his path, anxious to find Ruth.

When he saw the heaps of broken, unmoving bodies he feared the worst until he caught sight of her in a space against the wall, dazed, half-kneeling, a cut leaking blood on to her forehead. It looked like they would never get past the throng fighting to get out, but when the ship lurched crazily to one side they managed to hang on to a set of drapes while all the others near the exit were swept away.

The constrained space of the corridor made it easier for them to catch their breath. 'What the hell's going on?' Church was still disoriented after the Walpurgis's intrusion.

Ruth pulled herself along the wall towards the deck. 'I thought our progress was a little too smooth.'

They emerged into madness. Black waves soared up, some passing completely over the boat before crashing on the other side. The ship rolled in the wild water so violently that first one rail almost touched the churning sea, and then the other. The night sky was cloud-tossed and torn by lightning, with no sign of moon or stars. Church and Ruth had to grip on to the mast to prevent the howling wind hurling them into the turbulent ocean. Every time they inhaled they took in a mouthful of salty water; the very air was infused with it.

In a flash of lightning that froze the tableau in glaring white, they sensed movement above them. The next burst confirmed their fears. Something with the texture of black rubber gleamed in the light. It moved rapidly, but they recognised it was a tentacle, so large Church would not have been able to put his arms around it. Another lashed out of the water in an arc across the boat. The monster was trying to wrap itself around the entire ship to drag it down into the depths.

A further tentacle smashed into one of the crew, his body folding where no joints had been. Others skidded across the deck, fighting to keep control of the boat so it wasn't breached by the waves. And then, in another lightning burst, they caught sight of the bulk of the creature just off the port side, ten times as large as Wave Sweeper, something that was part-octopus and part-whale, with other, stranger inclusions too. It reminded Church of engravings he'd seen in old books about the mysteries of the deep.

'A G'a'naran.' Baccharus was beside them, answering Church's unspoken question. He was almost white, trembling from the shock of the attack. 'They breed on the ocean floor, grazing on the dreams of mortals. They rarely challenge ships, and never Wave Sweeper.'

'Then why is it here?' Ruth yelled above the storm.

Baccharus was steadying himself with a rope around his wrist attached to a nearby spinnaker. 'I fear it was summoned.'

'By whom?' Church could tell from the god's face some vital information was not being passed on. Baccharus's gaze grew hollow.

'What's going on here, Baccharus?' Church pressed.

The god might have answered, but in that instant a tentacle swept along the length of the deck towards them. Baccharus ducked at the last moment, but the tip of it slapped Ruth away from the safety of the mast. She hit the deck hard, stunned. Church barely had time to register what had happened when a wave crashed over them and Ruth was propelled by the thick, foaming surf towards the rail. At the same time the ship began to roll on that side. In shock, Church realised she was going over the edge.

Without any consideration for his own safety, he threw himself forward, allowing the surge of water to give him speed. It was futile. He watched in horror as the waves flung Ruth over the rail.

At the last moment her jacket snagged on one of the hooks used to secure the rigging and she was jerked to a sudden halt. Church was already moving fast with the force of the water and it was difficult to direct himself. He prayed her jacket would hold until he reached her.

Somehow she managed to buy a little extra time by clutching on to the carved rail, and then he slammed into the side with such force it knocked all the wind from him.

'Hang on!' he yelled.

The boat dipped down even further. Church thought he was going to pitch over the rail too, while Ruth's feet were now dragging in the bubbling cauldron of ocean. He could see the panic in her face, though she tried to bury it; her strength gave him strength.

They were a pocket in a universe of water, where it was impossible to tell up from down; when he breathed, there was only brine. The rest of the world was invisible through the constant stream.

Somehow he found her arm. He tried to tug, but there was nowhere to get purchase. Ruth would have been dragged to her death if the boat had not then rolled sharply in the other direction. The sheer force of the reversal sent them both flying: Ruth's hand wrenched from the rail and they turned in the water-infused air before slamming into the deck. It stunned them both, but soon helping hands were dragging them to safety. Baccharus and a group of other Tuatha Dé Danann lashed ropes around their wrists to keep them steady. Despite the worsening situation, Church grabbed Ruth tightly, overcome with relief.

She fell into him for a second, before pushing him away. 'I can help.' She turned to Baccharus. 'The storm is making things worse. If it stopped, can you do something about the monster?'

His answer was a gesture towards the poop deck where Manannan was floating a few inches above the boards, his hands making intricately complex gestures in the air, some so convoluted he must have dis- jointed his limbs to achieve them. Just beyond the cone of movement, starbursts flashed in the air, focusing and moving out in streams towards the dark bulk of the G'a'naran, where they exploded like arcing electricity, blue sparks showering into the water. 'The Master is doing what he can,' Baccharus said.

Ruth was already loosening the rope around her wrist.

Church grabbed her arm. 'What are you doing?'

'I can do a lot of things.' The look on her face scared him.

She heaved her way along the rolling deck, coughing out mouthfuls of seawater. Church lost her to the spray within seconds, but by then there were other things to occupy his mind. Tentacles lashed the boat with increasing ferocity, sweeping crew members into the boiling sea or crushing them against the deck. Church ducked the frenzied thrashing repeatedly, sometimes throwing himself flat on to the sodden boards.

The storm, too, was increasing in intensity. The lightning struck all around, freezing the conflict in bursts of white, the faces of those near him just skulls with black, terrified eyes. A tentacle swept by with the force of a boom. It narrowly missed crushing his head.

A cry drove through the howling wind. Baccharus had been pinned to the mast, the monstrous arm coiling gradually around him. Pain fanned out across his face as the pressure increased. Church was shocked to see the other Tuatha Dé Danann look on obliquely, then continue their tasks without any attempt to help; nor did Baccharus call out to them.

Church threw himself across the heaving deck, grappling the tentacle in an attempt to prise it free. The skin had the sickening consistency of decaying rubber, and it smelled like a compost heap with a few fish- heads thrown in. But it was too strong for him to budge it even an inch.

Then the strangest thing happened: in the middle of the creeping pain, Baccharus's eyes locked on his. At first Church saw confusion in them, then curiosity and finally something he couldn't understand at all, but it appeared to drive the pain back. A second later a scurrying sensation moved over Church's waist and quickly up his chest. He jumped back in shock as Baccharus's Caraprix scuttled on to the tentacle and clung on with spider legs, the silver orb of its body glowing in the gloom.

'Take it,' Baccharus yelled.

Church fought back his natural distaste and held out a hand towards the symbiotic creature. It instantly moved and changed, so quickly his stomach knotted in shock, slipping perfectly into his grip as it transformed into a cruel-bladed short sword, still brilliant silver. Church had seen the things' wild shapeshifting before, but it never failed to astound him.

At the moment before impact, the sword grew a row of serrated teeth that became a snapping jaw tearing into the rubbery flesh with remarkable ease. A shudder ran through the tentacle. Church struck again, this time with more force, then again and again until the air was filled with the flayed flesh of the G'a'naran. Finally the tentacle unfurled sharply, catching him in the chest. Winded, he slumped to the deck, but still found it within him to catch Baccharus as the god fell forward. Gratitude flooded his face.

'How are you?' Church asked.

'Not well, but well enough to recover. The Golden Ones are nothing if not resilient.' He smiled, and once again Church was surprised to see none of the usual arrogance of the Tuatha Dé Danann.

At that moment Church became aware of a change in the atmosphere, subtle at first, but becoming more apparent. It took him a second or two to realise what it was: the storm was gradually moving away, the lightning flashes becoming less intense, the winds dying down, the thunder no longer hurting his ears. Subsequently, the waves dropped and the inches-deep water on the deck flowed away. Within a minute the storm had gone completely; the sea lay saucer-flat, the night sky clear and sparkling with stars. The only wrenching motion came from the still-flailing tentacles of the G'a'naran.

Church peered along the deck to the aft where Ruth leaned against the rails, exhaustion hunching her shoulders. There was a faint nimbus of energy around her that disappeared so rapidly Church couldn't tell if it had truly been there or if it had been his imagination. He looked up at the clear skies, still not truly believing, but the rapidity with which the storm had receded had not been natural.

Baccharus levered himself up on his elbow. He was healing before

940

Church's eyes, muscle and bone knitting, energy levels rising. 'Look.' He motioned towards the poop-deck. 'Your intervention has swayed the battle.'

Manannan had doubled his attack, his attention no longer diverted by keeping the ship afloat in the face of the storm. There was a sound like silver foil rustling, then ripping. A smell of hot engines and baked potatoes. The air folded in, then ballooned out, a translucent rainbow rippling like oil in a roadside puddle. With a thunderous whip-crack, the light ripped towards the G'a'naran. Church anticipated some coruscating display of energy, but there was only the noise of the G'a'naran's flesh rending as a furrow opened up across the rubbery side of the creature.

Church saw no mouth, and there was no real sound, but suddenly he was driven to his knees by a high-pitched noise stabbing into his ears. When he was finally able to raise his head, there was only a sucking section of the sea where the G'a'naran had plunged beneath the waves.

Church dragged himself to his feet, shaky, and then Ruth was at his side, smiling wearily.

'You did it,' he said. He held out an arm and she slipped into it, coming to rest hard against his body.

'I wasn't sure I could, even at the last. But then when I opened myself up to it, it all came rushing out. It's like it's all battened down inside, things I've only half-heard but somehow fully formed. Fully remembered. Understood even.' Her eyes had grown wide and wondrous. 'The things I can do!' She caught herself, looked down modestly. 'I think. I mean, I feel I have a lot of potential.'

'What was it? A spell?'

She didn't seem quite sure herself. 'Remember when we were talking about magic being the cheat code for reality? It was like that, like I could suddenly focus to peel a layer back and move things around behind the scenes.'

Church kissed her on the forehead; that surprised them both. 'Maybe you can conjure up sausage, bacon and eggs for breakfast.'

They both felt the temperature drop a degree or two, and when they looked up Manannan was there. 'Sister of Dragons,' he said in his sea-tossed voice, 'you are true to your heritage.' He gave a little bow that, in his restrained manner, looked as if he was proclaiming her greatness to the heavens.

'Thank you,' she said shyly.

'And you, Brother of Dragons,' he continued to Church, 'you aided this Golden One in his moment of need. Wave Sweeper is the better for your presence.' He paused for a moment, then added, 'We must talk about great things—'

Whatever he was about to say was snapped off by a cry of alarm from the other end of the boat. There was a note of terror to it that shocked them all into immediate action. Church and Ruth sprinted until they reached the raised area where Church had earlier sat with Niamh. At the top of the steps one of the younger Tuatha Dé Danann was rigid, his normally plastic features shifting like smoke. Church pushed past him to get a better look.

Cormorel was slumped half over the railings, his eyes staring, blank. His body appeared to be breaking up like a cracked mirror. Where the fracture lines spread out across him, a brilliant white light shone through, taking consistency, shape, becoming something like moths that fluttered wildly around the body before rising up and up to become lost in the night sky. Hunched over Cormorel was the shadowy form of the Walpurgis, his bony hands clutching at the god's shirt, his hot coal eyes growing brighter than ever. His mouth was stretched wide, the jaws distended inches away from the body so he could suck up some of the flapping moths. They swirled around frantically before disappearing into that black maw.

Church felt sick to his stomach. He knew exactly what the Walpurgis was doing; Cormorel himself had said it: *the Walpurgis eats the souls of the dying.*

Manannan and the other Tuatha Dé Danann surged up the stairs. Church moved aside, fearful of the transformation he saw come over them. Their bodies were like knives, like light, like a maelstrom of howling faces. And the sound they made was terrifying: a screech filled with desolation and elemental fury. As they rushed towards the Walpurgis, the creature broke off its feeding, looked around briefly like a cornered animal, then ran towards the rails. He vaulted over them to the lower deck, hanging briefly like a sheet billowing in the wind. Within seconds he had disappeared through the door that led down into the bowels of Wave Sweeper.

Instead of pursuing him, the Tuatha Dé Danann gathered around Cormorel, his body now little more than fragments in a pool of white light. Church and Ruth couldn't bear to hear their howling grief, if that was what it was, and hurried back down the stairs to the far side of the deck.

Ruth had a disturbed, queasy expression. 'How could that thing kill him?' She looked around, grasping for understanding. 'I thought they couldn't die.'

Church shook his head, still trying to come to terms with what he had seen. He had witnessed Calatin's death and knew what a monumental thing it was; to all intents and purposes the gods went on forever, their vital energy unquenchable even if their forms were destroyed. It took something special to wipe them from existence.

'It doesn't make any sense,' he said. 'Why would the Walpurgis murder Cormorel? He would know he wouldn't get away with it.'

'Maybe he couldn't control himself. Driven by hunger . . . ?'

He turned and rested on the rails, looking at the reflected starlight glittering on the waves, thinking how much it reminded him of that disappearing essence of Cormorel.

'How's this going to affect things?' he said. 'At least we know we're going to die, even if we don't want to face up to it. It's no great shock. The Tuatha Dé Danann think they're going on forever. Seeing something like that, it's a blow we can't even begin to comprehend. What will it do to them?'

The question hung in the air, but after all they had been through it was too much to consider. Ruth stepped in next to him and again he slipped an arm around her shoulders. They both felt like they were huddling together for warmth in a world grown cold and dark.

CHAPTER FOUR

Empty Cisterns,

Exhausted Wells

The noises echoing around the ship that night were terrifying to hear: shrieks and howls, grunts and roars; at times it was as if a pack of wild animals roamed the cramped corridors, things not even remotely human loose on board. Church and Ruth chose to stay together in the same room for security, but they did not feel safe, even with a huge chest pulled across the door.

Although the sounds were impossible to track, they knew the Tuatha Dé Danann were hunting the Walpurgis into the depths of Wave Sweeper. But Ruth knew how futile that exercise was, even if the gods understood the twisted confines of their ship. And so the questing continued into the small hours until it eventually died away. The silence was bitter and they knew the quarry had not been located.

They woke in a beam of sunlight breaking through the bottle-glass windows, entangled like lovers, although they had only held each other for comfort. Their position brought embarrassment and they quickly hurried to opposite ends of the bed. Eventually, though, in the warmth of the morning sun and their relief that all was calm without, their legs were soon draping over each other as they chatted lazily.

'You don't think he did it, then?' Ruth asked as she brushed with crooked fingers at the tangles in her hair.

Church threw open the windows so they could look out across the foam-topped waves. 'There's something about it that's troubling me. When the Walpurgis was poking around in my head I got a sense of him. It wasn't quite a reciprocal thing – he had all my mind laid out before him – but I felt . . .' He fumbled for words. 'I don't think he kills, however black Cormorel painted him. He certainly feeds on souls—'

'So you think he found Cormorel dying?'

'I don't know.'

'Then who killed Cormorel? Who would have the *power* to kill him? What possible motivation could there be?'

Church held up his hand to stop her questions. 'You've seen all the wild, freakish things travelling on this ship with us. God knows what's lurking down there in the darkest depths.'

'The Malignos,' Ruth mused.

'There was plenty of opportunity in all the chaos for something predatory to attack. Perhaps whatever did it thought we were going down and it had nothing to lose.'

'I hope it's not going to deflect us from what we've got to achieve.' Ruth leaned on the windowsill, filling her lungs with the salty air. 'There's so much at risk, we can't afford any—'

'You don't have to tell me.'

The dark tone in his voice made her look round. 'What is it?'

'There's something else. When the Walpurgis was in my mind he pulled something out.'

'That's right – he said he had a message.' Her eyes narrowed as she scanned his face for clues. 'Something bad?'

'He kept replaying the scene just before Marianne's murder in our flat, the one I stumbled across in that time-warping cavern under Arthur's Seat. The same thing over and over again. Someone entering the flat, a shadow on the wall. It wasn't just images – I could smell it too, hear, feel. He knew exactly what he wanted to show me, but I think he felt it was important I found it out for myself.'

'More impact that way.' She chewed on a knuckle apprehensively; Church watched, wondering. 'So did you get it? I know how dense you can be,' she asked.

He nodded. 'Part of it anyway.' He weighed his thoughts, not sure how much he should tell her, then hating himself for even thinking it. 'One of us killed Marianne.'

'One of *us*?'

'Laura, Shavi, Veitch—'

'Or me?'

'Everything went pear-shaped before I had a chance to piece it all together. But I saw a shadow that I recognised. I smelled something—'

'What? Like perfume?' she said sharply.

'No. It was unusual. But familiar. Subtle. I don't know what it meant. Instinctively I was certain it was one of us. If I'd only had a few more minutes—'

'You're sure?'

He thought for a moment. 'I'm sure.'

She sucked on her lip. 'So who do you think it is?'

'I don't know.'

'Who do you *think*?'

'I don't know. Honestly.'

'Do you think it was me?'

He looked her full in the eye. Her gaze was unwavering, confident, perhaps a little hurt. 'I'm about as sure as I can be that it wasn't you.'

That pleased her immensely. Her mouth crumpled into a smile before growing serious a moment later. 'That ties in with what the Celtic dead told us about a traitor in the group. Whoever it was, they were there from the start.'

'We mustn't start jumping to conclusions.'

'No, but it makes sense.'

And he had to admit that it did, but it was too upsetting to consider. The five of them had been friends through the hardest of times. They had saved each other's lives. He trusted them all implicitly, knew them all inside out, or thought he did. None of them had the capacity to be a traitor on the scale implied, he was sure of it. But if he could be fooled through such intimate contact, what did that mean? That the traitor was truly evil, and truly dangerous.

He could tell Ruth was thinking something similar; she rubbed her arms as if she were cold despite the warmth of the sun. 'There's no point in guessing,' she said eventually. 'If we could piece it together from what we've seen we would have done it already.'

'I know, but . . .'

'What is it?'

'It casts a shadow over everything. I know that sounds stupid with what's going down, but the fact is, the five of us . . . six, with Tom . . . we were the calm centre, something I could rely on to make everything else bearable.'

'It's just the two of us now. *We're* the calm centre.'

Any further discussion was curtailed by a sharp knock at the door. It was Baccharus carrying a tray filled with cold meats, fruit and bread. 'I thought you might like to break your fast,' he said quietly.

They ushered him in, then refused to let him leave while they hungrily ate everything on the tray. They questioned him about what was happening elsewhere on Wave Sweeper.

'The Master has called a meeting of all who travel upon Wave Sweeper, on deck shortly. There is a feeling for . . .' He chose his word carefully. '. . . retribution.'

'Have you found the Walpurgis?' Church asked.

Baccharus shook his head. 'There are many scouring the boat, even as we speak, but it is . . .' He made an expansive gesture.

'How serious is this?' Ruth said.

'How serious? To the Golden Ones it is a crime against existence. We dance amongst the worlds; stars pass beneath our feet. We are a part of everything, of the endless cycle. We are not meant to be eradicated—'

'But it is possible,' Church said, remembering Calatin. 'You know that.'

'Anything is possible.' Baccharus's voice had grown even quieter. 'But there are some things that should not happen. One could imagine the whole of everything falling into the void before they came to pass. The eradication of a Golden One is one of those things. Cormorel may have appeared young to you. But he was enjoying his wild ways when your world was a steaming rock in the infinite dark. What you saw last night was something beyond your comprehension. A star exploding would not have matched one atom of its import.'

'I'm sorry.' Ruth rested a hand on his forearm. 'I know Cormorel was your companion. We know what it is like to lose a dear friend.' His expression brought her up sharp; it said she could never understand the slightest of what he – all the Tuatha Dé Danann – were experiencing.

'There are two issues here,' Baccharus continued. 'The Master is concerned that the Walpurgis had not only the power, but also the knowledge of how to use it to end Cormorel's days. And that he had the inclination.'

'Do you believe it was the Walpurgis?' Church pressed.

Baccharus looked at him thoughtfully. 'You saw as well as I—'

'I saw him drain Cormorel's soul. I didn't see him commit murder.'

Baccharus shrugged. 'The Master believes it to be the Walpurgis—'

'Isn't justice important?'

'Of course.' Baccharus's voice grew cold for the first time since they had known him.

'Well, isn't it?' Church pressed.

'Justice is above us all.'

An uncomfortable silence descended on the room until Ruth couldn't bear it. 'That thing which attacked last night—'

'The G'a'naran.' Baccharus was staring dismally across the waves.

'The G'a'naran. What was it?' She looked to Church. 'It reminded me of old stories, mariners' tales—'

'More race memories, things that slip between the worlds.'

'A sea monster?'

'The G'a'naran is unformed, from the age when all flowed freely, finding its shape,' Baccharus said. 'Its home is not beneath the waves, though sometimes it takes refuge there. It navigates amongst the stars—'

'Like you?'

Baccharus looked at Ruth. 'No, not like us.'

Church was troubled by Baccharus's description. 'I don't understand why it attacked the ship if it's not some kind of mindless animal, which I presume it's not. Is it a predator?' He was surprised to see Baccharus was concerned too. 'What is it?'

The god made to leave without answering, but Church dragged the reply from him. 'The G'a'naran would not have attacked Wave Sweeper unless it was provoked. Or summoned.'

'Summoned?' Church's head was thundering; connections were lining up, but not quite linking. 'What's going on here?'

Before the matter could be pursued further, a long, low mournful sound reverberated throughout the ship. It drew an overwhelmingly dismal feeling from deep within them; Ruth found tears springing to her eyes involuntarily.

'The Master is summoning.' Baccharus looked oddly distracted, almost dazed. When he realised they were still seated, he said, 'You must come.'

The sun was unbearably bright as they stepped out on to the deck, blinking. 'Tell me,' Church hissed to Baccharus in response to the silence that lay heavy over everything, 'when you were in trouble on deck last night, why didn't anyone save you?'

On the surface Baccharus's face appeared emotionless, but Church could tell there were deep but unreadable emotions running beneath. 'There is no recognition that we might not exist. Therefore there is no need to aid one in dire straits.'

'I thought you lot always stuck together.'

'You do not understand our ways.' It was a cold statement; Church knew there was no point pursuing the matter. By that time they had arrived in the midst of a crowd filling every foot of the ship's boards, some of the freakish travellers even clambering up into the rigging. Others were arriving behind them. Amidst the reek of alien scents, the pressing of skin that felt like carbonised rubber or gelatine, Church fought to focus his attention on the tableau unfolding on the raised area preserved for the captain of the vessel.

His face like an ocean tempest, Manannan overlooked the crowd, hands behind his back, flanked by other members of the Tuatha Dé Danann. Niamh was close by his right arm, her beautiful face troubled too. She stared across the waves, lost to whatever dark scenarios were playing in her mind.

A low muttering had risen in the crowd like wind over the water, but when Manannan raised his left arm, everyone felt silent. His gaze slowly moved across the masses; even at that distance Church was sure his eyes were burning. His face held an odd quality too, as though it were about to become fluid, transform.

'A crime has been committed against the very fabric of existence.' He appeared to be whispering, but his voice boomed over the throng, which grew visibly cowed. 'Something more valuable than the stars above you, more important than the entire weight of all your races, from the beginning to the end, has been torn away. This will not go unpunished.'

Church felt a pang of fear. Ruth's skin was unnaturally pale.

'The one who committed this atrocity is known to us, and though not yet within our grasp, know this: there is no escape from our unflinching eye. No hope. We will peel back the lies, strip away the moment and the mile, never rest, until we have it.' He paused, letting his words fall like stones. 'And know this also: our gaze will be turned on you, all of you, individually, even in your most private moments. And if we find any who have aided or abetted the committal of this monstrous crime, they will be punished.' Another pause. 'With the full weight of our wrath.'

He surveyed the crowd one final time, with many flinching from his eyes, and then slowly descended to his quarters, the other members of the Tuatha Dé Danann trailing behind.

Even when they had all departed and the door had closed, no one on deck moved, no one spoke, there was not even a rustle of clothing. Church smelled fear in the air and more than that, an awful dread that events were rapidly deteriorating. There was darkness on the horizon and none of them knew which way the wind was blowing.

'He's in here?'

Baccharus motioned towards the heavy wooden door with the black sigil. It was two decks down, at the heart of the ship so no wall was next to the cool, green water. Church moved his palm gently a quarter-inch above the surface of the door, testing the sensitivity that had grown in him since Tom had introduced him to the Blue Fire. His skin prickled. Inside the room he felt an unpleasant coldness that was the antithesis of that spirit energy. He didn't know why he had asked Baccharus to take him there while Ruth rested – or hid – in her cabin, but the urge had been insistent. He pushed his palm forward and the door swung open at his touch.

The chamber was in complete darkness. It smelled of some zoo cage littered with dirty straw, reminding him uncomfortably of his imprisonment in the mine deep beneath Dartmoor. He couldn't help but think a cruelty was being inflicted, despite everything his rational mind told him of deserving punishment.

Baccharus stepped past him holding one of the torches from the corridor and lit an extinct one fixed to the wall close to the door. Unlike the torches without, it cast only a dull, ruddy glare, barely causing the shadows to retreat. Baccharus nodded to him curtly, then stepped out and closed the door behind him.

'So you've found it in your heart to visit another soldier of the road, now sadly down on his luck.' The voice was infused with scorn.

At the far end of the room was an iron cage, barely large enough for a man to stretch out in. Straw was indeed scattered on the floor within, along with what resembled an animal's feeding trough. Callow squatted at the back of it, his peeled white eyes staring like sickly lamps. There was something about that unflinching gaze that made Church's stomach squirm: human yet not human. The parchment skin was a muddy red in the flickering glow of the torch, but the black veins still stood out starkly, a roadmap of hell.

'Don't get smart with me. You've brought everything on yourself.'

'Well, that's a fine attitude for such a noble man to take. Filled with Christian values. Do I hear the sweet tinkling notes of forgiveness? The vibrato of salvation? The teasing choir of redemption? Or perhaps we truly are brothers of the byway. When the ditch is your billet, you see life with a different perspective, is that not true? Not so noble then, is it? *Means to an end* is the phrase on every good man's lips.'

'Shut up, Callow. I haven't got the energy.' Church eyed the heavy padlocks on the cage door. The Tuatha Dé Danann were taking no chances with him. Perhaps he should be more cautious.

'And how is the lovely *Miz* Gallagher?' Callow began oleaginously.

Church's glare stopped him dead; it left Callow in no doubt that here was a topic where he could never trespass. Callow scrabbled around in the straw for a distraction like he was looking for a stray piece of corn from his meal; a chicken waiting to be harvested. But then he looked up with a cold confidence and said, 'Things have turned a little sour, have they not?' His thin lips peeled back from his blackened teeth in a sly smirk.

He knows why I've come, Church thought.

Callow's eyes were a vortex in the gloom. 'You're here to beg for my help. Oh, Glory be! My time has truly come!'

'Your time has long gone, Callow. But you might still be able to rescue a thin chance of saving yourself if you start acting like you don't want to see the whole of humanity eradicated.'

'Look after number one, my boy. You know that well.'

The jibe hurt Church even though he had managed to put his own selfish interests to one side. 'This is a new age, didn't you know? These days we look after each other.' Callow looked away. 'I may be wasting my time here in more ways than one,' Church continued, 'but I have to ignore my personal feelings if there's a chance everyone might benefit. And make no mistake, Callow, I loathe you. For what you did to Laura, and Ruth. For turning your back on the human race simply to achieve your own ends. You truly are a grotesque person. But it's still wrong the way the Tuatha Dé Danann are treating you like some animal.'

'We are all animals to them.'

'I know. They use us for their own ends, but this time we're using them.' Church felt uncomfortable trying to play Callow. A streak of madness that ran through him made him impossible to predict; Church still didn't really know what the Fomorii had done to him inside. 'I've got a feeling you know something that might help us. Where the Fomorii main nest is, where Balor is hidden, building up his strength. Some weakness—'

'Oh, you really are a prime example of hope over reality,' Callow snapped bitterly. 'I should give up my hard-won knowledge? For what? A chance to be seen as *good*?' He waggled his fingers to show the gap where he had sliced the one off himself. 'You forget, my little pet, the only reason I would want to take your hand is to harvest your digits.'

'So you don't know anything, then.' Church made to go.

'I know a great many things that would shock and surprise you,' Callow replied sharply, stung by the dismissal. 'I know what makes your eyes light up. And where the Luck of the Land lies. And I know what happened on this Ship of Fools last night.'

'How?'

'I can hear things through the walls. Through many walls.'

'I know what happened last night. That's not important to me—'

'You would think, wouldn't you?' Callow smirked again; Church couldn't tell if it was more petty tormenting or if he truly did know something of import. 'Now be off with you, and leave me to my peace and quiet,' Callow snapped, 'and don't return unless you have the key to release me from this foul den.'

When he reached the door, Callow called out to him again, 'Are you missing your friends? Do you feel lost without them? Too weak and inexperienced? What is it like to know they are all dead, dead, dead . . .'

Church stepped out and slammed the door hard so he wouldn't have to hear any more.

*

The first thought was like a candle in a room that had remained dark for an age. It flickered, dangerously close to extinction, but then caught. Slowly, the heat and the light returned.

For Laura, memories pieced together gradually and chaotically, sparing her the full horror of revelation in one devastating blow. Making love to Church. The joy she felt at finally finding someone to whom she could open up the dark chambers of her soul. Making love to Shavi, a friend who defied any insipid meaning she had given to the word in the past. Her hated mother, her pathetic father. Her friends. Her work: computer screens and mobile phones. One image returning in force: trees. The things she had fought for so many times with her environmental activism.

They gathered pace, memories clinging together, forming patterns in the chaos. The quest. The Quincunx, the five who are one. Brothers and Sisters of Dragons. Talismans and Blue Fire. Standing stones and old religion. Tuatha Dé Danann and Fomorii. And Balor.

And Balor.

Electricity jolted her body into convulsions. She recalled with crystal clarity the night on Mam Tor when she had taken the potion from Cernunnos and made the sacrifice that would end her life; for Ruth, for everyone. When she took Balor into her own body.

Another shock, dragging her from the recesses of her head. How could she still be alive, thinking? When Balor emerged from her it would have rended her body apart.

Gradually details of her surroundings broke through her confusion. She was lying on her back in a dark place; as her eyes adjusted she realised there was a thin light source filtering in from somewhere. The air was thick with the stench of decomposition. She choked, gagged, tried to breathe in small gasps that went straight to the back of her throat. She made the mistake of turning her head and looked into a pair of glassy eyes only inches from her. It was a woman, not much older than her. Beyond she could just make out irregular shapes heaped all around. They resembled bags of discarded clothing.

Closing her eyes, she took refuge once more in her head, but even there no safety lay. Her body was racked with pain. Slowly she let her hands move down her torso towards her belly, dreading the end of their journey. They were halted by sharpness and void almost before they had started.

Initially she couldn't work out what she was feeling, and then when she did, she refused to believe it. But there was no doubt. Her ribs were protruding on both sides like jagged teeth around the hollow from which Balor had erupted.

It couldn't be. She was dead. Dead and dreaming. Her arms collapsed to her side and her thoughts fragmented once more.

The next time she was aware, she let her hands investigate once more, praying it had been a hallucination. And this time there were no broken ribs and gaping wound, although her clothes around that area were shredded.

Her relief left her sobbing silently for several minutes.

Finally she found the strength to lever herself up on her elbows. From the air currents she could tell she was in some cavernous room, the ceiling and walls lost to the shadows. All around were corpses, piled in rolling dunes. Faces and hands and feet were pressing into her back and legs. So many dead. Hundreds. Thousands. Amidst the horror she was thankful for the small mercy that she was on the top and not drowning beneath the sea of bodies. And she was alive. Amazingly, astonishingly alive.

Then she cried some more.

In the Court of the Yearning Heart, laughter often sounds like the cries of the insane. The walls are never quite thick enough to prevent the noises coming through from adjoining rooms; whimpers of pleasure and pain, others a combination of both. Scents continually tease, each one subtle and complex so the passer-by dwells on them for minutes, perhaps hours. Every surface has a pleasing texture; it is impossible to touch anything once without wanting immediately to touch it again. Addiction can spring from the merest taste of the food to the tongue.

In comparison, the chamber designated for Tom was almost unpleasantly ascetic. He had stripped everything from it to minimise the sensory overload so that his life was, if not acceptable, then bearable. At least he no longer had to worry about accepting the food or drink of Otherworld; there was little hope he would be leaving the Court any time in the near future. Prisoner by his own hand, or theirs, it made no matter.

He sat cross-legged in the centre of the room, smoking a joint to dull his searing emotions: wishing he could smoke enough to shut down his thoughts completely. Despite the clothes that had been offered to him by the Tuatha Dé Danann, he still resembled an ageing hippie: his greying hair was fastened into a ponytail with an elastic band, the wire-rimmed spectacles had been fashionable in the late sixties, his too-washed T-shirt and old army jacket: they all grounded him in the experiences of the world he had left behind. And for the first time he felt the hundreds of years piled high on his shoulders. He had thought himself immune to the rigours of passing time, but now it felt as raw as it had in the first century or so of his transformation.

They had taken Veitch four hours ago. How long before they spat him out of the inner recesses of the Court where the miracles and atrocities occurred, torn apart and rebuilt into *something else*? Decades, as it had been in Tom's own case? Or longer? He winced, unable to stop the razored parade of memories of his own early experiences at their hands. After so long, they were still just beneath the surface, torturing every second of his life. He had already shed tears for the suffering Veitch would face in the times ahead, and he did so again, briefly and silently. Would Veitch grow to love his tormentors even as he hated them, just as Tom had? He thought he probably would.

Then Tom, grown emotional through the drugs, battled a wave of damp emotion, this time for himself. For the first time he had found kindred spirits, friends even, although he had never told them that, and all he had done was witness their appalling suffering. Now he might never see any of them again, not even Veitch, who would no longer be Veitch when he returned, in the same way that he was no longer Thomas Learmont. Against all that, even the destruction about to be instigated by the Fomorii was meaningless.

He took a deep draught of the joint, trying to decide if that thought was selfishness or some deep psychological insight; not really caring.

The door was flung open some hours later and Veitch tumbled into the room. Dazed and winded, he came to rest in a heap against the far wall. It took Tom a second or two to realise what he was seeing; even then, he barely dared believe it.

'So soon?' he said, puzzled.

'Don't just sit there, you old hippie,' Veitch snapped.

Tom scrambled over to help him to his feet. 'You're fine?'

Veitch examined his hands, then stretched the kinks out of his arm muscles, unable to believe it himself. His long hair was lank with the sweat of fear, his tough, good-looking features drawn with apprehension.

'What happened?'

Veitch was surprised at the bald relief in the hippie's voice after weeks of his curt, dismissive manner. 'I don't know what happened. When they took me from here I was brought before *Her Majesty*.' There was a sneer in Veitch's voice, but Tom knew it was there only to mask the fear of the Queen of the Court of the Yearning Heart, architect of all desire and suffering. 'She gave me some spiel about how I was setting off a *new phase of existence*. Didn't really know what she was talking

954

about, to be honest.' He examined his hands closely. 'Wasn't really listening.'

Tom remembered the same response: the fear of what lay ahead driving all rational thought down to its lowest level; not thinking, just reacting. He reached out a supportive hand; surprisingly, Veitch allowed it to rest briefly on his forearm; a small thing, but a sign of how deeply he had been affected.

'They took me through these red curtains into a room that was hung with tapestries. There was a wooden bench in the middle. They tied me to it. Up on the ceiling, there was something, a light of some kind. Only it wasn't a *real* light. It was like it had a life of its own, you know?' His description faltered under the limitations of his vocabulary and his unstructured thought processes, but Tom nodded in recognition. Veitch appeared relieved he wouldn't have to go into it further.

'And then whatever the light was, it made me black out. Next thing I knew I was looking up at the Queen and she was . . .' He searched for the right word. 'Furious.'

A tremor crossed Tom's face.

'Her face sort of . . . changed. Kept changing. Like . . . like . . .'

'Like it wasn't fixed.'

'Exactly. Like she was breaking up. Turning into something else. Lots of things. I dunno why. I mean, it wasn't like I'd done anything. I'd been out like a light. Next thing I know those jackboot bastards who always follow her around dragged me back here.'

Tom dropped back on to the floor, slipping easily into his cross-legged stance, his face locked in an expression of deep rumination; it didn't make sense, whichever way it was examined. The Queen would not have given up the opportunity to spend decades tantalising and tormenting a mortal for anything. He eyed Veitch suspiciously. 'Are you sure it wasn't some trick? Offering you the chance of hope, only to snatch it away. The pain is more acute that way.' The note of bitter experience rang in his voice.

'No, you should have seen her, mate. It was real. Scared the shit out of me.' Veitch grinned broadly, then cracked his knuckles. 'Fuck it. Who cares? Maybe there's a chance we'll get out of here.'

'The Queen will *never* let you go.'

'Don't be so bleedin' negative. You didn't see them. They were all like . . .' He made a dismissive hand gesture. 'Like I was something on the bottom of their shoe.'

Before Tom could consider the matter further, the door rattled open. Melliflor and the Queen's Honour Guard stood without, dressed in the freakish golden armour that resembled a mix of sea shells and spiderwebs, offset by silk the colour of blood; armour worn only for the most important occasions. Recognising the signs, Tom struggled to his feet. Veitch stepped in front of him protectively, the tendons on his arms growing taut.

Devoid of its usual mockery, Melliflor's face was contemptuous, hacked from cold granite. 'Our Lady of Light demands your presence.'

Demands, Tom noted. Not *requests*. All pretence of politeness had been dropped; they were no longer favoured guests, nor even figures of fun. 'How could we deny her?' Tom saw the dangerous glint in Melliflor's eye and knew he could afford not even the slightest mockery. He bowed his head and, with Veitch at his heel, followed the guard out of the room.

The Queen of Heart's Desire sat in the centre of a room where twenty braziers roared like blast furnaces. The air was unbearably thick with heat and smoke. Despite the light from the flames, gloom still clung to the periphery, beyond the thick tapestries in scarlet and gold that swathed the stone walls. It was oppressively unpleasant, yet still seared with sensation.

The first time Veitch had seen the Queen, she had been the embodiment of sexual craving, sucking at every part of him that *needed*; naked, splayed, prostrate, for him alone, yet still somehow above him, still in control. Even though he knew she was manipulating every pump of his blood, he couldn't help wanting her; even though the rational part of him had only contempt for her, he would have given himself to her immediately, done anything asked of him.

Now, though, she was enveloped in a brocaded gown and cloak that covered her from neck to toes; a headdress left only the smallest heart of face visible, and that was glacial. She wouldn't even meet his eyes. Despite himself, he felt broken-hearted, unwanted. He looked at Tom and saw the Rhymer felt the same.

Tom bowed his head. 'Have we offended you in some way, my Queen?'

She looked over their heads as if the voice had come from the shadowy corners. 'Fragile Creatures are always offensive.'

'What's wrong?' Veitch was shocked when the words emerged from his mouth, so rimmed with pathetic submission were they; he couldn't help himself, that was the worst thing.

'You are free to leave the Court of the Yearning Heart.' She addressed Tom directly. 'All compacts and contracts are rescinded. This is a gift given freely and without obligation.'

Tom kept his head bowed. 'We thank you for your hospitality, my Queen. And may I say—'

She raised her hand. Instantly Melliflor was at Tom's side, directing him towards the exit. The rapidity of their dismissal took them both by surprise, but Tom saw Veitch bristle before they had reached the door.

'Is that it?' Veitch hissed. Then: 'What's up with her?' When Tom didn't answer, Veitch thought for a long moment and then said, 'She just got bored, didn't she, like some fucking spoilt aristocrat.' He tried not to sound too hurt. 'She's found something else to interest her more. We're just . . . nothing.'

'Hush!' Tom cautioned with blazing eyes. 'If you want to get out of here alive—'

'True Thomas.'

A look of horror crossed his face at her voice. He turned sharply. 'My Queen?'

'The Quincunx are no more, True Thomas.'

Veitch saw Tom blanch. 'What's she on about?' he whispered.

'The shaman has moved on from the Fixed Lands.' A cruel smile lay comfortably on her face.

Tom bowed his head, this time for himself. 'And the other Brother and Sisters of Dragons, my Queen?'

She inclined her head thoughtfully. 'One of them sleeps in a charnel pit. I hear the other two travel to the Western Isles, True Thomas. And you know what that means.'

Veitch looked to Tom for explanation, although in his heart he understood the sense of the Queen's words. He stifled the rising panic, pretending he didn't believe them. Tom's face wouldn't allow him to wallow in the lie, and then Melliflor was once again steering them towards the door.

They emerged on to the summit of the Hill of Yews on an ethereal, late summer morning. Grey mist drifted amongst the gravestones and the clustering trees; the whole world was half-formed; fluid. It was cool and still, disturbed only by the occasional bird song and a wild fluttering in the treetops. They could hear no car nor plane nor boat on the nearby river. Their first thought was that they were the only ones left alive.

'Can you feel it?' Tom asked.

And Veitch did, though he was by far and away the least sensitive of them all: there was a sourness in the air.

'Balor is here,' Tom said redundantly.

Like a child, Veitch still refused to accept. 'Then why hasn't it all been wiped away?' His gesture took in the towering trees and the stones and the War monument and the glimpses of Inverness beyond.

'It can afford to take its time. Not that time has any meaning for it.' Tom drew in a deep breath of air, surprised he was still alive, stunned by how much he was glad to be back; he had thought he couldn't feel anything so acutely any more. 'It's waiting for Samhain, when its power is at a peak. But things are moving.' He closed his eyes and gave himself up to the sensations. 'Things are moving over the lip of reality, creeping here, eating away at the edges.'

Veitch kicked at the wet grass. 'That's why she threw us out. Suddenly she's got something more important to think about. She's like a spoilt brat who's been told she can't play with her toys because she'd got to do her homework.'

'You could be right. It would be unwise for the Tuatha Dé Danann to ignore the threat of the Fomorii. The Queen may well have been entreated to face up to her obligations.'

'Fuck it.' Veitch furiously blinked away tears that had appeared from nowhere. 'Shavi's dead.'

Tom nodded slowly. 'It appears so.'

Veitch's shoulders slumped until a new revelation dawned on him. 'But not Ruth!'

'Somehow she survived.'

'But if Shavi died, and we failed, who saved her?' His eyes narrowed. 'That bitch wasn't lying, was she?'

'No. She told us about Shavi to hurt us. If she could have hurt you more by telling you Ruth was dead, she would have done.'

Veitch punched the air. 'Yes! Jesus, yes!' Tom watched his emotions see-saw as he struggled to cope with Shavi's loss and Ruth's survival. 'But Shavi . . .'

'You were close to him. I'm sorry.' His sorrow was much deeper than his words suggested; without the five of them there was no hope. But that didn't make sense: he had seen the end, or part of it at least. That was the trouble with second sight: it never gave a true picture.

'I know he was a queen and all, but, you know, he was all right.' Veitch, never one to express sensitive emotions, looked like he was about to tear himself apart trying to find words to maintain his pride, yet show his true feelings.

Tom spared him. 'Come on. This isn't a place we want to tarry.'

Inverness was a ghost town. It didn't take them long to discover that technology had finally given up its futile battle to maintain a foothold in the world. The people they met looked uniformly dazed, as if they were walking through a dream, waiting to wake. But as the day passed, those who were determined to maintain some degree of normality came out of the woodwork. They found a café near the river where the owner had sourced produce from local farmers, but her face had the perpetually troubled expression of someone who worried how much longer it could last. Cash was still accepted; things hadn't yet broken down that much. Veitch and Tom had only a few pounds left between them in crumpled notes and coins, and they decided to blow it all on a big breakfast. Nothing tasted as vibrant or heady as the food in Otherworld, but, surprisingly, it was more fulfilling. Three weeks had passed since Lughnasadh and Balor's return, nearly a month of so-far gentle winding-down.

The breakfast passed in funereal silence. They should have been jubilant at their escape from Otherworld, but Shavi's death weighed so heavily on Veitch, nothing else felt important.

Over strong tea at the end of the heavy, fried meal, Veitch asked, 'So what do we do now?'

Tom blew on his tea, but even before he spoke, Veitch could tell he had no answers. That disturbed him; the hippie had always acted like he knew everything. 'Jack and Ruth are on their way to the Western Isles. There's nothing we can do until they return. *If* they return.' He spent a moment floundering around for words, then looked Veitch squarely in the eye. 'Everything has changed, Ryan. We cannot move ahead as we have in the past.'

'So we didn't stop the biggest Bastard of all coming back. We've had setbacks before—'

'No. It's worse than you understand. I know you find it hard to see beneath the surface – that's not where your strengths lie. But I think you realise everything we see around isn't the picture at all. It's a shop window decoration, a lie designed with a particular aim in mind. Behind it is a complex pattern of powers and relationships. Things work differently there. A single muttered word can have unguessed repercussions. Symbols weave through that pattern, across time and space, wielding powers undreamed of. There are rules none of us know, Ryan, a language we can't begin to understand.'

'What are you saying?'

'Five is one of those things that sends powerful ripples through all of existence, Ryan. Forget everything you know for a moment, if you can. Five is not a number. Let's give it another definition to point you in the right direction. Say, Five is a word we give to a nuclear generator, creating great energy that could transform the world, but also great destructive force.' Tom stared into Veitch's eyes, waiting for that familiar glazing over, but Veitch's gaze remained true, if troubled. 'There have to be five of you, Ryan. If not, the power isn't there. However much effort you expend, however clever you are, it will amount to nothing, because in the new language we're talking about, Three has a different meaning. It has to be Five. And it has to be the Five selected by whatever the unifying force is, whether you call it God or Goddess or the Voice of the Universe.'

Veitch looked dazed. 'You're saying it really is all over? I thought the message you were trying to drum into us all was that there's always hope? Because that's what I feel here.' He thumped his heart. 'So I know it's right. You taught us that, and I learned it well. So don't come here with your bleedin' mealy-mouthed talk of failure 'cause I'm not having any of it. Are you telling me we can't do anything?' He jabbed a finger at Tom's face. 'Are you?'

Tom finished his tea thoughtfully. 'I know things will come to a head. I know it will be a dark and disturbing time, but I have no idea if the resolution will be the one we all hope for. Perhaps we *can* do something.' At that moment he felt the weight of his great age.

One of the other early diners leaned over them on his way out. He was an old man in a dark, faded overcoat and thinning snowy hair above a similarly bleached face. 'Put a smile on your face,' he said in his lyrical Highlands accent. 'You'll be dead a long time. However bad it is now, think on that.'

'See,' Veitch said. 'Even he can bleedin' well see it.'

Rattling his cup in its saucer, Tom stood up and attempted to ease the strain from his limbs. The terrors of the Court of the Yearning Heart had shaken him to the core of his being; he needed time to find his true centre once more, his confidence. He truly didn't know which way to turn, but Ryan was relying on him, as they all had relied on him. He looked down at the childlike hope on Veitch's face and felt an abiding sadness.

'Come on, then,' he said. 'We'd better go and talk to the universe.'

The clear night sky was awash with a thousand stars normally obscured by the mundane glow of sodium lights, while the moon shone its brilliant rays through the treetops. The air was warm from the heat of the day and filled with the aroma of pine. The only sounds were their footsteps on the deserted road and the lapping of the waves in the loch.

Veitch couldn't stop looking up at the sky, feeling a small part of something immense and wonderful. Even a country boy would have thought it was special, but to Veitch, raised in a city where the night sky was a mystery, it was unbelievable. Even the thick shadows that swamped the hillsides running to the loch took a friendly cast.

'It's a good night,' Tom said, as if sensing his companion's thoughts.

'I've seen a lot of country over the last few weeks, but nothing like this.'

'There's still magic out there. Even with all that's happening.'

'Maybe it's become more powerful *because* of what's happening.'

Tom was surprised at Veitch's insight; it was rarely given voice, but when it did it came in inspirational flashes. 'You know what, I think you're right.'

'Yeah, magic. Something for us to plug into.' They walked in silence for a few yards and then Veitch added, 'Shavi would have loved this.'

Tom felt humbled by the aching loss he heard in Veitch's voice, but there was warmth there, too, of a kind Veitch had never before exhibited. During their journey north to the Court of the Yearning Heart Tom had learned to see his companion in a new light, more than just a caricature of muscles and South London *honour*; he was a good man, for all his faults, riven by neuroses, but with a decent heart. 'He was developing into a fine shaman. I was surprised how quickly he took to his abilities, always pushing back the boundaries, striving to better himself.'

'Yeah, that's it, innit? We all try to do the best we can, but it came natural to him. It's not fair he caught it first.'

'How do you feel about it?'

'Like I've lost my best mate.' Subconsciously he pushed himself a few paces ahead of Tom, head bowed, his hanging hair obscuring his face. 'I miss his advice, y'know. He always knew the right thing to say. I've never known anybody . . . sensible before.'

Tom was prepared to continue the conversation, but Veitch pushed on a little further, keen to be alone with his thoughts.

It had taken them most of the day to walk from Inverness, and even their hardened muscles were starting to ache. It would be just an hour or so more before they reached their final destination in Glen Urquhart, the valley running down to Loch Ness. For Veitch, the surroundings were still haunted by his memories of the hunt for the Questing Beast and the subsequent battle that had left him only a hair's-breadth from death.

They came up on the site Tom had identified on the map just before midnight; it was the place where Veitch had found the remains of one of the Questing Beast's victims, but the body was no longer there.

Corrimony was the home of a chambered cairn made of water-worn stone taken from the nearby river Enrick. It lay in green pasture at the foot of pine-covered hills, swathed in an atmosphere of abiding peace.

'Can you feel it?' Tom's voice was almost lost beneath the breeze.

Electricity buzzed in the soles of Veitch's feet, sending not-unpleasant crackles up to his knees. When he held up his hand, the faintest blue nimbus limned it against the dark of the landscape. 'Bloody hell,' he said in hushed awe.

'Since the Well of Fire at Edinburgh was ignited, this part of the land has come alive. At the right time, in the right atmosphere, it's quite potent.' Tom squatted down and stretched out an arm. When his finger was an inch from the sward a blue spark jumped between them.

'What are you going to do?'

'What Shavi would have done if he'd been here, only not as well. I learnt bits and pieces from the Culture, but not enough. I'm not a natural like he was. The Pendragon Spirit is an unbroken chain linking Shavi to the ancient races that set up these things, the ones who preserved their knowledge in the land. He was a lightning rod, attracting it all to him.' Tom dropped to his hands and knees and crawled into the claustrophobically low tunnel that led into the heart of the cairn. Veitch heard his voice float back, although the words were obviously not meant for him. 'I'm not much good for anything, really.'

Veitch followed until they were both sitting on the damp stone flags, backs against the rough rock walls, the stars scattered overhead.

'In times past you wouldn't have seen the night sky.' Tom's voice echoed oddly against the stones. 'There would have been a roof over us. Probably torn down by some stupid farmer to make his field boundaries. That brief journey through the tunnel into here is one of those symbols I spoke about earlier.'

'The new language?' Veitch thought for a second. 'The *true* language.'

'It was a mark of distinction, between the real world without and the Otherworld here, a shadowy place where the outside rules didn't hold. It was supposed to symbolise death, too, and birth, or rebirth. Here, we are reborn into a new world of mystery and magic.' He took out the tin in which he kept his hash. '*Here we are stoned, immaculate.*'

'I know that one,' Veitch said. 'The Doors.'

Tom slowly rolled a joint, crumbling a portion of hash into the tobacco. 'Then you had better prepare yourself for weird scenes inside the goldmine.'

'A mate of mine used to smoke all the time. Off his face, morning, noon and night. Didn't mind the odd one myself, like, just to chill, but I couldn't do it like he could.'

'Then he was a very stupid person. Would you buy a missile launcher and go out taking pot-shots? These drugs are sacramental. Those who use them for hedonism are like stupid children stealing the church wine.'

'What do you mean?'

'Crowley had it right.' Tom looked up from his task, saw the blank look on Veitch's face. 'Aleister Crowley. A self-styled magician a few decades back. He was actually quite good, though I'd never have told the arrogant bastard to his face. I spent a weekend with him at Boleskin House, his place here on the shores of Loch Ness. He summoned up what he thought was the god Pan. I think it was Cernunnos playing games with him, but I digress. Crowley had no time for people who used drugs like a few pints down the local, because he knew the power of them; their capacity for touching the sacred. Throughout history ancient cultures have used psychoactive substances for breaking the barrier between the real world and the invisible world. That's why I use them, and why Shavi used them.'

Veitch nodded thoughtfully. Tom thought how like a schoolboy he looked, taking a lesson from a stern master.

'So what's going to happen?'

'I don't know.'

'Jesus!'

'I told you – I'm no expert. I'm just trying to do the best I can. This is the right spot, a powerful spot. The drug will condition our minds. Then we'll try to make contact with something that can help us.'

Veitch cursed. 'I wish you'd told me this before. I wouldn't be sitting here with you now.'

'Why do you think I didn't tell you before?'

'You know what it sounds like to me? *The Deerhunter*. Bleedin' Russian roulette. All the things out there . . . Christ! You're saying we should call something in and take a chance it's something good. Shit!'

'If you put your faith in the universe, it often helps you out.'

'What, if you jump off a bridge something will catch you?'

'Now you're being silly.' He lit the joint, took a long draught, then passed it over to Veitch. 'This is a ceremony—'

'No more Doors, all right? Get with the decade.'

Tom slowly raised his eyes to the glittering stars. Beyond the cairn they could hear the wind shuffling through the trees. 'Old stories.'

'What?'

'Myths and legends are our way of glimpsing the true language of existence. In them we can see the archetypes. The real meaning of numbers and words and symbols. Those talismans you fought so hard for – they are not simply a Sword, a Spear, a Stone and a Cauldron. The

Sword is the elemental power of air and represents intellect. The Spear is fire, the spirit. The Cauldron is water, compassion. The Stone is earth, existence. We just have to be clever. Ignore the world-view imposed on us by the Age of Reason. We have to go back to sensing the mystery at the heart of life. That is the only way forward.'

'So we tell each other stories?'

'All of human society is based on stories, Ryan. They're not just words, they're alive; powerful. There's a theory about things called memes. In essence, they're ideas that act like viruses. You put an idea out into the world – tell it to a friend, get him to pass it on – and soon the idea filters out into society and everyone begins to alter their way of behaving to take the new idea on board. The idea – one person's idea – has actually changed the shape of society. That's the modern way of explaining it. Stories are memes, very powerful ones, because they speak directly to the subconscious using archetypes.' He watched Veitch's face intently, still surprised the Londoner could maintain his concentration; perhaps he truly was changing. 'Stories shape lives. People pick up little lessons from them, believe a certain way to act is the correct way, grow more like their heroes. If you have stories riddled with cynicism, the world will grow more like them, over time. Our myths today are Hollywood movies and TV. In America, in the eighties, there was a crime series called *Hill Street Blues*. The police who saw it started to mimic the way the characters acted, altered the way they went about their business on the streets. An entire culture was changed by one story. In ancient Sumeria the citizens took on board the worldview expressed by their archetypal hero Gilgamesh. He defined them.'

Veitch coughed and spluttered as the smoke burned his lungs. 'I get it. Down in Deptford I knew some villains – small-time wankers, you know – they saw that film *Lock, Stock and Two Smoking Barrels* and started dressing and talking like the geezers in it.'

'Exactly. Stories are our dreams, Ryan, and we dream our society and our reality. If we dream hard enough, we can make it what we want. If we dream hard enough.'

'Shavi said something to me like that.'

'Oh?'

'Not the same, really. But like it. He said if I dreamed myself as a hero I would be. If I saw myself as a sad loser, that's the way I'd stay.'

'Everything is fluid, Ryan. Nothing is fixed.'

Veitch rubbed his eyes as Tom appeared to grow hazy; he didn't know if it was a trick of the drugs or if it was really happening. His attention moved to the dark rocks of the cairn walls. Occasionally ripples of blue light flickered amongst them. In that place it felt like anything could happen. He steeled himself. Tom's quiet, lilting voice was like a magical spell, weaving an atmosphere of change around him.

'I know what you're talking about,' Veitch heard himself saying. 'You want us to dream up some of those old stories to show us what to do. Arky – what?'

'Archetypes. Symbols that take the shape of something we can understand. Things that speak with power.'

'Listen!' Veitch started. 'Did you hear that?' It had sounded to him like a hunting horn, echoing mournfully along the glen.

Tom was watching him like a raptor. 'What are you dreaming up, Ryan?' he asked softly.

'I don't know.' Had he really heard it? An image of the Wild Hunt intruded roughly on his mind and he began to panic.

Tom placed a calming hand on his knee. 'Something is rising from your subconscious—'

'Can this place do that?' The drug gave an edge of anxiety to Veitch's thoughts.

'The Blue Fire is the base stuff of everything, Ryan. It's there to be shaped and controlled, and this place was designed to focus that ability.'

'Things are happening.' Veitch chewed on a knuckle. He felt he could hear something moving through the deeply wooded slopes of the glen away near Loch Ness, although it was obviously too far for any sound to truly travel. 'I was thinking of Robin Hood. When you were talking about stories . . . It was something my dad read to me once . . .'

'The slightest thought, if focused enough, would be all it takes, Ryan.'

'But Robin Hood, like . . . I remember what Ruth said. That was one of the names for—'

'Cernunnos, yes. The gods are archetypes given form, but the archetypes are bigger than them.' He paused. 'I'm not making any sense, am I?' He took another drag on the joint, as if determined to make it worse. 'But perhaps that is the right archetype for this moment, Ryan. You may think the thought surfaced randomly, but there is no coincidence in this world.'

'Robin Hood.' Veitch's voice was heavy with anticipation; the atmosphere in the cairn was charged. The blue light had grown stronger, unwavering now, casting a sapphire tint over everything. He took the joint back and drew on it deeply. The sharpness of the rocks faded into the background and the light took on greater depth.

'Robin Hood,' Tom mused. 'The hunter in the deep, dark forest of the night. The rebellious force against the oppressive control of rigid authority. Wild creativity opposing the structured thought of the Age of Reason.'

The words washed over Veitch, whatever meaning they held seeping into him on some level beyond hearing. Another blast of the hunting horn, not too far away. Now Veitch could tell it was different to the sound of the Wild Hunt's horn; not so menacing, almost hopeful.

'But be careful.' Tom's warning sounded as if it came from the depths of a well. 'If you lose control of the archetype, its power can overwhelm you, tear you apart.'

'I wish you hadn't said that,' Veitch snapped. 'It's a bleedin' meme, isn't it? It's in my bleedin' head now.'

'At least you were paying attention.' Tom took several calming breaths; Veitch realised the hippie felt anxious too. 'My warning will focus your mind. You won't lose control.'

'Yeah. Keep telling me that.'

Feet rattled the stones on the road beyond the gate of the cairn compound. Rhythmic breathing that could have been a man's but was more like an animal's filled the air.

'He's here,' Tom said, redundantly.

Veitch felt his muscles clench with tension, barely able to believe it was something he had done, and with such little effort; but that tiny, out-of-the-way place felt so super-charged he was convinced he could do anything here.

'Speak to him,' Tom whispered.

'Me?' More panic; that wasn't one of his strengths, but then he thought how well Shavi would have done in the situation and that gave him the courage to continue. 'Hello.' His voice sounded too fragile. He tried again, stronger this time.

The sound of scrabbling echoed as something moved up the side of the cairn, seeking footholds amongst the tightly packed stones. A silhouette appeared over the rim, looking down at them.

'Hello,' he repeated once more.

The figure squatted on the roof's edge, watching them both sitting cross-legged on the stone flags. As it shifted, Veitch caught sight of a face filled with wisdom and kindliness, but also righteous defiance. There was certainly a beard, but while he saw the features, they were forgotten in an instant after his eyes lighted on them; this was all-faces, all humanity boiled down. The indefinable, tight-fitting clothes were of the Lincoln Green he had anticipated from his storybook of old, but at times they appeared to be vegetation rather than fabric or leather; and growing out of the figure itself. Strapped across his back was a bow of gnarled wood that also seemed oddly organic.

'I heard your call.' His voice, which came from everywhere at once, was comforting and fatherly; the tension eased in Veitch's shoulders immediately.

Instinctively, he knew how to talk to the visitor and what to say. 'We're looking for help. Guidance.' He was surprised to hear his own voice sounded disembodied too. 'We've got this big job to do. A big *heroes'* job. Saving the world and all that. But things have gone pear-shaped. We don't know what to do next.'

The figure stood up gracefully and walked slowly widdershins around the precarious lip of what remained of the roof. Veitch watched his progress until he grew dizzy. Then, after what felt like an age, the figure spoke. 'Every story is like a wave crashing against a beach, and there are as many stories as there are waves. There is the height when the sun sparkles on the white crest and the dark trough when shadow turns the water to slate. Each appears the end of something, but it is only when the surf runs over the sand that the equal importance of both can be seen in the journey to the shore.' He turned on his heel and began his circular journey in the opposite direction. 'In your story, times are unduly dark, but you maintain hope; I feel it shining from within you, and that is good for the heroes' work. I feel, too, your pain at the loss of one close to you.'

A deep silence fell over the scene; waiting.

'We need five of us to continue,' Veitch began. 'There have to be five Brothers and Sisters of Dragons. You know, the Pendragon Spirit. One's dead now. What are we going to do?'

'There are no boundaries.' The words echoed amongst the stones. 'The emerald silence of the green wood stretches on to infinity. You pass through wooded acres and appear to move on, to a new place and new sights, but it is the same wood.'

Veitch was struggling to understand, but he knew perfectly why the archetype was continually speaking in metaphors, the root of the true language.

The figure squatted down once more to look at them, as if invisible cycles had come into alignment, focusing its intent. 'The shaman is gone, but he can be returned.'

'Shavi?'

'You may fetch him back from the Grim Lands, the Grey Lands.'

'How?' Tom interjected. 'There is no return for our kind.'

'Special circumstances have seen fit to forge a pathway. The link still remains between the shaman's corporeal form and his essence.'

Veitch looked to Tom, puzzled but hopeful. The Rhymer pondered on this information briefly, then asked, 'What special circumstances—'

'Your patron has chosen to preserve his form—'

'Cernunnos,' Tom said.

'It resides in a bower, ready to be wakened.' The archetype rose and looked towards the dark horizon as if something were calling it.

'Where?' Tom asked.

'On the Hill of Giants, where the Night Rider awaits his challenges. But time is short. The protection is diminishing and soon the link will be broken.'

'How long have we got?' Veitch was afraid the information had come too late for them to act on it.

'Not long.'

It was a vague answer, but it was obvious the archetype would not or could not elucidate. It began to ease back down the slope of the cairn. 'Now—'

'Wait,' Veitch said humbly. 'Can I walk with you? Just for a while?'

The archetype paused, then held out a shadowy hand. It felt like velvet in Veitch's fingers. The archetype hauled him out effortlessly and they both slipped down to the ground. Veitch felt uplifted, sensing on some deep level the heroic essence. It felt more like energy crackling in the air than a person at his side, but when he cast a surreptitious glance, it was unmistakably Robin Hood. They moved across the road to the nature reserve beyond, keeping low like animals. Veitch was sure some of whatever constituted the archetype was rubbing off on him. His senses were sharpened, his spirit was soaring, as if he had consumed a quantity of drugs or was in the grip of some spiritual fervour.

When they had crossed a barbed wire fence into a field on the valley slopes, Veitch couldn't contain himself any longer. 'Show me,' he whispered like a child.

The archetype seemed to smile. In one fluid movement it took the bow from its back, fitted an oddly fashioned arrow and loosed it. Veitch heard the twang as the arrow neatly severed the top strand of barbed wire on the fence about thirty yards further down the field.

''mazing.' He *did* feel like a child again; a wizened memory of playing one of Robin Hood's Merrie Men in a Greenwich backstreet was given new flesh. It was the kind of feeling adults spent all their life searching for, but which he had convinced himself didn't exist anywhere in society. And perhaps it hadn't before; but now things were different.

The archetype appeared to read his thoughts. With an expansive gesture, it said, 'This night is magic, alive with potential. Here you are connected to the infinite.'

His feeling of exaltation grew stronger until every part of his body was tingling. He felt heady from the potency of the experience; it was truly religious, like he was about to turn towards the face of God. 'What does this all mean?' he sighed.

'This is how existence should be.' The archetype knelt on one knee to touch the grass gently. 'Dreams start within, then grow bigger until one can live within them. There are no boundaries; anything can happen. Fluidity, hope, expression.' He fixed a gaze on Veitch that was almost electric. 'Mythologies were never intended to be only stories. Dream hard enough and you can exist within them: neither reality, nor fantasy: just one realm of infinite possibilities.' He made another wide gesture. 'Look. The stories live. All of this exists within the age of heroes, as it was intended.'

When Veitch looked around, he noticed for the first time shadowy figures standing away on the field boundaries or amongst the nearby trees: old heroes, some he recognised, with shining swords and armour, crowns and shields, but many he did not; yet he *felt* he knew them all. The wonder washed over him in such force he was driven to his knees.

It was at least an hour later when Veitch made his way back to the cairn. A shooting star cut an arc across the sky. Tom was still inside, smoking the remnants of a joint while humming gently to himself.

'Weren't you worried about me?' Veitch said as he emerged from the tunnel, his face beatific.

'I knew you were in good hands. Did he give you an education?'

Veitch was unable to restrain his smile.

'Good,' Tom said. 'Make the most of your contact with the great beyond for tomorrow we have a life to save and choices to make which could wipe the smile from your face.'

Veitch didn't hear him; he was looking up to the stars, for the first time in his life feeling he was a part of something enormous; feeling that there really was hope for him.

CHAPTER FIVE

In League with the
Stones of the Field

Tom and Veitch stayed in the cool confines of the cairn until the sky turned gold and purple, and then a powder-blue. It was going to be a fine day. Veitch's mood had remained ecstatic as he babbled through the final hours of darkness about what he had experienced with the archetype. Tom could see some long-neglected part of him had been touched by the encounter. He was loath to bring Veitch down with discussion of what lay ahead, but it had to be done; the archetype had stressed time was short.

After a brief, unappetising breakfast of roots, herbs and edible flowers Tom had foraged from the surrounding hedgerows and fields, the conversation turned to Shavi. Veitch was surprisingly confident, his usual strategic caution stifled by his joy that there was still hope he would see his friend again.

'You know where Shavi is?' Tom chose his words carefully as he gently prodded the small campfire that had taken the chill off the early morning air. 'Not where his body is, but where *he* is.'

'The Grim Lands. Or the Grey Lands.'

'Two names to describe the same place. It's the Land of the Dead, Ryan.'

Veitch shrugged.

'Doesn't that fill you with dread? It's been a source of nightmares for the human race since the dawn of our people, and with good cause.'

'Don't start getting all negative.' Veitch's body language showed he didn't want to hear any of Tom's cautionary tales. 'Over the last few months I've seen and done things that would have had me screaming like a bleedin' idiot when I was just some chancer down in South London. Everything's a nightmare – that's the way it is these days. You just get on with it. So let's get on with it.'

Tom cursed under his breath. 'I knew it would be like this. You never listen to advice, do you? If you are not prepared before you go into the Grim Lands, they may never allow you to leave.'

'*They?*' Veitch's brow furrowed. 'Me?'

'Well, I'm not going in there. It's your responsibility, and besides, I don't have that wonderful Pendragon Spirit coursing through *my* system. And did you think the Dead would just allow some breathing, heart-pumping warm memory of lost times waltz amongst them and take away one they consider their own? The Dead have their own rules and regulations, their own beliefs, their own jealousies and hatreds. And the Grim Lands themselves are . . .' He looked down so Veitch could barely see his face. '. . . not a pleasant place for the living.'

Veitch shuffled into a sitting position, annoyed that his good mood had been driven from him. 'I'm sick of all this,' he said obliquely.

'I'm sorry for having to say this, Ryan.' Tom surprised himself at the sincerity in his voice. 'You need to know. The archetype told us what you always believed: that there's still hope. But the outcome is never assured in these things. You need to understand that the danger of entering the Grim Lands would be, for many, insurmountable.' He paused. 'But if anyone can do it, you can.'

Veitch brightened at the vote of confidence.

'But as I warned Shavi in Edinburgh, there is a great risk in allowing the Dead to notice you. A price might be demanded that could be too much for you to bear—'

Veitch waved a dismissive hand. 'There's no point telling me that sort of stuff. You know I'm going to do it. I've got to go in for Shavi. How could I leave him there if there's a chance I could bring him out? That's what it's all about for me. Yeah, we might be able to do something to stop everything going belly-up. But friendship, that's the important thing. You stand by your family, and you stand by your mates. Nothing comes up to that. Not even saving the world.'

Though he didn't show it, Tom was impressed by Veitch's sense of right and wrong, and his understanding of obligation, traits he thought had long been abandoned since the nineteen-sixties, the decade he most loved. 'As long as I know you're going into this with open eyes.'

'So how do I get there? Don't tell me there's some big doorway in the graveyard.'

'If only it were that easy. Firstly, we have to go to where Cernunnos has deposited Shavi's body for safekeeping.'

Veitch began his regular morning routine of stretching to help prepare his muscles for the day ahead. 'The Hill of Giants.'

'That is one of its names, though it is more commonly known as the Gog Magog Hills, just outside Cambridge.'

'Funny name.'

'In the old tales, Gog and Magog were the last of an ancient race of giants. They are supposed to sleep under the hills, with a giant horse along the way, and a golden chariot beneath nearby Mutlow Hill.'

Tom winced as Veitch cracked his knuckles, one after the other, oblivious to the Rhymer's displeasure. 'So, just to prove I've been listening, all these old stories you keep going on about actually mean something, though not usually exactly what they say.'

'They are an approximation, couched in metaphors.'

'So, what does this one mean? No *real* giants, right?'

'That needn't trouble you for now. I merely tell you this to underline that we will be travelling to a place of great power and significance. The ancient races were drawn to the hills for that power, in much the same way they revered Mam Tor. On the windswept summit is Wandlebury Camp where Boudicca and the Iceni plotted their revenge against the invaders. The Romans themselves took over the site later.'

'And that power's keeping Shavi's body safe?' A breeze blew along the floor of the glen, rustling the trees, making the phone wires sing.

'That and the fact that the hills have a guardian.'

'Yeah?'

'The archetype mentioned him – the Night Rider. In the legends he was supposed to have ruled Wandlebury Camp ages ago, and no mortal could ever defeat him. Those brave enough would ride out to the camp on a moonlit night and call, "Knight to knight, come forth!" He would ride out on his jet-black stallion and happily accept the challenge. A further story from Norman times claimed a knight called Osbert went out to try to put the legend to rest. He managed to unseat the Night Rider and even took the black horse home to Cambridge, but was wounded in the thigh in the process. The horse disappeared at dawn, and on every anniversary of the battle his wound opened up and bled as if it were fresh.'

'So what part of that load of old bollocks is true?'

Tom bristled at Veitch's typically irreverent reaction to the old myths and legends he held dear. 'I'm sure you will soon find out,' he replied tartly. 'The Night Rider has rarely been seen throughout the centuries – the Gog Magog Hills is a particularly lonely spot – but all who speak of him talk of a great threat which is not explicit in the stories. There is danger there, make no mistake. If such a powerful place requires a guardian, it would be a fearsome guardian indeed.'

'You expect me to be surprised?' Veitch kicked out the fire.

'I'm a little concerned that you're not taking this seriously—'

'I've had enough of taking things seriously. Since what happened to Ruth it's like that's all I've done. And if everything is going to end soon I don't want to end it like that.'

'Fair enough. Then the next question is—'

'How the hell do we get there in a hurry? I mean, Cambridge!' Veitch paced around anxiously. 'It's, what, five hundred miles away? No cars or planes or trains. That's crazy!'

'Horses,' Tom suggested.

'Still take too long.'

'A boat. We could sail up the Caledonian Canal, down the east coast to the fens—'

'No offence, mate, but I honestly don't fancy getting in a leaky old tub with you unless it's a last resort. I hate water.' He sighed. 'If it's the only option I'll do it, 'course I will, but it's still going to take too long.'

'Well, what do you suggest?' Tom snapped. 'We've gone back to the Middle Ages. A horse and a boat are top-of-the-range technology!'

Veitch chewed on his lip in thought. After a while he cast a sly glance towards Tom.

'What?' the Rhymer said sharply.

'Back at Tintagel when the crow-man forced us over the edge of the cliff, you did something—'

'No,' Tom said firmly.

Veitch squatted down next to him. 'Yeah, you did, you did. You moved us all the way from Tintagel to Glastonbury. What's that? A hundred miles? Just like that!' He snapped his fingers.

'No.'

'Stop saying *no* or I'll punch your head in.'

Tom couldn't decide if he was joking. 'What I did then was a one-off. I'd been taught the principle, but I'd never been able to do it before. I don't have the ability. I *don't*.'

'Then how did you do it?'

'The danger of the moment focused my mind. It was a subconscious act born of desperation. I couldn't repeat it if I wanted.'

'Maybe I should stand with my crossbow next to your head. Focus your mind again.'

Still Tom was unsure of Veitch's intention. His face was dangerously impenetrable, frightening in its coldness, with only the ever-present anger buzzing behind his eyes. 'That wouldn't do any good. Too staged.'

'Look, this is the answer, so we've got to make it work. Tell me about it. What makes it happen?' His eyes narrowed. 'From the beginning, and make it simple. No talking over the top of my head or I really will do you. This is important.'

'Make it simple, you say!' Tom cleaned his spectacles, an act of both irritation and preparation. 'The Blue Fire is the essential force running through everything – the land, trees and animals, you and me. We are

973

all part of the same thing. In ancient times it was fundamentally understood by all. The Blue Fire could be seen by everyone, and manipulated by many, particularly the adepts in a society, the shamen. Your society, certainly since the Industrial Revolution, has drifted away from the idea that man is a part of everything. Man is something special, *above* everything, is that not how it's seen?'

Veitch was concentrating on every word.

'The Blue Fire was forgotten. But it is as much about thought and belief as it is any subtle, flowing energy stream. Its source is in the imagination and the heart. It's a wish and a hope.'

'So it sort of dried up.'

'In your actions around the country over the past months you have been awakening the King of the World from his slumbers, but the task is not yet complete. The Fiery Network, it was called. Lines of the Blue Fire criss-crossing the country, the world, like the pulsing arteries in a body. The Chinese understood this perfectly. They called the force *chi* and mapped it out both on the land and in the body. In the latter it was controlled and refocused through acupuncture. On the land, the ancient sacred sites – the standing stones and first churches and cairns – did the job. But stones have been thrown down. In the last century, narrow-minded Christians who saw them as the work of the Devil rooted up whole circles. The Fiery Network fragmented; desiccated. If you imagine the land is a body, you would see some healthy arteries, an intermittent structure of veins and capillaries, and vast swathes of cold, dead skin.'

'So, it's like a machine that keeps the world running smoothly.'

'In a way.' Tom was relieved at his breakthrough. 'An ancient technology, if you will. A global machine that allows transportation across space, even across time, that allows one to jump dimensions. The manipulation of energy. That is the language of science, but this age's petty view of science doesn't even begin to encompass it.'

Veitch began to pace once more, the thoughts coming thick and fast. 'So, this is what you're saying, right? That you can move along these Blue Fire lines like roads, only, immediately, like a transporter beam on *Star Trek.*'

'Correct. Well . . . some people could. Not everyone. Even when the ancient races had the necessary skills to manipulate the Blue Fire, becoming one with the flow of energy was always fraught with danger.'

'Why?'

'Because it's possible to go in so deep you become lost. In effect, you give yourself up to the energy to which we all aspire. The Godhead. Our lives are spent trying to attain that, so why should we ever give it up when we have it in our hands? Imagine the troubles of life washing away as you become swathed in glory, in ecstasy.'

'So it's like a drug?'

'In a way, though that sounds too negative. Those who are skilled can skim along the surface of the Blue Fire, taking from it what they need. Others get sucked beneath the waves and happily drown in its wonder, never to be seen again.'

'And that's what you're scared of?'

'To go into the Blue Fire and never return would be a blessed release, indeed.' He wouldn't meet Veitch's eyes. 'To leave behind all this . . . shit.' He waved a hand dismissively around. 'No more struggle, no more tears and hatred and misery—'

Veitch looked around at the sweeping tree-swathed banks of the glen, listened to the bird song and the splashing of the river across the fields. 'But no more of *this.*'

Tom didn't appear to understand him.

'We've got a responsibility,' Veitch continued, 'to make things right for all those who can't go jumping into the Blue Fire.'

'Yes, yes, I know that!' Tom snapped. 'I'm simply saying I might not have the willpower to pull myself through it.'

This time it was Veitch's turn to be puzzled. 'You're not weak.'

'Yes, I am. Every day is a struggle to keep going. I'm ready to give it all up.'

Veitch mused on this a while as he looked out over the countryside. 'Nah, I don't believe it. You've got a load of faults, same as us all, but I know you, you old hippie. You'll always come through in a crunch. You just don't know yourself well enough.'

Tom was so surprised to hear this character assessment coming from Veitch's mouth, he was lost for words. Veitch laughed heartily. 'Anyway, we have a responsibility—'

'Stop using that word! I know you've just added it to your vocabulary, but—'

'—to the others. Whatever the risks, we've got no choice but to try. You're telling me you could live with yourself if you knew you might have been able to bring Shavi back—'

'All right, all right! Lord, you do go on.'

'You'll give it a shot?' Veitch didn't mask his surprise that he'd won the argument.

Tom snorted in irritation as he collected his haversack and stood up. 'Yes, but if I have to spend the rest of infinity with you, that Blue Fire will seem like the flames of Hell.'

*

975

The atmosphere on board Wave Sweeper was growing increasingly oppressive. The Tuatha Dé Danann had distanced themselves from the other travellers, retreating to a tight coterie around Manannan, who kept a firm grip on the running of the ship. The death of Cormorel had affected them even more than their aggressive response suggested; they were scared, Church could tell.

Many of the passengers confined themselves to the lower decks, taking food in their cabins or whatever shadowy area they inhabited. The ones who did rise to greet the sun kept their heads down and their eyes averted. Of the Walpurgis, there was still no sign, although the search parties departed daily at dawn, marching as far as they could into the infinite bowels of the boat before returning at dusk.

Baccharus, however, remained Church and Ruth's link with the Tuatha Dé Danann, repaying, perhaps, the kindness they had shown him since their first meeting. He spoke about his people's thoughts and their strategy without going into too much detail, and he stressed, on behalf of Manannan, that neither Church nor Ruth were under suspicion. They both knew that state of affairs could change instantly; the gods had loyalty only to themselves.

The ship skimmed the waves with great speed, even when the wind was low and the enormous sails scarcely billowed, but Ruth and Church were more concerned than ever that time was running away from them. It didn't help when Baccharus told them Wave Sweeper would continue to make its scheduled stops throughout the Western Isles before it reached its ultimate destination.

'I can't bear this,' Church said one morning as they leaned on the rail and watched what could have been dolphins rolling in the waves, but which made cries that sounded like shrieking women. 'Anything could be happening back at home.'

Ruth shielded her eyes against the glare of the sun off the water. 'It would be good to have a despatch from the front. Just to know we're not wasting our time.'

Activity further along the deck caught their attention. A strange contraption with a seat fixed at the end of a long, jointed arm was being dragged towards the side by a group of the plastic-faced younger gods. Once it was in place, the arm was manipulated over the side until the seat hovered mere inches above the water. With remarkable agility, one of the gods skipped up on to the rail then manoeuvred his way down the arm until he was precariously balanced on the seat, with no straps to restrain him and only providence keeping him from a ducking in the blue-green waves. A spear made from an intricately carved piece of enormous bone with an attached rope was lowered to him. He weighed it in his right hand, then poised to strike, concentrating on the depths.

'Do you think this is our sole reason for existing?' Church waited for something to happen, but the fisherman remained stock-still. 'The life we had in London, everything leading up to this point, it's like a dream sometimes. Not quite real at all. But the only thing that keeps me going through all this struggle is the thought that at some point, I'll be able to return to that life. If I thought this was all there was . . .'

'A lot of religions say we have one purpose in life. We just have to find it.'

'That's my worry. I don't want to have a life of nothing but sacrifice. When I used to read stories of the saints, and Gandhi, and Mother Theresa, I never found them uplifting. They always filled me with something like despair, because they were missing out on all the great things life had to offer: you know, fun and friendship and love and all that.'

Ruth brushed a strand of hair from her face. Oddly, she felt closest to him during his brooding moments, when all his attention was turned inward; a usually hidden fragility was revealed that made her want to protect him. 'Some people have to give up their lives so everyone else can enjoy theirs. I'm sure it's tough for the person in question, but that seems to be the way it works. Anyway, you know what Tom and Shavi would say – we can't ever see the big picture, so it's a waste of time for us trying to put something like that into perspective. Perhaps the reward is in the next world.'

'*This* is the next world,' Church said dismally.

'You know what I mean. *There's always something higher.*'

'Well, *I* want my life back when all this is over. I don't think that's too much to ask. I'll have met my obligations, done everything expected of me. I don't want to die an old man, still fighting this stupid, nightmarish battle.'

'Hmm, considering old age – that's optimistic of you. Me, I'm happy if I make it through to tomorrow.'

The water exploded upwards in a spout, followed by thrashing tentacles and the glinting of teeth. The fisherman struck hard with his spear, his face as calm as if he were lazing on the banks of a river, and then he struck again several times in rapid succession. A gush of black liquid soured the water. One of the tentacles lashed around his calf, and when it retracted, the flesh was scoured. More tentacles shot up, folding around his legs like steel cables. Church gripped the railing. It was obvious the fisherman was going to be dragged off the seat, yet none of the other gods who hung over the rail above him were in the slightest concerned.

'Dog eat dog.' The words at his left ear made him start. Standing just behind him was Taranis, Manannan's right-hand man, who oversaw the mysterious star charts by which the crew navigated. The face Church had chosen for him had a faint touch of cruelty, thin and sharp, with piercing eyes and a tightly clipped goatee. His presence made Church feel queasy. 'Fish eat fish,' he continued, by way of explanation for the scene they were observing. 'Bird eat worm, cat eat mouse, wolf eat rabbit.'

Church returned his attention to the fisherman and the crazed splashing that surrounded him. He was on the verge of slipping beneath the waves, clutching on to the seat with one hand while hacking mercilessly with the spear with the other. At the point when Church thought he would have to go, the spear bit into some vital point and he managed to wriggle his legs free and lever himself back up on to the seat. A few more choice hacks and an indescribable black bulk bobbed to the surface where it floated, motionless.

'Dinner?' Ruth asked distastefully.

Taranis gave a thin-lipped smile at the outcome. 'The way of existence,' he said.

'I'm heading back to my cabin for a bit,' Ruth said, before turning to Taranis. She motioned to the collapsible telescope made of ivory and inlaid sable and gold that hung from his belt. 'May I borrow this for a while?'

Taranis seemed taken aback by her request, and Church, too, was surprised by her forwardness, but the god acceded with a curt nod. Ruth weighed it in her palms, nodded thoughtfully, and headed towards the door that led beneath the deck.

Without Ruth to talk to, and with Niamh distracted, Church felt out of sorts. The other occupants of the ship made his skin crawl, even the ones that most closely resembled humans. There was nothing to see across the water, nothing to do in his cabin, little anywhere to occupy his time. He was reminded of Samuel Johnson's quotation: *Going to sea is going to prison, with a chance of drowning besides.*

As he made his way along the corridor towards his cabin, his nose wrinkled at an incongruous, sulphurous odour; it was powerful enough to sting his eyes and make the back of his throat burn. It appeared to be emanating from a branching corridor he had never seen before. In the back of his head an insistent alarm was warning him not to venture down it, but if there were a fire on board the alarm would need to be raised. He vacillated for the briefest moment before turning down the offshoot.

The corridor followed a serpentine route that made no sense, even doubling back on itself before ending at a double arched door made from seasoned wood. The handles were big enough to take two hands, made from blackened cast-iron. From behind it he could hear a thunderous pounding. The sulphurous stink was so potent now it almost made him choke.

Cautiously, he opened the door.

The room was stiflingly hot and the acrid smell hung heavily all around. His ears rebelled from the constant clashing of metal on metal, his teeth rang from the reverberations. It was almost impossible to tell the dimensions of the room, for it was as dark as night, with occasional pockets of brilliant light, ruddy and orange, or showering in golden stars. It was a foundry. On board a ship. Nothing in that vessel made sense at all.

The dull glow came from three separate furnaces. The sound of the bellows keeping them incandescent was like the turbulent breathing of a giant. He covered his mouth to keep out the fumes and prepared to back out, until his eyes grew accustomed to the dark and he realised he was not alone. Three huge figures worked insistently, pounding glowing shards of metal on anvils as big as a Shetland pony, plunging the worked piece into troughs of water, raising clouds of steam, moving hastily back to thrust tools into the red-hot coals.

Transfixed, he found himself trying to guess what strange implements were being constructed. He was woken from his concentration by a voice that sounded like the roar of another furnace. 'Draw closer, Fragile Creature.'

His heart thumped in shock, but it was too late to retreat. He moved forward until the glow from the furnace illuminated the shadowy form. It took a while for the figure to stabilise, marking out his position in the hierarchy of the Tuatha Dé Danann. Though none of it was real, Church smelled the stink of sweat, heavy with potent male hormones. The blacksmith had a rough-hewn face, marked with black stubble and framed by sweaty, lank black hair. He was naked to the waist, his torso and arms rippling with the biggest muscles Church had ever seen. His body gleamed, with sweat running in rivulets down to a wide golden belt girding his waist. In one hand he held a hammer as big as Church's upper body, poised mid-strike; in the other he clutched a pair or tongs that gripped a glowing chunk of iron flattened on one edge. Without taking his eyes off Church, he lowered the iron into the trough at his side and was instantly obscured by the steam.

When it had cleared, he said gruffly, 'We get few visitors here, in the workshop of the world.'

'I smelled the furnace. Thought there was a fire.'

The blacksmith's eyes narrowed. 'Are you the Brother of Dragons I have been hearing about?' Church introduced himself. The blacksmith gave a nod, his movements slow and heavy. '*The cry goes out across the worlds, in death and black destruction, the child answers, full of fury, yet finds no absolution.*'

'What's that?'

'A memory.' With a clatter, he dumped the tongs and the piece of iron on a workbench. 'In the times when my workshop armed your world, your people called me Goibhniu, known too, as Govannon.' He leaned forward and showed Church a ragged scar across his side. 'See my wound.' Church wondered why the god didn't lay down his hammer, but when he peered at it closely the edges of it rippled. Church couldn't tell if it were the heat haze from the furnace or if it were Goibhniu's Caraprix in the form that would help him the most. The god saw Church eyeing the tool and held it out before him. 'Three strikes make perfection. I can work the stuff of existence, shape worlds or insects. With these hands, anything can be made in a single day, and anything can be destroyed.'

Beyond him, in the shadows, Church could make out a tremendous armoury: swords and spears, things that looked like tanks in the form of beetles, and also enormous machines that served no purpose he could recognise.

'And weapons?' Church asked.

'Weapons from which none can recover. Weapons that can destroy the whole of existence.'

The words caught in Church's mind. 'Weapons that could destroy Balor?'

Goibhniu surveyed him for a long moment, then motioned towards the other figures, who had not paused in their work. 'My brothers, as your people knew them: Creidhne and Luchtaine, known as Luchtar, who works wood and metal, as well as the stuff of everything.'

Luchtaine had paused from his work at the anvil to shape an unusual piece of wood on a lathe that whirred like a bug. Creidhne was fashioning what appeared to be rivets made of gold. They both looked at Church with eyes filled with flame and smoke.

'Why are you here, on board this ship?' Church felt uneasy, as if he was missing something important and terrible in the scene.

Goibhniu's eyes narrowed; an atmosphere of incipient threat descended on them all. 'The Western Isles beckon. These are difficult times.'

'Difficult times? You mean the murder of Cormorel?'

Church shrank back as Goibhniu advanced with his hammer before him. Light glimmered off the head and shone like a torchbeam into the depths of the room; Church was shocked to see the beam of light appeared to stretch for miles. And it was packed with weapons as far as he could see. Near to the foundries was some hulking piece of machinery that dwarfed all others, but it was unfinished; waves of menace washed off it. The angle of light changed and the view was lost, but it had been enough.

Goibhniu continued to advance until Church's back was pressed against the door. Fumbling behind him, he found the door handle and flipped it open, almost tumbling out into the corridor. The last thing he heard before Goibhniu slammed the door shut was the god saying forcefully, 'Stay away from here, Fragile Creature. We have work to do.'

The sweat trickled into the small of Ruth's back as the full force of the noontime sun blazed through the open windows into the cabin, even though she was sitting naked on the floor. Her visit to the kitchen stores had been a success. It was a vaulted hall that went on forever, its air laden with the aroma of spices, fruits, cooking meats and steamed fish, and it was apparent from the demeanour of the dour-faced god in charge that she could find *anything* she wanted there. Even so, she was surprised to locate so easily such rare items, and ones that were not used in any dishes she knew; but then, who could guess the tastes of the other travellers on Wave Sweeper?

With a borrowed mortar and pestle, she had prepared the ointment in just the right way and now she was filled with a wonderful anticipation; it had been too long.

Soon after came the familiar sensation of separation from her body. There was rushing, like a jet taking off, and then she was out of the window and soaring up into the clear, blue sky. Once her mind had found its equilibrium, she looked down at Wave Sweeper ploughing a white furrow through the green-blue sea far below. The sails billowed, the deck was golden in the sunlight, the crew moving about like ants.

The exhilaration filled her as deeply as the first time she had experienced the spirit-flight in the Lake District, her limbs divested of earthly stresses, her mind glowing with a connection to the godhead. It would have been wonderful just to stay there, floating amongst the occasional wisp of clouds, but she had a job to do. 'Are you there?' she asked the sky.

In response came a beating of wings that was much more powerful than she had anticipated. When she turned to greet the arrival she was even more shocked: her owl familiar was a bird no more. It resembled a man, though with an avian cast to the features: too-large eyes with golden irises, a spiny ridge along its forehead, and its torso and limbs a mix of leathery brown skin like rhino hide and dark feathers. It beat through the air towards her on bat-like wings.

The breath caught in her throat. When she had just considered it an owl, albeit with a demonic intelligence, it had not been too threatening, but now it was patently menacing; she felt instinctively that if she did not treat it right, it would tear her apart.

'Is that your true form?' she asked hesitantly.

He smiled contemptuously. 'As if there is such a thing!' He could have left it there, but he took pity on her. 'It is the way I appear to you, in this place, at this time.'

She turned to look at the dim horizon. 'I need to return to my world, to see what's happening. Is that possible?'

'All things are possible when the right will is imposed. I told you that.'

She recalled their conversations in the cells beneath Edinburgh Castle when he had been a disembodied voice, passing on the information vital to her development in the craft. 'I can't believe I've learnt so much, so quickly.'

'Others would find it harder. You have been chosen for your abilities.'

'I still wonder how much I can actually do.'

'You will find your answer, in time.' There was a disconcerting note to his voice.

She allowed herself to drift on the air currents, overcome with apprehension. 'I'm worried I won't be able to get back here quickly enough.' Nina's warning of what would happen if the spirit did not return to the body within a reasonable time weighed heavy on her. 'It's so far—'

'Then you should waste no more time.' He moved ahead of her, heading higher, towards the sun, then dipped down and made a strange movement with his left hand that stretched his ligaments to their limits. By the time he had finished, a patch of air had taken on a glassy quality; Ruth had the odd impression that it was a pool of water, floating vertically. He flashed a piercing glance that charged her to follow him and then he plunged into the pool and disappeared. She hesitated for only a second before diving.

A sensation like icy rain rushed across her skin and then she was high off the coast of Mousehole, as if, for all their travels on Wave Sweeper, they had not gone anywhere at all. Everything seemed so much duller after her time in T'ir n'a n'Og, the quality of light, the sea-smell, the greens of the landscape beyond the shore. Her companion had once again reverted to his owl form, keeping apace with her with broad, powerful wing-strokes.

As she moved inland across the late summer fields, her apprehension became more intense. On some rarefied level she was sensing danger ahead.

Increasing her speed, she swooped over the landscape, uncomfortably eyeing the deserted roads and tiny villages that appeared devoid of life. And faster; Dartmoor passed in a brooding, purple-brown blur with memories of the Wild Hunt and senseless slaughter. In Exeter a fire was raging out of control. The grey ribbon of the M5 was a string of abandoned vehicles. And on through Devon, acutely aware how much the land had changed. No more comforting mundanity, supermarket shopping and boring commutes to work, daytime radio and bank managers and accountants. Even with the cursory glance she was giving the rolling greenery below, she could see it had become wilder, a land of mythology where humans were at the mercy of competing species with much greater powers. A place where anything could happen.

Over Wiltshire and Hampshire, closer to the source of the danger. Some towns and villages were wrecked and burning, others reclaimed by strangely wild vegetation. But there were still signs that people were there, either in shock or in hiding: cows, obviously milked and fed, here, clothes hanging on a washing line there. Little markers of hope; it was something. The faint, insistent tugging dragged her eastwards.

The owl had been keeping pace with her, beyond the ability of any true bird, but the beat of its wings began to grow slower until it had dropped back a way, dipping and diving with obvious caution. The reason was clear. On the horizon, London brooded. Although the sun shone down on its sprawling mass, Ruth had a definite sense that it hung in darkness. Her heartbeat speeded and anxiety began to gnaw at the back of her head; an aura of menace was rolling out across the Thames Valley.

It had to have been London, where it all started. The circle had closed.

Yet from that distance, nothing appeared out of the ordinary, apart from the stillness that lay over the approaching M4. She dropped back until she was beside her familiar, adopting its cautious approach. She listened: nothing, but not a serene silence: no birdsong at all. She sniffed the wind and caught the faintest hint of acrid smoke. As the suburban tower blocks and estates fell into view, that ringing sense of menace became almost unbearable, hanging like a thick cloud of poisonous gas over the capital. It was moving out across the land, barely perceptible in its slowness, but inexorable.

'Dare I go closer?' she asked the owl. When there was no reply she took it on herself to advance. She still needed something substantial to tell Church.

She knew she could be seen by the Fomorii in that form – they had spotted her as she watched their black tower being constructed in the Lake District – so she soared higher, desperately wishing for some cloud cover. And with that thought came the realisation that, if she wanted it, she could make it. Under her breath, she mumbled the words the familiar had taught her, making the hand gestures that activated the primal language: words of power in both sound and movement.

The wind changed direction within seconds and soon a few fluffy white clouds were sweeping in from the north. Not too many – she didn't want to draw attention to the sudden change in the weather pattern – but enough to provide a hiding place.

With a slight effort she sent them billowing towards the capital and slipped in amongst them. The air became filled with pins and needles; her heart was pounding so hard she thought she was having a coronary. 'It *feels* bad,' she said to her familiar, although she was really talking to herself, 'but it doesn't *look* too bad.'

And then the clouds cleared.

She was still beyond the suburbs, but from her vantage point she had a clear view deep into the heart of the city. At first it looked like the outlines of the buildings were rippling as if they weren't fixed. She wondered if it had somehow slipped into T'ir n'a n'Og, where things regularly looked that way. But as she drew closer, she could see it wasn't the outline of the buildings that were changing; something was moving across them.

A wave of revulsion swept through her. London was swarming. It looked like an enormous jarful of spiders had been emptied out on to the buildings and streets. The Fomorii scurried everywhere, at times as though millions upon millions of long-legged insects were racing chaotically over everything, then as if one beast lay across the capital, flowing like oil. Many or one, it didn't matter; London was subsumed. And at the heart of it, an abiding darkness pulsated: Balor, replete in its lair, growing stronger after the strain of rebirth, sucking in energy ready to consume the planet. Beating like a giant heart. Thump-thump. Thump-thump. She couldn't truly see it, had no real idea of its form, but it was there on a spiritual level, tendrils creeping out from the cold sore. She gagged, despite the fact her corporeal body was a world away.

What made her flesh creep the most was the way that vibrating black mass was pushing out from the centre, reaching into the suburbs, moving out across the country. Nothing could have stood in its path.

'All those people,' she gasped. The realisation of what must have happened made her head spin: an atrocity on a grand scale; perhaps millions dead, and more to come.

'We have to get back,' she said to the owl. 'We can't afford to waste any more time.'

But as she turned to depart, brutal reverberations crashed inside her skull and her body doubled up with pain. Looking back she saw, rising up above the skyscrapers of the City, an area of infinite darkness, blacker even than deepest space, cold and sucking. It was impossible to tell if it was truly happening in the real world or if it was a metaphor imprinted on a higher level of consciousness, but it filled her with utmost dread. It was alive, and it had an intelligence so vile her mind screamed at even the slightest brush with it.

Balor. The name tolled like a funereal bell deep in her head.

And it rose up and up, bigger than the city, bigger than all existence. *How can we beat something like that?* she thought with the bitter sting of despair. And still it rose, and washing off it came waves of malignancy. And then, as it had in the dream that was not a dream in Mousehole, an eye opened in that black cloud, an eye that was not an eye, though she characterised it as such. And it focused its attention on her and she thought she was about to go mad with fear.

It could see her there, hidden in the clouds, miles away. It could see her anywhere. But worse than that, it *recognised* her.

The shock dislocated her thoughts; it was already in motion before she registered it was coming for her.

A wide flailing disrupted the air currents next to her. Her familiar was thrashing and screaming, an owl, a ball of feathers, then the owl-man, and then something infinitely worse, moving rapidly backwards and forwards across the spectrum of its appearance in a terrible panic.

In terror, she attempted to flee, only to realise she couldn't move. The evil had her in some invisible grip, holding her steady like a fish on a line. Until it reached her.

Her consciousness finally burst from whatever spell it was under, and suddenly she was thinking at lightning speed. 'Help me!' she yelled, but the owl was already moving away from her, every wing-beat a flurry of desperation.

She tried to flee once more, but it was as if her limbs, or her mind, was pinned; no amount of effort could move her. Behind her, the monstrous gravity of the thing grew more powerful.

'Come back!' she screamed. 'You were supposed to help me!' The familiar was lost in the glare of the sun.

A freezing shadow had fallen across her, reaching through her physical body to the depths of her soul. It was creeping up her spine, deadening the chakras as it passed, crawling towards her brain. Incomprehensible whispers began to lick at her mind. In that contact she sensed the sickening presence of Balor, and she knew it was the reason why fear had been implanted in the human consciousness. The Celts had given it a name to try to contain it, but it could not be contained; it was bigger than everything.

Her vision started to close in, until there was only a tunnel of light towards the sun. A strain was being placed on the invisible cord that connected her with her body. One snap and she would be lost to the endless void forever. And then, slowly but relentlessly, the thing started to drag her back.

Just as she thought the darkness was about to engulf her completely, she caught sight of faint movement in that tunnel of light. Nothing. It was nothing. She slipped back further.

She was startled from her panic by the owl erupting from nowhere close to her face. Its bristling feathers obscured the whole of that tunnel of light, and for a second she was sure she had gone blind. But then it moved back slightly, changing shape back and forth as it had done at the height of its desperation. She could still feel its fear, but now behind it was determination and obligation.

The air pressure increased, iron filled her mouth and a weight built behind her eyes until she was convinced they were going to be driven from her head. Slowly, she started to move forward.

She felt like she was trying to push a truck up a hill; every agonising inch she moved was a triumph. Yet although the grip of the darkness didn't relinquish in the slightest, gradually her strength increased and she began to make slight progress. It was nowhere near fast enough, though; the tension zinged through her arteries.

With determination, she drove herself on until she reached a point where her speed began to build. Finally it felt like she had crossed some invisible barrier, and with a burst of relief she was soaring out over the golden-tinged clouds. The coldness left her head, skidding down her back to her thighs. Later she wondered if she had imagined it, but she thought she heard a howl of fury that was at once the movement of tectonic plates, the boom of cold water shifting in the depths of the Marianas Trench.

And faster still; hope soared in her heart at the same time as tears of fear stung her eyes. *She would never be so stupid again.* If she got back. A pain in her solar plexus told her time was running out. She had been away from her body for too long, and the flimsy spiritual bond was close to being broken.

The shadowy cold was still on her legs. Stupidly, she glanced back and thought her heart would stop. The entire sky was black, boiling like storm clouds, but not natural – sentient – and pursuing her with venom.

Fire filled her belly. Focusing all her attention on the flight, she propelled herself forward with a speed that made Dorset flash by in the blink of an eye.

Still the darkness didn't give up. She knew it would *never* give up now it had recognised her. She put the thought out of her head. Faster, faster, thinking of Church, giving meaning to her struggle; if not for her, for him.

Soon they were over the choppy sea and the owl was ahead of her, already turning itself inside out. The sky and sea swapped place, turned blood-red. And then they were soaring over Wave Sweeper and the darkness was nowhere to be seen.

She plummeted towards the ship as the connecting strand grew thinner by the second. It was just the width of a hair when she finally slid into her body, exhausted. Amongst the receding terror, one thing stayed with her: at the last, she had looked into her familiar's eyes. What she saw was a definite impression that *she* was now in *its* debt.

She recovered in her cabin for an hour or more, listening to the soothing wash of the waves beyond the open window. She couldn't believe how stupid she had been to venture so close, but until then she had not truly grasped the enormity of what they faced.

Once she had calmed herself, she made her way back to the deck, though she kept her shaking hands hidden from view. Taranis was at the rail, scanning the horizon. She handed him his telescope with a sly smile.

'How curious.' He turned it over in his hands. 'It is so very warm.'

'Hmm,' Ruth replied. 'I wonder why that is?'

Church had spent the time on deck, watching the crew go about their puzzling tasks. Few of the passengers ventured up from the depths in their attempt to keep a distance from the grim Tuatha Dé Danann, so that the ship had the dismal, empty appearance of a seaside resort in off-season. The atmosphere was so intense he had felt it politic to stay away from the gods himself, nestling in a heap of oily tarpaulins and thick ropes where he could watch without drawing attention to himself.

He had never seen the Tuatha Dé Danann so strained. Irritation gripped them because they had not managed to track down the Walpurgis, a failure that only added to their pain at Cormorel's death. Their aloof nature had always made them appear dangerous in a haphazard, detached way; now they were a constant threat, ready to take out their fury on anyone who crossed their path.

If the gods could not find the Walpurgis with all the heightened abilities at their disposal, there was little chance Church would be able to locate the creature he had increasingly convinced himself was not the murderer. Yet he felt a growing imperative to do so, for he was sure the Walpurgis had information of vital importance.

His thoughts were disrupted by a cry from one of the crew perched in the crow's nest. Everyone on deck stopped moving. Church couldn't tell if it was because of hope, or apprehension – or fear.

Across the pea-green sea he could just make out a purple and brown smudge on the horizon. *Here it is*, he thought, suddenly concerned himself. *The Islands of the Dead.*

CHAPTER SIX

Islands of the Dead

The waters were unnaturally calm as Wave Sweeper sailed in, leaving barely a ripple in its passing. Insects skimmed the surface of the ocean in the heavy heat, buzzing noisily. An unpleasant smell of stagnancy hung over everything, but it was the stillness that unnerved everyone the most. There was a feeling of death in the air.

As Wave Sweeper closed on the land, Church was surprised to see it was not one single mass, but an archipelago, the strangest one he had ever seen. Numerous small islands protruded from the sea like fingers pointing at the sky, rising precipitously to dizzying summits, many looking like they could barely support their own weight. They were gnarled with rocky outcroppings and fledged with twisted trees and tenacious bushes. Stone buildings perched on the top of the island towers, occasionally obscured by drifting plumes of cloud. However, on the loftiest, most twisted, most precarious island stood a grand castle of bronze and glass, the walls afire in the dazzling sunlight. Its enormous bulk atop the slim column was in direct opposition to any natural laws on Earth. But this was Otherworld.

Manannan's order to drop anchor drew the crew out of their trance. Church noticed Ruth had appeared beside Taranis, who was observing the peaks of the island through his telescope, his face as hard as the stone of the cliffs.

'What's wrong?' Church slipped in quietly beside them.

Taranis looked at him as if an insect had chirped in his ear. 'There has been no greeting,' he said distractedly, returning his attention to his telescope.

Church eyed Ruth, her face uncommonly tired and drawn, but she shrugged noncommittally. 'Who were you expecting to greet you?' Church pressed.

Taranis sighed. 'In the Fixed Lands she was known as Hellawes. She foolishly grew too close to Fragile Creatures during her travels and became afflicted with the weariness of existence. She retired here, to her island home, though whether she truly recovered, none know. Still, she provided a welcome for travellers. It was the Master's wish to dine at her table.'

Church followed the angle of the telescope to the castle that appeared to be floating on the clouds that drifted beneath it. 'Maybe she doesn't know we're here.'

Taranis snorted; it was obvious he was not going to give them any more of his time. Ruth caught Church's arm and led him away, eager to tell him what she knew of home.

'The Fomorii are already moving out across the country?'

'It won't be long before they're everywhere.' Ruth shivered at the memory of what she had seen.

Church's shoulders were knotted with tension. He watched the crew preparing the landing boat. It had an oddly shaped prow that curled up and over the rowers. 'Being here makes you feel detached from it all, even when it's buzzing away at the back of your head. I needed a slap like that to focus my mind.'

'I wish we could just get to where we're going.' She hugged herself, despite the heat.

He saw Baccharus and Niamh lining up to join the small band ready to go ashore. 'Maybe we can gee them along.'

He led her over to the boat as it was hoisted up above the level of the rail ready for the crew to climb aboard. Church pulled Baccharus to one side. 'We'd like to join you. All of this is new to us. We want to experience—'

'Of course.'

Church was taken aback by the speed of Baccharus's agreement, but he wasn't about to question it. He quickly climbed aboard, with Ruth behind him. Niamh was already seated at the aft. She gave him a warm, secret smile, hidden from the crew who silently filled the seats. Church was curious to see that they all wore the gold and ivory armour of the warrior caste.

Ruth echoed his thoughts. 'They're expecting trouble,' she whispered.

Even though her words were barely audible, Baccharus picked up on them. 'The greeting is always issued,' he said ominously, his darkly golden eyes flickering towards the lofty castle.

The oarsmen propelled them across the flat sea with powerful, seasoned strokes. Church had the oddest impression they were skimming the surface of a mirror, so disturbingly smooth was the water. Even around the base of the rocky islands there was only the slightest swell and no breakers. It was as if the ocean itself was holding its breath.

Ruth was driven to cover her mouth to block out the choking stagnant odours. Church passed the time swatting away the alien insects, some of which were like meat flies that had grown as big as his fist, others like minute, jewelled dragonflies, sparkling as they whizzed by.

At the base of the island was a tiny jetty. Once the boat had been made secure with a thick rope, they clambered out. There was barely room for them all to stand, so they progressed one at a time along an uneven path that wound upwards around the island. It was just wide enough for one person and dangerously precarious the higher they climbed. On the outer edge it was badly eroded by the elements; one wrong foot would have sent them plummeting into the waves or on to the protruding rocks. Church and Ruth held their breath as they fixed their gaze on the next step, but Baccharus and the other Tuatha Dé Danann climbed nonchalantly, oblivious to the drop.

The higher they rose above the flat, green sea, the harder it became to avoid feelings of vertigo. For distraction, Church found himself focusing on the wiry grass and diminutive yellow and white flowers that thrived in pockets on the rock face. His fingers gripped the stone until the joints hurt; behind him he could hear Ruth's laboured breath.

They climbed for almost an hour, until their thigh and calf muscles were fiery. Near the top, the buffeting wind threatened to snatch them off their uneasy perch so that even the Tuatha Dé Danann had to face the rock and edge around the path.

Finally they passed through cloud to reach the flat summit and an area the size of a tennis court leading to the castle's imposing gates. That close it was even harder to understand how the place had come to be built in that almost inaccessible position; how it continued to survive there. The bronze and opaque glass walls rose up high above their heads, too bright to look at in the seething sunlight. Windows looked out on every vista, but they were all too dark to see within. It was unpleasantly quiet.

'Maybe she's not in,' Ruth muttered.

'The mistress of this place never leaves its walls.' Baccharus looked up to the battlements, as impassive as ever, but troubled.

At the castle gate they considered their actions. 'A knock,' Church suggested.

Baccharus agreed. 'Cover your ears,' he said to Church and Ruth. They looked at each other curiously. 'Sound has power. Mere words, or the sound they make, can alter existence. You know that?' He read their faces, then nodded in approval before continuing; Church and Ruth both felt like children being guided by a knowledgeable parent. 'The reverberations from the striking of this door will send all Fragile

Creatures into a deep sleep, for—' he struggled with the mortal concept '—a long time.'

'How many *Fragile Creatures* do you get up here?' Ruth asked.

Baccharus returned his attention to the door. 'It is the way it is.'

Church and Ruth covered their ears, but even through their hands they could feel the strange vibrations of the struck door driving like needles into their heads, making them queasy at first, then drowsy. Baccharus shook them both roughly to keep them awake.

They waited for long minutes after they had announced their arrival, but all they could hear was the wind blowing around the castle walls, sounding at times like plaintive human voices.

Niamh, who had the position of superiority in the group, stepped forwards. 'We enter.'

Two of the guards put their shoulders to the gates, but they swung open easily, as if they could have been moved with the touch of only a finger. Beyond was a breathtaking hall soaring up to a glass roof that made the interior as bright and hot as a greenhouse. Within, they were assailed by numerous sensations. The breeze moved the most melodic chimes hanging in enormous trees that grew mysteriously out of the tiled floor, their tops almost brushing the roof. A white waterfall gushed down from an opening halfway up one wall, splashing in a cool pool that emptied out through a culvert in the floor. The smells were as complex and heady as any they had experienced in T'ir n'a n'Og. Church picked up lime, honeysuckle, rose and cinnamon before he gave up.

'It's beautiful.' Ruth was overcome by the sheer wonder after the air of threat without.

'It is the mistress's palace. Her sanctuary,' Niamh noted. 'She loved the Fixed Lands and wished to bring her memories of that place to life here.' She paused thoughtfully before adding, 'She loved a Fragile Creature—'

'Well, there's no future in that, is there?' Ruth ignored Niamh's pointed stare.

'And she retired here to nurse her broken heart?' Church asked. Niamh replied with a sad smile.

They pressed on through the hall into a maze of rooms decorated in different earthly styles: mediaeval, Celtic, Mexican, Japanese, Native American. Yet each felt as if an unpleasant presence had been in it only moments before, although there was no visible sign of recent occupation. Even the usually stoic Tuatha Dé Danann appeared uneasy.

Occasionally Church and Ruth glimpsed flitting grey shapes on the edge of their field of vision, accompanied by barely audible but insistent whispering, and a growing anxiety. Sometimes they caught sight of faces, most of them unknown, but one or two that were almost recognisable.

'Can you see them?' Ruth hissed after they had passed through a room where the shapes swarmed at their backs, disappearing the moment they turned round.

'They are the spirits of the dead,' Baccharus interjected. 'You will encounter them throughout the Western Isles.'

'Ghosts?' Church moved his head sharply to try to bring one of the figures to the centre of his vision, without much luck. 'Real ghosts?'

'Some of the dead are drawn here, Fragile Creatures with a yearning nature, unsettled, troubled. It has always been that way. The Western Isles are a destination for those of a questing nature.' The figures kept well away from Baccharus as he spoke.

'Are they dangerous?' Ruth asked.

Baccharus chose his words carefully. 'They can be. The dead bring their dark emotions with them. Many are fuelled by bitterness, resentful of those still living. Beware of them and their whispered words. They will wish to lure you to your doom.'

A chill turned Church's skin to gooseflesh. Another face he half-thought he knew. Ruth gripped his hand in hers, fixing her attention on the path ahead.

The lay-out of the castle was incomprehensible; they trailed from room to room without encountering anyone, constantly sensing a passing presence, always one step ahead.

'Maybe we should head back to the ship,' Ruth said. 'She's obviously not here.'

'But she *should* be here,' Baccharus said. 'She may be in need of assistance.'

'I thought you Golden Ones rarely helped each other,' Church said.

'We are not all the same.' It was a passing comment, but Church caught the briefest glimpse of something in Baccharus's face that gave him pause.

Before he had time to consider it further, one of the guards said curtly, 'In the next chamber,' although it was impossible to tell how he could know when the door was closed.

As one, the guards drew long golden swords from hidden pockets in their armour. They approached the door cautiously. Church's blood was pulsing loudly in his head; now he could also sense something, and although he couldn't pinpoint it, it set his nerves on edge. *In the room.*

993

He saw Ruth could feel it too. Her warning hand fell on his forearm, urging him back.

Niamh made a sign to the captain and the door was thrust open. The guards surged through, with Church so close behind, he ran into them when they came to a premature halt. They were so still Church first thought they were the victims of some enchantment until he realised they were staring at the corner of the room. He eased his way through until he had a better view.

The remains of a woman were slumped over a divan, her body breaking up just as Cormorel's had done on the point of death. Her body had been torn apart from neck to crotch. There was nothing anyone could do for her: the flight of golden moths had dwindled to a handful fluttering up intermittently to the ceiling, where they passed through it like wisps of light. Church guessed it was Hellawes.

Niamh thrust past him and dropped to her knees in front of the divan, an unnerving keening sound of grief emanating from her. She kneaded her hands together, dipped and raised her head, barely able to comprehend what she was seeing. Baccharus looked away, sickened.

'Cormorel's murderer—' Church began.

'No.' Baccharus eyed him forcefully. 'This crime was not committed by the same.'

'Who would want to kill a woman who lived like a hermit?' Ruth said.

The guards slowly moved backwards until they had formed a circle, swords ready to repel an attack from any direction.

'Remember: the mistress of this place was a Golden One,' Baccharus cautioned. 'To do this to her takes tremendous power, or specific knowledge.' The words caught in his throat and he raised the back of his hand to his mouth in disgust, unable to hide his feelings any longer.

'Who committed this crime?' Niamh wailed.

The nerves along Church's spine suddenly sparked. 'Something's coming,' he said hoarsely, feeling it acutely as he spoke.

Ruth looked up at him curiously. 'I don't sense anything.'

His left arm began to tremble uncontrollably. He gripped it at the wrist to steady himself. 'You haven't got a cocktail of alien shit in your blood,' he said hoarsely. He half-stumbled; Ruth caught him. 'Fomorii,' he wheezed. The taint of the Kiss of Frost was responding to the presence nearby.

The guards glanced at him, concerned, then at Niamh for guidance. 'Listen to him,' she ordered. 'He is a Brother of Dragons. He understands the Night Walkers.' She hurried behind their line of swords as the group began to back out the way they had come.

Before they were halfway across the next room, a guard's head split open. The blow had come so quickly no one had seen it. The Fomorii were all around them. To Church, they appeared to rise from the floor and drop from the ceiling, oil-black and filled with malevolence, armed with the cruel serrated swords. His stomach knotted at the waves of evil washing off them. The air was filled with an animal stink, the walls ringing with the echoes of their shrieks and grunts. He still couldn't bear to look them in the face, so all he got were fleeting impressions: darkness and shadows, moving fast, shapes continually changing, horns and bony plates, sharp teeth, ridges and staring eyes. But most of all, power.

The Tuatha Dé Danann responded with force. Their swords were a whirling golden blur, and while they had appeared delicate before, now they carved easily through any Formor who came close enough. The ferocity of the attack had obviously shocked the gods; more, the simple fact that the Fomorii had attacked at all. In their arrogance they had presumed the Fomorii would leave them alone out of fear. Now their very existence was at risk.

'What the hell are they doing *here*?' Church wished he had some kind of weapon to join in the fray, but the guards had formed an impenetrable wall between him and the Fomorii.

'It doesn't make sense.' Ruth was preoccupied, trying to find a space to concentrate so she could use some aspect of her craft, but in the mêlée it was impossible.

Another guard fell, split almost in two. Church saw none of the golden moths, so he couldn't tell if the victim was dead or not; there were still so many unknowns about the Tuatha Dé Danann, but there was no time to dwell on the puzzle. The Fomorii surged all around, black water shifting and changing, striking with venom, desperate to prevent the gods leaving the building. Church couldn't tell how many there were – a handful; a raiding party – but there were enough.

As they inched backwards through the next room, it became clear the Tuatha Dé Danann were prepared to respond with equal ferocity. Church had always seen the Fomorii as bestial and the Golden Ones as aloof and refined, but the guards hacked and slashed with a brutality that matched their historic enemies.

The Fomorii had one thing in their favour: a complete lack of self-preservation. Insect-like, they swarmed forward, attempting to overcome the guards with the sheer weight of their bodies. The floor was slick with the foul, acidic grue that spilled from the dead Fomorii. The guards slipped, then righted themselves, tripped over severed limbs, fought as hard to keep their balance as they did to repel the enemy; and still the Fomorii drove on.

The Tuatha Dé Danann paused at the threshold of the next door, blocking the Fomorii from circling behind them. The guards were an impenetrable wall, shoulder to shoulder as they lashed out, but the captain found a second or two to shout back, 'We shall hold them off. Go with speed.'

Niamh gave a faint, deferential bow. 'Your sacrifice will not go unmarked.'

Baccharus stepped through the door into the next chamber with Niamh close behind. She had gone only a few steps when she checked behind to ensure Church was following. 'Come,' she mouthed.

'Don't wait for us,' Church yelled above the rising cacophony as the Fomorii saw what was happening.

Baccharus and Niamh were astonishingly fleet – another ability they shared with the Fomorii – and soon they had outpaced Church and Ruth.

'What are the Fomorii doing here?' Ruth gasped as they sprinted through chamber upon chamber, trying to piece together their route back to the entrance hall. The grey shapes that dogged their route had grown frantic, shrieking silently on the periphery of their vision.

'It doesn't make sense. They should be preoccupied with our world before getting mired in a potential war with the Tuatha Dé Danann.'

They paused at a junction of corridors, peering up and down in desperation. From behind came an eruption of noise: the Fomorii had broken through the guards and were in pursuit. Church swore under his breath, selected a path and set off.

It wasn't long before they realised it had been the wrong choice. They were soon passing through chambers and corridors they didn't recognise, swathed in dark colours, deep carpets, black wood, purple drapes. The noises of pursuit were drawing closer; it was as if all the cages of a zoo had been opened at once.

'We're getting nowhere! They'll be on us in a second!' Ruth snapped, exhausted.

Church skidded to a halt next to a window criss-crossed with lead flashing. The glass was of a type that let light in while preventing any view out. When the catch wouldn't open, he searched around anxiously until he found a small stool, which he heaved through it. Smashing away the remaining shards with his elbow, he leaned out. They were about twenty feet above the main gate.

The animal noises were about two chambers away. With an effort he tore down one of the luxurious drapes and threw one end out of the window. 'Climb down,' he barked, bracing himself against the wall.

'What about you?'

'I'll be able to hang, then drop after you. If you get a bloody move on!'

She reflected for only a second and then clambered out of the window, lowering herself as quickly as she could down the heavy cloth. Church grunted as he took her weight. She dropped the final few feet to the ground, then beckoned anxiously for him to follow.

The cold hit him in a wave, frosting his skin with tracings of white. He sucked in a deep breath of air and his lungs were seared. Winter had stormed into the chamber. Shaking so much he could barely control his limbs, he turned to look towards the doorway. The Fomorii were surging through the next room, a black river sprouting limbs and fangs. One had separated from the mass and was gesturing towards him with strange movements that occasionally vibrated so fast he couldn't see them. More cold hit him with the force of a truck. His fingers contorted into talons; there was ice in his hair. He knew some of the Fomorii had control over temperature, but he had never experienced it himself. It was unbearable; his body was telling him to sink to the floor and seek respite in sleep. That was where warmth lay. Another shiver made his teeth rattle.

'Church!' Ruth's plaintive cry shocked him alert. A wave of darkness was sweeping towards him, rising up, ready to strike. No time to climb out; his limbs could scarcely respond anyway. Somehow he found the strength to shift his body weight, and then he was toppling out of the window, the air rushing past him, the cold dissipating as quickly as it had come.

He heard Ruth scream and then he hit the ground hard. There was a sickening crack and pain shot through his leg into the pit of his stomach. It was too much; he blacked out.

He came round only moments later to find Ruth shaking him, her eyes filled with tears. Pain filled his body. He looked down to where the worst of it writhed like a nest of snakes and saw a white bloody bone bursting from midway down his shin; another joint where one had not existed before. The sight almost made him black out again.

Ruth shook him harder. 'Church! You can't stay here!'

Above him he saw insectile swarming at the window. There was some kind of disturbance; he guessed the last of the Tuatha Dé Danann were making a final stand. At least it would hold up the Fomorii for a little longer. 'You'll have to help me.' Every word was like a hot coal in his throat.

He didn't know how he got on to his good leg, but then he was hopping like crazy, one arm round Ruth's shoulders, trying to stay conscious when spikes were being rammed through his body. With his head spinning and the sea and sky becoming one, they reached the top of the vertiginous stairs. He felt Ruth's tension through her arm, knew exactly what she was thinking: they would never make it down the stairs together, there wasn't enough room, they had to go one at a time.

'You go first,' he gasped.

'Don't talk so beered up.' She tried to ease him ahead of her, but he grabbed her and shoved her down the first few steps. She cursed, then said, 'I'll help you. Give me your hand.'

'No. I can do it. Go on. Go on!' He could hear the Fomorii at the gate, only seconds away. He clung to the rock face and began to hop down a step at a time. It was easier going down, until he made the mistake of steadying himself with his broken leg and felt pain like he had never before experienced. Somehow he kept going. He found a rhythm that kept him moving quickly, focusing on Ruth's pale, concerned face so that he didn't overbalance. How he did it, he had no idea; it was all down to his subconscious.

Through the pain he could hear the Fomorii just a few steps behind him. At least the path was so narrow they were also forced to advance cautiously, but he couldn't afford to slow up for even a second.

'Not far now, Church,' Ruth shouted encouragingly. 'Halfway down. More than halfway.'

His lungs and muscles burned from the exertion. He glimpsed the sky, brilliant blue through the clouds, the sea, a queasy green; spinning, merging.

'Church! Keep going! Concentrate!'

He looked back, saw something black snaking around the rock face towards him, attempted to push himself away from it, realised that with his damaged leg he had no sense of balance whatsoever. And then he was moving away from the rock, reaching out frantically for the dry grass, feeling it burn through his fingers. And then he was toppling backwards, over the edge, scrabbling for purchase, but he had only one good heel and that was not enough. Ruth was screaming and the air was thick with beast-smell and jubilant shrieking. And he was falling.

The world rushed by. He hit the water hard, gulping in a massive mouthful of salty, sickeningly pungent liquid that felt more like oil. His precarious consciousness fled once again, but the cold shocked him awake when he was several feet beneath the surface, wrapped in bubbles, feeling the sea flood his nose and ears. Panic washed him in its wake and he tried to strike out for the surface, but he was hampered by his leg, and anyway, he couldn't tell which way was up. The Otherworld sensations were too potent, the smell of the water too strong, the feel too greasy. His mind fizzed in protest. He was drowning, sweeping down towards the dark water below. And that wasn't all. Whatever thinking part of him remained alert had caught sight of movement in the water, heading towards him. Something as big as a car, with fins and trailing tentacles, undulating with the speed of a torpedo, a large black maw opening and closing in hungry anticipation. Beyond it, other terrible shapes darted in the green depths, smelling blood, sensing food.

Strength returned to his arms enough to make a few feeble strokes in what he hoped was the right direction, but the predator bore down on him relentlessly.

Just as he anticipated those enormous jaws crunching down on his legs, rending and tearing and dragging him down into the dark depths, his collar was gripped and he was hauled out of the water. Face down on wet boards, he felt the boat rock violently as the creature passed just beneath. Then Ruth was at his side, caring for him as he coughed up seawater, and, as he looked up, he saw Niamh watching him worriedly.

Baccharus was beside him, his sleeve wet where he had rescued Church. 'Quickly, now. You must help me row. The Night Walkers are close.'

Barely conscious, Church let Ruth help him into a seat where he clutched an oar feebly. Ruth and Niamh both joined them and soon the boat was moving slowly away from the island.

'I don't understand why they aren't following us,' Ruth said, glancing over her shoulder.

'They know we can be seen from Wave Sweeper. Any further pursuit would be futile.' Baccharus turned to Church. 'We will find treatment for you on Wave Sweeper, Brother of Dragons,' he said with surprising tenderness.

'Thanks for saving me.'

'I could not let such an honourable being die, Jack Churchill.' His words and tone were unlike any Church had heard from the Tuatha Dé Danann before. Closing his eyes, he leaned across the oar and reflected on what it meant as they drifted back towards safety.

Church woke in his cabin, the window thrown open to reveal the last sunlight of the day, mellow gold in a pastel blue sky, coolness on the wind. His leg ached with a rude heat beneath the rough blanket, but there was none of the agony that had consumed his body immediately after the break. Cautiously, he peeked under the sheet.

'It's still there.'

Ruth was sitting just out of his line of vision, keeping watch over him. 'Yes, but will I still be able to play in the Cup Final?'

'I'm glad you've retained your sense of humour. I lost mine when I saw that bone jutting out. Almost lost my lunch too.' She sat on the edge of the bed.

There was a splint fastened hard around his lower leg; it bit sharply into his too-taut flesh as he shuffled up into a sitting position. 'When I saw it I was convinced it was an amputation job. Luckily I didn't have much opportunity to think about it after that.'

'You were luckier than you think. Most ships of this kind have some old sawbones. But this being the gods and all, you get operated on by some self-proclaimed deity. Geltin, I think his name was. And did he work miracles! His hands disappeared into your leg like it was water, popping the bone together, fusing it. He slapped some poultice on and Bob's your uncle. With that and the Pendragon Spirit you'll be back to normal in a day or two. Even beats BUPA.' She took his hand. 'I was worried.'

He gave her fingers a squeeze.

She leaned over and kissed him gently on the forehead, lingering a moment, her lips cool and moist. When she withdrew she hastily changed the subject, as if embarrassed by her actions. 'They've been in conference ever since you went under. This murder, coming so hard on Cormorel's, has really shaken them up. I think they thought they were inviolate before. Now it's like any old enemy can knock one of them off whenever he feels like it.'

'And now they know how the rest of us feel.' Church instantly felt guilty for the harshness in his voice. 'I know it must be hard for them—'

'No, you're right. It's hard to feel sympathy when they have such little regard for other living creatures. It has really shaken them up, though. And just as much because this murder was committed by the Fomorii.'

Church tried to choose his words carefully, but after a moment gave up. 'I know this might sound cold-hearted, but this could really work in our favour. It's not just a murder. With the history between the Fomorii and the Tuatha Dé Danann, it's an act of war.'

'You'd think, but I could tell from some of the comments flying around the deck that they weren't exactly breaking a neck to retaliate.'

Through the window, Church watched a gull skimming the surface of the sea; the other islands must be nearby. 'I don't understand.'

'Neither do I. Who knows how their minds work?'

Church tried to shift into a more comfortable position, then gave up. 'Why would the Fomorii risk committing such a senseless act? The Tuatha Dé Danann, their arch enemies, were giving them free rein to wipe out our world.'

Ruth examined her palm for a while, then said, 'I think it might be me.'

'What do you mean?'

'When I did the spirit-flight to London, that awful thing I told you about . . . Balor, I suppose . . . followed me back, at least across our world. Maybe it saw us as a threat, sent out a killing party to wipe us out.'

'They'd have had to move quickly.'

'You know time means nothing to these freaks.'

Church grabbed her wrist and pulled her down on to the bed next to him so he could slip his arm around her shoulders. 'It's too confusing to try to work it out sitting here. Who knows what's going on? The important thing is I need to be up and about to lobby our case if I have to.'

She leaned down beside the bed and emerged with a cane, carved in the shape of a dragon. 'Voilà.'

'That's very fitting.'

'Yes, and they seemed to have it waiting for you.' Another mystery, but he had long since given up trying to comprehend.

There was movement in the corridor without, and a second later the door rattled open without warning. Church was about to castigate the visitors for not knocking until he saw their faces. Three members of the Tuatha Dé Danann cadre who always accompanied Manannan entered, but they were subtly changed. Their faces, which before had been impassive and waxy, now had a cunning and malicious cast at the edges of the mouth and in the eyes, barely perceptible in direct glance, but on another level, quite striking.

'The Master requires your presence,' the leader of the group said. His hand rested on the pommel of a sword Church had not seen in his possession before.

'The worms have turned,' Church muttered so only Ruth could hear.

They silently followed the guards, Church hobbling as best he could. On deck there was no sign of any of the other travellers, only small groups of the Tuatha Dé Danann, watching their passage with dark, brooding expressions.

In his expansive cabin, as large as a mediaeval banqueting hall, Manannan sat behind a desk of gold, carved with figures that appeared to move of their own accord a split-second after his attention left them.

Other high-ranking members of the Golden Ones were scattered around the room. Church spied Niamh behind a couple of thin, cruel-faced aristocrats, but she would not meet his eyes. The strained, icy atmosphere told him things were about to get much worse.

Manannan rose once they stood before him and clasped his over-sized hands loosely together in front of him. His face, too, was changed, though not as unpleasant as those of his guards; but it was harsher, certainly. 'Another of our number has been driven on.' His voice was as cold and hard as a sword-blade. 'The circling stars have been shaken, not once but twice.' The message was repeated almost for his own sake, as if he could barely believe it. 'Two times, in the fleeting memory of Fragile Creatures. Two abominations in the face of exist-ence.' Fury flared in his eyes, but his voice dropped to a whisper. 'Monstrous.'

Church didn't dare say anything for fear of retribution.

Manannan raised a hand to point an accusing finger at them. 'You Fragile Creatures brought this upon us.'

Ruth stirred angrily; Church fumbled for her wrist to restrain her, but she took a step to one side. 'The Fomorii—'

'—were brought to the Western Isles in search of you. Were driven to acts of vengeance by you. The Night Walkers are rough beasts, once prompted, rarely stopped. You must be accountable for this.'

'You're surely not blaming us for Cormorel?' Ruth held up her face defiantly.

Manannan did not answer.

'Scapegoats, then.'

The disrespect in her voice was a step too far. Manannan's face shifted furiously before settling into its original form. 'We have no interest in your feeble concerns.'

'The Night Walkers will attack you as soon as they've finished with us,' Ruth said, unbowed.

'And when they do we shall eradicate them as we did before. Until then, they are beneath our notice, as all creatures are.'

Manannan's tone and the mood of the other Tuatha Dé Danann filled Church with apprehension. The situation was worse than he had imagined.

'The time has come. It has been proposed that you Brother and Sister of Dragons are a threat to the good running of Wave Sweeper and should be wiped from existence before any further troubles arise.'

Ruth blanched. Church couldn't believe what he was hearing. 'You're going to execute us?'

'No.' Niamh's voice was filled with passion. She pushed her way past the other gods to stand before Manannan, her skin flushed to a golden sheen.

Manannan fixed his emotionless gaze on her. 'You speak in defence of these Fragile Creatures?'

'I do.'

'What worth have they?' one of the cruelly aristocratic gods said.

'You know their worth,' Niamh said directly to Manannan. Her words were strangely weighted.

Manannan nodded. 'Still, there is a need for discipline.'

'Do not be swayed by the voices of the dissenters.' Niamh bowed her head slightly so her hair fell around her beautiful face. 'In your heart you know—'

'Do you question the word of the Master?' The aristocratic god stepped forward, a dim fury flaring behind his eyes.

Curiously, Church watched. For so long they had pretended to be detached from most human emotions – truly gods. But they weren't gods at all, however much they pretended. His concern grew when he saw the flickers of fear cross Niamh's face; it was obviously a great transgression to question Manannan's thoughts.

'I do not question—' Niamh began, but Manannan held up his hand to silence her.

'I will listen to our sister, who speaks for the Fragile Creatures,' Manannan said to the assembled Tuatha Dé Danann before turning to Church and Ruth. 'You are fortunate to have such a powerful advocate.'

Church's relief was mingled with surprise that Niamh's voice carried such weight; he suspected Manannan was hoping to be convinced to change his opinion.

'Be warned,' Manannan continued, 'the eyes of the Golden Ones will be upon you from now on. Accept your role in existence, Fragile Creatures, and bring no more pain to this place.'

His attention was gone from them in the snap of a finger. The sneering guards – now strangely less malicious and cunning – herded Church and Ruth to the door. Niamh flashed Church an affectionate smile before she joined the others who were milling around in obvious annoyance at the outcome.

Outside, Ruth's eyes blazed. 'Those bastards!'

Church was taken aback by the vehemence in her voice. 'They're losing control. Looking for scapegoats. They can't believe they're not as all-round wonderful as they think they are.'

'And what was that witch doing?'

'Defending us—'

'Trying to get into your pants, more like. She never gives up, does she?'

She took a deep breath of the refreshing sea air, but her temper didn't diminish. 'What's wrong with you?' Church said. 'We were about to get summarily executed, but she got us off.'

Ruth turned to him, defiant. 'You know, when it comes to women, you've got a real problem.'

'What are you talking about?'

'The witch still thinks she's got a chance with you. Maybe she has got a chance, I don't know. But you just keep diving into all these relationships, stirring up a whole load of emotional mess, without once thinking about the repercussions.'

'I know I've made mistakes—'

'Well, sort yourself out.'

'I can't believe the world is falling apart and we're talking about this!'

'Oh, come on. You know this is the important thing. The rest of it is just stuff that happens.'

Church was lost for words.

'Do you want her?' she pressed.

'Niamh?' Ruth's gaze held him tight. He could finally read in her eyes all the truth that he had secretly known all along. 'No.'

'Are you sure?'

'Yes, I'm sure. I just get the feeling there's something else going on there, but I can't put my finger on it. Her feelings are so intense, they don't have any connection with how long I've known her. Everything feels completely out of balance.' He watched the gulls swooping around the masts. 'I don't like to hurt people's feelings, especially good people. And she does seem good.'

'Sometimes you have to be firm.' Her voice softened a little. 'You need to talk to her—'

'I've tried.'

'—be honest with her. She might be upset at first, but if she knows there's no point she can adjust. And then if you close all that down you can focus on your own future.' Her voice remained calm and detached, but there was a tremendous weight to her words.

'I just wish I understood her better—'

'Oh, for God's sake!'

She made to go, but he caught her arm. 'Let's not screw this up.'

Her eyes moved slowly across his face, reading every thought in his head. Eventually she nodded; the tension between them evaporated, leaving another tension beneath.

A universe away, the emotions that had been crushing Laura for so long had finally started to dissipate. The dislocation when she awakened in the charnel pit had brought shock, despair, horror, futility and a debilitating fear that had left her unable to move.

Eventually all that was left was an emptiness gradually filling with a near-religious relief at her survival. With an effort she pulled herself into a squatting position, squirming as the soft corpses gave beneath her or when she brushed against cold skin. The only way she could cope was by not thinking about it. Instead, she fixed on the faint light filtering in on the other side of wherever she had been dumped.

The journey across the bodies was sickening. At the far side of the room was a flight of brick stairs leading up to a partly broken door. Beyond it she could see grey sky.

Refusing to look back, she scampered up the steps and tried the door, which swung open at her touch. She was in a street running amongst dilapidated Victorian warehouses that rose up high overhead. It was eerily still and quiet. The damp vegetation smell of open water hung in the air, but there was nothing to give her any clue where she was.

But as she stepped out of the shadows of the building a detail caught her eye that shocked her. The skin of her right hand and forearm had a greenish tinge. It was only faint, but unnatural enough to worry her. Anxiously she checked the other arm and then her legs; it was the same all over.

Finding a window with an unbroken pane, she examined her face closely: another shock, this one uplifting. The scars that Callow had carved into her face were gone, the skin as smooth and clear as a baby's. There wasn't even the vaguest trace of the wounds. It made no sense to her, but her overwhelming joy wiped out any worries. Hastily fluffing her short blonde hair into spikes, she wiped some of the smeared dirt and blood from her face and then set off to investigate her surroundings.

The warehouses had been in use recently. In one there was the strong smell of cinnamon; others had been fitted with modern security systems. Ominously, several had open doorways leading down to cellars, from which familiar unpleasant odours rose.

One side-street led down to a broad, grey river. It took her only a second or two of scanning the riverside properties to realise it was the Thames; she was back in London. Heading along a road overlooking the water to the edge of the area of warehouses, she began to make out dim sounds of activity.

Just as she was about to emerge from the cover of the final warehouse she was suddenly grabbed from behind and dragged backwards, a hand clamped over her mouth. She fought furiously, but her attacker was too strong.

Only when her assailant had pulled her into the warehouse and flung her unceremoniously on to an oily concrete floor did she see who it was. 'What are you doing?' she raged.

The Bone Inspector levelled his staff at her, as if to frighten her into silence. His piercing blue eyes gave him a menacing quality, emphasised by the unkempt grey-black hair hanging lankly around his shoulders. He wore the same dirty cheesecloth shirt, baggy trousers and sandals Laura had seen him in the first time she met him at Avebury.

'Keep silent if you want to keep living,' he growled.

Laura dusted herself down as she flashed him a contemptuous look. 'I bet you get all your women this way. Let's face it, they're never going to compliment you on your dress sense.'

He grabbed her wrist roughly and dragged her over to a window, wiping away the dirt so she could peer out. Fomorii ranged as far as the eye could see, some carrying human bodies, others moving intently about some activity she couldn't discern.

'God.' Her throat had almost closed up.

'The whole city is their stinking pit now.'

Her fear was so strong Laura couldn't mask it; she stared at the Bone Inspector with wide eyes. 'So this is their base?' Then: 'They've killed everyone?'

The Bone Inspector took pity on her. He let go of her wrist and led her gently to a pallet where they sat side by side. 'It's a shock, I know.'

'You know what? Let's forget trying to describe things, because there just aren't the words.' She buried her head in her hands, shaking as all the repressed tension came out in a rush. When it had eased, she looked up at him suspiciously . 'What are *you* doing here?'

'Looking for you.'

This made her even more suspicious. 'How would you—'

'So I don't have to sit here answering stupid questions all day, I'll tell you. I came looking for your body. You made a sacrifice. It wasn't right that you were just dumped, forgotten.' He looked away to minimise the impact of what lay behind his words. 'Thought I'd take your bones back to somewhere fitting—'

'You're just a sentimental—'

He waved a threatening finger in her face. 'It's my job. I'm a guardian of the old places because I'm a priest of the land, if you will. I tend to

1006

the people who fight for it.' His eyes narrowed. 'But I don't have to like them, understand?'

'Well, God forbid you should show some sensitivity.'

'The earth energy's strong in you and your travelling troupe of hopeless cases. I can feel it even more now the changes you've wrought have started to wake the land.'

'So you followed your nose.' She looked back towards the window uncomfortably. 'But how did you get past all that?'

'It wasn't so bad when I came in. They were spreading out across a different part of the city, doing whatever foul business they do, and the eastern approach was pretty open. Even so, I had to move under cover. Took time.' He shrugged. 'Can't see how we're going to get back out, though.' He eyed her askance. 'So how come you're not a pile of blood and guts and bone? And why do you look like you've been sleeping in a compost heap?'

'You really know how to chat up a girl.'

'Well?'

'How should I know? I've given up trying to work anything out any more.'

They sat alone with their thoughts for a while until Laura said, 'Did it work?'

He knew exactly what she meant. 'You saved her life. Who knows, you might even have saved much more than that. I pointed her and that miserable leader in the direction of the Western Isles to try to get the Golden Ones on our side. They might even do it, if they can put a lifetime of failure behind them.'

'The others?'

'Don't know.'

There was another long silence before she asked the question they'd both been avoiding. 'So I've escaped a particularly horrible death to spend the rest of my life in a stinking warehouse with someone who doesn't know what soap is. Or do you have anything approaching a plan?'

He stared blankly at the dirty floor. 'No. No plans.'

Church and Ruth stayed in the cabin until night had fallen. The air was tinged with the fading warmth of the day and the scent of burning oil as the flickering lantern in the corner sent shadows shivering across the wooden walls.

All their attempts at making head or tail of the eddies of mystery and intrigue swirling around them had come to nothing, but so much was at stake they couldn't afford to just sit back any longer.

'We have to find the Walpurgis – he's the key,' Church said eventually. 'There's something very strange going on here, on this ship. These days I trust my instinct more than anything, and sometimes it's almost like I can feel deep, powerful currents moving just beneath my feet. I don't know if the death of Hellawes has anything to do with it, but Cormorel's murder *is* right at the heart. I don't understand why the gods in the furnace are stockpiling weapons, what the meaning is of all the strange looks and half-heard comments the other gods are making. Whatever it is, I *know* it's going to affect us, even if it's only that we're definitely not going to get any help from the Tuatha Dé Danann until the suspicion has been taken off us.'

'How do you expect to find the Walpurgis if Manannan's massed ranks can't?'

'I don't know, but I know I've got to try. He's down there somewhere.'

'I don't know.' She shook her head worriedly. 'The Malignos are still roaming around. You cross them, you won't be coming back up again.' She sucked on her lip thoughtfully. 'I'd better come with you.'

'No,' he replied forcefully. 'I'm not being chivalrous, it's just good tactics. If I don't come back, at least there'll be one of us left to try to hold it all together.' The shadows had pooled in her eyes so he couldn't read her expression. 'You still think it's going to end in tears?'

'Oh yeah.'

They were interrupted by a cry from the deck, strangely lonely in the still of the night. Church got up and peered out of the window. 'Another island.' A couple of lights glimmered in the sea of darkness. A rumbling ran through the walls as the crew prepared to drop anchor.

'More delays,' Ruth said with irritation.

Church watched the lights for a moment longer, then said, 'I think we should try to get on the landing party again. Any information we can pick up is going to help us.'

'Do you really think they're going to let us after the last one?'

'We can get Baccharus to help – he seems to like our company.'

'Or Niamh.'

Church agreed uncomfortably, 'Or Niamh.'

Ruth looked away.

'We have to—'

'I know.' Curling up on the bed, she rested her head in the crook of her arm and tucked her knees up to her chest. 'We have to do what we can to make things right, however unpleasant. It's war.'

The rocking of the ship changed its tempo as Wave Sweeper came to a gradual halt. Chains rumbled and clanked dimly, followed by a splash as the anchor hit the water. Then there was only a gentle swaying as the boat bobbed at its tether.

Church left the window and returned to the bed, sitting in the small space at the end that Ruth's long limbs weren't occupying. Her feet touched his thigh; she didn't move them away. 'Do you remember, just after Beltane, sitting by the campfire?' She shifted slightly, put her feet on top of his legs. 'That was a funny time. We'd already been through so much, had this massive blow, yet we felt—'

'So close.'

'Exactly. This year hasn't been like anything else in my life. I know that's stating the obvious, but I mean on an emotional level. It's been so . . . potent. I've never felt more alive.' He cupped the top of her pale foot in his hand. It felt so cool, the skin as smooth as vellum. 'And it makes me feel guilty.'

'What, we'd be better off moping around?' She stretched lazily. 'There was a lot missing from the life everyone led before. Nobody was *living* at all.'

'Now people are living, but they're dying too. That's not right.' He moved his hand up her leg to stroke the gentle curve of her calf through her jeans.

'We'd forgotten how to feel anything. We were wasting our lives, and it must be one of the great ironies of the moment that when there was a chance we all might lose everything, we finally started to appreciate things.'

'You don't know what you've got until you're in danger of losing it.' His hand moved over her knee to her thigh; she didn't flinch, or make any attempt to push it away.

'Let's face it: this is the place where memories are made. How many people can say that?'

'Is that enough?'

' 'Course it is.' She smiled, put her hand on the back of his. But instead of pushing it off her leg, she pulled it towards her, over her hip, on to her side, and up, until he was overbalanced and falling on top of her. She manoeuvred herself until she was on her back, looking into his face. Her smile was open and honest and for an instant he was back in those early days, just after Albert Bridge, when they had spent their time piecing together the first clues about the unfolding nightmare. And with that remembrance came a blinding revelation: he had felt strongly about her from almost the moment he had seen her, as if they were of one kind, one heart. But in his despairing mood after Marianne's death any emotion had been muffled. Even when that had finally cleared, his feelings had been in such chaos that nothing made sense. But now he saw it clearly.

He loved her.

And he could see in the opal shimmer of her eyes that she loved him too; secretly he'd always known it. But the difference now was that she could see his feelings as well.

She pulled his head down and kissed him gently on the lips; she tasted faintly of lemon, her skin smelled clean, her dark hair felt silky in his fingers. And her smile was strong, with so much in it; it was all so heady. She was right; the end of the world didn't matter, the conflicts and power games of other people, all the petty concerns of the outside world. Inside was all that mattered; inside their heads, inside their relationships. The places where memories were made.

Ruth felt like crying, she felt like laughing. She'd managed to convince herself it was a package of sensations she'd never ever appreciate, except by proxy, in books and films and the wilting, easily discounted conversations of friends: that ocean swell of the senses, filling her throat, her head. She'd told herself that failure to feel wouldn't be so bad; there were always things to do and see. And now she could see how ridiculous that had been. A life touched by this could never be filled by anything ever again; except more of it, and more, and more, and more. She could keep the fear at bay now; not a fear of being alone, in a holding hands in the park way; she was too strong and confident to need someone to fill her time. But of being alone in the human race; we weren't made that way, she thought.

And here it was. If the world fell apart, and the stars rained into the void, it was all right. It was all all right.

They stripped the clothes from each other with a sensuality that was slow and measured; unfocused passion would let it all slip through their fingers too quickly. It was something to be savoured, not just by the body but by the mind, and that was how they knew it was exactly right. Church wondered how he had never known that before.

They knew each other's shape from embraces, but the fiery skin beneath the clothes made it all new and different. They were each surprised at how hard their bodies were, freed of the fat of lazy living by their punishing existence on the road. As he penetrated her, they kissed deeply, filling each other with soft darkness illuminated by purple flashes that reminded Church of the view across space from the Watchtower. He moved slowly at first, then harder as she enveloped him with her legs, and her arms, and her kisses, and her thoughts. His mind had one brief instant of complete awareness and then it switched off so there was only everything he felt, wrapped tightly in the moment; as timeless as Otherworld.

They lay together in silence while the sweat and semen dried on their bodies, listening to their breathing subside, their hearts slow down. Their thoughts were like the movement of luminescent fish in the deepest, darkest fathoms, slow yet graceful under the gargantuan pressure, struggling with the immensity of what they had felt. After a while, Ruth fumbled for Church's hand and he took it. Two, as one, passing through time.

A movement somewhere in the shadows of the cabin roused them from their introspection; a mouse, they both thought. But then something that at first sight was a large spider scurried into the flickering circle of lantern light. It was a human figure barely half an inch tall. Ruth recognised Marik Bocat, the Portune she had encountered after escaping the Malignos.

She rolled over to cover herself. 'How long have you been there?'

'I have more to do than watch you make the beast with two backs,' he said sharply. He sprinted to the edge of the bed where he looked up at Church's bemused face. 'Ho, Simple Jack! Heave me up and mind how you do it!'

Church leaned down so Marik Bocat could clamber on to his palm. Once the tiny man was level with their eyes it was obvious concern lay heavy on his brown, wizened face.

'What is it?' Ruth asked.

'I come out of respect for fellow denizens of the Fixed Lands, and, of course, in respect for your exalted roles as champions of our home.' He raised one minuscule finger. 'A warning, then. Danger is abroad and your lives may be at risk. The door lies open, the cage is empty.' He paused while he looked from one face to the other. 'Callow is gone. The Malignos have freed him.'

Away across the water, the Islands of the Dead breathed steadily and silently and the night was filled with the terrible chill of their exhalation.

peine forte et oure

Marik Bocat told them little, although they were both convinced he knew more than he was saying. His people had the run of the ship, he explained, and witnessed many things: secrets and slanders, matters of great importance and minor betrayals. The freeing of Callow had been the latest example of their surveillance at work.

'The Portunes will, of course, maintain their vigilance, and if information regarding this situation comes to light I will relate it to you,' he said in an oddly formal manner.

'Why are you helping us?' Ruth asked.

'Horses and teeth,' he cautioned, before half-turning from them and motioning to be put back down on the floor. But as Church lowered him, his voice floated back: 'We are all fellows of the flesh in the Great Village.'

Church limped off the end of the bed and dressed, surprised at how quickly his leg was healing. He could already walk without the aid of a stick. 'That bastard will be coming for us when we least expect it, so we have to expect it all the time.'

'Like we haven't got anything else to do.'

A thought came to Church as he ransacked a chest in the corner where he had come across a number of sea-faring implements, including a bill-hook and a short dagger used for cutting rope, which he stuffed into his belt. 'Can you help me find the Walpurgis?' he said turning back to Marik Bocat.

'Now why would you be looking for that bundle of rags?' Church could tell from the suspicion in his voice that the Portune had some information.

'He can help us. He *was* helping us before he ran away.'

'I'll ask around.' He eyed Church askance.

'You *can* trust me.'

'So it seems.'

Church dug down to the bottom of the chest, but there remained only oily rags, sand and dried seaweed. When he turned back to prompt Marik Bocat further he discovered the Portune had already departed.

Ruth dressed quickly and a little nervously. Their bonding had been truncated and there was still so much they had to discuss.

Now was not the time, Church thought. 'We really need to find the Walpurgis,' he said redundantly.

Ruth easily accepted the rearrangement of priorities. 'Marik Bocat will probably be back once he's had a think about us. He's a suspicious sort.' She threw open the windows to let some cool night air into the stifling room, which was still filled with the scents of their love-making. The sparse lights of the island twinkled over the waves. 'I think he will come back,' she stressed. 'We need him to, really. It's even more dangerous to venture below decks now, with Callow on the loose as well as the Malignos. I've been down there, and believe me, when you get to the lower levels you can't tell what's a few feet ahead or behind you.'

'If I have to—'

She silenced him with a flap of her hand. The silence was broken by a dragging noise on deck. 'They're readying a boat,' she said. 'Looks like they're off to the island.'

'What, now? In the dark?'

'Hey, they're the Golden Ones. They don't jump at shadows,' she mocked.

Church said, 'We ought to go, you know. There might be something important out there.'

He looked reluctantly at the dishevelled bed and she laughed quietly. 'There'll be time enough for that. Come on.'

A cool breeze moved effortlessly across the deck, teasing out the heat of the day, bringing a hint of lush vegetation to the familiar aroma of salty water. The night was filled with the slap and rustle of the flaps hanging from the furled sails and the rusty hinge creaking of the rigging. Up on the mast, Ruth's owl glowed like a ghost, watching ominously. Although lanterns hung at regular intervals, there were still too many dangerous shadows lapping across the deck. Church and Ruth moved as quickly as they could to the small group of figures preparing for the landing party. Taranis was overseeing the activity as the crew prepared to lower the boat into the water, while Niamh and Baccharus hung back ready to board.

Taranis eyed Church and Ruth with cold suspicion, but Church ignored his gaze. Instead, he spoke directly to Baccharus and Niamh. 'We'd like to come with you.'

'You may accompany us, Brother of Dragons,' Baccharus said as Taranis opened his mouth to speak.

Surprisingly, Niamh looked unsure. 'There may be danger abroad,' she cautioned. 'The arrival of Wave Sweeper is always heralded by the denizens of the Western Isles.'

'And you've heard nothing,' Church noted. 'It could be the Fomorii again. Have you considered this is their first strike in a war against you, catching you off-guard as they work their way towards your most sacred lands?'

There wasn't the slightest flicker across the faces of the assembled Tuatha Dé Danann, but for the first time Church felt that unease was gestating deep inside them.

Wave Sweeper floated in silence as the landing boat was lowered to the waves. There was no sign of Manannan, or any of the thousands of strange creatures who occupied the lower levels. Taranis watched them impassively from the rail until he was swallowed up by the night, and then there was only the gentle lapping of the waves against the side.

As they neared land, Church was surprised to feel the air grow substantially warmer, as if each island had its own micro-climate. Here it was almost sub-tropical, the heat lying heavy on his lungs as his T-shirt grew steadily damp from the spiralling humidity. Their destination was more familiar than their last port of call; it reminded Church of one of the smaller Caribbean islands. From a rocky base where the spectral surf splashed, it rose up sharply through thick vegetation to a mountaintop lost in the dark. It smelled heavily of steaming jungles, rich and evocative, but tainted by an underlying corruption.

A small beach came into sight, at which point the crew had to fight to keep the boat steady against the heavy currents that swirled just off the shore. Church spied the tip of cruel rocks breaking the surface on either side and realised a delicate path was being picked; one miscalculation and they would have been dashed in an instant. As the currents grew more intense, the boat became a stomach-churning rollercoaster ride. Church and Ruth gripped the sides tightly, but the crew were in complete control at all times.

Eventually the shore came up fast and the rowers jumped out into the shallows to haul the boat up on to the white sand. A minute later they were all standing on the beach, allowing the adrenalin to drop while Church and Ruth surveyed the dazzling array of stars overhead. There, with the night sounds of the jungle at their back and the waves crashing before them, there was an exhilarating sense of paradise that outshone any South Pacific dream.

'Do you notice how each of these islands has a different feel?' Church whispered to Ruth.

'The last one was edgy,' she agreed. 'This one makes me want to kick off my shoes and run across the sand like some moron in a Bounty ad. So relaxing.'

'Come,' Baccharus interjected. 'We have a long walk, and it is dark beneath the trees. We must stay close together.'

'Who are we visiting this time?' Church asked.

'This is the Isle of Lost Lament,' Baccharus said, as if that explained it all. But then he added, 'Six dwell here. Kepta, Quillot . . .' He waved his hand dismissively instead of listing the remaining names. There was a strange undercurrent in his manner, but Church couldn't quite put his finger on it.

Once Niamh had given the word, the leader of the guards motioned them to move out, his men taking up positions behind and on either side. They quickly passed the tide-line on to the dry sand beyond and then into the impenetrable darkness beneath the trees.

It was claustrophobic under the cover of foliage in the hot, steamy atmosphere. The trees were clustered quite tightly in areas, their trunks oddly twisted, with branches resembling arthritic claws. They vaguely reminded Church of ones he had seen in the mangrove swamps of the South-Eastern US on a holiday with Marianne, only these trees had thick, fan-like leaves of a shiny green that served to keep the light out and the heat and moisture battened down against the ground. Vines as thick as Ruth's forearm trailed from the upper branches, clinging to their flesh with some unpleasant sticky substance when they brushed past. They weren't the only obstacle: scattered all around were thick bushes covered in thorns like razors; with only the slightest pressure, one drove through Church's jacket and shirt and into the soft flesh just above his waist. Away in the dark they occasionally saw colours glowing, dull scarlets and fuschias and sapphires, which they eventually discovered were disturbingly alien blooms, like orchids, only much larger; their perfume was cloying and sickly. They appeared to be straining for the faint moonlight that occasionally made its way through the vegetation.

When they had first crossed the forest boundary they had expected silence, but the jungle was alive with movement and sound. Their feet crunched noisily on the carpet of twigs and branches, sending things scurrying for cover ahead of them: the sinuous motion of snakes, and the creepily rapid and erratic motion of large lizards. Church saw one of them nearby; it resembled an iguana, but when it half turned away in the trees he thought he glimpsed a human face on its scaly body. Spiders as big as his hand dropped from the branches and scuttled across their path, their corpulent bodies coloured rouge and cream.

The screech of night birds, again distressingly human, echoed amongst the treetops. On several occasions, Church and Ruth thought they heard voices whispering comments, but when they looked round they saw only grey shapes fading in the strands of mist that floated around the boles; the dead were restless.

After twenty minutes of hard hacking, with the point men slashing a path through the thickest flora, Niamh dropped back until she was standing beside Church. Despite herself, Ruth tensed.

'You must promise me you will take care of yourself, Jack.' Niamh kept her head slightly bowed so her hair fell forward, obscuring her face. 'There is great risk here.'

'I always take care of myself, Niamh.'

Ruth was convinced she heard tenderness in his words, though he had managed to keep his face impassive. Despite everything he said, she knew Church still found his emotions as unknowable as the Tuatha Dé Danann; he could react to them on a superficial level, but he had no idea what was moving far beneath the surface. Ruth could see he felt affection for Niamh, against all his protestations. What was happening here? As Church said, they *had* experienced little contact, certainly no intimacy, yet sometimes, in little movements or looks, it was as if they had known each other for a lifetime. Now she had found Church, after all those years of looking and knowing *exactly* what she wanted without even coming close to finding it, she was not about to give him up. She would fight if she had to.

Church and Niamh were engrossed in a conversation about the jungle plants when they were shocked into silence by the sound of something enormous crashing through the trees about half a mile away. The loud splintering was followed by a wail like a crying baby; the effect made them feel sick to the pit of their stomachs.

'What's that?' Church asked anxiously.

Niamh looked puzzled. Ruth thought she spied a glimmer of fear.

The leader of the guards came back to hurry them along the path they were carving ahead. Church and Ruth tried several times to peer through the darkness in the direction of the sounds, but only once did they see movement, and that faded away in an instant.

'Large predators,' Church said to Ruth, one eyebrow raised comically.

'There's always something bigger.' She tried to lighten the mood, but whatever it was had upset them immensely.

Conversation dried up for the next fifteen minutes. It might have been their imagination, but since they had heard the creature, the

atmosphere had grown steadily more oppressive, until they were starting at every crack of wood or bird's cry.

Then, so sharply that Ruth broke out in goosebumps, they entered an
area of complete silence: no bird-call, no rustling in the undergrowth.
Even the trees appeared to be holding their breath.

Ruth shivered. 'What is it?' Her voice was a whisper, but it sounded
like a shout in the stillness.

Ahead, the lead guard raised his hand to bring them to a halt.
Although he couldn't see the reason for their stop, Church felt his
throat close up. The same anxiety was clear in Ruth's face. She looked at
him, said nothing.

A change in the mood of the Tuatha Dé Danann rippled back from
the front, like the first tremors before an earthquake. Anxiously,
Church pushed his way through the group until he reached the head.

It was the stench that assailed him first, so rich with fruity corruption
it made him gag. Across the path lay the carcass of some animal, a cross
between a zebra and a wart-hog. Yet the beast had not been killed by a
predator. The body was covered with deep, suppurating sores and a
thick, creamy foam frosted its mouth and eyes. Around the belly, the
groin and the neck, the tissue had liquefied into an oily black goo.

Church backed away until he found Baccharus. 'What's wrong?'

'The creature is diseased.' There was more to it than that, but
however much Church pressed, he would say nothing more. Neither
would Niamh make any comment, but there was evident concern in her
face.

'I don't know what's going on here, but they've certainly got the
jitters,' Church whispered to Ruth. 'Watch your back.'

After a few moments' reflection away from Church and Ruth, the
guards decided to cut a path around the carcass, but even when they
were several feet away, the stench still followed them. Not long after
that they came across another creature, this time a deer, small, with
sharp, furry ridges on its back. It had the same marks of awful illness.
The two discoveries in such close proximity only confirmed the worst
fears of the Tuatha Dé Danann. The guards were in two minds whether
to press on, but Niamh ordered them to continue.

'Whatever it is, it's not affecting the lizards or birds,' Church hissed.

'As long as we don't catch it.' Ruth kept her head down, watching
Baccharus's heels.

'I don't think the Tuatha Dé Danann would be carrying on if there
were any danger.'

'I'm glad you're confident.'

The incline increased sharply until they were slipping on the crumbly, peaty soil that quickly turned to mud in the humidity. Breathing was difficult and both Church and Ruth were sleeked in sweat, but at least the arduous progress kept their minds off the disease-ridden animals.

Cresting the slope, they came on to a broad, thickly forested plateau, and were hit by a sudden choking stink worse than anything they had experienced so far. Trees had been smashed down to create a wide clearing, their jagged stumps protruding from the ground like broken teeth. In the centre of the space lay a mound of decomposing flesh: the bodies of a score or more of the jungle's mammals, a range of species, all of them ravaged by disease and leaking the obscene black liquid that puddled and ran off down the slope.

Ruth took in the sight, then picked up trails on the ground. 'My God, they've been *dragged* here.'

'Maybe the local residents were clearing up to burn the carcasses. You don't want rotting animals all around your home,' Church suggested unconvincingly.

'Baccharus, you know what's doing this,' Ruth said sharply. 'Please tell us.'

He shook his head slowly, but kept his eyes fixed in the depths of the jungle. 'It is not the time. Or the place.'

The stench was so thick they couldn't stay there a moment longer. Covering their mouths, they bypassed the site as quickly as they could and continued on their upward path. In the eerie silence, the tension was almost unbearable. The lights hadn't been visible since they left the beach so they had no idea how much further they had to travel. The guards had grown particularly jumpy, and when the sounds started up close by, they formed a defensive posture.

'Keep moving,' Niamh pressed, but even in motion they were half-turned towards the source of the sound – breaking branches, snapping trunks, the noise of a large bulk moving through the vegetation. When the sickening wailing baby cry echoed loudly, they all knew they had not left the mysterious fearsome beast behind.

'Is it coming this way?' Grimacing from the sound, Ruth cocked an ear to hear the rise and fall of the cry, cut off for a moment, then appearing again suddenly. Her realisation dawned at the same time as the rest of the group. 'It's coming after us!'

The crashing in the trees grew louder, unmistakably surging towards them. 'What the hell is it?' Church asked hoarsely.

They were all frozen to the spot for a moment. It was impossible to tell from which direction the chilling noise was coming; distorting echoes bounced amongst the trees so that it appeared to be approaching them from every direction at once.

Baccharus was the first to move. 'Come, quickly!' Surprisingly, it was to Church and Ruth that he turned his attention, grabbing their wrists and dragging them on. 'The court is not far ahead – we can take refuge there!'

They moved swiftly, the guards taking up the rear, but before they had progressed far a terrible screeching erupted in the treetops above them. Suddenly the air was alive with frantic movement. Flashes of deepest black crossed Church's vision. A hard form swatted the side of his head. It left him seeing stars, and when he drew the back of his hand across the aching spot, a trail of blood was left behind. The sight of that scarlet line stunned him; he hadn't been hit that hard. Then he saw what was happening: winged creatures whirled amongst the trees, lashing out with claws and sharp teeth. Another one slammed against his head, his chest, his arm. He ducked and ran forward, trying to wave the attackers away. They were moving so quickly it was hard to see what they were; although he had an impression of bats with leathery wings, their faces were lizard-like.

He caught up with Ruth, her pale face also splattered with blood. The guards were on every side, slashing with their swords. The flying things plummeted from the sky in their tens, hacked in half. There was too much blood, like rusty rain, as if their bodies were bloated with the stuff.

Ducking and diving, now feeling the pain from many cuts, Church and Ruth managed to spy a tree with low, thick branch cover. They dived beneath where they could watch the scene. The bat-creatures were an air-borne maelstrom of fur and teeth, but the Tuatha Dé Danann stood their ground, their golden skin now an apocalpytic red, striking furiously, though their faces still registered no emotion. The bodies piled high around their feet.

It was soon apparent the bat-creatures had simply been disturbed during a period of heightened tension. Eventually those on the fringes began to flap away until only a few fluttered overhead, to be swiftly dispatched by the guards' swords.

Church crawled out into the bloody mire, Ruth close behind. 'What the bloody hell was—'

The screeching baby noise was so close, the words caught in his throat and his stomach did a flip. Trees crashed; they felt the tremor of the fall through the soles of their boots.

The guards hurried Niamh away through the trees. Baccharus ran over to collect Church and Ruth. 'If you stay here, you will join the beasts on the pile,' he said.

They ran with him, slipping on the slick, churned-up ground. Church had to haul Ruth up from her hands and knees, all her clothes now sopping with mud and the blood of the bat-creatures. Another baby-cry wailed close behind. It instilled in both of them a deep urge to vomit.

'It is slow,' Baccharus noted as he ran. 'If we move quickly we can evade it. For now.'

Church didn't like the sound of his final words, but before he could question him further they had broken out of the trees on to an area of clipped, green lawns, rising up gently to an imposing edifice of white marble built partly into the mountainside. Towers and minarets and columns formed strict lines of grace and power, like some odd mix of Greek and Middle Eastern architecture. Lights burned brightly within, welcoming after the seething darkness of the jungle.

They sprinted across the lawns, relieved that they had found sanctuary from the many terrors of the preternatural forest, grateful for the cool breeze sweeping in from the sea after the suffocating heat. But when they reached the building their relief evaporated. The front was a mass of glass windows offering panoramic views over the island beneath; all were shattered and the white muslin curtains billowed out into the night. The Tuatha Dé Danann slowed their run until they were once again advancing cautiously, swords raised. Niamh glanced at Baccharus, but said nothing.

The cry of their pursuer from just beyond the tree-line prompted them into action once more and they hurried through the broken windows into an interior which glowed white with the light from scores of lanterns, torches and candles, like some Byzantine impression of heaven.

The leader of the guards made several chopping motions with his hand and within seconds his men were in action. They dragged enormous stone tables and heavy wooden furniture to block up the windows, continuing ceaselessly until the blockade was several feet thick.

'Will that work?' Ruth asked.

'No,' Baccharus replied curtly.

'Now,' Church stressed, 'you've got to tell us. What's out there?'

'The Plague-Bringer.' Baccharus peered at the thin gap between the pile of furniture and the top of the window. 'Known in your land as the Nuckelavee.'

'It carries the plague with it, infecting all higher creatures in its path,' Niamh interjected. The baby-cry rose up again just beyond the

1020

wall; Church and Ruth started, then gagged; every aspect of the creature assailed the senses.

'Even you?' Ruth added once she had recovered.

Niamh looked away, but Baccharus answered for her. 'There are some who think the Golden Ones unassailable, the highest of the high in all of existence. That is not be my belief.' Niamh flashed him a curious stare and he changed tack. 'We have seen two Golden Ones eradicated. There is no doubt an ending can come to our race, though it is blasphemous to admit it. And it is told that that creature, the Nuckelavee, is one of the few things that can bring about that ending.'

The baby-cry again; Ruth covered her ears. There was a rough sound as if the Plague-Bringer was dragging itself along the foot of the wall.

'And it lives on this island? Near this court?'

Baccharus shook his head. 'Like all the Western Isles, this is a safe place for the Golden Ones. It was brought here.'

'By the Fomorii,' Ruth interjected. 'Specifically to kill your people. It *is* war.'

Baccharus nodded slowly.

They were interrupted by a cry of alarm raised by one of the guards. There was activity at one of the large arched doorways that led to the inner chambers. The guards were backing away hastily, half-holding up their swords, yet somehow unsure. At first Church could pick out only a long shadow cast along the floor, moving in an odd manner. A few seconds later a figure appeared in the archway.

It was unmistakably one of the Tuatha Dé Danann; the male's skin had the familiar golden tinge and he was wearing what Church perceived to be a white toga held by a gold shoulder clasp. Yet he was lurching from side to side, his legs buckling every now and then, until he caught himself at the last. The smell reached them a moment later. As he closed in, Church could see the terrible ravages of whatever disease the Nuckelavee carried: part of his face had been eaten away, revealing what should have been a cheekbone and part of his jaw, but instead there was only a golden light. An unsightly black stain scarred the front of his pristine toga and left a trail as he passed. He had one arm outstretched, in greeting or pleading, Church couldn't tell, and although he opened his mouth to speak to them, the only thing that came out was a stream of shimmering moths, drifting up to the ceiling.

Niamh's jaw dropped in horror; the guards looked to her for direction. Baccharus stepped forward and said firmly, 'Do not let him near.'

'But he's still alive!' Church protested. 'Surely you can do something to help him.'

Baccharus turned and there was a shocking emotion alive in his face. 'There is nothing I would like to do more,' he said in a cracked voice. 'He is a kinsman; we are all brothers of the same village. But if he comes near he will infect us all, and what is the good in that?'

Church watched the pitiful figure advance slowly, with a very human air of desperation. 'Definitely not gods,' he whispered.

'Hold him back,' Baccharus ordered. 'He is not long for this existence.'

Ruth was about to protest that Baccharus was acting too harshly when his face grew suddenly sorrowful. He ran forward until he stood as close as he could to the diseased god. 'Know this, brother. We are all *people*, all joined. I am filled with the great sorrow of the Golden Ones for your plight. Not because it is a crime against existence, but because of you. My brother. But, know this and forgive: I cannot let you near. You will take us all with you.'

The diseased god appeared to hear this, for he paused in his relentless forward motion. The weight of the decision Baccharus had been forced to make was heavy on his face, but he could only hold out his arms impotently as the guards stepped forward to drive the ailing god back. They herded him through the archway and then Church heard the slam of a heavy door and the piling up of more furniture.

When Baccharus trailed back to them, his face a lie of composure, Church laid a friendly hand on his shoulder. 'I'm sorry you were forced to do that,' he said.

Baccharus looked honestly touched by this gesture, and a warm smile briefly overrode the air of sadness. It was just one of many little incidents he had witnessed in Baccharus over the previous few days: cracks in the arrogant composure of the Tuatha Dé Danann that suggested something approaching humanity within, if that was not a contradiction. Perhaps he had been wrong in judging all the gods so harshly.

His thoughts were driven away as the bile rose in his throat at another bout of wailing just beyond the blockade. This time the heap of furniture rattled and a heavy oak chair rolled off the top and splintered on the marble floor.

'Can it force its way through?' Ruth asked anxiously.

'Seems like it's got some muscle. I'm going to take a look at it.' Church ran forward and began to climb the unsteady mound, Ruth's shrill warnings echoing behind him. It probably would have been safer to have kept his distance from the barricade, but if he knew what it looked like he thought he would be more able to contain his fears, and maybe even find a way to strike back.

But the moment he crested the rocking pile of furniture and wriggled forward on his stomach to peer over the edge, he wished he hadn't. His gorge rose as he peered down at the Nuckelavee moving backwards and forwards at the base of the wall, not knowing if his disgust was at what he saw or what he felt coming off the beast. It was as big as three cars in a row, with a barrel-shaped body and a snake-like head that lolled sickeningly from side to side, as if its neck were broken. It had no legs, instead dragging its slug body along on stubby, multi-jointed arms that looked too thin to support its bulk. Most foul of all was that it had no skin; there was only a thin membrane covering its body so the blood could be seen pumping through the network of veins as its muscles slithered and stretched like an obscene anatomy textbook.

Church allowed himself only a few seconds to take it all in before he turned his eyes away in relief. He retreated cautiously down the blockade and returned to the others, his pale expression telling Ruth everything she wanted to know.

'Is there another way out of here?' Church asked. Niamh and Baccharus were almost paralysed by what they had found on the island.

'No.' In the white light that flooded the room, Niamh's face was uncommonly pale. 'Perhaps the Master will send others to fetch us back.'

Baccharus eyed her with a curious expression. 'Or perhaps he will listen to the whispered words and sail away at dawn.'

A table flipped off the top of the barricade, forcing them to move aside hastily as it crashed into the floor. 'I don't think we have the luxury of waiting,' Ruth noted.

'We cannot run,' Niamh said. 'Nor can we confront the Plague-Bringer, or we will all be destroyed. What do you suggest?'

There was a brief, hanging moment of confusion until a shiver ran through Church: the gods were looking to him and Ruth for a solution. How could they have faith in *Fragile Creatures*? He turned to face the rocking barricade, feeling the cold weight of responsibility. They were saying there was nothing they could do; they were elevating him to a height beyond his capabilities.

Beyond the barricade, the baby-cry began again, but this time it didn't sound like it was going to stop: it rose higher and higher until his ears rang and his teeth were set on edge; mingled in it somewhere he was sure he heard a note of triumph.

In T'ir n'a n'Og, time moved fast, or slow, or stood still with no rhyme or reason, but in the Fixed Lands life crept on at its solemn, relentless pace. Veitch and Tom could not be frozen between moments or see the days and weeks flash by like the view from a train, but they both felt it was moving quicker than they could handle.

They had spent twenty minutes with their own thoughts, preparing for the trial that lay ahead, watching the birds or the swaying branches of the trees, but never straying too far from the cairn at Corrimony. It felt like sanctuary: the Blue Fire that could be tapped so easily there was both protector and energiser, filling them up and giving them purpose.

Veitch was still enthused with all the energies his encounter with the archetype had instilled in him; to him, he *had* met Robin Hood, a hero of Britain whose good deeds transcended time. Veitch barely dared admit to himself how much that excited him; and how much he wanted something similar. He wouldn't even mind dying if he could become a hero people would remember, wiping out in an instant the petty, twisted parts of his nature, the waste he'd made of his life.

For the first time in many years, Tom was feeling bewildered, and it wasn't from the two joints he'd smoked in quick succession as he ambled around the cairn, fascinated by the shape of the stones, their colour in the sun. He'd lived for hundreds of years. His memory was a vast library stretching into deep, subterranean chambers, but his own character he knew with weary boredom. Or thought he did. But Veitch, rough, uneducated, shallow, had made several sharp comments during the course of the night that suggested he didn't know himself very well at all. In his own eyes, he was compromised by the complexity of an age when things could no longer be seen in black and white. To Veitch, he was a hero, a conclusion born from observation, for not so long ago the Londoner had railed against his *mythological* status. What had Veitch seen that he couldn't see himself? It troubled him, yet excited him a little too. But it was a *frisson* nonetheless, and for anything that stirred his blood after such a long life he was eternally grateful.

When he finished his last joint, he peered over the top of the cairn and shouted, 'It's time.'

'You know you're not supposed to drive on that stuff,' Veitch said as he wandered over. 'I'm not so sure I want you in charge when we're throwing ourselves into the Universal Transporter.'

'Oh, shut up. We had a name for you back in the sixties.'

'I have a name for you right now. Get on with it.'

They crawled on their bellies through the symbolic tunnel until they were sitting cross-legged inside the cairn. After the previous night, when the stones had been alive with the crackling blue energy, the place looked flat and dead, but they both could feel the vitality deep down in the earth, waiting to be brought out.

'You're sure you're ready for this?' Tom said.

Veitch peered up into the blue September sky. 'It's for a mate. I'm ready.'

'As long as you know what you're letting yourself in for. Don't forget – this isn't a test. No trial runs.'

'In life or anything else. Just get on with it.'

At first Tom was annoyed that Veitch hadn't grasped the true dangers of what they were attempting, but as he watched the Londoner's face he saw that wasn't right; Veitch simply didn't care. The dangers paled into insignificance compared to what they might achieve: bringing a trusted, much-loved friend back from the other side of death.

'So what do we have to do?' Veitch asked blithely.

'We rip out our souls and throw them to the four winds.'

Veitch shrugged.

Tom shook his head wearily before taking in a deep breath to clear his head. The drug lifted him one step beyond day-to-day existence. Closing his eyes, he said in a dreamy, hypnotic voice, 'Stone has strange properties. It vibrates, did you know that? It collects and responds to the energies at the heart of everything. That's why so many ghosts are seen in places made of stone – castles and old houses and monasteries. The power affects the brain, raises the consciousness. Lets you see the Invisible World.' He took another deep, calming breath. 'These old, sacred places, these circles and cairns, were constructed out of stone for that reason, not simply because that was the only material to hand. The peculiar qualities of stone made it easier to release the stored energy our ancestors needed to *transcend*. All they had to do was make the stones vibrate. Do you know how they did it?'

Veitch was gripped by Tom's mesmerising voice weaving a spell around him.

'Sound. All these places are designed for auditory effect. Consider the fougou in Cornwall. The great chambered cairns. They have the sonic qualities of the best musical halls. The perfect pitch, the exact timbre. All are achieved within their confines. Yet they look so rough, just thrown together.' To illustrate his point, he made one low note, which bounced around the walls without losing any of its sharpness. 'When this place was complete, with a roof of stone to contain the sound, it would have been even more effective. Primitive woodwind instruments, carved from bone or wood, rhythmic chanting, the tools of the shaman the world over. Sound has power. Music has power – even on a mundane level. Yes, sound releases the energy in the stone, but it shifts something in our brain too, making us more receptive to the tran-scendent experience. That's why hymns are sung in church. The music provides direct access to the god-centre, helping us to see the wonder that is around us all the time.'

He waited for Veitch to make some deflating comment, but his companion was rapt. Tom hadn't expected that. He was only really using the rhythm of his words, the rise and fall of the sound levels, to make Veitch more receptive to the kind of sonic manipulation he was describing. And there he was, actually *listening*.

'So, it's like pop songs . . .' Veitch winced. 'Tell me if I'm being stupid, all right? But it's like some crappy little pop record. You hear it on the radio or somethin', and suddenly that moment that you heard it is . . . locked in. It's, like, more real than all the moments around it. Brighter, you can remember what things smelled like and sounded like, all the detail, even years after, when you've forgotten every other moment that got you to that point.'

'You have it.' Tom restrained a smile of deep affection. 'Now, say no more. Prepare yourself. Don't see or smell or touch. Hear.'

Veitch closed his eyes, surprised at how centred he felt. Even the anger that in recent times had become a constant background buzz had faded away.

Tom took another deep breath and when he released it, he made a low, rumbling sound deep in his throat, sustaining it until every part of the breath had been expelled from his lungs. *Soooooooooooooooooo*. Another breath, and then he repeated the sound. This routine continued, building up a mantra that filled the whole of the cairn. After a while Veitch felt confident enough to introduce his own chant into the breaks when Tom gathered his breath. It created a constant wall of sound swirling around the walls in ripples and eddies.

The first thing Veitch noticed was a tingling in his fingertips. Gradually that sensitivity progressed along his arms, while a similar force rose up from his spine, like a snake sinuously progressing round the bony stem, a sensation he recognised from the time Ruth had practised her sex magic on him. Flares burst at different points as the snake passed on its journey towards the back of his brain.

All around, the sharp edges of the stones were limned with the now-familiar blue glow. And it wasn't just in the stones, but in the ground, and in Tom, and in him, everything linked.

The snake passed his shoulder blades, wriggled its way up to his neck, ready to make that final leap. Veitch prepared himself for the rocket ride he had experienced previously.

Only this time it was different. At the final moment, he heard, or thought he did, Tom utter a word, one that he couldn't remember a second later, but which was filled with a tremendous weight of power,

1026

and then he felt like he was slipping into a warm bath. The tension was stripped from him in an instant; the tingling transferred to his groin; he felt as light as a leaf caught in the wind.

A tremendous sense of wellbeing washed over him. No problem was important, no financial worries, no argument with his friends or his family, no doubts about his own abilities; not even death. He was consumed with *perspective*, of being part of something enormous, that crossed the boundaries of time and space, life and death. From that vista, everything dragging him down was meaningless. The true meaning was all around.

He wanted to communicate this enlightenment to Tom, but when he opened his eyes again all he saw was blue. It wasn't a flat colour, more like a diffuse light, a glow, a liquid, warm and enriching, but he wasn't drowning or choking. Out of curiosity he tried to call Tom's name, but either his vocal chords wouldn't respond or sound wouldn't travel in that medium.

Where was he? he thought without any panic. *Floating . . . drifting . . . happy . . . content . . .*

There wasn't any sense of real motion. It reminded him of lying in the sun in the back garden as a teenager, floating in a ring at the lido on a Saturday afternoon. Cocooning. No need to worry about anything at all, ever again. In fact, all negativity had been thoroughly expunged from his thoughts; he couldn't think of anything unpleasant even if he tried. He found himself dwelling on the truly good things in his life: the moment he first saw the mermaid swimming next to the boat on the way to Caldey Island, his friends, particularly Church, his role model whom he admired more than anything; and then Ruth, whom he loved in a way he had never thought possible, so acute it was almost physically painful not to be with her.

And that thought did trigger something unpleasant in his head, just the faint tremor in the deepest reaches, but it was there. What was it? Why wouldn't it go away and let him enjoy the experience of floating?

What was it?

Something . . . something about Tom. No, something Tom had said. His head was stuffed with candy-floss, in consistency and sweetness; dredging up any kind of rational thought progress was a struggle. Ruth. Tom. Ruth.

And then he had it. Tom had warned him of the dangers of getting lost in the blue fire, of its seductive qualities that would make him not want to return to the real world. It *was* seductive, but if he didn't go back he would never see Ruth again; all the joys of the Blue Fire paled next to that.

The thought that he might already be trapped brought a bubble of panic, but the moment it surfaced he was moving. The blue sheen in front of his eyes still looked the same, but he could feel motion; he was shifting, faster and faster, until he felt he was speeding at a hundred miles an hour.

Before he could consider any further action, he sensed a presence beside him, Tom, although he could see nothing but blue when he looked around. More, he could sense his companion's mind, and what he saw there left him with a potent, bittersweet sensation. Laid bare was Tom's affection for all the travelling companions, which was both a shock, and humbling. But lying behind it all was a powerful self-loathing triggered by Tom's fear of what the Tuatha Dé Danann had truly done to him. He felt like an outsider, filled with a loneliness Veitch could not even begin to imagine; the only thing that gave his life meaning was the Brothers and Sisters of Dragons and the success of their mission.

Then he was moving again, only this time Tom was directing him. Soon he was whizzing faster even than he had before. A burst like TV interference crackled across his mind; another; and another; and then he was overcome with a monumental anticipation.

Another burst of static, and images began to flash across his mind so fast he could barely keep track. Some, though, were important enough to stick: Ruth, standing on the deck of a storm-tossed ship as black tentacles lashed through the air; Church, standing at a pool as the grim spectre of a woman rose out of the waters; Church and Ruth, sitting close beside each other on a cabin bed; the vampiric Baobhan Sith, grey and merciless, rising from the dusty ground; Laura, sitting in a damp warehouse, her skin an odd tinge of green, and a figure with white, papery skin scarred with inky-black veins looming over Church.

The images and the pure blue of the energy vanished with the feeling of passing through a membranous wall. For a brief moment an unending whiteness filled both his vision and his thoughts, and then he was thrust roughly into sensation: the wind and sun on his skin, the sight of trees and sky, the smell of fresh vegetation, made all the more powerful by their brief absence. It was followed by the realisation that he was several feet above the ground. He had no chance to prepare himself – he hit hard, winding himself. There was a crunch a split-second later as Tom landed beside him.

'Can't you do anything about re-entry?' Veitch sat up, irritatedly rubbing his bruised ribs. His annoyance was less to do with the pain of the landing than the fading memories of his overwhelmingly joyous experience in the Blue Fire; it had left him hollow and dissolute. He controlled his rumbling temper when he saw Tom was undergoing the same separation pangs.

The Rhymer struggled to his feet, obviously in some discomfort, plucking his spectacles from a bush where they had landed in the fall. They were on a gently sloping hillside in the deep shadow cast by heavy tree cover, although the sun burned brightly on a grassy path cutting through the wood nearby. There, the last Brimstone butterflies of summer fluttered amongst the burdock flowers. Bees buzzed lazily round the boles while midges danced in a sunbeam. The chattering of birds was everywhere. The air smelled dank and peaty from the leaf mould that covered the wood-floor, obscured in areas by patches of bramble and nettles and the occasional pile of coppiced wood.

'I saw things. Just before we got here.' Some of the images lay heavily on Veitch's mind, pregnant with meaning he couldn't discern. 'Church. And Ruth . . .'

'I noticed that the last time.' Tom grumpily checked his faded haversack to ensure nothing had fallen out. 'When you are about to exit the energy stream you pass through an area where you can see through time and space. Neither of those things are fixed anyway, except in your limited perceptions.'

Veitch checked his watch. Barely a second had passed since they had been in the cairn at Corrimony.

'You were right.' He stood up to see if he could discern their next direction. 'That was some smart bleedin' place. It was—'

'Heavenly.'

'Right. I didn't want to leave. But you know what? It didn't feel like that before when we went from Cornwall to Glastonbury.'

'Then you were panicking in the sea, blacking out, trapped in the mundane so you couldn't perceive the ultimate.' Tom readjusted his ponytail, then strode up the slope.

'You know where we're going?'

'Yes, out of the trees so I can get my bearings.'

Tom had retreated into his usual state of ill-tempered reticence, but Veitch wanted to talk about the many confusing thoughts the experience had engendered. 'That was amazing,' he said quietly as they walked.

'And dangerous.'

'You know what? I don't think it is. I reckon I've got it figured out.'

'My. Aren't you the smart one?'

'It's only really dangerous if you've given up on living.'

This struck Tom sharply. 'What do you mean?'

'You're all right as long as you've got something to hold on to in the real world. If you haven't got anything here, you give up, float away. If you have unfinished business, something important, you drag yourself back. You don't really mind leaving 'cause you know that sooner or later you're going to end up back there. You can wait.'

Tom thought about this for a long moment. 'And you had something to bring you back?'

'That's right. I've got stuff still to do here. But when it's all over, you know, when my number's up, I wouldn't mind going back there. Just knowing it's there changes the way you look at life, y'know?'

'Yes. I know.'

They emerged on the sunlit path and followed it up to a tarmac-covered route where an information board showed a tourist map of Wandlebury Camp.

'We made it, then. We could have ended up anywhere in that stuff, but we came to exactly the right place. We *thought* ourselves here, didn't we?'

Tom read the sign's notes on the historical background to the camp, then estimated their position from the noon sun. He pointed back down the slope. 'That way, but later. First we need to see if Shavi's body is here.'

Veitch shifted uncomfortably. 'What if something's got at him? Some animal?'

'Do you really think Cernunnos would allow that to happen?'

He set out along the path that curled around the eastern side of the low hill. A thick bank of trees obscured the top. The path drew tightly past a small nature reserve settled on a pond that was thick with rushes where jewelled dragonflies dipped and dived. Beyond, it took a sudden turn, cresting a slight rise to present them with a view of a magnificent mansion house, its grand eighteenth-century architecture oddly out of place on the flat-topped summit. The house looked out on to gardens given up to lawns where a flock of sheep nibbled aimlessly. A large, old-brick wall marked the boundary, beyond which thick trees rose up imposingly. There was stillness to the place, odd, though not unpleasant.

Veitch sauntered over to another tourist sign. 'Gog Magog House. Used to be a big place for horse-racing, breeding and all that. Funny old spot to do horse-racing, on a bleedin' hill.'

'People are instinctively drawn to these places of power.' Tom cleaned his glasses to get a better look at the ornate clock on the cupola mounting the stable-block. A gold weathervane stirred slightly in the breeze.

From the corner of his eye, Veitch caught the faintest movement, but it was enough to lock his muscles and still the breath in his lungs. Tom continued ambling around, surveying the scenery. Just to be sure, Veitch waited and watched, and when he picked it up again, he launched into action. Tom whirled in shock, but Veitch had already hurdled a low fence and was sprinting towards the stable-block. A figure lurked at the base of the wall, too slow to take evasive action before Veitch was upon him.

It was a man, short and plump, with a ruddy, wind-blasted face. He wore a checked flat cap pulled low on his brow and a gaberdine mackintosh fastened tightly over his broad belly. 'Don't hit me! You can have everything!'

'Chill out, mate.' Taken aback by the response, Veitch adopted an easygoing posture. 'You can't be too careful these days.'

The man composed himself, but still looked wary. 'You're lucky you caught me without my shotgun.'

'You live here?' Veitch scanned the courtyard and windows for any other sign of life.

'What's it to you?' The man backed off a few paces as Tom wandered up. He appeared to be considering whether he could make a break for it.

'We're not looking for trouble.' The edge of Veitch's voice suggested that trouble could, however, be on hand if necessary. 'We've got some business in these parts. We're not going to rob you or nothin' like that.'

'We're here to collect the body of a friend.' Tom held out a hand as he introduced himself.

The man took it, intrigued; his name was Robertson. 'A body, you say.' His eyes flickered towards the lawned area.

'Is that where it is?' Tom followed his gaze, but could see nothing.

Robertson rubbed his chin thoughtfully, then beckoned for them to follow him. He crossed the courtyard and entered the mansion. From the lonely air of emptiness, it appeared Robertson was the sole occupant. The wind blew through a broken window that hadn't been fixed and there was tracked mud across the tiled floor. Despite the grandness of the building, Robertson only lived in a couple of adjoining rooms that had a makeshift appearance, with furniture obviously dragged from other parts of the house. The first thing that caught their eye as he led them into his quarters was the strange array of items hanging around the door. Over the top was a large, ornate cross. Beside it were horseshoes, another cross made out of twigs of rowan, the old symbol for protection from witchcraft and fairies, the withered remnants of a mistletoe sprig for protection from thunder, lightning and evil, a bunch of St John's wort to ward off spirits, a roughly carved wooden swallow for insurance against fire, and many more.

Robertson caught Tom's inspection. 'Like your friend said, you can't be too careful.'

Once safely inside his room, he crossed himself and touched wood before offering them chairs next to the unlit fire. 'I'd make you some tea, but with the way things are I've got to conserve. Even water,' Robertson said. 'I hope they get the bloody thing sorted out soon. We can't go on like this much longer. Bloody government.'

'Do you work here?' Veitch asked.

'Nobody works anywhere any more, do they? Not in the old sense,' Robertson replied. He settled into a comfortable armchair within easy reach of the shotgun resting against the wall. 'I used to have a business down in Cambridge. Got out of there when the riots started.'

'What riots?' Veitch looked puzzled.

'What riots?' Robertson replied incredulously. 'I don't know where you come from, but round these parts it seems that's all there's been. When they brought in the fuel rationing. When the supermarkets stopped filling their shelves. Then when everything stopped working . . .' Suppressed emotions briefly turned his face into that of a child and he covered it with his hand until he had composed himself. 'I left the city when my Susie died. She was a diabetic, couldn't get her insulin.'

'I'm sorry.' Tom was honestly sympathetic.

'This place was abandoned so I moved in,' Robertson continued. 'I soon found out why they'd left. Still, at least there's no riots, and it's not too bad as long as you don't go out at night.' His eyes narrowed suspiciously. 'Strange things happen round here,' he said, obviously not wanting to go into detail. 'Never used to believe in those things, but now . . .' He nodded to the charms on the door. 'I don't know what's happened to the world. Do you find it's like a dream, where none of the rules apply? Where you can run as fast as you can but never get anywhere, and rooms are bigger inside than out? Sometimes I wonder if it's ever going to be right again.'

He sounded on the edge of a breakdown. Stress had brought twitches to his hands and a tic to a muscle beneath his eye.

'The body?' Tom prompted.

He nodded a few times too often. 'In the lawns out there, there's a large hollow. You can see it easily if you stand by the stable block. It's a dew pond, manmade, dates back to the Stone Age or something, according to the signs. If you go down there at certain times – sunset, sunrise – you can see it. Only not, which sounds a queer way of putting it, but that's how it is. The first time I saw it, it scared the living daylights out of me, but when I realised it came back regular as clockwork, just lying there, there was no point getting worked up about it. There are worse things.' He looked down at his hands, which he quickly clasped together.

'What do you mean, there only not there?' Tom leaned forward so he could read Robertson's face.

'How can I describe it? It's like it's half there and half not. If you stand at the right point, so the light's coming in just so, it almost looks solid. Take one step to the left or right and it disappears.'

'Can you see who it is?' Veitch asked.

'Looks like some Indian or something. Hard to tell. He's lying on his back, hands across his chest.'

Veitch looked at Tom excitedly, but the Rhymer kept his face emotionless. 'Can you show us?' Tom said.

'I can. But you won't see anything at this time. Sunset's probably the best time, but you won't be getting me out there then.'

'So what *is* out there?' Veitch asked.

Robertson rose quickly, suddenly uncomfortable. 'Well, I don't rightly know. And even if I did, I wouldn't want to be talking about it. They can hear everything that's said, you know. Take their name in vain, they'll make you pay.' He crossed himself, then once more for luck. 'You want to be careful what you say.'

'We don't bow our heads to anything undeserving,' Tom said curtly.

Robertson looked on them pityingly before leading them out, stopping briefly to touch all the charms around the door.

The September sun was warm on the backs of their necks as they wandered across the lawns to the dew pond. Robertson was right; there was nothing to be seen. The ground was hard-baked from the summer sun, the grass clipped close by the sheep.

Robertson looked up cautiously to check the sky. 'Two days ago there was a rain of frogs. A carpet of them all around here, hopping like mad. Do you think it was a sign?'

'Yeah, it was a sign we're all going to croak.' Veitch knelt down, brushing his fingers across the grass as he surveyed the area; it was too open. If they returned at sunset they would be easy targets. 'So what do we do now?'

'Now,' Tom said, 'we go to talk to the giant.'

the Sickness at the heart

The night was hot and humid, filled with the distant cries of alien birds. Beyond the barricade, the Nuckelavee roamed relentlessly, testing its strength with repeated attacks that sent furniture rolling off the top. Time and again the Tuatha Dé Danann guards clambered up to replace them, but it was a futile act. Sooner or later the Plague-Bringer was going to break through.

Church had led Ruth and Baccharus on a tour of the building to try to find something they could use to escape, but had given up after an hour. The rooms went on forever, filled with insane bric-a-brac and useless objets d'art. When they tried to retrace their steps the layout of the house had changed, just like Wave Sweeper, but after a while they passed through the chamber where the dying god had been imprisoned. All it held now was a noxious black stain on the floor to mark his passing.

When they finally made it back to the main area, the baby-cry was rising and falling until Ruth wanted to tear at her ears. She dragged Church to one side. 'What are we going to do?' Before he could protest, she added, 'You're the leader.'

'Don't worry, I know my responsibility.' He scrubbed his hand roughly through his long hair; he had only one option. 'We need a diversion. Someone to pull that thing over to one side so the rest of us can get out, get back, or—'

'Attack it.'

'You've got an idea?'

'I can do some stuff.' She tapped her head. 'It's all locked up here.'

'You've been trying it out?'

'Little things. Here and there. Just to get a feel for it.' For some reason she looked guilty, wouldn't meet his eyes.

'How much can you do?'

There was a long pause before she said, 'I honestly don't know. But it's like I've been made the receptacle for all the knowledge that exists about the Craft. It's like being super-charged.' Still not meeting his eyes, she added, 'Sometimes I feel like I can do anything.'

Church rested a hand on her shoulder, played with her hair. He was worried about how distant and troubled she appeared. Most of the time she had a blasé attitude to her new-found abilities, but it was obvious that behind it lay a deep-seated concern. 'What are you planning on pulling out of the bag this time?'

She peered at the thin gap of dark sky above the blockade. 'I have a couple of ideas.'

Church gave the back of her neck a squeeze before heading over to Niamh and Baccharus, who had been waiting patiently. 'I hate to ask this,' he said, 'but I need a volunteer to draw that thing's attention. There's not much chance of getting off alive. One of the guards—'

'I shall do it,' Baccharus said confidently.

'No!' Niamh's face crumpled with worry. 'There is no need—'

'There is every need. How could I ask another being to take such a risk if I would not do it myself?'

'Your abilities are needed. You have responsibilities.' Niamh's voice rose a notch.

Baccharus took her hand with surprising tenderness, the mark of deep friends. 'I have to shed my burden.'

Niamh nodded reluctantly. Baccharus turned back to Church. 'What do you request?'

'We need to move most of the blockade from the far end. When the Plague-Bringer moves up the other end, we kick over the last of it, and you make a break for the tree-line.' He paused. 'How close does it have to be to infect you?'

Baccharus gave a faint smile, said nothing.

Church spent the next half-hour fashioning a spear with a length of wood and one of the guards' swords. It was a paltry weapon compared to what roamed beyond the walls, but there was nothing else to hand that he could use. He longed for the mystical sword he had rescued from its hiding place underneath Tintagel; he had responded to whatever power it held, understood how it had been responsible for the coded legends of Excalibur. He had never seen himself as much of a fighter, but with that sword he had felt capable of anything.

Ruth spent the time meditating quietly in one corner. Church watched her serious face as the arcane knowledge gradually emerged from its secret chambers. Some of it brought a smile of surprise to her lips, others left her brow furrowed in concern.

When they were nearly ready, he knelt next to her, caressing the back of her neck. 'Are you fit?' he asked softly.

She flashed him an unsure smile. 'As fit as I ever will be. The way this thing seems to work is that I have to act on instinct as much as possible.

That means I can't plan. And if the instinct fails, I have no idea what I'm going to do.'

'You could always run.'

'That doesn't help Baccharus. Or you.' Her smiled faded. 'I'm not going to let you down.'

'I never for a minute thought you would.' He leaned over and gave her a gentle kiss.

'We can't afford to lose this, you know,' she whispered.

There was nothing he could say to that.

As he stood up, he realised Niamh was watching them from the other side of the room, her face impossible to read. She turned away when she saw him looking at her.

By the time they were ready, the Nuckelavee was rattling the blockade so hard it was rocking wildly, nearly toppling over. Church marshalled the guards, who obeyed him reluctantly, their eyes flickering in the direction of Niamh and Baccharus. When the beast reached one end of the row, Church dropped his hand and the guards hastily dismantled the barricade at the other end where Baccharus waited.

There was a moment of intense tension and then Church gave the nod; Baccharus silently slipped out into the hot night. The response was instantaneous. The cry rose up several notches, followed by the thunder of sturdy arms hitting the ground and the obscene slithering as it dragged its body behind it. The speed of the movement shocked them all. Church wondered briefly if his plan was already doomed; at the rate it was moving, it would reach Baccharus and be back on them before anyone reached the tree-line.

Once the Nuckelavee was far enough away, Church gave the signal and the guards demolished the barricade at the other end of the room. They were hurrying out into the moist dark before the last item of furniture was rolling away. Ruth blanched when she laid eyes on the Nuckelavee for the first time – there was something sickening about it beyond mere appearance – but then she caught herself and set off in pursuit with Church beside her while the guards hurried Niamh towards the trees.

'Why us, eh?' Ruth said with a tight smile.

'Cannon fodder. We know our place in life.' Church shouldered the spear, ready to throw.

Baccharus moved across the lawns like a shimmer of light cast by numerous mirrors, his form growing hard to perceive, but he was not fast enough for the Nuckelavee, which had surprising speed for its bulk and awkwardness. Church could see every bunch of its muscles, every pulse of its blood with each minor exertion.

At the tree-line, Baccharus came to a halt. Church had given him strict instructions not to take the creature into the jungle, where it would be hard for them to attack it in the dense undergrowth, but it was bearing down on him so quickly it was impossible for him to run in any other direction. He sensed this, for he brought himself round to face the Nuckelavee and drew himself up ready to meet his fate. There was something so noble about the way he stood – head slightly bowed, accepting the worst kind of death; even worse for the Tuatha Dé Danann, who thought they would never die – Church felt compelled to succeed. He hurled the makeshift spear as hard as he could, even though his plan had optimistically called for it to be used for the death-blow once Ruth had made her attack.

In the split-second before Church launched the spear, the Nuckelavee drew itself up and threw its grotesque head back, before making a silent belching motion. A barely visible exhalation rushed from the creature's mouth. It had little substance – Church could see the jungle and dappling stars through it – but Baccharus's face darkened as it raced towards him, and at the last moment he threw himself to one side. The cloud continued into the trees, where there was a sudden crash as an ape-like beast fell from the branches in violent death throes.

The sword-spear embedded in the Nuckelavee at the base of its skull; a fountain of dark-red blood gushed out. The creature went into paroxysms, the baby-cry turning into a shriek of agony. Near to it, it smelled like an old rubber boot that had been left in the rain.

The size, speed and hideous appearance of the beast were hypnotic. Church found himself rooted as it curled around on its slug-like body to examine him, the spear waving on its back with every violent tremor that ran through the torso. He took a step back and then became rooted once more when he looked into the Nuckelavee's pink-rimmed black eyes; what he saw there was cruel and alien, but undoubtedly intelligent.

'Church! Back off!' Ruth yelled.

He heard her words, but all he could do was consider the Nuckelavee's swirling gaze; it drowned out all his senses until the only thing in his world was the creature. Deep in his head came a skittering, like cockroach feet on the surface of his brain: the Nuckelavee's thoughts, reaching out to his own. The part of him that held the Fomorii taint *understood*, and somehow that was worse than anything.

Ruth saw Church freeze in the grip of the Nuckelavee's mesmerising eyes. It brought itself round, its mouth thrown wide to emit those stomach-churning cries, the disproportionately powerful arms dragging the body in lumbering jerks. It gave the illusion of slow, methodical progress, but Ruth had seen how quickly it had pursued the now-forgotten Baccharus, and the lightning-fast reactions when the spear had struck.

His life lay in her hands, and that was the fear that had gripped her from the moment he outlined his plan. She would never reach him in time. Even if she could knock him out of the way, they would be too close to the Nuckelavee to evade it. She wouldn't be able to utilise her Craft quickly enough.

But she *had* to do it or she would never be able to live with herself. She had to do it or nothing else would matter in her life ever again.

Seconds, that was all. Seconds.

She closed her eyes in an attempt to shut out all extraneous sensation: the cries that sounded like a war zone orphanage, the stink that made her nostrils flare and her throat close up, the wind in her hair, the sweat on her back, the nausea in her gut, the thunder of her heart. She closed it down like she was pulling shutters in her head. She was surprised how quickly it worked; accessing the Craft was predicated on *need* and at that point she needed it more than ever before. It came up like whispers from a deep, dark well. And as the images and sounds that shaped reality began to coalesce in her mind, she felt the power ignite.

And then she opened her eyes. Church was still rooted, the Nuckelavee rising above him, opening its mouth, ready to release the infection. Her concentration fragmented as desperation intruded.

She fought to get her focus back, her eyes fixed on Church, knowing he was about to die, knowing it was her fault, her stupid weakness, the shame and the guilt making it even harder to reach that quiet part of her.

Just as the knowledge began to rise again, there was movement like a flash of light on the periphery of her vision. It hit Church in a shimmer of gold and an instant later he was gone, just as the Nuckelavee's corrupting breath washed through the spot where he had been.

He reappeared several yards away, dragged by Niamh; and then was gone again. It wasn't as if the goddess was running, more that she was dropping in and out of reality, becoming, in the process, not human, something that was almost composed of light. They finally settled into her perception across the other side of the lawns, in safety. And then her shame was coloured by other, darker feelings: self-loathing, jealousy, irritation, then anger.

The rush inside took her by surprise, petrol on the bonfire of her emotions, more potent even than the exhilarating explosion of her abilities at the end of her tantric bout with Veitch. Fire filled her belly, her limbs, her head, until the world without didn't exist at all, only flame, blue, blue flame, and the feeling that she wanted to jump out of her skin and explode.

Shining across her mind with a blinding light were words her rational mind found incomprehensible, but which she instinctively understood. They leapt to her lips unbidden; she felt her mouth forming them as if it were someone else's. Her will became a spear, plucking the words and launching them into the night sky.

And then, spent, the fire cleared and she was overcome with a calmness that kept all sound from her ears. In the eerily silent scene, the Nuckelavee was rising up over her, veins throbbing, muscles glistening, eyes glowing. And beyond it, the stars were being eaten. Thick, black clouds rushed in from the north. Unnatural winds alive with rage tore through the trees. The Nuckelavee was buffeted back and forth, but Ruth stood calm in the eye; untouched.

The gale drew strength, flexed. Baccharus had lashed himself around a tree, the others were unseen. The Nuckelavee slid forwards against its volition, was driven down on to its bony elbows. The mouth still opened and closed, emitting the baby-cry that Ruth could no longer hear, too distracted to unleash its infection. Now bowed before her, Ruth thought she glimpsed a cast to its eyes, not of fear but of incomprehension. It was time.

More words in her mind, but this time they were surrounded by the coldness of deep space. She spoke, and whatever sound she made cut through the heart of the gale, reached up directly to the clouds that swirled overhead. Briefly they appeared to spin faster, a whirlpool of grey, until at the heart of them a hole formed through which she could not see the night sky, could see nothing at all. Lightning erupted from it, filled with a force beyond the control of nature. In the time between seconds it scorched through the air to strike the Nuckelavee squarely. There was a burst of brilliant light, a shockwave that split and folded around Ruth before moving on to blast the nearest trees, a smell of charged air that became the sickening stench of a butcher's shop on fire.

And when it cleared a moment later, there was only a circle of blackened grass where chunks of flash-fried flesh smoked or were limned with dancing, blue will o' the wisps.

Ruth was filled with an emptiness that made her feel weepy for something vital that had been lost. But when that faded, there was at first regret, then fear, and then horror at what she had done without even realising. For the first time she had a glimmer of what she was capable, of dark paths that lay ahead if she so chose, and she knew she must never let her anger get the better of her again.

Weakly, she staggered around, almost blank to her surroundings until she felt strong hands on her shoulders. Church pulled her close and kissed her. 'I knew you could do it,' he said in a whisper, tinged with relief, but also coloured by something that sounded like dismay. She saw Niamh sitting alone on the lawns, the guards gathered in a huddle far away, not wishing to approach her.

'The thing caught her,' Church said. 'She's been infected.'

Ruth couldn't begin to describe her emotions, although she knew she wouldn't be proud of them. Already aware of the situation, Baccharus rushed over. 'We are all in danger. We may already have been infected.' He looked coldly at the sullen guards and then, without a moment's thought, walked over to Niamh. She tried to wave him away, then fend him off as he dropped down next to her, eventually giving in and allowing her head to drop dismally on to his shoulder. Ruth was suddenly consumed with guilt.

'You must not come near me,' Niamh said directly to Church and Ruth. 'The Fixed Lands need you. All of existence needs you. You must leave me here.'

Church turned to Ruth and asked in an anxious, low voice, 'Can you help her?'

Ruth tried to read his face, wondering if she could be so evil that her choices would actually be decided by what she saw there, then feeling disconcerted by what she did see.

'Perhaps,' she replied, trying not to give her thoughts away. She knelt down next to Niamh, who looked up at her with an honest, open face that made her feel even worse. She wished she had seen bitterness there, or jealousy, or incipient rage, something that would blight the goddess's inherent goodness, or make her as distant and contemptuous as most of the other Tuatha Dé Danann. 'Lie down,' Ruth said a little too sharply; 'let me examine you.'

Niamh had obviously not caught the full force of the Nuckelavee's infection, but it was certainly there in nascent form; the golden skin of her forearm was mottled with faint blue rings that were spreading up to her armpit. Her body hadn't yet started breaking up, but Ruth knew it was only a matter of time. 'Alien viruses,' she muttered wearily. 'As above, so below. This whole place is a nightmare.'

She turned to Baccharus. 'I need you to send one of the guards back to the ship for supplies. You seem to stock everything there. I need some dainty weed ground ivy and wild celery to help with muscle cramps and vervain for an analgesic. That should help combat the side-effects of the virus. Then I'll need some rowan berries, mugwort and mallow to fight off any enchantment, as I suppose this thing doesn't act like any ailment we've come across on earth.'

'Will that do it?' Church asked hopefully.

Ruth looked up at him wilfully. 'No,' she said. 'Then it's down to me.'

Baccharus and Church carried Niamh back to the house, where they made her comfortable on a large divan piled high with sumptuous cushions. She was already growing weak. Once she was settled, Church brushed the hair from her pale face. 'Thanks for saving my life,' he said gently.

She smiled faintly.

'Why did you put yourself at risk for a *Fragile Creature*?'

'You know why, Jack.'

'You're not like others of your kind.'

'We are not all alike.' She paused. 'My kind have more differences than you could know.'

'But you gods see yourself as infinite, as much a part of existence as the stars in the sky.'

'More so.'

Church's expression grew more puzzled. 'You believe your continued survival is paramount in the rules of nature. I know what the concept of death means to you – a hundred times worse than it even means to us. I don't—'

She shushed him with a wave of her hand.

'But—'

'A small sacrifice.'

He smiled again, though it was a troubled one, and withdrew slowly until Ruth caught his arm on the other side of the room. 'Why don't you give her a big kiss?' she said and regretted it instantly. She'd always prided herself on her maturity and here she was acting like a stupid, jealous teenager.

The puzzlement on Church's face became comical until his expression darkened. 'Don't be an idiot.'

'Don't call me an idiot.'

'Well, stop acting like one. I'm not going to start mooning for her like some stupid kid just because she saved my life.'

'It looked like mooning to me.' She tried to bite her tongue; why couldn't she help herself?

'Look, she showed some nobility there.' His voice was low, filled with both hurt and annoyance. 'She was ready to sacrifice her life for another being, whatever her motivations. It's not about stupid relationship issues—'

'Relationships are stupid, are they?'

'I didn't say that.'

She marched away, regretting that Church would see it as some argumentative point-scoring ploy, but she only did it to save herself from saying anything further that would damn her. She was supposed to be smart, educated, and emotions had made her a moron in seconds.

She had planned to walk out of the room to get some calming night air, but to do that she had to go past Niamh's divan; the goddess motioned to her to come over. Reluctantly she perched on the end.

'I want to thank you for trying to help me, Ruth. I know my kind appear aloof to Fragile Creatures. But I hope you will accept I am very grateful.'

'Don't worry. I would have done it for anyone.'

'And that is why you are honourable and good. One of the best of your race.'

'No, I'm not. I'm typical, not good or bad, not stupid or smart. Just . . . just human.'

'You do yourself a disservice.' Niamh waved this part of the conversation away with a gesture and began, 'I know you are concerned about Church and me—'

Ruth stood up sharply and made to go.

'Please hear me out.'

'I don't want to talk about that.'

'Please—'

'I'm not used to having my emotions in this much upheaval.' *I've never been in love before*, she could have said. 'I don't want to say anything I might regret.'

Niamh continued to plead silently until Ruth felt she couldn't walk away. She sat down heavily and stared into the middle distance. 'I hold nothing against you, Ruth, for your feelings for Jack. I can understand them completely. He has a good, good heart.'

Ruth listened, but didn't respond.

'We are not rivals, Ruth. We are not fighting. There is nothing *we* can do. Jack will decide the direction of his own heart. The tragedy is that only one of us can benefit. That should cause sadness for both of us, not anger or jealousy.'

'When someone has a relationship, however new,' Ruth began, 'it's not considered very decent to try to break it up.'

'You do not know the whole story, Ruth.'

'Then tell me.' Ruth's eyes flashed; she was sick of being patronised by the gods.

Niamh chose her words carefully, which made Ruth instantly suspicious; there was something the goddess was trying to hide. 'You think my emotional response to Jack is some fleeting thing. After all, we have seen each other little, spoken to each other less. But that is simply your perception.' Ruth flinched visibly; Niamh noticed and caught herself. 'You should know by now, Ruth, that there is more than one way of seeing existence, and the way of the Fragile Creatures is the least apt. My love for Jack is not new and ill-formed.'

'I know you watched his development from when he was a child without interacting with him, but if you'll forgive me for being so forward,' she said tartly, 'that's both a little sick and a little pathetic. Love from afar, without any interaction, is worthless.'

Niamh's face remained calm, despite the sharpness of Ruth's words. 'I have loved Jack for longer than that, Ruth.'

Ruth snorted derisively. 'How can that be?'

Niamh ignored her. 'My feelings grew stronger as I understood his true nobility. He has a good heart. He is confused, directionless, has little confidence in his own abilities, but at his core he is good.'

Listening to Niamh, something struck Ruth sharply. 'Sometimes you don't even sound like your own kind. You sound like one of us.'

Niamh smiled, a little sadly. 'I have had a good tutor.'

Ruth watched her carefully, but Niamh wasn't giving anything away.

'Ruth, I will speak honestly to you. This is a vital time for my relationship with Jack.' Ruth wanted to yell: *You have no relationship!* 'If I cannot convince Jack to love me before the festival you know as Samhain then my love will never be returned. Therein lies my desperation, and my tragedy. Such a small window to convince a Fragile Creature to match the feelings of a god. If I lost Jack now it would be forever.'

Niamh had grown oddly introspective; the gods never usually appeared to have any real inner life. 'There will be no peace for him, Ruth,' she said quietly. 'That is not the path that existence has mapped out for him. Jack will have a life of struggle and strife, but that only makes love and comfort so much more valuable to him. He will have to seize it where he can, and cherish it, for it will be transitory.'

'What path *is* mapped out for him?'

'The same path all you Brothers and Sisters of Dragons must walk. You have been chosen to be champions of the vitality that runs through everything. That is a responsibility that dwarfs all. You must suffer for the sake of everyone else, everything else.'

'Well, isn't that wonderful,' Ruth said sourly, trying to ignore the panic flaring inside her.

'But is that not always the way? A few must redeem the many. If those with ability do not act, the darkness will win. There are few rules of existence open even to we Golden Ones, but that is one of them.'

'Yes, but why *me*? Why *us*?'

'Simply? Because you have what it takes.' A wave of exhaustion crossed Niamh's face; the disease was starting to bite.

'Take it easy,' Ruth said. 'The guard will be back with the supplies any minute and then we can get to work.'

Niamh smiled and took Ruth's wrist with her long, cool fingers. 'You have a good heart too.'

Once Ruth had the flowers and herbs she administered them to Niamh, although she had no idea how they would work on her constitution. The ones that worked magically appeared more effective than the simple medicinal ones, but it was still only a stop-gap measure. She had Niamh moved into a chamber where the lights could be darkened until only one candle-flame cast a dim light across the proceedings. The others were driven from the room so the atmosphere was calm and reflective.

The mottled blue rings had spread across the right side of Niamh's body and in places had grown black. In some areas the skin was fracturing.

'What are you planning to do?' Niamh asked weakly.

Ruth raised a chalice of water and kissed it gently. 'I'm planning on approaching a higher authority.'

'Higher?'

'When I met Ogma in his library, or court, or whatever you want to call it, I asked him if you really were gods. He said, there is always something higher. And now I have the knowledge gifted to me by my owl-friend I can see that's true. I have no idea what it really is, but I like to think it has a feminine aspect, like the triple-goddess that first led me down this path. Whatever it is, I feel close to it, because it's the source of the Blue Fire. And I, as you pointed out, am the champion of the Blue Fire.'

Niamh nodded thoughtfully. 'It is as I thought. Can you reach that power?'

Ruth's laugh came across as faintly bitter, to mask her inability to answer that question. 'Keep your fingers crossed.'

If she were honest with herself, she would really have preferred leaving the ritual to another day. Every time she utilised the knowledge of the Craft it took a great deal out of her, as if she was pushing herself beyond the limits of endurance, or psychologically beyond what her body had been created to do. But with Niamh's deterioration, there was no chance of delay. She would have to press on and deal with the repercussions later.

Baccharus had found some incense in another part of the house; Ruth burned it in a small brazier next to the divan on which Niamh was lying. Like everything in Otherworld, it had an unexpected potency, filling the room with heady aromas. But it was soothing and aided the concentration that her growing exhaustion made increasingly difficult. She closed her eyes and took a deep breath as the fragrant, sweet fumes enveloped her.

She began slow, rhythmic breathing, giving herself up to the shussh-boom of air, matching it with her heartbeat until it filled her consciousness, until she began to drift . . .

In T'ir n'a n'Og, Ruth could achieve things that would have been impossible at home, but it was still a struggle for her to break through the barrier. After a while, she moved outside time, so that her whole world was only the beat of her heart and the rhythm of her breath and the smell of the incense. Eventually, though, something appeared to crack in her mind, a hairline fracture running through a rock. She exerted pressure and the rift grew wider, and suddenly she was inside the protected area, and just as quickly rushing out, through her head, passing through the chamber where she could see Niamh lying sickly, through the ceiling and the upper rooms of the house and out into the night sky. And still upwards, until the green island lay like an emerald in a sea of ink, and up. And then through the sky itself . . .

What happened next came back to Ruth only in vague, fleeting impressions later. She knew she had entered some kind of blue, blue world, for the colour haunted her for days after, but of any other detail of the place – if it were a place – there was nothing. She sensed a tremendous presence, a sentience, so big it dwarfed the entire universe; even so, it appeared to recognise her. But the most striking impressions were abstracts: contentment so powerful everything else disappeared; connection; losing all her fears and worries in an instant. She didn't recall uttering a sound, never mind begging for what she required, knew instinctively she didn't have to.

And one other thing: an odd, fractured remembrance of Veitch and

Tom, so quick it could easily have been a memory leaking through from another time.

She came out of what felt like a deep slumber with Church's hands on her shoulders, feeling more refreshed than she had done in months. She took his hand and smiled beatifically; whatever he saw in her face appeared to shock him briefly. Then he said, 'I was worried when there was no sound so I took a peek in. I saw you slumped on the floor here, thought something bad had happened. Did I screw up?'

She turned to Niamh who was sitting up, rubbing her arms, looking faintly dazed, yet also slightly transcendent. The blue-black mottling on her arms was fading before their eyes, the strength returning to her limbs with amazing speed.

'You have changed the course of existence, Ruth,' Niamh said with deference. 'The alterations to the fabric spinning off from this point will be startling.'

Through her bliss, Ruth wasn't wholly sure she liked the sound of that.

Back on Wave Sweeper, an account of what Ruth had achieved passed swiftly through the crew and passengers. Ruth and Church barely had time to put their feet on the deck before they were ushered into Manannan's cabin. He stood next to his table, hands clasped behind his back.

'You have achieved a great thing, Brother and Sister of Dragons.' His voice appeared to come from all parts of the room at once. 'The gratitude of the Golden Ones is with you.' He moved around the table, still aloof, barely looking at them, but Church thought there was a surprising warmth somewhere far beneath it all. 'More than gratitude. You prevented another of our kind being stripped from existence. You have helped maintain one of the vital props of the way things are.'

'We see all life as equal,' Ruth said pointedly. 'That's why we helped.'

He nodded thoughtfully, as if, for once, he was actually listening, then fixed a curious gaze on them. 'This is indeed an argument that has raged amongst my own kind. I have never held strong views, allowing my opinions to be swayed by the voices of one side or the other, dependent on who was speaking. Now, I feel, I have made my choice.' He went to a crystal decanter filled with an unusual golden liquid. He poured three glasses and brought one each for Church and Ruth.

'Is it given freely and without obligation?' Church asked.

'Of course. Everything on my ship is given freely and without obligation. That is my way. And it is especially true for Brothers and Sisters of Dragons.'

He raised his glass and drained it in one draught. Church and Ruth followed suit, and were stunned by the immediate effect of whatever the drink was. The aroma was flowers and spices. The instant the drink touched their tastebuds, it created an explosion across all five of their senses, a bizarre synesthaesia, and as it passed down their throat it filled them with a warmth and light as golden as the liquid itself, infusing them with a transcendent feeling of wonder and excitement. Once it settled into their system their vision sparkled around the edges. Objects in the room took on a strange cast, as if the very essence of them was visible. Manannan appeared to be made of light, and when Church and Ruth looked at each other they saw the same illusion – if that was what it was – although the light was of a slightly different shade.

'What is this?' Church asked in awe.

'The drink of gods. The distillation of all there is.'

Church looked at Ruth again; they felt like they could read each other's thoughts; in one moment they could see the connections that bound them, something it often took couples a lifetime to discover. They would have embraced there and then, committed themselves to each other for all time, if Manannan's foreboding presence had not stopped them.

'Fragile Creatures have rarely tasted this liquid,' Manannan continued. 'Some of my kind consider it too rarefied for your tastes, that you are too rough to appreciate it and so should be denied it.' He took the glasses from them and returned them to the table. 'It can make you see like gods.' His voice drifted back to them, disembodied, yet filled with meaning they couldn't discern.

When he came back he took Ruth's hand and pointed to the mark left by Cernunnos. 'My brother, I see, has already come to his decision. Know this, then: you have an ally here too. I will take my stand with the Fragile Creatures.'

'Thank you.' Church made a slight bow. 'And can we count on your arguments to influence the minds of your brothers when we reach our destination?'

'I will do what I can.'

His mood changed abruptly as his attention focused on a number of charts unfurled on his desk, and it was obvious the audience was over. They thanked him, but he was already engrossed in new business.

Outside, they rested against the rail, pleased that the hot, humid microclimate of the island was no longer with them. The anchor had been raised while they were in Manannan's room and they were already speeding out into open water.

'You know what?' Church said curiously. 'I had a feeling there was a lot going on behind that conversation, stuff that wasn't said.'

'It's like he was talking about something important without telling us exactly what it was.'

'Maybe he thought we already knew.'

'These gods don't give anything away unless they have to, even when they're supposedly being friendly.'

Church pulled Ruth close, draping an arm across her shoulders; he still felt warm and fuzzy from Manannan's drink. 'I think it's time we stepped up our investigations.' She rested her head on his shoulder, enjoying the comfort of contact after the stress of the day. 'There's something very strange and disturbing going on here. We've been moving through it, seeing and hearing little parts of it. I think it takes in Cormorel's murder, and . . . lots of things.'

'Would you like to elaborate, or are you going to keep talking vaguely just for the hell of it?'

'I don't know what else to say. It's a gut instinct.' In his arms, she felt soft and hard and warm and cold all at the same time. 'I think if we don't find out what's going on, we're going to lose everything.'

'What do you suggest? An inquisition? You know they won't tell us anything.'

'I suggest it's time to go searching for the Walpurgis. Tomorrow. Just after dawn.'

An hour before first light they came upon the third of the Western Isles. Taranis summoned Manannan from his cabin and together they surveyed the rocky outcropping. A thick column of smoke rose from the island and settled in a pall across the area, the underside of it a dull ruddy-brown from the fires that raged there.

Manannan did not even bother dropping anchor. Taranis moved to mobilise the crew. The itinerary was dropped instantly and they set a course for the island they called the Green Meadows of Enchantment, with the certain knowledge that the vile corruption of the Heart of Shadows had extended to the very walls of their home.

'There weren't really giants,' Veitch said as they wandered down the hill from Gog Magog House.

'There were so.' Tom's face had grown sterner as the day passed. He had been quite rude to Robertson, who had refused to come with them to an area he claimed was cursed. 'Even in my time, before the Queen got her hands on me, there were still a handful of giants scattered around the island. Some died off, some wandered through to T'ir n'a n'Og. But they're not the kind of giants we're interested in right now.'

'So . . . what? These are short giants?'

Tom snorted with irritation, even though he knew Veitch was only trying to provoke him. '*There are giants in the earth,*' he muttered to himself. 'How little they knew.'

They crossed the path and made their way alongside a defunct electric fence that once kept sheep from the nature preservation area. The early afternoon sun was hot. Flies and wasps buzzed along the tree-line, while darting mosquitoes made brief forays from the pond. Under the trees the atmosphere had grown sweaty and oppressive. Tom picked his way amongst the brambles, scrambling over fallen trees and amongst the thorny bushes, with Veitch following easily behind.

'So, is it going to be a surprise, then?' Veitch continued to gibe. 'Like always. Blowing up in my face at the last minute. Like in the Queen's court?'

'You were warned about that.'

'Well, you didn't do a very good job of it, did you?'

'Sorry. I underestimated your stupidity.'

Veitch said something obscene, but Tom had already picked up his step until he arrived at an area where the topsoil had been cleared to reveal mysterious patterns on the ground.

With a puzzled face, Veitch attempted to make head and tail of them. 'Looks like one of those ink blots they show you when they think you're crazy.'

'The Rorschach Test,' Tom noted. 'That's quite fitting. Everyone who comes here sees in these patterns what they want to believe.'

'Not what's actually there?'

'Nothing is *actually* there, anywhere. You've not learned anything in all this, have you?'

Veitch stared at him for a long moment, then said, 'I've learned you're a—'

'Archaeologists have been digging around here for decades, ever since the famous antiquarian T. C. Lethbridge excavated this site on the south side of the ring in late 1955 and 1956.' Tom rested his hands on his knees so he could lean forward to get a better look. 'He pumped metal rods in the ground, claiming he found different depths, bumps, shapes underneath the surface which marked out this. He christened this the Gog Magog figure. All told, he claimed he'd discovered a sun goddess, two other male figures and a chariot.'

'You're talking like it isn't true.'

'Not in the eyes of archaeologists who came after him. All of Lethbridge's work here is steeped in controversy. Academics and the usual amateur historical sleuths who want to be seen as professional claim there is absolutely no evidence for Lethbridge's claim. All this is a figment of his fevered imagination. But if there's one thing we've learned, it's not to trust the establishment. Is that not so?'

'Too bleedin' right.'

'The occult groups always backed Lethbridge because they knew truth does not always come in facts and figures, quantifiable evidence.'

'You've lost me again.' Veitch's attention was drifting amongst the trees, searching for any signs of threat. For a while he had been aware of a deep level of unease that he couldn't quite understand. He was good at sensing obvious danger near at hand, or even more subtle signs of peril, but this was different; it was almost like the threat was there but not there, buried very deeply or watching from such a distant place it could barely be called a threat. But he felt it nonetheless.

'Whatever they say, there were certainly some hill figures carved on this site,' Tom continued. 'There are many antiquarian sources which confirm that. And with these hills bearing the name Gog Magog, and the house on the summit, it doesn't take a great detective to know who this sacred site was dedicated to.'

'Giants?'

Tom sighed, clambering on to the rough pattern and kneeling down so he could sweep it with his fingers. 'You should know by now, no one knows anything about the past. Every historian and archaeologist has *theories*, and yes, they can make convincing arguments. The ones who shout loudest set the agenda. But the clever man ignores their voices and looks closely at the evidence. And once he realises all of it is conflicting, he understands: Nobody. Knows. Anything.'

'But you know it all, right?' Veitch took the opportunity to check his weapons: the crossbow slung across his back, the sword secreted in his jacket, the dagger strapped to his leg. All in place, all ready for action.

'Who is Gog Magog? Who are *they*? They are there in the Bible, in Jewish and Christian apocalyptic literature. In one account, Gog and Magog are two hostile forces, in another Gog comes from the country of Magog. But the Bible is adamant they or he is a force for evil in the final battle between God and Satan. The Battle of Armageddon.'

'So they're evil?' Veitch had the blank expression that always irritated Tom.

'The Bible is a *book*, Ryan. The Church likes to pretend it's the word of God, but as we *all* know, it's the word of God as edited by men, by councils of the religion's great and the good for hundreds of years after

Jesus lived. Many of *God's words* were thrown out to present a more cohesive *story*. And man is flawed, so the Bible tells us. Ergo, the Bible is flawed and cannot be wholly trusted.'

Veitch chuckled. 'They'd have you dragged out and stoned for that in some places.'

'Then they would be morons,' Tom said sourly, 'mistaking intellectual questioning for blasphemy. It's all a matter of intent.' He stood up and stretched his old limbs. 'In the Guildhall in London are two wooden effigies of Gog and Magog, supposedly the last of a race of giants. And that itself is a mistake of history, for in ancient times they were statues of Gogmagog, a twelve foot Goliath, and Corineus, the Trojan general who threw him to his death. Or perhaps we listen to another story that says Gog and Magog are two mythical London heroes. Or Geoffrey of Monmouth, the mediaeval historian, who said Gogmagog was a giant chieftain of Cornwall. Or are we, indeed, talking about the giant oak trees at Glastonbury, sole survivors of an ancient Druid grove and ceremonial path? No one knows anything.'

'So is this the time for your catchphrase? Mythology is—'

'—the secret history of the land. Exactly. We read between the lines. We look for common threads. We search for the metaphors that all the old stories are reaching for. Giants in the earth, Ryan. A sacred site since the earliest times of man, their bodies buried far beneath our feet, along with a horse, the familiar metaphor for wild energy, for fertility, and the chariot of spiritual transcendence. People believed in this enough to keep the myth alive for thousands of years. Isn't that astonishing? Doesn't that shout out about the power that resides here?'

Veitch surveyed the light through the trees. 'Okay, enough talk. Get on with what you've got to do.'

'That's easier said than done.' Tom wandered around the pattern left by Lethbridge's excavations, swatting away the wasps that assailed him continually. Although to Veitch his meanderings looked random, Tom was actually following the tracings of Blue Fire in the land that Veitch had not yet learnt to see. The camp was a potent source of the earth energy, scything in sapphire strands across the grass, pumping through arteries as wide as a gushing stream, reaching through capillaries into the roots of trees and bushes. The Blue Fire added new shape and meaning to the barely discernible pattern Lethbridge had uncovered. The archaeologist had instinctively uncovered a figure that was spiritual in nature, rather than an exact outline on the hillside: a true representation of an ancient figure of worship, carved through ritual and prayer by the ancient people who first inhabited Wandlebury Camp, kept in focus by the Celts who followed.

But it wasn't just a figure. It was a mandala for reflection, allowing direct access to the spiritual realm, as well as one of the ancient people's landscape markers for a defence against incursions from Otherworld – and also a doorway. Near the top of the outline, at the large circle Lethbridge had identified as the head of the figure, the Blue Fire flowed back and forth between this world and the next. Tom knelt down, steeled himself, then thrust his hand into the current of flames.

'My body is the key,' he whispered.

From Veitch's perspective Tom's hand disappeared up to the wrist in the soil. For long minutes nothing happened, until soft vibrations began, growing into a deep rumbling and a shaking in the ground that made his knees buckle. A large section opened upwards like a trapdoor, trailing soil and pebbles. Beyond the mass of hanging roots, Veitch could see a dark tunnel disappearing down into the depths.

He made to duck into the opening, but Tom waved him back. 'This is for me,' he said. 'You must stay here to prepare yourself for what is to come. I will attempt to be back with the information we need by sunset. But if not, flee this place until the sun rises on the morrow. Do you hear me? Do not stay during the night.'

Veitch agreed silently. Tom nodded goodbye before diving into the hole like the White Rabbit. It closed at his heels with a thunderous shaking, leaving Veitch alone with a growing sense of apprehension.

CHAPTER NINE

Gods and Horses

A deep shiver ran through Tom as the ground closed behind him. He was far more fearful than when he had entered the Court of the Yearning Heart; another scare on the top of so many others. He had been afraid of losing himself in the Blue Fire, witnessing the deaths of the people he had grown to call friends, seeing the End of Everything. At times he felt fear was taking over.

Yet it was also uplifting, if it was not contradictory to view fear in that way. For so many centuries he hadn't been truly afraid of anything, hadn't *felt* anything at all, except for a brief period of enlightenment in the sixties. To know he *could* still feel was almost a price worth paying.

The tunnel drove directly into the heart of the hill, although he knew it was not a tunnel at all. The air was filled with aromas that soothed his heart: hashish, reminding him of warm Californian nights, red wine plunging him into a memory of a shared bottle with a pretty woman in a hippie dress at the side of the road in Haight-Ashbury, soft rain on vegetation, bringing him back to that first morning at Woodstock.

In the same way that it wasn't a tunnel, none of those pleasant fragrances were truly there; it was the reality, welcoming him with cherished memories, making him feel good.

So why was he afraid? Not because of some incipient threat, certainly, but because of immensity. What lay ahead was the infinite, the source of all meaning. And who could look on the face of God and not be destroyed?

Veitch sat on the trunk of a fallen tree, tapping his foot anxiously. Doing nothing felt like needles being driven into his body. He would rather fight one of the Fomorii than sit quietly; if he admitted it to himself, he actually enjoyed that pastime. While the others were talking their usual intellectual rubbish, he often reflected on the time beneath Edinburgh Castle when he had hacked one of the creatures into bloody chunks. He recalled the super-heated haze that fell across his mind, the adrenalin driving his limbs, the smell of the gore, the uplifting weariness that followed the exertion.

The fading image left an emptiness that disturbed him. Had he always been that way? Surely there had been a time when he could appreciate peace.

His thoughts were disturbed by movement in the branches overhead. Golden flitterings shifted quickly amongst the pattern of light and shade that made up the green canopy. At first he thought they were butterflies searching for the last nectar of summer, but there were too many of them and the activity was too localised. He counted twenty? Thirty?

It was the gossamer-winged tiny people he had seen before in tranquil places. The perfectly formed little men and women moved through the treetops with grace, like sunlight reflected off a belt buckle.

Searching for a position that allowed him to view the soaring creatures more easily, Veitch slipped from the trunk so he was lying on the ground with his head resting against it. Their flight, the wild shifts of light they engendered, was hypnotic. There was a definite calmness about them, but he was dismayed to find he was only aware of it in a detached way; he couldn't *feel* it, and at that moment it was all he wanted in the world.

'Come to me,' he whispered.

There was no way they could have heard his words, but they altered their flight patterns, some of them hanging in mid-air, as if listening, or musing. Veitch caught his breath, waited, but after a few seconds they returned to their rapid dipping and diving. Sadly, he closed his eyes, thinking of Ruth to cheer him, remembering when they had made love, the smell of her hair, the look of intelligence and sensitivity in her eyes. He loved her more than he had loved anything in his life. If he could have her, his life could be just as he had dreamed as a boy, when he had pictured himself as the storybook hero. A random tear crept out under his eyelashes, surprising him. He blinked it away hastily, not really knowing from where it had come.

When he opened his eyes one of the tiny golden creatures was hovering just above his belly, observing him with a curious expression. The fragility of it was profound, something that went beyond the construction of its body to the very depths of its spirit. He felt that if he touched it, its body would break apart and its soul would disappear into the afternoon breeze. Its eyes were large and dark and it blinked slowly, like a baby observing its parents. Its cheeks were high and refined, its hair long and flowing, like some nineteen forties movie star. The skin, golden from a distance, now looked like the glittering Milky Way.

'You're made of stars,' he whispered in awe.

The faintest smile crept across the creature's face. Here was ultimate innocence, supreme peace, a being not troubled by hate or anger or lust or desire for revenge. It held out a hand, fingers so delicate it was hard to imagine how they were formed, and as it moved the air shimmered around it. Slowly, so as not to scare it away, Veitch reached out one long, calloused finger until it was almost touching the creature's hand. He didn't go the final millimetre for fear of overstepping some unknown boundary, but the little figure merely smiled again and reached out the extra distance. When they touched, it felt like honey was flowing into his limbs. Suddenly tears were streaming down his cheeks, soaking into his shirt, and he had no idea where they came from either; there were so many it seemed as if they would never stop.

When they did finally dry up, the creature touched his finger once more and then, with a movement that might well have been a parting wave, rose up to its companions, casting regular backwards glances at Veitch's prostrate form.

Veitch watched them for the better part of an hour, his face beatific, but no thoughts that he recognised crossed his mind. And then, with the sun dappling his skin, he drifted into the first peaceful sleep he had had for years.

While he slept, the Woodborn stirred in their silent, leafy homes all around; knowing in his sleep they could not be discovered, they looked down on the still form, frail and insubstantial next to their mighty trunks. And, being spirits, they felt deep currents and saw more than eyes could ever see. After a while a soft shower of leaves fell from their branches all around the sleeping figure, like tears.

Tom thought of Van Morrison singing about 'Summertime in England', about Cream in 'The White Room', the Stones doing 'Sympathy for the Devil' and The Doors cranking up 'Five to One'. *Old man's music*, Laura would have called it, before rattling off a list of percussive-heavy songs that had been released in the past week. She missed the point. Music was the great communicator. It had nothing to do with fashion; it was part of the central nervous system, linking old memories and sensations and new ideas, joining everything of human experience up into one whole, a single bar releasing it in a torrent. Old music, new music, Gregorian chants, country and western tearjerkers or opera, it didn't matter; it was all power.

Right then, it was a barrier, blocking out all thoughts of what lay ahead. The best songs from his internal jukebox, the soundtrack to his life.

The tunnel curved down and up, and down again. Its serpentine progress reminded him of the tunnels beneath Arthur's Seat in

Edinburgh and the Fabulous Beast that slumbered there. Like that site, it was a direct access to the force that bounded everything, but unlike Arthur's Seat this place had – or at least he expected it would have – *presence*; intelligence; whatever it was that the Blue Fire encompassed. The Godhead, he supposed.

'Giants in the earth, you see,' he muttered, disturbed at how his words rattled off the walls with a force that changed their tone.

During his time with the wise men of the Culture, he had heard talk of the giants – the metaphor-giants, not the real ones that existed in times past. The Culture had understood the power of stories for communicating vital, instructive information, and how metaphors imprinted on the subconscious much better than bald facts. And this metaphor was quite transparent to the trained eye: something like men, only greater, stronger, more vital, something to provide awe and wonder, and a little fear too, responsible for great feats of creation, now sleeping beneath the earth.

How could he explain something so monumental to a man like Veitch, who thought deeply about nothing? Veitch hadn't even grasped the enormity of what was being planned. Crossing over to the land of the dead was not some weekend jaunt; humanity had been barred from it for a reason. And only a higher power could grant access.

'Thomas the Rhymer.' The voice shocked him, and not because it used the name by which he had moved from humanity to legend, now rarely heard. It was American, barely above a whisper and faintly mocking; and it was familiar.

The empty tunnel ahead filled with a faint, drifting luminescence, like autumn mist caught on a breeze, and when it cleared a figure was leaning against the wall, a bottle of Jack Daniels clutched in one hand.

'Jim?' For a second, Tom forgot where he was. The face, angelic, thick-lipped, framed by a lion's mane of hair, transported him back to the Whiskey on Sunset, when his bored wanderings had begun to show him a little meaning for the first time in centuries.

'They were good times, right, Scotty? Good times for poets. Peace, love and understanding. Not bread and brutality.' Morrison wandered forward shakily, his stoned smile unable to hide that troubling edge to his character. He tried to focus on Tom, but the cannabis-laziness of his left eye kept hindering him. It was the charismatic Morrison Tom remembered from their long, rambling discourse about life and the universe and politics, not the one who had died bloated and bearded in a Parisian bath-tub.

The sight was initially disorienting until Tom's razor-sharp mind cut through the shock. 'A memory,' he said dismissively.

'More than that, Tommy.' He proffered the bottle; Tom waved it away.

'A memory given shape.'

'You could be on the right road there. The road to excess.' He chuckled. 'Leads to the palace of wisdom, Tommy. But you still haven't hit that nail on the head.' Morrison lurched beside Tom and slipped a friendly arm round his shoulders.

Morrison's body had substance, and smelled of whiskey, smoke and sweat, just like the real Morrison had.

'I'm your . . .' He drifted for a moment while the drug-thoughts played across his face. 'Not a guide, exactly. Not a muse. I'm an angel to you, Tommy. Yeah, an angel in leather.'

Glancing at him askance, Tom caught sight of a blue light limning his wild hair, a halo, not golden like the ones the mediaeval Christian artists painted believing it more fitting for a sun-king, but its true colour. 'You're the voice of the Godhead. A form which my mind can communicate with.'

'Godhead? Yeah, well . . . whatever you say, Tommy. But I've gotta tell you, there's some serious shit a little way ahead. Blow your mind, Tommy. Better to turn back now. You sure you don't wanna drink?'

'I have to go on. I need information . . . more than that . . . a blessing.'

'It's your head, Tommy. I'll walk with you aways. You remember, you can turn back any time.'

'I need to speak to the giant.' There was a potency to the air – the effect of the Blue Fire, Tom knew – that made him almost delirious.

'No giants here, Tommy. But . . . yeah, maybe we can do that. Come on, let's go to the bar.'

There was a subtle shift in the air, as if paper scenery had been torn away in the blink of an eye. Suddenly Tom was standing in the Whiskey a Go Go, breathing in the familiar odours of stale beer and old smoke, thick with the LA streetlife of 1966. Krieger, Densmore and Manzarek were perched on stools at the end of the bar, chatting lazily with Elmer Valentine, the ex-vice cop who co-owned the joint. Tom looked around, dazed. The stage was all ready for the first set of the night – at that point in their career, The Doors were the house band, yet to record their first album. 'Incredible,' he muttered. It was just as he remembered, only more so. How could it have been plucked from his mind when he was seeing detail he was convinced he had never noticed before: the woman with the bright red hair and headband marked out with astrological symbols, the bikers near the stage, like barrels with arms of oak, blue from tattoos.

'This was the start of things,' Morrison said, quietly; his voice rarely rose above a whisper. 'For you, for me, for a way of life. The last time of innocence, Tommy. When this innocence died, the last chance of the world went with it. After that, everything was just livin' on borrowed time. There had to be a change.'

Tom nodded. 'There did.'

Morrison ordered two shots of Jack. Tom eyed his suspiciously before knocking it back with one swift movement. He didn't know what he expected – a taste like fluffy clouds – but it burned the back of his throat and made him cough. 'Real.' He held the glass up to the light. 'I suppose I should have been prepared. I've wittered on about the impermanence of so-called reality often enough.'

'That's right, Tommy. You wish hard enough, you can live in any world you want. Nothing is fixed. It's like . . .' He went druggy-dreamy, his hand floating through the air. '. . . smoke. You see shapes in it. A face. A dog. You look away, look back, see something different.'

'Christ,' Tom sighed. 'I hope I don't sound like this when I'm off my face.'

'You know, you got all these people whinin' about how the world is a pile of shit,' Morrison continued. 'Well, it's their own fault. They want it different, they should do something about it. You can't trust your eyes, you can't trust anything, and a big wish can change it all. *I am the Lizard King*, Tommy. *I can do anything.*'

Tom had to drag himself out of the seductive reality that had been presented to make him feel more comfortable. It was easy to slip into it, but wasn't that the point the Morrison-thing was making? People settle for the reality shown to them when there could be a better one just a thought away. With an effort, he managed to retreat from his surroundings to gain perspective, and then things did begin to make more sense: he was in a place that allowed direct access to the force that lay behind the Blue Fire and it was communicating with him. He couldn't allow himself to be distracted, or this fake reality to take over.

'I want to talk about that, Jim.' He called the barman for another shot, but this time he sipped it slowly. 'All this . . .' He gestured widely. '. . . it reminds me of the last true happy time in my life, perhaps the only really happy time, when I thought there were values that mattered all around. There was an alignment between the things I held dear to me and the world without. I was always a hippie,' he smiled ruefully, 'even when I was a mediaeval spy.' His face hardened. 'But now . . . now there is something worth fighting for. A world to change. That's why I'm here, to appeal for the rules to be . . . not broken, bent slightly. For a good cause. For something worth believing in.' The illusion that was not an illusion closed in around him again. He eyed Morrison, who was staring into the coloured lights above the stage where the roadies fiddled with the settings on the amps. 'You always were a spiritual man, Jim. When you weren't being a drunken oaf and a bastard to women.'

'I was a product of my times, Tommy. Hell, you remember the fifties! But we're all flawed, aren't we? Even the greatest. There are no saints in this world. You just have to make sure the balance tips on the side of the angels, that's all. With our nature, that's the best you can hope. No saints, no heroes, just people who try their best most of the time, and fuck up the rest.'

'And you think you did that?'

He stared into his shot glass for a long moment, then grinned broadly at Tom, downed the drink and ordered another. 'At least I can say I was trying.'

Morrison's voice had taken on such an odd quality Tom was drawn to stare deep into his eyes. He was mesmerised by what he saw: stars, whole galaxies, swirling in their depths. 'You're very good at making things real.'

Morrison's smile was oddly serious. 'There are no Fixed Lands, Tommy. Everything is spirit, you know that.'

'I suspected it.'

'It's all a matter of perception. You see things a certain way to make you feel comfortable, but there is no space and there is no time.' Morrison was altering before his eyes, although it was in such a subtle way – the cadence of his voice, a change of expression – Tom couldn't quite put his finger on it. He fixed Tom with a deep, unwavering stare that had the weight of the universe behind it. 'I told you, Tommy. You can wish things the way you want them to be if you know how. Is that predestination?'

Tom couldn't bear the weight of his gaze, broke it to stare at the optics behind the bar.

'We are all gods, Tommy.'

Tom's head began to spin. The words were delivered simply, but there was something hidden deep in them that suggested here was the most important message of all. His heart started to pound as he attempted to peel the true meaning from the heart of the comment, but before he could ask any further questions, Morrison held up his hand to silence him. He shook his head slowly; his eyes told Tom there would be no further discussion on that subject.

Tom was overcome with the drugged atmosphere; his thoughts ebbed and flowed and he was drawn continually to detail in the surroundings, instead of the heaviness that was building up in his thoughts.

'Tell me,' he asked hurriedly, 'the gods . . . the ones who call themselves gods . . . the Tuatha Dé Danann . . . do they speak for you? Are they part of you?'

Morrison smiled mockingly. 'Me?'

'You know what I mean.'

He thought about this for a while, his eyes glinting in the flashing coloured stage-lights. 'The gods reflect aspects of what lies beyond,' he began in his whispery voice. 'Some reflect it more than others, some better than others. But that light shines through all living creatures, Tommy. Even the smallest is a part of something bigger. It's all linked.'

Once more the grip of the illusion loosened slightly, as if he was caught in the ebb and flow of a supernatural tide. 'I'm running out of time, Jim. I can't afford these diversions. You must help me to stay on the path.'

Morrison nodded slowly. 'You want help.'

'I need to talk to the giant, Jim. The physical representation of the source. You must take me to it.'

'You know what you're getting into?'

'I know my mind might not be able to cope with it. It's a risk I'm prepared to take.'

'Yeah? But you know what you're getting into with the big shit back home. You know what I'm getting at?'

'Yes. I'm aware of it.'

'But do you *know*?' His eyes went hazy, focusing through the walls of the club, across Sunset and LA, across worlds. 'There are things moving out there that haven't been seen in your place for a long, long time, man. It's like when you move a rock and all these spiders come running out. They were born way out, and I mean *way out*. Right on the edge of the universe, where there's no light. They don't like the light. They're worse than your worst nightmare, man. You can't even *dream* these things.'

'My friends and I have no choice, Jim.' But a chill ran through him nonetheless.

'Just so you know, though.' He fumbled in his pocket and pulled out a small blotter with little pictures of Mickey Mouse and offered one to Tom. The Rhymer declined. Morrison swallowed one and washed it down with the Jack. 'I wouldn't be doing my job properly if I didn't do the warning thing. These are bad times, Tommy. It's the End of Everything. Some people would be running and hiding—'

'It may well be the End of Everything—'

'Don't listen to me, listen to them.' He motioned over Tom's shoulder. The Rhymer turned round to see The Doors, the roadies, the barflies had all disappeared. In their place were a mass of people Tom instantly recognised as Celts. Long-haired and dark of eye, some had distinctive sweeping moustaches. Others were prepared for war, their manes matted with a bleaching lime mixture that made it stick out in spikes like latter-day punks. 'I called them to announce sadness,' Morrison said with a faint smile.

One of them moved forward. He had a face of unbearable seriousness, framed by long hair, eyes limpid with emotion. Beside him were two women, sisters, skin like porcelain, hair shining black. Tom saw pride in all their faces, and strength. 'In the days before days they washed across the land like a giant wave from the cold, black sea.' The man's voice appeared from nowhere although his lips were not moving. 'We fought, and died, and fought again. And died. Many, many of us driven to the Land of Always Summer.'

'See?' Morrison said, tapping Tom firmly on the chest.

The Celt shook his head slowly from side to side. It moved jerkily, like an old movie rattling through a worn projector. There was the faintest smile on his face, despite the darkness of his words. Tom watched it curiously until he realised he was seeing defiance and self-belief and righteousness.

'The hand of bones comes for all,' the Celt began. He pointed at Tom. 'Fear is right, but fear must not rule. Death means the same to all, however they might die. But life has value. How you live, with fear at your back. What choices you make. Do you turn your back and live? Or do you face the threat and die? Which has more value? Which has more meaning?'

Tom looked at Morrison. 'You're not very good at presenting an argument.' Morrison smiled, unabashed.

'Know this,' the Celt continued, 'you know no fear like the fear you will know in times to come. Your death will be the worst death imaginable. But you will not die enfeebled. You will go as you should have lived, with the blood in your head and a song in your heart.'

Tom turned back to the bar and finished his mysteriously full glass. 'You're wasting your time. I'm under no illusions. Apart from this one. Remember, I can see the future. Not all of it, granted, but snapshots. Once you have that *gift* you stop worrying so much about what's to come.'

Morrison made a clicking song in his cheek and raised Tom's eyeline with a finger. On the periphery of Tom's vision, the bar was warping. The row of optics stretched into infinity, the lights above the low stage were running like treacle. The whole of it swelled, then receded as if it were scenery painted on the rubbery skin of a giant balloon.

'Is everybody in?' Morrison leaned in close to Tom and whispered in his ear, 'The ceremony is about to begin.'

Tom turned slowly on his stool, but the bar was already gone. Instead he was standing on a grassy area next to a wooden roundhouse with a turf roof in a night torn by lightning of such ferocity he bowed his head. There were other houses around, half-hidden in the unnatural gloom. A cacophony of frightened animal noises filled the air – pigs, sheep, cattle and horses. The boom of thunder sounded like cannon and there was a cruel wind making him stagger from side to side. But there was no rain, not even the slightest hint of it.

Morrison's eyes were lost to the acid. 'You see the future, you say, but you don't see everything.'

'Where are we?'

'The last time your world faced the End of Everything.'

The Celt who had spoken to Tom in the Whiskey staggered from the bar clutching a spear, naked and ready for battle. Others followed him, defiant, moving quickly. The quality of the lightning changed slightly, until it was more like flashes of gold, raging against the encroaching night.

'They called this in their legends the Second Battle of Magh Tuireadh.' Morrison was still whispering, but somehow his voice carried above the wind.

'The night of victory,' Tom said in awe. 'When Balor was slain.'

'One way of seeing it, Tommy. Or you could say it was a night of ultimate suffering. When the hills and dales ran red with blood and bodies clogged the rivers. This is why the Celts left their coded warnings hidden in the landscape, Tommy. This is when humanity looked into the face of the storm and almost became extinct.'

The atmosphere was loaded with tension. Tom felt his teeth go on edge, his stomach start to knot.

'You think you know everything, Tommy.' Morrison's smile had an unpleasant edge to it which Tom couldn't quite read. He raised his hand and pointed slowly to the roundhouse. 'Do you know what's in the hut? Do you want to look in there?'

Tom stared at the gaping door of the house, and felt what might have been dread, but wasn't quite; like fate come calling. Something he didn't want to see lurked just beyond the shadowy entrance. A part of him wanted to go in there, to see what was on the edge of his mind, but tantalisingly just out of reach. Another part of him knew it would break him to see it. Defeat in victory, he knew, and victory in defeat.

'Why are you trying to frighten me away?' he said to Morrison.

'Because you can't come in here and ask for the world without showing you really want it.' Morrison's smile was easier now. He clapped an arm around Tom's shoulder and shook him roughly, amicably.

'I wish you'd just tell me about Texas Radio and the Big Beat,' Tom sighed. 'Take me to GogMagog.'

The Celtic village had been replaced by the tunnels once more, although Tom still quietly yearned for the Whiskey; one more drink would have been nice, a time to rest. Morrison had not made the journey.

After about half an hour he noticed the quality of light was growing brighter, richer. At the same time the tunnel dropped into a steep incline, where he had to clutch on to the rocky walls to prevent himself sliding down into the unknown. The temperature rose rapidly; sweat soaked his shirt and dripped from his brow; the heated air choked his lungs.

Finally, he came out into a large cavern so bright at first he had to shield his eyes. In the centre was an enormous lake of bubbling, popping lava, occasionally shooting up in miniature geysers. The heat radiated off it, but there was none of the sulphurous stink that should have poisoned the air.

Covering his mouth with his shirt to prevent his lungs searing, he eased forward until he stood at the edge of the red lake. The air pulsed.

Tom wondered if madness were only seconds away. He knew it would be best not to be there, but how could he turn back? The others had put him to shame with their continued risk-taking, like he was a child, not the mentor. It was time to face up to his responsibility.

'I plead for help!' he said in a commanding voice, while at the same time bowing his head to show deference. It also helped to hide the fear in his face.

The pressure in the air ratcheted up a notch and he had to swallow to make his ears pop.

'I know that to look upon you could mean the end of me . . . I know that I'm not supposed to be here. But I have to. So much is at risk.'

Would it come? Or was he wasting his time?

'I'm prepared to sacrifice myself if that's what it takes. That the world should survive is more important than me.'

The pressure finally burst and a cooling wind rushed across his face, bringing with it a deep apprehension. His words had touched a chord. Something was coming.

The lava in the centre of the lake erupted, showering burning coals all around, although, miraculously, none of them touched him. Tom threw himself back in shock, dropping to his knees, one arm across his mouth. The lava bubbled up higher in a fountain of fire and smoke, up and up, gaining weight and consistency. And when it appeared it would finally come crashing down on him in a tidal wave, it stopped, hanging silently. It stayed that way for just a moment and then the lava shifted until shape came out of its globular form: an oval, indentations folding out of it, two slits halfway up, an elongated one running vertically and a horizontal slash below. Within seconds a rough-hewn face had grown from the glutinous lava, appearing remarkably like one of the statues that looked to the endless horizon on Easter Island.

Tom climbed to his feet, but a deafening roar burst forth from the lava-thing, knocking him back to his knees, his ears ringing. This time he stayed there.

For a long moment he didn't dare speak. The cavern was filled with ebbing sound, dull and reverberate, as if the thing was breathing.

'Are you the Godhead?' Tom whispered. His voice carried with remarkable clarity. 'The source?'

'I am GogMagog.' The voice was the eruption of a volcano, an earthquake turning the ground to fluid. Tom knew he wasn't *really* hearing it; it was something else prepared for his limited perception. And he also knew this wasn't the Godhead either; he had been presented with another intermediary, albeit a much more powerful one. He felt both relieved and disappointed at the same time. 'You have been judged,' the force continued.

'But I haven't made my case yet,' Tom protested. 'Please—'

'We see through you. Your shell, to the essence inside. We see it all. Saw it as soon as you crossed over.'

Tom's spirits plummeted. It saw through him, just like that; picked the worthlessness from his soul, the cowardice, the indecision, the hopelessness, all the things he had tried so hard to hide. He had failed.

'You shine. A star in miniature.' The voice became richer, less elemental. Tom looked up curiously; the face could almost have been smiling. 'Stand tall, little light. You do good work, as do your companions. You do the work of existence.'

'I do?' Tom felt befuddled. 'I expected to be presented to the Godhead.'

'Do you really wish that, little light?' The lava glowed brighter. 'There is no going back from that. Only forward, only forward.'

'I hoped—'

'Your mission has been recognised. You need to return to the world.'

A part of Tom still yearned for the bliss of giving himself up to the spiritual source, and he accepted that some of what drove him to follow the path underground was akin to a death-wish. But what lay beyond had saved him from himself by interposing GogMagog at the last moment. That affirmation was both surprising and affecting; he could feel it warming the cold, dark parts of him.

'The path you have chosen is fraught with danger,' GogMagog said, 'but it is the most important path. Many things hang in the balance, both now and in the years to come. In the great cycle, a change has taken place. There will be no peace until the period of transformation has passed and the new order has been established.'

'I understand.'

'No. You do not. The Adversary awaits on the edge of everything. Choosing his time carefully. Preparing for the ultimate battle.'

'Balor?' Tom asked. 'But he—'

'That is but one small part of the Adversary. A fragment of shadow within the greater shadow.'

'There's something else?' Tom's heart fell. 'Something worse?'

'There is always something more. Your kind must always be on its guard. There is no peaceful home on this side of the inviolate boundary.' The lava rose, then receded.

'When?' Tom asked. There was no reply. After a while, Tom put the matter to the back of his mind to concentrate on the issue at hand. 'A friend must cross into the Grim Lands to bring back someone vitally important to ridding the world of the evil now occupying it. This friend is not dead, nor is he alive, but his spirit is trapped in the Grim Lands. That itself is a transgression of the rules. I ask that you allow my agent to cross over. And to return with our friend.'

There was a long silence, filled only with the sighing of the heated air currents in the cavern. The more time passed, the more Tom feared rejection. But then GogMagog spoke: 'The inviolate boundary may be traversed. Your agent can make the voyage from which your kind may not return.'

'Is he given safe passage?'

'He is.'

'And for the return?'

'Yes. But know this: your agent faces great peril. He may cross the inviolate boundary as the rules say.'

Tom thought about this for a second, until realisation suddenly dawned with a cold chill. 'He might die?'

Another silence, the shush-boom of the lava breathing. 'Night is drawing in. The beast is preparing to snap at his heels.'

Tom cursed quietly; had Veitch not obeyed his order to vacate the camp at nightfall? 'Then I must return to help him.'

'Also, beware: when he crosses the inviolate boundary, the dead will be waiting. You know what that means?'

Dismally, Tom nodded. 'How can the doorway be opened?'

'Here, I will give you knowledge.' A tendril of lava extended from the lake just below the swaying head, slowly covering the gulf between them. The super-heated smell of it was powerful; his skin bloomed when it wavered in front of his face. Like a snake, it started, striking the centre of his forehead. He yelped in pain and recoiled as the flesh sizzled, but in that moment the information he required was transmitted.

'Know this also: you have seen more than any of your kind in an age. Carry this memory with you, but never return. There are boundaries that must not be crossed, and information that must never be learned, until your transformation . . .'

The last word was drawn out like toffee as the cavern receded at great speed. Tom's head spun with the sudden warping effect, and then he was lifted on a blast of super-hot air, flying backwards out of the cavern and up the tunnel so fast the breath was crushed from his lungs. He hurtled through the Whiskey, with Morrison smiling at him mockingly, through the Celtic village, and then the pain in his lungs became unbearable and the dark folded around him sharply.

Veitch emerged from a deep sleep, disoriented and aching; some hidden branch had been digging in his back and his thighs felt like they'd been stoned. A string of drool soaked his cheek. It was not a sudden awakening; his dream still had its talons in him – an upsetting scenario of Ruth telling him something he couldn't bear to hear – leaving him feeling irritated and out-of-sorts. As he came to his senses, he was aware of a chill in his limbs. The patches of warming sunlight had departed, taking the tiny flying creatures with them. Colour was slowly leeching from the vegetation as twilight took hold.

'Shit, how long have I been out?' He dragged himself awkwardly to his feet, shaking his arms to get the blood flow moving.

In the half-light, the woods appeared less idyllic. Unease scurried under rustling nettles and made branches sway wildly when there was no breeze. Shadows crept along the ground menacingly from the boles of trees, clustered under bushes, waiting. Rubbing his wrists, Veitch wandered down the slope a little way to a path. From there he could see the sun so low on the horizon it was really just a glow of red and gold.

Tom's warning came back to him, but he had never given it serious consideration – he had faced too many bad things to run at the first sign of trouble. Even if he did heed it, where would he go? And what if

Tom returned from wherever he was, only to find himself alone, at night, in a place he considered dangerous? He might be a miserable git at times, but he deserved better than that.

Weighing his options, Veitch decided to return to the mansion to sit with Robertson while the superstitious squatter rubbed his mojos till dawn. He strode out through the forest, the chill in the air telling him the deceptively warm season was slipping out quietly. Unsure of his direction, he paused at the system of paths leading from the car park around the hill. Everywhere looked different in the growing gloom. He still hadn't adjusted to the dramatic change the night brought to a land free from electric lights: deep, still darkness heavy on the countryside and the stars so bright overhead it was as if he had never seen them before. The last few midges drifted away to wherever they spent the night, pursued by the flitting shape of a bat darting from the trees across the open areas. The jarring screech of an owl echoed away in the woods. All the night creatures were coming out to hunt.

At a fork in the path, Veitch took the one he thought he remembered, but it was soon apparent he'd taken a wrong turning. The Tarmac gave way to stones and then hard-packed soil as the path became a thin trail amongst the bushes. Ahead of him he could see the outline of the house silhouetted against the night sky; it didn't appear too far away.

The path bore down steeply until Veitch found himself in a strange, broad ditch that looked as if it ran around the circumference of the hill. He vaguely recalled Tom muttering something about the fortifications of the old Iron Age fort, but, as usual, he hadn't been paying much attention. The bottom of the ditch was flat, some six to eight feet wide, and obviously used regularly as a footpath from the hardness of the soil. On either side the banks rose up steeply. Clustering firs formed a natural roof that only added to the gloom. As his eyes adjusted he made out festooning ivy, chest-high nettles and thick banks of bramble that made the sides of the ditch impenetrable. On the house side there was also some kind of high wall or fence at the top of the bank.

Sooner or later there would be a path up to the truncated summit, he guessed, so he set off clockwise round the fortification. The low level of the ditch and its flat bottom against the steep banks reminded him of a racetrack, and he briefly fantasised about scrambling round on a motorcycle; just another thing he missed with the passing of technology.

At intermittent points, crumbling flint walls protruded like ghostly fingers from the bank, while gnarled roots snaked out of the ground, threatening to trip him. He kept his eyes down, his ears alert and walked slowly; the last thing he needed was a broken ankle.

The first sign that something was wrong was a wall of cold wind that came from nowhere, raising goosebumps on his arms before continuing along the ditch behind him. It was starkly unnatural the way it clung to the bottom of the trough; the vegetation on either side never moved and the trees that hung overhead were still. Even when he could hear its whispering disappearing far behind him, the goosebumps remained. It felt like a sign delineating a change, as if something profound had shifted in nature itself; the old time had gone, the new time was near.

He found it disconcertingly eerie there in the darkness of the ditch, where the banks were so steep his only way of escape was forward or back. The place was intensely still and each footstep sounded like the crack of a whip. Perhaps it was the odd acoustics of the place, but no sound came from outside the ditch, not even the cries of owls. An unpleasant loneliness hung over all.

Veitch started having second thoughts about his choice of route, but it was too late to go back. His bravery took a further knock when he heard a long, low noise; he couldn't tell if it came from ahead or behind, nor what kind of animal had made it. After the heavy silence, it was deeply unnerving. It rolled along the bottom of the ditch as the wind had done, suggesting something akin to the whinnying snort of a horse, but different enough to raise the hairs on the back of his neck.

He turned slowly, full circle, trying to pinpoint the location, while his mind raced to plan a course of action.

Just a horse, he told himself. The place used to be famous for horse-breeding and racing; that was the rational explanation. But he couldn't forget the story Tom had told him about the Night Rider.

It's coming. The words jumped into his mind unprompted.

Just ahead of him, the left bank was cut through with a path that ran down the slope of the hill. Hurrying up it to get a better view, Veitch saw only thick vegetation and open fields ahead; nowhere to hide if he was pursued. His best bet was still to get to the house and bar the door; suddenly Robertson's superstitions made a lot more sense.

Back on the floor of the ditch, the silence had returned, now weighted with anticipation. The familiar pressure drop that always accompanied some unnatural event left his ears humming, and he could taste iron at the back of his mouth. Almost loping, he moved forward, trying to avoid any twig or stone that might give his location away.

A hard, clicking sound brought him up sharp: hoofbeats, slow and measured; just a few and then silence, as if whatever was out there was also advancing and listening. It was still impossible to identify the location. The *clack-clack-clack* appeared to circle him, loud and crystal clear in the stillness. Cautiously, Veitch withdrew his crossbow and carefully fitted a bolt. The dark would make it hard to get a clear shot, but he felt more comfortable being able to launch an attack from afar.

Clack-clack-clack. This time he was sure it was behind him. Veitch peered into the gloom, waiting for the sound to stop. Only this time it didn't. The horse was coming towards him at a measured but relentless pace. Now he was convinced it was ahead of him. He turned back, raising the crossbow until it was lined up for anything advancing along the ditch.

Clack-clack-clack-clack-clack.

He continued to wait for the dark to peel back, until, with a sudden *frisson*, he realised the sound wasn't ahead of him at all. He spun round to see a creamy cloud filled with sparkling stars twisting and turning as it hurtled along the path right at him. A buzzing like a swarm of angry bees filled the air, setting his teeth on edge.

Expecting a horse, the sight caught him unawares. The cloud rushed towards him at great speed, then, just as he decided to loose a bolt, it winked out; the disembodied hoofbeats continued thunderously.

Veitch paused for a split second before his instinct kicked in, then he was sprinting along the bottom of the ditch, not sure if he could outrun it, knowing there was no other way out.

Twisted roots threatened to trip him before retreating back into the shadows, but his reactions were electric-fast. Behind him the storm-clatter of hooves grew louder and louder, matching the beats of his heart. Twenty feet away, then ten, then at his heels.

From out of the dark, an obstacle rushed at him: a pile of hard earth forming a bridge-path between the two banks piled as high as his head. He went up it with what felt like snorts of fire burning the back of his neck, threw himself down the other side and rolled into a ball. A large form tore over his head and landed with a heavy crash before pounding on for several yards. Looking up, he saw a shimmering in the air like malleable glass rein itself to a halt, then whirl round, catching the light with pools and glints. The limning of moonlight indeed suggested a horse with a bulky figure on its back before it was lost to the dark. The hooves began to pound once more, building up speed.

Veitch waited until the last moment before throwing himself back over the bridge-path to perform the same manoeuvre. Again his pursuer passed overhead. This time he launched himself to gain a few vital yards before the Night Rider could round.

As the horse rattled down on him, he whirled and rolled, loosing a bolt in the same motion. A second later a tear of fire appeared in thin air, followed by a cry like a metal crate being dragged on a concrete floor.

He had no time to discover how much damage he had wrought, for the sound continued to bear down on him. He threw himself to one side at the last moment, but it was not quite far enough. His jacket and shirt tore open, his flesh mysteriously burst as a raw red line rushed up towards his neck. He just had time to jerk his head before the invisible blade could rip through his jugular, and then he was rolling backwards against the bank, his shirt growing hot and wet.

The pain sharpened his thoughts. When he moved, the rest of the world felt like it was frozen; he was scrambling to one side, rolling, ignoring the pain, reloading the crossbow, readjusting the balance of his body like a machine.

He landed on the balls of his feet, poised to attack, but though his eyes and ears were charged to pick up even the slightest sound of his attacker, there was nothing. The bottom of the ditch was still; even the faintest hoofbeat would have sounded out loud. Not even a hint of movement, the barest shift in air currents.

His blood thundered in his head. Where had it gone? He turned slowly, but the thing really had disappeared. Perhaps the bolt *had* caused some damage.

He waited for a few seconds longer, just to be sure, and then set off at a slow lope around the ditch. He was under no illusion that the Night Rider had gone for good, but its absence might just provide him with the time to find a route to the house.

His feet padded on the hard-packed mud as he ran, his breath ragged; the night air was chill and fragrant. Every sensation was heightened. The enveloping trees that made the ditch feel like a tunnel instilled an oppressive claustrophobia in him; he was trapped, like an animal. The thought brought a burst of adrenalin and he threw himself up the side of the ditch, feeling the thorns of the brambles tear at his flesh, the nettles stabbing with their poison needles. Somehow he made it to the top, but the trees there were impenetrable, and beyond them the brick garden wall was too tall to climb. He still tried to force his way through, but the trees acted as if they were alive, forcing him back until he was slipping down the slope to land on his back at the bottom of the ditch once more.

As he lay there while his breath subsided, tremors ran through the ground into his bones: rhythmic, powerful. He was up in an instant, running once more. This time, when he actually heard the hoofbeats, it was almost hallucinogenic; they faded in and out of his hearing, the rider here, then not here. And then they disappeared completely again, leaving only silence.

A moment of clarity overwhelmed him. Tom had spoken of *liminal zones* where the boundaries between this world and T'ir n'a n'Og were blurred. The camp must be such a place, he realised, and the Rider was shifting in and out of the worlds as it pursued him.

Veitch whirled, crossbow at the ready. His nerve-endings prickled as he slowly surveyed the scene. His pursuer could be anywhere. How did it make itself invisible? Or was that its natural state? Yet he knew now what he had to do: attack at the moment it was fully in this world, when – he hoped – it would be most vulnerable.

Another low whinny drifted along the ditch. It sounded unimaginably distant, but it brought back the gooseflesh. And then, as it wound its way through the undergrowth on the ditch banks, it began to change; slowly at first, but definitely, losing its equine characteristics. The sound became shorter, broke up into linked sounds; became words.

That eerie noise made the snake around Veitch's spine pull the coils in tighter. 'What the *hell* is that?' he hissed.

He was already moving when the words rattled around him like pebbles on a frozen lake, devoid of emotion, but threatening. 'Run fast, run fast, at your back.'

They were barely audible, could almost have been the distant echoes of hoofbeats, but the chill they brought to his blood drove him on. Faster and faster still, with the rumble of pursuit building behind him. He glanced over his shoulder as he hurdled a twisted mass of root: nothing yet. The words were all around him, some indecipherable, hidden in the snort of a horse, others barely registering on his consciousness, but disturbing him nonetheless.

As he rounded the curve of the ditch, running faster than he ever had in his life, an arching shape loomed up out of the night. The mass of trees had thinned out and the light of the moon revealed a brick bridge across the ditch. He was sure he would be able to scramble up the side to get to it and then it would be only a short sprint to the house. With the thunder of hooves almost at his heels, the sight gave him enough of a filip to drive himself that little bit harder.

But just as he thought he would make it, his foot caught one of the roots that had threatened to trip him ever since he had ventured down there. He hit the ground so hard all the air was driven out of his lungs; the pain in his chest felt like someone had swung a hammer there. At first he was stunned, but then his mind scrambled in panic. It was too late.

He looked back and was briefly hypnotised by the strangest thing: little flames, like will o' the wisps, alighted at ground level, drawing towards him. It took him a second to realise what it was: invisible hooves striking the flints that were scattered across the ditch.

The moment locked. He wondered what it would be like to be trampled to death; wondered if anyone would mourn him.

And then he was transfixed by something else. As the little flames closed on him, the air above shimmered and began to peel back. It looked to him like the Night Rider was shedding his skin: at first there was nothing, then the translucent glassy substance, until that slipped away to reveal the true form of his pursuer, or as true a form as his perceptions would allow. The first shock was that the picture he had created in his head was so wrong: this was no mediaeval knight with a broadsword or a lance on a black charger. There wasn't even a man and a horse. What bore down on him in a rage of clattering hooves was both man *and* horse, the two forms constantly flowing together, never staying the same for too long. A head that had the flowing hair of an Iron Age warrior, becoming a wild mane, the face growing longer, nostrils flaring, blasting clouds of steam in the chill night; two legs, then four, then two again. It wasn't like a classical centaur, but was half-formed, or still forming, or never-quite-forming; continually halfway between the two in the same way that the sounds had appeared to be coming halfway between here and there.

The intoxicating shock was riven out by a burst of blood in Veitch's brain. Suddenly he was ready to move. He tried to fling himself to one side, but even as he was moving, the futility of it was strangling his thoughts. The Night Rider was on him, rising up, iron-shod hooves glinting in the moonlight. One of them caught Veitch on the temple, knocking him back to the ground where stars flew briefly.

When they cleared, all he could see was the creature's terrible face framed against the night sky. It was filled with all the fury of the animal kingdom, wild and unfocused, the eyes ruddy and smoky as they branded him. Its musk was thick and choking, blanking out all his senses, yet behind it all Veitch sensed something resolutely human; once a man, and now greater than a man.

'I ride the courses between the worlds.' Those stony words again; Veitch wanted to cover his ears at the unbearable force of them. Everything about the thing was so *vital*. 'I am the power and the fecundity of the stallion, the speed and the strength. Worlds are dashed beneath my feet.'

Veitch snatched his head away as the Night Rider brought a hoof down sharply. It slammed the ground an inch from his ear, jolting his head upwards so powerfully he knew his skull would have been crushed if contact had been made. With the next blow, sparks burned his cheek. He was trapped beneath the body of the creature, with no way of wriggling free.

'This sacred place belongs to the Machan who made me. Totem of Rig Antona, our Great High Queen, who made the sky and the stars and the green grass on which we run.' The words reminded Veitch of a recorded announcement programmed to be delivered to intruders in the earliest of days. 'In this place, where the barrier is thin, the wild, untamed spirits of the horse gallop to the Grey Lands and back.'

Another hoof came down in punctuation, this time clipping Veitch's shoulder; a bolt of pain shot down his arm.

'No one but the Machan may ride here betwixt sunset and sunrise. That is the law.' The horse had human features, but the Night Rider's face was now wholly that of a demonic horse with blazing red eyes, an alien conqueror who would brook no trespass on his domain. Veitch felt swallowed up by that scarlet glow, forced to accept his place in the scheme of things. *You are nothing,* it said. *Insignificant in the face of a higher power. You will obey, and you will die.*

It meant nothing to Veitch. As the Night Rider rose up high, its hooves tearing at the air ready for the killing blow, Veitch brought the crossbow up and loosed a bolt directly into the creature's belly. That unmistakable metal-on-concrete roar erupted from its wildly shifting face as it threw itself into a furious downward drive at Veitch's head.

But the bolt had unbalanced it. In a sinuous movement, Veitch pulled out the short sword from his belt and drove it upwards at the same time as he kicked himself backwards. The sword ripped into the belly and tore upwards. 'Nothing scares me any more,' Veitch growled defiantly.

He was too busy doing a backward roll to see the results of his attack, but he could hear the Night Rider's hideous cries. And then he was sprinting for the bridge, scrambling up the bank at the side of it, his feet slipping on the weeds, but gaining enough purchase to propel himself to the top.

Only when he was on the bridge did he allow himself a glance back. There was neither blood nor intestines, but the Rider was lurching from side to side in obvious discomfort, his head held back, roaring his pain to the night. Once his gaze fell on Veitch, the face changed once more to the demonic horse's head and, with the eyes shining like red lanterns, the Rider overcame his agony to spur himself into pursuit.

Veitch paused to give him the finger, then flipped over the wall of the bridge and landed on the Tarmac path that curved around the trees into the flat summit of the hill. *Nearly there*, he thought breathlessly, energised by his escape and his defiance. For a moment he felt indestructible, until he heard the Night Rider thunder effortlessly up the side of the ditch and the hooves clatter on the Tarmac surface.

Veitch weighed up the prospects of loosing some more bolts, but he estimated the effect would be negligible. It was now all down to his fitness and his energy reserves. He followed the curve of the path until he saw the lawns laid out before him, silver-grey in the moonlight with the dry dew pond at the centre. Before him the dark bulk of the house loomed up. The comforting golden glow of candlelight illuminated a square on the courtyard from the window of Robertson's quarters.

Behind, the rumble of hooves came on like a runaway train.

I can make it, Veitch told himself.

He ran as if caught by the north wind, hurdling the small fence and pounding across the courtyard. The hooves grew closer, only yards now. He couldn't out-run a horse, but the house was close enough to reach before it got to him. Past the stable-block with its silent ghosts of horses past. Their energy was everywhere, he thought.

Now he could hear the beast's breath, explosive bursts punctuated by the gnashing of its teeth. He waited for the hot bloom of it on the back of his neck.

He slammed into the door, sending the panes ringing in their frames. Fumbling around, he caught the handle and yanked. Locked.

'Robertson!' His throat was torn by the yell.

Robertson appeared at the window, his face pale and desperate. Veitch was already reading the signs, recalling the man's nature. 'Come *on*, you bastard,' he said under his breath. The sound of hooves was deafening; Veitch forced himself not to look. As Robertson took in the situation in a glance, an expression of revelation crossed his face; and the revelation was that the world was the hell he had always imagined, where reason didn't exist and superstition crushed lives at random. He backed away rapidly, waving his hands in front of him.

From behind, there was a hiss like escaping steam, loaded with a note of triumph.

Veitch cursed under his breath and turned, the house heavy at his back, the enclosing walls of the courtyard too oppressive; nowhere to run.

The Night Rider had slowed his speed, revelling in the cornering of his prey. In the candlelight, Veitch could make out more details of his pursuer. The rider's legs went directly into the body of the horse, not just fused there, but utilising the same muscular and vascular system. The rider's arms disappeared into the mane, the horse-hair wrapping round, becoming part of the human flesh; and still the features on both the heads were hideously changing places.

Nowhere to run.

The rider came to a halt. Slowly one hoof dragged along the ground, raising sparks. The head at the front lowered, the rider leaned forward.

Still a chance to move, Veitch told himself optimistically. *Don't give up. Never give up.*

Before he could break away from the door, a voice boomed across the courtyard. The tone and volume made Veitch jump in shock. It was in a language he didn't comprehend, but the words – if that was what they were – made his ears hurt just by hearing them.

It had an effect on the Rider too; he paused as he prepared for the charge, cantered round, backed off. Veitch noted the mutating appearance had speeded up; the features were now just a blur, suggesting uneasiness.

For a time the whole of the world hung in abeyance. With his heart in his mouth, Veitch saw movement in the shadows surrounding the stable-block. Whatever had spoken was there. Veitch wanted to flee to a secure hiding place immediately, but the figure was now emerging from the gloom. The Night Rider, too, appeared to be waiting with something like apprehension.

When the figure stepped into the moonlight, Veitch was shocked to see it was Tom. He was staggering a little, as if exhausted, but the most curious detail was that he was smoking, as if he had been singed by a blaze. The Rider focused all his attention on the slight figure. When Tom was ten feet away he made a strange hand movement which appeared to involve another set of joints in the wrist. It was followed by another word; Tom whispered it, but it crashed like the peal of cathedral bells.

The Rider responded as if chastened by a whip. The front of the horse bowed down, bending its front legs until its head was almost on the ground. The Rider followed suit with a similar act of deference. Then it rose back up and, without a second glance at Veitch, calmly cantered off.

Veitch remained tense for a few seconds, barely believing what he was seeing, but then his shoulders relaxed and he turned to Tom with a broad grin. 'You old bastard! Like the bleedin' cavalry!'

Tom marched over and stabbed a finger into Veitch's face. 'I thought I told you to get off the hill at nightfall!'

Veitch's expression soured. 'Since when did I do what you say, you senile old bastard?' The adrenalin still pumped deliriously around his system. 'Hang on a minute.' He turned and launched a hefty kick at the door, which burst off its hinges, shattering all the panes at once.

Tom recognised the expression on Veitch's face, the consuming rage that he carried with him at all times. 'Now, steady on—'

Veitch had already marched inside. There was a loud crashing within and a moment later he emerged, dragging a writhing Robertson behind him. The squatter was almost insane with fear, his eyes rolling, his jaw sagging.

'Ryan! He's scared!'

'Yeah? Well, here's something to be scared of.' He thumped Robertson so hard on the side of the head, Tom was afraid his neck had snapped. He slumped to the ground in a stupor.

It took fifteen minutes before Veitch had calmed enough to have a reasonable conversation with Tom. Robertson had scurried back indoors, barricading the doorway with furniture. Even then Veitch couldn't sit and spent the time pacing in circles around Tom, who sat cross-legged, drawing on a joint, unable to hide the shake in his hands.

'What was that thing?' Veitch asked.

'This place has been linked to horses much longer than the racing fraternity realised. Back in the earliest times, it was dedicated to Epona. Her name derives from the Celtic word for horse and she was one of the greatest goddesses of the Celts. All riders – warriors, travellers, whoever – bowed their head to Epona. In Wales, she was known as Rhiannon, in Ireland Etain or Macha.' Tom let the smoke drift into the wind. 'She was the patron of journeys, particularly the most important journey of all: from this life to the next. She was usually pictured carrying a key that unlocked the door to Otherworld.'

'Yeah? Then it ties into this place. The doorway to the Land of the Dead, and all that.'

'Yes. Amazing how it all fits together.' Veitch didn't appear to notice the sarcasm in Tom's voice; he was lost in his own childlike amazement. 'The Night Rider was her avatar. Once he was probably a man like you or me, perhaps a man who even lived at this site. But at some point he became infused with the essence of Epona, became, in a way, the totem he worshipped. And so he eternally guards this sacred spot were she canters back and forth between the worlds.'

'Horses.' Veitch kicked a stray stone across the yard. 'Don't see the bleedin' attraction. Smelly animals.'

'Horse worship persisted from the earliest times of the nomadic people in this land. To them, the horse was a symbol of fertility, energy and power.' Dreamily, Tom nodded his head to some inner soundtrack. 'Worshipping is wishing by any other name, and if you wish hard enough you can create something from nothing.' Words from another world came back to him.

'What's that, then? You're saying all those folk gave her the powers. Made her. She's one of the Danann bastards, right?'

'Yes and yes and yes, and no and no and no.'

'Oh, shut the fuck up. I'm not going to talk to you any more when you're smoking.' He marched irritatedly into Robertson's apartment.

The chill before dawn brought a deep ache to their bones. They sat on a bench, watching the moon scud across the heavens, the sky slowly turn from midnight blue to pink and gold, the grass growing from grey to green. An affecting peace lay over everything. When the birds came alive in the trees that ringed the lawned area, Veitch turned to Tom and smiled. 'It'll be all right, you know.'

Tom nodded noncommittally.

'What happened? You know, when you met the giant?'

Tom considered how to put the experience into words, then simply shook his head. 'That's a story for another time. All you need to know now is you've got the necessary permission to bring Shavi back.'

The sun came up soon after. The diffuse golden light glimmered through the branches, eventually making its way across the lawn until it reached the dew pond. At first nothing happened, but when the light was just right they could make out a shimmering image of Shavi's body lying in a flower-bedecked bower. It was insubstantial, fading in and out like a poor hologram. He appeared to be sleeping; only the stark paleness of his skin gave a clue to his true state.

Tom thought he saw the glint of tears in Veitch's eyes, but the Londoner looked away before he could be sure.

'We better do it,' Veitch said solemnly.

'Are you sure? This is your last chance to back out.'

'Yes.'

'You understand where you're going? What lies ahead? What it could do to your mind? You know you might not be coming back?'

Veitch fixed a cold eye on him. 'Just get on with it.'

A pang of guilt clutched at Tom's heart. He *knew* what lay ahead, and he knew Veitch could not even begin to guess the extent of the horrors that lurked in the Grim Lands. How could he send the man to face that? But even as he thought it, he knew he had no choice; only Veitch stood a chance of bringing Shavi back. And therein lay the tragedy.

On the edge of the dew pond, Tom knelt down and kissed the damp grass. When he stood back up, he had composed himself. 'Are you ready?'

'Bring it on,' Veitch replied in a cod-American accent.

Tom closed his eyes and attempted to access the knowledge Gog-Magog had implanted there. He had already used the secret words of power to dismiss the guardian. Now there was one remaining: the key to the door. He couldn't reach it in his memory by normal means. He simply made a space, and then it leapt into it. He didn't remember speaking, but when he opened his eyes, Veitch was clutching his ears and grimacing.

There was a sound like a jammed door being wrenched open and the air over the dew pond peeled back. Through it Tom could see thick grey fog, swirling in the wind.

Veitch made to say something, but couldn't find the words. Instead, he grinned, winked and then launched himself through the hole in the air. The wrenching noise echoed again as the door closed, leaving Tom alone to stare at the fading visage of Shavi.

CHAPTER TEN

Below

'It's time.' Church tried to sound more confident than he felt, but Ruth was not about to be fooled.

'I still think I should come with you.'

He shook his head firmly. 'I'm not trying to protect you like some big macho idiot. You'd be the first person I'd want alongside me in a fight. But I told you, one of us has to be here to see things through.'

'You're not being very consistent. You made a big thing about how you felt all five Brothers and Sisters of Dragons had to be together to get a result. Now you're saying I can do it on my own—'

'I hate having smart people around me. Okay, I'll be back. Did that sound like Arnie Schwarzenegger? Sorry, I wasted the eighties at the movies.'

'You're so low-brow.' She put her arms around him and pulled him to her, planting a wet kiss on his lips. 'Be back soon. We have a lot of lost time to make up for.'

In the constantly changing corridors where the flickering torches never cast enough light, the kiss brought an ache to his heart. More than anything, he wanted to stay with Ruth, secure in their new-found world, but he knew that was an illusion. He had to journey down into the deep, dark bowels of the ship where there was no security, no softness. He drew his jacket around him, resting one hand on the cold short sword that hung at his belt.

'Life's good as long as you don't weaken,' he muttered, repeating the credo he had once only half-jokingly spoken aloud. 'Please don't weaken.'

The ship grew icier and smelled danker the more he progressed, as if he were journeying beneath the earth itself. He had adjusted to the constant gentle rocking, but the creak of the timbers was like the background chatter of a hundred voices, obscuring other subtle sounds that might come as a warning. The hiss of the torches brought sweetly perfumed smoke to his nose, but the underlying odour of dampness could never be hidden.

After a while he started cautiously trying the doors on either side. Most were locked, some rooms were empty, but in one something that was a mass of tentacles and snapping jaws rushed towards him squealing insanely. He slammed the door and hurried on, vowing not to open any more.

The ship went on forever. More than anything, Church feared getting lost down there, spending the rest of his life wandering around in the dark, living on rats (although he had not seen any vermin – perhaps something else was already feeding on them), slowly turning pale and mad. But he had a gut instinct that the ship was sentient in some way he couldn't explain, and that while the corridors behind him might close and move, when he returned, they would lead him back to the upper decks by one route or another.

At that point he began to wonder if he was really on a ship at all; if the spy he had encountered in Edinburgh had been right and all this was a warped perception brought on by some outside force using drugs or deep hypnotism, for whatever reason. As this thought entered his head, he was convinced he heard the throb of machines and the hubbub of men's voices through one of the doors; it troubled him inexplicably and he chose to hurry on.

Further on, the corridors took on a different appearance, so that it was no longer obvious he was on board a ship. It might have happened so gradually he didn't notice it, or in the blink of an eye, but suddenly the walls were in part limestone, in others, rough-hewn timbers, peppered with holes of varying sizes. It smelled differently, too. The saltiness that had permeated everything had been replaced by a faintly sulphurous odour of dust. The heavy echoes of his tread had taken the place of the constant creaking, nor was he even aware of the ship's rocking. Other sounds were more prevalent now, through the walls or further along the corridor: movement, fast and light like the scurrying of vermin, or slow and laboured as if enormous creatures were shifting slowly.

He was startled at one point by the sound of small feet near to his ear. He turned sharply to see a blur passing quickly across a hole in the wall at head height. One of the Portunes, he guessed, spying on him. The little people were everywhere, the eyes and ears of the ship. But why were they always watching? What did it benefit them?

As the atmosphere became less like that onboard ship, the more the air of tension rose; it was enough to warn Church he had moved into an area of more immediate danger, rather than the general background threat of the upper decks. There was a quality to it that made him queasy. His palms grew slick around the handle of the sword, his knuckles aching from holding it.

His eyes, by now well-accustomed to the gloom, felt sore from continually probing the shadows ahead; so much that at first he thought the flickering shapes he occasionally glimpsed were just the tremors of an over-worked eye muscle. But gradually he came to realise there were things moving just beyond the light of the now-intermittent torches, darting around corners at the last moment. He was sure they weren't the Malignos; as Ruth had described them, they would not be so restrained. It could, of course, be Callow, playing some sneaky little game, waiting for just the right moment to attack. But still—

Church almost jumped out of his skin when a hand protruded from an unnoticed branching corridor to his left, reaching for his arm. It was just a glimpse out of the corner of his eye, but he was whirling instantly, lashing out with the sword. His reactions were perfect, but the hand became a blur of golden lightning. Before Church had time to launch another attack, Baccharus stepped out sharply, motioning for Church to remain silent.

Church's angry face passed on all the fury of the curses he wanted to yell out at Baccharus's unthinking approach, but Baccharus, as usual, was oblivious. They hurried several yards along the branching corridor until Baccharus turned and said bluntly, 'You must turn back.'

'I'm starting to worry about you, Baccharus,' Church snapped. 'Do you spend all your time hanging around down here? You know, is it the Tuatha Dé Danann equivalent of the street corner where the furtively smoking teenagers hang out? Or do you just wait in the shadows until Ruth or I come along?'

Baccharus gave several long, slow blinks while staring into Church's eyes. Eventually he said, 'You must—'

'Yes, yes, I know. Turn back. I know it's not a saunter through Covent Garden—'

'You do not realise the extent of the danger.'

Church sighed, running his fingers through his long hair. 'Baccharus, I really do appreciate you looking out for me. It's such a rare trait in your kind I'd be a fool not to recognise it. But this is something I have to do. There's so much at stake here for all . . . all the Fragile Creatures. And at the moment only Ruth and I can do something about it. I wish someone else was having to do the business, but that's not the way it is.'

Baccharus's stare was still intense. 'How does your journey here, in the depths, bear upon your mission?'

The question was curious, the fact that Baccharus was asking it more so. 'How did you know I'd be here anywhere? Have you been spying on me?'

Baccharus appeared a little taken aback by the question, but not hurt or irritated; the emotions of the Tuatha Dé Danann were so difficult to read he might simply have had no idea what Church was talking about.

Church thought a moment. 'The Portunes. Running through the walls. That one was with you when you saved Ruth. So why are you particularly interested in us?'

Baccharus, in his usual honest manner, did not attempt to bat it away. 'A long story.'

'And when we get back topside you're going to tell me. But right now—'

'You must not continue. The danger is out of control. The Malignos are preparing for something unpleasant. Your fellow Fragile Creature, the one tainted by the Night Walkers—'

'Callow.'

'—he has whispered secrets to them, given them guidance. My associates are searching for them now, but they can wrap the night around them.'

Something was jangling deep in Church's head. '*Your* associates? Why isn't Manannan doing something about this if it's such a threat?'

Baccharus didn't answer.

'What's going on here, Baccharus? The five of us, the Brothers and Sisters of Dragons, we've been run like rats and had our lives ruined by your people. I'm not having any more of it. I feel like some massive thing has been going on all the time we've been on this ship, but Ruth and I have seen only a tiny part of it. Used when your people feel it suits their needs. Ignored or barely tolerated the rest of the time.'

'No.' Baccharus's voice was firm. 'If you knew the truth, you would not say that.'

Church searched his face; something sharply human hung there, something few of the other Golden Ones carried. A faint sound echoed nearby. Church glanced over his shoulder. 'This isn't the time. I have to find the Walpurgis.'

'I will take you to him.'

Church's attention snapped back. 'You know where he is?'

'If it will prevent you blundering into the areas of greatest peril, I will accede to your request.' He strode out along the branching corridor, then turned right down another branch that Church hadn't noticed. Church was rooted for a second, but then he skipped into step behind the hurrying god.

Church lost track of how many junctions they came up on, and the constant branching made his head spin. When he had set off below-deck, the corridor had stretched on and on with no other side-route, but Baccharus found a myriad, lurking in shadows, or disguised as hanging drapes. At first Church fired numerous questions, but when the god refused to answer any of them, Church fell into a steady silence, trying to make some sense of his topsy-turvy thoughts.

Eventually Baccharus came to a halt before a stretch of corridor that was lit more brightly than most of the others. The wall in this area was of wooden timbers, uneven and nondescript. He rested one hand on it, fingers splayed, bowed his head and muttered something under his breath. The wall became like the running water of a waterfall. Baccharus strode through it. Church jumped behind him, expecting to get soaked, but it felt like the overhead hot air heaters some shops treat their customers to on a wet winter's day.

On the other side was a large chamber, comfortably fitted out with thick rugs, heavy tapestries on the polished wood walls, chairs and tables bearing a few half-filled goblets and trays of dried fruit and nuts. Several figures were scattered around. They broke off from what appeared to be intense conversation to stare at him. There were a few members of the Tuatha Dé Danann Church recognised by sight, but whose names he didn't know, a smattering of Portunes scurrying around like mice, and one or two of the odd figures he had glimpsed at the banquet. At his gaze, these moved back into the shadows where the torches did not reach.

'What's going on here?' he asked suspiciously. His hand moved towards his sword as the half-thought entered his head that Baccharus might have led him into a trap.

'We are all friends here.' Marik Bocat squatted on the back of a chair, shouting, although his voice sounded barely more than a whisper.

'Then why are you hiding away?'

'The situation is complex,' Baccharus said. 'Perhaps it is time to unveil it to you.' He turned to the others. 'This is Jack, Brother of Dragons.' All those who had not been introduced to Church before bowed their heads.

'Maybe later.' Church walked to the centre of the room and looked around. 'First, I want to talk to the Walpurgis.'

A fluttering bundle of rags emerged from the gloom at the back of the chamber. Beneath the broad-brimmed hat, the hot coal eyes glowed as intensely as Church recalled. 'I am here.' His voice was a chill wind over a graveyard.

Church put the confusing scenario to the back of his mind. There were more important subjects. But first he had to know if he was right. 'Did you kill Cormorel?'

'He did not,' Baccharus interjected.

'I want to hear it from him.'

'I do not kill.'

Church nodded thoughtfully. 'You said you were a Messenger. With a message for me. A message that was very clear.' The Walpurgis stared, said nothing. 'What is the message?'

'Do you not want your dream examined?'

The Walpurgis was talking about the hidden memory of who had really killed Marianne; the identity of the traitor amongst them. 'Yes. More than anything. But first, this.'

The Walpurgis came forward, pushing cold air before him that raised the goosebumps on Church's arms. When he was only a few feet away, the tattered creature intoned gravely, 'You will find no peace in this world. For some, that is the way it must be.'

Church's heart fell. The Walpurgis's words were like a death-knell, tolling out his deepest fears.

'But you must not lose hope.' The Walpurgis reached out a papery hand. 'You must never lose hope. You are part of something much larger than what lies around you. Many will benefit from your sacrifice.'

'Do you think that's enough?' The bitterness in Church's voice shocked even himself. He looked around the gathered faces and was unnerved by how they were hanging on his every word. 'All the pain I've already had. My girlfriend . . . my love . . . the love of my life . . . murdered. All the grief that followed, beating myself up because I thought she'd committed suicide, that I was *responsible*. Laura . . . the young Marianne . . . all the other ones I've seen die.' Ruth's face flashed into his mind, followed by a sharp pang of regret that was almost painful. 'And now I can see a way out, some kind of good life ahead for a change, and you're telling me it's not going to happen? No fucking way.'

The Walpurgis took another pace with his outstretched hand, oddly comforting now, but Church waved it away.

'I don't want to hear it.'

'These things are written, Jack.' Baccharus's voice was sympathetic too.

'What do you know about it?'

'You are a Brother of Dragons—'

'Yes, I know my responsibility and I've accepted it. But once I've done all I can do, that's it. No more Fabulous Beasts, no more *waking the sleeping king* and all that Arthurian shit, no more Blue Fire. I'm getting my life back.'

'Then you think you can actually do something? In the face of such overwhelming odds? That *a life* still awaits you?' Baccharus's words, as always, were calm and measured.

Church turned back to the Walpurgis. 'Now. I want to know who killed Marianne.'

'There is always something bigger, Jack.' Baccharus's voice sounded closer and more intense, although he had not taken a step. 'Bigger powers. Bigger plans.'

'Show me,' Church said harshly to the Walpurgis.

The Walpurgis began to move. Church felt butterflies in his stomach. This was it: the final, bitter revelation. He put his head back, closed his eyes and waited for the Walpurgis to push his fingers into Church's mind.

Something was nagging at him as he waited. Not the silence in the room, so heavy he could almost feel currents flowing through it. Not the way the hairs on the back of his neck were prickling, the way his gut was knotting in dread at what he would discover. He felt his nostrils flaring and that triggered recognition; smell, the least developed of all his senses, the reason why he had not been able to pinpoint Marianne's killer. Smell.

An odour was shifting gently through the room, caught on the subtle movements of air caused by the heat from the torches. The primal part of his brain kicked into gear, generating memories before he had even identified the source: the adrenalin, wild, wild action and then the rush of terror that was so all-consuming it could only come from one source. The stinking, zoo-cage smell of them.

'Fomorii.' The word was on his lips before the thought had found purchase in his head. It appeared to be a word of power, for in the instant that followed, very many things happened at once: there was a rushing through the chamber like a mighty wind; the smell grew suddenly choking; his eyes snapped open to reveal faces frozen in disbelief; and movement, all around, so rapid his eyes at first couldn't focus on it, like the shadows in the room were breathing.

The Walpurgis was framed in his field of vision, hanging in that single moment like everything else in the room. Church took in the seething red eyes, which glowed brighter, as if fanned by the breeze, the wide-brimmed hat, the tattered black rags of his body. And in the next instant they started to come apart. Scarlet lines were being drawn across the figure. A section across the arm here, across the torso there, underlining the head, pointing up the waist. Spaces appeared between the segments; a hallucinogenic moment filled with fascination. The Walpurgis was falling apart.

He snapped from the moment as if someone had punched him in the face. The room was in turmoil. The occupants dashed here and there searching for an exit as dark shapes moved lethally amongst them. For only the briefest time, Church focused on the remains of the Walpurgis scattered across the floor before him, consumed by the immensity of what had been snatched away from him; wondering how his future life had been changed by that one moment.

And then he was moving instinctively, just as some heavy object whistled past his ear. One of his fellow passengers with tentacles where his face should be lay in chunks under his feet. He skidded on the remains before finding his balance, propelling himself toward the place where he had entered the secret chamber.

The Fomorii were all around, moving so quickly it was impossible for him to estimate how many of them there were.

His thoughts were cut short by a heavy axe that splintered into the wooden wall next to his head. Thinking would be the end of him; he gave himself wholly over to instinct. The chaos of fighting bodies, flashing weapons and striking limbs became a series of frozen instants through which he could dart and dive. All his reactions had improved immeasurably in recent times, more than just learning from experience; it was the Blue Fire, or Destiny, or whatever he wanted to call it. He was changing.

He dodged another Fomorii attack that increasingly appeared to be directed towards him. The Tuatha Dé Danann were fighting back ferociously. Church slid towards the entrance through a stinking, poisonous grue washing across the floor. But it was a solid wall, and he had no idea what Baccharus had done to make it accessible.

The stink and shadow overwhelmed him before he glimpsed any hint of movement; then he realised an axe was swinging down with such force it would likely cleave him in two. Reacting instantly, his hand was on his sword, whipping it up sharply. The blade just caught the handle of the axe at such an angle that it managed to deflect the strike slightly, but the impact jarred his bones so much he thought his teeth were coming out of his head. He went down on one knee. The Fomor was already raising the axe for the killing blow.

A flashing motion crossed the beast's throat and its thick, stinging blood came gushing out. Church threw himself out of the way at the last moment, watching as it sizzled into the wooden floor.

Baccharus stepped forward as the creature slumped down, wiping a small, sharp blade. 'Now, quickly.' He made a hand motion and muttered, and the wall became like water.

Church was just about to dive through when a figure burst out of the shimmering wall, knocking him to the ground. Others followed, and in a second he and Baccharus were surrounded. They were not Fomorii, but they were misshapen, lithe and reptilian, with scales and slit eyes. *The Malignos*, Church guessed. As they huddled around, bending over him with forked tongues darting, he felt so destabilised the only thought in his head was that they smelled like wet grass.

He saw a glint of teeth, sharp talons, and then the circle of them parted and in stepped a maliciously gleeful figure.

'Now we shall find a balance for old wrongs,' Callow said sardonically.

The voice sounded like the rustle of brown paper just beyond the window, where only the sea spray lived. Ruth had been dozing intermittently on the bunk, but she woke sharply when the familiar tones insidiously infected her drifting mind with memories of cells and chains and torture. Throwing open the windows to the crashing waves of a burgeoning storm, she frightened the owl, which fluttered upward towards the deck like the ghost of a bird in the gloomy night. Yet its words stayed in her head like a bad taste: 'The war has begun.'

A tremor ran through her; a premonition, perhaps. She riffled in the chest and came up with a long, thin dagger, ideal for poisonous court intrigue, but little use in any fair fight. But it was easy to secrete upon herself, and she had other weapons for confrontation, locked away in her brain. An insurance policy, nothing else.

Her familiar's warning could have meant nothing at that time, but she thought she ought to discuss it with Baccharus at least. Yet as she made her way to the door she heard an unidentifiable sound without that brought a shiver to her spine. She rocked briefly on the balls of her feet, then hurried back to the bunk, glancing round for somewhere to hide. Not so long ago she would have dismissed her instinct as stupid and childish; now she trusted it implicitly. She realised there was no worthwhile hiding place in the cramped chamber. She flung open the windows again. Beneath her the waves crashed crazily, topped with white surf. The boat dipped and rose sharply. Lightning crackled along the horizon as the storm rushed towards them.

A slim wooden spur ran around the boat, slightly below the level of the window. It was slick with spray, barely wide enough to get a toe-hold, but an oily rope stretched above from which members of the crew could hang if they needed to make repairs.

Don't be stupid! the rational side of her brain yelled at her. The ship rolled from side to side. *You'll be off there in a second.* And if she fell into the tossing sea, she would be lost in a moment. No one would even know she was overboard.

She looked back at the door. The strange noises, both rumbling and slithering at the same time, were closing on it. Steeling herself, she launched a leg out of the window, clutching at the rope and swung on to the ledge. With her other foot, she kicked the windows shut.

This is insanity. You really have lost it. But the warnings sounded like the faint, dying voice of the old Ruth, who had been supplanted by someone smarter, braver, more in control.

Outside the comfort of the cabin, the full fury of the night assailed her. The spray lashed against her like ice bullets, while the ship bucked on waves that appeared to grow fiercer the instant she stepped outside. Bracing her feet against the spur, she hung on as if she were about to abseil down the side. Self-preservation took over all thought processes; nothing concerned her beyond the strength of her arms and the intensity of her grip, on which her whole life depended.

Through the smeared panes, she could just make out the golden-suffused interior of the cabin. It looked warm and comforting, and safe.

She leaned over to get a better look and had to fight to prevent herself sliding off the rail. Steadying herself with one hand on the sopping boards, she tried again, just as the door eased open. Through it came a shadow with substance that still made her gorge rise however many times she saw it. The Fomorii were onboard.

After the shock, her initial thought was for Church. She prayed that however the Fomorii had got on, they had focused their attentions on the upper decks where the Tuatha Dé Danann were, and not surprised Church in the dark below.

The Fomorii swept into the cabin and turned everything over. The smashing and rending should have alerted someone, but when no one came after a full five minutes of destruction, Ruth feared the worst.

Suddenly she thought that they might see her through the window. She pushed herself back a little too animatedly, throwing her careful balance awry; both feet slipped off the rail. For an instant she was like a cartoon character, frantically scrambling for purchase on the side of the boat, her feet kicking over the drop into the waves that clamoured for her.

Her toes slid and slid, and then she dropped. The arm that clung on to the rope took the full force of her weight, jerking her like a puppet. Fiery pain shot through her tendons and muscles into her armpit. Her fingers felt like they were going to snap; they slipped around the rope, barely holding. Wildly, she lurched out with the hand that had been leaning against the boards, missed, tried again, missed.

All she could see was wet wood and spray and the hungry waves below. Her fingers slipped a little more, barely holding on now. An unbearable heat was burning in her knuckles.

Finally her free hand caught hold, but she was still hanging tight against the boards, slamming into them with every roll of the ship. Any second now, she would be knocked off.

Four months ago, it would have been too much of an effort to save herself: too much pain, not enough desire. She would have hung there until her knuckles finally gave way, feeling the skin strip from her fingers as they slid down the rope, and then the long drop into the hard, cold, suffocating depths.

But she *was* a different person; her suffering at the hands of the Fomorii had seen to that. Somehow, for all the agony, it had brought out the best of her, given her a reason to live beyond all else; a dichotomy too great for her to ponder.

With tremendous willpower, she clamped her fingers tight on the rope. Flexing her muscles, she rocked back and forth, bouncing off the boat, but with a bigger and bigger space between her and the wood until she could bring her feet up to plant them on the side. Then it was only a matter of inching up slowly until she found the rail again.

Finally she could peer through the window to see the cabin was empty. Shaking from the shock, she managed to hook the window open with her foot before swinging in on the rope to land hard on the bunk. It winded her, but she felt exhilarated at her victory over death.

It faded too quickly, to be replaced by that familiar unease. Cautiously, she approached the door. No sound came from beyond except the usual creak of the timbers. How many Fomorii were there on board? And where were they now?

After a moment's reflection, she gripped the dagger tightly, eased open the door and slipped out into the dark corridor.

The mists had a disturbingly cloying texture that felt like wet cotton wool slowly being drawn across the skin. For Veitch, that wasn't the worst thing, although it was unnerving enough. Nor was it the chill that reached deep into his bones, even though the air itself was not particularly cold. It wasn't even the way the mists occasionally cleared to reveal brief glimpses of a terrifying scene, different every time it happened, too quick to ever settle on any detail, but enough for the subconscious mind to know it was shocking. It was the feeling of someone constantly at his shoulder, about to draw icy fingers down his neck, but whenever he turned round, there was nothing but the subdued echoes of his footsteps.

His destabilisation began the moment he stepped into the Grim Lands and discovered the door through which he had passed was no longer there. How would he ever find his way back?

But there were many things to do before he even had to think about getting back, and it was possible he might not have to worry about it at all, so, true to his nature, he simply put it out of his mind.

Occasionally the mists cleared enough to provide a view of the lowering gunmetal sky. Oppressive enough, he also glimpsed black shapes sweeping across it; birds, he guessed, but of a size that made him think of pterodactyls. Perhaps it was their unnerving silence, but there was something immensely threatening about them, although he never saw them in enough detail to decide if they were raptors. But that gave him pause. If he was in the land of the dead, were they dead too? Or did the Grim Lands have its own life? Dead life.

Thinking about it made his head hurt. He wished Tom had given some directions. A *Rough Guide of the Grim Lands*, with a nice tourist map. Avoid this place, especially after dark. You'll get a good welcome here. And here you'll find Shavi.

But he was on his own, as always. He went for the simplest option: keep walking and something would turn up; then adjust your path accordingly. He just wished that terrible feeling of something at his heels would go away.

The uneven terrain alternated between hard rock and shale. What he could make out of the landscape was featureless, with no markers for his journey there or back. Nor was there anything to judge the passage of time, so it was impossible to tell how soon after he entered the Grim Lands that he heard the noises. At first it was like scratching, as if a dog were trying to claw something out from beneath the shale. This came and went for a while, continuously matching his progress, and then, gradually, it mutated into the sound of footsteps, echoing near at hand, then far away, then disappearing completely. He had to accept there was something out there and it was tracking him.

His hand went to his sword for comfort, though he knew it would be useless in that place. He tried not to get distracted; head down, keep going, a mantra he repeated over and over.

And then, as if they had been commanded, the mists parted and a figure emerged from them. It was a woman, her face blank, her skin a pallid grey, clad in an ankle-length, colourless dress of some harsh material. Long blonde hair hung limply around her face. Her head was held uncomfortably towards one shoulder and she moved awkwardly, as if her limbs were not used to any activity. She paused a few feet away from Veitch, swaying slightly.

'Hello?' he said tentatively. A beat had started to pulse deep in his brain.

Instead of turning her head, she inched her whole body round until she was facing him. He expected to see some kind of terror, some severe intelligence in her eyes, but they were cold and dead and that was even worse. Slowly, she beckoned for him to follow her.

For a second or two, Veitch hesitated as Tom's words briefly tapped a warning: the dead hate the living. They were jealous and bitter. Yet he could see no threat in her, and following her was preferable to wandering aimlessly; any presence, however strange, was a respite from the awful sense of foreboding gathering all around.

'I'm looking for someone.' His voice, so vibrant and full of life, sounded jarringly out of place. He modulated it so it sounded less expressive. 'A friend.'

She turned towards him with those eyes that showed no glimmer of thought, gave nothing away, then shuffled back round silently and continued slowly on her way.

'So, are you ignoring me? Or can you talk? Who knows what the bleedin' rules are in this place?' He eased a little as the minutes passed without event and slowly he warmed to the sound of his voice, like a flame in the deep, dark night. 'I hope this isn't a wild goose chase. For all I know, you've got no sense left at all. You're just a shape or something. And I'm acting like a right twat talking to you. No change there, then.' He smiled to himself. 'This isn't as bad as I thought. The old bastard built it up into some big, bleedin' fright. Thought I'd be fighting for my life the moment I crossed over here. And look at us. Having a nice stroll. Shame about the scenery.' He paused thoughtfully. 'Still better than Greenwich, though.' His chuckle rolled out through the mists, eventually coming back to him distorted into the growl of a wild beast.

They continued until the ground sloped downwards and became littered at first with stones, and then with large boulders. Veitch had to pick his way through them carefully, but the woman moved effortlessly, almost oblivious to the obstacles.

'You really better not be taking me for a ride.' He clambered over a rock with lethal-looking fractured edges, as sharp as razors.

Beyond the rocks, passage became even steeper and it was necessary to take a winding route down to avoid careering out of control. Veitch was disturbed to realise his journey was like a distorted analogue of the landscape he had left behind in the real world: the flat summit, the thickly forested rim, the sweeping hillside; instead of lush vegetation there were only dead land and dead people. He wasn't taken with many thoughts of reasoning or perception, but at that moment one came to him that excited him with its novelty. Perhaps all the words – T'ir n'a n'Og, the Grim Lands, and whatever lay beyond – were just like his own world in layout, only altered to fit whatever rules of the place abided. It was a big notion, and there were too many questions building up behind it to consider it for too long, but he felt a remarkable sense of achievement that he had thought it in the first place.

As he made his way down the hillside, the mist cleared a little. What he saw wasn't as disturbing as on the summit, but it still brought troubling questions. At one juncture, he seemed to be looking out over London, only it was transformed by shadows shifting along the streets with a life of their own. Later he saw a Spitfire sweeping across the sky, and then a tribe of fierce men and women in furs and leather.

And in one particularly upsetting moment, he even saw himself, or thought he did, but it was so fleeting he couldn't be sure. Yet in that half-moment, he was overcome with a consuming horror. The expression he saw on his face had the look of a man who had peered into the depths of Hell and saw it was even worse than he could possibly imagine; broken, filled with despair, and more, an almost inhuman self-loathing. It made him sick to his stomach at the thought of what that vision meant, but try as he might, he couldn't put it out of his head.

It troubled him enough to lose his commonsense briefly. Suddenly overcome by doubt that his guide was taking him no closer to Shavi, he hurried forward and grabbed her arm. He regretted it instantly. The flesh felt as dry and lifeless as sandpaper. At his touch, a tremor ran through the woman and she turned once again to fix that blank gaze on him. Once more he tried to see some meaning in those implacable eyes, but there was only a defiant idiocy there. He retreated quickly and didn't speak to her again for the next half hour.

By then his thoughts had started to move on to more questions about his surroundings. Did all the dead stay in that place? If so, why was it so empty after the long spread of human existence? Or was it like a waiting room before the departed moved on to somewhere else?

'Maybe this is it, just you and me, and everyone else has already passed on,' he mused. 'The only living boy in the Grim Lands and his dead girlfriend.'

'Oh, there are more.' He jerked in shock at the sound of her voice, like a file on metal.

'You *can* talk.' All his carefully constructed conceptions were shifting under his feet. His mind raced to get back on track; he was thinking, *If she can talk, what else can she do?* but by then it was too late.

The remaining mist swept away, although he could not feel any breeze. It was an eerie sight, billowing across the bleak landscape like a reversed film. As it did so, she was turning to face him once again, only this time she was fundamentally changed. Her posture had become more upright, but it was most evident in her eyes, no longer dead, no longer stupid.

He thought: *She tricked me.*

The tinge of a cruel smile appeared. 'Welcome to the Grey Lands. May you never leave.'

She made an expansive gesture. Hesitantly, he turned to look, although every fibre of him was screaming that he didn't want to see.

They were behind him. Dead people, as far as the eye could see, line upon line, column upon column, stretched across the grey stone land beneath the grey sky. Figures leeched of colour, of expression, of body language, bereft of life in all its signifiers. But not bereft of emotion. Although their faces were impassive, he could see it in their hateful eyes. A thousand, thousand unblinking stares radiating darkness, silently roaring that they wanted to tear him limb from limb; to punish him for the crime of living. The planetary weight of their gaze made him feel sick.

As he scanned them slowly, he began to understand. Here were the ones who had not yet moved on, but also the ones who *could not* move on; those trapped by hatred or fear or shock. He came across the face of Ruth's uncle, whom he had shot down in cold blood, and felt a terrible, crushing guilt. To understand the awful repercussions of the murder had been traumatic enough, but to be faced with the cold, accusing eyes of his victim was infinitely worse. He quickly looked away, knowing he would never forget what he had seen in that face. But there were others he had seen slain during the long, hard days of his youth, when he first started to move with the wrong kind. The ones nearest were unknown to him, but he could still read the harshness of their existence in the lines on their faces, the sour turn of their mouths.

It was a strange, hanging moment of complete silence; he was look-ing up at a tidal wave the instant before it crashed down. And then they moved.

Veitch launched himself across the rocky ground as the wave broke. In the instant of his turning he had glimpsed them all shifting as one, a single grey beast of hatred and retribution bearing down on him with outstretched arms, wide, staring eyes and silently screaming mouths. A million dead, hunting. If he survived, he knew it was a sight that would haunt him for as long as he lived.

As he passed the treacherous spirit that had guided him to that spot, she spat like a wildcat and lashed out with sharp nails that raked open the side of his face. Without breaking his stride, he cursed and returned the blow with his sword. Her bloodless arm fell to the ground.

The fear and adrenalin took conscious thought from his head. Instinctively he recognised his only hope was to run faster and longer. But could the dead tire? And he had already been pushed to his limits by the Night Rider.

The ground passed in a blur beneath his feet, the featureless, rocky landscape streamed on either side; he was locked into the beat of his heart, the surge of his blood, the pump of his muscles. Through it all he could feel the weight of them pressing at his back, just a hand's-width from him, constantly reaching. One wrong step and they would have him.

And he ran.

The silence was the worst thing. His ears told him there was nothing there, seductively teasing him to stop, but the primal part of him sensed them, responded to them as his ancestors would have done. He had reached the foot of the hill, crossed the first two miles of a flat plain that reached to the horizon. But he was starting to tire. The constant pounding on the hard rock sent spikes of pain from his knees into his groin and a knot had formed in his gut. Fire was creeping out in a web across his lungs.

He slowed, almost imperceptibly, but it was enough. Some fluttering thing brushed the back of his jacket. He propelled himself forward to escape it, but he didn't have the energy to maintain the spurt. When he slowed this time, the touch on his jacket was as sharp as a knife. He pressed forward again. Stars burst across his vision. Winding down, nearly over. A pinching sensation seared his shoulder like red hot pokers. The hairs on the back of his neck were prickling from nearly-contact.

He would never give up. Death or glory.

The rock fell away beneath his feet. For one frightening moment he was pedalling thin air, and then he reconnected with the ground hard, skidding on his heels down a pebbled scree-slope, windmilling his arms to maintain his balance. Dark walls rushed up around him and shadows clustered far below. A fissure of some kind, invisible until he was upon it.

Gravity dragged him faster, barely able to keep his balance. A boulder leapt out of nowhere, but he had no control of his momentum to avoid it. He clipped it and did a forward roll in the air, crashing down on to the stones and shale, twenty knives in his back, ripping his flesh. Faster and faster, the shadows looming up, impossible to tell what dangers they hid. His head slammed against the rocks and he lost consciousness for the briefest instant. He awakened to realise the sucking shadows were close at hand. The force propelled him over a rock ledge into the heart of them.

He awoke in so much pain he was convinced something bad was broken. Blood slicked his clothes from a deep gash on his head and numerous other cuts across his body. He wiped a puddle from his eye and loosed the splatter with a flick of his wrist. Cautiously, he tested his limbs. Apart from a searing pain in his ribs, he appeared in one piece; he guessed that was probably bad bruising rather than a break.

After the initial stupefaction, he came to awareness sharply, jumping to his feet to flee his pursuers. He was alone on a flat stone floor. High overhead he could see a sliver of grey sky and, as his eyes adjusted to the gloom, the shapes of the dead moving down the walls of the fissure towards him.

Exhausted and brittle from the pain, he headed along the floor of the fissure into the dark.

It continued much further than he imagined. At the far end he found stone that had definitely been worked into blocks. It formed a doorway around a black hole leading into the ground. With the relentless grey shapes drawing in on him, he had no choice: he dived in.

Inside he was surprised to find more worked stone lining the walls, floor and ceiling. He had no idea who was responsible – surely not the dead – but it gave him hope it might lead to a way out. Fumbling for the matches he always carried in his pocket, he struck one and saw the walls were covered with primitive paintings, inexplicable in·design but which resonated uneasily with him. The match also illuminated a dead torch. It was dry as a bone and lit quickly.

Glancing back, he could just make out hints of movement at the other end of the fissure. There was no time to proceed with caution. His footsteps bounced off the walls of the tunnel as he ran.

After five minutes the tunnel led into an enormous room that must have been carved from the bedrock and then lined with stone blocks. The ceiling was lost in the shadows far beyond the reach of his torch.

The effort that must have gone into its construction stunned him: the wall paintings were now the size of three men, and there were carved effigies all around, squat, misshapen figures with no human character-istics, and tall, spindly forms that loomed over him like grotesque children's doodles. He couldn't help slowing to a walk to mask the echoes of his feet; suddenly he didn't want to make any sound that would bring attention to him. The scale of the place suggested no human sensibilities, nor did the jarring lines of the alien and unsettling architecture. It reminded him of a temple. Did the dead have their own gods? Did they pray for relief from the bitterness of their grey reality?

The grey shapes were again visible where he had entered the cavern-ous chamber. He hurried on, hoping he hadn't taken himself into a cul-de-sac.

But the more he progressed into that place, the more he felt an oppressive dread, even worse than the feeling when he had first entered the Grim Lands. Something was out there, lurking in the shadows, perhaps, or even further afield: just beyond the spiderweb veil that separated the worlds. Close enough to reach out and swallow him whole.

Do the dead have their own gods?

He couldn't shake the question from his head.

Before he could consider skirting the perimeter in search of an exit, he found himself at a slightly raised area. At the centre of it was a short column on which stood a foot-high egg, its surface swirling with shades of sapphire and emerald. The moment he laid eyes on it, a part of him told him to avoid it, keep moving by. But there was something hypnotic about the thing that sapped his natural caution. He took a step on to the dais and realised obliquely it was even more than that: the egg was actively blanketing his fears to draw him in; he could feel it tinkering on the edge of his consciousness. The time when he could have ignored it had already past, and so he found himself approaching the column with trepidation.

Three feet from the egg he passed through some invisible boundary. The air wavered briefly and then he was inside a bubble where every-thing was green-tinged, the chamber beyond unreal, all sounds muffled. The egg was pulsing slightly, although it was certainly not alive in any true meaning of that word.

Tentatively, he reached out. The air itself gathered a charge, hum-ming like an electricity pylon. A second later he felt a dull jolt and the bubble transformed. He was in the centre of a three-dimensional view, so real he might as well have been amongst the ruins of Urquhart Castle on the banks of Loch Ness, looking down at himself being charged by the Questing Beast. The detail left no doubt that it was a true view, across time and space. Had it been plucked from his mind, he wondered? And if so, why that moment? He had a vague answer to that: it was the moment when he felt he had really, truly failed, not only everyone else, but also himself.

The repercussions of what he was seeing began to worm its way through his mind. On a hunch, he thought of Ruth and what she was doing at that moment. The 3-D view shifted and he was on the rolling deck of a boat in the middle of a night-time storm. The rain was flying horizontally, the sails flapping so wildly it was almost deafening. A figure crept in the shadow of the raised cover to the hold, its long hair flattened to its head and back. As he watched, Ruth looked around, her face grimly determined. The first thing Veitch noticed was how much her features had changed in the short time they had been apart. A hardness made her appear, if not a little older, then certainly more mature; some of the innocence that softened her features had gone.

Seeing her brought a damp wave of emotion inside him, but in an odd way it invigorated him too; here was all the motivation he needed. Focusing his mind, he pushed Ruth out of it and thought of Shavi.

There was only the briefest period of transition before the image around him showed a strange, hopeless landscape of yellowing grass and twisted, leafless trees. Shavi sat on a stone box of some kind, staring deeply towards the horizon. Veitch couldn't tell if there was anything wrong with him or if he was simply lost in thought.

'That's a start,' he muttered. 'Now show me how I get to him.'

He was now looking down on himself standing at the egg, only the shadows all around had cleared to reveal several tunnels leading off. The angle of his view highlighted one directly ahead.

Cautiously he walked backwards until he stepped out of the bubble with a faint pop. Away from the magical cocoon, he felt suddenly exposed and hurried towards the tunnel, pausing at the threshold to look back. Curiously, the dead did not appear to have pursued him; he would have expected some of them to have arrived by that time. Something else was in the chamber, though far away. He could hear the dim echoes of the movement of an enormous shape. With an involuntary shudder, he hurried along the tunnel.

Laura lit a small fire in the corner of the warehouse while the Bone Inspector foraged for food. The last time he came back with cans for just the one meal. She berated him enough that he wouldn't make the mistake again, stressing that a choice between meatballs resembling glutinous chunks of mud and fatty steak pie filling was really no choice at all.

In the cavernous warehouse, the fire provided little warmth, particularly at night when the chill radiated up out of the concrete floor. For some reason she felt the cold more than she ever had.

She pulled the packing crate closer so she was almost on top of the flames and rubbed her hands together. She found it amazing she still hadn't given in to despair. The Fomorii now appeared to be everywhere in the city. They'd climbed up into the roof of the building to peer through broken slates across the capital. There were swarming black shapes as far as the eye could see. The sheer volume was sickening, drawing on the basic human revulsion for anything insectile. At times they would disappear to some lair, possibly beneath the ground, in an eerie, silent exodus. The Bone Inspector had suggested fleeing through the deserted streets at that time, but the beasts were never gone for long and the thought of being trapped as they swarmed out of the sewers filled Laura with dread.

In the firelight, her skin looked even greener. Earlier she had cut her wrist on a rusty nail. The blood – green blood – had flowed freely for a second before performing a startling u-turn on the back of her hand, returning to the wound, where it proceeded to seal it as if it had never been there.

The Bone Inspector had stared in amazement, but nothing shocked her any more. She'd died and come back; after that anything paled into insignificance.

She was a freak in a world that no longer made any sense. What was the point in considering it for even an instant? Instead, her thoughts were for the others: Church, of course, Shavi, Ruth, Tom, even Veitch. She missed them in a way she never thought she'd miss anyone. More than anything, she wanted to be sitting round a roaring campfire in the cold night, laughing, teasing, mocking; the company of good friends made life right.

The army of Fomorii on every side told her it would probably never happen. Samhain was coming up hard, the world was going to hell, and they were scattered God knows where.

She wondered what was to become of her; what was to become of all of them.

The rope bit roughly into Church's wrists and his joints ached from having his arms dragged so tightly behind him. He'd been in this position before, looking up at a sneering Callow pacing maniacally and triumphantly back and forth, and it had made him sick to his stomach then; of course, on that occasion Callow hadn't looked like someone had injected printer's ink into his veins. Now his nightmarish appearance made the situation even worse, as if Church had found his way into a Goya painting.

The Malignos kept to the shadows – they'd extinguished several torches to feel more comfortable – and the Fomorii were now nowhere to be seen. Baccharus was next to him, bound just as tightly, but the rest of the room's occupants had been dragged somewhere else, out of sight, possibly out of the chamber.

It was obvious what his own eventual fate would be, but Callow was determined to get some kind of payback for the suffering that had been heaped upon him; agonies which he blamed on Church and the others, but which had come only from his own will.

'These are the ways we live our life,' Callow was saying, not making much sense any more. 'In fear of this and in fear of that, never quite knowing the wherewithal and the whywithal. It makes us broken, like dogs in the yard. But you wouldn't know about that, would you?' He turned and spat in Church's direction, the lamps of his lidless eyes bright and terrible.

'Take a stress pill, Callow.' It was childish, but Church couldn't resist it, even knowing the reaction he would get.

Callow hovered for a long moment, then threw himself forward wildly to swing a vicious kick into Church's gut, as if he were planting a football the length of the pitch. Church snapped shut, retching, before two of the Malignos ran forward to haul him back up. The pain was so acute he cursed his stupidity, fearing something had ruptured and his stomach was now filling up with blood.

'Violence is unnecessary,' Baccharus interjected gently. 'You fail to see we have a common enemy.'

'Oh, you're *so* superior,' Callow mocked in a pathetic singsong voice. 'I have no friends, I have no enemies. That makes it easy to understand how things work. No surprises.' He bent down until his face was inches from Church's, the rotten-meat reek of his breath blooming, his features hideously distorted by the tear-blur in Church's eyes. 'You and your filthy little followers destroyed everything. I had plans for my life. I had a way out of the misery of my existence. Unlike you and your favoured brood, there have been no opportunities in my life. No pleasant acts of chance that lead me on to the sunlit uplands. It has been hard toil and suffering. And when I found a way out of that, you spoiled it for me.'

'Quisling,' Church said through gritted teeth. 'You tried to sell out all of humanity just to get some grubby little advantage for yourself.'

'You say that like it's a bad thing.' Callow jumped back, his eyes rolling like a madman. 'Life is brutal and short and we need to take what we can to make ourselves comfortable before the jaws of night close around us forever.'

'Fine. As long as no one else gets hurt in the process.'

'Oh, why qualify it? Will it matter you made a few people cry when the worms are crawling in and the worms are crawling out?'

'Look at yourself, Callow. Where's your self-analysis?' The sharp pain had turned to a dull throbbing. 'Has that philosophy worked for you? At all?'

'There is only hope,' Baccharus interjected, 'if you look beyond your petty concerns, to the needs of your fellow Fragile Creatures, to the needs of all things of existence. Everything is—'

'*You* should not preach goodwill to your fellow man.' Callow danced around him, but couldn't bring himself to strike out.

'So you've teemed up with those things now?' Church nodded towards the Malignos. 'Are they the only ones left who'll have you?'

'The Malignos recognise the opportunities for personal gain in any situation. They always loved their hoards of gold. And their human flesh, of course.'

'But you're helping the Fomorii again, after all they've done to you!'

'I may not be able to forgive, dear boy, but I am incisive enough not to antagonise the eventual winners.'

Church snorted bitter laughter. 'You think they're going to take over like any other invader? They're going to wipe out everything, you mad bastard! They're not interested in gold, or any other creature comforts.' He laughed again at the stupid pun. 'They're driven by the need to eradicate all of existence. They're a force of nature. A hurricane—'

'Oh, well, you've won me over. Of course I'll help you,' Callow mocked.

He wandered over to converse with the Malignos. Church seized the opportunity to talk to Baccharus. 'How did the Fomorii manage to get on board the ship without anyone knowing? I thought it was completely under Manannan's control?'

'The power of the Heart of Shadows is growing. The Night Walkers can achieve things they never would have been able to do before.'

'Do you think this might actually motivate your people to do something about it?' Church asked acidly.

'It may already be too late for that.'

'What do you mean?'

'If the Night Walkers can strike at the heart of Wave Sweeper, they can strike anywhere. They might have already launched their assault on the Court of High Regard.'

'If only you'd done something before.' Church caught the negativity before it spread. 'The first thing we have to do is get out of here.' He looked over at Callow, who was performing a mad little dance around the Malignos. 'Before that bastard slits my throat. Or worse.'

'Then you are fortunate to have friends in low places.'

The voice was barely audible, but Church recognised it instantly. It felt as if a mouse was scurrying around his hands. Marik Bocat was hard at work severing his bonds with a tiny implement that occasionally pricked his flesh. A surge of hope rose in his chest, but he kept it from reaching his face.

After a few moments, Callow returned, loping like a wolf. 'The arrangements have been made.' His eyes slithered from side to side while he rubbed his hands oleaginously. 'Once this filthy little skiff has fallen, then it's the turn of your happy little palace of dreams.'

Church felt Baccharus stiffen beside him at the news that the Fomorii had not yet moved on the High Court of the Tuatha Dé Danann. Still hope. Always hope. 'What now, Callow?' he said. 'Is this where you get your kicks?'

Callow slipped his hand into his threadbare jacket and pulled out a knife whose blade was smeared with dried, brown blood. Church tried not to look at it, but he knew it was the blood of his friends. Callow weighed it in his hand, smiled.

His bonds gave suddenly. He kept his face emotionless, his arm muscles taut. *Pace yourself,* he thought. *Wait until he bends forward.* His eyes flickered towards the Malignos; they were too far away to stop him if he was quick enough.

Callow struck like a snake. Church didn't even see the blow, but he felt his forehead rip open and hot blood bubble down into his eyes. He cursed, threw his head back, but Callow, in his crazed state, was sweeping in with eager blows. Church dodged one, but another took his cheek open. The next one might hit his jugular.

He threw himself forward at the same time as did Baccharus, whose own bonds had been sliced. They piled into Callow, who folded up like a sheet on a line, and then their impetus carried him with them as they drove towards the door. The Malignos exploded into a frenzied activity of snapping jaws and flashing limbs. One of their talons caught Church's other cheek and it burst open as cleanly as if it had been sliced with Callow's knife. Their speed was frightening. With reptilian sinuousness they had swept round to attack Church's and Baccharus's exposed backs, but by that time the two of them had reached the door. Baccharus shouted a word, twisted his left hand and the wall shimmered into the waterfall.

They rolled into the corridor with Callow screaming before them, his face contorted with rage. Church silenced him with a sharp headbutt; not wholly necessary, but it made him feel good. Then he grabbed Callow by the collar and hurled him into the path of the approaching Malignos. They fell backwards in time for Baccharus to seal the door.

'That will not keep them for long,' he said.

'Doesn't matter.' Church fingered the sword that Callow, in his arrogance had failed to remove. 'We need to raise the alarm—'

The words died in his throat as the ship came to a sudden, lurching stop. Baccharus's expression told him all he needed to know. The Fomorii had seized control.

CHAPTER ELEVEN

GRIM LANDS,
GREY HEARTS

It was a graveyard, though why there should be a graveyard in the land of the dead made no sense to Veitch at all. It stretched as far as the eye could see: stone crosses, gleaming white like fresh-picked bones, or chipped and mildewed, some standing proud, others bowed and broken as if they had been forced from the earth; single standing stones and ancient cairns; mausoleums styled with fine carvings of angels; rough built stone tombs. Mist drifted languorously at knee-height. The sheer weight of the monuments brought an air of severe melancholy.

As he emerged from the tunnel into the city of the dead, the view triggered all his primal fear of death. His more immediate fears were more prosaic: what if each of those graves and tombs and mausoleums contained one of the dead, ready to rise up the moment he walked amongst them? His heart beat faster.

There was no alternative. He placed a foot next to the first grave and waited for a hand to grab his ankle. Nothing. He proceeded to the next one.

After several minutes the tension was starting to tell. It felt like walking through a minefield. He couldn't let his concentration slide for a moment: if the dead were present, they would choose the moment he least expected to strike, when he was in the midst of the graves with nowhere to turn. He looked around slowly; there *was* nowhere to run. A million graves, packed so tight he could barely move amongst them.

The direction he had chosen – from the view presented to him by the egg – proceeded past one of the largest mausoleums in the vicinity. It haunted the edges of his vision and he found himself drawn back to it continually. Its size made it out of place in the surroundings, but there was another aspect that did not feel *right*. As he approached it, his gaze snapped back, and back again, on the heavy, marbled door, waiting for a crack to appear, on the way the mist appeared to be drawn towards it. A few feet away he was convinced he could hear something dimly scrabbling within, like an animal, but not.

When he was parallel with it, a small droplet of sweat trickled down his back, like water off a glacier. Even when he had passed by, his anxiety did not diminish, and he could feel it on his back for many moments after.

Eventually, his attention was drawn by what appeared to be a giant crow, sitting on a low, stone box. Shavi had his eyes fixed on the horizon, as Veitch had seen him in the vision presented by the egg. It didn't seem right that he was so still. He wanted to call out to his friend, but the thought of his voice, loud and hard in that place of whispers, filled him with dread.

And so he hurried on, his heart beginning to soar, hardly daring to raise his expectations. His mate, his pal, his buddy, his best friend; alive.

As he neared the unmoving form, he finally found the courage to speak. Shavi's name drifted across the final feet between them, as dry and insubstantial as the spindly trees that poked up amongst the graves. At first there was no response. Veitch's heart started to beat faster: it was all another stupid game, dangle the prize, then snatch it away at the last minute, laughing at how foolish the *Fragile Creatures* were.

But then a shiver ran through the hunched, dark form, as subtle as wind on long grass.

'Shavi?' Veitch repeated hopefully.

Another tremor. Slowly Shavi's head began to turn. Veitch caught his breath. Would he see something terrible in that face? The eyes of someone driven insane by the experience of dying?

Shavi's limbs moved with the gradual adjustment of a man waking from a deep sleep, and when he did look round, Veitch was relieved to see his old friend as he had always looked. Shavi blinked long and slowly, squinting slightly as he focused on Veitch.

'I was having the strangest dream.' His voice was strained, as if he hadn't spoken for a long time.

Veitch ran forward, beating down his surging emotions, and awkwardly put a celebratory arm round Shavi's shoulders before quickly pulling back. 'You're all right, mate. It's all going to be all right now.'

Shavi smiled faintly, brushed a lock of hair from Veitch's forehead. Veitch didn't flinch. As his waking became sharper, his attention was drawn to his surroundings. 'Where are we?'

'Don't worry about it,' Veitch said hastily. 'I know it looks like the biggest bleedin' graveyard you've ever seen, but you're not dead, all right?'

Shavi's brow furrowed. 'A graveyard? Is that what you are seeing?'

Now it was Veitch's turn to be puzzled. 'Don't you?'

Shavi covered his eyes, then slowly ran his fingers through his long, black hair before letting them drop cautiously to his chest. He tentatively probed the area around his heart. 'Callow. He stabbed me.' He examined his fingers for any sign of blood. 'The pain was . . . intense. Like needles being forced through my veins.' He looked up at Veitch with panic flaring in his eyes. 'He killed me.'

'Calm down, mate—'

'Lee was here.' He looked around wildly. 'He brought me into the land of the dead—'

Veitch took his shoulders roughly. 'Pull yourself together, pal. You're not dead. One of the freaks – the big, horny-headed bastard – he saved you. Well, not quite, but he kept you sort of half-alive and half-dead. I'm here to take you back.'

'This is not still a dream?'

'I'm here. Hit me if you want. But I'll hit you back, you dim bastard.'

Shavi smiled, calmed. 'Just a different kind of dream, then.'

'You can't wait to start talking bollocks, can you?' He helped Shavi to his feet. 'We've got to get you back to your body—' Shavi stiffened. 'Your body's not here.'

Shavi thought about this for a moment, then nodded in understanding. 'My essence has created this form to house it. There is so much to assimilate. You need to rejoin my essence to my body.'

'We don't know how much longer you can carry on like this before you really do peg out.'

Shavi took a few shaky steps, his legs quickly regaining their poise. 'The others?'

'Tom's with me. Don't know where the others are exactly. I think they're fine.'

'Ruth?'

'She's okay.'

They looked at each other for a moment, then broke out in broad grins, the telepathy of old friends replacing the need for talk.

'Then,' Shavi mused, 'the question is, how do we return?'

Unsure, Veitch surveyed the cluttered landscape of cold stone. 'I reckon we head back to the place where I came in, if we can find it. We'll find it,' he added positively.

They had to walk single-file to pick their way amongst the grave markers, but Veitch could still tell Shavi was distracted. 'What's wrong?' he asked.

'I was thinking about Lee.'

'Your boyfriend.'

'When he died that night in Clapham, I thought I had seen the last of him. My heart was broken, but also I was consumed with guilt because I was sure I could have done something to save his life. When the spirits in Edinburgh sent him back to haunt me as the price I had to pay for gaining their secret knowledge . . . I was almost pleased.' Veitch turned to stare at him, surprised by this new information. 'It was terrible – psychologically, emotionally – but I felt I deserved it. And even at the point of my death, he was there, ushering me across the boundary for more suffering.'

'So where is he now?'

'That is exactly what I was thinking. I do not really know what happened to me in the period that followed my death, but I do know that in some way I have come to terms with Lee's death, and my involvement in it. And now he is not here. It is almost as if the way I felt about myself turned *him* sour.' He paused thoughtfully. 'We make our own Hell, Ryan. In many ways, many times a day.'

Veitch continued his measured pace. 'You just be thankful you're shot of him.'

The hand closed round his ankle with the speed of a striking snake. It took him a second or two to realise what was happening, his gaze running up and down the pale limb protruding from the rough, pebbly soil of the grave, and by then movement had erupted all around.

'Shavi!' he yelled, but the word choked in his throat at the shock of what he was seeing.

The ground was opening up in a million small upheavals, mini-volcanoes of showering earth and stone. Across the vast graveyard, bodies were thrusting out on locked elbows, alien trees growing in time-lapse photography. Veitch, as brave as any man alive, felt his blood run cold.

In sickening silence they surged from every side. Hands clutched his arms, his hair, pulled at his jaw, slipped into his mouth. Odourless, stiff and dry, they dragged him down to the hard ground. He tried to see Shavi, but his friend had already been washed away in the tidal wave of bodies.

Even that thought was eradicated when he saw where they were dragging him: to the mausoleum that had haunted him from the moment he saw it.

It loomed up among the mists, only now its door hung agape and the interior was darker than anything he had ever seen before.

Tom smoked a joint as he watched the sun come up over Wandlebury Camp, but even the drugs couldn't take the edge off his anxiety. Veitch was sharp, a strategist, a warrior: there was no one else he could have despatched into the Grim Lands. Yet the decision was still a crushing weight on his heart. Despite his constant ferocity, Veitch was, to all intents and purposes, a child and the Grim Lands was the worst battlefield in the worst war in the history of the world. Tom winced at how he had fooled himself that his protégé was operating under free will. Veitch had no capacity to make a rational choice.

Some people have to see the big picture. Tom had utilised that mantra many times during his long life and it had kept the beast locked up on most occasions. But increasingly his guilt was getting out of the cage. He'd been around the Brothers and Sisters of Dragons too long. Why did they have to humanise him? How could he be a general sending the innocents off to war if he felt every death, every scratch?

Some people have to see the big picture. All of existence is at stake. Against that, no individual matters.

He sucked on the joint, then let out the draught without inhaling, spat and tamped out the hot end. He had taken on the role of teacher, an archetype demanded by the universe, but he didn't feel up to it at all. The others might see him as all-knowing, but in his heart he was the same romantic fool who had fallen asleep under the hawthorn tree in the Eildon Hills. Whenever anyone described him as a mythic hero, he felt faintly sick. A man. Weak and pathetic like all men, crippled by insecurities, guilts and fears. Not up to the task at all. But like all men he put on a brave face and pretended to the world he was the one for the job; it was a man thing, as old as time, and it involved pretending to yourself as much as everyone else.

But still, in his quiet moments, when he dared look into his heart, he knew. Not up to the job, Thomas. Not up to it at all. Smoke some more hashish.

He stood up just as Robertson was approaching fearfully from the shade of the house. A bruise marred his cheek from Veitch's attack. He glanced at the sun now beating down on the lawns before he dared speak, 'Your friend—'

'I haven't got time for that now,' Tom snapped. 'Show me the stable-block. I need some horse dung, some straw where a mare has slept, and then I need you to leave me alone for the next hour.'

Robertson stared at him blankly.

'Don't ask any questions.' Tom pushed by him. 'Or I'll do to you what my good friend did.'

Veitch was fighting like a berserker within seconds of being swamped by the wave of dead, a few limbs lopped off here, a skull or two split there. By the time the sword was knocked away from him, he was already aware how worthless it was.

He tried to yell Shavi's name to check his friend was okay, but dead fingers drove into his mouth like sticks blown off an old tree. Sand-papery hands crushed tight around his wrists and his legs, pulled at his head until he feared they were going to rip it off. He choked, saw stars, but still fought like a wild animal.

And the gaping black mouth of the mausoleum drew closer.

Dead hands passed Shavi from one to the other across the angry sea. It was impossible to get his bearings, or even to call out, and any retalia-tion was quickly stifled. From his occasional glimpses of Veitch he knew the dead were not treating him as roughly as his friend. Perhaps they considered him one of their own.

Veitch was thrown roughly into the mausoleum first. Shavi was pitched at head height into the dark after him. He skidded across the floor, knocking over Veitch, who was clambering to his feet in a daze.

Before he could say anything, Shavi noticed his pale hand was slowly turning grey. At the entrance only a thin crack of white mist and grey sky remained. As he threw himself forward, the door slammed shut with a resounding clang.

'Are you okay?' Veitch whispered.

Shavi felt a searching arm grab his sleeve, hauling the two of them together. 'Bruised.'

'Bastards.' A pause. 'Is this the best they can do? We'll be out of here in no time.'

'How?'

A long silence. 'How solid can this thing be?' Another pause. 'It's not like it's meant to keep things *in*. We could jemmy the door—'

'Wait.'

'What?'

'We are not in here alone.'

'What do you mean?'

'Hush.'

There came the sound of a large, slow-moving bulk dragging itself at the far end of the mausoleum.

'What the hell's *that*?' Unease strained Veitch's voice.

Shavi felt the hand leave his sleeve as Veitch scurried in the direction of the door. Several moments of scrabbling and grunting followed before he crawled back, panting and cursing.

Whatever else was in there was shifting towards them. Shavi had an image of something with only arms, dragging what remained of its body across the floor. He couldn't help but think it was hungry, probably hadn't been fed for a long time.

'I've still got my crossbow.' The note of futility in Veitch's voice suggested he wasn't about to use it. 'I thought this was just the land of the bleedin' dead.'

'Ryan. Hush.'

After several minutes, the dragging noise died away. From the echoes, Shavi estimated it had halted about fifteen feet away. All that remained was the sound of breathing, slow, rhythmic and rough. Although there wasn't even the faintest glimmer of light, he couldn't shake the feeling it was watching them with a contemptuous, heavy gaze; sizing them up, dissecting them.

At his side, Veitch's body was taut. Neither of them knew what to do next.

'The rules of this place were formed long before your kind emerged from the long night.' The voice sounded like bones rattling across stone. Its bass notes vibrated deep in Shavi's chest; he felt instantly queasy, not just from the tone of the voice, but from the very *feel* of whatever squatted away in the gloom. 'No warm bodies, no beating hearts, no words or thoughts or ideas.'

'No. There's a deal. I was allowed to come here,' Veitch protested cautiously.

'You were allowed to *cross over*, but the rules of this place can never be transgressed. The living are not wanted. The dead rule here. And they will have no warm bodies spoiling the cold days of this land. They will have punishment.'

Shavi waited for it to attack, but there was only silence. He pictured it savouring its taunting before the inevitable. Here was not only intelligence, but also cruelty, and hatred.

'What are you?' Shavi asked. The hairs on the back of his neck had snapped alert.

'This is a place without hope for those who do not leave. Where behind is too terrible to consider, and ahead is an unwanted distraction. This is desolation, and despair. Misery and pain.'

'A land for those who prey on those things,' Shavi said.

'Here, the dead have their own existence, their own rules and rhythms, their own hierarchies and mythologies, fears and desires.'

The dark was so all-encompassing Shavi was beginning to hallucinate trails of white sparks and flashes of geometric patterns. The atmosphere of dread grew more oppressive.

'What are you?' There was no bravado in Veitch's voice. Shavi really wished he hadn't asked the question again; he was afraid the answer would be too terrible for them to bear.

'I am the end of you.'

Those simple words made his stomach clench. They were flatly stated, yet filled with such finality, hinting at a fate much worse than death.

Slowly it began to drag itself forward, an inch at a time.

'Wait,' Veitch said sharply. 'I *was* allowed to come here – you can't get away from that. And Shavi here, he's not dead—'

'He will be.' A blast of cold air.

'But he's not now. He shouldn't be here. What I'm doing . . . yeah, it might go against your rules – but against the bigger rules I'm doing the right thing. I'm taking him back. I'm making everything all right again.'

For a long period the mausoleum appeared to be filled with the soughing of an icy wind. Then: 'There is the matter of trespass.'

'What do you mean?'

'The dead want no reminder of the living. It makes them aware of what they have lost and what they have yet to gain. To remember makes their suffering even greater.'

Veitch sensed a chink in the seemingly inviolate position. 'So they want some kind of payback,' he said, warming to his argument. 'We can do that. Then you let us go, and everybody's sweet.'

'No!' Shavi gripped Veitch's wrist; the memory of the price he had paid for the deal with the dead of Mary King's Close was still too raw. 'You never know to what you are agreeing. Words are twisted so easily.'

Veitch shook him off. 'We have to cut a deal – it's the only way. There's too much at stake.'

'Ryan! You must listen to me—'

But Veitch had scrambled off in the dark. 'Go on then.' His disembodied voice filled Shavi with ice. 'What's the deal?'

There was silence from the brooding presence. Shavi couldn't work out what that meant, but he felt like it was swelling in size to fill all the shadows.

After a moment or two, Veitch repeated, 'What's the deal?'

'A hand,' the rumbling voice replied.

'Ryan, please do not do this. We can find another way.'

'A hand?' Veitch's voice was suddenly querulous. 'Cut off my hand?'

'A small price to pay for your friend's life.'

The price is too high! Shavi wanted to cry out, but he knew his voice would only tighten his friend's resolve. The sense of threat in that confined space felt like strong arms crushing his chest. They both knew their lives were hanging by a thread.

In the silence that followed, he could almost hear the turning of Veitch's thought processes as he considered the mutilation, what the absence of his hand would mean in his life, what the absence of Shavi would mean. There was an awful weight to Veitch's deliberations as he desperately tried to reach the place where he could do the right thing, whatever the cost to himself. *Do not agree, Ryan*, Shavi pleaded silently.

'Okay.' The word sounded like a tolling bell.

Shavi tried to throw himself between Veitch and the dark presence, but he misjudged his leap in the dark and crashed into the wall.

'Don't worry, mate. Really,' Veitch said. 'I know you'd do the same for me. Whatever you say, I know that. We've got bigger things to think about. That's what Church always said. I can do this. For everybody else.'

Shavi bit sharply on his knuckle to restrain his emotions. All he could do was make his friend feel good about his choice. 'You are a true hero, Ryan.' Shavi knew it was what Veitch wanted to hear, what he had wanted from the moment he had got involved with them.

Veitch didn't reply, but Shavi could almost feel his pride. 'Get it over with,' the Londoner said.

Veitch was trembling, despite the bravado he was trying to drive through his system. He still couldn't quite believe what he had agreed to, but from his position the lines appeared clear-cut: Shavi was the better man; the world couldn't afford to lose *him*. What did his own suffering mean against that? Once they were back in the world, he'd take it all out on the Bastards. Bring on an army of them.

He threw off the shakes, set his jaw, and extended his left arm.

The first sensation made him shiver with disgust. Hot air on his hand, rushing up his forearm, then something wet tickling the tips of his fingers, brushing his skin as it enclosed his hand. The flicker of something that felt like a cold slug on his knuckles.

He closed his eyes, despite the dark.

The sharpness of needles encircled his wrist. The pain increased rapidly until the sound of crunching bones brought nausea surging up from his stomach. The noises that followed were even worse, but by then he had already blacked out.

He lost consciousness for only a few seconds, and when he came round there was heat in his wrist and the sickening smell of cauterised flesh. His left arm felt too light. Amidst the shock and the nausea, thoughts flitted across his head without settling.

And then he did capture one, shining more brightly than all the others: he had saved Shavi. Through his sacrifice, he alone.

'That's my part.' He didn't recognise the ragged voice as his own. 'Now you've got to let Shavi go.'

The wet, smacking sound churned his stomach even further, but he wouldn't allow himself to accept what was happening. When it had died away, the rattling bones voice returned, flat, almost matter-of-fact: 'Then he may go.'

A wave of relief cut through the shakes that convulsed him.

'But you must stay.'

Veitch couldn't grasp the meaning of the words. Shavi was yelling something, trying to grab at his arms, getting knocked away by a figure, more than one figure; not the monstrous presence, which was dragging itself back into the depths of the mausoleum.

He drifted in and out, his left arm by his side, trying to move his fingers.

Movement all around. Shavi was being dragged away. He fought himself back to clarity, knowing it was vitally important, but he still felt wrapped in gauze. At some point he realised he could see, although he couldn't guess the light source; the illumination was thin and grey, like winter twilight.

The dead had come back in. Shavi was against the open door, hands clamped across his mouth, head and arms. Veitch could just make out what appeared to be a large rough box, the lid open, next to a gaping hole. His shock-addled brain couldn't put the information into any coherent shape.

Then the dry-wood fingers of the dead were in his clothes, pulling him forward. He had no strength to resist. They bundled him into the box, which was just big enough for him, and then the lid swung shut with a bang. That jarred his mind into life: with a surge of panic he realised what they were planning.

'No!' In the dark again. He punched the lid with his remaining hand; the splintered wood grated into his knuckles.

The box was lifted into the air. Yelling his protests, he threw himself from side to side, but it didn't overbalance. A brief moment of weightlessness, then a crash that jarred his head so sharply he lost consciousness again.

The next thing he heard was a rattling on the wood. Smell pebbles. The slush of gritty soil falling on the lid, kicked or thrown in. Then the occasional slumps turning into an insistent fall. He screamed and shouted, hammered on the lid and box walls, but there was no room to get any purchase, barely any air to breathe. The stones and earth fell faster, but grew more and more distant.

Finally he couldn't hear anything at all, apart from the sound of his own hoarse voice, growing weaker by the moment.

With the dead gripping him tight, Shavi watched Veitch buried alive. His empathy made him feel acutely the choking claustrophobia and rising hysteria; horror, almost as much as he could bear. As soon as the hole was filled in, he was released, but the dead formed an impenetrable wall between him and the grave; they were not going to allow him to save his friend.

'This is not fair!' he raged to the shadows at the back of the mausoleum, but although they pulsed slightly, there was no reply.

Flailing around, Shavi wandered out into the thin grey light. The area that Veitch had seen as a graveyard, but which he saw as a battlefield spanning the entire history of human existence – trenches and barbed wire, iron age earth defences and mediaeval fields of sucking mud – was deserted. With retribution achieved, the army of the dead had returned to wherever their homes lay.

He couldn't leave Veitch, but what could he do? Sacrifice himself to save his friend? Perhaps that was what the dead truly wanted: a never-ending cycle of sacrifice and suffering, the best punishment of all for being alive.

As he paced back and forth in distress, he noticed a figure about fifty feet away, almost hidden in the cotton-wool mists. A chill ran through him as he instantly recognised the body language: Lee, back to haunt him.

His first thought was to ignore the spirit of his dead boyfriend; at that moment it was too much to bear. But then he changed his mind and hurried over until he was a few feet away. The mists folded around Lee, providing only the briefest glimpses of him.

'I need you now,' Shavi said. The words hung in the damp, misty air. 'I have paid my dues to the dead of Mary King's Close.' He caught his breath. 'I carried a burden of guilt for what happened to you, Lee . . . that I could have done more to save your life. But the truth is, I could not do anything. I remember you in life. I loved you, I think. I loved your values, your beliefs, your gentleness. You were never a man who would want to see anyone suffer.' He let the words flow from his heart without any interference from his mind. 'The pain you caused me over the last few weeks, I think . . . I am sure . . . that was not through any desire of your own. It might have been the Edinburgh dead, but I believe it was probably me, punishing myself. Whatever the cause, that lies behind us now. Now I want your help.'

The coffin had grown unbearably hot from Veitch's rising body temperature. It was also becoming increasingly harder to breathe. His chest felt like rocks had been placed upon it, and there was a prickling sensation in his arms, regularly obscured by waves of pain washing up from his missing hand. He tried to suck in some of the air tainted with the odour of rock dust and soil, but there wasn't enough to fill his throat.

After the swinging emotions that surrounded his sacrifice, the adrenalin had died down and panic had started to set in. He recalled how terrible it had been trapped in the tiny tunnel beneath Edinburgh Castle, and knew that if he gave in he would go crazy, tearing futilely at the wooden lid until his fingernails were broken and bloody.

He rolled round as much as he could to test the lid with his shoulder. It wouldn't budge. Trapped; powerless. Another wave of panic. His throat almost closed up. Flashes of light crossed his eyes.

Dying.

Trust in the others. He tried to focus on something Church had told him. *Have faith. It's out of your hands now.*

The dark closed in around him and the panic rushed up through his chest into his head and then he was yelling until his throat was raw.

The blood trickled from Tom's nose into the corner of his mouth. The ritual had been an awful strain; he felt as if his life had been sucked out of him, and part of it probably had, but he felt good about himself, for the first time in a long while.

Robertson had fled back into the house and buried himself beneath a pile of furniture once he saw what was happening. The stable-block door had been torn from its hinges. Intermittent smoking pitholes marked a trail across the courtyard to the sweeping lawns, where another route of churned mud continued to the dew pond.

Tom hoped he had done enough. More, he prayed he had not made things worse.

The stillness was like the moment after the final exhalation of breath. Shavi thought that place had been that way for as long as time, and would probably remain in that state of suspension until the end of existence. So when the ground shook and the sky cracked with thunder, it really did feel like everything was coming to an end.

Shavi spun round, his heart pounding. The thunder was tearing towards him through the thickening mist. The vibrations drove nails into the soles of his feet.

Was it some kin to the thing that lurked in the mausoleum, sucking up the despair of the dead? The notion chilled him.

He knew there was no point in running. As he waited for it to present itself to him, he became aware of a prickling on the back of his neck, a familiar sign of warning from his supercharged subconscious. When he turned, the sight was so shocking he couldn't help an exclamation. From nowhere the dead had appeared in force, a silent army of thousands forming a grey barrier around the mausoleum. All their eerily staring eyes were turned towards the direction from which the thunderous noise was approaching.

The vibrations were now so powerful the nails had reached Shavi's knees. There was a rhythm to it; not thunder at all. The sound of hoofbeats. All other thoughts were lost as he turned to stare alongside the dead.

The mist usually drifted with a life of its own, but now it was sweeping away rapidly. Unconsciously he cupped his hands over his ears against the deafening noise. The dead remained impassive.

Shavi was buffeted with a warm wind filled with the stink of stables and the musk of sweating, over-worked horses. When the intruder appeared, he was instantly overcome with the swirling destabilisation of perception that always accompanied the most powerful of the Tuatha Dé Danann. This was worse than anything he had experienced before; his mind revolted at the image his eyes were attempting to present to it. After a few seconds, the sensation eased slightly, to be replaced by a succession of rapidly changing forms: a beast that looked more serpent than animal with gleaming black scales and a pointed, lashing tail, a voluptuous woman oozing sexuality, a pregnant mother, blissful in her fertility.

The uneasy flickering eventually settled on one form that his mind found acceptable. A woman, naked apart from a silver breastplate and a short skirt of leather thongs, long, chestnut hair flowing in the wind behind her, riding a stallion of inordinate vitality. Her beautiful face was filled with pride and joy, power and defiance. In her raised right hand she carried a wooden spear tipped with a silver head, while in her other hand she held aloft a gleaming silver shield. Shavi thought of Boudicca, of the power of womanhood, strength and sexuality so potent he could almost taste it.

'Epona,' he said beneath his breath.

Her terrible gaze snapped towards him as if she had heard him, and the sheer force of what he saw there made him look away. Here was a power he had never experienced before, one of the oldest gods, the most primal and powerful, not far removed from the archetypes. Her form had resonated in the belief system of mankind from the earliest time.

The horse reared up before the ranks of the dead, its hooves striking the air. She let that withering gaze move slowly across the army of the dead. It was apparent they were not going to allow her through.

From the way she was directing herself towards the mausoleum, Shavi guessed she was there for Veitch, although he had no idea why. She took her charger back and forth across the frontline of the dead in search of access.

At one point she paused to address the dead in a language Shavi had never heard: wild shrieks that disappeared off the register, interspersed with the snortings of horses. Whatever she suggested, it had no effect.

Why can she not force her way through them? Shavi wondered. But from what he remembered from the stories Tom had told him of the Tuatha Dé Danann, one of her obligations had been the Grim Lands, or at least where it bordered with the world of the living. Perhaps she served them as much as she dominated them, in the way that Cernunnos had a similar dual relationship with the *Fragile Creatures*?

The delay cranked up his anxiety. How long could Veitch survive in the shallow grave with the air running out? What terrible things would be going through his mind?

No air was left in the coffin. Veitch wheezed like an asthmatic old man. The weight on his chest was crushing him. There was blood under his fingernails and his head swam with shifting lights and the sensation of tumbling down a neverending well. No one was coming for him. It was the end; life was being sucked out of him, one breath at a time.

'Lee! I need you! You must help me!' Shavi turned towards the spirit of his boyfriend once again, but the place where Lee had stood was empty, and in the vast crowd of the dead there was no hope of finding him.

Perhaps he could force a way through so Epona could follow. He started to push through the stiff, unmoving bodies towards the front-line, but before he was halfway there he noticed movement not far from Epona. The army of the dead was parting like grey waters before the power of God.

Shavi used his elbows to drive his way towards the path. Epona had already started to trot down it towards the mausoleum. He slipped in behind her before the dead closed ranks.

As Epona moved before the mausoleum door, Shavi caught sight of the reason for the dead's change of heart. Lee waited in the shadow of the stone building, and for the first time that day Shavi saw his face. It was not terrible and frightening and filled with the horrors of death as it had been during the long days and nights following his return in Edinburgh. It was the Lee he remembered: gentle, thoughtful, smiling. For one fleeting moment, things passed between them: acknowledgement, gratitude, friendship, love. And then Lee was moving away towards the grey horizon; not walking, but simply appearing further and further back, as if there were shifts in Shavi's perception. For one instant he appeared to glow like a star, and then he was gone.

Shavi's eyes filled with tears. Lee had achieved his own salvation; he would never have to walk in the Grim Lands again.

He barely had time to think what that meant before he was jolted by a resounding crash as the flinty hooves of Epona's mount broke down the mausoleum door. Although she had appeared too tall to pass through the doorway, a second later she was inside. Shavi ran in behind her.

Close to Epona he felt faintly queasy, his teeth on edge as if he were standing in an electrical field. The goddess moved beyond the rough grave and faced the shadows that still pulsed at the rear of the chamber. From the outside, the Mausoleum appeared twenty feet long, but peering into the gloom, Shavi had the unnerving feeling that it continued forever.

He didn't wait to see what the goddess was doing. Throwing himself on top of the grave, he tore at the shards of rock, the pebbles and soil, with his bare hands. Within seconds the blood streamed down his fingers until his palms were covered with a brown sludge of rock dust and grue.

'Ryan!' he yelled. 'Hold on!'

From the corner of his eye, he could see movement in the shadows. Epona's horse reared up to face it; the goddess issued a warning in that half-shrieking, half-equine cry.

The response was not in that deathly voice Shavi had heard before, but an incomprehensible bass rumble filling him with dread. It was followed by the dragging sound of the huge bulk moving across the stone floor. The shadows swelled forward.

Shavi threw the contents of the grave wildly in all directions. It was loosely packed and easy to move, but it was still taking too long.

'Ryan!' he shouted again. 'Ryan!'

This time he heard a muffled response that spurred him on.

On the edges of his vision he realised Epona was glowing with a faint blue light that lit up their end of the mausoleum, but made no inroads into the advancing shadow. The rumbling sound emanated once again from the dark. This time Epona altered in shape, becoming almost opaque, then something that Shavi didn't recognise. Crackling blue energy washed off her up the mausoleum walls. The shadow stopped sharply before responding with what at first appeared to be a black lightning bolt, or could have been an arm, or a tentacle, lashing out furiously. Epona fended it off with the silver shield, but the force of it drove her back a pace.

No one else would have been able to hold back that thing, Shavi knew. Whatever reason she was there, it had given him the only chance he might have had of saving his friend. He could no longer feel his swollen hands as he tore through the rubble, but eventually the sound of his scraping changed and he realised he had reached wood. Frantically he ripped out the remaining stones while Epona and the unseen presence conducted a ferocious dance in the background. Blue light and black shadows flashed wildly around the mausoleum.

Thrusting his tattered nails under the lid, he wrenched it free. Veitch shot upwards, gulping air, clawing at Shavi's shirt with his one good hand. Shavi was sickened to see the charred black stump that flailed behind.

Even when his lungs were full, Veitch continued to choke. Shavi grabbed his shoulders and held him tightly, stroking his hair until the panic subsided. 'You have survived,' he whispered. 'You are the stronger for it.'

The battle in the background came to a sudden halt. The dark throbbed around whatever it contained. After a moment the bass rumble began, at first so loud it hurt Shavi's ears, but then it changed to words in the chilling, boneyard voice they remembered. 'You have broken the pact. Transgressed the rules of this place. In times to come you will discover you cannot evade your punishment, and it will be inflicted not only upon you, but upon your world.'

'Our world is already suffering,' Shavi muttered.

'There are worse things than the Night Walkers. Worse than the Heart of Darkness. Beyond the edge of existence, the void is stirring. Soon you will fall beneath its unflinching eye. And then it will move towards you.'

Shavi levered himself to his feet, still holding Veitch to his chest. 'We will face it as we have faced everything else. With dignity and hope and faith.'

The shadows began to drag towards him, but the pulsing light around Epona flared and it withdrew. Shavi stared at it defiantly, then turned and helped Veitch out into the thin, grey light.

Epona led the way across the blasted, grey land to the slope on which Veitch had first appeared. She kept a way ahead of them, sometimes disappearing in the mist, but they were always aware of her presence. Now that the conflict was over, there was something eminently soothing about her that raised even Veitch's spirits. They found bread and fruit in her path, which they devoured hungrily; it quickly made them replete and relaxed and imposed a warm sensation of abiding safety that for some reason reminded Shavi of his mother.

The goddess slipped into a state of flux now that the warrior side had been put away. Sometimes when Shavi glimpsed her, she was a young girl on a pony, then a plump mother on a mare, and finally an old, old woman with streaming white hair, on a similarly ancient white charger. Shavi recognised the sign instantly: the triple goddess, mother-maiden-crone, one of the most powerful of feminine symbols. Just like the goddess who had manifested to Ruth.

The more he considered this, the more it gave him pause. He couldn't understand why some of the Tuatha Dé Danann were so close to humanity, both sources of worship and symbols of all that was good, while others had provided the template for the mischievous and malicious sprites and fairies who held humanity in contempt if not hatred. It didn't make sense.

When they reached the summit, Epona cantered round it clockwise three times and the doorway appeared, shimmering in the mist. The goddess turned and briefly acknowledged the two of them, with something akin to the respect of a wise matron. Then, proud and aloof once more, she drove her horse through the doorway and was gone.

Tom was waiting for them when they crossed over. As Veitch emerged, the bier bearing Shavi's body fell into stark relief. Tom's face crumpled in a broad beam as he clapped eyes on Shavi sitting up in a daze. It was the greatest joy they had ever seen him exhibit, but then he noticed Veitch's stump and his jubilation was replaced by an equally intense horror.

'Epona?' Shavi asked.

Tom couldn't take his eyes off Veitch's mutilation. 'I called her to help you.'

'How long was I over there?' Veitch's weak, gravelly voice was on the edge of delirium.

'Two hours.'

Veitch bowed his head. 'It seemed longer.'

Shavi explained to Tom what had happened in the Grim Lands as they both helped Veitch back to the house to recover. He was particularly troubled by the loss of Veitch's hand.

Eventually he brightened enough to say, 'We must not lose sight of the great thing we have achieved this day. You have been brought back from the edge of death, a victory over some of the most powerful rules of existence. That is symbolic of the great power, and hope, invested in the Brothers and Sisters of Dragons.'

'Hooray,' Veitch croaked.

'Now we must find the others and prepare for the battle that all your lives have been leading towards.' He nodded thoughtfully. 'Five once more. Amazing. Perhaps we can carry ourselves with a little more hope than the situation would suggest.'

CHAPTER TWELVE

Infected

Church and Baccharus hurried along dark, twisting corridors with the expectation of an attack at any moment. They had left the vicinity of the Walpurgis's secret hideaway rapidly, and Callow and the Malignos had so far failed to catch up with them. At some point they had expected to come across the Fomorii occupying force, but the lower decks were strangely free of them. Wave Sweeper was still stranded in the same spot, tossing and turning on waves that were obviously being whipped up by the growing storm. Church wondered what that meant for Manannan, whose will alone appeared to power the ship.

At his cabin, he darted inside and then into the wreck of Ruth's room, but there was no sign of her. He threw off the first bolt of despair: Ruth was resilient; she would survive, he told himself.

As they reached the steps up to the deck, they realised how presumptuous they had been. Through the open door, framed against the night sky, they could see the swarming silhouettes of the Fomorii. From their perspective it was impossible to tell how many of the Night Walkers were loose on deck, but it was obvious they had control of Wave Sweeper, and Manannan, if still alive, was probably a prisoner in his cabin. A little guilt crept up on Church as he secretly relished how the Tuatha Dé Danann would feel at being the prisoners of beings they considered less than bacteria.

Cautiously they retreated along the corridor until they had reached a point where they would not be overheard. Baccharus watched him silently, until Church realised the god was waiting for him to decide a course of action. 'What?' he said uncomfortably.

'You are a Brother of Dragons,' Baccharus replied, as if that answered everything.

Church shook his head disbelievingly. 'Okay, okay.' He fidgeted with the sword at his side, then said, 'We've got to move soon. Callow and the Malignos could be upon us at any moment. Callow's got a bastard's tenacity; he won't give up until he feels he's paid me back for ruining his life. But we can't go forward. There's no way we'd ever get past all those Fomorii on deck. They'd cut us down before we made one step out there, like . . . like Butch Cassidy and the Sundance Kid or something.' Baccharus continued to wait on his words. Church pedalled furiously. 'So . . . so . . .'

'We have to find another course of action.'

'Exactly.' And then he had it. 'The first time I was down here I was searching around and I came across another secret room . . . at least I think it was secret. And there were three Golden Ones in there – Goibhniu—'

'Creidhne and Luchtaine, as they were known in the Fixed Lands. The room *was* secret, but it would have opened itself to you because of your heritage.'

Church felt too weary to question what this meant. 'They were making weapons,' he said instead. 'What was that all about?'

'That must wait until later, when there is time.'

'If the room is still there, if the weapons are still there, if Goibhniu and the others are still there—'

Baccharus was already moving along the corridor. Church kept up with him, still amazed to see branching corridors appear as if from nowhere. Five minutes later they passed through the door into the foundry, with its familiar smell of sulphur and smoke. The furnaces were cold, the room silent. Hammers lay where they had fallen. Iron remained partly worked on the anvil. In the gloom beyond, Church could see the mysterious weapons stacked in heaps, untouched.

Baccharus traced his slim fingers along the edge of the furnace. 'I do not think the Night Walkers found this place. The three smiths would have gone to the aid of the Master once the interlopers were discovered.'

'So it's still just us.' Church investigated the first pile of weapons. The uses of most of them were impossible to divine. 'Do you know how to use these?'

'Some. I am not a warrior.'

Church picked up a sword with twin parallel blades. It was extraordinarily light, made of gold and silver, useless in battle. A blue gem was imbedded at the top of the handle between the blades. Casually, Church brushed the jewel with his thumb and was instantly shocked by a sucking sensation deep within him that rapidly grew stronger until it felt like his innards were being pulled out. The sword jumped like a living thing in his hand, so powerful he could barely control it. Before he could fling it down, he noticed coruscating blue energy crackling between the blades near the base, slowly rising up towards the tip as it grew stronger.

Baccharus stepped in quickly and touched his thumb to the gem. The energy died away and Church's jolted body returned to normal, although he could still feel faint vibrations running through his skeleton. 'A Wish-Sword,' Baccharus said. 'To be used with caution.'

'You're telling me.' Church placed it back on the pile, wary of touching anything else. 'Is there anything a little less apocalyptic?'

Baccharus mused for a moment before pulling out a leather thong with what appeared to be a Japanese throwing star tucked in a fold. The star had six points in the shape of extended teardrops, cruelly tipped with barbs, and was made of the same silvery metal that was a constituent for most of the weapons.

Baccharus weighed the weapon in his hand a moment, then slowly began to whirl the thong around his head. Unnerved, Church took refuge behind one of the furnaces where he could just see Baccharus building up speed. When the weapon was a blur, Baccharus snapped his wrist and the star went flying out of the thong. It ripped in an arc through the air; a primitive if effective weapon, Church thought. But then Baccharus nodded his head towards a heap of unformed metal and the star jumped unnaturally in the air to follow the direction of his gaze. It tore through the metal like it was made of sand. Baccharus moved his head sharply two more times and the star obeyed him exactly, making two more cuts through the pile, which fell with a resounding clatter. The star spun back to Baccharus, slowing and hovering slightly so he could pluck it out of the air with his thumb and forefinger.

'That's amazing.' Church snatched the star and examined it closely. There was nothing to show why it should act in such a manner. 'Can anyone use it like that?'

'Anyone with a will.' Baccharus smiled.

'It's still not going to help us if we have to face the massed ranks of them, but it's a start.'

'What do you suggest?'

Church shifted uncomfortably. There was one avenue he had been resisting, but he didn't see how he could ignore it any longer, however detestable it was to him. 'The Fomorii corruption your people all sense in me,' he began, 'has a side-effect. The taint was left after the Kiss of Frost almost took me over, and soon after my life was saved by the liquid I drank from the Cauldron of Dagda. Whatever it was gave me some essence of your people too, so inside me I've got Fomorii and Tuatha Dé Danann fighting it out. The result is that sometimes, when I really try, I can sense what's going on in the Fomorii mind. It's not like I can read thoughts – at least I don't think it's like that. I don't even know if the Fomorii *have* thoughts. It's more a vague impression. But if I really concentrate on it, I'm convinced I can get right inside their heads to work out what's happening. I have to be in close proximity, though.' He winced. 'It feels like my head is filled with spiders. But that's not the worst of it.' He paused as he tried to find the words to express his fears.

'What is it?' Baccharus obviously saw something in Church's face for he rested a steadying hand on his friend's shoulder.

'I'm afraid I could get lost in there. Somehow . . . it's like their minds are all linked. Lots of different bodies, but one being. I've only had the briefest hint of what's inside them, but even then it felt like a rushing river. Of oil, black and so cold. It was tugging at me even then.'

Baccharus nodded. 'I understand. You must do what you feel you have to do. No one will judge you.'

Somehow that made things even worse for Church. 'I've got to stop being such a wimp. What would Tom say?' He grinned defiantly. 'Come on, then. Let's get us a guinea pig.'

They crept back to the foot of the stairs that led to the deck, constantly checking for any sound of Callow and the Malignos. A cold, heavy wind buffeted them and through the doorway they could see swirling clouds occasionally lit up by flashes of white lightning. In the storm, the ship pitched so much that Church had to clutch at the wall to remain upright. At least the pounding thunder would hide any noise they made, Church thought.

The view through the doorway was occasionally obscured by a large shape lumbering slowly by. A guard, Church guessed, to prevent any of Wave Sweeper's passengers interfering with whatever was happening on deck. Even though they had discussed the plan – and it was a simple one – tension still tugged at his neck muscles. One mistake and they would bring the whole of the Fomorii force down on them.

'Are you ready?' he whispered.

'Yes.' Baccharus's voice was characteristically cool.

Church held the throwing star gently, keeping his fingers well away from the razor-sharp barbs. 'You sure you wouldn't be better off using this?'

'You have the ability. And I am faster than you.'

'Okay,' Church said. 'I'm set. Go carefully.'

Baccharus smiled shyly, then loped towards the stairs. Church backed off along the corridor and round a bend. His breath was fast, his heart beating hard. With nervous hands he loaded the star in the thong and held it at his side, rolling on the balls of his feet, ready to move in an instant. Despite Baccharus's vote of confidence, he still doubted his ability, even though he'd had several practice attempts with the star. It responded to his thoughts remarkably easily, almost as if it were a part of him, but the Fomorii were fast when they had to be. Were his reactions sharp enough to build up the velocity and release the star before the beast was on him? Before it could raise the alarm?

Don't think, he told himself. *Just act.*

In his mind's eye, he saw Baccharus sneaking to the foot of the stairs, sliding up them sinuously on his belly, waiting for the guard to pass to the furthest reaches of his path, hoping there were no other Fomorii anywhere near. Tossing one of the coals from the furnace so it rattled on the wet boards just beyond the doorway. Sliding quickly back down the stairs and retreating to the shadows while the guard investigated the sound easily discerned by its magnified perceptions.

Church held his breath and listened: nothing but the wind.

And now Baccharus would be hurling another coal to the foot of the stairs and retreating again. This time Church thought he heard the rattle of the coal. The guard would be advancing down the stairs like the onset of a winter night.

Church couldn't breathe. He shifted from foot to foot as the adrenalin made his body shake with repressed anxiety. Slowly he began to twirl the thong around him, taking care not to clatter the weapon against the walls. Swish. Swish. A gentle breeze.

Another coal tossed from the security of the shadows. This one rolling almost to the guard's feet. Now it had a suspicion of what was happening. But it was not scared. It created fear, it did not know it.

Events happened like a house of cards collapsing. Baccharus appeared round the corner, a blur of gold, not slowing as he approached Church, ducking beneath the whirl of the weapon in one fluid moment. Church suddenly spinning like an Olympic discus thrower, faster and faster until he feared his vision would be too blurred to see the Fomorii approaching. The star singing to him, a plaintive tune. And then the shadows at the bend becoming filled with something even darker than shadows; that sickening stink, the roar of a jet taking off punctuated by a monkey-shriek. Something so huge it filled the entire corridor, moving with the speed of a racehorse; a shape that had tentacles, then teeth, then silver knives, fur then scales, then nothing but an absence of everything.

Church whirled one final time, then snapped his wrist to release the star. The weapon was like a glimmering light in the void as it tore through the air. It ripped through where the creature's arm should have been and something heavy fell to the floor. The monkey-shriek grew more high-pitched.

Church's mind was clear of everything but the star. Back and forth, up and down, he chased the pin-prick of light, tearing the beast apart. Things fell; the floor grew sticky beneath his feet. The smell was unbearable, part of it the odour of his boots being corroded by the thing's essence. His heart zinged as relief flooded in; he was actually doing it. But he had to be careful. Not too good. He had to keep the thing alive, at least long enough for him to get into its head. A pang of guilt hit him at the suffering he was inflicting on another living thing.

The shrieks were cut off and the beast crashed to the floor. This was the most dangerous moment. It was still alive, but he didn't want it so alive it could still kill him with its dying blow.

Baccharus brought up a torch so he had a better view of the sickening havoc he had wreaked on the body. He tried to avert his eyes, but it was all around.

'It is time.' Baccharus's words gave him a gentle push, but were at the same time supportive. He steeled himself and stepped forward.

His sizzling boots slid in the grue. A tendril flapped wildly before curling around his legs. In a moment of panic he kicked out wildly. The tendril flew off and continued to judder aimlessly.

He had no choice but to climb on the body, which was sickeningly resilient beneath his feet. His boot slipped into a hole that felt like a sucking bog. He withdrew it with an unpleasant slurping sound.

Finally he reached the point where he guessed its head would be. There was certainly a raised area with what appeared like eyes rolling back and forward in its dying spasms, but they were as black as oil, glinting with an inner light which was inexplicably black too, but of a different quality. Fighting the nausea, he bent down and brushed his fingers against the skin. Although he couldn't begin to describe the texture, it felt so unpleasant his stomach rolled and he truly thought he was about to be sick. When the queasiness had passed, he placed his hands near those shivering eyes, closed his own lids, and concentrated.

He was caught aback by the speed and severity of the reaction. One second he was fighting back his disgust at his surroundings, the next he was sucked violently into a surging river of crude oil, immersed in a vile stench that was part-chemical, part-excrement, feeling revulsion in every fibre of his being at what his senses told him. It was such a totally overwhelming experience he felt he was living it; the corridor, the Night Walker, Baccharus, all disappeared from his mind.

He was swept along in the black stream, choking, not from a lack of oxygen, but from the sensation that his body was being suffused with such Evil his very spirit recoiled. The abstract was given form by his mind as a complex mix of feelings, strangulation, a feeling that something vile, like human brains, was being forced into his mouth, that his skin was being touched by the innards of a loved one's corpse. The rush was amphetamine-fast, pulled this way and that so dramatically he didn't have a second to think. He was fighting, for his life, for his sanity, sure he would never get out again.

And then he felt the full force of what had only been hinted at before: the awful, alien intelligence that linked the Fomorii. Spiders burrowed deep in his brain. There were no words, no images that made any sense to him, but there was an intense *impression* of that thing's thoughts. He was swamped with a soul-shattering despair as it cruelly disseminated the point of view that there was no meaning to anything, no reason for anything to exist, that it would be better if nothing existed at all.

He saw through multi-faceted eyes London cast in negative: bodies piled in the streets and the Thames running thickly, white shadows reaching into buildings and hearts. He glimpsed the world from a hundred thousand eyes, and more, the Lake District, the Welsh borders, the South Coast, the Midlands, moving out with the tramp of an infinite marching army ringing all around.

Even more sickening was that the longer he was in it, the more he could control, picking eyes here, then there. And eventually he saw through eyes that looked out over Wave Sweeper and soaked up the oily impression of intent.

His body prickled with cold sweat. He *was* Fomorii, and it would never, ever let him go. The vibrations that convulsed him grew stronger and stronger, until he thought he was beginning to shake apart . . .

He hit the floor hard, driving the wind from his lungs. It took a second or two for the black oil to drain from his mind, but daemonic voices still rang in his ears, even when he saw Baccharus's face above him.

'Jesus.' He choked; a mouthful of bile splattered on the sizzling ooze that ran from the now-dead Fomor.

'Find peace, Brother of Dragons.'

'I was one of them . . . I couldn't get away . . .'

'Your face told me what was happening. I thought I would never be able to break the spell.'

Church took several deep breaths, then put his head between his knees, but he couldn't shake the squirming in his brain.

'I know what they're going to do,' he gasped.

Baccharus helped him to his feet. 'You saw?'

'Saw . . . felt . . . whatever.' He heaved in another breath, trying to keep the nausea at bay. 'Are they really a part of me? Is that it? For the rest of my life?'

'We are all a part of everything, and everything is a part of us.'

'That doesn't sound like one of the Tuatha Dé Danann.' He rested on Baccharus as the god led him away from the corpse. 'I saw something . . . a structure . . . a geometrical shape that seemed to disappear into other dimensions . . . glowing ruby, then emerald.'

'The Wish-Hex.' Baccharus's voice was suddenly so dismal, Church snapped alert.

'But it wasn't just that,' Church continued. 'I got a hint of something about disease . . . a plague . . .'

Baccharus turned away so Church couldn't see his face.

'What is it?'

'The Wish-Hex is a construct of unimaginable power. The Night Walkers used it to break the pact and sever the bonds that chained them to the Far Lands. It decimated my people. Some were contaminated by the essence of the Night Walkers, some—'

'. . . were driven into exile and some fled. I know the story.'

'The Night Walkers must have sacrificed much to focus it again.' He bowed his head and put a hand to his temple. 'But to bind one of the great plagues into the matrix . . .'

'That's even worse?'

He looked up at Church with liquid eyes. 'My people will not be exiled. They will be destroyed, in the worst way imaginable. Eaten away from within.'

'They're going to convince Manannan to take them to your high court, and then they'll unleash it there.'

Baccharus shook his head. Church thought he was going to break down in tears.

'It's not done yet, Baccharus. The ship is still stationary. They haven't broken Manannan.'

They were both disturbed by a scuttling across the wooden floor behind them. They whirled to see a silver spider disappearing into the shadows: a Caraprix, one of the symbiotic creatures shared by the Fomorii and the Tuatha Dé Danann. It had vacated the cooling body.

'Quick!' Baccharus said.

Church whirled the thong and loosed the star, but it simply raised a shower of splinters from the floor. The Caraprix was already en route to the deck. They both chased around the corner to see it disappearing out into the night.

Baccharus grabbed Church's arm forcibly. 'We must flee. The alarm will already have been raised. They will be on us in moments.'

As if in answer to his words, a shocking outcry of animal noises tore through the night. It was followed an instant later by the thunder of forms rushing to the lower decks.

Church and Baccharus turned as one and sprinted away along the endless corridors.

The cacophony of pursuit dogged them for fifteen minutes, but Baccharus took them down hidden tunnels which, from the cobwebs that festooned them, appeared not to have been used for years. After a while, the silence lay heavy again and they could both rest against the wall to catch their breath.

'Now they've found their dead comrade they'll be fanning out across the ship,' Church noted. 'There's no element of surprise any more.'

'We cannot hide forever.' Baccharus was unusually anxious.

'We're not going to be hiding.'

'Then what do you suggest? Two of us, against an army . . .'

'There're more than two of us, Baccharus.' Church smiled at the god's curious expression. 'You seem to know the ship well.'

'Very well.'

'Good. Then there are some places I want you to take me.'

Liquid echoes and dancing splashes of light reflected off the oily water below. The stink of rotten fish and seaweed choked the air. Church and Baccharus hurried through the gloom along a wooden walkway that hung shakily over the black, slopping contents of the bilge tanks. They were vast and deep, filled not only with the buoyant seawater, but also the run-off from the kitchens. This was only one of many, but Baccharus had convinced Church it was the correct one.

It was also one of the most rundown sections of the ship. The walkway was creaking and bowing, and in some areas vital planks were missing so they had to jump gaps, or edge along a strut with their backs to the wall.

Two Fomorii who had pursued them down there entered the tank when Church and Baccharus were about a hundred and fifty yards along the walkway. Church felt the chill rippling out from them long before he looked back to see the looming shadows. 'This better work.'

The Fomorii closed the gap quickly. Baccharus could move faster, but he was holding back to stay with Church. Church was feeling the strain of the exertion; his chest hurt and his legs occasionally felt like jelly. A bout of weakness overcame him just as he was jumping one of the gaps in the walkway; his toes caught the edge, but began to slip back on the slick, broken boards.

'Bacch—' was all he had time to shout before he slid off the edge and plummeted through the gap. At the last moment he jammed out his elbows and wedged himself between the two supporting struts. Peering down, he could see his boots were dangling only two feet above the water. The Fomorii were coming up like a train, now only thirty yards away.

Suddenly there was a frantic splashing in the water sweeping towards him. A second later golden fish with enormous jaws and twin rows of razor-sharp teeth were leaping from the bilge, snapping at his feet. One came within half an inch of his toes; if those monstrous jaws closed on him, the thick leather of his boot would amount to nothing.

He kicked out wildly, but before any more of the fish had a chance to go for him, Baccharus's iron hands closed on his shoulders and hauled him effortlessly out of the gap. Lacking the breath even to gasp thanks, Church drove himself on. He did not have to run far. The walkway came up against the end of the bilge tank with no sign of any other exit.

Church and Baccharus turned to face the approaching Night Walkers, who slowed as they realised their prey was cornered. The walkway creaked beneath their bulk. In their shadows, Church could see armoured plates and bony spikes, constantly shifting. They carried the cruel serrated swords favoured by Fomorii warriors, rusted and blood-stained.

'No way out now,' Church said. He didn't take his eyes off the approaching warriors.

Baccharus dipped into his pocket and pulled out a lump of clinker from the furnace, which he tossed over the side. It splashed loudly in the dark waters, sending out ripples and wild echoes.

The Fomorii paid no attention. Church watched as their centre of gravity shifted, ready to strike.

The water beneath them began to boil. Big white bubbles, rainbow-streaked, burst on the surface. Church would have been forgiven for thinking it was more of the razor-toothed fish, but it was soon obvious whatever was rising was much, much bigger.

The Fomorii gave it only a cursory glance. They realised the mistake they had made when they saw the grin break across Church's face. An instant later, a long, rubbery object lashed out of the water at lightning speed, smashing through the walkway between the Night Walkers and Church and Baccharus. The Fomorii teetered on the edge, but before they could regain their balance, the enormous bulk of the Llamigan-y-dur burst from the water on its bat-like wings and smashed into them. One of the warriors was clamped in the jaws of the grotesque toad-creature, while the other toppled into the tank where there was the sudden white-water of a feeding frenzy.

Church had a brief glimpse of the first warrior being ripped apart by the Water-Leaper, named by Cormorel at the banquet before his death, and then the toad disappeared back beneath the waters. The fish finished their meal soon after, and then there was stillness once more.

'How did you know it wouldn't go for us?' Church said, eyeing Baccharus suspiciously.

Baccharus smiled. 'It is not only the Golden Ones who detest the Night Walkers. Low beasts like the Malignos may walk the same path, but most denizens of the Far Lands despise those foul creatures.'

Church leapt the gap in the walkway before pausing to look back at the oily waters. 'A giant toad. With wings. And a tail. Yes, the Age of Reason is well and truly dead.'

They spent the next hour probing the darker recesses of the lower decks. As a member of the Tuatha Dé Danann, Baccharus commanded a respect amongst the other travellers that Church would never have had alone. Arrangements were made. Some refused; many agreed.

The kitchens were a relief after the stink of the bilge tanks, rich with the aromas of spices and herbs, the smells of cooking meats and roasting fish drifting. The room stretched the size of four football pitches; Baccharus told Church it was only one of several. Clouds of steam rose from abandoned pots bubbling on the iron ranges that crackled and spat from the well-stoked fires roaring in each one. Bunches of dried herbs hung from the ceiling, releasing scents as they brushed against them, mingling with the wood-smoke from the fires. Pots and pans gleamed brightly in the light of scores of torches. The most unnerving thing about the spacious room was the way it magnified even the smallest echo as they crept down the aisles.

They knew it was only a matter of time before the Fomorii found them there, and sure enough, three entered at the same time, two through one door, another on the opposite side of the room. The Night Walkers made no attempt to approach cautiously. They launched into a charge, smashing over bins of vegetables, sending pans and cooking implements flying; the sound of crashing metal was deafening. They didn't waste time following the aisles, instead jumping on to the ranges, filling the air with the stink of their searing flesh.

It was a terrifying sight, but Church stood his ground coolly. He loaded the star in the thong, whirled it round three times and loosed it, taking out one of the pair in a shower of black rain. It was too late to reload for the others who bore down on them with swords raised.

The Afanc rose up from where it had hidden itself in one of the aisles. The half-sea beast had mistimed its entrance so it was too close to one of the attacking Night Walkers. The beast swung its sword in an arc, slashing the Afanc's chest to the bone. It should have been a killing blow, but as quickly as it appeared, the wound closed. Cormorel had been right: the Afanc could not be killed by normal means.

The Night Walker paused in surprise at this revelation. The Afanc grinned, although it was more like a grimace on its extended face. It brought up the strange, twisted spear it had been carrying low and with its powerful arms thrust it right through the Fomor's body, from the gut to the top of the spine. The Afanc backed off quickly while the Night Walker yanked at the spear. Although it looked mundane, it was another item from the secret weapons store. There was a soundless burst of blue light and the spear clattered to the floor as burning chunks of Fomor rained across the room.

Church and Baccharus ducked the smoking missiles as the last Night Walker launched its assault. It leapt on to the range and swung its sword at Church. There was no time to use the star; the Afanc was too far away.

Baccharus grasped a large clay jug from the side and hurled its contents at the warrior. The golden oil sprayed the Night Walker from head to toe, splashing on to the range where the flames licked through the hole in the top. A second later the beast was burning with a furious heat. It fell backwards off the range, then blundered clumsily around as it feebly attempted to damp the conflagration. Before long, it crumpled into the aisle, filling the kitchens with an oily black smoke and an unbearable stench. Church and Baccharus hurried for the nearest door, covering their mouths.

'There are weapons,' Baccharus said brightly, 'and there are weapons.'

'Smokin',' Church added in his best Jim Carrey impression. 'You do realise I've got a humorous saying for every eventuality? That won't be very irritating, will it?'

The wine and beer store was cool and musty, long and thin and low-ceilinged, with enormous oak barrels in lines on opposing walls. The floor was stained with a million wassails; it smelled sour and sweet at the same time, reeking of happier times. There were too many deep shadows, too many places to hide. It was perfect.

Church and Baccharus made no attempt to disguise their entry from the three pursuing Fomorii. As they sprinted between the barrels, the echoes of their footsteps took on a strange deadened tone, like nails being driven into hard wood. Halfway along the store, they loitered briefly in a puddle of light from one of the few flickering torches, just to make sure they were seen. Once they had slipped into the encroaching folds of darkness, they dropped to their knees and crawled under the barrels, scraping their hands and face on the rough wood, drinking in the even more potent aroma. As the Fomorii thundered over the boards, they wriggled like snakes under the next few barrels until they reached a point where they could clamber up the back and lie on top of one for a better view.

The Fomorii hadn't seem them. The Night Walkers knocked the taps on several casks as they passed so the beer and wine foamed out into the gulleys. When the two leaders were about twenty feet from Church and Baccharus's hiding place, there was a sigh and a faint breeze. The two Fomorii continued, only now they were missing the top third of their heads. It took them several more feet before they realised this important fact and then they crashed down hard in the aisle, sizzling like cooking bacon where their blood met the beer and wine.

Church was stunned. When Baccharus had described the Whisper-Line's abilities, he couldn't quite grasp how something as thin as cotton could cut through any object. Even the demonstration – remote-triggered from what appeared to be a yo-yo to whisk out and slice an anvil in two – hadn't wholly convinced him. But here it was.

The Night Walker who was a little behind came to a halt when he saw his fellows drop. Slowly it sniffed the air currents, its rough breathing like the rumble of an old engine. Church was convinced the thing knew exactly where they were.

He needn't have worried. The cry that echoed along the store was enough to jar even the Fomor. Part-bird, part-animal, part-human, Church realised the dread it must have invoked when it had been heard echoing amongst the lonely hills of Skye.

From out of the shadows at the other end of the store emerged a large, lumbering, human figure, the torso heavily muscled, the arms like the branches of an oak. Bloody furs of goat and sheep hung from its waist where they were bound by something that Church didn't want to examine, but had definitely started out as human. The smell was as vile as the first time he and Baccharus had spoken to it.

Roaring, the Fomor launched an attack. Unconcerned, the Baiste-na-scoghaigh stepped into the light; the lethal-looking horn protruding from its forehead cast strange shadows. It waited, yellow eyes glowering. At the last moment it ducked down beneath the cleaving sword, drove forward like a bull and buried the horn deep in the spot where Church presumed the Night Walker's belly to be.

The battle was furious, the noise of roars and squeals and shrieks deafening. Barrels were smashed, drink flooded everywhere. The

Baiste-na-scoghaigh took several nasty wounds to its arms and chest before it smashed the sword in two, but they didn't seem to bother it. The Fomor then proceeded to change shape in the unnerving manner that always reminded Church of stop-go animation, adopting razor-sharp thorns, snapping jaws and at one point what appeared to be giant lobster claws. But the Baiste-na-scoghaigh was so ferocious it simply powered through every offence, tearing with its horn, its enormous fists coming down unceasingly with the force of jackhammers. The Fomor was soon trailing most of its innards, but still fighting on, even when it collapsed. The Baiste-na-scoghaigh didn't relent, not even when the Night Walker was unmoving: it proceeded to pound every last inch of its prey into a thick paste.

Church and Baccharus left it there, slamming its fists over and over again into the floor.

Church and Baccharus had considered playing a part in the map room and library, but there didn't seem much point. Instead, they secreted themselves behind some enormous volumes heaped on the floor where they could watch the proceedings unobserved.

Hundreds of torches and lamps lined the walls or sat in the middle of the reading desks, but even the smell of oil and smoke couldn't stifle the warm aroma of old, dry paper and papyrus. After the gloom of the store and the bilge tanks, it was refreshingly light and airy.

The room was oddly detached from the storm that raged without. There had been so many of them in recent times; certainly the Fomorii had something to do with it. Windows along one wall allowed a vista on waves rising up higher than the ship. Lightning filled every corner of the room with brilliant illumination while the rain slammed in a constant, violent rhythm.

Yet the charts and books covering every table, desk, chair, shelf and most of the floor were not thrown around. It was almost as if they were watching the storm from some distant place, which Church suspected was probably true.

The Fomorii came in about ten minutes later. They acted unnerved by the light, wandering around the room with uncharacteristic caution, prodding potential hiding places with their swords. Church was surprised to see that in the glare of the torches they looked diminished; quite literally. They were smaller, their gleaming sable forms no longer holding so many surprises: two legs, two arms, a head.

As one of them passed a bookshelf packed with maps, it didn't notice a column of mist, fading in and out of the light. The haze curled around the Fomor, then moved away as if it had been caught on a breeze. For a second or two the beast froze. Then slowly it threw its head back and released a terrible cry that was immediately and surprisingly recognisable as despair. The Night Walker lashed out wildly, demolishing the bookcase with one blow, then began to run backwards and forwards in a frenzy, tearing at its eyes and ears. Black gunk splashed on to the pristine white of the charts.

'What's happening?' Church whispered.

Baccharus shrugged slightly. 'The Spriggan has whispered a secret.'

'Christ, what kind of secret?'

'One that can drive anything insane.'

What this could possibly be disturbed Church so deeply he decided not to consider it further.

The other Fomorii grew as animated as monkeys in the jungle at their fellow's demise by its own hands, but they didn't back off. Opting for a tight defensive formation, they moved cautiously through the vast room in search of the invisible enemy. Church couldn't identify the Spriggans either, and he had suggested areas where they could secrete themselves. He knew of the legends surrounding them long before Cormorel had pointed them out. The ghosts of giants, supposedly, haunting the standing stones of Cornwall, but in actuality they had the shapeshifting abilities of many denizens of T'ir n'a n'Og. Often they appeared as insubstantial as morning mist, but when they took on substance they were even more grotesque than the Fomorii.

Despite their fearsome reputation, they respected Church for his links with the Blue Fire, which apparently calmed their violent natures.

The Fomorii were growing irritated with their inability to locate the enemy and had taken to hacking randomly at shelving and piles of books. But as they passed near heavy purple drapes flapping in the breeze from one open window, there was sudden movement. The drapes folded back and out of them – out of the air itself – came the Spriggans, now solid, and monstrous in their rage. They descended on the Fomorii like frenzied birds, intermittently fading so the Night Walkers could never get a handle on them.

If there had been fewer than the eight Spriggans Church counted, the Fomorii might have stood a chance; as it was the Night Walkers managed to bring down one with a lucky blow while he was solid. But the white-hot rage of the Spriggans drove them on relentlessly. Soon the torn bodies of the Fomorii lay heaped in the centre of the room.

In the light of what he had seen, Church was wary of emerging from his hiding place, but Baccharus was quickly out to thank the Spriggans with a taut bow. They were shifting anxiously around the corpses, as if they were considering feasting. Rather than see what transpired, Church thanked them from a distance and quickly exited.

For the next hour and a half, the attacks proceeded relentlessly. Here the tearing claws of the thing that resembled a griffin, there the ferocity of the Manticore analogue. Losses amongst the ship's passengers were relatively few – a couple of Portunes crushed by a falling Fomor, something that had a body covered with sharp thorns, like a human porcupine – but the Night Walkers were decimated. Once Church and Baccharus had convinced themselves no others roamed the corridors, they moved speedily towards the deck.

They emerged into the face of a gale as sharp as knives. The rain was horizontal, bullet-hard, and mixed with sheeting salt water. Lightning tore the sky ragged with barely a break between strikes. Below deck, they had been aware of the ship's movements on the waves, but had somehow been protected from it. There in the open they faced the full force of the wild pitching that almost tipped Wave Sweeper from end to end. Even shouting, they could not be heard above the explosive force of the thunder. Purchase on the streaming boards was almost impossible to find. They skidded from side to side, clutching on to rigging or railing to prevent themselves being thrown overboard. At one point, Church was hanging on by only his arms, his legs dangling out at near-right angles to the deck. Strangely unaffected by the yawing, Baccharus hooked a hand in Church's jacket to keep him anchored until the boat began to turn the other way, and then they hurried to the next safe point.

After fifteen minutes, the door to Manannan's quarters loomed agonisingly close. Church clung to a spinnaker, ready to make the final dash. Just as he was about to put a foot forward, lightning painted the deck a brilliant white and from the corner of his eye he caught sight of an incongruous shadow. He whirled and dodged with a second to spare. Talons like metal spikes turned wood to splinters where his head had been.

Another flash brought a face into stark relief only inches from his own: slit pupils turning to a black sliver in the glare, reptilian scales, a flickering tongue, flaring nostrils steaming in the storm's chill, the bone structure of the skull ridged and hard.

Church thrust hard and the Maligna flew on to its back and rolled down the deck. But he was not alone. The lightning flashes created an odd strobe effect, freezing then releasing, before freezing again, as the rest of the Malignos attacked. It was a surreal scenario, the creatures leaping like lizards from railing to rigging, caught in the light, untroubled by the wild swings of the ship. And at the back, clutching the jamb of the door that led below deck, was Callow, his face as furious as the storm.

The Malignos were flitting shadows until the lightning caught them, and then it was apparent why they were so feared. Their bodies were lithe yet packed with muscle, efficient machines with only one brutal purpose in mind. The speed with which they moved made it impossible for any prey to avoid them in open pursuit, while their reputation as flesh-eaters made them even more fearsome.

Church was caught between running for cover and standing and fighting his ground, but in the violently tossing ship it was impossible to do either; the most he could do was hang on to the spinnaker for grim life.

There must have been six or seven of the Malignos, but it was impossible to pin down the exact number because of the speed of their movement and the force of the storm. They were coming at him from both sides, but shifting around rapidly to confuse him like a pack of hunting wolves.

Baccharus was yelling something, but Church couldn't hear above the wind. In that instant, the Malignos struck. A ball of flailing, wiry limbs slammed into Church head-on. He lost his grip on the spinnaker and went down hard. Another Maligna flashed by just close enough to rake him with its talons. Warm blood seeped out through the tears on his jacket. The first one planted itself astride him, raising up one arm ready to tear out his throat. Church frantically tried to throw him off, but the creature was too strong. The talons curled; the arm came down.

Baccharus caught the Maligna with the back of his hand, a blow of such force Church felt the vibrations in his bones. The beast flew down the deck. Baccharus managed to get Church to his feet. The god was still trying to tell Church something, but before Church could decipher it, another Maligna crashed into his back. The deck tipped, his feet left the boards and he was flying down the length of the ship, careening off the rigging, bouncing off the railing, inches from going overboard into the savage sea. He slammed into the wall next to the door leading below deck, and for a second lost consciousness.

When he came to, Callow was over him, a rusty razorblade clutched between thumb and forefinger, ready to slice into Church's jugular. His hideous face glowed white in the lightning, the black veins standing out in stark relief. Church suddenly flashed to Callow's attack on Laura in the back of the van, to what he had done to Ruth in Callendar, and he was overcome with fury.

Church came up sharp, catching Callow on the jaw with the top of his head. Callow stumbled back; the razorblade was washed away. Spinning round, Church faced the Malignos and knew what Baccharus had been telling him to do. From his side, he pulled up the Wish-Sword that he had been saving for the final assault on Manannan's captors; Baccharus had warned him the effect it had on his spirit would mean he could only use it once in a day, but there was no other option. He thumbed the gem in the handle and waited as the blue fire crackled between the twin blades, building from the handle towards the tip.

The Malignos were almost upon him. They leapt as one from different directions, but they were a second too late. The energy leapt from the blade in a sapphire flash; lightning brought down to earth, it jumped from one Maligna to the other, seizing them in a coruscating field so bright Church had to look away. When his eyes cleared, all of the attackers were gone, with not even the slightest remains to indicate they had ever existed.

Weary, Church slumped back against the wall. He felt as if a vital part of him had been lost, but Baccharus had told him the debilitating sensation would pass.

Nearby, Callow was shakily making his way to his feet. Church didn't know if he would have the energy to repel another attack.

When Callow saw Baccharus approaching, his expression grew sly and he pointed accusingly, mouthing something over and over. The insistence in his face suggested the importance of his unheard words, but they were snatched from his lips the moment they were born. Church was drawn magnetically to the shaping of that mouth, divining the syllables. Again. And again. He almost had it . . .

The wave must have been twenty feet high, the water as grey and hard as stone. It came down with the force of an angry god swatting flies. Church grabbed hold of the door jamb the moment he saw it rushing towards him, screwing his eyes and mouth shut tight. For a brief moment a new universe closed around him and he was convinced his arms were going to be torn from his sockets. He held fast while his fingers felt like they were breaking, and when the rush passed and he opened his eyes, Callow was gone.

There was little point searching overboard; even if Church could spot him in the turbulent waters he would have had no way of getting him back on to the ship. He didn't feel any sense of victory at the loss; he didn't feel anything at all. The weariness that had afflicted him since using the Wish-Sword reached into his very bones and although it had eased slightly in the passing moments, he wondered if he had any reserves left to face what lay ahead.

They paused at the door to Manannan's quarters briefly before stepping inside. There was no guard waiting for them; the remaining Fomorii still expected their forces to be swarming on deck.

A moment later they stood outside Manannan's private room. Through the thick wood came the muffled growls of the Fomorii, but there was no other recognisable voice. Church wondered if Manannan was still alive, and Niamh too, but his real thoughts were for Ruth.

'Give me the Wish-Sword,' Baccharus whispered, pulling Church a few paces back from the door.

'What am I going to do?'

'Rest, and watch my back. What I can provide the Wish-Sword will not be as powerful as you, but it should suffice.'

'So, what? We just barge in there?'

'An act of surprise may win the day.'

They exchanged a look that underlined their mutual respect and trust, paused to gather their thoughts, and then rushed the door.

The scene inside the vast cabin was shocking enough to take the edge off their charge the moment they crossed the threshold. The Tuatha Dé Danann had been herded to one end of the room, where they were guarded by several prowling Fomorii. The Golden Ones were on their knees, humbled, eyes fixed dead ahead. The scene reminded Church of old pictures from the Second World War, of Nazis guarding brutalised POWs. Niamh was at the front, pale and worried, but there was no sign of Ruth.

The attention of the gods was fixed on Manannan – at least Church presumed it was Manannan – and at the glowing geometric shape he had seen when he had probed the mind of the Night Walker. Three Fomorii had Wave Sweeper's Master bound across the enormous desk, where several monstrous implements appeared to have been used to torture him. It was impossible to tell the exact use of the instruments, which resembled bear-traps and hand drills, but they had obviously had a profound effect on the Master. He had lost his familiar shape. The body was blurred and pulsing, leaking light in dazzling beams, and the face was like a running mixture of oil and water.

Church couldn't believe the Fomorii had overwhelmed Manannan, one of the most powerful of the gods. The only explanation was that he had been forced to succumb because of the Wish-Hex; yet he had still patently resisted attempts to coerce him to take Wave Sweeper to the Court of High Regard.

Even to glance at the Wish-Hex made Church feel queasy. It looked like a system of interlocking cubes and triangles and pentagons made of light, hovering in midair, but at some point all the elements seemed to disappear into a different dimension.

By the time he took this in, the Fomorii were aware of their presence. Five of the Night Walkers rushed at once, the others preparing to follow.

Church looked to Baccharus to use the Wish-Sword. To his horror, he saw the god's thumb wavering over the gem. *Why is he holding back?* Church thought until a shocking thought ripped through him. Perhaps Baccharus was a traitor. In the pay of the Fomorii. He was going to give Church up to the enemy. Was that what Callow had been trying to tell him?

At the last moment, Baccharus did thumb the trigger. The blue fire built quicker than it had with Church, but it did not burn so brightly. It surged through the Fomorii, creating a chain of blue balls of light where it passed through the Night Walkers' chests. Four, five, six, all writhing in the brilliant arc-light. But with each one it possessed, the light grew a little dimmer, and then Church realised Baccharus's strategy: he had been waiting for the Fomorii to get close enough for the force to strike them all. Eight, nine, ten. The light dying now.

Come on, Church prayed silently. *Only five more.*

Twelve, thirteen. But after it had passed through the fourteenth, the light faltered, then died. The corpses of the Fomorii fell to the ground, crumbling into a black dust.

The single surviving Night Walker was already moving. He reached the Wish-Hex before anyone in the room could react.

Niamh dashed over to Manannan and loosed the shackles. As she helped him up, his body and features gradually returned to the form Church knew, but his body was still leaking too much light. He didn't have the strength to help.

The Night Walker positioned himself with one arm on either side of the Wish-Hex. Church removed his sword and weakly moved forward, hoping he didn't look as impotent as he felt.

'Hold.' Baccharus waved Church back frantically. 'The foul beast will trigger the Wish-Hex if you approach.'

'It can't hope to get anything. What's it going to do? Commit suicide?'

'It will destroy us all, and itself, in the blink of an eye. But it does not want to waste the Wish-Hex. The Fomorii will not be able to create another one in the near future.'

'A stand-off.'

'We will never take this foul beast to the Green Isles of Enchantment.'

Niamh was speaking with pride. 'We will see ourselves wiped from the face of existence first.'

The Night Walker appeared to understand her words, for he brought his hands closer to the Wish-Hex. It began to throb; the light turned scarlet, then black. A faint tremor ran across Niamh's face, but she did not back down.

The Wish-Hex glowed brighter and brighter. The unease it radiated became more intense, turning Church's stomach, making him inexplicably want to cry. *This is the end?* he thought in disbelief.

And then the strangest thing happened. The Night Walker tripped backwards. The light surrounding the Wish-Hex began to die. The Fomor fought to get back to the weapon, but it stumbled, and then it propelled itself in the direction of Church.

In that moment, the empty space where the Night Walker had been was suddenly occupied. Astonishingly, Church realised he was looking at Ruth, her face anxious, fearful, but with a rising note of triumph.

The Night Walker turned at speed to rush back to the Wish-Hex. Church didn't even think. He drove his sword into the base of its skull, cleaving the beast's head in two. And then when it hit the floor, he waited for a second before splattering the Caraprix the moment it left the corpse.

A cry rose up from the assembled Tuatha Dé Danann – not just triumph, but also gratitude, directed at him, and Ruth. Directed at *Fragile Creatures.*

He threw his steaming sword to one side and rushed over to Ruth, throwing his arm around her waist.

'Well, aren't you Mr Testosterone.' She held her head back from him, grinning. 'See, even the sensitive ones can't wait to let it out.'

'What was that all about? How did you do that? Where did you come from?'

'I am a woman of many talents and great fortitude and you are very, very lucky to have me.'

While the Tuatha Dé Danann tended to Manannan's wounds, feeding him the strange drink Ruth and Church had sampled earlier, the two of them sat next to the window where they could watch the storm.

'It was something the familiar taught me,' she said as she cupped his hand loosely between hers. '*To avoid being seen in plain sight.* But you can't keep it up for long, and it doesn't really work if anyone is actively looking for you, but—'

'How much more have you got in your bag of tricks?'

'I don't really know.' She fixed an eye on him. 'What's the matter? Scared?'

'Should I be?'

'*I'm* scared.'

'That's understandable – it's powerful stuff. But Cernunnos and his partner wouldn't have invested it in you if they didn't trust you to do a good job with it.'

This comforted her a little. 'We're all *becoming* something, aren't we?'

'I think we're achieving the potential we always had. I think everybody has great potential, but necessity is the greatest motivator for discovering it.'

'Stop it. You're starting to sound like an optimist.' She smiled shyly. 'I was worried about you.'

He gave her hand a squeeze. 'It's made things worse.'

'What do you mean?'

'Before, I had only myself to worry about, and let's face it, I didn't worry too much. Now I can't stop worrying about you. All the time.'

'You're saying that's too much of a price to pay?'

'No. I'm saying it's given me even more of an impetus to find some way out of this mess so we can get back to our lives.' He felt a deep yearning for the normality he had once taken for granted. 'I want to lie in bed on Sunday morning with you, wander out for a lazy lunch. I want to feel what it's like just to do nothing with someone you love.'

She looked surprised. 'Do you love me?'

'Yes.' And he realised in that moment, for the first time, that he truly did, and that it was a feeling as potent as he had had for Marianne.

'Brother and Sister of Dragons.' The interruption came from Baccharus, who was bowing formally. 'The Master requests your presence.'

'Oh, we're back to *requests*, are we?' Ruth said under her breath. From the colour of her cheeks and the brightness in her eyes, Church could tell he had touched her deeply.

Baccharus led them to Manannan who rested in a large, high-backed chair. The light no longer broke out of his form, but his face had a weary cast. Even so, he brightened perceptibly when he laid eyes on Church and Ruth. It was strange to see any emotion on that normally impassive face, never mind something as subtle and human as gratitude.

'Brother and Sister of Dragons, you have my thanks for the part you have played this day. Amongst the Golden Ones there is a hard-held belief that we are the pinnacle of creation, a part of the fundament of existence. And with that belief is the certain knowledge that all other creatures lie beneath us. Some would argue this is reason enough to treat all other races with contempt. They are beasts of the field, and we are shepherds. But you have shown this day that Fragile Creatures are not so fragile, that you have the facility to climb the ladder of existence, even to rub shoulders with the Golden Ones. The signs are true. No more the centre path. This is my belief. And I mark it with this.' Manannan beckoned them forward, then gently took their hands in turn. His fingers felt like cold light; insubstantial, ghostly. There were faint sounds of surprise from some of the gathered gods, but when Manannan levelled his heavy gaze slowly around the room, the murmurings died away sharply.

'You will have my support in your undertaking, Brother and Sister of Dragons. My voice carries weight. The Golden Ones shall heed your call. This is the day the seasons have turned once more. This is the time. The Night Walkers shall be cleansed from existence.'

He spoke with such authority, Church almost believed him.

CHAPTER THIRTEEN

All Stars

'This is crazy! We can't sit here forever!' Laura hurled the empty baked beans tin across the warehouse.

The Bone Inspector winced at the clattering echoes bouncing around the vast, empty space. 'What do you suggest, then? Going out there and asking them nicely if you can go home?' He snorted contemptuously, wiping the bean juice from his mouth with the back of his hand.

Laura paced around the embers of the fire, her irritation turning to curiosity at the unfamiliar emotions growing inside her. For months she had been arguing with the others about running away from their obligations; now she couldn't do it even if she wanted. 'The responsibility's on us to find a way out,' she said firmly. She realised the Bone Inspector was watching her with a strange expression. 'What?'

'Nothing.' He slurped some more beans. 'I always thought you were the weak link who'd bring everything down.'

'You and me both.' She wandered over to one of the dirty windows. Smearing a patch clear, she watched the Fomorii scurrying along the banks of the Thames as they went about their mysterious tasks. The view was sickening, but strangely hypnotic. In another moment or two, though, another notion began to creep in. She turned to the Bone Inspector with a confident smile and said, 'Okay, here's the plan.'

The river had the dank, sour smell of rotting vegetation. Under the night sky, the water looked almost black as it lapped languidly against the creaking wharves. A hint of frost sparkled all around; it was the coldest night so far. Laura lay on the sodden boards and held out a hand so the Bone Inspector could steady himself. It had taken them three hours to find something they could use. The boat was holed and filled with a couple of inches of water; it looked like it had been abandoned for months. But it was big enough for them to lie in the bottom while it drifted in the strong currents out of the city and towards the sea.

After ten minutes of splashing and cursing, the Bone Inspector finished plugging the hole with the oily rags they had brought from the warehouse.

'Do you think it'll hold? I don't fancy swimming in this weather.'

'How should I know?' he snapped. 'I'm not a shipwright.'

'No. What you are is—'

'Just get in the boat.'

She lowered herself down to the tiny pebbly beach where plastic bottles and old ropes formed a trail along the water line. She was still amazed they had managed to avoid the Fomorii. They had encountered several large groups of them moving silently through the dark streets, but had always had time to find cover. She hoped it was a sign luck was on their side.

Once they had baled out as much as they could, they pushed the boat out into the freezing shallows, then jumped aboard. Water had already started to trickle into the bottom.

'We should stay near the banks,' the Bone Inspector said.

'There'll be too much chance of being seen.'

'This river has powerful currents. If we go down in the middle of it, we won't stand a chance.'

'All right. But if we get caught, I'm blaming you.'

They guided the boat into the current with a broken plank and then lay down in the bottom, watching the stars pass overhead.

Manannan recovered quickly enough to take back control of Wave Sweeper and soon they were speeding on their way. By the time dawn was breaking the sea was calm, the sky poised to turn a brilliant blue, free of even the smallest cloud. Soon the gulls were clustering around the mast and a cry was rising up from the watcher in the crow's-nest. The Green Fields of Enchantment came up quickly on the horizon, a sunlit haven of rolling, emerald downs dotted with crystal streams and cool woods.

From his position at the prow, Church watched in growing wonder. There was something breathtaking about the place that went far beyond its appearance; it was in the air, in some too-subtle signs that only his oldest senses could perceive, but it left his nerves singing and his stomach filled with tremors of excitement. Some deep-seated part of his mind was registering recognition of one of the oldest archetypes: a place of miracles and peace. Heaven.

Wave Sweeper sailed into a small harbour built of gleaming white marble. There were no other ships in sight and the dockside was deserted, apart from two of the younger gods manning the jetty. They took the ropes Taranis's men threw out and fastened them to iron spurs, but Church had the feeling Wave Sweeper would have waited there like a faithful dog anyway.

The Tuatha Dé Danann were allowed to disembark first, while the other strange travellers congregated below deck ready to begin their search for some meaning in their lives. Church and Ruth, however, were given pride of place at the front of the column with Manannan and Niamh.

They marched along a dusty road, baking in the heat, which wound briefly along the golden beach where the blue sea broke in white-topped waves before ending amongst the soothing shadows of the trees. Flowers bloomed in clusters of blue, red and gold. It reminded Church of Andalucia, or Umbria, an unspoiled rural climate designed for dreaming.

Manannan was borne on a gold chair carried sedan-style by four young gods. He was still weak, but he cocked his attention to Church and Ruth often enough for them to know they lay heavily on his mind. Niamh watched Church surreptitiously from beneath long lashes; it was impossible to tell what she was thinking, though her praise in the aftermath of the rescue had been fulsome, for both Church and Ruth.

The Court of High Regard lay in a shallow valley beyond the wall of soaring black pines, surrounded by pleasant grassed slopes where the breeze moved back and forth soothingly. If the first sight of the island had taken Church's breath away, the Court of High Regard was a hundred times more affecting. Tears of sheer awe stung his eyes; it was in the very fibre of the place, majesty in every atom.

Unlike the Court of the Final Word, it was more of a town – if not a city – than a court. The buildings were all white stone, so that the whole was almost impossible to view in the sun. In the architecture, Church glimpsed touches of the Middle East, of ancient Greece and Rome, Japan and the heavy Gothic stylings of mediaeval France. There were domes and towers, cupolas and obelisks, Doric columns and piazzas and sweeping boulevards where fountains tinkled pleasantly. Clusters of cultivated trees provided shade to talk and think.

'It's beautiful.' Ruth blinked away her own tears. 'Now I know why the stories said visitors never wanted to leave.'

They entered through gates of ivory and glass. Once within, the Tuatha Dé Danann dispersed into small groups conversing quietly but intently.

Church and Ruth were left alone next to a statue that resembled the god Pan, but every time Church looked at it, it had a different face. 'Now what?' Ruth said.

After ten minutes Baccharus returned with a tall, thin god with flowing black hair and sculpted bone structure who resembled an aristocrat in his late twenties. 'The Master has already announced your presence to the court,' Baccharus said. 'A decision will be announced soon on when you may make your case. In the meantime, I have discussed your needs with Callaitus, Provarum of the sector of Trust and Hope, who will make the arrangements for your stay.'

Church took his hand and shook it. 'Thank you for everything you've done for us, Baccharus.'

Surprisingly, Baccharus appeared humbled by this. 'I will be along shortly. There are other matters—'

'I understand,' Church said knowingly. 'We'll talk later.'

Callaitus took them to a light and airy chamber, far removed from the cramped quarters of Wave Sweeper. At the window, the most delicate linen blew gently in the breeze. There was a large bed covered with sumptuous cushions and deep, soft blankets. A small wooden table held a bowl of fruit and a crystal decanter filled with sparkling water.

'Married quarters,' Ruth said, looking round at the furniture and space.

'What?'

'On the ship they put us in adjoining cabins. Here we've got a room together. How very presumptuous of them,' she added with mock-affront.

'They're good at looking beneath the surface.'

She eyed him studiously, remembering his words on Wave Sweeper, saying nothing.

'I wonder where I'll find the Pool of Wishes.' He threw himself on the bed and slipped his hands behind his head. The soothing atmosphere made him feel instantly sleepy.

'I wonder what you'll find there.' A dark note rang clearly in her voice.

'What are you inferring?'

'You know how these things work. Everything comes with a price. You want to get rid of something big. That's got to be balanced out.'

He threw an arm across his eyes. 'I don't think I can take any more sacrifice.'

'Let's have none of that.' He felt the bed give as she climbed on. There was a rustle of clothing, more movement, and then she straddled him. He looked up to see her naked to the waist. She laughed silently at his expression. 'Remember your mantra: *Life's good as long as you don't weaken.* So stop thinking about all the sacrifice and suffering. Focus on the good stuff. That's a rule for living, Churchill.' She slowly ground her hips on his groin, smiling now, gently teasing.

Sleep was going to have to wait.

When he woke, dark had fallen. It was still warm, and fragrant with woodsmoke and the heady perfume of night blooms. There was a sense of magic in the air. He eased his arm out from under Ruth, who stirred and muttered, but didn't rouse, then dressed lazily before stepping out. The evening was alight with flickering torches gleaming off the white buildings. Faint, melodic music drifted across the jumbled rooftops, and somewhere he could make out the excited chattering of many voices. He leaned against the doorjamb and breathed deeply, enjoying the peace.

Across the piazza, a shadow stirred, then separated from the surrounding shadows. Baccharus made his way over from the bench where he had been sitting patiently.

'You needed to rest,' he said by way of greeting.

'Have you been waiting long?'

'It is not waiting if you are engaged in something important, and I was enjoying my time here in the Court of High Regard. I could have sat there until light.'

'You missed this place?'

'It is where I feel comfortable.' He placed a hand on Church's shoulder. 'Come, there is much we need to discuss, and this is not the best place.'

The streets wound round and back on themselves, diverged, became vast boulevards, then a network of interlocking alleys; briefly Church felt like he was back on Wave Sweeper in the endless corridors. He mentioned this to Baccharus, and for a second or two he had the odd impression he was lying on his back looking up into a brilliant, phosphorescent light. It faded into a gentler luminescence that flickered over a studded oak door. Baccharus pushed open the door and beckoned for Church to step through.

It was an inn, low-ceilinged, straw on the floor, lots of tables and stools nestling in the comfortable shadows of nooks and crannies. A large fire roared in the grate despite the summery warmth, yet the temperature remained agreeable. The drinkers were a mixed group. Church recognised many of the travellers he had seen on Wave Sweeper – some of them even nodded to him as if they were old friends – but there were many strangers.

'None of your people?' Church said.

'This place is for the benefit of others. The many who come to visit us, seeking the gratitude of the gods, seeking direction or redemption.'

There was a raucous group of muscular men with red beards, so they headed to a quiet table under the overhang of a staircase. It was pleasantly dark and secluded. Baccharus returned from the bar with two pewter mugs filled with ale that frothed over the edges.

'Given freely and without obligation?'

'This is a place for visitors,' Baccharus replied. 'Everything here is given freely and without obligation.'

Church took a sip. It felt like light and colours were streaming down his throat; a faint buzz of exhilaration filled his veins. 'You're trying to get me drunk before you tell me what you have to say?'

'No. This is the drink of welcome, to put you in a receptive frame of mind.'

'That's what I said.' Church took a long draught, then looked Baccharus directly in his deep, golden eyes. 'What's the true story?'

'That is unanswerable. You strip away one story and another lies behind it, and another, and another. You will never find the true story that lies behind it all, for there lies the truth of life. All is illusion, each illusion as valid as any other, until you reach that final level, and to find that is to know how everything works. To know the mind of . . .' His words trailed off and he ended his thought with a gesture suggesting something too big to comprehend.

'You're as bad as Tom. Ask a simple question and you get a philosophy lecture.'

'The Rhymer is a good man.'

'That's not the point. In *this* story' – his sweeping arm took in the whole of the bar – 'there are a lot of illusions, and now it's time for the truth. Like why you murdered Cormorel.'

Church expected some kind of surprise from Baccharus, or guilt perhaps, or even anger that he had been uncovered, but there was nothing. 'I pay a price every day for that act.'

'You were *friends*.'

'More than that. To lose Cormorel was like losing part of myself. My existence is forever tainted.'

'Then, why?'

'How long have you known?'

'Don't change the subject.' He softened slightly when he saw Baccharus was telling the truth about his hurt. 'It came to me just before we disembarked. No blinding revelation. Just a gentle understanding that that was what must have happened. You were arguing at the banquet just before he died—'

'Cormorel and I held contrary positions of a kind that you would find hard to grasp unless you were a Golden One.'

'Try me.'

Baccharus finished his beer, then signalled for the barman to bring over two more. 'Then I will tell you of the things I brought you here to understand. Of truth, of a kind. Consider: the view held by the Golden Ones of Fragile Creatures.'

'That we're the lowest of the low.'

'There are many of my kind who would disagree.'

Church was taken aback by this. 'I know some of you are closer to us than others, but I thought all of you at least vaguely held the same view. Veitch defined it: you're like aristocrats looking down on what you consider the lesser-born. Some of you despise us, some of you hold us in contempt, some of you mock us, and even the ones of you who think we're okay still think we're way beneath you.'

'I can understand how you might think that, for that is the view of some, but not all. No, some of us believe the Fragile Creatures are in an exalted position; even above the Golden Ones in the structure of existence, for in their arrogance the Golden Ones have embraced stagnancy, while you Fragile Creatures continue to rise and advance. Within your kind lies tremendous potential. The Golden Ones no longer have potential. This view, as you might expect, is tantamount to blasphemy in some quarters. Indeed, the Golden Ones are riven. But for those of us who are concerned with the great sweep of existence rather than the narrow perspective of our kind, the future of the Fragile Creatures is very important indeed.'

At the bar, the red-bearded men had started to punch each other hard, while laughing heartily. Some of the other drinkers were moving away hesitantly. 'That would be quite a turnaround. Riven, you say. Like a civil war situation?'

'It is very close to that. The Golden Ones have always seen our position as unassailable. Yet to suggest we are not all-knowing, all-powerful, would weaken our position and allow us to be supplanted. A contradiction that gives the lie to the former. I think the latter is not only inevitable – for it is the way of existence – but also to be desired, again, in terms of existence.'

'I remember the first time we met you and Cormorel at the campfire,' Church mused. 'The two of you had a disagreement about whether humanity could ever evolve into gods.'

'At that time, Cormorel did not know the extent of my beliefs, although he was aware of the fractures forming amongst my people. I was influenced by others who have had more contact with the Fragile Creatures across the turning of the ages.'

'Niamh?'

'And the one you know as Cernunnos, and his partner. Ogma. And many more.'

'The three smiths on Wave Sweeper? Were they preparing weapons for a civil war?'

'Perhaps.' Baccharus was uncomfortable. 'Or for a war against the Night Walkers. We would have launched one independently, if necessary. It was, as you pointed out, inevitable. To pretend otherwise was the height of arrogance.'

'Goibhniu wasn't very pleasant to me.'

'He is new to our beliefs, brought round by Niamh, who knew he would be an important asset to our side. He accepts the way things are, but he finds it hard to break from past feelings for Fragile Creatures.'

Church stared into the dark depths of his beer. 'Tom knows about all this?' Comments Tom had made, which at the time had been cryptic or just plain strange, suddenly fell into a new perspective; Baccharus nodded. 'So this isn't just about saving humanity from a big threat, it's about preserving the future of life, everything?'

'True Thomas knew the Golden Ones would have to be resisted as much as the Night Walkers if you Fragile Creatures were to prosper. He is an adept at politics.' Baccharus smiled. 'I like him immensely.'

What had been a quiet conversation about Baccharus's motivation for murder had suddenly taken on a terrible significance that he couldn't absorb all at once. 'What are you saying exactly?'

'I am saying you are all stars. Each Fragile Creature bursting with the potential of a god. Given the right situation, that potential could easily blossom, and from what I have seen of you and the other Brothers and Sisters of Dragons, you could far surpass the Golden Ones. You could all become greater than everything that ever existed. For you love and cry, you are tender, and caring—'

'—and hateful and murderous.'

Baccharus shrugged. 'It is there within you. The light burns very brightly. Brighter than my own.'

'You're talking about a long period of time—'

Baccharus lowered his head so shadows pooled in his eyes; a skull in the play of light and shade. 'These events you find yourselves in are a catalyst that could propel you – all of your kind – into the next phase of development. My people know this – some will deny it, but they know it somewhere within themselves – and they seek to prevent you achieving your destiny. You will have to fight for your future.'

'That makes a change.' Church pushed his stool back on two legs and rocked, tipsy now. 'So, trickery and deceit right the way down the line. Situation normal.'

'There are manipulations ahead,' Baccharus continued. 'You need to know what is at stake so you can act accordingly; when lies are told to you, when seemingly simple choices are asked of you. Do not allow anyone to make you believe you are lesser, unimportant.'

'I never did.'

Baccharus smiled. 'I always admired your confidence, Brother of Dragons.'

'I saw some of the splits on Wave Sweeper. Many were angered that Manannan offered us his support.'

'The Master had always steered a calm path between the troubled waters. I felt his sympathies lay with you and your kind, but with his position amongst the Golden Ones, to openly endorse our stance would have caused too much upheaval.'

'But now he's going to do it?'

Baccharus nodded slowly.

'This must be the first time that gods are servant to the people who worshipped them.'

'All should be in servitude to others, and all should be free.'

'But this split amongst your people . . . is it really so bad?'

Baccharus gave a thin-lipped smile. 'If there is to be war amongst the Golden Ones, you will find many fighting for the future of the Fragile Creatures.'

'You'd do that? Against your own people?'

'This concerns much more than one severely limited perspective, even if that vista belongs to the Golden Ones. We are all servants of existence, and we must do what we can to ensure the best possible state for all.'

'So let me get this straight – humans have the potential to become gods—'

Baccharus winced at the description, waved it away with a lazy hand.

'—greater, then. Than we are now. To achieve the massive potential—'

'—encoded in your very make-up.' Baccharus nodded emphatically. 'You were made with the powers of stars inside you. All sentient creatures are formed to rise and advance. That is the reason for all this.' He made an expansive gesture.

'The Golden Ones have stopped advancing, for whatever reason. Some fatal flaw. But they don't want to be supplanted by Fragile

Creatures and so they will do everything they can to keep us down. To prevent us achieving our destiny.' Church looked dreamily towards the bar where the red-headed men were still punching each other, though their laughter was now more forced.

Baccharus smiled proudly at Church's expert summing up of the complex matters he had raised. He raised a finger. 'One more thing: the lie is given to my people's assertions of superiority by the mere existence of the Court of the Final Word.'

Church grew cold at the mention of the Tuatha Dé Danann court supposedly devoted to healing, but where more sinister things happened in its deepest recesses. 'What do you mean?'

'For many generations of your people the Court of the Final Word has been *investigating* mortal children.' Baccharus pronounced the word carefully. 'My people wish to know what innate part of Fragile Creatures is the key to their advancement.'

'So they can steal it for themselves!' Church grew rigid at the repercussions that spun out of Baccharus's comment. 'That's why Tom's Queen was so adept at taking him apart and putting him back together!'

'Oh, my people know every component part of Fragile Creatures. They know how every molecule interlocks with every other molecule. But they have still not found the source of your potential.' His eyes sparkled. 'And they never will.'

'This is too much for me to take in right now.' Church held up the beer. 'This doesn't help. But you're right – it puts me in the correct frame of mind. I thought I'd get everything laid out in my mind about what we were fighting for. Now it's even bigger stakes. Not just survival, but our . . . evolution? Crazy.'

'These are monumental times.'

'You're telling me. Wait till Ruth hears about this.' He leaned forward once more and peered back into his beer. 'Now tell me about Cormorel,' he said quietly.

Baccharus stared at one of the flickering torches for a long time. 'It is said my people feel nothing like you Fragile Creatures feel. But I loved Cormorel. I think, once we see things from your perspective, we learn to be how we perhaps once were.'

'Then how could you kill him?'

'It was not my intention at the time, but in the instant before I acted, I knew it had to be done. Cormorel had discovered there was a conspiracy afoot. That is his word. Conspiracy. Niamh, myself, certain others, had taken the decision to confound those who attempted to block the chances which might come the way of the Fragile Creatures on their path to enlightenment. Niamh and I had formed an alliance with some of the other creatures on Wave Sweeper—'

'The Portunes.'

'And others. And in the eyes of my people, associating with such lowly creatures against our own kind was the ultimate crime. Cormorel was preparing to expose us. The Portunes and all the others would have been eradicated. Niamh would have been despatched to the Court of the Final Word, where she would have suffered. Immeasurably.' He bowed his head even further. 'I pursued Cormorel on to the deck during the upheaval of the attack—'

'That was the Fomorii's first strike, right? Not you?'

He nodded. 'I was pleading with him. He would have none of it. In fact, he took great pleasure in the pain he saw he was causing me. For all that he considered himself above the emotions of Fragile Creatures, he was filled with cruelty.'

'How did you do it?'

'There is a manner known only to my people.' Church wouldn't have dreamed of asking, but Baccharus added, 'It cannot be revealed to any outsider.'

'And the Walpurgis was caught with his hand in the biscuit tin, having a final meal.'

'Destroying the evidence. If he had succeeded, my people would have believed Cormorel was simply washed overboard during the attack and would have turned up sooner or later.'

The weight that lay on Baccharus's shoulders was palpable. Church rested a supportive hand on his forearm. 'You did the right thing. Under the circumstances. There was too much at stake.'

'But that does not diminish the pain I feel, for I committed a crime against existence itself. While striking a blow for existence. I have wrestled with the conundrum every hour since then and still made no sense of it. Did I do the right thing? Can an act of such terrible negativity create something worthwhile?'

The questions were not rhetorical; the weight of emotion in Baccharus's voice showed he was asking for guidance. The fact that he felt Church somehow had the wisdom was shocking; how could Baccharus possibly perceive him as someone who had a grasp of such things? 'Time will give you the answer to that, Baccharus.' He hoped it didn't sound like too much of a platitude.

They were disturbed by a blast of warm air as the door swung open. Ruth walked in, looking around curiously. Church called her over.

'Typical. First chance you get, you men are straight down the pub,' she said in a faux-chiding voice.

'How did you find us?'

'A little bird told me.' She wrinkled her nose as she looked round at the raucous activity at the bar. 'So let me guess. I've got a choice of beer, beer or beer.'

'I'll see if I can get you a lady's glass.' Church dodged away before she could hit him. She turned to Baccharus. 'So what were you two talking about so seriously?'

'Death. Conspiracy. The rising and advancing of the spirit.'

She rolled her eyes. 'Oh, how we laughed.'

'It could have been worse.' Veitch huddled closer to the fire. In his weakened state, the chill October night bit deep into his bones.

'In what way could it have been worse? The Grim Lands were a particularly unpleasant experience.' Shavi took a sip of the bright green absinthe they'd picked up in a deserted off-licence before passing the bottle on to Tom.

'I could have had to give you the kiss of life.'

'And how would that have been worse?'

'Because you'd still be lying there!' Veitch chuckled.

'Well, you seem to be getting better.' Shavi eyed his friend warmly. He had been worried Veitch was going to crack under the shock of losing his hand – certainly the first few hours after their return from the Grim Lands had been very hard – but since then he had regained much of his equilibrium. However, there were still too many worrying signs for Shavi to relax: a wildness in the eyes, exaggerated movements, overreactions. He hoped the Blue Fire would work its magic before things started to fall apart.

Veitch took the absinthe from Tom.

'You know you're not supposed to drink it neat,' Tom said, with a little too much contempt. 'You mix it with water, a spoon of caramelised sugar. They say you'd have to have half a brain to take it without watering it down.'

Veitch grinned, waving the bottle in front of Tom's face before taking another slug.

Tom gave him a sour stare. 'It's got hallucinogenic properties, you know. The active ingredient from cannabis.'

'Oh yes . . . you're right.' Veitch pretended to waver. 'I can see things! It's amazing! You look . . . almost human!'

Tom snorted and waved him away.

Veitch let his chuckles die away before rubbing his hand thoughtfully over his three-day stubble. He looked over at Shavi curiously.

'What?'

'How you doin'?'

Shavi gave a questioning shrug.

'You died, or nearest thing to it. That must have done your head in. How do you come back from something like that?'

'So you do care.'

'Just checking you're not going to go psycho with an axe in the middle of the night.' His smile gave the lie to his words. He threw another log on the fire; it cracked and spattered, sending sparks shooting up with the smoke.

'I actually feel better than I did before I died.' Shavi pulled the blanket tight around his shoulders, his breath white. Winter was not far away. 'You may find that hard to believe. But I have made my peace with Lee. I have seen the other side of death and returned to talk about it. I have been reborn, bright and new in the world. It was a redemptive experience, highly spiritual, uplifting.'

'Yeah, but can you still get a stiffy?' Veitch leaned back against his rucksack, laughing drunkenly.

'Don't be talking to him,' Tom said sternly. 'You won't be getting any sense out of him tonight.'

'You are implying I get sense out of him at any time.' Shavi didn't see the boot coming; it hit him on the side of the head.

'Yessss! One-nil!'

They had embarked on a meandering route west after leaving Wandlebury Camp, careful to keep a good distance from London. The darkness in the south was growing with each hour, like night eating the day. The cinders in the breeze were more pronounced, and there was an overall sense of despair hanging in the increasingly cold wind. The world was winding down.

With Samhain approaching rapidly, a deep anxiety had gripped them, amplified by the certain knowledge that there was nothing they could do alone. They needed Church to succeed in his mission. They needed Ruth and Laura too. Sometimes it was almost too hard to hope, and that was when the depression set in.

But their abiding friendship, forged through hard times, kept them going and ensured the evenings around the campfire were filled with light talk and humour, lifting spirits dampened by the day's sights of deserted villages, frightened people hiding in their homes, or children and old people begging for food.

It wasn't as if they had any plan except to find Church and Ruth and Laura. That lack of direction left Veitch feeling strained and irritable.

He was not a person who coped well with inactivity, particularly with time running out, when there was so much that *needed* to be done.

Shavi, however, guessed Tom knew more than he was saying.

'Do you think we'll find them?' Shavi said, breaking the rule of keeping the conversation light. Next to him, Veitch snored loudly in a drunken sleep.

'I think there is always hope.' Tom enjoyed a joint as he stared into the fire.

'But you are True Thomas. You can see the future. You must know something.'

'I try not to look. What will be, will be.'

Perhaps it was the drugs or the drink affecting him, but for the first time Tom's cool exterior was not impervious. Shavi caught a glimpse in the Rhymer's face of all the things Tom was not saying, and he was uncomfortable with what he saw.

'What if you really did see everything?' Shavi suggested. 'What if you knew exactly what was going to happen, bar a few minor hiccups here and there. What if you knew who lived and who died?'

Tom raised his head sharply to fix a stare that was so cold Shavi felt a chill in his bones. 'Then,' Tom said, 'my life would be damned.'

At the heart of the Court of High Regard stood an enormous tree with a trunk as far around as an office block and a top lost high overhead. All around it spread an area of distortion that left Church continually disoriented; buildings were never quite the same each time he looked at them. Some were substantially altered, one moment a sweeping dome like St Paul's, the next a thrusting tower of Middle Eastern design. At times Church would glimpse rapid movement from the corner of his eye, the hint of crystal birds flapping across the sky, but when he looked there was nothing. People came and went as they crossed a piazza, or appeared in a haze on a corner, while the dead appeared to be everywhere, dazed, beatific, unthreatening.

'This is where our heart beats, the closest to the fabled home of our deepest memory.' Niamh's voice trembled with awe. Church was struck by how young and girlish she appeared, not alien at all. Now Baccharus had explained the distinction amongst the Tuatha Dé Danann, Church was amazed he hadn't seen it before. It was as simple as those who felt and those who didn't.

'Have you always been like this?'

She looked at him curiously with her large, innocent eyes. 'No,' she said after a moment's thought, 'once I was a true daughter of the

Golden Ones, one of the confirmed rulers of all existence, above all else.'

'Then why did you change? When you hold such a position, it must take something phenomenal to turn you around.'

'I was taught, over what your people would consider a long period of time.'

'Who taught you?'

She smiled a little sadly, but did not answer.

They continued their tour in silence for a while, until Church broke the restrained mood by asking about the enormous tree.

'It is the World-Tree,' Niamh said, looking up into the distant branches. 'It is at the heart of all worlds. Its roots go down, its branches reach up.'

'Linking Heaven and Earth. This is an amazing place.' And it was. Wonder brought every nerve alive, just breathing air, looking round at the fluid scenery. It was filled with magic, the thing his life had always lacked.

'Once the Fixed Lands had the same power. Everything was alive, constantly changing. But your brethren stopped believing, or believed in the wrong things. You wished your world to be something lesser.'

Church examined a fountain where the water turned into tiny diamonds. 'I keep hearing that phrase, about wishing the world a certain way.'

'Nothing is truly fixed. The Fixed Lands are only such because they are sleeping. All is illusion, and all illusion is fluid. Belief is a powerful tool. Creatures great and small – life – is at the centre of everything, and they can shape things as they see fit. Nothing has to be accepted.'

'If you just wish hard enough,' he mused. 'I was never happy with how things were in my world. There was always something lacking. And it was getting worse. The people I didn't like, the ones interested in money over everything, and personal power, they seemed to be driving things their way. It wasn't a world for people like me.'

'You gave up your responsibility, Jack.'

'What do you mean?'

'The people you despised were wishing harder, setting the world the way they wanted. They are the Night Walkers, whichever form they take. People like you, Jack, people who truly believe, have a responsibility to take a stand and wish the world the way it should be. To wake the land, to dream it real. Belief is stronger than anything the Night Walkers have.'

The crystal birds were still flying around the edges of his vision and there was faint music on the wind, still powerful enough to make his emotions soar. What Niamh was saying echoed deeply inside him. He realised she was staring at him intently, and when he turned to her he was shocked to see tears in her eyes.

'I have made my peace with the way things are, Jack.'

He took her hand, concerned. 'Don't cry. What's wrong?'

'The Golden Ones have always used their power without responsibility. They have achieved their ends by force. I would never do that, for I have learned it would be valueless, and the thing I strive for has too much value to be wasted. I see now we will never achieve the love that has filled my thoughts since the darkest days of the Fragile Creatures.' She gazed into the middle distance, her eyes full. 'I had hoped, once it came to this time, your heart would have opened to me, as mine did to yours so long ago. But I see clearly now your love for the Sister of Dragons is true; that indeed it is worthy of a love that transcends all time.'

Church felt truly sorry for what he saw in her face. 'We can still be friends, Niamh.'

She smiled wanly. 'And that enriches my existence, but if you only knew what lay before this point . . .' Her words drifted away.

'What do you mean?'

Her smile became a little brighter, to hide her thoughts. 'I will always love you, Jack, and in time you will understand where that love comes from.' She cupped his hand in hers. 'I have always had your best interests at heart, but from this moment on I dedicate myself to helping you achieve your aims, whatever it may cost me.'

He gave her hand a warm squeeze, overwhelmed by the level of emotion that was being expressed. 'You're a good woman, Niamh.'

'Now, come, I have many sights to show you. Wonders beyond your imagining.' She brushed her tears away, her smile gleaming. 'These days will stay with you always.'

The tour was indeed as amazing as Niamh had predicted. Some of the sights were so startling his mind could barely cope within them, and within the hour the reality of them began to fade until they took on the warmly comforting but intangible quality of dreams that would haunt him forever.

But even though time meant nothing in that place, he was acutely aware of events running away from him. The real world seemed so far gone, but what he might find when he returned filled him with dread. Each moment wasted could mean another death, another life filled with suffering. And it felt like he had been gone so long.

But when he returned to his chamber, Baccharus informed him that approval to enter the Pool of Wishes had been granted by some higher authority. It was finally time to act.

As twilight fell across the Court, thousands of torches sprang into life like summer fireflies. Baccharus, Niamh and Ruth gathered in the main piazza with four horses. The beasts were powerful, snorting and stamping loudly on the shimmering marble; at first glance they appeared normal to Ruth, then she noticed the hint of Otherworld in their eyes where a disturbing intelligence burned.

Church had spent the previous hour in his room preparing himself; he had enjoyed the tranquillity after spending so long with Ruth discussing the shocking repercussions of what Baccharus had told him in the inn. Baccharus had also warned him that the Pool of Wishes was not something to be taken lightly, as if anything in that realm was. He would be forced to journey deep inside himself to locate the taint of the Fomorii, Baccharus said, and if he was not at ease with himself, the experience would drive him mad.

And so he spent the time thinking of his life, of Dale and his friends in London – where were they now? – of Marianne and his love for her, of the terrible grief he had felt at her death, of his parents, and his studies, his dreams and fears, of Laura and Niamh and Ruth, and at the end of it, it still didn't make any sense.

Finally he was ready. The other three were already mounted when he took the long walk across the piazza, his footsteps echoing solemnly. Their greeting was just as serious, a simple nod, a faint smile, and then they were away through the labyrinthine streets of the Court towards the green countryside beyond.

Baccharus led the way, with Church behind, then Ruth, and Niamh taking up the rear. As they passed, Church glimpsed strange faces watching him from the darkened windows, some of them golden and alien, some of them terrible and dark. The buildings grew more solid as they approached the outskirts, jumbling tight up against themselves like the oppressive weight of ancient habitation that lay crushed within Jerusalem's walls.

Once the Court was behind them, green fields lined by thick, old hedges rolled out. They passed intermittent copses and trickling brooks that made their way through culverts under the rough road. But then the country became wilder, the trees taller and darker, pressing hard against the roadside, forming a roof above their heads. Baccharus held up a lantern as they rode and they were all grateful for the flickering golden light that flooded ahead.

Church occasionally heard movement, although in the thick shadow it was impossible to discern what was amongst the trees; some seemed too large for any animal he knew, others were small and fast, some came far too close to the circle of light, which increasingly felt insignificant. Eventually the road all but disappeared and the trees came up so hard they could have reached out and touched them on either side if they had so wished. Church spent so much time attempting to probe the woods on either side, he nearly ran his mount into Baccharus on more than one occasion. The undergrowth was thick with bramble and bracken, which would have made the going hard if they had strayed from the path.

To Church's relief, as the going became steeper the wood eventually gave way. When they finally emerged from the trees, he realised they were on the foothills leading up to snow-capped mountains, although he couldn't recall seeing them from the ship as they approached the island.

'Are we going right to the top?' Church asked.

Baccharus put a silencing finger to his lips. 'There are things around here that appreciate silence,' he whispered.

The road – now barely more than a track – became rocky and the horses had to step slowly. Boulders piled up on either side, cracked and patch-worked with moss. The air was much cooler. Church pulled his jacket around him, oddly wondering what the weather was like back home.

After a little while longer, Baccharus reined in his horse and nodded towards a group of pine trees separated from a thickly forested slope by a rocky outcropping on three sides. A distinct path wound its way into the centre of the copse.

'In there?' Church asked quietly.

Baccharus nodded once more.

Church jumped down and advanced several paces before he realised the others were not behind him. 'From here your journey must be alone,' Niamh whispered in reply to his quizzical expression. That brought a sharp chill to his spine.

In the trees, it was even cooler, but the air was beautifully scented with pine and the tang of the mountain snows. Overheard, a stunning full moon glowed white and misty butterscotch, framed by icy, glittering stars. His breath bloomed; a shiver ran through him. Thankfully Baccharus had allowed him to bring the lantern to keep the shadows at bay, although his movement made them jump and recede as if they were alive. Pine needles crunched underfoot, but beneath them the path was oddly well-made, with large flagstones worn by age.

The first thing he noticed when he entered the copse was the soothing sound of tinkling water. The path opened out on to a broad, still pool, black and reflective, with trees all around it. On the opposite side was a jutting rock, face-down, over which white water cascaded, churning the pool just beneath but obviously carried away by some underground stream before it sent waves lashing out across the surface. The air was heavy with a feeling of deep tranquillity, but as Church stood and drank in the atmosphere, it changed slightly until he sensed something jarring uneasily just beneath it. As he gave in to his instincts he could feel a dim electricity in the air, waiting to be awakened. This was the place.

He played the lantern back and forth and noticed the stone flags disappeared around the back of the waterfall. With anxiety tight in his throat, he stepped cautiously around the edge of the pool, half-expecting something to leap out and drag him in. He paused briefly next to the waterfall before darting behind.

It was like crossing over into a place completely detached from the other world. It was a grotto, with barely formed stalagmites and glistening walls where the lantern made a million sparkles dance, and reds, greens and yellows shimmered in the wet brown of the rock. It was small, barely a couple of car lengths across, and within lay another pool, a mirror image of the one without, only without the waterfall the water was even darker. The flagstones gave out to a small, rocky path that ran around the edge, at some points barely wide enough to walk around. Echoes of gently lapping water rolled off the walls, distorting but peaceful. He set down the lantern and kneeled to peer into the depths.

He expected to see the pebbled bottom of the pool easily, at least around the edges near the lantern, but the black water appeared to go down forever. He didn't really know what to do next. Baccharus had told him simply to wait, stressing that 'the pool would see' and know what was needed. Yet the surroundings felt so normal it felt silly sitting back waiting.

There was a certain odd oiliness to the quality of the water, so he reached out a hand to stroke his fingers across the surface. At the last moment he withdrew; something was sending alarm bells ringing in his head. He slumped back against the wall, hugged his knees and waited.

It was less than a minute later when he perceived – or thought he did – some activity deep below. Now on all fours, he pressed his face close to the water's surface to get a better look. Something was swimming. The perspective it gave him was shocking, for the pool went down more than twenty or thirty feet, and even then he couldn't see the bottom.

Whatever was there was striking out for the surface. The lantern light brought reflected glints from its skin, at times silvery, at times flesh-tone. It was certainly a trick of the distorting effect of the water, but it gave him the impression that the pool's inhabitant kept changing back and forth from a fish to a human. Or was somehow both at the same time.

And still it rose, until it was obvious it was human, long arms reaching out, feet kicking, but the face was still obscured by shadows. It covered the last few feet very quickly, but stopped short of coming completely out of the water. Instead, it hovered patiently, looking up at him, only an inch or two beneath the surface, and in that instant he was overcome by a deep dread. The face he was looking into was his own, his long hair drifting in the currents, only it was changed very slightly, in the way the features were held or in some sour experience that had left its mark, so that it was darker in essence.

For long seconds they were locked in that connecting stare, and then there was a flurry of rapid movement in the water. The Other-Church's arms shot out of the pool, clamped on Church's shoulders, and before he could resist, dragged him under.

In the shock, he didn't have time to grab a breath of air. The cold water rushed into his mouth and up his nose before he clamped his lips shut and struggled frantically to push his head up above the surface. But though he fought wildly, turning the pool into a maelstrom, his other self was far too strong. Further down it hauled him, and down even more, until the light from the lantern was too dim to illuminate the water and his lungs seared from the strain. He struck out futilely a few more times, the blows so weak they barely registered, and then his mouth jerked open and the water flooded in, filling his throat, his lungs. Fractured thoughts flared briefly in his mind, but the abiding sense was that it wasn't supposed to be like that.

Except that one minute later, he realised he was still breathing; inexplicably. His brain fizzed and sparked, somehow found a state of grace that allowed his thoughts to grow ordered once more. He wasn't dead; he was breathing water.

The Other-Church released his grip, although his face still had that mean cast; Church thought how much older and unattractive a state of mind could make him look. He signed for the Other to tell him what was happening, but it gave an expression of slight contempt before turning and swimming away. Church had no choice but to follow.

The experience had the distorting feeling of a hallucination. Briefly he wondered if he was dead and this was some final, random activity in his dying brain, but then he noticed a strange sheen across the whole of the pool that resembled the skin of a bubble. The Other swam into it, and through it; Church couldn't see anything on the other side. He hesitated, then followed suit.

The bubble gave slightly as he touched it, then eased over his body, finally accepting him with a slight give. Emerging on the other side, he was shocked to realise there was no water at all; he was in midair and it was dark. Suddenly he was falling, the water shooting out of his lungs. The sensation lasted for only a few seconds until he found himself standing on a broad plain covered in stubby grass, beneath a star-studded night sky and ringed by black mountains. Before him was a pile of rocks fused into a pillar that rose three feet above his head. The Other-Church stood on the far side of the pillar, the same distance from it as he was.

'What is happening here?' His voice resonated strangely in the wide-open spaces. As he spoke, the Other-Church mimicked him silently.

The pillar of stones began to hum with a low, bass note. Church couldn't take his eyes off it; the atmosphere was heavy with anticipation. As the Other-Church continued to glower at him, movement became visible within the pillar and gradually a figure stepped out of the solid rock.

Church's stomach flipped. Marianne looked exactly as she had when she was alive, not the gaunt, spectral figure sent by the Fomorii to torment him. His shoulders sagged; conflicting emotions tore through him: doubt, terrible sadness, a touch of joy. 'Marianne.'

She smiled at him weakly.

'You're another hallucination of this place.' He rubbed a hand across his face, but when he looked back up she was still there.

'I'm here, Church. At least, a part of me, a part they couldn't get to. An echo.'

Tears flooded his eyes. 'Really?'

'Really.'

He made to move forward, arms outstretched, but she held up a sudden hand to warn him back. She shook her head strongly. 'We can't.'

'Why not?' Almost a plea.

'There are rules, Church. Things going on that you can't imagine, beyond what you see here, or there, or anywhere. I can't tell you . . . can't explain. I'm not allowed.'

'Not allowed by whom?' Her face grew still. She took a step back towards the pillar. 'No! Okay, I won't ask any more about that!'

She smiled, brighter this time. 'It's good to see you, Church.'

For a brief while, he couldn't see for the tears. 'Thank you,' he choked as a delaying tactic, 'for the contact you made in the house . . . on Mam Tor . . . The writing . . .'

'I had to do something, Church. I couldn't bear to see you so broken.'

'You could see me?' No answer. 'Okay . . . the part of you the Fomorii have—'

Her face darkened; she hugged her arms around her, a mannerism he recalled her doing when she was distraught; when she was alive. 'It feels like it's tearing my heart out.'

His voice grew rough and fractured. 'I'm going to save you, Marianne.'

Her expression was, if not quite patronising, then certainly pitying.

'I am.' Reassuring at first, then defiantly: 'I am.'

His emotions felt they would break him in two. He wanted to ask her about her death, about who had killed her, how bad it had been, whether she had really suffered as he always imagined, but looking into her face where the Marianne he loved still resided, he couldn't bring himself to do it. There were a thousand questions, but his overwhelming desire was for the one thing every bereaved person wished for above all else, but could never, ever achieve: to tell her how he truly felt.

As he was about to speak, she silenced him with a raised finger. 'I know how you feel, Church, and I always felt the same about you. You were the only person I ever loved.'

He covered his eyes.

'I know your thoughts now, Church. I know your hopes. And that's a good thing, truly. In the days that follow, remember that. And I know about Ruth, and that's okay. She's a remarkable person. You've made a lot of silly mistakes since I died, but she was the right one. You stick with her, she'll stick with you.'

A sob choked in his throat. 'I miss you.'

'I know. But you should have learned a lot of things by now. That nothing is truly fixed in the Fixed Lands.' Her use of words he had heard before brought him up sharp. He blinked away his tears and started to listen. 'You see things from your own perspective, but in the broad sweep of existence, things look very different. When you know the rules, everything changes. Things are switched right around when they're put in context: what seems a bad experience becomes good, good, bad. I can't explain better than that at the moment, but you can't judge now, Church. Just accept things, and know there's something more.'

'I know, I do.'

'But sometimes it's hard.'

He nodded.

'Feel it, don't think it. The Age of Reason is long gone.'

'I feel so tired, Marianne. I want a rest from all this.'

Her smile grew sad. 'There won't be any rest, Church.'

'I heard that before.'

'It's true. No rest. But there'll be a balance. You'll know why there's no rest, and though it'll be hard, it'll make you feel good to know that what you do is valuable.'

'Life's good as long as you don't weaken.'

She laughed, and he was surprised at how wonderful it sounded, even in that place. 'That's the kind of person you are, Church. A good person. Someone for people to look up to—'

'You haven't been watching very closely over the last few months, have you?' Church moved around the circle a few paces to get away from the glowering stare of the Other-Church, but it matched him pace for pace.

'—you shoulder your burden and still focus on what's important in life. It won't grind you down. Life's too good.'

He shrugged. His surroundings had started to intrude and so he asked, although he didn't want to, 'What are you doing here, Marianne?'

'You called me.'

'No, I didn't.'

'Yes, you just don't know you did.'

He turned his thoughts over rapidly, trying to make sense. 'I'm here to get rid of the Fomorii corruption that's eaten its way into me from the Kiss of Frost that you – that Calatin made you – give me. That's why I'm here. At least, I think that's why. Nothing makes sense any more. Nothing ever has.'

There was movement in the shadowy distance, high above the mountains, against the sky. At first he thought it was clouds, but it looked briefly like a Caraprix, only enormous, hundreds of feet larger than the tiny creatures the Tuatha Dé Danann and the Fomorii carried with them. It was gone so quickly he could easily have dismissed it as a bizarre hallucination, except that he was convinced it had been there. The part of his back brain that always attempted to make sense of what was happening told him he had glimpsed something of a much larger truth, although what it was, and why the Caraprix *felt* so at home in that place, was beyond him.

'Church.' Marianne called his attention back. 'The symbolism is bigger than the reality. In the wider sweep of existence, symbols tell the truth. I'm the cause of all your misery, Church. I'm what's holding you back from achieving your destiny. The stain of the Night Walkers is minor compared to that, and it wouldn't even be there if I wasn't holding it in place.'

'What do you mean?'

'Do you want to talk like smart people?' Her expression was teasing. 'Or shall we carry on as we always have done?' He motioned for her to continue. 'Thanatos, the death-urge. When I died, you were consumed by it. That's what infected you. It made your days black, your thoughts worse. You couldn't see life, you couldn't see yourself. You've pulled away from the worst part of it, but it's still there, a little black cancer of the soul. A mess on that Fiery Network that makes up the real you, stopping the true flow. Making something so vital and powerful grow dormant. You have to wake the sleeping king if you want to save the world.'

'All that Arthurian stuff is a metaphor. For waking the Blue Fire in the land. Nothing to do with me.'

'As without, so within. This whole business is about celebrating life in all its forms, Church. Seeing death as part of a cycle: life, death, rebirth. You've been through the damn thing yourself, as have most of your merry little group. Haven't you got the picture yet?'

'I have to let go of you, is that what you're saying?'

'You don't have to *forget* me. Just remember the good parts. Don't let death rule your life.'

The Other-Church's expression was even darker now, murderous. 'Am I really seeing you?' Church asked. 'Or is this some hallucination, some part of my subconscious speaking to me?'

'You should know better than to ask questions like that by now.'

'Then what do I have to do? It's one thing saying I won't obsess about death, but it's a subconscious thing—'

'Just wish, Church. Wish so hard it changes you from inside-out. Kids know best how existence works. We unlearn as we go through all those things the Age of Reason saw fit to throw at us during our formative years. The Celts never had that, all those ancient people who shaped the world. You know I'm not some stupid, anti-progress Luddite. But the truth is, we took a wrong turn and now it's time to get back to how things should really be. A time to *feel*. The world's been waiting for this for a long time.'

'For all the death and suffering?'

'No, of course not. It's your job to minimise that. But it's not your job to take things back to the way they were. You've got a bigger destiny than you ever thought, Church. It's all down to you to make things better.'

His lips attempted to form words, but nothing would come.

'Just wish, Church.' A whisper. 'Just wish.'

He closed his eyes. And wished; not with a thought, but with every fibre of his being, and he found power was given to that wishing from somewhere else, either deep within himself, or without, in the distance where strange things moved against the sky.

And when he opened his eyes, Marianne was smiling. 'If you could only see yourself as I see you. We're all stars, Church. All stars.' She drifted back towards the pillar of stones.

'Is that it? Have I done enough?' His question was answered by the Other-Church, who began to fade, slipping back into the shadows that had gathered around the area until he was no longer there.

'From here it gets hard. Harder than anything you've been through so far. Pain and death and suffering and sacrifice and misery. It'll be a trial, Church, but you always knew that.' Parts of her became misty, merging with the rock. 'If you stay true, you'll see it through. Have faith, Church, like I have faith in you.'

The tears were flooding down his face now; he had never cried so much since he was a child. 'Thank you.' His voice, autumnal. 'For this, and for everything else you gave me. I'll never forget you.'

'Until we meet again.' The smile again, filled with long, beautiful days, fading as she was fading. And then she was gone.

It was like a rope tied around his waist had suddenly been attached to a speeding truck. He shot straight up into the air, that strange place disappearing in the blink of an eye, the sky and the stars whizzing by, rocketing so hard he blacked out.

And when he woke, he was sitting on the edge of the Pool of Wishes.

He made his way back along the worn path in a daze, trying to separate reality from hallucination and to make sense of the true weight of what he had learned.

When he reached the others, Ruth said curiously, 'What's wrong?'

'What do you mean?'

'You've only been gone about five minutes. Isn't there anything there?'

His smile gave nothing away. He climbed on his horse and spurred it back down the slope, feeling brighter and less burdened than at any time before in his life.

*

The Palace of High Regard lay at the centre of a confusing geometric design of streets, laden with symbolism. Church and Ruth's winding progress along the route was an intricately designed ritual, affecting their minds as well as their hearts; it was an odd sensation when simply turning a corner resulted in a flash of long-lost memory or insight, a fugitive aroma or barely heard sound. By the time they reached the enormous doors of ivory and silver, it had worked its magic on their deep subconscious so their heads felt charged with a disorienting energy, as if they were about to embark on a drug trip.

Baccharus was waiting to admit them. He carried a long staff carved from black volcanic rock. When Church and Ruth paused ten feet away, as they had been instructed, he tapped the doors gently with the staff. The resultant echoes were so loud Ruth put her hands to her ears.

The doors swung open of their own accord. Within was a hallway flooded with sunlight from a glass dome a hundred feet above. There were columns and carvings, niches filled with statues and braziers smouldering with incense. The floor had an inner path of black and white tiles, but on the edge was a pattern Ruth remembered from the floor tile at Glastonbury, with its hidden message that had pointed them towards T'ir n'a n'Og.

They waited for an age at the second set of doors, eventually being admitted to a room so large it took their breath away. It resembled the Coliseum in size and layout: rising tiers of seats in a circle around a vast floor area that made them feel insignificant. There was enough distortion of perception around the edges that Church wondered what it really looked like. The power of the Tuatha Dé Danann was focused there in all its unknowable, fearful glory. Ahead of them, the highest tier of gods was obviously seated, but the golden light that came off them was so forceful Church couldn't look at it. At the centre was the being the Celts had called Dagda, the Allfather, and around him others of the oldest and most powerful branch of the Golden Ones. On the perimeter he could just make out the ones the Celts had characterised as Lugh, and Nuada, whom he had first met on Skye when he had been brought back from the dead.

The air was crushing down on his shoulders and deep vibrations ran through him. It made him feel queasy, and he didn't know how long he would be able to endure it; it was apparent Fragile Creatures were not meant to be in that place, or to spend time in close proximity to those potent gods.

They waited, uncomfortable beneath the oppressive attention of the Golden Ones; the weight of all those fearsome intellects focused upon them was almost palpable. The debate started soon after. Nuada rose to deliver a speech to the assembled mass, although they couldn't understand a word he was saying; it sounded like a song caught in the wind, lilting and beautiful, with occasional threatening notes. Others spoke: some from the rank of the highest, many from the lower levels. Back and forth the discourse ranged. It felt odd to be under the scrutiny of such powerful beings, having hopes dissected with the very fate of the world hanging in the balance, but Church refused to be cowed by it. He held his head high and looked every speaker in the face.

Eventually Manannan rose, but instead of making his speech from the tier of the highest, he descended to the floor and stood beside Church and Ruth. He spoke with a passion and belief not previously visible in his reticent nature. Standing next to him, his ringing, incomprehensible voice resonating in the cavities of their bodies, they had an even deeper sense of the power around them.

Though Manannan never acknowledged their presence in the slightest, they knew he was arguing their case powerfully. The Tuatha Dé Danann hung on his every word, and when he finished speaking, a ripple of obvious disagreement ran around the arena. The tension in some of the comments that followed suggested that even Manannan's involvement might not swing the Golden Ones' support behind humanity.

But when the notes of dissent threatened to become a tumult, a hush suddenly fell across the arena. It was eerie the way it went from noise to silence in the merest moment. Church turned, searching for the source, and saw a large shadow fall across the arena. Cernunnos strode forward, his partner at his side. As she moved, her shape changed from that of a young, innocent girl, to a round-cheeked, middle-aged woman to a wizened crone and back again.

They stopped beside Manannan, and when Cernunnos spoke in a clear, booming voice it was in words Church could understand. 'No more. The seasons have turned. The days of holding on to faint beliefs have long since passed. Some of us have been wiped from existence for all time. Is this not a sign that it is time to act? How many more Golden Ones must lose the shining light before a reckoning comes? You have heard my brother speak of many things, of the warp and weft of existence, of reasons and truth and change, of the rising and advancing of spirits. Yet at the last, it must come down to this: do we sit proud and true and wait for the Night Walkers to bring their foul corruption to our door – even to this hallowed place itself – or do we fight as we have done in the past, for what is ours and for our place in the scheme of things? We aid these Fragile Creatures in their task, and thereby aid ourselves. The greater questions that trouble you need not be considered at this time. This is about the Golden Ones, and the Night Walkers, and the age-old history of lies and treachery and destruction that lie between us.'

He paused as his voice continued to echo around the vast chamber. There was no other sound; every god was listening intently to what he had to say. A swell of hope filled Church's heart.

'The Golden Ones have always been fair-minded, and we have always come to the aid of those who have aided us,' Cernunnos continued. 'These Brothers and Sisters of Dragons freed us from the privations of the Wish-Hex, and they prevented an even more heinous crime being inflicted, one that might well have wiped *all* of us from existence.' Mutterings of disbelief ran round the hall. 'They acted freely, and without obligation, and the Golden Ones should repay that debt. There is no longer the taint of the Night Walkers upon this champion. We are free to act at his behest.' He paused once more and looked slowly round. Briefly his appearance wavered and instead of the creature that Church saw as half-animal, half-vegetation, there was something almost angelic, but it was gone in an instant.

'I stand here with my brother, the two of us shoulder-to-shoulder. We say the old ways of non-involvement must end now. Risen and proud, the Golden Ones were always a force to be feared. The time is right.'

Complete silence followed his plea. Church's heart fell; his words had not stirred them at all. He looked around frantically, wondering if he should speak himself, but before he could decide, Baccharus had gripped his arm and was leading him and Ruth out of the hall. 'The case has been made,' he whispered.

They were deposited in an annexe where a crystal fountain gently tinkled. Baccharus refused to answer any of their questions, but they had only to look in each other's faces to confirm their private thoughts: they had failed.

Baccharus returned to them an hour later. At first they couldn't read his face, but when he was close it broke into a broad and unlikely grin. 'They will ride with you. The Night Walkers have been designated a true threat, and the feeling is that an agreement of cohabitation is not enough. It is time to eradicate them completely.'

Church jumped to his feet and hugged Ruth. 'We did it!'

'We need to thank Cernunnos and Manannan,' Ruth said.

'There will be time enough for that later,' Baccharus replied. 'The decision has been reached. The Golden Ones will act swiftly and we must be away at dawn. But first there is a ceremony to be enacted.'

'What ceremony?'

Baccharus ignored Church and motioned to the door. In the chamber, Cernunnos and Manannan waited patiently on the floor, but around them were gathered some of the highest of the gods, with only Dagda and those whose form was most fluid still remaining in their old place.

'Your hearts are true, Brother and Sister of Dragons,' Cernunnos said. 'An agreement has been reached that rings across existence. Not since the most ancient times of your people has the like been seen.'

He raised his right hand and the crowd parted to admit Lugh, leading four of the younger gods. Each carried one of the ancient artefacts Church, Ruth and the others had located to free the Tuatha Dé Danann from exile: the Stone of Fal, the Cauldron of Dagda, the Spear of Lugh and the Sword of Nuada Airgetlámh. Lugh himself carried the Wayfinder, the lantern with the flickering blue flame that had pointed them in the direction of the mystical objects.

'The Quadrillax,' Cernunnos intoned, 'are yours once more. Use them well and wisely.'

Church could barely believe what he was seeing. The four objects were so powerful, such a part of the traditions of the Tuatha Dé Danann, that he could never imagine an occasion when they would have freely given them up. But he could tell from the way the other gods looked to Cernunnos and Manannan that he knew who to thank.

He bowed. 'The Brothers and Sisters of Dragons thank you. And we shall use them well and wisely.'

Barely able to contain himself, he walked over to the sword that was resting on a cushion of strange, shimmering material. He had once seen it as a rusty, crumbling artefact. Now it gleamed as if it were made of silver and gold, and looked as sharp and strong as if it had just been forged. A shiver of anticipation made him pause before his fingers closed on it. But then it was in his hand and once again the power rushed through him; it felt warm and alive, comforting, against his skin. 'Now we'll see some justice,' he said in hushed tones.

Church sheathed the sword in a leather scabbard presented to him by Baccharus, while Ruth took the spear that she had used to such good advantage when freeing Cernunnos from Fomorii control in South Wales. The other artefacts were placed in a golden box that the young gods would hold until directed by Church.

Once they were on their own in their room, Church dragged Ruth on to the bed and hugged her tightly. 'A result,' he grinned, 'on every front.'

'So where's that familiar pessimism? Come on, you're the man who manages to drag misery from every victory.'

'I'm still pragmatic – I know it's still going to be near-impossible. But at least we have the two things we need: the support of the Tuatha Dé Danann and the Quadrillax. That's a chance, and I'm going to seize it with both hands.'

'Oh, get away from me. You're not the real Church. You've been possessed in that mysterious pool.' She playfully attempted to push him away, before relaxing so he could fold into her. 'Go on, there's got to be *something* on your mind.' The flicker across his face gave her answer. 'Spit it out.'

'Okay, there's one thing that worries me, and it's a big thing.' He rolled over so he was lying next to her, staring at the ceiling. 'Everything was tidied up nicely on the ship, except for one thing. You've seen the Tuatha Dé Danann. You know what they're capable of. And now they have the Wish-Hex.'

CHAPTER FOURTEEN

Like a Serpent play'd
Before them

Water began to flood in around Laura as she shivered in the cold beneath the insipid dawn light. The Bone Inspector attempted to force the rag back into the hole, but it only made matters worse. 'We're going to go down like a brick,' he hissed.

'I can get a bit further if I throw you overboard.' She leaned up just enough to peek over the rim. They hadn't even made it as far as the Dartford river crossing. Nearby, gleaming mudflats lined the bank. There was no movement anywhere, nor was there any sound, not even birdsong. The stillness was unnatural.

'If we drag it over to the side, we might have a better chance of plugging it up again,' she hissed.

The Bone Inspector grunted before rolling over the side into the waist-deep water; he appeared oblivious to the cold. Laura allowed him to drag the boat close to the flats before she jumped out to help it across the last few feet.

Once they'd beached it, the water drained out and the Bone Inspector could attempt the repairs a little easier. But it was soon apparent why the previous owner had abandoned the craft. As the Bone Inspector worked the rag in tightly, his hand went right through the bottom, taking out a chunk of rotten wood about a foot square.

'You ham-fisted git!' Laura slapped a shaking hand over her eyes. 'Now what do we do?'

The Bone Inspector ignored her attempts at blame. Quickly surveying the area, he pointed toward some streetlights beyond an expanse of waste ground. 'The Fomorii may not have spread this far out of the city. If we proceed cautiously, it would be quicker to use the road to put the city behind us.'

Laura wrapped her sopping arms around her. 'All right. But you go first.'

The wasteland had been used as a dump. Burst dustbin bags lay around amidst broken bottles, empty milk crates, a burnt-out car and decaying furniture. It smelled of chemicals and excrement. The road beyond was deserted, apart from a jackknifed petrol tanker.

'Looks safe,' Laura mused after ten minutes in the shadows of the hedgerow. 'Shall we chance it?'

'No choice.' The Bone Inspector sniffed the air, then stepped out on to the pavement.

They'd gone only a few yards down the road when Laura experienced a prickling sensation. Looking back quickly towards the city, all she could see were a few birds swooping in the grey sky. She attempted to dismiss the nagging feeling, but if anything it was growing stronger. She took a few more paces and only then realised that since she had woken in the charnel house she had not seen any birds at all. With a shiver of dread, she turned back.

The dark smudges had moved much closer in the seconds between looks, and now she could see they were far too big for birds. Their uncanny speed held her rapt for a few seconds and by then she could see they were winged Fomorii. 'Shit. I didn't know some of them could fly.'

The Bone Inspector turned at her strained voice, before grabbing her arm to propel her back the way they had come.

'Away from them!' she yelled.

'There's no cover.' His voice was remarkably calm, although his body had dropped into a low, loping posture that reminded her of a hunting wolf.

He was right; their only chance was to attempt to hide and hope the Fomorii couldn't see where they were going, but there was hardly anywhere in the flat open landscape.

The only place in view was the jackknifed tanker. It offered little protection, but if they could crawl beneath it they might be able to scurry into the ditch beyond where the Fomorii would have trouble reaching them. In the heat of the moment Laura didn't have time to consider how sickeningly short-termist that was.

The Fomorii had the terrifying speed of jet fighters. The tanker was still yards away when the wash of driven air buffeted Laura and the Bone Inspector. There was a smell like rotting meat and what sounded like a power drill. Their peripheral vision was filled with constantly changing horrors; a deep, arctic shadow fell across them. The Bone Inspector knocked Laura to the ground and threw himself across her.

They both felt the breeze as the Fomorii tore through the space where they had been. Despite his advancing years, the Bone Inspector was on his feet in an instant, hauling Laura up behind him as if she weighed nothing.

Amidst the frantic activity and danger, Laura was surprised to find an area of deep serenity in which she could step back to observe herself.

What she saw surprised her: just weeks ago she would have been paralysed by fear. Instead she felt calm and focused and, if it hadn't sounded so incongruous, brave.

She was thrown out of the moment by a hard impact to her right shoulder. Relieved that the Fomorii had missed clubbing her to the ground she continued a pace before an object came flying past her to skid across the road. It was an arm. Her arm.

The shock of the sight brought her to a halt. Her vision wavered a second; impressions rushed towards the front of her mind, but didn't coalesce. She was dimly aware of several shapes converging on her.

The Bone Inspector was in her frame of vision, yelling something she couldn't hear. A second later she was being lifted across his back as he ran the final few yards. They dived beneath the tanker as the road erupted at their heels.

Laura came out of her daze, aware of a dull ache at her shoulder. She didn't look at all. Shards of metal clattered across the road as the Fomorii tore frenziedly at the side of the tanker to get at them. 'Keep moving,' she croaked. 'I'm fine.'

The Bone Inspector cast a searching eye across her face, and then scurried into the ditch. Laura followed, keeping low, feeling brambles tear at her face and hair, not really caring.

The Fomorii continued to attack the tanker. 'Stupid bastards,' Laura said under her breath.

The two of them had managed to crawl three hundred yards away when the inevitable happened. The tanker went up in a massive explosion that rained burning debris all around them. They had just crawled in a culvert that ran beneath the road as the hedgerow disappeared in a blur of flame; trees turned to charcoal and the field beyond disappeared in red and yellow smoke. For a second or two, Laura couldn't breathe, until fresh air rushed in to fill the vacuum. Her ears rang from the blast.

She slumped back against the culvert, suddenly convulsed in tremors. The Bone Inspector was at her side in an instant, ready to bandage her shoulder with his shirt. When he paused suddenly, she gasped, 'I know. Green blood.'

'And not much of it.' He pressed the shirt against the protruding socket joint and torn arteries. Despite his comment, it quickly grew wet.

'It had to be the right one,' she said miserably. 'Now I'll never beat Veitch at darts.' Her attempt at humour sounded pathetic. She let her chin slump on to her chest, listening to the roar of the inferno.

'We'll rest here for a while,' the Bone Inspector said. 'We'll start moving again when the fire dies down.'

'Good idea,' Laura murmured. 'I feel so tired.' She closed her eyes and drifted away.

'I'm just saying it's bad strategy, that's all.' Veitch finished up the last of his plate of rabbit stew hungrily and eyed the black pan on the old range with a measure of hope. Through Tom's judicious herbal treatments, he had recovered from the shock of the amputation and appeared back to his old irascible self; a piece of white cloth he washed obsessively was tied around his stump.

'Ryan *is* our strategist, after all.' After his dinner of steamed vegetables, Shavi gnawed on a raw carrot, his dessert, much to Veitch's disgust.

Tom furiously dunked his home-made bread in the last dregs of gravy. Before he could launch into a bad-tempered tirade, Davenport, the farmer who had taken them in earlier that day, poked his head round the door. He was wearing a dirty, shapeless hat and old coat, protection against the evening chill as he finished up the last of the jobs around the farm. 'Everything all right, lads?'

'It was a very enjoyable meal, Mr Davenport,' Shavi said. 'Our compliments to your wife. And we offer you our thanks for feeding us, when we have nothing to offer in return. We know there are shortages—'

Embarrassed, Davenport waved him quiet. 'We've got enough to go round. I'd be worrying if I was one of the big boys. They won't know what to do now they can't get hold of their pesticides and chemical fertilisers. But I've been organic for a few years now, so, cross fingers, we should be all right for a while.'

His wife, Rowena, pushed in next to him. She was in her late thirties, attractive, though weary-looking. 'Go on, Philip,' she said, nudging her husband in the ribs, 'ask them.'

'I'm not going to ask them.' Davenport shifted uncomfortably.

'If you don't, I will.'

He sighed with irritation. 'The wife wants to know if you're the heroes—'

She slapped him on the arm. 'Don't say it like that!'

He wiped his nose with the back of his hand. 'If you're—'

'Oh, get out of the way!' She pushed past him. 'People are talking about a group of men and women going round the country trying to put right this awful thing that's happened. The farmers have been talking about it for weeks. They keep saying how some of these people helped out a farmer down in the West Country who'd got one of those spooks or goblins or whatever in his house. That's the story, anyway. But then we heard it from somebody else . . . a woman in the village.

She's part of this parish pump news grapevine that's being set up to let everyone know what's going on. And one of the stories passed down the wire was about this group up in the north somewhere who fought against all those horrible things and saved an entire village. And they were doing all sorts of other . . .' Her voice faded away as she realised she was starting to ramble. She looked at her husband and added, 'And yes, they did call them heroes. Said they could do things no other people could do. Said they were special.'

Veitch tried to appear nonchalant, but he was fighting against pride. The woman noticed his fidgeting. 'It is you, isn't it?'

'We are not special,' Shavi said. 'Not really. We are simply trying to do the best we can in a very difficult situation—'

'I told you they were the heroes,' the woman said to her husband. She turned back to them excitedly. 'What are you—'

Her husband pushed her out with undue roughness. 'They don't want to be bothered by us!' He shuffled around uncomfortably. 'We'll leave you alone now, lads. I know you'll have important stuff to talk about. But if you've got a moment before you take your leave—'

'We'll fill you in, mate.' Once he'd gone, Veitch said conspiratorially, 'Can you believe that? They're talking about us!'

'One should never believe one's own publicity, Ryan,' Shavi said wryly. He eased back in his chair and sipped on his boiled water.

'Yes, control your ego before your head explodes.' Tom collected the plates together and put them in the sink. 'It's not important—'

'It's important to me. Nobody's ever called me a hero before.'

'And this lot wouldn't either, if they knew you,' Tom snapped. 'To get back to the matter at hand—'

'Your strategy's all wrong.'

Tom picked up his chair and banged it down in irritation. 'So you said. Then what do you suggest?'

'You're the big bleedin' psychic. Shav here can talk to the birds. Can't you find out where the others are – exactly – so we can link up with them? We haven't got the time to keep wandering around. I want to be there the moment they roll up, ready to ride on London.'

'And do what? Shake your stump at them?' Tom recognised it was a cheap shot the instant the words had left his lips but he refused to be contrite, although he wouldn't meet Veitch's eyes.

Veitch wasn't upset. He leaned forward, resting his elbows on the table so he wouldn't look so combative. 'You know I'm talking sense here. We need a plan. There's only a matter of days until Hallowe'en . . . Samhain . . . that's all. There's not even a guarantee Church and the others are coming back.'

1178

'Then we're lost,' Tom said sharply. 'Separately, we are nothing.'

'Sometimes you're so bleedin' pathetic.'

'They will be back,' Shavi said. 'I have faith.'

'Then we can get down to the fighting.' Veitch adjusted the cloth around what remained of his wrist.

'You all appear to be forgetting something vitally important.' Tom spun the chair around so he could lean on the back. He looked at Veitch accusingly. 'Church will not have forgotten.'

'What?' Veitch looked from Tom to Shavi.

'The land,' Shavi said.

'Exactly.' Tom took out his tin and made a roll-up with his dwindling supply of tobacco. 'Wake the land. The primary mission, encoded for generations in myth and legend. There will be no defeating the Fomorii, no future for Britain – or the world for that matter – unless the land is woken from its long sleep.'

'Like Church did in Edinburgh,' Veitch said, 'when the Fire helped blow those Bastards in their lair to kingdom come. But, yeah, it *helped*. Why's it so important?'

'The Tuatha Dé Danann would not have beaten the Fomorii before if the power in the land had not been vibrant.'

'I do not remember you telling us that before,' Shavi said suspiciously.

Tom sucked on the roll-up a few times to get it alight. 'The power in the land, at its height, weakens the Fomorii. The Blue Fire – and what it represents – is the antithesis of the Night Walkers, and what they represent.'

'So it's everywhere—' Veitch began.

Tom had no patience left. 'It is powered by belief and faith and hope, by humanity and nature in conjunction. By all that is good in us. And for generations it has been slowly growing dormant. Several hundred years ago humanity took a wrong path. We gave up all that was most important for the promise of shiny things, home comforts, *products*. There was a time we could have had both, to a degree. But the ones who shape our thoughts, in politics and business, and the fools who invested their faith in science alone, convinced us to trade one off for the other. And without the belief of the people, the energy slowly withered, like a stream in a drought. Not gone for ever, just sleeping.'

'But you know how it can be woken,' Shavi said. 'You have always known.'

Veitch watched Shavi's face and then turned his narrowing eyes to Tom. 'Another thing you've kept from us. You can't be trusted at all, can you, you old bastard? We could have done it weeks ago and saved us all a load of trouble.'

'The time was not right then. Church was not right. The Fomorii corruption in him would have brought failure. And to fail once would have meant failing for all time.'

Shavi watched Tom carefully. 'What else do you know?'

'More things than you could ever dream.' Tom was unbowed. 'Some have to be learned through hardship and ritual – they can't be imparted over a quiet cup of tea. Others, well, the telling of them could alter the outcome of what is being told. I ask you to trust me, as I always have.'

'We do trust you,' Veitch said irritably. 'That doesn't mean you don't get on our tits half the time.'

'At least we have some common ground,' Tom said acidly. The strain of events was eating away at all of them.

'Then what needs to be done?' Shavi asked. 'And can it be done in the time that remains?'

Tom sucked on the roll-up thoughtfully; they couldn't quite divine his mood: dismal or hopeful? 'The energy in the earth criss-crosses the globe, interlinking like the lines of latitude and longitude, only not so uniform. The Fire is not a straight-line thing. It splits and winds in two strands around a central point, so that from above it resembles the double-helix, the map of life, or perhaps the caduceus, the age-old symbol of two serpents coiled around a staff. Imagine, if you will, power-points where the energy rushes in, or is refocused and driven out into the network. The Well of Fire at Edinburgh was one, and Stonehenge and Avebury and Glastonbury Tor. The last three are important for they all fall on the divining line for Britain.'

'The St Michael Line,' Shavi noted. 'A ley running from Carn Les Boel at Land's End to St Margaret's Church at Hopton on the east coast in Norfolk.'

'Along that line are many of those power-points. They feed the whole network. For the land to come alive with the earth energy, the St Michael Line must be vibrant and powerful. But it is fractured in part, sluggish in others, a trickle in many places.'

'And to wake it?' Shavi asked.

'On the tip of Cornwall there is an ancient and mysterious place known as St Michael's Mount. It is the lynchpin of the entire line. I have spoken in the past about the Celts and the other ancient races encoding great secrets in the earth itself. At St Michael's Mount is the greatest secret of all. Locked under that place, Church – and Church alone – will uncover the key to bringing the line, and the land, back to life. Or he will find death.'

Veitch tapped out a monotonous beat on the kitchen table with a teaspoon. 'They'll have the place well-defended,' he said, staring into space. 'Those tricks and traps they lined up to guard the spear, sword and the rest of it were bad enough. If this is their biggest secret—'

'Exactly,' Tom said.

'Then,' Shavi said, 'we need to get Church to St Michael's Mount as soon as we can.'

In a quiet orchard at the back of the farmhouse, with the yellowing, autumn leaves glowing spectrally in the moonlight, Shavi sat cross-legged and listened to the sound of the night. Amongst the surrounding vegetation, eyes glittered – a fox, a rabbit, a badger, several stray cats – all of whom had come to see the shaman at work. The ritual, his first since leaving the Grim Lands, had been wearying, necessitating some of the tricks of concentration he thought he had become too experienced to need. But it had worked.

A few feet above the ground, the air was boiling as what appeared to be liquid metal bubbled out and drifted down; it was accompanied by the familiar smell of burnt iron. Behind it came one of the bone-white, featureless creatures Shavi had summoned before, a human-shaped construct used by one of the denizens of the Invisible World. It pulled itself forward and hung half-in and half-out of the hole in space.

'Who brings me to this place?' Its voice was like the wind on a winter sea.

'It is I, Brother of Dragons.'

'I know you, Brother of Dragons. Have you not learned your lesson, of reaching out to the worlds beyond your own?'

'I know my place, and I know yours. I seek guidance.'

'You did not heed our words before.' The creature put its head on one side in a faintly mocking style.

Shavi recalled the prophetic message one of these creatures had given him about his murder at Callow's hands, but it had been couched in such cryptic terms he had not realised its meaning until it was too late to do anything about it. 'I chose my path. And I am here to hear your words again.'

'There is a price.'

Shavi ran a thumb over the rough pad of his left hand, now criss-crossed with a score of tiny scars, chose a spot, then slit it with a knife. The blood dripped on to the damp grass.

'You give freely of your essence, Brother of Dragons.' An underlying note of warning.

'Another Brother of Dragons, our leader, known as Church, is currently abroad in the Far Lands. Firstly, how does he fare?'

'He fares well. You have achieved all that you desire, but what you desire may do more harm than good.'

Shavi noted this subtle warning, knowing there was no point attempting to get the construct to elucidate. 'Then he will be back shortly. My second question: where will he arrive?'

'He will return to the Fixed Lands at the point from which he departed, where Merlin's Rock marks a doorway between worlds.'

Shavi didn't recognise the name, but he guessed Tom probably would. 'Then I thank you for your guidance. Return safely to the Invisible World.' He paused. 'No final words of warning?'

Although the construct had no features, Shavi was convinced it was smiling. 'No warning would ever do justice to what lies ahead for you and your Brothers and Sisters.'

And then it was gone.

Tom and Veitch sat around the range in the candlelight, drinking home-made beer. They were used to Shavi's ragged appearance after making contact with the Invisible World, but were eager to discover what he had learned. As he had expected, Tom knew the location instantly.

'Mousehole,' the Rhymer said gruffly. 'Then he joined Manannan's sick crew.'

'Where's that, then?' Veitch swilled the beer down rapidly; six large mugs in a quarter of an hour.

'Cornwall.' Tom stared at the red coals in the open door of the range. 'In the furthest tip. The part of the country where the Celts buried their greatest secrets, and subsequently the most spiritual part of the land.'

'Bloody hell, it's going to take us ages to get down there.' Veitch took another swig, then looked up suddenly. 'You could make another jump.'

Tom waved him silent, his eyes still fixed on the fire, deep in thought. Shavi asked what Veitch meant and the Londoner spent the next five minutes attempting to explain how they had slipped into the energy flow between Scotland and Wandlebury Camp. Shavi was enthused by the entire concept and excitedly questioned Tom about it.

'Didn't you hear me say the St Michael Line is fractured?' he snapped. 'If we attempt to travel along it and hit a dead spot we will be unceremoniously spewed out into the world. Perhaps over a gorge or a cliff-face or above a river in torrent. Now what good will that do?'

Veitch examined the deep lines of Tom's face, the fix of his eyes, until Tom could no longer pretend he hadn't seen him. 'What?'

'You're thinking about it.'

'No, I'm not.'

'Yes, you are. I can see it in your face, you old bastard. And I know exactly what you're thinking. You're thinking it's too much of a risk for all three of us, but one of us needs to try it because we're running out of time.'

Tom was particularly irritated at Veitch's sudden insight.

'I'm right, aren't I?'

'Oh, shut up.' Tom rose from his chair and went over to the window to peer out into the dark. 'It has to be me because only I can give Church the guidance he needs. Only I can point him towards St Michael's Mount.' A few beats of silence. 'And the two of you are too valuable to risk. Five of you are needed to put this square. Any less . . . if any of you don't make it through the next two weeks . . .' He made a dismissive gesture.

'Then what should we do?' Shavi asked.

Tom was already gathering his things together in his haversack. 'You must make your way to a meeting place, somewhere just beyond the reach of the Fomorii influence on the outskirts of London. I would suggest the west—'

The door crashed open and Davenport lurched in, his face pale and drawn. Shavi helped the farmer to a chair. Veitch's eyes went instantly to the door and window; the farmhouse was sprawling, impossible to defend.

'Down at the pub,' Davenport gasped between juddering breaths. 'I was talking to some bloke about you lot. Never seen him before. He was asking a lot of questions. I thought he'd just heard the stories, like the rest of us—'

'What happened?' Veitch gripped Davenport's shoulders and had to be prised off by Shavi.

'After I told him you were up here, his face started to change . . . melt . . . I thought I was going mad. Then I thought I was going to black out. One of the other blokes down there was sharp. Chucked a pint glass at him. I got away, still thought I was going to puke my guts up.'

'Fomorii,' Shavi snapped.

'There were more of them,' Davenport continued. 'I saw as I ran up here. They were following me—'

His sentence was cut off by a crashing at the front door.

'No time,' Tom said. 'We will find each other in the west, along the M4 between Reading and London.' He nodded to them all, then darted through the back door where he snatched Davenport's bicycle from its resting place against the wall.

'Hide,' Shavi said to the farmer. 'They are after us. They will leave you alone.' He saw Veitch's fixed expression and knew he was considering a fight. 'This is not the time. We cannot afford to fail now.'

Veitch backed down, and then they were both out of the door, running across the orchard and into the fields beyond.

His joints aching, Tom pedalled as fast as he could. The evening was alive with monkey-shrieks, dark shapes flitting across the fields towards the farmhouse, the candlelit rooms surprisingly bright in the sea of night. He desperately hoped Veitch and Shavi would escape – if anyone could, they could – but he had his doubts for Davenport and his wife.

That the Fomorii were still looking for them had taken him by surprise. He had thought that in the aftermath of their great success at bringing back Balor, the Night Walkers would have little time for failed insurrectionists.

He narrowed his eyes and concentrated until the thin tracings of Blue Fire rose from the shadowy background, like silver filigree glinting off the blades of grass in the fields. It was not strong in that area, but he could still pick out the ebb and flow. Driving himself on as fast as he could, he searched for a confluence on the St Michael's Line.

An hour later he found himself in the Hertfordshire town of Royston, at a point where the ancient Royal Roads of Britain, the Icknield Way and Ermine Street, crossed. The town was still, although candles glowed in many windows. The moment he saw the town name, he knew where he was heading. The old stories enshrined the mythic power of certain locations so they would never be forgotten by the adepts, however much locals became inured to their mystery.

A grating in the pavement showed his destination, but it took him a while longer to raise one of the residents to point him in the direction of an old wooden door. Taking a candle, he made his way along a tunnel to a thirty-foot-high, bell-shaped chamber cut into the solid chalk lying just beneath the street. He remembered how one of the Culture had told him of its rediscovery in the eighteenth century when a group of workmen digging a hole found a millstone sunk in the earth; beneath it was a shaft that led into the cave.

Tom held up the candle and the walls came alive; carved pictures swelled and receded in the flickering light. Here *Sheela-na-Gig*, one of the old fertility goddesses, there Christian images of the crucifixion, and then a mix of the two, with St Catherine holding the symbolic eight-spoked wheel of the sun disc. It had the same resonances as Rosslyn Chapel, where Shavi and Laura had freed the mad god Maponus, and like that place, it had also been a haunt of the Knights Templar, the old guardians of secret mysteries and the last people to truly understand the earth energy.

Cautiously he set down the candle and sat cross-legged in the centre of the chill cave, allowing its symbolism to work its magic on his subconscious. The shape of an inverted womb and the female images on the wall showed it was a place where the Earth Goddess was honoured by the ancients; more, it was a place where the life-giving power of the earth was celebrated.

The atmosphere was already crackling, setting the hairs alive across his arms and neck. He closed his eyes, breathed deeply, and prepared for his trip.

The deep dark of pre-dawn clustered along the coastline as Wave Sweeper sailed in to the sleeping land. The waves crashed in bursts of white along the rocky coast and the salty scent of seaweed filled the air. Church stood at the rail, filled with excitement at the prospect of returning home after too long in the strangest of strange lands. Behind it, though, was apprehension at what lay ahead.

Ruth gave the back of his hand a squeeze with a reassuring smile. Her hair had been tied back, but the force of the wind still lashed it around. 'Ready for the final act?'

'I don't like the way that sounds.' He slipped an arm round her shoulders, comforted by her warmth.

All around them the deck milled with the Tuatha Dé Danann readying the ship for landing. The decks below were crammed with even more of the force: horses, and strange, gleaming chariots with spiked wheels, an entire deck of armaments prepared by Goibhniu and his brothers, plus tents and supplies and all the other minutiae needed by an army on the move.

'I wonder if we'll see the others?' he mused.

'When. It's only a matter of time. We were drawn together in the first place, and it'll happen again.' Her thoughts turned to Veitch; she quickly drove them out.

'It's funny that it's going to end in London.' The spray flew up around him. 'We've come full circle.'

'The Universe speaks to us in symbols, that's what Tom would say. I still can't get over how much we've all changed. If the stakes weren't so high, that would be . . . an achievement in itself.'

'You feel better for it all?' He gently touched the space where her finger had been.

She only had to think for an instant. 'As stupid as it seems, I do.

Between this and the rest of my days stretching out in a safe but mundane legal world, there's no contest. It's such an obvious thing, but we never, ever grasp it: life's short, so why spend it bumping along in a secure existence that stops you feeling anything? Life should be about snatching as many great experiences as you can before you die, trading them in for wisdom. But if you want that, you've got to take the risk of great lows as well. Any sane person would say there's no contest, but we keep doing it.'

'It's society. Conditioning. That's what we all need to break.'

She laughed. 'Life in the Age of Reason isn't all the brochures say.'

'Reminds me of an old song.'

'One nobody else has heard of, I suppose.'

'I guess.' As they neared the coast, he picked out a few lights in Mousehole; either early risers or the night watch.

Ruth watched the shadow of thoughts play on his face. 'What's wrong?'

'Just wishing the Walpurgis hadn't died before he could tell me what he knew.'

'About the one of us who's going to sell all the others down the river?' She kept her eyes fixed on the shoreline.

'I just hope that wasn't a turning point, the one moment when we could have saved everything, only to lose out by a hair's breadth. And Callow's treachery.'

'No point worrying about it now.' Her face was dark, unreadable. 'We've just got to play the cards as they fall. That, and other clichés.'

If the residents of Mousehole knew an alien ship was disgorging some of the most powerful beings of all existence in their midst, they never showed it. Doors and windows remained resolutely closed, despite the clatter of metal and the grind of wheels on stone and the whinnying of horses that looked like any other until one saw the unnaturally intelligent gleam in their eye.

Yet there was one figure, waiting near the pub where they had stayed on their arrival. He was wrapped in a voluminous, extreme-weather anorak, the snorkel hood pulled far forward against the chill so his features were lost to shadow. Even so, Church recognised him in an instant from the stance, at once relaxed, yet, conversely, taut.

He ran across the road and threw his arms around the figure. 'Tom!'

The Rhymer pulled back his hood to reveal a face worn by exhaustion, the edge taken off it by the flicker of a smile. 'If you knew the trouble I'd had to get here—'

'We wondered if you were dead!'

'If only.' He blushed as Ruth bowled up and planted a large kiss on his cheek before throwing her arms around him. 'Enough of that.' He tried to recapture his grizzly demeanour, but they could both see his true feelings. 'We have serious business ahead.'

He filled them in quickly before motioning towards three horses he had tied up at the side of the pub. 'We can be at St Michael's Mount soon after dawn, if we hurry.'

'And what do I get to do while Mr Hero goes off and does all his testosterone business?' Despite her tone, Church knew Ruth wasn't offended that she had to sit it out; she was afraid for him and wanted to help.

'It'll be okay,' he said. 'I have to do it alone. It's a destiny thing. You know, like the old stories. Except this time they've got me instead of King Arthur. Bummer, eh?'

Baccharus sauntered over when he saw the three of them conversing. 'Greetings, True Thomas. I knew you would not let hardship come between us meeting again.'

'Baccharus. So your people have finally decided to stir themselves into action, I see.'

'The Golden Ones like to conserve their energy so they are more effective when the time is ripe.'

Tom tried to read his face, but the god gave nothing away. 'You better watch yourself, Baccharus. Humour? What's next: laughter, tears and broken hearts? They'll be drumming you out of the Arrogance Club for good behaviour.'

'Oh, I can still be arrogant, True Thomas. When one is highborn, one does not lose that trait.'

Tom shook his head, stifling a grin. They told Baccharus that they would have to take their leave, without giving him details of their mission, in case news leaked out to those of the Tuatha Dé Danann not sympathetic to humanity.

Baccharus shook their hands in turn. 'Then I wish you all well, for you have been the best of companions. We shall meet again before battle is joined.'

As the three horses left the mêlée behind, Church felt sad. Baccharus had proved both a good comrade-in-arms and a friend, despite his difficulty in expressing emotion. But soon the night closed in around them and all thoughts turned to the dangers that lurked beyond the black hedgerows.

The village of Marazion was peaceful in the pale, early morning sunlight. Tom, who had amassed several lifetimes of knowledge, gave them a potted history of the oldest chartered town in Cornwall, its great age marked by the twisty-turny thirteenth-century streets running down to the wide stretch of sandy beach.

Ahead of them, St Michael's Mount rose up majestically, a throne of stone in the bay bearing the crumbling castle and ancient chapel silhouetted against the sky; it had been the source of dreams for generations. Legends clustered hard around the bulky island, hazy in the morning mist; stories of giants and angels, lovers and redeemers.

Ruth reined in her horse, closed her eyes and put her face up to the sun as she took a deep breath of the cool, soothing air. She wrinkled her nose thoughtfully. 'It's weird. It's only been a matter of weeks, but already it smells different . . . sweeter.'

Church knew what she meant: no traffic fumes, no faint aroma of burning plastics, no hint of the modern world that made all the senses recoil, but that everyone had simply grown to accept. He followed the sweep of golden sands to the break of surf on the edge of the blue sea. 'We've got everything here that makes life worth living. So tell me again why we need to go back?'

Tom slid off his mount and tied it to a tree. 'Leave the horses. From here, we go on foot. Like pilgrims.'

He led them across the dunes to a rough stone causeway. The tide was out so they could walk easily to the Mount. Despite the time of year and the salty sea breeze, it was peculiarly warm, reminding Ruth of the same unseasonal weather she had appreciated at Glastonbury. 'I feel safe here,' she said.

As they walked, Tom spoke in a dreamy monotone, describing the history and symbolism of the place that now towered over them. The beat and tone of his words made it almost a ritualistic chant, lulling them into deep thoughts born in the dark subconscious.

· 'In the old Cornish language this place was called Carreg Luz en Kuz, translated as the Hoar Rock in the Wood. In the ancient Celtic language, hoar often refers to a standing stone. There is no standing stone now, but who knows? You now know what the stones mark . . .' His words were caught by the wind, disappeared. When they picked up his monologue again, he had changed tack. 'Once this place was known as Dinsul, or Citadel of the Sun. This is where the wise men of the Celts called up their god of light. There is a very clear tradition of sun worship at this site. Then the cult of St Michael grew up in the Middle Ages after a vision of the saint filled with light appeared atop the Mount. So the old ways were passed on through the Christian religion where the site became dedicated to St Michael, a saint who became a symbol associated with light. In the language of symbols, there is no differentiation between the old religion and the new. The same source, different names.'

Tom's words had begun to nag at the back of Church's mind; it wasn't just travelogue. 'Why are you telling us this?'

Tom ignored him. 'Christ, too, another symbol of light, in legend is believed to have landed with his uncle Joseph of Arimathea at St Michael's Mount before making his way to Glastonbury. He began to sing softly, ' "And did those feet, in ancient times . . ." '

Church glanced at him uneasily. 'I said, why are you telling *me* this?'

'St Michael – some writers once described him as the Spirit of Revelation, and that is a fair description,' Tom said. 'For if he stands for anything, it is this: there are mysteries heaped on mysteries and nothing should be taken at face value. Religions, all religions, are ninety per cent politics and ten per cent belief. The belief continues eternally, only shaped by the politics to appear this, or that, but it always is as it was. One thing; one belief.' Tom took a deep breath. 'Old stories,' he said with pride; he thought of the Mount's legends of giants in the earth, as there had been at Wandlebury Camp.

'In Cornwall,' Tom continued, 'there's a legend that St Michael sleeps beneath the land, waiting to be woken.'

Church felt a shiver down his spine as the threads of disparate ancient stories drew together to reveal a pattern behind the chaos. There were similar threads drawing together different religions, all leading back to the same source, though he was sure many worshippers of those faiths would refuse to see the connections. Yet it was all there for anyone who chose to see it. What did it mean, that was the question? Possibly the most important question he would ever have to consider in his life: a pattern behind everything. That was the message that had underpinned every step of his journey around the country since that cold night beneath Albert Bridge.

They reached the end of the causeway. A steep path wound upwards in the shadow of the mount. By the time they were halfway up, they were sweating in the morning heat.

'All these secrets hidden in the earth, buried in old stories, it makes me feel queasy,' Ruth said.

'That's because you are being spoken to in the true language of symbols, the ur-language, but you are not yet educated enough to understand it.' Tom rested briefly to catch his breath. 'Yet your sub-conscious hears and it grasps the importance, if not the meaning. The signals it sounds out to your forebrain causes conflict, upsetting your equilibrium. Secrets and mysteries – hints at the true universe that lies behind the one you see.'

They fell silent, meditating on his words, until they reached the summit and the ancient buildings. Church suddenly felt heady and had to reach out for a wall to support himself.

'You can feel it?' Tom asked.

He could: a tremendous surge of the earth energy, running through every stone, as if the place were an enormous battery. His flesh tingled and there was a corresponding tightness across his chest that eventually eased, to be replaced by euphoria.

'What a rush.' Church laughed; he could see Ruth was experiencing it too.

'This is why people take drugs,' Tom said, 'to attempt to reach this state that they only have a vague race memory of, from the days when their ancestors could manipulate the subtle energies at the ancient sites. But nothing earthly can ever come close to it.'

They moved slowly in the long shadows of the castle until they came to an ancient stone cross rising out of the ground. At first glance it was nothing special, but once they drew closer they saw a double-swirl of the Blue Fire continually flowing all around it.

'This is where the lines all draw together,' Church said. It was so potent he almost felt like kneeling before it.

The mood was broken when, from the corner of his eye, he caught sight of a dark figure away to his left. He whirled, half-drawing the sword, only to see a man dozing in the sun on a low wall, his dog collar just visible beneath a lightweight blue cagoule. He was in his late sixties, his face sun-browned and lined, his hair a shock of white. He stirred, as if Church's gaze had disturbed him, and then jumped to his feet, straightening his clothes with a mixture of embarrassment and anticipation.

Once he had calmed he looked penetratingly into their faces in turn. 'Is this it?' he asked with a note of excitement. 'Is this the time?'

'It is the time,' Tom said, stepping forward. Church and Ruth looked at him curiously.

'That's a relief, you know. After all that waiting and waiting. Of course, when I saw the signs . . . the failure of technology and all that . . . I supposed it *must* be the time. But when the message has been lying around for hundreds of years . . . longer, of course . . . it's difficult to believe it's actually going to happen in *your* lifetime.' His cheeks coloured at the realisation that he was rambling. He held out a cautious hand and greeted them in turn. 'I'm Michael.' He smiled at what some would have considered a coincidence. 'Watchman of St Michael's Mount.' He paused. 'Chief Watchman, of this time, and this land. There. That seems so odd to say, after thirty years of never being able to say it to anybody. When the obligation was first passed to me, it felt such an honour . . . the mysteries that were opened to me! . . . and I can honestly say that has never diminished with time.' He stared into Church's face so deeply Church felt uncomfortable. 'Is this the one?'

'It is,' Tom replied.

'Yes. I can see it. In his eyes, always in the eyes. The one good man.' He cupped Church's right hand in both of his. 'May God go with you, my boy.' Then he did the most curious thing: he dropped to his knee and gently kissed Church's hand.

Ruth, who had been watching the scenario intently, inexplicably grew angry. 'What's going on here?' she snapped.

Church looked around puzzled. 'That's a very good question.'

'It's time, Jack.' There was a strange cast to Tom's face that Church had not seen before, and it took him a second or two to realise what it was: Tom's features were unguarded; completely open.

Church was a little disturbed by this out-of-character intensity. 'What do you mean?'

'Time to tell you something I've been keeping a secret ever since I've known you. A big secret.'

Church thought of the Celtic dead talking of the traitor in their midst and his hand instinctively went to the sword.

Tom smiled and shook his head, as if he knew exactly what Church was thinking. 'A big secret, Jack,' he said softly. 'So big you might not be able to take it all in. From the very beginning, this has all been about you, more than anything. You're on a journey to enlightenment. You think you've been doing one thing, but instead you've been doing this.' He took a deep breath; there was a faint tremor in his voice. 'You need to gain illumination for what lies ahead, to prepare you for the next step. The biggest step of all. There will be a long period of trial, but after that . . .'

'So what are you saying? That he's some kind of Messiah?' Fury waiting to burst forth was buried in Ruth's voice.

'That's a particularly *stupid* way of putting it,' Tom said sharply.

'But it's essentially true.' There were tears in her eyes. *What is she thinking?* Church wondered.

Tom dismissed Ruth with a curt wave of his hand and turned to Church. 'Jack, you have died and been reborn. You have the essence of the gods in your veins. *You* are the next step.'

Church felt sick; his head was spinning and he couldn't breathe as the full weight of what Tom was saying finally crushed down on him.

'What you are about to embark on is the final stage of your trans-formation.' Tom's words were droning like flies. 'This is what the old alchemists were talking about. You, Jack. The transformation of lead into gold was a metaphor for what you are undergoing.'

'This was all about *me*?'

'The future of humanity, the rising and advancing of our race towards the next stage, depends on you. The prophecy has been with us since the earliest times. *In Britain's Darkest Hour, a hero shall arise.* You will arise, Jack. You will awaken the land, and through your tribulations you will make the next step of spiritual evolution that will lead humanity from the shadows to—'

'Godhood?'

'Perhaps. The Watchmen were established to help defend the land against incursions by the old gods, but they were also brought together to see this through. To find the one on whom the whole of the future rested, and to help shape him.'

'I've been manipulated by the Tuatha Dé Danann, the Fomorii and now humanity?' Church felt like he was going to be sick. It was too much, both of comprehension and responsibility. And it was stupid! So many people had called him a hero, but he knew what he was like inside: flawed, unsure, conflicted. And now they were trying to thrust all of humanity's future on to his shoulders. Who could cope with that?

'Not manipulated. You had a choice every step of the way. You still have a choice. No one would blame you for turning away from this. But you need to know what rests on your decision.'

'Am I going to change?'

'Physically? No, it's much more subtle than that – the great leaps forward always are, at the time. But inside, you will change, and you will wish that change in all humanity. It will move through people like a virus, altering their thought processes, making them look up from the gutters to the stars—'

'It's not fair!' The hurt in Ruth's voice was almost painful. 'How can he turn away? Who could throw down that responsibility for selfish reasons?'

She was right. He tried to comfort her, but she was having none of it.

'We just wanted to be together, to appreciate what we've got now, to appreciate life, if we ever sort out this mess we're in. That was always the slim hope that kept us going, but now what you're saying means there's never going to be any rest! Not for Church, who deserves it the most. Not for me.'

'Some things are more important—'

'Don't give me that!' Her eyes blazed, and away on the mainland a wind rushed wildly through the trees. Church stealthily signalled to Tom not to anger her further.

'We've all sacrificed so much! We deserve a break!'

He tried to take her in his arms, but she fended him off. 'Ruth, it's okay—'

'It's not, Church. It's not okay, and it's never going to be okay. This is like some stupid, sad old story where the heroes go through hardship and end up sacrificing themselves so everybody else can have a good life. It's just not fair!'

Her tears were flowing freely now. She couldn't bear to look at any of them. She wandered away and faced the sea, her head bowed as if she had been struck.

'Why couldn't you tell me all this before?' Church said to Tom.

'You wouldn't have reacted the same way in your trials if you knew they were trials. All your achievements are wholly your own. Your choices were made by your own sense of goodness.'

Church rubbed his eyes, overcome by what he had been told. 'Baccharus told me the gods were afraid humanity would come up and take their place.'

Tom rested a friendly hand on Church's shoulder. 'They know. Thousands of years have led to this one point. Millions of variables falling into line. No coincidences, Church. Make no mistake, there are no coincidences. The gods may not have known you were the one, but they knew the whole game was coming to a head—'

'It isn't a game!' His voice broke.

'I'm sorry, that was the wrong word.' As Tom shifted, the sun fell behind him so Church could not see his features in the dazzle of light. 'But I knew you were the one, Church, from the very first moment I met you. As Michael said, you can see it in the eyes. I knew you were the one, good man.'

The note of respect and friendship in his voice brought a swell of emotion in Church. He looked over to Ruth, frail against the rugged surroundings, and he felt both love and sadness at the same time. More than anything he wanted to spend the rest of his days with her, but the obligation was too much. He had no choice. He never had a choice from the moment he was born.

'Ruth.'

She ignored him, wrapped her arms a little tighter around herself.

Standing behind her, he hesitated briefly before putting his hands on her waist. 'Don't do this.'

'Why not? You're going to do it.'

'Of course I'm going to do it.'

'That's typical of you. No doubt at all.' Her voice trembled. 'You're throwing us away.'

'I'm not going to do that. You're more important to me than anything.'

A long pause. 'You never said that before.'

'There are a lot of things I've not said. I'm not very good at expressing my emotions in words. But I do love you, Ruth.'

Another pause, and then she turned slowly and rested her head on his shoulder. 'This thing isn't like anything else. It's too big. Christ, the responsibility for leading humanity into the Promised Land!'

'You're mixing your Biblical stories.'

She took a deep breath to regain her equilibrium, then cuffed him gently on the shoulder to break the mood. 'They'll never let you back after this. It's like the Mafia. You're a Made Man. You don't get out alive.'

'I believe things have a way of working themselves out.'

'That's a very childish and naïve view of existence.'

'Sure. What's wrong with that?'

She hugged him tighter, her fingernails biting through his clothes. 'I'll do whatever it takes to make sure I'm with you when all this blows over.'

'Cross mighty oceans?'

'Yes.'

'Climb the highest mountain?'

'Yes.'

'Travel the length of time and scour the universe?'

'Yes and yes.'

'You're a lying git, but I love you too.' He could feel her tears soaking through his T-shirt. She gave him another playful hit on the arm and then stepped back. 'Go on with you, then. Just make sure you're back for lunch.'

Tom was sighing loudly and shifting from foot to foot when Church returned to him. He made to speak, but Church silenced him with a jabbed finger. 'Don't say a word.'

Michael stepped in and motioned towards the chapel. 'It's this way.'

Church could feel the lines of force buzzing through the soles of his boots; he could have found his way to the destination blindfold.

Outside the chapel door, Michael paused. He looked both unsure and ecstatic. 'This is it, then?'

Tom took Michael's hand and shook it firmly. 'Well done. You've discharged your duty well. The long watch is over.'

'Well, I don't quite know what I'll do with my time.'

'Be patient. And pray to your God for success.'

Tom slapped him on the shoulder to send him on his way back to Ruth before stepping into the chapel with Church at his heel. Inside it was cool and dark, filled with the ages-old smell of damp stone.

'What am I going to find?' Church asked.

'You'll know when you get there.'

'You're a great bloody help, aren't you?'

The very air was charged with the earth energy; from the corner of his eye, Church could see blue sparks, like stardust.

'There are realities upon realities,' Tom said. 'You can't rely on anything you see, hear, smell, touch, taste. But that's always been the way. The only thing that matters is what's in here.' He levelled his fist at Church's heart.

'Nothing is fixed in the Fixed Lands,' Church said, repeating the words that had haunted his thoughts.

'Exactly. There are realities that may not be to your taste.' He was looking at Church in such a strange way it was troubling; Church tried to make sense of the unease he saw behind Tom's eyes, but it wouldn't come; something else the Rhymer wasn't telling him. 'Sour realities. Pinched and mean. Places where there are none of the values that make life worth living – friendship, love, honour and dignity. Where there is only power and greed and money. You don't have to accept them, Jack. Wish the world better. Everything is illusion. You just have to wish hard enough to shape it.'

He looked as if he was about to hug Church, but he caught himself at the last. In the end he stepped aside and pointed to a small stone stairway not far from the altar.

'What's down there?'

'A tomb about nine foot square cut out of the rock. In 1275 the monks here came across the bones of a man eight feet tall. A giant.'

'Who was he?'

'Not important.'

'The place is important?'

He nodded.

'Are you coming with me?'

'No. This is something you have to do alone.'

Church sighed, tried to force a smile but it wouldn't come. Without another word, he put his foot on the first step.

CHAPTER FIFTEEN

Waʀ ıs Ðeclaʀeð anð
Battle Come Ðown

Blood thundered in Church's head as he made his way down the steps
to the chill interior of the tomb. Trepidation filled every part of him,
but it was tinged with relief that finally there would be some kind of
revelation after so many mysteries.

Inside the bare tomb was a powerful sense of *presence*. Narrowing his
eyes, Church allowed his deep perception to take over until the walls,
floor and ceiling came alive with a vascular system of Blue Fire, interlocking at pulse-points, drawing together at one section where the
depth of blue glowed in the shape of a hand. He steeled himself, then
placed his own palm down hard on the spot. There was an instant of
hanging before the wall juddered apart to reveal a dark tunnel beyond.
Church slipped through quickly and the rock closed behind him with a
resounding clash.

The tunnel reminded him of so many others he had experienced in the
dark, secret places beneath the earth, although he knew that description
was not wholly correct. The Celts and the people who came before them
understood perfectly the symbolism of the routes they had established;
indeed, it was probably the main reason for their location. He was
entering the womb, going back to the primal state.

After a few minutes, the tunnel opened on to a wide corridor filled
with different coloured light filtering through a gently drifting mist;
near the roof it was golden, near the ground the rich, sapphire tones of
the Blue Fire, and in between were flickers of red and green and purple.
The mist gave the place an ethereal quality that was deeply soothing.
The air smelled like dry-ice.

For a while he hovered anxiously, concerned that it was impossible to
see what lay ahead. Knowing he had no choice, he strode out, feeling
the unnatural sensation of feathers on his skin as he entered the mist. If
it resembled the other secret places he had visited, somewhere ahead
would lie a puzzle with a particularly lethal sting; if Tom's description
of the place was correct, this one would be worst of all.

Within the mist, he lost all his bearing. After a while, a dark smudge
appeared in the drifting white, quickly forming into a figure. The Sword

was in Church's hand in an instant, electric against his skin. It was a man, dressed in the armour and white silk of a Knight Templar, the red cross on his chest glowing eerily. His face was drawn, his eyes hooded above a drooping white moustache. He rested on the long sword the Templars favoured.

Church waited for him to adopt a fighting posture, but the Knight simply motioned for Church to continue along the corridor. There was an air of deference about him, but his face was dark and threatening. Inexplicably, Church shuddered as he passed.

Further on, other figures emerged from the mist. These were Celts ready for battle, naked and tattooed, their hair matted, spiked and bleached with a lime mixture. They stood against the walls on either side, watching him with baleful eyes. Some broke away, loping past him in the direction from which he had come. Again he felt the same old mixture of wariness and reverence, but his fear of a sudden attack had started to wane.

As he progressed, representatives of the races that preceded the Celts floated in and out of the mist, but most of them were swallowed up again before he got good sight of them. At some point, a troubling noise had started up, so faint at first he hadn't noticed it, but it built until it was pulsing through the walls with steady, rhythmic bass notes that resonated in the pit of his stomach. It sounded like war drums, or the beating of an enormous heart.

And then, suddenly, the mist cleared and he was looking at something so incongruous it was at first hard to take: a large window, and beyond it people in modern dress stared back at him with hard, uncompromising expressions. Before he could see any more, the mist closed in once again. There had been something dismal and threatening about the scene, although he couldn't quite put his finger on what it was. He hurried on and didn't look back.

Finally he was out of the mist. The corridor was even wider at this point – enough for ten men to lie across – but the most curious thing was that the floor was a mass of intricate patterns carved into the hard bedrock. There were the familiar spirals and cup-holes he had seen at prehistoric sites during his days as a working archaeologist, but also the detailed interweaving designs of the Celts. The patterns of hundreds, if not thousands, of years were portrayed there.

The swirls and fine detail were almost hallucinogenic, but there was no time to waste examining the iconography. He put one foot on the edge of the pattern.

A spike burst from the ground, through the sole of his boot and into the leather uppers. A bolt of red agony filled his leg and he howled, wrenching his foot off the iron nail with a sickening sucking sound. The spike disappeared back into the design the moment he was free of it. Feeling sick from the shock and the pain, he crumpled down hard on the cold stone, tearing off his boot. The spike had torn the flesh off the insides of his big toe and his second toe, but luckily, had done no further damage.

As he laced the boot back up, he surveyed the floor pattern: a trap. The spikes were obviously buried along the length of the design: step on the correct place, you were fine; make the wrong move and you were impaled. The pattern stretched out in delirious confusion. How was he supposed to divine the path through it?

He retreated a few paces to see if the change in perspective offered any clues, then moved in close; it was a miasma. From a distance, it was a mess, meaningless; near to, the design hinted at great meaning, but none of it made any sense in any context he understood. Sighing, he sat back, trying to ignore the pain stabbing in his foot. He took comfort from the knowledge that all the previous puzzles they had encountered had been soluble if seen from the cultural or philosophical perspective of the Celts and the earlier people who had originated them. His university studies helped him a little in understanding their world-view, but he had never studied in depth the group that seventeenth-century romantics had designated a unique people. He knew the Celts were a fragmented collection of tribes, originally rising from a broad area centred on India, but common threads tied them together, of which their view of life and spirituality were probably the strongest.

He thought back over the previous puzzles and their odd mix of threat and spiritual instruction: the one at Tintagel, where sacrifice was the key, or the clues at Glastonbury that demanded Shavi, Ruth and Laura search for the 'signal hidden in the noise', the truth buried in the confusion, a metaphor for life. There it was. Quickly, he crawled forward to the edge of the pattern. The Celtic design showed serpents – or, he thought excitedly, dragons – flowing in a spiral pattern that progressed from side to side along the floor. And the Spiral Path had been the Celtic metaphor for both the journey through life and a ritual procession that allowed access to the Otherworld, like the spiral path carved into the slopes of Glastonbury Tor.

Was that it? He had no way of knowing for sure until his foot was on the design, so in the end it came down to an act of faith; in himself and his own abilities.

He cracked his knuckles, then took a deep breath. It was time to embark on the Spiral Dance and move from this life to the next.

With the air leaden in his lungs, he stepped on to the stylised Celtic serpents. Every muscle hardened. When he realised nothing had happened, he relaxed a little, but the path was barely wider than a kerb, a tightrope winding its way through a sea of danger. What happened if he slipped? A spike ripping through his sole, sprawling across the design, spikes punching into his body wherever he landed. With the blood thundering in his ears, he took his second step.

The path took him from wall to wall, forwards then backwards, in slow progress along the length of the corridor. Sweat soaked through his shirt, ran in rivulets into the nape of his back. His head hurt from staring at the tiny pattern in the half-light. Follow the serpent in the earth to enlightenment. As the ancient Celtic inventors had undoubtedly intended, his stark concentration brought a deep meditation on what he was undertaking; the metaphor of walking a thin path through constant danger did not escape him.

At one point, he paused briefly to rest his eyes. It was a mistake, for he instantly started wavering and almost pitched forward until he threw out both arms to steady himself. It only just did the trick, but it was enough of a scare to focus him even more sharply. He did one final spiral, more complex than any of the others, and then, abruptly, the design had gone and he was back on safe stone flags. He collapsed on to his back, sucking in soothing breaths.

He rested for only a moment before following the corridor once more. The Spiral Path had been some kind of transition, for within a few yards the corridor had been replaced by a wall of trees, their tops lost high up in the shadows. Church had long since forgone trying to apply logic to his experiences in such areas, but the sight was still oddly disturbing. The underground wood appeared healthy enough, with full-leafed oaks and ash and hawthorn, with bracken and brambles growing beneath them. An odd green luminescence filtered amongst the trunks, but Church could not identify its source; it was enough to illuminate the way ahead, and gave the impression of first light or twilight.

The density of the forest added to the deep foreboding that had crept up on him. Anything could be hiding amongst the foliage. As if to echo his suspicions, rustling broke out in the undergrowth. A second later, two rows of sheep emerged from the forest and passed him on either side. The ones on the left were white, the others black, both lines walking in perfect step. The bizarre sight became even more unnerving when one of the white sheep bleated, for then one of the black sheep wandered over to the white queue and immediately became white. The reverse happened when a black sheep bleated. Church looked round to see where they were going, but there were none behind him. When he peered back, the last few sheep emerged from the forest and were gone.

He was sure it meant something, but he had no idea what, and the image continued to haunt him as he began his journey in the quiet, green world.

The atmosphere amongst the trees was so ethereal it was difficult to shake the notion that he was dreaming. Odd sensations began to make their way through his body – a tingling in his legs, a feeling that his hands were no longer hands – and a moment later the weightlessness that had crept up on him became palpable. It was not a hallucination, for he really was drifting a little way above the ground. He called out in surprise, only to be shocked that his voice sounded like the cry of a bird. His eyes were astonishingly sharp and his arms were wings, covered with thick, brown feathers. He was a hawk, flying up into the branches, and up and up.

There was no time to question his transformation, for he was immediately confronted by another hawk with blazing yellow eyes. 'You are one with the birds of the trees,' it said in an unsettlingly human voice.

It swooped down at him, talons raised in attack. Church panicked, losing all control of his form. The hawk raked claws across his back and a shower of brown feathers flew all around. He attempted to steer himself, crashed against a branch and went into a downward spiral.

The hawk didn't give up its attack, shrieking loudly as it bore down on him. Once more the talons tore through his back, and this time the pain almost made him lose consciousness. But he recovered slightly, and his mind was focused. He didn't fight against the messages that were coming from instinct, and after a slow start, where he only narrowly evaded another scarring, he found he could move swiftly amongst the trees.

He wasn't about to stand and fight – he didn't see the point of it – so he flew as swiftly as he could, before a weight pressed down hard on his shoulders and forced him to the ground. His wings gone, he hit the turf hard, tumbling athletically.

Barely able to catch his breath, he rolled to his feet, which were now grey paws. 'You are one with the beasts of the field,' a rough voice said. He looked round to see a large grey wolf away amongst the trees. It was watching him with the same hateful yellow eyes of the hawk.

It moved, but Church was quicker, loping through the trunks, leaping the clusters of vegetation, avoiding the pits and hollows with ease. As he ran, he moved further off the ground and his paws became hooves, while a sharp pain in his forehead signalled the sprouting of antlers like those Cernunnos sported.

The hoofbeats of his pursuer continued to thunder across the soft ground. And then Church was back on his own legs, and in his peripheral vision he could see his own hands; his lungs burned from the exertion. Church didn't know if he had truly transformed or if it had been a hallucination. He tried to look over his shoulder and awkwardly caught his foot in a root, stumbled, and slid down a slight incline.

What he saw made his blood run cold. There was no man behind him, as there had been a deer, a wolf and a hawk. At first it was a stark white glow, before he realised that what he was seeing was a pack of dogs, savage and alien, filled with their own brilliance.

He picked himself up and ran as fast as he could. The beasts' crazed howling made him sick with primal fear. They were not like the dogs of the Wild Hunt, which were fearsome enough, but were filled with an unbridled ferocity and, he was convinced, controlled by one mind. He risked another backwards glance and saw them bounding amongst the trees like spectres, there, then gone, moving on two flanks to capture him in a pincer movement.

He jumped a stream, almost skidding down the opposite bank, then hurdled a fallen log. The pack was relentless, and drawing closer; he would not be able to outrun them. Their howling became even more blood-crazed as they sensed this.

He came out of the forest so fast he barely realised he had left the last of the trees behind him. The land fell away sharply, becoming hard rock again, and the roof had closed once more twenty feet above his head. In the distance he could make out a brilliant blue glow. Slipping on the rock, he tumbled, cracking his head hard, but he was up and running in one fluid movement, wiping the blood away that had started to puddle in his left eye.

He had hoped the pack would remain behind in the forest, but now their shrieks were echoing off the walls, growing more intense, more terrifying. If he looked back, he knew he would see them snapping only inches from his heels.

As he ran, he pulled out the Sword once more. Legend said it could kill anything with a single blow. Swinging it behind him without slowing his step, he felt it connect with two hard forms. A terrible howling rang up from the whole pack.

He carried on that way for a few minutes more, but his arm muscles were soon burning and his joints ached. There was no time for an alternate strategy: the path ahead of him ended abruptly at a cliff edge, and beyond was a lake of the Blue Fire, the energy rising up in coruscating bursts like the bubbling of lava.

A few feet from the edge he spun round, lashing out wildly with the sword, but the pack had already halted a few yards away. All the dogs were watching him with their sickly yellow eyes, their mouths open to reveal enormous, sharp fangs; drool ran out in rivulets to splatter on the rock where it gave a hot-fat sizzle.

Breathless, he waved the Sword at them while attempting to look over his shoulder to see if there was some exit he had missed.

'There is no escape from here,' the dogs said as one. 'You have reached the Chapel Perilous. Your life is now over.' They advanced a step in perfect, unnerving rhythm, like some drilled Roman legion.

'No,' Church gasped. 'It wouldn't end like this. There has to be a way out or there's no point to the trial.' He looked all around quickly, but could see no exit. 'I'm missing something.'

'No escape,' the dogs repeated. 'This is your death. Behind you is the source of everything. One step and you will be swallowed up, eradicated. Here we stand, ready to tear you to pieces. To turn your meat to fibres and your bones to dust.'

'I can fight,' Church said.

'You can,' the dogs said, 'for you have already killed some of us. But do we seem any less to you?'

The pack appeared to go on forever. 'Where there's life, there's hope,' Church said.

The dogs advanced another step.

He wiped the blood away from his eye, his heart pounding. The Sword handle was slick with sweat.

The dogs moved four paces in rapid procession. He waved the Sword wildly. Only a couple of yards away now, the white of their coats was almost blinding. Their jaws moved in unison – *click* – their eyes rolled as one.

Perhaps this was the trial: to fight and fight and fight, until he was down to his last reserves. But against an enemy that could not be killed, or even weakened? What was the point in that? Sooner or later they would overwhelm him.

He gripped the Sword with both hands and adopted a fighting stance.

What was the meaning in that?

And then it came to him. It took only a second or two to weigh it up, and then he sheathed the Sword and spun round. The blue looked so inviting: relief after his long, arduous struggle. He closed his eyes and stepped off the cliff.

He expected burning, but there was no sensation at all for a long time, just a world of blue overwhelming everything. He also expected his consciousness – his sense of self – to be broken up within seconds of contact, then dissipated amongst the blue waves, to be returned to the source, but that didn't happen either. He remained who he had always been, since the beginning of time.

When sensation began to return, it was fitful, and quite alien. He felt the beating of mighty wings coming from his own arms; he saw with crystal-refracted vision through serpent eyes; he felt the blast of flames pass his lips, the stink of smoke in his nostrils.

'You are one,' a voice from nowhere said.

He was looking at blue, but the shade was much softer. It took him a few seconds to accept the change in hue, and then a fluffy cloud drifted into his vision and he realised he was staring at the sky. He closed his eyes, smiling, enjoying the heat of the sun on his face.

Sitting up, he found himself lying on the causeway that joined St Michael's Mount to the mainland. From the position of the sun, it must have been around noon; he had been gone barely any time at all.

Ruth's cry stirred him from memories of flying; reluctantly, he realised they were fading rapidly, but the sense of freedom didn't go. She came running along the causeway towards him, her hair lashing in the breeze. She grinned with relief and joy. He jumped up and took her in his arms, overjoyed that she was with him.

'I saw you from the top,' she said. 'How did you get here?'

'Look at that,' he said, pointing over their heads.

A Fabulous Beast swooped on the air currents, the sun glinting brightly off its scales, reds and golds and greens. Church was overcome with a sense of wonder. The Beast was otherworldly and lithe and graceful as it gently circled the top of the Mount, but it was what it represented that truly affected him: a world where anything could happen, a world where the mundane had forever been stripped from life.

'It's the old one, from Avebury. The oldest of them all.' Tom was at their side, craning his neck to peer beneath a shielding hand. 'You've done it. It wouldn't have left its home if the Fiery Network hadn't been brought back to life.'

'Then I really did it?' Church asked, barely believing. 'I woke the sleeping land?'

'There are more of them,' Ruth marvelled. 'Loads of them.'

Church counted ten, then gave up; they were coming from all directions to converge on the Mount. Some were smaller, some obviously younger, their colours slightly different, but they were all flying with abandon, rolling and gliding and looping the loop, so that there was an unmistakable feeling of joyous celebration.

'We did it,' he said in awe.

That night they made camp on a hillside overlooking St Michael's Mount. Tom had already located tents and sleeping bags before coming to meet them at Mousehole, and they lit a fire to keep out the autumnal chill that came down with the night. He had also found a bottle of whisky to drink to their success.

The cleric, Michael, had met them briefly after Church's return, but he was eager to get back to his parishioners to spread a message of hope. The deference he had shown Church had been almost embarrassing.

'How do you feel?' Ruth asked Church hesitantly, once Tom had gone off to build up their wood supply.

It was a question he had avoided, for he was almost afraid to examine himself. 'Good,' he said.

'Don't think you're going to get away with that. Do I have to kiss your hand every time I meet you? Are you going to walk on water for your party trick?'

He tapped his head. 'Up here I feel pretty much the same as always. I mean, I think the same way. I'm definitely the *me* I always was, which is good because I had this feeling I'd turn out like a reformed smoker or Born-Again Christian, turned off by half the things I used to be in my old life.'

Her smile showed relief; it was obvious she had felt the same way.

'But in here,' he said, tapping his chest, 'I feel amazing. I feel . . . I don't know, the best way to describe it is *right*. I feel at ease with everything. Positive. Confident.' He thought hard. 'I feel at peace.'

She was looking at him with an expression that suggested she wished she felt that way too. She took his hand and gave it a squeeze.

'I expected it to be earth-shattering,' he continued. 'But it's so subtle. I don't feel like the man who's going to lead humanity to the next level. In fact, I cringe at the thought of it.'

'Maybe that's the point. Maybe you were like a jigsaw with one piece missing. Now you've found it you can be the person you always might have been.'

He shook his head, laughing quietly. 'Now I know how I feel, I'm taking it all with a pinch of salt. Tom gets so wrapped up with these predictions and prophecies. They're all so vague they can mean virtually anything under any circumstance. Who knows? Maybe Veitch is the big saviour.'

'But what does it mean? For us?' Her eyes shimmered brightly in the firelight.

'I'm carrying on with my life as it was. I'm not thinking about tomorrow. I'm not thinking about the big picture. I'm making the most of each minute and I'll deal with whatever's thrown at me, as and when it happens. And I'm doing it with you.' He pulled her forward and kissed her tenderly.

They were interrupted by Tom's irritated muttering. 'You've got time for all that spooning in the privacy of your tent,' he said.

'You're only jealous because you're not getting any,' Ruth replied.

The night was clear and bright and filled with a deep, abiding magic. The full moon brought silver tips to the waves, their gentle lapping a soothing symphony accompanied by the occasional breeze rustling the goldening leaves; the perfect soundtrack to Church's thoughts. Stars glistened everywhere they looked; they felt peaceful for the first time in months.

'It could be like this all over,' Church said, his arm around Ruth, the two of them watching the light on the waves.

'And I thought I was the hippie,' Tom said. 'Don't start going soft. This is a little oasis. The real world is out there and it's thoroughly unpleasant.'

'Can't we just enjoy the moment?' Ruth protested.

'You go right ahead.' Tom prodded the fire with an annoyance that matched the sneer in his voice. 'We'll just forget about all those bodies getting torn apart and eaten, all those lives being ruined, land being blasted, cities razed to the ground, rivers polluted. Oh, and while we're at it, let's forget the end of the world in just a few short days.' He punctuated it with a tight smile.

'I didn't mean that.' Ruth's eyes blazed. 'But we can't do anything right here, right now, so do we have to continue flagellating ourselves? We've worked hard. We've achieved something . . . Church has achieved something. We should celebrate our victories.'

'I simply wanted you to remember—'

'Of course I remember! I know what we're up against! And I know what our chances are, even with what Church has done today.' Tom flinched. 'Yes, I can see it in your face. Even if we win we aren't all going to make it through alive, right? So I just want to enjoy this quiet time with Church and my *friend* because it might be my last.'

Tom shrugged. 'Point taken.' He gave a slight grin that punctured the mood.

For the next half hour, they did take it easy, enjoying their company with jokes and gossip while handing round the whisky. Even so, they found it impossible to bury the momentous events of the day and soon they were chatting animatedly once more about what had happened. Church couldn't bring himself to discuss what he had felt once he had given himself up to the Blue Fire – it had been too personal, a spiritually transcendent moment that would be devalued by being discussed. That infuriated Ruth, who was eager to understand.

'But I don't see what he *did* to bring the land alive,' she said. 'It wasn't as if he unblocked a channel or something.'

'He gave it his life, his spirit, in honesty and openness, and the Blue Fire gave it back to him, but not before that vital surge had brought the whole of the system alive.' Tom was lying on his back, watching the stars through his cloud of smoke. 'It is fuelled by belief, and Church believed in a way that nobody had for centuries. Not just believed in the Fiery Network, but in himself, in humanity and the universe and hope, and childish things too, like dreams and wishing.'

'So he's just one big battery.'

'The only battery who could have done it.'

'I don't get it,' Ruth continued. 'You talked about *waking the land* as if it were a big thing, but apart from the Fabulous Beasts we saw earlier, everything looks the same.'

'Maybe you're not looking in the right place, or the right way. Maybe you're not *feeling*.'

Ruth hurled some mild abuse at his patronising attitude. He sighed wearily and dragged himself to his feet. 'Do you remember that night at Stonehenge when I gave you the first sign of the Blue Fire?' he said.

'No, I don't,' Ruth said, 'because I was fast asleep. You saved that demonstration for your favourite son here.'

'Yes, I remember,' Church said. 'It was amazing. Like something I'd been looking for all my life.'

'The power of Stonehenge made that easier,' Tom said, 'because it's a node in the network. Look around – do you see any standing stones in the vicinity?' They agreed that there weren't any.

They waited for him to continue, but all he did was smoke, and check his watch and the moon and stars, until they were convinced he'd slipped into a drugged stupor. Ruth shifted impatiently, made to speak, but Church placed a restraining hand on her forearm. She looked at him curiously; he put his finger to his lips.

After fifteen minutes, Tom said, 'Now.' He dropped to his haunches and placed one hand flat on the cool grass. 'The time has to be right. The mood has to be right. Everything has to be right, and it's not been righter for centuries. You even need the right eyes for this – not everyone can see it – but you should be ready now. Watch carefully.'

Around his hand, tiny sparks began to fly. They had a life of their own, dancing and jumping into the grass, surging towards the nearby trees. Other strands ran to Church and Ruth, infiltrating them with a prickly thrill; they both felt a sudden surge of euphoria.

'It's in everything,' Ruth gasped.

'You think that's good.' Tom smiled. 'Watch this.'

The ground erupted with Blue Fire. It shot out in lines across the land, towards the sea and under the waves, intersecting at regular points where tiny flares burned. And then it suddenly burst upwards in a tremendous, breathtaking rush, hundreds of feet high, a dazzling cathedral of lights like the one Church had seen at Stonehenge. A paler blue light shimmered between the connecting strands, turning opaque, then clear, like protective walls. Only this cathedral was not the only one. An even bigger structure covered St Michael's Mount; and there were more beyond, stretching right across the land. It was dazzling in its potency. Caught up in the sheer wonder of it, there was no doubt the whole of the land had become infused with the vital force.

'How did you do that?' Ruth gasped.

'Sometimes when things fall into alignment it becomes more active. I simply helped you to see it.'

'This is why the ancients put up the stone circles,' Ruth said in awe.

'And the standing stones and cairns and other places of sacred power.' Tom was now sitting cross-legged on the grass, watching the display with a beatific smile. 'To channel it, to help it to live, and to reap the benefits it provides.'

'It heals,' Ruth said.

'It heals the body, certainly. But more importantly, it heals the spirit.'

'I want to feel that.' Ruth looked from Tom to Church. 'You've both had experience of it. It's changed you both, I can see. I *need* to feel it.'

'There'll be time,' Tom said.

'Will there?' Ruth replied. The note in her voice infected them all, and gradually the astonishing display faded.

Church put his arm tightly around her shoulders. 'But it's worth fighting for, isn't it?'

Veitch and Shavi escaped from the farmhouse, but only with a helping of guile and a good serving of luck. They kept to the hedgerows, hiding in ditches at the slightest sound, barely moving, barely breathing.

The Fomorii were out in force, scurrying along the roads all around the farm. Veitch and Shavi were in no doubt the Night Walkers still considered them a threat. At times when the beasts drew a little too close, Shavi used his shamanic abilities to direct various field animals to cause a distraction so they could escape. Since his return from the Grim Lands, he was even more adept at the things at which he had previously excelled.

Eventually they were faced with open countryside; as dawn began to break they were moving as fast as they could towards the west.

Over the following days, they kept as far away from any roads or centres of population as possible. They slept in trees or ditches, wrapped in dustbin bags and other items of rubbish, like two tramps. Sometimes they found a hollow where they could light a fire without being seen. Veitch cooked rabbits or birds, while Shavi satisfied himself with any autumnal berries and fruits or roots that he could scavenge.

On a day that began cold and overcast with light drizzle sweeping across the countryside in gusts, they made their way over fields towards the rendezvous point. Ahead lay a rise where they expected a good vista over the rolling valleys that led down to the Thames; the outer reaches of the London sprawl was not far away.

When they came close to the ridge, they dropped to their bellies and wriggled up the remaining few yards, their clothes already sodden and thick with mud. Peeking over the summit so they would not be silhouetted against the skyline, they witnessed a sight that made their blood run cold.

London lay beneath a thick bank of seething clouds that formed no part of the surrounding weather system. Occasional bursts of lightning punctured the oppressive gloom so they could see that, somewhere in the centre of the capital, a large black tower had been raised up. It was still incomplete, and the edges were indistinct, as if roughly constructed. It reminded Shavi of pictures he had seen of enormous termites' nests in the African veldt. Ruth had spoken of a similar tower she had seen in the Lake District, constructed from the detritus of humanity: abandoned cars, plastics, bricks and girders, old washing machines, anything that could be reclaimed and stacked. And all across the city, fires blazed, sending up thick gouts of greasy smoke to join the lowering clouds.

There were things buzzing the tower with the insistent, awkward motion of flies. The distance was too great to tell exactly what they were, but there were clouds of them, black and threatening. And from the periphery of the city, across the surrounding countryside, swarmed what at first glance appeared to be ants. The Fomorii scurried back and forth, thousands upon thousands of them, sweeping out in wider and wider arcs as they spread across the country. Their movement looked chaotic and meaningless, but that only masked the complexity of regimented actions designed to scour and destroy. It was a scene from Hell.

Veitch watched the panorama for long minutes, his face heavy with hatred and repressed anger. 'How the fuck are we going to fight something like that?' he said in a cold, dead voice.

In the shadow of the M25, Laura and the Bone Inspector sheltered amongst a tangled maze of wrecked and abandoned cars. Through gaps in the vehicles they could make out waves of Fomorii fanning out across the Essex fields.

'We don't stand a chance,' Laura whispered. 'They're everywhere.' She still felt sick from the shock of losing her arm. Pressure was building deep in her shoulder, as if her blood was about to gush out of the gaping socket, despite the stained shirt she had pressed against the wound; she still couldn't understand why she hadn't bled out.

'They're searching for us.' The dismal note in the Bone Inspector's voice told her he agreed with her assessment. Their luck had run out.

'What do we do? Stay here?'

'Nowhere to run. They're all around now.' He tapped a syncopated rhythm with his staff.

Laura rubbed at her shoulder joint; the pressure was growing unbearable.

'We can't stay—'

Her words were drowned out by the sudden rending of metal. Cars flew on either side, as if they were made of paper. Laura flung herself backwards in shock. The Bone Inspector raised his staff in defence, his face drained of blood. Eight or nine Fomorii ploughed through the vehicles with ease, tossing aside what they could move, rending apart what they could not.

Laura thought: *Shit. What a way to go.*

The noise of crashing metal was so loud neither of them heard the hunting horn, and so they were surprised when the first of the Fomorii dissolved in a thin, black rain. To Laura, the world appeared fractured: frozen frames, sudden temporal jumps. The Fomorii were turning as one. Red and white dogs leaped through the air, their teeth tiny yet so very sharp. Spears tipped with cruel sickles sliced into the Night Walkers, the beasts falling apart at the slightest touch. Drifting through the grey rain were men on horseback, swathed in furs and armour, their eyes hidden by shadows.

In less than two minutes the Fomorii were gone, their remains steaming amongst the shattered cars. The Wild Hunt reined in their horses and cantered around the area as the one of their number with the most fearsome face dismounted. As he walked towards Laura he began to change; antlers sprouted from his forehead, fur and leaves intermingled across his body. Cernunnos passed the Bone Inspector as if he were not there and dropped to his haunches before Laura, his wide-set, golden eyes calm and soothing.

'Daughter of the Green, I greet you.'

'I thought you only came out at night in that last form,' Laura gasped, not really knowing what to say.

'The world has changed. Many rules are falling like autumn leaves.' Then he did turn to the Bone Inspector. 'Guardian, you have moved beyond the bounds of your calling on this occasion. You sought this one out at great personal danger, and you have protected her to the best of your abilities. I look kindly on you. A reward will come your way.'

The Bone Inspector bowed his head slightly. 'I seek no reward.'

'Nonetheless, it shall be yours.' Returning his attention to Laura, he trailed his long, gnarled fingers gently through her hair. 'Frail creature. *Fragile* creature, yet filled with wonder.'

Laura lost herself in the swirling gold in his eyes. He held her gaze for a moment, then rose. 'Come, this place is corrupted. We must find safe haven.'

All Laura could remember of the journey from her seat on Cernunnos's horse – although he wore the hideous form of the Erl-King as he rode – was a blur of green fields and grey road. They came to a halt in no time at all on the fringes of Brentwood, where the Essex countryside still rolled out peacefully.

In a thickly wooded swathe of the South Weald country park, the Hunt dismounted and let their horses wander amongst the trees. The Erl-King became Cernunnos once more and led Laura off to a quiet area where he could talk to her privately.

'What's going on?' she said weakly as she lay against the foot of an enormous oak.

'Events move faster as they rush towards the point of greatest change. You are caught up in the flow, Sister of Dragons, as you were from the moment existence came calling for you. This is your time, your destiny.'

'What use am I going to be?' The pressure in her shoulder made her stomach turn. 'My arm—'

'Remove the rag.'

Laura hesitated, afraid to see the tangled parts that remained after her arm had been torn off. He urged her once more, gently. She dropped the stained shirt and looked away. The pressure in her shoulder grew unbearable and she was forced to ram her fist into her mouth to stop herself screaming. But within a moment the pressure had broken, to be replaced by another disturbing sensation: it felt like everything inside her was rushing out of her shoulder. It was impossible not to look.

What she saw made her mind warp. The dangling tendons and skin were moving of their own accord. Before her eyes, cells multiplied and grew into long tendrils that twisted and knotted, then fused, became bone and muscle and gristle. The stump of an upper arm protruded from her shoulder. The process grew faster, reminding her of time-lapse film of sprouting plants. The tendrils lashed so quickly her face was buffeted by the air currents they made. An elbow formed perfectly. A forearm and wrist. The palm came together in a blur, and finally the fingers, the nails added with a flourish.

She couldn't take her eyes off it. Slowly, she turned it over, examining it from every angle. It was *her* arm; she knew the patterns of light and shade from the muscle structure beneath the skin. Her stomach flipped and she thought she was going to be sick, but as she brought her hand to her mouth she noticed the circle of interlocking leaves Cernunnos had branded into her flesh on the eerie island in Loch Maree. 'The green blood, green skin . . . What did you do to me?' Thoughts trampled through her head. Her hands went to her stomach. 'I didn't imagine it. I was ripped open when that thing came out of me. And I. Mended myself?'

Cernunnos made a strange growling noise deep in his throat that was almost sympathetic. 'You are a Daughter of the Green. Within you is the potency of nature in all its fury and wonder.'

'What did you do to me?'

'Your old form had reached the end of its days—'

'You killed me?' Her mind was reeling.

'There is no life or death. All things have no beginning and no end. For the immutable laws, you only have to look around you. Seasons turn. Things fall into the earth, then rise again. New forms are made, but the essence remains the same. The rules have always been laid bare for your kind to see, but in recent times you have been blinded by arrogance. You saw yourselves as special. You thought that, for you, with death there came an ending when everything around you told you otherwise. It trapped you in your forms, made you truly into frail, fragile creatures. It prevented you reaching out to existence or utilising the greatness that lies within you.'

She examined her arm once more, not sure if she should feel horror or wonder. 'I can grow bits of myself? Like a plant?'

'This gift is not given lightly, Sister of Dragons. You are of my essence now. You are part of the greatness of nature, you are a vibrant branch of my bountiful family.'

Laura nodded; slowly it was starting to feel right. If Cernunnos hadn't changed her she would have died when Balor had been reborn into the world. But more than that, she felt something indefinable yet all-consuming, as if she had finally come to a place she was always meant to be.

'All things are open to you now, Sister of Dragons, Daughter of the Green,' Cernunnos continued. 'The sunlit uplands stretch before you. All is possible.'

'Why me? There were others, Shavi—'

'Your heart was given to the green long ago.'

He was right: in childhood, she had always been drawn to nature; as an adult, she had devoted herself to environmental activism. It had always been the most important thing in the world to her. 'Ruth got the same mark from you, but she didn't get the same treatment.'

'As my daughters, you each have roles to fulfil. She echoes a different aspect of my essence. The force that cannot be stopped.'

'She's the sledgehammer, I'm the stiletto.' She felt uncomfortable using weapons as a metaphor for abilities that were so life affirming.

'Yet there is danger for her. The gift I have given her is great. It fills her being, shifts the balance of her day and nightside. She must learn to encompass it or it will consume her.' Cernunnos began to roam around her, tearing at the turf with his hooves.

'Will she be okay?'

He remained silent for a little too long. 'The greatest danger lies at the place where all things converge. If her will fails her, the power will drive her down darker lanes.'

Laura subconsciously flexed her new fingers. 'The power's eating her up. She's losing control.' She felt a pang of worry for the woman she had disliked for so long. 'Can't you do something?'

'It is her gift. To intervene would make it worthless.'

Laura ground her teeth; the shock of losing then regaining her arm had ebbed and she was overcome once more with urgency. 'I need to get back to the others. Time's running out.' She stood up shakily. 'So Ruth gets all the big-shot powers. I'm just indestructible.'

'You can do more. Much more. Let me show you.' He smiled and held out his hand.

Church and Ruth had been intrigued by Tom's account of how he had used the lines of Blue Fire to travel vast distances, and were eager to utilise it to get closer to the rendezvous point. He refused flatly, emphasising the many dangers.

'It's not like catching a train, you know. Whatever you might think, the chance of getting lost in it is high. You need skills taught over the course of a lifetime to follow the channels and flow. I could look after one of you, but two . . . that's too many. Imagine diving into a white water river gushing through a ravine over rapids – that is what it is like. If it is a life or death matter, I will attempt it. But after coming so far, we can't afford to throw it all away by losing one of you. Time *is* short, but in my opinion the best option is to take the horses and ride them hard.'

Reluctantly, they agreed, and within minutes of sunrise they were riding fast across the rugged Cornish landscape. They picked up the A30, eventually following the route on which Ruth, Laura and Shavi had been pursued by the Wild Hunt, crossing the M5 to bypass Bristol, where they joined the M4. It was still eerie to see the motorway devoid of cars. Already thick weeds and long grass had sprouted in the central reservation, and birds strutted defiantly across the lanes. At one point they disturbed rabbits gambolling lazily in the fast lane, enjoying their freedom from the tyranny of humanity.

They ransacked the motorway services for any food that had not spoiled, giving the horses water and rest, taking the opportunity to doze in the dry air of the cafeterias. But the closer they got to London, the more the atmosphere became depressive, the more they felt an unpleasant anxiety building in the pit of their stomachs. The skies were darker, filled with charred matter blowing in the wind. The stink of burning was everywhere. Their instincts told them to turn back to seek out the green fields and sunlit lands of the West Country, but they forced themselves to keep on.

With only two days to Samhain, they finally parted company just past Reading, with Tom heading on to find Veitch and Shavi, while Ruth and Church continued to the camp of the Tuatha Dé Danann. Although none of them gave voice to it, they all dreaded what the coming days would bring.

CHAPTER SIXTEEN
Semper Fidelis

Twilight was already heavy on the land when Church and Ruth wearily crested a ridge above the rendezvous point. What they saw made them rein in their horses in astonishment. After the long grey shadows, they were confronted by a sea of light filled with the noise of activity and a complex range of smells. Spread out before them was what appeared to be a mediaeval tent city, but it covered vast acres. Campfires showered columns of sparks amongst the billowing tents, some small, others of marquee size, while torches flickered with yellow-white light, marking paths and meeting areas. The air was fragrant with incense, spices and perfume, but there was also the powerful musk of horses and the aromas of cooking food. The hauntingly seductive music of the Tuatha Dé Danann rose from numerous quarters, but instead of conflicting, it came together in a symphony that made their spirits soar. For a while they were entranced by the gods walking, talking, preparing weapons, making merry.

'I don't remember this many on the ship,' Ruth said.

'They must have been joined by some of the other Courts.' Church tried not to be engulfed by the wonder of what he saw, but it was impossible. Whatever he might think of the gods, they were a source of remarkable magic.

They urged their exhausted mounts slowly down the slope, but they hadn't gone far when they heard a sound like wind in a mountain pass. A second later there was movement all around. Figures barely more than ghosts separated from the dark landscape to form a barrier between them and the camp. They were lower-born Golden Ones, in strange shimmering armour offset by red and white silk, with helmets that looked like enormous seashells.

'Fragile Creatures,' one of them said to the others.

'We are a Brother and Sister of Dragons,' Church pronounced. 'We are here at the behest of the First Family.'

There was sudden activity beyond the ranks. The guards fell roughly aside as another god strode through. From the more intricate designs of his armour, he looked to be of higher rank, but he had a cold, cruel face that Church instantly disliked. When he laid eyes on Church and Ruth, he gave a dark, cunning smile and did a bow that could easily have been mockery. 'Greetings, Brother and Sister of Dragons. Your reputation precedes you. I am Melliflor, of the Court of the Yearning Heart. I welcome you to this place, though it lacks the charms of our home.' He stepped aside and motioned to a path that had opened up between the guards. 'Come, let me take you to my Queen. She will be eager to learn the latest from the world of Fragile Creatures. You will be able to rest and eat and drink your fill—'

'Hold, Melliflor.' The voice was stern and a little threatening.

The guards moved to one side as another group marched up, their silver armour bearing designs based on an avian motif. Their leader's face gave nothing away, but it had none of the unpleasant qualities of his opposite number.

'Greetings, Gaelen. I was about to lead these two weary travellers to partake of the hospitality for which the Golden Ones are famed.'

Gaelen barely looked at Melliflor. 'I think the Brother and Sister of Dragons would rather be spared the hospitality of your Queen.'

Melliflor bristled. 'Step carefully, Gaelen. My Queen would not—'

'I have orders to take these two directly to the Lady Niamh. That is the desire of the First Family.'

Melliflor appeared to consider challenging this, but eventually backed down. He gave another dislikeable smile to Church and Ruth and bowed once more. 'Another time, then. I hope you do not regret missing the comforts on offer, nor the information my Queen could have imparted.' He turned on his heel and marched away, with his guards trooping behind.

Gaelen nodded curtly before leading Church and Ruth slowly to the camp. They dismounted on the outskirts where one of the guards led their horses away for food and watering.

Within the camp their perceptions became increasingly distorted. They felt like they were drifting through a dream where everything was fluid, strong enough for them to wonder if they would remember any of it once they left. Their senses were stifled beneath the constant assault of sounds, smells and sights. As they passed, eyes turned towards them, some filled with contempt, others accompanied by a smile of greeting. They saw no one they recognised. Many of the gods were of the lower caste, but on two occasions they caught sight of burning golden lights unable to stay in one shape.

Gaelen halted at a large purple tent made of a heavy material that resembled velvet. Over it fluttered a flag showing two dragons, red and white, either in embrace or fighting. The god pulled aside the flap and bid them enter.

The inside was cosy with sumptuous cushions scattered on a richly patterned carpet. Lanterns hung from poles at intervals around the perimeter, but the flames were turned down so the light was soft and hazy. Baccharus slumped in a low chair, his legs stretched out before him, drinking from a wooden flagon studded with four rubies. He lifted it in greeting, but didn't rise.

Niamh stood next to a trestle table in the centre of the tent, poring over a large map that had previously been rolled around large brass spindles. She hurried over to Church, smiling broadly. She made to embrace him, but when she saw Ruth, her face lost its sheen and she turned away sadly.

'You completed your mission, then, Brother?' Baccharus said.

'I did,' Church replied. 'The land is alive again. That should at least give us something for the fight.'

Baccharus sipped from his flagon. 'We can feel it. It is a powerful defence. Even my kind fear the force of the Blue Fire.'

Church and Ruth flopped wearily on the cushions while Niamh sent out for food and drink, 'all given freely and without obligation', a statement that told Church this was a Court of the Tuatha Dé Danann in all but location.

'You've already agreed a plan?' Church asked as he ate his fill of fruit and bread.

'The Golden Ones you know as Lugh and Nuada have overseen the battle planning,' Niamh said. 'The Night Walkers are well-established in their den and it will not be easy to unseat them. The dark ones are a foul infestation. They swarm everywhere. But a direct assault on several fronts should weaken them. We come from the North and the West. The Master will lead Wave Sweeper along the river to split their force in two.'

'What about us?'

Perhaps it was a trick of the flickering lanterns, but she suddenly looked deeply sad. 'Though some of my kind refuse to admit it, you are the key to defeating the Heart of Shadows. You must find a way into its lair and use the Quadrillax to wipe it from existence.' She turned away, pretending to unfurl another map.

Ruth's hand fumbled for Church's and gave it a squeeze. 'We'll do our part,' she said.

Baccharus and Niamh left them alone to eat and doze in the warm atmosphere, but they were too tense to get much rest. Four hours later, the tent flaps were roughly thrown aside. Church automatically jumped to his feet, his hand on the Sword hilt, but he was almost bowled over by a large figure that crossed the tent in seconds and threw its arms around him tightly.

'Ey, you bastard!' Veitch lifted Church off the ground and hugged him until he felt his ribs were about to crack. 'I thought you'd have done a runner by now.'

'You can't get rid of me that easy.' He clapped Veitch on the shoulder, more pleased to see him than he would have believed.

Shavi slipped in behind, smiling quietly, and then Tom, looking tired and irritable. Veitch turned and waved the stump of his wrist at Shavi and Ruth. 'Beat you both, as bleedin' usual.'

Ruth stared in horror for a while, then followed his gaze down to where the finger was missing on her hand, and over to Shavi who sported the same gap. They all burst out laughing together.

But then Veitch could control himself no longer. He marched over to pull Ruth to him tightly, burying his face in her hair to hide the emotion that rushed through him. After a few seconds, he pulled back to kiss her gently on the head. Ruth went rigid in the face of his show of feeling, knowing it wasn't the time to tell him about Church, unsure what to do, but Veitch didn't appear to notice her reticence. She flashed a glance at Church, who gave one quick shake of his head.

Veitch smiled with a mixture of affection and embarrassment. 'Sorry about that.' His eyes were fixed on hers, wide and childlike; there was a flush to his cheeks. 'I've missed you.'

Ruth smiled back awkwardly, but said nothing. The moment was deflated by Shavi who hugged Church and Ruth in turn, his emotions also close to the surface. 'It feels good to be together again,' he said quietly. 'Now all we need is Laura.'

There was a moment of uncomfortable silence before Church said, 'She's dead.'

'No, she's not,' Veitch said, puzzled. 'Shavi was the only one who was dead.'

They looked from one to the other blankly.

It was hard for any of them to believe they were back together again. Each of them felt, at times, overwhelmed; and then they would simply sit and listen to the others talking, enjoying the motion of faces, the animation of limbs, the energy crackling amongst them. Elation overwhelmed them all, completely wiping out any thought of what the morning might bring. There was drinking and raucousness, jokes that made light of their hardships, and the warm glow of old friends brought together again.

Veitch held up a flagon marked with a design of a Fabulous Beast. 'You seen this?'

'Isn't that the one with the pellet with the poison?' Church laughed, but Veitch completely missed the reference.

'No, no,' Shavi said, grinning, 'that is in the chalice with the palace. That one is the brew that is true.'

'You lot haven't bleedin' changed,' Veitch muttered.

Veitch was mesmerised by every movement Ruth made, as if he could barely believe she was there before him. Part of Ruth felt uncomfortable at the depth of emotion she sensed, yet she was excited by it too. That conflict made her uneasy. She knew she loved Church, so why was she responding to the attentions of someone else, in particular a man with whom she had so little in common?

When the conversation became a heated debate about Laura she was thankful for the opportunity to distract herself from her thoughts. Neither she nor Church could believe Laura was still alive; Tom and Veitch were adamant she was. It was left to Shavi to argue that they now lived in a world where anything could happen.

The conversation moved on. Ruth tried to stay out of the limelight, but Veitch brought her in at every opportunity, rapt at the tales she told.

'You hung on the outside of a ship in a storm? You're a crazy girl!'

'At least I didn't manage to lose a hand,' she said wryly.

'Maybe we should get ourselves a little Amputation Club going.' Veitch chortled; he was drinking too much, too fast. Beneath his upbeat exterior, they all could see the strain the loss of his hand had brought in him.

'That'd exclude me,' Church said, 'so in defence I'm proposing the Born Again Club.'

Veitch furrowed his brow. 'What's that, then?'

'Well, I died and came back.' He nodded to Shavi. 'So did you. And Ruth did, fleetingly, just before Laura took the seed of Balor from her.'

Veitch snorted. 'You're not counting me out, you tosser.'

'Do not worry, Ryan,' Shavi joked, 'there is plenty of time for you to meet your maker and come back down to earth.'

'Right. And I'll do it in style. With a choir of bleedin' angels!'

Tom muttered something indecipherable, but patently irritable. Veitch swore at him playfully, laughed when Tom bit, then broke open another amphora of wine.

'You know, I miss technology less than I thought,' Ruth said, lounging back on one of the enormous cushions. 'But one thing I could do with now is a CD player, or a tape deck . . . anything that gives music.' She eyed Church with *faux* contempt. 'As long as I don't have to listen to any Sinatra.'

He laughed. 'Shame. I could come up with a good soundtrack for all this.' He thought for a moment. 'How about "That Old Black Magic" from *Come Swing With Me!* followed by "It's Nice To Go Trav'ling—"'

Ruth covered her face.

'No, no, something soulful. Spiritual,' Shavi said. 'Curtis Mayfield. Perhaps Van Morrison—'

'Geezer music,' Veitch said. 'I never thought I'd say this, but I wish Laura was here. She might have been a pain in the arse most of the time, but musically she kept you musos in your pen.'

Shavi looked towards the tent flap. 'I still expect her to walk in at any moment.'

An outcry outside brought them all to their feet. They rushed out into the cold night to see the Tuatha Dé Danann in a state of excitement around one of the campfires.

Church grabbed one of the gods by the shoulder. 'What's going on?'

The god was shocked that he had been accosted by a *Fragile Creature*, but he appeared aware of Church's reputation. 'The Norta has been seen! And her sisters too!'

'What's that?'

The god struggled for the right words in his excitement. 'The one your people called the Morrigan.'

A hand fell on Church's shoulder and he turned to face Baccharus, equally animated. 'A great portent, my friend. The Morrigan is one of our own, but she prefers her own company, or that of her sisters, Macha, Badb and Nemain. They have not been seen by the Golden Ones since the first days after the pact. But they are drawn to war . . . and . . . and bloodshed . . . and . . .' – he attempted to speak in a manner Church could understand, but he struggled with a word that was still alien to him – 'death. The Dark Sisters are fearsome, both in what they represent and in their prowess. The Morrigan and her clan helped us win both battles of Magh Tuireadh. Undoubtedly, her appearance is a good omen.'

'Where is she?' Church scanned the campsite, eager to see a figure of such reputation.

'The Dark Sisters will not come into the light.' Baccharus raised his head to the gleaming moon. 'Macha, Badb and Nemain were seen circling the camp earlier. They wore the armour of war.'

'And the Morrigan?'

'There is a stream nearby. In it she was seen washing the heads of those who are to die in the forthcoming battle. The Morrigan keeps count of those who move from existence.'

Church flashed back to a cold February night before he had any inkling of the terrible change that had come over the world. It was the Morrigan he had seen washing his own head in the Thames. His throat closed up when he thought how she had turned and looked at him, with a face that appeared like death itself. But another worry crept up on him: was that portent referring to his previous *death* on Skye or was she revealing what lay in store for him in the Battle of London?

'Tell me,' he said, 'did your people see the heads?'

Baccharus knew exactly what he was asking. 'I cannot lie. There were Fragile Creatures.'

Church's blood ran cold. 'Who was it?'

'No!' Tom strode over, his face cold and hard. 'Do not tell him! It would not help for anyone to know they are going to die. Hope is the engine of success.'

Church studied his face carefully. Tom didn't meet his eyes. 'You know who's going to die, don't you? You've always known.'

Tom fixed an eye on Church that made his stomach turn. 'Yes. Pity me for it.' He turned and marched away without another word.

Church felt sick. He looked round at the others, who were talking to another of the Tuatha Dé Danann; none of them had heard the exchange. In that instant he understood exactly what Tom was going through. He couldn't tell them one of them was destined to die; it was a burden he would have to carry himself.

The sadness came up quicker and harder than he anticipated as he watched the people who had become his best friends over the last few months. He couldn't imagine being without any of them, even though that had been a constant from the moment they had banded together. Unbidden, his thoughts turned to which of them he would miss the least, and that made him feel even worse.

Dismally, he turned back to Baccharus, who deftly changed the conversation. 'True Thomas is a good man. Do not blame him for being the bearer of bad news.'

'We never got on at the start. I thought he was manipulating us. That he was cold and patronising and arrogant. I wish I'd been better to him.'

'True Thomas has accepted his responsibility. He does not expect anything from you.'

'That makes it even worse.'

A whistling like an incoming missile passed overhead. Church looked up to see the terrifying form of a woman pass by, her hair as wild as winter, her black clothes streaming off her in rags, her mouth torn wide as she made the anguished noise. He shivered as her shadow passed over him.

'Badb, Queen of Crows,' Baccharus said.

'I'm glad she's on our side.'

He watched the other figures moving across the sky for a while, but the night was too cold to stay for long. Returning to the warmth of the tent, he found the others already in deep conversation, though Tom was nowhere to be seen. Their faces showed the mood had darkened.

'We were talking about the traitor,' Ruth said as he entered.

'I don't want suspicion causing any rifts at this critical stage.'

'Yeah, but we've got to be on our guard.' Veitch was repeatedly unwrapping, then rewrapping the cloth around the stump of his wrist. Church knew his mind was working through numerous strategies, dismissing some, rethinking others. He was still drunk, but he was now brooding, and it was easier to see the anger that always lay just beneath the surface. 'We've come through all this shit together, trusted each other. If I found out one of us had been playing the others just to sell them out, I'd kill them.'

'Ryan!' Ruth said.

'I find it hard to believe one of us could be a traitor.' Shavi looked around them, as honest and open as always. 'We come from different backgrounds. We are all different people, with nothing, superficially, in common. Yet we have seen into each other's souls. We are good people, all of us, at heart. I trust my instinct implicitly. I cannot see anything in any of us that suggests betrayal.'

'Exactly.' Church sat down close to Ruth, then became aware of Veitch watching him curiously. He shuffled away an inch or two. 'I can't pretend it hasn't bothered me, but we all know how much the dead love to twist things. Who knows what they really meant?'

Veitch took a knife and diced an apple into four quarters. 'I'm still going to be watching my back.'

The conversation drifted to lighter subjects, but they never caught the uplifting mood of celebration again. Just after one a.m., when the sounds of revelry from the camp had died down, the growing quiet was disturbed by the distant blast of a horn. It was barely audible, but it brought a chill to them all. A second or two later it sounded again, much closer to hand, followed by the fearsome baying of hounds.

'The Wild Hunt,' Shavi said.

Ruth fingered the mark that had been imprinted on her hand. 'Cernunnos is joining us. That's good news.'

'Right. He's obviously on the side of us *Fragile Creatures*.' Even so, Church couldn't shake the fear he felt at the god's Erl-King aspect. He would never forget how the Hunt had torn through the revellers leaving the pub on Dartmoor: so brutal, yet cold, like a force of nature.

They fell silent with their thoughts until they heard the sound of two pairs of footsteps approaching the tent. They waited for the flaps to be thrown back, but the visitors slipped in quietly. The tall one at the rear was the Bone Inspector, his greying hair matted with grease and filth hanging loosely around his shoulders. His cheesecloth shirt was covered with green stains.

The shorter one at the front wore a cloak with a hood pulled over her head, but Church immediately knew who it was. His stomach flipped; a shiver ran up his spine. 'Laura.' The word was barely more than an exhalation.

She threw back her hood with her typical flair for the dramatic. They were shocked to see Veitch was right about the tinge to her skin, but that the scars Callow had inflicted on her face were mysteriously missing shocked them more. 'Church-dude. You look like you've seen a ghost. Instead of just the walking dead.' She looked round at the others, who were rapt. 'Well, that's the kind of wild reception I always expected from this little group.'

Church jumped up, looking deeply into her eyes for a long moment, before putting his arms around her. She smelled of spring leaves and summer flowers. He didn't know what to say, so he led her to a space and sat her down.

Ruth leaned across the circle. 'I want to thank you—'

'Don't. We've all made sacrifices. That's what we do.' She nodded to the Bone Inspector. 'He's the one you should thank. If not for him I wouldn't be here for all that mystical five symbolism baloney you need to do the big job.'

'Somebody had to do it,' the Bone Inspector said grumpily. He shifted around, uncomfortable with the attention. 'Where's the Rhymer? I need to sort something out with him.'

When they said they didn't know, he left in a bad temper to scour the camp. Their attention turned back to all the confusing emotions Laura's reappearance had raised.

'We were just saying we could not believe you were truly dead,' Shavi said with a smile, reaching out to take her hand. She smiled back, sweetly, without a trace of the bitterness that had always characterised her.

'Don't get me wrong, hon. I *did* die. And now I'm back, the same, only different.'

Another one, Church thought. *What does it all mean?*

'But how did you survive?' Ruth was pale and troubled. 'I had Balor in me. I know what it felt like, what would have happened when it came out.'

Laura lifted up her over-sized T-shirt to reveal a rapidly fading jagged white scar, running from her belly to her sternum. 'Something like this?'

Ruth couldn't help gasping. 'That would have killed you!'

'It would have if I wasn't already dead. This is the key.' She showed the back of her right hand where she sported the mark of Cernunnos, the circle of interlocking leaves. 'You know how screwed up I got about all the changes taking place in my body . . . the green blood that had a life of its own? It was such a shock at the time.' She traced her finger around the mark. 'I had no idea what he'd done to me . . . could never have guessed.' She looked around them. 'I died that day up at Loch Maree when he marked me with this.'

Church shook his head in disbelief, but she silenced him with a wave of her hand.

'I died, and then he remade me in his own image. For the rest of you time was frozen. But for me . . . well, I don't know how he did it.' She shook her head, barely able to summon up the words. 'I'm not human, I'm a plant.'

There was a hanging moment when they all tried to work out if she was joking. She laughed to herself, silently, at their expressions. 'Okay, maybe that's not the right word. Physically, he turned me into something that has the characteristics of flora rather than fauna. I don't need to eat or drink or breathe, not in the same way you do. I can survive under water. I can survive where there's no air at all. And when I get hurt, I repair myself like a plant. That's what happened with Balor. I'll tell you now, I don't remember much about it, apart from the fact that it was agony. That's one thing he didn't sort out. It tore me apart. It wasn't pretty. But I put myself back together. And—' she held her arms wide '— I did it better than before.' She pointed to her face. 'No scars. Not on my back, either. So I've got a slight skin problem, but that's a small price to pay. At least I don't pollinate or any of that shit.'

Her flippant manner made it difficult for them to assimilate what she was saying. Church's brow furrowed. 'So all the time we were together—'

'That's right, Church-dude – you were having sex with a plant.'

'A nature spirit.' Shavi leaned forward excitedly. 'He distilled the essence of what you already were, and made you an avatar.'

'Well, he might have asked.' Her smile was relaxed.

'Are you okay with it?' Ruth asked, concerned.

'It's better than being a nobody. And it's better than being really, truly dead. I think the same, I feel the same. I'm still the same gorgeous, wonderful, witty and charming Laura DuSantiago. Apart from the fact you have to water me twice a day.'

Church leaned forward and touched her forearm. The skin felt exactly the same as it always had done. She took his hand with honest affection. 'I'm okay. Really.'

'You seem different,' Ruth said. 'I mean, as well as all that—'

'I have my flaws, but stupidity isn't one of them. When somebody shoves a big, fat, old lesson in my face, I make sure I learn from it.' She looked down at her fingers as she knotted and unknotted them. 'I've found peace, I guess, if that doesn't sound like some stupid, navel-gazing New Ager. It was always there, I just couldn't see it. I don't hate myself any more.'

Her words were simple, but Church felt a swell of affection; he knew how deep her pain really went. If Laura had found some kind of redemption, there was hope for all of them; for everyone. The others recognised this too. As she looked round, for the first time she felt accepted.

'Then we really are all back together,' Shavi said. 'As it was intended.'

'Yes, yes, yes, the stars are aligned, and God is looking down on you from his heaven.' Tom was standing in the entrance with the Bone Inspector. 'Now I suggest you get some rest. For tomorrow, as the saying goes, you may die.'

Veitch slipped into a drunken sleep quickly; Shavi had a remarkable ability to nap instantly, wherever he was. Tom and the Bone Inspector sat at the table, talking quietly, their faces stern. Ruth tried to stay awake as Laura and Church chatted, but even her faint jealousy couldn't stop her eyelids from drooping.

Laura watched the regular movement of Ruth's chest for a moment or two before turning back to Church. 'So I'll ask you again: have you and little Miss Frosty done the monkey dance yet?'

'Laura—'

'You still don't know me, do you?' There was a trace of sadness in her smile. 'In most cultures that's known as humour.'

'Are you really okay?'

'Yes, I am. For the first time in my life. So don't go giving me any pity or I might be stirred to be my old catty self.' She put her fingertips on his sternum and pushed him down.

'I'm sorry I wasn't better to you. And that's not pity. What you did to save Ruth . . . that showed a side of you I never knew, and I feel bad for that. I jumped to conclusions, just like everybody else.'

She rolled on to her back, her hands behind her head. 'It's all in the past now. We learn, we move on, and all that shit.' She looked at him from the corners of her eyes. 'I'm still sorry it didn't work out between you and me, but I've finally got a good injection of reality. It wasn't the right time, maybe we weren't the right people, but I was so desperate I was trying to force it.' She nodded to Ruth. 'You and her, you're the real deal. She's a good person, for all her many, many problems. And you, well, you're Saint Church, aren't you? Mr Walks On Water.'

He watched Ruth's chest rising and falling and wished he was lying next to her. 'Is it that obvious?'

'It was obvious to everybody right from the start. You were the only one who couldn't see it. Because, let's face it, when it comes to emotion, you're damaged goods.'

'And you're okay about it? It's important to me. Really.'

There was a brief pause in which he dreaded her answer, but then she said, 'I'm okay with it. All I really wanted was somebody to stand by me shoulder-to-shoulder. I've never had that. But I was, like, where's the dog and the white stick? It was all around me. It's stupid. The world's falling apart and right here I've got the best friends I could ever wish for. You, the Shav-ster, even Miss Icy Knickers. We'd have got on okay if I hadn't been the Bitch From Hell from the get-go. Veitch, well, he's about as fucked-up as it gets, but if it came to the crunch I know he'd come through. I just hope I haven't learnt my big old life lesson too late.'

He fumbled for her hand and gave it a squeeze. 'It's a lesson we've all had to learn. When you're looking for meaning in life, don't look at the big picture, look at this. Look at your friends and your life and your loves – you need no meaning other than people.'

She yawned theatrically. 'You're getting up your arse again, aren't you? Just enjoy it, for Christ's sake. And don't screw up your love life this time. If she doesn't kill you, I will.' She watched him for a minute, her eyes shining, and then she smiled, still a little sadly, and rolled over to sleep.

As Church shuffled down to rest his head on the cushion, his gaze fell on Veitch's still form and for a fleeting moment he thought the Londoner was still awake. The notion disturbed him, but as he slipped into sleep he couldn't quite work out why.

The cry ripped through the camp, snapping them all awake in an instant. It was the sound of a woman shrieking, filled with such desolation and horror it left them frozen in shock. The cry rose, becoming more hysterical, louder, until they thought their ears would burst, and then, just as suddenly, it snapped off. The ringing echoes of it persisted for several more seconds.

'What the bleedin' hell was that?' Veitch's face was drained of blood.

Tom pushed himself back from the table where he had been resting his head. 'La Belle Dame Sans Merci.'

'The Banshee, to you and me,' the Bone Inspector said, bleary-eyed.

'Bummer.' Laura crashed back on to her cushions. 'Bad omen-a-go-go.'

Church looked to Tom. 'Is it as bad as the legends say?'

'You don't need the Banshee to tell you it's not going to be a walk in the park tomorrow.' The Bone Inspector slumped back on to the table.

'Some stories say anyone who hears it will die,' Ruth said. Church wished he could comfort her, but Veitch appeared to be watching them both closely.

'You're all going to die,' Tom said. 'Sooner or later.' He lay back down on the table.

'Thanks for the morale boost, old git,' Laura said sleepily.

'It doesn't mean death for anyone who hears it,' Tom said wearily. 'But it does mean death. And destruction and suffering and devastation on an epic scale.'

'Situation normal, then.' As Veitch lay down, Church steeled himself and surreptitiously moved next to Ruth.

The others assimilated the information and after a few minutes somehow managed to go back to sleep, but Ruth was aware Church was still lying awake.

'What are you thinking?' she whispered.

His words were given greater weight by the long pause before he replied. 'I'm thinking, where are they keeping the Wish-Hex? And when are they planning on using it?'

They were woken at first light by the sound of stirring across the camp. The smell of cooking drifted into the tent, teasing pangs of hunger from their sluggish forms. With an effort, they dragged themselves out into a cold, clear morning, their breath pluming; they were forced to bang their arms against their sides in a futile bid to keep warm. It was a beautiful dawn: a full-hearted swell of gold and purple before the sky slowly turned a pale blue; a day for hope and love and great things, not a day for war.

The lesser gods had gathered in the various large clearings amongst the tents, eating at long wooden tables. Church still wasn't sure that they really *needed* to eat, but they relished experience with a hunger that belied their status, as if searching for something valuable they had long since left behind. They certainly ate with gusto, shovelling down platefuls of food, swilling it down with flagonfuls of a hot, fragrant liquid.

All of the gods appeared to be in high spirits. They called Church and the others over with hearty shouts and made a space for them at the end of one table with much back-slapping and camaraderie. It was so out of place that all of them felt uncomfortable. Platefuls of dried fruit and spiced meat and several loaves of bread were brought to all but Laura and Shavi, who were given an odd but tasty bouillabaise of tomatoes, mushrooms and peppers without having to ask. Laura admitted that although she didn't *have* to eat, she too, like the gods, still enjoyed the sensation.

As they ate, their spirits rose, all except Veitch who remained sullen and uncommunicative. 'They look like they're eager to get off to war,' Ruth noted.

'For all their many claims to a wonderful life, they lack much colour in their existence,' Tom said, dipping a sausage into an egg. 'Quite simply, they are bored.'

'Despicable bastards, the lot of 'em,' the Bone Inspector muttered as he gnawed on a chunk of bread. 'Like a bunch of upper class idiots whipping themselves up before a rugby game, without a single thought for all the suffering that's going to happen. With any luck a few of 'em will meet their maker.'

'That is a little harsh,' Shavi said.

'Might teach 'em to appreciate life a bit more.'

'I still don't get why you're helping us.' Church sipped on the hot, invigorating liquid.

'That's because you're a moron.' The Bone Inspector threw the remainder of his bread to a group of ravens that had ventured fearlessly into the camp.

'I can see why you and the old git get on so well,' Laura said under her breath. 'Both graduates of the Finishing School for Irritating, Miserable Bastards.'

Shavi pushed out his chair and stretched his legs. 'I would guess the Bone Inspector is simply following his office as a guardian of the land's old places. If the End of Everything happens on the morning after Samhain, there will not be many old places to guard.'

'Well, aren't you the smarty-pants.' The Bone Inspector was watching the ravens intently. 'Ready for carrion,' he mused.

'*Carry On To The End of the World*, maybe,' Laura said. 'With Kenneth Williams as the dark god Balor and Charles Hawtrey as the Guardian of the Old Places.'

The Bone Inspector eyed her so darkly Laura realised she couldn't chide him in the same way that she toyed with Tom.

Shavi was laughing. 'Oh, yes. And you would be Barbara Windsor,' he said to Laura. 'And Church would be Sid James—'

'Bwah hah hah,' Church said flatly. 'So what's going to happen after we've stuffed our faces?'

'In half an hour there will be a meeting to outline the strategy,' Tom said. 'As the spearhead of the attack, we must be there.'

'The generals sending the disposables in first?' Veitch said sourly.

'Something like that,' Tom replied. 'They have their agenda and we have ours. As long as we are not swayed, who cares what their motivations are?'

'But they have the Wish-Hex.' Church made the comment quietly so none of the gods could hear.

'Yes,' Tom said, 'which is why we shall have our own meeting first.'

After the meal they wandered off separately, agreeing to meet fifteen minutes later. Ruth had not gone far when her arm was grabbed sharply enough to cause her pain. She whirled angrily. It was Veitch. She could tell instantly from his threatening expression what was on his mind.

'You couldn't wait to get off with him, could you?' There was pain in his voice beneath the anger.

'I'm sorry you're upset, Ryan, but—'

'Upset? I'm upset when my team loses on a Saturday. This is like a kick in the bollocks, and another one in the face for good luck.'

She bowed her head, sorry to see him so hurt. 'I didn't want you—'

'No, you didn't want me. I put my life on the line in Scotland – for you. Not for all this end of the world bollocks. I couldn't care less if the whole miserable place went belly-up tomorrow. But, you . . .' He shook his head, his long hair falling across his face. 'I nearly died for you. I took risks to get down here – for you.'

She was shocked to see the rage lighting in his face; there was a seething glow in his hooded eyes. 'You've got so much anger in you! Were you always like this?'

Her words appeared to strike him hard. He rubbed at his temples furiously. 'Stop talking about that!'

'I tried to be honest to you about how I felt, Ryan. I think you're a good man. I admire you. But there was never going to be anything between us.'

'Never?' She flinched as he bunched his fist but instead he smashed it into his side. There were tears of hurt in his eyes.

She went to comfort him, but he backed away. 'Ryan, don't hate Church and don't hate me. We love each other. And we both care about you, really.'

'You're only saying that to keep me on the team. Afraid I'll go running off to join the other side?'

'Don't be stupid! None of us would ever think that. You said you always wanted to be a hero. Well, you are, Ryan. You are. And everyone here respects you.'

He looked away towards the horizon, blinking off the tears. 'Yeah . . .'

'That must mean something?'

He nodded. 'But not enough. I always thought it was the most important thing. I've never had that . . . never had any respect.' He jerked a thumb over his shoulder. 'One of them was talking about how they'd all learned something important from all this shit. Well, I have too. I've learnt you're the most important thing to me, and if I can't have you I might as well be dead. So I can go into this with no fear 'cause I've got nothing to lose. They'll remember me as the biggest bleedin' hero of all by the end of it.' The anger disappeared briefly and all she could see was the face of a hurt child, but then he turned sharply on his heel and marched away.

She called after him, but he didn't look back.

They met in their tent while the Tuatha Dé Danann were away making their preparations for battle, although Baccharus and Niamh were there, much to Veitch's suspicion. The first thing they did was distribute the Quadrillax. Church kept the Sword and took the Way-finder lantern, while Ruth reaffirmed her hold on the Spear. Veitch agreed to carry the Stone of Fal and Shavi took the Cauldron in a pack on his back. Laura was happy to have nothing to do with any of them.

'If the Wish-Hex is here, its location has been kept from us,' Niamh said when they had gathered around the table. 'Those of us who believe in the destiny of mankind would never allow such a thing to be used, and certainly never in this form, adulterated by the Night Walkers.'

'It would be good,' Tom said, 'if all your brethren felt the same way. But many believe this is too good an opportunity to pass by: two irritants wiped out in one fell swoop.'

'And the prime position in the evolutionary pile secured for the

Tuatha Dé Danann,' Church noted. 'We need you to find out where the Wish-Hex is being kept, and when it will be used,' he said to Baccharus and Niamh. 'We'll have to find some way to neutralise it.'

'The aim would be to unleash the Wish-Hex in the core of the Night Walkers' lair, close to the Heart of Shadows,' Niamh said. 'The Night Walkers are more resilient than Fragile Creatures. They need to be closer to the release.'

'We just get wiped out in the plague fall-out,' Church said bitterly.

'We will uncover the intention and pass it on to you as soon as we can,' Niamh said. 'We understand what is at stake.'

Veitch appeared not to have been listening, and had spent the meeting carving his name into the wooden table with his knife. Then he said, 'I'm worried we're spreading ourselves too thin,' and Church realised the Londoner had instead been carefully weighing all the strategies. 'We'll be driving forward on more than one front, and this thing will be coming up behind. We're not going to be in a position to split our attention.'

'What are you saying?' Church asked.

'Sounds like a recipe for disaster to me.'

Church thought for a moment. 'It might help if one of us found a back way in.'

'What do you mean?' Veitch said.

'I've been thinking about this . . . about a lot of things. There's been important stuff that's been there right in our face before and we missed it.' He turned to Ruth. 'Like Maurice Gibbons.'

'The civil servant who was murdered under Albert Bridge the night we met. So?'

'We got so wrapped up in *what* he discovered, we never thought about *how*—'

'He saw one of the Fomorii changing—'

'But why was he under Albert Bridge on that particular night?'

She opened her mouth to answer him, but no words came. 'Okay, smarty-pants.'

'Why was that Night Walker there too?'

Her eyes narrowed. 'You've already worn out your dramatic build-up, Church.'

'The Fomorii were already building their base under London. And Gibbons had somehow found one of the entrances to it. He was investigating when that thing came out and killed him.'

Veitch was already ahead of them. 'So if we could get to it, we might be able to get straight into their base before they know it!'

'But the danger of us all going together is that it is easier to stop us with one well-timed strike,' Shavi noted. 'They would be able to target all their resources at us.'

'Good point,' Veitch mused. 'All right, we split up. But we do our damnedest to get to where we're going, even if it means leaving all those golden-skinned twats behind.' He nodded to Niamh and Baccharus curtly. 'No offence.'

'And we all know where we're going,' Laura said. 'That big tower they're throwing up near the City. I saw it up close. That has to be the place.'

'At the ritual in Scotland, when we summoned the dead for guidance, they told us we needed to find the Luck of the Land before we could beat Balor,' Shavi noted. 'Do we have any more of an idea what that means?'

Tom shifted uncomfortably. 'That is not a matter to concern us now.'

'Why not?' Veitch asked suspiciously.

'Heed me.' Tom's voice was unduly stern. 'When we are closer to the confrontation.'

Church noticed Ruth was deep in thought. 'What's on your mind?' he asked.

She looked at him with a curious expression. 'What you said about Maurice Gibbons. It made me think how much else we missed that was right in front of our eyes.'

The war council took place in a heavily guarded marquee of purple silk, deep in the heart of the camp. It was at the centre of an area where all the higher-born gods had congregated, and the sense of dislocation as Church and the others entered was palpable.

Many gods were already waiting in the tent, communicating quietly, and in some cases, silently. Church recognised Nuada Airgetlámh, his almond eyes like razor blades in his golden face, and Lugh, with his long mane of black hair and his torso bearing the scars of battle; both of them exuded power. But there were many Church didn't know. Their faces shimmered and changed as his gaze passed across them. He saw famous generals, renowned political leaders at times of crisis, a bully he recalled from school, the hardened casts of terrorists and revolutionaries, but eventually their images settled down into distinctive personalities, all of them grim. Church had the unshakeable feeling the important things had already been discussed and agreed.

'I offer the greetings of the Golden Ones to the Brothers and Sisters of Dragons, who have served us so well in the past,' Nuada said, seemingly unconscious of his patronising attitude. 'You know me as

Fragile Creatures have known me in the past: Nuada Airgetlámh, wielder of Caledfwlch, which in my wisdom I have gifted to you, Dragon-Brother. Your people have also known me as Nudd, of the Night, as Llud, and Lud, founder of this place on whose doorstep we stand – Londinium. This is my place where, in the Fixed Lands, I stand supreme. This is where Fragile Creatures bowed their heads to me, made offerings of the little things that had importance in their brief lives. Where blood ran, where my heart beats.'

Lugh's eyes were fixed on his Spear, which Ruth held tightly to her side. She felt uncomfortable at the attention, as if he were desperate to wrest it from her.

'You Brothers and Sisters of Dragons have proved your worth,' Nuada continued, 'and it has been deemed that you should wield the Quadrillax on our behalf. Only with those objects of power will the Heart of Shadows finally be wiped from all existence. But the path to it will be hard. Too hard for Fragile Creatures. And so the Golden Ones have agreed to drive a route through the shadows, to protect you from the attacks of the Night Walkers, until you are in a position to carry out the act required of you. Does this meet with your agreement?'

All eyes turned to Church. 'It does.'

'Then this is what is suggested. There will be three lines of attack into the city, until the Heart of Shadows' location is established. I will lead the drive from the north. My brother, whom you know as Lugh, will bring our forces from the west. And the Master will take Wave Sweeper along the river into the centre of the city.'

'And that will be the most important,' Church said, 'because it will take us directly to one of the entrances to the Fomorii lair.'

Nuada's gaze was incisive. 'You have access to secrets, Brother of Dragons.'

Church gave nothing away.

Tom stepped forward. 'May I speak?'

'Your exalted position is recognised, True Thomas.'

'Then I would suggest the Brothers and Sisters of Dragons divide into teams to ensure the best chance of success. Ruth and Ryan will join you in the attack from the north.'

Ruth went cold. Surreptitiously, she glanced over at Veitch, but his gaze was fixed firmly on Nuada.

'Shavi and Laura will come from the west with Lugh,' Tom continued. 'And I and the Bone Inspector will accompany Church through the secret tunnels. Though he is powerful, he is also young, and we have the experience to guide him through the darkest turns.'

Nuada nodded. 'Your views are acceptable, True Thomas.'

Laura smirked and whispered to Church behind her hand, 'Fun day out with the senior citizen club for you, boy. Hope you don't get in any fights or there'll be zimmer frames all over the place.'

'Use the Quadrillax wisely,' Nuada said. 'You have already drawn the Sword from the stone of disbelief. Now is the time to fire it with your heart. And the others – each must be used at the right time, in the correct manner, with the full weight of your essence behind you, and even then victory is not assured. Much death and suffering lies ahead. This is a period of pain that will be remembered when the stars go out. Go well, Brothers and Sisters of Dragons. Your world turns with you.'

They left the tent to prepare themselves for what lay ahead. The joy of their initial reunion had dissipated, to be replaced by an oppressive sense of foreboding. There were no jokes or smiles; they were lost to their own thoughts as they wrestled with their secret fears or searched for the depths of strength that would get them through the coming hours.

Veitch was the last to leave. Before he had gone ten paces from the tent, Nuada called him back.

'We have seen your sacrifice,' the god said, motioning to Veitch's bandaged wrist. 'I know only too well the pain of such a wound.' He removed a glove that covered an ornately crafted silver hand that looked like it had come from some futuristic robot. 'The scars go much deeper than the skin.'

Nuada's eyes felt like they were going right through him. 'I had to do it to bring my mate back. I'm not bitter about it.'

'Not bitter, no.' Nuada smiled knowingly. 'Still, I understand your heart, Brother of Dragons. Listen, then: if you are to be effective, you will need a new hand. Would you like that?'

'Can you do it?'

Nuada indicated the silver hand again. 'We are gods. We can do anything.'

The tent was the deepest red, so that within even the air had the hint of blood. It was enormous, bigger even than the marquee where the war council had met, with numerous annexes and branching passages so it was impossible to see all of it from one view. Nuada presented Veitch to Dian Cecht, who wore robes of scarlet. He carried himself with bearing, his features as aristocratic as his manner: a high forehead above a Roman nose, sharp, grey eyes and gunmetal hair tied in a ponytail.

'We have little time,' Nuada said, as Dian Cecht gently unfastened the material on Veitch's wrist stump.

'It is a simple operation on a Fragile Creature.' Dian Cecht examined the burnt flesh, then shrugged and turned away, motioning for Veitch to follow.

They came to a room set with several tables. Cruel-looking silver instruments were laid out on small trays next to each table. Dian Cecht nodded for Veitch to lie down, then busied himself at a large cabinet at one end. He returned with a wooden box inlaid with gold, which he placed on the tray next to Veitch. Inside, on a velvet inlay, was a silver hand the exact replica of the one Nuada wore. 'A spare,' Dian Cecht said with a smile.

Veitch felt a faint flutter of excitement; the thought of being whole once more was seductive. Dian Cecht gave him a foul-tasting potion to drink, which instantly made him sleepy. After a moment he was drifting in and out of hallucinatory waking dreams, filled with strange, disturbing images, including one of a black and a white spider fighting furiously over him. He was vaguely aware of Dian Cecht working on his wrist with a long knife with three rotating blades; the smell of blood filled his nostrils with surprising potency. A glimmer of silver in the corner of his eye told him the hand was about to be fitted. He watched with the curious detachment of a drug trip as Dian Cecht placed it against his stump, now soaked with blood.

At the instant the blood touched the pristine silver, three arms snapped out of the hand and poised erect; on each one was a row of sharp silver spikes. Veitch only had a second to consider what was going to happen next before the arms suddenly sprung down, driving the spikes deep into the bone and muscle of his wrist. Even through the sedation, he screamed in agony, but there was more pain to follow: something within the hand was burrowing into his arm, wrapping its way around ligaments and tissue, bonding with nerves and veins.

Veitch's throat grew raw from screaming and a moment later he blacked out.

Church and Ruth stood behind their tent, embracing each other silently. The weight of what they wanted to say was too great, crushing them silent. Ruth blinked off tears as she pulled away. She forced a smile.

'We'll be meeting again soon,' Church said gently. 'In the hideous lair of the one-eyed god of death. How about that for a one-off?'

'Oh, very romantic. Every girl's dream.'

'At least you'll never forget it.'

Neither could bring themselves to discuss the possibility that they might not see each other again; the occasion called for sweeping optimism and hope and faith.

They pulled away, ready to meet the others, but Ruth turned and caught Church's arm. 'Be careful,' she said with a quiet intensity that moved him.

Tom poked his head round the corner of the tent. 'For God's sake, get a move on! They're not going to hold up the end of the world for you.'

The others were waiting quietly. Veitch looked pale and drained, but his new hand was a source of wonder and he appeared proud of it. The others were not so sure. 'What did they demand in return for that?' Tom asked harshly. When Veitch told him nothing, he said, 'I'm very disappointed in you,' before walking away.

'Just be careful, Ryan,' Church said to him. 'They can't be trusted. And they're not known for their charity.'

' 'Course I'll be careful.' Veitch couldn't help examining the hand in the light. 'I'm whole again. That's what matters.' He was patently oblivious to the foreboding that filled the rest of them.

At that time, though, they couldn't hold it against him. They hugged in turn – even Veitch and Tom. They knew each other well enough not to need to say anything more.

Once they were all on their horses, Church couldn't part without adding something. 'This is what it's all been leading to, all that pain and hardship and suffering. We've been to hell and back and we've come through it. Of all the people who could have been here at this point, I'm glad it's you, all of you. You're the best there is, and I'm proud to be one of you.'

Veitch looked to the horizon, his cheeks flushed. 'Yeah, well, we're not going to let you down, boss. Death or glory, and all that.'

'Just glory,' Laura corrected.

In the moments before they departed, Church found himself turning over the wild parade of events that had led them to that place. At the start it had seemed so simple: a straight fight between good and evil for the sake of humanity. Instead, they had found themselves probing the very mysteries of existence, travelling through worlds where reality and illusion intermingled until it was impossible to tell what was real and what was not. There had been so much hardship, pain and death on every side, yet, ironically, it had been the best time of his life. He had become a better person because of it, although he knew he still had a way to go.

Now it was back to being a simple fight once more: humanity against all the alien powers that were attempting to deny its destiny. And all to be decided in two short days. He hoped they were up to the obligation that had been placed on their shoulders.

They rode over a slight rise to see a massive army spread out across the countryside in the wan October sunlight. As the call went out somewhere at the head, a charge of excitement ran through all of them. A grin jumped like wildfire from one to the other. After the weariness of all the build-up, the culmination came like a jolt of energy. Veitch gave a triumphant yell and then they spurred their horses to join the others, lost to the pump of the blood in their heads.

When they were finally in motion, it looked like a sea of gold was sweeping across the countryside towards the capital. Within it, Church and the others felt enveloped in a dreamy, yellow haze, where figures and horses faded into the background, to be replaced by an amorphous feeling of wonder.

The journey passed in a blur, faster than they could ever have galloped on normal horses. They only slowed when London hove into view, and in that instant all brightness drained from them. In the centre of the city, the monstrous black tower rose up, its summit lost in the clouds that swirled continually overhead. Greasy black smoke lapped up towards them from the fires that burned all around. There were things flying, and things moving on the ground, but Church didn't focus on any of them.

All he could think of was the prophecy of him watching a burning city that had haunted his nights since his visit to the watchtower between the worlds. It had felt like the ultimate in desolation, and as he sat there, watching the scene for real for the first time, he understood how true that feeling had been.

CHAPTER SEVENTEEN

[Don't Worry]
if there's a hell Below

Despite all they had seen, Laura and Shavi were still overwhelmed by the incongruous sight of an army of otherworldly beings trooping along the M4, where tourist buses and cars and articulated lorries had once trundled bumper-to-bumper. Occasionally they passed an abandoned vehicle, windows smeared in thick dust, that only added to the sense of dislocation.

There had been a brief flurry of activity as they came into London past the now-silent Heathrow Airport. A group of Fomorii had attacked, shrieking and howling, but it had been half-hearted and directionless, and the attackers had drifted off once their casualties had started to mount. The Tuatha Dé Danann were armed with a terrifying array of weapons constructed by Goibhniu and his brothers in their secret smithies, some of which could deal death at a great distance, but it did not appear that this show of strength was the cause of the retreat. Many of the Fomorii had disappeared into the houses that lined the motorway, while the flying Night Walkers had retreated into the bank of thick clouds.

'I expected greater defiance,' Baccharus said as the road wound past Osterley towards Brentford. 'They will not allow us to drive directly into the heart of their nest, where their most sacred thing resides.'

The atmosphere didn't help the growing apprehension. When the wind blew in the wrong direction, Shavi and Laura had to cover their mouths and noses with scarves to keep out the choking smoke filled with sickening chemical undertones. It was cold, too, the sun mostly obscured by the clouds; they were wearing several layers of borrowed clothes beneath their old jackets.

The fires blazing near to the motorway brought little warmth, but cast a hellish red glow across the empty houses, shops and business premises. Homes stood with doors torn off and windows smashed. In some the roof had caved in, while in the worst places entire streets had been demolished. Although many areas appeared relatively untouched, it was almost impossible to imagine the Fomorii occupation, and how terribly the residents must have suffered.

Shavi continually scanned the buildings on either side, until Laura said, 'Can't you do something? You're supposed to be the big magician.'

'Any abilities I might have are shamanic. I prefer a quiet space to meditate, something to put me into the right frame of mind.'

'You set all those animals on the Bone Inspector at Rosslyn Chapel. Can't you send an army of . . . I don't know, badgers, on ahead?'

'Badgers?'

'You know what I mean. Anything.'

He coughed into his scarf as a swirl of smoke engulfed them. 'We would need a Ryan or a Church to offer any true resistance to a direct assault by the Fomorii. Or even a Ruth, if what I hear of her advancing abilities is true. This is not the best situation for us.'

'Speak for yourself. I've learnt a few new tricks myself since I became the Chlorophyll Kid.'

'Oh?' He eyed her curiously. 'What can you do?'

'Mind your biz. And hope I don't have to show you.' She tied her scarf tighter so she resembled a Bedouin riding into a sandstorm.

The lack of resistance was unnerving even the Tuatha Dé Dannan now. They were moving more cautiously, watching the surrounding cityscape for any sign of movement, Goibhniu's bizarre weapons levelled for a quick strike.

Baccharus rode up next to them once more. 'The Night Walkers are an underhand race. We fear an attack from the side or rear, rather than an honourable face-to-face confrontation.'

'An ambush makes sense,' Laura mused. 'Veitch made a smart suggestion for the two land teams to use the motorways to get right into the city quickly, but it does make us sitting targets.'

'The Golden Ones,' Baccharus said self-deprecatingly, 'are too proud to hide.'

Ahead of them the Hammersmith Flyover rose up as the houses and shops fell away on either side. As they passed over it, Laura could see the edges of the roundabout under the bridge way below, and the rooftop of the Hammersmith Odeon. 'At least we're above the snipers now.'

'Not for long,' Shavi noted. 'The road drops down quickly towards Earls Court.'

'Thanks for wrecking my one tension-free moment of the day.' Movement away to her right caught her eye. 'Look at all those birds. What are they? You know, I haven't seen any pigeons yet. Do you think they've all moved out to the country?'

Shavi watched the flock swirling around one particular rooftop.

'Crows,' he said, and the moment the word had left his lips, he knew. Anxiously, he turned to the Tuatha Dé Danann. 'Beware—!'

His warning was cut off by a deafening explosion. The ground beneath their feet rolled like water, then dropped suddenly. Shavi was still watching the birds fly into a tight formation that made the shape of a man when he realised he was falling.

Laura was yelling and fighting with her horse, which was frantically attempting to gain purchase on the crumbling road surface. They were all engulfed in noise: the panicked whinnying of the horses, the yells of the gods, the crack and rumble of the shattering flyover, the booming bursts of more supports getting blown out, a roaring cacophony that threatened to burst their eardrums.

They were lucky all the supports didn't go at once. Instead of dropping in one block, the bridge concertinaed, twisting one way, then the other, so those who were on that section slid back and forth as they moved towards the ground. Shavi and Laura were best-placed. On the area where they had skidded it only fell sharply for the final ten feet, but that was enough to fling them both from their horses as they were showered in rubble.

Shavi blacked out briefly, and when he came to there was a large chunk of concrete crushing down on him. With an effort he managed to drag it off, but he could feel the blood soaking through his clothes; nothing appeared to be broken, though. He staggered to his feet, calling Laura's name. The air was so choked in dust and smoke, it was impossible to see more than a few feet, but what he could discern was bad enough. Many of the Tuatha Dé Danann had been torn apart or crushed by the falling sections of bridge. Horses lay dead or dying all around. A few of the gods staggered to their feet in one piece, and a similar number of the horses had survived.

The smoke and dust cleared enough to reveal the rest of the army in a chaotic mêlée on the remaining part of the flyover, desperately urging their mounts to move back along the motorway towards the slip road to ground level. It was exactly as Laura had foreseen: there were too many of them fighting for too little space. They were easy targets.

A sound like wind rushing through a derelict house filled the air. Mollecht was on the edge of the building, the crows that made up his body flying in ever-faster formation. The crows increased their speed until they were just a blur, and then a hole opened up in their centre. The sound of rushing wind became almost deafening. There was a flash as a fine, red spray erupted out of Mollecht's body, sweeping across the gulf to the Tuatha Dé Danann struggling to get off the bridge.

As it fell across them, the reaction was instantaneous. Black, mottling patches sprang up across any exposed skin. Foam burst from their mouths and their eyes rolled as they clawed at their throats. Those nearest to the shattered end of the bridge staggered backwards and plummeted to the ground, bursting open like sacks of jelly. Shavi had only an instant to reflect on what could have had such an effect on near-invulnerable gods before the thick smoke rolled in again to obscure the rising tide of panic on the flyover.

'Laura!' he yelled again, moving amongst the rubble.

'Here.' Her voice was muffled. He found her struggling out from a thick shelter of vegetable manner that had kept the worst of the masonry from crushing her. 'The wonders of green blood,' she said by way of explanation.

He offered his hand to drag her out.

'Well, that didn't take long to go pear-shaped,' she said bitterly.

'They were too arrogant. And we should have trusted our own judgment more.'

Some of the gods staggered in a daze out of the swirling smoke. A few attempted to rein in the horses cantering around wildly. Laura watched Shavi's face grow serene; a moment later all the horses had calmed.

Baccharus came stumbling over the broken tarmac and twisted girders. 'Move quickly,' he yelled. He caught three horses and herded them towards Shavi and Laura. The other Tuatha Dé Danann were already mounting their own steeds.

Shavi and Laura had barely taken the reins when a gust of wind cleared the smoke and dust to reveal a sight that rooted them to the spot. All around, silent and unmoving, were the Fomorii, their monstrous faces turned towards Shavi and Laura. It was an eerie scene, as if they were robots waiting to come alive. The pile of broken masonry on which they and the Tuatha Dé Danann stood was a tiny island in a sea of black.

Shavi and Laura jumped on to their horses, casting around for a way out. A breeze rippled across the immobile sable statues. They began to move.

The shrieks and howls that rang out were deafening, the sight of the Fomorii sweeping forward in a tidal wave enough to drive all conscious thoughts from their minds.

Baccharus threw Shavi a strange sword with twin blades and a jewel embedded in the handle. 'Press the jewel,' the god yelled.

Shavi looked at the weapon in incomprehension.

'Press the jewel!'

The Fomorii were surging forward. One of the Tuatha Dé Danann tried to fend them off with a sword, but sheer force of numbers dragged him from his horse, and both he and the mount were swallowed up by the sickening tide.

Laura lashed out at Shavi's arm, shocking him alert. 'Press the jewel, you moron!'

Shavi thumbed the gem. He felt a subtle sucking sensation deep in the heart of him as a blue spark began to crackle between the twin blades. The Fomorii appeared to recognise what was happening, and obviously feared it, for their forward motion halted and the shrieks died away with a ripple of apprehension. The Blue Fire burned a little higher up the blade.

Then, Shavi understood. He closed his eyes and focused his concentration on his heart, his spirit. The effect was remarkable. He jolted as an electric surge rushed through him, and when he opened his eyes, the Blue Fire was burning brighter than he had ever seen it. It tore up the remainder of the blades in an instant.

He thought he heard a whisper of terror rush through the Fomorii, and then the sapphire energy exploded from the sword like a summer lightning storm. The force almost knocked him from the horse; for a moment the whole world was blue. He heard Laura's exclamation of wonder, and when next he looked there was a massive blast zone around them where lay the charred remains of many Fomorii. Beyond it, the other Fomorii were backing away frantically.

Shavi felt so exhausted he could no longer sit upright. He slumped against the horse's neck as the sword slipped from his grasp. Laura caught it. 'I think we'll save this for later, don't you?' She slipped it into an empty scabbard fixed on Shavi's saddle.

Baccharus was at their side, his skin so pale there was barely a hint of gold in it. 'Come, we must not tarry here. The Night Walkers will not hold back for long. Although they fear like beasts of the field, their individual existence is meaningless. They will give themselves up happily for the will of the collective.'

A pitched battle was raging along what remained of the flyover and the stretch of the M4 they could still see. The Fomorii were clambering over the edges of the motorway, getting torn apart by the array of Tuatha Dé Danann weapons, then coming back for more. And on the rooftops Mollecht was unleashing more of his plague-blasts.

'We won't be getting any help from them,' Laura said. She looked round and pointed to a path that had been cut through the Fomorii.

They had no idea where they were going, knew there was little hope for such a small band riding ever deeper into enemy territory, but there was no chance of them going back. Even so, they refused to countenance failure, and thoughts of their deaths never entered their minds.

The only route open to them was along Hammersmith Road. They soon left behind the main mass of Fomorii, more concerned with defeating the Tuatha Dé Danann army than with hunting a few stragglers. Yet there were still random bursts of movement in the buildings on either side.

Baccharus was accompanied by nine other gods. They all looked stunned, as if they'd taken a detour into a world they never dreamed existed. Baccharus, however, had best overcome the blow and was now leading the group; they obeyed him blindly, glad that someone else was taking the responsibility.

The road led on to Kensington High Street. It was snarled with discarded cars, trucks and a burnt-out bus, forcing them to ride on the pavement. Names from another age reached out to them: Smith's, Boots, Barker's department store.

The smoke was thicker towards the eastern end of the high street. Kensington Palace was still burning, its roof collapsed, the walls blackened and broken. The huge security gates that had closed off the road leading to the palace had been torn down and lay mangled and barely recognisable in the street.

'I wonder what happened to the Royal Family,' Shavi mused as they passed.

'Those sort of people always have a bolt-hole. *The Great and the Good.*' The contempt in Laura's voice was heavy. 'The secret service probably spirited them off to a cushy estate in Scotland long before all this came to a head. And I bet they never told any of the *little people* that Armageddon was coming to their doorsteps.'

Ahead of them the green expanse of Kensington Gardens stretched out towards Hyde Park, silent and eerie in the drifting smoke. Baccharus reined in his horse uneasily and scanned the stark trees towards the Serpentine. 'Some of my people used to come here on summer evenings,' he said. 'They would steal children and take them back to the Far Lands. Some would stay, some would be returned.'

Shavi closed his eyes, letting himself read the atmosphere. 'It is a liminal zone,' he said. 'Green space in an open city. The boundary between here and T'ir n'a n'Og is fluid.'

'I tripped here once,' Laura said. 'It was summer. Everything was yellow and green. Me and a friend dropped a tab up near Temple Lodge, then went out on a boat on the lake. Just drifting along. It was . . . peaceful.' The memory jarred with the landscape that now lay before her. She shivered. 'I don't think we should go in there.'

Behind them the sound of pitched battle grew more intense. Someone was screaming, high-pitched and reedy, so despairing they all wanted to cover their ears. Another explosion sent a booming blast of pressure over them.

Shavi noticed shapes moving in the doorways across the street. Fomorii were emerging slowly. They looked wary, as if they knew of the sword even though they had had no contact with the other group.

Laura fought back another wave of nausea when she looked at them. 'God, this place is disgusting! It's *infested*.' She turned to Shavi. 'Are you up to using that super-cool sword again?'

He shook his head. 'It is powered by the spirit. It will take a while to bring my energy levels back up.'

Baccharus pointed along Kensington Road towards Knightsbridge. 'The Night Walkers are attempting to cut us off. Moving across the road ahead, coming up behind us.'

'Then we go across the park,' Shavi said. 'Perhaps lose them in the smoke. We cannot afford to move so slowly.'

They spurred their horses and headed into the disquieting open space of Kensington Gardens.

The smoke was even thicker there, blowing in from the palace, and from another large fire burning somewhere nearby. They kept their scarves tied tightly across their mouths, but it was still choking them; their eyes teared so much it was often hard to see the way ahead.

It was Shavi who first recognised they were no longer alone. His ears were attuned to the shifting moods of nature and he felt the pressure drop rapidly. It was followed by rapid footsteps padding in the grass all around, moving back and forth. Although the smoke was too dense to see what was there, he had the unmistakable feeling that it was hunting.

'Be on your guard,' he said quietly.

And then they all could hear the running feet, sometimes ahead, sometimes behind. They reminded Laura of a group of preschool children at play. There was no other sound; not the shrieks of Fomorii, no voices at all.

Baccharus motioned for the other Tuatha Dé Danann to bring their horses close together. They urged their steeds to step lightly, but every now and then the hooves would hit a stone with a clatter.

'What are they?' Laura whispered.

Shavi shook his head. The footsteps moved closer, as if their owners had begun to get their bearings. The Tuatha Dé Danann reined their horses to a stop and drew their swords.

The throat-rending, bloodthirsty cry behind them made Laura

almost leap from her saddle. The Tuatha Dé Danann whirled ready to lash out, but it was too late. One of them was torn from his horse and thrown to the ground, where a squat figure about five feet tall stooped over it, its muscular arms rending and tearing with a frantic clawing motion. The agonised screams of the god were sickening, but the sheer brutality of the attack froze them in place.

Laura was nauseated to see the figure was wearing a hat made out of human body parts – she thought she saw half a face there – and its tangled, black hair was matted with dried blood. It turned and bellowed triumphantly. Its bloodstained teeth were large and broken, its features monstrous, but its skin was green and scaled in part. Laura felt a wash of cold.

Another launched itself from the smoke towards one of the Tuatha Dé Danann. Its huge hands were grasping with long, jagged nails as it roared ferociously. The god reacted quickly, swinging his sword down to split the beast's head open. It fell to the ground, twitching and vomiting.

'What are they?' she gasped.

'You were ill in the van when they attacked before,' Shavi said. 'In the Lake District. They are called Redcaps. Tom said their natural enemy is man.'

'Mollecht's favourite brood,' Baccharus said, with something approaching contempt.

Others emerged from the smoke – Laura counted eight of them – and these were carrying short swords that were chipped and soiled. For the first time they saw Shavi and Laura, and the transformation that came over them was terrifying to see: savage before, they were now Berserker, ignoring the Tuatha Dé Danann to drive towards the two humans.

Baccharus barked an order in his natural alien language and the Tuatha Dé Danann formed a barrier between Shavi and Laura and the attacking Redcaps. Although the gods hacked and slashed in a constant blur of weaponry it did little to repel the ferocity of their attack. While they came at the gods, they were also continually circling to find a route through the defences to the two humans. Laura's heart beat even faster when she realised the Redcaps never took their eyes off her or Shavi for an instant; the look in those eyes was ravenous hunger.

The assaults continued relentlessly for fifteen minutes until it became obvious even the Tuatha Dé Danann would soon be worn down. One of the gods eventually made a slight error in his parrying that was punished instantly. A Redcap dragged the sword from his hand, oblivious to the deep gashes it was cutting in the creature's fingers, while the one closest to it dived in and ripped out the god's neck with its talons. He had been torn savagely limb from limb before he hit the ground.

An instant later the air was filled with the fluttering of golden moths. The rest of the Tuatha Dé Danann saw them and froze, their faces registering unspeakable dread. The Redcaps sensed their moment and prepared to move.

'This is insanity,' Shavi hissed, his guilt over the dead god almost painful. He turned to Laura. 'Follow me.' He dug his spurs sharply into his horse's flank and it shot off in the direction of the Serpentine. Laura was behind him in an instant.

Their escape stirred the Tuatha Dé Danann, who were soon following in their tracks. Shavi glanced over his shoulder and was shocked to see how fast the Redcaps were moving in pursuit. Although they were only on foot, their leg muscles were unbelievably powerful. They weaved around trees and rubbish bins without slowing their speed at all, and were soon passing the Tuatha Dé Danann, who were urging on their terrified horses even more.

Laura noticed the Redcaps approach too. 'Jesus, what powers those things?'

'Hunger. And hatred.'

'Any idea where we're going now?'

'We could attempt to outrun them. Or we could find a place that will offer us sanctuary, somewhere to rest and lick our wounds.'

'In this place?' She laughed mockingly. 'Maybe we can take in some sights while we're at it.'

The smoke rolled across the surface of the Serpentine where the abandoned boats bobbed and drifted. Shavi pressed on along Rotten Row until Hyde Park Corner came into view. The roundabout was choked with dead traffic, much of it blackened and twisted in the aftermath of a flash-fire that had raged through the area. It still smelled of charred oil and singed plastic.

'They're closing,' Laura gasped as she sent her horse along the pavement until they found a space to get through the traffic to Constitution Hill. The high brick wall of Buckingham Palace lay to their right.

Their manoeuvres had slowed them considerably, while the Redcaps merely powered over the heaps of blackened metal.

'Shavi,' Laura said, 'this is the time for your big idea. You have got one, haven't you?' The jungle cat-snarling of the Redcaps was now close behind.

Shavi guided his horse in close to Laura until there were barely two inches between them as they pounded down the centre of the street.

With his left hand gripping the reins, he fumbled with his right for the twin-bladed sword, then held it out for Laura.

'What am I supposed to do with that?'

'It is easy to operate.'

'Get lost. You're the one with the big soul-charge. The only spirit I've got is vodka and Red Bull.'

'Take it.'

Uncomfortably she accepted the sword and immediately thumbed the jewel in the hilt. The Blue Fire began to build. 'Now tell me how I ride while facing backwards.'

'Have you never seen Hopalong Cassidy?'

'Uh, no.'

'The Lone Ranger?'

'Get real.'

'I am sure you will pick it up.'

Laura swore at him violently, then half-spun round in her saddle. The yell erupted from her lips unbidden. Three Redcaps were so close behind they could almost touch the horse's tail. She could smell the rotting-meat reek of their breath. When they saw her face, their eyes flared hungrily with a red light.

One of them threw itself forward. The charge leapt from the sword like a missile, tearing through the Redcap's face in a blue blast. When her eyes cleared, all three creatures were headless, still twitching on the road as their bodies struggled to catch up with the news. The other Redcaps had stopped and were blinking stupidly at this strange development.

'That'll teach them to wear hats out of season,' Laura said weakly. This time it was Shavi's turn to catch the sword and steady her with the other hand as she threatened to slip from the saddle. 'Shit, I feel like I'm coming off a six-day bender. Is this how it was for you?'

'I feel a little better now, but it will take a while to recover completely.'

Baccharus rode up and then past them, urging them on. 'Come! They will be on you again in a moment!'

Laura somehow managed to get her horse moving again before resting against its neck, hoping it would find the right direction by itself. Shavi once again took the lead. But they had barely got out into the wide open space surrounding the Queen Victoria Memorial in front of Buckingham Palace when a harpoon trailing fire tore through the air to impale one of the Tuatha Dé Danann, who fell from his horse.

Fomorii were swarming over the roof of Buckingham Palace, where they had sited an odd weapon that looked like a cross between a mediaeval siege machine and a piece of WWII artillery. Five Fomorii were loading it with another harpoon that mysteriously burst into flame the moment it was in place.

'They're changing the guard at Buckingham Palace,' Laura said ironically.

The harpoon rocketed into the Queen Victoria Memorial, which exploded in chunks of stone.

'They are slowly picking us off.' Shavi's face had grown dark with anger. 'We must not allow this.'

Laura felt a tingle run down her spine when she saw the Tuatha Dé Danann were waiting on the two of them for orders. 'This is about as weird as it gets,' she muttered.

When she looked back, Shavi had his head bowed and his hands over his face, one of the rituals he regularly used when he was meditating.

'Quickly,' Baccharus insisted. 'The Redcaps will be coming.'

When Shavi looked up, Laura thought she saw blue sparks leap from his eyes. 'Church did a good job,' he said, moving his horse on.

'What do you mean?'

'The Blue Fire is all around now. So easy to see, I barely need any concentration.'

Almost the instant he said the words, Laura realised she could see it too: in some areas just thin capillaries of sapphire, in others like a raging current beneath the ground, as if the road surface was made of glass.

'Trippy! So this is what it means . . .' Her words trailed off, unable to capture the depth of what she was feeling.

'Then this city is not dead to us,' Shavi said. 'Church suggested the force would be a weakening power for the Fomorii. They hate it, and what it represents. And here we can see the lines leading to the most potent sources.'

'Come, then.' Baccharus's voice was strained, his eyes darting all around.

'What is it?' Shavi followed his gaze, but could see nothing.

'Can you not feel it?'

The moment the words were uttered, he could. Against the background of rising anxiety like a deep bass rumble, something unpleasant was stirring. The roar of the Redcaps bouncing off the buildings disturbed Shavi before he had time to analyse the sensation, and then the feral creatures surged into view with renewed vigour.

Baccharus, Shavi and Laura spurred their horses, with the other Tuatha Dé Danann following a split-second later. Shavi, who had his perception fixed on the flow of the Blue Fire, took the lead.

The unbearable speed of the Redcaps was the least of their worries. They had barely broken into the once-serene environment of St James's Park when Shavi realised what it was he had sensed. When the smoke and icy mist cleared to present a view of the sprawling city, he had the unnerving impression that it was altering its shape like a Night Walker. The edges of the stately buildings along Whitehall, of the sedate and cultured pale stone blocks of The Mall, of those further away in the West End, were continually moving, like some bad, speeded-up animation. When he realised what it was, his blood, already chilled by where he was and what he had seen, became even colder.

Thousand upon thousand of Fomorii were emerging from their hiding places, moving out into the city, across rooftops, down walls; all the sickening, alien activity of a disturbed ant-hill. The speed of their waking suggested some call must have gone out on a level only those hideous creatures could understand.

'They're coming for us.' Laura's voice was drained of all life.

Behind them, the ferocious roaring of the Redcaps drew nearer. 'No way back.' Shavi spurred the horse on faster. 'Only forward.'

'This is what they wanted,' Laura said dismally, her words almost drowned out by the thunder of the hooves. 'To separate us. To get us into a place where there wasn't the slightest chance we could fight back.' She gulped in a mouthful of air to stifle the rising emotion. Then: 'Do you think they've got the others?'

Shavi wasn't listening. The sea of black, roiling bodies moved in rapidly on either side; soon they would be submerged in the deluge. Dread formed a lump in his throat. *Always hope,* he told himself, a calming mantra repeated over and over. *Focus on the source of the hope, not the source of the fear.* Gradually the black, oppressive world faded away into the background until all he could see were the streams of brilliant blue. And the deepest, fastest and most brilliant of them blazed a channel between the enclosing darkness. Shavi guided his horse on to it and prayed.

The scorched grass, blackened trees and thick layer of grey ash that blanketed St James's Park passed in a blur. The jolt of hooves on hard road. Great George Street. Then the wide open space of Parliament Square, the statue of the great war leader Churchill reduced to a broken stump. Westminster Bridge shattered, ending after only a few yards in broken concrete and twisted iron girders. The Houses of Parliament seething, across the roof, through the smashed windows, bubbling out towards them. The Fomorii that had the ability to fly on leathery bat-wings swarmed across the Thames like angry wasps.

'All around!' Laura yelled. 'This is it!'

The Fomorii surged down Whitehall and Millbank into Parliament Square, black, gleaming bodies as far as the eye could see. Shavi guided his horse round until the dark, majestic bulk of Westminster Abbey rose up in front of them.

'There,' he said.

They raced their horses to the western entrance, where Shavi saw the Blue Fire swirling into a coruscating pillar of energy, lighting up the ornate columned front with its imposing twin towers. Three of the Tuatha Dé Danann jumped down to try the handles before putting their shoulders to the heavy oaken doors without budging them in the slightest.

'Locked,' one of the guards said. Panic bloomed in his face. The Square was completely obscured now; the relentless torrent was almost upon them.

'Who's there?' The voice was timorous, broken.

Shavi leapt from his horse and threw himself at the door. 'Let us in! We need sanctuary!'

There was one hanging moment when they feared whoever was within had left them to die, but then came the sound of heavy bolts being drawn.

The Redcaps were ahead of the driving wall of Fomorii, jumping and leaping like crazed tigers. One of the Tuatha Dé Danann guards attempted to fend them off to give the others more time. They fell on him in a frenzy.

The door swung open and a voice shouted, 'Quick!'

Shavi led them in, horses and all, and then the doors slammed shut with a sound like the tolling of a bell.

Within the Abbey there was an abiding stillness. The thick stone walls muffled the noise of the terrible force without, but all Shavi was aware of was the thunder of the blood in his brain. The entire building was filled with the iron tang of the Blue Fire, too potent, he was sure, for the Fomorii to attempt to enter. Yet as he came to terms with the amazing fact that they were safe, he gradually took in his surroundings and was overcome with surprise.

The vast body of the Abbey was filled as far as he could see with pale, silent faces. Men and women, old, middle-aged and young, babies and children, all looking up with expressions riven by fear. They stood shoulder-to-shoulder, turned towards the new arrivals, or slumped on pews or on the stone floor, at first glance barely human; sheep, he thought, even less than that.

But there was humanity behind the fear, although it was of a pathetic kind, of people desperately trying to cope with a paralysing disbelief that everything they understood had crumbled in an instant.

'Who are you?' It was the voice of the man who had spoken to them through the door. He was in his early fifties, stylishly dressed, with a sallow face, cropped grey hair and designer glasses. He appeared to notice the Tuatha Dé Danann for the first time. 'Who are they? Are they—?'

'Friends.' Shavi rested a calming hand on the man's shoulder. He glanced once more at the expectant mass. Around the edges of the nave were empty cans and boxes, the remains of whatever food supplies they had brought with them, but many of the faces looked hungry. 'How long have you been in here?'

'From the moment it all blew up. It took everyone by surprise. We scrambled in here with what we could grab, a few provisions, not enough . . . How in heaven's name did you manage to get here? We thought everyone else must be dead by now.' His voice died; there were tears in his eyes. 'We can't go outside. A few tried it, to get more food.' He shook his head, looked at his shoes.

Laura pulled Shavi over to one side. 'This is a nightmare. They're either going to starve or go outside and get slaughtered.'

'We are in the same predicament.'

'Yes, but they're not like us. They're normal people. That shit is part of our job description, not theirs.'

Shavi still couldn't comprehend how much she had altered. Not so long ago she would have been advocating self-preservation at all costs, and now she was urging them to accept their responsibility. Could someone really change that much? 'You are right,' he said, smiling. 'We owe them what little hope we have, at the very least.' He turned to the sallow-faced man. 'Are you in charge here?'

He shook his head. 'You want Professor Michell, I suppose. He's not really in charge. But he makes decisions. Any decisions that need making.'

'Then,' Shavi prompted, 'could you take us to him?'

The nave was beautiful and awe-inspiring, with fabulous monuments on either side. An air of solemnity hung over it. As they passed through, brief hope flared in the eyes of the refugees. Some held out their hands like the Victorian poor, silently begging for food. A Nigerian woman, overweight in a too-tight coat, offered a tentative smile, her eyes flooded with tears. Children stared blankly into the shadows. A girl in a blue dress, Sunday-best smart, as if she'd been on her way to a special function when her life had been arrested, said, 'Have you seen my mummy? I'm waiting for her.' Babies shuddered with sobs drained of tears. Shavi and Laura tried to offer reassuring smiles to the first few, but the emotional cost was too great and they averted their eyes for the remainder of the long walk.

To distract herself, Laura nodded to a monument in the centre of the nave. 'What's that?'

'The tomb of the Unknown Soldier.' Shavi had stood in front of it before, but this time it was laden with meaning. 'An unidentified British soldier brought back from a French battlefield during the Great War. He represents all the victims of that great tragedy, indeed, all the lowly warriors who have since given their lives in conflict.'

Beyond the nave were the aisles to the choir, which was also packed with refugees. Shavi paused to examine the monuments that lined the walls. Now everything he saw was filled with so much meaning, the emotion was welling up and threatening to overflow. 'This is what we are losing,' he said gravely. 'Not fast cars and computers and mobile phones. *This* is what truly matters.' He pointed to each monument in turn. 'Elgar. Purcell. John Wesley. William Wilberforce. Charles Darwin.' He pointed towards the south transept. 'Down there, Poets' Corner: Chaucer, Auden, Shakespeare, Shelley, Blake, Keats, Dryden, Spenser, Jonson, Milton, the Brontës, Wordsworth, Tennyson, Coleridge, Dickens, Kipling—'

'Don't get maudlin on me, Shav-ster,' Laura said gloomily. She wandered off ahead.

Eventually the sallow-faced man brought them to St Edward the Confessor's Chapel, the sacred heart of the abbey where its most precious relics lay. Here a man in his sixties, with shoulder-length, straggly grey hair, sat wearily in a Gothic, high-backed chair. He was painfully thin, his wrists protruding skeletally from the fraying arms of an old, woollen overcoat. Behind his wire-rimmed glasses, his face suggested a man burdened by the greatest of worries, but underneath it Shavi saw integrity and intelligence.

The sallow-faced man hurried over and whispered in his ear. Without looking up, the Professor gestured exhaustedly for Shavi and the others to approach. When they were in front of him, he cast a brief eye over them, but if he felt any shock at the sight of the Tuatha Dé Danann, he didn't register it. 'More strays sheltering from the storm?' His voice was achingly tired.

'We are here to confront the invaders,' Shavi said.

He counted them off silently. 'So many of you. Did you really need to come so mob-handed?'

'We're only part of it,' Laura said. 'The best part, sure, but there are others. Lots of them. There's a war going on.' She gestured towards the Tuatha Dé Danann. 'These—'

The Professor acknowledged them with a nod. 'Old gods made new again. I expected they were around, though I haven't seen any of them till now.'

'Who are you?' Shavi asked.

'The wrong man in the wrong place at the wrong time.' He removed his glasses and rubbed his eyes for a long period. 'An academic. Just what the world needs now. Even better, one versed in anthropology.' He laughed bitterly.

'So how did you get the top job?' Laura watched the sallow-faced man slope away.

'Someone had to do it. Not that there's anything to do, apart from preventing everyone from killing themselves. Though even that may be an exercise in futility.'

The Tuatha Dé Danann shifted awkwardly until Baccharus silently motioned to Shavi that he was taking them back to the horses.

'So, introductions. My name is Brian Michell. And you are?'

Shavi and Laura introduced themselves before briefly outlining what was happening in the city. Michell listened thoughtfully, nodding at the correct moments. When they had finished, he said, 'When I first saw those horrible things out there I knew they were the template for all the worst things in our old myths. There was something inexpressibly ancient about them, something laden with symbolism. It was only a matter of time before the ones responsible for the other archetypes appeared.'

'You'd get on well with our own old git,' Laura said. 'Same language, same old bollocks.'

'I still haven't worked out why they haven't come in here to tear us apart.'

Shavi explained as best he could about the Blue Fire, but Michell picked up on the concept quickly. 'Good old woolly-minded New Agers. I always knew they were on to something. The spiritual wellhead, eh? Then I suppose it's only natural this place is a potent source of it. It's been a sacred spot for as long as man's been around, so the legends say. A divine island in prehistoric times, bounded by the Thames and the two arms of the River Tyburn that's now buried in pipes. The old Isle of Thorns, sacred to the Druids. Later, sacred to Apollo, where his temple was sited. Home of numerous other now long-lost religious monuments. And still giving up all it has to our generation. Amazing.' He forced a smile.

'What have you been doing for all those people?' Laura asked.

'Ensuring the little food we had was distributed fairly. Not much to do in that quarter now. In the early days, mediate in disputes. Try to keep them from taking their frustrations out on each other. They turned to me because they thought, being an educated man, I know about *things*. Now isn't that a laugh? I haven't even been able to look after my own life. The wife, God bless her, left long ago. Sick of all my cant. And the booze, I suppose. Haven't had a drink since I came in here. Now isn't that a thing? They should have examined my curriculum vitae a little more closely.'

'Whatever you say, I am sure you are the right man for the job. You have held them together,' Shavi said. Michell shrugged, wouldn't meet Shavi's eye. 'I would like to talk to them,' Shavi continued.

Michell chewed on a flayed nail, his eyes now fixed on Shavi's face. 'And say what to them? I don't want you making their last days any more miserable.'

'He's not going to do that.' Laura grinned. 'Shavi here's the preacher-boy. He's going to uplift their souls.'

'I want to tell them there is still hope.'

The Professor winced, shook his head. 'I think we've all had enough fairy stories.'

Shavi rested a hand on the Professor's thin fingers, which felt unbearably cold. 'I ask you to trust me.'

A tremor ran through Shavi as he ascended to the pulpit and looked down at the array of pale faces turned towards him. There was too much emotion there. It made him feel he wasn't up to the task, not even slightly. *I am just a London boy*, he wanted to say. *Not a shaman, not a hero, not a saviour.*

But after a moment, his heart took over and the words flowed to his mouth without any thought. 'For centuries, this has been a place of miracles . . .'

They made their base in one of the Sir Christopher Wren-designed twin towers on the western side. Outside, night had fallen; without any lights in the city, the Abbey felt like it was suspended in space.

The Tuatha Dé Danann settled easily in one corner of the gloomy old room and rested their eyes. Shavi was still not sure if they actually slept.

'That was a good thing you did,' Laura said quietly as she, Shavi and

Baccharus sat around a stubby candle from the Abbey's store. 'You could see it in their faces. What you did for them . . . amazing. I couldn't have done it. No one else could have done it.' She gave Shavi's thigh a squeeze. 'You missed your calling, preacher-boy.'

'Hope is a human essential.'

'Hope is essential for all things in the sweep of existence.' Baccharus stared at the flickering candle flame. 'It is common currency, too often in short supply.' He looked up at Shavi. 'And to give hope is the greatest gift of all.'

'Oh, don't. His head's big enough already.' Laura rested on Shavi's shoulder. After a moment she said, 'So what are we going to do? We can't sit here forever.'

'I fear we have been removed from the conflict,' Baccharus said. 'Unless my people can fight their way through to us, or one of the others achieves something remarkable that changes the situation, there is little we can do.' His voice suggested he didn't expect it to happen.

'But it's so pathetic,' Laura protested. 'We didn't do anything! We barely got into the city!'

'No,' Shavi said. 'I have to ensure the cauldron is there for the final battle. Laura and I both *need* to be there. We have to find a way.'

Baccharus held out his hand in equanimity. 'But there is nothing we can do. We are surrounded by a city of Night Walkers where we cannot move the slightest step without being cut down. The wise one accepts when events are beyond control.'

Laura looked from Baccharus to Shavi. 'So we sit here waiting to die?'

'Or,' Shavi said, 'waiting to live.'

At some point the quiet conversation became a distant drone and Laura's eyelids grew heavy, although a dim part of her was amazed that she could even consider sleeping. When she next stirred she realised the talk had stopped. Baccharus was lying next to the guttering candle, his eyes closed. Shavi was nowhere to be seen.

She stood up and stretched, although since her transformation her limbs no longer really ached. But she did feel the cold more, and her breath was clouding. She pulled her jacket tightly around her, the chill of the stone flags rising through the soles of her boots.

She found Shavi in an adjoining corridor lined with windows that looked out over the city. She might not have seen him in the pervasive gloom if not for a brief instant when the smoke and mist cleared to allow the moonlight to break through. Then he was limned in silver, like a ghost, leaning against the wall.

As Laura approached quietly, she was disturbed to see a strange cast to his face. It was heavy with dark thoughts and deep troubles, and she suddenly wondered whether his experience in the Grim Lands had affected him more than they thought. What if it had twisted a part of him, and even he didn't know?

She was considering retreating when he looked up to see her. His warm smile instantly dispelled all her doubts.

'Planning a suicide mission?' she asked.

He held out an arm so she could slide in next to him. 'I was thinking about the others.'

She felt warm and secure wrapped against his body. The smell of him brought back memories in a rush and she was surprised how happy they made her feel, but there was an edge of sadness to them as well. 'That time we did the monkey dance in Glastonbury,' she began, 'I was being a little manipulator.'

'I know.'

'Not in a bad way. I just wanted to get close to you. I thought nobody would do that if I didn't try to play them. Anyway, I'm sorry. I should have been more honest.'

'Why do you feel the need to tell me this now?'

She thought about this for a moment. 'If I screw up . . . if I'm not up to what you expected of me . . . I just don't want you thinking I'm all bad. Too bad.'

'I could never think badly of you, Laura.'

'Yeah, well, you don't know what lies ahead. I might run off screaming at a vital moment. Or something.'

'I have faith in you.' He gave her a squeeze. 'I wonder where the others are now. Ryan and Ruth should have realised how dense the Fomorii forces are in the city by now. I hope their regiment of the Tuatha Dé Danann had more success than ours.'

'The worst thing is that we might never find out, just be stuck here while everything winds down, not knowing if the people we care about are alive or dead.'

'And Church—'

'Church will be fine.' She nuzzled into Shavi's shoulder. 'He's got God on his side. Too damn decent to screw up.'

'It must hurt you to still love him.'

'Not really. Yes, I still love him. But I've got my head round the fact that we're never going to be together.' She put on a fake voice. 'It's just one of those terribly tragic love stories.'

'It is not the end, you know.'

She laughed silently. 'That's a good thing to say in this predicament.

But if we're just talking about our stupid personal lives, then I know you're right. For the first time I feel optimistic about me. About what I could do. Which is ludicrous when there might only be a day left, and I've got green blood running through my veins. But, you know, I feel . . . hopeful. And I never thought I'd feel that in my life.'

Shavi rested his head against hers, smelling her hair, relishing the new aromas she generated since her change. Above all, he was happy for her, even if there were only hours left. 'What do you want to do now?' he asked quietly.

'I just want you to hold me here like I was some pathetic child. And I want to watch the dawn come up with you.'

Silence draped across them in the deep dark, with only the occasional soughing of the wind to remind them there was a world beyond their own sphere. And there was peace for both of them.

When dawn rose in intermittent bursts of gold and red through the shifting smoke, Laura was asleep on the floor in Shavi's arms. His thoughts had been too troubled to sleep himself, but the magical colour ignited in the corridor by the light through the stained glass was enough to lift his mood.

'A beautiful day.' Michell was standing in the doorway. 'I'm sorry – irony doesn't go down too well at this time in the morning.'

Shavi slipped out from under Laura without waking her and wandered over to greet the Professor.

'I just wanted to say thank you for what you said to everyone last night,' Michell continued. 'It did them the world of good. I'm a little too cynical to say I was affected by it myself.'

'I am glad I could be of some help.' Shavi glanced out of the one window he had left open the previous night. 'Has the food gone completely?'

'There's a little left. For emergencies.'

'Then I suggest you divide it up amongst them this morning.'

Michell searched Shavi's face and then nodded slowly, chewing on his lip. 'I'll arrange it. Do you have any plans for the day? Any sights to see? I thought I'd work on a few lectures myself.'

Shavi smiled. 'No. No plans.'

Behind them Laura stirred and yawned loudly, eventually making her way to them, still sleepy-eyed. A racking shiver brought her fully awake. 'When do you think the end'll start coming down?'

'It should not be too long.'

'How do you know that?' Michell asked.

Shavi pointed to the open window. Laura and the Professor peered out together.

The Fomorii stood shoulder-to-shoulder everywhere they looked, packing the main drag of Victoria Street and every surrounding street to the dim distance. The entire cityscape gleamed an oily black in the wan sunlight. None of them made the slightest sound, nor did they move an inch: an army of sable statues. And all their faces were turned up to the window where Shavi, Laura and the Professor stood.

Waiting.

CHAPTER EIGHTEEN

Down to the River to Pray

'Are you going to talk to me at all?' Ruth had been keeping one eye on Veitch long enough to know he was fighting to ignore her.

She instantly regretted speaking when he flashed her a glance that was so harsh it jolted her. 'What do you expect? Happy smiles and blowing kisses?'

'Not from you, no.'

His long hair, lashed by the cold north wind, obscured his face so she couldn't read his response, but she had watched his eyes made darker by a brooding brow ever since they had picked up the last leg of the M1. His handsome face had been transformed by the icy set of his features. Sometimes, when she saw him like that, he frightened her.

The Tuatha Dé Danann who rode in front, behind and on either side had added to her loneliness by alienating her ever since they had left the camp. They had taken to Veitch immediately, encouraging him to strip off his shirt so they could examine with delight the fantastic tattoos that covered his torso, so she knew it wasn't because she was a *Fragile Creature*. She had endured enough similar ignorance from men during her working life not to take it to heart. With what lay ahead, she could have done with a friend for support and she hated Veitch a little for not being there for her, even though she had no right to ask that of him.

At the end of the motorway they took the North Circular. It gave her a strange *frisson* to be riding a horse along deserted roads on which she had queued irritatedly in backed-up traffic so many times. At least the Tuatha Dé Danann force gave her some confidence. There were hundreds of them, maybe thousands, armed with bizarre weapons that made her blood grow cold just to look at them. They stretched as far back as she could see, and fanned out slightly on either side ahead so the force resembled an arrow driving into the contaminated heart of the city. Lugh and Nuada led the way, both of them enthused with a warrior spirit that sickened her. She didn't take any pleasure in fighting, certainly not in killing; it was a job that they had an obligation to fulfil, but that was all. And she also despised the jealousy, or contempt, she felt coming off the two gods at her possession of the Spear. The weapon rested on her back in a specially made harness Lugh had grudgingly handed over, its power warming through her clothes to invigorate her spirit.

They broke off from the North Circular, passing down North End Road until they arrived at Hampstead Heath. The expanse of greenery was looking a little washed-out in the October chill, but it had been protected from the ash falls by its lofty position above the city and the direction of the wind.

From the heights all they could see was the pall of thick smoke and mist that drifted along the Thames Valley. Occasionally, though, it shifted enough for the black tower to loom up ominously in the east.

A blast from a strange horn resembling a conch shell brought the force to an abrupt halt. Ahead, Ruth could see Lugh and Nuada in deep discussion. After a moment they beckoned to Veitch. It was noticeable that they were ignoring her, but out of bloody-mindedness she spurred her horse to keep pace behind Veitch.

Both of the gods kept their eyes fixed on Veitch's face as they spoke. 'We are debating crossing this heathland,' Nuada said. 'It is a wide expanse that could be dangerous.'

Veitch scanned the heath. 'If there are any of the Bastards out there, there can't be many. There aren't that many places to hide.'

'The Night Walkers are a cunning breed,' Nuada said.

'I say we continue,' Lugh said. 'It would not do to waste the hours following the edge. And if there are Night Walkers, they will fall before the might of the Golden Ones, as they always must.'

Veitch rubbed his chin. 'Well, I don't know. I wouldn't like to be caught out there.'

'I heard you were a mighty warrior,' Lugh gibed. 'That strangest of things, a Fragile Creature who is not fragile!'

Ruth willed Veitch not to be swayed, but after a moment's thought, he shrugged. 'It's your call, then. Let's get to it.'

Ruth sighed, but none of them looked towards her.

When they returned to their positions, Ruth said to Veitch, 'Why did you give in to them? You know better than they do. You're good at what you do, Ryan. You should have more confidence in yourself.'

He grunted unintelligibly, but renewed his effort to scan the heath. Clusters of trees dotted the rolling grassland, with thicker woodland to the north. They were aiming for Parliament Hill, where they could press down speedily into Kentish Town, and then on into Camden, Islington and finally the City. Ruth was dreading the final leg of the assault where the winding streets and soaring buildings would make any mass approach impossible. She expected a long, gruelling fight to their destination, and if the Fomorii could hold them off for just thirty-six hours it would end in failure. If only there were a better way, she thought.

The Tuatha Dé Danann fanned out across the heath, giving Ruth an even more impressive view of their numbers. So concentrated were they that her perception could barely cope; the gods lost their individuality, became the untarnished power that lay at the core of them, merging into one, bright glow. It reminded her of a sea of gold, licking up to an oil-stained beach. The sight was comforting and she relaxed a little. The Fomorii wouldn't stand a chance.

They moved across the heath slowly. Nuada and Lugh were leading cautiously, constantly scanning the terrain. Veitch kept his eyes on the tree-line.

Briefly the sun broke through the thick cloud cover, warming Ruth's face. She closed her eyes and went with the gentle rocking of her mount, enjoying the aroma of greenery the breeze brought from the north. In her mind she pictured a perfect autumn day, walking with Church amongst a wood turning gold, red and brown somewhere peaceful, Scotland perhaps, or the New Forest. Her mind plucked a soundtrack from her memory that had been pressuring to come forward since the journey began.

'What are you thinking?'

She opened her eyes to see Veitch watching her suspiciously. 'I can't get an old song out of my head. It's sort of gospelly, traditional, but it was in a George Clooney film a while back. It's called—'

In the blink of an eye, the Fomorii were there. They rose up out of the ground, not there, then there a second later, an opposing army created from thin air. By the time she had realised what was happening, chaos had erupted.

Ruth was caught in a hurricane. Her nightmares of the forthcoming confrontation had suggested it would be as sickeningly ferocious and bloody as any mediaeval battle, but what she saw around her was much, much worse. The Fomorii wielded their ugly, serrated swords like propellers, hacking and slashing in a relentless whirl. Limbs, heads and other body parts showered all around, filling the air with a blizzard of golden moths.

The Tuatha Dé Danann were just as brutal. Their weapons were unleashed in furious rounds, turning the Fomorii into a mist of black droplets or a thick sludge with only the hint of component parts. And where the fighting was too close, they resorted to their swords, jabbing and hacking as fast as their enemy. In the fury of movement and the ear-splitting din of combat, with the mud and grue covering all, Ruth could barely tell them apart.

Veitch was matching them all for ferocity. His sword whisked around with the efficiency and blurring speed of a machine, while he somehow managed to manoeuvre his horse back and forth to attack and retreat, even in close quarters. It was a staggering display of instinctive ability that left Ruth breathless. That was why he had been chosen: he wasn't just good at the role that had been presented to him, he was the ultimate warrior.

The Spear was in her right hand – she didn't recall withdrawing it – and she clutched the reins with her left. Numerous Night Walkers fell at the touch of the weapon, but she was nowhere near as good as Veitch. In fact, she felt a liability. Her own abilities were useless in that kind of situation, while the sheer senseless slaughter left her unable to think clearly.

Veitch appeared to sense this for he suddenly spurred his horse round to her side. 'Let's get out of this fucking hell-hole!'

With his sword cutting down any opposition he drove the horse in as direct a line as he could to the open ground beyond the battlefield. Ruth was quick to follow in his wake, bracing the Spear against her side to take down any opposition Veitch missed. By the time they had forced their way through the final ranks, her ribs felt as if they had been beaten with metal bars.

Veitch continued until they had put a hundred yards or more between them and the fighting, then he rounded to survey the scene. 'Shit. Look at that.' His voice was barely more than a whisper.

From their new perspective the true horror and brutality of the fight could be seen. The Fomorii and Tuatha Dé Danann never turned from a confrontation, driving on from one fight to the next until they eventually dropped. The heath was thick with the essence of both of them – hundreds had already been slaughtered – but the Fomorii had a slight advantage in that they had no concern for their own preservation; one would sacrifice itself so another could gain a better position in a fight. The shimmer of golden moths over the scene added an incongruous touch of beauty to the horror, so that after a moment Ruth felt she was watching a strange, detached cartoon, shifting in a syrupy slow-motion as golden snow fell languorously.

'Are they going to fight to the last man?' she said when she couldn't bear to look any more.

'They're not men.' Veitch was seized with a cold anger. 'They've forgotten the job. We're going to lose everything because they're locked up in their own stupid, bleedin' rivalry.'

Before Ruth could answer, their attention was caught by frantic movement in the air down in the valley. Rising from the drifting smoke were black shapes that looked like flies from their perspective. 'Fomorii,' Ruth said. 'Flying ones.'

It was never easy to get a fix on the fluid shapes of the Fomorii, but Ruth was sure she could make out wings like a bat, but gleaming and rigid, as though they were made of metal. As the creatures fell down towards the heath, their insectile body plates shifted, folded out and slotted into place until they were covered with a hideous ridged and pitted armour. Numerous horns rimmed the skull while the eyes glowed a Satanic red from deep within Stygian orbits.

As Ruth and Veitch watched, a pair of the flying Night Walkers broke away from the formation and targeted the two of them. 'Come on!' Veitch turned his horse in a bid to outrun them.

The flying Fomorii were like small jets, flattening their wings against their backs to build more speed. As their shadow fell over Ruth, she threw herself to one side. It was enough to avoid a killing blow from talons of black steel but she still felt a ringing impact on the side of her head, knocking her from the horse. She hit the ground hard, seeing stars, feeling a wetness seeping into her hair.

When she next looked up, the two creatures had zoned in on Veitch. They hovered, avoiding his blows, then diving in between his sword thrusts with the speed of hummingbirds. Even so, they'd only managed to land a couple of minor blows on him; blood trickled from a cut on his temple, another on his cheek.

As Ruth pushed herself dazedly to her feet, she saw Veitch feint and then rip his sword along one of the creature's bellies. Thick, black liquid gushed out, steaming in the cold air. It narrowly missed Veitch, splattering on the grass where it sizzled like acid. But in the Fomor's dying spasm it had knocked Veitch's sword from his hand, and the other one was preparing to sweep in for the kill.

Though her head felt like cotton wool, Ruth acted on instinct. She snatched up the Spear from where it had fallen and hurled it with all her strength. As the creature dived down, the Spear rammed through its skull, neck and out of its belly. It dropped to the ground like a stone.

Veitch snapped round towards her. At first his face was unreadable, but then a grin crept across it. 'So you can be as big a nasty bastard as the rest of us.'

After reclaiming the Spear and Ruth's horse, they only had a second or two to consider their options before they realised a section of the Tuatha Dé Danann force was rushing towards them. The flying Fomorii were wreaking havoc amongst the outer reaches of the Golden Ones, but hadn't yet progressed to those fighting in the thickest of the mêlée. It was obvious they had tilted the balance firmly in the direction of the Fomorii.

Lugh and Nuada patently recognised this for they were in the forefront of the retreat. The conch-like horn sounded insistently above the clash of battle and the bloodthirsty screeches of the Fomorii. The Tuatha Dé Danann attempted to extricate themselves from the thick of the fighting. Many fell in the course of the retreat.

Soon Ruth and Veitch's horses thundered across the heath. The airborne creatures continued to harry those at the rear, but away from the battle there was more room to use Goibhniu's weapons. Once a handful had plummeted from the sky the other Fomorii hung back, waiting for the right opportunity. Dropping back further, the Night Walker forces regrouped to drive the Tuatha Dé Danann eastwards; once the gods hit the built-up areas, their retreat would fragment.

Ruth could see this was not lost on Nuada. His face was drained of the arrogance that had turned his earlier smiles into a sneer; a stony cast hid his concern.

Veitch knew it too, was probably aware of it before anyone else. 'We can't keep running!' he yelled above the pounding of a thousand hooves.

'Then what do you suggest?' Nuada snapped.

The thoughtful expression that crossed Veitch's face brought a smile to Ruth's lips; she recognised it instantly. 'There's one route that'll take all this lot, horses and all, right into the heart of where we want to go,' he said.

'Then why was it not proposed earlier?'

'Because it's probably bleedin' dangerous.' Veitch turned to Ruth. 'The tube.'

Ruth was struggling to keep up, but Veitch's suggestion gave her added impetus. 'Of course! The whole city's got tunnels running under it everywhere!'

'Not just the train tunnels. There's other shit down there. Secret passages for the Government and the army. Disused lines and everything.'

Nuada reined in his mount; they had reached the eastern edge of the heath. Within a couple of minutes, the rest of the Tuatha Dé Danann would be milling around them, jammed into a bottleneck and ready for the slaughter.

'Make haste! There is little time!' Ruth thought she sensed a hint of respect in Nuada's voice.

'Okay, here's the deal. If we all head to the nearest station the Bastards'll follow us down and pick us off. But what they really want is you, Lugh and the other top dogs. Me too, probably. We're going to draw some of them off, try to lose them. Ruth's going to lead as many of your lot as she can to Archway station and then move up with some more to Highgate.' He winced. 'The rest are going to have to fend for themselves.'

'Agreed. They can honour themselves by holding off the Night Walkers until we reach our destination.' He made to go before turning back to Veitch. 'You are a true champion of your kind, Brother of Dragons.' And then he was away, passing on the plan to his lieutenants.

The flush of pride rose up in Veitch's cheeks and he tried to turn away before Ruth could see. She rode up to him and placed a hand on his shoulder so she could pull him closer to whisper in his ear. 'You're the hero, Ryan. Everybody knows it.'

He looked deep into her face, unable to find any words that could express his thoughts. Instead he pulled her closer to kiss her just once, on the cheek; it was a kiss for old time's sake. And then he spurred his horse to round up the men he needed.

Veitch, Lugh and Nuada led a band of about thirty eastwards through the pleasant streets that bordered the heath. Within a couple of minutes they were at the place Veitch had identified from his encyclopaedic strategic memory. Highgate Cemetery brooded behind stone walls and chained iron gates, a maze of paths amongst the crumbling Victorian monuments to the dead, festooned with ivy, shadowed by clusters of dark, overhanging trees.

Lugh smashed down the main gate with one blow of his boot. They drove their horses deep into the heart of the cemetery where they dismounted. Veitch knew he had made the right choice: plenty of places to hide amongst the stones and mausoleums, the groves and hollows and mounds that gave no clear line of sight.

Yet he couldn't help a shudder when he looked round at the stones. It was the Grey Lands all over again. Images of the dead beneath his feet rose unbidden into his mind, and however much he tried he couldn't stifle the thought of them listening and shifting, gradually clawing their way up to the light.

Before he made any further move, he climbed into the low, twisted branches of an ancient yew. Through the thick greenery he could just make out the cemetery perimeter. He had been right there too: the Fomorii were milling around in the streets beyond, confused. Their hive-mind was good for any obvious confrontation, but anything involving guile and difficult choices left them at odds. It helped that he could not see any that stood out as leaders. No flapping crows, no enormous, powerful warriors like the one that had pursued them from Edinburgh.

After a moment the main body of the force set off to track Ruth through the trees, but they had hesitated long enough for her to have a good headstart. A large group turned towards the cemetery. A chill ran through Veitch as they flowed over the walls and amongst the stones like shadows at twilight. Several of the flying Fomorii joined them, swooping low over the graves, searching for any sign of their prey.

Veitch dropped from the branches to Nuada and Lugh. 'You know what guerrilla warfare is? We split up into ones and twos, pick off as many as we can while we make our way across the cemetery. We meet up on the other side and head to Highgate station.'

'What about the horses?' Nuada asked.

'We scatter them. They'll confuse things.'

Nuada and Lugh barked something to the others in a language Veitch couldn't understand. A moment later they had slipped into the surroundings like ghosts.

A film of sweat covered Veitch's entire body despite the cold. He stepped out from behind the lichen-streaked obelisk towering over his head into plain view of three Fomorii, who moved cautiously along the path two hundred yards away. They heralded their discovery with a barrage of monkey-shrieks.

The other Fomorii nearby were too distracted by the wildly galloping horses to heed the call. The mounts ran back and forth along the winding paths, in sight just long enough for their presence to be registered but disappearing before the Fomorii could see if there was a rider on their backs.

Veitch's heart thundered as the Fomorii started towards him. They moved so much quicker than their bulk suggested: efficient killing machines filled with unquenchable energy. There was something hypnotic about their power that kept him rooted and they were dangerously close by the time he had turned and was running over the lip of the hill. He knew he wouldn't be able to out-run them for long.

The strain of the last few days was beginning to tell as he darted from the path amongst the stones in the hope that it would slow down his pursuers. Exhaustion brought a dull, aching heat to his thigh muscles, his usually bountiful reserves of energy close to empty.

The Fomorii veered from the path, smashing down grave markers that had stood for a hundred years with a flex of their leg muscles or a sweep of their arms. The wind picked up the thick, unpleasant musk of them; every time Veitch smelled it he felt sick to his stomach. Now he didn't even have the strength to combat the queasiness. He hurdled a tilting cross, ripping his calf on one of the arms, then landed awkwardly back on the path. He was convinced he had broken his ankle, but after he limped a few more paces he realised it was probably only a twist, but it was enough to hamper him.

A chunk of old stone crashed against a statue of an angel, missing his head by only an inch. He rounded a bend in the path and came up on a large mausoleum covered with so much ivy it looked like a natural formation.

Gripping the ivy hard, he hauled himself on to the roof to leap to a tree branch beyond. His reactions were still sharp enough to catch the shadow falling across him. The talons of one of the flying Fomorii raked the air where his head had been. Quickly he lashed upwards with his silver hand. Nails extracted as Nuada had showed him, slicing through the creature's left leg. It lost control of its flight and he hacked again, half-severing a wing. It crashed down amongst the graves, still alive but badly wounded.

He didn't have time to catch his breath. The Fomorii were now dragging themselves up the mausoleum, but they were slowed by the ivy, which was being pulled away by their bulk; they were still managing to find enough of a foothold to progress.

Veitch leaped for the branch and swung, dropping down on to another path. Pain flared in his ankle as he landed. He stifled a yell, clutched at it and hobbled off as the path wound round into a dense thicket of trees.

A minute later the Fomorii were there. But as they turned into the shadowy grove they were confronted by Nuada and Lugh poised on either side of the path.

Veitch was leaning against a tree, taking the weight off his ankle. 'Could be worse,' he said with a shrug. 'You could be dead.'

The Fomorii were still struggling with their surprise as Lugh stepped in and gutted one, while Nuada lopped the head off another. As the third started to transform into something more offensive they both swung their swords to dismember it.

'Oh, well.' Veitch eyed the steaming corpses with a confident grin.

Across the cemetery, golden shapes flitted like autumn shadows. The remnants of gleaming sable bodies hung from crosses and angels, were strewn across stone boxes or were slumped against the walls of mausoleums where the ivy flapped against their caustic cavities.

Veitch guided it all with a consummate eye for detail, and when he was convinced enough damage had been done in the limited time they had available, he directed the Tuatha Dé Danann to depart. They slipped amongst the stones to the perimeter wall, and even with Veitch limping, they were not seen once.

Ruth waited in the shadows of Highgate Station ticket office, watching the loosed horses canter along the road in the fading afternoon light. Hundreds if not thousands of the beasts were now roaming through the streets of North London, covering their tracks with great efficiency.

Barely a quarter of the Tuatha Dé Danann force had streamed down the cramped winding staircases of Archway tube station under her guidance before she had decided to move on to avoid the Fomorii. Many more now waited at the foot of the terrifyingly deep shaft at Highgate, the deepest – if her memory served correct – on the entire tube network. Without any of the lifts working, it had taken them an age to filter through the tiny station and on to the stairs, clutching makeshift torches from any wood they could find in the vicinity. And all the time her heart had been in her mouth, expecting the Fomorii to sweep down on them when they were in no position to defend themselves.

But somehow they had done it, leaving her to wait alone in painful anticipation for Veitch and the others to arrive. She clutched the Spear close to her side for comfort, feeling the warm pulse of it, the soothing heat. Strangely it appeared slightly different from when she had first received it, less rough, with more delicate inlays of brass and silver.

She hadn't given a thought to what the next twenty-four hours would bring; indeed, if she were honest with herself, she would have admitted that for several weeks she had anticipated a terrible end for all of them. It didn't frighten her any more. When things were so likely, you made your peace with the outcome and moved on. As she stood there, she was surprised and a little disturbed to realise the worst thought that crawled around her head was that Veitch would not make it. Had his uncontrollable anger driven him to make some stupid mistake? Had his overweening bravado left him lying in a pool of blood in some Godforsaken backstreet? She was afraid of examining the subject too deeply for fear of what she would find.

She loved Church – she knew she did – but a part of her still had deep affection for Veitch; more than friendship, less than *amore*, not enough to make a song, more than enough to fill her with a consuming sadness that she might never see him again. Even her emotions had been so much simpler before the big change; now she couldn't even count on herself.

When she saw the glimmer of gold skin in the grey streets, and Veitch at the centre of them, dark hair flying in the breeze, she wiped her eyes, heaved in several deep breaths and turned towards the stairs.

'You're falling apart, Ryan. Losing a hand, now twisting an ankle.' Ruth held the torch higher. The darkness receded along the walls of the stairwell like a living creature.

'We all heal quick.' Veitch limped down the steps heavily, clutching on to the rail for support. Behind them Nuada, Lugh and the other Tuatha Dé Danann traipsed silently.

Veitch's mood had turned dark once more. Ruth saw it in his face the moment he had entered the tube station. Once he had passed into the gloom of the stairwell he locked himself off even further, his replies to her questions clipped and curt. There was something ineffably dangerous about him. In its milder form it was attractive, but when he got like this she was glad he was on their side.

By the time they reached the platform, Ruth's heart was pounding and her breath was short. She was surprised and disturbed by how much the claustrophobic darkness was affecting her; even with the torches, it was impossible to see more than a few feet. Although she'd been on that platform several times before, in that state it was oppressive and alien. She was acutely aware of the massive weight of earth piled up over her head. The air was stale without the circulation system working and it smelled of damp and burnt oil. It was also extremely cold. With an effort, she fought back a desperate urge to get back to the light.

'Where's the rest of them?' Veitch asked.

'I sent them down the line to rendezvous with the others at Archway.' Her voice sounded strained, with incipient panic tightening its grip around her airways.

'You know it's a bleedin' maze down here. They could get lost—'

'Sorry,' she snapped, sarcastically. 'I foolishly thought there wasn't any time to lose.'

'All right. I suppose we just have to take chances.' He lowered himself down and slid off the lip of the platform on to the tracks.

Ruth hesitated a moment before following suit. She moved in close to Veitch. Lugh and a couple of the other Tuatha Dé Danann led the way cautiously, while the rest guarded the rear.

At the end of the platform, the black hole of the tunnel loomed up in the flickering torchlight; a mouth ready to swallow them, Ruth thought. Her skin grew cold as she stared into the darkness and she was overcome with a sudden premonition of a grave and none of them ever seeing the light again.

'What's that?' Her heart rattled frantically when she glimpsed a fleeting movement on the edge of the light.

Everyone froze. 'Didn't see anything,' Veitch whispered.

'There's definitely something there.' Her voice was taut.

Lugh had found some oily rags on the tracks, which he tied into a large knot and lit with his torch. He whirled it once round his head and hurled it along the tunnel in front. The shadows rushed fearfully along the arc of the tunnel, but what was caught in the light for the briefest moment made Ruth shudder.

A sea of rats were frozen in the sudden glare, from wall to wall and as far as the light carried, their eyes glittering coldly. The sickening tableau was there only for an instant. As the burning rag fell, they retreated frantically, one brown-furred mass, rippling sinuously, until a second later the entire area was clear. The sound of scratching on metal rails faded away down the tunnel.

'Good job we have light,' Veitch said. 'They're fierce little bastards when they're hungry or cornered. I wouldn't fancy our chances against them in the dark.'

'There were so many of them!'

'These tunnels were always infested. The whole city was. They used to say you were never more than three feet away from a rat. I expect it's worse now, with all the bodies and everything.'

The image conjured by Veitch's comment made Ruth sick. 'You know there's a danger some of the tunnels could be flooded,' she said, changing the subject. 'None of the pumps are working.'

'That's the least of our worries.'

'Do you think the Fomorii are down here?'

'They might use some of the tunnel system, but they'll be going about their business. They won't be looking out for us.'

Ruth thought about this for a moment. 'Are you sure? They've always been pretty smart in their planning. Second-guessing us, setting up all those back-up plans if the main one didn't work. I know Calatin's gone, but there's always Mollecht and God knows what else—'

'Well, you be the bleedin' strategist, then.'

'I'm just offering an opinion. I'm allowed to speak, you know.'

'That's all you bleedin' well do.'

'Get lost.' She shoved him hard so he fell on to his injured ankle. He cursed vehemently and turned, his face transformed by fury, his fists bunched. It was so terrifying she dropped the torch, which sputtered and fizzled but didn't go out.

'Give me that!'

'No!' She fended him off and snatched up the burning wood.

'If the torches go out we're screwed!'

'I know that!'

'Well, keep a hold of it then, you stupid—'

'What?' She rounded on him.

'Nothing.' He realised he'd overstepped the mark.

'What were you going to say?' Her voice was edgy and shrill.

'Come on.' He marched on ahead sheepishly. 'Don't do this here,' he said under his breath, 'not in front of them.'

'Who cares what they think?'

'I do.'

They continued in silence for several minutes while Ruth's seething temper calmed. Finally she said, 'You should see a therapist about all that repressed anger. The slightest thing and it comes bursting out.'

He wasn't going to answer, but then he said quietly, 'It never used to be a problem.'

'You've had it as long as I've known you. And let me tell you, it's a liability. You fly off the handle at the slightest thing and you stop thinking rationally—'

'All right.'

'We can't afford that—'

'I said all right!' He realised a second later that he'd done it again, but instead of apologising he speeded up his step until he caught up with Lugh and the point men.

They continued that way for half an hour, with Ruth wrapped in a shroud of loneliness, listening to the unforgiving echoes bounce crazily around, hinting at strangers nearby but never quite revealing anything. No one spoke; the atmosphere had grown more intense the further they progressed into the tunnels. Ruth couldn't shake the feeling there was some terrible threat lying in front of them, staying only a step or two ahead of the advancing torchlight.

Veitch kept his head down, but she could tell from his rigid shoulders that he was aware of her behind him. She wondered if she had been too harsh on him; the strain had been making her increasingly snappy. The niggle of guilt she felt told her it probably wasn't as one-sided as she had pretended. Veitch had performed an exemplary service; if only the stupid emotional side didn't keep getting in the way, she would be able to give him the whole-hearted praise he really deserved.

As they passed through Archway station, the torchlight flared up over the tiled walls and a nagging doubt grew full-born. 'Where are the others?' she asked to no one in particular.

Veitch hesitated before turning round. 'Probably took a wrong turn somewhere,' he replied. Ruth thought he sounded a little abashed.

'With a whole army traipsing through here, you'd expect to hear some echoes. Wouldn't you?'

They all halted to listen. There was nothing at all; the air felt dead. 'Maybe they accidentally crossed over to the northbound tunnel,' Veitch suggested. 'Who knows? There might be a whole load of service tunnels we don't even know about. In the dark back there anyone could have taken a branching track without knowing.'

Veitch could easily have been right, but the weight on their hearts grew heavier nonetheless.

Ruth lost all track of time. The only sign of the passing minutes was the growing ache in her legs and the dull parade of platforms that had once meant nothing more than a commuter liminal zone between work and home. Now they were stations on the road to Hell, their names emblazoned on her mind: Tufnell Park, Kentish Town, Camden Town, Euston, King's Cross, Angel. She knew the next one would be Old Street and then they would be in the heart of the City. And by that time, she guessed, they would know exactly what troubles they were facing.

At one point, near King's Cross, they had heard the dim sound of clashing weapons and shouts echoing from one of the myriad tunnels converged there. They presumed it was the main Tuatha Dé Danann force encountering resistance somewhere.

Nuada was keen to reunite with his comrades to offer support if needed, but Veitch argued fiercely against this. The tunnel system was so complex the chances of locating them were slim – they could spend days wandering around down there, he stressed. And time was not on their side; at least some of them had to reach their destination.

After a heated debate, Nuada once again gave in, though Ruth could sense his patience with a *Fragile Creature* was growing thin.

Veitch came back to her side once Old Street and Moorgate stations were behind them. The air had grown several degrees colder and there was a deeply unpleasant smell that Ruth didn't want to examine too closely.

'Back in your good books now, am I?' she asked tartly and instantly hated herself, but she had been unable to resist the gibe.

This time it washed over Veitch; he had other things on his mind.

'Bank next. We'll have to go up top soon.' He paused. 'That fighting we heard must mean there *are* Fomorii down here. We've been lucky not to meet any of them.'

'Luck doesn't begin to explain it. I can't believe they've left one of the main routes into their most sacred places completely free from guards.'

Lugh hurried back, hushing them into silence.

'There,' Ruth hissed childishly, 'tempting Fate again.'

Distant sounds carried to them from ahead. It suggested many bodies on the move; the occasional foul stink caught on the air currents told them it was the Fomorii.

'They're going to push us all the way back to Moorgate before we can find somewhere to lie low,' Ruth said dismally.

'Shit!' Veitch looked around like a cornered animal. 'We can't waste the—'

One of the Tuatha Dé Danann was motioning to a shadowy area on the eastern wall. They hurried over to see a small tunnel wide enough for a couple of people. Veitch dived in to investigate. Less than a minute later he was back, grinning broadly. 'It leads to another tunnel. We can hide in there.'

'Haste, then,' Nuada said. 'They are almost upon us.'

They bustled in as silently as possible. They had barely vacated the Northern Line when they heard the heavy tramp of many feet drawing closer. From the noise and the time it took them to pass, Ruth guessed there must have been at least five hundred, possibly on their way to fight the Tuatha Dé Danann. She hoped that meant the Fomorii forces they were joining were doing badly.

At one point, it sounded like the Fomorii were coming down the connecting tunnel so they all hurried several hundred yards away and flattened themselves against the wall, desperately trying to shield their torches. After a couple of minutes, Ruth's pounding heart subsided a little.

The tunnel had patently not been used for a long time. Most of the tracks had been torn up, and the occasional signs appeared to date back to the earliest days of the tube system in the late nineteenth century. Ancient junction boxes rusted against bricks covered in the white salt of age and damp. Where the rails should have been there were numerous hummocks and rough piles that Ruth guessed were the dust-covered detritus of work on the other tunnel.

Once all the sounds of the Fomorii had faded away, they relaxed. 'God, they smell so bad!' Ruth protested.

'They are being driven by their Caraprix.' Nuada was looking back and forth along the tunnel. 'When the Caraprix take an active role in direction it stimulates a powerful aroma.'

'Even in you?' she said acidly.

'We, of course,' he said with a smile, 'smell divine.'

They set off back the way they had come, but after they had been walking for five minutes it became apparent to Ruth they had gone past the connecting tunnel in the dark. 'We must have missed it,' she called out to the others.

'I didn't see anything,' Veitch said, much to Ruth's irritation. 'Let's carry on a little way.'

Three minutes later their torches began to illuminate irregular shapes in the distant gloom. 'Look, it's a station,' Ruth sighed when they were closer. 'I told you we'd gone past it.'

Veitch held up his torch to read the sign over the platform. 'King William Street?' he said. 'Never heard of it.'

'It must be one they don't use any more,' Ruth said. 'There are quite a few, aren't there? But you're right, I've never heard of this one.'

Veitch's torch illuminated dirty, broken tiles and some torn, peeling posters. One said *Light's Out!* Another, *Loose Lips Sink Ships.*

'Looks like it was used as an air raid shelter in the Second World War,' Ruth said.

'We need more wood,' Lugh said. 'The torches are burning through quickly.'

'There might be some here,' Veitch said. 'Send your men in to check.'

Lugh eyed him darkly; this sounded very much like an order, but then he motioned for three of the Tuatha Dé Danann to investigate.

'What time do you reckon it is?' Veitch said, leaning against the edge of the platform.

Ruth shrugged. 'My body clock says eleven . . . midnight . . . Maybe later.'

'We should rest.'

Ruth was glad Veitch had raised it. She felt exhausted, but she was afraid to bring it up herself in case the others thought her weak. Nuada nodded in agreement and passed the information to his followers.

'We're close enough to spare a couple of hours,' Veitch continued. 'And we'd be no use to anyone if we turned up at the Big Bastard's door completely knackered.'

'You don't have to convince me.' Ruth clambered wearily on to the platform and found a spot against the wall at one end. Behind the windows of an old office she could see the torches of the Tuatha Dé Danann moving around like lazy fireflies as they searched for wood.

Nuada, Lugh and the others sat quietly at the other end of the platform, talking in low voices. Ruth was surprised when Veitch sat next to her; he didn't speak, but the fact that he was there was a loud statement. He closed his eyes and was asleep in an instant. Ruth wished she could rest just as easily, but by the time the thought had entered her head she was out.

She stirred uncomfortably, irritated by the cold surface of the hard platform floor against her behind. As her eyes flickered open when she tried to shift into a more comfortable position, she realised she couldn't have been asleep for very long at all because lights were still moving behind the office windows, beautiful, like a golden snowstorm, lulling her back to sleep.

She was so tired, enjoying the comfort of rest. Her limbs felt light and airy, after the leaden weight of the long march. Her troubled mind was cocooned in a fuzzy, yellow warmth. Yet as she tried to snuggle back into her pleasant state, she was annoyed to feel something nagging at the back of her mind. With annoyance, she tried to damp it down, but it wouldn't go away. The warmth slipped further away. Finally she realised the only way she was going to get any sleep was to examine it; something about what she had seen.

She opened her tired eyes again. The platform and track was quiet and still. The Tuatha Dé Danann sat in close conversation. Veitch was beside her asleep. Nothing out of the ordinary.

She tried again to get back to sleep, but it was lost to her now. The feelings of alarm wound up a notch. There *was* something there. What was she missing?

She looked around once more before settling on the light in the windows. She pulled herself shakily to her feet. Still half asleep, she focused hazily on the light shimmering through the panes. Earlier she had thought of it as fireflies, and now it seemed even more like that. Through her daze it was hypnotic in its dreaminess. Fireflies. No, more like butterflies. And then she had it. At first she felt shock, and then a deep iciness, before she was running along the platform to raise the alarm.

A face loomed up against the glass, hollow-cheeked, contorted with terror, a sight made worse by it being the face of a god. The eyes bulged, pleading with her, with anyone, and then it snapped away as if it was on elastic.

The clouds of golden moths ebbed and flowed, fluttering against the glass, caught in the torchlight.

'No more!' Lugh was yelling. 'How many Golden Ones must depart this day?' All the Tuatha Dé Danann looked on in horror, paralysed by

1274

the realisation that even away from the field of battle their kind were being wiped from existence in a manner they could never have realised in all their time.

Veitch powered past Ruth, his sword already out. 'No rest for the bleedin' wicked.' He levelled a flying kick at the office door. It burst from its hinges.

The three Tuatha Dé Danann lay dying on the floor, their bodies slowly breaking up. All around grey shapes flitted, although at first Ruth thought they were shadows cast by the flickering torches that lay where they had fallen.

While she was transfixed by the activity, Veitch was backpedalling along the floor where he had fallen and then propelled himself to his feet with undue haste, his sword waving in front of him. 'Shit,' he muttered.

'What is it?' Ruth asked.

Four figures burst from the doorway, their mouths held wide in an eerie silent scream, grey like mist, and at times just as insubstantial before there was the faintest shift and they took on a terrifying substance. They moved like light reflected off mirrors; Ruth only had an instant to take in their appearances: all women, beautiful in a haunted way, dressed in shrouds, their hair flying wildly behind them as if they had been caught in a storm. Ruth had a flash of talons like an animal's, of too-long teeth, sharp and pointed, and then they swept by her and she had only a second to throw herself out of the way.

The talons caught in her hair, ripped out a chunk, but she had avoided being caught; she had evaded those teeth.

'The Baobhan Sith!' one of the Tuatha Dé Danann said in fearful awe.

But Ruth didn't need reminding of the bloodsucking creatures that had attacked them on the lonely Cumbrian hills when Tom had betrayed them.

'They *did* have bleedin' guards posted!' Veitch threw himself out of the way of clutching hands, rolled and jumped to his feet. He lashed out with his sword, but it either passed through the creature or the Baobhan Sith avoided the blade so quickly Ruth didn't see it.

Veitch grabbed her wrist and pulled her out of the way of another of them. He chopped with his sword again. This time the spectral woman became mist as the blade cut through her, reforming as it passed.

'Christ, there's no fighting them!' He yanked Ruth hard and they both fell off the platform, landing with a bone-jolting impact on the hard stones of the track.

The Baobhan Sith moved up and down the platform wildly, twisting and turning in an imaginary wind, avoiding any attack the Tuatha Dé Danann made with any of their weapons. As Ruth watched in horror one of the creatures distended its mouth seemingly wider than its head and the razor sharp teeth folded out like kitchen knives. It flew towards one of Lugh's soldiers and clamped on his neck, the teeth snapping through the substance to suck up the god's essence; and however much he threw himself around or lashed out with his sword it could not be removed. A moment later the golden moths began to fly.

'Let's get out of here,' Veitch said quietly.

'We can't leave them!'

'We stay here, we die. There's too much at stake.' He could see she was still unconvinced and added, 'They'll soon catch up with us.'

The Tuatha Dé Danann already had formed a phalanx and were backing rapidly across the platform. One of the Baobhan Sith tore another from their midst.

'Look at that,' Veitch said. 'No point dragging our heels. Just bleedin' run.'

He made to grab Ruth's hand again, but she had jumped up to snatch a torch from the edge of the platform where it had fallen. Then she was sprinting at his side, glancing over her shoulder. One of the Baobhan Sith had left the platform to pursue them. 'They're coming!' Ruth gasped.

Their breath formed white clouds in the cold. Ruth was afraid she wouldn't have any energy left to escape. The ground was uneven, threatening to trip them, and the motion put the torch in danger of going out so that she had to shield it with her body. She didn't dare look over her shoulder any more because she couldn't go any faster if she tried.

'Which way? Where's the other tunnel?' Her thoughts fell over each other in her panic. *This is a nightmare.* The words blazed white against the background darkness of her mind.

'What's that?' Veitch was pointing into the shadows ahead; the edge in his voice turned her panic up a notch.

No more, she prayed.

There was movement on the ground ahead, not just in one spot, but in many. The soil and stone of the track floor was moving in little piles. Obliquely, Ruth realised it was the strange hummocks she had taken to be building rubble.

From one of them, a grey hand rose slowly.

Ruth couldn't restrain a brief shriek. They skidded to a halt. The hand became an arm as the stones and soil sloughed away. Across the myriad other humps the same scene was being played out as the

Baobhan Sith emerged from their resting places. Earth showered from their wild hair and fell from their open mouths as they levered their shoulders up, then their torsos. Their faces turned towards Veitch and Ruth, all of them shrieking in silence, scattered from wall to wall and away into the shrouded distance. Ruth was too terrified to consider how many of them were waiting there in the tunnel.

The sheer weight of terror elicited by the Baobhan Sith emerging left Veitch and Ruth rooted for an instant. But then Veitch shoved Ruth forward and they were sprinting once more, throwing themselves into a wild dance away from grasping hands.

Behind them, the first to emerge were already on their feet, shaking off the lethargy of slumber, flitting in pursuit. Ahead, the hummocks in gradual upheaval stretched on forever.

The Baobhan Sith rose up with increasing swiftness, and however fast Veitch and Ruth ran it was obvious they would soon be surrounded. Talons bit deeply into Ruth's ankle. She yelped as Veitch's flashing sword forced the creature to become insubstantial. They continued to drive forward, knowing that if they slowed an instant they would be lost, but already the Baobhan Sith were massing ahead of them.

A few seconds later the route ahead was blocked with shimmering bodies. 'Shit.' Veitch ground to a halt and whirled round, his eyes feral. The Baobhan Sith swept up from all sides.

Ruth jabbed a finger excitedly. 'There's the tunnel!'

To get to it would mean passing through the flickering creatures. Veitch gave Ruth a reassuring smile. 'Head down. Stay right behind me. Don't let them get a hold of you.'

He barrelled into the mass of them, lashing his sword in front of him. Ruth kept exactly in his step, her heart thundering as hands clutched at her clothes; some caught but were pulled free; others ripped through her hair without getting any purchase.

Just as they were about to dive into the tunnel, one of the Baobhan Sith latched on to Veitch. Ruth saw the transformation from mist to solid form as its mouth tore wide to expose the unbelievably pointed teeth. The powerful jaw muscles heaved as the head swept down to Veitch's neck.

At the last moment Ruth jabbed the Spear into the creature's mouth. The fangs smashed down on it and the thing shimmered into nothingness. Veitch dragged Ruth into the small tunnel.

Though breathless, they couldn't slow down. They could feel the presence of the Baobhan Sith at their backs like an icy shadow. In the main tunnel they headed southbound, acutely aware that they might run into more Fomorii and be trapped between the two forces.

The torch cast barely enough light to see, and it was hard running across the uneven tracks without tripping, but the Baobhan Sith drove on ceaselessly.

'They're not going to let up, are they?' Ruth gasped. 'What do we do – keep running until we're face to face with Balor?' At the mention of the name the air temperature noticeably dropped several degrees and a deep, resonant rustling, like whispering voices, rose up on the edge of their hearing. Ruth resolved not to say that name again.

'We've got to lose those grey bastards before we can do anything.' Veitch spotted another side tunnel, this time leading to the northbound tracks. He headed towards it. They continued southbound, both beginning to flag. A hundred yards further on they came upon a doorway leading to the conduit for power lines and fibre optics. The Baobhan Sith were almost upon them as Veitch wrenched the door open, thrust Ruth inside and slammed it shut behind him. He jammed his sword into the frame and twisted it so the handle wouldn't open.

They could sense the Baobhan Sith moving beyond the door as they collapsed against the wall and sucked in mouthfuls of air. 'That should hold them until they raise the alarm.' Veitch rubbed his tired eyes. 'Good job they're morons with no initiative.'

'We better get moving before the Fomorii turn up,' Ruth said. 'I tell you, I could do with a sleep.'

'We'll get some downtime once we find a safe place to hole up.'

'I suppose we've lost the others?'

'We can't go back for them, can we? They'll be there.' A heavy pause. 'At the end. You can count on it.'

The conduit lay beyond another door. It was lined with cables and wires, but they could walk along it at a stoop. Every time they came to a branching conduit, they turned, right, then left. After half an hour they found another inspection door and exited into a tunnel.

'Well, I have no bleedin' idea where we are now.' Veitch headed left, hoping it would lead them back towards the City.

'All we need to do is find another station.' Ruth eyed the torch worryingly; the flame was burning very low.

They continued along the tunnel for a little way until their path was blocked by a large, dark object: a tube train. 'Don't worry – we can squeeze by it,' Veitch said.

But as they edged along the side of the train, Ruth looked up and cried out in shock. The torchlight revealed the dirty windows were streaked with blood in explosive, paint-gun patterns. Inside she could just make out the shapes of bodies. It was hard to tell from her perspective, but they didn't appear to be in one piece. The sour-apple stink of decomposition was thick in the air.

Veitch noticed it too. 'The doors have been torn off,' he noted.

Ruth could just make out small figures too, and frail, old ones. She fought back tears; the terrible waste still tore a hole in her heart. 'The Fomorii must have moved out across the city through the network when their leader was reborn.'

Veitch peered in through the ragged doorway. 'Poor bastards. Didn't stand a chance.'

From ahead came the tramp of many feet. Ruth and Veitch were halfway along the carriage, squeezed tight against the dirty, oily walls. They wouldn't be able to make it back to the open tunnel before the Fomorii arrived.

'In here,' Veitch whispered. He crawled up through the doorway into the body of the carriage, pulling out his handkerchief and pressing it against his face. Ruth shook her head furiously in primal disgust, but she knew it was the best option. She screwed her eyes shut, covered her nose and mouth and followed Veitch in.

He guided her along the floor away from the open doors, but even with her eyes shut she had a visceral image of the scene around her. She brushed against hard and lifeless things that swung or shifted dramatically with a soft, wet sound. The floor was puddled with a thick, sticky substance; though her mouth was covered, the stench made her retch. Her stomach heaved time and again, and she didn't know how she managed to keep it silent, but then her eyes filled with tears at the thought of what had happened and somehow that helped.

Veitch took the torch, which was so low it barely cast any light, and said he'd shield it with 'something he'd found'; Ruth didn't ask what that was. They'd barely ended their exchange when the carriage rocked madly as the Fomorii barged past on either side. The two of them slid backwards and forwards on the slick floor. Ruth had to jam her hands and feet against the sides of the seats to stop herself skidding back towards the doorway. She almost lost her grip when Veitch slammed his boot-heel into her face, but a moment after that the violent movement subsided. They exited the carriage a little sooner than safety would have suggested, but even then they couldn't escape the stink from their fouled clothes; nor the thought of all the atrocities that had been committed.

A little further on they smelled smoke, and as they progressed they realised they could make out a faint glow tinting the tunnel walls. They moved in closer to one wall and edged forward cautiously. The smoke grew thicker, the light brighter.

Round a bend in the tunnel they glimpsed several fires burning. After so many hours of darkness it took a while for their eyes to adjust to the glare, and when they did they pulled back quickly. Several Fomorii were moving amongst piles of burning rubbish. It was obviously some kind of checkpoint or guard camp.

Veitch cursed quietly. 'We're never going to get past that.'

'I bet they've got camps like that all around the perimeter of their core area.'

'There was a door further back. We *will* find a way past the bastards.'

'I wish we could get some of that fire.' Ruth examined what remained of the torch.

They retraced their steps to an unmarked door almost lost in the gloom. Veitch used his dagger to smash the lock and they slipped into a clean corridor that led on to a large thoroughfare. It had a hard Tarmac surface and there were military-style stencils on the wall pointing to locations obviously written in code.

'These must be the tunnels the Government set up in the fifties and sixties in case of a nuclear strike,' Ruth said. 'A good way to save all the great and good and leave the poor bastards to die. Probably a favour. Who'd want to live in a world filled with politicians, the military, businessmen and the aristocracy?'

'We're well and truly bleedin' lost now,' Veitch said angrily. 'Why did it have to be me who fucked up again?'

When he was like that there was no consoling him. 'Pick a direction,' she said dismally. 'It'll take us somewhere.'

His anger grew more intense as it became obvious they were moving off the beaten track. The well-tended road gave way to rough ground, the tunnel became unfinished: bare brick, then girders and scaffolding, before they came to a thick barrier of sleepers and planks.

Veitch smashed his fist against the wall, as hard as if he was punching someone in the face, but his rage wiped away any pain he might have felt. When he turned, Ruth could see his knuckles were ragged.

She cowered as he stormed around searching for something to attack. 'We fucked up!' he yelled.

'We can go—'

'No! We! Can't!' His furious face thrust an inch away from hers. Suddenly she was terrified; she couldn't see any sign of the funny, gentle Veitch she had known from the quieter times they had shared.

She took a step back, but didn't show her fear. 'Pull yourself together.'

'What?' His eyes ranged wildly as though she wasn't there.

'I said, pull yourself together. You're the hero here—'

'Hero! I'm the bleedin' loser! Same as I always was!' He flailed his arm, obviously some sort of primal gesture to wave her away. But instead he caught the torch and knocked it from her weak grip. It smashed into pieces on the floor, the flame now a faint flicker along one of the shards.

'Ryan!' Ruth dropped to her knees desperately, but there was nothing to save.

'Oh, fuck! Now look what I've done!' He ran over and kicked the wall hard.

Ruth only saw what happened next from the corner of her eye as she bent down trying to pull the remaining pieces of wood together to keep the flame going. Weakened by his punches, the wall collapsed. Veitch plunged forward into a gulf beyond and a shower of rubble fell down re-closing the opening.

Ruth covered her head until the fall had ended, but none of the debris touched her. She looked at the faint flame and then slowly took in her surroundings.

'Oh, Ryan,' she whispered. And then the tears came in force.

When she finally regained control of her emotions, Ruth wiped her eyes and resolved to find a way out of her predicament. She wasn't going to be beaten. She certainly wasn't going to die down there. Balor had to be beaten, humanity had to be saved and, more importantly – she had to laugh at that strange truth – she had to see Church again. Even if she had to crawl along pitch-black tunnels to find a way out.

The flame was barely more than a candle's height on the splinters of wood. It became trimmed briefly with blue and then began to gutter.

Here we go, she thought. *Prepare yourself.*

Then, as the flame finally began to die, she became aware of other lights in the dark. At first she dismissed it as an optical illusion caused by the sharp contrast of shadow and light on her retina. The flame became the size of her fingernail.

Almost gone now.

But the other lights remained; tiny, glittering stars sweeping across the firmament. She scanned them curiously, and then, just as the flame finally died she realised what she was seeing and her blood ran cold.

Darkness swept up around her and she heard the sharp skittering sound as the first rat moved forward.

*

Veitch fell fifteen feet into freezing water, slamming his head hard on the way down. The cold and wet kept him conscious, but the dark was so all-consuming he couldn't tell up from down. The water came up to his thighs and by stretching out slowly on either side he realised he was in some kind of small tunnel or gully as wide as the span of his arms. He spent ten minutes trying to find where he had fallen and attempting to climb back up, but it was impossible to see, and more rubble kept falling. Dejected and afraid he might be pinned by another collapse, he began to wade wearily forward.

He continued for what he guessed was around an hour, pausing occasionally to rest against the wall and catch minutes of microsleep. He couldn't even feel his lower legs and he wondered how long it would be before hypothermia set in. But whatever set him apart as a Brother of Dragons made him resilient, helped him to heal; he'd keep going, he thought dismally. He hated himself. He hated himself so much he considered lying down in the water and drowning himself, but it wasn't in his nature. So he had to continue with the infinitely worse burden of his guilt, thinking about what he had done to Ruth, punishing himself by images of her wandering along inky corridors until the inevitable end came. It had all been his fault; he could almost have scripted it.

The water began to rise soon after, a half-hour later it was up to chest height. He was racked by convulsive shivers, drifting in and out of a fugue state brought on by the cold. Gradually he became aware that the tunnel was becoming increasingly steep. By the time he had grasped how sharply it was falling away, his feet would no longer give him purchase and suddenly he was sliding down. He barely had time to take a breath before the water washed above his head, and then he was rattling down an incline, faster and faster, until it became a vertical drop.

The rush of water burst out into thin air. He could vaguely feel his legs bicycling as he plunged thirty feet into more water, deeper this time and rushing in a torrent. One random thought flickered through his head: Ruth's beautiful face as she told him about London's old River Fleet, now buried beneath the city as it rushed down towards the Thames. And then the impact stole his consciousness and the water closed over his head.

CHAPTER NINETEEN

In the Belly of the Beast

Wave Sweeper was moored not far from Southend when Church came sweeping down from the north-west with the remainder of the Tuatha Dé Danann force. The journey skirting Greater London and through the green fields of rural Essex had passed in a golden blur. He was accompanied by Tom, the Bone Inspector and Niamh, but he didn't recognise any of the other gods, although he sensed many of them were not sympathetic to the cause of the *Fragile Creatures*. He wondered why his particular task force was burdened with more dissenters than the other two, but Tom wasn't too concerned when he raised the matter.

On board it felt strangely good to be back in the familiar detachment of Otherworld with its heightened sensations, away from all the suffering of the real world. There was an atmosphere of stillness that eased the anxiety coiled in his chest; even the sun was shining brighter than on the shore. He made his way to the rail where he quietly enjoyed the tang of the sea and the warmth on his skin, until Tom joined him.

'You're going to bring me down, aren't you?' Church said without looking round.

'I'm the last person to advocate an injection of reality, but—'

'I know: responsibility, obligation, and all that. Is this the standard pre-crisis pep talk?'

'Something like that.' Tom leaned against the rail, facing the sun, his eyes closed. 'You know, I can remember the days of my youth as clearly as if they were yesterday. Hundreds of years – although it's not really, not by Otherworld time. But it's still a long, long time and so many experiences.' He took a deep breath. 'I smell the blossom in the garden of my childhood, so powerful, like incense and fruit wrapped up together. I remember distinctly the way the sunlight caught the dew on a spiderweb in an old yew tree, one dawn when I had crept out of the house before anyone had awoken. The rosewater on the neck of the first woman I ever loved. The touch of her fingers on the back of my neck.' He shook his head dreamily. 'Amazing.'

Church watched Tom curiously. He had never heard him speak so tenderly, nor talk of any of the happy times in his human life before his transformation at the hands of the Tuatha Dé Danann Queen. It was as if he had wanted to keep them secure from the horrors that had assailed him since.

'Now I begin, for the first time in many years, the memories come thick and fast.' Tom's eyes glistened in the sun. 'Days of tenderness, composing songs and poems. Nights watching the stars over the Eildon Hills. My mother and father, at Christmas, leading the singing before the fire. My best friend James, playing hide-and-seek in the kitchens, then later courting the girls from the village together.' He turned fully to Church with no attempt to hide his tears. 'Remember your own bright moments, Jack, and hold them in your heart. They will keep you warm in the coldest nights.'

'Why are you telling me these things?'

'Nothing I could say would help you to comprehend right now. You will understand everything presently.'

Church tried to glean some insight from Tom's face, but he was taken aback to see it was packed with complex emotions. For so long, Tom had appeared to have no feeling in him at all; as inhuman as he always believed himself to be. It felt like a sea-change had come over him, even in the last hour. 'What's happened to you?'

'Time has come a-calling. Finally.'

Church could see he was not going to get anything out of the Rhymer; infuriatingly, his friend's unexplained words worked their way deep into his mind, where they set off a troubling resonance.

While he wrestled with his thoughts, he scanned the deck where the crew busied themselves for departure. The main Tuatha Dé Danann force had all disappeared below with their weapons. Manannan stood at the wheel, overseeing the activity. He raised a hand in greeting when he saw Church.

'I hope you're telling him what a pathetic little runt he is.' The Bone Inspector's gruff voice shattered the mood in an instant. He leaned on his staff, the wind whipping his grey hair.

Tom snapped, 'No—'

'I was talking to him.' The Bone Inspector nodded towards Church.

'Don't start with your useless prattling.' Tom eyed him murderously.

'You may have been honoured by the Culture in the times of my ancestors, but that doesn't mean I can't give you a good whupping with my staff.' The Bone Inspector underlined his point by twirling the staff around his arms as if it were alive.

'Great. Two old people fighting,' Church muttered. 'It'll be like watching your granny barge her way into the bread queue.'

'Don't forget,' Tom cautioned the Bone Inspector, 'the Culture dies out with you.' He smiled sadistically.

'Well, that's where you're wrong. I've been making some plans—'

'Don't you think that's a little premature?' Church said.

'You shut up and concentrate on your job, you lanky-arsed weasel.' The Bone Inspector returned his attention to Tom, nodding superciliously. 'Yes, I've been thinking. Now the seasons have turned and all the materialistic, logic-obsessed bastards have had a rude awakening, it might be time for a reflowering of the Culture. I can see the colleges now, maybe at Glastonbury and Anglesey, like we used to have in the old, old days. Passing on the wisdom to a new generation of bright-eyed—'

'You think you'd make a good teacher?' Tom sneered. 'After all that time sleeping in ditches they'll need to hose you down with industrial cleaning fluid just to get somebody in a room with you.'

The Bone Inspector scowled. 'At least I know my arse from my elbow.'

'Yes, but do you know your arse from your mouth? I think not.'

Church sighed and made to pacify them, but they turned on him so venomously he backed away. 'Okay, go ahead, knock yourself out,' he said tartly. 'Literally, if possible.'

The bickering ended when Niamh walked over. Tom gave a restrained, deferential bow, but the Bone Inspector simply looked away, as if he were alone on deck and lost in a reverie.

'The Master is preparing to sail,' she said. She glanced round to ensure she could not be overheard, then added quietly, 'Taranis oversaw the arrival of a container brought aboard by Nuada's personal guard. It was stowed in a section of the hold where access is restricted only to the Master and Taranis. Those faithful to Nuada stand guard without.'

'I think I saw it,' Church said. 'Was it a large wooden chest with bands of iron around it and a gold clasp?'

'That may be how you perceived it.' Niamh looked from one to the other. 'I believe it to be the Wish-Hex.'

'They won't even let you near it?' Church asked.

She bit her lip. 'I could attempt . . . It would cost . . .' She shook her head. 'No matter. There is too much at stake.'

Church looked to Tom. 'When do you think they'll detonate it?'

'When it's close to Balor and they're well away.'

'Not on board ship?'

'Good Lord, no!' Tom looked horrified. 'And lose Wave Sweeper? This isn't just a collection of timber and nails, you know!'

Church took Niamh's hand and led her to one side. 'I know this is hard for you, working against your own people, but if there's anything you can do—'

'Do not feel you have to ask anything of me, Jack. I do what I do freely because I believe in the rightness of this course. And I believe in you.' She looked down at where her slim, cool hand still lay in his. 'You have changed my existence, Jack. And to one of the Golden Ones, who are as constant as the stars, that is a humbling and profound thing.'

'I don't see how I could have, Niamh,' he protested. 'I'm nothing out of the ordinary.'

She leaned forward to kiss him gently on the cheek. 'Things are coming to a head, Jack. All will be made clear soon.'

Her smile was filled with such deep love he was left floundering. She turned and drifted away amongst the frantic activity of the crew, an oasis of calm and dignity.

The ship hove to soon after and made its way into the Estuary. Though it still remained a tranquil place, the strain on all who sailed was apparent. Tom rejoined Church at the prow, looking around nervously. 'Now if we can get to that pep talk without any interruptions from that old curmudgeon . . .' He pointed to the makeshift rucksack hanging from Church's shoulder. 'You have the Wayfinder?'

Church removed the old lantern with the flickering blue flame that had guided him through the earliest days of the mystery to show him. 'But I don't know what use it's going to be. I was thinking of leaving it here. I don't want to be carrying any more weight than necessary.'

Tom shook his head furiously. 'There is still one talisman to find.' His smile suggested this was another long-kept secret he was relieved to be revealing. 'The biggest one of all.'

'Where is it?'

'Somewhere near our destination. You recall when we summoned the Celtic dead for guidance in Scotland? They said: *You must find the Luck of the Land if you are ever to unleash the true power of the people.*'

'Yes,' Church said suspiciously, 'and you said you had no idea what they were talking about.'

'At that *exact* moment, I did not. But it came to me soon after. There was only one thing it could be.'

Church bared his teeth. 'And you didn't see fit to tell me until now?'

Tom shrugged dismissively. 'The time was not right.'

'Tom . . .'

'All right,' he snapped. 'I wanted only you to know. And I left it to this late stage because I did not want you to confide in any of the

others, as you undoubtedly would have done with your various romantic liaisons,' he added sniffily. 'And then it would have been all over the
place.'

'All right. No need to act like my granddad.'

'It is my role to be—'

'All right, all right! What is the bloody Luck of the Land?'

'The Luck of the Land is the severed head of Bran the Blessed. He was
a great hero, and the closest of the Golden Ones to humanity. He knew
about the destiny of the *Fragile Creatures* and he was even prepared to
sacrifice himself to see us achieve it. The old stories tell how he was
murdered by a poisoned arrow. On his deathbed, he told his followers
to cut off his head, yet even removed, it could still eat and talk. It was
brought back to London and buried beneath the Tower, where it
became the source of the land's power. Of humanity's power. Another
myth said King Arthur sought it out as the source of his own strength.
You can see the symbolism.'

'So it's linked directly to the Blue Fire? That's what all the Arthur
myths mean, isn't it?'

'Correct.'

Church looked out at the quiet, dead countryside that bordered the
river. 'But what can it *do*?'

'The Celts revered severed heads, believing them to have great
magical power. In their view, the head is the source of the soul. They
knew the truth at the heart of this legend. And don't forget . . .'

'. . . myths and legends are the secret history of the land. I'll be
happy when I don't hear that phrase again.'

'The head has great power, both in real terms, and symbolically. It
encompasses everything you have discovered about the Blue Fire.'

'So, in the day and a half we have left, we have to avoid Balor and
about a million Fomorii in the heart of their power, locate this head
somewhere under the Tower of London – like it's going to be just lying
around ready to be picked up – and then find some way to use it or
activate it or whatever the hell you're supposed to do with it?'

'Well, you didn't expect it to be easy, did you?' Tom said curtly. 'If
you only had to waltz in there and chop off a head or two they could
have got anyone to do it.'

'I'll take that as a vote of confidence,' Church said moodily.

All that remained of the Thames Barrier flood defence system were
columns of concrete and twisted steel jutting out of the slow-moving
water. It looked as if it had been smashed into pieces by a giant fist.
The rubble just beneath the surface formed a treacherous defence that

would have sunk most ships coming up the river, but Manannan's magical skill picked the only path through. It slowed them down a little, but they were still on course to be in the heart of London by noon.

As they progressed further into the eastern fringes of the capital, the mood on Wave Sweeper darkened considerably. The pleasant sunshine was soon blocked out by continually rolling black clouds whipped by the powerful winds circulating the city. It brought the temperature down several degrees while adding a permanent gloom to the cityscape. Vast swathes of south-east London were burning, bringing huge clouds of smoke rolling across the river. Church fastened a scarf across his mouth, but the foul smell of charred plastics and rubber still stung his throat.

As he saw the city up close for the first time, Church thought of all the people he knew who lived there, his old friends, like Dale, who had done so much to try to lift his spirits in the dark weeks after Marianne's death. Had they survived? Had they suffered? It was too depressing to consider, and he was almost pleased when Tom grunted, 'Not as bad as the Great Fire.'

'Things always were better in the good old days, weren't they?'

The ship suddenly lurched dramatically to the starboard. Church gripped the rail to avoid being thrown into the grey waters. A second later it was swinging back the other way. 'What's going on?' he shouted over the wild activity that had erupted on deck. The crew struggled to restrain any item that wasn't lashed down, while Manannan fought with the wheel to keep Wave Sweeper steady.

Tom pointed into the water further upstream. A black, sinuous shape stitched white surf into boiling water.

'Their guard dog,' Tom said.

'Dogs,' Church corrected. Two more serpentine shapes rolled in the waves. Their attacks were throwing up so much backwash the ship was buffeted back and forth. They were tiny compared to the monster that had attempted to sink Wave Sweeper in Otherworld, but their speed and random, darting movements made them equally dangerous.

The ship sloughed towards the north bank before executing a sharp turn towards the south, rapid manoeuvres that no real-world craft would ever be able to complete. Members of the crew sprawled across the desk, clutching for handholds. Church and Tom were drenched by the eruptions of water as the serpents threw themselves against the sides, either in an attempt to hole the ship or to turn it over.

A shadow fell across them. Church knew what it was before he looked up. The serpent's head towered over them, the same terrifying features he had glimpsed in the sea off Skye: a flattened cobra head, yellowish eyes glowing with an alien intelligence, strange whiskers like a catfish tufting from its mouth, which contained several rows of lethal teeth.

It hovered for a second or two, during which time Church felt the faintest contact with an intelligence that fizzed in the back of his head. He knew what it was going to do before the head darted down towards them, jaws prised wide. Church rolled over and pulled the Sword from its scabbard, jabbing it upwards towards the descending darkness. It impaled the head as if it were slipping through crude oil. The serpent made a high-pitched mechanical whine as it thrashed madly. Church felt an electric jolt in that deep connection the serpent had made with him. An instant later it transformed into a searing scream. Caledfwlch's particular powers ensured that death always resulted from the slightest injury it inflicted.

Church tried to retreat from the bond the serpent had made with him, but it was locked in place. He felt its life force flare briefly, then dwindle down into a dark tunnel before finally winking out. Its body slipped back into the water, lifeless.

The shock of feeling the beast's final moment left Church dazed and distressed. Tom shook him roughly to bring him round, but the sensations stayed with him like a shadow in his subconscious.

Wave Sweeper continued to lurch from side to side. By then the Tuatha Dé Danann forces had made it on to the deck with several silver weapons resembling harpoons plugged into grenade launchers. Three of them manhandled one to the rail and launched it.

Lightning crackled out across the water. It headed towards the north bank, and then made an unnatural dogleg to the right to strike one of the serpents as it attempted to dive. The creature burst from the water, stinking foully as it charred. A moment later, its shrivelled form drifted downstream.

The remaining serpent was retreating as the Tuatha Dé Danann struck. It was eradicated just as quickly.

Tom saw Church eyeing the weapons cautiously. 'Yes,' he said. 'They are too powerful to be in hands that cannot be trusted.'

Manannan forged on quickly along the centre of the channel. Church watched the banks intently, but he could see no sign of any Fomorii threat. Yet the air of incipient danger grew more and more intense until deep, rhythmic vibrations began to run through Church's legs; it was accompanied by a distant noise, almost too low to be heard beneath the wind. Something about it made his stomach turn. 'What is that?' he asked.

Tom stared into the water darkly. 'The beating of Balor's heart.' The wind whipped at him.

Soon after the smoke and river fog closed in around the ship, limiting vision to a few yards ahead. Manannan let Wave Sweeper drift slowly. The crew remained silent, listening intently for any sound of attack.

Thoom. Thoom. Thoom. The beating had grown a little louder. Church felt it in the pit of his stomach.

And then the obscuring mists parted and Church's blood ran cold. A black tower soared up from the northern bank, its top lost in the clouds above. It rested on the remnants of the Tower of London, the ancient fortress that symbolised the defence of the nation, and was constructed like a termite nest from rubble, crushed vehicles, plastics, household refuse, girders torn from other buildings and anything else that came to hand. Slowly Church looked up the structure as far as he could see. Fires blazed at various points, some inside seen through ragged windows, some on the surface where the leftovers of the twenty-first century still burned. It was a sinister mockery of the gleaming skyscrapers that rose out of the City's financial district only yards away, another source of unbridled power.

As he watched, there was movement through the windows and a second later winged Fomorii burst out in a massive swarm. They swooped up as one, then hurtled down towards Wave Sweeper.

The Tuatha Dé Danann were prepared. The harpoons that had made short shrift of the serpents were hooked upwards and unleashed. Lightning crackled across the sky, tearing holes in the Fomorii swarm before the harpoons were drawn back, reloaded and fired again.

Some of the Fomorii made it through and engaged with the Tuatha Dé Danann in fierce fighting across the deck. Church ran into the fray wielding Caledfwlch. Wherever he went the Tuatha Dé Danann stepped aside deferentially. The Fomorii he encountered shrivelled in the air like dry autumn leaves and fluttered into nothingness on the wet boards.

But the Fomorii were proving too numerous. Many of the Tuatha Dé Danann were driven over the rails into the river or carried off into the black tower to meet an undoubtedly hideous fate. Others were torn apart as the winged menace descended on them like raptors. Manannan kept the ship going at full speed, steering it as far towards the south bank as he could without running aground.

A difficult course had to be navigated through the remains of the shattered bridges – London, Southwark, Blackfriars and Waterloo – but eventually they rounded a bend in the river and the swarms of Fomorii began to fall back.

Finally, the aerial assault ended. Church slumped against the mast, exhausted. 'I can't believe they've left us alone.'

Tom, who had kept well out of the trouble, replied, 'It is just a lull, a regrouping. They will be back in force soon.'

'Then we better get to where we're going quickly.'

The parade of broken bridges continued apace: Westminster, Lambeth, Vauxhall, Chelsea. But then the familiar site of the Battersea Park Peace Pagoda loomed up out of the smoke, reminding Church of Sundays spent walking there with Marianne. Finally the remains of Albert Bridge came into view, as misty as the day when it all started for Church so many months before.

He felt a brief *frisson* as the images flooded into his mind: the figure washing his head in the water, the first meeting with Ruth, the trip beneath the bridge and his first encounter with one of the Fomorii before it murdered Maurice Gibbons.

'If I'd known then what I know now . . .' he said.

'Be thankful you *don't* know what lies ahead,' Tom said darkly.

As they prepared to drop anchor, Church headed below deck to find Niamh so he could say goodbye to her; he felt he owed her that at least. He searched for fifteen minutes with a number of Tuatha Dé Danann pointing him this way and that. Eventually he saw her emerging from a cabin in an area set aside for the Tuatha Dé Danann force. He called her name and was instantly surprised by what he saw on her face: unmistakable shame. She attempted to walk away as if she had not heard him, then thought better of it.

'What's wrong?' he asked, honestly concerned.

She forced a smile before leading him away from the door a few paces. 'I will be allowed to accompany the small group Nuada has placed in charge of the Wish-Hex.'

'To Balor? I don't think I like that. You'd be better off here.'

'Why? Because you think I have not been in a dangerous situation before?'

'No, because I don't want you to get hurt.' He shrugged, uncomfortable at the open way she was watching him. 'The others I don't care about—'

She placed a hand on his forearm to stop him. 'That makes it all worthwhile, Jack. There is no need to say any more. But I must come, for the Wish-Hex is now my responsibility, and your survival is my responsibility. If I am not there, you may die.'

'Maybe—'

'That is the way it is.'

The door swung open on the cabin Niamh had just exited and one of Nuada's lieutenants swaggered out. He cast a glance at Niamh, then moved lazily towards the stairs.

Church looked from him into Niamh's face, but he couldn't find the words to express the thoughts that were suddenly falling into place.

She saved him the trouble. 'We all do what we can, Jack.'

Deeply troubled at what he had forced upon her, Church made his way back to the deck where Tom and the Bone Inspector were waiting for him. They would be going ashore with a small group of Tuatha Dé Danann briefed by Nuada before he'd left with Lugh and Veitch. Another group would remain to guard the entrance to the tunnels so no Fomorii could come up behind them, while the remainder would stay on board Wave Sweeper to take the fight back to the enemy, as a distracting ploy more than anything.

'I want to know who's in charge,' the Bone Inspector said. He patently wasn't going to accept any answer that included the Tuatha Dé Danann.

'The Brother of Dragons will lead the way,' Taranis said in his usual aloof manner. 'However, the Golden Ones who will be accompanying you must be free to follow their own hearts if the need arises.'

Church knew what that meant – they must be free to sneak off to unleash the Wish-Hex.

While they prepared for a boat to be lowered, no one noticed the dark figure slip out from the place where he had been hiding for so long, living on the blood and meat of rats and other foul creatures. Nor did they hear the faint splash as he slipped into the cold water and swam quickly to the shore. Callow had bided his time well and now things were working out better than he could have dreamed.

The area beneath the bridge gave Church an uncomfortable feeling. Despite the fact that most of the span was missing, it was still uncommonly dark. An unpleasant atmosphere set his nerves on edge.

The Tuatha Dé Danann stood back to allow Church to search for an opening. They gathered protectively around the large chest that he knew contained the Wish-Hex. Niamh was with them, pretending to be aloof from the *Fragile Creatures*.

'I don't know how I'm going to find this,' he said after five minutes wandering around the featureless area.

The Bone Inspector swore profusely. 'Call yourself a leader of men?' He marched past Church and rammed his staff against a stone set into the wall on which the bridge's foundations were set. The ground fell away with a ghostly silence. 'After you,' he said sarcastically.

The tunnel was rough-hewn, dripping with water that ran in rivulets along the edges. It was only wide enough for two people to walk side by side, though the ceiling was high enough to accommodate the Fomorii bulk. It sloped down quickly into deep shadows. Tom lit a torch they had brought with them, as did one of the Tuatha Dé Danann.

Then, when they had all steeled themselves, Church and Tom led the way, with the Bone Inspector close behind and the rest coming up at a distance as if they were barely connected.

When the tension of entering enemy territory had ebbed a little, the thought that had been troubling Church the most rose to the surface. 'I've just been talking to Niamh,' he whispered to Tom. 'I got a hint she knows what's going to happen.'

'They all do.'

'I don't get it. How does that work? Even you, you're always talking darkly about what the future holds like you know it inside out.'

Tom said nothing, but Church wasn't prepared to let it lie. This was fundamental.

'If everything is set in stone,' he stressed to get a reaction, 'what's the point?'

'It isn't like that.'

'Then what is it like?'

Tom sighed. 'It is beyond your perception.'

'Then put it in simple terms. For a stupid old country boy.' Church thought about adding a few choice words, but decided it would be unproductive.

'Those who can see the future – although that's really not the right term for it – see it as a series of snapshots, not as a movie. Sometimes there is no context. Sometimes the photos are out of order. Reading meaning in them is a dangerous business. You recall, I described it once as catching glimpses from the window of a speeding car.'

'But it's still fixed.'

'Nothing is fixed. Anywhere.'

Church cursed quietly. 'Just give it to me straight, instead of packaged around your usual—'

'Everything can be changed by the will of a strong individual. One man. Or woman. There are no rules, not at the level the great thinkers of humanity examined, anyway. Only the illusion of rules. The future runs right on like a river, but it can be turned back by someone with the right heart and drive and state of mind. What the old storybooks laughingly call a hero. The Tuatha Dé Danann pretend they know everything that's going to happen and that has happened, pretend it even to themselves, but you can see from the way they've been acting in the last few hours that in their hearts they know the truth. What they perceive might not turn out to be the way it appears, or perhaps they have missed part of the equation. Or perhaps someone like you will come along. There is a reason for free will, Jack.'

Church thought about this for several minutes. It gave him a deep feeling of comfort, although he couldn't quite tell why. 'Then you don't *really* know anything.'

Tom remained silent for a long, uncomfortable moment. 'That's not quite true. Some things are so weighed down by the monumental events around them that they might as well be set in stone.'

However much Church questioned him about this, he would say no more. But Tom's words had set other thoughts in motion. Barely daring to ask, he said firmly, 'Do you know who's going to betray us?'

Tom kept his eyes fixed firmly ahead.

'You do, don't you?' His anger rose quickly. After all the months of worry, Tom could have told them at any time. 'Why didn't you say something? You know it could mean everything might fall apart! You've got to tell me!'

'I can't.' Tom's face was unreadable.

'Even with the potential repercussions? Why not? Do you want to see us suffer?'

Tom rounded on him furiously. 'Of course not! I can't tell you because there's too much that might be changed.'

'How long have you known?'

'I've always known.'

'Always?'

'Always. And if you'd been paying attention, you would have known too.'

The words were like a slap to the face. In the space between seconds, a million memories flashed across his mind as he turned over everything he had seen and heard over the previous months. Had he missed something? Had he screwed up again? 'I guess I'll know soon enough,' he said with bitter resignation. 'I just hope you can live with yourself when it comes out.'

The tunnel followed an undulating path, the changes in the air pressure telling Church it regularly ran under the river. He had taken to holding the Wayfinder permanently aloft so the walls were painted with a sapphire wash. The tiny blue flame gave him a measure of encouragement in that dark place, and raised the spirits of Tom and the Bone Inspector too. The flame pointed dead ahead.

'Why didn't it lead us to the head before?' Church asked.

'Because it is responding to what you hold in your heart,' Tom replied.

'It's alive?'

'As much as anything can be said to be alive, yes.'

When they'd been walking an hour or more, the Wayfinder flame began to grow brighter. At the same time, the unnerving background beat became rapidly louder. Within ten minutes it was coming through the walls all around – BA-DOOM, BA-DOOM – a war drum marking their passage to disaster.

Two and a half hours later, the tunnel rose up, while at the same time becoming more formed, with props and stone lining the walls. The Wayfinder's flame had started to point away from the main route of the tunnel so that when they came to a large oaken door Church was prepared for it.

'Looks like we're here,' he said. The door was locked, but Caledfwlch sliced through the rusty iron mechanism easily. Church looked around at the others. Tom and the Bone Inspector were grim-faced, the Tuatha Dé Danann impassive, Niamh concerned and colourless; they all nodded.

He yanked open the door.

It felt like they had walked into a foundry. After the chill of the tunnel, the heat was stifling, the air suffused with the smell of acrid smoke that caught the back of their throats. The thunder of Balor's heart was almost deafening.

The stone walls and flagged floor suggested they were somewhere in the lowest level of the Tower of London. The Bone Inspector breathed deeply, despite the atmosphere. 'Can you feel it? Ancient power, even though those bastards have tried to pervert it. I haven't been here for years – too many people. Should have come back sooner.' He looked at Church. 'This place was sacred long before they threw up this mountain of stone over the top of it. If any place can be called the heart of the country, it's here.'

The Tuatha Dé Danann set the chest containing the Wish-Hex down in the middle of the room. 'What *is* in that box?' Church said mockingly. Nuada's lieutenant didn't reply, didn't even acknowledge he had spoken. Church caught Niamh's eye as he turned back to the others and she gave him a secret nod. 'We need to move quickly,' he continued. 'They might already know we're here—'

'The Wayfinder will blind Balor's perception to you, at least for a while,' Tom said. 'And if you hadn't brought the energy flow back to life at St Michael's Mount you wouldn't be here at all.'

Church made to follow the lantern's flame until he saw the Tuatha Dé Danann were not moving. 'We shall wait here,' Nuada's lieutenant said.

'I'd say we've got even less time than we thought,' Church said under his breath to Tom and the Bone Inspector as they left the room.

The seething heat had them all red-faced and soaked in sweat before they had got very far along the maze of once-dank corridors. Church had visited the Tower before and had never seen any sign of that area, so he guessed it must lie beneath the zone normally open to the tourists. He had the Sword at the ready, but the entire lower level was deserted.

'They're all up top throwing rocks at the boat,' the Bone Inspector said, but Church wasn't convinced.

The Wayfinder led them to a short corridor that ended in a dead end. At first sight there was nothing out of the ordinary, but then Church allowed his perceptions to shift until he could see the lines of Blue Fire running through the stone like veins, converging into the circular design of a serpent eating its own tail. He steeled himself, then placed his hand hard on the pattern. The wall ground open to reveal a shaft plunging down into the earth, the bottom lost in shadows.

The Bone Inspector leaned in to inspect it. 'There are handholds cut into the stone.' He tucked his staff into the back of his shirt and levered himself over the lip. 'Don't know why they made these things so bloody lethal. One slip and there'll be a mess on the floor.'

The Bone Inspector had disappeared from view and Tom was just about to follow when they heard the faintest sound behind them. They spun round to find the corridor filled with Fomorii. And at the head of them was a frantically fluttering mass of crows.

Church had sheathed Caledfwlch to open the doorway, but it was back in his hand in an instant. Before the first Fomorii could move, he was advancing quickly, swinging the Sword back and forth in an arc. His target was Mollecht, the leader, the most powerful. Faced with the enemy, the Sword was even more alive in his hands than he recalled. Its subtle shifts of weight forced his hand in different directions to make the most exacting of strikes, while at times he felt it squirm so hard it almost leapt from his fingers.

But before he had gone three paces, the Fomorii had closed around Mollecht to protect him. They were obviously aware of Caledfwlch's abilities, but they showed no sign of self-preservation at all. Church carved through them as they flooded forwards ceaselessly, the bodies falling then shrivelling to nothing at each cut of the blade.

Sweat rolled off him as he hacked and lunged in the sweltering heat. Eventually he began to make some headway. Soon he could see Mollecht once more, directing the Fomorii silently. It was enough to drive him to renew his efforts. He hit one high, spun round and caught another low, and then took out three with one blow. And then Mollecht stood before him once more.

But the hideous creature was prepared. As the final Fomorii fell away, Church saw the birds moving aside to open a hole that revealed the entity inside; his mind was as unable to accept it as the first time he had witnessed it at Tintagel. The energy inside the hole was already swirling and on the brink of erupting.

Tom thrust Church out of the way. The blast hit the Rhymer full on and within a second the blood was starting to seep through his pores. Church had no time to help. The Sword was tugging at his hand, as aware of the opportunity as Church himself. Mollecht had drained himself. It would be a moment or two before he had the strength to make another attack, or even to defend himself. The hole was already closing. Church drove the Sword horizontally towards the centre of it. The creature would be skewered, finally.

The dark shape exploded out of nowhere. Church only caught the briefest glimpse out of the corner of his eye before it slammed into him with force, knocking him to the hard stone floor. Caledfwlch went flying from his grip.

'Do I have to do everything round here?'

The voice stunned Church just enough to hamper his reactions, and by that time a figure had jumped on to his chest, pinning his arms over his head. He found himself looking up into the monstrous black-veined face of Callow. He was gloating in every fibre of his being.

'I want your finger, Mr Churchill, and I want it at the knuckle. I've decided to make a necklace,' Callow said gleefully.

And then the Fomorii were all around him, swamping him in darkness.

Church came round in a place that was dark and so unbearably hot he thought he was going to choke. Twisted leather bonds bound him to a splintered table fastened to an iron gear system that angled it forty-five degrees from the upright. Aches and bruises buzzed in his limbs, but beyond that he was in one piece. Scant, scarlet light was provided by a glowing brazier in one corner. As his eyes grew accustomed to the gloom, he saw with a sickening chill where he was. Cruel, sharp implements hung from a rack on one wall, reminding Church how adept the Fomorii were at torture.

The thought was knocked aside by the blunt realisation that he had failed, at the very last, after so many obstacles had been overcome; and that it wasn't even he alone who would pay the price. It was all of humanity, everyone he had ever loved.

He tore at the bonds until he was disturbed by a low groan away to his right. The figure lay like a bundle of old rags in a slowly growing pool of blood. The moonlight glow of his skin, tinged blue at his fingers, told Church he was dying. 'Can you hear me?' Church asked gently.

There was no reply or movement for a second or two and then Tom tried to lever himself up on his elbow before slipping back. He made two more attempts and then managed to roll on to his back so he could look at Church. His face was covered with blood still seeping from his pores. Church felt a wash of despair.

'If there's anything you want to get off your chest, now's the time to do it,' Tom said gruffly, though his voice could barely be heard above the thunderous heartbeat.

'You saved my life.'

'Lot of good it did you.'

'I'm sorry,' Church said, 'I let you down. If only I'd moved quicker.'

'Nonsense.' Tom coughed violently. 'You have exceeded my wildest expectations. From the first time we met I could see you were the right man for the job. Oh, I know I never said it – couldn't have you getting a big head – but you were the best possible choice, Jack. The very best.'

'I wish you'd said that before.' Church closed his eyes, trying to deal with all the acute emotions bubbling through him. 'I've still failed, though.'

'You're breathing, aren't you?'

A thought sparked in Church's still awakening mind; he looked around as best he could. 'Hang on. Just you and me?'

'So it seems.' There was a note of caution in Tom's voice not to say any more.

Church knew how resilient the Bone Inspector was. If he had managed to evade the Fomorii, there was still a slim chance. 'How long was I out?' he said with renewed enthusiasm.

'I would say it's getting on for dawn. Not long to the feast of Samhain. The gates will be opening soon. The Heart of Shadows will get all the power he needs.' He coughed then added quickly, 'Don't mention its name. Not here, not this close to it. The repercussions might be . . .' His voice faded.

'The Sword?'

'Behind you. And the Wayfinder. They can't touch them, you know, even with the massive advances in their power. They have to rely on Callow.'

'That bastard. I was convinced he'd died on Wave Sweeper. He's like a cockroach – stamp on him and he just keeps on running.'

'If you get free . . .' Tom gave a hacking wet cough '. . . you must use the Wayfinder.'

'To find what? The head?'

'No. Think of the symbolism. What it *means*. It is a lantern that will light your way to the true path. It has a direct access to the source of the Blue Fire. I always told you to keep it close to you because . . .' Another cough; something splattered on the stone '. . . it's more important than you thought.'

Tom fell silent; Church couldn't even hear his ragged breathing any more. 'Tom?' he called out, fearing the worst.

'Yes. I'm here. It's nearly time.'

'For what?'

'Remember what I said to you. On the ship. About keeping your memories close to you. They're your Wayfinder, Jack.'

Tears stung Church's eyes. 'Just hang on—'

'No. This is no surprise to me. I've had the chance to prepare myself.'

Church forced himself to keep his voice steady. 'How long have you known?'

'A long time. Longer than you've been alive.'

Church couldn't begin to imagine how that could have been: to know when your death would be, to have the shadow falling over your whole life, yet still managing to keep going, to make friends, to care for people. It threw all of Tom's difficult character into a new light. Church was overwhelmed with guilt at the bad things he had thought of his friend, certainly in the early days, and all the harsh words he had ever said. There was so much he still wanted to say. Despite their prickly relationship, Tom had been an excellent teacher, and a father-figure and the best of friends; he had made a deep and lasting impact on Church's life.

Tom appeared to know what Church was thinking. 'I've had a long life, Jack. Too long. Too much pain and suffering. I'm looking forward to moving on.'

'I'm sorry these last few months have been so hard for you.'

'They have been hard, but they have also been some of the best months of my life. I've learnt a lot from all of you, Jack. You reminded me of all those things I thought I'd lost when the Queen got her hands on me. For centuries I thought I'd become less than a man. But you – all of you – showed me the truth. And now it doesn't matter what the Queen's *games* did to my body, because the thing that really counts, my humanity, comes from somewhere else. And it's still there.'

Tom coughed again, and this time it sounded like the fit wasn't going to stop. When it did finally end, he was noticeably weaker. His eyelids fluttered half-closed; his skin grew ashen.

'Tom,' Church pleaded futilely. He had always been so flawed and weak compared to the heroic legends of Thomas the Rhymer, but in truth his heroism was even greater; deeper and more complex than the shining, courageous myth, infinitely more worthy, because it came from the best of humanity.

'The spiderweb.' The Rhymer's voice was a papery rustle. 'Diamonds all along it. Little worlds.' Another cough, slow and laboured. 'Beautiful, little worlds.'

And then there was silence and a heavy stillness.

His eyes burning, Church rested his head on the hard wood. He would miss his old friend immeasurably.

His sorrow had turned to a cold, hard anger when the door swung open and Mollecht entered, flanked by three Fomorii guards. Behind them, Callow danced a little jig. Mollecht led the Fomorii to the array of torture tools, ignoring Church completely.

'They're going to punish you, you know.' Callow moved across the floor in a manner that reminded Church more of an insect; insanity burned bright in his eyes.

'I'd call you crazy if it wasn't stating the obvious,' Church said. 'Throwing your lot in with these bastards again, after all they've done to you. Do you think they'll give you what you want?'

Callow cast a sly, admiring glance towards the mass of flapping birds. 'Oh yes, oh yes. My new best friend.'

'I had some sympathy for you, Callow, but it was misplaced. You aren't how you are because you didn't get the breaks in life. There have always been too many people like you, blaming everybody and everything for their suffering because they're too weak to face up to the selfishness or the greed that drove them into bad situations. Doing the right thing is difficult, and there's always some kind of hardship, but it pays off – for yourself, for society, for humanity. You were just too lacking to do down that road. Too pathetic. You wanted things for yourself and you wanted them quick and easy. Face up to it, Callow. All your misery in your life is because of the choices *you* made.'

'No!' Callow protested childishly. 'Nobody looked after me! I never had what others had!'

'You said it yourself, the first time we met. Longfellow, wasn't it?' Church drove the nail home harder, enjoying every blow.

'Shut up!' Callow covered his ears.

'*In ourselves, are triumph and defeat.*'

'No!' He ran over and kicked Tom's body hard, then looked to Church for a reaction.

'He can't feel it, you know,' Church said. 'He's away taking a rest from this big mess. It's all of us left behind who still get to feel the pain.'

Callow scuttled forward to Church's side so he could whisper in his ear, 'And that's just what you'll get, old boy. Once he's finished with you' – he pointed to Mollecht – 'I'll have my finger.'

Mollecht completed whatever task he had been carrying out on the other side of the room and turned back. Church couldn't tell if it was his imagination, but the crows appeared to fly even faster, like a heart speeding up at the anticipation of pleasure.

'Enjoy it while it lasts,' Callow whispered gleefully.

The three Fomorii guards were each carrying one of the cruel-looking implements; Church tried not to look at them, nor to think what damage they could wreak on his frail body.

Close up the sound of flapping wings was deafening, the smell of the birds potent. Church couldn't comprehend how they could fly so fast, so close together without once crashing.

Callow sloped back to the far corner of the room, obviously unnerved by Mollecht, even though he considered him an ally. The Fomorii guards roughly flipped the board back so it was horizontal, and Mollecht moved to stand at the head, where his presence was oppressive, but only partly seen. Two Fomorii positioned themselves on Church's right, one over his knee joint, the other close to his hand. The third Fomorii moved in on his left and held a rod tipped with a corkscrew over his groin; Church remembered that one well from the tunnels beneath Dartmoor.

Something was happening with Mollecht, although it was impossible to see exactly what. Church had a sense that the birds were moving their formation slightly; he could feel the air currents from their wings on his forehead. A moment later an unpleasant sucking sensation throbbed deep in his head, though he was sure it was not physical.

He writhed on the table in an attempt to shake it off; but it grew more and more intense until he felt something deep in him rushing out. There was a moment of utter darkness and then the torture room was gone, although he felt his body still lying in it. Everything was infused with intense, smoky colours, unreal, like a distorted Technicolor film from the sixties. A large, armoured insect appeared to be crawling around the inside of his head. His whole being recoiled; it was the mind of Mollecht.

Church had flashes of a nightmarish landscape where threatening creatures loomed up before receding in speeded-up motion. There was a shift and he glimpsed a building as big as a mountain made of black glass. Another shift and he was inside, in a room as dark as the deepest well despite a brazier glowing a dull red in one corner. One of the Fomorii stood hunched over the hot coals pouring some dust on to them from a glass philtre. This Fomor – whom Church knew was Mollecht – was a half-breed, just like Calatin, but while Calatin had more of the Tuatha Dé Danann in his physical appearance, Mollecht was closer to the grotesque Night Crawlers.

As the dust fell on the coals, a cloud of smoke rose up in purples and reds. Church had a sudden sense of a great Evil, greater even than Balor, lying somewhere on the edge of the universe. He felt its attention turn on him/them, and was convinced he was going to die from dread.

The smoke billowed with a life of its own. Finally it folded back and out of it flew the murder of crows, although there was something sickeningly alien about them; they were much larger, their eyes glittering red, and Church could sense in them an awful intelligence. They fell on Mollecht, pecking at his skin with blades as sharp as razor blades, tearing through flesh and bone.

As Mollecht fell to his knees, he howled in the insane monkey-gibbering way of the Fomorii, but there was nothing he could do to fend them off. At the same time as they ate him alive, they spun a chartreuse web, like spiders, that coagulated, folding within his body to make another form. As he shrank, it grew, not as large but more powerful, and when he was completely gone, it lay there, infinitely more hideous, both within and without. It was so fragile it threatened to fall apart in an instant, but the crows began to fly, faster and faster, weaving a binding spell that created a network of restraining energy. And when it opened its eyes . . .

The shock jolted Church out of the trance-state; he would never, ever forget the sickness of seeing the world through Mollecht's eyes.

Mollecht retreated from his head and moved to where he could direct proceedings.

'Have you lost hope yet?' Callow jeered from the other side of the room.

'Mollecht belongs to something else,' Church gasped. 'He wants to challenge Balor.'

All the Fomorii stopped; Callow dropped to his knees whimpering. The air pressure in the room fell; a wind rushed through it. Church was aware of a presence in the room, unbearably threatening; fear surged through him. It was only there for a second or two before moving on, but it left deep scars on his mind.

Somehow he forced himself to speak. 'Where is—'

'Don't say the name!' Callow pleaded.

'Where is he?'

Church thought Callow was going to cry. He looked around in terror. 'Don't you know? You are inside him.'

Church had no time to ask what that meant. The crows that made up Mollecht shifted their formation; a signal. The Fomorii moved in with the torture instruments.

Before any of them could hurt him, there was another drop in air pressure, only this one felt different: Church's nerve-endings tingled, warmth flooded into his limbs. The Fomorii felt it too, for they looked towards the door as one. Mollecht backed away.

The door was growing a dim blue, distinct in the darkness of the room, and it was from there that the electric atmosphere was flooding. Mollecht let out a series of barks and yelps. The Fomorii guards threw away the torture instruments and pulled out their swords, but before they reached the door, the blue glow became noticeably brighter and a resonant hum filled the room. An instant later the door exploded in thousands of shards. Church was close enough to the blast to have been torn to pieces by the flying wood, but nothing touched him at all.

When he looked back he was confronted with a miraculous sight. On the stone floor outside the door was a severed head. It was the source of the brilliant blue glow that now flooded the room. The head of Bran, the Luck of the Land; the god who had sacrificed himself for the sake of humanity. Church could make out long, flowing hair, but where the eyes and mouth should have been there were only holes out of which the blue light streamed. The most unnerving thing was that the head appeared to be still alive. Its mouth moved, the muscles on its cheeks twitched, the eyes grew wider and then narrowed.

The Fomorii guards hesitated, but another command from Mollecht drove them on. They barely had time to move. The light became a river of surging Blue Fire rushing towards them. Church was mesmerised as he watched it burn away everything down to the skeletons, and an instant later they were gone too.

In the corner, Callow was shrieking. Church's attention was drawn to the door as a tall silhouette slipped in. The Bone Inspector hurried over, his face drawn in pain. Church saw that his hands had been charred black.

'Too hot,' he said in a fractured voice.

Somehow he managed to undo Church's bonds, although Church could barely look into his face at the pain he was experiencing. 'You did a good job,' Church said.

The Bone Inspector grunted. 'I've suffered worse.'

Once Church was free, he dived behind the table and snatched up the Sword. Mollecht was pressed against one wall, unable to leave the room while the head was there. Even so, the birds were shifting formation ready to unleash another of the plague-attacks.

Church knew how fast they came, and this time he didn't hesitate. Bounding across the room, he began to thrash wildly with the Sword. Black feathers showered across the room. Deep puddles tinged with red formed as the crows' bodies fell heavily all around.

There was a sound that made Church's gut turn, and it was a moment or two before he realised it was Mollecht screaming. The remaining birds had to fly harder to maintain the binding pattern, but every time the Sword nicked one it plunged to the ground.

Church lost himself in a storm of black and red until there was only one bird flying frantically around the hideous shape that lay within; the thing he still couldn't bring himself to look at. He paused briefly, took a deep breath, and then struck the last crow.

The bird hit the stone flags, followed by the thing within. It thrashed and shrieked wildly for a full minute, and then slowly it began to break up, then melt away. Eventually there was only a black sludge on the floor, and soon that, too, was gone.

Church rested on the Sword, shattered from fear and exertion, and in that moment Callow broke his frozen position and darted for the door. He skirted the head, glancing back once at the threshold.

Church pointed at him. He didn't need to say a word, and he knew from the look of terror on Callow's face as he disappeared that his message had been received.

Church hurried back to the Wayfinder, lying on its side behind the table. 'What do we do now?' the Bone Inspector croaked. He was resting heavily against a wall.

'I don't know. But this lantern is going to show me.' He sat down and pulled it upright before him. 'I hope.'

Closing his eyes, he focused on the Blue Fire as Tom had taught him at the foot of Arthur's Seat in Edinburgh. The Rhymer had been a good teacher; it took him only a second or two to reach the necessary state of heightened perception.

The lantern flame surged and the energy crackled into his fingers, his hands. For the first time on his own he saw in the flames the tiny faces and minute bodies he had witnessed when Tom had introduced him to the earth-power at Stonehenge. He knew what they were now. 'All stars,' he whispered.

Things fell into alignment.

It seemed to him that the Wayfinder had moved deep in his head, and the flame was now blazing as bright as a lighthouse. It was a direct connection with the source of the spirit-fire, wherever that might be. Church felt it flare in his head, in his heart, as a doorway opened, and then the Blue Fire was streaming out of him.

Veitch awoke on a mudflat next to a grille that looked across the Thames. Next to him the River Fleet rushed out on its journey to the sea. He felt like he was dying: too cold, too exhausted, broken-spirited.

On the south bank he could see the dawn light painting the buildings in beautiful pastel shades. It was only a second or two later that he realised there was a corresponding light in the culvert in which he lay, only that illumination was a deep sapphire; and it was coming from him, from his very pores. With it came not only a tremendous sense of well-being, but also renewed vigour.

He clambered to his feet, stamping the last remaining cold from his limbs as he cracked his knuckles. 'Bleedin' hell,' he said in awe.

Then he was at the grille, attempting to prise it open.

The Fomorii marched back and forth at the camp in the under-ground tunnel, oblivious to the foul-smelling smoke rolling off the burning piles of rubbish. They were long used to the foraging rats that ventured close before scurrying back into the shadows, so they paid scant attention to the movement further along the tracks.

It was only when the activity refused to recede, indeed began to move closer than any of the rats had dared before, that they looked up, and by then it was too late.

A torrent of undulating brown bodies swept towards them from the dark, covering every square centimetre of the tunnel floor. The rats surged past the perimeter bonfires up on to the Fomorii, biting chunks out of their forms, tearing their way into any orifice they found. Their relentless speed and vast numbers belied the weakness of their size;

however many the Fomorii crushed or swatted away, there were a thousand more to take their place and within seconds the Night Walkers were lost beneath the deluge.

Walking amongst them was Ruth, her eyes blazing with righteous fury. She was untouched by the scurrying creatures that moved exactly where she wanted, did just what she required. The information had been there in her mind, ready to be accessed, all part of the detailed lore she had soaked up from her familiar while imprisoned in Edinburgh. She had always thought she might be able to control one, perhaps two, maybe even three, but the extent of her abilities stunned her. She felt able to do anything.

As she passed the camp, the Blue Fire surged into her limbs, driving out the exhaustion so her physical strength could match the overwhelming confidence she had discovered. She had a sudden, deep connection with Church, and knew he had made it through to his destination. Now all she had to do was join him.

Muttering beneath her breath, the rats responded, surging on beyond the camp, with tens of thousands more coming up behind her.

'Did you feel that?' Laura's jaw sagged in cartoon style as the electric jolt jerked her limbs.

Shavi held up his hand towards the end of the corridor where the dawn light had still not penetrated. A ghostly blue aura could just be made out around his fingers. 'It is Church.'

Laura closed her eyes in relief. 'Good job we're not all losers.'

Shavi looked back out of the window at the army of silent Fomorii staring back. 'We have to join him. All of us need to be there.'

'That's all well and good, Shav-ster, but I'm still waiting to hear the cunning plan. Maybe the one that turns us invisible so we can waltz past the hordes of Hell.'

As the sunlight slowly moved across the rooftops, the deathly silence was suddenly broken. From somewhere in the distance came the dim but instantly recognisable sound of a hunting horn, low and mournful, but drawing nearer.

And the Blue Fire rolled out across the city, joining up with the Fiery Network, and with it flowed Church's thoughts and hopes and prayers. The Wayfinder had lit the way for the very essence of his being, the part that had been transformed from base lead into gold by his experiences at St Michael's Mount. Deep in his subconscious, encoded in his spirit, was the link he had with the vital energy that flowed into everything. He was, finally and truly, its champion, the Brother of Dragons. He was One.

When he had achieved what it became apparent that he had to do, he broke the link and put the Wayfinder aside.

'Tell me that did some good,' the Bone Inspector said.

Church looked up at him with bright eyes. 'The Fabulous Beasts are coming,' he said.

the place Where all
things Converge

Shavi and Laura hung out of the window high up on Westminster Abbey to get a better view. At first it looked like birds moving across the rooftops, until they saw the drifting smoke and mist rolling away mysteriously before them. The occasional breaks in the cloud cover became a broad swathe, allowing sunlight to flood in across the ancient monuments and modern office blocks of London, spotlighting what they could now see were figures on horseback preceded by a pack of baying hounds.

'The Wild Hunt,' Shavi said, recalling the last time he had seen them at Windsor, shortly before his death.

The unearthly red and white dogs bounded effortlessly across tiles, leaping the gulfs between buildings as if they were nothing. The Hunt thundered behind, Cernunnos in his Erl-King aspect at the head, blowing the horn, the horses galloping an inch or more above the roofs.

And the Hunt was not alone. The Dark Sisters, Macha, Badb and Nemain, swooped like ravens across the skyline, and beyond them Shavi could just make out the Morrigan, harbinger of war.

'Look.' Shavi pointed to a commotion amongst the Fomorii near the Government offices off Great George Street. Black Shuck, the devil-dog that always heralded the Wild Hunt, tore through the Night Walkers with huge jaws that could rend metal.

The Hunt descended on the gathered Fomorii army, ripping back and forth until they had cleared an area where they could stand and fight. The Dark Sisters swooped from above and the Fomorii fell wherever they chose to attack. But it was the Morrigan that chilled Laura's blood the most. She walked amongst the Night Walkers as if she were strolling in the park, and whichever beast she passed crumpled to the ground, dead.

Laura and Shavi looked at each other; neither of them needed to speak – they knew the attack had given them the opportunity to break out. The Professor, who had been about to return to the detritus of humanity sheltered below, understood too. 'How on earth do you propose to get out there?' he said in horror. 'You'll die. Of course you'll die.'

'Thanks for the pep talk, granddad. That's got me all jazzed up.' Laura snickered to herself as she ran her fingers through her hair to spike it up.

'These times demand more of us,' Shavi said, smiling. 'From our conversation last night, I would guess you never imagined you would be a leader of men, a rock that holds a desperate community together.'

'I'm not a leader.' Michell looked out at the now-raucous fighting. 'No, you're right. I was shaping my life to end it in the dustbin.'

'And now you feel better about yourself. Now there is hope.'

He nodded. 'How strange that it takes a world falling apart to make us become better people.'

'The life we were leading seduced us away from the things that mattered,' Shavi said. 'We thought society, technology, money, were offering us something better, but instead we ended up indolent, bored and depressed. This has been a terrible time, but if we find a way through it, something good will come out of it. A better life.'

'There's something undeniably sad that we can't get back on the tracks without experiencing such suffering.' The strain had made Michell emotional; tears flecked the corners of his eyes.

'It is the human way. But we do learn. Good does come out of bad, although at the time of suffering it is impossible to see what good there might be.'

'If you two are going to keep talking, I'll just wander off and slit my throat. Jesus, analyse, analyse. Start living, for God's sake.'

Shavi flashed a secret smile at Michell, who winked in return. 'Come on, then,' he said to Laura. 'I guarantee you won't find it boring from here on in.'

'Are you sure you know what you are going to do?' Shavi asked as they stood at the Abbey door with Michell ready to swing it open.

'Why don't you patronise me a bit more, you big, poncey shaman?' Laura's face was moody, with a hint of apprehension. 'Offer to do somebody a favour and what do you get? Nag, nag, nag.' She squatted down and bowed her head, balancing herself with one hand in front of her. 'Okay, granddad. Put those creaking joints to use.'

The Abbey was suddenly filled with the deafening clamour of battle. Laura knew if she looked up she would be too terrified to act; for all that Cernunnos had transformed her, she was still the frightened, unconfident woman she had been for most of her life.

She surprised herself by containing her fears; necessity was a great motivator, she thought. In her meditative state she had no problem accessing that corner of her mind she characterised as a brilliant green screen. It gave her a great sense of pride to see it, a feeling that she was doing the right thing. Environmental activism had been all she had ever truly believed in, and the thing she felt might actually balance out the weighty debit side of her life. And now, she thought, nature had paid her back by giving her a reason to live.

It started small. Hairline cracks ran out from her fingers where they touched the stone. Beyond the Abbey walls, they grew into fissures in pavements and roads; further on, a street lamp swayed, then crashed to the ground. The Fomorii nearest to her were thrown this way and that as the ground went into upheaval.

From the long-hidden soil beneath, green shoots sprouted, rapidly growing into a tumbling thicket of vegetation that moved as if it had a life of its own: bushes and vines, brambles, flowers, reeds, and then saplings that became trees, rowan, oak, yew, hawthorn.

Shavi gaped in amazement. As the abundant flora became thicker, the Fomorii were driven back and a path formed within the greenery, now stretching across Parliament Square. 'Can you keep this up?'

'Not for long. It's knackering. But I can do it enough to get us through the worst of it. Then, I'm sorry to say, we'll have to run. Unless you can call up some badgers.' She looked up finally and smiled with pride at her achievement. It was quickly replaced by a dark determination. 'Okay,' she said. 'Let's go.'

They glimpsed the carnage the Wild Hunt, the Dark Sisters and the Morrigan were inflicting on the Fomorii forces, but then they were across the Square and heading along the Embankment. After all the choking smoke of the city, the aromas of the vegetation were invigorating, and died away too soon, but the streets beyond were empty and Laura was already growing weak.

Shavi put an arm round her shoulders to support her as she shakily came to a halt in the middle of the road. 'I'll be fine in a moment.' She could already feel the Blue Fire working its wonders in her limbs. 'You know what? If we get through this, I think I'm going to come back and turn the City into a garden.'

Shavi gave her a hug, but he knew as well as she that the chance of them coming back were still very slim. Ahead of them lay the deep shadow cast by the ominous black tower rising out of the east. With a shiver that had less to do with the cold, they moved into it.

The journey through the tunnels to Tower Hill tube station passed in a blur. Before, Ruth had found that when she was using her new abilities she became so focused the real world was almost a distraction. Now the power was sucking her further and further from life into a place that was like a waking dream, where she could do anything; where the power defined her completely.

But as she gradually made her way up the frozen escalators, she began to slip back to how she had been. The realisation of the near-fugue state that had taken her over terrified her, as did its implications, but it was wiped away in an instant by her disgust that she was standing amidst a carpet of brown, writhing bodies that stretched as far as she could see. She closed her eyes briefly to compose herself, then continued on her way, but she couldn't help her shudders every time one brushed its cold fur against her feet.

Whatever she had done to control the rats began to diminish with her return to awareness and by the time she reached the top of the escalator they had begun to thin out. A few torches flickered in the ticket station, but Ruth was puzzled that she couldn't see any daylight. As she approached the doorway she realised the tower she had seen from Hampstead Heath had been built over the top of the tube station. The door that normally led out to the gardens overlooking the Tower of London now exited directly into a dark structure constructed out of compacted steel and melted plastic. In the walls amongst the twisted girders and building rubble, she could make out bits and pieces of the things that had been used in the building: computers, cash registers, mobile phones, cars and vans and motorcycles, part of a London bus. It was suffocatingly hot and filled with what sounded like some mining machine pounding away rhythmically nearby.

Broad steps ran up and down, with warren-like rooms on either side. She hesitated, unsure which way to go. A wave of panic flooded through her. Earlier she had sensed Church had made it, but what if he was now dead? What if she was the only one left? The responsibility was so vast she could barely comprehend it. What was she supposed to *do*?

As she agonised she caught sight of a faint blue glow above her that ignited a desperate hope. Holding the Spear before her, she took the steps two at a time. Her heart beat faster as she almost stumbled across the remains of several Fomorii, and then she rounded a corner into an intense blue light.

Church and the Bone Inspector were climbing ahead of her. She was shocked to see the illumination was streaming from what appeared to be a severed head, hanging by its hair from the same hand in which Church held the Wayfinder.

When he saw her his face broke into such an open expression of relief she had to run over and throw her arms around him. He held the head and Wayfinder away, although she didn't sense any danger from them. 'Where's Ryan?' he asked.

'I don't know. Don't know if he's alive or dead.'

'He'll get here if it's humanly possible,' Church said confidently. 'Tom?'

Church's expression told her all she needed to know. Her spirit sagged. 'I thought he'd go on forever.'

'This isn't the place to stand around talking,' the Bone Inspector said curtly.

They began to move cautiously back up the stairs. Occasionally one of the Fomorii would wander out of an adjoining room, only to be despatched in an instant by Caledfwlch or by a flash of searing energy from the head.

'I presume you know where you're going,' Ruth whispered.

'No. But if you stop and let yourself *feel*, you'll know you're going in the right direction.'

As he spoke she realised she could sense a palpable *pressure* in the air that was slowly squeezing the life out of her chest; and it was getting stronger the more they climbed. A corresponding feeling of dread was eating away at the edges of her mind; all she could think of was the hideous thing she had seen during her spirit-flight from Wave Sweeper. 'What are we going to find?' Her voice suggested she hoped for some comfort, although she knew there would be none.

'I always expected it to be something like Calatin or Mollecht, only bigger. But I don't think it's going to be anything like that at all.'

'Worse?'

'What do you think?'

'Hasn't Frank got a song for an occasion like this?'

'Yes, "Get Happy". As the lyric goes, *Get ready for the judgment day.*'

'Thanks. That's dismal.'

'No, no, it's positive. Really. *We're going to the Promised Land.*'

There was something so naïve about him, even in the face of such terrible surroundings, Ruth felt a surge of love. 'We'll get out of this,' she said gently.

Her words were lost as a shadow crossed Church's face. 'Did you hear that?'

She hadn't heard anything.

Church was suddenly consumed with anxiety. He dashed up a few steps and threw open a door on the outside of the tower. It was empty apart from piles of burning rubbish before irregular windows looking out over the Thames. Flying Fomorii were zipping around without, diving down on something that was below their range of vision. A tremendous shock rocked the entire tower. Liquid flame gushed past the window.

Church tried a door on the inner wall of the stairway. It was locked. 'I've got to look in here,' he said anxiously.

'We haven't got time,' the Bone Inspector replied harshly. He was continually peering up and down the stairs for any sign of attack. 'It's already morning. The gates will be opening in a few hours.'

'There's time for this.' Church tried to force the door.

'I told you not to be so stupid. The hour's almost here!' The Bone Inspector made to drag Church away, but Church knocked his blackened hand off. They squared up to each other.

'This isn't helping,' Ruth pleaded. 'Why is this room so important?'

Raw emotion flickered across his face. 'Marianne's in there. I heard her.'

Ruth stepped in before the Bone Inspector could began a rant. 'You have to let him do it,' she begged. 'There'll still be time.'

After a moment, the Bone Inspector relented. Overcome with apprehension, Church stepped back and levelled the Sword at the lock. It burst with a resounding crack and the door swung open.

The room was not like any they had seen before. It was spacious, about fifty feet square, with smooth walls lined with black stone. A single torch burned on the far side. The flagged floor had been marked out with an intricate pattern of lines and geometric shapes, along with bizarre symbols that suggested an alien language. The effect of the relationship of the various elements was so intensely disturbing it made Church's head spin. A large block of black stone stood in the centre of the design, and on it was a stoppered green-glass bottle.

'Be careful.' The Bone Inspector held out a hand to stop Church stepping over the threshold. 'Don't go blundering in.'

Church scanned the room one more time. 'Can't see anything that might be a problem. What makes you worried?'

'Instinct.'

Church fixed his eyes on the bottle. 'That's it. That's where she is.' He set down the head and the Wayfinder, but held on to the Sword. 'I'm going to have to chance it.'

'Bloody stupid. All this at stake and you're taking risks,' the Bone Inspector muttered.

'It's an obligation to someone I loved. Don't you understand that?'

There was a long pause before the Bone Inspector replied quietly, 'Maybe.' Then: 'Get a bloody move on! Time's running out!'

In the room the temperature was inexplicably below freezing.

Church's breath clouded, his body protesting with shivers after the intense heat. Church let his foot hover over the design, but couldn't think of any other way to reach the bottle. Slowly he brought it down.

'You okay?' Ruth called out.

'Fine. No problem.' He took another step.

'Just keep that big head and big mouth in check,' the Bone Inspector growled. 'And stop dawdling.'

As Church took the third step, he felt a strange tingling sensation in his extremities. Ruth noticed his surprised reaction. 'What is it?'

'Nothing. Just the cold. It's like the Arctic in here.'

With the next step, he lost the feeling in his fingers and toes. He shook them for warmth and was surprised to see them glisten in the torchlight.

'Tread . . . careful—' The Bone Inspector's voice was oddly distorted before disappearing completely. Church was too fixated on the bottle to be concerned about it. All he could think about was Marianne and everything she'd suffered because of his unwitting involvement in the events now being played out. He had made her a promise to free her spirit and he would not fail; his own redemption was tied up in his success.

The words of warning and encouragement from Ruth and the Bone Inspector had ended; they must have realised he was doing okay.

Several more steps passed unnoticed, so much did the bottle fill his mind. Memories of Marianne and the time they had spent together traipsed across his head until the black stone chamber almost faded from his perception. He was there with her, happy, as they always had been.

It was only when he realised he was having trouble moving forward that he jolted back to reality. What he found was so shocking it took him a few seconds to assimilate. His arms and the parts of his body he could see were strangely white. His dulled thought processes eventually told him the truth: he was covered in rime-frost. It sparkled across his limbs, so thick his joints would barely work against it. Even his eyelashes were heavy with the weight of it, shimmering so that he found it hard to see past the glare.

If he had not had the Blue Fire coursing through him, he would most certainly have been dead; even now he was close to it. If he turned back there was still a chance he might actually survive. Yet the bottle was only a couple of paces away. How could he leave when he was so close? He couldn't abandon Marianne.

In his mind, there was no choice. He forced another step. Almost there. He couldn't feel any of his body now; his mind was disembodied, recalling a dream of being trapped in a person. Oddly, that helped him. With no physical sensations to distract him, his thoughts were pure and strengthened. He slipped easily into the perception where he was aware of the Blue Fire, and was surprised to see that even in that awful place the spirit-energy still flowed, though much weaker.

By force of will, he drew some of it to him; a little but it was enough. He took the final step and swept the bottle off the stone with the back of his hand. It shattered on the floor to release the gentlest breeze; he could feel it even through the thickening frost. With it came the scent of a woman he once loved, of a hot day in the Caribbean and a warm night on a boat on the Thames when they had kissed. And something else: the faintest touch of an intelligence, like a lover reaching out to reassure themselves their sleeping partner was still there in bed, still breathing. It was a small thing, but filled with so much. Church felt enormous gratitude that swelled his emotions, and admiration for him and his abilities, and forgiveness; and love, but not the love of a young couple, a spiritual thing that sent his soul soaring.

Emotions that had been held in stasis for so long finally rushed through him; it felt like someone had plunged a hand deep within him and dragged out every shadow, every shred of misery, every tear. The burden that shifted left him as light as air. Finally, an ending for something that had manacled him for so long.

She was free. And he was finally free of the burden her death had placed upon him. A tear squeezed out of the corner of his eye and burned a path through the white down his cheek.

After that the getting back was easy, despite the cold and the weight of the frost, both of which appeared to be increasing. The shock of the heat outside the room made him lose consciousness for a moment, and when he came round he was lying on the floor, his clothes soaked, with Ruth wiping his face. Her concern was unmissable, but it faded when he forced a smile.

'It was the Kiss of Frost,' he said, recalling the Fomorii spell that had almost destroyed him on the Isle of Skye. 'Mollecht had obviously left it there for me, knowing I'd undoubtedly attempt to free Marianne's spirit. To remind me of how I screwed up last time. His final malicious act.'

'Well, you showed him, didn't you?' She brushed his hair away from his face. 'How do you feel? About Marianne?'

He knew what she was saying. 'It made me realise how much I love you. The relationship I had with Marianne was strong, but it's all in the past. What I felt in there was about something different.'

'Care to elaborate?'

Church looked at the Bone Inspector, who appeared to be considering whether he should clout Church with his staff. 'I don't think this is quite the time.'

He pushed himself to his feet, pleased at the recuperative powers the Blue Fire gifted him. What lay ahead would be much, much worse.

After Veitch had torn the grille away from the stone, he stumbled out into the cold waters of the Thames. The mist and smoke that had blanketed the city for so long was drifting away, leaving a sky that was golden and pink. The rooftops of the buildings along the south bank gleamed in the early morning light. Everything hinted at a beautiful day.

The quickest way to his destination was obviously to swim; he was thankful he now felt curiously immune to the chill. He kept to the shallows where he could not be seen from the bank and let the current push him along.

The spirit-energy had raised his spirits, but there was still a dark area at the back of his head where all his worst traits lay. It was there where the self-loathing multiplied at the thought that he had failed again, not just Ruth, but Church, everyone, the world, and that was such an enormous failure he couldn't keep out the seductive fantasies of suicide. And it was there, where his consuming anger generated a dull heat.

Eventually the black tower was in view. He rounded a bend in the river to see Wave Sweeper launching an attack on Balor's lair. Bizarre flashes of energy lanced out from strange weapons positioned around the deck. The flying Fomorii dived and soared like crows over food, but the Tuatha Dé Danann didn't allow them the slightest opportunity to get through.

As he drew closer, an enormous shadow passed over him. He craned his neck expecting to see another Fomorii creature, and was transfixed. A Fabulous Beast glittered like a jewelled brass robot in the sunlight, wondrous and terrible at the same time. It swooped down towards the tower to release a blast of fire that atomised a host of the flying Night Walkers. More of the serpentine creatures were approaching from all directions; Veitch had never dreamed there were so many. Columns of searing flame lanced down across the capital. As he drifted in the current, he saw the financial district engulfed in a fireball, Docklands decimated, pillars of billowing black smoke shoot up from the West End. Wherever the Fomorii had made their nests, the Fabulous Beasts sought them out.

Though he would dearly have loved to have joined in the simple battle of black and white, good versus evil, he passed unseen. He entered the Tower of London at the foot of the black tower through a riverside gate that opened on to a sandy area and a flight of stone steps where so many important men and women had trod before him.

Veitch still had his dagger, but it was little enough defence against what lay ahead. As he reached the top of the steps he came across a pile of items obviously discarded by the Fomorii as worthless. Amongst the broken doors and ripped tourist guides, jewels shimmered brilliantly. It was only when he fished out a crown bearing a remarkable diamond that he realised he was looking at the Crown Jewels. He considered – for a brief moment – prising out the diamond to slip into his pocket, but then his eyes fell on an ornate sword protruding from the bottom. He dragged out the Curtana, the Coronation Sword of Mercy. It was blunt, but it would still be a better weapon than his dagger.

As he made his way through the Tower, he was almost disappointed that he didn't meet any Fomorii. He was desperate to release some of the anger burning away inside him, an unpleasant sensation that was only getting worse.

At some point he left the historic castle and found himself in the black tower that circumscribed it. There, a pitched battle was taking place, and at the heart of it were Shavi and Laura.

Veitch was so overjoyed to see his friends, he rushed in with a whoop, whirling his sword around his head. His intervention cheered them immeasurably for they had reached a point where they feared they might be overwhelmed. Vegetation tangled everywhere, but Laura hadn't learnt enough to utilise it in close quarters. Shavi used a sword hesitantly, but his hatred of violence hampered him severely.

Once Veitch had hacked a Fomorii warrior into a pile of seeping chunks, the battle turned, although both Laura and Shavi were a little concerned at the glee with which he despatched his enemy.

Yet it was a short-lived victory. More and more Night Walkers began to stream in from outside. 'They're trying to force us downstairs,' Veitch said. 'That means we go up.'

It was easier for them to hold their ground as they fought while edging backwards up the steps. The Fomorii could stand only two abreast and as every one fell it made it harder for the others to clamber over the bodies.

'I hope we do not meet any more coming down,' Shavi said.

'I'm more concerned about what happens when we get to the top,' Laura replied.

Church was beginning to wonder exactly how high the tower soared above the cloud cover. It felt like they had been climbing for an hour or more, although the heat hadn't diminished at all. Increasingly, explosions rocked the construction to its very core; chunks fell from the ceiling and walls. Through the windows he occasionally caught glimpses of Fabulous Beasts laying waste to the city and was stunned by both their number and diversity. He had never seen so much grace and power in one form, so many gleaming colours. How could humanity have traded them away, and all the wild magic that came with them, for the brutal rationalism of the twenty-first century?

The Fabulous Beasts provided an uplifting counterpoint to the oppressive presence of Balor looming darkly. The rising sense of threat was putting a huge psychological strain on all of them. There was a perpetual feeling of Balor always standing one pace behind them, ready to strike.

In a sense, that was true. Church could feel Balor's essence throbbing in the very walls; it was all a part of him. The dark god of the Fomorii was an amorphous evil that pervaded everything, even the very air; Church could taste the sourness when he swallowed. The atmosphere was almost painfully pregnant; despite the power it already held, Church knew the Beast was waiting for the Doors of Samhain to open so it could claim the undreamable force it needed to destroy all life. It could afford to wait; they were insignificant beside it.

The steps opened out on a wide, flat area covering the entire floor space of the tower. It was the first time they had come across a room like it, but they could tell from the windows around the circumference that it wasn't the top. After the claustrophobic gloom, they were pleased to see the rough holes cut in the walls provided a pleasant amount of sunlight, but there was still not enough to illuminate the shadows at the centre of the room.

As they tentatively crossed the floor in search of the next flight of steps, they noticed a figure sitting hunched in that dark zone, next to a shimmering motion in the air. With weapons at the ready, they approached until they saw it was Niamh. Church laid down the head and the Wayfinder and hurried over, but she was so locked in her thoughts she didn't see him until he was almost upon her.

When she did look up, her face was filled with such a terrible grief that Church stopped short. The movement all around her were golden moths rising up to the ceiling. On the floor lay the gradually disappearing bodies of the Tuatha Dé Danann guards.

Church dropped down and put his arm around her shoulders. She rested her head against him, oddly frail for such a powerful being. 'I'm sorry for your people,' he said. 'Did the Fomorii hurt you?'

'There were no Night Walkers.'

'Then what happened?'

She raised her head to look at him deeply, her face haunted, her eyes damned. 'I happened.'

As her meaning gradually dawned on him, he looked around at the brutally slain bodies uneasily.

'Do not think badly of me, Jack.' Every part of her was shaking. 'I have committed a crime that will ensure my name is despised by my people for all time. I never thought I had it within me to commit such a monstrous act. But I did, Jack, I did.'

Church tried to console her, but she would have none of it.

'I did it for you, Jack. For all Fragile Creatures. I did it for all existence. And I have lost myself in the process.'

Church looked round until he saw the chest a little way away. 'The Wish-Hex?'

'I attempted to prevent them unleashing it. They ignored my pleas. And so I . . . I . . .' Her face fell into her hands; her sobs were silent and racking.

'I know it's a terrible burden,' Church said gently, 'but you did do the right—'

'You do not understand, Jack. I failed. The Wish-Hex has been set in motion.'

He stared at the chest, suddenly cold despite the heat. 'In motion?'

'There is no stopping it now. Soon, very soon, it will begin.'

Church fought back a wave of despair. The odds had always been incalculable, but now it truly was hopeless. He began to ask her how long it would take for the energy to drive the plague across the world, then caught himself; it didn't really matter. The Tuatha Dé Danann would get what they wanted: a universe free of competition.

He helped her to her feet. 'Don't worry. You did your best.' He looked across at the others, wondering whether to tell them that whatever they now did was futile.

Niamh took his hand. 'There will be an ending, Jack, but it might not be how you imagine,' she said as if she could read his mind.

'But what can we possibly—'

He was interrupted by the sound of violent fighting rising from the stairwell. Ruth rushed over to investigate before calling back excitedly,

'It's Shavi, Ryan and Laura.' The hope in her face made him feel even worse.

'We need to keep going,' he shouted.

The Bone Inspector sniffed the air like an animal. 'I think we're nearly there.'

'Then they'll do anything they can to try to stop us.'

'Time's running out,' the Bone Inspector continued. He looked more worried than Church had ever seen him. 'Not long left now.'

'Will you stop it with the countdown!' Church snapped.

Laura and Shavi emerged at the top of the steps. Veitch was just below, holding back the Fomorii. 'There's bleedin' millions of them now!' he yelled. 'They're not bothering with the ship any more. They just want us!'

Ruth came running up to him. 'The next flight of steps are just over there.'

'Okay, shout down to Ryan. When he reaches the top of his steps, he'll just have to run for it.' He turned back to Niamh, who had lifted the chest easily. 'What's the point in taking that along with us? We might as well leave it here now.'

'I am afraid of it falling into the hands of the Night Walkers. They created this Wish-Hex. They may know some way to ensure it destroys only Fragile Creatures.'

'I appreciate what you've done, Niamh, more than you can know.' Her sad smile told him how much his words meant to her.

He called Ruth over to help Niamh with the chest while he reclaimed the Wayfinder and the head; its blue glow was coming out in waves, accompanied by a dim but insistent hum. The features continued to move; Church had the unnerving feeling the head had been listening to them.

At the foot of the steps, he waited, urging the others up ahead of him. Eventually Veitch came sprinting past.

'You all right, boss?' he said with a grin.

'Fine and dandy.' As he leapt on to the steps at the rear, Church threw one backwards glance and was instantly chilled. Flooding the vast room was what appeared to be a river of shadows. He knew it was the Fomorii, but it was like one entity, of one mind. It moved and spread with such speed he guessed there must be hundreds, if not thousands, of the Night Walkers pouring in.

Then the awful sight was wiped out in an instant by a blinding revelation. 'What's that foul smell?' he called out.

Ruth's voice floated back. 'It's the Fomorii. Nuada told me that when the Caraprix is in control it stimulates that stink.'

Church felt sick and shaky as numerous troubling thoughts slotted into place. It was the same smell he recalled from the Walpurgis-induced vision of the night Marianne was murdered; and he had smelled it, too, when Tom had been driven to betray them in the Lake District. His pounding heart threatened to burst.

The traitor amongst them was being controlled by a Caraprix. That was why he couldn't imagine one of his closest friends selling them down the river; any acts of betrayal would be against type, and therefore unexpected. The Fomorii must have implanted the parasite months ago. Their scheming was unparalleled: back-up plan after back-up plan, and now this, the final defence to prevent their defeat.

He glanced up at Veitch taking the steps two at a time, thought of Ruth and Shavi and Laura. Which of them was it? It could be any one of them. And when would they be forced to make their move? He would have to watch all of them now, at a time when all his attentions should be focused on the threat without.

With a heavy heart, he pressed on, holding the head out behind him to deter the advancing Fomorii.

Gradually the circumference of the tower narrowed as they neared the top. When they finally thought they could climb no more it opened out into another large room that took up half the floorspace. There were no windows to provide light, but they could just make out building debris scattered all around.

'I can't stand here holding the rest back forever,' Church said impatiently. More explosions brought a shower of debris from the ceiling. As he jumped to one side to avoid it, he was struck with an idea. Directing Veitch and Shavi to collect rubble, girders and beams, and anything else they could lay their hands on, they flung it down the stairwell. It didn't take them long to jam it.

'So we won't be going down in a hurry,' Laura said dismally.

'It won't take them long to get through that,' the Bone Inspector said.

Veitch glared at him before venturing to the edge of the barrier. 'Can't hear anything on the other side. I reckon they've fallen back.'

'Now why would they do that?' Ruth laid down her edge of the chest and Niamh followed suit.

'They probably think we're a lost cause.' Church almost had to shout over the echoing beat of Balor's heart.

A large stone wall bisected the floor, with an oaken door placed in the middle; it had looked unusual from the instant Church emerged from the stairwell, but up close he could see it was seeping a viscous, black liquid. The gunk oozed down into a gully and then ran through the wall and down the side of the building, adding to the tower's skin.

Church moved his ear towards the wall to see if he could hear any sound from the other side. As he neared the stone his stomach turned; radiating through it was a sensation of unbearable evil that spoke to his most primal fears.

He staggered away quickly. 'In there.' If it was that strong without, he thought, what would it be like when they entered?

The others must have noticed his expression when he was against the wall, for Laura said, 'Are we up to this?'

'There aren't any other candidates. We'd better get the Quadrillax together.'

They each gave up the artefact they had protected until the Sword, the Spear, the Cauldron and the Stone stood in front of the door. As the pieces came in proximity, a faint metallic singing rang up, melodic and strangely soothing in that awful place. Church realised that the Wayfinder and the head would be needed too. All were linked, and while they appeared as objects they all recognised, Church knew that they were not seeing their true forms at all; what they really were, he guessed they would probably never know.

During the frantic activity the futility had been put to one side, but in the lull it returned in force. He didn't know why they were there. They might as well have vacated the tower and enjoyed their final hour together, as much as they could. 'How much longer with the Wish-Hex?' he asked. When there was no reply, he looked round and could tell from Niamh's face that it was almost upon them. Yet oddly he didn't see any fear there, just a deep, painful sadness; she forced a smile, and somehow that made it worse. 'Then we had better get moving.'

He walked up to the door. Ruth, Shavi, Laura and Veitch followed without any prompting, although the fear was obvious on all their faces. He was suddenly aware of a deeply moving feeling of gratitude that he had been allowed to spend time with them; they were the best.

A faint glow began to leak out of the Wish-Hex chest; the air pressure dropped a notch. *It's beginning*, he thought. He stooped down to pick up the Sword and something crashed against the side of his head, plunging him into unconsciousness.

The first Ruth realised was when Laura yelled and leapt back. Church was sprawled on the floor with blood seeping from a wound on the side of his head. Standing over him was Callow, his eyes baleful and filled with hatred. He was clutching a lump of rock, one end jagged and as sharp as a knife.

With a strength that belied his size, he grabbed hold of Church's jacket and began to drag him away into the shadows. Veitch dived forward, his ceremonial sword at the ready, but Callow moved as fast as a snake, yanking up Church's head and jabbing the rock against his throat.

'Anatomy lesson, little boy: the carotid artery,' he said. 'One slight cut and there's not a thing you can do. His beautiful heroic blood will wash across this dirty floor and it will all be over.'

'You're bleedin' crazy!' Veitch raged. His temple pulsed; his expression suggested he would hack Callow to pieces at the bat of an eyelid. Callow merely smiled, which infuriated Veitch all the more.

'Please,' Shavi said. 'There is no—'

'There is every need. If you win, I will be lost.'

'If we lose, you'll be lost, you wanker!' Veitch advanced another step.

Callow dug the rock into the pulsing artery. 'Can't you understand? Humanity is weak. If we don't ally ourselves with greater powers, we are nothing. Do you think the working classes ever got anywhere on their own? This isn't a world for the powerless.'

'Excuse me. Pathetic loser alarm.' It was the first time Laura had seen him since he had clambered over the van seat to slash her face with a razor. Even the torments inflicted on his body didn't assuage the hatred she felt for what he had put her through.

'What lies on the other side of that wall is the greatest thing this puny little world has ever seen,' Callow continued. 'He will take me and give me the position I truly deserve: as a leader of men, not someone crushed by the yoke of an uncaring society. You're not going to take that away from me. This is my time that's coming. Your time is gone.'

Ruth held up her hand and waggled her fingers at him so he could see where one was missing. 'I was nice to you the first time we met in Salisbury. I thought you were down on your luck and maybe you just needed a helping hand. You showed me the truth when you did this. Everything I've seen over the last few months has shown me how much greatness there is in humanity. But you, you're the flip-side. You're everything that drags humanity back: selfishness, and greed, and a belief that any act, however vile, is justified by your own needs.'

'You seem to forget I'm the one holding your boyfriend's life in his hands.'

'Yes, you are. And that's your big mistake. In Cornwall, and on the ship, I was ready to get my pound of flesh from you, Callow. And the only thing that stopped me was Church, because he's decent, and he believes in second chances and forgiveness. I don't.'

Laura stepped to her side. 'Who'da thought it? Me and Frosty with something in common.'

'So who's going to speak up for you now, Callow?' Lightning flashed in Ruth's eyes. 'Who's going to stop me?'

A shiver ran through Callow. His unblinking gaze left Ruth's face only to take in the flinty defiance in Laura's features.

A wind blew up from nowhere, rushing through the room violently. The force of it buffeted Callow a few paces backwards. 'I'll kill him!' he screamed.

Ruth made a sweeping gesture with her right hand and Callow flew several feet across the floor as if he had been struck heavily. The rock went spinning away into the shadows. He jumped to his feet, looking frantically from side to side like a cornered animal. Laura squatted down, one hand on the floor. Before Callow could flee, vegetation burst up from minute seed particles buried amongst the stone flags and lashed itself around his legs, pinning him tight. He wrenched at them, screaming and cursing insanely.

Ruth was filled with an otherworldly fury, though on the surface she appeared completely calm. 'Revenge does nobody any good,' she said. 'But sometimes you have to punish yourself.'

Veitch took a step away from her, shocked by what he saw. As the tempest screamed around the room, she appeared – although he didn't know if it was an illusion – to rise a few inches above the floor.

Church came round with his head ringing and blood seeping down to his neck. When he saw Ruth, the pain was instantly replaced with a panic that slowly changed to despair. That unrecognisable cast to her face told him everything he needed to know, the one terrible fact that destroyed his life in an instant. With the route his life had taken since the gods had started to manipulate it, he could almost have forecast the traitor would be the one person who meant more to him than the world. There had been signs before, he knew, but like a child he had avoided the harsh reality of investigating them too closely. He had pretended, and in truth had known he was pretending.

The one thought that saved him was that he wouldn't have to deal with it. The light leaking from the crate was now intense; the faint hum had become an insistent throb.

Laura's head was bowed in concentration. The vegetation had bound Callow like a mummy to his neck. When she looked up, she was in two minds about whether to continue, though her anger was still clear on her face.

She looked up at Ruth for guidance and saw her friend was not going to back down. Ruth was changed; the terrifying elemental forces crackling around her appeared infinite, reaching deep into the heart of creation. Though she looked exactly the same, the others were convinced it was no longer Ruth, but what had replaced her, they were not sure.

In that instant, Laura knew it was the moment of which Cernunnos had warned. If Ruth gave in to her hatred and killed Callow she would be lost; the immense power she had been gifted would be corrupted and would consume her.

Laura had only a second to act. She threw herself at Ruth, knocking her down hard. The lightning Ruth had been calling up erupted from the ceiling and missed Callow by a hair's-breadth.

And then Ruth turned her attention on Laura. Her face was unrecognisable, her eye black and empty like space. 'Mine,' she hissed.

Terror washed through Laura. Ruth began to focus the power towards her.

Laura had only a slim chance to defend herself. Instead, she rolled round towards Callow and concentrated until green vegetation rippled from her fingers across the floor, lashing up Callow's body. As he ranted and raged, it twirled briefly around his neck and then jerked. The head came free and bounced away into the shadows.

Laura waited for the blow to strike her. When nothing came, she looked back to see Ruth slumped in a daze, her eyes no longer black. 'Thank you,' she said weakly.

Church could feel Ruth's eyes on him as he rose, desperate for comfort after her experience, but he couldn't meet her gaze. And then it was too late. The room was quickly filled with twisting flashes of yellow light. The throb became a constant drone.

They all stared at the chest blankly: they had overcome so much, over so many months, and had still failed at the last. The light washed over them, almost soothing in its way.

Before they could say their goodbyes, Niamh flicked open the chest and removed the Wish-Hex. It was so bright it hurt their eyes and they were forced to turn away.

Church was closest and only he heard Niamh say, 'This is the way it must be.' It was a simple statement, but it brought a shiver to his spine. She pressed the Wish-Hex to her stomach until the light began to dim. He was shocked to see that somehow it was disappearing inside her. The sight was too strange to comprehend, but he knew exactly what she was doing; she had told him, in her own way.

When the Wish-Hex was finally gone, for the briefest instant she stood exactly as he remembered her from that first, misty appearance in his childhood bedroom. Her face open and honest and filled with unconditional love.

The droning noise ended. For a second her body shimmered and distorted, as if he were watching her on an out-of-tune TV, and then she was replaced by a massive cloud of golden moths that soared up into the shadows of the ceiling, twinkling like stars before slowly fading out.

Like Tom, she had known the moment of her death, Church was sure of it. That was part of her desperation that their love affair bloom. Somehow he knew she believed that if it happened, the course of events would be changed; that she would have a happy life.

He recalled the moment he told her they would never be together. How would that have felt? Not just rejection by the one she truly loved, but the announcement of her death sentence. And she had not complained, or attempted to change his mind.

And even after all the heartache he'd dealt her, she had still sacrificed herself so alien, weak, violent, spiteful, greedy, deceitful *Fragile Creatures* could move along the road towards their destiny.

Her act was humbling, but she had shown him an important lesson: that no race should be judged by the worst elements. That however bad humanity was at times, it could always be redeemed by the best.

Ruth was at his side, her arm around his waist. 'She did that for us? God, I feel so guilty!' She appeared honestly shaken by what she had witnessed.

Church looked down at Ruth in growing dismay as the repercussions of Niamh's actions slowly fell into place. They had been given another chance; now he couldn't simply let things run their course to a bitter end. He had to take whatever action was necessary to ensure their success, and that meant dealing with Ruth when she attempted to betray them. What would he do? Kill her? He had faced that terror when she had been a host to Balor, but that was before he had realised the true depth of the feelings they had for each other.

Ruth grabbed his hand. 'Look at you – you're shaking,' she whispered. 'Don't worry, we're all scared.'

'This is like Ten Little Indians,' Laura said morosely. 'Bags not being next.' She looked round and fixed on the Bone Inspector. 'Oldest first, I say.'

He gave a dark, triumphant smile. 'Ah, but I'm not going in there. That's your job.'

In his sly way, he had pointed them back on track. They turned as one and stared at the door, then looked to Church.

'Okay,' he said. 'Let's do it.'

As they collected the artefacts in silence, they were constantly aware of the door, like a sentient creature watching them malignantly.

'What's the plan?' Veitch asked Church.

'We have to use the talismans as soon as we get in there.'

'That's a plan?'

'We might not even get a chance,' Ruth said. 'He's so powerful he could strike us down in a second.'

'The talismans should offer us some protection.' Church was aware he had to sound as positive as possible. 'Individually, they're powerful. Together they'll be incredible. And with the head, the Luck of the Land . . .' He shrugged.

'So, we're winging it, right?' Laura's grin eased the mood a little.

'Just remember the legends,' Church said. 'He was always described as having a single eye – if he turned it on you it would cause death in an instant. I don't know if that's for real or symbolism, but there's a reason it was passed down the years. Keep it in mind.'

'So what's it like in the land of the dead, Shav-ster?' Laura asked.

'It's like Jamaica, but with free drink.'

'Really?'

'No.'

'You could have lied, you know.'

As they turned to face the door, Veitch stepped in close to Church and said quietly, 'I'm glad I'm with you, boss. You've done right by us all the way down the line.'

His face had the same childlike innocence that had made Church warm to him in the first place; for all his flaws, and there were many, that saved him.

'I'm okay, you know,' he continued. 'About you and Ruth.'

Church winced.

'I feel like I've been stabbed in the gut, but that's not important. I want her to be happy. And I want you to be happy. Whatever happens here, I'm going to be a winner. For the kind of life I've had, that's the only thing that matters to me. And I've got you to thank for it, mate.' He took Church's hand and shook it forcefully, hesitated a second, then stepped in and gave him a stiff hug. The others pretended not to notice.

'Will you lot get a move on.' The Bone Inspector marched around anxiously. 'The gates will be open any moment, and then it will all be—'

'Make sure you cheer loudly so we can hear you from way back here,' Laura said acidly.

Finally, it was time. Church gripped the door handle. Before he swung it open, he cast an eye on Ruth. Her move would undoubtedly be made at the worst possible moment. But could he face up to Balor and watch for an attack from the back as well?

The answer would come soon enough. He opened the door in one swift movement and stepped over the threshold.

The room was as silent and still as night. Darkness clustered on every side, but the sapphire glow from the talismans gave them enough light to see by. The pounding of the blood in their head drowned out all thoughts and sensations for the first few seconds before everything fell into stark relief.

They each had their own idea of what monstrous form Balor would take, so they were all left floundering around when their eyes fell on a small boy, standing with his arms behind his back in the centre of the huge, empty chamber. A shock of black hair tumbled around an innocent, smiling face. His clothes were Sunday School-best, his posture polite and upright like a dutiful Victorian son.

'If I'd known we could just have spanked him, I wouldn't have got so worked up,' Laura said breathlessly.

'A boy, right?' Church said. 'We're all seeing a boy? You know that's only the form our own perception is putting on it.'

'But why a boy?' Ruth's voice had an edge of dismay to it.

It was only then that the finer detail of what they were seeing broke through. Unimaginable dread pressed like a boulder on their chests, choking the air in their throats. A deep, primal part of their sub-conscious recognised what lay beyond the physical: a race memory of unbearable evil that demanded they flee or lose not only their lives, but also their souls. And then they saw his eyes were completely black, as immeasurable as the void.

The shock of the image kept them rooted for a second too long; they had already missed the opportunity to act. Something was happening to the boy. A horizontal crack opened slowly in his face. The top and bottom folded back gradually to reveal a twisting geometric shape made of brilliant red light so complex their minds couldn't make sense of it.

'The eye!'

They scattered at the sound of Church's voice; he was the head, they were the vital, component parts of the body, the reason why they worked so well together. In the instant the face opened completely they felt something as dank and chill as the grave brush past them. Church saw Shavi turn white, fight to control himself before moving off. He dabbed at his own ears and found blood on his fingers.

The thing with the body of a boy was already turning to focus on them.

'Keep moving!' Church shouted.

They scattered amongst the shadows just as death swept through them again. It whispered by a hair's-breadth away. An ache sprang up deep in Church's bones. The thing was too fast, too powerful; they wouldn't have an instant to lay out the talismans. The worst thing was that Church knew it was using only a fraction of its power. Most of it was maintaining the integrity of the tower, overseeing the Fomorii forces, preparing for the gates to open. They were a distraction, nothing more.

They ran back and forth as the boy turned this way and that. Each time the icy, whispering wind rushed out it came a little closer to them. Laura appeared to have lost the use of her left arm. Veitch was bleeding from his nose.

Yet there was a moment between attacks when the eye needed to focus, and in that time Ruth snatched up the Spear. It was the kind of smart, brave move he would have expected of her, but all he felt was panic. *This is it!* he thought.

Ruth hurled the weapon, but not at him. It shot like an arrow, much faster and stronger than she could have propelled it herself. It would have driven through the eye, but at the last instant, the boy folded like a paper figure. Instead, it rammed through his chest. White light exploded across the room like gouts of molten metal and there was a shrieking that came from everywhere at once.

Laura was already crouching, her good hand resting on the floor before her. Vegetation sprouted madly along a rapid path between her and the boy. Thorns of the hardest wood burst through its legs, vines and brambles snapping round and round like steel wire.

Church seized the moment. He turned for the talismans, but Shavi was already scrambling to lay them out. Church dived in to help him, aware of the agonies Balor was going through behind him, knowing how futile it really was. It was a shock to feel the talismans writhe and twist beneath his fingers, subtly forcing him to put them in the right place. The head sat in the centre of the array, its mouth opening and closing as if it were barking orders. Yet Church didn't feel scared by it; there was a deeply comforting warmth rolling off the objects.

Finally the five talismans they still had were laid out. Instantly they began to change. No longer were they a Sword, a Stone, a Cauldron, a Lantern or a severed head, but something that Church couldn't begin to get a fix on, yet they were undoubtedly one *thing*, unified, beating powerfully; it was like he was staring at a storm cloud through a heat haze.

One part was still missing; he could *feel* that intensely. He had to retrieve the Spear. All he needed was Veitch to launch one of his brutal attacks to keep Balor off-balance and he would be able to do it.

Shavi was already moving towards the Heart of Shadows, but Church pulled him back; it was his responsibility, his risk. Secure in the knowledge that Veitch would instinctively know what to do as his exquisite strategic skills came into play, he ran towards the creature that no longer resembled a boy, now as unknowable as the talismans, growing and changing all the time.

Laura was still drawing the greenery out of nothing, swathing Balor in bark and leaf, but as his form changed he was rising above, sucking in the true power that he had dissipated throughout the tower, perhaps even throughout London. And from the corner of his eye Church saw Ruth utilising all the power Cernunnos had gifted her to attack Balor, and he wondered why, at the end, she had turned away from betraying them.

And then he was within Balor's sphere, sickened by the power and the evil, his thoughts fragmenting with the chaos that swept around him. Somehow he managed to grab the Spear; it squirmed in his fingers as he dragged it out.

White-hot pain exploded in his side. The shock snapped him away from the Spear as his mind struggled to understand what was happening.

Ruth?

He staggered backwards, blood flooding into his clothes. Scarlet flashes burst across his mind. In the madness that engulfed him, the world seesawed sharply: he saw Balor looking down on him dispassionately, its attention already moving elsewhere; and he saw Ruth, her face torn with anguish.

Somehow he found himself on the floor near the talismans, and Shavi was over him, desperately trying to staunch the wound. He tried to strain towards Ruth, but all he could see was Laura continuing her attack on Balor, her face as white as the moon. Slowly the Beast was driving her back.

Veitch drifted into his fractured frame of vision, and the maelstrom of insanity grew infinitely worse. His silver hand was dripping blood. Church's blood. Veitch stared at the prosthetic dismally as it clenched and unclenched, seemingly beyond his control. Suddenly it lashed out of its own accord, smashing with the force of a hammer into the side of

Shavi's head. Shavi flew across the floor, droplets of blood trailing behind him. Blood, everywhere. More on Veitch's face, trickling from his nose, mingling with the streaming tears. The blood that did not come from an injury inflicted by Balor, as Church had thought, but was the mark of a Caraprix in action.

'Bastard!' Veitch hammered his fists against his temple, his face scarlet with the strain. 'Bastard, bastard, bastard!' He bucked at the waist as the rage consumed him.

Church looked down hazily; the pool of blood around him was so large! He never dreamed he had so much blood in him. The blue light streaming off the talismans was reflected in it, as he watched those tracers in the dark he had a moment of clarity. Veitch's anger, always so close to the surface, so terrible when unleashed, was the product of his subconscious continually struggling against the subtle influence of the Caraprix. They had judged him by that anger, all of them, and they had been so wrong.

'Fight it, Ryan.' Church's voice cracked; cold spread along his side. 'I know they stuck one of those things in your head.'

'Not one! Two!' His nails tore deep furrows in the sides of his head. A scream ripped from his throat. 'I didn't know! I knew! But I didn't know!' He jack-knifed at the waist again, still fighting. 'Those golden bastards stuck one in first so I'd do all their dirty business to get us all together!' A sob; more tears. 'I'm sorry!' He threw his head back and howled. 'I'm sorry! Church, for Marianne! Oh Christ, I'm sorry! The others, Shavi, mate! Shavi!' And then he was crying uncontrollably.

Horrific images shimmered across Church's mind: Veitch bludgeoning Shavi's boyfriend to death in a South London street; Veitch murdering Laura's mother while Laura lay unconscious on the floor; Veitch gunning down Ruth's uncle in the building society rage.

And then he was back in the sequence the Walpurgis had played over and over in his head. The flat, comfortable with a woman's presence. The acid jazz CD playing. Marianne humming as she moved into the bathroom. Dread surged through Church; he didn't want to imagine any more. But just as it had with the Walpurgis, the images came thick and fast: the gentle click of the front door that Marianne never heard. His heart boomed. The strange smell he now knew was the Caraprix at work on Veitch; the familiar shadow. Veitch slipping through the flat like a shadow, his eyes glassy. The knife glinting in his hand. Her voice, as clear as day: 'Church? Is that you?' And then Veitch in like thunder. A merciful blur of limbs and steel and blood . . .

'Ryan . . .' Church felt he was swimming away from the world.

'Then those Fomorii bastards did it too! You didn't even think it through!' Veitch's voice had the shattering pain of a child who had been failed by a parent. 'They dragged Tom off and stuck one in his head when we were in those cells under Dartmoor! And I was there first – why shouldn't they have done it to me?'

Church felt sick; he had never considered it for even a moment. He *had* failed him, failed them all.

Laura and Ruth fell back as Balor grew; to Church's warped perception the Beast appeared to be filling the entire room.

Veitch was sobbing now. 'The Queen – that witch that screwed Tom – she kicked me out because she found out I was tainted. Useless. Just thrown away. Too much of a loser to fight back. Doing everything they made me do. Useless! A part of me always knew that shit was in my head, and I couldn't tell anybody! Couldn't even tell the part of me that did the thinking!'

There was a noise like metal sheets being torn in two. Behind Balor, a doorway had opened in the air presenting a vista on to shimmering stars hanging in the cold void. Streams of sparkling dust began to drift out of it into Balor; the final power he needed.

'Not fair.' Veitch was on his knees, whimpering. 'Not fair.'

'The gates are open, Ryan. You can stop it.' Church felt like he was calling up from the bottom of a well.

'I can't do it. I'm too weak. I've always been too weak.'

'No, you're not. You've just got to see yourself. Have faith in yourself.'

Veitch shook his head, blood splattering from his nose. He was still fighting it, but his heart wasn't in it; he'd already given up.

Anger flashed across his face. Against his will, he lifted the silver hand to drive it into Church's chest.

A long, low moan emanated from the glowing head of Bran the Blessed. Light flowed from it into Church's mouth, soothing, invigorating; whispers crackled across his head; the god was telling him the secrets of the infinite. A word that was not a word was branded in sapphire letters on his mind. A word of power from a language before language. A symbol that could change reality with a single utterance.

Church fumbled to one side. Caledfwlch jumped into his hand of its own accord. With a tremendous effort, he drove himself up and forward. The Sword punched through Veitch's gut, ripped upwards. For one moment they were locked together, in body and in thought.

Veitch retreated into the depths of his head. In the end he had amounted to nothing; despite all his hopes and dreams, he hadn't wished hard enough. Briefly, his eyes flickered towards Ruth, as beautiful as the first time he had seen her. He remembered them making love in a warm room, recalled the way her hair reminded him of the liquorice sticks he had as a child; the way she made him feel he was more than what he was; the deep peace she had given him in his soul for the first time in his life. Through all the violence and bitterness and despair, he could hold on to that sparkling moment of transcendence.

Life gushed from him; the room grew slowly dim. And then he was in a slow boat drifting to an island off the Welsh coast, watching a mermaid swim in the waters beneath him, seeing her wave at him and smile. And he was lying on the warm ground looking up at tiny, golden figures flitting through the trees on gossamer wings; one of them coming down to see him; to say he wasn't so bad after all.

Life filled with wonder. Moments of peace he could count on one hand.

If only . . . If only . . .

Shavi watched his friend's face grow pale. His heart broke in two. Laura stared, wishing it was her. And Ruth cried gently, tried to catch his eye to give him some affection to take with him, to say he was forgiven his sins; to say he was a good man and a hero. But he didn't see her.

Church saw the despair flare in Veitch's face, saw his dreams shatter and fall into nothing. There was one instant when life flickered in his pupils, an instant later there was nothing. He slumped to the floor, dead.

Church could barely see for his own tears. He was aware of the sucking power of the gate, and Balor rising up, ready to usher in the End of Everything. And it *was* the End; for him.

With the last of his strength, he ran forward. The word of power burst from his throat and the whole of existence turned inside out. Blue Fire leapt from the artefacts to each of the five – including the prone form of Veitch. Tom had been right; there had to be five, the final element in a spell as old as time. The energy rose up in a column in the space amongst them and then rushed towards the Heart of Shadows. For the briefest instant, Balor was drained of every shred of dark power. Church seized the moment. Caledfwlch, known as Excalibur, known as the Sword of Righteousness, drove straight into the Beast. Church saw terror etched on a boy's face, saw a sharp-suited man recoil in horror, saw a general roll his eyes in despair. And still he pressed on, driving Balor back towards the gate.

The effort was too great, but then they passed a certain point and the dreadful vertiginous pull of the beyond took over. The flesh felt like it was being ripped from Church's body. Balor went first, his form compressing as the power was sucked back out of it; and then he was folding becoming nothing, less than a child, less than the enormous black insect he resembled for a fleeting moment, and then he plunged into the gate, blocking its pull briefly.

Church had time to turn. His eyes fell on them one after the other: first Veitch for whom he grieved as if he had lost a brother, and then Shavi, and Laura, as close to his heart as he could imagine. And then Ruth, who *was* his heart.

He was dying, even if the gate didn't have him in its pull. His regrets at doubting Ruth were driven away the moment he looked into her face. All he wanted to remember was the love he saw there, mingled with the terrible pain.

'I'll love you.' Ruth was shouting, her voice torn apart by an unbearable grief. 'Always, Church. Always.'

She loved him, she loved him, she loved him, and it wasn't fair.

She saw his face one final time, just as she remembered that first night under the bridge, filled with decency and honesty and all the best things she had ever wanted in her life. Slowly the haze that swirled at the gate's entrance folded around him. One word drifted back to her: '. . . forever . . .'

And then he was gone.

CHAPTER TWENTY-ONE

Samhain

Over London, the Fabulous Beasts swooped on heated currents rising from the raging flames that had eradicated any taint of the Fomorii. In their grace and serpentine power, in their glittering like jewels in the setting sun, they were inspirational. Hope and wonder soared with them, and on their backs rode a new age, free of the hated old ways and the tyranny of mundanity. Again, as it once had been, it was a world where anything could happen.

Of the Fomorii there was no sign. Whether they had followed their god into oblivion, or simply retreated, broken-backed, to T'ir n'a n'Og, no one knew, but no trace remained of them in the world. All the places they had made their own burned in the flames of the Fabulous Beasts: the financial district, the Palace of Westminster, Buckingham Palace; and of the black tower that had been the source of their power, nothing at all remained, not even rubble.

Ruth, Shavi, Laura and the Bone Inspector had escaped, carrying the body of Veitch, before the ultimate destructive force of the Fabulous Beasts had been unleashed on the tower; indeed, it had almost been as if the serpents had waited for them to vacate before attacking.

They made their way north through the city, skirting the areas of greatest destruction. For the main the journey passed in a blur; they were in shock, too distraught by the blows that had been inflicted on them to comprehend the scale of their victory. It was a triumph they had never imagined in their wildest dreams, but it didn't feel like one. Occasionally the Tuatha Dé Danann could be glimpsed like flitting golden ghosts, moving out across the land. Survivors, but not victors; that title belonged to humanity, thanks to the Brothers and Sisters of Dragons, and the sacrifice of people who cared.

The Bone Inspector slipped away respectfully while they buried Veitch by torchlight on the heights of Hampstead Heath overlooking the city. None of them really knew what to say; the loss was too acute, the atmosphere of broken dreams too oppressive. As they started to throw the clods of earth back into the hole, Shavi finally broke down.

'Goodbye, my good friend,' he said, the tears streaming down his face. 'You brought something to all of us. And you did your best, often despite yourself, and that is more than enough. I will miss you more than you ever could have believed.'

And then they were all crying, not just for Veitch, but for all the ones they had lost, and for themselves, who would have to deal with the world left behind and the lack of their friends in it; and none of them tried to hide their tears, not even Laura, who surprised herself with the weight of the emotion pouring out of her.

When all their tears were gone, and the mound of brown earth stood complete and alone in the rolling green, they turned to face the uncertain times ahead.

The night felt subtly different. The lamp of the moon cast a beautiful white light from a sable sky now devoid of storm clouds. The sourness in the air that had arrived with Balor's rebirth was gone, replaced by the aroma of green vegetation in an atmosphere slowly ridding itself of pollution; it smelled like hope.

Beneath the stars, Shavi, Ruth and Laura huddled together around a bonfire against the October chill. The Bone Inspector leaned against his staff and watched the city thoughtfully. They sensed the spirits of the Invisible World were beginning to venture abroad, as they always did on that night that had come to be known as Hallowe'en, yet the small group felt no sense of threat.

'How are you doing?' Laura said to Ruth after a long period of silence, punctuated only by the crackle of the fire. Her voice held a real tenderness that made Ruth even more emotional after their long period of rivalry.

'At the moment I feel dead.' Distractedly, she prodded the grass with a stick, before releasing a juddering sigh. 'And I know it's going to get worse before it gets better. I know we won . . . I know the whole world benefited . . . but the price we paid seems so high.'

Laura tossed more wood on the fire, though it hardly needed it. 'You can talk about Church, you know.'

'Thanks. Really.' Ruth wiped away a stray tear, smiled. 'It seems so unfair. Personally, I mean. I'm being selfish here and I know anyone else would tell me to get some perspective—'

'That is not how grief works,' Shavi interjected.

'It took us so long to get together,' Ruth said, 'but when we did I felt happy, truly happy, for the first time in my life. Church was always talking about searching for meaning, and for me that was where I found meaning in my life: in my love for him. Does that sound vomit-inducing?'

'Yes, but keep going. I need to make a space for dinner.' Laura's gibe was gentle and Ruth couldn't help laughing.

'It would have been perfect for me if we'd stayed together into old age, and I know it's a childish thing, but sometimes you think that's reason enough for it to keep going. But life has its own plan. I think that's when you know you've grown up – when you can accept you have no control over anything. Church told me the Tuatha Dé Danann believe everything is fluid. I suppose the mind has complete control over everything, and that if you wish hard enough you can change reality. Well, I wished and I wished. And he still hasn't come back to me.'

Laura fumbled for her hand and gave it a squeeze. Shavi slipped an arm round her shoulders. Overhead, a shooting star blazed across the heavens, reminding them of other times, when they had been all together.

'All I think now is what would he have wanted me to do,' Ruth said. 'And the answer's obvious: keep doing the right thing, make the world a better place, ignore what anybody else might tell you. Emotionally, it will be hard for me, for all of us, but that's a good reason for living. Don't you think?'

They all agreed.

'You know, I don't really want to think about this,' Laura said, 'but, do you reckon he suffered? I mean, he'd been stabbed and all, I know. But that gate he was sucked through—'

'I don't know. But even if he did he would probably say pain is transitory and there are better things to look forward to.'

'You believe that?'

'I do. Now. I'll see him again one day, I know it.'

Laura remained silent for a long moment, then said, 'You know Veitch and me didn't get on. He scared me. But I think the real reason was because we were so alike. Two losers trying to escape the past that held them back. I feel bad that I'm here and he's not.'

'Don't feel guilty.' Ruth gave her arm a squeeze.

'No, Ryan would not want that.' Shavi leaned forward into the firelight. 'Ryan did the best he could, but he was a victim, and that is the great tragedy of what happened to him. Under other circumstances, he would have found his redemption, as you did.'

'Those bastards took it away from him,' Laura said vehemently.

'Exactly. We were all manipulated by higher powers, run ragged and forced to suffer, yet in the end we – humanity – still won. Despite everything inflicted on us. That is our great success.'

Ruth watched the sparks flying high in the smoke. 'When do you think the Tuatha Dé Danann first stuck that Caraprix in Veitch's head?'

'I do not know,' Shavi replied, 'but they were manipulating us from the moment we were born. They knew they needed the Brothers and Sisters of Dragons together ready to free them if the Fomorii ever got the upper hand. And to achieve our destiny we all had to experience death at first hand, so they utilised Veitch to engineer that state. With the Caraprix driving him, he set off on his murderous spree. I wonder how that must have affected him? His conscious mind did not know, but it was there in his subconscious, eating away at him.'

'Why Veitch?' Ruth asked. 'Why didn't they get you or me to do their dirty work?'

'Because Ryan was perfect for the job. His life already contained violence. He had crossed a barrier that the rest of us would have found hard to deal with.'

'So he did exactly what they wanted,' Laura said bitterly, 'you'd have thought they'd have left him alone after that. But they gave him that silver hand to do Church in at the end.'

'That was the faction that didn't want humanity to become a threat,' Ruth said. 'They were scheming all the time, both the Tuatha Dé Danann and the Fomorii. Plan after plan, manipulation after manipulation. We were like kids in comparison, so trusting.'

'It did not do them any good,' Shavi said. 'In fact, it was their arrogance that did it for them in the end. The Fomorii never saw us as a real threat. They had implanted their own Caraprix in Ryan's head, but it only came into play right at the end when it actually looked like we might stand a chance. If they had set Ryan to pick us off one by one over a period of time, they would have won. But we were just *Fragile Creatures*, beneath their notice.'

'That'll teach the bastards,' Laura said. 'It's like the French Revolution all over again.'

Ruth stretched, the aches of the past few days finally coming out. 'Liberté, fraternité, égalité.'

'Look. What's that?' Laura pointed to a light that suddenly flared brightly in the sea of night.

As they scanned the darkness, their breath caught in their throats, others glimmered faintly across the city. It was such a simple thing, but after so long it seemed like an act of God.

Shavi thought for a moment, then said, 'An emergency generator has come on.'

They were all silent for a long moment, barely daring to believe what it meant. It was Ruth who gave voice to it: 'Technology is working again.'

'What's left of it.' With a fake dismissive shrug, Laura played up to what they expected of her. 'No web, no MP3, no ER. What's the point?'

'Technology and magic, side by side,' Shavi mused. 'Interesting times lie ahead.'

They spent the next half hour talking animatedly about what the coming months would hold as humanity crawled out from the wreckage of society and attempted to make a new life out of the devastation. Power lost, industry destroyed, food distribution ruined, transport in tatters, and how many dead – thousands? Millions? How long would it take them to get even a modicum of organisation up and running again? In the short term the hardship would be intense, but they all agreed there was hope. After all, mankind was now on a new road, one rising to a glorious future.

Eventually they decided to wander away from the fire for a while, to stretch the chill from their legs and be alone with their thoughts. Ruth found herself drawn to a dark copse; even before she had entered the trees she sensed an old magic in the air: a deep musk and the snorting of an animal that was not an animal. Antlers were silhouetted against the moon.

Cernunnos roamed through the undergrowth, his breath steaming. Beyond him, Ruth could see the woman who had haunted her during those early days after the world had changed: at first glance a wizened old hag, then a middle-aged mother, and finally a young woman, filled with vitality and sexuality.

'You called to me,' Ruth said. In the branches of the trees above, her owl hooted eerily.

Cernunnos loomed up before her, his power daunting but tempered in that aspect by a subtle gentleness. 'You have overcome all challenges, as I knew you would. And now you have reached your blossoming there is no longer any need for my guidance.'

'I don't know who I am any more.'

'You are a daughter, not of my flesh, but of my spirit. And a daughter too, of my bright half. You are a guardian of the old ways, a champion of the moon, the sum of all the potential carried in the essence of every woman. Nature will bend before you. The grass will plead for your foot, the air for your lungs.'

'Yes, but what does it *mean*? What am I supposed to do now?' Her voice was strained with emotion from the stresses tearing her apart.

Cernunnos snorted once more and prowled amongst the trees as if he was doing a strange, ritual dance. When he returned to her, he said, 'You will be a light in the dark, showing the way between old days and new, between summer and winter, day and night, sun and moon, man and woman. Many trials lie ahead. But you will not walk the path alone.'

'Who's going to be with me?'

'Let the seasons turn, and take them as you find them.'

Ruth thought about this for a moment; she felt strangely comforted that there was some sort of direction planned for her. It would give her something to immerse herself in so she didn't have to think. 'But where do I start? Where do I go from here?'

'Let the seasons turn.'

'Something will turn up, I suppose. It always does.' She made to go, then turned back. 'Thank you. For giving me something to believe in. Something . . . more.' She couldn't find the words to adequately express the depth of what she had discovered since her change, and so she simply bowed her head and left. She had no doubt she would see him again.

As Ruth walked away, Laura stepped from the shadow of the trees. 'She doesn't realise exactly what she can do yet, does she?'

'Do you?' Cernunnos said.

'I have an idea.'

'You will watch her? Ensure she overcomes her pain?'

'Yeah, I'll be her shadow,' Laura said. 'I'll be a friend, and I hope she'll be mine.'

'Winter may be approaching, but this is a time for all growing things. The two of you will be needed as the heart of nature begins to beat strongly once more. Through the harsh days before the seeds that have been planted come forth, you will be needed more than ever. Existence has changed in more ways than you can comprehend. There are new rules. Old magic is loose in the land. Nothing will be the way it was.' He raised his head to make a strange, throaty call to the moon. 'When next you encounter the Golden Ones, they will not be how you recall.'

'How will they look?'

Cernunnos ignored her question. 'Unchanged for so long, my people have now had change thrust upon them. They, too, must deal with the new rules.'

'There's certainly going to be a lot of bad blood amongst them. This whole business has split them in two. Will you all go back to Otherworld?'

'Some. Others will retreat to their Courts to lick their wounds. A few will remain abroad in the Fixed Lands. The success of the Fragile Creatures will have consequences even the Golden Ones cannot foresee. We will no longer see this land as our territory.'

'I bet a few of you are going to hate us for what happened. There'll be trouble. And how are we going to cope with all the other crazy stuff that came out of Otherworld? That'll still hang around – the Fabulous Beasts and the Redcaps and the Baobhan Sith and all the rest of the shit.'

'The Fragile Creatures are a resilient breed.'

'Not so fragile, eh?' She looked up at the owl as it beat a path towards Ruth. 'So Ruth and I have got our work cut out. We'll be a good team. I've got the mouth and the looks, and she . . .' Laura was surprised at how excited she was about the prospect of what lay ahead, an opportunity to do the kind of good she always dreamed of doing '. . . she'll be the best there is.'

'So you're some big-shot shaman?' The Bone Inspector leaned on his staff, examining the theatre of stars. His burned hands miraculously appeared to be healing.

'So they say.' Shavi was smiling in the dark at his side. He liked the Bone Inspector; all his curmudgeonly ways and his difficulty with human relationships only added to his appeal.

'I've heard lots of people say that. They couldn't do anything.'

'Hmm.'

'At least you haven't got a big head like some of your associates.' He fiddled with his staff uncomfortably. 'Do you know what you're going to be doing after this night?'

'Not yet. Travelling, I suppose. Seeing how the landscape now lies. Finding out what I can do.'

'I could offer you a position.'

'Oh?'

'You've heard talk of the Culture?' Shavi said he had. 'The Culture were the original wise people. In society from the earliest days, from when man had just a few sticks to hack out a life, I reckon. The Egyptians sailed to these shores for guidance from us about the pyramids. The Celts revered us. We knew all the lore of the land, how animals and birds acted, trees and plants grew. We knew about the stars and the planets. The spirit-fire. We knew *everything*. And then the damn Romans came. Slaughtered some, drove the rest underground where we couldn't do the job that we were meant to do. The colleges at Glastonbury and Anglesey were destroyed. It was hard to pass on the knowledge. And then, thanks to that God-awful Age of Reason, the Culture gradually died out.'

'And you are the last,' Shavi said.

'Now wouldn't it be a shame for all that thousands of years of knowledge to die out with me?'

'What are you suggesting?'

'The land needs the Culture. The people need the Culture – especially now when they need to learn a new way of living to cope with what it's going to be like out there.' He faced Shavi, his eyes sparkling. 'I want to start the colleges up again, pass on all the knowledge I've got before I'm gone. Build a new Culture.'

'And you want me to help?'

'I want you to be the first to learn. And then I want you to help me pass it on. Maybe set up at Glastonbury, I don't know. What do you say?'

Shavi's face was so serious as he considered the offer that the Bone Inspector was convinced he was going to refuse. But then a warm smile crept across his face. 'I think that would be an excellent idea.'

When they returned to the fire, thoughts of what lay ahead were put to one side, and once more they were old friends enjoying each other's company. They remembered the ones they had lost and thought about the times they had spent together, and they cried a little. But as good friends should, they helped each other along the rocky path, and after a while they even found the strength to laugh.

Lying back beneath the sweep of stars, there was some sadness that they would soon be going their separate ways. But though they might not meet again, they would never forget all that they had shared, and everything they had learned: in the midst of hardship they had discovered the best that life had to offer, both in the world, and in themselves.

And though there were undoubtedly hard days ahead, they had been forged in the worst of times, and with hope and optimism in their hearts, the road would always rise before them.

Church woke on a hard, cold floor surrounded by the smell of wood smoke. A deep ache suffused his limbs, though slowly fading; his stomach turned queasily. Strange dreams had paraded through his head, of people in dark suits and army green, but the last vibrant thoughts he had were of the dying light in poor, tormented Veitch's eyes, of the desperate love in Ruth's face, and of plunging into nothingness in the company of a deep shadow. He was still clutching

Caledfwlch tightly. His free hand moved to his side where Veitch had torn him open, but there was no blood, no wound. It made no sense.

He levered himself up to see he was in a dark, round room constructed from wood. The only light came from a fire smouldering in the centre, the smoke drifting up to disappear through a hole in the turf roof. It was undeniably primitive, filled with the aromas of animals and damp vegetation.

His thoughts careered. Where were the others? Where was Balor? As his eyes grew accustomed to the dark, he realised with a start that he was not alone. Jumping to his feet anxiously prompted a shriek from the dark shapes huddling across the other side of the room.

Moving past the fire, he could see a woman was protecting her two children. She had long dark hair that framed a face hardened by harsh living. The children, a boy and a girl of around seven or eight, had the same dark hair and eyes. They were all terrified.

'Don't worry. I won't hurt you,' he said gently, but his voice only agitated them further.

The woman jabbered in a language he didn't understand until he caught one word: *Samhain.*

As he repeated it, the woman froze, her eyes widening. 'Samhain,' she said again.

And then the elements began to fall into place: the house, the basic peasant clothes of the woman and children, the language. Somehow the gate had flung him into the distant past, amongst one of the tribes that modern scholars had lumped together under the catch-all title of Celts.

He closed his eyes and rested on his sword as he fought the rising panic. His first thought was that it couldn't be true, but everything he saw, heard, smelled, told him otherwise. Then the impressions came thick and fast: isolation, utter loneliness amongst people who would consider him an alien or a madman, the brutality of life in those times, of Ruth, whom he would never see again, of his friends, and his world. Slowly, he went down on to his knees, unable to bear the weight.

His torment was disturbed by the woman gradually advancing. She pointed tentatively. 'Nuada?'

She was indicating the Sword. He held it up, nodding. 'Nuada Aigetlámh.' It was the god's sword; of course she would be familiar with it.

She suddenly pointed towards the open door and jabbered once more, excitedly this time. There was little else for him to do but follow her direction.

Outside, a wild electrical storm lit up other roundhouses clustered nearby. Frightened horses and cattle added to the deafening cannon-fire of thunder. A terrible wind tore across the landscape, though there wasn't even the faintest hint of rain; in the gale was the familiar stink of corruption that had surrounded Balor.

He looked round, overcome with the strangest impression someone familiar had only just left the vicinity. Despite the grinding sense of disconnection, he felt uncannily good, and he knew why. His deep perception showed him the Blue Fire was stronger in the land, and the buildings and the animals than he had ever seen it before. That was why the wound in his side had healed. As a Brother of Dragons he had tapped into it.

And with that realisation came another thought: he recalled Tom telling him there were no coincidences, no accidents. Then why had he been saved? There was no obvious answer, but he had the strangest feeling that somebody had wanted it to happen for him.

As he tried to decide what his next move would be, he became aware of a faint golden glow approaching across the dark, storm-torn country-side. It was Niamh. His shock was palpable until he accepted this was long before she had sacrificed herself to save them all.

She came up to him sharply, an unfamiliar contemptuous expression inscribed on her face. 'Fragile Creature!' Her words were the arrogant bark of someone used to complete deference. 'Is that the Sword of my brother?' As always, he understood her words in a way that transcended language.

It was intriguing to see the difference in her. Here she was more like the worst of her kind, cold and aloof with a hint of cruelty. 'It was once. It's my Sword now.'

Fury tinged her features. 'How can a Fragile Creature dare to touch so powerful an object? How can you dare to take it from my brother, and now, when he needs it most?'

'I'm a Brother of Dragons.'

This puzzled her a little. 'I have not seen you amongst that dismal brood.'

His spine prickled as connections began to be made. 'What's happening?' he asked, listening to the noise that was almost masked by the storm.

'You do not know? It is the Second Battle of Magh Tuireadh. This night the future of the Golden Ones will be decided, when the Night Walkers are finally driven into the sea after their bitter rule.'

'And the future of the Fragile Creatures,' he added wryly.

She didn't deem his comment worthy of any acknowledgment.

And then everything fell into place, with a *frisson* that was so acute it shocked him. The mysterious comments that he would not find rest at the end of his struggle. The hints that he had a wider role to play in leading humanity towards the next level. Tom telling him to use his memories as a source of warmth in troubling times.

He steeled himself, letting the obligation settle into his bones. Then he said: 'Take me to the battle.'

'You mean to fight?'

'I intend to do what I can. And to be there when Balor is finally destroyed.'

She appeared quite taken aback by his bravado; a little warmth broke into her frosty features.

'My name's Jack.' His heart was already soaring as he realised the solution to his predicament. 'I think we're going to become good friends.'

'Friends? With a Fragile Creature?' she snorted.

After the battle he would return to the home of the gods T'ir n'a n'Og, where time could pass much slower than it did in the real world. And while he aged only slightly, the centuries would tumble by in a mad parade until he could once again step back into the world to take Ruth in his arms and meet their future together. The paradox made his head spin. For a while he would exist in two places at once: in the *real* world, where he would be born and grow to maturity; and in Otherworld, waiting for the culmination of the confrontation with Balor so he could step back into the Fixed Lands to reclaim his life. Could he sit idly by in Otherworld, knowing the suffering that would be inflicted on humanity during the Age of Misrule? Could he wait there when he might be able to save Veitch's life? Or would he cross over earlier, to meet his younger self and change the course of history? Was that at all possible, or would existence come crashing down around his ears? It was a conundrum that would have to wait.

Now he knew why Niamh had appeared in his childhood bedroom, guiding him along the path he had eventually walked, why she had been filled with such a deep love that had made no sense for the little time they had known each other. Between now and then, they *would* become friends, and he would bring humanity to her, and she would in turn convince other members of the Tuatha Dé Danann to come over to the Fragile Creatures, something that would have such great import so many years down the line. And eventually, although he would aim to prevent it, she would learn to fall in love with him.

In the meantime he had so many things to do: establishing the reputation of the Brothers and Sisters of Dragons, convincing them to prepare for the return of the Fomorii, ensuring the first steps were taken on the path to godhood.

And then one other thought came to him that filled him with warmth. In just a few brief centuries' time he would see Tom again. Tom, who had kept so many secrets, hidden his character and his emotions for the sake of those around him. They would become the best of friends and he would finally pay the Rhymer back for saving his life.

'Come on,' he said to Niamh, 'let's go to war.'

His one hope was that the world he eventually returned to would not have been bequeathed to the worst of humanity; that the old, bad ways had simply slotted back into place. 'I'm wishing,' he whispered aloud, his eyes closed. 'I'm wishing for a place where the good things have the upper hand: love and honesty and friendship and wonder and hope. I'm wishing enough to change the world.'

In a bleak room filled with hard men, a cold wind blew. For as long as anyone could remember they had dreamed the world their way; and it was a world filled with lies and power and money, of subtle manipulation and limpid promises, where *Fragile Creatures* were held in place by a little of this and a little of that, but never anything that mattered. Yet beneath their arrogance lay fear, for sooner or later the scales might fall.

A lie was needed to cement their rule. A Big Lie. Lives were shattered in the telling of it, families torn apart, good men and women twisted out of shape. But the hard men were right to be afraid, for even in the worst of all worlds, good men and women aspire; and inspire.

With that same arrogance, the hard men believed no one could be moved by a world without money or power; dreams were for children; dreams had no power. And so they released the means to their downfall. The Lie proved more seductive than the world they had wished; it was filled with love and wonder and friendship and hope and faith; and meaning; a world where anything could happen.

A wish was all it took; because if you wish hard enough you can change the world.

The Lie became the Truth, and everything that hadn't happened, had happened. Five people quested through untold hardship; they plumbed worlds beyond imagination, rubbed shoulders with gods and beasts; and in the end brought the magic back home.

This is how it was, and is, and will be.

The cold wind blew the bad things right away. The hard men no longer existed. The hard men never existed. Their world was just a bad dream; and only bad dreams have no power.

The Blue Fire is in everything.

And the world turns slowly towards the light.

Bibliography

Baigent, Michael, Leigh, Richard and Lincoln, Henry *The Messianic Legacy* (Corgi)

Bently, Peter (ed.) *The Mystic Dawn: Celtic Europe* (Time-Life)

Bord, Janet and Colin *Mysterious Britain* (Thorsons)

Briggs, Katharine *An Encyclopedia of Fairies* (Penguin)

Brydon, Robert *Rosslyn – A History of the Guilds, the Masons and the Rosy Cross* (Rosslyn Chapel Trust)

Bulfinch *Bulfinch's Mythology* (Spring)

Bushell, Rev William Done *Caldey: An Island of the Saints* (Lewis Printers)

Campbell, Harry *Supernatural Scotland* (HarperCollins)

Celtic Mythology (Geddes & Grosset)

Carr-Gomm, Philip *The Druid Way* (Element)

Coghlan, Ronan *The Encyclopedia of Arthurian Legends* (Element)

Cope, Julian *The Modern Antiquarian* (Thorsons)

Cotterell, Arthur *Celtic Mythology* (Ultimate Editions)

Crisp, Roger *Ley Lines of Wessex* (Wessex Books)

Crossing, William *Folklore and Legends of Dartmoor* (Forest Publishing)

Davies, Margaret *The Story of Tenby* (Tenby Museum)

Dunning, R.W. *Arthur: The King in the West* (Grange Books)

Earl of Rosslyn *Rosslyn Chapel* (Rosslyn Chapel Trust)

Fitzpatrick, Jim *The Book of Conquests* (Paper Tiger)

Graves, Robert *The White Goddess* (Faber & Faber Ltd)

Hadingham, Evan *Circles and Standing Stones* (William Heinemann Ltd)

Hardcastle, F. *The Chalice Well* (The Chalice Well Trust)

Hicks, Jim (ed.) *Earth Energies* (Time Life)

Hicks, Jim (ed.) *Witches and Witchcraft* (Time Life)

Hopkins, Jerry and Sugerman, Danny *No One Here Gets Out Alive* (Plexus)

Kindred, Glennie *The Earth's Cycle of Celebration* (Self-published)

Knight, Christopher and Lomas, Robert *The Hiram Key* (Century)

Knight, Christopher and Lomas, Robert *The Second Messiah* (Arrow)

Lamont-Brown, Raymond *Scottish Superstitions* (Chambers)

Larousse *The Larousse Encyclopedia of Mythology*

Mann, Nicholas R. *The Isle of Avalon* (Llewellyn Publications, USA)

Matthews, John (Ed.) *The Druid Source Book* (Brockhampton Press)

Matthews, John & Stead, Michael J. *King Arthur's Britain: A Photographic Odyssey* (Brockhampton Press)

Michell, John *New Light on the Ancient Mystery of Glastonbury* (Gothic Image)

Michell, John *Sacred England* (Gothic Image)

Miller, Hamish & Broadhurst, Paul *The Sun and the Serpent* (Pendragon Press)

Porter, Roy *London A Social History* (Hamish Hamilton)

Radford, Roy and Ursula *West Country Folklore* (Peninsula Press)

Richards, Julian *Beyond Stonehenge* (Trust for Wessex Archaeology)

Rutherford, Ward *Celtic Mythology* (Thorsons)

Seafield, Lily *Scottish Ghosts* (Lomond Books)

Siefker, Phyllis *Santa Claus, Last of the Wild Men* (McFarland & Company, Inc)

St Leger-Gordon, Ruth E. *The Witchcraft and Folklore of Dartmoor* (Peninsula Press)

Stewart, Bob & Matthews, John *Legendary Britain* (Blandford)

Stewart, R.J. *Celtic Gods, Celtic Goddesses* (Blandford)

Tabraham, Chris (ed.) *Edinburgh Castle* (Historic Scotland)

Tabraham, Chris (ed.) *Urquhart Castle* (Historic Scotland)

Various *Folklore, Myths and Legends of Britain* (Reader's Digest)

Westhorp, Christopher (ed.) *Journeys Through Dreamtime* (Time Life)

White, Richard (ed.) *King Arthur in Legend and History* (Dent)

Wilde, Lady *Ancient Legends of Ireland* (Ward & Downey)

Zink, David D. *The Ancient Stones Speak* (Paddington Press)

Many on-line resources were a valuable source of reference. Since my research, some have closed, the ones remaining are:

Celtic Deities and Myth – *www.eliki.com/ancient/myth/celts/*

Kaleidoscope – Celtic Mythology – *www.softanswer.com/hans/celtic/mythology.html*

Knights Templar – *www.brjeffreys.freeserve.co.uk/knights/knights.htm*

Knights Templar Index – *http://homepages.enterprise.net/paulmagoo/index.htm*

London Underground History – *www.starfury.demon.co.uk/uground/*

Mythology – *www.exotique.com/fringe/mythology.htm*

The Megalith Map – *www.megalith.ukf.net/bigmap.htm*

Neopagan – *www.neopagan.net*

The Official Rosslyn Chapel Site – *www.rosslynchapel.org.uk*

I am indebted to all of the people behind them.

Acknowledgements

World's End
Bob Rickard and the Gang of Fort; John Charlick and Sean Devlin at Trebrea Lodge; Coach and Horses, Salisbury; White Hart Hotel, Okehampton.

Darkest Hour
Roman Camp Country House, Callander; The Point Hotel, Edinburgh; Kingsmills Hotel, Inverness; Warren Ellis.